ALIEN REFORMATION

BOOK ONE OF THE HYDRO-CARBON STRATAGEM

MICHAEL O' DWYER

 **New Generation Publishing**

DID MANKIND COME ABOUT BY ACCIDENT OR DESIGN? WERE HUMAN BEINGS CREATED FOR A PURPOSE THAT MAN IS YET STILL UNAWARE OF? DID HIS KIND OCCUR BY CHANCE OR WAS IT A NORMAL PROCESS OF THE EVOLVING UNIVERSE?

CHAPTERS

PROLOGUE

In the beginning; before the creation of everything, evolved intelligences glorifying in their accumulated wisdom devoutly believed; there was supposed to be nothing in existence prior to that initial moment. To these knowledgeable societies; there had only been a vast colourless and soundless emptiness. But paradoxically, like their maker, other things predated the afterglow of creation.

One such phenomenon became conscious in the precise instant of conception. It was a whisper or fragment of whatever set the momentous process in motion. In a fraction of a nano-second after the colossal big bang had created the initial physical content of the Universe; this malignant trespasser had passed through from the fabric of nothingness. This trans-dimensional traveller now faced new perceptions that were previously unknown to it; mainly time and space. Where once there had been nothing but emptiness, swathes of energy were now converted into dense matter. In a split second, this new reality instantly inflated from been smaller than an atomic nucleus into a fiery furnace of sub-atomic particles millions of kilometres across. As the course of creation accelerated; Spiral, Elliptical, Cluster and Irregular Galaxies appeared from this shock wave of Omnipotent instigation to fill in the immense vacuum of vacuity. As the ageing Cosmos inexorably cooled down from the incipient gargantuan blast, billions of boiling Suns with Planetary Solar Systems were now formed in massive collisions of localised space debris. Each of these uniquely fashioned dependant actualities was bound by the physical laws of gravity, mass and velocity. The phenomenon that had passed through from emptiness was a principle unlike these other laws, but a part of this newly emerging conception, none the less. As the Universe matured over tens of millions of aeons; it expanded with exploding Star's spreading the building blocks of life in their wake. These Celestial furnaces became red giants, yellow stars, red and white dwarfs and finally black holes. Instinctively, it hitched a ride on this Cosmic highway of creation. It became aware that travelling by the route of this interstellar Stardust, its goal would be eventually achieved.

FOR THIS ENTITY WAS BESET OF MORE THAN A MINDLESS EXISTENCE.

IT WAS BEGINNING TO REALISE THAT IT HAD A PURPOSE.

So, it kept pace with the evolving Cosmos, feeding on the scant scraps the emerging Universe provided. In adherence of the physical laws of this emerging actuality, it had an opposite. It was aware of its divergent, but it cared little that its rival might have passed through from the same emptiness as itself. In keeping with its nature, its opponent was deemed to be of little consequence. Ultimately, the Planets cooled and hardened. On Worlds with magnetic poles, iron and crystal cores, basic forms of life took hold in their liquid and gaseous seas. It drifted along the path of stellar creation until eventually higher forms of intelligence evolved. It preyed on these infantile minds with the promises of greatness. Then it thrived, delighted itself with its growing influence and prospered. It was of little matter that it destroyed countless Civilisations; the real jewels of Creation in its immature rampage through the Universe. Because of this Entities selfish nature, only its existence counted and it would preserve that circumstance at any cost. After the destruction of each culture, many from nuclear holocausts, it moved on seeking new victims. It grew ever more complex and seemed unstoppable until it encountered the ancestors of the exiles in the fifteenth billion year of the Cosmos. (This was their measurement of the age of the Universe when this magnitudinous event occurred.) They were peaceful and enlightened seekers of knowledge and had named themselves before their encounter with the Entity; the ASCETIC'I. A placid society of Scholars and Scientists, this race based their entire scriptures on the assumption.

"The Creator had constructed the Universe from the ultimate equation."

These believers in the "Great Mathematician." had no concept of the destruction that was about to be unleashed upon them. Like those before them, the malignant force brought them to their knees and to the threshold of near extinction. But this supposedly weak race had a resolve that none of the phenomenon's victims had before. At their nadir, the disembodied manipulator discovered it's opposite.

It was HUMILTY.

The phenomenon's method of seeking out praetorian individuals from an encountered society and corrupting them was thwarted by the necessary development of a communal society. It was this unique suppression of the self by the ASCETIC'I which manifested in the acceptance of a Queen who became immune to the temptations of the singularity. This course of action saved them from the brink of final destruction. Those who had not succumbed to the Entities enticements linked their minds; shared their thoughts, ideas and dreams and became one with the "Mother." This was a barrier the phenomenon could not surmount. It was diffused, broken and scattered around the Universe, where it lurked in its weakened state of limbo waiting for the opportunity to triumph again. Its main staples of selfishness and pride had been taken from it.

It was the E G O.

Countless millennia passed.

Disembodied and lacking substance, it lay frustrated and inactive. Barely surviving within this indeterminate state; it waited. As in the cycle of things; its time had come again. Because of the Corruption's original assault, individuality had crept into the psyche of those who had rendered it ineffective. The oneness that bound the ASCETIC'I together began to erode. A Conclavi of Patriarchi had evolved to put forward doctrine and law. Minuscule cracks appeared in the Commune and this slight whisper was enough. Where there was a hint of distrust, disaffection or envy; it eagerly pounced. Subsequently, the EGO had found one that could restore it to its former glory and with a little prodding of its newest dupe; it would be stronger than before. This inquisitive mind that solicited it would make it whole again. Between the two of them, the Entity and its pawn would create a new race that the gluttonous force would sate itself upon. After all, this was the sole purpose of its being. What really made this a moment to savour for the EGO was the fact that this pitiable individual was one of the hated race which had banished it into near oblivion. With its willing servant's help; a dis-satisfied being named Zebulan, the ASCETIC'I machines were transformed and rose up against them. In the ensuing holocaust, it nearly destroyed his race and separated them from their Queen. But another one among them had been too clever for it and once again it failed to unmake them completely. Those that escaped from its well-practised mayhem fled their destroyed Worlds and way of life, leaving the corruption ensnared with their Matriarch. But the life-giver of their species neutralised its devious impact and held it captive within the sphere of her influence; thus giving her children time to escape. While the EGO lay trapped for aeons alongside the Queen relentlessly probing the confines of its cage, it had time to ponder its origin and the reason for its existence. Eventually, it realised that whatever brought this dimension into creation must surely have the ultimate sense of self-esteem and it must have once been part of this fantastic actuality. Contact with that instigator of this Universe would be the fulfilment of its destiny. The Entity had found a new resolve while in this indeterminate state. It had come to the conclusion that it had become bored and weary of the same repetitiveness of this existence. In the mist of this imposed reasoning,

A NEW PATH HAD OPENED UP TO IT.

It had become aware that the only way to achieve its destiny was to return to the state it had been in before the creation of the physical Universe. Over the billions of years it existed, it had always a profound sense of loss at the separation from the source from where it originated.

THE EGO ARRIVED AT THE EVENTUAL CONCLUSION THAT IF A COLOSSAL EXPLOSION CREATED THIS UNIVERSE; THEN AN EQUALLY EMMENSE DETONATION WOULD UNDO THE FABRIC OF THIS CREATION. THIS TRAIN OF LOGIC BEGAN TO

CONSUME IT UNTIL IT BECAME THE ENTITIES' MASTER AND NEW PURPOSE. IT STARTED TO PUT THE NECESSARY PLANS TO ACHIEVE ITS GOAL INTO MOTION. DESTRUCTION OF THIS UNIVERSE WOULD BE THE NEW PURPOSE AND ITS SALVATION. ONCE THE EGO ACHIEVED THIS, IT COULD FINALLY RETURN TO THE WHOLE THAT IT HAD BEEN INEXPLICITLY SEPARATED FROM.

The ancient force had found its ultimate propose and the reason for its nature. All it had to do was to escape from the Queen's ambuscade that it was ensnared in.

DESTROYING THIS REALITY IN THE PROCESS.

Over the next few millennia, the trap was beginning to fail from its persisting efforts at escape. The EGO perceived that it would be freed eventually; it was a certainty and only a matter of time. Time was of no impediment to a phenomenon that even counted the long lives of the ASCETIC'I as short-lived and inconsequential.

What did become of the remnants of those who had escaped from the fate envisioned on them by the Entity. Once, long before it had sought them out again, every individual of that learned race knew what another compatriot experienced. There had been a great sharing of minds, thoughts and ideas. As the EGO crept into their psyches, individual personalities developed and they began to keep knowledge and secrets from each other. An enforced hierarchy developed and the feeling of individuality increased as the oneness of the former commune evaporated into the globes of history. The survivors of this transposed and much altered race fled their Home Worlds and their older cooler red dwarf Sun and travelled through the frozen wastes of space to newer Galaxies with warmer gaseous Stars. It was during this flight that they became known as the Exiles (Or in their own tongue, the ALASTHA'I.). Their tryst with the EGO had changed them forever and far from its wrath they planned a revenge on it. The former tranquil race had made a vow to their abandoned Queen that they her beloved offspring would explore every method possible to free her and to return home to their precious Worlds; even if it meant using the very tools of their destroyer. Finally some of them accepted this "Great Paradox". These few individuals understood that the only way to counter what they designated as the "INIQUITY." was in fact for their peaceful race to embrace and surpass the belligerence of the Entity. These altered Beings were no longer quite what they had been before their unwitting encounter with the EGO and so something unique and wonderful had been lost forever to the Universe. This malicious detriment was a Cosmic event as similar in magnitude to a Star blinking out of existence and it was no less profound in the overall scheme of Creation.

I.

NORTH-WESTERN EURASIA 19,000 BC.

"Are we a figment of the imagination of a greater intelligence or do we really exist independently of his ministrations, no matter how illogical they are?" pondered Cetheren surreally.

If he was uncertain about that blasphemous consideration; he was absolutely in no doubt about his next one.

"Here I am standing atop an icy cliff edge on a World that is not my own and one that I fervently hope will never be."

The naked Alien stood with his wide back to a bleak and desolate windswept plain that belonged to the furthermost westerly fringes of the largest Continental mass. The white frosty vista around him bore no comparison to the orange expanses of similar latitudes back on his abandoned Crystal Sphere. Still, he accepted the reasons for his predicament.

"This was a site chosen for its apparent isolation, so that the plans of our race can develop unhindered until they eventually come to fruition."

Both of his two metre long sinewy arms were out-stretched in a cruciform posture in preparation for his next actions. His broad wings had not been fully unfurled from his extended appendages when a sudden and unannounced temperamental gust, born within the volatile climate of this Planet nearly knocked him from his feet. The much faster spin of this sphere created winds and vortices in far greater profusion, intensity and spontaneity than on his cherished, but long forsaken Home-World of CRYSTALIOS. The irritated mortal swayed from side to side and then steadied himself, mindful that his exertions were turning the recent fall of frozen liquid to slush beneath his exposed feet.

"It's amazing that some things on this harsh and unforgiving World can be so fragile."

The ever constant bright light over his head; an integral physical part of his kind remained static; reminding him that he had lost his main train of thought during his struggle to balance himself. In response; he mind-uttered, it was more of a curse than a researched statement.

"This place is a cauldron of extreme contrasts. Even the vaporous climate and explosive geology of this World is in a violent hurry. It is far different here than in our placid Solar systems. It feels that this Planet wants to complete its life cycle as quickly as possible and return to the solar dust that created it."

Just after the dawn as the rising Sun began its speedy assent into the Northern sky, their kind, now known as the ALASTHA'I needed to absorb surplus minerals from the atmosphere to survive on this marginal bio-sphere. It was a circumstance of their unique biology and forecasted cloudy and overcast mornings were always chosen for this practice of inhalation. Cetheren like everyone else was aware of the quantities.

"In this very different environment far flung from the place of our origin, the units of solar radiation gathered are equivalent to one calorie per sq. centimetre, far less than the sphere of our birth where this life sustaining energy was seventy times that."

The habitually chronicling Aliens gave this place no name; to them, it was an uncharacteristic discretion in case their enemy found them by just one of their kind mentioning a designated title for it. Some among them believed it to be.

"A foolish and illogical precaution."

But, they prudently obeyed the directive anyway. To pass away his enforced non-mobility, Cetheren mulled over their reasons for their choice.

"Our cherished race has chosen this blue sphere that orbits around the harsh yellow Sun in this obscure solar system as a temporary base, mainly because this third Planet of nine contains the seeds of our plan to regain what has been lost to us. Another advantage of using this World as a refuge is because of the unlikely hood of a large asteroid strike which would almost certainly destroy our chosen schemes; whichever one was favoured. Four enormous gaseous giants would still protect this tiny World if the deflectors our experts installed on the ice rock in the outer fringes of the Solar System failed to do their work."

To either side of him, as far as the limits of his perception could make out, lay thousands of his exiled kind holding the same posture as himself. The assembled host were about to partake in a lunar routine. At this hemisphere, the comfort of the large intense moon gave each of them the illusion of a larger and familiar sphere that was lost to them now. All of the off-Worlder's were fanned out at eight metre intervals along the rim of a long vanished body of saline liquid. The deadly fluid had since departed leaving behind the frozen terrain that existed now. That long vanished and much greater seabed had been formed when the land and water above it had been vaporised from the impact of a comet fragment millions of years ago. Thousands of aeons of exposure to the natural rhythms of ice, wind, sea currents and rain resulted in its present geological appearance. But in this recent cycle of the Planet, the current ice age was waning, its huge glaciers were inexorably retreating north and south and the sea was gaining in magnitude each year. Mountain tops of chiselled bare rock caused by enormous weight and movement were beginning to protrude in the wake of the ice sheets retreat and outcroppings of exposed stone were also forming in the growing seas. It was on these emerging islands that the ALASTHA'I had formed their bases and it was on such a recently issuing landmass that Cetheren now stood. Another intense updraft that tore up the cliff face unsettled him. Again, he steadied himself and he had the perverse conviction.

"I am the only one that is getting knocked about."

Even though, his body needed the inhalations, he wanted to get off this exposed ledge as quickly as possible.

"If the climate allows me!"

Normally, vaguely transparent shrouds of light protected their bodies from the unfamiliar pressures of this Planet, but the personal shield had to be lowered during this time of ingestion. There were two months during the high summer where this practice was cancelled, when the billions of swarming insects made it impossible to inhale nutrients without clogging up their intake systems with nauseating solid matter. The winged Aliens could tolerate the chemistry of this World without this covering in these northern latitudes for a brief respite. But closer to the equator, the intense heat made these safeguarding shields inefficient, not that any of them ventured there anyway. Down below in the frozen tundra the true indigenous lifeforms of this World toiled for their accepted masters. The repulsive "Primates." as the advanced new-comer's categorised them were clothed in the skins and furs of other dead life forms and infested with all manner of living and non-living matter. The bipeds scampered about industriously and were overseen by other lesser winged forms that were not taking sustenance. These Alien charges were adding the finishing touches to hundreds of earthen mounds which had been constructed all over the north-western edge of the largest Continent. However, large roughly hewn stones far beyond their capacity to lift or align stood in regimented precision and were waiting patiently for erection on top of the nearly completed earthworks. This reminded Cetheren of a recent mind-conversation with another exile about his assumptions on that topic.

"Soon by the measure of their short lives, generations in fact, the ice sheets will retreat and as an integral part of our scheme, the ever encroaching sea will cover some of their final efforts and all of ours."

The other had understood the reasoning for such a venture.

"Our CRYSTALOID'I could easily accomplish all of the work in a fraction of the time."

"Of course."

"So the purpose of this exercise is to convince these low intelligent bipeds of the notion that the conception of mound building was their idea and it will remain imprinted in their collective memories for aeons to come. So, in the course of their advancing history, the true natives of this World will believe that they were the original creators of these earthen structures and therefore will strive to attend to them."

Both knew that preservation and ultimate usage of what was under these constructions of dead matter was one of the ALASTHA'I designs. Another integral part of this Alien deception was the falsifying of the ending of this period of glaciation. In the Primates future; those knowledgeable among them would believe that in this part of the Globe; it had actually ended five thousand years later. These highly advanced beings wanted to conceal their presence at all times from those they were about to alter profoundly. Cetheren continued his private theological debate.

"Was it luck or divine providence that we have stumbled across this World which is abundant in killer organisms? If it is the latter, then this supposedly supreme intelligence of creation has a strange way of running the Universe. I am no longer certain that there is there some higher life form than us in the Cosmos. Take the dominant life forms on this Planet for instance."

From crystalline ridges under his extended arms and along his side, light filament patagium began to expand. He paused as his frame began an involuntary action. His long iridescent wings slowly unfurled. Once these flying appendages were fully unfolded, the Alien brought both of his arms up ninety degrees and formed a complete circle. Every other body standing side by side on the frosty ridge mimicked the unveiling of this living gossamer dish. It was a time of concentration now, the battering air drafts could easily knock them over the edge and they would have to make their way back up again. Alien frames welled up like balloons in the expectation of mineral intake. A heedless Cetheren continued his musing as his crystalline ribs expanded.

"These ignorant life-forms look upon us as immortals or in their own uncouth speech; Angels. It is a word of power among their species. To them, we are creatures from their spiritual places and should only be encountered after death. Our normal colouring tells them that. They struggle to explain why we have left the realms of the dead and are here now. The Primates cannot comprehend that our life spans consist of millions of yearly cycles of their Planet. Their short-lived ancestors told them that we have always been here and will always be. But we have only been here for eleven thousand cycles of their Planets orbit around its Star. Still, that is an immense time for their limited comprehension. No wonder they think we are divine or in some instances, messengers of the Gods."

Cetheren and his kind lived half-lives, much like the degradation of a radioactive isotope. The Alien crystalline chemistry of their autonomy decayed in half-lives of ten million Earth years. He laughed suddenly; this was exemplified by a change in colour in the light above his head and the widening of his intake orifices.

"Besides our obvious longevity, there are two other reasons why the Primates look upon us as Angels. The Primates first grounds for this assumption are primarily because of our wings. But the second is more significant. It is a supposition based on the white circular nimbus that is forever projected above our crowns. The Primates call these shimmering lights Halo's. Ha; these bright circles of cryo-lumineance are not heavenly symbols of divine beings as the indigenous natives think. No; they are only the pinnacle of an advanced technology way beyond their limited

comprehension. These are our Preceptor- Bands. The crowns of light are only a tool of communication and not a sign of divine existence. But as it keeps the ignorant Primates in awe of us, we maintain that deceitful deception."

Cetheren's race was no longer pure, but still, most of his own people were uncomfortable with this duplicity.

"If the Primates only knew?"

He shuddered slightly causing his wings to tremble in anxiety and not as a result of the wind currents. The Alien could feel the intensity from the stares of the Primates locked on him and his fellow mineral ingesting ALASTHA'I.

"Always watching us with their curious eyes. They would tear us apart in seconds, if those infant minds discovered the truth. If, they only knew how brittle and timid, we really were, then these Primates would no longer see us as their superiors. And, that certainly would be the end of us. Of that, I am a hundred per cent certain. It is a dangerous game that we play."

Abruptly, the wind ceased to a slight atmospheric ripple. Its fierce intensity had been reduced in an instant. The sudden waning nearly caused him to fall backwards. Watching Primates were wide-eyed.

"They probably think that we had something to do with that. And if I had fallen, their oral legends would say that I took the power of the elements into me."

He shook his oblong head.

"Foolish life-forms."

Cetheren was a member of the faction that had taken a radical path in the suggestion of using other organisms that had survived the rigors of evolution on harsh Worlds to resist the legions of the "INIQUITY.". These bipeds with a limited intelligence from the third Planet circling the uncomfortable Sun were a prime example. He and a few others of his race agreed.

"They are ferocious beasts that can be easily moulded into our requirements."

As the off-Worlder mulled over their relationship with the Primates, he never questioned why these lesser life-forms had a need for a tangible Deity. If the winged Alien had, he would soon realise that the endemic bipedal species craving for the justification of a Creator was far different than the requirements of his far wiser race. These planet-bound creatures needed all powerful, vengeful and punishing Gods; who demanded total obedience to their whims and that was something, which this once totally passive race could not deliver. The Primates of this volatile blue sphere were bipeds like Cetheren's kind, but that's where any similarity according to the extra-Terrestrials ended. No items of clothing concealed their Alien aspect, exposing bodies totally devoid of hair follicles. The ALASTHA'I

13

stood on average around three metres tall and hobbled along the ground in a similar manner to the avians of this Planet. This was partly due to the heavy atmosphere and their unaccustomed reversion to walking, especially along the difficult terrain that constituted the surface of this rock. Back on their Home-World, short journeys were always made by self-powered flight. They did however share the attributes of limbs, toes and fingers. The Aliens had six digits of equal lengths at the end of both extremities. Their digits at the end of broad palms were inter-laced with similar crystal webs to their wings; it was a remnant from the time that they controlled their technology by the physical means of electric impulses. Cetheren's race had large oblong faces with large bulbous craniums that culminated in a point at the chin. Their wide visages were of a whitish blue, a colour that was once unknown to this World and punctuated with countless black macula. These small blemishes of discoloured crystal covering their entire forms expanded and contracted when required. In addition, a built in reflex system filtered out any unrecognised molecules when they came in contact with the macula. These bodily orifices also had a flimsy cognitive flexible lens that allowed multi-facet perception that displayed emotions to those who understood the meanings. As with all of their kind; they had no mouth or ear orifices as neither of these primordial receptors were needed for communication or mineral inhalation. They conversed by telepathy and digested by symbiosis. These blue/black Aliens saw this biological World through a continuous frosty band of white flickering receptor molecules that circumvented above their entire head. Two large macula; three quarters the way up from their pointed chin gave the Hybrids the false impression of eyes. This hovering receptor interpreted the physical sensations for them, such as sound, sight, taste, touch and smell and it also enabled them to communicate in their mind-speech. Cetheren's fragile crystal skin itched as he started to absorb the scant minerals from the Planet's atmosphere. This regular routine was necessary as most of their required intake of life sustaining chemical nourishment lay buried in the poisonous soil, which took time and effort to extract. As the bright ball of the yellow Sun rose higher in the sky, its growing heat caused thermals to create a soft breeze. Its gentle air played the mineral muscles of their wings in a rising symphony that was unrelated to this World. To the Primates below, this opus was a celestial ballad. All of the banished Aliens were of male persuasion and the louder and the more vibrant the sound, the fitter and healthier the male. As the libation of the off-Worlder's increased, so did the rippling rhythmic vibrations of their wings. Their inflated chest cavities expanded as the empty space within the Alien frames contracted. Wind borne trace elements were converted into mineral reserves in stomachs that were not designed on this World. A living aurora borealis became profiled on the horizon.

For the ALASTHA'I were Aristocrats of light technology.

These advanced Beings, not of this World could bend, warp, channel light waves and the Cosmic plasma to do their bidding. They discovered, like the "Great Mathematician." had during the creation of the Universe that spheres were the ultimate method of focusing that celestial force. The Primates below fell on their knees in adoration as they witnessed the Alien spectacle.

"It always has this effect on them. Their limited minds will never accept it as anything other than their Gods demanding veneration. Still, its operates for us and keeps them in awe of our kind. And that can only be a beneficial arrangement."

On this misty winter morning in this primeval time, all these vaguely familiar Humanoid shapes taking in substance stood together against a background of countless dull metallic shaped obelisks. The usually pristine silver hulls of these craft were covered with the filth of the Planet as its constant weather patterns and the harsh rays of its yellow Star battered them continuously without respite. Winged raptors that had acclimatized to these latitudes devoid of trees also used the craft as a vantage point to scan the terrain for prey, defiling the ships with their excretion. When a force shield was activated to protect the transport craft's hulls, it incinerated a number of these flying predators. The taking of any life was anthemia to these passive beings. So after much soul searching and recrimination, the ships were left to their degrading fate. These were the craft that ferried them up and down from the Mother ship to this dirt ball of a rock. This vast star traveller lay deactivated and hidden behind one of the huge ringed Planets moons in case of detection from the enemy. Pointing up towards the heavens in a trajectory aimed at that hidden location; the ferrying craft mirrored the general longing of the ALASTHA'I of leaving this Planet and never returning. For the owners of both of these type of craft were going against their nature and creating something on this World that would only lessen them forever. To ensure the continuation of their species, some of them had even embraced this "Great Paradox". To Cetheren's immediate left stood his sibling Cathbad. The two shared a bond that made them much closer to each other than any other groupings among their race, both having been split from the same larva. This was a remarkably rare occurrence in the long lived race and because of their present circumstances; it could be an event that might not happen again. Both were extremely tall, even for their kind, standing over the normal three metres at the shoulders. As Cetheren's strength gradually returned from the slow intake of minerals, he returned to the same conversation they seemed to become embroiled in every time the two brothers came in proximity to each other. Although neither spoke audibility in a frequency that cut vibrations through the atmosphere, they resumed the heated debate about the preparations that their race had carried out in their unique mind-voices. The Primates had never heard the Angels speak, so they believed, the musical ambience of flexing wings was naturally, the language of the Gods. Both of the conversing Aliens knew that the centuries of effort neared completion. To the brothers, their retaliation against the "INIQUITY." had been narrowed down to two alternatives and soon one of these would become the paramount objective. There was a third choice of passiveness, but Cetheren more that most was adamantly against it. With these undecided options in mind, both had uncontained desires that it would be their scheme that would be selected. A mist that just blew up with the wind bothered Cathbad, the slightly taller of the two and who was also the eldest (Only by milliseconds.). As he wiped the numerous droplets of moisture that began trickling down his abnormally large forehead which was even prominent for one of his race, he turned towards his brother and spoke telepathically.

"Is everything prepared for tonight's CONGREGATION?"

Cetheren who was suddenly distracted by a number of shapes and a hovering opaque white beam of light on a distant lower hillside replied sharply.

"By the globes of our ancestors, yes! The Elder has everything organized and you are well aware of his abilities."

Cathbad, the placid brother still had not got use to these growing and characteristic outbursts from his sibling. He rightly assumed that this World of violence was having an effect on him.

"My brother, what disturbs you? If it is the wind or the infernal liquid, we can exchange places." Volunteered Cathbad; shocked at his brother's malediction.

If Cetheren were possessed of calcium teeth like the Primates, he would have clenched them in anger. Venomously as much as one of their race could muster, he spat out the words in his mind-voice.

"No, it is not that. That's just a minor inconvenience. No, it's because some of Zebulan's followers are observing and monitoring our progress. A number of the DEFILED are concealed by that huge boulder down in the valley. And I am certain that the tainted ones are obviously planning some mischief."

Cetheren's Preceptor-Band focused in on where he saw the crouching figures. But his brother remained indifferent. Calmly, Cathbad reassured his angry sibling.

"Don't be bothered by them. They have been watching us since we first started erecting these new set of mounds. Some of us are already aware of them."

Aghast Cetheren stuttered in his mind-voice, but Cathbad who shrugged with total disregard interrupted him again.

"There is nothing the DEFILED can do. We will put wards in place. Then none of them or any of other of our race can enter the mound without the proper forms of access. When the exodus continues anew, the retinue of

Zebulan will follow as they have always done."

An instant wave of nausea, sudden in its intensity overwhelmed Cetheren as he recalled the decision of the CONGREGATION that Cathbad was to remain behind on this forsaken World when the others left. It would only be a few thousand more cycles of the Planet's elliptical orbit around its Star that these Aliens had scheduled their departure for; but this was an instant for such a long-lived race. No matter which of the two final plans were chosen, it was their judgement that he would oversee its progress. It was ironic that if the third scheme was selected, which neither of them wanted, then they would not be separated from one another. Trembling with visible emotion knowing that his outburst was futile, Cetheren mind-exclaimed in distress.

"Why can I not be the one that remains in your stead? You are too gentle in nature to stay behind on this hostile rock."

"It was the resolution of the host, a vote taken freely by all and I was chosen. Anyway, this place is having a perverse effect on you, so, it is better if you go and settle on a more benign sphere," replied the other to his question.

Feeling proud from his brother's offer, for self-sacrifice was not in their nature; Cathbad knew that their shared grief bound them as one. Basking in the glow of his twins love and admiration, his mind remembered. These two ALASTHA'I had been more than siblings, even since before their eleven millennium enforced exile on this World. They had almost become one person and now within ten more revolutions of the Planet's orbit around the yellow Sun; they would be separated for an unknown length of time. None of the two could accept that neither of them would be physically united together again until the enemy was overcome. Silent now lost in abstract thoughts, both of the Aliens resumed their scrutiny of the mass of workers below. A low buzzing sound; an effect of the heavy atmosphere startled them out of their stillness. The white nimbi above their heads glowed brighter and a spectrum of swirling frequencies danced within their mass. The growing luminance formed into a projection that shot off from the circle of light and began to coalesce into an energy disturbance directly in front of the two off-Worlders.

"A Missive comes," informed Cathbad.

It had been addressed to him, but the sender was well aware that the two inseparable brothers were more than likely together. Both of the nutrient absorbing Aliens stood to formal attention as the air in front of them began to shimmer and warp. They had both recognised the signature tune of the member of the Conclavi which the receiver confirmed.

"It is the Patriarchi Celtairs."

Abruptly the landscape and the horizon ahead of them blurred; then vanished as it was replaced instantly with a huge image of a floating torso, one which was topped with a most regal face. This was a private communication and none of the thousands of other ALASTHA'I gathered on the cliff edge bore witness to the image. On seeing the two proud brothers sharing some of their short remaining time together, Celtair mind-sighed momentarily. His stern features became soft.

"It grieves me that these two have to be separated, but they both know that sacrifices have to be made if our race and indeed the fate of the known Universe is to prevail."

"Greetings esteemed one." The two siblings gestured in unison.

Witnessing the two brothers soaking up minerals, the incorporeal presence from the other side of the Missive said.

"It is good that you are taking sustenance, you will need your strength over the coming days."

"Cut to the more sustainable wind currents. To what do we owe this pleasure of your presence?" Demanded Cetheren interrupting accepted protocol with a question tinged with petulance.

A mortified Cathbad interjected hastily.

"Forgive him Patriarchi, for he knows that we must part soon."

"His anger is expected. We are changing and I understand his quandary; for have I not been in the same position as Cetheren. I have also left the closest of my kin behind on a distant Moon."

Celtair was speaking about his own brother, the Patriarchi Assirah and ninety-nine other ALASTHA'I who had been left behind on a base on a small planetoid. This previous separation of kin was a result of a time when the exile's Mother-ship had been orbiting that rock for over a millennium while they replenished their stocks, hid from the "INIQUITY." and discussed their strategy. The solar system was ideal for the regeneration of their Star-Traveller and their sparse reserves. Their huge ship had to remain static and in close proximity to its Sun as it renewed its power supply. Numerous moons of its thirty satellites had similar crystal constituents to their requirements. Three outer ice bound rocks had an abundance of life giving inhalants, so starvation was diverted for another few millennia. The stocking up process took over two hundred years. Close to the eve of their departure, one of their curious kind discovered to their horror that a primitive life-form similar to the reptiles of this World had become depended on the waste products that were ejected regularly from the Mothership. The natural evolution of the creatures had been circumvented and now it went hand in hand with the dumping of their waste products. At a hastily convened meeting of the CONGREGATION; one of the investigating Patriarchi announced.

"In our ignorance we have unwittingly made this life-form dependent on us. And if we just departed, we would be leaving the creatures to an unknown fate. And my esteemed colleagues, that is identical to doing the work of the INIQUITY."

There was an universal agreement among the host. To them, it mattered little that it had been an unforeseen accident. The problem was discussed and it was decided to leave a group of their brethren behind to solve this unfortunate dilemma. The hundred would follow in another smaller ship after them when this crisis had passed. At the time, Celtair's brother had been chosen along with the others to remain behind. Like everybody else, the Patriarchi expected them to catch up with the rest of their race in the foreseeable future. Cetheren pleaded apologetically as the ejected bitterness evaporated from his system. His new found sense of anger and injustice was always short-lived.

"Of course esteemed one. I am sorry; forgive me, for grief has clouded my thoughts. You most of all understand my predicament"

"There is nothing to forgive." Said the Elder diplomatically ignoring his transgression.

"Now to other matters. As you know, it has taken a long time and much persuasion for our kind to even agree to use the Primates as manual labour. Now the reasons for that decision will become clear. Tonight our exploitation of them will proceed to the next level or we will be forced to abandon this project all together and devote all our efforts to one of the other solutions. And neither of us believes that the other plans will succeed. Cathbad is your report ready for the CONGREGATION?"

"It is completed wise one." Replied his student.

An excited Cetheren interjected.

"If the host agrees with our plan, then Assirah can abandon that ball of lunar dust and leave his charges to their own devices."

"He will not agree to that." Stated his brother.

"That is my sibling's nature and such a thing is worth preserving. I will leave you both and prepare the finishing rays to my own speech."

Celtair gave an impromptu wink that was achieved by his band of light receptors going dark for an instant. It was preceded by a wry smile as his macula widened briefly. The Elder's image blinked for an instant and disappeared. The air crackled in front of the two brothers and the beam of light energy flashed back to the nimbi above their heads. The swirling colours faded and they were restored to their normal white frequency. The horizon and the drop to the iced over landscape below reappeared and the two of them were left with a strange empty and foreboding feeling which neither could dispense with.

"What was that about?" Enquired a troubled Cathbad.

"What do you mean?" Asked his sibling.

"That wink and knowing smile of his macula." Replied the other.

"You have a perception of him and his little quirks. Still, I have a nasty feeling that he and you know who have a surprise planned for the other factions at the CONGREGATION. One that he has not even divulged to us. For certain, it is going to be an interesting meeting of the assembled brotherhood, one that will be remembered for aeons to come."

19

They both laughed and nearly choked because of their sly mirth. The two of them were still taking in nourishment and the brief widening of their macula allowed unusable molecules into their respective digestive systems. As they cleared their intake systems, Cathbad realised sadly.

"Yes, we are definitely changing. If my brother is becoming quick to the unfamiliar traits of anger and impatience, then Celtair is certainly flirting with the trait of deception."

Then in a sombre tone; infused with fierce passion, Cetheren began to lecture his older twin about his belief.

"Those who oppose the use of these Primates are wrong. Granted, they have the desired level of aggressiveness we require, but there is more to them than that. This life-form is a survivor; they have evolved on this harsh rock where only the strongest and fittest organisms prosper. For knowledge sake, even if we do not interfere with them, they will still become the pinnacle of evolution of this World. As proof of their durability, our Scrying globes did a scan of their recent past. Did you know that shortly after our arrival on this Planet, about 50,000 cycles ago, a massive volcano erupted in the Southeast and it caused a global winter? Many hardy species that had existed for millions of cycles up to that time; perished. Our Primate was reduced to about a few thousand in number. By all rights that should have not been enough for them to survive as a species. And now they are thriving again, their numbers are in the millions once again."

By now, the yellow Star had risen fast and all of Aliens began to sweat profusely as the air temperature increased with its ascent. Puddles of water formed at their feet. All along the line of basking nutrient infusers, clouds of gathered molecules also began to plume from their crystal bodies. Without their filaments of protection, the host who were not created in this Solar System could only tolerate the glare of these circumstances for a short period of the morning and evening. It was time to head back to the coolness of their spherical city. With their mood lighting and their appetites sated, the two Aliens leapt from the crater rim and soared into the morning sky. These masters of that medium glided towards their destination that was the permanent base of the ALASTHA'I on the Planet. Exhilaration swept across their outstretched wings as they rode the heavy air currents. The ever-watchful Primates gaped in stupefied awe as flight among bipeds was the sole preserve of the "Angels". Normally, flying or soaring in the dense atmosphere of this World was a mighty effort for those who had not evolved in tandem with the heavy stratosphere of the Planet and was usually done only in exceptional circumstances, either if danger threatened or to impress the natives. But when they were fully sated with absorbed minerals, like now, it became a pleasure. As the two shadows glided towards their distinct Diadems, other ALASTHA'I dropped from the cliff edge randomly. These individuals had also satisfied their hunger and they equally soared effortlessly into the awaiting sky. Visibility now deteriorated with the approach of heavily laden rain clouds that had formed out in the large Western Ocean. A sign that the climate of this Planet was steadily changing, for now there were many more periods of falling liquid hydrogen (Rain.) than ones of solid flaky ice crystals (Snow.) since they first arrived on the blue sphere. The worsening weather now caused the host of mineral taking Aliens to depart the cliff-edge on mass. The intense fluttering of wings caused a group of Primates watching the spectacle to cower and scramble for cover. It was a subconscious memory from when their even more primitive ancestors hid from large flying predators that regularly snatched them from treetops in the equatorial jungles. Even now, some of these killer raptors were still able to seize away their young.

"Winged killers dropping from the sky. What an obnoxious circumstance that the beauty of flight should be used as a tactical advantage." Mind-thought a disgusted Cathbad.

The more prudent exiles reason for leaving the cliff was because of what happened to one of their kind called Gluteen. He had been dozing while he took in minerals and had his macula fully opened. The falling combination of hydrogen and oxygen in their liquid state had entered his vapour ingesting system and effectively drowned him. Now, most were unwilling to take the risk of ingestion during a downpour. Automatically the luminance of the individual Diadem's that made up their exiled city enhanced themselves to compensate for the deteriorating weather. On their lost Crystal Worlds, this adjustment would have been unnecessary, but here the moisture density of this sphere far exceeded the one on their Planets. Through the advancing mist, the globes of light from the singular domes appeared from their height as festering blisters of white exposed on rough skin. Not unlike the kind of disfiguring pustules some of their kin received when caught unawares or by accident in the equatorial parts of the Planet under the harsh glare of the unforgiving yellow Sun that this sphere orbited. It was a painful lesson indeed and under enough exposure, it would become a fatal one. At a glance the globes of their exiled city might appear extremely fragile and delicate, but each seemingly translucent structure was designed to with stand an asteroid impact or even a direct hit from a nuclear detonation. The ALASTHA'I in keeping with their passive nature could not confront the minions of the "INIQUITY." directly. So on their long voyage through space; their engineers developed a cohesive defensive strategy. If the Corruption found them, they would hide behind their indestructible globular shields. Niggled, Cathbad glanced back towards their spacecraft as he sailed through the turbulence of the darkening vista. Suddenly veins of bright lightning tore from the murky sky impairing his vision and as he turned away, he was left with the imprint of neat lines of the silver vessels in his memory. He wondered gloomy.

"Why am I left with the impression of hundreds of tomb markers laid out in neat parallel lines?"

He instantly regretted the comparison as the inevitable bang of thunder followed seconds after the bright flash of light and the fall of liquid hydrogen and oxygen grew heavier. He hoped that this vision of doom would not prove a metaphor for their civilisation. The loud crashes and tingling flashes of the turbulent weather systems was an event that their race had got used to, but some still cringed when an unpredictable bang caught them unawares. Cetheren was not one of these, but the same could not be said about his brother whose Preceptor-Band continually winced after each and every detonation. In response to his uncomfortable situation, the latter hurriedly suggested.

"We have to get out of this. This turbulence could smash us against a solid object."

"Follow me. I want to show you something first." Insisted the other.

The stark symbols of death were still lingering in the taller brother's private thoughts. Caught up in this depressing chain of thought, he spied a bunch of Primates running for shelter from the downpour, making their boisterous way towards a frosted overhang in the steep sides of the cliffs that had once marked out the coast of the long forgotten sea.

"Is this the depths to which we have sunk? Are these filthy primitive creatures our salvation? When we, the seekers of knowledge find something unknown, we analyse it with advanced technology. But these Primates just stick it in their mouths and taste it. If it is good, they swallow and if it is bad, they spit it out. That is the limits of their experimentation"

If their solution was the one chosen at the CONGREGATION, then it was Cetheren who would be the one charged with turning these savages into the end result. But, it would be up to his brother to mould them over the coming centuries. So this is why he had asked his companion in flight to take an unscheduled stop to view the Primates in their unnatural setting. His brother agreed reluctantly as he wanted to be out of the weather system before it got any worse. The two flying Aliens banked away from their Exiled City and glided west until they had cleared the inclement weather. Landing on a damp hill of mush, they shook the clinging moisture from their wings and folded them away. Static now, both of them activated their personal translucent weather shields as squalls blew up without warning. A thin film of transparent light immediately encompassed them. Then Cetheren pointed to a large group of Primates. As they watched the inferior life-forms go about their tasks, a loud screeching sound shattered the background noise of the rumbling storm that was making its way eastwards. It was a signal for the Primates to cease their exertions. The natives of this place filed into rank and marched towards a covered area of flickering light at the other side of the flat tundra. Fascinated Cathbad barely registered Cetheren's mind words.

"Impressive, is it not? They can be disciplined and controlled, but only for the promise of a reward."

His brother nodded in appreciation.

"Observe and perceive what happens next."

The mind-speaker felt sated with a touch of disgust and a trace of horror as he had witnessed what was about to occur on many an occasion. Still focused on the drama below, the watching Aliens saw that the overseeing CRYSTALOID'I had signalled for a break, so that the host of Primates could take nourishment. These Alien intrusions on the tundra were one type of the robotic machines that carried out the various tasks assigned to them by their programmers. The artificial constructions came in all shapes and applications; in essence they were the workforce of their race. Once made from every manifestation of the natural elements of their Home-Worlds, these automations had carried out a multitude of tasks. Now the number of these machines was not sufficient, billions had been left behind during their Diaspora; with good reason. The process of constructing new types from the limited resources of this solid orb was tasking and time consuming, but slow progress was been made with the new materials. A quirky member of their race had given his opinion of these new constructs.

"With their many limbs and solar gatherers, they look like large versions of the invertebrates of this World to me."

Still this impediment of increasing their numbers was actually a boon to the two brothers and the Patriarchi Celtair's argument. Those of their kin that were involved with the other scheme were been hampered by that fact. These specifically designed multi-limbed CRYSTALOID'I below them had been programmed with the primitive speech of the Primates and the ALASTHA'I via the mind-voice used these automations to convey any requests to them.

"The command for ingestion originating from them is transmitted in a pitched frequency that only the Primates can discern. And they have subsequently worked out what it means. That shows a modicum of intelligence."

Wanting to turn away, Cathbad could not. Riveted to the unfolding spectacle happening in front of him, he became aware of the newer robotic machines, now completely constructed from elements found on this Planet moving on silent appendages approaching the now squatting multitude. The Primates babbled excitedly, for they knew what to expect. Their vocal sounds filled the air with wispy water vapours. This reminded Cetheren of the time when a first inspection was carried out on these life forms. One of the exiles named Qentant had theorised.

"These fluffy exhalations is the basis of a primitive language, one that we will decipher."

He had been partially right, the cooling vapour was an effect of their pronouncement. But none of the ALASTHA'I could have imagined back then, the harsh guttural vibrations of their communication method. With their large solar absorbers that mimicked the Aliens own wings, the new types of automations lined up a few metres away from the squatting host. Each machine began to dispense large quantities of foodstuffs from containers on their backs with large mechanical arms; it was as if their creations shared the same revulsion at been so close to the host of Primates as their makers did. The Aliens always kept a healthy distance between themselves and any life on the Planet as the heat perpetuating off an organics biology had a perverse effect on their crystalline forms. The two not of this Bio-sphere's ways watched as the machines extracted large decaying lumps of flesh from some other unfortunate creature of this World and placed them on the ground between groups of clustered host. Both brothers felt uneasy, for this was one of the major taboos from their society that they had managed to cross. Rudimentary implements of tempered metal had been given to the Primates from which their cleverest had quickly converted into weapons to hunt. That was the aborigine's nature, they were co-operative killers.

"Well, given to them is incorrect. They were left around for the Primates to pilfer." Amended Cetheren. *"That eased our consciences over the uses that they put them to."*

"I am beginning to understand more." Said his brother.

This calculated interference enabled the Primates to gather sufficient quantities of prey to feed the growing workforce that the ALASTHA'I needed to complete their tasks. Hunting parties went out and returned with great quantities of meat. Cetheren imparted recent findings on that subject.

"It is a positive boon that the mounds will be completed soon, their flesh gathers have to roam further and farther away."

At first, the waiting Primates watched the victuals and then each other warily. Then as if responding to some unheard signal, the entire host scrambled at a rush to the waiting food. The biggest and strongest reached the nourishment first. With threatening gestures and fierce snarls, the weakest were held back while they took their fill. One of the inferior males who was lower down in the social scale overstepped his station and got too close to the food. He was set upon and quickly beaten to a pulp by his betters. One of the watching Aliens sighed and commented.

"That's another one for the infirmary. This many Primates are not yet socially evolved to co-habit together. It is already over flowing with the sick and the injured."

Cathbad could only agree; the spectacle of instant violence had frightened him.

"We are duty bound to care for the Primates. After all, it was us that gathered them all together in such a small territory."

His sibling also imparted a detail about their behaviour that he had recently become aware of.

"When our advanced medical treatment fails to preserve the life of one of the injured Primates, some of its kind take the body away and perform a funeral ritual. There is genuine grief at the liturgy and the fact that they believe in an afterlife shows that the natives of this World are not such dumb life-forms as most of us assume. As the Patriarchi Celtair constantly reminds us, they show promise of better things."

The rest of the weaker ones held back a safe distance while the dominant ones devoured the meal voraciously. In between hurried mouthfuls of food; they hissed and spat at their inferiors. More machines arrived to balance the diet of the Primates and dispensed familiar fruits and vegetables and even untreated glacial water. Like the rest of the previous offerings it was consumed greedily and when the strongest had sated their appetites, these significant males moved away to rest. The subservient ones seeing their chance rushed in to finish off what remained. Although, Cetheren had witnessed this ritual many times, he always felt sickened and revolted at how another life-form could kill, shred, dismember and consume the body of another living organism.

"So abhorrent compared to our process of ingestion. Still, it is their callous ways that we need now."

When, the weaker and socially inferior Primates had finished their repast, they joined the dominant males for rest, while some of the alpha males indulged in procreation with the females. Older males and females slept in close proximity, heedless of the groans and grunts from the cavorting couples. Others idled about scratching their cranium cases, this constant habit caused more than one sarcastic Alien to comment.

"It is as if they have to keep checking that their brain is still there."

Another siren sounded, its resonance rippled within their Preceptor-Bands. It signalled the return of more machines burdened with latrines which they deposited in neat rows in front of the Primates. With an air of puffed up self-importance the dominant ones moved to the cubicles to relieve themselves. This was another aspect of life on this Planet that revolted the Aliens, the fact that many life forms on this World carried the undigested remains of meals; once living things still in their stomachs until a need arose to eject the disgusting organic mess. The thought of such things made the ALASTHA'I queasy to their pores. With much banter and humour, they performed their absolutions and then grudgingly were forced back to continue the appointed tasks given to them by their Gods.

"Those portable organic collectors were definitely one of your better ideas. Do you remember before they were introduced and the Primates just defecated anywhere that suited them." Observed Cathbad.

"Yes and the whole valley was littered with digested remains and our pores itched constantly with the decaying waft." Replied his sibling.

"Where does it go now?" Asked the other.

"Large CRYSTALOID'I with deep interiors remove it to another valley far away, where it is piling up into another mound that would rival this one. Each deposited collection is covered with a layer of other decaying matter. We should let the carrion and scavenging animals have it. Then its removal and burial would be one less burden for the overburdened machines. They have to be purified after every trip and that is time consuming."

"And make the same mistake we made on the World that Patriarchi Assirah is managing." Warned Cathbad.

"It is not the same; this Planet is far different than the rock that the Elder is stranded on. We have not introduced an alien substance. What we are disposing of, is already a part of this bio-sphere. The animals of this World already consume each other and small micro-organisms are probably already breaking it down. It would not be against the natural order that has already been established here. In fact, the organic waste is probably helping life to thrive here and no species will die out when we leave." Reasoned, his brother.

"Unlike what we are doing to these Primates. We have given them the tools to wipe out endemic life-forms."

He did not miss the sarcasm that was evident in the others mind-words.

"As much as we hate it. It is necessary for our survival." Insisted Cetheren.

"Two inaccuracies do not make a right."

"Agreed, but this is the only flight-path left to us. After all, we require them more than they need us."

"I know; that is the Great Paradox." Uttered his brother with regret.

A really loud boom infringed on their conversation and a rumbling from the south west promised that a really intense storm was approaching.

"Even the elements of this atmosphere are in constant confrontation. The hot air clashes with the cold air. What a place."

Sensing his brother's growing disquiet, Cetheren suggested.

"Come let us proceed to where the vista is more pleasing."

"What a good idea."

Cathbad felt his dark mood dispersing like the vapours from his macula. Nothing cheered him up more like the idea of visiting the "Contentment Diadems." and its respite from the outlandishness of their existing circumstances. Both of them unfurled their wings; downed protection shields and took to the air once again. The flying Aliens arrived at their destination well before the storm hit. These domes recreated aspects of their Home Planet of CRYSTALIOS and the Queens chamber before the Holocaust of the "INIQUITY.". Inside this haven, images pulsated with frequencies comfortable to their receptors. Entwined in its embracing remembrance of things gone, it was a sanctuary where any of

26

the exiles could re-enact the mating ritual with the virtual image of the Matriarch of their species or glide through vanished landscapes before they were melted into oblivion. The polychromatic colours of their birthplace shone as a beacon of remembrance, the soft octiums, calsums, silcolums and plisums had their last visual representations in here. The immensely pleasurable place was built using enormous reserves of energy, which could have been put to a more practical use. But as it kept all of the ALASTHA'I sane, it was judged to be well worth the expenditure of those valuable commodities. Strangely, Celtair never ventured into these recreations of their former existence and when Cathbad had asked him.

"Why not?"

The Elder explained.

"On the last morning of our forced exile, I happened to be at my home under the blue Chopila Mountains. Alas, I had little inclination, it was to be my last sapphire sunrise over those majestic heights. If I had known then of the events of that day, I would have cherished that moment and might have stayed behind and perished. No, I will keep that final image of my Home World in my mind. It reinforces my resolve to regain what we have left behind."

His student was well aware of the retreat under the Chopila heights; it was the paramount place for meditation and contemplation. High altitude methane rain popped in soft chemical reactions along the 12,000 metre towering mountain chain, eroding the mineral landscape and causing an abundant flow of nutrient diversity to cascade down their slopes into a sea of condensed chemicals. This potent rainbow coloured lake wafted a concentrated mist of sustenance that invigorated the ASCETIC'I. This chemical soup of inhalation enhanced the clarity of the mind and when an individual struggled with a solution to a conundrum, it was the place to visit. The memory of that lost beautiful place also hurt Cetheren deeply. So he acknowledged with an old adage of their race.

"I think Celtair is correct, it is better to let inactive CRYSTALOID'I stay switched off."

As Cetheren and his twin entered the dome, they left behind the drab colourless World of rock behind them. A welcome blast of petrified air, rich in the minerals of their natural diet swayed his dark mood. The slightly older of the winged Aliens exhaled a sigh of relief. He now experienced the once familiar sensations of his lost World, a symphony of majestic harmony compared to the harsh crackle, he had left outside. Once, he had told one of their kind.

"I am convinced that the sounds of this Planet are in effect nothing more than Primate excretion."

The other had laughed at his observation till the vapours filled his macula. Once inside, Cathbad's sibling had chosen to glide through the meagre orchards of fragrant Pulpa fruits, their frosty and shiny oval produce glistening with the promise of delicious inhalation. Painful remembrance made Cetheren mind-utter.

"Back home on my lost World, you could cavort among the plantations for hours on end; gliding along while inhaling a variety of fragrances. Here, resources are desperately scarce and all you have is a modicum of those expanses."

Someone had programmed in an aspect of their climate. The plants swayed in recognition of the artificial methane rain that mimicked the real circumstances of the Home Planets. In reality, huge drops of liquid methane began life in the cooler upper atmosphere and fell rapidly to the surface. But because of the increasing heat near the Planet's crust, the bubbles evaporated at three metres above ground where patient receptors of crystal flora reached for them. Because of their instant diffusion, the falling drops were known as puffballs. Similar to the ALASTHA'I wings, the crystal plant's appendages were formed throughout millions of centuries of evolution as their long sinuous tendrils flicked from plant stems and snatched the methane drops from the atmosphere, before the liquid bounty evaporated. In this recreation, the soothing red Sun had just reach the zenith of a Summers day and millions of crystal insects, 300mm in length floated among the vapour orchards, proudly exhibiting their rainbow magnificence. In here, their numbers were in the low thousands. If the heat of the powerful Star of this Planet intruded on this piece of paradise, then all the flora and fauna in the Contentment Diadem would solidify and shatter into brittle glass shards. Cetheren watched as three CRYSTALOID'I plucked blue crystal pomegranates from the sleek branches of the fruit trees. These gifts from the plants would be distilled into the finest digestion fragrances. He idly picked one of the fragrant fruits himself and infused its mineral fullness. This pure reminder of his Home World intoxicated him and his mind drifted back to where Silicon Avians and Crystal-like Mammals ran carefree among the vines of lost forests, where pools of methane vapour held the most exquisite aquatic creatures. This was a place free from predators where all sustenance was inhaled from its existing life-forms. Crystal beaded rivers of silica flowed from far away mountaintops, meandering towards Methane Seas. He yearned for a sight of the vast schools of giant fan tailed mineral gatherers that trawled the gooey Oceans back on CRYSTALIOS, splendid in their vast rainbow fans fluttering in the gentle breezes near to the shore. That was only a distant memory now. But the expenditure of energy needed to create this spectacle had been judged to be too high. Also, the Contentment Diadem could not re-create the plastic polar seas or the magnificent equatorial globular Tree City of Chist. Its multi-coloured globes hung like crystal pomegranates from an inter-locking crystal stem towering over a 1,000 metres into the bright methane clouds. Strangely, the allure of the lost Worlds had little impact on him today and he felt that he had lost something within himself. He peered through the green glow of the day towards the globular capital where Cathbad had chosen to spend his time. The majestic city of multi-coloured refracted crystal, gone now and in its place, an aggregate of vitrified glass shards. Melted now were the grand helix spirals where individual Diadems meandered up their great ridges of crystal. Living quarters started at the bottom and rose one by one each day giving the occupant a different view of the city. When a globe reached the top of a ridge, it again descended one by one each subsequent day until it reached the ground and started the process over again. This was an artefact from their communal past; it ensured that every ASCETIC'I got an equal view of the magnificent city. Celtair once commentated in a moment of sarcasm.

"There are flightless avians on the icy southern Continent of this rock that appear to do the same thing. They constantly shuffle around."

Cathbad on the other hand had elected to visit the Queen's Helix supported chambers. The perpetual Mother of their race chambers was not in fact a truly enclosed space. In the centre of Campus, the capital city of CRYSTALIOS, there stood a tall twisted slender pillar of five interlocking strands of gleaming white crystal. It had been crafted from five distinct pieces of the same mineral and rose a hundred metres into the green sky. Attached to its top tilted like a solar ray collector and perfectly balanced at its forty-five degree angle was the conclave platform where the propagator of them all dwelt. From this rotating perch, she could take in the vast amount of minerals which she required for her daily intake. The replica created on this Alien World by her exiled offspring was a recreation in exact detail of the mating venue where their beloved Mother still dwelt. The Queen's body was colossal, over two hundred metres long. She was in fact, a massive grub like creature, uniformly blue and devoid of adornments and vanities. This enormous organism had only one desire, the propagation of her race. She was in essence, a baby-making machine. But, she was beautiful to her male offspring. Nobody knew how the Mother had evolved from a race of male lineage. Strangely from a society of knowledge gatherers, it was a question that was never asked, her presence among them was an accepted fact. The Queen had many sexual receptors, as she was the sole female among them when they were the ASCETIC'I. After their birth, her children underwent a genetic transformation that altered their chemical make-up. This enabled those who were born from her to become the fathers of another generation. Her male offspring performed the sexual act lined up at her receptors like piglets of this World suckling their mother's teats. This constant injection of male fluid was processed through her reproductive system, fathering new generations. Each new offspring was born on a yearly cycle of the Planet CRYSTALIOS (Twins were the rare exception.) and each new life had been a joyous and welcome celebration. One became a sibling of another when the birth came in sequence. So when one ASCETIC'I had been born, the next years grub was his immediate relative and the year after was the latter's brother. But, the first and the third bore no kinship other than been born from the Queen. So in this long-lived race, an individual had one sibling and no more. Because of the Corruption's ministrations; this newly named race of the ALASTHA'I had never fathered offspring as the matriarch which satisfied their needs was now only a simulation; not the real thing.

NOW, WHEN HER CHILDREN NEEDED HER THE MOST, SHE WAS LOST TO THEM.

Hours later unlike his brother; Cathbad left the Contentment Diadem feeling completely refreshed and invigorated, he proceeded to his private quarters for a well-anticipated sleep. Like most life-forms, including the Primates, the winged Aliens also needed this period of recuperation. It was one of the mystery's that still eluded the savant race. Those that studied this field knew.

"In all forms of life that we have encountered, sleep allows the body to repair muscles and tissues, crystalline or sinew. This less active state enables the brain to process information and organise thoughts. But its deeper purpose still eludes us."

These crystalline bipeds did not dream however. They just shut down and then rebooted hours later, awakening with no recollection of that period of existence. Here on this hostile, stressful and ever changing World, the duration of sleep needed exceeded the length required on their Home Worlds. His brother had left earlier, his desire unfulfilled because of the constant interruption by the dark thoughts of his assignment. Unknown to himself, Cetheren was changing faster than the rest of the ALASTHA'I and had developed a rebellious nature. In fact, the twin had voluntary embraced the challenge that he had been given. With the newly evolved trait of stubbornness firmly entrenched into his macula, he could see no other solution to their predicament than his own factions scheme.

"No more fleeing from the Corruption and its minions, I will stand and resist the lure of the INIQUITY in memory of our lost brothers and our tragic Mother. Her supreme sacrifice will not be in vain."

Locked into this giddy frame of mind, he knew.

"Cathbad would be horrified at this vow. He would know that it is an outburst aimed at our kind and their inherent weaknesses. But still, I feel elation, not despair, for Celtair has promised to gain an advantage at the next meeting of the CONGREGATION."

The Patriarchi had hinted to the two brothers that he had a design that would sway the gatherings vote in their favour. They also had a plan B, for the three deceivers had a dark secret which none of them revealed to their fellow ALASTHA'I. It was a plot shrouded in such deceit that would shock their exiled community to the core.

"And, if the others found out about our deception; my brother, myself and Celtair might also be declared as DEFILED or even something else. But, it has to be a risk worth taking for the salvation of our people. And if we three are the only ones capable of this step, then so be it."

But inexplicably, the consequences of discovery of their dark enigma did not induce the same level of fear as it once had. Because, if they were discovered; then at least their separation would not occur, as Cathbad would not be allowed to remain behind on this dirt-ball of a Planet to supervise a plan that would then be rejected.

"Although our freedom will be curtailed by an edict from the Conclavi, at least we can be still together. So it seems that for once, I might have the choice between the lesser of two evils."

A wicked mind-laugh that no longer disturbed him issued forth from Cetheren's soul, but nobody heard it as the cautious ALASTHA'I had his room dampers on. Still, if his outburst of merriment had been over-heard, the listener would have come to the conclusion that another of their race had joined the ranks of the shunned. But, whatever direction the disgruntled exile was heading in, the developing Alien was certain that he was not taking the flight-path of the DEFILED.

"Yes, I am taking a course that could easily dam me and my kind more than the path the renegades have taken. But it is the correct course."

The surprising thing to him was that he was no longer in denial and he was gradually coming to terms with his decision.

"Yes, we are definitely changing." Amended Cetheren.

II.

EIGHT LUNAR CYCLES OF THE UN-NAMED PLANET'S MOON EARLIER

The ALASTHA'I used the time measurement of a second. This initial calculation had no connection to the rotation of their Home World or the extent of its orbit around its Star. Their finest Mathematicians based this computation on the duration of 9,192,631,770 periods of the radiation corresponding to the transition between two hyperfine levels of the ground state of the caesium-133 atom. The atom had to be at rest and approaching the theoretical temperature of absolute zero. So on every World in their experience, these space-travelling gatherers of scientific knowledge had an inbuilt compulsion to standardised time with this dimension and create a calendar. On this latest stop of their continued exile, sixty of these seconds became one hour; twenty-four hours became one rotation of the blue Planet on its own axis and three hundred and sixty-five of these rotations equalled one orbit of the Biosphere around its Sun. Their experts in this field had to make a slight adjustment during every fourth orbit of the Planet around the Star. By a bizarre coincidence, these local measurements of time nearly equated with those of the Queen's World of CRYSTALIOS. The difference in time estimation between the vastly different spheres was of so fine of a fraction that it became invalid. It was one welcome and familiar comfort on this strange and hostile place. In total contradiction to his changing beliefs; Cetheren for one saw this similarity as a sign that his race had chosen the right base for their ministrations. It was an assumption that had no basis in science.

As the entire community of the ALASTHA'I was confined in the temperate domes of their globular city during an unusual balmy day for the brief summer of the northern latitudes, the Aliens went about their tasks oblivious to the discomfort of the outside heat. The general consensus on times like this was.

"That bright Sun is always too big in the sky."

More serious opinions were circulated too.

"The background radiation emitted from our own Cosmic furnace is the equivalent absorbed by one individual of our race. What this Star gives off corresponds to twenty of our crystal based bodies."

All of these Aliens from a small red dwarf solar system did however concur.

"It seems that this yellow Star is waiting to pounce at any moment and devour the entire Planet along with ourselves and everything on it."

It was an irrational fear, since their scientists had calculated that their refuge would endure for another fifteen billion cycles of its orbit around the Sun. Away from their glowing Diadems, CRYSTALOID'I of various purposes kept the Primates under control during this preferred period of confinement. The automations masters rarely ventured outside during the inclement weather and when the ALASTHA'I did, it was in translucent and encrusted suits of light. Such apparitions only confirmed their divinity to the bipedal natives. On this mid-Summer day, normal routines were broken as a Missive sent to the whole population halted every pursuit. In a sparkle of imposed inference, every individual's personal communication device was over ridden. Preceptor-Bands buzzed to the one frequency and the single event that the exiled community had been anticipating with expectant pores for centuries was about to commence.

The long awaited and predicted moment had finally arrived.

Each enthusiastic individual received an image of the entire Conclavi of Patriarchi. One of the sombre governing body told the bated population.

"Four important Missives were about to be sent."

Each light based communication was to be considered in private or among friend's and then open minds could decide which one they favoured before the formality of the next meeting of the CONGREGATION. Their esteemed council shimmered briefly and was replaced with an image of six ALASTHA'I. The image of Trelix and those of his faction appeared to everyone. Trelix mind-spoke for them.

"MISSIVE ONE.

Memorandum for the return of the old ways and the use of a non-aggression pact. Dated in the thirty-first millennium of our imposed exile from our Mother Planet.

Proposed by Trelix.

Reasons for the use of passive resistance.

As the CONGREGATION will note, our race has no comprehension of actually committing physical destruction. We have not the knowledge of weapon making and even if we had, the genetic block would not allow us to take life. We propose that our cherished race flee to the other end of the Universe, find suitable Worlds, rebuild and maybe one day, we will have transformed enough to send a rescue force back for our beloved Mother. This is the ideal option for our race as we are not strong enough to confront the "INIQUITY." and its minions yet and will never be. So to sum up, here are the reasons for our solution to the quandary of our people.

1.We have not the construction capability of the lost manufacturing factories. We could not produce enough machines to confront the CRYSTALOID'I legions. And if we choose this method, we will use up enormous resources during their construction that could be used for continued flight and concealment. In fact life will become even more unbearable.

2.The genetic block is still in place. We would be just slaughtered again and this time there might be no survivors. Imagine the loneliness of our Queen, if that event was to occur.

3.Finding suitable Planets at the edges of the known universe is the ideal option. It would take an eternity for the malfunctioning CRYSTALOID'I to locate us and the advantage lies with us.

4.And certainly the most import factor is that some of us have already interacted far too much with the endemic life-forms of this World. And this should be stopped now before it proceeds any further.

Missive ends."

Trelix's short speech came to an end and his image dissipated. One viewer told his two confidants.

"Most of the older generation of exiles will favour his argument."

After a decent respite, the droll Alien was replaced with an image of Celtair, Cathbad and Cetheren. The two brothers appeared humble and unassuming. Their mentor spoke in his confident mind-voice for the trio. His two students had no problem with the Elder putting forward their scheme. No ALASTHA'I could do justice to a debate, more than this Patriarchi. Many of the exiled population would be swayed to their opinion, just by the fact that Celtair backed this audacious scheme.

"MISSIVE TWO.

Memorandum for the use of the Primates as the weapon to confront the "INIQUITY."

Dated in the thirty-first millennium of our imposed exile from our Mother Planet.

Proposed by Celtair, Cetheren and Cathbad.

Reasons for the adaptation of the said Primates for our purpose.

As the much learned CONGREGATION will have noted, the survival of a species on this World depends on the prowess of the strongest and most prolific. Although, there are many more powerful predators than the Primate on this Planet, we have chosen this genus for our needs. Other sub species from this group contain Lemurs, lorises, monkeys and apes, but none of those perform to our requirements. Even recently, it has rid the Planet of the last of the semi-intelligent bipeds. The top predator in this chain is this homicidal Primate whose aggression is instinctive and brutal. It is nearly unique in that it will kill for pleasure unlike other species of animal that will kill only by instinct or because of food or competition in its need to reproduce. With no perceivable threat, our chosen life-form will kill on impulse. This is its bellicose nature. Other factors have also been taken into account and are listed.

1. The Primate has a highly developed brain. (Compared to any other life form we have thus far encountered.) It has the basic understanding of using abstract images

for an accumulation of complex memory storage.

2. It has limbs that contain opposable first digits. (This will enable them to use our modified technology.)

3. It lives in small family orientated social groups, which are the beginnings of more complex social relationships. (It will be easier to mould them into a vast resistance force.)

4. It has developed a basic language.

5. Its females can breed all year round. It is capable of producing enormous numbers.

6. It can be genetically altered to suit our needs.

7. It has enormous potential for aggressive violence.

8. It has a concept of justified revenge. If a member of any other lifeform loses an individual to predators, it just continues on with its life cycle. But the Primates will actively seek out the perpetrator and try and end its existence. This can be used against our machines.

Celtair halted his oration, took a deep breath through his macula and announced.

"Missive ends."

Most of the exiled host could not believe what their audio and visual senses were telling them. Of course, they had their suspicions; but to have them confirmed was another thing. This was an unheard of and profound step for their once non-interfering race to be taking. It was completely against their former ethos. But, it would find acceptance with the younger generation of exiles.

Following soon after the second Missive, there came a third one. The receiving Alien host had barely got their inhalation pores around the previous communiqué. Celtair's image was replaced by a large ALASTHA'I with a rotund face. It was the exile known as Naisi. He was the author of the third scheme and the Patriarchi Celtair's main opposition. With similar designs to the Elder, he was advocating his own plan. The exile spoke to the listening throng.

"MISSIVE THREE.

Memorandum for the use of robotic CRYSTALOID'I as the method for confronting the "INIQUITY."

Dated in the thirty-first millennium of our imposed exile from our Mother Planet.

Proposed by Naisi.

Reasons for the continued research into converting robotic machines for our purpose.

1.   The Corruption already uses transformed machines, turning them from peaceful tools

into killing objects. In view of its success, it would be prudent to follow a solution

that has already been proven.

2.   This World has an abundance of resources to produce them, it will take time and effort.

But we will be able to manufacture enough of them, if we devote all our priorities to this.

3. *By employing such machines we keep the moral high ground of not exploiting an existing*
     species.
4. *We remain in control of the CRYSTALOID'I, unlike with a genetically modified organism.*
5. *CRYSTALOID'I composed of artificial elements would be more superior in strength, durance and longevity than any biological life form.*

Smugly, he signed off.

"Missive ends."

Naisi deliberately kept his presentation short and concise to promote the belief that he was supremely confident and assured of his proposition. He told his nearest companion in private mode.

"Unlike the wind sac Celtair."

He had purposefully taken the middle ground between his two opponents and was certain that he would pilfer votes from both of them. His portly figure was replaced by the image of the Conclavi of Patriarchi and one of their number addressed the exiled throng. This fourth communication was a rare event, because it was sent by the united council of the Elders, this Missive was called an Encyclical. The last one had been sent aeons ago on the Mothership. It usually heralded a crisis in the lives of the now nomadic ALASTHA'I.

"MISSIVE FOUR.

An Encyclical from the Conclavi of Patriarchi.

Memorandum for the three sides of the debate for the solution to the crisis of our imposed exile.

Dated in the thirty-first millennium of our imposed exile from our Mother Planet.

Forwarded by the Conclavi of Patriarchi.

As all three parties have finalised their millennium long preparations, a gathering of the CONGREGATION will convene and finally decide on this, the most important issue of our race.

Memorandum ends.

An enormous wave of titillation swept through the ranks of the exiles; excited individuals contacted each other in a buzz of unprecedented mind traffic and began to take sides or try to convert one of their kind to their choice. It was finally up to the CONGREGATION to make the final decision of their race. For once; all of the exiled Aliens agreed that this would be an epic and unprecedented meeting of the esteemed gathering and one that would be remembered as long as their cherished race existed. The record of its events would be studied again and again as long as the last ALASTHA'I inhaled nutrients. Not far away from the exiled city, another winged Alien and former Patriarchi waited for news of the great debate that he would not participate in. This being would never be invited to give his point of view, not that he wanted to anyway. For he served the thing that had driven them from their Home World's in the first place and he had only thoughts of their destruction; not their salvation.

III.

"How do I know where Mescal has gone? He probably does not know where he is himself. For all that I am aware of; he might not even be on this liquid hydrogen of a ball. More than likely, he has gone cavorting around the Solar System." Mind-asked Cetheren of himself ill-temperedly.

It was on the sultry night of the three Missives along with the Encyclical from the Conclavi and his wings had just been ruffled. All of the ALASTHA'I were still comfortably nested in their temperate domes and he was the exception bar one. He had just left the Patriarchi Celtair and his brother Cathbad in the Elder's Diadem on this fool's errand after he had been asked that question concerning the afore mentioned Patriarchi's absence. His mentor's room dampers had been on all through the night while the three of them had been discussing their perceived assumptions to the reactions of their Alien brethren to recent events. Not wanting to be abroad in the continuing and disagreeable weather; his first excuse was.

"So, he is not answering our personal Missives. We half expected him to join us, but he has not shown up. Don't tell me that either of you are surprised at that?"

Celtair still asked of him.

"Go and see if you can locate the wayward Patriarchi anyway. We need his input on this."

He countered in a huff.

"You should be so fortunate."

Still, he went anyway. Cetheren had already noticed that these wilful disappearances of his new mentor were becoming a more frequent event. He was now searching for him because of Celtair's request and would check the missing exiles usual haunts.

"Where would you be; Mescal?"

At the utterance of the Weapon-Masters name, the winged Alien was set on a path of reminisce through his recent past, back to tens of centuries earlier when he was aboard the vast Star-Traveller that had brought them here after their long flight from the "INIQUITY.". The immense vessel, the ark of their species was aptly named.

"EXPECTATION."

But in private conversations among some of the reluctant travellers, it was known as.

"The Spacegrub."

This was due to its larval shaped appearance. The huge one hundred and fifty kilometre long vessel had an outer skin of light gossamer which protected layers of crystal and metal on its inside. It voyaged from one Star-System to another by folding space. An ancient ASCETIC'I Engineer named "Dimensi." had found.

"This is the shortest route between two points and not a straight line as

was the norm on three dimensional Planets."

This Star-Traveller was the Mother-ship and it held the last of the remaining survivors of the exiled race, just over a hundred thousand strong. It was during this long space journey that the character of the ALASTHA'I had irreversibly changed. After recovering from the shock of forced exile, their species had altered mentally and could now contemplate theories and ideas that were once unattainable. The traumatisation of their forced ostracism had hardened them slightly and one Patriarchi debated privately.

"Would it be enough to overcome the INIQUITY?"

It was on-board this sprawling craft that the survivors had passed from the boundaries of fear and cowering and into the beginnings of organised resistance.

In Cetheren's remembered past; he and Cathbad were making their way back to their living quarters on board the craft. A half-hour before, both brothers had just left another fruitless session of the regularly convened CONGREGATION, which had been recreated on a much smaller scale on board the expansive ship. They had been frustrated at every turn by the antagonising and eloquent speaking Naisi. He was a vocal opponent to their plans and their most outspoken opposition. On leaving the great debating chamber, their main opponent infuriated them further by gloating in his mind voice, which only the two brothers could perceive.

"Where is the sanctimonious bore that usually speaks for you two? You should have brought the Patriarchi with you. What was he thinking in leaving you two grubs to debate with me? He must be slipping into his dotage."

If Cetheren was capable of an act of violence, he would have surely have decked the haughty upstart, but all he could do was stutter a failed retort. Naisi just laughed into his Preceptor-Band and left him standing there fuming. His brother clasped his broad shoulder above his folded wings and advised.

"Just ignore him."

On exiting the floating tubes at the level of their living quarters aboard the huge space vessel, the still annoyed brothers proceeded down the crystalline corridor in agreed silence. On entering Cetheren's private quarters, the disappointed duo were confronted by an ecstatic Celtair whose macula were flared in open titillation. Seeing the excitement etched into the honest visage, they both gaped in bewilderment.

"What is he so pleased about? This was the worst session yet. Naisi made us look like fools." Demanded Cethern.

Celtair and the two twins switched into personalised mode, so that only the three of them could communicate and not be overheard by anyone. This underhandedness was a sign of the times that now prevailed among the savant race.

"I not sure, but by the smug look that's on his Preceptor-Band, I am assuming that we will soon find out." Answered his brother, speaking as if Celtair could not perceive them conversing with each other.

"We can mind-speak openly. I have already activated the cabin dampers. For I cannot contain my joy any longer at what I have discovered. You both know that I have been missing from the CONGREGATION for a few days of ship time." Implied Celtair with an edge of suspense.

Days onboard the travelling bubble of their World were still measured in a standard revolution of the Queen's Planet, as day and night had no physical reference on the giant ship as it voyaged through the black empty spaces between Star-Systems.

"Yes. We sorely missed your debating skills at the debating chamber." Interjected Cetheren slyly.

In his excitement, the Elder missed the sarcasm directed at him and unable to contain himself, he blurted out.

"Another Patriarchi has survived the holocaust. I have been in contact with him."

This simple statement stunned both brothers.

"Who?"

The question came simultaneously; as visions of various missing Patriarchi's flashed through their awareness. But they were not prepared for the answer.

"Mescal!"

Sudden joy, in a bitter instant became tangible disappointment. Aghast, both siblings stared at Celtair, but they remained silent. Their mind voices became subdued and their macula remained inactive. Such was the level of stillness; there was no need of the room's dampers. Finally, Cathbad managed to mind-speak in stuttered anger for the both of them.

"This is the worst possible news that you could have given us. Mescal is a minion of the Corruption and not perceived in a good light. He should be captured and isolated like his fellow cohort Zebulan. Together, those two deviants formed the axis of iniquity that nearly destroyed us forever."

Nobody wanted to be reminded of the prisoner kept below in an isolation chamber, the one who had betrayed them to the ministrations of the "INIQUITY.". It was perceived among the less enlightened ALASTHA'I that just mentioning Zebulan's name might convert you to his dark cause. Most mind-thought that it was an irrational fear, but others of the host were still out on that theory. A distressed Cetheren cut in.

"Certainly. I agree with my brother. He is equally responsible for the destruction of our beloved Worlds and the slaughter of millions of innocent souls."

Before the horrific events than nearly destroyed them, illness and death though rare, did visit the ASCETIC'I. Expiration was seen as a gradual fading from one state to another, but the brutally of instant death and finality of the Holocaust had shaken these long-lived beings to their very core. Most of the old beliefs were been systematically eroded as a result of this unwanted flirtation with extinction.

"Break off all contact with him immediately." Insisted Cathbad.

His twin agreed with a statement that once would have been beyond their reasoning.

"Put him and Zebulan in an escape pod and direct it and them to the nearest boiling hot Sun."

Fortunately or unfortunately, nobody was capable of that course of action yet.

"No, hear me out. We were erroneous with our judgement. All the facts were not available to us at the time and so we have done Mescal a great injustice. Everybody has condemned him falsely. I truly believe this." Acknowledged Celtair with genuine sadness.

"What do you mean?" Enquired Cathbad.

He was one who required all the facts before he committed himself to a decision.

"Who do you think saved us? This last remnant of our beloved race. Who made ready this craft and provided the means for escape? Who saved the Queen and trapped the INIQUITY and rescued Zebulan from the clutches of the Corruption? Not I, nor any of the other Patriarchi."

He paused for effect as the two brothers became intrigued.

"No. It was not Mescal who betrayed us. Of all of our entire race, he was the sincerest believer in good. He never gave up trying to put the corrupt Patriarchi back on the path of righteous. No, he kept returning to the moon of banishment where we isolated Zebulan, always believing that the next visit would prove rewarding and our lost brother would renounce the evil taint and return to the fold. But alas, he never realised that the one he was trying to save had chosen the dark path freely and he had plans of his own, One, which included the subversion of the unfortunate Mescal. He never knew that the "Evil." and our lost brother had fused into the one being. On the eve of our destruction, Zebulan imbued with the Corruption requested a meeting with Mescal. The Patriarchi of course agreed and when he arrived on the moon, the Zebulan/INIQUITY thing displayed none of their usual arrogance. Using all of their guile, the melded being convinced him that he had reformed and the presence of the amoral taint was gone. Mescal was over joyed and the gullible Patriarchi believed that our lost bother had truly repented because he really wanted to. Convinced that the returned soul would be no threat, security was relaxed and Zebulun was given the freedom of access to our Archives."

"A fatal mistake" Concurred both twins.

Celtair continued.

"Mescal's naivety in the ways of deceitfulness became our downfall. He

never realised that his devotion to good could be equalled or even surpassed by another embracing this unfamiliar trait of evil. Thus, the prisoner escaped and plotted the path of our downfall. When he discovered the enormity of his decision, the wise Patriarchi had gained some conception of the depravity among us. Mescal tried to rectify his actions and trap the "Evil." and been the epiphany of goodness; he attempted to rescue Zebulan again. But, he also made ready the escape ship and fitted it out with archives of our entire knowledge. Then he lured us there, thus saving us and this remnant of our civilisation. For if we had been in the CONGREGATION on that fateful day, we would have certainly perished along with the rest of our kin."

"So it was him who mimicked the call of the gathering and lured us to the Mother-ship." Cathbad realised.

"That is the only logical explanation." Agreed the Elder.

Both brothers reappraised Mescal and sadly bonded with the misguided Patriarchi, while Cetheren alone whispered.

"So Mescal was betrayed more than any of us."

"Nearly as much as our Mother." Added his sibling.

"Such is the way of the defilement." Stated Celtair.

The three of them reassessed the implications of this new information and one of the brothers stated the obvious.

"We must introduce him back to the CONGREGATION. The host must know the truth. I am sure he would make a big difference to our plight when the others realise that he is innocent of the great betrayal." Said an excited Cetheren.

"Yes, the scale of his knowledge is invaluable. He is still the greatest mind among us." Established Cathbad.

"No! We will leave him where he is." Replied Celtair as a peculiar tinge of compassion caught in his mind-voice.

The other two looked at the Elder strangely. Both became perplexed at his unusual outcry and mind-asked in unison.

"What?"

"We cannot let his presence be known." Said Celtair.

"Why not?" Asked Cetheren, mind-speaking for his brother as well.

"He has become our redemption." Stated Celtair.

"How is that possible?" Exclaimed both siblings.

"Mescal has been inside the "INIQUITY." and understands its goal. He has retrieved vital data that will help us in our struggle. As he had been unwitting involved in our downfall, the Patriarchi could now be our saviour." Answered Celtair.

"That would be ironic." Said Cathbad.

"That is more of a reason to bring him back." Implored Cetheren.

"Come let us converse with him. Then you will understand why he must remain hidden." Advised the Elder.

The two brothers still unbalanced by Celtair's revelation agreed to accompany the Patriarchi. Like the rest of the existing ALASTHA'I, both of them had never realised who they had to thank for their narrow escape during the Holocaust. Like all of the ragged survivors, they remembered the confusion when the false call of the CONGREGATION had brought them inside the hull of the "EXPECTATION." and not the revered debating chamber. The memory of standing around inside the great ship where bafflement was rife and heated debates began was still strong in the collective memory. All the immediate controversy was cut off in stunned disbelief as destructive beams of light alighted from near orbit and erupted in huge flashes of brilliance. Having never witnessed warfare before, the ASCETIC'I had no comprehension of global destruction. As they stood around stupefied watching the liquefaction of all that they had known, the engines of the vast Star-Traveller suddenly ignited and it rose from the ground. In response, their age-old inbuilt system of self-preservation rendered them comatose. Well before the hundred thousand souls that had been lured aboard had regained their senses, the accelerating ship reached orbit and set off on the course that had been pre-programmed. Thus, these shipbound remnants of their race had been saved from the total destruction of everything they had ever known and the fate of those who had been left behind. The ships communication systems continued to receive images of hell. All across their Worlds, cityscapes had been dissolved into the consistency of melted toffee and when the structures re-hardened; it left a landscape of tortured and twisted angles. Eventually, its passengers recovered and received these dreadful depictions. In their growing panic, the ship's systems were over-ridden and the shell-shocked survivors sped faster away from the annihilation of everything they had ever known. Now tens of centuries later, Celtair and his two bemused companions left Cetheren's living quarters and re-entered the crafts transport tubes. The Patriarchi voiced their destination and the three of them floated downwards. The brothers looked at each other; they were more than slightly confused at the Elder's choice of destination. It was to a part of the ship, that no exile had reason to venture. During the half hour-long descent of the asteroid-sized starship, Celtair began to fill in the gaps about how he had discovered that Mescal had not perished during the holocaust. The mind speaker began his narration sure that none of their race could eavesdrop on them down here.

"After a few months on the ship and still recovering from the terrible events that had occurred and no longer numb from the initial shock, which fortunately had gradually loosened its depressing hold on me. I realised that I had been totally remiss in my duties."

The twins appeared mystified and he explained while giving Cetheren a challenging glare of his Preceptor-Band.

"I am our races Intercessor with the creator of the Cosmos."

43

His listener's repeated Celtair's sign of peace and knowledge as the Patriarchi said the Almighty's name, even though all three were aware that Cetheren was having a hard time at the moment in the belief of the Supreme Being. Still, the Elder believed.

"The younger twin's faith is still intact, although it is severely strained. And he is unlike Zebulan who has found himself a new God."

Celtair privately took a little comfort in the latter's circumstances.

"Although each of us can exist for tens of millions of years due to our slow crystalline metabolism, we are not immortal. And because of our ideology, we accept that our actions in this life are accountable and when each and all of us encounter our maker, we will be judged. While Zebulan only believes in living for the moment and its short lived pleasures. The betrayer of our race believes that because of the long life span that he was endowed with, expiration appears an eternity away. But, it will eventually seek him out. That is the one certainty of our existence, because even Stars and Galaxy's die. And when that final moment does arrive, none of my brothers will welcome it. But unlike Zebulan we are not consumed by the overpowering terror of it. Even if our betrayer destroys us all and succeeds in his aims, I still believe that he will still have to confront that one certainty the Universe still contains."

He paused dramatically and in a mind-whisper proclaimed.

"Death!"

Celtair continued in his normal tones.

"As High priest of the faculty of religious studies, I gathered together all the surviving Clergy and assembled the population records from before the holocaust and we set to the task of putting the dead to rest. Each of us took a vast selection of the deceased and began our work. My first task was to seek out the souls of the departed Patriarchi and help their tormented souls to leave the void and journey on to the Creator. Firstly I tried to contact Mescal's soul to ease his transition.

I failed!

I thought nothing of this because of the countless people the INIQUITY/Zebulan had sent on their way. As you have realised, the amount of transitions during this difficult time was unprecedented in our long history. I had only witnessed a handful of such transitions before and believe it or not, this was my first as intercessor. Who would have thought that my first duties in this capacity would be to send millions of our brothers to the next plane and I never had done one such rite before? Taking the lead from the Scrying globe of my first such event, I began the proceedings. This was in stark contrast to the first such ceremonies. They were holy and sanctified experiences and this had to be done on an industrial scale."

The Patriarchi sighed.

"So many dead to find and where to start. I turned to find the soul of

my close friend Cryus."

He choked, but did not falter.

"I found him easily enough and performed the sad rites. His soul cried out for release from the dark place he had found himself cast into. Then in quick succession I discovered the souls of Uzziah, Hezekiah, and Hiram and sent them on their way. Ending with Nadab and Azariah. Eventually, we the Clergy had found all our lost brothers; except Mescal. We tried and tried, but it was to no avail. Though exhausted, I resumed my search for the missing soul and all my efforts resulted in an erratic signal. Perturbed, I blamed my failure on tiredness. Loath to desist, I decided to rest and continue the search when fully refreshed. I fell into a deep sleep and in my inactivated state; mind-voices came to me."

"Mind-voices!" Exclaimed Cathbad.

The Elder shrugged his wings.

"Well, whatever they were, they dragged from my slumber with a start. I then knew the reason for my failure to contact Mescal's soul.

It was simple!

Mescal had not passed on to his eternal reward. No, the Patriarchi was still alive. For two centuries, I tried to contact him, but it was to no avail. It is only recently that he made himself known to me."

"Then why did he not contact you before. Has he been left behind on our ravaged World afraid to communicate with us in case the "INIQUITY." sought him out?" Asked Cathbad with an involuntary shudder at the thought of been all alone on a World of stalking and deranged CRYSTALOID'I.

"No. The Corruption would be unable to do that. For the Patriarchi is aboard this ship. Did I not say we were going to him?" Replied Celtair sounding as if the mind-words hurt him deeply.

"One moment esteemed one. We assumed that we were on our way to a concealed communication device?" Said Cetheren.

"Always jumping to conclusions my student." Admonished the Patriarchi.

It was this impulsive behaviour that endeared him so much to Celtair.

"But that still does not answer my question why we cannot reveal his presence. Is he afraid that we will still hold him accountable for our near destruction?"

"Negative."

"Was he injured?" Certain, he had found the answer for Mescal's reluctance to rejoin the fold.

A look of utter helplessness appeared briefly on the Patriarchi's features. But he quickly turned away from them and neither brother was sure that they had seen his twisted macula or the slight change of his Preceptor-Band. Composed Celtair swivelled back and said.

"Again negative. No it is much worst that that."

Highly vexed, Cetheren insisted.

"He has not perished; he is not lost and not hurt. So what in the Great Mathematicians name could be more awful than any of those three fates?"

Celtair had been avoiding it up to now, but he knew.

"I will have to tell them eventually."

He paused for effect and then in a high updraft, he said.

"The Patriarchi has become insane. He has acquired a disorder of the mind from his necessary contact with the INIQUITY."

Celtair's normally strong voice then quavered.

"His great mind has been irretrievably damaged. This contamination would have been enough to push him over the edge and into madness. Then add that with the choice he had to make. Don't forget, he had to choose on who to save and who not to. This burden carved an erasable mark on his soul. He blamed himself for every life that perished in the destruction of our World's."

Those final words reverberated in their minds as both brothers were stunned into sympatric silence. The enormity of that last sentence sunk in. Their race existed for the sole quest of seeking peaceful and beneficial learning. In pursuit of this a logical and functioning brain was paramount. To be denied a rational and coherent mind was incomprehensible to any of their race. Even when Zebulan was debated, it was explained.

"He is not insane; he just sought knowledge in the wrong place."

The ALASTHA'I believed inexorably in the adage.

"I question and reason, therefore I exist."

To be suddenly deprived of rational thinking was akin to a lesser being losing any of its range of senses. But the comparison ended there, while the lesser life-form might adapt due to its never-ending struggle in a hostile environment, these finely-toned intellectuals could not. (But how could they be certain, for Mescal was the first of their race that this unfortunate malady had happened to.) Countless millennia of a non-aggressive existence had seen to that. Surviving in a permanent state of a non-functioning mind could only be guessed at by the trio. The silence prevailed until Cathbad's logical mind asked the inevitable question.

"How can a damaged mind help us?"

Celtair became enigmatic.

"This will be revealed soon and only the three of us must know that Mescal lives. You will discover something profound. Yes, even beings such as us can still find surprises in this Universe. Some things have to been perceived to be believed."

"Like the unimagined destruction of entire Worlds and all that was on them." Suggested Cetheren without a trace of sarcasm and he instantly regretted it.

The atmosphere remained thick with mystery as the downward moving tube came slowly to a stop. The liquid crystal door of the descending shaft shimmered and dissolved and the three of them stepped out into a murky corridor. Celtair waved his large hands in front of where he envisioned a light emitting diode to be located and the gloom was shattered. But the welcoming light failed to remove a slightly carbolic smell that offended the scent pores.

"Nobody ventures down here anymore, except of course, the ships maintenance CRYSTALOID'I, hence no perfumed air and the primitive light source." Offered Celtair in the way of an explanation to the two wary brothers.

However, he added in consolation.

"On the bright side, we are alone."

Just as his two companions were muttering injustices their discomfort, he amended slyly.

"We also have a long walk ahead of us as the corridors are too narrow for our wings."

As they both groaned, Celtair turned away in the direction they were to proceed, hiding a smile that was gradually becoming broader on his amused features. To the three ALASTHA'I; the long shadows cast by the rarely used ancient light source mocked their true appearance causing demonic caricatures to be cast on the metallic surface of the maintenance tunnels walls directly in front of them. The shades were cut off in non-comprising points where the light failed to penetrate the impregnable darkness ahead of them. The path in front of them lay in complete blackness, as only the part of the corridor where Celtair waved his hand, had illuminated for a designated distance. He urged them forward and they moved reluctantly. When out of range of a sensor they had just passed, it switched off automatically, plunging the passage behind them into complete darkness. This combination of been englobed in a bubble of slow shifting light was a mockery of the technology available to them and the rapidly increasing temperature rising in the claustrophobic tunnel caused two of the three to believe they had entered the netherworld. A jittery Cathbad mind-voiced to himself.

"Surely Mescal had perished after all and this is the realm of the deceased."

Each one of them increased the pace so they could be out of the uncomfortable tunnel as quickly as possible. The Patriarchi noticing the other two's growing apprehension continued with another narration so as to distract them from their growing agitation.

"As you know this ship was constructed over aeons and is old even by our measure of time. Its immense size and the effort of constructing another every time an innovation of new technology arrived would probably have bankrupted our economy. So when a new advance was made it was simply incorporated in to the body of the craft. Think of it been similar to the brain of our crystal bound ancestors evolving until those

creatures became us. Even though there is no comparison between the two, our cranium still contains a basic foundation from that primitive brain. It is similar with this craft; though these lower levels are seldom used by us, they are still part of the ship none the less and are still needed in a tiny way in the running of the "Expectation".

Cathbad, who was not convinced, was just about to voice his opinion on the Patriarchi's assumption, when he was halted by a low rumbling sound that reverberated through the tunnel and echoed through the points of light above their oblong heads. As the three ventured forward, the booming intrusion grew louder. Both brothers froze in their tracks, not willing to move one step forward.

"What is that noise?" Questioned a highly disturbed Cathbad.

"Oh that. It's only the sound of the ships engines." Replied Celtair as a matter of fact.

He did not divulge the detail that he too had been terrified when he first encountered the rumbling noise. All alone in the tunnel, he had nearly bolted. But the desire to reach Mescal overcame his fear. Even now it unnerved him, but he understood.

"I can remain strong; otherwise, my two companions will not accompany me any further."

The Patriarchi concealed his encroaching fear with a confident reply.

"There are no sound dampers at this level of the ship. That's another comfort that is neglected down here."

The Elder was now aware.

"It's time to tell them that the real trial lies ahead."

Keeping his mind-speech at an even level and disguising his private thoughts, he spoke as calmly as he could under the circumstances. He amazed himself that his voice did not betray the anxiety he was feeling.

"As I have already explained, Mescal has lost his mind, but it has left him far from stupid. He has moments of fantastic rationality and he has developed a cunning trait and an instinct for self-preservation that will amaze you. To protect himself from discovery, he has tampered with the lights of the tunnel for the next five hundred metres and we will be in total darkness until we reach his clandestine abode."

Cetheren whistled through his pores that one of the Patriarchi could actually commit a deliberate act of vandalism. He felt a warm sensation flow along his tall frame unlike any other experienced before. There was a slight pause for this revelation to sink in and then it was broken by a nervous Cathbad.

"It would be best if we returned later with a couple of service CRYSTALOID'I to repair the broken illumination. Then we can continue on in assured safety."

But instead of agreeing with his twin, Cetheren replied with an insight that thrilled their Mentor.

"No my beloved brother. We have to leave the lights extinguished. For if Mescal is truly our saviour, as Celtair believes, then he must remain hidden from the rest of our kind. Because, who do we know for certain among us that still serves the "INIQUITY.". So alas, we must proceed through the darkness without the benefit of luminance."

Celtair was proud of his protégé. But then again, Cathbad's brother was always a quick study.

"It can be done. I have already conquered it." Agreed the Patriarchi.

The previous light source had reached the limit of its influence and extinguished automatically and their Preceptor-Bands went out in conjunction with that occurrence. The trio were left in total impenetrable darkness as their floating auroras need at least a modicum of light to operate. Down in these depths, the blackness surrounded them like a shroud, suddenly enveloping and suffocating them. The two brother's wings beat in alarm and scraped the sides of the confined corridor. Cathbad lost his nerve and fled back to where he assumed the final light source had been. Frantically, the panicked ship dweller waved his crystallised hands to reignite it, but he had passed out its sphere of operation. Overwhelmed with fear, his mind screamed.

"I am going to perish. How was it possible for me to get in to this predicament?"

An image of Celtair in his capacity as intercessor performing the rights of his soul's transition came into his incoherent mind. Feeling the weight of the unknown and the darkness crushing him, his long wiry legs that had always seemed too frail to support his muscular body suddenly gave way. Falling to his knees sobbing, his unfurled wings flapping in distress and finding himself isolated from the other two threatened to squeeze his life force in to oblivion. Then, thank the Creator, the light returned and his Preceptor-Band was functional again, but it was flashing erratically. A strong hand helped him to his feet.

"My brother has saved me."

Still shaking, he took several deep-racking inhalations through his macula from the stale environment of the tunnel, uncaring now as his ordeal was over. When the frightened ALASTHA'I had regained most of his composure and as his mind-voice returned, he pleaded with him.

"You have to continue without me."

No amount of persuasion would change his sibling's opinion; so he left him behind basking in the safe glow of the light source. Cetheren cursed inwardly at his brother's show of weakness, but he knew it was not entirely Cathbad's fault. Again he swore, this time at his ancestors.

"What was your intention? Was it to breed an entire race of weaklings? Any hint of danger or take us out of our safe environment and we become doddering wrecks? You have created a race of weaklings and when faced with a threat, we cower and accept our fate. No wonder Zebulan took a

49

different path. "

But deep within his soul, he knew that some of their race were beginning to overcome the genetic block. (Including himself.) Armed with this thought, he marched uncaring into the gloom and sensed that Celtair had stopped ahead in the distance.

"Still afraid after all of his bravado. " Muttered a disgusted Cetheren.

As he caught up with the Patriarchi. Celtair spoke suddenly.

"Be careful Cetheren, the tunnel turns at a ninety degree angle and we don't want you walking in to the wall of the tunnel. Like I did the first time. The shock of it scared me half to death and I fled as if the "INIQUITY." was after me itself. Fortunately I had become disorientated and ended up in Mescal's place of concealment. Luck was on my side for if I had run back the other way where we entered, I would never have come back through the darkness again. "

Trembling with apprehension and forewarned of the extreme change of direction, Cetheren gingerly raised his hands, slowly stretched them out and proceeded forward. His twelve fingertips brushed against a solid cool surface, which he knew to the metal of the wall. He withdrew his hands instantly as if he had accidentally immersed them in acid, though in reality he was only in contact with the wall for a microsecond. But it was enough to cause him to come to a complete standstill and take a few deep swallows of the stale air. He turned around ninety degrees and resumed walking at a much slower pace. Then, Cetheren heard Celtair's impatient mind-call.

"Hurry up! I can perceive the end of our travels in the near distance. "

Encouraged by this welcoming news, he tentatively increased his steps and squinted his Preceptor-Band to pierce the darkness ahead. What he could make out only confused him. Instead of a brightly-lit area, all that was visible was a slight lifting of the gloom. A small transition into visible light that was barely discernible. Not the old fashioned lights that had illuminated the rest of the maintenance tunnels that he expected. His growing uneasiness gave way to utter despair. The nervous ALASTHA'I was geared up for a sudden transition from darkness to light, but he was ill prepared for the slow fading of the blackness into the ultimate terror of life fluid red luminance. Cetheren found it impossible to tell where one light source began or where the other ended. Both degrees of light melted in to each other like the familiar embrace of two passionate lovers. He had a wry mind-thought,

"Now, is precisely the time to test his theory that we are gradually over coming our conditioning and are able to confront unaccustomed challenges like this. "

Cocooned in this delirium of fear, Cetheren began to notice that the temperature had risen uncomfortably in the narrow duct and some abstract feeling told him that it would soon become intolerable. Armed with the knowledge that the Elder had made it through on several occasions, he finally achieved the conviction that he would also overcome this test. He quickened his pace and caught up with Celtair outside Mescal's secret abode. Basking in the unfamiliar euphoria of success in the face of adversary, Cetheren abandoned all protocol and warmly embraced the Patriarchi. His expression was a mask of pride as he exulted more with relief than joy.

"I have done it. I have really done it."

"There is more to come." Said Celtair sobering him instantly.

As if in a dramatic response to his words of warning, a truly ancient quartz door swung slowly open engulfing them in an icy blast of air that held the oppressive heat of the claustrophobic maintenance tunnel at bay. It was far cooler that what would be considered pleasant and it numbed every sensitive nerve in their crystalline bodies. As both of them absorbed this new onslaught, a manic laugh which scared an already twitchy Cetheren half to death shattered through the steady background hum of the ship's engines. The two winged beings leapt into each other's arms in fright. The mad chuckle was followed by an equally crazy voice that roared gleefully.

"Randy Grubers."

This was a reference to the unfounded rumours circulating among certain ALASTHA'I that some had sought sexual solace among themselves, now that genuine physical access to their Queen was denied.

"Did you both steal down here to satisfy your perverted needs? Afraid your members are not up to standard, is that it? So you both skulked down here to grope each other instead of attending the Pleasure Diadem?"

"Patriarchi. What are these words he mind-speaks?" Asked a baffled Cetheren.

"They puzzle me also. We will need to study this more." Came the others mind-reply.

Again came the weird high pitched cackling sound. It continued for a few minutes and then ceased abruptly. The two of them were certain that the owner of the screeching had met with the Creator. Suddenly loud slurping noises replaced the silence, these sounds mimicked the unmistakable sounds of mating with the Queen and it was followed again by the manic laughter. A look as close to unadulterated rage that one of their kind could muster appeared on Cetheren's features, but he overcame the fury with pity.

"Surely he is afflicted with a disorder of the mind. Come Patriarchi let us shun him and his corruption and leave him to wallow in his insanity."

"His madness is not contagious" Rebuked the Patriarchi.

Still stinging from the chastisement, a slow smile crept across Cetheren's macula. It as if he had solved the most difficult theory in the entire Cosmos at the first attempt. Even though, he had been fighting fear with every step through the darkened tunnel, his logical mind was still working away in the background. He was not able to contain his excitement.

"I got it. The vandalised light sources, the profanities and the mocking of our sacred rite. He is able to overcome a measure of the genetic block." Said Cetheren as he began jumping up and down in the cramped tunnel.

The Elder shared his student's excitement and he said.

"You are correct and more importantly, he has made primitive weapons to defend himself."

His companion's reaction to this incredible news surprised the other. He had expected looks of joy, puzzlement and of course amazement, but not the expression that was staring back at him now.

Fear!

"What is the matter now?" Demanded, the Patriarchi in consternation, now that Cetheren had ruined the moment.

"Patri- Patriarchi."

Those mind-words and his next ones were forced out.

"Ca-Can he? Because, he can do the other aggressive things."

A confused Elder halted his student.

"For knowledge sake. What are you trying to say?"

Shaking now because of the assumed danger that now loomed behind the closed door, Cetheren fired out the mind-words without pausing for breath.

"Can the irrational Mescal harm us Patriarchi? It would seem likely because of the fact that he is able do those other destructive things."

Celtair faltered as if he had struck the plastasteel wall of the service tunnel, the colour drained from his Preceptor-Band and he replied in a strained mind-voice.

"By the Great Mathematician. In all the times I have been alone with him; it never entered into my calculations."

Startled by this revelation, the now wary two noticed that the door of Mescal's hideaway had opened wider, it's crystal hinges jerked with a sudden loud groan. The one who they were seeking produced a chilling roar that could only have originated from a stalking predator and it scared them witless. It was followed by another bout of hysterical laughter. The mad Patriarchi decided that he had enough of this silly game and in a lucid voice invited the two unfortunate companions into his abode. Not the best quarters, he had ever possessed. Cetheren looked wary but Celtair entered without hesitation, so he followed and when they crossed the threshold, the door shut with a loud groan, trapping them.

"Come. Enter my humble home. Forgive my rather lame joke about the two of you coupling." Entreated Mescal in a raucous manner.

Still, they both failed to enter the space fully. Both of the two rational ALASTHA'I stayed rooted to the spot, beside the closed door, armed as they were with the revelation they had just made and the potential danger either of them now faced. Even though Mescal could never feel the fear that the other two shared, his voice softened in regret in some remembered past. He felt sympathy for them. He tried a coaxing tone delivered in a soothing lilt, but his harsh rasping tone ridiculed the attempt. Seeing that his two guests were still immobilised, his hoarse voice belittling his concern, he was fast losing his patience.

"If I intended in harming you. I could have done it at any time."

Those words melted their nervy resolve and they relinquished their reluctance with a supreme effort and came deeper into the room. In a brief moment of lucidity, Mescal thanked them for trusting him and then lost it as a string of profanities escaped within his mind voice. In the mist of this outburst Cetheren quickly surveyed the room and mentally came to the conclusion that they had entered the realm of madness, for everywhere he scanned, chaos leapt out at him. To the ALASTHA'I in their new guise, who were forever proud of their sense of order, of striving towards perfection and enlightenment, the state of Mescal's room seemed to deliberately mock them. Ever since the crazy Patriarchi took up residency here, Cetheren was positive that no service CRYSTALOID'I had ever found its way here.

"He could have at least left one machine operational." Thought the fastidious Cetheren.

The sour smell wafting through his macula of Mescal's hidden abode alone atoned for that. In fact, the first time visitor perceived that functioning machines of any type were noticeably absent. How this isolated Patriarchi took nourishment was anyone's guess. Where there should be holographic libraries holding holo-globes suspended in neat chronological order, there were what appeared to be crude plasta quartz shelves. Even the presence of old fashioned storage units meant nothing out of the ordinary, as some of the truly ancient Elders preferred them. No, these racks were constructed from battered sections of the tunnel lining and some things that were momentarily unrecognisable. Becoming insightful, Celtair's student realised.

"If there had been luminance in that section of tunnel where Cathbad had feared to enter, the artificial light would reveal that this metal had been ripped from its walls."

What was on those shelves gave more concern. Scattered about on their ledges were thousands of pieces of every type of artificial material known from their industrial labours. Having no access to the technology of the corporeal globes, Mescal had reverted to a primitive storage system. All of the scavenged material had been formed into crude information units. Some stood upright in the correct position, while others lay horizontal, seemly just there to prop others up and some lay at oblique angles with their titles upside down. All the script had been etched on with some kind of fine burner. In every other library, such was the ALASTHA'I reverence for knowledge, not one information source touched another and a thin light shield protected each volume to last indefinitely. Mescal's crude data sources were covered in dust and the Creator forbid even ingestion stains. On every shelf and piece of crude literature, this patchwork of intermittent dust and stains prevailed and spread around the room like some expanding organism. If the shelves made them uncomfortable, then the flooring was something else to behold. Strewn all over the floor's surface lay the cannibalised remains of service CRYSTALOID'I. Their crystal bodies were mangled and scavenged for useful materials. Crude quartz pages lay cut and severed, torn from volumes as if destroyed in fits of anger and frustration. Where the perpetrator had apparently lamented, the leaves had been crudely rejoined and hastily stuffed back into their respective volumes, but many protruded from their crystal covers. It appeared that the floors original sheen would never be seen again from the amount of refuse cemented upon it, though in reality a few maintenance CRYSTALOID'I would have it habitable in a few hours. (That's if the machines survived Mescal's attacks.). There was some furniture made with the same crudeness of the shelves. These functional items seemed to predate the conquest of space. (Very old indeed.). But these objects were no lovingly restored museum exhibits, just a simple attempt at construction with the limited tools at hand, for a purpose that the hidden Elder though necessary. Celtair disturbed Cetheren's inventory of the living space on his individual thought mode so that the other could not discern his words.

"He wantonly breaks the tunnel walls for material for his etchings knowing that the CRYSTALOID'I will come to repair the damage, then he ambushes them, destroys them and uses their body parts for materials."

After witnessing all this degeneration of their most esteemed values, it was the abomination that sat on the crude chair and staring at them that unnerved Cetheren the most. Before the "INIQUITY." came into the ALASTHA'I realm, that thing that was now studying him, grinning inanely and muttering incomprehensibly would have been an apparition from his worst imaginations. This wretched form that sat in the glow of the red fluid coloured light was indeed a Demon from some underworld, for it was no longer one of their kind. The last time he had seen the Elder was well before their exile and while he was no heavyweight like Naisi, he had been sturdily built. Now, their saviour had become anorexic, a shadow of himself and as he stood up from his seat and approached them, Cetheren got a good look at the former member of their race and it astounded him. He was certain.

"He cannot be one of us. This individual before me is from another species altogether."

Mescal had grown shorter in stature and was attired in some sort of crystal-textile as if he was ashamed of his nakedness. In fact, he was bent over double and had unexplainably grown a hunched back, which the frail frame seemed unable to support for any length of time. The hump protruded grotesquely through the filthy garment in a mockery of his former perfection. He lacked the graceful motion of his race, he moved in a slow lethargic manner, then in a blur switched to a hyperactive frantic motion and then again he reverted to the slow motion. All the time between these varying speeds of movement, he was suffering from a shortness of breath. His Preceptor-Band was displaying frequencies of an unknown wavelength. As the Patriarchi came closer, the vibrant blue hue of his crystalline skin, a sign of good health and vitality had eroded away to reveal a sickly yellow parchment of wrinkles. This was a result of living in the dark depths of the ship and a poor diet of minerals. To add argument to his decline his intake pores had become inverted and sunken into his frail frame. He was actually showing signs of great age that was setting a precedent for their long-lived species. Cetheren was certain that if the isolated Elder unfurled his wings, there would be no vibrant shimmering. Celtair approached the mad Patriarchi and touched Mescal on the forehead in ritual greeting and in a wheezing voice the latter regained a measure of sanity.

"Welcome old friend." Announced the deranged Elder.

Then, the former Patriarchi began to weep minerals from his pores in anguish. The insane Elder turned to Cetheren to repeat the gesture but the student involuntary flinched at the touch of one so repugnant. Acknowledging this; Mescal flipped and lost his tenacious grip on reality, grabbed hold of the astonished Cetheren's private parts and pulled them violently. Mescal fled back giggling to a dark corner as his victim fell gasping to the floor. His wings had unfolded reflectively and were flapping wildly. His assailant ran amok and began the familiar ranting and raving that they were becoming accustomed to. Then a crazy squeal was followed by an unmistakable taint of a sour odour.

"Preferred that posterior pores." Came the twisted mind voice of the long lost Elder.

Something inside Cetheren snapped, he folded his wings away and stood up. The changing ALASTHA'I was exasperated with everything that happen him since he, his brother and Celtair had alighted from the transport tube and been assaulted by the crazy Mescal became the final straw, Cetheren even surprised himself, when he retorted.

"Dim your Preceptor-Band; you old fool. I've had enough of your insults, which are incidentally incorrect. You have little comprehension of the new jargon that is propagating among the exiled host. It's anus pores, not posterior pores. You anus pore!"

Mescal refused to be intimidated and became very excited by this turn of events and he mind-uttered gleefully.

"New profanities, by the Creator. Celtair; if your student could enlighten me with more such mind-words. I will help you with your little problem."

As Mescal ranted, he glanced at the Patriarchi's waist and broke into bouts of merriment.

"Please forgive my private jest? Ha Ha."

This finished him altogether as the laughing Elder thought about the statement he had just uttered. His laughter increased in intensity.

"Come, Cetheren. We will achieve nothing while he is in this frame of mind." Declared Celtair regretfully.

He was painfully aware of previous encounters with the fluctuating moods of the mad Being. The two of them left the tormented soul to himself and as both of the disgusted souls exited from the room, the laughter ceased and a coherent Mescal shouted.

"Don't forget our arrangement."

During the ensuing silence, a grave Celtair turned to his student and said.

"I want you to let him take you under his wing and work with him. In his sane moments, Mescal will be of great use to us. He has a great knowledge of the Corruption and if we are to survive, we will need to coax it out of him. It is the only way to confront the INIQUITY."

An astonished Cetheren could not find an answer. So the Patriarchi found the mind-words for the flabbergasted exile.

"I do not need a resolution now, take your time and come back to me with your decision."

Then, the mad laughter returned to haunt them as they re-entered the absolute darkness of the section of vandalised corridor. But this time the absence of light held no more terror for Cetheren. They emerged from the gloom and into the light where Cathbad had remained, unmoving and still shaken. The deserter was extremely relieved to see his companions return from the shadows of a perceived netherworld. Looking into his sibling's expression, he noticed that his bearing radiated a strength that had never been there before. He realised something profound had occurred deep down in the darkness where he had be afraid to venture. Cathbad knew with the understanding of a twin that Cetheren would never be the same again. The troubled soul enquired of his brother.

"What happened down there?"

"Not now. Come let us leave this filthy place. We will converse about it later." Was the only reply he received.

Keeping his own counsel, the Patriarchi Celtair had mixed feelings about this arranged meeting with Mescal. But he was confident that his student would assume the mantle of the insane Patriarchi's confidant.

"But at what price. Would my pupil exchange his morality and honesty for the knowledge to save us from oblivion? If so, would he be resilient enough to overcome the trials ahead and not end up like the deranged Mescal."

The esteemed Elder did not like the logical answers to these un-inhaled questions. Celtair re-entered the floating tubes with these sobering thoughts that he kept repeating in his private mode.

"Troubling times ahead indeed."

The two brothers were also locked into a swirl of mixed emotions. There were no mind-words conversed between the trio during the time it took the ascending tube to reach the level of their living quarters. Curt and brief goodbyes were uttered as each of them entered their separate cells. The conspirators had much to think about. Celtair did not see Cetheren again until a week of ship time had elapsed. His student entered his cell in the middle of the day and said simply.

"I have discussed your proposal with Cathbad and we both concur, but with reservations. I will be Mescal's understudy. I will learn everything about the "INIQUITY." from him."

"I am pleased that you have taken on this task and I am confident that you will be up to it."

Cetheren's Preceptor-Band flickered in agreement and then he gave the Elder a perceptive look that was followed by a question.

"There is one thing that bothers me and I think that you can enlighten me."

"Ask away." Replied the Elder.

"When the three of us went down to visit Mescal, you already knew that the lights were non-functional."

Celtair nodded.

"As I informed you, I had been there already."

"So why did we not bring a portable light source?"

A sly Patriarchi gave his student the answer that he had been expecting.

"Call it a rite of passage, like the trial of flight you took when you were young. You passed the test while Cathbad failed. That is the reason that I want you to be Mescal's understudy."

So began his training as apprentice to the Weapon's Master. Mescal was the first ever ALASTHA'I to ever merit that title and now he even had an assistant. Then his new student found out the true portent of his mentor's plan. The mad genius told him.

"The "INIQUITY." used resources that were already there; it just moulded them into its designs. We will do something similar, but different."

Cetheren did not understand the paradox. His teacher explained.

"We will find a World with severe conditions for life. The rock Planets close to yellow Suns will be ideal. Anything that thrives in those hostile conditions will be suited to our purpose. And like the "Corruption", we will mould it to our designs."

As the "EXPECTATION." passed Planetary Solar systems in its long flight of exile, certain individuals monitored the Worlds close to yellow Suns. Celtair's faction had won the hard fought argument to begin preliminary investigations into that course of action. Then after countless failures searching for an ideal life-form, an excited Mescal found the Planet, they were searching for. It was located in a barred Spiral Galaxy of that was a hundred thousand light years across. There was a broad band of stars in the lens shaped structure. The insignificant yellow Sun that the orb rotated around was on a spiral arm exactly 32,000 light years from the Galaxy's centre. Images from their Scrying Globes showed a Biosphere that abounded in aggressive species.

IT HAD BEEN THE WORLD OF THE HYBRID'S.

The rest was recent history. Now many centuries after his initiation to this course, Cetheren's mind-thoughts returned to the present. The night was growing steadily warmer, but the translucent shield that he had donned deflected its uncomfortable effects. His search for the missing Elder was proving fruitless. These bouts of abscondment were becoming an increasing occurrence and a nuisance. He had the obnoxious feeling that Mescal had developed the distasteful habit of spying on fornicating Primates. In recent years, he was focusing too much on their release of sexual energy. The spying Alien even watched their births; it was such an intense violent affair as the new life-form came into existence accompanied by the wracking convolutions of its mother. The mad Patriarchi's student was beside himself with worry when Mescal came whizzing by in a borrowed flying Platform of Light. Cetheren ducked and the gliding craft missed him by millimetres. Its maniac rider had the magnetic thrusters turned up to maximum, just for the hell of it. Cetheren's blue features turned nearly as pale as a Primate's face at the near miss. Mescal making an acute turn came back towards him and stopped at the last moment. There was a look of unadulterated frenzy and abandonment etched into his features. The cavorting Elder was also without his protective film; he wore the crude fibres that he always had. His sane student urged him.

"Get out of sight, you will be seen."

"By who, they are all inside cooling their broad posteriors."

Cetheren was used to Mescal's odd behaviour by now and so one sane and another crazy Alien proceeded to the mound. Under the earthen structure, these two who were now the new hope for the exiled race mixed the science of weapon making with the sexual and genetic make-up of the Primates. The mad Patriarchi stayed true to their experiments for the next eight lunar cycles. One day Cetheren became frustrated at the lack of progress in their experiments and shouted at a lucid Mescal.

"These Primates are englobed in pride. All they think of is themselves; these selfish life-forms will be of no use to us. We will never mould them into our desired outcome. They will never form a cohesive force. It would be going against their original creation."

"No, my limited thinking student, you are incorrect, this is preciously

58

what we are striving for." Said Mescal inexorably. *"Think of the Primates as a virus against the Corruption. Just like venom becomes anti venom. The "INIQUITY." will be confronted by a force much stronger than itself and be destroyed. And believe me; the poison circulating in the make-up of the Primates is extremely potent indeed. For I know, have I not been there?"*

This simple reduction of their plan opened his student's awareness pores to his teacher's mind. His glimpse at the magnitude of the corrupted Elder's scheme overwhelmed him. If he had been the old Cetheren before the enforced exile, then he would have been sick to his pores.

"I understand at last. Everything is crystal clear." Said a jaded Cetheren.

From then on, their experiments proceeded with alacrity and much progress was made. The only blot on the horizon was the returned Patriarchi's increasing bouts of madness. But, his moments of brilliance occurred when he entered these phases and more often than not, the mad Elder had to work alone as his student had little comprehension of the profound ideas in his teacher's mind. But the constant exposure to these dark experiments was beginning to have a negative influence on Cetheren's inner being. He often wondered.

"Have I become as unfunctional as Mescal?"

Then, the mad-beings understudy always came to the same conclusion.

"Only time will tell."

Now, the eagerly awaited juncture had arrived; tonight would be the time of the most important CONGREGATION in aeons and Cetheren knew.

"If we are denied our scheme, then I will find another way."

The seed of rebellion within his soul was growing strong indeed.

IV.

Like the blink of a macula; the brief warm season had ended and the climate shifted instantly into favourable Winter. Towards the encroachment of dusk; Cetheren left his individual Diadem with a strong sense of purpose. He literary leaped out into the growing night and joined the droves of his fellow host that were now converging on the CONGREGATION Dome. Their destination was a form of a "Mind-Auditorium.". Each one of the off-Worlder's walked at this time of year as a metre or more of the mix of frozen hydrogen/oxygen covered the layer of decayed matter that constituted the surface of their Exiled City in warmer times. In the short Summer, all of them with one exception were reluctant to make contact with the remains of the dead life-forms, so they used the smaller versions of the hovering Platforms of Light to go about their business. Although there was still a fair amount of the falling frozen moisture flowing over the contours of his personal shield, surprisingly, Cetheren was strangely upbeat. Most of the Alien throng were abroad at this time and wearing they're translucent weather shields, making them appear as flickering fireflies in the dimness. Dusk was all of the exiles favourite period of the twenty four-hour day. There was always a general mind sigh of relief when this side of the World turned away from the harsh yellow Sun. Of course the long colder season of this hemisphere was the most pleasing time of all for them. The reason why the ALASTHA'I walked some of the time on this Planet, especially during the hours of darkness was because flying in this heavy atmosphere was mineral draining and not to mention, exhausting. Only in the few hours after dawn inhalation did the weaker Sun enable them to glide facilely without inflicting any harm to their brittle bodies. Gliding Platforms of Light were used on longer journeys across the uncompromising terrain of this forever changing landscape, no matter what the time of year. As the blue Alien made his nocturnal pilgrimage, the negative feelings of a few hours ago; of them losing the great debate were washed away with a sense of purpose. To try and lighten his mood, he let his brother convince him to visit the recreations of their World once again. Somehow lately, a visit to the "Contentment Diadem." always left him unfulfilled and dejected at the sham of the false pretence. This was a contrary feeling that Cetheren had already surmised,

"It is because, I know that the total experience is artificial and the boundaries of the spheres are extremely limited."

He had spent the day in a melancholy remembrance of their Home World. The winged exile pined for the real green sky of CRYSTALIOS and the huge puffballs of methane that fell slowly from the sky and evaporated before hitting the warmer ground. The beauty of the geological forms of hardened crystal of many refraction's that were an equal to the strength of any substance that issued from the bowls of this inferior Planet also played heavily on his mind. The mountains and plateaus of sculptured volcanic glass, reflecting their rainbow hues had brought a sigh of grievous loss from his pores. But most of all, Cetheren longed for his abode of reflection that overlooked the Endless Sea. That enormous body of methane on his Home World covered a plane that was at least three times the entire surface area of this tiny orb. (Gaseous and crystal type Planets tended to be much larger than rock based ones. Scholars among them found no plausible explainable reason that their own small Red Dwarf Star had larger habitable Worlds that most yellow or white Suns). Unlike the dense and deadly saline Oceans of this Planet, its bobbing expanse invited him in, to bathe in its soothing embrace. Outstretched wings enabled him to soar through its liquid mass as effortlessly as gliding over the pink air above. He was at peace with the Cosmos when he trundled along at high speed under the emerald surface of the Methane mellifluous and then made the transition from one magnitude to the other. In a wondrous instant, he would find himself soaring over the green waves of the Endless Sea. Then, he would glide in the assisting wind currents to the shore of multi-coloured jaspers, lie in the silicon-beaded quartz mass and soak up the comforting glow of the pallid scarlet Sun. He had been at that wonderful place when he had received Mescal's false call to attend the CONGREGATION. Remembrance made him melancholy.

"If I had known then that was to be my last time cavorting in the green Sea, it would not be an understatement to say that I would have certainly savoured the moment more."

Another of the Home Worlds wonders that he sorely missed were the gelatinous volcanoes of the equator that spewed out a cold black viscous mucous of slow moving lava flows. This then reminded him of the high mountain ranges where mere's of pink bitumen were trapped in semi-heated lakes and where methane fell from green cloud formations. The various sized falling viscous bubbles exploded on contact with the bitumen and their remnants crawled across the inky surface like something that was alive. Their stark flowing beauty was timeless. Then, there were the white rusty deserts of uniaxial crystals, devoid of cloud cover, where endemic life-forms displayed enormous solar gathers to take full advantage of the exposed Sun. The list of his Home World's physical beauty was boundless. Even the yellow efflorescent plains of the Polar Regions that still supported life were a blessing compared to the unfamiliarity landscape of this rock. Two huge chunks of both hemispheres were nothing more than a bland whiteness for most of its cycle around its Sun. Cetheren sighed theatrically at his fond remembrances.

"And now millions of light years away from my beloved retreat, I am close to a deadly alien Ocean and in another Galaxy. Thankfully, the afore mentioned is frozen over for most of the year. I have also turned to

Mescal's dark path. Still, if it means a return to CRYSTALIOS and one more swim in its alluring Seas, or once again to soar over its mountain peaks then it is a flight-path worth taking. For either of those lost pleasures I might embrace the 'INIQUITY' itself."

Regretfully, he cast the painful images of the past aside and concentrated on immediate events. In the mist of this intellectual progression that was making its way through the strict grid system of the temporary city, (Their base had only been there eleven thousand cycles of the Planet's orbit around its Star.) he felt the captive call of the CONGREGATION.

A call that supposedly none of the Aliens could resist.

It was a clamour that grew more intense, the closer an exile approached. While the high pitched stringy sound of the gatherings summons endured, it turned the ALASTHA'I into almost automated replicas of their pre-programmed CRYSTALOID'I. As he rounded a non-descript globe of light, his crystallised muscles and filaments hummed in sequence with the fluctuating Diadem. Cetheren like his brother; who was a head taller than most peered over the teeming masses. The falling wetness had now abated to a slow drizzle as the promised storm of falling hydrogen and oxygen never reached its threatened potential. It still flowed off his flickering shield causing sharp flashes of energy where the moisture made contact. The tempest subsided and through its disappearing mist, it gave a glimmering profile of the largest Diadem in the globular city. This colossal convex globe was at the epicentre of the exiled community, both physically and spiritually. It was the nerve centre of their endeavours on this World. No plans or indeed enterprises of any type could proceed unless they were approved in this dome. This was an ancient fallacy; there were un-consulted and nefarious schemes about now. For example; only four of the exiles knew of Mescal's existence (Including the irrational Patriarchi himself, though sometimes, he forgot whom he was.). But in theory, only two of them knew the particulars of the real scheme that the mad Elder was concocting and even then, one only knew its full extent, Mescal. (And he only remembered sometimes.). Cetheren mind-laughed at the farce of it all.

"None of us are sure what is really happening. And we are the superior race? Ha!"

The CONGREGATION Dome was a monument and a legacy to their sacred communal past. It was a benefaction from a period of sharing that belonged in the history archives and a time before most of the present species abroad in the galaxy had evolved to their present states. There was none of the ALASTHA'I existing that still remembered its original conception. They're Queen did however and that was a measure of how long this ideal had been in existence. Changed opinions concluded without hints of regret.

"Not anymore. The bond that has united us from time immemorial is broken. There are too many lies and deceptions among us now. Some even seek higher office on their own terms. I have often wondered if it was this Planet that changed us, but now I realise that the lies and ambition began far out in deep space and possibly even before that."

Cetheren was becoming quite comfortable with the concept of individual thinking and needing no approval from the collective. He was even doing something that he would have once thought impossible and one that hurt him to his crystallised core.

"I am even keeping secrets from my beloved brother."

Not only was the sphere of debate and discussion different in measure or stature than the other globes of light, beside the call it beckoned with. It also changed the complexity of its colour, the nearer the converging flock got to it. The demanding sphere flickered on and off in a harmonious throbbing rainbow of colours that forced them all to approach in a trance like manner. It was an in built insurance that none would miss the great debate, as all of the truly devout ALASTHA'I could not resist the antiquated summons.

The call of the dome still worked its magic on the former ASCETIC'I.

Cetheren arrived at one of the curves of pulsating light and found his twin Cathbad waiting for him. He remembered the shrouded thoughts he was keeping from him and felt a twinge of guilt. His twin gestured a greeting and the two brothers entered the dome together. A beam from their Preceptor-Bands shot out and kept a portal of the glowing light barrier open. Their weather protection nimbi were shut off as they entered another space, a bubble of reality which was divorced from the outside World of the Primates. Once inside the CONGREGATION Dome, its Atrium spun dizzyingly upwards to a height that could not be contained inside its perceived space, if one had the inclination to measure the height of the exterior from the outside. So used to the bewildering transition, it never bothered any those summoned that the inner space was warped. The few experts of this calibre of light technology among the banished host knew exactly the method of converting the internal space to a multiple far in excess of what it should contain. If they were asked to explain, these confident individuals would answer.

"The matter contained inside the volume of this temporal distortion is at a higher ratio and is indirectly proportional to the surface area of the outside and so there is no cohesional equilibrium in translating from the two dimensions.

To those ALASTHA'I not involved in that field, these individuals did know whether they shrunk or the dome grew when one interfaced from the outside. It was exactly the opposite experience when one left the interior and contended with the exterior landscape. All that was accepted was the simple fact that the volume of space contained on the inside far exceeded the amount of what it appeared externally. In all of their Diadems, the internal temperature was pleasant and non-fluctuating. The coolness of the inside reminded him of the new name that the younger generation gave to the transitions into their own environment; they called it "Chilling out.". The atmospheric conditions of this hostile World were forever banished by a steady and unchanging replica of the climate of the Mother's Home Planet.

"Another pleasing titbit to keep the masses content," thought Cetheren bitterly.

But, he knew deep inside his crystal make-up.

"This place is a necessity and not a luxury like the Contentment Diadem. If this were taken away from us, then our race would no longer be what they were."

This pleasant surroundings, so different from the outside was reminiscent of the Queen's World of CRYSTALIOS and this feeling was further enhanced because the entire ground floor of the globe was a revered requiem containing all the treasured artefacts of the lost Worlds.

"All except our beloved Matriarch, that is."

This invaluable legacy was waiting as patiently as the ALASTHA'I to be re-established back on their abandoned Planet's, once the "INIQUITY." was defeated. This would come to fruition when the refugees returned home and once again became the ASCETIC'I. This was the only hope that they had.

PARADISE WILL BE RE-CREATED, ONCE AGAIN IN THE HOME SYSTEM OF WORLDS AND OUR EXILED BROTHERHOOD WILL RETURN TO WHAT THEY WERE BEFORE.

But many now perceived that this would not equate. New experiences of the exiles would never allow them to be what they were once before. The entire crystal based flora and fauna, the geography, the plans of their wonderful mathematically precise cities and their laws and art were amassed here. In effect, this was where the attributes of their genius were stored. Cetheren knew of the significance this place had on some. He had confided in his brother once.

"Some of the less adaptable of our brothers spend all their time here, loathsome to be in the harsh outside of the Alien planet. These misguided souls even preferred it to the replica of the Queens mating chamber and its sexual delights. Some of these misguided fools even wanted to construct enormous viewing scopes, so they could see our lost Worlds at a whim. Thankfully, we did not have the resources for that type of endeavour."

"You are incorrect my brother. They know the Mother is lost and they cannot bear to look at her representation. It brings moisture seepage to their macula. They prefer to remember her as she really is."

"Out of perception, out of mind. That is no solution."

Cetheren had given up on those specific individuals; they might as well be dead. He told his sibling.

"Celtair should perform the transition rite on them. They have lost hope of ever returning home and are excepting the scant comfort of this mausoleum."

The Alien knew that this unforgiving Planet with its contrasts of extreme heat and temperate cold was a challenge that they must adapt to, if they were to succeed. Cetheren and his brother crossed this wonder or curse quickly and entered a small chamber located beneath the transport tubes that ascended to the upper levels of the CONGREGATION dome. This was where one had to be sanctified before going up to the upper levels. In ages gone by, those who partook of this ritual firmly believed in its ability to cleanse the soul. But now, especially among the younger generation of ALASTHA'I, it was only a routine, a necessary chore to be dispensed with swiftly. They entered opaque cylinder containers called "Fonts.", where one proceeded to cleanse themselves, physically and spiritually. Those that really believed took time with the ritual, those that did not, hurried through the motions. Once inside the Font, the opaque doors melded into the whole form and a dense sweet tasting colourless vapour issued forth from numerous nozzles imbedded in the surface of the Fonts. Amazingly the winged host could ingest this concoction. To those who still believed, they emerged totally purified and at one with creation. Cetheren had been waiting impatiently outside for his brother; he had hurried through the ritual in reflex actions. The vacuum tubes that gave access to the upper levels stood directly across from the Fonts. The two brothers entered one and Cathbad selected the desired level, which in this case was the debating floor. Not that it mattered, as there was no other option available to them tonight. There was a slight swishing sensation and they glided effortlessly upwards to the debating floor. On reaching their destination, the whispering vibration ceased and the two brothers hesitated a brief moment before the vacuum tube's chamber doors opened. They had just entered their second most revered space in their society; the mating chamber of the Queen being paramount. One glance of the inside suggested why these fleeing Aliens had chosen this corner of the World for their base over three thousand years ago. When the tools of their first encounter, the Scrying Globes surveyed this land on their initial inspection during the brief summer of northern latitudes, the surveillance spheres found that a tiny chlorophyll plant that abounded in the short lived grass meadows of this hemisphere that resembled the depiction of the sacred debating chamber. Great euphoria gripped the exiled population at this discovery.

"Surely the Creator is still with us; he has given us a sign."

When Cetheren brought the news to a lucid Mescal, his mind-utterance was blasphemous.

"It will be the first time in aeons that our God has sided with us."

However, dismay set in soon afterwards, when the winter season encroached and the plant withered back into the soil and was covered by a thick covering of frozen hydrogen/oxygen. But it reappeared again the following summer when the confining blanket thawed out. It was such a physical metaphor for their plight that found favour with the more desperate.

"Ironic that such an advanced race still holds sway with superstition." Noted a sceptical Cetheren.

"But it gives the host renewed hope and their efforts have increased substantially." Argued Celtair.

The debating floor of the sacred chamber was laid out in the shape of three inwardly curving seating amphitheatres that were approached down a long narrow central aisle. An individual coming down this exposed corridor could be viewed by the entire seated CONGREGATION. A permanent orange mist wafted in its confines. Seats were in the form of floating platforms of condensed light. Those with the topics of utmost interest entered down the floor last, keeping the gathered assembly in total suspense. Back in the city of Campus, on the Planet of CRYSTALIOS where flying was effortless and commonplace, it was a sign of deep reverence and respect to walk down the narrow aisle of the debating chamber. That observance was kept here, light years away from the original concept. The two siblings marched down the aisle. Their proud and confident manner was an act to those whose vote might still be swayed at the eleventh hour. They took their allocated hovering seats in the faction supporting theirs and the Patriarchi Celtair's memorandum. The chamber was nearly three-quarters occupied and a steady flow of ALASTHA'I was still filling it up. When the entire host had settled into their hovering seats, the excited throng waited for the entrance of the Conclavi of Patriarchi. The Elders were always the last to come into the debating chamber. This was another break from the initial commune when every individual entered together and tonight those of a higher station were greeted with a general feeling of sombre anticipation. They sat in their allocated places in the section that fronted the three amphitheatres. Even, they were unusually sombre as this promised to be the greatest debate in living memory among the exiles. It was very unusual for a Patriarchi to be participating in and fronting a project. Celtair would receive a large backing for his side, just because of his involvement. Then, the nearly one hundred thousand minds present communicated across the chamber as each and everyone realised that one Elder was conspicuous by his absence. A gradual hush swept over the floor until there was complete mind-silence.

"By our imprisoned Queen, where is he? He is always first up on the podium." Whispered Cathbad.

"I told you he had something planned." Answered his brother.

Cathbad was alarmed.

"I anticipated a surprise, but not one of this magnitude."

"Well it has certainly got the attention of the CONGREGATION." Stated Cetheren.

"Maybe, something has happened to him?"

"Have patience, brother. I have total confidence in our mentor."

The compelled assembly waited and waited until the suspense intensified, until nobody could hold the silence any longer.

Still, there was no sign of Celtair.

From a slow murmuring, the babble of mind-voices reached a growing crescendo. The debating chamber matched this uncertainty as circles of transitional light flashed around in an erratic sequence as it appeared that one familiar to it had ignored its summons.

"He is not coming. That is impossible." Said a disbelieving Cathbad.

"Celtair will come." Replied Cetheren, but uncertainty was creeping in within him also.

However, in a hot flushed moment of despair, he was not so sure about his absolute confidence in his mentor. The fluttering mind-voices of the assembly that began at the top echelon were certain.

"The impossible has occurred; never in our long history has a brother failed to answer the call to the CONGREGATION."

No one except Celtair, Cathbad and Cetheren knew about the crazy Mescal's ability to ignore it and when it came to the DEFILED, those gathered here firmly believed.

"Even those impure individuals have no ability to disregard it. They are disguised and present somewhere in the hall."

But because of the mad Patriarchi, at least two now in attendance knew that they were not here. Then, the doors of the vacuum tubes opened in a dramatic sparkle of energy. Everyone present stared aghast as Celtair strolled nonchalantly down the hallowed aisle as if he had no care in the Universe.

"He is definitely becoming quite the performer," thought one of his students.

Cetheren's and Cathbad's mentor took his place on the hovering podium, met the two brother's stares and winked. This physical action was perpetuated by a swift buzz of energy across his Preceptor-Band. There was a slight sheen of perspiration on the Elder's visage, the result of the battle with the call of the CONGREGATION. Celtair's faction stood up and mind-voiced their approval. Looking around at a shifting of positions; Cathbad said in amazement.

"There are some who had previously decided to vote against our scheme have now switched to our side. And some of the neutrals have also followed suit."

His main opposition tonight was Naisi and Cetheren stole a glimpse in his direction. Delighted at the others expression, he whispered.

"Our adversary is highly vexed after witnessing Celtair's late entry. It was something that he did not expect."

"Did any of us?"

Boosted by his supporter's fate in him, the last arrival fluttered his wings in a confident posture, then clasped a small orb in front of him and began to address the gathering. He began with an entreaty for the safety of their imprisoned Queen.

"Let our beloved Mother be safe and well."

This would be the only time during the ensuing debate that the whole community of the ALASTHA'I would be in complete agreement. Even the DEFILED wished no harm to the Matriarch. The entire assembly alighted from their hovering chairs and fell to their knees in abject humility and recited the following oath.

"By all the power contained within us, we promise to endeavour to free our Mother and overcome the "Corruption" that has plagued our race. We will rid ourselves from its evil taint."

"Amen." Chorused the exiled host.

When the prayer/promise died away, Celtair did not hesitate; the great debater pounced on his audience. He would prey on emotions that would be still raw from the recitation. His enhanced Dias linked mind-voice punctured the aptitudes of those present.

"Fellow venerables gathered here in our sacred hall; this great debating chamber of our race. Tonight on this World of our enforced exile, I will explain to you a way of removing the INIQUITY from us, once and for all. My delayed arrival was a ploy. It was to show you that we can achieve anything if we put our great intellects to it. And a way has been found to rid ourselves of the thing that drove us here. Will I tell you my reasoning?"

He paused for effect and then answered when a shout of encouragement came from a pre-planned direction.

"We will fight combustion with combustion."

There were interruptions of approval and disapproval from the host; the great debate was in full flow. When the CONGREGATION was up and going, everyone present had an equal voice (A legacy from their communal past that was still rigidly adhered to.). From the lowest acolyte to a revered Patriarchi, each had only one vote. When an ALASTHA'I was outside the revered hall, mind communication could only take place between ten different individuals at the most. Inside its hallowed halls, the entire host of a hundred thousand souls could converse simultaneously. The combination of the sanctification taken below and the incandescent orange mist which permuted all over the chamber allowed this mass communication. Celtair's great booming baritone mind-voice reverberated in the minds of the gathered host as he began with a rehearsed litany. First he would tell them about what they had lost and then how to retrieve it. The Patriarchi was certain.

"By the time I am finished with them, the majority of the present gathering will favour my scheme."

Celtair the performer was born for this night. The speaker continued, his mind-voice had divested itself of his opening enthusiasm and was now full of sorrow, regret and loss. Supporters and hecklers halted their outbursts.

"Our Worlds are silent of joy now, only the slow hum of twisted CRYSTALOID'I in our charred cites mingle with the rage of the contained Corruption. It has been imprisoned with our Queen on the paramount world of CRYSTALIOS, in the revered city of Campus. Our Life-giver is alone now and she still fights for her beloved children while she clutches the repugnant INIQUITY to her bosom."

Tears of mineral evaporation flowed from the macula of most of the gathered CONGREGATION. Strangely Cetheren was not one of them; Cathbad was. This display of grief would be costly; many hours of standing exposed to the unruly elements of this blue sphere would be necessary to replenish this loss of nutrients. Mention of the Queen's plight always hurt them deeply. Celtair paused; he let his words sink in and continued with his requiem for a dead World, a separated Mother and a lost way of life.

"There are no more landscapes of orange, green, blue and colours not perceived on this World. No slowly falling puffballs and their caressing evaporation. No great cities of Crystal or orchards of pomegranates. Why? Because of the INIQUITY. It has taken command of our peaceful creations and turned them against us. Machines that produced beauty and everyday practicality, now scavenge among the broken shards of our dead. It forced us to flee the desolated Worlds of our beautiful solar system and end up here far from home."

The Patriarchi's mind-voice began to rise in anger and resonation.

"With one Starship, we fled to this nitrogen snotball of a sphere and we left over ten million of dead brethren behind in our wake. We witnessed the death of the first CONGREGATION. Alas how we grieve."

Now his mind-voice fell in tandem with his diminishing rage until he was barely audible. Then the tremor of his words began to rise very slightly in growing octaves with every syllable.

"Well my fellow members of this venerable gathering; I for one have had enough of accepting our fate."

As if he thought that he had not been heard, Celtair used the full might of his impressive mind-voice and thundered.

"Did you perceive me?" I said that I have had enough, do you agree with me?"

There was rapturous applause from his faction. Even Cathbad and Cetheren got carried away and his Preceptor-Band flashed exuberantly.

The Patriarchi who now held a captive audience in the fold of his wings continued.

"Tonight you the CONGREGATION will decide which method we will take against the INIQUITY. And I am sure you will choose wisely."

He made as if to leave the podium and join the other Patriarchi when a substantial figure stood up from the opposing schism and approached the Dias. Standing directly beneath him, the figure gestured towards Celtair. It was Naisi, their constant antagonist. He was the author and leader of the third faction that were of the opinion that no lifeform should be taken and moulded into an opposition against the legions of their former constructions. They proposed that the ALASTHA'I take the same strategy as the "INIQUITY." and use CRYSTALOID'I similar to the ones the enemy used except that this time the corruption would not be able to override their programming. Celtair detested Naisi because of his naked ambition to become a Patriarchi above everything else. Also, the vain exile had begun wearing shimmering crystal rings on his fingers, a sign that he was different from his kin. Celtair firmly believed.

"Our corpulent adversary always has his own interests first."

The Elder always vetoed the vote for his election every time it was proposed. A fact that Naisi was well aware of and loathed the one responsible for it. To be elevated to this high rank required an unanimous election by the Conclavi and usually it was only Celtair's vote that decided the outcome. Because of this, the fat ALASTHA'I was rejected time and time again. But undeterred, he kept trying and the Patriarchi was certain.

"If my opponent has one redeeming quality, it is his stubbornness."

Naisi in his irritating mind-voice whine that annoyed Celtair so much informed the CONGREGATION.

"Nothing has been decided yet!"

Celtair smug with the knowledge of his presentation and by the fact that he had goaded Naisi to approach the podium without been requested grinned and answered the challenge.

"Of course my learned colleague. It is up to the gathered host to decide on the outcome. All that we can do is to put forward our ministrations on the best flight-path. Then it is up to our learned assembly to choose."

The fat leader of the opposition was highly vexed at this condescending attitude.

"It was as if I did not know the procedure of the gathering and the Patriarchi was explaining it to me as if I was nothing but an immature grub."

Then Celtair rubbed bitter salts into his macula with a hint of sarcasm.

"If you please, I will continue with my presentation. It is not your turn yet."

For the gathered host's benefit, he added.

"If I am allowed?"

This was received with spontaneous laughter, the loudest from his faction. It was if he had decided not to leave the Dias after all. The sly Patriarchi knew his false attempt to sit would draw the rash Naisi to break protocol and interrupt. Celtair refused to have his wings ruffled by the overweight exile and had never intended to leave the podium at all, so he continued his presentation much to the others consternation. Humiliated, Naisi returned to his hovering seat. In the middle of the seated throng, Cetheren whispered to his brother.

"Our mentor had no intention of sitting down. He anticipated Naisi's interruption. He just wanted to annoy him and he took the bait. Our shrewd colleague has a lot more of his presentation left yet."

Up on the floating lectern, Celtair continued.

"Though our race unanimously abhors the use of violence, we will have to change and alas we have no choice."

There was an uneasy shuffling of wings at that utterance, but a sizeable amount of those present concurred. After all, the two main factions agreed on confronting they're nemesis, it was the different methods which divided them.

"Our ancestors did pursue the craft of CRYSTALOID'I creation for the improvement of our race. These machines were extremely useful in the development of our civilisation. But alas, the Corruption easily took control of them and turned them against us, their makers."

The assembly was unanimous in agreement; even Naisi's faction could not dispute that fact.

"That is why we cannot rely on our constructions again."

Now things got vocal, there was conflicting views among the host. Naisi sensing the turn of the CONGREGATION towards Celtair's Schism interrupted again and shouted at the figure on the podium. This time from his hovering chair.

"That is incorrect. What you said about our old models is correct. But as everybody except you is aware of is that our engineers have developed newer prototypes that the INIQUITY cannot infiltrate. These current and more advanced CRYSTALOID'I will easily overcome the older models."

His faction now laughed at the Elder's apparent ignorance. Celtair fed up with this constant, but expected heckling from his clever disputant suddenly roared with scorn.

"Enough, I say. We have seen what the machines of our past achieved and these new ones will be no better. It is now time to do it another way."

He played on the emotions of the host once again.

"How many here have lost kin or friends to those tainted machines?"

(Every exile present had in fact lost somebody dear). Because of the extraordinary reproduction system of the Queen's womb, the ALASTHA'I had technically only one parent and that was her. The accumulated life creating fluids of the males produced during sexual activity was stored in a

71

communal reservoir and tapped into when required by the mother of their race.). Siblings were produced by a system of consecutive fertility. It was when she used the same male sex infusion to fertilize one or more eggs. It was never more than two and individuals of this male based race only had one brother. The sympathy of the host was now with him. The over confidant Naisi had been drawn into the debate and had not been given time to present his scheme skilfully. Celtair had seized the initiative, the Patriarchi pointed to a visual display globe that he had just activated and he challenged the gathering.

"Look and learn. You are about to view a micro-cosim of events compressed on a single Scrying-globe."

The faucet of opaque light shimmered and expanded; its increasing radiance became sharper than the light of the chamber. A scene of the grassy steps far to the south appeared into view within the spheres circumference. A gently flowing stream that measured half way up its earthen banks split the plain in two as it meandered westwards to a bigger tributary of the largest river of the searing hot Continent. The CONGREGATION shuddered, as the heat of the Sun seemed to flicker out from the image and enter the debating chamber. Some of those nearly activated their shields in response to the non-existent danger. On one side of the flowing watercourse, there lay rooted tall grasses of the type that thrived so near liquid and on the other side of the stream lay an abundance of the food staples that the Primates used as their basic form of nourishment. A tribe of closely related black skinned hunter/gatherers were down on their hands and knees uprooting the plants and placing them in woven dried grass baskets that were already filled to the brim. The nomadic Primates, some who were clothed in a single piece of animal pelt and others who were entirely naked were singing merrily in praise of their God's that they had encountered such a bountiful and unharvested site. All in all, it was a scene of Primate bliss that the Alien host was witnessing. The harmonious vocalisation was accompanied by the false call of bird mimics which intruded on the natural rhythm and were watching the group with eager eyes. Small burning fires were been tended in expectation of prey. Cetheren knew this because of the simmering pots of liquid above their glow and the fact that the heat of the day meant that intense combustion was not for warmth. Some of the females not involved in the gathering or preparation of food were suckling their very young while they peeled the leaves from the grasses that were already gathered and put into the communal baskets. The larger males stood in the shallow ripples with pointed sticks, ready to stab at any passing fish that got into their range. Cathbad shuddered, he remembered with fondness, the sport of angling on the Home World of CRYSTALIOS.

"Back there, it was a gentle game of patience where both the Cryo-trawler and his flying prey participated in a contest of matching wits.

Gentle suction pads with titbits of infusion would attach themselves to the Cryo-organisms without inflicting the slightest harm. Once the bait was taken, the snared participant was gently released to continue with its normal routine. On this competing orb of consume or be consumed, it is a brutal ritual that always ends in blood and gore and the consumption of something. Even some species of the desired cold blooded vertebrates lie submerged in wait for some hapless thing to stray within their reach and that included the hunters themselves."

He had a moment of clarity, a scene of fondness from his last trip in the equatorial region of his lost Planet. In that zone of high temperatures, it regularly reached a humid nought degrees centigrade: a heat variance that was now laughable. Huge fan-tailed gliders of lengths that reached fifty metres and more used the hotter winds to soar endlessly along the central meridian. These enormous hovering and siphoning organisms of inert gas never touched the solid ground during the course of their long life spans. Other creatures took advantage of this and used their flat frames as permanent or temporary bases to exploit the rich veins of minerals that flowed along the wind currents. More daring life-forms dangled from the gliders undersides and used the shade of their living perches for protection. It was from these encrusted microcosms and drifting vantage-points that the ASCETIC'I had once sat on and Cryo-trawled. It was where in the infancy of their technological race that the idea of the Platforms of Light had originated.

Cathbad was snapped out of his reflection as the recording sphere switched to the tall verdant grass on the opposite bank from the contented Primates, from where the false birdcalls were originating. Crouched down and hidden amongst the reedy grasses from those on the facing bank, lay another group of Primates that had their faces and naked bodies grotesquely painted with abstract symbols. The colorant had been concocted from the crushed seeds of a mustard plant that was mixed with raptor eggs and semen from their own bodies. It was assumed that their own virility would make them powerful hunters. The painted faces made the Primates appear three-dimensional to the viewing devices of the ALASTHA'I. Cetheren had to stifle an insane urge to laugh.

"Their shadowy profiles remind me of the crazy Mescal."

Some of these hidden Primates were armed with long thin sticks of green wood that had razor sharp triangular pieces of flint attached to their tops and held in place with animal gut. Others were carrying large sections of polished animal bone or bark stripped tree limbs fashioned into crude clubs. Back on the opposite bank, some of the young and adolescence Primates finished their toil and waded into the cool stream to cavort. The bushwhacker's concealed in the tall grass had waited patiently for this opportunity. They now stood up and charged with howls of glee towards the isolated young and their startled adults. Before anyone reacted, the attackers had snatched up a fair number of the shocked young and fled, not before the ambusher's had set the tall dry grasses alight. Too late the members of the clan went for their own weapons. The warriors of the tribe gave futile chase, but lost the kidnappers in the arid smoke and poor visibility. As the shock of discovering that twenty-eight children were missing set in, there was much lamenting at their loss and the temporary camp resounded with the wails of grief the entire evening. Listening to his clan's misery while sitting at a fire to ward off the chill of the night, the Chief of the tribe had come to a decision.

"I have failed the tribe as their leader and it is up to me to put things right."

His fearless cold black pupils reflected the firelight and he rose. Arming himself with a huge war hammer made from scavenged hippo bone, several flint blades, a bow and arrow with a full quiver of feathered shafts, he was going to give chase. The leader also equipped himself with a woven reed basket with a strap that allowed it to be swung over his shoulder. It contained enough life sustaining foodstuffs for his journey. A cluster of hollowed out speckled ostrich eggshells contained all the water he would need. The shells had a hardened clay stopper and they could be replenished along the way. Satisfied with his preparations, the leader of the tribe went off into the night without a word; he did not ask for or require company. The lone tracker picked up the tracks of the kidnappers beyond the edges of the blackened grass. The Chief followed the trail relentlessly for five days until he discovered a grisly sight. In the dawn of the rising heat, he found a blackened firepit that revealed the scant remains of two children. His worst fears were realised.

"Those that I chase are cannibals."

All of the watching Aliens shuddered. To them; the consumers of their own species were the ultimate nightmare of this blue Planet. Within the contours of the Scrying Globe, the Chief increased his speed and three days later; he located his quarries encampment. Hidden by a high hollow, he hunkered down and watched. There was great excitement and boisterous shouting in the man-eaters compound and to his horror, the searcher found the reason why. He found himself staring at what remained of five child sized bodies on a roasting spit over a fire in the village centre. Holding back his revulsion, he done a quick scan of the grass hut filled site and he located the other children. They were imprisoned in a small, but sturdily built wooden cage and were under guard by a couple of armed men. The Chief waited until nightfall, too disgusted to eat and then made his move. With silent ferocity, he despatched the two sentries with horrendous blows of his war hammer. The guards crumpled to the ground with caved in skulls; they fell and died without alerting the rest of the encampment. The twenty-one captives looked at him in wide-eyed shock, before they knew him. He quickly cut the ropes of the cage and rescued the children. Urging them to be silent with hand gestures, he led the youths of his tribe to safety. Great rage over the fate of those he had failed to rescue overcame him; he took out two flints and a prepared torch. A spark from the striking stones ignited his brand and the vengeful tribe leader set the Cannibal's huts alight to give the eaters of flesh a taste of their own medicine. In instant burning tinder dry grass huts lit up the black sky and howls of panic and rage faded into the background as he escaped with the children. Many of the Cannibals died in their beds and others perished from been mistaken for attackers in the ensuing confusion. The image inside the scrying Globe shifted to accommodate a passing time span. The Chief was greeted as a hero when he returned home eight days later with most of the abducted children. The now very alert tribe had posted lookouts and these sentries were the first to see them approach and they quickly alerted the rest of the clan. Although there was much grief over the few dead, he had secured the tribes future and on this harsh World, that was all that counted. Even the watching ALASTHA'I felt the Primate's actions were justified despite the horror of his response. In a flight of fantasy; Cetheren, for one wished.

"I had the same resolve."

The image of the satisfied Chief dissipated and Celtair feeling the movement of the host in his direction told the CONGREGATION.

"Despite the fact they are efficient killing organisms; the Primates have a sense of righteous and can triumph over any adversary or challenge."

Someone from the neutral faction stood up and disagreed. He was planted there by Naisi.

"This proves nothing. So, your subject was victorious against a few dumb Primates. Those filthy animals could never overcome our advanced technology. The twisted CRYSTALOID'I would make short work of them. The hopes of our continued existence cannot rest on these inferior creatures."

All across the great debating area, there were loud mummers of acceptance of his words, especially from Naisi's faction. Their shouts of disapproval about what they had seen were the loudest and most boisterous. Celtair's opponent rubbed his hands in glee; the Patriarchi had now played into the fold of his wings. Smugly, he began to refute the speakers claim. Then, Naisi rose from his floating seat and once again marched up to the hovering Dais. Now it was his turn and he would take the path of the air currents with favoured him the most. Standing on a podium that emerged alongside Celtair, he addressed the throng.

"Before I begin, I must go against the esteemed Patriarchi's statement that his delayed arrival into this great chamber was a feat. I myself assume that it was just tardiness and an insult to our ancient beliefs."

Murmurs of assent came from his own faction and most of the oldest ALASTHA'I. In a daring ploy, the corpulent speaker now switched from

75

his accepted view of the primitive life-forms.

"Does the CONGREGATION realise that what you have been shown supports my true argument? The speaker who interrupted the weaker argument is correct about the intelligence of these Primates, but he is also incorrect about them remaining inferior creatures. The fact is that these lesser evolved bipeds have a sense of right and wrong. They can understand consequences and that means these lower life-forms can make moral decisions. These are no dumb organisms with a one-track programming. This species can reason, but most of all, there is another aspect of their behaviour that argues against us interfering with them. They have started to bury their dead and perform rituals over their corpses. The Primates also inter them with objects and tools to make the afterlife more comfortable for the departed souls."

Privately, Naisi mind-thought.

"They are of course dumb life-forms that will not evolve any further on the evolutionary ladder."

But he was not going to divulge this opinion to the enraptured assembly. With a mind-command; a Scrying Globe of his own design flickered on. On an island in a sea free of ice there was a sombre gathering of a hundred Primates of all ages. A body had been placed in a hole with his possessions and what he would need in the next life. To all of the watching host, it was unmistakeable to them that a ritual was been performed. As the image dissipated, shocked silence flooded the Alien-debating chamber. All of the mind-voices ceased, even the learned Celtair was aghast.

"By the unknown formulas of the Great mathematician, I never expected my opponent to go down this path and praise the emerging intelligence of a life-form that he is privately known to revile and despise. He is well aware that a belief in the afterlife signifies that we are dealing with a sentient being."

His two prominent supporters were just as upset. Cetheren raged.

"He is turning the hovering tables on us."

Naisi feeling as if he was floating on a high updraft continued with his deception.

"These so called primitive life-forms are also in the process of developing a sophisticated language and culture. Eventually writing will be available to them; granted it will take about a million cycles of the Planet, but so what. Who are we to intrude on their natural development?"

He raised his mind-voice.

"We have no right. We do not have the moral high drafts."

The decision of the CONGREGATION shifted again, this time in Naisi's favour. His faction swelled in number. Sensing victory, he became egoistic. He then stood up and augmented his argument.

"The new CRYSTALOID'I is the way to go."

Now it was Cathbad's turn to foster rejection of a proposed scheme. From the audience, he challenged.

"Even if what you state about the new models is correct. We have not the capacity to produce them in sufficient numbers."

Members of his faction backed him up and were joined by a growing clamour of other opinions that agreed on that. Far from having his wings ruffled, the smile of Naisi's macula grew larger.

"More trouble." Cautioned Celtair.

The esteemed Elder was correct in his assumption. The fat ALASTHA'I activated another Scrying sphere. It's enlarging luminance displayed an enormous underground chamber under another set of mounds. To Celtair's consternation and his two students dismay, it showed millions of constructed CRYSTALOID'I. All were in pristine condition and made of materials of this World. The gloating Naisi said.

"I am sure that my learned friend is mistaken. As the CONGREGATION can perceive with their own Preceptor-Bands, it is simple enough to produce the machines."

Celtair was contacted by the two brothers on personal mode.

"That is impossible. They could not have produced such numbers."

The Patriarchi agreed.

"It is a deception; he is using multiple images of the same mechanoids."

There was an eager mind-ripple as the weight of the host shifted to Naisi's side. Cetheren's respect for the large exile grew. Then Celtair decided.

"It is time to set my own indissoluble formula in motion."

Underhandedly, he activated another globe. There was a slight disturbance at the entrance to the debating chamber. As one, the entire host of ALASTHA'I glanced backwards. Some stood up from their hovering seats to get a better view. Others at the back were tempted to hover with their own wings, but they stayed rooted to the floor of the sacred chamber. Celtair had re-activated the imaging device; he wanted everybody to see this. The Scrying Globe showed an amazing scene from the back of the chamber.

An inferior Primate had achieved the impossible.

It was actually present in the sacred hall and among the gathered host. This was an unprecedented event in the annuals of their history. Never before had a different life-form witnessed this gathering. (They were wrong with that assumption, the EGO had.) Mind-gasps filled the assembly chamber as astounded members rose to their feet, too outraged to be afraid. Even though every Primate looked similar to the off-Worlder's, most present recognised the native of this World as the one they had just witnessed in the images from the hot Continent. Celtair had the appalled throng now; he spoke over the buzzing multitude and called for silence.

When he had got some measure of what he desired, he voiced.

"Now you are able to see the truth of my predictions. You have just witnessed the ingenuity of these Primates. They are like a rough crystal with impure facets, ready to be shaped by us. No CRYSTALOID'I could have entered here of its own accord. Even the ones that ended the CONGREGATION back on CRYSTALLIOS were programmed by one of our own race. Imagine with our assistance, what they will be able to achieve. If we are to survive, we have to cast away our former beliefs and philosophies. Our continued existence in the Cosmos and even our return home depends on this lowly life-form. Choose the Primate and we might survive, choose the CRYSTALOID'I and we will perish. Our past has already confirmed that."

"We cannot control them." Came an obscure mind-voice.

"What's to stop them destroying us?" Said another from the same faction.

Celtair acted, he left the podium and strode down the aisle towards the hostile life-form. The dangerous looking Primate turned to meet him. As the Patriarchi neared the confused Chief, he unfurled his wings a pre-calculated gambit.

"I must be mad to accept Mescal's guidance, this had better work."

The bewildered Primate fell to his knees at the sight of the Winged Angel. He had already accepted that he had perished and had entered the realms of the God's, but the bewildered Chief could not remember how he had departed the physical World. The Patriarchi pointed at the descending transport device. The Primate who had already been conditioned by Mescal reacted to his programming and went back into the tubes and disappeared from view. The mad exile was waiting below and took the bewildered Primate away. There was an audible sense of relief from the assembly and wonder at how easily one of their own had controlled the volatile life-form. Then, in the mist of these unprecedented events, Trelix took his place on the Podium and called for attention. But now little of the gathered throng listened to him after Celtair's impudent and heroic act. Few were in the mood for pacifism. He rushed through his policy, but knew that his opinions were useless. He finished and went back to his floating seat. Still believing himself to be undefeated; Naisi knew that when he had taken the stand, he had given his finest oration. He was certain his efforts were not in vain and he managed to convince a sizeable proportion of the audience to his side. But Celtair's act of audacity sealed the vote in their favour and Naisi's schism was defeated. It was a close call; they had won by four thousand, nine hundred and twenty votes. Most of the younger generation had voted for Celtair's scheme. Just as the result was declared, the image showing Naisi's enormous legion of CRYSTALOID shifted and when it returned in an instant, there were only a thousand of the artificial constructions, his boast had been a sham. Fuming, Naisi left the chamber as he realised his desire to become a Patriarchi had failed once again with the CONGREGATION rejecting his plan and the mockery that followed when his ruse was revealed. Celtair smiled smugly as he witnessed the departing upstart. He privately mind-murmured.

"Now the salvation of our race and the return to Campus lies in the hands of an untried youth, a mad Patriarchi and a most unpredictable tool."

He had a flash back of his lone confrontation with the Primate.

"I wonder if I have not become a little mad myself."

Cetheren and Cathbad rushed over to congratulate their mentor. Their uncontained joy was evident in their Preceptor-Bands and expanded macula. the victor mind-spoke to them.

"Now we know the correct flight-path to take and I hope this is not a solution for disaster."

Cetheren decided that this was a joke on Celtair's behalf, but Cathbad was not so sure. Later on that night, the three victors were celebrating their triumph in Patriarchi's quarters, (Mescal had been excluded as he had entered a potent bout of irrationally). But, not before he had disclosed.

"I was responsible for correcting the false image of Naisi's legions."

They were inhaling some fine pomegranate vapours from a pre-exile vintage. The chilled crystal container was unsealed and it's much anticipated contents wafted into the confined space of Celtair's private quarters. The normal blue hue of the room became a radiant green, a sign of the age of the ancient vintage. In this sauna of vapours, the three were in good humour as their macula absorbed the fine treat.

"This is exquisite." Noted Cathbad.

He fancied himself to be quite the connoisseur on such blends of crystal pomegranates. Their mirth was enhanced after a bout of merriment caused from something Celtair said while preparing the very rare concoction.

"I have kept this unusual inhalation for a special occasion and I surmise that if Naisi knew that we were enjoying this rare vintage, it would probably hurt him as much as losing the great debate."

"It is rumoured that he was trying to appropriate every last pre-exile vintage."

"Well I know for a fact that he won't be acquiring quite a few."

"You mean; he will not be invited into your private vapour collection?" Asked Cetheren innocently.

"What do you think?"

The three of them laughed hard and at that precise moment, the room dampers were switched off, so Naisi might perceive them. Gloating was another nasty trait that had crept into the ALASTHA'I make-up. The time of one been part of the whole were buried long in the past and some among the host might have said.

"Good riddance."

"Is it this World or our long journey here that has made us so callous?" Wondered Cathbad on his personal mode.

If Mescal had been lucid, he would have told him.

"Inviting the INIQUITY among us is what has changed us forever."

It was then that the three celebrating victors of the great debate received some really shocking and sobering news. A communal Missive flashed into their Preceptor-Bands. There had been an enormous explosion in the great mound and it had ripped the earthwork apart. Plumes of obnoxious gases vented from a great rip in its grassy side. Scores of Primates had been killed and injured and were hastily rushed to treatment centres by automated CRYSTALOID'I. Then more reports came in stating that the underground chambers under the mound had escaped undamaged. Accidents rarely happened to such a technically advanced race; so an investigation uncovered that a Primate had been responsible for the destruction. However, the three companions knew who had really been accountable.

"It can only be the DEFILED!"

"But how have they overcome the genetic block? How can they use another life-form for destructive ends and also ignore the conditioning of the CONGREGATION?" Asked a perplexed Cathbad.

Celtair had no answer for him. But a few days later, after examining the scene of the scorched earth and the gory remains of the deceased Primates with the only one who could tolerate the scene; he came up with an answer of sorts.

"Mescal also believes that the servants of the INIQUITY somehow convinced a Primate to carry in the explosive device. I have discussed this with him and he said without detailed explanation. They are infants compared to me, but the DEFILED are beginning to understand the true nature of the Corruption and used the basics of the same method as myself. Whether or not, they will grow in its ways, is up to them."

"Did he explain how it could be done?" Enquired an intrigued Cetheren.

"I questioned him more, but our insane Patriarchi said that he could not define it to me. He just laughed and added, you either got it or you haven't." Replied the Elder.

"What does that mean?" Asked an infuriated Cathbad.

"I am not certain. But he also said that we were fortunate that this had not happened before the great debate. Otherwise, our brethren would have rejected our plan outright. Even now, there are some who are asking for another session of the CONGREGATION."

"But that will take time and we better soar ahead with our plans."

"Affirmative." Replied the Patriarchi.

This insight into the minds of the outcast's left Cetheren frustrated, but he hurried to the mad Mescal to try and pry some scraps of information from him about how they were making ever increasing inroads into breaking their races genetic conditioning. Also, he decided to study Celtair's vengeance seeking Primate in more detail and see if he could gain additional insight into the hypothesis of aggression. Seven cycles of the Planet on its own axis had passed when the production facilities for the construction of the new CRYSTALOID'I were shut down. This left Naisi who had never before been so humiliated in total despair, he had no idea how or who revealed his deception to the host. The broody Alien had heard Celtair's, Cetheren's and Cathbad's mocking laughter on the night that he was defeated in the great debate and the fat ALASTHA'I vowed.

"I will make them regret their untimely laughter."

Thus, the disgruntled exile made his plans.

IV.

ZEBULAN'S BASE (DUN AENGUS; ARAN ISLANDS) THREE LUNAR CYCLES AFTER THE DECIDING CONGREGATION

"Campus, Campus, how I miss that city of wonder on the banks of the purple Bituminous Flow. Oh, how I long to be back there on the Queens World to fulfil my destiny. To build a new marvel of change and to father the stronger race that was promised to me. That is my destiny after all." Declared the one whose true nature was darker than a lunar eclipse.

This tall winged Alien was embellished with a flawless blue visage that reflected his supreme arrogance. In conversation with his minions, he never mentioned this desire or the fact that the magnificent city that he longed for did not exist anymore or that he had been directly responsible for that state of affairs. The assertive mind-thoughts were meant for nobody, but himself alone. His frozen expression was devoid of any macula and even his Preceptor-Band responded to the same symmetry. Zebulan had just left his private quarters of his concealed globe; it was hidden only a few hundred kilometres from the globular city of the despised ALASTHA'I. He strode outside in the pleasant coolness of the northern night air. More than all of them, he hated the Sun of this World with a fearful passion. Oddly; this Alien like Mescal was also clothed. The once Patriarchi Zebulan had become a nocturnal creature and only ventured out during the hours of darkness. It was the only sign of weakness from him that his underling's had noticed; though wisely none cared to mention it to his cold sterile countenance. He was anxiously waiting for reports from his recent convert who was unknowingly to his hated kin once deeply involved during the debates of the CONGREGATION. It had taken him three lunar cycles to convince that one to defect from the main host of exiles. Zebulan despised those weaklings from his race with a passion. It festered in him like a malignant sore.

"They name me and my followers; DEFILED. But I am more inclined to designate myself; ENLIGHTENED."

At first he was wary to come this close to the hated enemy for fear of recapture and humiliation. But now he was supremely confident here in his well-constructed and concealed fortress. His secret lair was situated just over two hundred kilometres westwards from the Exiled City, the inconsequential landmass it was perched only became an island during the short summer months when the main body of the northern ice sheet retreated briefly. In that short warm season, it was then surrounded by the dreaded seawater that would reduce their kind to nothing in a matter of minutes. The lethal saline liquid had a dissolving effect on their crystalline constituency and would excruciatingly melt them into unrecognisable globs. On this periodic isle, Zebulan had constructed a structure that resembled a creation of nature. Built with five convex shaped walls, all of which were coated with light based camouflage that not only fooled the Scrying devices of his hated kin, but the delegations of the local Primates that he allowed to worship him. The endemic natives called the visible rippling effect of the walls, magic. A phrase that had become familiar to Zebulan.

"It is in essence their explanation for any phenomenon the stupid beasts do not understand."

The fortress was located at the edge of a narrow peninsula on the perpetual isle, whose other three shear sides fell dizzily away to the foaming white tops below. The first shield wall was the widest, its solidness crossing the entire breath of the peninsula and there were four more walls with each diminishing in length as the isthmus narrowed. This forsaken jutting limestone shelf at the edge of a lethal Ocean was the base of the paramount servant of the "INIQUITY." amongst the DEFILED. He was not inclined to find humour in the fact that he was stranded on a rock in a rock. Zebulan was the Corruption's first committed disciple among those who were once defined as the ASCETIC'I. The vain being had been easily converted to the darkness as he was already disgusted with their finite ethos well before he came in contact with his new master. But the Conclavi of Patriarchi had become aware of his divergence and managed with great difficulty to incarcerate him. The act itself was against their nature. (Zebulan had been the first of their race to ever be imprisoned.). The Elder's deplored this situation and called his circumstances "Reflective isolation.". To them, their misguided kin had just been encouraged to live on the barren satellite that he was forced to call home. He was actively planning to thwart them from his place of confinement when the "INIQUITY." caressed his thoughts. The Entity promised him.

"I WILL RELEASE YOU FROM YOUR ENNUI AND FULFIL ALL YOUR DESIRES."

Thus it was relatively simple for the Corruption to slip into his mind and make him its own. The willing convert would never forget the precise moment when in his prison on the small barren moon, the master had come into his awareness and freed him from those pathetic recreants. For Zebulan, one of the exiles own race, whom many considered a charismatic genius without peer and second only to Mescal in learning had been a highly respected member of the Conclavi. But unlike the former, he had delved into places of forbidden knowledge. His insatiable quest took him to proscribed areas where he should not have ventured. The EGO was lurking in those disturbing regions for just such a curious mind. This significant meeting between the two occurred during his second millennium of banishment while he was researching an obscure and long forgotten archive. This seeker of diverse knowledge came across a tiny fragment of translated prose. It originated from a civilisation whose World had vanished aeons ago. It had been found by inquisitive expeditions to other Star Systems that the ASCETIC'I had sent out around their Galaxy. So disturbing was its content that in a unique precedent, it had been censured. Its predominant feature was that.

IT CONTAINED A DIRE WARNING FROM HISTORY.

The artefact should have been left where it was. But there was a challenge in that archive the savant could not ignore. Zebulan attempted to activate the ancient vestige. The archive was badly damaged, distorted and composed in a rhythmical language that was extremely difficult to translate. It had taken his best efforts to activate it, but eventually the genius succeeded and an image appeared within the confines of his Scrying Globe. A tall sticklike regal being of synthetic orange origin with what seemed a fatalistic demeanour stared back at him from the displayed archive. Through a large orifice in its head, it spoke in a sad musical singsong tone which Zebulan's Preceptor-Band converted into mind-speech. The Alien began to recite.

"Come with me to a time when we thrived."

"When we were masters of land, sea and sky."

"Oh, this was a time to be alive."

"But then, it came among us, we do not know why."

"Who called it from its deep slumber?"

"Who of us was to blame?"

"For it tore our lives and World asunder."

"Alas now, we are a forgotten name.

In the background behind the grieving Alien, fantastic cities of coloured metal and glass disappeared in enormous mushroom clouds as the lamenting mantra was repeated over and over in the background. With traces of moisture streaming from three sight appendages above its vocal orifice; the weeping Alien trailed off with words of finality. There was no rhyming now.

THIS IS THE LAST EPITATH OF AN ARROGANT RACE.

IF YOU FIND IT, DO NOT LET IT SEDUCE YOU. DO NOT___.

The archive that had crossed time and Star Systems, ended abruptly.

For two cycles of the moon's orbit around the Planet it circumvented, Zebulan lay entrapped by this discovery. He became intrigued at what had caused such unimaginable destruction. The images of the spoliation were intoxicating. Lost in his conjecture, the banished ASCETIC'I in his arrogance ignored the warning of the orange coloured being. He was little aware that slight tendrils of the EGO slithered among those words. He never realised that his soon to be master lay lurking in these forgotten places, patiently waiting and probing into Zebulan's pretentious mind until it finally made their new relationship clear.

"MASTER AND SERVANT."

The faithful encounter occurred one night (For the prison moon twisted on its own axis, so while it had gravity and an atmosphere, it also had night and day.) when Zebulan finally admitted he was perplexed at how the race in the archive contrived its own demise. He was unable to discover what had turned such a passive race into global desolaters. With a bleary Preceptor-Band and exhaustion, the interested scholar decided on long needed sleep and rose from his addictive study. The lone inhabitant of the moon rose from his viewing globe and proceeded to his sleeping quarters and settled into much needed rest. He drifted in and out of slumber and something extraordinary occurred, he began to dream. Tall Aliens, angry and pleading in the forefront of mushroom clouds haunted his rest. Then, he witnessed other strange beings lamenting lost Worlds. Echoes of violence became the norm. The images built into a maddening clamour until suddenly, a disembodied voice probed at the shadows of his drained mind and demanded attention in the midst of the chaos. Startled, he cried out.

"Who are you?"

An incorporeal timbre defied him.

"I AM WHAT YOU ARE SEEKING. I AM THE EGO."

Zebulan awoke transfixed. The uninvited mind-voice assailed his senses, for the malignant Entity had found, the more intelligent a race had become, the easier it infiltrated them and carried out its dark deeds. It asked enticingly.

"ARE YOU NOT NAUSEOUS OF THE COLLECTIVE SOCIETY THAT YOU ARE PART OF? DO YOU NOT LONG FOR INDIVIDUALISM AND CONTROL OF YOUR OWN DESTINY?"

These were precisely the mind-words that opened the gateway of Zebulan's conversion. The banished Patriarchi was not the only child of the Queen it had corrupted (No, far from it. But he was the most pivotal.) The glue that held the communal race together was beginning to come undone centuries earlier. The EGO was using their emerging greed, ambition; their pride and all new negative emotions to enter their souls and claim them for its own. But still, the Entity had only made scant inroads into the new society of the ASCETIC'I and now, its salvation was at hand. This new aspirant was truly him, because his soul embraced the duplicity wholeheartedly and without reservation. It reinforced a heretical thought that the corrupted Elder had been engrossed with over the centuries. It told him that it was possible and it had the means to accomplish it. Zebulan would fundamentally change the sexual production of his race. Only he and none else, not even his offspring would mate with the Matriarch. He would achieve a semblance of their only parent and be on an equal status with her. This promise of success to his ambition was the twisted goal that won him over to the master of deception's side.

He aspired to be the male version of the Queen.

Through its agreeable means of access, it worked with various temptations to ensnare others. Then, the impossible happened; the Patriarchi Mescal was converted to their cause by the force of the entities will. During their many discussions, the hovering tables were overturned and the good doer became what he had tried to exorcise from the other. One minute, his long-time adversary was struggling with the force of the Corruption and his inhalations became heavily laboured. The next instant his Preceptor-Band flickered in transition and the once force of goodness had lost the battle. Mescal became one of the DEFILED.

"Oh, how easy it had been or so I had thought."

The EGO gave their new convert instructions and the eager devotee hurried away to do their bidding. As a result of that conversion, Zebulan finally believed in his implied destiny. Every minute of every day, he allowed the malignant force to probe his willing mind until eventually it melded with him. The Entity had manifested itself into a physical form as it merged with its willing host.

TOGETHER, THEY BECAME THE "ID.".

This new life form took control of the moon's systems; it had fostered a new ambition. They were now both part of the one mind and body. The EGO/Zebulan Being that was now the "ID." freed themselves from the prison moon and escaped into space in an unguarded craft. Zebulan was astonished at how easy it was. (As it was mentioned, the ASCETIC'I had never incarcerated anybody before and they foolishly believed that Zebulan accepted his circumstances as a form of repentance. So, in his isolation, he would regret his contrary ways and be welcomed back into the fold.). The "ID." eventually reached the industrious Planet where the CRYSTALOID'I that carried out all the mundane tasks for their requirements were constructed. It was an enormous giant uninhabited crystal orb of various hazes where every element needed for mechanoid construction was stockpiled.

Most of the material was imported from around the Galaxy without leaving a six digit footprint. A huge artificial luminous ring that surrounded its circumference a hundred kilometres in upper space contained all of the factories. It was a single giant organism devoted to issuing completed constructions in a vastly different manner than the method used by the Queen in producing her offspring. This manufacturing complex was connected to the planet's surface by thousands of transport conduits that physically joined it to the surface. Raw materials and completed constructions travelled up and down these transport arteries, then underwent various stages of fabrication until they emerged as completed creations designed for a specific purpose. The melded creature docked with the enormous elliptical construction and slaughtered the hundred living controllers; it had other more sinister projects in mind. Zebulan's mind was shut away while the EGO took care of this dirty work.

But in the fringes of the melded being's awareness, the now DEFILED felt a trace of its actions. On a second-hand plane, the altered Patriarchi became the second murderer of his race. There had been an accidental killing of a single soul before by an ASCETIC'I named Cani. After finishing the carnage, together they broke the encryption codes and re-programmed the CRYSTALOID'I production lines, constructing machines that would now destroy instead of creating. Zebulan had found a stock of exotic and contra-banded inhalations and proceeded to enjoy these as the foul scheme proceeded. Intoxicated and on another plane of deprivation, he embraced the growing scheme with gusto. The "ID." concealed the fabrication of these new and lethal machines with elaborate security precautions so that everything seem normal and nobody knew about their interference until it was too late. From this base, the melded being infiltrated into all aspects of ASCETIC'I life and took control of suptial minds with childish simplicity. It had already initiated that kind of interference, the existence of the narcotic inhalations bore testament to that. Eventually; they were ready for the final solution. On the day of the greatest celebration in the predominantly male races calendar; the Queen's birthday, the "ID." launched its premeditated attack. Their twisted machines devastated the entire collective of Planets. Every cherished World was obliterated with millions massacred. All of the crystalline flora and fauna scorched from blackened spheres until only the Mother World of CRYSTALIOS remained undefiled. In orbit around the first World, Zebulan's mind voice issued the EGO'S final decrees and if they complied, their lives would be spared in exchange for fidelity to the "ID.". It was a lie; the melded being had no use for these weaklings, but it found pleasure in tormenting its victims. All of this race would all be eliminated and its dupe would mate with the Queen to create a new ethos with more aggressive tendencies. The last remaining detonation shocked ASCETIC'I debated in the CONGREGATION, but unsurprisingly refused to yield to this new order. The "ID." had infiltrated their systems and transmitted images of the destruction of the other Worlds to the gathered savants. Aghast, the entire assembly stared in shock as uncomprehending scenes flooded in. Bright traces loaded with destruction crackled down from orbiting spacecraft towards their beautiful cities. They watched in transfixed horror as the white-hot beams melted each and everything into dense globs of cullet. All across the Planet's, silent flashing strobe bursts brought instant obliteration. Then landing craft launched from the orbital craft above hovered over crystal cities while disgorging millions of the deadly corrupted CRYSTALOID'I, there seemed to be no end to them. The horrified assembly watched as the once creative machines slaughtered and dismembered their victims. The wanton instruments even killed great numbers of their own kind. Many of those beholding the butchery dropped dead on the spot as assessing minds registered what their disbelieving

Preceptor-Bands were witnessing. Alas to their detriment, those who were deliberately kept until last were next to have the horror visited upon them. For now it was their turn. But unknown to them, the EGO/Zebulan could not afford to destroy the Mother Planet outright as the warped creature feared for the safety of the Queen. The dark force had promised the great betrayer that he would be the only one to mate with her, so he could begin a new more powerful race. The now completely encircled World, seeing the other Planets fate pleaded for outright mercy. It was then that Zebulan came to know the real master, who he had given his soul to. Inside his mind; the EGO took complete and absolute control. Using its host's mind-voice, its terrifying concise mind-chords reverberated around the ancient debating hall.

"I AM SURE THAT YOU ARE UNDER A MISCONCEPTION. I ONLY OFFERED MY ULTIMATUM ONCE. YOU ARE REFUSED YOUR PITIFUL REQUESTS. PERMISSION DENIED."

Those below gasped in denial and some pleaded for a second chance, but it was to be of no avail. Mind-voices filled the medium of communication like tormented spirits crying for release. The "ID." turned to the new phenomenon of "War Machines." and gave the command with a mind-word that had disappeared from the ASCETIC'I collective.

"ATTACK!"

Thousands of landing craft sped down to the surface and legions of other killer CRYSTALOID'I flowed from them on their mission of annihilation. When the evening came, only the capital city remained untouched and unmelted. The CONGREGATION now reduced to babbling grubs watched in abject fascination as the ancient doors of the debating chamber were blown in and their un-mitigating doom approached. Some on their knees closest to the detonation were scattered into lumps of sharded mangled crystal. Others present even broke with sacred protocol and tried to fly away within its confines. They lit up like melting candles as light beams found them. When the smoke from the dead cleared, the arrogant Zebulan\Ego being entered the chamber. Everyone present was aghast at what they were witnessing. One of their own kind was clothed and had what seemed to be a weapon in his hands. An Alien presence dominated the former prisoner's features and this unnatural being killed anyone that was not cowered by his spectacular entrance. Nonchalantly; the "ID." strolled up the central aisle dealing death with beams of light. The melded being who had grown in stature then sat on the hovering speaking chair and in a voice that could not be his own; Zebulan ordered the cowering Conclavi of Patriarchi's to approach him. He also commanded the murderous CRYSTALOID'I cease firing. The vapour-thirsty machines powered down in compliance. There was an unreal silence across the shattered chamber as the killer mechanoids hummed down. In one instant, the revered place of debate and wisdom had become a place of dread, death and horror. The sacred hall had become tainted and reeked of corruption. Evil death had never entered these hallowed halls before. One of the oldest Patriarchi who was in deep shock over the immediate events staggered up to the highly amused "ID." and in an outraged decree, mind-spoke.

"This is forbidden. You have broken the ancient sanctity of our sacred chamber. How dare you?"

In a never before witnessed flicker of a Preceptor-Band, the receiver of the strong mind-words, replied.

"MY, MY! IT SEEMS THAT AT LEAST ONE OF YOU SPINELESS COWARDS HAS ACTUALLY GOT SOME KIND OF BACK BONE AFTER ALL. THERE IS HOPE FOR MY PLAN YET?"

Malignant macula hardened and met the senses of the challenger.

"AND I DO DARE."

Before the detonation shocked Elder could elaborate, the incensed speaker was cut off as the Ego/Zebulan causally be-headed him with a swipe of an armoured hand. Without even a look towards the falling body and the puff of vapours emitting from the huge hole in the Elders trunk; the twisted being smugly glanced around the cowering survivors. But deep inside the monster, a feeling of dismay encompassed the part of it that was Zebulan. He had committed himself fully now and he knew that there was no way back. In the mist of acceptance, the monstrosities glee turned to outrage as it mentally done a head count. Fully half of the Council of Patriarchi was missing; including the other one who had converted to their cause. Confronting the EGO from the back fringes of his mind, its host demanded.

"He is not here. You were confident that he was one with us."

Then, he made a very foolish mistake. Zebulan actually demanded of the presence within.

"Why is the Patriarchi Mescal not present and waiting for us?"

An excruciating wave of pain flooded through every crystal sinew of its host's body, dropping him screaming in agony to his knees. Red-hot needles of pain touched every orifice in his flaying form. Black spots danced in the swirling light of his Preceptor-Band. Those still remaining alive in the CONGREGATION chamber and conscious enough made the sign to ward off evil. All of the survivors were convinced that a Demon was among them and these cringing beings were not incorrect.

"DO NOT QUESTION ME AGAIN?" Commanded the EGO to the wailing Zebulan.

The intense pain was switched off like a vapour outlet and the black spots faded into white light once again. The afflicted soul gasped in between body racking spasms.

"Yes, yes master."

He convulsed again before he could finish.

"I will not question you again."

He now knew where the real power lay. By the strength of their mind, the "ID." drew a member of the cowering throng to them as if he was a piece of ferrous metal attracted to a magnet. As the terrified member of the diminished assembly floated into hands reach; he was picked up with his feet dangling in mid-air and unable to touch the floor. A chilling mind-voice demanded of him.

"WHERE ARE THE OTHERS?"

The terrified ASCETIC'I answered it.

"We do not know. We were debating that fact before you came. Nobody should be able to resist the call of the CONGREGATION."

The "ID." realised that the squirming Patriarchi was really baffled on the whereabouts of the missing members. The combined being cast him away with such ferocity that the flailing individual crashed to the floor with such momentum that he shattered into hundreds of glassy fragments. In a bubbling lava mind-voice, the "ID." with a malicious glint in its Preceptor-Band at the remaining souls and then the physical manifested entity gave a command to the impatient machines that hovered in the background. Powering up on its decree, they waited for another instruction.

"THE REST OF THEM HOLD LITTLE INTEREST FOR ME. EXTERMINATE THEM."

As the melded being sauntered back down the hall stepping over glassy body parts, it paused and spread out the full raiment of its wings. In its regal splendour, it assumed a thoughtful pose and mind-uttered in a moment of flighty decision.

"OH, SLOWLY AND PAINFULLY BY THE WAY."

Then, there was a cruel bout of laughter. This was a sound that had never before been picked up by the ASCETIC'I receptors in their millions of years of existence. In the midst of that wicked jingle, laser torches were ignited among the machine host. The melded being left the chamber as the killing creations piled in and the slaughter began anew. Leaving the dying debating sphere to the pleasant sound of wails and pleading, which were abruptly severed and replaced with shrieks of agony, they stepped out into the only unbroken city on the Planet. Outside in the once perfumed air, now tainted with the odour of a melted World, the EGO/Zebulan stood in the only intact area of habitation on the Planet; (Minus its living souls). The physical manifestation of the joined being mind-spoke aloud in glee and not a little madness.

"NEXT STOP; THE QUEENS PALACE."

The "ID." hopped on a Platform of Light and made its way through streets deserted of the endemic population which were filled with roaming killer CRYSTALOID'I intent on more victims. But when the physical entity arrived there, its joy and anticipation was short lived. At the entrance to the palace, the melded being was confronted with a sight that made

Zebulan's rage surpassed even that of the EGO'S. Mescal the betrayer was waiting for them.

The "ID." was going to enjoy the assumed convert's account on why so many of the now obliterated CONGREGATION were missing, thus avoiding the fate that they had planned for them. It was going to demand an explanation before it smashed his crystal body into oblivion. The Patriarchi went down on his knees, folded his wings in subjugation and abased himself as the two in the one body approached. Perceiving the malevolent Alien expression in Zebulan's Preceptor-Band, a thing that was older than time; Mescal knew deep within his soul.

"I have made the correct decision and the immense weight that I carry is a little lighter now. I never converted to their twisted logic. It had been a lonely ruse as the Conclavi of Patriarchi would never have believed my deliberations. So I acted alone."

The wise Elder knew what he had to do. He grovelled for his very existence. This blunted the Zebulan\Ego's anger as it appealed to their vanity. Mescal spoke in the mind-voice, hoping that they would believe his lies.

"The others must have somehow got the air-currents of our plan. They somehow got the courage to flee off World. Forget about them, they are insignificant. The way has been prepared master. The Queen is waiting. Your destiny has arrived."

Impatient to begin the mating; the "ID." would deal with him later. With an arrogant wave of dismissal to the grovelling Patriarchi, the melded being entered the palace compound and made its way to the Matriarch's chamber. The mass murderer gazed at the slender spire and unfolded its wings. It needed his host's physical strength now as it had a new race to father. The only benefactor of the demise of the ASCETIC'I flew up towards the Queen's platform and landed alongside her just as blackened green clouds of methane began to bubble up in the overhead sky. Inside the melded being and knowing that he was on the verge of greatness, Zebulan was contemplating the changes he was going to make as the father of a new dynasty when from nowhere, a multi-coloured beam of light enveloped them. The mysterious luminance shrouded the "ID." just as they crossed the threshold of the Queens chamber. The fixating beam froze them in place and it formed into a matrix of confining light. Instantly knowing, it had been double-crossed, as it was the master of such deceptions; its incredible survival extinct took over. The EGO furiously cast out Zebulan's physical presence from the trap and flashed towards Mescal's mind. A warding had been put in place and none but the author could undo it. But the strength of the devious trap drew the Entity away from Mescal's soul and towards the unwelcome embrace of the Queen, but it was still too late for the Patriarchi. He had been briefly inside the darkness and became tainted with the corruption. Zebulan still dazed from the severing of his joining had been cast over the edge of the spire. He tumbled towards the ground with folded wings, unaware of the impending impact. Mescal flew up and caught the unconscious deviant a few metres before he smashed all over the base of the spire. Still muddled from the iniquitous influence, he gently placed Zebulan on the floor. The accomplice to the slaughter of his own kind recovered quickly. The confused traitor's analytical mind took account over riding his usual shrewdness.

"My master and the Queen are lost to me unless I destroy the author of the warding."

His master was frozen in the same place as the Mother, but its will was stronger than the Matriarch's and it could still contact its servant. The screams of rage and frustration were deafening and the promised threats to who was responsible were frightening. By the strain on Mescal's features, a reflection of his own torment, Zebulan knew he had guessed correctly who was responsible for the separation.

"You! What have you done?"

The false convert was the culprit that had ensnared the EGO. But there were still lingering traces of the corruption within its host. Zebulan could still put an end to the Patriarchi's existence. He started to rise and carry out his threat. But the dark part that had been cast out of his mind had now recovered fully and its voice in his mind distracted him totally.

"THE MORE I TRY TO BREAK OUT OF THIS TRAP; THE MORE I AM ENSNARED. GO MY DISCIPLE AND FIND THE OFFENDER. FREE ME!"

Mescal was still reeling from the backlash of the Entities mind and the momentary hesitation in the servant listening to his master was all that less muddled Patriarchi needed. He struck him with a powerful sedative. A waft of vapours engulfed the other. With a glint of total surprise in his Preceptor-Band, Zebulan collapsed to the floor. Foolishly believing that he had freed his compatriot from the evil force, Mescal carried the unconscious deviant to a waiting transport platform. It would bring them to a hidden spacecraft that would catch up with the missing Patriarchi's and the other surviving CONGREGATION members. After that, the already fleeing ship would take them far from the EGO'S wrath.

"The trap that I and our Queen have woven will not last forever. Our valiant Mother will endure, but even her great resolve will be overcome eventually. That is the way of the Corruption."

The Life-giver of their race had agreed to the sacrifice, if it was the only way to save her children. He put the insensible Zebulan on a salvaged Platform of Light and made his way to the hidden Spaceship. When the transporting contrivance caught up with the Mothership; ten solar systems away; Mescal found that all the surviving ASCETIC'I that he had rescued had been rendered comatose. The call of the false CONGREGATION and their inability to comprehend his duplicity had done this to them. Their saviour had sealed them away on the ship and none could answer the hail, this reflex action had saved their sanity. Mescal also locked the unconscious deviant away and reprogrammed the ship. He had set a course for deep space, to a different quadrant and further than he had originally anticipated. Remnants of the "INIQUITY." still infringed on his mind, so the affected Patriarchi retreated to the bowls of the Star-Traveller. He remained there to suffer alone from his inflicted madness until Celtair had found him. When the hundred thousand escapees recovered, they found a Scrying Globe showing them the full horror of the holocaust. Bewildered, shocked and terrified, they quickly came to the conclusion that they must keep on fleeing. The survivors had to get as much distance as possible away from the instigator of the mayhem.

Then, Zebulan was discovered.

When the author of their destruction came to, he found himself aboard an accelerating ship with the rest of his race that Mescal had saved. He tried to enforce his will on them, but failed. They somehow had gained a resistance to his enticing's and he remained locked away once again. This time, it was easier and there had been little remorse. Each of the ship's passengers had all been handpicked by Mescal as they were the best candidates at resisting the Corruption. Realising that their Worlds and civilisation were no more, his race now called themselves the ALASTHA'I.

"Always labelling and cataloguing." Noticed their bitter detainee.

They gave him a title too; DEFILED. The fleeing craft had taken him far from his master and the distance grew with every second. But the EGO was still in the fringes of his and another's mind and the fleeing exiles had unknowingly taken a lethal viper into their midst. But, he had become fangless as the distance between his master and himself increased. The ability of the deadly act of taking a life had waned and once again, the original compulsion of his despised race had returned. But his resolve remained steadfast and he would lead his master to his captors and regain what was promised to him. Light years passed by as the flight of exiles entered its second millennium and the journey through the stars found a new purpose. It was then that the Patriarchi Celtair noticed an emerging concept.

"As Zebulan's pacifist nature reasserts itself to a lesser degree; some of our reluctant voyagers aboard the Spacecraft have not notice that their own defiance is increasing in tandem with his decrease. Though the changes are not exactly comparable, they are significant enough."

Without Mescal's insight, those who were not changing now assumed.

"Our prisoner is nearly free of the taint and he will soon be welcomed back into the fold."

No actual record of his physical part in the slaying of the majority of their race survived. The rest of the ship travellers truly believed.

"It had been the twisted CRYSTALOID'I that had been responsible. Zebulan was only to blame for their unfortunate programming. It was an experiment that had gone erroneous."

Throughout the long journey in frozen space that took them to this forsaken World, the deceiver had slowly but not entirely regained a slight measure of trust. Unknown to the new Conclavi of Patriarchi, Zebulan had now converted a small number of souls to his master's side and they supplied him with information. In orbit around this dirt ball of a Planet, he learnt of the ALASTHA'I plans to resist his master's automated legions. Once, he would have found this knowledge a source of great amusement, but he also knew.

"Still, I had been one of them. Who was to say that another among them could not change like I have. They now find themselves in a new and challenging environment and, of course, the unpredictable Mescal is still around and he is certainly an unknown quantity."

Curiously none of his informants knew of the existence of the Elder, but a tenuous connection told him that the destroyer of his scheme was present.

"And I know where you are."

Except for the mad Patriarchi, he was certain in his arrogance that they would flounder in their attempts to thwart his master and would fade meekly away into oblivion. He also took comfort in the fact that Mescal unlike himself had been unable to contain the force of his master's will and now hid away below in the bowels of the Mothership, unable and unwilling to make contact. The smug DEFILED had no idea about Celtair's plans. During the circling of the Blue sphere Zebulan became so focused and absorbed on the problem of recontacting the EGO that he ignored the memo about the World below; a lapse that he would pay dearly for. The Missive listed the composition of the iron core Planet.

"The crust of the Planet contains oxygen, silicon, aluminium, iron, calcium, sodium, potassium, magnesium and titanium. The atmosphere contains 78.10% nitrogen, 21% oxygen, 1.00% argon, 0.2% carbon dioxide, hydrogen, inert gases and water vapour that forms a vast amount of compounds with the hydrogen element. These Hydro-carbons are the basis of life on the Planet below."

The memo also warned of the dangers below. It stated.

PRECAUTIONS ON EXISTING ON THE PLANET'S SURFACE.

1. The atmosphere is nitrogen based, but breathable. Protection shields will be needed, but inhalation of nutrients without its safeguard can be sustained for short periods.

2. Preceptor-Bands will have to be adjusted to counteract the intensity of the yellow Sun. This will require a period of mental meditation.

3. The equatorial region with its powerful sunshine is deadly, but the ice bound northern and southern hemispheres are habitable.

4.   The water of its oceans is even deadlier than the stars light, covering sixty per cent of the surface; it would dissolve our Alien integration on contact.

5.   Most of the Planet's fauna will attack on the perception that you are a threat or prey. Avoidance of such species is a main priority.

Oblivious to the directive, escape only on his mind, Zebulan now gathered ten converts together. The renegades stole a landing craft and fled to the Planet's surface to thwart the exile's schemes. His outright contempt for their schemes had waned slightly and he began to take a slight modicum of concern that they might be a niggling threat to his plans. But something went wrong with the descent of the transferring craft and instead of landing in the bearable northern latitudes; it crashed a thousand kilometres north of the equatorial zone. Crawling from the wreckage Zebulan and his corrupted servants were disorientated and stood up in full view of the midday Sun.

"Oh, how I will never forget that day." Uttered the voice who remembered it all too well.

On this Planet, the betrayer of his race was introduced to real pain and the intense sensations of agony. Fully exposed to the strength of the noon rays of a yellow Star, the crystal skin of their Alien bodies began to blister and smoke in burning plumes of white hissing steam. The excruciating pain scorched him with a power that encompassed him in an agony that made his masters previous efforts at chastisement appear as a mild telling off. Such was the intensity of the ordeal, that his screaming mind-voice was heard by every exile onboard the Mothership. All, but one shuddered, the Patriarchi Mescal took immense satisfaction in the deserters torment. The leader of the DEFILED began crawling towards a nearby cliff overhang that formed a cool cave and the promise of a reprieve from this incredible torment. His ice cool crystalline blood began to thicken and his brain boiled causing a flotilla of surreal mirages to sail around the shadows of approaching madness. Gripped in the throes of searing affliction, he remembered every millimetre of the horrendous crawl. As he inched his way across the blistering ground, sharp pinnacles of cracked rock punctured his fragile crystal skin. Zebulan was vaguely aware of others suffering similar atrocities to their bodies. These whimpers of agony danced at the edges of his vision, but he ignored them in his effort to reach the cave and relief from his own crushing pain. When he finally reached the salvation of the shelter, the suffering off-Worlder collapsed in a regeneration sleep unaware or uncaring if any of the others followed him. When the Sun scorched Alien awoke three cycles of the Planet later, he nearly wished that he had not survived. The physical pain was gone, replaced with an unbearable mental anguish. But he was no longer Zebulan the beautiful, his two magnificent wings were in tatters, his handsome visage and impeccable blue/black skin was covered in white festering noodles. His only boon was that his Preceptor-Band had powered down and had escaped largely untainted. Still, he now avoided his reflection; the shimmering pristine glow mocked the tattered remnants of his frame. He knew that given time (A few thousand years of this Planet's orbit around the Sun.) he would repossess his lost beauty, but as with everything, the EGO'S servant blamed the ALASTHA'I for his predicament.

"One especially, Mescal."

Even in his pain; Zebulan was certain.

"You are still alive and have tampered with the landing craft's controls."

He was indeed correct; it had been his adversary that caused his affliction. His love and passion for his people and the brief joining with the Corruption had finally made him overcome the genetic block. Some part of his victim admired the one responsible; he had crossed the barrier that he could not traverse without the melding of his master. His cohorts had survived and it was annoying that most of them had suffered less damage to their forms than him. To cover his ruined body and face, he now wore an unrevealing garment and the blue crystal face. His minion's visages had remained largely untouched, so they only wore the concealing apparel.

The servant of the EGO returned to the present. Now thousands of cycles of this Planet later, Zebulan naively believed.

"I have reached the same proficiency as Mescal."

The DEFILED was greatly mistaken. He had no conception that the mad Patriarchi could now actually take life without been consumed by the EGO. The willing student of the "INIQUITY." could now manipulate other life-forms to commit murder. This feeble shadow of the insane Patriarchi retreated to a shadowed cliff overhang to wait for his infiltrator to return with news. Just then, the bright yellow Sun began to rise in the eastern sky. The cursed orb was still athma to his ruined body. He had another hour until its glare became unbearable and he mind-spoke in disgust.

"How I miss the pale blue orb of our smaller Star and the cool soothing comfort of its radiance, so unlike the harsh glare of this large yellow sun. The thing evens rises in the east instead of the normal west."

These nostalgic remembrances evaporated with regret as he perceived someone desperately trying to contact him on his individual thought mode.

"Who is speaking?" Questioned Zebulan, though he knew quite well who it was.

"I beg your forgiveness Lord, but it is I, Setantana and my companions returning with news of our strike against the weak ones. Please lower the protective umbrella so as we can land our Platform of Light safely." Pleaded the mind-voice fearfully.

Zebulan seemed to be oblivious to their danger and asked in a controlled voice.

"Has the conclusion of your mission been concurrent with my desire for the destruction of that accursed mound and whatever is concealed in its depths?"

After the success of the first attack over three cycles of the moon ago; the leader of the DEFILED had sent his subjects on the same mission. Setantana fearing the wrath of Zebulan's anger trembled and avoided a direct answer as he replied.

"There was a great explosion from the mounds interior after the Primate unwittingly carried the volatile chemicals inside. So we can assume that great damage was done."

"We can assume. Can you imbeciles do anything correctly?" Mocked their leader.

Seantanta interjected hurriedly.

"But the Primates did exactly what you predicted, they did not learn from the first time. My lord, we have other news, another among the ALASTHA'I has returned with us."

The one with them mind-spoke; he sounded haughty.

"Zebulan. After much reflection, I have decided to come over to your side. With my assistance, we will accomplish great things."

"Yes, he can help us with your plans, my Lord." Added Seantanta.

Feeling annoyed that one of his kind thought that he was an equal to him, calling himself an ally and not a servant, Zebulan decided to pick his irritation out on one of his followers.

"It is time to teach the newcomer, something I have learned from my Master."

He mind-spoke acidly.

"Seantanta, I can forgive your folly at the mound, but not your constant interruptions."

Suddenly, the receiver of his mind-words stood up involuntary, somewhat like a puppet on a string, clutched his head and screamed silently. All in the flying craft could hear with frightening clarity through the shared mind link; the racking sobs as he pleaded for mercy. Under the mind-assault, he then started to twitch spasmodically. His tattered wings flapped unintentionally and he abruptly fell in a heap to the floor of the gliding platform as if his imaginary strings had been severed. The extra passenger and newest turncoat gasped in wonder at this display of unforgiving power.

"Yes. You have seen a taste of what I can give you and you think that you understand. But you are aware of nothing." Declared a pleased Zebulan to himself.

Naisi had been fearful to approach the destroyer of the Worlds; it had taken three months to convince him. Even that subtle persuasion would have not been enough, but for his fall in standing among the rest of his kind. Withering in the depths of failure and ridicule, he finally succumbed to the approach of the one who promised him power and respect. There was aloud buzzing noise as the umbrella quickly receded and the Platform of Light hovered above the concealed fortress. Then the craft slowly descended and landed a few metres from the red dome that dominated the centre of the last enclosure. Six DEFILED and a new convert alighted and four of the former passengers carried the unconscious Seantanta between them while the other remained aloof as if that task was beneath him. The loud buzzing noise returned as the umbrella was restored and the shield closed them in complete security in Zebulan's haven. The traitor knew that escape was now impossible.

"His wards are in place."

A quick study told him that he was on the edge of a small island of rock that was enclosed on three sides by dreaded sea water and a shimmering line of barriers of Zebulan's make on the front. He was also acutely aware that the seawater was a hundred times more potent to their crystal bodies than the dreaded rays of the yellow Sun. The turncoat stepped from the craft, glad to have his feet on the rocky ground devoid of dead matter and away from the terrifying sight of the foaming ocean below. Away from the magnetic clamping of the Platform of Light, the wind began to buffet him.

"If my wings were unfolded, I would be swept over the edge and at the mercy of the wind currents."

The fat Alien did not like those thoughts at all, especially as he would be over the dreaded Ocean. He then groaned in disbelief as the tall figure of a covered Zebulan materialised at the cliff edge and gestured for him to join him. The newcomer had wondered why the other DEFILED had been wearing such coarse artificial protection. He had asked his escort's why, but they were non-committal. But Naisi was a quick study and rightly guessed that they had somehow been disfigured. With all the stubborn control which he could muster, the former member of the CONGREGATION tried to approach to the vicinity of the sheer drop. To add insult to injury, the wind speed picked up as he neared the edge of the cataclysm. Standing tall and trying to appear calm, he failed and he fell to his knees in terror. On his six digit hands and feet; he crawled to the edge and dared to look over. Down below the breaking ice sheet showed great yawning maws of the salient azure sea water that eagerly wanted to dissolve him like some type of nutrient. The ALASTHA'I retreated to a safe distance instantly; his wings flapped in distress from his ordeal and nearly pushed him towards the edge. He retracted his flying appendages immediately. Zebulan shook his head in disdain and removed himself from the edge and strode towards his new convert.

"Still, he has done better than the rest."

From his kneeling position, his visitor glanced up into the image of unblemished beauty. But on close inspection, one could tell that he was wearing an artificial construction. He mind-gasped in the realising shock that the flawless face apprising him was in fact a mask of wafer thin blue crystal. The artefact was manufactured of quartz from the mines of his former prison Moon. So fine was the workmanship that it might as well have been a new layer of crystallised skin. His mimicking visage was full of false vigour, but contained no macula. It gave the EGO'S servant a sinister looking appearance. Naisi reappraised his situation once again.

"Zebulan must have some significant resources available to him if he was able to manufacture that here on this mud ball. Still, he was unable to incorporate any Macula; I can help him with that."

He then realised that none of the others wore such an adornment; he had been shocked when he first perceived the damage to their crystal forms. The defector came to the conclusion.

"By the moons of CRYSTALIOS, he must be more deformed than the rest."

Angered at the look of pity held in the flickering light above Naisi; Zebulan impacted the full force of his will on him. The tainted ALASTHA'I felt a great weight crushing him and a primeval power that could snap him in two like brittle crystal. Unable to withstand it, he still refused to grovel as Seantanta had done and just as he was been forced to his knees, his tormentor released his grip and mind-spoke.

"Welcome Naisi. At last I might have found someone worthy of serving me."

As the beads of gaseous perspiration diminished, Naisi thought inwardly.

"What power. This is what I want. I will give him my servitude, but not my loyalty. He will inadvertently teach me. And then when I am his equal, all things will be possible."

But, he mind-replied.

"I hope I am worthy of the honour my Lord?"

He had spent time in the Archives studying Mescal's original reports on Zebulan and had found the designation.

"My Lord."

He assumed correctly that this would please his new ally and the others use of the word had confirmed this. However an insightful Zebulan knew.

"Naisi's outward demeanour might fool most of the weaklings into thinking that he was a slouch, but behind the bland exterior there is a clever and devious mind."

Cathbad, Cetheren and Celtair had found this out much to their detriment. Naisi had become aware that Zebulan desired subordination and the leader of the DEFILED answered him.

"Indeed you are Naisi. Even though you could be too ambitious for my service."

Taken aback, the overweight Alien's hovering light paled.

"Am I that transparent my lord? Has he perceived me that easily?"

99

His newest convert's feet-inhaling had not fooled Zebulan. The EGO'S menial had seen the naked greed displayed on the fat exile's features on witnessing his power.

"You will be mine soon."

With totally concealed glee, he mind-insisted.

"Come let me introduce you to the rewards of serving our Master."

Naisi did not miss the emphasis on our master's service. Zebulan believed him fully committed. His new disciple opened his mind to the images but was careful to block out his covert thoughts. Every desire he could have thought of and some he could not of had flooded into his intoxicated conscious. This unlimited reservoir of promises, pleasures and most important of all, unrestricted power, threatened to unleash itself and tear down the boundaries of an unprepared mind. There was more displayed to him than his wildest fantasies could have produced.

"More, more. Show me more."

He cried in longing, lost in this never before encountered possibility. It was a World where only he counted. Zebulan knew he now had him forever in his thrall. Stopping the flow of promises, he casually motioned his newest adherent to accompany him.

"Just like one of those four legged canines that follow the Primates everywhere." Muttered his new master as Naisi stepped into line and trailed after his new leader.

"This is ironic. I have just fed him some scraps, just as the Primates do to their tame mammals and he is mine."

In the personal telepathic mode he told Naisi. (He was tempted to say the mammal.)

"Let us proceed to my study and discuss what you have learned about those weaklings and their plans."

Then, he amended himself.

"I also have to be careful with Naisi as the Primates pets are known to sometimes bite the hand that fed them."

Inside Zebulan's private study, the thin inner film of the dome revealed a surprising vista. It opened out to a memory of the landscape of the barren moon where he spent his imprisonment. Naisi shifted uncomfortably as he viewed an image of a dense shellac dawn and where moons were bigger than Stars in the sky. The owner of the living quarters smiled at the others embarrassment.

"Just a little reminder of my incarceration."

But it was really a remembrance of where he had first met his master. Zebulan pointed to a table made of inferior quartz and as his hand caressed the polished surface; he motioned for Naisi to sit on a hovering chair. As he did, his eyes were drawn like iron attracted to a magnet to a tray of odd-looking capsules that lay on its surface. These concoctions cried out to be sampled. He wanted to break them open and inhale their fragrant plumes.

Feigning boredom Naisi traced his podgy ringed fingers along the coarse edge of the table and advised Zebulan.

"The crystals of this rock are so ugly and lack character. I have brought equipment that can reproduce the best crystal formations from our Home World."

"It is not quartz." Replied Zebulan with an unusual glint in his Preceptor-Band.

"No. Then what is it made of?" Asked a bemused Naisi.

His new master had a desire to upset the arrogant newcomer. But feeling especially tolerant towards the cocky Naisi, he mind-spoke as if he was admiring a fine work of complex equations.

"Do you know the woolly mammal with the large tusks that inhabits these northern latitudes, the one that the Primates hunt for nourishment?"

With a growing insight that bordered on the horror visiting his soul, Naisi's voice dropped as he stammered.

"Ye-Yes."

"Well these are the calcium bones and tusks of its skeleton. Cut and polished of course. All my own creation. Is it not beautiful? One has to keep his mind occupied on this rock. Do you not think so?"

The only thing Naisi was considering was to remove himself as far away as possible from the fore mentioned table and flee the study. But he stayed put because his curiosity about the capsules contents outweighed his extreme discomfort at been in such close proximity to the remains of an expired life-form. As if in answering his growing dilemma, his host turned away from him; opened his synthetic clothing and in a concealing manner ingested an unbroken capsule. His Preceptor-Band became a strange hue for an instant and then returned to its normal shade. His method of nutrient intake went against the grain. Intrigued, Naisi's quizzical and gluttonous nature got the best of him.

"My Lord why do you take nourishment in this manner, instead of absorbing it like the rest of us."

Zebulan's deformed macula beneath the artificial mask darkened briefly for the Sun of this orb had seared away the outer membrane of his body thus making the normal process of ingestion extremely painful. His ruined body could not absorb the scant nutrients from the Planet's atmosphere. He regained control, Naisi was well known for his intemperance. Zebulan's Preceptor-Band glinted mockingly and he became his master incarnate.

"Come my new convert. Try one of these delights and afterwards, the finest inhalations will taste like bitter crystal shards. This is another of the pleasures I have promised you."

What the wiling transgressor was not about to reveal to the unsuspecting Naisi was that this was the final part in the transformation of an ALASTHA'I into DEFILED. The fat exile never could refuse an offered treat; he lifted up a single capsule with extreme delicateness and carefully examined it like one of the Primates receiving a new plaything. Tentatively, he placed it on one of his orifices and let it slowly dissolve directly into his bloodstream. Naisi moaned in exquisite delight as if all of a sudden he had grown new sensory organs. When the initial euphoria had waned to a level of comfort; he confirmed to his obliging host.

"You were telling the truth. This is the ultimate inhalation."

"Did you ever doubt me?"

"No!" Lied Naisi.

Then his providers tone became fanatical as he elaborated. Taking one of the capsules in his covered hand, he explained.

"And because of these, we no longer have to stand out in the open and inhale nutrients."

Now Naisi surmised.

"That is why the Scrying Globes have never picked up the DEFILED performing the ritual of inhalation."

Zebulan looked pleased and offered him another. Lost in exquisite sensations, he heard his host ask him.

"Tell me what has been going on over in that city of fools."

An inebriated Naisi told him everything.

"There were three proposals for debate and acceptance. Trelix said that we should flee. I took example from you and said that we should use CRYSTALOID 'I."

"Yes, they would be the best option."

"You would think so! But neither was chosen. They went for the Patriarchi Celtair's scheme."

"And what was that?" Asked the other in a bland mind-tone, not wanting to display his growing interest.

"To use the Primates against the might of the CRYSTALOID 'I.

"Primates!"

"I know what a ridiculous idea?" Giggled Naisi.

"I agree. And what made them accept that solution?"

Zebulan became very intrigued. He had already begun to study the native bi-peds and became attracted to their spectacles of violence. Naisi told him about the emergence of the Primate in the CONGREGATION chamber and the revelation of his own duplicity. His listener's Preceptor-Band darkened slightly as he confirmed in private mode.

"Mescal! That degenerate is behind this. But what does he see in this flight path? I must study this more."

To Naisi, he said.

"I have business to attend to. Stay here and enjoy more of the capsules. It is my gift to you."

Zebulan left him alone and he began to sample the delights on the hovering table with increasing gusto. As always, because of his nature, he overindulged. Much later after consuming a vast amount that even he had to stop himself, he rose from the table turned a sickly pale colour and completed an act that earlier in the day, he would have said was impossible for one of his race. The corpulent ALASTHA'I regurgitated almost everything he had ingested and promptly passed out, but the damage was done. A new chemistry had entered his crystalline constitution. What was more important that once Naisi had sampled the concoctions, he would crave for them always. For Zebulan had tampered with their makeup and unknown to the first time inhaler; he would develop an addiction.

A confusing twilight rose and fell in a bewildering conflict which formed into a cloudy dawn as his slumbering conscious regretfully gave up its comforting sense of oblivion and confronted the horrifying brightness of the globes artificial light. Patterns of patchy haze focused in to the painful light of awareness as faint outlines of a strange room's furniture flickered on and off in a maddening regularity. While Naisi was passed out; his body was affected deeply by his new intake as rouge vapours acquainted themselves with his internal chemistry. Strange images of violence, supremacy and lust came to him.

Then, he awoke.

Coming out of the trance, he began to rise; but every crystal muscle in his fat body groaned inwardly as his physical being refused to obey the impossible demands of his muddled mind. Normally the Preceptor-Band of an ALASTHA'I powered down during periods of recuperation. Brain patterns would go into hibernation during this spell of inactivity, but Naisi knew that his awareness had been going as fast as a speeding Star-ship. After what might have been several lifetimes, he eventually achieved in getting his rotund frame into a sitting position. Just then a bout of dizziness receded and he allowed himself a grunt of satisfaction.

"That was a mistake!"

Unbridled sour nausea nearly choked him and he gagged out the mind-words with considerable effort.

"By the five moons of my Home sphere. I must have passed out. I do not remember going to sleep."

Feeling as close to death without actually dying, his receptors gradually focused on another piece of bone furniture that was situated provocatively at the outer limits of his painful vision. Another series of spasmodic eruptions racked his body, as he perceived another tray of capsules sitting harmlessly on the dead table. As this renewal of convulsions slowly receded, Naisi vowed never to succumb to the temptation for a sweet and exquisite short-lived delight and then to suffer this agony the next day. He noted sagely.

"After all some pleasures are best forgotten about and the best pomegranate vapours would not do this to me."

Summoning all the resolve his aching body could muster, the unsteady exile strove to rise into a standing position. From his stationary place, vertigo assailed him like a lost lover. It was as if these two metres could be equated with the pinnacle of the sea cliffs which surrounded this insignificant isle. He collapsed immediately in an unseemly heap and complained as if it just hurt to mind-speak. He vowed.

"There's no way I am able to stand up. I will just stay on the floor."

The door to the room shimmered open and one of Zebulan's disciples entered. It hurt to look at him, but as his Preceptor-Band focused, he recognised Seantanta. Naisi was amazed at the others remarkable good health and quick recovery from his ordeal the previous time they had met.

"After all, he had been unconscious, when I last saw him."

He motioned for the shunned one to help him to his feet. His visitor came to his aid and lifted him easily into a standing position. Amazement at Seantanta's unusual strength was washed away as realisation dawned on him.

"How do I know it is the next revolution of the Planet?"

Fearfully, he questioned his helper.

"How long have I been slumbering on this sleeping platform."

Seantanta smiled inwardly as if he possessed some secret knowledge which had to be cajoled from him. Waiting until Naisi's full attention was on him, he answered, pausing for impact.

"About ten cycles of this Planet turning on its own axis."

Naisi lost what little composure he had left and groaned.

"That long. It cannot be."

Hurt clouded his false pretence of having recovered. The pain of humiliation threatened to overcome reason and he once again collapsed back on to the beckoning floor. Feeling deflated of all of his normal stubborn resolve, Naisi did not resemble the arrogant former member of the CONGREGATION. Seantanta left the other's side and snatched up the tray of capsules and returned to the huddled heap on the floor and as if treating a child admonished.

"Quickly you must consume some more of these capsules. Do it now, before it is too late."

The suffering exile was shocked out of his comatose and stared aghast at the mind-speaker.

"Surely, I am losing my mind-perception. Or is it diminishing as I am slowly slipping into unconsciousness. Or else Seantanta is around his master long enough to become as crazy as him."

Turning his baffled visage diagonally towards the now confirmed dysfunctional, the groggy defector decided to humour him and surprising himself at the control in his voice, he asked calmly.

"Are you completely bereft of your senses? I would rather expire this second than consume anymore of those infernal things. Those confounded mixtures are the reason that I am in this state."

Turning away in dismissal, the distressed mortal barely registered the others detached reply.

"You will certainly perish if you do not re-ingest these."

Thrusting a few capsules into his unfeeling hands, he repeated the statement. Naisi was beginning to lose him in a slow uncaring paralysis, but was shocked back into reality as the powerful Seantanta grabbed the astounded exile by the scruff of the neck and forced two capsules into one of his swollen opened pores. The much stronger Alien was under no illusions what punishment Zebulan would dish out if anything premature occurred to his charge. Within a few heartbeats of receiving the prescribed treatment, a wondrous change engulfed Naisi. Gone was the trembling, the slow paralysis, and the dripping moisture from his macula. He felt born again. This sudden regaining of his composure forced him to venture a quizzical look of his Preceptor-Band towards the now relieved Seantanta. The latter saw Naisi's look of bafflement and became a little arrogant, after all the after effects had not compromised him as much. But then, he had not taken as many as the gluttonous one.

"Surely our master explained the consequences of taking the capsules."

Seeing no acknowledgement in his blank features, he continued in an extremely condescending manner that was clearly becoming a lecturing tone.

"Those capsules are of a special formula devised by the master to enhance an aggressive behaviour."

His tone became passionate, as he continued.

"Because of those concoctions. We will not be weaklings anymore. One day, we will overcome the forbidden barrier. But there is a side effect to them, discontinuing the capsules will result in a slow painful expiration."

Hot flushed realisation dawned on Naisi like an abrupt slap in the face. Instead of been dismayed, he could see a prominent position for himself in the new order. Always the pragmatist, he mind-spoke aloud.

"I am his. It seems that our new master is experimenting on us just like Celtair is with the Primates."

Because of Seantanta's loyalty to his lord, it was hardly likely that he would believe that his master had tricked and manipulated Naisi, thus resulting in service or death.

"Naisi; do not judge Zebulan too harshly. For he too undergoes the same treatment as us. Our master has been ingesting the capsules ever since he recovered from his ordeal, when we crash landed on this Planet."

Then in a conspiring whisper in the individual mode, he added.

"Some say that is the source of his power and it was revealed to him by the true Master before our exile."

"Seantanta, stick to the real World. You do not believe that ridiculous fable concocted by Zebulan to explain his past deeds." Scorned Naisi.

A dark look crossed the others flickering feature and he mind-replied.

"I swear to you by our Queen that I do not lie. You will see for yourself for our leader seems to favour you above his longest followers."

His mind-voice betrayed a hard trace of envy as he saw how much Naisi was taken aback by those forced words. His chaperone, in foolish arrogance absolutely believed that those stories about Zebulan's divine communication with a depraved Entity was a clever ploy to guarantee him absolute power among these gullible fools. It allowed him to cover up the horror of him going beyond the pale and nearly slaughtering an entire race by re-programming their machines. At first Naisi with good reason had been very reluctant to approach this destroyer of Worlds, he had actually been trembling with fright with the prospect of meeting with the annihilator of all that he had ever known. But Zebulan clouded in lies had explained that the CRYSTALOID'I had been responsible for the slaughter.

"It had been an anomaly in their programming."

That much was true.

"And because of their infallible belief in the perfection of their own technology, the other Elders blamed me for their own failings."

That was completely false.

Besides Zebulan made it clear that he needed him to repair the damage, so they could return in triumph with newer and better models, and be acclaimed for their efforts.

"Still, there is much work to be done before that day."

It looked like he had more immediate concerns. On seeing the rage contorted on Seantanta's Preceptor-Band over his remarks concerning Zebulan's perceived nature and remembering the ease in which he had lifted him from the floor, he decided to keep his ideas to himself. With him not pursuing the subject any further, Seantanta's anger receded and he advised him.

"Make ready as the two of us must witness a ritual that is carried out every full cycle of the Planet's moon."

His curiosity was aroused and pepped up by the new intake; he motioned the other to guide him. Leaving the chamber, not before gathering a few capsules, they both proceeded outside the globe. After a brisk walk across the uneven bare rock terrain as Zebulan did not allow flight due to his handicap, Naisi was still suffering and felt shaky from the unaccustomed exercise. The heavy Alien rarely flew and like his kin, he only took to the air after been sated with mineral intake. It took him longer than most. He flew then, mainly because that it was the most practicable option in getting back to his quarters. Otherwise, he went everywhere by a Platform of Light. The two walking Aliens reached the cliff edge and Seantanta halted. Mustering enough courage, (Were the capsules working already?) Naisi looked over the precipice where the other had led them to and was shocked to see the dreaded sea had receded and formed an extremely long sandy beach. His much taller guide pointed to a long narrow stepped limestone path that hugged the sides of the cliff.

"We must travel down the path for a short distance. We cannot fly, Zebulan has forbidden it." Informed Seantanta.

"Not that I would fly over the open Ocean anyway. The wind currents are treacherous. Is this another test?" Questioned a sceptical Naisi.

"No. It is the only way to get to our destination."

"Are there no buffers put in place."

"No, we do not have the energy for such things."

Naisi decided to persevere. As he hurriedly gulped down two more capsules, something came to his attention.

"Those horrible infusions must have given me a measure of audacity. Zebulan is correct."

The new DEFILED took tentative steps and the stranger to this journey became relieved when he noticed a primitive hemp fence running parallel to the trail and following its meandering path to the bottom. Grabbing hold of the tightly twisted dead matter, he stepped over the abyss and slowly began his descent. He felt violated at the touch of the exposed clumps of decayed guano matter and ferns that the angle of the cliff path revealed, but he refused to show his disgust. Noticing his companion's baleful expression as he unsuccessfully failed to avoid the offending gunk. Seantanta explained.

"We cannot interfere with the islands makeup and remove this mess, in case a Scrying Globe reveals our presence to the weaklings."

Naisi who liked to have all the available facts wondered.

"If you are so brave, then why does your master fear discovery?"

Zebulan's new disciple was annoyed to see the speaker ignore the descending aid and skip pass him. A few metres on, his overtaker halted and when Naisi caught up with him, the puffing fat exile made out the faint darkness of a cave that was completely hidden from above. On entering the hidden opening, they were greeted by a low ceiling and a space that was lit by some unknown light source. He asked Seantanta about it and received an indifferent reply.

"The master has had to improvise, not having access to all of our science. Only he fully perceives the source of its operation."

From somewhere below a chill wind funnelled through the tunnel, bitterly cold maybe to the inhabitants of this latitude, but not to these creatures from another World. Naisi embraced the chill with a glad heart. His spirits picked up from the cold blast, which he found invigorating. His companion increased the pace until they came to a fork in the tunnel. Seantanta took the lead and without hesitation chose the left hand passage much to Naisi disappointment as the blast of invigorating cool air came from the right. Even more baffling was that they now faced a blank wall of stone whereas the other subterranean channel had been free of obstacles. His guide went to the wall and spoke what felt like gibberish to Naisi. But he revised his estimate of the former when the fabric of the wall seemed to liquefy and shimmer in the form of an open entrance. He was impressed for he knew that Zebulan lacked the resources that were available to the rest of their race. Naisi again marvelled at its making and got the same reply.

"Only the master knows the source of its operation."

He had a silent mind-thought.

"I would really like to throttle him."

Astonished by the focus of his thinking, he stopped suddenly causing the other to walk straight into him.

"By all of creation. I am actually contemplating violence. No wonder Zebulan surrounds himself with these imbeciles. It enhances the tendency towards aggression."

What Naisi had yet to realise was that his new master's concoction was still flowing through his crystalline veins. The two subterranean travellers came to a small alcove cut into the limestone walls and his guide ushered him inside. Hanging from the wall on rusty coated metal was numerous dull black robes of synthetic make. (Zebulan had not got the means to produce perfect crystal elements yet.) Naisi was instructed to wear one of the outfits. The robe was woven from a coarse plant of this World. He wanted to ask.

"I am not disfigured. Why should I have to wear this ugly thing?"

He was also mystified by the contrast of the superior technology of the lights and the concealed door and the corroded metal and the items of basic clothing. That was not the strangest thing that Seantanta requested of him. The other Winged Alien handed Naisi a fleshy mask of moulded synthetics etched in the image of a Primate face and told him to put it on. Now, the overweight Alien had a million questions. But he had learned to keep his queries unspoken, as he would undoubtedly receive the same monotonous response.

"Only the master knows the answer."

He adorned the primitive cloak, it felt extremely uncomfortable and his macula itched uncontrollably. But it was nothing compared to the distaste he felt when he looked at his fellow Alien dressed in the Primate mask. Seantanta was gesturing in an impertinent manner for him to hurry up as he was fearful both of them would miss the spectacle Zebulan had ordered them to attend. Flinching, Naisi donned the coarse mask of Primate mimicry and increased his pace, not out of any compassion for his companion and the consequences if they were tardy, but because his curiosity was multiplying tenfold. As the tunnel narrowed and the light mechanisms became more frequent, his breathing became ragged as he was unaccustomed to this much exercise. Their momentum carried them into an enormous natural cavern. The entire underground space was bathed in an uncomfortable brightness. Even the far above ceiling was exposed to the reach of the blinding light. His attention was drawn to a protruding shelf of granite remarkable because of the way it lay detached from the overall effect. Crude eroded steps led from the sandy beach that was exposed by the ebbing tide to a shelf of stone that appeared to all intentional purposes to be a hastily erected podium. Standing where there would normally be a speaker of the CONGREGATION; stood Zebulan. The leader of the DEFILED was also covered entirely in a suit of the coarse hemp. He wore a similar mask that also branded an imitation Primate face. On noticing Naisi, his mind-voice demanded that the newest member of his faction join him on the dais. Having no choice, the last arrival clutched at the false bravado of the inhalations and quickly crossed the sandy floor. He climbed up the slippery steps been very careful not to touch the rock as little hollows in its soft surface bore the shallow indentations of the lethal seawater. The overweight ALASTHA'I had never moved so fast. With wide opened macula, he alighted alongside the irritated Zebulan (Who was extremely vexed, because the forthcoming ceremony reminded him of his frizzled wings and the temporary loss of flight, still, he had to endure.). Swallowing his annoyance, but still giving Naisi a bitter glance, his new master told him.

"After what you will witness here, you will be convinced of my actions. When I give the mind word, remove that crude robe for our arriving guests and unfold your wings. So, they can view us in our whole splendour."

Naisi could feel the hot venom in the others voice as he arrived at the conclusion.

"Zebulan requires my unblemished body for some performance."

He was correct, for all of his deviants were scared at some degree when they had become exposed to the blazing Sun. Swallowing a feeling of superiority; he met his new superior's Preceptor-Band and smiled defiantly. But the other cut short his pleasure with a far superior smirk as he pointed to the outer entrance of the cavern. The curved opening was partially blocked by the outline of an irregular boulder giving the natural breach a tuber shape. Concentrating on the space of the outside entrance that allowed his nimbus to penetrate, Naisi perceived the approach of something more terrible than the equatorial sun. He mind-exclaimed.

"Dreaded seawater!"

The lethal liquid rushed in to fill the vacuum between the boulder, then retreated with an agonised slowness and then sped back again devouring ever more sandy beach with each crash of its foaming waves. The chunks of the lighter frozen water surrounding the isle had vanished since he first arrived; it was a complete liquid that came at him. The effects of the inhalations must have worn off as Naisi stood rooted to his spot as every splashing, foaming and frothing wave seemed like a rabid beast of this World intent on devouring him in an acidic grasp. Vaporised plumes of misty seawater rose effortlessly from the boiling liquid mass and danced tantalisingly at the edges of where they stood. Shuddering at the imaginary screams from the scarred stone as the seawater flowed over it; Naisi forced himself to turn away from the hypnotic attraction of the liquid. He glanced towards Zebulan whose Preceptor-Band gave the appearance of him been untroubled about the nearing doom. Then, the turncoat realised that they must be safe up here on the shelf of rock, so he regained some of his fleeing composure (Not for the first time that day.) Waiting until the salt water lapped against the bottom step, Zebulan then energised a light barrier that protected them from harm. Naisi relaxed when told what the enclosure was for.

"He saves his energy for other things."

After the light barrier shimmered and became invisible, Naisi's new master activated a hidden recording device. A rhythmic primeval vibrating sound of pounding drums that sent a shiver through his wings filled the enclosed cavern. Wisps of sweet smelling incense issued forth from concealed vents, masking the smell of the salt laden sea. Naisi looked towards the cavern opening; the seawater had reached a level around the rock that partially blocked its entrance, giving the new diminished space an appearance of a cracked egg. The sounds and smells must have been a signal as boatloads of painted Primates rowed through the reduced sea opening in crude hollowed out tree trunks as it they had been born from the illusion. In each craft, one primitive biped stood taller and prouder wearing a parody of the ALASTHA'I wings. Zebulan's mask took on a personality of its own; it began to mimic Primate actions. The mouth, lips, nostrils and especially the eyes adapted movement. The newcomer to the ritual wanted to laugh, but held himself in check.

"These life-forms copy our appearance and we mimic them. Has the Universe mislaid its common sense?"

On first impressions Naisi knew.

"These Primates are vastly different from those that toil on the great mound and other constructions."

On their floating craft displayed in full view were bone caskets, containing an offering to the Gods. He realised.

"Us! We are their Deities."

To his horror, it looked like the blood of other unfortunate Primates; a fact bore out by the crude red painted silhouettes of primates killing one another on the caskets sides. The salty metal tang of the blood offerings permeated the incense odour and wafted into the Alien's pores. Naisi was now doubly glad of the protective barrier. All the DEFILED shuddered, except their leader as the winged adorned Primates leapt out of the crude boats into the dreaded seawater with an exaggerated splash and marched towards them. There was no melting of flesh, no hissing of steam. Each of the off-Worlder's present on the landing (Including Zebulan.) backed up a few steps, while failing to keep their dignity intact. This was an unnecessary reaction from the Winged Aliens as the unseen barrier still protected them from the water and the Primates. If the killers that paid homage to them understood one thing, it was fear. Callous eyes scrutinised their God's actions, some could have been looking for other signs of weakness.

"Quickly, show yourself." Hissed Zebulan to Naisi in the mind-voice.

With urgency in his fumbling six fingers, the fat ALASTHA'I let the coarse robe he wore slump to the grey steps. The Alien insightfully unfurled his magnificent wings and rose a metre above the floor. The approaching aborigines halted, then gasped in awe and fell to their knees in adoration while averting their eyes from one of the Gods. Those Primates still on the steps shouted in their coarse language to the others who were still in the boats. These additional bipeds leapt from the boats, waded through the frothy water and brought the gifts of blood to the bottom of the natural steps. The gift bringer's had learnt the prudence of not approaching the invisible shield after previous encounters with its zapping pain. The other Primates used long slender wooden poles that fitted into the rims of the bone caskets. The timber shafts had come from the warmer south; there were no trees at these latitudes. The uncouth natives touched their heads to the stone floor, which Zebulan had learned to be a sign of reverence. Once the precious "Gifts to the Gods." had been unloaded, the Primates rushed back into their sea craft and rowed from the cavern. There would be some tales told around their campfires tonight, not many beings got to meet with their God's personally.

Then, the winged Aliens were alone again. All of the fierce looking Primates had departed as quickly as they had come. The rhythmic chanting ceased as Zebulan operated a small globe and turned off the sound mechanism. Two Platforms of Light arrived to take away the gifts. The leader of the DEFILED motioned for Naisi to accompany him, as he told Seantanta and the other underlings.

"Load the contributions of the natives onto the hovering platforms and take them to my private lab."

The newcomer was aghast at seeing other members of his race do menial work. When the flying contraptions were loaded, they set off on a pre-programmed course that made its way out through the sea opening and straight up the cliff escarpment. Walking back up to the surface, Zebulan started filling Naisi in on his plans for using the Primates to thwart the growing schemes of his former kin.

"You have seen what these Primates are capable of. Celtair is on the correct flight-path, because in their recent evolution, the Primates reduced their consumption of leaves, nuts and berries and the flesh of other animals became the main staple. To hunt and trap game that is extremely larger than themselves, their brains and cunning increased in tandem with their bloodlust. I have come to the conclusion that it is the life fluid of lesser

111

animals that increased the Primates aggression and so it will be with us. I am using these bipeds to bring me offerings of other Primate blood. If we keep infusing this potent cocktail, then finally we will remove the weak trait that our cursed forefathers left us with."

Naisi had just heard Zebulan's plan and he was intrigued as much as he was repelled. He wondered if the leader of the shunned had lost his sanity. But the fat Alien had witnessed the others power and reason told him that he was on the correct path. Then Zebulan cautioned his adipose disciple.

"Be cautious Naisi, These life-forms have to fear us, that is the secret with them, otherwise these habitual killers will tear us apart. That is their only solution to perceived weakness."

"Yes master."

Naisi was now fully in the Diadem of the DEFILED and he wondered.

"Have I over flew myself? How am I going to make these bestial and primitive life forms fear me? My powers of argument would be lost upon those savages. The art of logical reasoning is beyond them. It would be the equivalent of asking them to fly to this Planet's single satellite and step foot on its craterous surface."

VI.

Why had the ALASTHA'I been persuaded to choose this unassuming World for the first battle in resistance against the "INIQUITY."? To all intents and purposes, the Blue orb was an unavailing Planet with one natural satellite, third from a medium sized Sun at a distance of 149,600,000 km. It was not even an impressive specimen of creation with a mass of 5.976 x 10 to the power 27g and a volume of 1.083x 12,756km. Basically, their decision had all been down to the cycle of carbon that was the driving factor of life within its blue confines. When the first Scrying Globes from the Mother-ship had circumvented the globe and returned with their gathered data, it soon became clear how the cycle of life operated on this World. The information gathering modules discovered that it is an ever changing caldron of transformation where.

CONTINUED EXISTENCE OF A SPECIES IS BASED ON THE CARBON CYCLE THAT GOVERNS LIFE ON THIS WORLD.

Every type of organism existing on the Blue Planet was a carbon based life-form and each living thing gathered this major element as well as other lesser particles such as hydrogen and oxygen in any possible manner to sustain its existence. All of the major species, like the ALASTHA'I did inhale some vapours, taking in a liquid combination of hydrogen and oxygen. But these acceptable intakes were insufficient for their continued efforts, so each individual organism looked for other available sources to satisfy their needs. In this aggressive ecology, this meant proteins, fats, vitamins, minerals and carbohydrates. The majority of these methods of accumulating organic molecules resulted in the violent demise of the host or of using decayed matter of other life-forms that covered a thin layer of the outer mantels surface. So species at the lower end of the food chain occurred in unfathomable numbers to increase their chances of survival. Some organisms did use a sustainable method of cropping and left their food source to endure. But in times of geological stress, this was neglected and the prey species was devoured completely. Most organisms also reached towards the glare of the bitter Sun; without it, they would not survive, especially most of the Flora. So, plants that relied entirely on photosynthesis were the main producers of energy. Herbivores were the primary consumers of these plants while Carnivores became secondary consumers of the plant eaters and all ensnared by this competitive system were reduced by the decomposers which in turn were reused by the plants again. One such cycle of this accumulation and dispersal of carbon was used as the basis for this prognosis. On the wide savannahs on one of the large landmasses close to the equator, many species of herbivores gathered in packs of millions. Drawn together, the huge herds of beasts consumed their entire food source without reservation and some inbuilt sense told them that the seasonal rains were falling to the north and would provide more nourishment. The falling mixture of hydrogen and oxygen would rejuvenate the scorched earth and replenish the green chlorophyll plants that were their main food source. A vast migration began. This exhausting journey caused the weak and injured to be picked off by large predators and scavengers who gained their intake of organic molecules from these unfortunate animals. When the herd came to a large course of liquid hydrogen and oxygen, specialised ambush predators waited. These land, water and even ariel-based scavengers extracted large amounts of stored up energy from the herd. Through many digestive systems, the predators and their prey excreted solid and liquid waste on to the grasslands. This was further used by countless beetles and other insects to gather their crude intake; while they aerated the soil. The organic waste of all of these lifeforms re-nurtured the earth and the chlorophyll plants grew again when the liquid hydrogen and oxygen downpours returned.

The ALASTHA'I when they went by another name had their own cycle of life on their lost system of Worlds that was based on sublimation and fusion. The structure of their crystalline forms required a regular array of atoms, ions and molecules. The necessary sustenance produced within their internal chemistry occurred when substances passed from gaseous phases to the solid phase by the process of evaporation. These intakes cooled and solidified giving them the building blocks for functionality. What interested some among them now was the brutal taking of life that abounded on this Planet and not the constructs of biology. The built in violence of this World was what the peaceful Alien race required now. If their much depleted race were to continue and survive what would soon hunt them, then they had to harness this evolved aggression and put it to their use. Thus, the Primate suited their needs best. It had the advantage of basic cognitive intelligence over the rest of the other candidates. Study showed that, it was a result of the adults and children spending a long time together. The long period of co-habiting enabled any acquired knowledge to be passed on. The Aliens knew that given enough time, the Primates would evolve far quicker than every other organism on the Planet. So, some decided to exploit this trait of growing aptitude and Mescal was the one being of their race capable of doing just that.

It was early morning and the rising Sun began to power the chemistry of the blue Planet. As the stellar furnace began to remove the slight chill of the daybreak, the large Golden eagle confident in its supremacy; ignored his customary observation point and lazily flew to the tall tapering stones, which protruded out of the spongy grass on top of the experimental mound. From there, the sleek silent flying killer could scan the surrounding terrain with its sharp hearing and eyesight for any movement or tell-tale signs of its prey. Its favourite quarry was the small brown lemming that thrived in these northern latitudes, but it would take anything that it could handle and that was most things. It was even known to take the unattended very young of the Primates. Back in his large eyrie, hidden in an icy cliff edge, his mate and a never sated brood of young waited eagerly for his return. As he prepared to land on top of the artificial perch, the killer avian knew that this location would prove to be a productive site. Its large outstretched wings banked to slow his descent. The bird's razor sharp talons touched the tips of the ancient limestone and the unsuspecting raptor was incinerated in an invisible flash of pulsating energy. The once majestic bird had not even time to even squawk in alarm. Its demise happened in the blink of a macula. The charred remains of the raptor fell to the ground to join a pile of other hapless flying predators of night and day. Back in the craggy Erie, his mate would wonder why her partner never returned and why their young would go hungry this day. Soon the female would realise that her seasonal spouse was not returning and she would have to leave her young cold and vulnerable, while she went off and hunted. If the lone parent chose the same vantage-point as her unfortunate mate, then her young would perish from the bitter cold, well before starvation crept in. The real irony of this situation was that the raptors prey were having a bountiful time with the carcasses of their predators that lay rotting around the base of the towering stone. This recent petulant and random slaughter and reversal of the order of things was Mescal's doing. The mad Patriarchi was becoming more unstable and irrational. His bouts of coherency were few and far between. In one rare moment of lucidly, he begged Cetheren to go ahead with his plan without him. Mescal's polarised vision was to create a Hybrid race from the Primate gene-pool. He and his accomplice would take the path of divergent evolution. This interference in the natural order of the Planet would have been once impossible to commit for those who were in all manner and outlook; the ASCETIC'I. But Mescal had been under the influence of the "INIQUITY." and Cetheren had a resolve stronger than all of them. The tall Primate; Celtair's creature that these two of the Alien race had chosen would have its genes impregnated with the technology of the ALASTHA'I. Mescal would change the makeup of their specimen's electro-chemical brain, speeding up and altering its focus. Improved synaptic connections would enhance the intelligence retaining pathways and produce a far improved thinking creature. Cathbad had always been amazed that every living thing including themselves had a precise genetic code that reproduced itself under the appropriate conditions. How and when these codes functioned was proof enough to him of the Creator. Now, his race was deliberately altering the work of the Great Mathematician. This step was as significant to the ALASTHA'I as the Primates discovering faster than light space travel. During his private experiments, Mescal located the stem cells, which controlled aggression and acumen and amplified them. The microcondrian cells and D.N.A strands of the Primates were epigenetically altered; these new traits would affect the behaviour of their descendants. The biped's evolution would be speeded up a hundred fold and it would become a bigger, stronger and smarter end product. It would be essentially a Hybrid life-form.

AN ORGANISM NOT ENTIRELY BORN FROM THE PLANET.

Cetheren totally wrapped up in the scheme, agreed. So, he met Celtair in private and both of them decided that it was time to implement the plan. The Patriarchi had commandeered a small spacecraft and flew with him to the small ice bound Planet's at the edges of the Star's influence. Out here on the fringes of the solar system, far from the power of the yellow furnace, its vistas of frozen seas were quite pleasant for both of the exiles. The small orb of the Star in these heavens even bore a slight resemblance to their far distant Sun. The two of them were out here cloaked in shimmering shields with the pretence of monitoring the asteroid deflectors. It seemed apt; that the final go ahead for the mad Patriarchi's scheme was given in the cool tranquilly of this tiny Planet. But if Celtair knew the real plan that Mescal had concocted, it would be doubtful that he would have given the final authorisation. Little did the wise Elder realise that,

IT WAS A SCHEME BORN FROM INSANITY AND DESPERATION.

Under Mescal's growing influence, Cetheren began to lie to the gatherings of the CONGREGATION. He gave them false reports and these were inspected and approved. Ever growing in the art of deception, the two hid their real experiments and agenda from everyone. Mescal's plan was to incorporate his separated being into pieces of an Amulet that were to be given to the newly created Hybrids. It had many advantages, chief among them was that abnormal Patriarchi physique would be diluted and the madness would dissipate. All projections showed that the re-assembly would make him whole and rational again. The mixture of his knowledge, his flirtation with the "INIQUITY." and the increased aggression combined with the new intelligence of the Hybrids would make a formidable weapon indeed. None but Cetheren had even an inkling of the chaos and the madness of Mescal's ambition. But the student was also been lied to by his mentor.

The Lab for the creation of Hybrids was off limits to every exile, except Mescal and Cetheren. Even Celtair and Cathbad never dared to visit. This was a place of deep rumour and none could comprehend the terrible things that were been shaped in its subterraneous depths. It was far down in the belly of the earth, covered over with a lesser mound as if to hide it from the other ALASTHA'I. The Alien technology that powered the deception relied on the performance of two main types of crystals. First there were the uniaxials, tetragonal and trigonal. These types had refractive indices displaying double refraction. Then there were the bixials, orthorhombic, monoclinic and triclinic. These types had three principal refractive indices. When beams converged and electrons spun, mysterious light webs spun in the depths. The luminance moved like swirling waters; conduits open to the air sucked in cosmic plasma. Bubbles of white light flowed through the Lab's unearthly space as if each individual spark had captivated the viscosity of liquid. Ribbons of light flowed from one three-dimensional closed surface to other throbbing spheres connected in sequences that only their makers understood. Strange globular tubes of focused actinic light fed hundreds of transparent cryostats that were interlined with crystal globed accumulators. Each frozen vessel contained a swirling gaseous mixture that enveloped a single Hybrid that occupied each one. Though those creatures that were harmlessly in-cased, looked like Primates, they were no longer so. Their intelligence and physiology make up had been tampered with. Far more extreme than the CONGREGATION could envisage. The Hybrids had become the tools of a member of an Alien race and a mad individual at that. This underground Lab concealed a dark secret that Cetheren and Mescal were keeping from every exile, including Cathbad and Celtair. No one could know the full extent of the work carried out here. If they did, their whole race would be aghast and the plan would certainly be halted at once. For both of the deviants were using secret and corrupted knowledge which Mescal had stolen from the "INIQUITY.". This Lab had now become the factuality for the Arcane. The disturbed Elder had finally eroded Cetheren's will using the formers new sense of passion and injustice to convince him that this was the only way to save their ancient society. Their race were going against the Creator's vision and using the Hybrids souls for their own purpose. The soul originated from light and it required its own type of nutrients to feed it.

Emotions!

Both of them now harnessed these essential energies of emotional chemistry that the spirit needed to nourish it. Been in close proximity to these mental pulses had pushed Cetheren over the edge and into Mescal's camp. In their need, the two ALASTHA'I used these emotions of the new Hybrids and interfaced them with the advanced Alien light technology of their race. The frequency of their enhanced creations brain waves was insufficient for direct mind connection to their advanced craft, so the Hybrid's main advantage, its opposable thumb was incorporated. Even then, five digits became an unseen handicap. The short lives and daily struggles of existence made the Hybrids souls more potent. In fact the harsh elements of this place made them a product of an environment which would eventually build a tougher race than the constructed CRYSTALOID'I of their softer Home Worlds. In fact, the mad Patriarchi seemed to be in affinity with this upside down biological reality. Because to the consideration of the exiles, the normal propagation of species that they were familiar with did not apply here. Every type of organism on their lost Planets, no matter how ineffectual their part in the greater scheme of life had a Queen that only bred with selective males. But here, males could have different partners, producing countless offspring. In some bizarre instances, males just released their sperm on millions of eggs without any physical contact. So this Planet created an abundance of individuals because such a small percentage survived. (Because of this reality, Mescal had gone out and gathered more Primates for his experimentation and found that those who had settled in the harsher places were better suited to his tampering. It was ironic that what Primates considered unkind environments were in fact pleasant places to the exiles). Thus the possibilities of tampering became endless.

Huge solar reflectors focused beams of light on to the gaseous containers containing the selected bipeds. This interface would be accented by the Mescal/Amulet. It would be the catalyst, when far into the Hybrids future these new creations reached their genetic potential. This was the main reason, why Cetheren desired to remain behind instead of Cathbad, so he could supervise their creation. But, the Conclavi of Patriarchi had no inkling of the extremes his task had reached and they needed him, as the likely hood of finding more semi intelligent life-forms in the vastness of the Cosmos was certain. He was now their supreme manipulator of inferior species and the Primates of this World were to be his first experiment. Celtair's noble savage had been their inspiration. The two ALASTHA'I scoured the Planet for more Primate Specimens to form the basis of their experiments and there were no shortage of senseless killers among the bi-pedal populations. Scrying orbs flying all over the surface witnessed the Primate's savage nature, watching and recording individuals and groups killing other species and even its own kind. Sometimes the murder was carried out, just because the Primate could do it. As far as the two observers could tell, this animal killed for sport. A trait that was unique among any life-forms the off-Worlder's had encountered on their vast journey through the frozen wastes of space. The globes got up close to the selected Primates and a whiff of a knockout gas rendered them unconscious and harmless. Waiting pre-programmed CRYSTALOID'I aboard Platforms of Light would deliver them to the lab for the creation of Hybrids. Cetheren began his day in an optimistic frame of mind and entered the experimental chamber to find a rational Mescal. He was relieved as the Patriarchi was having one of his now rare bouts of lucidity. These instants of rationally were becoming few and further between. Mescal's capacity for aggression and violence was increasing. As was borne out by the sterilizing automations that were cleaning some smashed piece of equipment. The two manipulators toiled long and hard that period, the Elders aggression gave him renewed impetuous for twisted creation. The next day, Cetheren uplifted by the previous week's efforts was abruptly brought down to earth when he entered the Lab. There was no sign of Mescal and more to the point, a number of sealed cryostats were empty of their occupants. Panicking, Cetheren desperately tried to contact the mad exile, but to no avail. The absconded Elder was ignoring every

Missive that was sent to him.

"What is he up to?"

A few hours later, the Patriarchi returned without the missing Hybrids. Surprisingly, his mentor was rational. Cetheren always knew when the other was lucid as his back straightened up, while the rest of his presence, including his wings took on a different bearing. A haunted looking Mescal looked his student square in the light perceiving Preceptor-Band and said simply in the mind-voice.

"It is time for the meld. I have realised why my affliction is growing. The INEQUITY has escaped from the trap. Our Queen was no longer able to contain it. The Corruption is now free and roaming CRYSTALIOS. But it is yet unaware that I am conscious of it. It is occupied with something else at the moment."

"We must inform the host. We must warn them." Insisted Cetheren as the implications of Mescal's mind words sunk in.

"All in good time, we must first present them with a completed solution." Replied the other with a hint of slyness.

Not missing the devious expression, his student confirmed to himself.

"The Patriarchi's bouts of madness are growing more astute; he has been surely touched by the dark force."

Unknown to his student and his rational self, he had completed designs of such depravity and destruction which were increasingly becoming more alarming and negative. The Elder had already incorporated them into their scheme. This sustenance of degeneracy that had its beginnings in the embrace of the EGO had taken a life of its own and had warped beyond the wildest imaginings of the ALASTHA'I. The now fully schizophrenic Mescal would have made a far better host for the Entity than Zebulan. What the momentary rational being was proposing was the final solution of their efforts. His siphoned psyche would be merged with the emotions of the Hybrids by channelling and funnelling his altered form into a receptor. His entire physical profile would be manipulated with lasers, compressed in a light press where his soul and transformed being would be retained in the silica of an Amulet whose chemistry was not born of this Galaxy. Mescal's transmuted form would begin to bond with the Hybrids make-up and they would share his knowledge and craft. This meddling of the original Primates did not go against the new principals of the ALASTHA'I, as the Hybrids did not expire during the operation. No, the Aliens had just accelerated their evolution a thousand fold and had improved them enormously.

"Are you completely certain that it is time?" Questioned a sceptical Cetheren. *"After all it will still take the corrupted legions millennia to get here. Surely we have more time."*

"Without a doubt. But it is for my sake and the inception of our scheme that we need expediency. I have done something terrible. An action so vile

that the part of me that I once was is so horrified by it that I cannot continue in this state any longer. Where do you think I've been?" Insisted his unequal partner in deception.

Cetheren could see that this bout of lucidly from Mescal was about to come to an end, his frame was bending slightly. But, he noticed that the Patriarchi had a sharp edge of grief etched into his macula and his Preceptor-Band had taken on a sombre tone. He noted.

"Something is different."

The emaciated being raised his thin arm and advised.

"Watch and judge."

A viewing globe floated over and with a command from Mescal, the imaging globe displayed a Platform of Light, which was gliding along at a high velocity while all the time hugging close to the frigid ground of the tundra. These hovering devices were still the Aliens main method of transport on this or any other World. These flying machines travelled only across the frozen Northern Hemisphere of packed ice and connecting landmasses. No one was brave or foolish enough to fly the contrivances over the salty seas, not even the crazy Mescal. The Patriarchi was mad, not stupid. The flying apparatus was speeding along a rugged eroded trail that cut through the steep slopes of a frozen gorge. The meandering path had been beaten down over centuries by some large herd animals migrating to their winter and summer grazing areas and these types of trails were in common use by the Primates. The floating platform contained Seantanta and all of the shunned. To the astonishment of the watching Cetheren, Naisi was there too. Only their devious master was not present in the image.

"Naisi has taken the path of Corruption." Mescal informed him after witnessing his student's reaction on seeing his former antagonising opponent among the DEFILED. Cetheren was shocked at this revelation and he also noticed.

"They seem bigger, more bulkier."

"My opponent is meddling with the forces of nature too."

The mind-thoughts of those aboard the gliding Platform of Light became audible to them. Its passengers were in heated disagreement about the mission that they had been sent on. Zebulan at the limits of frustration had ordered them to find out what was going on beneath a mysterious mound. (It was the earthworks above the lab for the creation of Hybrids.) It was as if the probing tendrils of the EGO was been focused there. Something happening underneath it was drawing his full attention there. He informed them of his plan.

"As false supplicants, you are to return to the fold and beg forgiveness for your misguided actions. To them, it would appear that you Naisi have convinced the others to return to the host and redeem themselves. The stupid Conclavi of Patriarchi's will only be too willing to re-accept the

strayed members of their flock back into the fold. From there, you have a greater chance of disrupting the weakling's plans."

Naisi greatly admired his duplicity.

"It is a simple scheme based on the Patriarchi's gullibility."

The discussion brewing among the DEFILED was ended abruptly, when Mescal stepped in front of the low flying craft. The speeding contrivance stopped suddenly unwilling to crush the Elder. On seeing the Patriarchi, Naisi reacted in shock; he was looking at a ghost. His mind-words echoed his confusion.

"But you are expired."

"Do I look departed?" Asked Mescal in a mind-voice laced with scorn.

Then he ruined his dramatic appearance by swearing and fluttering his wings in a bizarre fashion. Always a quick study, Naisi guessed the truth and whispered it to the others on their private mind-modes. All onboard the flying platform laughed loudly. Naisi raised his jewelled-fingered hand and ordered the others to cease their mirth.

"What can we do for you, mad one? Is this the best the weaklings can manage?"

He looked at his companions while pointing at the mad Patriarchi. Naisi was becoming quite bold; he had been infusing Zebulan's capsules with an increased appetite. But like a connoisseur of fine Pulpa inhalations, the fat DEFILED preferred the blood of the fiercely territorial boar. He and the others had a supply of Zebulan's capsules to bide them over during their mission. The others on board the Platform of Light snickered even more at Naisi's audacity.

"We have no reason to converse with you. Go back to the other recreants or we will show you something we have learned from our master." Threatened Seantanta.

The cocky deviants had just made a fatal mistake; you see their leader never divulged to his underlings that Mescal had overcome the genetic block. Why? Was it because Zebulan could not tolerate anyone been more superior to him? No, it was for the arrogant reason that their master had no inkling of the full extent of Mescal's transformation. In a schizophrenic twist, the Elder got his act together; his mind-voice became rational and icy cold.

"I have a Missive for your foolish leader and his true master. Unfortunately, you will not be capable of delivering it. But, he will know its full portent. It is something that I have learned from the thing that he idolises." Replied Mescal with an even madder than normal glint in his features.

Then, the crazy exile swore and laughed at them, he was becoming quite proficient in the face of adversary. He had learned this from conversing with his experimental Hybrids, for they had a capacity for expletives that went far beyond the mad exiles experience. The DEFILED inside the stopped craft were shocked into silence with the colourful mind-language; the mad Patriarchi was using. Naisi knew there was little hope of getting a rational argument from Mescal and he was just about to order the Platform of Light to go around him. However, Zebulan's second in command foolishly decided to use the mind-tool to cower the living obstacle in front of them. Naisi truly believe that he was becoming gifted with that mental contrivance. Focusing, he entered the unstable mind of the Patriarchi and instantly regretted his imprudent action. The hefty figure drew back in a horrified moment and the expression on his features said it all. His Preceptor-Band fluctuated wildly and he was actually oozing solid vapours from his pores. Naisi's trembling increased when with a dramatic flourish, Mescal pointed to the hillside above them and to the horror of the shunned; a huge boulder could be seen careening down its slope. To the transfixed watchers, the descending stone was flawless and circular in appearance and could not have been carved by any Primate. The piece of the Planet's outer surface was accelerating in its descent and it was been chased by a group of excited Primates. Their titillation evident by the plumes of warm breath wafting from opened mouths as a result of their boisterous yelling. An instant before impact, Mescal pointed a device at the DEFILED and to their dismay, the light shields that shimmered around them weakened greatly. The plummeting missile crashed into the static platform and the collision sent shattered crystal bodies tumbling through the frosty air. Mercifully, more by luck than design, Naisi and Seantanta were thrown clear and landed a little bruised and deeply shocked, but mainly unharmed. In moments, the two defenceless Aliens were going to wish that neither of them had survived the original attack. Unfortunately for them; Mescal's interference in their transparent shields ensured that the now flimsy membrane would not deflect any blow. Naisi's and Seantanta's waking nightmare had just begun. The group of Hybrids who had sent the boulder careening down the slope advanced on the hapless duo. For effect; Mescal had divested them of the clean plant fibre garments that they wore in the Lab and they now sported the scraped and bloodied skins of other dead species. The biped assailants looked familiar to Cetheren and then he knew why. The observer in the lab closed his eyes to the approaching horror.

"These perpetrators of violence have been freed from their chambers by Mescal to perform this terrible deed. I am a part of it now."

This bunch of Hybrids had instilled the belief that if they consumed the Gods, then the power of the immortals would be conveyed to them. So the attackers proceeded to do that to the dead and the two still living victims. Cetheren begged his teacher to turn off the horrible images and sounds of Naisi and Seantana been torn apart while they were still alive. In real time, Mescal had an irrational mind-thought.

"It is an unusual and lasting timbre for an ALASTHA'I to make; even

during the holocaust I never heard such high pitched utterances."

The murderous Hybrids chopped off the fingers of the still breathing and screaming Naisi and fought over his precious rings. The sphere went opaque and Cetheren was spared the horror of the grisly feast. Recovering gradually from the broadcasted atrocity, Mescal's student got a firm grip of himself and demanded in a forced mind-voice.

"Why have the Hybrids not been returned to their cryostats?"

He would never be prepared for the mind-answer he received.

"I have disposed of them. I gave them a lethal concoction, they have all expired."

Cetheren stared at Mescal in absolute horror.

"Why?"

"It had to be done. Those Hybrid's became aware that they were able to murder their Gods easily. Their next step would have killed us all. These primitive beings cannot lose their awe of us."

A petulant Mescal then threw Naisi's severed hand on the floor of the lab. The crystallised limb landed with a dull hollow thud that appeared to thunder around the confines of the Lab. Cetheren knew they were his former antagonist's digits because his rings were still attached. The murdering Hybrids had expired before any of them had removed the finger adornments.

"Now do you believe that it is time?" Challenged Mescal.

His student did and he fled from the underground chamber with his wings flapping frantically as if the "INIQUITY." had been in his presence. He would have been correct in his assumption, but the appearance of the Entity would have been in a different wizened form and not recognisable to Zebulan. Back in his island base, the leader of the DEFILED had felt the cold sliver of fear throughout his ruined macula. He had witnessed the carnage instigated on his adversary's behalf, but vestiges of his master's slaughter on his own kind had made him queasy only when his own life was threatened. Still he had lost useful tools and he had seen the container of precious capsules sail through the air and lie undisturbed in the emerging undergrowth. His actual terror came from the fact that Mescal was still alive and very much capable of orchestrating death. This terrorised the EGO'S servant.

"That one would certainly use the Primates to slay me if he found my secret base?"

For the first time since his chastisement by his master, he became deeply afraid of another living Being.

"It is time to move my base farther south, into the hot places where he would never search for me."

Been a witness once again to recurring murder by a familiar winged form made him first envious, then whimsical and finally callous.

"Oh, how I long for Mescal's power. Still, seeing the fear and utter

realisation that he was doomed, in Naisi's features has nearly made his loss worthwhile. Most of the others fate has not even been an inconvenience. Those fools can be easily replaced.

However, Zebulan was not privy to the fact that the ALASTHA'I were ready to depart from this Sphere. His fear of Mescal was also misplaced and premature as this one capable of organising murder was soon to lose not only his physical presence but his identity too.

He would be caught in a dilemma, whether to follow them for more converts or stay and try to destroy the hydro-carbon weapon that was been created on this Planet. Meanwhile, after witnessing the massacre and the mounting terror of the doomed DEFILED, Cetheren knew for certain that it was time for the transformation of the mad Patriarchi.

"If the Conclavi and that includes my mentor Celtair get a whisper of the slaughter of our estranged kin, then they will insist on an end to our efforts. This World will be quickly abandoned out of fear.

Thirty-six hours later after his hurried exit, Cetheren returned. He was not completely recovered from his revulsion. With grim determination, he faced the waiting Mescal and mind-spoke without emotion.

"Let's proceed."

The mad Patriarchi's features flickered with a glint of no return. His student mimicked the others expression with a large intake of the Lab's atmosphere into his macula. These long-lived Star travelling observers had noticed in their thorough examination of all details.

"Highly respected individuals among these primitive aborigines carry sacred Amulets named "Churinga.". These are the designations that they give to items of perceived power. Made out of natural materials, they are supposed to have a connection with their spirit places. These objects are precious to them and are always treated with great respect and care."

This was to be the foundation of their plan. Mescal's brain patterns were to be imprinted photochromically on to a now very rare form of an epoxide crystal that was only to be found in the depths of one Cryo-volcano on the cool equator of the Queen's World. This incredibly dense element had the unusual property of absorbing, retaining and reconstituting the physical body and mind of a living ALASTHA'I. When the task was completed, it would be substituted for the Hybrid's precious amulets. The living focus of this process divulged his garments and stood in the middle of the operating area. His student was shocked at his emancipated frame. The cognitive light above Cetheren's oblong head glowed as bright as a miniature Star as he initiated the program. He powered up the arrays of crystal machinery in the Lab for the Arcane. Shielded photo cells of frosty light, far brighter than the Sun's rays illuminated the dark depths of the space that lay beneath the layers of strata. The ultra violet rays that bathed this World had a far greater aggressive potency than the similar beams that CRYSTALIOS absorbed. Today, as the light above heralded another dawn, this event deep below the ground was going to circumvent the natural way of things. This reversible change was their solution, Mescal's being was bathed in channelled bright light and through the action of photolysis, he would decompose and all of his molecules would transfer on to the special element. Once embedded in the pearl of light, his altered structure would reform and become one with the non-living substance. The merged form would then become a living thing.

From now on, it would be known as the APOCRYPHA'I. (The hidden deception.).

In the mind-language of the winged Aliens, this meant obscure and unproved knowledge that should not be availed of. Celtair had inadvertently pushed them into this flight-path when he had confided in them.

"These times are chaotic and desperate beings must alter their original conceptions whether they like it or not."

Whiteness shrouded the Patriarchi, the rays of luminance encompassing him began to bubble like agitated liquid and his form began to disassemble, until it coalesced into a beam of rainbow coloured luminance. It adhered to his form like a lucent epoxy. His essence hidden among other undertakings was now contained in a single palm sized globe. The next part of the procedure was to take the living object to Guidex's lab where it would be etched into the epoxide crystal. He was a dour individual, totally wrapped up with the complexities of new engineering. Once lacking imagination, he for one could not comprehend how Zebulan had circumvented the programming of the CRYSTALOID'I. But now after their long flight; even he had come up with innovative designs that would be incorporated into their scheme. Unlike the lab of Hybrid creation, this place was a hive of communal activity. Here, the globe containing Mescal's being would be integrated within the brain patterns of their subjects. It was causing the Alien Engineer and his colleague's enormous problems to calibrate their advanced technology with the patterns of the primitive neural networks. But eventually through tenacious effort and comprise; solutions although not completely satisfactory to the perfectionist were worked out. Cocooned in deceit, a very nervous Cetheren stood over them as they performed the operation.

"They must not discover the erratic presence of Mescal within."

He did not bear to think about the consequences if it happened. Suffused in the state of high anxiety, the alarmed student had no contingency plans for that occasion. Gudiex and his assistants bonded their craft with the unassuming globe and incorporated a tracking device that would trace it into the future of the Hybrid's, whatever that was going to be. Relieved that his and the entombed deception of the Patriarchi went undiscovered, the elated deceiver brought the solid form back to his underground lab. He never realised that the anomaly was missed because, these logic thinking individuals could not detect something that they had no comprehension of. The two deceivers had formed a protection device much like an acoustic shadow and it would only be located if one had a reason to probe into that range of frequency. Once inside his own space, Cetheren exhaled with deep relief. The returned presence of the Elder interfaced with the viewing globes and his semblance urged.

"Make haste, I need to be in close proximity to the Primates. Perform the final solution."

Cetheren was about to comply when the disembodied image of his mentor warned.

"Before I become lost in this disassembled form, there is a matter of paramount importance that I must broach with you. The separated parts of my being will have their own agenda. Re-assembly under one Hybrid host with be their single minded objective. Nothing will stand in the way of them trying to achieve their destiny. If our observers need to influence critical events, they will have to manipulate the Hybrid's hosts brain patterns, not mine. We do not know how my madness will proceed. I may resist your diagnosis. So, I repeat, do not contact me until I become whole again. Only then, will we know if my sanity has returned."

A dense white crystal prism emitting solid light used the arrays of advanced technology and split the APOCRYPHA'I seamlessly into seven small pulsating globules. Refracted wave lengths of the visible spectrum then coated all of the epoxide forms forming a separate tinted image of Mescal in each of them. The student found himself studying multi-hued replicas of his tutor. Each entrapped form was an exact likeness, only the various shades made them indistinguishable from one another. The features of Mescal gradually faded until only the colour of each globe became dominant. The metamorphous was complete and as he was locked into the glare of the transmuted forms; his transformer knew.

"The essence of Patriarchi is contained in each one."

Taking each piece reverently, he opened a specific Cryostat containing a Hybrid host. For selfish reasons explained only to himself, he now altered the plan. This un-consulted modification of their scheme, one that Mescal never even anticipated would have far reaching consequences. The disturbed ALASTHA'I only placed six of them around the necks of each unsuspecting biped. As Cetheren clutched the violet piece that he held back, he mind-uttered.

"When the Hybrids awake from their time with the Gods, they will have forgotten the experience, but they will cherish their Churiangas."

One of the chosen hosts was the Primate who sought out revenge and rescued the young from the cannibals. Far into the future, he was going to be the progenitor of the one who would assemble the lost conscious of Mescal. These Hybrids were now left with in stasis, complete with their new possessions, so that the evolving connection between two such different Life-forms could commence and strengthen. When the bond was judged to be sufficient, the hosts would be put aboard Platforms of Light in an unconscious state. Then they and their precious cargo would be scattered to the ends of the Planet. Each segment of the living jewel would co-exist independently of each other until the moment when they would be reunited. Mind-thoughts of the schemes advancement caused Cetheren to speculate.

"It would be then up to my brother. Cathbad would begin to monitor crystal arrays that would display the brain patterns from the hosts of the segments of the APOCRYPHA'I and follow their generations through time. But he will not be alone."

However Cetheren's dabbling in independent thought had a dark side. The misguided Alien was continually pre-occupied with his withheld piece of the Mescal/Amulet. His grief-clouded reasoning for such an act was simple to his own twisted thinking.

"Once we are aboard the Mothership, just as its huge engines are started and we are about to depart this Solar System. I will approach the Elders and tell them about my deception. They will have little choice, but to let me return to the Planet in a shuttle. Then Cathbad and I can supervise the experiment together."

He paused and continued with a mind-thought that Zebulan would have appreciated.

"And if they refuse I will return without their consent. I will defy them."

Cetheren left the mound, extremely relieved that he had found a solution to the problem of been separated from his brother. The pore turning grief that had always been on the edges of his awareness had been banished into a sad memory. To the Patriarchi and the other ALASTHA'I, it was impossible for them to understand the bond between the two twins. Cetheren remembered their first flight. It was under normal times, the only hazardous event in the life of an ASCETIC'I. When they were about to leave their adolescence and enter adulthood, each individual had a rite of passage. This ritual had been put forward as a means of progressing past their passive past. The test was designed to breed a more resilient race. Its main architect had been Zebulan and it was to be a great honour for the two siblings as the wise Elder was present today. Climbing to the top of the ten kilometre high sacred cliff that encircled and dominated the chief religious city of "Sedulous.", an individual had to leap off and for the first time in their young lives, use their wings that up to that time were bound by light laser strap. At this stage in their development, there were many failures, compared to the rare success. The inbuilt genetic block against harm was very strong at this early age and passing this test resulted in high office. Those that lost their nerve retook the trial, but at much lower levels. All of the Patriarchi had passed the trial and it was considered mandatory for them. Both brothers reached the top of the sacred summit and found a hooped platform that projected out over the edge, the width of the circular walkway was exactly a metre wide. As the two youths contemplated the test, the Red Dwarf Sun came above the mercury clouds to reveal the lowlands far below. To the reminiscer, that long lost crimson and green experience could never be produced to the same effect in the Pleasure or CONGREGATION domes. Taking deep inhalations through their macula, both of them stepped onto the crystalline structure. And at their touch, a pulsating sequence of the spectrum began running around the circumference of the projected structure. Whichever wave length of the active gamut was under an individual's feet as they leapt off the suspended dais would be the defining colour of their lives. Finally, just as both siblings had finished their mental preparations and decided to spring from the flickering perch, a solitary and extremely dense methane cloud blocked out the Sun's rays momentarily. Cathbad faltered and was unable to leap; he stood petrified at the edge. His brother held his hand firmly and on his urging, they jumped together and fell towards the ground. Then in a moment of magic, they began to rise. It was their first flight and the twins became poetry in motion. Never before had the watching Patriarchi's seen such a display of agility; one even felt a modicum of jealously. But if it were not for his brother, Cathbad would not have made the leap of faith. Even though, they had always been inseparable, things had changed with that jump. For as they alighted, Cetheren had leaped from a red facet, while Cathbad had departed from a green one. This was the first time in their existence that something different had occurred to each twin.

Now hundreds of centuries later with many unshared secrets and different flight paths, Cetheren met with Celtair on a night when the Planet's only satellite appeared large in the night sky. The moon's frosty nimbus looked breath-taking and each of them were aware that the Primate's worshiped that chunk of space rock. The primitive bipeds believed that there was a huge Primate face etched into its surface and it was looking down on them, scrutinising their every move. The younger exile began to reveal most, but not all of the conspiracy to the Elder. Only he and Mescal knew the full extent of the tampering with the Hybrid race. Without revealing that startling fact, he disclosed what the latter had mind-told him.

"The INIQUITY is abroad."

"Then, it begins."

The Elder noticed that his students Preceptor-Band remained undimmed. It was in fact bright with enthusiasm. His confidant mind-responded.

"It already has. Mescal's being has been absorbed into the inanimate objects and taken around the Planet by the Hybrids. Each segment is already making air currents into their psyche and when the time is fitting, one of them will unite the whole and lead the violent host against the

CRYSTALOID 'I.''

"You must call a meeting of the CONGREGATION, I will address them. They will know that we are finally ready. "

This was not an unusual request as any individual could call for a gathering of the host, if a Patriarchi supported them. Celtair's mind reply was cautious.

"We are gliding on heavy-air currents, so we must disclose every element of our scheme."

"Agreed. " Replied Cetheren, but he knew. *"All will not be revealed. "*

Days later; he stood in front of the hastily convened gathering of the ALASTHA'I with Celtair and his brother at his side. Taking turns on the podium, the three of them informed the assembly about Mescal and his involvement in everything. There was disbelieving mind-gasps all over the gathering. Then as the assembly frantically debated, Cetheren dropped the bolt from the blue.

"We have to leave this World, before he was melded into the Amulet; Mescal notified me that the INIQUITY has freed itself. It is sending out probing tendrils and will find us. And when it does, it will send its legions of destruction here. "

Celtair added.

"At least our Mother is now free of the contamination. "

This news made the CONGREGATION decide to depart the Planet as soon as possible. Preparations began in earnest. In the mist of the exiles meticulous arrangements for departure, Cathbad approached Celtair and advised the Patriarchi.

"Since we have now crossed the boundary of interference in another life-forms evolution, should we now send a message back to your brother and the thousand to join us? After all what they are doing is irrelevant now. "

The Elder disagreed.

"No my student. You must perceive, they are the only uncorrupted among us. They still adhere to the old ways. We will let them be and when their mission is completed, they can re-join and bring some of the good of what is lost to us, back into the fold. "

Over in his western fortress, Zebulan's deliberations were also made up for him. His freed Master had been probing the Blue Planet after been drawn there by an occurrence that flashed around the Universe like a directional beacon. Through its resumed contact with him, it had learned about and had become intrigued with the Primates. It ordered its disciple to discover more about the murderous life-form. So the DEFILED was forced to remain behind even if the ALASTHA'I departed. But, he now decided that it was too risky to remain this close to Mescal, he had no idea of the latter's transformation. A month later, the Alien instruments deep below the Diadem City registered a huge explosion to the west. Scrying Globes revealed a distorted energy draining light shield, three shattered convex shaped stone walls and part of an island that had fallen into the sea of ice. Nobody knew for sure what had occurred; but Celtair mind-stated wrongly.

"The leader of the DEFILED is covering his flight-paths and is ready to join the continued exile. As much as he hates us, he still cannot exist without been close to us."

At last the long awaited or feared day had come upon them. Cathbad stood with his ninety-nine kin who had remained behind with him and watched the ships streak into the morning sky. His brother and soul mate along with the Patriarchi Celtair were on one of those ships and exhaled nutrients of grief seeped from his macula. He admonished himself.

"Such a wasteful use of energy."

The memory of his last night with his twin was etched forever into his soul. In the privacy of his Diadem, he had nearly embraced his brother, like the Hybrid's and other Primates did. The soon to be parted siblings spoke of passionate promises that they would not be separated for a lengthy duration. Something in Cetheren's demeanour hinted that the split would not be as long as his brother thought. His confidence encouraged the other. What Cathbad did not know was that his twin was not going along with the next stage of the ALASTHA'I plan. Onboard the shuttlecraft, he was already making designs of his own. As the ships vanished from sight, he and his kin went below to their invisible hideaways. Those left behind now proceeded with the next stage of the plan.

All of the Hybrids that had been experimented on woke from their slumber and found themselves back in the bosom's of their tribes. In the darkest of northern nights, the sedated males had been loaded abroad hovering Platforms of Light by CRYSTALOID'I and brought to their destinations. They're people greeted them as favourites of the God's, for these were the first that returned from the underworld. Each of the heavenly returnee's clutched their precious Churiangas and in a miscalculation on the Alien's part, each of them actually remembered their time with the Gods. These divinely appointed leaders were the undisputed leaders of their tribes and around blazing campfires, they told tales of their wonderful time in paradise that would live on in oral tradition.

"A place of many colours where I felt no pain or want."

These were legends that were soon embellished by those who passed them on. So began the new mythology of the Hybrids and one that would endure for as long as the tampered life-forms breathed. Platforms of Light became chariots of fire, Preceptor-Bands became Halo's and the off-Worlder's themselves became supernatural beings. The exiles scheme evolved and some of the Hybrids that bore the pieces of the Mescal/Amulet already gave the impression that they had become smarter and more advanced than their unaltered brothers had. In the following centuries, it was these chosen receptacles of the ALASTHA'I and their inheritors that kept the momentum of Human kind's advancement in a forward motion. Man's rapid rise from been virtually, a grub eating savage for five million years to the beginnings of civilisation that only took ten thousand years after the interference was not for the benefit of his own species, but for another's. Man in his growing perception and awareness knew that he was been used and all across his domain, people began to know these users as God's. Six such perceived living Deities went from benign to evil as the bouts of madness overtook them. The internal voices caused their listeners to commit acts of righteousness or depravity as their encased minds fluctuated during the long wait for the fruition of the Alien plan. As time flowed by and mankind progressed, the Hybrid's still continued in the adoration of their new God's. This unflagging trait of divine creation became a very useful tool for the resolute Zebulan in his attempts to thwart his fellow exiles.

VII.

BURIED GLOBE OF CETHEREN, THE HILL OF TARA, 17,000 BC.

Nearly all of those who had not been guests, but forced exiles on the blue sphere; had departed. In the measure of these long lives, it had only been a brief respite during their long flight from their lost Worlds and the malevolent force that searched for them. Some of the more sceptical among them knew.

"It is a journey through the Cosmos that might never come to an end."

The winged Aliens had left a hundred of their brethren behind and a substantial amount of their advanced technology in the hope that the chosen scheme would succeed. In the uncertainty of the resumed voyage, most had their doubts about accomplishing that event. To one of those who had engaged in a painful separation, he now had an understanding of how long the perception of time seemed to be for the Hybrids. Each new moment without his brother was a bitter slice of eternity. Some among the host were reluctant leavers, but the over-whelming majority of them had been delighted to abscond from the hot hostile Planet that regularly became unbearable to their crystal-based autonomy. Most of the space voyagers now looked forward to a nice cool World with a familiar Red dwarf Sun type, as their next destination. Their uneasy tenure had lasted, thirteen millennia of the orb's celestial path around its harsh yellow star. On the morning that the ALASTHA'I had departed, the patchy weather around their lift off site produced melancholy drizzle that was so light; it did not even produce a puddle. It was a grey day, one that the superstitious Primates believed was sent up from the netherworld. Some of these awe-struck natives were now watching the exodus of the God's who they believed were returning to Heaven. But not all of the exiles had left, more than one of their kind remained behind.

It was more than one cycle of the Planet's orbit around its Sun after the bulk of the winged Aliens had departed when several silhouetted figures with glowing circular bands above their oblong heads emerged from below ground and began preparations to launch a new version of the Scrying orbs. These "Vigil" Globes as they were designated were the means of studying the progress of their experiment (The Hybrid's.) who had already been out in the World for five centuries. Thousands of these multi-coloured spheres of light would fly to an orbital path around the limits of the blue Planet's gravitational field and circle, increasing in acceleration until their speeds approached the velocity of light. These speeding orbs would eventually break the time barrier and re-emerge in the future. Using the new technology of the segments of the APOCRYPHA'I, this master of light technology could only manifest images and mind-thoughts along both directions of the time line. These extraordinary spheres which were at the pinnacle of their technology could not transport physical objects. As the "Vigil Globes" were connected to the Mescal/Amulet pieces, the monitoring orbs could slow down and drop out of their time travelling at certain periods and record and transmit data back to the past, just in the twilight days of the Ice Age. The tallest of the Aliens who was now designated as "The Watcher." stood in the autumn dimness between day and night as thin wispy pink clouds trailed across the shadow of the large bright moon. The stranded being watched as the windows into the future sped into orbit to begin their assault on the timelines. Then he went back underground to the rest of his brotherhood. Infant Stargazers among the biped natives were baffled that the newly appearing celestial lights had come from the Earth and had not fallen from the Heavens. As this was a reversal of their long held understanding of these matters, a lot of bad omens were predicted And who was to say that these primitive astrologers were not wrong in their assumptions.

The wind currents of time shifted, until.

14,053 BC.

A "Vigil Globe" dropped out of orbit.

The blue World that held a small contingent of Aliens proceeded along its relentless orbit around the yellow Sun. The stellar furnace continued to give light, heat and power to the multitude of life within its influence. But the Watcher's main preoccupation was with the Hybrid life-form that his race had created. The Planet's once dominant polar ice sheets and glaciers had dwindled as the Sun entered another Cosmic Cycle, thus heralding an era of mild climates on the ever-shifting World. Turquoise sea's had risen from the bleached ice melt and the land where the ALASTHA'I once dwelt had become an emerald island again. Now in these new temperate and moderate elements, the hundred Aliens who had stayed behind were confined in their underground spaces; unable to venture out except during the coldest of times. They now kept a low profile; their days of interacting with the Hybrids in a visible manner were long over.

It was that season again just after the ever lengthening Summer, but not quite winter when the plant life of the Northern Hemisphere that did not die went into hibernation. Almost the entire flora and the majority of the fauna at this hemisphere needed this duration of dormancy to exist in these newly colonised latitudes. The era of the large herds of huge tusked grass eating herbivores that fed on the short frantic chlorophyll growth of the northern latitudes were fast coming to an end. Forests and Hybrid predation would soon push those species over the edge and into extinction. Many of the newly arrived mammal species were fattening themselves and showing the first vestiges of their thick winter coats as they prepared to go into dormancy with the promise of rebirth after the long winter. The panorama had changed as thin islands of meandering trees had made inroads into the sea of grassland that had first appeared in the wake of the retreating ice wall. Eventually these much more imposing plants filled the majority of the landscape and the sea of grasses had all but disappeared. Deciduous plants were also shedding needle fine leaves in this season of preparation. It was a time of mists, yellow fruits, brown nuts, black cones and mottled hair coverings. The flying creatures who had made the most of the brief summer were also making their way south to warmer climes and would return when nature had turned a half a circle from autumn to late spring. High up in the towering mountains of the Continent, the last of the gravity driven snowmelt that flowed down to the lowlands encountered hardy mosses and colourful algae imbedded in its stony beds that filtered the icy water of impurities. These elevated mountaintops had always protruded above the lairs of ice; they were there to greet the Aliens when they had first arrived. Now, in a different cycle of life, vast forests of deciduous and evergreen trees relied on this bounty of fresh water. The seasonal tundra that had once crept up to the edges of the ALASTHA'I Diadems had been replaced with a new landscape of forest; flowing rivers and countless tree lined lakes as the global temperature rose by an average of ten degrees Celsius. The underground being not of this World observed the land above as an acorn fell from its parent tree and dropped down towards the leaf covered floor of the now matured forest. Quick as a lighting strike, the woody plants promise of a next generation was snatched up by a foraging squirrel, who bounded away in delight with its prize. It would add it to its winter hoard. In its eagerness the bushy tailed animal never saw the shadow of the big-eyed flying predator that snapped him away, just as he had taken the acorn. The large dark brown seed slipped from a nerveless grip and fell undamaged to the floor below. There it lay forgotten, except by the Alien observer who waited until the following spring, when it sent tiny sprouts of greenery skyward. Seasons passed and the insignificant shoot became a strong sapling. Years went by and the sapling became a young tree. Then after a few centuries it had matured into a giant that shrouded a great expanse of the forest floor. The exile watched, as a newly arrived tribe of his principal assignment moved into the land where his adopted giant ruled. He had tracked their northern migration and it was here in the vicinity of the mound that they settled. On a bright clear prehistoric day, the nomadic Hybrid's cut the huge Oak down and built crude structures out of it. The bits of the tree that they did not use were cast on flames to provide them with warmth and fuel. The Alien observer felt saddened at the tree's demise, but he realised.

"This destruction is in the Hybrids nature and this disparaging trait is the goal of our race; after all."

All sorts of game were plentiful in the forests and the newcomers prospered. Cathbad had now become the millennia watcher, for what was the passage of time to a race that had it in abundance. With his fellow ninety-nine souls going about their tasks around him, he sat in front of an array of crystal machinery contained in rotundas of spherical light not far from where the globular City had been, all the time scrutinising his plan of action. The city of the ALASTHA'I had been removed from the surface of the Continent and stored in one of the holds of the vast Mother-ship. But enormous vestiges of it remained below in the depths, hidden until the time for it to be revealed again had arrived. Feeling alone in his enforced isolation (This had been the CONGREGATION'S decision.); he still missed his brother and the painful forced separation stayed with him every waking moment, but it had become almost bearable. The ninety-nine others that had remained behind with him did not produce the same bond. Cathbad had ample time to reflect on what his race had achieved since their narrow escape from the "INIQUITY." and its minions. The contemplating Alien arrived at an astounding conclusion.

"My brother had been correct. We as a race; have indeed altered. Much faster than our brightest intellectuals thought possible. New ideas and reasoning have come to us, while the threat of annihilation hovers over us. We are still infants in the science of aggression, but our kind are beginning to choose our own wind-currents. And that must be a good thing. Our time on this World has changed us forever."

The task that had been given to him was to follow the future through the Hybrid subjects with the marker genes and the seven pieces of the Mescal/Amulet. He had informed the ninety-nine.

"We will monitor the progress of the tampered life-forms through the future and if they stray from becoming the perfect killing machines, they we will have to correct any transgression. Scanning the future through the marked Hybrids will be time consuming and could take tens of centuries until the true inheritor of the completed APOCRYPHA'I appears on the scene. The ethereal tracer can only follow the path taken and we cannot fast forward to the moment when a Hybrid accepts the completed Mescal/Amulet. The course has to be watched by us in case an element of incorrectness slips into the genetic line."

During his initial scrutiny, he found one of the first markers in a deep valley between two Continents. His village lay under the precarious barrier of an eroding natural weir and ominously that land would form a new Sea.

"He is a descendant of the Primate with the sense of justice that tracked down the tribe of cannibals that had slaughtered his people. After been responsible for the demise of a lot of them and rescuing the offspring, he returned to his tribe. But Mescal had used him and lured him into infiltrating the CONGREGATION. And then, the irrational Patriarchi had chosen that Primate amongst others as a receptacle for the living amulet."

Unaware of the scale of deviousness; Cathbad smiled at the memory. He would have checked his mirth, if he had known that was Mescal had poisoned some of his original selection. The Watcher's crystal array told him that the marker genes in that one were correct; the influence of the piece of the APOCRYPHA'I was progressing nicely. He searched the four corners of the Planet and eventually located six other parts of the Mescal/Amulet. The violet piece was causing unforeseen problems, his instruments only detected a slight whisper of the living object; itself. He was slightly disturbed at this anomaly, but knew that the self-adjusting technology would sort the problem out.

12'109BC.

A "Vigil Globe" dropped out of orbit.

Cathbad sped along the time line following the altered bipeds line of descent, watching patiently as generation after generation of their creations lineage spread all over the Globe. The Hybrids genetically interfered make up quickly dominated the Primate population.

He followed their lineage until they had become technically superior to any of their ape like cousins. The Hybrids growing in importance renamed themselves "Humans.". With their much larger brains, they discovered easier methods of producing fire, turned their crude weapons of flint and bone into more efficient hunting devices. Along with these discoveries, improvement in their manufacture of warmer clothing enabled those Humans to move into colder climates and their race multiplied. Still, the desired gene markers were correct and present in enough numbers of the Hybrids population and the scheme of the ALASTHA'I was progressing on the desired flight path. Then something unexpected happened to a member of the exiles; seven thousand years after they were separated from their Star travelling kin. Culupix was one of the last of their race to be born on CRYSTALIOS and he had become quite fearless and adventurous. The deadly salinity of the sea caused little anxiety within the fold of his wings, so he made his way down to the Southern Continent to supplement his mineral intake. Miraculously, he was able to cross the short stretch of boiling liquid between two Continents on a Platform of Light. Culupix knew that the minerals were purer down there. But on one of his trips, the Alien disappeared forever and a batch of "Vigil Globes" sent down there failed to discover his gliding vehicle or his fate. It was assumed that he fell into the acidic sea and had dissolved. But the failure to locate his travelling contrivance was a real mystery indeed. The Aliens number had fallen to ninety-nine individuals.

9'000BC.

A Vigil Globe dropped out of orbit.

Eventually more waves of the migrating Hybrid's reached the north and discovered the mounds that still stood above the sea with their standing stones still proud and erect. Collective memory induced by the ALASTHA'I kicked in and these places were cleared of trees and scrub and became revered sites to the worshipping newcomers. Everything was progressing correctly, but then two blots appeared on Cathbad's horizon.

One of the ninety-eight informed him.

"The migrating Hybrids are slaughtering all of the endemic species that they encounter and when the sum total of their prey decreased, then the hunter's numbers went in tandem with their decline."

Cathbad realised.

"The required numbers of the interfered with Primate needed to battle the legions of CRYSTALOID'I will never be achieved unless other resources are exploited."

Their problem was solved by the green segment of the APOCRYPHA'I. Through the sub-conscious of its male host, a solution for the required numbers was initiated.

AGRICULTURE.

From the Hybrid's perspective, their God's had advised them of this wonderful boon. Then to the Aliens horror, the Hybrid's transferred the skill of crop husbandry to certain animals. They bred the livestock on a vast scale and then killed the unfortunate beasts for food consumption. One of the ninety-eight mind-voiced his revulsion.

"Is it not a perversion that our tools can easily gain the complete trust of another species and then butcher it for nutrients?"

"Still, this is what we had designed them for." Bemoaned the Watcher.

Grasping the advantage delivered by a false source; the main stream of the Hybrids relinquished their hunter/gathering life style and settled into small settled family groups. As the Human's mastered the wild Flora and Fauna, they increased their yields of crops and domesticated livestock. As a consequence, the numbers of Hybrid's increased a thousandth fold. These new prosperous communities now supplanted less productive societies to encompass the entire globe. This bountiful increase in the production of foodstuffs, basic textiles and small-scale industry exploded the population of Human's again. New waves of more aggressive Hybrid migration displaced the tribes that had settled where the mounds had been built. But these new warrior farmers worshiped these holy places with a newfound vigour. Cathbad watched as this new breed of spiritual Hybrids began to construct their own imitations and bury their royalty in them. Legends from their time under the supervision of the Extra-terrestrials; especially after the attempted sabotage by the DEFILED had these new mystical leaders pronounce.

"In the age of our creation, the God's had taken our dead ancestors below when a flash of thunder had killed them. Some even returned to us."

This cult lasted thousands of years, until it finally got so absurd that it culminated in colossal stone pyramids. One of the Watchers colleagues found a favourable windfall in these antics.

"Still, this bizarre cult serves one useful purpose. There are now so many mounds spread over the northern continent that our ones are indistinguishable from the Hybrid constructions."

The second problem was more serious and Cathbad explained his reasoning to his brothers.

"The violet piece of the APOCRYPHA'I that we know to be in the frozen Southern Continent is beginning to give a more erratic perception. While the signal from the piece remains scant, but true, we still have no representation of its host. And now, our "Vigil Globes are failing to operate over the ice sheet. Something puzzling is impeding them."

As this was where Cupulix disappeared from, nobody gained the courage and was willing to go down there and investigate. The wry Watcher surmised.

"We haven't changed that much. But, I know that if Cetheren was still here, he would go down to their and solve our quandary."

The Alien compliment spent many long years on the problem, but they did not have all the facts to solve their dilemma. Failing to solve the conundrum, Cathbad concentrated on the remaining six pieces and the host's that had possession of them. He calculated.

"The missing segments bearer or its ancestor will reveal itself again and that will be a problem for another time."

He was also privately aware.

"The pieces of Mescal's being have attained the madness and are issuing instructions depending on each division's state of lucidity. Strangely, one piece seems to have divested itself completely of the lunacy, it is the red piece. But, the knowledge contained within its fabric is erratic and minimal."

As the Hybrids need for trade grew, their small villages became towns, which in turn developed into cities. Cathbad still watched and was content that events were progressing in the correct sequence, despite the missing host. All in all, everything was mostly going to plan and as the mad Mescal would have told him.

"After all, what we are doing is unprecedented, so it is not an exact science."

7,OOOBC.

A "Vigil Globe" dropped out of orbit.

Over the next few centuries, conflicts between societies of Hybrids were rare, as there seemed to be adequate resources available to the World population. But as the centuries progressed and their numbers kept increasing, small-scale conflicts erupted around the globe. Whenever a calamity struck one group, such as famine or disease, they immediately coveted their neighbour's resources. To protect their interests, City-states evolved into Nations. These distinct states were ruled by royalty, priests and soldiers. Each of these administrators were so certain of their own rightness, they all began trying to extend the scope of their influence. Armies grew in size and craft; cities became magnets to the rural peoples with their promises of walled security, wealth and food. The urban notion prospered with its characteristic features of a complex division of labour, literacy, monumental public buildings, management of resources, political and religious hierarchies and a right to rule by divine right. Nations in turn became Empires and war became the natural order of the Hybrids. The World of the Alien creations now abounded with numerous small realms until one strived for the first global empire.

The schemes of the ALASTHA'I were still on the most favourable flight-path.

In a burst of creativity, the Hybrids developed a written language and Cathbad felt proud for their creations, much like a father would with a clever child. The winged Alien knew that the production of a written script was a profound step on the path to enlightenment. The first Empire began as a city-state, which was nestled between two enormous rivers in the desert plains of the Near East. Using the new science of irrigation, its engineers turned the arid ground into fertile pains. With metal ploughs and new inventions especially the wheel, these industrious people built vast cities of exquisite beauty. They ruled an empire called Mesopotamia. These Mesopotamian's had a rival Empire on the African Continent that co-existed in an uneasy peace alongside them.

A land ruled by Pharaohs.

Both Empires regarded each other with open hostility and created the largest armies the World had ever seen. Advances in technology enhanced their war-craft. The two Empires eventually declined, but newer and more vigorous ones supplanted them. Then came the time of the four great kings of the Near East, these were the Egyptians, the Babylonians, the Assyrians and the Hittites. But all of these Empires of power also faded into obscurity. However, Cathbad was contented.

"Our plans are succeeding and in a few thousand of the Hybrids years, we will have a force capable of confronting the army of CRYSTALOID'I.

During this time of Alien scrutiny, an intriguing image unfolded in a "Vigil Globe". The Patriarch of a small tribe who was also the current orange bearer gave his favourite son, a multi coloured cloak and more importantly, his piece of the living amulet. The Watcher from another reality was intrigued; it was as if the giver was trying to replicate the shimmering protection of the ALASTHA'I.

"Is the fragment of Mescal's presence within interfering?"

Another contemporary event drew his attention and the Alien switched his focus. When he returned to his scrutiny, the receiver of the coat had become an important ruler in the Egyptian hierarchy. This current amulet bearer had shown great initiative, so he would pay close attention to this line. It was during this time that Zebulan organised a huge maritime force with the explicit instruction of wiping out Cathbad and his remaining host. It landed on the emerald island and began heading towards the buried Diadem. But the deviant's scheme ran aground. Under the threat of a foreign army, the diverse tribes of the island united under one king, the Ard Ri and defeated Zebulan's army on the plain above the Alien base. The invaders were wiped out to a man and they're bloodied heads, along with their dismembered bodies adorned many a wooden spike around the perimeter of the mound. Those underground witnessed the carnage while shaking their oblong heads at the brutality of the natives, not for once realising that they were the objective of the invading force and that the resident Hybrids had saved their crystalline compositions. Raging in defeat, the EGO'S servant never tried this type of action again. He had come to realise that failure was seen by his servants as un-godlike and to a defenceless being like himself; that perception could be fatal.

800BC.

A "Vigil Globe" dropped out of orbit.

Something disturbing occurred among the Hybrid's that revealed itself in the shades of the recording device and it did not fit in with the ALASTHA'I scheme. In an area where the sea had split two Continents, a new state emerged straddling the edges of both landmasses and in its bosom; a new idea was evolving.

Democracy.

This alarmed Cathbad, as some among the Greeks, the name by which they were known were now advocating new ideas. He was snared in a paradox of his races own making because it should have been his sworn faith to protect and nurture these seeds of goodness. These commendable rights of freedom, democracy and new sciences were unfortunately incompatible with his races goals. The Watcher's peers had wanted a killing organism; not something moulded in their own image. As if to make matters worse, these Greeks had overcome the greatest war machine of that age, the Persians. The Alien observer found it curious that these defeated Hybrids from the east thought that the dreaded sea water was demonic.

"Is the presence of Mescal making itself known again?"

The victors had formed a large Empire and were on their way to regional domination. As he fretted and pondered this new problem from his base thousands of years in the past, it was taken out of his hands and solved for him. With the aid of a red carrier of APOCRYPHA'I named Philip of Macedonia and his son Alexander who took the Greeks and their allies on a war of World conquest, the Hybrid's regained their bloody nature. The young Macedonian and his generals formed a promising Empire, but it disintegrated into fiefdoms and it soon passed into history and failure. This was becoming frustrating for Cathbad and his growing disappointment was passed on to his fellow exiles.

"The Hybrids capability for warfare and brutality is increasing, but no Empire capable of unifying them into one force is lasting any length of time."

Then when things were at their nadir, a new system of government rose from the death of another that seemed made to order.

The Roman Empire.

It was everything the off-World meddlers desired. The Romans mixture of technical brilliance (Though tremendously crude compared to the masters of light technology.) spiced with extreme brutality and the vast landmass they controlled was deemed to be the ideal solution. But its rulers became depraved (That itself was not see as a problem.), it was their erratically that finally convinced the ancient watchers to neglect them. Cathbad's hard pressed technicians inadvertently helped one of their Emperors and changed the path of the Western World for the next two thousand years. A "Vigil Globe's" receiver malfunctioned and the ALASTHA'I who repaired the device inadvertently caused the blurry image of a number of mineral inhaling Aliens to rebound into the future. The radiant echo of the outstretched winged figures bounced off a cloud and were seen by the Emperor Constantine. Convinced that he was looking at a divine sign, he adopted the Christian religion as his own. Although, the Roman Empire existed far longer than the others had, it too was doomed to failure. Cathbad became perplexed at these turn of events and became even more depressed as for the next thousand years the Hybrids began to withdraw into small nations and all attempts at Empire building was forgotten.

"But still, there is one bright outlook, the Hybrids war craft is advancing in tandem with their brutality." The Watcher noticed.

What the observer from the past failed to understand was why his schemes were failing. The answer to why his mechanisms were unsuccessful was simple. It was one undisclosed fact that the species manipulator could not integrate into his calculations. Unknown to him; Zebulan was still at large and because of his immense longevity; he was actually present in every age thwarting Cathbad's meddling from the past. On the day of their exodus, the naïve host had left a craft behind capable of reaching the Mother-ship and foolishly believed that their tainted brethren would avail of it and follow them out to the Stars. But Zebulan's master, now freed from Mescal's trap had become curious at these Hybrids ability to absorb its probing tendrils and let it wash over them with little effect.

IT BECAME INTRIGUED WITH THE HUMAN DIMENSION.

Meanwhile, on the Blue Sphere, the last servant of the "INIQUITY." had finally worked out what was going on and he was amazed at the audacity of his former kin.

"Those weaklings have circumvented the natural order of evolution of the Primates and have engineered a new species. It is entirely possible that the sense of self of these Humans is on par with my Master and they are the manifestation of itself in this reality."

That worried the Corruption's disciple more than it fascinated him. This was the reason that the emerging Entity had ordered the leader of the DEFILED to remain behind. It was a good thing too; Zebulan's interference was hindering the progress of the ALASTHA'I creations. Only for his meddling, the altered bipeds could have been two thousand years more advanced. In a memorable instant, a curious Hybrid had found a primitive battery that the clumsy Seantanta had inadvertently lost. The brown Middle Eastern man took it back to his home in a red clay bricked city called Baghdad to study and possibly re-create the device. But, he lacked the means to manufacture the crystal globes, so he made them out of hardened earth instead to mimic separate cells. The industrious Hybrid filled the clay pots with sulphuric acid and copper sulphate to try and make an electric charge. This innovation would have been a serious advancement for the Hybrids, so Zebulan ordered an assassination party to dispose of the clever Persian. The murderous squad succeeded and returned the original battery to their master. This was the beginning of a cult of assassination among his worshipers and a device that the false God would use to good effect in the coming centuries.

1AD- 16OOAD.

A "Vigil Globe" dropped out of orbit.

Where the Watcher interfered with the Hybrids evolution from the past, he had a great disadvantage by the fact that Zebulan's meddling was in real time. The minion of the "INIQUITY." had formed a sect among the Hybrids who believed he was the "Supreme Being." and he used them to further his ambition. Then a real irony in Cathbad's ignorant battle occurred when his opponent; the advocate of aggression discovered an obscure holy man in a remote region of the Asian Continent. Through this seeker of enlightenment, he tried to convert his races creations into pacifists. The tainted servant reckoned.

"If I can curb the Hybrid's aggression, then these creatures will be easy meat for my Master's CRYSTALOID'I legions."

Cathbad believing it to be a natural occurrence counteracted this peaceful tendency among the Hybrid's by using tribes of marauding barbarians who found these pacifists easy prey. Then an era began where both of the Aliens began to use varying degrees of Prophet's to further their own goals. Then events occurred that disturbed both of them. Three holy-men emerged on to the World scene that seemed independent of their ministrations. Even the DEFILED who appeared to them found them incorruptible. These non-conforming holy-men were the Prince from the east, the Carpenter from Galilee and the Prophet from the sands of Arabia. This trio of self-reliant Seer's built up great followings among the Hybrid's populations. Then to Cathbad's joy and Zebulan's dismay, the followers of the Carpenter and the Prophet formed two vast armies that tried to convert each other to their supreme cause by the sword. The Watcher was now certain.

"The victor in this religious struggle will have the capability to confront the approaching legions of killing machines."

But the conflict dragged on for ten centuries. During this discord one side obtained a black chemical from the Far East which they turned into a deadly weapon. The Hybrids called it Gunpowder and their capacity for destruction increased tenfold. The combustible mixture gave rise to muskets and cannon. Unlike the bow and arrow, this now meant that most of their creations could kill from a great distance with little training or experience. Cathbad took account.

"The Hybrids are now numbered in the hundreds of millions; they have vast disciplined fanatical armies and now have explosive projectile weapons. They are certainly becoming a match for the CRYSTALOID'I armies. But the Hybrids are still short the leader to unite them into a coherent force."

Zebulan on the other hand was disturbed yet again. Although, the DEFILED was still unable to take life personally, he could still command others to do it for him. Using infected mules among his followers, the Alien sent out deadly diseases concocted in his laboratory to destroy the Hybrids. In a fortified city under siege on the Black Sea coast, his followers inserted the plague virus into the rotting corpses of Hybrid's and animals, which were then lobbed over the city walls. In a few weeks the city became infected with what became known as the bubonic plague. Rats carried the pestilence around the Near East and Europe and its consequences were devastating on the Hybrid populations. However, Zebulan's plagues had little effect on the bipeds overall numbers. This was because of their rapid changing genetic makeup and vast numbers. Still, millions of Hybrid's died horribly from his biological pestilences, but their populations recovered and became immune to his cellular ministrations. The Hybrids resistance to disease grew and subsequently their numbers increased. Realising that he was only creating a more resilient species, Zebulan withdrew this tactic.

Over the next few centuries, Cathbad discarded two vast Empires. An enormous realm in the east built a vast wall around itself and isolated its people from the rest of the World. The disgruntled Alien dismissed this Hybrid trait of non-aggression.

"They will hide behind their walls and suffer the same fate as our race; someone will eventually come and destroy them."

The other dominion in the west blamed or appeased their Winged Gods with ritual blood sacrifices. The implications of this gave Cathbad many a restless sleep period.

"Memories of the ALASTHA'I should have disappeared aeons ago."

The Watcher's "Vigil Globes confirmed that the brutal ritual was started by an insane king who had his amulet piece stolen and in his paranoia; he had the chests of victims ripped out in his search for it. When he died, his descendants twisted the murderous rite into appeasement to their Gods. But their viciousness was turned inwardly and the rebuffing Watcher concluded.

"They will probably eliminate their entire population if left to themselves. And these practitioners of ritual death only answer to a CRYSTALOID'I army would be to offer up thousands of unfortunate victims."

One incongruity that did intrigue him and demanded more study was the fact that all across the Globe; the Hybrids had built large pyramidal structures. Independently and at different time periods, several unconnected civilisations had piled great effort into these huge constructions. It was a perplexing puzzle that would demand further examination by the winged Alien. Again, he was inclined towards the imbedded pieces of Mescal's mind causing these anomalies. Another thing that was brought to the Watcher's attention in this time period was the strange case of a man from Province in France. This seer was making highly accurate prophecies. To the logical mind of Cetheren, it seemed that this individual had somehow tapped into the "Vigil Globes" and the information of the future was been sent back to him. Aware of the harmful consequences of this prophecy, the Watcher lacked the ruthlessness of Zebulan and the seer was left unharmed. He never solved the mystery as the Alien had more pressing problems at hand. One enigma, the Watcher did resolve was the reason why so many Hybrid Civilisations build various types of pyramids. The logic behind it was now self-evident as he explained to a colleague.

"They have some remembrance of our Diadems and our constructions of dazzling light were a thing of wonder to them. So the Hybrids are trying to imitate them with their own versions using their limited technology and the materials at hand."

1600AD-2100AD.

A "Vigil Globe" dropped out of orbit.

Then circumstances started to get dire for Zebulan, when a new candidate for the unifier cropped up. He came from a small nation that had ideas of World conquest. His name was Napoleon Bonaparte. This little Dictator was on the right track, but he too failed to build a great Empire. Cathbad became dismayed as he looked back at the Hybrids progress.

"Their armies are getting larger, their weaponry is becoming more advanced, but they are missing the great leader which we are seeking. All of the Empires throughout history have failed to produce the one. Classical Greece under Alexander, Imperial Rome under the Emperors, the hordes of Mongols under Genius Khan, the Holy Roman Empire under the Popes, the Armies of Islam following the words of their Prophet, the French Empire under the Dictator Napoleon, the Ottomans, the Tsars, etc. The list of potential leaders is endless. All of them have failed to unite the Hybrids

into a unified global fighting force."

The ALASTHA'I was rightly mystified, but he existed in hope.

To these masters of silent technology, the sheer noise of the nineteenth, twentieth and twenty-first centuries was over bearing.

"Surely the escaped "INIQUITY." will easily perceive this incredible resonance."

Then over a hundred cycles of the Planet's orbit around its Star after Napoleon's defeat, a cycle of violence took place that showed the Hybrid's great capacity to persevere against adversary. They called it the "Great War." and all across stagnant lines of dirt and wire, the Hybrids slaughtered millions of its own kind. Cathbad addressed the ninety-eight with his findings.

"The Hybrids have developed the art of war on an industrial scale. The manner in which they discard lives for their respected Monarchies shows that finally, we have created a host to match and surpass the might of the CRYSTALOID'I legions."

One sober mind-voice added.

"But they might poison the Planet first."

Throughout his vigil, Cathbad had always expressed distaste at the Hybrids methods of providing the raw materials for their advancement. Across the ages, their creations hacked or blasted the required minerals out of the Planet's surface in violent and destructive methods, unlike their advanced society who coaxed or teased their requirements from their crystallised Home Worlds.

"Still, that is the nature of the beast."

Then in the early decades of the twentieth century something profound happened to the Alien's plan; the ideal leader which the ALASTHA'I desired appeared on the map of history. His name was Adolph Hitler and he was the leader of a political sect called the Nazis. Their use of the Eagle, mostly with wings spread as the symbol of their regime suggested to the Watcher.

"A significant amount of the other failed candidates also used winged creatures, real or imagined to display their identity to others. Is it another link to us?"

The leaders of the Third Reich became reminiscent of the mad Patriarchi Mescal; they too used the dismembered parts of their victims for raw materials. Cathbad would have been certain that this was the one, the regime was perfect and its capacity for brutality on an immense scale was only matched by its sworn enemy (Joseph Stalin.) to the east of its annexed borders. But the genetic markers were not sufficiently present in these two antagonists and the former was abandoned and left to his fate. The man that showed so much promise was vanquished and his ally in the Far East was defeated in a manner that switched the initiative to Zebulan.

The Watcher and the ninety-eight nearly faltered.

145

In a remote part of the Arizona desert, the stupid Hybrids had discovered the power of Suns. The weapons of mass destruction were of no threat to the technology of the ALASTHA'I, but the erratic Hybrid's might obliterate themselves from the face of the Planet. Then all the efforts of his race would be in vain. Cathbad became aghast when he witnessed a flying machine called the "Enola Gay." drop its lethal load on an island city and it wiped out hundreds of thousands in an instant.

"Our creations have no limits on the amount of destruction that they can cause. Have we gone too far? Have we created something that is possibly more destructive than the twisted CRYSTALOID 'I?"

Cathbad had noticed other things during his long vigil.

"Any technological progress made by the Hybrids has a detrimental effect on the harmony of the Planet. And also that superior power blocks use subordinate peoples to do their dirty work. Is this type of delegation something they have learnt from us?"

Another thing that cropped up was the astounding fact that some societies among their pawns had recreated the ALASTHA'I system of measurement and by some incredible unknown factor had even named these increments exactly as their Alien interferes. Metres, litres and grams had the same meaning in both conceptual societies. It was too outrageous to be a coincidence and the Watcher often queried of himself.

"What else have they taken from us?"

In the dark depths of loneliness and frustration of his task, he became certain that the Hybrids would surely destroy themselves and the Blue Planet long before the legions of the "INIQUITY." arrived. Needless to say Zebulan sensed an opportunity in this destructive trait and all his efforts were aimed towards that goal of nuclear annihilation. He was becoming an alter ego of his master. Two Superpowers emerged from the ashes of the second global war. Both seemed intent on destroying their ideological enemy and if so, the entire Planet. But the Federation from the East collapsed from within as the World hovered on the threshold of nuclear annihilation. Others challenged the victorious power that appeared outwardly peaceful as the century closed. Some of its enemies were ruthless, but they lacked the numbers and military expertise the ALASTHA'I desired. In the dying days of the twentieth century one Empire that had shown some promise at its beginning (The British Empire.) had passed on, only to be replaced by one that would soon retreat into isolation. Then the Hybrids reached for the stars in violent explosive rockets; the residue of decayed life-forms. The advanced Alien was not surprised by their method of leaving the Planet, but there was a nasty surprise waiting for them up there. But then again, it might not work, for there was one thing that the Watcher had concluded.

"The Hybrids thrive on decimation, like the crystal weed of our Home Worlds, they come back more potent and numerous. And eventually, they

will overcome our last defence. We left the weed alone and did not interfere in its life cycle; maybe we should have done the same with the Hybrid's."

In the latter half of the twentieth century, one point that came to the Watcher's attention was carefully noted. The Hybrids had increased their proficiently in the science of aviation. Their primitive technology had achieved enough capability that these instruments were beginning to detect the signature of the "Vigil Globes". The Hybrid's became very interested in them. Their scientists called them U F O'S and tried to discern their origin. Another item of their existence that Cathbad found interesting was the Hybrid's invention of a very basic "Vigil Globe". They called it television and the Watcher in a rare burst of humour decided.

"I and my remaining colleagues have become the ultimate reality T.V viewers. After all we scrutinise the daily lives of a whole World."

It was around this time that a major shift in the Hybrid way of life occurred. In the year 2023 AD in the measure of their creation's time, the greater numbers of them now lived in densely packed urban districts. The Alien's conceptions were well on the way to becoming a well-organised and cohesive force. Zebulan was at his wit's end in trying to halt the Hybrids progress in fulfilling the ALASTHA'I plans. His schemes for global nuclear destruction had gone awry and in the localised conflicts that ensued around the Globe, individuals began to self-terminate in blasts of chemical explosion's; in pursuit of their many aims and convictions.

"My Master's robotic legions cannot equal that sort of single mindlessness."

Then an idea came to him that was brilliant in its simplicity. The scheming servant of the Corruption began to use the Hybrids own physiognomy against them. His followers infiltrated every major power block and insured that their leaders or regimes exhibited the characteristics that he needed for his new plan to succeed. Charismatic paranoiacs were the one Hybrid genre that he coveted and those who exhibited this trait were encouraged into the corridors of power. Centuries later in the latter half of the twenty-ninth century of the Hybrids measure of time, Zebulan was virtually triumphant; the scales of balance had been tipped in his favour. The whole Hybrid race had withdrawn into deeply suspicious power blocks with very little contact with each other and always tethering on the verge of hostility. With no sharing of ideas' each state had regressed or stagnated in technical progress. All the major power blocks became isolated and he was now convinced.

"The Hybrids will prove to be little more than a hindrance to my Master's legions. They would be picked off and exterminated at leisure."

While the schemes of Zebulan were coming to fruition, Cathbad's on the other-hand seemed to be falling apart. There was one Hybrid trait that had not figured in the ALASTHA'I calculations. When things were going smoothly for their creations, they retreated into a lifestyle of complacency and acceptance. It was in this situation that their creations resisted the urge to improve themselves. Most had divested themselves of that Greco-Roman construct of democracy and either blatantly or in disguise, reverted to totalitarian regimes. It was ironic that this one circumstance was part of the Aliens scheme and for a race that thrived on individual input, it was to their detriment that they now depended on a form of ethos that spoke with one absolute voice.

The Hybrid's stagnated.

Now, the most important Power blocks of the Hybrid's had slipped into the acceptance of the status quo. Cathbad thought about influencing a great religious war, this had always worked in the past. But now conditions were different.

This was an unevenly balanced World.

Wealth and resources were not distributed equally. Only in the most poor and depressed places of the Planet did the belief in God and the next life prevail. Initiating a religious war would be of no consequence against the atheists with their superior technology and armed forces. His calculations indicated that they triumph easily and even if the believers of God became victorious, past experience showed that they would settle into a belief of a peaceful Deity and existence.

For now Zebulan was in the ascendancy or so he thought, for there was one Power block that was back in the murky business of controlling neighbouring states and demanding tribulation from them. It too displayed the image of a fabled winged creature, the Phoenix. Its rulers also had plans born out of a warped inherited ideology, gifted to them by beings not birthed on this World.

A new order was beginning and still the "Vigil Globes." kept their attention on the Blue Planet for their Alien observers who nevertheless existed far back in the past. To the concerned Watcher, the success of their scheme was still in the fold of the wings of the mad Patriarchi as various Hybrids inherited, stole or just came across the six pieces of the living amulet. The whereabouts of the seventh piece was still a mystery that he was nowhere near solving. And so, near the dawn of the 31st century, the present holders of the pieces of the APOCRYPHA'I continued with their ownership, oblivious to their real purpose. If mankind knew about or even believed in an external threat, then it was in no shape to confront it. The ALASTHA'I creations would be totally at the mercy of the CRYSTALOID'I host.

148

VIII.

NORTHEAST AFRICA 1875AD.

The once tall candles of solidified animal fat that had given him adequate light during his fascinating study had melted into squat blocks of implausible shapes. Their oily wicks had finally burnt out, but wisps of their pungent odour still lingered and infringed on his short sleep. Conscious of his strained eyes, he longed for his bifocal's. He mumbled in regret.

"They have been lost a long time ago and it is not as if I can make an appointment with a Harley Street optician to replace them."

He was far from Western civilization and modern innovation. It was as if he had been dropped into a medieval existence.

"Still, I have certainly endured worst places."

He had been up all night, the journal was riveting and the explorer could not take his weary eyes from the aged parchment that he had been drying over his open fire. The musty smell of steaming hot paper was a necessary encumbrance, if the mouldy pages were to be read once again. The leaves of the artefact were bound in red leather and it was the detailed gold etching of an Angel on the cover that had initiated his interest. He longed for a smoke of his pipe, but the convalescent had traded that and the last of his tobacco for the written artefact. This subject of Queen Victoria must have dozed off at some time before the exchange of night and day, for the sunlight of the bright Ethiopian Sun shone through the wooden blinds of his sleeping quarters, striking his closed eyes. It enticed him to rise and he stirred the embers of his dying fire, before adding more fuel to ward off the early morning chill of these high elevations. He replaced a black battered kettle full of questionable water to brew an herbal tea that assuaged his recovery. Hopefully, the crackling green timber would also frighten away the spiteful mosquitoes before they became active as the morning heated up. During the night, the pesky insects had crawled under his body-heated blankets and pepper dashed his flesh with itchy red blemishes. He scratched his tender spots with one hand while the other still had the ancient red leather tome clutched tightly in his callused fingers; its writings contained the clues to his most coveted wishes. From a bowl of water, he washed the scales of sleep from his orbs and dressed fully in what he considered a necessary modicum of civilization. Then he rose, eager to re-immerse himself in the ancient tale. The impatient reader knew for certain.

"Somewhere in this bizarre story, I will find the solution to fulfil all my desires."

For the aged parchment told a fantastic tale of events wiped from the pages of history; of an assault on the holy city of Jerusalem that had never been recorded until now. There was one major hitch however, pages had been ripped from its binding and someone's name had been scratched out. But this was not a problem; he knew from Egyptian scholars that some ruler's cartouches were treated in this manner by succeeding Pharaohs. But the reader sensed that this long dead author feared that if he mentioned the missing name, then servants of that monarch would find him and hunt him down.

"Anyway, both are long gone from this World and they matter little now. The only important thing is this legacy that they have left me with."

After his first initial reading of the scroll, he had found an additional page written in the Coptic script of a monk. He asked a member of the monastery to translate it. It cost him his reliable time piece, but it was worth the exchange. The head of the scriptorium told him.

"The author like you sought refuge among this religious community hundreds of years before. This person died mysteriously and was found hanging in a cell and that by the manner of his death, he could not have done it himself. The mystery was never solved."

Those ancient circumstances suited him fine; he now firmly believed.

"I am the only living soul that knows of this lost place described in the incredible tale. I have my doubts that the writer could have passed on his knowledge before his untimely demise. The lost city with its fantastic riches will be still there; though abandoned and ruined, but waiting for me to reveal its wonders."

The water had boiled enough; he poured it into a tin mug and stirred it. Through the steamy haze and a refreshing gulp; he began to read his treasure once again. It began with the proclamation in larger than life flowing script.

"THIS IS THE LEGEND OF THE FOUNDERS OF OUR ORDER; THE KNIGHTS OF THE WINGED ONE."

JERUSALEM 1206AD.

After a few weeks of bloody siege and during a filthy day of persistent rain, the flailing Trebuchet's of the besiegers finally made a substantial breach in the formidable walls of the Holy City. A few days before, the machine's loaders had tired of filling the buckets with rotting excrement and dead carcasses (Both Human and animal.). The use of these grisly contents was a strategy designed to spread plague and panic among the city population, but if there was sickness behind the formidable walls, then it was proceeding too slowly for those that surrounded the stout buttresses. Word might get out and a massive Saracen force might rush to relieve the siege. So haste was the main priority of the attacking forces and armed with that knowledge; craftsmen among the huge armies entourage had been tasked to carve smooth round projectiles out of hard basalt blocks. It took three sturdy men to load a single shot into a waiting wooden bucket. Each loader wore tough leather skinned gloves smothered with animal fat to prevent friction burns from the moveable ropes of the machines. But these slippery finger protectors made it awkward and time consuming in loading the polished stone projectiles. Once the bucket was packed and the ropes cranked tight, the order was given to launch. The soldiers of the besieging army scattered as the counter lever of the Trebuchet pendulumed back as its swinging bucket delivered its deadly load in a high arc to smash against the thick walls of the Holy City. Many a man, unaware or unlucky had been crushed by the swinging action of the throwing machines during this and previous campaigns in the Holy Land. By sheer luck or skill, the siege engineers had struck the same weakened spot in the cities defending walls with five enormous blocks of the circular stone over the last few days. A loud creaking noise heralded the collapse of that section of wall. As that fraction of the stout barrier began to shudder, resounding cheers broke out among the encircling army. Much to the besieger's delight and to the starving defender's dismay, the formally impregnable wall crashed down in slow motion to the corpse-strewn ground; crushing the charred remains of siege engines and a few of the attackers, who had been feigning death under the wall and waiting until nightfall to make their escape away from vigilant archers. All the efforts of the defenders were to no avail, from the reinforcement of the walls with earthen banks, to the hastily battening down of the city's drains with iron grates. If the siege weary citizens of David's citadel thought for one instant that they would be exchanging one set of masters for another, then, they were sadly mistaken. For this was no army of chivalrous Knights, who followed the code and measure that was about to enter the doomed city. Years of brutal crusading in getting to this place had eroded nearly every virtue; the armies of the Papacy had once cherished. The invading hoards of European Knight's and lesser men at arms from the coastal Crusader states poured through the break in a mad scramble over the still dusty rubble, not to free the Holy City from the God forsaken Saracens, but for the reward of rape and plunder. This had been a shock and rapid attack in total violation of an uneasy truce between the Christian and Muslim armies. This lightning raid had been ordered by someone in the higher echelons of the invading forces and most of the mob were willing to oblige. Rampaging soldiers passing through the huge earthen embankments piled high against the wooden gates, scoffed that all the hard toil of their construction had been to no avail. The abandoned mangonels of the defenders were quickly cleared of their dead loaders and turned facing back into the city that they had once had protected. Fireballs crackled overhead, the manmade conflagrations soon found wood and thatch as eager flames leapt from house to house. The rampaging Christians trampled the brightly coloured pendants of the defending army into the muddy ground. All the appalling hardships the rampaging host had endured up to this moment were going to be extracted in blood from the mostly unsuspecting population. And those pouring into the holy city were in no mood for forgiveness. Chief among them sought after the holy relics of Christendom, which had not been found in pillaged Byzantium. The devout Knights of the Crusade longed for the glory of finding the Holy Ark of the covenant, the Holy Grail or even the crown of thorns that once adorned the head of their Saviour. Any such relic was guaranteed to bring wealth to ones town from visiting pilgrims and thus ensure the finders position in that society. While any object connected to Christ's life was the Knighthood's goal, the ordinary rank and file would settle for food, drink, coin and women. Belief was strong that the chief relics held mystical powers. Each sect within the Knighthood searched for a particular item. The supposedly pious Knights excuse for this covert assault on Jerusalem was to keep the holy places Christian, to protect the Church of the Holy Sepulchre and to convert the heathens to the true faith. Unfortunately for the city inhabitants these believers in Christ converted by the sword and for those that survived this night, wearing a cross was no insurance against rape or murder. Look what they had done to the beautiful Christian City of Constantinople, where the populace had been slaughtered and its wealth carried back to western kingdoms. Its once revered art and sculptors now adorned the churches and squares of the newly emerging banker states of the west. The power of the Byzantium Empire was no more. Now, the once fabulous city was reduced to an impoverished city-state trapped between two opposing religious beliefs. A thousand years of learning, the last vestiges of Ancient Greece and Rome turned to dust in a night of rampage.

Jerusalem became no exception.

Its Saracen defenders, its Jews and even its own Christians were raped and butchered in the uninhibited frenzy that followed. From all parts of the smoke blackened city came the cries and wails of its victims. Jerusalem was no stranger to spats of bloody murder like this. Throughout its long history, nights like this occurred spontaneously. These narrow streets had seen carnage on a greater scale before when the Roman legions burnt down the second temple of Solomon, but tonight's murderous events would run a close second.

"What was it about walled cities that brought out the worst in the besiegers once the deadlock was broken" Wondered the Templar Knight Baldwin De Courcy as he led a detachment of his mostly armoured and determined brotherhood through the narrow streets in a special quest. He was a member of the order founded in the year of the Lord in 1118AD to protect pilgrims making the journey to Holy Jerusalem.

"This night, I have a very different mission."

De Courcy and his men at arms blood-splattered armour gave them a demonic appearance as if his band of Knight's and footmen had been cast out of hell and made to roam the tortured city. Tattered and blood stained white tunics with their large red cross only gave credence to that assumption. His company had started out with a force of two hundred strong, but ambushes, confrontation and bitter street fighting in the narrow thoroughfares had withered them down to eighty men. The grim statistics made De Courcy curse in a laboured breath.

"One hundred and twenty good men lost. I hope it is worth the cost."

He and his men made their way by foot, for many reasons. Most of their horses had perished in battle or went lame on the journey to the Levant. The starving army had even eaten some of their valuable mounts. Another incentive for leaving their few and precious steeds behind was that Jerusalem was a city of narrow lanes, countless steps and open sewers. The shallow culverts were treacherous and it would be easy for a horse to break its legs. Experience also taught them that cramped streets were deadly to mounted men. But the Knights still did not tarry, there was urgency in the warrior's actions, they had a specific goal in sight. Although long denied access to the sacred sites by the stronger armies of the successors of Saladin, there had been a few truces. During these cessations in hostility, their agents had made contacts inside the Holy City. So now they had spies behind those once formidable walls and one such man accompanied them. He was one of the two unarmoured men that was cocooned behind the Templar Knights shield wall, which was paying its way in blood and sweat as it progressed through the narrow claustrophobic streets. The man born in the besieged City had given them; the name of "Simon.". A good name from the holy bible. Along a fragile chain of communication stretching from Jerusalem to their chapter house in faraway Normandy, thousands of leagues distant, there had come an unbelievable tale. While the other sects searched for tangible relics, De Courcy's hardened veterans now picking their way down the narrow and treacherous streets had a clandestine quest that made all the others pale in comparison.

BELIEVE IT OR NOT, THIS BELEAGURED COMPANY SEARCHED FOR A LIVING ONE OF GODS OWN ANGELS.

The Templar knights had to be vigilant in this unearthly quest, not just from the enemy defenders, but from other sects in their own army. An hour ago, a group of the Teutonic orders tried to follow their path. But the German Knights were beaten back by a horde of maddened Saracens that had come between the two parties. Both groups of combatants just hacked away at each other until somebody went down; this was medieval warfare at its most precocious. His company had left the sound of the clash far behind, heedless of the outcome. This small band had pressing matters of their own. De Courcy was a tall lean man, the fatness of aristocracy toned away by the hardships of this desolate land. A harsh and unforgiving place, it was so different from the gentle greenness of his homeland. The big Knight longed for his pastures more pleasant and green, where even the cattle were healthy and vigorous, not like the scrawny beasts of this land. On bitter hindsight; his semi fortified Donjon seemed more of a palace now, unlike all of the defensive buildings, he had called home during this

Crusade that had been blessed by the Holy Father. His six feet two frame that was once was topped off with a proud mane of fine black shiny hair had been severely cropped to rid himself of the parasites that thrived in this filthy place. His face that instantly defined him as one of the nobility had a long inkvine scar (A gift from a dead Saracen.) that betrayed itself by a lengthy thin line across his cheek and into his goatee beard. He refused to shave it off and suffered the lice that he combed out of it every night. His face had aged and had become browner under the Middle Eastern Sun. The Frenchman looked far older than his thirty years. The battle hardened Knights within the group were puffing in their heavy metal armour; the smell and fumes from charred and burning timber caused stinging tears that could not be wiped away by gauntleted hands or armoured forearms. Most of the Paladins had scavenged parts of armour from other fallen Knights. Ill fitting, helmets, breastplates and greaves were their uncomfortable lot. Their own shining armour was a distant memory. The men at arms wore conical helmets with wide flat rims; as much as for protection as identification of their station. Even they donned tattered white tunics with the large emblazoned red Cross, the plain fabrics only prominent feature. The bitter road from Constantinople along the coast of the eastern Mediterranean lay dotted with graves marking the final resting-place of many a Christian soul. With dented shields that were held in front and raised over heads by weary arms, De Courcy's band advanced slowly through the murderous lanes; four aside and twenty deep. Completely encircled within their metal turtle was the citizen of the Holy City, Simon, who had come over to their side months before the Christian army had camped outside the walls. This man of small stature born in the mysterious bosom of this place knew the whereabouts of the Angel. While they halted for a breather, De Courcy paused and studied the features of the small squat man as much as the burning fires of the city would allow. During this brief respite, their metal shield wall was peppered with missiles that reminded him of falling hail on a tin roof. Then, their unseen assailants managed to drop large stones or broken masonry and already stressed elbows jarred with the heavy impact. The man under his scrutiny looked like all the inhabitants of the Holy Land. None were as tall as the Europeans or of fair complexion. The man boasted a swarthy skin. His head was covered by some type of black headdress, but his brown eyes and prominent nose could still be made out in the light of the fire-ravaged city. The calm demeanour of the man hinted at a God given confidence or a strong personality. De Courcy found that while he trusted nobody in this land; but he did admire this fellow.

"I know what the inquisitors have put him through, those fanatical torturer's had stopped at all out maiming. This Simon had been interrogated, threatened with torment in the iron maiden and burning at the stake by the best persuaders in the Holy Church, but astoundingly he *stayed true to his incredible story. And those bastards could get you to say that your own Mother had fornicated with Satan, beasts and all of his minions."*

The synod of the Templar's came to the decision that this fantastic story must be looked into and that was why; this group of decimated warriors were fighting their way through the narrow streets. While De Courcy was the military commander of this punitive group, a fanatical Padre, simply named "Juan" was the overall leader of the expedition and he was responsible for reporting everything back to his superiors. When the company had started out, this Priest was the second unarmed man in the middle of the shield wall. But he had picked up a fallen weapon on the way and was using it to good effect. He wore a tight red skullcap over his head, a sign of his order. Unlike most of his immediate brethren, he carried his weight in a stout frame and puffy red cheeks. It seemed that the dubious Cleric enjoyed the good life and did not suffer the rigors that most of the Christian invaders had over the last few years. He was clean shaven and even had the audacity to even look healthy. Some of the Knights still under his command were to say extremely sceptical about the mission and many times this night they advocated within close earshot.

"Cut the dammed Priest's throat and abandon this foolish assignment."

But, De Courcy was acutely aware.

"If any of us return without our religious appointee, then it will be each of us who face the Inquisitors. Besides, the men of my troop are a desperate lot. Many of them believe that the completion of this mission will absolve them from previous barbarous actions."

The Templar had an instant dislike for the Priest, there was a religious fanaticism that surrounded his manner and for all his holy zeal, Padre Juan had betrayed himself and shown a hint of his true nature. It was while the detachment were making their way through the early stages of the bitter street fighting and came across a few Frankish soldiers raping a young girl; who was not even out of her puberty. With genuine disgust, he uttered.

"The age of chivalry is long dead. "

The Priest however was not able to contain a look of naked lust that crossed his face at the sight of her terror and exposed olive flesh. His expression made him appear even more devilish as it was highlighted by the orange light of the crackling flames and burning timber of the cities dwellings. The crucifix hanging between her adolescent breasts did not save her from molestation and eventual murder. Scenes like this no longer sickened the Knight De Courcy. Alas; he had become much too familiar with them.

"Yes, he is like the rest of us. He is no Saint. " Revised the warrior of Christ.

The leader of the armed detachment had learned from bitter experience.

"Wailing children draw rapists and murderers like shit drawing flies, for those scum have learned that most mothers and young girls will not abandon their infants."

The compassionate side in him hoped that many a terrified woman would keep the children silent tonight. The pelting of the crossbow bolts that were glancing from their shields abated and despite his men's laboured breathing, he ordered them to proceed. The weary men at arms progressed through narrow lanes at a greater speed and this pleased their charge. Occasionally a maddened Saracen came out of the shadows and flailed futilely at them shouting all the time in Arabic, only to be cut down by their remaining marksmen. As they passed over the fallen warrior, a sword thrust or a knife made sure the assailant was finished off. The Padre carrying the nasty looking studded mace that he had appropriated had no scruples in smashing the head in of any fallen enemy. The hypocrisy of the Priest at blessing the deceased, even when he had just brained one, sparked fury in De Courcy. The Knight of God wondered.

"What is the church was coming to. This is no toil for the clergy; it should be left for her men at arms. We have always carried out the dirty work."

A short while later, they paused again to take another breather and to lick their numerous wounds. Suddenly, there came the sound of a lone rider, the clipping of his mounts iron shoes on the narrow stone lane ringing out in an approaching challenge. The mounted and mailed Saracen, who was in full gallop crashed into their shield wall and both man and beast fell from the impact. The horse and its rider lay in the narrow cobbled lane with their necks twisted and broken. De Courcy, who cared little for the slain man looked at the dead white stallion and mourned.

"What a waste of a magnificent steed. I would have loved to bring him back to France and bred his offspring."

The rider and the horse's valiant efforts caused the packed formation to buckle and the rigid shield wall had opened slightly. A lucky or well-aimed bolt that came between a gap in the screen of metal ended his musing as the barbed shaft took a man at arms under the armpit. The fallen man was his squire and his inadequate armour had failed him. An answering hum from one of their own crossbow men resulted in a shrill scream and a Saracen fell from a rooftop with the iron bolt embedded in his forehead. His falling body hit the cobbles with a palpable crunch. The impact with the ground drove the shaft completely through the archer's head and a pool of blood formed around the matted hair of the body. De Courcy with vindictive outrage; hoped it was the fellow who had gravely wounded his servant. Then just as he was about to decide to halt and take care of his squire's injury; the decision was taken out of his hands. Padre Juan knelt down beside the wounded man, removed his helmet and whispered the last rites to the gasping man. Still reciting, the Priest drew the squire's own blade across his throat. Red blood flowed from the gash and the sharp intakes of breath became a gurgling sound and then silence. De Courcy became outraged, he was well known for his fiery temper. The enraged Knight turned on the killer of his man, his voice quavering with menace.

"Have you a death wish, Priest? If so, by all the saints in Heaven, I will surely grant it. We could have saved him."

Possessed with religious fever, the Squires killer challenged.

"You, Sir Knight know most of all that nothing can interfere with this holy quest. He would have been only a burden that we could not afford. "

Seeing death in De Courcy's eyes, the Priest said hurriedly.

"We dare not leave him. You know what the Saracens would do to him, if they came across him wounded and helpless"

Reluctantly and privately, the furious armoured man was forced to agree.

"I have seen the bodies of captured Knights whose families failed to pay the ransom that the Saracens demanded. There is no such offer for the rank and file of the Christian army. Besides, after the slaughter that has been visited here tonight, any prisoners taken, even nobility will be killed out of hand. A wounded soldier of the Church is certain of a heinous death, if the Heathens discovers him."

His loyal squire's life fluids mixed with the lather of the open drains and flowed in the direction that they were to proceed in.

"A road maker etched in blood. How many of those have I seen? Too many I'd wager."

De Courcy ordered his troop to move on and out of the corner of his eye, he saw the Priest smirk. He promised to himself.

"That one will not see out this night alive."

His squire's body disappeared into the murk and as the advancing troop continued on the route that their guide was showing them. The screams of the dying city became more intense. The silent man who alone knew the route took them down a series of narrower and more secluded back alleys, until finally they were only able to walk one abreast. The highly alert company had been steadily going downhill for at least fifteen minutes. Eventually overhanging buildings enclosed the streets entirely, closing out the noise of destruction while at the same time protecting them from attack from above. All they could hear now was the trod of heavy footfalls, clinking armour and labouring breaths. Then all of a sudden, Padre Juan's expeditionary force found themselves in an incense torch lit tunnel that was much wider than the one that they had come down in. The soldiers were grateful for the purifying odour, as its fumes also blocked out the gut wrenching stenches from the blackened smoke of the burning city. The troop halted and stillness ensued.

"More than silence disturbs this place." Thought De Courcy as he felt a sudden chill down his spine. As their eyes met, he knew the Priest shared

his opinion. There was a feeling of the unknown in the very air of the tunnel. A few of the surviving party blessed themselves. That action became contagious and those that had not; did so now. Strangely, Padre Juan never made the sign of the cross. Simon urged them with his accented voice and the column moved on, it was as if the Semitic man had taken charge. At the end of the passageway, the hesitant group of armed warriors was confronted with a large stout iron banded wooden door that measured at least ten men abreast and three high. The huge shut entrance had a bell rope hanging from the wall at its side. Unperturbed their guide pulled on the tarred hemp in a sequence that was only known to him. Instinctively, the battle experienced leader of Templar Knight's knew.

"If those sounds had been made incorrectly, then we would all have died instantly."

The peals of the bell died away and a few seconds later, though it seemed an eternity, the huge door swung open effortlessly and silently. Nobody had moved it and there was no sign of any mechanisms to move such a weight. To those that witnessed its movement, it spoke of the supernatural. Guardedly and cautiously and with a threat from De Courcy, the battered group pushed on through the opened door into a large open courtyard. The quantity of fresh air within the enclosed place was disorientating and from atop its encompassing walls, the exhausted soldiers were suddenly greeted with loaded crossbows. Every man that appeared above was aiming a mechanical weapon at the Christian soldiers. All of the Crossbow men had their face cloaked in a black Haik.

"It's a trap. Defend yourselves. Form a shield wall." Yelled De Courcy as he grabbed their betrayer. His men complied with his shouted command, but he found himself outside the hastily erected defensive barrier with a knife pressed against Simon's spine.

"No! You are safe here." Shouted their guide as he felt the point of the blade in his unprotected back. Simon then bellowed in a Semitic language that was unknown to any of the Crusaders and some of those above lowered their cocked weapons. He removed his cowl and again he shouted for compliance in his own tongue and those who had not lowered their weapons, did so now. He raised his hands in submission and as he felt the pressure on De Courcy's blade ease a fraction. He whispered softly.

"It was a misunderstanding. These men have sworn an unbreakable oath and have the right to be cautious. But they now know that Gods messenger sent for you. Listen to me Knight De Courcy, I swear by the Winged One. Your siege engines did not bring down the outer wall. No offence, but it would have taken years to collapse, if we had not lent a hand. The Angel of God gave us magical contrivances to burn the earth and stone under the wall. It was us that sanctioned your entrance into the Holy City of David. "

Speaking as he cupped his right hand in a pleading gesture, Simon implored.

"You must believe me."

Going against the grain; the leader of the Templar Knight's did. He commanded his fighters.

"Lower your swords."

De Courcy had seen the firmness of command in the man's voice when he had ordered the crossbow men above and in an exasperated tone scolded those of his company who had not lowered their weapons in response.

"It is not a trap, these people have helped us."

His own men nodded in agreement and sheathed their steel, knowing full well that they were at the mercy of the crossbow men on the wall. Simon gave him a pleased look and De Courcy got the impression.

"This Simon could have easily got free from my grasp, if he had really wanted to."

His original opinion of the Semitic man had increased enormously and gone up a few notches. Behind them, the door of the hidden courtyard closed soundlessly; again his men murmured oaths and blessed themselves. De Courcy did not believe their assumptions about magical devices, but guessed that these men had indeed some ingenious mechanism for opening and closing the door. Then their guide spoke.

"Come. They will protect our rear."

He led them to the back of the courtyard to another door, much smaller in size. Before they entered, Simon told the leader of the Templar's.

"I have been the keeper of this wonderful miracle since the time of the Emperor Vespasian. And the secret had been passed on to me by my predecessor. And he had been born in the time of the Pharaoh's. Long before the Ptolemy's."

De Courcy like all members of the aristocracy was well educated in the Greek and Latin histories. He did a mental calculation and then looked at Simon to see if he was ridiculing him.

"That Emperor ruled shortly after the death of Christ, from 69AD to 79AD. He is saying that he is over a thousand years old. But, he is not mocking me; the truth is emblazoned in his eyes."

On a night of shocks, the Christian Knight predicted.

"There are more to come and I pray that he will see this day out."

This new door moved open with the same ease as its predecessor and it led down a spiral stairs to a hidden Serdab. The very impressive mortuary temple was framed by stone carvings that depicted Angels. The detailed images of God's messengers were shown in flight and in holy contemplation with outstretched wings. Bright glaring Halo's adorned all the heavenly representations, but oddly the divine circles were not just white, but of many colours. Three lighting torches hung on either side of the sculpture. Their guide who had now definitely taken command removed two burning brands from their iron sconces, snuffed one out and replaced both brands back in alternative brackets. A second later, a section of the wall vanished before their disbelieving eyes. This time, the doorway did not open, one second the wall was there and in an instant it was gone. Again there were whispers of disquiet among his men. A frigid breeze coming from the magical opening froze them in their tracks, as all of them shivered uncontrollably with the sudden drop in temperature. The armoured Knights were the most effected by the chill as their chain metal attracted the cold like a magnet attracted ferrous metal. Then wide-eyed and fearful, the awed company filed pass the portal, only Simon knew what to expect. On the other side of the entrance lay a short passageway whose roof arched a few feet above their helmeted heads into a semi convex curvature. Both sides of the tunnel held smokeless lights that were embedded solidly in the masonry. The illumination did not flicker or cast shadows, its brightness was uniform, cool and vivid. The Christians gasped in wonderment as the lights snuffed themselves out one by one as the last of them passed through. The extinguishing glows seemed to be herding them towards another space. As each light went out, there was no smell of smouldering pitch, oil or tar.

"What devilry or trickery is this?" Mouthed an offended De Courcy.

"It is not chicanery; this is the work of God." Whispered the Priest hoarsely, he had been unusually silent up to now. He was incorrect; their maker was not able to withstand the sulphours concoction that powered the normal light sources. The overawed Christians crossed into what could only be described as another hidden Sepulchre. There was a small door in the side of the Crypt and it could only be entered by a polished bronzed gate in a railing that surrounded it. Simon led and the tall European's hunched over, so they were able to pass through the small opening into the burial chamber. Squeezing in one by one, the Crusaders were on the other side, where they instantly forgot about the freezing cold. All of them now stood frozen in cataplexy. For the inside did not make sense, its impossible proportions affronted them. Madness had surely overcome them or had they unknowingly died and were now walking the halls of the after-life. The enormous blue space of the chamber inside the tomb dwarfed the greatest Cathedral in Christendom. Unlike the venerated halls of Saint Peter's basilica or the vastness of Saint Catherine's in Constantinople, it had no lines of parallel pillars to disturb the view of the vast enclosed space. It also had no massive columns that were topped with huge arches to support and bear the enormous weight of the roof. Its great height and fantastic depth showed no conceivable means of construction and its gaping magnitude was impossible to grasp. The frozen air of its space was azure coloured and the chamber had the feeling of perpetuity, making those that just entered measured their time in the World as a candle in the wind compared to this enormity. Its vast floor was a carpet of permafrost and there was a heady smell of incense. Someone cried out in disbelief.

"How is this possible?"

"God and his holy works." Replied the Priest in a trembling voice.

Everyone turned to the man of God; he might be able to give them answers. He obliged.

"Don't you doubting Tomas's understand? Only the Lord of Hosts could imagine or build such a wonder. This must be the fabled temple of Solomon. It was not above ground, but below."

De Courcy gave the Priest a black look as his troops were already seriously twitchy and ready to bolt. The Templar was also unsure whether the Priest was correct or not. Suddenly Padre Juan was drawn towards movement in the frigid cobalt shadows; then he saw the apparition, a spectre at the edge of his vision. His trembling voice was rising towards a howl, but suddenly ceased as his eyes widened in adoration. He fell to his knees and began praying. Every eye shifted in the direction that had caught the penitent's eye. All of the men except De Courcy fell to the floor in unison and stared in reverence at the eidolon that began to materialise in front of them. As one they proclaimed.

"The Angel of God."

Shimmering, shifting, his gossamer wings flapping in a rainbow kaleidoscope of colours, Zebulan gazed down on the Hybrid's that were mostly cowering in his presence.

"It's wonderful that I never tire of that." Mind thought the ostentatious Winged Alien.

His full grandiloquent magnificence had regenerated and for the first time in thousands of years, Zebulan had his full raiment returned. The false Angel no longer had the tattered sickly appearance or the frizzled wings. It had taken thousands of years of this Planets orbit around its Sun and more than a little help from the constant and never ending blood infusing to rejuvenate his once marred body. But more importantly, he now wore a crystal mask crafted into the semblance of the Hybrid's features and floating above it was his Preceptor-Band. Those who now bore witness saw an Angelic face that was flawless and immaculate. However, his body with its macula had to remain hidden and the most realistic projection of unblemished blue skin that he could fabricate enveloped his frame. To the Hybrids, he was a true image from Heaven; a holy Cherub topped with a halo as blinding as newly fallen snow. The Priest was the first to regain his speech and he begged of the supernatural being.

"Servant of the Lord. How can us worthless mortals serve you, one of God's holy Angels?"

Simon who was about to chastise him over his misconception was halted by an unheard command from his God. Vexed at been called a servant, but wise enough not to anger this band of cutthroats, Zebulan went through his well-rehearsed routine. It was always in the fringes of his mind, what had happened to Naisi, Seantana and the others. Due to his single mind-set and poor resources, he had not developed the necessary protection to shield his body from attack. Initial attempts in this direction interfered with his false appearance and this was no use to the Hybrid manipulator. The DEFILED had taken a gamble with only Simon present and the disguised Alien knew.

"These warriors would not respect me if I was surrounded by a company of armed Hybrid's and the invisible shield in front of me will not withstand a persistent assault from their steel. I must be careful; for the one without the metal covering is lurking at the edge of madness. It is an irrational trait of the Hybrid's that I still cannot comprehend or plan for. But, this is one I can use."

Padre Juan was rapidly losing an internal battle. He had never truly believed in what he preached. The Cleric had always used his position for influence and advantage. His next words flowed out as sobs.

"And now it is all true. I will have to face my Creator in the end."

The bogus practitioner of the faith remembered all the sins that he had committed. The now shameful list was substantial.

"There is not one of Gods holy commandments that I have not broken. I will burn in hell for eternity."

Padre Juan felt the closeness of imaginary flames. His voice stricken in dismay, he pleaded, while weeping tears of repentance.

"Please intercede with our Lord for forgiveness for my sins. I am a wretch and I beg for clemency. I entreat you, ask him to forgive me."

He snatched out his hidden dagger and prepared to immolate himself. Behind his crystal mask, Zebulan's Alien receptors of circular macula locked on to the miserable creature, all the Hybrid saw was two false intense and unreadable humanlike orbs, the master of deception exulted.

"Always, these Hybrids with their melodramas, but I have him now. He is mine."

The DEFILED spoke directly into the Priest's mind.

"The Lord forgives you my son. For is he not known as the lord of mercy. He only asks that you serve him with all that you possess for the remainder of your life. Then, he shall reward you in Heaven."

To the abased Priest, Zebulan's mind-voice sounded like all the choirs in Heaven. His breathing tortured and his vocal chords oddly subdued, Padre Juan shone with religious euphoria. The new man of God had an expression of holy zeal etched into his face. This time, he had truly been converted on the spot. He knew for certain that the line here between Heaven and Earth was very thin indeed. Witnessing the Priest's reaction, De Courcy shuddered, but then the Angel's gaze sought him out and the same disembodied melodious voice caressed his mind. It sounded like the second part of an echo. The others did not hear the shifting words; they were for him alone.

"You are the greatest of all of Gods Knights and it is his will that you

serve him. For, your Lord has a great test for you. The Lord's followers have lost the true path; it is up to you to find the new faithful. Like in the time of Noah, the lord of hosts has decided to save the few and be done with the rest."

The shock of those words played De Courcy like a lute; he fell to his unworthy knees and pledged obedience. The Templar removed his Anlace, a short dagger with a broad tapering blade that every Knight had strapped to his waist and raised it with two clasped hands to his lips. As his heavily callused hands tightened around the steel, De Courcy swore his allegiance to the servant of the Creator. He as a Knight had just made an oath to serve one of God's Angels. A promise that could only be broken by God himself. The rest of his subordinates abased themselves and swore the same pledge.

THE FORMER KNIGHT'S OF THE HOLY SEE HAD MADE A COVENANT WITH GOD AND WERE PLEDGED TO PROTECT THE SECRET OF THE WINGED ONE UNTIL THE LAST BREATH EXPIRED FROM THEIR LUNGS. DE COURCY, THE PRIEST AND THE REST OF THEIR GROUP HAD FORMED A NEW CHAPTER OF THE CHURCH. THEY HAD BECOME THE SACROSANCT KNIGHTS OF THE WINGED ONE.

The object of their adoration noticed that some of the Hybrids were oozing life fluids onto the floor of his living space. The noxious vapours were irritating to the Alien, so he instigated a procedure to mend the injured. On his command, light rays targeted the warriors, bathed them, then sealed the cuts and gashes and removed the damaged blemishes leaving no trace of an injury. When it withdrew, the men were healed completely. Even De Courcy's ink vine scar had vanished. In the mist of their wonderment, the Priest confirmed after witnessing the spectacle.

"God's Holy radiance has washed over us!"

What Zebulan wanted with these Knights was explained by the fact that a rare conjunction between three of the Sun's orbiting Planet's had knocked out his backup systems. His hiding place would soon be revealed and though he might be able to prevent this occurrence, it was just getting too crowded around here with all the wars and such. The Alien had remained hidden with his followers and completely safe during the Jewish revolt of 79AD when the vengeful Romans had practically levelled the city, but that time his protection devices were fully operational. This city had become a magnet for the erratic exuberance of the Hybrids and it was becoming the focus of too much unwanted attention. It was a repeat of the events surrounding Zebulan that happened over three thousand years before, when he had courted a King to the Southeast and received his complete adoration. That stupid ruler had renounced the old Gods and went into the deep desert with his people. There, he founded a new capital away from Thebes, devoted to the one true Deity; Zebulan. He had been the Pharaoh of Egypt; Akhenaton Aton was his new name. But the followers of the old religion of many God's turned against him and destroyed him and his city. Many future scholars would look at inscriptions that had been hacked off or covered in acidic resin and rightly assumed that they had to do with this despised King. What they would not know was that the cartouche of the "Winged One" was also deliberately erased and this rewriting of history suited the Alien who needed a low profile. Zebulan fled Northeast with a few followers and found refuge in Jerusalem. The Winged Alien had been here ever since. But to confound his other problems, there had been a lot of seismic activity lately and it was playing havoc with his experiments. So now it was time to move on again and find a safer base from where he could thwart the plans of the ALASTHA'I. That is why the Winged Alien needed the protection of these battle hardened warriors. The Saracen fighters were too devoted to the Prophet and their God, besides Simon had advised him.

"My Lord, these Christian Knights are the best and most brutal of soldiers."

Zebulan told his new converts what was to be done. Two days later as the Sun went down over a smouldering city; a large palanquin carried by eight burly armoured men and flanked by more than a hundred red crossed Knights in their new guise was used to conceal the Angel on their escape from the devastated city. Simon released a concoction given to him by the God and it left a trail of red pestilence in their wake. Thousands died as its wafting vapours were inhaled. The Winged Alien could still only kill second handily. He had manufactured the poison but could not release it. Behind the hefted drapes, Zebulan carried all of his technology and himself in globular spheres. As the heavily armed procession passed through the Crusaders lines, no sentries questioned why the palanquin was been hoisted by the nobility, for in the chaos of these times, it was hard enough to survive, never mind asking stupid questions that might get you killed anyway.

A month later, the ruler of the coastal states met their Islamic counterparts in a desert tent. The antagonists agreed that the rash attack on Jerusalem was caused by a few rogue orders and it would be best for both sides if the incident was forgotten. Both sets of leaders believed that the red mist which spread a trail of agonising death from the bowls of the Holy City was a judgement from God over the broken truce. If either of their many followers supposed that it was they who had incurred the wrath of the Supreme Being, then they would be both history. The Christians paid a huge bribe in golden ducats to the successors of Saladin. The bloody affair was removed from the annuals of history and the murderous attack on the city of God was never mentioned out in the open again.

A HUNDRED YEARS LATER.

The Christian Knight's last foothold in the Holy Land was under siege by the fearsome Mameluke. Every twang from the besieging Muslim army's catapults tore the courage from the citizens of the coastal Crusader city of Acre. The Templar Knight De Courcy turned to the Priest; Salvador and said.

"It is time to leave; we will bring the agent of God back to France."

The Cleric formally named Padre Juan agreed. He, like De Courcy had not aged a day since their incursion into the Holy City; it was a gift from the Angel of Heaven. The former Priest had even shed his fatness and it had done him good. He now displayed a thick neatly trimmed goatee beard and had reverted to his family name as a precaution against anyone recognising him. This was highly unlikely, as all that were born in his time had passed from this World. The two men knew that they would not live forever as the Semitic Simon had passed away three years ago. But he had lived an incredible life span. Both of them were now the guardians of what was called the "Divine Secret.". When they had fled the Holy City with their precious trophy, it was brought before the leaders of the brotherhood. Zebulan used his thousand year old expertise of manipulating the Hybrid's and the inner circle of the order devoutly agreed to protect the servant of God. This station still vexed the vain Alien, but he was prudent enough not to upset the status quo. But given time, he would change their perception of him.

"After all, they are an inferior species."

The rulers of the coastal enclave had constructed secret tunnels under the coastal fortress, the order was given and the Knights fled the city. To the victorious Muslims, it became known as the "Flight of the Templar's". With the Seraph safely in the palanquin, De Courcy's group joined the exodus. In the dark tunnels, desperate women pleaded with them offered their wealth, jewellery and even their virtue to take them along. But the Priest laughed.

"As if they could tempt us with earthly vices. After all an Angel of God watches over us now."

De Courcy thought.

"He is a changed man."

The former Templar Knights and servants of the Holy Roman Emperor escaped the doomed city and took Zebulan back to France by ship and kept the secret among their sect for over a hundred years. The protectors of the Angel made their base in a castle above the town of Arles in Provence, which was in view of the frozen shadow of the alpine range. But rumours spread about them having the Holy Grail or the Ark of the Covenant and the covetous Holy Roman Emperor turned against them. At the request of King Philip; Pope Clement 1V abolished the sect and they became

Heretics. Their order was eventually suppressed in 1312 AD and they were declared enemies of the realm. Like the Cathars of Montaillou who suffered the inquisition and those from Montsegur who threw themselves on the fires of their besiegers to guard the secret they too had taken from the Holy Land, the Knights of the Winged one fought back with a similar lack of fear. But, the order was too few in numbers to triumph against the might of the Papacy and most of their sect were hunted down and slaughtered. Some were captured and suffered horrendous torture, but none gave up the secret of the Winged One; they took it screaming to their graves. From the agony of burning flames, some were heard to utter a strange name. Only two leaders of the sect survived the purge, the Knight De Courcy and the former Padre Juan. Zebulan had extended their life spans; this was the main source of rumour among the Sects protagonists, as their seemingly eternal youth spoke of possessing the Holy Grail. And others in power coveted this. With those that were not imprisoned or killed, they fled to the deserts of North Africa with their "Divine Secret". Even though Zebulan despised the hot climate, the Alien had no choice, as his new base was so remote and unpopulated that it would be ideal. His followers called their new city "Sanctum.". In the passing years, his fanatical minders had begun to grown large wing shaped moustaches and allowed their hair to mature into long flowing locks. It was not to the false messenger of God's taste, but he learnt the wisdom in allowing the Hybrid's to have their traditions. Zebulan and his few remaining subjects set up a new doctrine and from there over the next five centuries hidden under a mountain shield beneath the searing Sun, the last of the DEFILED plotted.

WESTERN CHAD. 1880 AD.

A caravan of sorry looking single humped Arabian camels meandered south-westwards across the bleak expanse of the open desert hardpan. The crunch of the ungulates splayed hooves on the hard packed sand contrasted with the jingling of the metal utensils draped over their hairy mammalian bodies. The tiny Caravan was made up of an Explorer, two ex-British soldiers, one Batman and their native bearers. The Europeans were outfitted in white suits, neck ties, trousers and white straw rimmed Panama hats with a black band around their middle. Some among the white men held their leg ware up with sturdy leather braces. Their Arab bearers wore traditional white and black headgear and robes. But the contrasting mix of western and eastern clothes had now become a universal dusty brown colour, a result of the desert around them. Once again ex-Quartermaster George Pamerstown, formally of her supreme majesty's Royal Engineers wiped the sweat that trickled down from underneath his Panama hat. As he brushed the dust off his garb with exaggerated hand movements, the former solider was beginning to believe.

"I probably smell like one of the unwashed natives of our bearer party."

The sleeve of his drab non-military styled outfit was stained from uncountable wiping's. When the sweltering heat had dried the fabric once again, he wondered not for the last time.

"How did I agree to go on this crazy fool's expedition? Why did I resign my comfortable commission for this insane quest?"

A desperate giggle explained his predicament.

"The answer is simple; any bloody fool can see it. I have finally lost my marbles. It is as simple as that."

Been a large overweight bullnecked man with a long handle bar moustache and equally enormous sideburns, Pamerstown was not suited to the rigours of frugal travel, a severe touch of gout and a sore backside testified to that. His deep-set eyes gave him the baleful appearance of a basset hound, which gave his mockers extra ammunition for ridicule. The mixed bunch had made their way from the shared British and Egyptian territory of Sudan and crossed westwards into French Equatorial Africa. Bribing and dodging ferocious tribesmen, they had made it this far, without loss. He and his travelling companions were weeks out from the last French outpost of Fort Lamy. While replenishing their supplies at that bleak stony coloured garrison, (The citadel was deemed the last proper outpost of civilisation.), the hardened soldiers of the Foreign Legion just shook their heads at these crazy Englishmen. Some of the desperate Legionaries counted the few blessings they had, for these wretched soldiers told each other.

"Those madmen will never be seen again."

General Vadim Clichy, the forts commander had questioned the Englishmen in case they were spies, But when he found out their objective, the officer agreed with his men and left them on their way. An honourable man, he would have loved to have confiscated their weapons. Two of the pieces were brand new bolt action, breach loading .30 calibre American Springfield rifles. However, the piece de resistance was another breech loading side action Winchester repeating rifle carried by the most dangerous one among them. Clichy knew a killer when he saw one.

"It is not strange that these Englishmen favour these weapons."

As he stood on the baked ramparts with a junior officer, the garrison commander was also aware.

"If those crazy adventurers stand the slightest chance of survival, they will need those rapid firing rifles out there."

His subordinate added wisely.

"For our sake, I hope that some flea bitten desert nomads do not turn up at the fort armed with those particular rifles."

Against his better nature, the French officer wished that he had a few

167

adventurous men like them. Then, he relented.

"Maybe some of my command were like them until this soul killing place ground them down."

His last sight of them through his binoculars going towards the terra incognita caused him to utter.

"C'est la guerre."

Sweltering under his umbrella (He was thankful for bringing this one item of civilisation.) on top of a particular temperamental camel, Pamerstown searched for the man who persuaded him with the temptation of fabulous riches and the acclaim of the legendary Royal Geographical Society.

Eminent explorer and philanthropist, Richard Clyde.

Unlike the rest of the Europeans, Clyde wore an Arab headgear as if born to it. To Pamerstown this seemed strange, as the other had nothing but utter contempt for the natives. He had heard the rumours circulating around Cairo about this enigmatic man, that their leader was an archaeologist, explorer and most of all a treasure hunter. His cantankerous beast snorted as if the animal was agreeing with him that he had made the biggest mistake of his life in teaming up with Clyde. Three months was all that he had known the man before the explorer had convinced him to make this journey. Pamerstown had met him in a bar; he frequented on his nights off. At first, the quartermaster thought it strange that a man of Clyde's age still stayed on in Africa, he appeared to be in his fifties, but as he got to know him more, he understood the man's reasons for not returning home. The bar was a rather seedy den located in the native quarter of Cairo. The Quartermaster preferred this establishment as the proprietors of the premises afforded him a sense of importance unlike in the officer's mess where the seasoned veterans of her majesty's forces looked down on the lower class military clerk with thinly veiled contempt. Pamerstown was a career soldier from a humble background who had climbed the promotional ladder; unlike the other officers who came from upper class families and instantly gained their rank. He also had a lifetime touch of gout and his gammy leg had prevented him from active service. This suited him fine, for he was no chivalrous hero. Under the influence of the establishment's wares and the heady perfume of the belly dancers and the other exotic delights that were on offer, Clyde had ignited a sense of exploration in him; he knew that he never had. But the promises of hidden wealth and most importantly fame and respect enticed him to go off on this wild goose chase. Unwisely, they were travelling during the blistering heat of the day for two reasons. The first was, as the caravan was travelling through unknown territory, they needed the light of day, so that none of their pack animals were injured because of unseen terrain. After all these beasts of burden carried nearly all of their water and supplies. Their Arab levies carried the rest of the precious liquid on their lean backs. The second reason was as important as the first, Clyde needed the stars of the night to collate his sextant and match their direction with a map that he guarded jealously. The explorer never showed them the contents of the chart. Pamerstown was now wallowing in misery as he swatted at another biting fly with the feathered cords of his camel stick. The uncomfortable man was careful not to kill it, for Pamerstown had acquired the strange belief.

"If I did, then hundreds of its kin would turn up for the funeral and I would become the main refreshment at the wake."

Clyde, himself, Major Wesley and his batman, Hughes (Their other civilised travelling companions.) and their Arab bearers, along with their pack animals had become a boon for the desert insects, who having no prejudice found all of their bodies a welcoming feasting ground.

"I am definitely going mad."

From cracked and swollen lips, Pamerstown took a swig from his tepid water bottle and nearly fell off the swaying camel as he was also trying to support his precious umbrella. Not for the last time, the former army man cursed.

"I should have stayed in my drab, but cool office. But then what would have become of me after the army was finished with me? Ha, a petty pension and maybe a small hovel to spent my remaining days."

That familiar hovel did not look so bad now. Pamerstown had worked hard to become an officer and he needed the wealth that Clyde promised to earn the respect, he craved. He saw the explorer glance over at him. The leader of the expedition looked at the pen pusher with barely concealed disgust.

"This is not the type of man, I normally would have chosen for such an adventure, but then I had no other choice."

His accolades and more importantly his monetary rewards from the Geographical Society had run out. The jack of all trades had tried to sell contraband to the natives, but this had left him penniless, close to death and imprisonment. But while he was recuperating in an Ethiopian monastery after a skirmish that left only one survivor, himself, he unearthed extraordinary images in their dusty Scriptorium that spoke of the ultimate discovery. One that for once and all would set him above his peers as the greatest explorer of all time. He had befriended the monks and gained their trust. In their library, isolated from the other buildings in a cave high up one a sheer cliff edge, he discovered the ancient red sheepskin scroll. The only method of gaining entry to this storehouse of knowledge was by a basket, which was hauled up by a primitive winch. The well-travelled man knew.

"All monasteries kept their treasures in such high places. I have seen round towers in Ireland that echoed this style of defence."

For a pipe and a pound of tobacco, the monks foolishly let him borrow and read the ancient manuscript, as these adept men of a different society could not read the indecipherable script. But Clyde had a good understanding of it. The writing was in Medieval Latin, a language; the Ethiopian monks would be totally unfamiliar with. The parchment revealed a fantastic tale, a lot of it had been missing, words were lost, but in between two pages that had been cleverly bound together, he found a tantalising hint on a scribbled note.

"Unwittingly, I have been the servant of the false God, Lucifer himself. The manifestation said he was an Angel of Heaven. Those words echoed true, but like all of his lies, the arch deceiver never revealed that he was the one that was cast out of paradise. We dwelt in a miraculous city of advanced machinery deep in the desert, between blood red Mountains, that jutted out from the desert floor. Nestled in their bosom was a vision of splendour, whereas Knights, we done his bidding. Two golden giant statues of winged deities plated with precious stones guarded the entrance to this city of wonders. A city called "Sanctum". Golden statues and fountains with beds of sapphires surrounded by gardens of exquisite beauty adorned its bountiful acres.

The scroll went on to describe the wonders of the incredible place and then the writer's proud words, echoed bitterness.

"As a trusted follower, my fellow Knight's invited me into their initiation ceremony. Unknown to me, it was a black mass of blood sacrifice and ritual slaughter. Then, I became aware that I was part of a Cabal of evil and their so-called God desired to end the glory of man. With great difficulty, I hid my thoughts from him. I stayed among them waiting for my chance to redeem myself, and then I saw my chance. I tampered with the fantastic machinery and as I fled, a huge explosion destroyed the city of deception. No one could have survived the massive detonation, including the demon himself who was sent back into the underworld. I have left a map, so maybe far in the future someone will heed my tale and mankind will not be fooled by Satan again when he returns to tempt man once again."

In growing excitement, the reader turned over the parchment and found the crude map. The search had become paramount. For Clyde coveted fame and recognition more that any member of the party. Ever since his first attempt at discovery had failed miserably. His failure was compounded when he returned back to Egypt and discovered that John Hanning Spake had beaten him and Richard Burton to the source of the Nile.

"How were we to have known that there were two dammed rivers?"

That was in eighteen fifty-eight, now thirty-two years later, the Dark Continent had very few secrets left. Clyde had been twenty-three back then and now at the age of fifty-five, he knew that this was his last chance at grabbing the fame; he knew that he richly desired.

"But, by God, this discovery will rock the fifty year old Geographical

Society to its pompous core. My bust with its marble plinth will dominate its marbled halls. I will laugh at their gold medal. They will have to come up with a higher accolade. The rest of its venerable peers will be nothing compared to me."

This magnificent quest and its final outcome was the only reason it was worth putting up with this pathetic excuse of a bureaucrat. The inept Quartermaster was the only person who he was able to persuade that could finance and equip such a venture at such short notice. Clyde had no doubts that this was the ultimate challenge and all others would pale in comparison. He then looked at the third member of their party, another who held the Queen's commission, but in another regiment, the Royal Fusiliers. The thirty-year old Captain Horatio Wesley was a small man, he stood at five foot six tall, but he was a true member of the upper class; if there ever was one. He was undoubtedly a professional soldier and an expert marksman even though he still wore a large Calvary sword at his side, which he explained by.

"A rather good tool in close quarters for chopping up any opposition, as they say old bean."

His reason for joining the expedition was.

"A rather unfortunate incident old chap. Some fellow made a rash statement, old boy. Had to sort out his impertinence. As they say."

Clyde wondered.

"Who the Hell are they?"

The explorer had heard the rumour about a duel that ended in murder, which was doing the rounds around the city of Cairo just when the Captain volunteered himself. It had been about some woman's honour and her husband had died in the pistol fight. Duelling was forbidden among her Majesties subjects, particularly in her armed forces and especially with one that ended with a death. The punishment would be severe indeed, no matter who the participants were. Clyde despised the upper class snot as his own background was suspect. His father, a hardworking, but poor Scottish Presbyterian had married into a middle class English Roman Catholic family, but he did not disclose his Anglo-Scot lineage to the other two. There was another white man in their party, but he was Wesley's Batman and to Clyde, the manservant counted as little as the natives. His name was Hughes (Nobody had asked or cared what his first name was.) and he did all of Wesley's mundane chores. Every night the Welsh man erected his master's tent, served him meals and even cleaned the officer's boots. One evening when Clyde noticed Wesley was sitting and the manservant was shaving him. As he then proceeded to trim the Captain's moustache, the upper class twit had said to him.

"We have to keep a modicum of civilisation out here old chap."

Been one of the only four armed men, his pistol was out on his lap and guns lay within instant reach. Clyde wanted to bring along a few armed native levies with them, but Wesley had argued.

"Not a good idea to have blackies with guns along with us, old fellow. There would be nothing to stop us from getting chopped, if they decided to run off, as they say. And in my experience, they usually do old boy."

Pamerstown agreed with the Captain, so the explorer did not pursue the matter. Clyde glanced up at the hazy, but vengeful sunlight and it appeared to press closer, trying with all of its might to crush the party into the sand.

"No bloody wonder they call the open desert, the Sun's anvil. I feel like a piece of metal been pounded between the Sun and the sand."

He took scant comfort that Pamerstown was suffering more than him and became annoyed that the popinjay Wesley seemed totally unaffected.

"But then, by God, I much prefer travelling during the heat than resting during the cool of the evening and listening to that pompous bore. Especially, when we made camp for the night with him under that ghastly parasol and his collapsible small chair that he says is the requirement of every civilised officer."

Watching him one night, Pamerstown had told Clyde.

"I am certain that all of this unnecessary baggage is to emphasise that he is true upper class and both of us were just peasants."

After Hughes erected his civilised quarters every evening no matter the conditions, the officer insisted on boring them with his new-fangled phonograph. It was a recently contrived expensive invention that Clyde could live without and to make it more annoying, Pamerstown enjoyed it. Still, he had the comfort of a pipe and a large pouch of tobacco. The Quartermaster shared his affinity with the weed and both of them took a slender lightening brand from the campfire and puffed away contently. On the other hand Wesley preferred cigarettes. He took these out from an ornate silver case, tapped them against its face and then proceeded to smoke. In these times of freedom from his master's service; Hughes, a tea-totalling non-smoker used to take out his well-worn black leather Bible and read passages silently from it. The God fearing man always paused at the first inside page and read the inscription. It stated in handwritten script.

To our loving son Paul. May this book of the Lord keep you in good stead in the lands of the heathens. Let it be a reminder of those who love you and pray for your safe return every day.

Your loving parents Mary and Tom. Cardiff, June 1870 AD.

True to Wesley's prediction, most of the native bearers scattered one evening after encountering a caravan of fierce desert riders earlier in the day who were engaged in the thousand-year-old practice of the salt trade. A cavalcade of contrasting wonderment, they appeared first as shimmering blurs out of the fuzziness of the desert dawn as their meandering path vectored towards them in the vast emptiness. The Nomads had changed direction after spotting them and headed towards the smaller group.

Gradually as they neared, the hazy and indistinct shapes of man and beast detached themselves from the desert heat. Clothed in white flowing robes, whose colour was now drab from the blowing barren sands. The Nomads were in stark contrast to their highly colourful camels that they rode. Their saddles were just brightly coloured blankets with two layers of tassels hanging at the edges. Equally colourful baggage packs were tied securely on the backs of the beasts of burden. A headband of even brighter coloured tassels adorned the head of each camel. Their chief overseer who always wore his deep red Fez was a devout Muslim. The nervous fellow cast a prayer to Allah as he saw these ferocious fighters near. He too was beginning to think this journey had been a dreadful mistake and the sight of the wild desert tribesmen convinced him even more so.

"These crazy Europeans. They are not as normal men. White men see an impossible journey over rugged and isolated terrain and ask how much water and supplies would it take to reach such a place. Even when local people knew it was madness, they set off anyway and either succeeded or perished in the attempt. Allah please protect me. I am only doing this for my family. For we desperately need the money."

He blessed himself in the Muslim way, hoping these desert wanderers were faithful servants of Allah and saw his devout gesture.

"The white men can fend for themselves if the Nomads attack."

From the mounted camels, the Tuareg assessed the travellers, for these fearsome riders of the desert sands were known to dabble in the slave trade, if the opportunity presented itself. Noting the steely eyed looks directed at them from the white men and more importantly the highly prized modern weapons held casually in their grips, the Tuareg approached with their hands held away from their bodies, to signal they were not a threat. They had instantly realised that the four white men had equipped themselves with a batch of very modern rifles. A breech loading, bolt action magazine weapon. The Tuareg leader told his fellow tribesmen.

"We are more than matched, out here in the open, so no threatening gestures. Our old-fashioned smooth bore muzzle loading ornate muskets are no match for those modern rifles. We will converse with the armed men; let them pass and double back later. Then we will ambush them for those modern guns which are priceless out here. Even one of those weapons will buy many camels or make a proper dowry for our female children.

On seeing the approaching Nomads, Clyde had ordered Wesley, Hughes and Pamerstown to dismount while he went through the pretence of checking a split in his shoe. The Tuareg saw at once that this was no easy prey. The desert warriors took note that the white men had put their camels between them with their rifles causally slung over their saddlebags and pointed in their direction. On receiving instructions from Clyde, the head bearer bravely went over to the Nomads, well aware that the Sahib's had him covered. Knowing a little of their tongue, he asked them after the Muslim greeting.

"Do you know of mountains to the Southwest that spring from the desert floor? At their base, there are two large statues probably ruined now."

The desert natives looked to where he pointed; the camel riders became very agitated and argued in another unknown tongue. Ignoring the startled overseer, the Tuareg called out to Allah to protect them, then slapped their mounts and moved off in haste to resume their once yearly journey. The chief overseer who was left spluttering in a cloud of dust returned to the white men and said while dusting himself down.

"I am indeed perplexed Sidi. The desert men were mighty fearful of the place we are going to. And these riders are great warriors. They do not frighten easily."

"Stupid native superstition." Replied Clyde with a snort of disdain.

That night, some of their bearers who understood a little of what had spooked the camel riders, deserted. The fleeing bearers scattered with the vast majority of the expedition's supplies and had even taken a very distressed Hughes beloved Bible. However, there was one bright outlook on the Horizon; the renegades had smashed Wesley's phonograph into tiny pieces. Only Clyde's and the officer's light sleeping, a product of their combined years of travelling in hostile lands had saved them from having their throats cut. At least Wesley was happy; he had managed to bag a couple of the "Blighters." with his trusty rifle as the bearers had fled into the night. They found their bodies with neat bullet holes, the next morning. Hughes searched the dead for his treasured bible, but none of the corpses had it.

"Dam those wogs." Said a distraught Pamerstown as he realised that some of the comforts he also enjoyed had vanished with the cowards. The only thing that Clyde missed was his binoculars. Ten of the natives had stayed loyal including the head bearer as these fellows probably reckoned their chances of surviving lay with the white men. Only two days after the desertion, the mother of all sandstorms blew up. It began with instant dust devils as the wind velocity suddenly increased. The sandstorm kicked up blinding and stinging particles of sand and grit and the party lost sight of each other. The chief native believed that the only reason for the sudden maelstrom's existence was for it to exert all of the mustered might of nature's weather extremes that it had gathered during its long path from the sea and to rid from the exposed surface of the desert floor; these arrogant travellers. Strangers, who been from soft lands had not enough respect for the Empty quarters vastness. It wanted to show how insignificant their presence was and how easily, they could be removed. As the power of the wind chafing tempest increased in vigour, the white men donned heavy orange-glassed goggles, their natives had to make do with their

headscarves. But luck was with them, the desperate men managed to find a line of sand scoured rock that jutted up from the unprotected sandy floor and it saved them from certain death. Caught in the beginnings of the tempest, the travellers would have never seen the salt encrusted stone, only for it rose up from the sand like slashed skin exposing bare bone. With its shelter at their backs, the remainder of the expedition hunkered down behind the tough leather skin of the camels that were placed in front of them. This undoubtedly saved their own hides from the scouring sand and grit. A vindictive Pamerstown fervently hoped.

"Those run away natives have not been so fortunate."

The storm threw its tantrum at the sheltering creatures for two days and nights before it relented its attack on the party; leaving with a grudging respect for the huddled Humans. Stiff and sore from the days of sitting uncomfortably, they rose and stretched inactive muscles. A slight breeze, the remnants of the sandstorm still carried in the air, but it was light enough to proceed on. The white men mounted the camels and moved on with the few trudging native bearers following in their wake. The next day, the explorers realised that the dust driven storm had been a boon, for it revealed a sight that they would have surely missed. As the fine sand in the air gradually dissipated, they discovered two dried up riverbeds that had their origin in an obscure line of distant hills. Clyde was ecstatic, for it corresponded with his map, for the two parallel lines of distortion that scraped the desert surface were the colour of sepia. Precisely the same effect on the original mural, he had thought that this was just a fanciful addition, but it was a precise representation.

"The omens look good" The delighted scroll owner muttered to himself.

Something did not feel right about the look of the soil and scree that lay within the parameters that marked the occasional river. Clyde ordered his camel to lower him to the ground and after dismounting; he hurried to the deep red blemish on the desert surface. In the shadow of the scant depression that would once again be a riverbank when the sparse seasonal rains came, if they ever came, he knelt down and scooped up a handful of ruby dirt. Incredibly, at a hand's depth, it was saturated with water. Pamerstown remembering the last time he had questioned Clyde's eccentric behaviour and the tongue lashing that followed, still could not help himself as he stated the obvious.

"The soil is ringing wet. How is that?"

"Is it a water hole old man?" Asked Wesley.

"No. The whole dried up river bed has water flowing under the top strata." Replied an amazed Clyde.

"But that's impossible." Challenged Pamerstown.

"Impossible or not, old boy. It is a fact," Agreed Welesy as he had also dismounted and cupped a handful of the gritty soil. Clyde went back to his

camel and rooted through one of the leather bags lashed to the animals yellow hide. He took out a large brass telescope and traced the furrowed etch of the baffling enigma to distant outcrops. He rubbed his eyes in disbelief as he imparted what he had seen.

"There are moving black wisps of dense smoky mist hovering about their summits. It can only be falling rain."

"Out here, old man? I don't think so." A sceptical Wesley enquired.

"Where do you think the flowing water comes from then?"

The officer had no answer and shrugged his shoulders. A smug Clyde fiddled with the instruments knobs gaining closer scrutiny. He suddenly realised with glee.

"Not clouds, but enormous flocks of birds."

This was just as promising and he passed on his experience to the others.

"Such a vast amount of flying creatures circling means only one thing. Surface water in large quantities; a boon for Human travellers and wildlife alike."

Euphoria gripped Clyde; laughing with abandon, he embraced a startled Pamerstown. Caught up in the explorer's bout of merriment, the bulky man threw his kepi that he had purchased off a foreign legionnaire into the desert sky. Pointing towards the distant hills, the cause of this excitement shouted to anything that would hear his boasts in this empty land.

"By her Majesty's corsets. I have done it. Do you hear me? I have done it. This is for your smug arses in faraway London. What have you stuck up twits have to say now?"

Pamerstown was miffed at his insulting reference to Queen Victoria.

"We are still subjects of her Majesty, no matter where we find ourselves. And after all, she might rule this God forsaken place one-day."

The man that he rebuked smiled broadly and unapologetically replied.

"After this, she will. I guarantee you."

Wesley also caught up in the infectious humour, laughed alongside him and asked.

"What the deuce is the matter, my good fellow. Why the jolly waltz?"

Clyde handed the telescope to officer and told him.

"Look up there and tell me what you see?"

The flocks of birds had settled and the professional solider had missed them.

"Nothing, old boy."

The explorer ran back to his camel and jumped on to the sitting beast. The animal snorted at this sudden unexpected liberty and spat a glob of mucus at him. But the spit never reached the man. Indignantly the ship of the desert was forced under protest to rise with its burden. When the camel stood erect on its broad padded feet, its passenger still in good humour produced a riding crop and slapped its hind quarters. The beast gave an

176

angry snort, but done it's master's bidding and cantered away over the burning sand. The others had remounted as well and soon all were cantering towards the mysterious hills. Wesley caught up in the moment shouted.

"Tally ho! Toodle pip what?"

Half way across the sandy plain and as the hills loomed larger, the camels sniffing the air, broke from their cantor into a heady run. Again Clyde roared with glee as he and the others grasped the pommels of the camel's saddles and clutched the reins tightly, so they would not fall from the speeding beast's backs. The native bearers had little choice but to run after the mounted men and the chasing men were soon left far behind. They began hollering in protest at the perceived abandonment. Oblivious and uncaring, the leader of the expedition challenged his white counterparts.

"Can you feel it? Don't you sense it?"

"Sense what? Old chap." Shouted a trailing Wesley.

"Water. By God. Lots of it."

The mad gallop ground to a halt as the panting Humans and animals stared at a sight that defied nature. A mist licking at the hill's base made it appear that the entire edifice in front of them floated on air. But as the four mounted adventures cautiously neared the incredible sight, the mist began to dissipate and the illusion vanished. They searched along the cliff base for a way up to the top. A bright gleam in the cliffs shadow revealed two enormous golden, statues of winged figures, both stood vigil with folded wings over a narrow crevice that led upwards. Wesley dismounted in a fluid movement and went over to the right hand statue which like its twin was twelve feet tall. He produced a bayonet and scraped it along the figure's torso.

"By Jove, it is real gold all right."

Then something strange happened, the wings of the idol flipped over to reveal their unseen backs. The former officer whistled as the once bland wings were now encrusted in diamonds, sapphires and emeralds and other precious gems that the astonished men had no name for. Even the stolid Wesley was startled for once.

"By Jove. These stones make the crown jewels look like cheap trinkets you would give to a native whore, old chaps."

He for one had believed that Clyde's yarn had been a ripping tale and had only went along until the furore of the murdered officer died down.

"We are rich, we are rich." Shouted an ecstatic Pamerstown while slapping Hughes on the back, now believing that the horrible journey had been worth it. All his misgivings vanished in a cloud of greed. But then, pragmatism cut soberly into his euphoria.

"We should just take these statues and cut and run. We can chop them up and live like Kings with these. There is no need to take any more risks."

"Pamerstown, you boring Bureaucrat. Have you lost your mind? Think man, this is only the entrance. Imagine what treasures lie up there. There are mountains of that stuff there for the taking." Challenged Clyde, his face flushed in anger and another expression that could only be described as,

"You will not deny me."

Their humped beasts shattered the impasse as they began to bay frantically in eager anticipation of forthcoming water. The noise of the camels was deafening. Wesley urged the panting natives, who had caught up with them, to silence the anxious animals. He admonished while pointing up to the hills summit.

"Somebody up there might hear them."

The Anglo-Scot laughed with genuine humour.

"If their bones are capable of that feat, then by God we shall really see wonders. Whoever lived up there last saw breath hundreds of years ago."

For Clyde, the reader of the journal in the Ethiopian monastery explained as he waved his map around.

"This is why. The author of this parchment destroyed those that once dwelt there."

"Why did he do that?" Asked a nervous Pamerstown.

"Who knows?"

He had lied and then he added.

"Believe me; no men live up there now."

The explorer's arrogant words would prove on hindsight to be very prophetic indeed. For their small group was been watched at this very moment by a creature that was not completely Human and it obeyed something that was not even slightly manlike. For the being that ruled here had diluted the make-up of man with another beast. From high above, the watcher with slight traces of feline genes observed the trespassers. The unfolding of the God's sanctified images had triggered an alarm. In a non-Human like sound, he growled.

"More of my brothers are on their way, but I do not need them."

This diminutive sentry was adorned in multi-hued armour with wings attached. He also had a large similarly shaped moustache and was a descendant of the Templar De Courcy among others. For unknown to the men below, they had invariantly discovered the hidden fortress of the Cabal of Knight's who served the Winged One and for them, that was certainly not good news at all. As the Knight watched, the travellers locked in his scrutiny began a heated debate. Clyde was the most vocal and adamant. He argued with a ferocious gleam in his eyes, daring anyone to contradict him.

"Dam it, if there was anybody up there. Then we would see the smoke from the fires that those people would use for their cooking and heating. Believe me, locating concealed smoke is a forte of mine and I have never *been wrong before."*

Wesley could have debated.

"If you are so sure of your abilities old boy, then how did you become penniless and forced to seek our help for this expedition?"

The cunning officer had also noticed the silence of their mounts.

"Our camels have suddenly become skittish and uneasy at something that the beasts can only smell. Hopefully, it is only a mountain cat or a pack of wild dogs that startled them. Better be wary old man."

Clyde lost on the verge of promised immortality failed to observe this. But then, neither of them knew anything of the Alien technology that provided for those above, there were no fires on the plateau. As if he felt foreboding on the wind channelling through the rock crevices, Wesley thought it prudent to give voice to his fears.

"All the same old chap. There's some not so jolly feeling in my water. A gut feeling tells me that we are been watched old boy."

Pamerstown tried to hush the veteran soldier, but it was too late. There was a slight pause from Clyde and then the customary outburst followed.

"Nonsense old boy. Who is the seasoned explorer here? If I tell you that nothing but the dead and their bones live up there? Then by Christ and his resurrection, you had better believe me, old boy."

The furious speaker had laid emphasis on the "Old boy." bit.

"You are right of course. It's just the jitters. As they say." Replied Wesley as he reached into a pocket and removed a small hip flask. The officer took a swig of brandy from the flagon, the warm infusion failed to rid him of a shiver the lay lodged along his spine. After a short broody silence, Clyde magnanimously accepted his apology. But all the same Wesley kept his rifle uncocked and close at hand, even if it was only for mountain lions. Just then, the greedy and cowardly Pamerstown said to the two seasoned men.

"I am staying here to guard these splendid treasures, I don't trust these natives. Those heathen would up and take off with them. The jewels I mean."

The normally silent and subservient Hughes broke protocol and spoke to his master in his deep Welsh baritone without been asked.

"If you don't mind sir, I'd like to remain down here too."

"A jolly good idea old boy." Decided Wesley.

Leaving the camels, Pamerstown, Hughes and all of the natives except the head bearer began to organise the lifting of the two priceless statues. Three men entered the portal between the cast divinities and began climbing up a steep hill that led into a valley that was surely carved by the devil himself. But the eager trio heard the promise of flowing water ahead. As the trepid explorers drew near to the source of cascading liquid, they were taken aback by the waters appearance.

It was blood red.

179

The nervous head bearer called silently on his deity again.

"Allah, be merciful?"

But the promise of fantastic riches drove him on. None of the three men were geologists, so they did not know that the cliff face on which the water flowed down had a high iron content that made it appear that blood was seeping from its insides. The wary group moved on unaware that they were still under those watchful eyes, which had now been joined by others of his Knighthood. Leaving the valley behind, the three men climbed higher and entered a hellish landscape of burning fire and boiling brimstone. There was the eye stinging smell of rotting eggs in the air. Clyde's brow furrowed as he said full of conviction.

"This is a ruse, a deception to discourage us. We will press on."

"Well it is a dammed pretty good one, my man" Stated Wesley.

Their nervous Arab bearer muttered another prayer to Allah, but greed was getting the better of him. They proceeded across the forbidding plateau and at its other side, the mirage shimmered and evaporated, they had passed some kind of barrier. The blinding white saline and sulphurous springs with their obnoxious smells instantly evaporated and the men were confronted with a white marble stairs that was surely a stairway to Heaven.

"See! What did I tell you?" Shouted an ecstatic Clyde.

The unworthy climbers reached the top in great enthusiastic strides and were greeted to a vision of Eden. An avenue of trees led up through a bountiful forest of fruit bearing crops. Trees and well maintained bushes were weighted down with the fruits of many varieties. Golden coloured apples were in close proximity to succulent oranges, peaches, grapefruit and lemons. All lay under the shadow of tall palms branches, bending with the amount of brown figs under their broad leaves. Wesley exclaimed.

"By Jove! Quite extraordinary old boy!"

Clyde was euphoric.

"Did I not promise you this?"

The perceptible Wesley noticed.

"These plantations are well tended and that means people. Strange for a place that was supposed to be deserted."

He released the strap on his holster and he was just about to call Clyde's attention to his reasoning.

Too late!

As the amazed trio of adventures gazed at this wonder of greenery, they were quickly overpowered and taken prisoner by a bunch of small men with large wing shaped moustaches. But one of them did not go quietly. There was the sharp sound of six cracks from a pistol. The professional soldier who was a master at close quarter fighting had pulled out his prized American revolver (Not standard British army issue.) and had got off those shots before it was knocked from his grasp. With his hand still stinging from the blow, Wesley drew his heavy blade from his white-leathered scarab and faced another dozen opponents. The dashing officer uttered.

"That was not nice old boy."

One of the strange men advanced and swiped at him. Wesley lost his normal calm demeanour and with a vicious roar, he blocked the man's blade and gutted him. That's when he was taken out with a heavy blow, but not before he had managed to despatch four of their attackers. When the British soldier came to, he was brought in front of a fantastic creature; the experienced fighter knew he was still alive as his head hurt like hell. He was also in a blue lit chamber.

"My word, old boy. That buffoon Clyde had been right. This is certainly the greatest discovery of all time, as they say."

For this was the place where Zebulan and De Courcy's surviving Templar's had fled to. They had found "Sanctum." where a new brotherhood had been formed. The new Knights of the Winged One had mixed they're old Religion with a different one. Each warrior of the new God wore a black cowl. The followers of the DEFILED had been bred shorter in stature, but it was their heads that singled them out. Large winged shaped moustaches adorned their faces while their altar boy shoulder length hair was uniformly black with a centre at the crown that was entirely blonde. This haloed effect was achieved during their initiation at a sacred ceremony that replaced baptism with water with two coloured dyes. The voice of the Knight's focus of adoration entered Wesley's very soul and offered him great rewards for his allegiance. As the professional soldier had slain a quartet of the Cabal's Knights, (No mean feat.), and more importantly the latest Preceptor; the Alien wanted this Hybrid's services. From the dawn of civilization Zebulan knew what these Human's ultimate desire was. The off-Worlder then offered the Hybrid a specific reward and of course, a practical Wesley settled on that one. The former British solider could not resist the tantalising glimpse that was offered to him. A Knight took his hand, this time there was no retaliation as he began to remove him from Zebulan's presence.

"Welcome brother." Simply said the strange looking man as he gently led him away.

Wesley asked his escort.

"What about the others that came with me?"

"The Winged God has no use for them. Their lives are already forfeit." Replied his new companion.

"That's a dammed shame old chap. He was a bit dull, but Hughes was a really efficient Batman. It is a bit of a dash bad convenience to lose him. Still that's life old man."

For once his "Old man." bit was in the correct theme, the Knight that stood before him was over three hundred years of age. Three hours before Wesley's meeting with the Winged God; Pamerstown, Hughes and the native bearers were captured while trying to pry the precious stones off the winged statues. They had been quickly surrounded by strange small men in glittering armour. In their greed, no rifles were at hand. The Quartermaster had an urge to run, but one of the bearers beat him to it and died from the attempt. An expertly thrown heavily ornamented blade of a repeating motif had ended his miserable life. That had finished what little resolve he had. Pamerstown was dragged babbling before Zebulan. Whimpering and shaking in terror, he was pleading for his life.

Then, he saw the Winged God.

The bureaucrat stood transfixed in mounting terror as the fluttering apparition moved towards him. The supremely confident Alien had still not perfected his defensive shield as any improvements would greatly curtail his movement. Fear and awe was still his favoured way of protecting his crystalline form. Pamerstown suddenly sneezed and the approaching false Deities nimbus was covered in a spray of mucus. Beneath his Hybrid guise, the Alien cringed. The prisoner toppled in a dead faint as he saw the monstrosity tower over him and he literally crapped in his pants. Zebulan had noticed the Hybrid's defective leg and cowardice, but most of all, the vented gases and solids that trailed down to the floor. The DEFILED spoke to the two guards in his mind-voice.

"He is no use to us. I will not have him sour our sacred gene pool. Take him away for the offering. And bring more incense."

Fierce looking Knights with much larger moustaches than him took the unfortunate and oblivious Pamerstown away. It was certainly a good thing that the unconscious man did not hear the bit about the sacrifice; he would more than likely have fainted again. Hughes and the bearers suffered the same fate; the latter's belief in Allah made them refuse to accept the Demon's promises. The last member of their expedition was in a bullish mood. Clyde had been aware the whole time during his march to meet whoever was in charge of the wonderful place. As he was escorted down a long narrow corridor built into a hillside, he noticed the lustrous enamels and inlays, again depicting Angels. The superb artistry and rich authentic details brought the artwork alive.

"It's like as if the artist had really seen these heavenly creatures."

Then Clyde was brought into the frozen chamber, his head already pounding from the accolades, he was going to receive and of course the newspaper headlines.

"What is the source of the petty Nile compared to this? I will make the front page of every broadsheet. I will be famous all over the Empire and the rest of the civilised World. I have found the lost city of Atlantis. It was never an island in a sea, but in a desert; Plato had been wrong or mistranslated."

To him, a really lifelike statue of a winged deity lay at the centre of the chamber.

"Such fine workmanship. What other wonders is there to discover in

this fantastic city? I must compose the greatest acceptance speech the Geographical Society has ever been privileged to hear."

The Anglo-Scot's man was oblivious to the danger he was in; the explorer was lost in delusions of grandeur and not a little madness. The statue moved slightly in a manner that could not have been mechanical.

"My God, it's alive!"

Clyde stared open mouthed at what his mind had just registered.

"By God, an Angel. I will amend that. This is the greatest discovery ever in man's history. And I am its finder."

Now the reader of the ancient parchment knew.

"That is why certain pages and words had been ripped out and covered up."

He could see his marble bust clearly now, it was gigantic. The bronze effigy of him could no longer be contained in the Geographical Societies hallowed halls. A new square in every city throughout the Empire would be named after him. Shiny polished bronze plaques would proclaim in each revered space.

RICHARD CLYDE. THE GREATEST EXPLORER IN THE WORLD.

THE FOUNDER OF AN ANGEL.

A MAN HONOURED IN HIS OWN TIME.

A voice intruded and entered his mind, offering him choices. At the edge of ever growing delusion, Clyde had no doubt what he wanted. High up on his imagined pedestal, the explorer demanded.

"You will travel back to London with me. I will show you to the civilised World. They will know that man is not alone."

Although, Zebulan could never mimic a Hybrid's open-mouthed gape, the Alien thought that he must have come close to it. The Winged God perceived the madness in the life-form before him.

"The one has no fear of me. He wants to use me as an object for his self-gratification. This is beyond belief."

In his thousands of years of meddling in Hybrids affairs and receiving their unrelenting devotion, the DEFILED had never been treated like this. Images of Naisi and Seantanta's grisly end flashed into his mind. His personal shield could still be penetrated by a sustained assault.

"This irrational Hybrid might even attack me."

Hurriedly, the false God told the two guards who had brought Clyde into his presence. In the inaudible mind-voice, he said.

"His mind is tainted. He is no use to me. Take him away."

Clyde knowing that his requests were been denied screamed as the two Knight's dragged him away.

"No, you cannot deny me, my destiny. You are mine, I tell you."

As the two strong servants of Zebulan brought the struggling Clyde to a courtyard, the man who had gone over the edge saw the dangling bodies of

Pamerstown, Hughes and all of their remaining natives. The Muslim bearers failed Zebulan's choice, as always, the followers of the Prophet would not renounce their God. The devout Christian Welshman found himself in a similar predicament. Each one of the swinging bodies had their throats cut and a tube of some transparent material was filling containers of the same stuff with their blood. Their red fluid was a libation from his followers to the Winged God. Zebulan's converts had twisted the words of the New Testament into.

"YOUR GOD SHALL DRINK OF THE BLOOD OF MAN."

Strength born from madness and denial enabled Clyde to break free from his captivity. Surprised by his abnormal strength, he clubbed the guards to the earth and fled in a daze of insanity through Sanctum. Incredibly, the great survivor managed to escape from the hidden city without been captured. A furious Zebulan deplored failure and the two guards who failed in their duty joined the swaying bodies. The doomed men had no regrets; their blood would feed their God whom they had failed.

TWO MONTHS LATER.

A cry of alarm came from the watchtower facing the desert; a bedraggled figure was approaching the fort. Sergeant Jacques Piers, a veteran of twenty years, who was in charge of the early morning watch, raised his telescopic eyeglass and the oncoming figure staggered into focus causing him to utter aloud.

"Sacra blue."

"What is it?" Asked the legionnaire alongside him.

"I am looking at one of those crazy Englishmen that passed through here over three months ago."

"Saint Denis." Exclaimed the other.

It was Clyde. Somehow, he had escaped and survived the desert crossing. Sunburnt, delirious and rambling, the explorer was deemed crazy by the fort's entire garrison. Luckily for him, a relief column had arrived with fresh men and supplies and they were taking the severely wounded back to the coast. As the westward travelling column skirted the British territory of Nigeria, the relieved French troops handed over the lunatic to a passing border patrol who was reluctant to take the madman.

LONDON, SIX MONTHS LATER.

A fully recovered Clyde marched up the processional steps and strutted through the book-laden hall of the Geographical Society. Today was to be the moment of his triumph. Looking splendid and distinguished in his top hat and tails, he went straight for the podium. In his arrogance, he never

184

met the curious and expectant stares of the gathered assembly. One of its venerable members introduced him.

"Esteemed and learned Gentlemen of the geographical society, I give you the explorer Richard Clyde."

There was a polite applause. Niffed at this unenthusiastic reception and the lack of respect, he thought,

"You will soon regret that when you hear my fantastic story, then you will be sorry. But I will forgive you when I receive my accolades."

Clyde gazed at his learned audience and began his tale. It started out normally enough, a typical tale into the darkness of unexplored Africa. When the winged creature and the lost city was mentioned, curious and amused looks soon turned to ridicule and scorn. Voices broke out in outrage and the chairman's heavy black gravel was thumped so hard on the beechwood table that it nearly broke. He tried to restore order.

"Gentlemen, gentlemen, please, please."

Silence was re-established as a prominent senior member of the society got the floor. The barrel chested man stood up and exclaimed.

"What foolish nonsense is this? Does Clyde think us some medieval monarchs to be impressed by fabulous tales of a non-existent World? Well Mister Clyde, you might not have noticed, but we are in a modern society at the pinnacle of scientific and engineering advancement and we do not believe in your far-fetched tales. There is a travelling circus in Soho, go to it and regale the ignorant masses with your tales of fantasy."

The speaker was accompanied by cries of.

"Here, here!"

From there on, the meeting became a farce, until Clyde's fanciful tale was flatly rejected and was eventually laughed from the building. Les that counted to him, he never taken seriously again. It broke him. The explorer ended his days in a mental asylum for the insane in the London Borough of Whitechapel. The chief psychiatrist of the institution's filed report stated.

"The foundations of Clyde's sanity have collapsed and he lives in a World of illusion, it is more delusion and grandeur. His constant craving for fame could not exist alongside all of his failures, so he came up with this incredible tale that he actually believes to be true."

Clyde spent that icy winter in a cold cell and wished on numerous occasions for the dry African heat. One morning during the warmth of the following summer, the ridiculed explorer was found hanging outside his cell in strange circumstances, the wall of his prison had fallen away. He was dangling with a strange presumptuous smile emblazoned on his face. Unknown to his keepers, he did not die by his own hand. His demise was ordered by a servant of the Dark Angel; Wesley himself. The upper class twit had responded to his accusation.

"You sold out to the winged monstrosity. You have swayed from your loyalty to the crown."

The Winged One promised me eternal life old man and you know how much I like to enjoy myself."

His younger looking eyes glinted mischievously.

"And you're the price old boy for that delicious reward."

Zebulan had indeed offered him eternal life, but the Alien could not deliver it. That would have taken the combined craft of the ALASTHA'I and even then that would be suspect. But the false God had the resources to give his newest servant at least a thousand and five hundred years of life. The devious Alien needed someone of Wesley's competence as his two loyal followers, De Courcy and Salvador had perished during the early stages of this century and the DEFILED required somebody of Wesley's character to replace them. The God knew that his new convert might react badly when he realised that the promise of eternal life was false, but the long-lived being surmised.

"By then the Hybrid will probably perish on some mission that I send him on. After all, most of them do."

The Semitic David, the Frenchman De Courcy and the Spanish Priest Salvador had already died without knowing the full extent of their longevity. But still they had lived fantastic life spans in any case and all of his followers would confirm that to his latest recruit. Giving Wesley the same promise was a calculated risk that the Alien could take. The former British subject had been commanded to track Clyde down in case anyone would credit his unbelievable story. After all, the Winged God had told him during one of his audiences.

"Humans are a curious lot and someone might believe him."

But the Deity need not have worried; Clyde had been put in a straightjacket, after a violent incident that evening during supper for the inmates. He had nearly killed one of them who had ridiculed him and he was now completely helpless. A sudden silent explosion had removed the back wall of his five-story cell. His attackers had used small hovering devices to reach the place of Clyde's incarceration. All of them had night vision refracting crystals which were extremely helpful and overcame the problem of Victorian London's dim gaslight and constant smog from soot filled chimneys. This technology was proof to the former British soldier of the Winged Ones offer of eternal life. The certified lunatic looked at Wesley and his strange appearance and rightly assumed in a moment of lucidly.

"So you have been tempted by the Devil and his false promises. I knew that you would return. There is no chance that you would verify my story before you do what you have to do."

Wesley shook his head in the negative and with an exaggerated yawn cupped by his raised hand, he said.

"Sorry old chap; that would be a tad difficult. I cannot accommodate you there."

"I thought as much."

"Chin up now, like a good fellow."

The new Knight turned towards the six of his brotherhood that accompanied him on the God's request and commanded them.

"Carry on there, like good fellows. Make it quick. Even thought he was a prat, don't make him suffer."

While some of Zebulan's servants held him in a secure grip, one of them tied a rope around the unresisting Clyde's neck. The two that had immobilised him picked up the now silent man and threw him over the broken wall of the cell. The other end of the rope was secured around the inmate's bed on which the other three Knights sat upon. The iron frame shifted a little as the former explorer sailed over the precipice. Richard Clyde was a man who always assumed that he was right. As the doomed man flew towards his fate, he had a final conviction, just before his neck snapped.

"I have now had proven those quacks wrong, because if I had been insane, then how did seven of the Angels minions track me down and murder me in my secure cell. Let them chew on that one."

Darkness engulfed him as he passed into oblivion; His last heard sounds were of Wesley's irritating drawl as his once companion lamented.

"Sorry about this old bean. Nothing personnel mind you."

Then the new servant of Zebulan laughed out aloud and in between bouts of mirth, he told the doomed man just after his neck broke.

"Strange the way faith works old boy. I dreamt of doing this to you when we were travelling through the desert. You were a pompous bore. And as they say, it worked out pretty well in the end. Toodle pip what."

The next morning, as the lingering smog thinned with the arrival of an easterly wind, the clear day revealed Clyde's dangling body to passers-by. Instead of the usual bulging features of a hanged man; there was a self-satisfied smirk on the dead man's face. His sneer would have been wider, if he had learned that the next morning, the asylum's doctors had planned a lobotomy for him and it could be argued that Wesley had done him a great favour indeed. The Asylum's authorities had no conceivable explanation for the night's events and it was quickly hushed up. For if anybody in their staff discussed the mysterious occurrences, then they would end up incarcerated as one of their own inmates. Due to the peculiar circumstances of his death, Clyde's name was removed from the sanatorium's register and he was buried in an unmarked grave in its pauper's grounds. Such an unambiguous ending for one whom dreamed of greatness. There was no fine statues of bronze or engraved plaques for him, not even a paupers cross and his name passed out of history. It was if he had never existed at all, only his birth certificate in an unfashionable Presbyterian Church in Glasgow testified that Richard Clyde had ever walked the Earth at all. Wesley returned to the desert city and he was now the enamoured of his

God and fellow Knights. A lavish ceremony was held in his honour and the Winged God presided. So it came to pass that at least one member of Clyde's entourage received the honour and accolades that one of them had craved all of his life, but it came from a totally unexpected source. The reward had nothing to do with the cravings of the dead explorer, it had not been one of wealth or respect, but something more important than those triflings. He had received the gift of immortality and the trust of a God.

IX.

The Alien observer back in the frosty past addressed a particular swirling globe that had instantly materialised in front of his oblong head and proceeded to give his assessment of the time period that he was now monitoring. His mind-words which would be etched into its multi-hued fabric were for ALASTHA'I posterity.

"Concerning the Hybrids. This is not the sparsely populated sphere that my brothers have left behind. Our genetically engineered creations are now dominating every species of the Planet and have settled on every landmass, no matter how extreme the conditions for its survival are. These self-centred bipeds have taken unjustified liberties with nature and have reshaped entire ecosystems that now suffer under pressure from their massive population explosion. Whole species of flora and fauna have been eradicated for their selfish requirements in desiring a World suited to their short-perceptive nature. The industries of the Hybrids and the cycle of the yellow Star have caused the saline Oceans to rise from forty per cent of the Globes surface during our initial time on the Planet to sixty-five per cent in this time in their history.

Thus altering the character of this World forever.

The Hybrids have formed into complex societies, the vast majority into urban concentrations and they now number in the tens of billions. That part of our scheme is still on the correct flight-path. Our creations are sub-divided into numerous political, economic and ideological Power-Blocks that consist of Hybrids of many varying sizes, colours and races. The once relentless path of globalization has irreversibly broken down and Nations have turned inwards and are mostly ignoring what was happening outside their borders. This part of our scheme is failing. As a consequence, levels of advancement across the Globe are not on an equal wing-span. The gap between the affluent States is increasing exponentially. Although, it is the latter days in the twenty-ninth century in their measure of time, some States remain at a twentieth century level and many are even unable to achieve even that. Isolated from each other, their main staple for advancement, ideas and resources are not been shared and this is the reason for the inconsistency. I will keep recording and pray to the Great Mathematician that events will improve."

THE SARAJEVO CONTRIB, THE ANSCHLUSS 2951 AD.

On the Continental mass where the relieved ALASTHA'I in their silver ships had departed from thousands of years before, new forces were now in the ascendancy. To some specific individuals who were concerned by such broadcasts, it was doubtful that the state controlled media's weather announcement of the upcoming but uncommon event of a storm would

189

commence on time. The looming day was promising to turn out fine and clear as it could be in this immense metropolis. The ever present stratus of low hugging milky white cloud brightened slightly as shadows of blustery twilight diffused into the soft light of day. It was another short-lived victory for the brightness over the darkness of the previous night. A constant discord that had been waged in the Heavens ever since the Planet first coalesced into an irregular sphere; orbited around the Sun and began spinning on its own tilted axis. A five billion-year-old battle, that would be forgotten forever when the expanding yellow Star consumed this unfortunate World to oblivion. The fleeting conflict passed over every area of longitude and latitude that fell in and out from the Sun's life giving rays. On the geographical point directly below where the dark melted into light and underneath the patchy and formless cloud, there lay a colossal urbanised metropolis. This city-state stretched unbroken across five time zones of the Planet. However, this geographical fact was denied to the majority of its citizens who existed in one single time frame. Those who had created this vast power block named it.

"The Anschluss."

It was a word derived from one of the old and eradicated languages of the Continent. The present leader of this ruling shadowy political identity was a critic of the first man to have used that designation. He often belittled the failings of that short-sighted Dictator.

"He failed miserably, we will not."

For all of his importance, the Watcher ignored this man. His Vigil Globes had been drawn towards another soul who would from first appraisals seem to be less significant. In a seemingly deserted street between two parallel lines of tall narrow derelict buildings in a sector in the centre of this city-state that was soon to be demolished; a rubbish strewn pavement moved of its own accord. The shifting dirt began to form into the indentation of two Hybrids; making it seem as if they had appeared from nowhere. These two males of the interfered with species crawled along the built up area, hugging the shadows and dark recesses. Each of them blended with the insignificance while inching their way towards a secluded doorway of a dilapidated building. Their actions were well calculated and orchestrated. Once, they were under the shadow of the facade, both men, one slightly taller than the other crouched and huddled together in the shadow of the abandoned structure. In this covert position, the two figures once again blended back into nothingness, becoming one with the urban landscape. They were not as still and unmoving as the dead concrete, for every so often one of them glanced up ominously at the darkening sky praying for the promised weather. Paradoxically, the two would have preferred a hot summer's day, as the water vapour discharged from billions of solar powered units created a pea soup of a fog that obscured visibility to within a few feet.

"Still a storm would do." Wished one of them.

A sudden or prolonged squall would have another benefit as the two were aware that the government of their Anschluss enemies had a secret and highly covert force called "PREVENTIVES." who were unknown to the vast majority of the population. These two camouflaged subversives were absolutely certain that members of this punitive agency were trying to pinpoint them right now. All within their organisation called them, "The Filth."; a name that their leader had instigated. The State had its everyday police force with their black, blue bulky uniforms and conical helmets with a sharp vertical point that protruded from their crowns; reminiscent of the ancient Prussian armies that once existed on this Continent. These protrusions were no fancy adornment; they were loaded with high tech devices of a thirtieth century organisation. These visible and regular law enforcers known as "Conicals." carried out the normal duties of any law enforcement agencies, but the sinister PREVENTIVES belonged solely to the person that watched them now from the murky skies above. Those been observed were also aware of these unmanned drones and foolishly believed themselves protected from any aerial scrutiny. This clandestine figure who had access to the silent hovering aircraft had unknown to these two, already located them. Several soundless two metre flat disc shaped drones that were called by those in the know as "Wraiths." and that was a tiny percent of the population were already in the vicinity. These zealously discounted flying machines were loaded with surveillance devices and lethal armament and their most disturbing quality was what was called the "Perceptive effect.". This in essence was a silent vibration that was focused on the awareness and co-ordination of its targets. The unsettling probes made their prey feel edgy, scared and unsure of themselves. The level of striking paranoia they metered out dependent on the desires of the inflictor. But at the moment, the watching machines had been commanded to observe and not to interfere with those under their inspecting actions. One of the men below continued his train of thought.

"High winds would hamper any passing aircraft's efforts and make this a lot easier."

He did not realise that it would have little effect on the hovering spies and their ability to follow them. These surveillance craft had no problem penetrating the permanent gloom that hovered over the urban areas. Somebody must have answered the silent speaker's pleas as he felt the first few drops of the vanguard of the approaching weather system. These droplets were much colder and larger than localised precipitations. Denser squall clouds gradually filled up the sky and blocked the watery Sun from transmitting its revealing light to these back streets. The growing darkness shifted among them, embracing the two into its bosom as its own. They became concealed along with all of the street's ground level. In this abandoned sector, no artificial street light's switched on in response to the near darkness; leaving a murky World where those up to no good lurked. It was doubtful that anyone running this vast metropolis should care about the unfolding events in this sad excuse of a district, but the eyes in the sky were still eagerly watching the upcoming drama. The chief observer was the ultimate pariah of these two. This, the most powerful of individuals would not interfere with their mission; he had reasons of his own.

"Come, deeper into my web. The strands are tightening and there will only be one outcome, mine."

Safe and in opulent comfort, hundreds of kilometres away, this tall shadow of a man sniggered, secure with the knowledge that the two been viewed and recorded unwittingly done his bidding. Oblivious that their covert movements and precautions were to no avail, the two men now satisfied that they would remain unobserved picked themselves off the debris-strewn doorway, leaving any newly gained spattering of dirt and filth attached to their clothing. This street scum would supplement the growing camouflage which the two secretive men coveted. The armed duo had been waiting for over twenty-four hours and both were still highly alert due to the cocktail of hypersensitive drugs that they had taken. The artificial substances fooled the central nervous system and suppressed the need to sleep, eat and the necessity of toilet functions. Designed by the group's leader, these pills also negated the mental effects of the flying Wraiths. However, they were unaware that this protective effect was not needed. They moved off in a prearranged direction to complete their covert mission, circumstances which the unseen puppet master allowed. Both of them belonged to an outlawed terrorist organisation whose goals were to replace the atheist system of government with their own desired structure and ideology. These non-conformists who harboured a vision of an ideal state were the discontented within the Anschluss and that made them public enemy number one. Members of their post-scribed group were known to those citizens that feared or secretly admired them, as "RE-INSTATOR'S.", the name their leader had chosen. This illegal societies stated reason for existence or its straight to the point manifesto of "Four Points." was.

1. The removal of the established regime.

2. The reduction of the unsustainable population.

3. Dismantling of the huge urban areas and a return to smaller independent communities.

4. The right to worship a Deity and the establishment of a clergy.

The last demand, the key element of their charter was a belief which had been eradicated from the general population over the centuries and only groups of fanatics still believed in the existence of a God. The RE-INSTATOR'S were such a force and like all extremists, they were supremely confident in their own righteousness. They were quite capable of blindly enforcing any orders given by their superior. Its members would

192

strike suddenly and ruthlessly and melt back into the anonymity of the huge City-State. Kidnapping and assassination was this group's trademark. Bombings, even executions had been carried out by these two for their beloved movement. One of the slogans of their pro-scribed society stated.

"The disease of the Anschluss is so repulsive and rotten to its core that any means justifies its destruction."

The general populace feared these murders and assassins, but the masses would be certainly amazed at how little they troubled the higher echelon of the Anschluss. Oh, those at the top of the pyramidal structure had a vested interest in them, but they had little fear of this tiny opposition. The organisation was as irritating as a fleabite was to an elephant. As one of the ruling elite always quoted when necessary.

"There is no way we would cede part of our Anschluss never mind giving it an entire overhaul. Four points my arse."

The Anschluss state began life as the European Union over nine hundred years ago with the goal of transforming the World of man and ushering in a new era of tolerance, prosperity and enlightenment. It was an ideal that was in total contrast to the growing instability that existed all over the Planet at that time. Despite their historical differences, many Nations on the European mainland came together to rid themselves of a destructive past and set an example to the rest of mankind. If these warring nations who were responsible for two major World conflicts could do it, then, so could the rest. Like some Frankensteinian monster, it now bore no resemblance to the vision of its original creators. Encompassing an area of millions of square kilometres, it stretched from the sea wall, west of the Aran Islands (Zebulan's former base.), to the great land wall in the East that straddled the Black Sea. Its boundaries went south from the warm Mediterranean Sea and North to the windswept Finnish Arctic circle. Huge walls had replaced the natural embankments of sheer cliffs; wind shaped dunes and sandy beaches that normally formed at the seas edge. In a great public works programme that lasted over seven hundred years, most of the mountains of the Continent were levelled in the largest construction project the World had ever seen. There were a couple of exceptions to the removal of the heights, notably the southern volcanoes around Naples and Sicily and the mountain ranges of the sparsely populated northern zone. In the south Vesuvius and Etna were harnessed for electrical power. In other places, natural valleys were covered over with huge concrete and steel platforms and the manmade caverns became hidden power stations. Infrastructure was built on these vast floating rafts, concealing what lay below. Almost every height and depression within the urban sectors had been filled in to create a manageable landscape. The once imposing Alps had been decapitated in what was considered as one of the greatest environmental acts of vandalism of all time. Massive explosions and an army of huge earth moving machines ate greedily into the chiselled heights and loaded any unusable spoil into endless lines of rail transport. The tracks made their way to the coast and from there it was loaded into gigantic barges and taken to the site of the new sea wall. Every load of reclaimed spoil was guided to its final destination by global positioning satellites. These reusable substances; the fabric of the ancient Continent itself formed the base for the massive sea wall that eventually sat on top of it. The concrete for the barrier was made out of the limestone and granite of the former mountains. The once rugged coastline of bays, inlets and coves had been softened. These irregular projections carved by tides and currents had been redeveloped with the mountain rubble into bland linear forms that stood fifty metres above sea level. In some parts between this monotonous coastline and the sea wall, there lay a channel of only ten kilometres. The Anschluss isolationists had put the proverbial moat on the inside of their great wall. There were slight geographical inclines, unnoticed by the population that allowed most of its ancient rivers to flow but a new demographic of water courses flowing south from the artic regions had been instigated. Due to the disposal of the huge spoil heap of billions of tonnes of rubble, among other reasons, the islands of Sardinia and Corsica now lay in the centre of a reclaimed landmass that connected the former named nation of Spain to Italy. The geographical Italian boot was no more. In fact the whole of the Italian peninsula now lay in the middle of newly recovered land that stretched from Iberia to the Balkans. The former seas of the Aegean, the Adriatic and the Tyrrhenian Sea had been turned into a vast agricultural plain that produced all of the food staples for the huge population. Curiously the island of Sicily remained unaltered, it still lay surrounded by the sea, but the shifting delights of Venice had vanished, as it was now an inland region far from its constant flirting companion, the sea. Other islands remained as they were, such as Cyprus and Malta, simply because it was impracticable to build land bridges to them. Some smart arse among the ruling elite had named this new reclaimed land, the Atlantis sector.

"After all, have we not brought back the land under the sea?" Was her quip.

A female of this same individual's line had once wanted to remove names that signified where a person originated from, such as Van, Mac, O' De' etc. This was calculated to enforce the homogenising of the power block, but the protocol was largely ignored by the masses and proved impossible, even for the totalitarian government to enforce. With the demise of the heights, most of the smaller rivers and streams had vanished. Large inland reservoirs formed the source of most of the major rivers. But, the paths of these ancient waterways had straightened and deepened and their old names had been changed. Rivers like the mighty Rhine now became known as Water Course one, etc. In this period of one-sided enlightenment, all types of roads were ripped up and added to the accumulating reclaimed areas. From now on, there would be no freedom of private transport. Controlled Rail transport was going to be the new arteries of movement around the Anschluss. From the diminishing ice fields in the north to the Mediterranean seawall in the south, this was the enormous landmass overseen by the Anschluss. Most of the population lay crowed together in a vast urbanised sector of swollen cities that straddled the centre of the Continent like an orange rash made from many blemishes. From east to west, this immense metropolis was divided into local Conturbations that echoed most of the ancient capitals that thrived throughout the European landmass for the past three thousand years. Differences of culture that had made each former nation ideologically distinct had been eradicated in an effort to form one homogeneous mass.

It was now, a tamed Continent.

All the old city names had the prefix "Contrib" added to them. So the ancient name of London became "The London Contrib." As in any period of the Continent's history, each Contrib had its own regional accent of the common language. At the heart of the Continent lay the "The Geneva Contrib.". It was situated on top of a kilometre high plateau that had been artificially formed when the Alps had been quartered in height and where necessary filled in to achieve the desired level. This thousand square kilometre citadel looked down on the rest of the city-state in a remembrance of medieval hill towns. It had been a massive undertaking had taken three hundred years of constant excavation. This plateau based Contrib was the political heart of the Anschluss. It was the only real elevation left in the middle of the Continent and anyone doing business there could only reach the top by the large magnetic driven lifts that straddled its sheer sides. These access conduits were known as Vert-levs and their use was confined to the privileged elite. All of the former alpine lakes now served as reservoirs and their once pristine wildness was reduced to massive ornamental ponds. Every Contrib in the Anschluss melted into one another to form one huge urban mass and if the departed ALASTHA'I had returned and circumvented the Northern Hemisphere at night-time when the murky cloud cover was less dense, the Aliens would now witness a myriad of lights not unlike a miniature version of the Milky Way galaxy. All of these Contribs were connected together in a vast hub of transport conduits. The network of electromagnetic linear rails polarised with alternating current spread out like veins across the Power Block. These ultra-speed rail links were the backbone and lifeblood of the Anschluss and the floating polarised engines and carriages sped across the Continent at high speed making the longest destination accessible in a matter of hours. This transport system was known officially as.

"The Mag-lev."

Mag-lev been an abbreviation for Magnetic Levitation. The ordinary citizen called these conduits.

"The Pipes."

These noiseless and sleek engines of this transport system flowed through glass cylindrical tubes of a diameter of twenty metres. These frames were supported on large steel stanchions spaced every two hundred metres apart. Along the glass frame, circular bands of polarised boosters assisted the Mag-Lev's velocity. These accelerators were spaced in conjunction with the steel supports. The speeding craft floated along on a cushion of air within the tubes. Hundreds of these Perspex like tunnels and bridges crossed its manmade inland seas in feats of brilliant engineering. Each Contrib had its own localised shuttle system that inter-connected with the Mag-lev. The local shuttle network was supplemented by a third level of transport; moving escalators otherwise informally called.

"The Stand Ons."

All major streets had their own moving platforms that allowed alighted citizens to reach almost any point in their Contrib to within walking distance. Most inhabitants of this vast enclosed Anschluss had never heard of private transport, but they had seen flying craft of a sort. The valid argument for the non-existent aircraft was put down to the blanket of water vapour that permeated over the City-State. To prove their point, the government set up demonstrations every few years that resulted in the destruction of the craft and its aircrew. Disappointed citizens watched their video screens in silent regret, hoping that the next time, someone would succeed. The two before mentioned methods of transport by flight and private vehicles did exist, but they were the sole secret of the ruling elite. This information was kept hidden from the majority of its citizens as a deliberate method of curtailing freedom. The biggest obstacle against the banning of private transport was ambulances, fire tenders and other emergency services. But this was solved at great cost by constructing a separate shuttle line that spread throughout every street in the Anschluss. This emergency duct allowed high-speed medical shuttles packed to the brim with specialised equipment and highly trained staff to access every building in minutes from area bases that were spaced in a radius of every twenty kilometres. The leaders of the paranoid state had flirted with APS technology (Anschluss Positioning Systems.) and tagged every citizen, but the system became overloaded with the continuous transmission from eight billion souls. Everyday systems suffered, so those in power relented and only those individuals connected with the states operating functions were tagged. The once burgeoning global internet connections were severed, they were not alone in pursuing these measures; most nations adhered to this policy. Virtual traffic now only flowed within the internal conduits of the isolated states. Southward from the central metropolis sector lay another vast area given over to the production of food crops and livestock to feed the Anschlusss billions.

This was the Agriculture sector.

These staples of Human requirements were grown in abundance. In huge greenhouses, some necessary tropical plant hybrids were nurtured, mainly coffee, tea and cocoa. Animal husbandry was confined to huge factory enterprises. Beyond these food production areas and nestled between them and the sea walls lay huge dock-lands that were off limits to most of the population. Strategic ports and hidden airbases around the Southern seawall were the only exits from the Power Block to the outside World. From here sea going vessels set off with the purpose of trade with other lands, for the Anschluss was not so isolationist, as its indifferent inhabitants believed. To the north of the urbanised concentrations that straddled the middle of the Continent lay the Industrial Sector which produced the manufactured goods the Anschluss deemed sufficient for the masses. Further north again of the Industrial Sector lay the huge green belt of the regenerating northern forests, the main supplier of wood to the hungry urban sectors. The sea wall encircled all of the Anschlusss coasts from the frozen wall in the north, right down the Atlantic sea (It lay a mere ten kilometres offshore.) where it joined with the Mediterranean sea wall and proceeded to cut that narrowed body of water in half. The Baltic Sea, the North Sea, the Irish Sea, the Bay of Biscay and all of the Atlantic trapped behind the wall became a vast reservoir that supplied desalinated water for industry. This adjusted inland sea was stocked with a huge variety of seafood. Genetic advances and seafood management had brought back near extinct levels of fish, edible crustaceans and other delights to an abundance never seen before. The numbers of cod, plaice, whiting and tuna were in such vast quantities that it was boasted that a person could walk across the Inland Sea on slimy forms without ever touching water. The earliest incarnation of the Anschluss had practised managing the scarce sea resources by making their own fishing trawlers stay at home for a certain period of the year. But other nations plundered the dying fish stocks on their migration routes, now this closed in sea was only for the Anschluss's use. Deliberate strain like openings in the wall allowed tidal movement, but not fish migration between the artificial sea and the deeper blue ocean. Huge wind/water wheels that dotted the entire length of the western sea wall were spread out every ten kilometres. Tidal and wind movement rotated these giant machines, which in turn were connected to enormous generators that harnessed the power of the ocean for this population of eight billion. But this was a deception; the real energy that ran the Anschluss was provided by secretive nuclear power stations which were located in every Contrib. Most of the citizens thought that their power came from their solar power units or volcanic heat extraction, but the pea soup of the constant mist made the former method of producing energy impractical. All the Atomic suppliers of electricity were hidden in disguised buildings under the hidden valleys. Another consequence of the life style within this power block was that individuals now aged better than their forebears of a thousand years ago. A person now in his forties looked the same as a person in his thirties did back then and life spans had also increased in tandem. If this constant and unchanging system sounded like paradise, then an observer could not be more mistaken.

For every citizen had a station in this society.

The most coveted status was of course the ruling elite, but the ordinary person had little comprehension of the quality of life of such a position. Next in line was to be a member of the Anschluss's security services, followed in descending order by the civil services who were charged with the everyday running of its gigantic bureaucracy that kept it functioning. Then came the industrial, agricultural and marine workers. Bottom of the heap came the majority of the populace, who were transitional labourers and spent most of their lives unemployed. These citizens were commonly known as "Plebs.". Thus the size, location and quality of your living quarters depended on your status at the time. The Anschluss had total control of the media and information, its citizens were only supposed to know what it wanted them to. An allowance given every month allowed the population to avail of foodstuffs, clothing and other essentials from government run department stores. Every person had a credit card and it was topped up each period with an amount that depended on your status. This system insured that poverty was a thing of the past and many such people in difficult situations around the World looked upon this land with envious eyes. Like every system of people management since the dawn of civilisation, it was not infallible and there were those who lived alongside it who did not operate within its rules, but after all the wall that stopped unwanted people from entering also kept those in who desired to leave. The Anschluss elite ruled with an iron hand, but they allowed the general population some freedoms to stop the pressure cooker of urban living from exploding. No citizen was actually allowed to own property, this belonged to the state, but it could be rented off it. The ruling elite had learnt the mistakes of total totalitarian regimes of the past. An individual was allowed to acquire wealth through inheritance; small businesses allowed a hidden middle class and mobile information monocles (M I M's.) allowed private communication. (But this was easily monitored by the secret services.) All of the composite and numerous coloured transmission devices were in the shape of a circle that was 10 cm thick, and its circumference depended on an individual's ear size. The disc was clasped to the full rim of the biological audio receptor for most of a person's daily routine; left or right appendage was a private choice. It could be taken off at will, though some people left it on permanently. When it was required for use, (A beeping noise indicated an incoming call.) its operator twisted the circle anticlockwise and this released a thin circular wafer, 5 mm thick. Another clockwise twist released a twin. Both of these optical monocles were then self-adhered in front of each eye. The audio disc remaining in the ear had a cursor and by manually activating this indicator; video and sound frequencies were reflected into the wearer's pupils and ears giving a two dimensional image. In a pretence of privacy, the concave lens could absorb silently mouthed words and communicate them on to who they were intended for. On moving the solid ear cursor by hand to displayed icons, selected functions would be exhibited in the lens. When finished, the monocles were twisted back into place and became a single earpiece again. Most of the Plebs called the M I M's.

"Frogs Eyes."

Mass television (This was censored from above); computerised video games and football matches between teams from the different Contribs were what many a citizen lived for. Competitiveness in any sport was encouraged and only second to the football contests was a challenge called "The Span.". This was a speed contest that entailed crossing the length of the Anschluss by foot. The endurance race was all about setting off from the coastline in the Lisbon Contrib and planning the quickest route through the Metropolitan sprawl to the wall at the Kiev Contrib. It was a test of speed, planning and staying power. The Span was first undertaken by a Lisbon Contrib Pleb named Vasco Figo in 2553AD and increased in popularity until every citizen of the Anschluss made it their life ambition. The present record of thirty days was held by a mysterious masked competitor, who was rumoured to be a member of the ruling government. Then there was the extreme version of the sport "Parkour." so named by its legendary founder Sebastian Foucan. This dare-devilling run was done along rooftops by leaping from building to building at high speed wearing boots fitted with high tensile steel. It was a banned sport as competitors often fell and killed innocent and unaware citizens below. Another extreme sport was named "Base." which consisted of leaping off of high rise buildings with rippling winged suits that trapped air and making a getaway before the authorities apprehended you. Practitioners of these outlawed sports were seen as role models and heroes among the strictly regimented populace. Though, it had its delinquents, many of the Anschluss's naive citizens believed that its criminal and justice system was just and fair. Petty criminals were sent to re-education centres and after serving their allotted time, these repentant individuals were released back into society away from their original Contribs. Taken away from the environment that had caused their infractions, they would become model citizens and not re-offend. It was accepted that murderers, rapists and sex offenders were removed from society and imprisoned for their natural life span. But this was far from the reality of the situation. If the petty criminals re-offended continuously, then these non-beneficial people were executed by lethal injections. The violent offenders were assessed and if they failed the criteria, they too were also terminated. Those killers that past the examination were drafted into the ranks of the PREVENTIVES. This was just one example of the Anschluss that had many layers of deception hidden in its unblemished front.

Back in the Sarajevo Contrib, the falling precipitation of this misty morning was uncannily similar to the one that Cetheren and Cathbad had seen at their final parting all those millennium ago. Maybe it was a descendant of the storm that now sprayed its moisture down on the inhabitants of this urban sector and on these two Humans, one of whom was a direct descendant of a line of Hybrid chosen by manipulative Aliens. The ALASTHA'I had more than a vested interest in this being and his lineage. This twenty-five year olds name was Naomh Lynch and his one year older companion in stealth was called Cahill Burns. The two men were wearing doctored M I M's which had filters attached. Both were walking arsenals, each carrying at least twenty weapons of varying degrees. From steel blades to automatic pistols which could be produced in an instant, if either were required. Their main weapon was a unique piece; it was highly portable and was called by its designer, Naomh's uncle.

"A Flatpack."

As their outlawed group dealt in subterfuge, concealment of weapons was the name of the game. When they travelled incognito, all of the guns were of a slender linear shape no more than 75mm in circumference and covered with an obscuring sheen that went undetected by most security systems. If the weapon was required, a gas canister increased the volume of the weapon at the push of a button. A scope, screen and stock could be speedily added. In these days of adequate body armour, all of their guns were made from light, durable homogeneous plastic. Each inflated piece had large muzzle bores that allowed snub-nosed projectiles to spin within their wide spirally grooved barrels with enough velocity to penetrate the standard projection of the Anschluss security forces. These squat scatter guns had large circular magazines which contained over two hundred of these large 12mm rounds and over twenty high explosive shells. When the trigger was pulled the muzzles of the weapons rotated in the opposite direction of the round magazines. The latter barrel spun clockwise while the former spun anti clockwise, while the stock of the weapon remained unmovable and sturdy. There were no shell cases for the projectiles as the high-powered oxygen that fed naturally into the weapon chamber propelled them at a high velocity. Discharged rounds made a sharp crack that was loud enough to identify the sound as a lethal source. Silencers impeded the accuracy of the Flatpacks, so they were discarded. These weapons also had the advantage of shooting around corners, keeping its holder out of harm's way from responding fire. All of these weapons functions were processed by a complex internal computer that was accessed by a toughened L.C.D screen that also issued voice commands. During this covert mission, each one of their voice recognition projectile weapons had its automated voice telling its bearer that it was activated or switched off. This in-built metallic voice, if operational told its bearer how many rounds of what type were left and if there were non-functioning parts. After all, on this night the weapons owner did not want the metallic voice of their automatic arms betraying their presence. Similarly, if they had to break radio silence, then they would use their designated Code-names, "Tyro." and "Bonkers.". The use of these pseudonyms over the air-waves prevented the Anschluss security forces from identifying them; all of the RE-INSTATOR'S were labelled so. Naomh was called Tyro as he was the second in command and the inheritor of the organisation. He was judged by its leader to be still unready to assume overall command. Cahill was known as Bonkers because of his berserker reactions in moments of real danger. His slightly wide head fit in with his competitive streak and need to win. Moving forward one at a time, while they took alternate turns to cover each other's advance, the armed men slowly progressed to the doorway of an already reconnoitred building. This row of derelict structures was once again in the cycle of a dire need of a new coat of paint. It was hard to believe that they were once opulent places of abode in the long vanished Austria-Hungarian Empire, a ruling dynasty that these two knew nothing about. The buildings faded hues of yellow and white had been rejuvenated many times, but now some nameless official in the housing department had finally gotten around in listing them for demolition. The huge sprawling Anschluss was awash with decrepit structures such as these and its rulers had no place for nostalgia. Not been students of history, the two RE-INSTATOR'S had no idea that a kilometre away from them and nearly a thousand years before, a lone gunman named Gavrilo Princip had killed the Archduke Ferdinand and his wife, the heirs to the Hapsburg throne. That single occurrence had changed the face of Empire and the Nations of Europe had never been the same again. It was an event that led to the successful overthrowing of the old establishment, much like these two gunmen desired. The facility had been made safe by a previous operative and his brother from the Madrid Contrib. This meticulous individual insisted on "Dummy Runs.". That person had already deactivated the security lock on the main entrance door, dirtied it up again and replaced it back on the frame to avoid arousing anybody's attention. Looking through the shielded eye slits of his head covering and breathing deeply into his anti-chemical mask, Naomh removed the useless lock and they crossed the threshold into the lobby of the presumed vacant premises. Once they were safety inside the building, he shut the door and both of them removed their masks. Without hesitating and full of purpose, both crossed the floor and made their way up a darkened and cluttered stairway. The cones of light from their weapons, which were now switched on, pierced the gloom of the forgotten stairwells ahead. In a break with protocol Cahill swore in unison with his companion as the stairs creaked alarmingly and he whispered.

"I hope it will bear our combined weight."

"It will, look."

He saw two sets of dusty footprints on the steps where Naomh had pointed and because of the size of one pair, he knew it would hold. Looking into each other's expressions, knowing that each of them had been thinking the same thing caused both men to articulate wide, but unseen grins. Climbing seven flights of musty steps and landings, the two-armed men navigated their way to the corridor of a long abandoned penthouse. The floors and walls of the upper passageway were streaked with white layers of pigeon excrement and pruned feathers. There was a recently deceased bird on the floor; its carcass was still intact, as the prowling rodents had not found the ready-made feast yet. Gaping holes in the ceiling allowed the cooing of nesting birds to penetrate below. Hardly out of breath; one of them checked for a mark that would have been left by their comrade and on finding it, both men breathed a sigh of relief. Naomh opened the door in front of them slowly and stealthily, while Cahill pointed his rifle towards the room. The beam of light emitted from the weapon revealed an empty living space, which had surely seen better days. Mercifully, its ceiling was intact and they were spared the mess of the outside corridor. On entering, the stench of the long unused room became overpowering making them grateful for their masks. Cahill cursed silently as he saw a number of small dark rodent shapes scurry across the floor. Musty cobwebs lay broken and draped from wall to ceiling. Other spiders had constructed webs that were supported from flaky paint, which sagged in large paper-thin sheets from the wall. Out of date furniture, stained white by fungi still sat in the exact place when the owner of the apartment had closed the door for the final time. Expressing his distaste visually, Cahill stuck to gestures and hand signals from sheer habit, as you never knew if the Anschluss listening posts were focused on this area. The operative had clearly been here as the faint impression of his boots tracked across the dusty floor to an imposing window space that had been shuttered up years before. Crossing the decaying deck carefully and silently, so that none of the ancient rotting floorboards creaked or caved in, they reached the window that overlooked the target. Just as the two RE-INSTATOR'S sank to floor in a fluid motion, an antique tapestry whose irregular frayed edges had long since ruined the symmetry of the decorative wall mount; chose that exact moment to fold over and fall to the ground. Both men reacted with amazing reflexes to the sudden disturbance and had their inflated rifles aimed in the direction of the noise before either realised what the real cause of the commotion was. Hormone induced muscles relaxed as the sound was identified and logged as non-threatening. The light from two guns revealed clouds of dust from the slumped artwork that danced madly in billions of sparkling particles, before fading away into oblivion. One of them broke silence.

"After all the time that has hung there, why did it decide to fall now?"

Whispered Naomh.

"I don't know, but it's a pity it didn't stay intact, a thing that old would have been worth something." Replied Cahill.

As the dusty powder settled, his companion shuddered and hoped that it was not an omen of doom. Matching twin decaying purple drapes of a much sturdier material than the wall covering that hung over the window impeded a complete view of the target area. But countless moth-holes of every size allowed narrow pinpricks of flickering street ambience to penetrate the darkness of this depressing room. This was good news at least as the lights worked on the street that they were to observe, unlike the other concourse where they lay hidden the previous night. While the lack of luminance had been a boon before, its presence would be beneficial now. Cahill's hand inched upwards to the drapes that were twisted at their tops in some long forgotten style and with extreme delicacy he parted them for a better view of the target area. The forced cleft revealed two broken timber window frames; neither construction had one intact piece of glass. Despite their face protection, they were thankful for that as at least a tiny bit of fresh air penetrated the staleness of the room. The frames were barely fastened together with a corroded brass latch. The remaining shards of glass left imbedded in the sashes suggested that it must have once been a remarkable piece of stained glass. Naomh found himself amazed that somebody was once well enough connected to possess such a magnificent window. (He had no conception of individual wealth.) The prowling RE-INSTATOR reassessed the rest of the room in a new light. He warned himself.

"Enough of these distracting thoughts. I hope our other covering units have taken up position as well."

He turned his attention back to the job in hand. Finding two dust-covered blankets beside the wall; they warped themselves in them. This would provide warmth and even extra cover from any Anschluss surveillance squads, as the decaying gases emitted from the blankets would mask any Human presence. Adjusting an outdated hand held pair of infra-red laser viewer's over his slightly bumped Roman nose, Naomh peered through the parted rotten drapes and got his first glimpse of the target building and the reason for this covert mission. Inside the equally run down warehouse across from them; his beloved uncle Rory was trying to secure a deal to buy modern and state of the art equipment for the movement, to scale up their low grade war. He was promised the weapon of the PREVENTIVES, the Ernst2930. This was a triple-action up to date gun. Like his Flatpack, its projectiles needed no shell cases. It could shoot through normal walls, around them and its smaller squat magazine could hold up to three hundred smaller but equally potent rounds. Its laser sights connected directly to the owners M I M which was also more efficient, making reaction times quicker. Their leader's argument was.

"Even though the Flatpacks are ideal for our situation, they have one minor flaw. Ammunition. It takes too long for our support teams to manufacture it. This way, if we use the guns of our enemy, we will never run out of bullets or parts."

It was a sensible point. Rory Lynch was the present leader of the RE-INSTATOR'S and his designated code name was the "Gaffer.". Naomh was uptight as his paternal relation was in that warehouse with minimal protection while he was negotiating the arms deal. He and the Bonkers were part of the "Exit strategy.", if things went wrong. Rory and Naomh behaved more like father and son than uncle and nephew. Ever since the Anschluss had brutally murdered his parents (He was too young to remember them.) Rory had taken care of him. His uncle never spoke of his parent's deaths, but he heard that both of them had died together under government torture. The Gaffer was the only blood relative that he had ever known and the relationship grew more paternal as the years rolled by. So his edginess was understandable. He knew that other back up teams were situated all around the adjoining buildings in case of betrayal. But deep inside, he was well aware that if anything were wrong those within the warehouse would not have a snowballs chance in hell of evading injury, capture or worse, death. His uncle was the leader of the struggle and would not even consider letting anyone else risk their hides doing this deal. His nephew had argued for days in vain to take his place as the movement could not survive without his leadership. It had taken a direct order from his superior; the Gaffer, for Naomh to reluctantly cease his constant protests.

"Besides. It is only like going to the local store to pick up a few items." Said Rory half-jokingly.

His nephew relaxed and laughed.

"Well don't forget my favourite beer then."

The ice broken, his uncle agreed to have Tyro and the Bonkers as one of the back-up and extraction teams.

"As if I would have anyone else?" Acknowledged Rory.

Cahill and Naomh absolutely beamed. Their leader took four other operatives on the mission. The first two were from the Warsaw Contrib and went by the codenames of "Producer." and "Speedy.". The former had made a documentary that was not approved by the Anschluss census and was on the run, the latter got his name because he never stood still. The second couple of minders were from the Oslo Contrib and their designated titles spoke for themselves, the "Mouth." and the "Leech.". Naomh became edgy as he sighted his optical Viewer at the crumbling brick façade of the warehouse that was revealed in a background of digital numbers and letters. He could not escape a nagging feeling that all was not right. A veteran of many missions, he had always returned unharmed and the others were sure he had a sixth sense. Because of this reputation, many of the group's operatives wanted him along, but he always chose Cahill. Lately, though his friend had been picking someone else. Gripping his assault rifle too tight, a movement that did not go unnoticed by his companion, who slightly raised his hidden eyebrows into a questioning glance? Uncharacteristic like, Naomh loudly broke the silence and said in a tone edged with worry.

"Something is not right. I can feel it in my bones."

Cahill knew better that to ignore at his peril his friends "Gut feelings." So his concentration became more intense.

"You old fool. You should not have led this mission. Have you not risked your life enough times already?" Demanded Naomh of his uncle in his silent thoughts.

But as the minutes passed, the uneasiness was growing more intense. Soon, it was overwhelming; he had got cold feet about this operation. He knew with certainty what he must do.

"Quick Bonkers. Break radio silence. Tell them to abort the mission." Pleaded Naomh.

"Tyro; are you crazy? I don't think that is a good idea, we cannot break protocol. If I do this, then we will definitely break our cover and alert the Anschluss. Then, we will look like right idiots." Stammered Cahill, not entirely convinced at the wisdom of his companion's words.

Naomh distracted by other concerns might have thought this strange, for his friend had always been the impatient type and could change his focus in a split second. But at this moment of crisis, he stood rooted to the spot and hesitant. He on the other hand removed his face protection. Seeing the anguish on his mate's face, Cahill overcame his anxiety. He took a deep breath and cursed. Then, he activated his doctored M I M and it began frequency hopping until it settled on a random channel that would be picked up by a similar system. He shouted into the audio receptor.

"This is Bonkers. Abort, abort the mission. I repeat again, this is Bonkers, abort the mission."

To himself, he thought.

"Shit I'm in big trouble if Naomh is wrong."

He heard his friend scream helplessly.

"Too late!"

As if his roar of anguish instigated it, the entire overcast evening sky lit up as beams from Anschluss observation positions and unseen Wraiths that hovered silently above focussed in on confirmed targets. Wailing sirens vied for supremacy alongside the sound of incoming explosions and their high-pitched shriek. Highly audible muffled thuds mixed with the dull mechanical symphony of heavy calibre machine gun fire. All of the vibrations of battle combined to sound like an archaic recital performed by a demented being. The entire district shook and the jarring of their building shook them from their inaction. The last few fragments of glass were finally released from the window frames long time grip and fell on the sill or to the street below, to begin another journey. On some other level, Naomh wondered why such a covert force always announced its attack in such an unrestricted manner, especially when they had the upper hand.

"They probably think that it terrifies their opponents. Well, they should think again."

Experience took over; he gave an assertive command.

"Let's go Bonkers. Our people need our help."

Shaken by the sound of instant battle, Cahill looked at his comrade and asked.

"How did you know?"

His friend never gave him an answer. Re-establishing their face protection, both of them discarded their mucky camouflage, it was left with the broken glass, the dust and the cobwebs. The time for stealth was over. Weapons held ready, the two-charged feline like out the apartment door. Unnoticed by either of them, the heavy curtains by the window dropped back together as if by reflex, the drapes wanted to shut out the chaos across the street and return to the timelessness of the room that existed before these two Humans rude interruption. Down the flight of rickety steps, both of them bolted, not caring this time if the stairs collapsed beneath them. Pigeons that were not disturbed by their entrance now went ballistic and against their nature broke out into the night sky. The whirring vibrations of the frightened birds was louder than the sound of the hovering "Wraiths" above. Heedless of the panicked creatures, the two descending RE-INSTATORS crashed into four Anschluss PREVENTIVES exiting from the room directly under the one that they had occupied. Not knowing who was more startled; the two companions reacted quicker and despatched the shocked soldiers with sudden bursts from the swivelling muzzles of their silent firing rifles. Naomh had reacted to the slight whisper of a metal boot on the wooden surface of the landing; Cahill had responded a micro second later, that was why they had the jump on their adversaries. The slain soldiers had been too focused on the radio traffic coming through their earpieces to hear the racket their killers were making as they careered headlong down the stairs or the sound of the falling tapestry before that. Standing over the bodies, both of them knew that the time for radio silence was long over. Besides, Cahill had already broken it. Studying the bodies, he muttered.

"Nice one."

These two words always came out of his mouth when things were going from bad to worse. Naomh called for his uncle to acknowledge, his voice loaded with urgency.

"Come in Gaffer. This is Tyro. You must respond."

He roared into his mike, with more desperation than the latter. No answer! Cahill was at the end of his tether. Again, he demanded.

"Come in Gaffer, come in Speedy, Producer. Come in anybody?"

Still there was silence on the private channel. Naomh's rounds had taken two of the enemy in the head, while Cahill's bullets had slammed into the other two's trunks. The more accurate shooter bent down by the bodies of the two men he had just slain and received an angry look from his companion; who berated him.

"This is no time to admire your handy work."

A look of total exasperation was returned.

"No you idiot. The uniforms. Strip them and put them on."

"But if we go charging in there, our own will mistake us for the enemy."

Cahill got a blunt answer.

"Our own inside that warehouse are either dead or captured."

"Then what about our own sniper positions, they will definitely take us out, when we are out in the open."

"Take off our head gear, we will just keep on our M I M and filters, they will recognise us. Look Bonkers, we have no choice. We have to find out what happened to the Gaffer."

Realisation dawned on the other and with no other disagreement; he bent to the task of stripping the bodies. As the two killers went about the grisly work, one of the men Cahill shot groaned in pain.

"Shit! This one is still alive." Said Naomh.

His friend's rifle bore swivelled again as a single sharp crack filled the stairway and he replied.

"Not anymore."

Bonkers had gone into berserk mode. Speedily, both men donned the deceased uniforms and Cahill pumped another burst of fire into the sprawled figures.

"Just to make sure."

"Hurry, we have lost loads of time." Urged Naomh.

In reality, they had only wasted five precious minutes in dealing with the four Anschluss PREVENTIVES and relieving two of them of their uniforms. They left the more efficient Ernst's 2930's of the slain behind, those guns were accustomed to the fingerprints of the dead. It would take time and effort back in a safe house to reuse them and carrying the useless excess weight at this moment would be suicidal. Cahill shook his head in regret at leaving the all-purpose and multi-calibre weapons behind. He reloaded his own inadequate gun with a fresh circular magazine and hurdling over the riddled bodies the running combatants descended the rest of the stairs reaching the ground floor without any other incidents. Gasping for breath with adrenaline pumping in the bloodstream, they swallowed two more performance drugs and put back on their filtration masks. Taking deep mouthfuls of untainted oxygen from their own personal supplies, the reinvigorated men charged out of the building, hugging the sides of buildings, both praying that their own units recognised them. Rain began to fall. Kicking up puddles of stagnant blood soaked puddles or sewerage water; they focussed on running towards the mayhem. Both leapt the crumpled bodies of dead protagonists as they zig-zagged across the wide street, dodging whistling tracer rounds that struck the ground all around them. Bullets smashed into walls in sheets of firepower and there were causalities everywhere. Cahill put a voice to his thoughts.

"Shit! There are a lot of dead bodies here. What the hell is going on?"

Another nagging feeling told Naomh that this was all wrong; the enemy was overreacting to a simple arms deal gone sour. Neither of the men did not spare a moment to check if the bodies were friend or foe, their own safety was paramount. Miraculously, the weaving men reached the now blown open doors of the warehouse, one door screaming on one hinge while the other lay in pieces discarded on the ground. In that instant, a PREVENTIVE staggered out of the doorway, his face covering had been torn off to reveal haunted eyes and a bloodied face. The demented man had his machine pistol levelled at them. Naomh froze.

"Shit. This Filth has got the drop on us."

Helpless, Tyro saw death in the man's eyes, his own and Cahill's. In a spray of red vision, their manic foe's head exploded and both of them were showered with clumps of brain and blood.

"One of our own got him." Shouted his companion with a relieved laugh as he took a second to wipe the gore from his goggles. Naomh also realised.

"I am still alive."

He muttered a quick thanks to their unknown benefactor and moved on, they had no time to analyse events or thank their lucky stars. Things could get more dangerous yet. Inside the smoke filled warehouse, the two entering combatants found a confusing sight within.

"What the fuck happened here?" Demanded Cahill.

Although, both of them breathed filtered air, they were certain that it still smelt of cordite and death. The former depot was littered with a great many Anschluss dead, all torn apart with looks of abject horror portrayed on what was left of their faces. Body parts were scattered everywhere. One headless trunk sat rigid at a seat. It might have looked normal, if it had not been minus its head. The blood on their vision goggles only enhanced the demonic scene. Stunned, they're eyes followed the trail of dead towards a huge opening torn from the frame of the warehouse. The gap had not been blasted from the wall, ripped or torn seemed to be the right word. It led out into a small alley. Returning to the scrutiny of the warehouse, both uneasy men discovered the bodies of the two of their comrades that had accompanied Naomh's uncle, the Producer and Speedy. Both had clean shots to the head and the latter would now be still for ever. But there was no sign of Rory or the other two that had been with him, dead or alive.

"The Anschluss must have them." Said Cahill.

Naomh grabbed armed comrade by the jacket and shoved him towards the shattered wall and spoke through his communication filter.

"They have escaped. Why else would that huge hole be in the wall. Come on Bonkers; let's go after them."

Cahill jerked his friend back as he moved to go through the shattered gap.

"God dam Tyro. You're right, but something weird has happened here. I have never seen the like of this before. Judging by the dead outside, the Gaffer must have had more back up teams."

Naomh looked at the speakers face in bewilderment but continued to proceed to the rent in the wall. Locating his uncle was his first priority. But, his confidant roared at him, causing him to stall.

"No, wait, the bodies. Look at the fucking bodies."

"What so special about the dead. I'm sure you have seen corpses before." Replied Naomh in a voice loaded with sarcasm.

Once again, the same question was repeated by his friend.

"No their dead. All of them look like they have been through a meat grinder."

"So?" Asked Naomh impatiently.

"Our two friends died normally from gun shots. The Filth; they did not. Something else did that to them."

Shocked silence from the other.

"I don't know of any weapon that only targets certain individuals and makes mincemeat out of them. Do you?"

"We will find our answers out there." Said Naomh as he pointed at the hole in the wall. For once, his jittery comrade agreed.

"I don't like it, but it makes sense."

Both of the now wary men clambered through the powered brick into the alley hardly perceiving that the drizzling rain had abated. Eyes and weapon beams focused warily on the ground ahead. The anxious men noticed that it was covered in a thick grunge of unknown metallic origin. They had stepped into the slime unwittingly and smoking vapours escaped into the chill night air from their military grade footwear. The acidic gunk had also formed into a trail.

"Shit, have the Filth got a secret weapon?" Wondered Cahill in a voice touching hysteria.

Naomh remained silent, knowing that his voice would also betray him. He could not answer his friend's question because logic now told him that if there had been such a thing, then their side had used it.

"And our side means my uncle Rory."

Following the alien trail, the vigilant RE-INSTATOR'S came to an intersection with the trail of slime going off to the right and two sets of distorted footprints going to the left. Now faced with a dilemma, they had to make decision. Coming to it quickly, Naomh charged Cahill with a task.

"You got to get back with the information of this new terrible weapon to the rest of the organisation. They need to know what we are up against."

However, this was a cover story, because he felt unsettled and something told him that he did not want his friend to discover what lay ahead. Another one of his gut feelings told him.

"No whatever, I am about to encounter is for my eyes alone. I definitely do not want anyone around when I find out what is going on."

To his relief, his comrade concurred and offered up no argument. He urged his friend to be careful as they headed off in opposite directions.

"Be careful too, Tyro." Said Cahill, his voice fading in the distance.

On his own now, he became extremely alert and put his rifle sight to his shielded eyes and proceeded down the narrow alleyway scanning his vista all the time through his weapon. Noticing a weird multi-coloured glow emitting from the end of this run down and depressing back street, he made his way towards it. He glanced up for a street name, for a point of reference, but this forgotten backwater had none.

"Not a good sign. "

He meandered through the increasing number and larger sized puddles of acidic slime which he was encountering. The gunk appeared to culminate in a mini rainbow of colour at the end of the alley. That's where he found his objective. Naomh's throat tightened, he felt like some ones fingers were crushing his windpipe and slowly suffocating him. He eventually managed to gasp out aloud.

"What in God's name is this?"

Naomh had located the Anschlusss secret weapon and he came to the wrong conclusion.

"This must be one of those rumoured mutants that they use for their dirty work. But something must have gone wrong, because it has torn its own people apart. The Gaffer must have affected that?"

The RE-INSTATOR now wished piously.

"I should not have followed the weird trail that ended in this alleyway. Shit, Cahill should have stayed with me too."

Now the tightening in the pit of his stomach matched the distress of his gullet. What he laid eyes on was not Human, although it might have been once. It was a rainbow hued lump or blob of larval flesh completely shattered and torn apart. Littered with bullet holes and jagged shards of twisted shrapnel protruding from blackened punctures, the thing was still alive. The gleam of the metallic perforations imbedded in its body contrasted with the seeping slime that oozed down from the metals razor sharp edges. He had witnessed horrific deaths before; one incident especially stood out. It was when a bomb had detonated prematurely and engulfed the person who was carrying it, blowing the beautiful girl to smithereens. Her severed head did not look so pretty then. It was in that moment he found out that death comes in a precise instant, whether it is expected or not. Despite its devastating injuries, he noted.

"This monstrosity does not look as if it is dying. No, on the contrary; it looks as if it is been born. And what in hell is that shimmering iridescence that glows around it?"

A rancid stench, not even vaguely Human in origin penetrated his protection filter and assailed his senses. Naomh nearly gagged. In his horror and fascination, he thought he saw the thing wobble a fraction. While having the upper hand, he stood rooted to the spot not daring to breathe.

"Yes, I am certain that it is trying to turn over."

A slow trembling began at one end of the broken body and rippled along the frame until it became a violent shaking. He exclaimed.

"That thing is definitely still alive!"

The modicum of movement testified to that. Surprisingly, he felt an acute awareness of the incredible pain that coursed through the wrecked Alien body. In tandem with this, some enforced pity for the thing took control of his being. As if in a trance, a remembered bond caused him to kneel down beside the hulking form and gently caress it. The blob responded to the touch, for it recognised one of its own. The end which Naomh had felt started a slow spasmodic transformation as the leathery membrane that cocooned became elastic and transparent. The shocked witness lost his grip on the composite handle of his Flatpack. Naomh's weapon fell from his twitching fingers as the full shock of what he was seeing registered. The rifle dangled from a leather strap that connected it to his belt and stopped it from laying forgotten on the slimly ground. In agonised slowness the tormented visage of his beloved uncle eventually superimposed itself under the skin of the thing.

Or was it a ludicrous caricature of the former Rory.

He now had no doubt.

"It is or was my uncle, because the ever present and unique amulet of his is around the things bloated neck."

The red jewel's chain had somehow expanded in size. The nose became the size of the entire face; the lips blossomed becoming like puffed up balloons. Small eyes bulged grotesquely and the head was devoid of ears. The out of proportion facial features only enhanced the overall comical appearance of the pantomime like figure. Only Naomh did not feel like laughing, well maybe a hysterical bout would suffice. The misshapen parody of his relation opened its eyes in a scream and any doubt that it was not his uncle evaporated. All that had been Rory remained forever etched in those haunted orbs. Wiping away a traitorous tear that became trapped under his eyelids, he remembered the kindness and the passion, and the fear, and the anger and the love those eyes had formally held.

Now, there was only distress and madness.

Bathed in pain, the thing tried to smile, but the effort remained a grimace. Words and sentences lacking coherence sounded from it. It seemed as if it was taking the first steps in mastering a language. Halting and inhaling a ragged breath, it then spoke clearly for the first time in the most alien of accents. As the words came out, the features of Rory became more pronounced.

"Not a pretty sight, am I lad?"

The monstrosity saw the horror in Naomh's face and the thing spoke for its nephew in its heavy rasping breathing.

"Yes, it is me."

Rory's voice was no longer the charming lilting brogue that regularly enchanted the ladies, speech that had known the joys of living on the edge, now wreaked of decay and insanity. Each word that was spoken from its swollen mouth was followed by a vulgar belch and a waft of foul feted stinking air that overwhelmed Naomh's filters.

"Don't be afraid lad? I know this might seem strange."

The voice faltered from the mother of all belches and a sickening mucopurulent mixture of white slime flowed down the corners of the huge mouth. Naomh lost all pretence of control and suddenly his disbelief found a hysterical voice.

"Strange is a fucking understatement. What the fuck is going on. What on earth are you? Your one of those fucking mutants the enemy has, aren't you? That's what you are. The last time I saw you, you were a Human, now you're a bloated worm."

"I am still me. You know my voice." Said the thing.

"Did you kill all those dead Filth? Their fucked up bodies were everywhere, inside and outside the warehouse. It's a slaughterhouse back there."

"Most of them were killed by their own. They panicked and began taking out everybody.

"Can you blame them? One look at you would scare the shit out of anybody."

"I did not look like this in there."

"Again I ask what are you? A fucking maggot or something. Look at me I am talking with a large larva." Giggled his nephew inanely

"That's enough of your babbling. Calm down. I am regenerating. In a couple of hours I will return to my normal self." Voiced Rory with such power that he stopped his relation amid his profanities. It then commanded.

"As you can see, I am helpless. You will have to protect me until then. Take up position at the entrance to this alley."

"I'll not watch over you. I don't even know what you are. I'm out of here. Look after yourself. Whatever the hell you are?" Wailed Naomh.

As he made to depart, the next words that he heard impacted on him like a bang of thunder. His ultimate shock did not come from the non-use

212

of their Codenames.

"You will stay dam it! I'm your father, Naomh. Don't you understand? I'm your Father? My name is Rory. Can you not feel it? I never had a brother. It would never allow that. You are me, Naomh. My own flesh and blood."

"No. You are not even human. You cannot be my Father" Cried his newly named son as he went into self-denial.

"But, I am!"

"No, you are not. I have photo-scans of my parents. They look normal like a real person. One of them has black curly hair like me. You cannot deny that."

"They're a complete fabrication. I made them up." Replied the thing with certainty.

Naomh staggered trying to flee from this nightmare, but his legs betrayed him. They would not move. His newly found parent/thing realised.

"Shit. I'm losing him."

His father's mind sought out his offspring's and with the strength of a gravitational pull, he locked into his son's consciousness sharing all the information within. The intrusion completely overpowered his unnerved target and no resistance was offered. The flow of his parent's memories started as a trickle, then as a stream and finally turned into a raging torrent. The receiver's fury mounted at all of the cherished memories that his father had denied him and his anger welled up. But then, the thing panicked as its strategy backfired. Naomh's will became stronger and leeched every iota of memory from him including things his father wanted hidden. His son's awareness was pulled firmly towards one disturbing echo from the past. He devoured the scene with a ravenous hunger. Tears of rage poured down his face at what the monster had taken from him. He saw an extremely beautiful woman with a wonderful smile. Then, there was a brief struggle, a bang and she lay dying on a familiar floor. His supposed parent was standing over her with the irrefutable murder weapon still in his hand. Naomh was now engulfed with a cool anger.

"You bastard. You killed my mother." Said her son rhetorically.

The thing had been caught in a trap of its own making; it looked for an avenue of escape.

"No Naomh. It was not me." Insisted his parent.

Searching for time to diffuse his child's anger, the grotesque figure lied.

"It was you. She died in child birth."

"Shut up. I have seen the murder. She died at your hands. You killed her, no one but you." He raised his forgotten weapon and armed the launcher on it. The metallic voice of the weapon broke the stand-off.

"Grenade launcher activated. There are ten projectiles remaining."

The thing panicked, it saw the intentions in the tormented green eyes.

"No, for pity sake, you have got it wrong Naomh. She was an agent of the Filth. She was going to kill me and flee with you back to her Anschluss masters. You would have become one of them."

Rory was about to tell him.

"The PREVENTIVE agent who shot me back at the warehouse had the face of your mother and that was the second time that I have killed her."

Even in his larval state, he had been aware of that incident and somehow had kept it secret during the siphoning of his memories. However, for the moment, he decided against it.

"That would tip my son completely over the edge. I have to stall for time."

But Naomh was not listening. The thing knew his son's final intent; he saw his offspring's fingers press the firing button and in desperation screamed.

"It told me to do it Naomh. You don't understand. You have no idea what mankind will be losing. For pity's sake. Nooo-."

Another metallic voice interrupted.

"One explosive projectile discharged, nine remaining, eight remaining, seven-."

Rocket after rocket slammed into the bloated body until he had emptied the weapon. The mechanical voice that had counted each discharge and said with finality.

"Explosive rounds chamber emptied, please reload."

But none of the rounds detonated on impact. Each explosive round just plopped into the forms oily mass and vanished. The wormy bulk shuddered and with a final shout of despair and resignation, it said.

"It's finally betrayed me. After all these years it's found somebody else to take my place. Don't trust it my son. If it thinks that you are a liability, then it will seek out another host to do its dirty work."

Then, the thing that had Rory's voice uttered its final words as it imploded,

"You are no longer Tyro. You are in command now."

There was an intense flash of blinding light and a wave of searing heat as shreds of charred flesh filled the night sky. The Gaffer had died from a weapon of his own design and by one he would have never thought capable of the feat. His killer stood over him. Where bits of Alien fluids and gore splattered his combat gear, the acidic mucus caused whispering tendrils of smoke to float on the damp air.

"Got you. You murdering son of a bitch." Shouted a vindicated Naomh.

He had avenged the death of a mother, he had never known. But he did not feel right. As the perpetrator of patricide stood there shocked, bloodied and head bowed, something had flown from the exploding body and hit him in the chest. A quick scrutiny revealed that he had no apparent injuries.

"My body armour must have taken the blow?"

Oblivious to the profound implications of that event, Naomh departed the smoking dead end; in abject despair and growing madness. Leaving behind an alley that smelt and looked like a makeshift abattoir, the distraught RE-INSTATOR took one final and lingering look. Through a light-headed blur and sodden vision, he noticed that of the remains of his father had liquefied and blended with the sudden downpour that had just erupted. The grisly clumps of flesh were been washed away down the drains.

"There will be no evidence of that thing remaining for the hygiene vehicles when they go about their work.

Then he amended.

"That's if they ever pass this way?"

Suddenly an erratic thought born from his bewildering situation crossed his mind. Naomh remembered something that the man who he had always considered his uncle had told him years ago when a good friend of his was killed.

"There is an old superstition from those who we were descended from that said, if you died when it rained; then God was weeping for you. The harder the downpour then the more he grieved. This was a sure sign that you would go straight to Heaven. And the longer the rainfall lasted, the more exalted the position of the deceased would be when they arrived in paradise. Just in case they were correct, I hope that it is raining when I die."

"Well, you got your wish." Spouted his killer in bitter malice.

But on reflection, Naomh decided.

"I don't believe that large bloated worms went to paradise and if they do, then I certainly do not want to go there."

Back in the distant past, Cathbad had not been surprised by the larval transformation, he had encountered it before, but it still disturbed him. Naomh did not hear the Alien voice of the Watcher whose bitterly disappointed mind-voice echoed from a point in the time-lines.

"Another failure. I had great expectations for that Hybrid. This one can be rejected at once, his time will be short-lived and I can proceed to the next bearer."

X.

THE AMSTERDAM CONTRIB 2951AD.

At this exact moment, a well inebriated and somewhat indisposed Naomh just didn't give a dam. His mind was awash with ridiculous possibilities.

"Or is it my mind?"

That was one of the absurdities going through his muddled head.

"I haven't just received an unbelievable body blow. No! I feel like I have been kicked in the teeth, over and over again."

A gut wrenching feeling of hopelessness and despair; even the unusual circumstance of helplessness racked his entire being. His foggy brain was clouded over, much like the constant vapour barrier that hovered over the urban and industrial sectors. But one inescapable fact shone through.

"Rory is gone; the Gaffer and my assumed parent has died by my hands."

His son and killer was suffering guilt-ridden remorse for his actions. The murdered man had always been such a strong presence in his life and now he was no more. Naomh raged at the injustice of it all.

"All through my childhood and my precarious adult life, he had been my mentor. He was my rock! And for a few incomprehensional minutes, I had a father of some sorts; then I killed him. No, not a Father, a fucking worm."

Realising that these recent events were just too bizarre, another line of reasoning flirted in between the only solution and sanity. The disturbed man began to assume.

"The Anschluss Filth must have dosed me with some powerful hallucinogen as the events of last night are just too fantastic to be believed. No! That would be the simple solution."

But Naomh was well that the crazy events of last night, December the 10th were no delusion, they had really happened. After the weird incidents, the utterly confused RE-INSTATOR had found the nearest Mag-Lev line and fled by the Pipes to the Amsterdam contrib. From his beginning in the Sarajevo Contrib, he had sped towards his destination via the central hub of the Geneva Contrib. As he passed the sheer granite plateau with its despised government perched on top of its base, he wished that he could blow the whole fucking thing up and watch its glittering towers come crumbling down. Through the transparent plastic by his window seat, he watched the rising and descending of the Vert-Levs up and down the plateau's sheer sides, a method of travel that he had never been privileged to experience. Before, he had boarded the first Mag-Lev; the perpetrator of patricide had already rid himself of his stolen PREVENTIVE paraphernalia and Flatpack. He discarded four unused circular magazines and most of his weaponry. But he kept his body armour, one concealed automatic pistol and a razor sharp blade; just in case. Both of these coated weapons would evade most detection devices, but not a close inspection by hand held equipment. He had recovered clean clothing from a drop off point close to the night's events and donned the common jumpsuit it over his body armour. His choice tonight was of a plain blue colour, it was a non-descript hue and he would not draw anyone's prolonged gaze. There was also a quick cleaning kit, complete with a hygienic smelling container of water, a drying towel and a perfumed air fragrance. He used the enhanced toiletries to hide the stench of his crawling around in the gutter, the chemical residue of weapon proximity and to remove any remaining blood or ooze that still clung to his skin. The masking deodorants also had the advantage of cloaking any unusual smells that might draw attention to him. He could do nothing major with his jet black hair except wear a common enough hood over it. The disturbed twenty-five year old had been amazed that he had been thinking with such clarity. This cleaning act after a mission whether it was successful or not was standard procedure for all RE-INSTATOR operatives and instinct had taken over. But for the first time in his recollection, he broke with strict protocol, by not going to the appointed safe house in the Prague Contrib immediately. He had by passed it and switched off his Frog Eyes. He was deliberately out of contact. Now, none of his comrades knew where he was or even if he was still alive. Since the extraordinary revelation from the creature, he had done what he knew best in times of crisis. He had got roaring drunk. But during this bout, there was a difference in his actions; he was by himself and not having a good time. Naomh was never a loner; he had always the company of his associates. He had discarded his circle of close knit friends for preferred, self-company as he frequented bar after bar along a neon strip in the Amsterdam Contrib, showing strangers a side of himself that his friends would not recognise. Anyone that crossed his path saw a gruff hard eyed young adult with shoulder length black hair who was well inebriated and was sensibly avoided. He also was without his M I M; an unusual circumstance. Experience told them.

"This drunken Pleb will soon be picked up by the Conicals and locked up to cool off for the night or worse."

Heedless of that threat, he sat at automated drink dispensers paying with false credit information that ironically was used by Anschluss operatives to fund their own covert operations. The "Lenses.", a valued member of his faction had discovered this unlimited source of funds while infiltrating the governments master computer archives. He spoke in gratitude to the hacker's aid with a simple salute.

"Cheers to you my good hacker."

He looked hard at his drink in the dank and dour establishment that he had ended up in. His distorted reflection in its plastic face made him look like the thing that he had killed. As he got more inebriated and sullen, the same litany pounded his brain during each mouthful of gulped liquor.

"What am I? What the Hell am I?"

Once, even a few days before, he could have easily answered that simple question with the words.

"I am a freedom fighter, whose sole aim is to overthrow the corrupt system of the Anschluss by any possible means."

Now, he wasn't even sure if he was Human. He sat in stool after stool, in bar after bar, often ignored by other patrons and staff. All had seen the imprint of madness in his eyes and nobody had the inclination to bother him. Now in his last premises, he glanced at a digital time-piece on its wall. It was 3.30 pm. Naomh wondered why other people in the bar were drinking at this time in the afternoon. Was it for pleasure as throaty laughter came from somewhere in the smoky background or was it just a means of getting through the day? Perhaps some of them were like him; they needed to be surrounded by comfort during a bout of dark depression.

"What the fuck am I thinking? I'm positive that none of them have the same reason as me. That's for sure. How many of them have just found out that they have a great fucking worm for a parent? I bet that they would have something to talk about then."

He chuckled insanely as he downed a straight whiskey in a single gulp. A fished up memory recalled some words his Uncle/Father had once told him.

"Lots of things are not exciting Naomh, that's why we like them. We are comforted by their normality."

He said aloud, fervently wishing that he had now lived a boring and uneventful life.

"Amen to that."

A brave or stupid barman overhearing the religious reference approached and told him.

"You've had enough drink consumed. Go home. Things will look better tomorrow, they always do."

"I don't think so."

The barman was insistent, thinking that some lover must have dumped him.

"Believe me, it will."

He returned Naomh's swipe card with the false name of Anders Borg, which he had left in the drink's dispenser credit unit and kept up the insistence that he go home. The drunken RE-INSTATOR placed his card back in the drink unit and told him bluntly.

"Go fuck yourself. Mind your own business. Leave me alone."

The barman deciding to nip trouble in the bud signalled to two huge bouncers with a hand sign that Naomh had noticed. One of the large men was delighted, he remembered the sullen man from another place and the memories were not good. He whispered to his companion about the infraction.

"Six months ago, over in Joe's place, he had been in the company of an enormous man who had beaten the crap out of me and four other Plebs."

Now that this Pleb was alone, he cracked his knuckles in anticipation of one sided violence. The two taller and extremely bulky men approached the young drunk confidently, deciding that they could easily handle this slight youth who was about 185cm tall and weighed about ninety-five kilos. Without his big friend, he would be no match for them. One of them, armed with a broad smirk put his hand on the tormented soul's shoulder and gripped him tightly while the other opened his coat to reveal an illegal stunner that he was about to use.

"Do as the barman says, go home."

Naomh shrugged off the one gripping him in a fluid movement and rose unsteadily to his feet. The bouncer that had been easily thrown off approached him again. He was now red faced with anger and was about to take it out on the drunk who had evaded him so easily. He told his friend who had out the taser.

"No, not that way. I want him."

"The Pleb is all yours."

He addressed Naomh.

"I was hoping you would do that. You don't remember me do you?"

The object of his fury stared at him blank faced.

"Well, let me give you a reminder."

The bouncer stopped his movement towards revenge when Naomh deliberately opened his jumpsuit top with his left hand. He put his right hand on the trigger of his lethal pistol. The two usually clued in men had never seen such a high powered weapon before, but they instantly realised what it was. Both backed off quicker than an inter-Contrib bullet shuttle. The snatches of conversion that had floated around the bar ceased, only to be substituted by low murmurs of speculation as the other patrons had seen the two bouncer's back off as if bitten by a deadly snake. But none except the strange young man, the barman and the two security men knew why. Deciding, he had gone too far in producing a highly illegal weapon, Naomh resealed his jumpsuit and looked at the barman. He smiled sheepishly.

"I think you are right. I have had enough to drink. I am leaving. So no hard feelings, eh."

A somewhat composed Naomh left the premises, the staff more than the patrons heaved in relief. The junior doorman said to the barman.

"What are you waiting for Fritz, call the Conicals."

"No Alan, that will bring unwanted scrutiny down on the business."

"Fritz is right and if he is lifted, that Plebs friends might return looking for him. Besides, did you see the piece he was packing? You know what that makes him and you don't want to get involved with those bastards."

Alan was a quick learner.

"That's for sure. I definitely do not want to see the big man again, especially if he is armed and one of you know who."

The wave of halted conversation began again; it was as if he had never been there. Outside in the glittery street, Naomh did not care about his performance in that nameless bar, for he would never see those people again in this urban sector of billions. A few hours later, by a roundabout route, he arrived in the Prague Contrib, only to be greeted by a cold sharp drizzle. He made his way to a roof directly opposite the safe house where he and Cahill were supposed to have rendezvous after a successful mission. His head covered by his hoodie, he began to pace up and down the rooftop; not caring if anyone saw him and thought he was practising for an illegal run of Parkour. He laughed at the idea while threading through the liquid puddles that seeped from the solar units on the roof. The pools of water were rising in volume as the night's rainfall added to them. Soon, the centre of the roof was one large miniature lake, as its blocked water outlets were letting the water drain slowly away. Naomh splashed about on the rooftop in a highly agitated state.

"Who can I trust to tell what I have found out?"

He answered his own question.

"Nobody. Not even Cahill. They would all think me mad."

His whole existence had been shattered in less than twenty-four hours.

"Only a day, was that all?"

Oh, he knew deep down that his World might come crashing down one day. Always in the end of his fantasies, it was the cold comfort of death, never the humiliation of capture for he and a few fanatics had poison pills concealed in their teeth. It was a safety net provided by a technically gifted member of the organisation. The lethal tablet had a safety mechanism built in, in case of accidental use. A certain rhythm of teeth gnashing would only set it in motion.

"That's it. I will bite down on the pill and end it all."

The drink and the enormous shock of the revelation were taking their toll on his depressed state. He was not thinking rationally.

"What the fuck. I'm going to do it. Nobody must find out that I am a monster, a maggot like him. This way the movement will continue on oblivious to the thing that controlled it."

He shrugged in acceptance of megalomania, then bit down in the correct sequence to disperse the lethal poison. Naomh waited for the bliss of death to take away the pain and horror of what he was. Oblivion was slow in coming and his confused mind drifted. He was a RE-INSTATOR and could have imagined his own demise, predicted the death of loved ones, his comrades, but what had transpired forced his mind to scream.

"What happened to the glorious death, I envisioned? My body lying broken and smashed by Anschluss bullets, while giving my life for the

cause. Or maybe capture and the expressions of fury on the Filth's interrogators as I broke the poisoned tooth and deprived them of my torture. It would be only be physical pain not this mental anguish that is destroying me now."

Alone on the building, something twigged in the corners of his brain.

"How am I still having this conversation with myself? I should be dead by now. Maybe I bit down in the wrong pattern. I will try again."

But he could not; the capsule had already been broken, he had felt the lethal liquid flow down his gullet. Incredulity overrode his anguish. The suicide pill must have been harmless and he had great faith in its provider.

"Another lie."

He swore in frustration and then instantly to his dark depression.

"I am not a monster."

Tears flowed over his moving lips. Then, the distraught Naomh had an irrational thought.

"What would my corpse look like? Would it be a big bloated worm like Rory?"

He had always believed that he would have made a great looking dead martyr, but another dark thought intruded.

"I forgot, there is one at the body recycling facility and I would not like him to get his hands on my dead body. It will have to be a bomb, to make sure there is nothing left."

A vision of the beautiful girls severed head flashed by. Naomh faltered. He looked over again at the safe house. The lonely RE-INSTATOR could imagine the twin beacons of light from the safe house over the street promising warmth, food and companionship from this God forsaken night. But this was an illusion, as he knew that no light would be allowed to break free from the confines of the safe house.

"Anyway, they don't want me. I am a monster."

He ceased his pacing and squatted down on the silver mineral covered roof and became lost in his cloak that enveloped him like a shroud, his solid squat appearance belying the raging torment within. The temperature dropped and the rain turned to sleet. It became the only sound as if ran off his waterproof garment and where it met the rooftop, it formed sharp glittering rivulets of ice. The freezing chill had no effect on him and it would soon melt as the watery cloud of the ever-present murkiness absorbed the weather system. The pleasant quietness was broken by the gurgling discharge of a waste water outlet and it depressed him that people were going about their normal night's business oblivious to the suffering of his soul. Again the voice of doom interceded.

"Go on. Walk to the edge of the roof and fall. Do a base jump without the wings. End it now."

But the slightly saner part of him replied.

"No! Not like this. It will still be the glorious end for me."

He found a little comfort in that solution and vowed.

"Tomorrow in the harsh reality of daylight; I will seek out a passing Anschluss police patrol and die in a hail of bullets."

His change of heart with the bomb idea had gone with the remembered visions of the severed head. Immensely satisfied with that decision, he relaxed and with a calmness of the condemned, he began to sing the words of a favourite song. The words came slowly at first, but soon the comforting melody gave him the courage to face the storm within.

"Where I was, I had wings but couldn't fly."

"Where I was, I had tears but couldn't cry."

"My emotions, frozen in an icy lake."

"I couldn't feel them, until the ice began to break."

"I have no power over this, you know I'm afraid."

"The walls I built are crumbling"

"The water is moving, I'm slipping away."

"I throw myself into the sea, release the waves, let them wash over me."

"To catch the myth, I once believed, that the tears of the dragon were meant for me."

It was a highly apt tune, given his circumstances and it was a favourite of his uncle/father. The two of them had always debated in good nature whether it was.

"To catch or to fetch the myth."

He had gone for the former. It was a verse of a song that had survived from the twentieth century and forbidden like all ancient music by the anonymous watchdogs of the state, as further on into the lyrics, the vocalist mentioned a place called Sao Paulo that was not within the Anschluss boundaries, but in another part of the unacknowledged World. He was always amazed at what survived from the past and what did not. Lost in the repetitive litany of the song, he opened the Velcro strip of his jumpsuit and his hand went inside his jacket and under his shirt. He idly scratched the tender spot where unknown to him, his father's amulet had struck him. The words of the song died slowly on his lips fading away into the lost realms of his mind; there to be retrieved when desired again.

"My father! How strange that word had become after all these years. My father? Was he some mutation planted by the Anschluss to destroy the movement? No! That does not make sense, he was the movement. It would not have existed without him. He would not have destroyed something he loved. But then he did murder his wife and my mother."

Now, he began to wonder what life would have been like with her around. Instant bitterness assailed him because of all those lost years; the two of them could have truly shared without the deception.

"Why did you kill her? Did she find out you were a mutant?"

Still clutching the spot where he had been struck in the alleyway, Naomh became alarmed to feel a piece of protruding solidness there. He thought it strange that he had not noticed it before, even when he changed his clothes. He then put that down to his high anxiety and his proceeding drunken binge. Gripping the irritating object tighter he felt a warm wetness on his fingers. His digits came away dripping with redness.

"My own blood, no doubt."

He tried to pluck it from his wounded chest; but he knew it would not come away without doing some fearful damage. Opening his jacket to confirm what harm had become him; he discovered that a pulsating bead of sparkling red energy had been imbedded in his chest.

"It must have been in deeper and only now broke through the flesh. Wait a minute, I know what this is."

Strangely, Naomh recognised the piece of jewellery.

"It is my uncle's amulet."

He corrected himself.

"No, my father's."

Rory never took it off or allowed anyone to examine it. His former mentor had always been vague when he was questioned about the red jewels appearance and origins. He would remove it from view and just answer.

"It is a simple bauble and is of sentimental value."

Then, that would be the end of the conversation about it. Naomh had always thought that weird. The Gaffer would never allow anyone else to wear any sort of jewellery, he decreed.

"It would be an easily identification mark. It would twig the memory of any enemy operative."

It was the same with their Frog Eyes, the communication devices were of the plainest and non-descript type. They were also traceless. When Rory had worn it, the jewel had been a dull and opaque red, now it seemed to be alive; pulsing like a living heart and his own blood coated some of it. Equally bizarrely was that he felt no pain from its jagged penetration into his flesh.

"What in Hell is this made of? It must have hit me when that worm thing exploded."

Absently, he stared at the scintillating surface coated with a thin film of his dried black clotted blood; the stark contrast between the two seemed fitting. For a long time, the amulet lay captured directly in the line of his vision. It was as if, he could make the thing pop out of his chest of its own accord, so he could stand on it and shatter the peculiar object with his boot. He released his stare from the offending piece of jewellery and was about to attempt its removal.

"Put your hand on me and concentrate."

The metallic voice came from nowhere. The Alien sound starling him so much that he jumped up violently and whipped out his concealed firearm. The edgy RE-INSTATOR looked around with a hunted look for the owner of the strange utterance. There was nobody else on the roof with him.

"Shit, I am so wound up that I'm hearing voices." Decided a jittery Naomh.

Disturbing images of what his father had become flickered in his memory and a feeling of losing something vitally precious from his life smothered over him. The weird voice sounded again.

"You should treasure those memories Naomh. Your father was a great man. He was unique among Humans."

Naomh's mouth gaped in suppressed shock, for he was now sure the voice was coming from the Amulet.

"I must be going crazy. For a minute there I was certain the thing was talking to me."

He shook his head violently to clear the madness from his battered being. Again came the insisting exigency of the disembodied voice.

"Hold me tightly. I need to resume contact with you."

This red segment of the Mescal/Amulet was the only one that could communicate directly with its host. Because it was a distinct part of a separated whole, the Alien presence did not credit a appellation until completion. In this time period, he was referred as an inanimate thing. The other pieces wormed a way into their pawns conscious and made their voice seem as if it was the hosts own. Naomh's unwittingly acquired piece of the APOCRYPHA'I normally took its time with its integration of previous hosts, but now urgency was required. Again it urged him to grasp it. But the living Amulet sensed that its former host's offspring was reluctant to handle it, so it began to cool itself down until it shone with a brilliant piercing blue light. Only for the calming effect of the hypnotic luminance, Naomh stood rooted to the spot; otherwise he would have fled the scene screaming as loud as his own vocal chords would allow him. The one piece of the Mescal/Amulet felt that the Hybrid was beginning to falter and it pressed even more firmly for its new intended host to hold it and concentrate.

"No, I will not become a monster like my father."

Naomh panicked and went into hysteria. His gun was activated, another voice, the once belonging to the composite piece told him so. A mad struggle began, he tried to raise the weapon to his head, but he himself was resisting the impulse. His face became strained and his muscles quivered with the effort, but he could not point the weapon at himself. He let it fall from his fingers with a curse.

"Fuck, I cannot do anything right. First the pill and now this."

The piece of the living Amulet began to dismay, never before in all the previous millennia since its conception had it encountered such stern resistance from a bearer. Some vague whisper told it that the other parts of itself had not either.

"By the oneness of our Queen, I cannot hold the Hybrid. I am already weak from distilling the toxin from his bloodstream."

Unknown to Naomh, the reason for the failure of the poisoned tooth was due to the heroic efforts of the living Amulet in keeping him alive while it flushed out the lethal liquid from his system. Gathering up the last vestiges of its reserves of power, it made ready to cast one final bust of energised light when it felt the Hybrid weaken. Stalking Naomh like a silent predator, (The Mescal/Amulet was truly unique among its species.), it waited for the right moment to strike. A sudden increase in the flow of seeping blood provided the catalyst. The instant had come; the Hybrid's resolve had weakened another slight fraction and he unwittingly touched the Amulet to stem the flow of his own life-fluid. This momentary contact was more than enough, the Alien artefact filled with a strong resolve and a built in desire for preservation. After all, the fate of its race depended on it. In the moment of his indecision, the ancient and non-Human awareness within the red jewel pounced. Naomh stood transfixed in a parody of a mannequin except that he had a mouth and teeth that were opened in a silent scream. The Amulet's unheard pulsing gathered growing momentum. In an instantaneous climax, his whole World changed and by definition, you could say that everyone else's future did as well. A pure needlepoint beam of multi-coloured light exploded from the thing, but it seemed an eternity before it struck him on the forehead. Naomh staggered in preparation for a mighty blow, but the rainbow spectrum of light lifted him in to an erect stance with both of his feet twitching in the air a few centimetres above the solid rooftop. His forgotten pistol dangled from a wrist strap and hung lower than him. Locked in this paralysed posture, the unwavering beam kept him upright and the slight warmth from the light felt like the slight wetness of a lover's kiss. As the glow was absorbed into his brain, Rory's successor felt a short sharp stab of pain that was both excruciating and comforting. His mind filled with every colour and none. From his cranium, the light flowed through his synaptic nervous system, his blood carrying veins and arteries. The intelligent ray was searching for the familiar genetic code.

"God, the agony or is it the ecstasy." Moaned Naomh.

The investigating presence of the Amulet travelled around his physical body to every extremity, from the internal organs to the hair follicles on the outer skin. In an increasing crescendo; it began to experience a wild elation.

"This is the Hybrid; I have spent aeons seeking. The perfect genetic code that my and Cetheren's toil ultimately desired matches with this single life-form. The genetic markers are so concentrated that this is surely the one."

A sigh of almost sexual in its intensity escaped from the now merged Alien presence. One part of Mescal's being became more aware. In the Patriarchi's voice, now the Amulet's as well, he spoke.

"At last!"

Its final reason for existing came to the fore. It knew what had to be done. Now it was time to search out the rest of itself that was incorporated into other segments. These six other pieces lay scattered across the blue globe, disguised as other pieces of Hybrid adornment. When they were all gathered and assembled, then he could move in to the final stages of his programming. The seven parts of the Mescal/amulet were not what they seemed to Human eyes. Every one of them looked like an unusual piece of body piercing; slightly warm to the touch, but a common enough type of body decoration none the less. But each was part of a living breathing sentient being and it was the ultimate creation of the Weapon Master's program. Locked within each living core was one fragment of the essence of the once mad Mescal's mind. An intellect that had once touched the "INIQUITY." and learnt its corrupt ways. That combined with the age old knowledge of the ALASTHA'I, made it a commodity that far surpassed anything their creations could envision and when it completed itself with the other six parts, then this Hybrid's potential for unlimited aggression would be earth shattering. Now struggling to hold on to the momentarily control of this one, the one piece of the Mescal/Amulet forced it to reaffirm the life sustaining connection. It took a few minutes of fierce effort and finally, its newest host was under its disposition. Its pawn was allowed to gaze at the transformed life-force. The once solid object a become a watery shimmer, it seemed more fluid and vivid than before and more importantly, it had merged with the skin between his breast bones.

It was a part of him and was not.

Satisfied, the one piece of the Mescal/Amulet allowed the Hybrid to close his jacket. Naomh fumbled with the Velcro strip of his blue jumpsuit. Still dazed and confused, he slowly buttoned up and sealed the red piece embedded in his broad chest away from the bitter night. Then as the last miniature hooks locked, the one part Mescal/Amulet sealed the connection. From within, micro-filaments of light spread along the tendrils of its host's physical body until he became a thing of luminance. He would have been a highly visible spectre through the continuing fall of sleet to any astonished observer. For his being radiated with the entire spectrum of light and with the passing of a few seconds, long wisps of spiralling brilliance traced a jagged outline on the night sky. Where these energised coils contacted with any moisture in the air, bursts of short-lived electrical dynamism exploded into plumes of white vapour. The flashes were accompanied with loud plopping sounds and then the noise trailed off into nothingness. A lingering presence in the night air spoke overwhelming that something ancient and corrupt was prowling the rooftops of this sector of the Prague Contrib on this very night. The mounting build-up reached fever pitch and then suddenly it came to an abrupt end, when all the fantastic hues were snuffed out like a candle's feeble flame been exposed to the full force of a gale. Naomh shook, trembling all over and in a final orgasmic climax, a thundering blast of pent up energy shot from his body and rose vertically to the heavens above. (He had no idea that he was connecting to a Vigil Globe.) The strings of light holding him were suddenly cut. As the released Human dropped to the flat rooftop, his weapon made a dreadful clatter. Naomh collapsed into a heap as the one part Mescal/Amulet withdrew into his deeper conscious leaving its comatose host to fend for himself.

"Let the Hybrid recuperate, for my programming has just begun."

Its whispered remnants echoed in Naomh's subconscious and then its host drifted into oblivion. The one part Mescal/Amulet temporarily retreated from the Hybrid's full awareness, but it was still in the background, ready to react if a situation arose. Minutes later, Naomh came too, he was totally ignorant of what had passed, but faint traces of his ordeal floated on the verge of revelation. But these fledgling whispers of the impossible could not be recalled. Feeling as if he awoke from a great sleep, Naomh realised that his clothing was saturated. Thinking that he had fallen into a drunken slumber on the exposed rooftop, he cursed.

"What a weird night. What am I doing up here. I could have caught pneumonia. Shit that's enough drink for me for a long while."

Naomh was taken aback that he had no trace of a hangover after the amount of alcohol he had consumed. With a surprisingly clear head, he decided to make his way to the safe house that should have been his intended destination in the first place.

"Better late than never. After all, I have comrades there and they are probably worrying about me?"

The one part Mescal/Amulet had done its work well. All thoughts of suicide had vanished from the Hybrid's memory. Naomh was not totally convinced that something was left unfinished as haunting glimpses of troubled dreams tugged at his thoughts. The euphoria lasted an instant. He was starting to lose it again, a trembling began and he fell to his knees. The disturbing echoes were cut off by a shout from a troubled Cahill.

"Tyro. Are you alright?"

A short time earlier, his best friend had been sitting before the electrical fireplace in the safe house sipping boiling coffee from a chipped mug. It had been given to him by the other occupant; she had been waiting for him here. The safe houses were assigned by the Lenses; he supplied them with false names and histories and if they were intruded on by the security forces, their documentation would prove valid. As the recently returned RE-INSTATOR blew on the hot liquid before every sup, he was unaware of its taste as conflicting thoughts wrestled for prominence among the sound of the artificial flames. He picked up a remote control and then turned down the volume of the programmed sound of crackling, splitting, and burning wood. Still feeling cosy, he mouthed

"That's better, now I can think."

But, he did not like the thoughts that filled his worried head.

"Naomh has been out of contact for over twenty hours now."

He argued internally for the thousand time.

"I should go back out and search for him. For all I know, he might have been killed or taken prisoner. I also need to know whether the Gaffer is alive, captured or even dead too."

Cahill silently mouthed protocol.

"I cannot make contact with Naomh in a time of crisis. When a mission is aborted, all bets are off and everybody has to make it to a designated safe house without breaking communication silence. There you stay until contact is made. That is the directive after all, not to go on a bloody wild goose chase.

The location of the haven was contained within the memory of their M I M's. But once it was called up, it self-erased. The internal battle raging within; on whether to stay put or go out was gradually been eroded as the hypnotic three dimensional flames and the radiated warmth of the heater lulled him towards the loving arms of Morpheus.

"But what if the Gaffer has been killed? Who gives the orders then? Shit, I don't know what to do."

He was caught between a rock and a hard place and with no mobile communication been permitted, all devices had to be switched off until the following morning. His own inactivated Frog Eyes lay on the floor beside him. On impulse, he was half tempted to break protocol and call his missing friend. But he refrained. With all his heart, he hoped that Naomh had found Rory unharmed and they had made it to another safe house. He finally decided.

"Tomorrow will tell."

With heavy eyelids, Naomh's best friend gently lowered his half-empty unenjoyed beverage to the floor and ignored his M I M. He succumbed to the temptation of sleep. Greta, his female companion smiled to herself as she walked across the room to remove the mug from her exhausted lover, she scratched his mane of red hair and received a non-comitial grunt.

"If those Anschluss security forces could see their feared adversary now, sleeping like an innocent child. They would not call him Bonkers now." Asserted Greta.

The intriguing female was tall for a woman. At 182cm, she was a statuesque vision of an Aryan ideal. At twenty-nine years of age, she was slightly older than Cahill's twenty-six. She was an unusually serious woman, robust with others and when she smiled with her ice blue eyes; it was always at someone else's expense. A generous mouth with a natural ruby red pout enhanced her braided coifed blonde locks. Her jutted chin enhanced her tenacious will and a quality of not giving up easily. She was easily the most beautiful woman that many after encountering her; became instantly jealous of Cahill. But, she was a flawed beauty, there was coldness in her dealings with those she did not know and a cruelty to those she hated. Her enemies knew this as bodies of their comrades were left with shocking exit wounds. Greta filed her projectiles to a blunt point, to inflict horrifying injuries on them. When it came to the PREVENTIVES, this killer of them had a downright mean streak. Cahill more than most understood her hatred for them. When asked.

"How they you meet?"

He would remember with sudden clarity, his first encounter with his beautiful lover four years before. The RE-INSTATOR had been on his way to meet five of his comrades in the Warsaw Contrib for a prearranged mission. Sitting in the Mag-lev and trying to appear inconspicuous, he nearly left his indifference slip as he spotted what he thought was a high priority target. He was amazed; the man appeared to be alone and nonchalant. He needed to confirm his suspicion. Cahill had to act, he had a fully loaded concealed weapon and he or one of his outlawed group might never get such a golden opportunity again. Not in the least looking out of place with the rest of the commuters, he activated his tampered M I M with a confident hand. Expertly without revealing himself, he took the man's image. Using his communication device, he sent a coded transmission to the Gaffer about his discovery. Thirty seconds later, an answer returned.

"Bonkers, the target is confirmed. Follow him and see where he is going. He might lead you to someone or somewhere very interesting. Do not make a move without confirming it to my approval. I will try to get you some assistance, so keep your head and don't do anything foolish. Gaffer out."

The man got off at the Berlin Contrib and transferred to the local shuttle network. In the crowed transport system, the unassuming Cahill kept his target in view. The Anschluss agent left the network and went onto a Stand On. The beginnings of a slight mist gave his tail the advantage as most people on the moving walkway covered up. The man would not know he was been shadowed. For two kilometres along the busy walkway, he followed and then his enemy got off in a sector scheduled for demolition.

"Nice choice of scenery"

Now Cahill had to be careful, people were now few and far between. Suddenly, the man he was following halted and turned around. The RE-INSTATOR had just ducked out of sight in a corner between two buildings. As he gulped a deep breath, he was certain.

"A split second slower in my actions and I would have been spotted."

Breathing heavily, the rain dripping down the wall from broken gutters convinced him after a few minutes to move on. Taking his heavy and squat weapon and inflating it, the wary man moved from the corner he had hidden in. His target had disappeared. Slowly, he advanced up the deserted street and something drew him to a break in the wire fence surrounding the half-demolished sector. Having little choice, he entered the open space on the other side.

"Shit! I am a sitting target."

With these circumstances in the forefront of his mind, he moved swiftly to an intact building that showed a glimmer of light from its insides. Once at the structures edge, he peered into the interior. What he discovered enraged him; there was no sign of the man he pursued. However, he instantly forgot about him as something much worse than he could have imagined was going on. Cahill had found the one that would become his love been brutally raped by a rowdy bunch of four of the Filth. The blonde woman was spread eagled on a plastic table, her clothes torn in disarray and her breasts were exposed. A man with dropped trousers was thrusting into her opened legs while another male and a female held her two arms. The fourth stood in the foreground busily sharpening a knuckled handled knife. Slumped in the background were the bodies of her family. (She told him this later.) Her parents and two male siblings had been badly mutilated, before a single bullet to their temples had dispatched them. As one of the rapists was pounding into her, he shouted with glee.

"You remind me of a superior that I hated, bitch. Her name was Liben."

Another of his mates pulled him off and took his turn. He shouted at his fellow rapist.

"I always wanted to have a go off Liben."

As, he took over, this guy panted, he asked of the woman he was raping.

"Do you prefer me my precious Liben?"

Cahill had experienced so much rage at the sight of the girl been violated, he forgot to contact the Gaffer and ignored his warning about not doing anything foolish. The maddened man went into psycho mode and charged in. Full of blind fury, he attacked those that were abusing her. Projectiles flew from his Flatpack as the muzzle and magazine swivelled in opposite directions. The rapist that had been forcing himself on his helpless captive died as his head erupted in a spray of blood. The one who had abused her first still had his pants down; he tried to run, fell over and died too. The two that were holding her down were defenceless and as they released their prisoner, both held their hands in surrender. Cahill took no heed of their actions and riddled them with a burst from his weapon. Then, there was complete silence. Their victim pushed away the dead man that had fallen on top of her and the body slumped to the ground. Rising unsteadily, she made a feeble attempt to cover her modesty. The red haired man's heart went out to her. The traumatised victim had the look of the recently condemned who had suddenly been reprieved, for she had no doubt that she would have been killed after they had finished with her. Still groggy, she straightened up as a fierce look filled her expression. The dishevelled woman picked up a discarded weapon and attempted to fire it into the bodies of those who had abused her. But her unfamiliarity with it caused the gun to remain silent. Cahill came over to her and gently put his arms around the shocked woman, at his touch she nearly bolted like a frightened rabbit. Delicately, he took the Ernst 2930 out of her hand and put it into the grip of one of her dead assaulters who was slumped over the up turned table. As he looked straight into her tormented eyes; a metallic voice said.

"Weapon activated, please select projectile choice."

He selected rapid fire for her and he received a grateful look. Clutching the dead man's trigger finger, the gorgeous blonde woman riddled the dead bodies, not stopping until the magazine was empty. The three bodies articulated movement from the projectile impacts. She forced the gun hand of the Ernst 2930's owner to point at his already ruptured head and blew the rest of his face away. In a frenzied moment; she picked up a discarded blade and removed the flaccid penises from the dead men who had had defiled her. In that terrible moment of revenge, she had changed forever. Her blood covered hands flung the offending pieces of flesh into a darkened corner and she hoped that the rats would feed on the grisly remains. Then, the false energy of revenge abated. Deflated; she went over to her dead family and clutched each one of them while sobbing uncontrollably. Her saviour felt tears well in his own eyes, but expediency prevailed.

"We have to go, their backup teams will respond soon."

The grief stricken woman made no attempt to leave, but somehow he eventually managed to persuade her. As she reluctantly left, she wailed at her dead kin.

"I will avenge you."

Her red rimmed blue eyes met Cahill's and she entreated.

"You will teach me, won't you?"

He nodded thinking that she had got a head start already.

"Of course."

Then as an afterthought, she added shyly.

"My name is Greta."

"I'm Cahill."

He had rescued her and they had become lovers. In gratitude, she had embraced his cause, unlike most of the other members who had been handpicked by Rory. The striking woman followed Cahill heels like a loyal puppy that adored its master. But like the afore mentioned, Greta would bite the hand off anyone else who took this as a sign of weakness. The Gaffer had asked her to give herself a codename. She mulled it over and then replied with venom.

"Those Filth as you call them were taunting me with the name Liben when they were raping me. As far as I am concerned, my past never existed before that. They have wiped it out. That name will do and it will be one they will not forget. I will leech the blood from their bodies; yes it is a good codename and one that will come back to haunt them."

The name Liben became a constant reminder of the day her World changed and consequently her potential state of mind. Eight months later, Rory explained to Naomh.

"Greta had this new life thrust upon her by terrible events, she had not chosen it. But she has become as fiercely committed to the movement as if she had joined it herself."

Although some, who were initially wary of her, changed their opinions after hearing Cahill's account of the brutality inflicted on her. Soon, she was accepted without reservation.

"Surely, the tall blonde woman has suffered more than any of us have?"

The once novice embraced their rebellious life and became a very efficient member of the group. She lapped up her training and soon was one of the best among them. But vicious hatred always clouded her reasoning as she made some bad judgements about taking hostages. Cahill always apologised for her afterwards.

"She just didn't!"

So Greta had been really pissed off when Rory refused to let her accompany them on the fatal mission of a day ago. He had given her his steadfast judgement.

"You are too volatile. This time, I need level heads around me during these sensitive dealings."

Earlier on, she had told her lover.

"I'd bet we would not be wondering if the Gaffer was still alive, if he had chosen me to guard his back."

"Without a doubt." Declared her convinced soul-mate.

An insightful Greta who knew he was no coward had also asked him.

"Why did you leave Naomh all alone?"

He could not answer her; the reason about going back and alerting the others seemed so lame now. All, he could say was.

"He wanted to go after whatever it was alone. Something in his voice caused me to obey. You know his instincts. He told me to follow the other two's trail. Still, it did not matter, I lost them as well."

"It's weird. You did not see anything strange." Enquired his partner.

"Except for that glowing oily slime, no."

Greta rubbed her sleeping partner's head, then went to the kitchen and emptied the remaining contents of Cahill's cup down the liquid recycling chute. A flash of light through the one way windows caught the corner of her eye. The visual disturbance was merely a flicker and it came from the direction of the roof of the neighbouring building. Dismissing it as a reflection of a flash of lightning, she returned to her chores saying to herself within the earshot of her partner.

"After all it is a nasty night out there."

Like him, she herself appeared glad to be inside in this cosy room. The female RE-INSTATOR turned on the cold water faucet as the dammed hot one was broken. She decided.

"The Lenses is not as clever as he thinks he is. He could have easily provided a better equipped safe house."

The shock of the freezing liquid over her hand occurred simultaneously with an icy feeling that ran down the length of her long spine. She returned her sight to the adjacent rooftop just as it exploded in a cauldron of unfamiliar colours. Unnerved with goose bumps tingling throughout her flawless skin, Greta urgently shouted for the sleeping man in the other room.

"Bonkers. Wake up. There are a lot of weird flashes coming from the rooftop next door."

He had already been on his feet, pistol in hand, reacting on instinct, the moment he had heard her shout. He cursed at his instant reaction and the one who had disturbed him.

"My enjoyable sleep is ruined by a silly woman scared by the extremities of the weather. Does she not know that sometimes weather patterns mixing with the ever-present blanket of cloud causes strange colours in the sky?"

For her ears, he explained.

"For God's sake Greta. It's only the thunder and lightning. We do get that sometimes. And I was just nodding off as well."

The blonde woman did not relent, her tone changed to one of command.

"Get out here this instant!"

By now, Cahill realised to whom he was talking to. This was certainly no flighty woman scared by strange lights. Furious at his words, the tall woman had stifled a bitter retort and instead, she explained patiently and stressed some words as if talking to a novice.

"You don't understand my love? What I saw were no flashes of lightning that I've ever seen. Nothing has colours like this. There's no sound or crash of thunder after each flash."

As the words of her cool assessment of the situation sunk in, apprehension replaced complacency in a moment of cold fear. Cahill grabbed his Flatpack that was always within reach and he crossed to the window that Greta was staring out of. As he took in the confused scene through the thin laminated glass, he let out a strangled gasp.

"What the hell. The Filth must have found us."

The spectacle of light intensified and the bursts of colour multiplied as the underside of the clouds reflected the growing light show. His confused frame of thinking implied that the countless flashes of brilliance were from some secret PREVENTIVE weapon that was patiently intent on destroying them. Then with a sickening feeling, suddenly he knew.

"Not us. Naomh!"

Concern for his friend overrode his anxiety. He made for the door, but not before throwing a hoodie over his face. Running from the apartment, down the flights of stairs, he had ignored the lift in a crazy dash of emotion. With the sound of his female companion's breath resounding directly behind him, Cahill was out into the bitter night breathing plumes of white vapour from the sudden intense exertion. Without hesitation, Greta who also masked her features had also snatched up her weapon, a stocky piece capable of a tremendous explosion of fire in a single pull of the trigger. The thought of his lover rushing with him into danger never cast him a second thought and it certainly did not slow him down. She could have her life snuffed out in an instant, but he would never order her back. If he did then Greta would despise him. Sighing in resignation, Cahill quickened his pace and he was heartened that his female companion did as well. The two-armed lovers, deeply concerned for their friend ran across the street to the opposite building from where the flashes originated. They found the main door locked, but it only temporarily denied them access. Greta barely halted; she took aim with her stocky weapon and blew most of the door with its electronic lock away in a single burst of automatic fire from her gun. They both entered the lobby through the shattered door. The hallway was empty. This building was an exact copy of the one that both of them had just come from, so neither of them had a problem with direction. Heading up the stairs, taking three steps at a time, the charging duo reached the top breathing heavily. Cahill glanced behind and noticed that Greta had faltered and had halted on the final flight of stairs. Crouching behind the only door to the roof, his gun butt caressing his face and tucked into his shoulder blade, he turned his attention to what was happening outside. His armed comrade had not stopped because she was scared or exhausted. No, female logic had taken over. From the second, the outlawed woman fighter had witnessed the out of the ordinary spectacle, an inconsistency nagged at her. As she was running, things were been worked out in her insightful mind and processed. Firstly, it was the nature of the beams.

"Is it some secret weapon?

As a committed member of the RE-INSTATOR'S Greta knew more than most about Anschluss weaponry and supposed.

"It is doubtful that the Filth have acquired some new soundless laser."

She had dismissed these assumptions instantly as she reasoned during the headlong dash.

"The direction of the tracer fire was wrong. Its trajectory was from the

rooftop to the heavens, not from the expected direction".

Casting aside her gun she made a supreme effort and a split second before Cahill opened the door, she tackled him. They both landed heavily on the concrete steps. Her unarmed lover rose first, his face twisted in rage at this attack from an unexpected quarter. However, his mask of fury turned into astonishment as he realised whom his assailant was.

"What the hell?" Came Cahill's strangled gasp through a bloodied lip.

Greta motioned for silence with a gesture of a finger on her own red lips. In a low whisper, she spoke.

"This isn't as straight forward as it seems my love. There are odd forces working here."

Cahill whispered back in a clenched voice.

"Of course it's not, Liben. Tyro is having a picnic out there and fancied some fireworks."

He was on the edge of ignitable hysteria and retrieved his weapon. He had also reverted to using codenames, due to the fact that they were masked and armed. Biting his lips in frustration and bringing tears to his eyes, he looked into his lover's calm blue eyes. His rage subsided slightly as he heard her say.

"No. Something's not right."

His retort exploded from his mouth.

Of course something's wrong; Tyro could be dying out there."

The fury returned, but his tantrum was halted by a sharp slap across the face from Greta. His hysteria ceased, not from the force of the blow, but from the shock of her action.

"Bonkers, get a grip on yourself. Think for a minute. When have you seen explosions like those? They are not been fired at the rooftop from above or below, but from the rooftop to the sky. And what kind of noise is that."

She was talking about a tremendous ear-shattering explosion that had just occurred.

Although he had been glued to the events that were unfolding the entire time on the roof, something suddenly dawned on him. That was the first real noise that either of them had heard. He had enough.

"I'm going out there, Liben."

She nodded, glad that he was still focused enough to use her code-name.

"Ok. I'll cover you. But do it carefully." Chastised Greta.

Bursting out to the roof with weapons targeting any movement, no matter how bizarre, the two RE-INSTATOR'S discovered suppressed darkness, silence and a distraught Naomh kneeling down in the wet roof. The one part Mescal/Amulet's calming of its host had only lasted briefly. The Hybrid had remembered again. All of its energy sapping work had been undone in an instant. The comrade who they were seeking glanced up with haunted eyes at the two's intrusion and the colour drained from his face when he recognised them. Their friend's eyes reflected the insanity that he had become the master of. Something in Cahill's and Greta's stunned looks rekindled a horrified remembrance in him and without any provocation; he burst through his astonished two friends, knocking them aside. He shouted something incomprehensible at them as he fled screaming down the stairs. The unrecognised words were.

"They know what I am?"

Both of the lovers gaped at each other in astonishment. There had been a menacing edge of genuine madness lurking in their fleeing friend. As he vanished from sight, a sombre Cahill thought he understood. He nearly choked on the words.

"The Gaffer didn't make it. He's dead!"

"How can you be sure?" Asked a disturbed Greta.

"Believe me, my love. I have known Tyro all my life. His uncle is dead. The shock has overwhelmed him."

Cahill stood transfixed, unsure what to do next. His girlfriend put her arm around him.

"Come my love. Let's get off this roof and out of this area, before the Filth arrive and investigate what the hell has happened here. We definitely don't want to be around for that."

The two confused suitors returned to another safe house in the next Contrib before the security forces swarmed all over the area. Both of the sweethearts were unaware that the a shadowy figure had seen Naomh's whole performance on the rooftop via his unmanned drones. The big man who had just finished viewing the "Incident." that had been relayed live into his office rubbed his hands in glee. He mouthed in his deep throated artificial voice.

"My my! That was highly interesting. I knew that there was something special about him. But I never figured that he was more unusual than his father. My devices could never perceive his image. And unlike his son that made him a dangerous and unknown quantity."

The supreme ruler of the Anschluss then pressed a button on a panel in front of him. A voice answered immediately.

"Yes. Mr Chairman."

He gave his personal secretary the location of the apartment block in the Prague Contrib; this man did not like loose ends.

"Get a special team of PREVENTIVES down there and sort out any witnesses. Make it something exceptional."

"As you command Mr Chairman." Answered the secretary and then was gone to carry out his orders. The communication link to the outer office was cut off. An hour and twenty minutes later, from his vantage point, he saw the massive explosion away to the North-East. The next afternoon when Cahill and Greta awoke after finally catching a little sleep

in another safe house, the news announcer on the video unit told the City-State.

"A mysterious explosion that has destroyed a city block in the Prague Contrib. Seventeen apartment buildings had collapsed and five thousand and fifty people had perished, men, women and children. Initial government reports are blaming the atrocity on the outlawed movement called; the RE-INSTATOR'S."

All of the crushed and blackened bodies were laid out in neat lines on covered stretchers and public opinion was outraged. Connected spokespeople came on to condemn the atrocity. A shocked Cahill realised.

"From the pictures, it appears that the centre of the explosion has originated from the exact building that we and Naomh had been on the night before."

In fact it had happened forty minutes after they had boarded the Mag-lev to the Parisian Contrib. They had no words; both of them just held each other and thanked faith for their lucky escape. Even their first choice of the adjacent safe house had been levelled with no survivors. At first, both of them wondered if Naomh something to do with the unfortunate events and the large loss of innocent life. But, then Greta added with hindsight.

"If he had not been on that roof with all that commotion, then we would have stayed in the safe house and died along with them."

"You are right, my love. It doesn't bear thinking about."

While still in the clasped embrace that Cahill had initiated, both verbally and reluctantly agreed to the obvious conclusion.

"It is foolish thinking about ifs. The Filth have used another secret weapon in an attempt to wipe us out. Naomh has saved us by forcing us to leave the apartment block.

As usual, their state controlling enemies had failed in their efforts to kill them. But on the other hand, it looked like the Filth had finally removed a thorn from their sides. Back in his private office, the instigator of the action was in fine mettle. As always, when the leader of the RE-INSTATOR'S was about, his instant transmitters had failed to work. So, he had been unaware of transpiring events during the fake arms deal until a recovered concealed video among the gruesome remains of an operative showed him the events. He had seen Rory go down, presumed dead. A few days later, he received confirmation from a reliable source that it was true. To his delight, Naomh's uncle Rory, alias the "Gaffer" was no more and the sadistic ruler had even played a cruel trick with his mind before he had met his end.

"Did you enjoy seeing her once more in the flesh?"

He answered for the dead man with a malicious laugh.

"I doubt it. Still, you must have enjoyed killing her again; I know that if our positions were reversed. I would have had."

The movement was now without its influential leader and lacking him, it was doubtful that it would survive. One very significant person of his staff who was on the inside understood.

"It will tear itself apart; with a little help from my meddling, of course."

Back in his office in the heart of the Geneva Contrib, the Chairman's glee was slightly tempered by the fact that Rory's body had vanished. With no corpse to put on display; it meant that he had no proof to give to the masses of the leading terrorist's demise. This man born to the World of political expediency knew from history.

"Rumours of a dead man not proved to be dead will always come back to haunt you. Just look at what Jesus did to the Roman State. He changed them completely as they were overtaken by a movement that they should have eradicated."

Then, he laughed out loud, the death of his antagonist had put him in a good mood.

"But then again, we are not ancient Roman's and Rory was certainly no heavenly saviour."

The Alien Watcher back in the past would have agreed with him.

XI.

THE BRUSSELS CONTRIB 2951AD.

Once again; he became the frantic observer of his own torment. Seeing himself in feverish distress, but helpless to intervene, the witness became even more agitated as the unstoppable events progressed. He squirmed as little creeks of perspiration filled all the hollows of his tepid skin. On another level, this dreamer knew.

"Sleep is a two edged sword, it can fulfil your wildest fantasies or in this case, my worst nightmares."

The dream was always hauntingly similar and the inevitably of it always sent goose bumps throughout his damp and feverish body. These physical sensations of anxiety were soon forgotten as on another plane, a veil of swirling supernatural mist parted once again and his reluctant spirit flew towards the inevitable drama. Perambulated colours of abrupt electric luminance flashed in a fluctuating sequence until a random choice was made. This time, the apparition settled for a vista of black and white.

"After all, what colour are ones dreams?"

The panorama below englobed a limited World; a stage and set just large enough to act out the oncoming events. It was a battle of a war, a minor skirmish, somewhere in the lines of the past. The reluctant voyeur wondered.

"Am I personally taking part in these unveiled events or is it a whisper of another person's remembered memories that I am sharing?"

In this limbo World, the mist parted and the dreamer always found himself in the rear-guard of an attacking force that was advancing covertly between the countless trunks of a natural tree cover. It appeared to be an unbroken forest of the Northern Hemisphere, boasting many an ancient tree, many of which flaunted life spans in thousands of years. The knobbly wood was splendid in a bounty of Oaks, Elms and Larch's that were intermixed with the occasional slender evergreen. So vivid were the mental images that he could smell the sweet mustiness of the forest floor, hear the soft crackling of half-rotten timber and the crunch of decayed leaves as his alter ego stepped on the litter of the canopy above. Each footfall and every sound seemed to be amplified. He paused at a very fine specimen of a Douglas fir, took a strong breath and got the heady smell of its decaying pine needles. The strong fragrance from the enormous tree got deep into his sinuous and the producer of the vision wondered abstractly.

"It's amazing that I can experience sound and smell."

How the dreamer knew the classifications of these trees never seemed strange to him. He had spent many an hour in the manmade parks of the Anschluss and never bothered to learn their names. To him they were just big trees that offered shade or shelter from the elements. To his mostly urban and nature controlled society, the expanse of tightly clustered trees was a natural figment from the past. Oh, he had heard of these dense woodlands, but he had never actually been in one. Even though, he had never had the pleasure of been in the factory forests of the north, he knew that those plantations were not the same. His only experience outside the concrete jungle of his usual habitat were the manicured Contrib parks with their pitiful remembrance of the ancient forests and the mono-cultured plantations that produced foodstuffs for the masses. The almost gothic arch formed from the trees entwining branches revealed a gloomy lit living corridor that was his path ahead. The nearly complete darkness was broken only by pencil thin; sharp piercing shafts of dusty light that penetrated through the canopy from above at irregular angles. These rays of unknown origin made it through to strike the moist laden carpet of decaying leaves that shrouded the forest floor. Insects of various shapes and sizes which had made their home under the dying soup of discarded foliage fled in a mad directionless scramble as the trampling feet of the Humans destroyed the protective hemisphere of the only World they had known. The engaged men gave no thought to the fleeing invertebrates and the destruction of their habitat. Still, if one of them died here, the scavenging beetles and their like would have their revenge and feast on the forgotten body. Above and foolishly aloof from all of this were the ancient forests mainstay. These encrusted trees that towered over last year's foliage were showing new buds that hinted a shoot of virgin green. The infant leaves eventual fate, becoming brown and brittle lay below them on the forest floor. He saw a parasitic vine that had been ignored by a giant of a tree; the copper beech was now a dead shadow of itself. The vine had sucked out its insides and now used it for support. When it was finally of no use, it would move on and find another host.

"Just like those that we left into our country. That's what they will do to us if we stand by and let them."

He rested briefly against a scaly bark and felt the spongy leaves rub against his forehead. Then he moved on. As the party reached the line of the ancient timberland, he now remembered his name. It was Naomh not Tyro, but this realisation did not make things easier. He knew what was to come. Circumventing through the forest had not been a pleasant experience. Even in the dense city blocks of his actual existence, there was a certain amount of clearway ahead; here there had been only a few metres of a twisting trail. This enhanced the confining and claustrophobic nature of his imaginary circumstances. Finally, he stumbled clear of the woodland, down a black earthen bank that marked its boundary. Protruding roots gave the appearance of half rotten bones and he cursed.

"Not a pleasant comparison."

Images in front of him shifted, but the ominous brooding horizon always remained static. Free at last from the view blocking foliage, he raised a sighting device to his eyes to scan ahead. This time it was a lightweight pair of infra-red laser optics. In other dreams or memories, it had been a bulky brass telescope, or even his own two green eyes. In one rare scenario, it had been a pair of green and brown binoculars. There was always a fortification to be assaulted on the edges of his vision. This time it was a reinforced concrete bunker. Other times it was a medieval castle or sometimes a wooden palisade. All the defences and military paraphernalia of history echoed simultaneously as the visions blended together in dream after dream. The lonely trek through the forest ended as his loyal comrades packed against him. It felt strange that he did not recognise any of them, but every one of them seemed eerily familiar. In numerous repetitions, he raised the optical devices/his hand above his eyes to his artificially blackened face and focussed in on the object of his scrutiny. His attention was on a lone concrete bunker/a stone castle/ a timber palisade. Each alternating fortification had a flag of the invading enemy fluttering in the strong breeze, the flying pendants were a sure sign of their arrogance. The bunker had the look of sheer white granite, the castle of cool grey limestone and the palisade of dry tarred black. All of the fluctuating fortifications stood solid and unforgiving in the centre of the fragile moisture soaked environment in where his dreams or remembrance randomly cast him. The wind picked up and pelted his group as they left the protection of the tree mass. Through the deteriorating visibility, he adjusted the oil based lens of the laser sights/twiddled with the screws of the telescope/squinted with his eyes and made out a scattered line of faded dark shapes in the distance who were crawling up the fortification's hillside. The covert group were out of sight from its defenders and converging relentlessly towards the targets. Those advancing men were his compatriots and among them was one that he cared deeply for. The climbing men were now close enough for an attack, having got into position unobserved. Naomh lowered his optical assistance and sighted his automatic rifle/flintlock musket/clutched his heavy sword and prepared himself for imminent violence. He clung to the familiar and comforting feeling of the icy cold metal of his Henrick-Gruber 2020 laser sighted rifle/the timber stock of the musket, both were pressed against the hollow of his right shoulder blade and pressed against his cheek. While the cloth wrapped around the hilt of his sword touched his face for no apparent reason than just to mimic the other two scenarios. After all, the dreams had to have a main thread of consistency; why he did not know. But a controlling presence in the background had the answers and would not divulge them. A veteran of many missions like this, Naomh was forever fearful for a person in the vanguard of the attackers. This fretted over individual was always a close relative, a father, a brother or an uncle. A prevailing sixth sense or because he knew the outcome of the recurring dreams told him that something terrible was occurring. A nagging feeling

241

of doubt mixed with overwhelming fear caused the adrenaline to pound like drumbeats of apprehension throughout his distressed body. The scene would shift in a queasy blur and then all of a sudden, he would be alone. All of his comrades that had emerged at the border of the woods with him had vanished. Then another expected blur would occur and in the temporal shift, at least one of his true companions materialised in the vision. Somehow, it was always his favoured and loyal friend; Cahill. Suddenly his confidant would appear alongside him in a dug out, how they got from the tree line to here, he never knew. He would study the well-known features, the neatly trimmed red hair, his fierce blue eyes and the bland nose. He would nod in acceptance, glad to have his slightly taller companion alongside him. This scrutiny of his friend always gave the dream a familiar substance and an altogether brief moment of comfort. Then, seconds after the precise moment of Cahill's appearance, his fear for his relative would increase and this new urgency made him shout in an echo of another reality.

"Quickly! Call them back, something does not feel right. Our comrades are been set up."

The receiver of those urgent words, who had often been saved by Naomh's gut feelings never hesitated. He shouted into his microphone/sounded his trumpet/ waved his flags to signal the retreat. Naomh would always roar helplessly.

"Too late."

Suddenly, the overcast sky would light up as bright as a sunlit day. Then the battle would begin in earnest. Chaos reigned, mayhem triumphed as demented sounds and flashes lit up the background. Naomh turned to Cahill and uttered the same words time and time again.

"Come, they need our help."

The two soldiers would leave the dugout and charge up the slope of the hill through puddles of stagnant rainwater. Then as the incline of the hill increased, they advanced up through the less watery spongy bog land. All fear of the unknown was disappearing as they entered the familiar sights and sounds of the battlefield. On and upwards, the running men stumbled until the two of them miraculously reached the perimeter of the bunker complex/the castle/the palisade unscathed. Immediately after crossing the enemies' perimeter into the manufactured hell, Naomh always felt a minute tingle of a beam/ tripwire. He would ask his companion as they dodged tracer rounds/musket balls/barbed shafted arrows.

"Did you feel that?"

Then, the two men would throw themselves into a recently formed crater/natural hollow, just as a fragment round/cannonball/Greek fire landed in front of them. Experience always told them that a projectile rarely landed in the same place twice.

"Feel what."

Cahill always responded after landing in the hole. As the flying dirt of the explosion showered superheated metal fragments that hissed as they quenched in the damp conditions, he would answer.

"I felt it as we crossed over their lines. Our foes have installed a new warning system and they have been alerted to the attack. Our comrades are under heavy fire, they must retreat. They will be wiped out to a man."

The enemy in the dreams always seemed to have an extra trick up their sleeves and had the upper hand every time. Then Cahill would rise up and with lightning speed, shoot off a rapid burst of gunfire/ musket balls/ a flight of arrows into the acrid mist caused by the battle. Then reacting with the same quickness, he always dropped back into the hole as numerous missiles of varying degrees whizzed by, just where his head had been an instant before. With laboured breath, Naomh's comrade would mutter.

"Great. That's all we need. We must get up there and warn them. Let's go."

The two men would rise from the shell hole/natural hollow and charge into the haze and get separated in the low visibility. Naomh always tried in vain to find his companion as the air in front of him ignited with sporadic flashes of painful light. Suddenly, he would find himself thrown in the air; flapping helplessly. In each vision, he landed heavily and tumbled down the muddy hill until he came to a stop at the bottom. He'd find himself unaware of transpiring events and convince himself that he was lying face down in a pool of murky water purely as the consequence of a drunken stupor. Wondering abstractly, if he was the owner of the blood that stained the surface of the puddle, he would look up in to the smoke filled landscape. Still concussed from the jarring blow he received, Naomh would wipe the sordid water into his eyes and when confronted with the unreal landscape, he always became certain that he had perished and crossed the threshold to the next World. His retreating comrades constantly appeared as mist shrouded spectres. Evil shadows that danced at the limits of his vision floated by and then clutching hands would begin to drag him away to reap the consequences of a violent life and failure to save his kin. Completely bereft of his hearing as a result of the detonation and heavy fall, he did not hear the familiar voices of his comrades as they hauled him away to safety. His temporary loss of sound was a blessing in disguise, for if he could still hear the shrill wailing and whining of incoming fire, he might have associated it with the pleading of lost and tormented souls. Misguided as he was, Naomh was certain that death himself was dragging him away. He passed out; he always gave himself up to unconscious with a long sigh. It was another brief moment of comfort.

Then the scene shifted again and he found himself awake and struggling frantically with fear until he grasped reality. His sight cleared and he found himself looking into the disturbed eyes of Cahill. The two of them were the only one's about, they were both frozen in a moment of dream time. He always knew that some length of time had passed since he had went flying through the air, because he found himself way behind their lines and far from the short lived and disastrous skirmish. There was nothing but stony silence. Holding on to the realisation that he had been brought to safety, he focused on his friend and the effort hurt his head. Expecting to see Cahill's smiling face etched in relief and then been scolded at how he was always saving his worthless hide. Instead, he found himself looking into a face that was twisted in horror and revulsion. It was a frightening stare that said.

"I've just bore testimony to my worst nightmare and more besides."

Startled, both in and out of his dream, because Naomh knew Cahill had witnessed some of the worst atrocities of man's inhumanity towards his own species. In the repeated visions, both of them had seen stoning's; burning's, impalements and crucifixions, all the time remaining unfazed. But now, in this frozen moment, he had never before seen such a distorted look on another person's features. Fear, anger and silent brooding were present, as what was normal when a comrade had succumbed in battle. Naomh always wore a speechless expression wrapped in trepidation, fearful at what he was about to hear. The other always stood immobile as granite, frozen in shock with an edge of madness lurking behind his staring eyes. Those fixed pupils betrayed an internal battle, which if lost would release the small grip he was reputed to have on reality during engagements like today's. Feeling Cahill's reluctance to talk and still slightly dazed from his recent ordeal, Naomh would demand.

"For pity sake. Are you all right? What happened to you?"

Countless possibilities of fatal occurrences played havoc within his mind and then he knew what was troubling his friend. Naomh would lower his voice to a barely audible level as if he feared to be heard or understood. He choked out the next words.

"It's; it's."

He faltered. With slow dread his speech stumbled. Then finding a great resolve, he would finally ask.

"My father/ my brother/ my uncle. Where is he?"

The others eyes glinted dangerously, but he always held his silence. Because of the inseparable bond he shared with Cahill, he knew his friend was holding something back and his anger always flared at his companion's reaction and reluctance to part with that information. Once again, he would demand.

"Where is he?"

Each time, the question was asked in a very slow and deliberate manner, defying the mute man to refuse him an answer. The reaction from his best friend always made him jump back as if a snake had bitten him. Even though, he invariably heard the same reply from his comrade, it regularly and completely unbalanced him every time. He could not believe it. Cahill would be actually shaking, but he would utter no words to explain the state he was in. Bewilderment constantly gave way to astonishment and Naomh would mumble.

"Ok. Have it your way. Take me to him.

At last a sign of life echoed from the other. He would return a look that spoke volumes. Naomh might have as well have asked him to go over to the enemy's side and embrace their general like a long lost friend. Then, his comrade would speak. Bitterness emblazoned on his features, as if his whole life had been suddenly betrayed, Cahill always rasped.

"Naomh. You and your father/brother/uncle, what in God's holy name are you?"

Every occasion those words faded, the owner of the visions would be confronted with an automatic rifle/ musket/ bow and arrow pointed menacingly at him. Shocked betrayal was repeatedly Naomh's only reaction. Again Cahill would repeat the question, his voice growing steadier as he regularly realised he had the upper hand on his friend.

"I said. What are you?"

Now it would be Naomh's turn to be astounded and his visage became a mask of reflecting pain that moments ago contorted the others face. Cahill receiving no reply, released the safety catch of the rifle/ uncocked the musket/ tightened the string on the bow. Naomh just gaped. How could his lifelong friend turn his weapon on him?

"What the hell is going on inside his head?"

Unknown to the two hostile men, a family of foxes lay frozen in cataplexy under a bush that still miraculously retained its green foliage, unique on this ghostly landscape. It was as if it had been an added prop. The thicket was only a metre from them. The two Humans had unwittingly cut off their only means of escape. Trapped by the nearness of hated people, the animals stayed nervously put in their hideout. But the beasts combined nerve constantly failed and they always bolted from their haven after a yell from Naomh.

"Cahill why are you pointing that weapon at me? What in God's name is going on? Answer me, Goddam you."

The family of brown canines forever ran directly into the men's path. Scared witless, the small pack of brown furry shapes crashed into the hapless Humans. As the two men crashed to the ground, Naomh would seize the initiative and leap on top of his sprawled ex-comrade. But the others quickness enabled him to roll away and twist himself into a standing position far faster than his rival. Using the rifle/ musket/ bow and arrow like a club, Cahill repeatedly advanced on the still sprawled Naomh, fully intent on hammering him into the muddy ground. Lying spread-eagled in the dirt, the focus of his furious attention fingered the hilt of a concealed dagger. An expert with the blade, he could finish off the enraged Cahill with a flick of his wrist. But he was unable to do this to his lifelong companion.

"I cannot kill him."

Smiling grimly, he rose partially to his knees, still gripping the concealed dagger and by the look on his advancing opponent; he guessed that his life was in immediate danger.

"I know how to stop this without killing him, but it is going to have to be the best throw of my life."

The career warrior never hesitated and flung the heavy blade towards his friends exposed forehead. The flying blade somersaulted while moving through the air and the blunt hilt smashed into Cahill's temple, instead of the razor sharp point. The struck man collapsed heavily into an unconscious heap. Every time this occurred in each vision, Naomh would utter out aloud.

"Bloody marvellous."

Taking no more chances, the knife thrower constantly recovered the fallen weapon and would cautiously approach the slumped figure of his friend.

"After all if I had the proverbial trick up my sleeve. He'd have one too."

The scuffle had invariably opened a shallow wound on Naomh's face. As blood dripped down his chilled cheeks; he would search for a dressing. Locating one, he pressed it against the wound. Regaining conscious with blurred vision, Cahill was not helped by the intermingling of the coppery taste from the blood that trickled down his own face from the dent of the thrown knife. Frustration on realising the tables had been overturned caused a frigid sweat to glisten on his pale skin and the cold reality of a rifle/musket/arrow pressed against his head did little to ease his discomfort. As he raised his throbbing head to behold the stern presence of Naomh, his companion's frosty expression did not offer any salvation either. His friend had a standard military bandage pressed against his forehead, while keeping his weapon trained on him. Blood dripped freely from underneath the edges of the absorbent pad and flowed as tiny tributaries over the contours of his face. The life supporting fluids were eventually lost to the dried corners of his mouth or dropped forever to supplement extra content to the ever-changing texture of the ground. Naomh was certain that a grin that broadened on Cahill's features was a rash gesture caused by the gravity of his situation. The man with the upper hand would lower the red stained bandage and aim a questioning look at him to explain this sudden mirth. Every time in every vision, Cahill would exhale a joyful laugh and proclaim.

"Thank God. You're bleeding. You can be hurt."

A disbelieving look of anguish always passed from Naomh's countenance at his friend's rash statement and his expression regularly turned to anger at this final insult from his captive. His finger invariably

246

tightened on the trigger/string. The man under the shadow of his weapon had threatened, attacked and was now taking the piss out of him. It was too much to bear. Red mist parted and something that explained Cahill's abnormal behaviour flashed into perspective.

"Of course, the suspected traitor."

The alarm bell rang.

"All of our recent operations have been complete failures. People whisper to each other that there must be a turncoat. All efforts to find the traitor have failed. It is logical that Cahill has revealed himself to be the one; by his actions towards me. Who would have suspected him? The guilt of so many betrayed deaths must have finally unhinged his mind."

Naomh full of resolve knew this menacing animal must be put down. But the dreamer's watching self knew that this could not be true. He screamed a futile warning across the dream barrier. But, he was not allowed to interfere. As the fantasy continued, the author of the visions always saw Cahill cry out in synchronization with his own yell.

"For God's sake Naomh. You have nothing more to fear from me. Listen I will take you to your father/brother/uncle. Then you will understand."

Naomh never failed to motion for him to rise, continually relieved at delaying the termination of life long companion. Cahill would rise and start to speak.

"Naomh; I----;"

But he was cut off abruptly every time.

"Save it till we reach my father/brother/uncle."

He would make the others suggestion, his own idea.

"But you don't understand. He is not what you think."

His voice sounded like ice.

"I've seen death and injuries before."

"Not like this."

This last voice trailed off as other figures emerged wraith like from the surrounding mist. A new scene began to be acted out in the dreamscape. A new cast appeared. Naomh regularly and instantly recognised the converging group as comrades in arms. He always became relieved that he would soon be alleviated from carrying out the execution of his prisoner, friend and now traitor. Then he would thrust the rifle/musket/arrow into the small of Cahill's back and after taking an indrawn breath of relief, he always spoke sharply.

"Move towards the rest."

Although his former friends words that he was no longer hostile played seductively in his mind, he kept the weapon pointed at his prisoner. As a result of the growing weariness from recent events, coupled with ever increasing heaviness of the rifle/musket/bow and arrow, he would still refuse to give into that temptation to ease his fatigue. Those watching from the circle that had been formed around the two should have seen a strange sight. One of their comrades was holding the other captive. The prisoner standing proud and erect, the captor bent and ragged. But none of the converging men at arms were surprised by this event, because of what they knew. From the shadows of another level, Naomh screamed a warning to his dream self. But again, the cry was ignored as angry and fearful curses flowed on the wind.

FROM THE EDGES OF THE DREAM, NAOMH AGAIN TRIED TO WARN HIMSELF, WHAT HE WAS WALKING INTO.

His dream self knew he had some explaining to do, under such circumstances. So he was not unduly concerned when all the groups' weapons were pointed in his direction. But what really confused him were all the hardened looks of hatred, the same expressions that had lined Cahill's face earlier on. Each despised stare was directed at him, not his prisoner.

"He does not know." His captive would say simply.

The main participant of the dream always misunderstood his friend's words. He would try to cut off the speaker as he clubbed him to the ground and put his weapon to the head of the sprawled form. Naomh was forever losing control of the situation and shaking visibly, he constantly stammered.

"You got it wrong, he is the traitor. Not me."

He would then nudge the kneeling man as if to emphasise this. Another bout of profanities regularly followed and one beardless youth that had always hero-worshipped Naomh would shout.

"He is a companion of Satan. Kill him."

Guns would be armed, muskets would be cocked and bow strings would be made taut.

Each time the words uttered by the youth struck him with the force of a blow. He always flinched as more curses along similar lines followed. Consumed with conflicting emotions and now disoriented, he would question some of them in their new found belief in religion. Disbelief gave him renewed vigour, passion eclipsed fear. Naomh always screamed violently at the mob, for he knew that their purpose was to judge him and by the grim expressions on the grimy faces, they had already delivered a guilty verdict. In growing desperation, he continually demanded.

"For the last time where the hell is my father/brother/uncle?"

The mob would be held at bay by the request and a hushed silence always struck them dumb. Some would cross themselves; others always spat in his direction. It was too much, Naomh gaped every time, too stunned to move or reply. In each dream/vision Cahill constantly took full advantage of this and with a swipe of his arm, he would disarm the devastated and unmoving statue of a man. The mob always roared in triumph and pressed eagerly forward and feeling very brave, now that he had lost his teeth. Naomh would go down under the onslaught as he was pummelled with fists, boots and rifle butts or were they spear's that inflicted the hurt on him. As the doomed man raced towards oblivion, he heard every time.

"Finish him off. Put a bullet/ball/shaft in him."

"Why? It done nothing to the father/brother/uncle. He just laughed at us."

"Burn him." Said another.

"No! Drown him. That's what is done to witches and they're familiars."

In another reality, he would scream for the scene to shift, but the assault continued unabated. Finally as he went hoarse from his pleading, the unwanted images shifted and he was back in the forest again, where the Human shadows warped into trees. Before, he could breathe a sigh of relief, towering plants that were devoid of leaves, just skeletal limbs began reaching for him. He screamed at their foul touch. Another blur and men returned to torment him. His watching self-cried out in final anguish at the treatment of the mob, for he had now recognised many of his attackers. The crowd parted and his dying, broken and bloodied body lay spread eagled in futile protest of what had happened to him. His dead form always had a red jewel splayed across his chest. He had no idea how it got there. The presence of the object always caused the sleeper to be shocked out of the dream time, knowing that if he perished in the vision, he would not wake from it. When he awoke, he still found himself grieving at the betrayal. Every revelation ended the same and he knew them to be a portent of impending events. Finally, the visions began to make sense. These dream tears of warning were obliviously an inbuilt caution, not to reveal to anybody what was happening to him in real life.

THE DREAM WAS A PROPHECY OF SIMILAR EVENTS, WHICH WILL OCCUR IF HIS DREADED SECRET GOT OUT, FOR HIS IMAGINARY KILLERS HAD THE FACES OF HIS FRIENDS AND COMPANIONS.

Naomh had a prophetic sense that if his own death occurred, he would witness the slow decaying process of his rotting body left on the moor. First, he would see, the larger mammals tear him apart, then the scavenging birds and finally the bugs. His spirit would not leave that place and he would experience every excruciating attack on his body. Then, he had the chilling premonition.

"What if they buried me? From my vantage point, I would be a living cadaver. Then it would be a slow decay of years. I would be aware of the suffocating darkness, the helplessness as the hair of my dead body still grew. My fingernails and toenails would continue growing. Then the slow decay of flesh as parasites attacked from the inside and invertebrates worked from the outside."

If he had been asleep, he would have awoken with a scream as the skin peeled away to reveal his flesh beneath. Over the next few weeks, the nightmares continued and each progressive one started to become confused and nonsensical. In one specific episode, there was an imaginary event where his friend "Tim the hat man." appeared outrageously dressed in a time period that was not compatible with his attire. Tim walked the streets of the twentieth second century Oslo Contrib dressed as a fifteenth century courtier of the Parisian court accompanied by another close friend called Goulash. The fat man from the Budapest Contrib had inexplicably become a brightly coloured Jester who ridiculed their outlawed group's attempts at overthrowing the establishment. Like these two surreal popinjays, his other comrades also appeared as other bizarre characters in equally strange circumstances. Always lurking in the background of his twisted dreams, there were flapping noises. Again, he was puzzled; at how could he remember sounds in his dreams, so vividly. But, he soon identified the troubling noises that passed so clearly into his waking moments.

"Wings!"

Somehow, the dreamer knew that those whirring vibrations were not a natural sound of his World. Finally, the shock of revelation gradually eased away as the Amulet worked its magic. The presence within slowly took his fears away. It made recent events seem normal, but a few nagging doubts remained as less and fewer flashbacks dogged his waking memories. The one piece Mescal/Amulet had done its work and the enormity of recent events found a rightful place within Naomh's physique and he grudgingly accepted his legacy. It was time for a fresh start and a different approach to overthrowing the Anschluss. The red jewel, an inheritance from his dead father would give him the means to do just that.

XII.

It was a fairly humble sized apartment and its current shabby state spoke volumes about the general tidiness of the owner. It also told that this individual lived alone. Still, too many of the lower class citizens of the state; namely, the Plebs, this assigned living quarters would be spacious enough to raise a large family. So it had more than ample room for a single bachelor of twenty-eight years. Naomh and his companions knew the holder of the apartment by the pseudonym, the "Clerk". In fact, the owner's real name was Victor de Mere and he was presently at work in the Logistic Department of Transport or LDT. (This arm of civic administration was just concerned with the running of the Mag-lev, the local shuttle networks and the Stand Ons.) It had been fairly easy enough to assign him a code name. Although, de Mere had despised being called a Clerk, this new slant on its meaning made him revel in it.

Now, he was proud of the name.

He was smaller than either Naomh or Cahill, at 179 cm. Even Greta had the advantage of a centimetre over him, but he had an even fairer shade of hair than hers. This made his green pupils shine like two refracted emeralds. His blonde flared eyebrows went well with his love of drama. The Clerk's living space was one of those condominiums usually given to the Clerical class, a constant employed citizen that dominated the Brussels Contrib. People assigned to this social scale were more than one step above the normal Plebs on the advancement ladder and you would assume that they were contented with their lot in life. De Mere had become disillusioned with his place in the Anschluss machinery as he had been constantly passed over for promotion or never offered a new and exciting challenge. He would complain to anyone who would listen to him about his escape from bureaucratic drudgery with a sense of finality.

"Fat chance of that?"

His constant brooding about the state of his circumstances was the main architect of his woes and in time, his growing boredom turned to hatred. Rory with his gift of finding disgruntled individuals approached him and found a kindred soul. Initially, he had joined the RE-INSTATOR'S mainly for mischief and excitement. But, after hanging out with them, he began to realise how drab and mundane his existence had been before and he began to extol the Gaffers vision. In time, the Clerk realised.

"I have not been living life. I was just plodding through it; time was pilfering away my dreams. I would have gone to the recycling plants without a whimper against being nothing more than an organic part in an endless system of accountability. My new friends have more vigour, excitement and most importantly, a goal."

The orphan from the Brussels Contrib began to believe in their aspirations and eventually, he reasoned.

"Even if I am killed, then so what? My six years in this outlawed organisation more than makes up for a prospect of spending my life in my former tedious existence."

The Clerk's single occupied abode was located just on the outskirts of the bureaucratic Contrib of Brussels. This vast hub were the living and working place for all those involved in the everyday administration of the Anschluss. His apartment was lost among the myriad of newly constructed and drab looking blocks of functional housing that had mushroomed up all over this sector in the last few decades and where non-descript architecture was the norm. Each building was constructed of modular cells that were pre-fabricated in the manufacturing zones and transported to the site for erection. On arrival, each self-contained unit was slotted into place like some giant hollow brick. All across the Anschluss, tower cranes worked tirelessly as a testament to this new form of convenient construction. Old and dilapidated buildings were coming down in droves. Even in this modern urban sprawl of a billion or more habitats, some forgotten structures that had not been preserved deliberately were still over a thousand years old. They had been given countless make over's during their many reincarnations. Some that were far older than that and not judged threatening to the establishment were given the same treatment. The Clerk's apartment lay on the fifteenth storey of a typical floor plan, where one could only tell the outside of an individual's apartment from the number on the entrance. All the doors were painted in the universal chosen colour scheme; Drab grey. This dour colour was repeated on the outside facades of the buildings and it fitted in unequivocally with the demeanour of most of the block occupants. Only within the cramped living spaces of each apartment were the residents allowed to express an individual identity with their own chosen decor. Inside number fifteen hundred and twenty-eight on the fifteenth floor; the contrast between the outside and the inside could not have been more pronounced. The gloomy grey of the corridor was banished into forgotten distaste when a visitor was invited over the threshold. (This was a rare occurrence indeed.) Then, the unwelcome guest entered another dimension and immediately longed to retreat to the normal confines of the corridor. It was as if the occupant of this flat was resisting the orderly drudgery of his everyday existence and this was where he was making his last stand against conformity. Bright garish paints pepper dashed the plastered walls of the apartment. There was no accepted form of decor; it was random, haphazard and totally unfinished. Where one deranged colour scheme ended and where another began was only the owner's guess. The ceiling reflected the apparent madness of the walls and shined with a brightness that really hurt the eyes; if one stared at it for any length of time. Electric wires lay on the floor like rubber parodies of vipers huddled together in hibernation, unmoving until stirred into action. Only the Elite of the Anschluss had access to wireless technology, mainly because of the cost and installation, but mostly because of security issues. Some of the metal alloys required for wireless communication were scarce enough for the needs of a population of eight billion souls. The vast majority of these rare elements were invested in the public mobile information units. Besides most of the RE-INSTATOR'S falsely believed that by using wired electrical outputs, they avoided been detected by the security forces and their no wires technology. Surprising, the clutter of unwashed cutlery and stained drinking vessels with their unfinished contents that lay piled in the sink and on the tables screamed out in protest at the blatant contrast with the functioning mind needed for this person's occupation. Away from the kitchen area, this heedless disregard was reinforced with the mountains of reading and entertainment chips that tethered precariously, always millimetres from the brink of collapsing into a flattened heap. When the piles inevitably buckled and fell over, you could be sure that they would not be tidied up. In the centre of this dishevelled living space, an unshaven body lay on a rumpled settee lost in a fatigued misery. The couch as far as the non-elite knew was the latest air vacuumed model, designed to fit every contour of the sitter's or in this case, the sleeper's body shape. The person lying on it still wore their flat body armour and heavy-duty combat boots, thus confusing the moulding programme of the chair and giving it an untidy appearance which funnily enough co-existed happily with the distorted décor of the place. Discarded liquor bottles still lying at the foot of couch only added to the general clutter. The Pleb who had consumed this cocktail of oblivion to excess was not the allocated tenant of the apartment and he was still on his drinking binge.

That person was Naomh!

This was where the tormented soul had fled to after storming passed Cahill and Greta on the building that was no more. Last night had been akin to the previous two that he had already spent here. Fortified with liquor, he had tossed and turned in a fitful sleep the entire night and had the same bewildering dreams. His internal struggle was unlikely to be helped by the general untidiness of the apartment; it was as if his physical being tried to discard the unwanted memories of the previous few days and revelled in tormented dreams. In these troubled visions, Naomh had replayed the confrontation with his parent and the fact that his suicide attempt had failed, over and over again. Somewhere during the internal replays, the dreams twisted and had become downright peculiar. He had wept, then laughed and cried again. In the mist of these clashing emotions, he had no recollection of the passing of time as the two conflicting attitudes competed against each other for ascendancy. As he fought the many sentiments that vied for dominance, a semblance of normality returned. Naomh had descended to the nadir of hopelessness and now the only way to go was up. At last as the dawn of the forth new day neared, he finally began to drift off into an aspect of comfortable sleep. So he was really pissed when Cahill awakened him with a gentle grip on his broad shoulders. For once his training had let him down; he had never heard his friend enter the apartment. Focusing his half-open tired red rimmed eyes; he gradually became aware of his surroundings. Lost in that confusing transition from deep sleep to gradual conscious, the awakened sleeper suddenly sat up with an abruptness as if a bucket of ice cold water had shook him out of his pleasant slumber. He remembered the recent past, all of it.

"No. It had not been a nightmare. Those events had really happened. But now I can accept them."

He stretched his arms and his breath reflected off his hands; the stench staggered him, he nearly gagged. As if to add credence to his tear induced sleep, his face was stiff with the lines of dried mucous; his throat was incredibly dry and his voice sounded hoarse. Feeling the state he was in, the awakened man longed to return to oblivion. But he knew with a gut feeling that any rest would be denied him this day. He heard Cahill's words.

"Shit Naomh, there is some stink in here and it is not the normal stench of the place. Did you even put on the air extractors?"

His friend sought out the control panel on the far wall and reset the air conditioning program with a voice command. Swallowing a mouthful of stale air that spoke volumes of another's living quarters, not believing that he was the cause of the lingering odours and still vexed at been woken, Naomh demanded sharply from his unwanted visitor.

"What is it Cahill? Did Victor tell you where I was?" Thinking that his disturber's presence had better be for a good reason. Cahill did not reply to his friend's question at first. The other man went over to a portable video unit whose battery had gone low and the device was crying out for recharging like a hungry cat mewing for food. He had also noticed that there was no music or video devices on. It made the room feel cold and sterile. Satisfied with his adjustments, he noticed something about his out of sort's friend.

"Shit, why are you still in your combat gear?"

Naomh guessed that he must have put them on during a drunken binge. As he remembered the strange tormenting visions, he silently reassessed his reasoning.

"The dreams, that's why I am like this?"

Not answering the question, he retorted with one of his own.

"What did you come for? Could you not let me alone for a few more days?"

"Never mind the fact that we were worried and considering that you have deactivated your Frog Eyes for the last few days and not received any transmissions, it was only natural that I tried to find you." Was his

254

concerned reply.

"Well you found me." Said his less than thankful friend.

"I'll cut straight to the chase then. We have a major problem Naomh."

The other man in the room rubbed his half-closed sleep filled eyes and riposted sarcastically remembering what he had endured in the last few days thinking that it was him alone that had the mother of all troubles.

"You're not serious, are you?"

Cahill cleared his throat nervously. He still did not fully understand why his lifelong friend had fled the other night and why he had looked at him and Greta as if they were two rumoured mutants before he ran away screaming into the relative darkness of the urban night. For the last few days, he replayed the encounter on the roof over with the tall blonde woman again and again not really finding a conclusive answer. The Gaffer had also vanished, but that was not unusual for him.

"It must be the disappearance of his uncle that has caused Naomh's weird behaviour."

Ignoring the other's vicious temper and foul mood, he informed him of the bad news.

"Things have moved on since yourself and the Gaffers absence. Every Cell commander has been ordered to attend a provisional council. It looks like somebody is making a bid for the leadership."

Naomh's green eyes glassed over. He hesitated and then spoke slowly and unmistakably.

"The Gaffer is dead."

Cahill's stunned look was as equally vacant. Somehow, he found the words through emerging tears.

"He is dead? How can you be sure?"

"I was with him at the end, just before he died in agony."

Hearing those words from his own throat nearly bowled him over. A sinking feel of absolute despair threatened to revive the tears. His consoling friend became adamant.

"Then we must retrieve his body. We will get on to our man in the body recycling plant. He will know when the Gaffer passes through."

Cahill for one hated dealing with their slimly contact who worked in that soulless place. No sooner were the words out, he realised.

"They will put his corpse on show first. A public display for the masses."

"That will not happen." Replied Naomh, knowing that his remains would never be found.

"Why, that's what they do. Don't you remember the Madrid cell leader and he was nowhere near as important?"

He lied convincingly.

"There is no body. The Filth used a chemical weapon that dissolved it. That was the glowing slime we saw."

255

"Those bastards. Is there is no end to their atrocities?"

During the following brooding silence, Naomh now realised that with the demise of his father/uncle.

"I am now the new head of our cell. No, not just that, but the whole movement. The Gaffer had always made it clear that I was the next in the line of succession."

(Unknown to anybody though, Rory always believed that he was perpetual and would never be replaced.) To all of the others, the Gaffer seemed eternal and indestructible; his presence was the mortar that held them together. But, now the impossible had happened. More tears betrayed Naomh as they flowed unabashed down his cheek. He was not the same man since the revelation and said with grief-induced insight.

"I can't do this Cahill. I need time to get over this. The last thing we need is for the other faction leaders to see me in this state. Any sign of weakness from us and they will pounce. You know that as well as I do."

"Look Naomh. To cry over a loved one's death is not a sign of weakness. Later on, I will probably bawl my eyes out knowing that the Gaffer is not going to be here anymore."

"Yes, but you have Greta to comfort you."

"I am here for you."

"It's not the same."

Seeing Naomh's fill in again; Cahill became convinced.

"I have to get him out of this circle of self-pity, if our cell is to be saved."

So he hardened his voice and ordered the man who was now effectively his superior.

"You got to snap out of this circle of depression. There is no immunity from this. Any cell commander not at the meeting will be deemed a traitor to the movement. And you know the consequence of that."

Naomh realised the implications immediately.

"Alone?"

"Not Exactly. Each commander is allowed to bring a token force of five minders, all unarmed of course."

His lingering traces of grief dissipated instantly as he became all business on absorbing the full intent of Cahill's words. He would not stand idly by while another robbed him of his legacy. Pulling himself together as much for himself as his friend, he told the other.

"It is up to me now."

Cahill seeing the change in his lifelong friend decided at that moment to broach the question that had been plaguing him and partner for the past few days.

"Naomh, why did you run from me and Greta the other night on the roof? Of course, I now know you were traumatised by the death of your uncle. As am I, for I was just as close to him as anybody. But, he told us

that it could happen to any of us. And there was a look of complete madness on your face; it looked like you did not recognise us."

"What are you talking about? It was just the shock of the Gaffer's death. That's all. What else could it be?" But Naomh's eyes betrayed the lie as they refused to meet Cahill's look. His troubled orbs stared at the uncarpeted floor of the room.

"You know what I'm talking about. Something weird happened to you that night." Insisted his friend.

"Do you not trust me? Remember our pact. We promised that we would be there for each other no mattered what happened."

Brushing aside the question, Naomh pleaded.

"My friend, you have to trust me or have you decided not to hold to the pact anymore."

Cahill's eyes hardened slightly as he answered.

"I gave you my oath. You know I will stick with you till the end. I would sooner cut off my right arm and beat myself to death with it."

Naomh absorbed his companion's words, but to the others discomfort and surprise, he cried out in sudden anguish.

"Things have changed. I am absolving you from that promise. And believe me you will be better off."

His lifelong friend looked dumfounded. Not for the first time since this encounter, he was speechless. But after a few moments Cahill regained his voice.

"You cannot do this. I won't let you."

Never in a million years did Cahill expect the maddening insanity of his reaction.

"Look, you don't understand. You haven't a fucking clue. You poor deluded fool. Do you really want to know what you are getting yourself into?"

The never dormant red piece of the Mescal/Amulet stepped in quickly and calmed his confused host, before he revealed too much. It used the Hybrid's own internal chemistry to do it. Naomh had got used to the intruding voice believing that it was enmeshed within his own disturbed state. Cahill too tried to mollify him.

"Calm down Naomh. Relax."

The receiver of his advice started to shudder violently. Equally shaken by these events, Cahill could not bring himself to believe.

"This entire behaviour from Naomh has been brought on by the death of his uncle. Shit, our whole lives have been spent flirting under death's shadow and members of our cell have an extreme fatalistic opinion of surviving the Anschlusss wrath in the long term. That's why we carry the poisoned tooth."

He put things in perspective for his grieving friend.

"Rory is not the first of your family to be killed by the Filth. True, like *me, you did not remember your parent's slaughter, but others have seen the demise of entire families and they carry on with life. Take, Greta for instance. She saw her own kin executed in front of her and was in the process of been gang raped alongside their bodies until I intervened and saved her."*

The man that he was trying to comfort became incredulous.

"And according to you, after you dispatched them, she took a knife to the dead Filth's private parts and with a savage ferocity mutilated them."

Remembering her subsequent treatment of PREVENTIVE prisoners and those she had killed personally, Cahill raised a hand and jokingly acquiesced.

"Ok! Bad example."

Naomh did not see the humour. Realising how much the other needed his genuine reassurance, his best friend affirmed.

"As I have always told you; up to my final breath, I will always be there for you and no matter what happens, I will stand by you."

But once again, the other unsettled him.

"You don't know what you are promising."

Shouting back at his friend, it was now Cahill who became annoyed.

"What do you want? Do you need it in writing? For the last time, I don't break my word once it is given. You of all people should know that."

It was as if he had returned to the context of the dreams. But this time, his loyal companion was on his side. Satisfied with his friend's answer, he appeared contrite and told him in a subdued voice.

"Thank you my friend. I always believed you. I just needed to be reassured, that's all."

However, he secretly suspected.

"If you found out the truth, I really doubt that you would keep your rash oath?"

Then, the man who had just reaffirmed his loyalty literary hit him with a bombshell to prove that no matter what Naomh would do or had done; he would always remain true.

"That building you were on a few nights ago was destroyed along with nine other structures around it. Even our safe house was obliterated. Thousands of people died. It has been on the information units for the past few days. The Authorities said it was our organisation that was responsible. If it had happened to just one building, maybe. But nine, I don't think so. We do not have that kind of firepower. No, it was none of us. And those strange lights, what the hell were they? The News reports never mentioned them."

There was a stony silence as the words sunk in. Naomh looked at his friend to see if he was kidding. But Cahill returned a hard stare that said; he was not fabricating some incredible story.

"Nine buildings and you are not pulling my leg? As you said; none of

our factions have that destructive capability. It had to be the Filth."

"Precisely, but what were they trying to cover up."

He joked.

"Maybe, those scumbags thought I was still on the rooftop and that would be the sure way of eliminating me. They must be that afraid of me to take an action like that."

In his binge drinking and mixed up state, Naomh had avoided the everyday news and he had always passed out before the Clerk returned from work. There had been little coherent conversation between them; especially since the verbal lashing he had given him the first time the other had tried to wake him. But now, he was unsure that he was not somehow responsible for the slaughter of so many innocents. He struggled inwardly and demanded from his internal advisor.

"Was it me? Did I do this?"

The one part Mescal/Amulet replied matter-of-factly.

"It was not you."

The metallic voice made its bearer believe it. He looked at his companion, his gaze unflinching and said.

"But why would they destroy several blocks just to get at me."

"I don't know, Greta and I thought you might have the answer."

"Well believe me, I don't." Lied Naomh to his pal.

Ending the conversation, before anymore awkward questions were asked, he rose then from the makeshift bed where he had spent much of the time curled up in a foetal position. Leaving his surrogate womb, he stretched his arms and yawned with an exaggerated effort. The recovering man turned his head away from his friend and grimaced painfully as he cracked the mucus of the dried tears which had become etched into his skin. Going to the clean-room, he turned on the cold water tap, cupped some of the flowing water into his filthy face and washed the stains away. Naomh wished that all the hurt of recent events that he had endured could also be banished down the drain like the soiled tap water. Those thoughts helped to strengthen his resolve to come through this. Then deciding that he needed to be cleansed thoroughly, he removed his soiled clothes and entered the air shower. His outfit was put in a similar contraption. Water showers were an extravagance that only the Elite could afford or got designated to them. In his perverse nature, Rory had a water shower in his apartment that scandlessy-wasted litres of water. This was one luxury; he had in common with the rulers who he hated so much. It was one of his quirks and it had never been detected by the appropriate authorities. The Gaffer had used some clever tricks to conceal it. As the perfumed blowers went about their business, Naomh noticed.

"I have acquired several large scrapes and bruises, how and when I got them, I don't know."

He knew their purple blemishes had already turned black and over the next couple of days the dis-colourations would turn yellow until the injured skin would lighten and fade into obscurity. While in the air shower, he popped two teeth cleansing tablets into his foul smelling mouth. He nearly gagged on the fizzy motion. Switching focus, Naomh had no inkling that this new strength to persevere had come from the Alien artefact which was quietly working away internally on his mentality. If he had been completed, Mescal would have thought it ironic that one disturbed being was in the process of assisting another in that department. With this small comfort, his host suddenly realised that he was famished. He had not eaten properly for several days. He remembered eating a bag of pretzels, shards of their gnarly wooden like lengths still littered the couch and the floor. Now, his fully awoken stomach growled in protested hunger. Again this was because of the one part Mescal/Amulet's interference. It had to make sure the Hybrid was functioning properly and the taking in of substance was part of that development. Coming out of the clean-room, Naomh discovered a compact kitchen that was even more untidy than the living and dining areas. Its once glossy and clear blue composites with their curved and bevelled edges had also been mutilated by what the Clerk called art. With Cahill's help, he found a fridge full of food and cupboards hidden in the wall that were crammed full of clean utensils. The hungry man approached the fridge and its front became translucent, displaying its contents. With a smile, he asked the other.

"Do you fancy something to eat?"

"Why not?"

He and Cahill proceeded to cook a huge breakfast that consisted of bacon, sausages, eggs and a large amount of toasted bread. They washed down the meal with a bitter coffee that neither had tasted before. Naomh asked.

"Where did he get that from?"

"No idea. But you know him he can get anything."

That widely drunk beverage and other staples such as chocolate were also lies of the Anschluss. These three commodities had to be traded for across the globe, although they were produced under huge greenhouses in the Agriculture Sector, they could not be grown in sufficient quantities in the temperate climate of the northern power block. But as was the norm, the vast majority of the population were unaware of that circumstance and accepted that they were home grown produce. The meal was digested with little conversation and most of the noise exchanged was of food gulped hungrily down. Enough fare had been prepared for four people, but they both normally had hearty appetites and disposed of the meal in record time. When the two men finished the repast, they found the utensil cleaner filled to the brim. The sated eaters added their used dishes to the growing pile on the sink board. Seeing as they had put a considerable dent in the fridges contents, Cahill called up its display icons. Choosing from its menu, he ordered replacements that would be transferred from an assembly point below by a delivery chute. After all, he thought.

"It's nice to be nice."

While he was doing that, Naomh excused himself and went to the toilet. The state of it was shocking, but he could not decide whether he or the Clerk was responsible for the place. Simply because, he was mostly unaware of what had occurred during the time he had spent here. It had become a blur. Setting the self-cleaning program into motion, he left the toilet. Invigorated and refreshed with newfound enthusiasm, Naomh issued his first command.

"Ok, Bonkers, let's go to this meeting and find out who is trying to usurp my rightful position. We will sort this out once for all."

"Let's meet our lot first. We might need them, don't you think?"

"Oh yeah, that would be handy? We are good but not that good." Laughed Naomh.

The one part Mescal/Amulet was working overtime.

"Now, the Hybrid is too self-assured. With their kind, that always leads to a fall."

The Alien intelligence within had completed its immediate work and decided for the moment it would halt its interference in the Hybrid's internal chemistry. The returned confidence was not all of Mescal's work. Both RE-INSTATORS entertained undoubted assumptions that belying his youth, Rory's nephew was the only choice for leader, as he was now the heir apparent. The temporary user of the apartment looked around the room and found what he was searching for; his Frog Eyes. He clipped it to his right ear and changed the frequency to his normal everyday one. If anybody contacted him or heard him on it, he was now Naomh. A quick alteration and he would be Tyro again. The man who would be the new Gaffer left the Clerk's apartment accompanied by a whistling Cahill. After enduring the commotion of the previous week, both men had no idea of what would lay in wait for them when they showed up at the provisional council. But the two of them were confident enough in their own abilities. Before closing the main door of the vacated abode, Cahill glanced back at the messy interior with a smirk. The door to the Clerk's apartment slid shut and its non-essential electrical systems would shut off automatically as soon as the apartment's computer realised that it had become unoccupied. The red haired man left a chuckle escape as the grey portal slid shut. His companion gave him a quizzical look.

"What's tickling your balls?"

"I have a perverse urge to tidy the place up and to witness de Mere's expression when he comes home and discovers it spotless."

The two friends began to laugh out aloud as they entered a packed elevator at the end of the corridor. Both men received some strange looks from its occupants. It was as if laughter was forbidden at this hour unless it was carried out behind the closed doors of your own abode. The looks of consternation directed at them only increased their merriment. They made their way out from the Clerical sector by taking a "Stand On." to the nearest intercity shuttle link. Both had imaging deflecting hoods covering their faces, this had become a popular dress code of the ordinary young Plebs. Like all teenage generations, this was their attempt at rebellion against the system. The authorities detested it for obvious reasons, but there were too many participating and it would have been impossible to incarcerate them all. It suited the RE-INSTATOR'S fine; it kept them hidden from prying cameras or so they thought. There were even some rumours that Rory had started this craze among the Anschluss youth. The two men waited for the next shuttle to take them to their secret cell headquarters in the Dublin Contrib. The normal half-hour long journey took them several hours. As first, they went to the Paris Contrib, and then they doubled back to the Copenhagen Contrib. Then, from there the two travellers made their way to the Manchester/Liverpool Contrib. Finally after convincing themselves that they had thrown off any pursuit; imagined or real, they went to the London Contrib and then took the Mag-lev to their final destination. Once inside that Contrib's local shuttle network they made a few more unnecessary changes, in case any of the local security had inadvertently caught sight of them. On the first leg of their marathon, they used their illegal doctored M I M's to contact the others who would be accompanying them to the meeting. A prearranged coded attachment also told them of the Gaffers death. After sending it, Naomh confided.

"That's one I thought I would never send."

"And me. Still, it will give them time to get their heads around it."

Eventually, the travel weary men arrived at the secret base of their faction. All loyal members of the cell were in attendance including a worried looking Greta and the owner of the apartment that they had come from. It was a small gathering indeed, a pitiful fifty. The tall blonde woman gave one of them a quick look of her concerned blue eyes. Her lover nodded briefly indicating that everything was fine. Naomh did not miss the exchange; he was pleased that Cahill was not the only person worried for him. All in all, it was a shocked group that had gathered here. They had contingency plans for losses, but nobody had expected to lose Rory. The rest of the cell approached Naomh and commiserated him on the death of their leader and all vowed to fight on. On his turn, the Clerk gave him an embarrassing look and hastily explained.

"I had to tell him where you were. He made some vivid threats about what he would do to me if I didn't tell him."

Naomh smiled at the smaller blonde man.

"I can well imagine."

As he backed away, Cahill whispered.

"My threats didn't work. It was only when Greta took out a sharp knife

and started telling him what she was going to do with it, that's when he spilt the beans."

"I can see how that would have done it?"

The rest of those in attendance had already been briefed about the impending conference. What surprised Naomh was the fact they had already chosen his five accomplices without consulting him. A slight cough coming from the Clerk halted any further discussion from him. The bureaucrat formally addressed the gathering.

"To call a provisional council at such short notice is highly irregular and unusual. I have never heard of a meeting called on such a hurry. Also by the way the message was worded; it had an urgency that is most curious. The only thing that explains this is that somebody is definitely making a bid for the leadership of the movement and it is not one of our faction. They must also know that the Gaffer is dead."

As the Clerk was speaking in his business tone, the only female in the room voiced her misgivings and added weight to the argument.

"It must be a set up."

"Going unarmed is madness." Interjected another one of the gathered group.

They were mostly unanimous in that view, but the Clerk stated protocol.

"If there is a call of substance, then everybody attending the meeting is under truce and any differences or actions taken during the discussion could not be acted upon for twenty-four hours. This is a founding principle of our sworn charter. If there is intended betrayal, then every other faction will turn against those who committed the infraction. It would be suicidal for anyone attempting such an action."

"We still don't have to like it." Came the same dissenting voice; it was Greta's

Others echoed her sentiments and she added in her normal superior tone.

"Anyway, we will be alright. Who in the other factions can match us in close in unarmed fighting? None I think?"

There were many nods of agreement at her statement and the arguments for not attending eroded in confidence. Naomh regarded the blonde woman in quite awe.

"That last assertion from her has effectively silenced any opposition from the rest of the cell who believe that attending the meeting is not in our best interests. Like her, everyone present in the room is certain that we are the elite fighters of the movement. After all, the former Gaffer had handpicked each of us."

Cahill, Greta, the Clerk and two others accompanied Naomh to the Conference. The first of the two was the Lenses and the other was an ordinary foot soldier from the Budapest Contrib, nicknamed "Goulash.".

The Lenses whose real name was Peter Kaliningrad was slightly younger than Naomh, at twenty-four years of age. Originally from the Warsaw Contrib, he now lived in the same building and floor as Rory had. The Gaffer for his own reasons; always wanted him safe and close by. He was a brown haired slim man with permanent pink eyes, so he always wore his Frog Eyes in public. His thin frame, his height of 178 cm and slender build of 68kg made one think that he always needed a good meal. He lived on coffee and cigarettes. It was highly extraordinary for him to go on a mission, but then these were unusual times. He was their hacker and the odd colour shade of his eyes was an occupational necessity. A man of pale features, the Lenses found the virtual world more interesting and spent most of his waking hours scanning the Anschluss's computer network. Most of the time he went into forbidden places and gleamed very secret and dangerous information. Finally, he had slipped up and drew very serious attention to himself. Rory had saved Kaliningrad after he had broken into the most secret of files and was unaware that he had failed to prevent himself from been located. He was instantly traced, a squad of PREVENTIVES was about to lift him. But Rory had got to him first. Unlike the others, his normal identity was lost for ever and he normally stayed rooted in his apartment. But without the Gaffer, they now needed his technical expertise. Goulash on the other hand was a chef and worked covertly in a government department. Tomas Kund was a stout thirty-five year old man with a chubby face from the Budapest Contrib. He was good-humoured fellow whose face had a smile never far away. He was famous among his peers for the local delicacy of his Contrib, hence his name. From his rotund and portly frame, it was apparent that he sampled most of his creations. Why this jolly and quirky man was one of them, only the Gaffer knew. Goulash never volunteered the information, so nobody asked. Naomh left orders to be adhered to, while the group of six was gone. He was secretly relieved that they had accepted his commands. The sextet went to the nearest conduit station and worked out a travel plan to get them to the London Contrib. This time, it would be direct. Within twenty minutes, the six RE-INSTATOR'S had travelled the three hundred kilometres in a sleek shuttle and arrived at the main London Contrib station, Heathrow. Naomh's group then transferred onto the local shuttle network and reached their intended destination, a square now devoid of its famous pillar. There, the six left the station and split up into two groups while each party ignored the other as they loitered outside the entrance, waiting for a contact. Normal urban activity ignored their presence. A street-cleaning machine hovered two hundred millimetres on powerful air jets above the pavement, sucking any litter into its metal body. Inside, their insatiable metal and plastic stomachs, the rubbish was sorted into various compartments for recycling. Nothing was wasted in these modern times. The hovering cleaners were the closest things to flying machines that ninety-nine per cent of the Anschluss's citizens would ever see during their lifetimes. A multitude of people passed by, ignoring them like the machines. After a few minutes, a street hustler accosted them vying for their patronage to some seedy and illegal back-street show. Offended, Cahill shoved the man who was drawing unsolicited attention to them away and advised him.

"You are looking for a deserved thumping."

The culprit muttered a few choice profanities, but sensibly backed off. Only someone who was looking for it would have seen the small package that was thrust into Cahill's hands during the brief scuffle. It was a coded chip, which was then handed to the Lenses; only he had the skill to decipher it. He inserted it into his Frog Eyes. The information device magnetically connected to the disc in his ear, he touched a lot of icons on the displayed screen and activated it. The chip contained directions to the meeting place. It was to be held in one of the more luxurious apartment blocks on the South-bank that faced directly onto Watercourse 223 (The Thames). It was only a short trip on a mobile walkway and so the six RE-INSTATORS proceeded in that direction. All along the entire mobile river walk, spaced every fifty metres lay fine specimens of Planes and Popular trees, some were reputed to be a thousand years old. The Clerk thought that highly unlikely. It was a fact that every Contrib had streets lined with its favourite tree. A futile attempt at trying to keep a separate identity from the whole. A quarter of an hour later and across the water course, the sextet were outside the front of the tower block, it was located on Southwark Street not far from the third reincarnation of the Shard. This thoroughfare like many others around the various Contribs still followed its ancient course. The names of streets had only been changed, if they had born testament to a proscribed reference. There were some things that the Anschluss did not alter. Somebody behind Naomh whistled in appreciation on seeing the impressive condition of the building. Cahill grinned and cracked.

"We must be in the wrong faction."

Goulash gave a large belly laugh. There was a murmured agreement from the impressed group. Scanning the neighbourhood, the stout man noticed one of the most bizarre buildings he had ever laid eyes on. Nestled between the modern high rises was a construction that must have been inspired by a history chip. The odd structure appeared to be assembled from ancient black timber surrounding white alabaster squares of a different wood. It only rose to a height of an incredible two stories. (Extremely rare in the densely packed Anschluss.) But it's most noticeable detail was an old fashioned hand written sign that advised them that beer was sold there. The Lenses quickly typed something into his M I M and then explained.

"It dates from the late sixteenth century and the local Guide say's that

it would be worth a visit."

Seeing that Goulash's gaze was lingering, Naomh suggested.

"We should have a few beers to celebrate my impending election. After all we have a couple of hours to kill."

The others had no problem with that suggestion and included in the chip the acting tout had given them was a swipe card that would enable them access to the building at any time. The forged access chip was very exact, because the computer recognised the eye pattern of each member of the group as occupants of the fancy building and would allow them in. Inside the gloom filled interior of the ancient inn and in an isolated booth, all except their soul female colleague drank a few beers and acted like day-trippers to the London Contrib. Greta never participated in the consumption of alcohol, she disliked its taste and its effects. In the pleasant atmosphere of shared companionship, a strange event occurred. The giddy Clerk blundered, when he asked Goulash.

"Why did you become one of us?"

The Lenses had already set up a short-lived disruption device that would hide their immediate conversations. The fat man deep brown eyes appraised them and actually opened up. He clapped the questioner on the back and began his revelation in a hushed voice.

"You are right my friend. We should have no secrets from each other. My father was a better chef than me and had a plush job in the Geneva Contrib. He was drinking one night with some high-ranking official and an argument broke out about something. All I know, it was food related. In his arrogance of his expertise and to prove that he was right, my father foolishly obtained some imported contraband. He produced his creation and confounded his critic. But his rival had been cleverer than him; the man had set him up."

His listeners knew what was coming next.

"He received a visit from you know who and questioned about the procurement of the illegal contents. After that, he was never seen again. It was then that I asked myself, what kind of government disposes of people because of their cooking. I was watched for a while, but they had nothing on me. When the heat died down, the Gaffer found me."

The Lenses raised his glass and his lips silently mouthed.

"A toast to the Gaffer."

His sombre friends followed suit and a few tears, helped by the alcohol escaped. When it was nearly time for the meeting the colleagues reluctantly finished their drinks and proceeded to the entrance of the building, where it was to take place. The pre-arranged meeting was to be held on the top floor. Because of the chip, the six of them entered the building as if they were occupants. The Lenses remained on guard with the Clerk in the lobby, these two were secretly armed. The other four went into the elevator; its interior reflected the luxurious décor of the lobby. The chip was inserted into a control panel, but it refused to move. With a laugh, Cahill realised why.

"Somebody needs to tuck in the stomach."

Goulash's belly was blocking the sensor, the fat man tucked it in and the doors closed, blocking out a few good natured sniggers. The doctored chip allowed them to reach the top floor. The lift's occupants were alert now as the elevator stopped at its programmed destination and when the remaining four exited, they found themselves in a corridor that said in one word; opulence. There was only a single penthouse at this level and its door was a massive affair, easily the size of three normal ones. It was flanked by four openly armed security personal; none known to them. One of these gruff men proceeded to frisk them, while another scanned them for hidden lethal objects. His device would pick up any of the composites that could constitute a weapon or traces of fired projectiles. The guy doing the searching with his hands made an error of judgement when he tried to frisk Greta. The offender ended up on the floor doubled over and clutching his groin. Cahill looked to the ceiling for inspiration and said.

"I can't bring her anywhere."

Things were starting to get out of hand when one of the security personal prudently suggested.

"The scan was satisfactory and it says that there was no way she could be carrying a concealed weapon."

The guard rubbing his tender spots agreed.

"Just give us your Frog Eyes. That will be sufficient."

They removed the circular devices from their ears and were allowed access to the living quarters and in the background Naomh heard one of the security personal mouth.

"Arrogant bastards."

He turned around and gave the man a dark look that instantly silenced him. The size of the penthouse caused the quartet to exchange looks of envy and annoyance. It fully encompassed the entire floor area of the top floor. It reminded Cahill of what the derelict one on the fateful night of the Gaffer's death must have looked like in its prime. On entering into the reception area, they could see that most of the faction leaders and their entourages were already present. Looks of agreed compliance were directed at them. Goulash whispered urgently to Naomh.

"They have made up their minds about something already."

"I agree."

"Be careful, I don't trust this lot. Some of them look very smug." Hissed Greta.

She had no time to finish his words as a door opened from a shadowed corner and suddenly three of them understood. A very tall lean man with an uncombed beard emerged from the dimness. The other faction leader's beams of self-satisfaction increased as the giant came fully into the room.

Naomh now knew that all in the apartment were a party to the upcoming events. For the man that entered was known as the "Hellfire Preacher." and believed devoutly that the organisation's only reason for existing was to bring back the proscribed religion of Christianity. He was a faction leader from the Iberian sector and his real name was the non-descript Tobias Escobar. This Pleb privately hated Naomh's uncle Rory with a passion and thus anyone loyal to him. Once, he believed that it was his natural destiny to succeed the latter as the movement's next leader, but the Gaffer showed no sign of relinquishing control. The most important obstacle to his leadership challenge was the fact that Tyro had been named as his successor. The Preacher believed that decision to be pure nepotism. Others had thought along the lines of the man from the south, but the Gaffer's number two convinced them as they realised that he had a natural aptitude for leadership. The man with the holy vision was not fond of any of the metropolitan zones and based himself mostly in the agriculture sectors. He rarely left those; anyone wanting to see him had to go to him. "So it was a massive surprise for them to see him here, in the middle of one of the largest urban Contribs." Ghoulash whispered.

"It must have taken a lot of effort to get him here without the Filth picking him up."

The Preacher's outlook on the future without the Anschluss government was more severe and demanding than any proposed by any other faction of the movements following. He wanted to replace their pagan symbol with the crucified Christ. He wore his usual enormous black-rimmed hat, which topped off the large man and his massive body frame. Escobar was a person who always wore a black garment, which completely shrouded his body and it forever intimidated any person unlucky to be in his presence. Due to a quirk in his beliefs, his undergarments were always white and the lining of his jackets were also of a pallid sable. Rory had been heard to comment.

"His dress code is inside out. The white should be on the outside and his hidden dark-side underneath."

In keeping with this demeanour, he always wore a very inky shaded pair of reflector glasses, which allowed no inkling of what his features betrayed when one was in conversation with him. Because of his height, most people had to look up at him and this always gave him an advantage. Rory had always been un-phased by this; a long haired friend of his used to describe him as.

"A figure that loomed out of the past, he is like a biblical prophet with shades man."

Feeling that he was encouraged, he would go on.

"He despises the Anschluss's atheism and is intransigence with its use of machines and artificial intelligence. He says that they have taken away mankind's soul as he no longer does an honest day's work. He is the

268

Luddites reborn."

Now as Cahill studied the Preacher, he silently uttered.

"I am glad that we have left you know who behind. We have definitely chosen the correct personnel for this meeting; otherwise the rest of us would now be watching our backs as well."

Of the four of them present, only Greta had never encountered Escobar before. She had heard of him through conversations and despised his opinions on a woman's role in a man's World. You were always left with a feeling of uneasiness in the Preacher's presence. When he spoke it was almost in an effeminate voice as his speech level never rose or fell, but always remained at a disturbing monotonic tone. At one of his friend's request, the guy who he was glad that was not here now, Naomh had attended one of his sermons once and true to the nature of the orator, it was all hellfire and brimstone. He had left bored, much to the orators chagrin. Escobar had been privately convinced.

"Once Tyro has my words revealed to him, and then Rory's nephew will be convinced to join my divine cause, step down and eventually name me as his successor."

One part of the Preacher's seemingly never ending sermon had told of his own favourite lesson. It was about his most cherished hope, the demise of the Anschluss. The oration began thus in his high pitched voice,

"One day, the Holy Father caused a light wind to blow up and the flurry of creation carried within its bosom, the spores of a lichen. Protected by the gentle arms of the breeze, the spores alighted on a virgin roof and flourished in idyllic conditions. The lichen grew and attracted a community of aphids. Each of these dependent life-forms formed a symbiotic relationship and thrived. The lichen grew taller and heavier and the aphids multiplied and fattened in the shelter of the expanding plant. And for both, life was good."

The Preacher always paused here for effect.

"Existing only for their satisfaction, they cared nothing for their Creator; the one who had made them. But the combined weight of the two life-forms made their once ideal World unstable. Then on a quite blustery day, a wind just with enough power snapped the plants roots and their tenacious hold on the roof. It blew the two communities over the edge and into oblivion."

He finished with an explanation.

"Its doom was caused by a simple fact. The two life-forms had become victims of their own success and belief in their arrogance. They only saw their small part in things and never planned for acts of God."

The Preacher devoutly believed.

"The Anschluss will with God's blessing, eventually fall in a similar and dramatic way. And only those who practised the true faith will survive."

269

Rory had incurred the Escobar's wrath when the latter had asked him once in an attempt to gain his patronage.

"Did you think that I used a good metaphor for the Anschluss's demise?"

Naomh's father always thought that the Preacher's words were lost on those from the Urban Sectors. If pushed, he would say.

"The simple reason for this is not because he misunderstands the city dwellers. It is just because Escobar despises them."

Rory had no time for that bigoted attitude. So he used the same type of metaphor as the great orator, highly laced with sarcasm, it must be said, just to annoy him.

"What I don't understand is that the aphids would have devoured the plant long before it was blown from the roof. They did not produce anything. Maybe you should mean that, it can be destroyed from within. I think that the Anschluss is more like a piece of rotten wood, riddled to its decayed core and slowly festering away. Then someone, maybe they are like us, comes along and picks the timber up and the smashes it to smithereens and all the scattering louse are its naive citizens. You should tell the ordinary Plebs that this will be their fate eventually and only those who are with us will survive."

The Preacher had become incensed at his blatant plagiarism and mockery. However Naomh's fathers main reason of detestation against Escobar was because he was a suicide bomb fanatic. The supposed man of God recruited among the disillusioned, the depressed and the easily influenced. Many who came under his wing threw away their lives in an instant of horror. All for the promise of an eternal reward.

"Of course, he would never blow himself up. He leaves that to the poor fools that fall under his deceptive theology." The Gaffer would say to Naomh every time such an indiscriminate attack was carried out. Because of Rory's hostility to his questionable tactics, the Preacher boasted of these attacks with the name of another organisation called November 2553. (This was the month and year that the practice of religion was banned completely from the Anschluss and the Papacy was sent into exile.) Because of the exploding outrages, public opinion forced the PREVENTIVES to react in a more brutal manner and that secretive organisation wiped out numerous cells as a result of the Preacher's heavy-handed tactics. A smug Escobar addressed them with an unusual tremor.

"I see the blasphemers have arrived."

He went on the offensive straight away. His voice began to rise as he found the righteous words. His covered eyes lingered on Greta, he was well known for his opposition against women fighters and having them in places of power.

"I always knew your uncle could not be our leader, for there was something heretical that always floated around him. You all thought I

coveted his position. But you were wrong." The lying and ranting Preacher removed his glasses to reveal small beady eyes and he pointed at Naomh. Locked in religious frenzy, he screamed in a triumphal and if possible in a higher pitched voice.

"At last by the grace of God the almighty, I have obtained the proof that I strived for. Yes, it has been revealed to me that his uncle is not one of us. By the demons of Hell, he isn't even Human. The fires of Hades will freeze over before I will let these devils rule our organization and our path to the true faith. They are a serpent among us and the Gaffer is chief among them."

A disgruntled roar from Cahill cut off the speaker.

"What the hell are you ranting about? His uncle was the best of us."

With a howl of ecstasy, the Preacher roared back.

"Hell is precisely what I am talking about; minions of the Devil. His uncle was seen before he escaped. He is a mutant. We have witnesses that saw him with their own two eyes."

Escobar raised his voice.

"Enter."

Another side door opened and two more figures emerged. Naomh's blood ran cold.

"These two were among those that accompanied my father to the fateful arms transaction."

To make matters worse, both of them were from the Preacher's faction and they were completely in his thrall. Almost fainting in the knowledge of what these men were about to reveal, he glanced around the room and noticed that except for his companions, all the others in the luxurious pad had hostile glares directed at him. An insightful Goulash hissed.

"This is a kangaroo court. They have already made up their minds about us."

One of the two accusers, Paplo Peres alias the Mouth pointed at Naomh and fearfully shouted.

"I was there with the Leech when his Uncle was shot. He was sitting at a table with the Producer and Speedy negotiating the deal. One of the dealers had a funny looking glass eye, but his uncle had only eyes for the female that sat next to him. The Gaffers face had dropped. It was as if he knew her somehow and the memories were not good. He started shaking and then he looked straight into the artificial eye of the man and said. You think you are clever, but you are just evil bastards. They must have been undercover Filth; the woman whipped out a pistol and shot the Gaffer directly in the head. She said something about poetic justice. We were in complete shock as he and the chair he was sitting in crashed to the floor. Glasseye just laughed and then pointed the pistol at Speedy and blew him away. The Producer received the same treatment; the slug took him straight in the forehead and went out the back of his head."

Naomh weighed his options.

"This Pleb is not called the Mouth for nothing. He remembers everything. I'm goosed."

The speakers face turned grave and his voice shook, but he continued.

"Then the others pointed their weapons at me and the Leech. We thought that it was all over, they were not taking prisoners. Then, there came some unholy rumbling. Glasseyes's face muscles froze and the others fingers loosened on their triggers. From under the chair where his uncle had fallen, a monster moved. His uncle's body was making weird noises. No-one knew what was happening, man. The smile on Glasseyes's face froze even more and before he could react, the thing left out a blood-curdling yowl. It moved with astonishing speed. Believe me, it tore Glasseyes's fucking head from his shoulders. It happened so fast that the fucker still had the stupid grin on his face as his headless body slumped to the ground. His eye rolled across the floor like a marble. The woman agent reacted and nearly got away. But, the thing had picked up a fallen weapon and riddled her; it did not stop until the gun was empty. She took a hundred rounds man!"

The Mouth faltered in the telling of his account, but the Preacher urged him on.

"What happened then? Tell them, man."

The other man known as Gruber or the Leech had a determined look across his face. Some called him the Squealer due to his attention seeking approval of his superiors. He filled in for the disturbed Memoriser.

"All hell broke loose. Everybody's weapon was discharged at the thing, including our own. But the mutant went through the Filth like a combine harvester. The thing took a load of hits, but it didn't matter, it did not stop it. As bits of bodies flew everywhere, we panicked and made our escape through a hole in the wall. We heard the screams from the Filth as we ran. That's something I will never forget even if I live to be two hundred."

The Memoriser regained his voice.

"Like us they were shit scared and started blowing everybody away, even their own. We were all trying to get away from that thing."

The Leech interrupted.

"Then we heard it following us, but we came to an intersection and lost it."

Naomh's eyes darted around the room as it began to spin for he knew the two had spoken the truth and it all began to fit together.

"I am a mutant, just like him."

The one part Mescal/Amulet's recent work was becoming undone rapidly. Too stunned to reply, Naomh stood motionless and speechless and this must have compounded his guilt, for he was suddenly looking down the barrels of six Flatpacks. The worst parts of his repetitive dreams were becoming true. The Preacher had broken the charter and his people had smuggled in weapons and every prohibited gun was pointed at his group. The man who was now in control ordered his companions and the other faction leaders.

"Step away from them."

Cahill who had been listening to the whole cock and bull story came to the conclusion that this was a crazy ploy by the Preacher so he could discredit Naomh's family and seize the leadership of the movement. He declared in genuine truth.

"You're all deluded. I have known Tyro and the Gaffer all my life and I'm sure as hell would have found out if they were some of these so called mutants."

With a cold sense of intent the Preacher repeated his previous words to all but Naomh's group.

"I said that he is a mutant. Move away from them or you will die with the four of them."

The main focus of his assertion still did not react. He stood frozen in place, the enormity of him been a mutant just like his father was crushing the life from him. He was dimly aware of the rifles sounding their metallic warning in near unison.

"This weapon is activated. Select projectile type."

Whenever there was the prospect of violence, Greta's normal beautiful and vulnerable appearance changed. Her features took on an icy mask of cold preparedness. She looked to her lover; a glance that told him that she was ready to do something. Seeing that his lifelong friend was not about to defend himself, Cahill prepared himself to be galvanized into action as well, but he knew the gunmen had the drop on them. Especially as he heard, *"Rapid fire selected."*

Looking at the hatred flickering in the Preacher's eyes and the triumph in the armed men at catching them defenceless, he knew for certain.

"We are going to be whacked."

But out of the blue, a panicky Mouth startled them all by screaming.

"You fools. Your guns won't kill him, that was already tried. He will react like his uncle and tear all us apart."

Convinced that his deluded outburst was been ignored, the terrified man broke for the door and once again made his escape. It was enough of a distraction for Cahill to act. Still, he was not fast enough, but fortunately Greta was. She raised her arms and two very strange squat pistols appeared in her hands as if by magic. The doubly armed blonde woman caught the gun toting men unawares, for the six men were sure they were the only ones carrying weapons in the room. A strange hissing noise erupted from the odd guns, very different from their usual Flatpacks. In the pace of two heartbeats, four of the gunmen fell back clutching where their life-blood seeped away as her bullets smashed into unprotected necks and foreheads. One fatally wounded man's blood sprayed from his body with the sound of him gurgling on his own fluids. Cahill shoved the inactive Naomh to the floor and instinct took over as he automatically found cover behind a sturdy metal table. Back in control, he wondered about the unfamiliar sounds coming from the recoil of Greta's gun. The two remaining gunmen open fire with heavy thuds and someone behind Naomh was not as lucky as he heard a gasp of pain. Unknown to him, Goulash had been mortally injured. Greta had also dived and twisted away from the arc of fire, another hiss from her strange weapons saw the two remaining gunmen collapse with gaping chest wounds. She had terminated all the armed men with extreme prejudice. As the sound of flying projectiles petered out, they became aware that all of the unarmed bystanders were cowering behind any cover any of them could find. Some were not so lucky as sprawled bodies twisted in death testified; they had taken bullets meant for them. The guards outside rushed in after hearing the commotion, only to be instantly disarmed. They seemed amazed that he, Cahill and Greta were still among the living. Naomh got up as his two living comrades ordered all survivors to line up against the wall. The Preacher was among those. He had grabbed the Leech during the brief but deadly firefight and used him as a shield and the unfortunate man had been riddled with bullets from a gun that Cahill had appropriated. He was still clutching the dead man's body and let it slump to the floor, streaks of blood trailed down his black garment. Naomh questioned the weapon carrier, also the one that had saved their lives. The blonde woman boldly replied.

"After all Tyro, you don't come unarmed to a gun fight."

Bursting with pride, Cahill backed up his lover by saying.

"You know what the Gaffer used to say? It is better to have a gun and not have to use it than not having one and suddenly finding that you need it. We even kept them secret from you, as I knew that you would not break protocol. We sensed something fishy about this."

He then realised something.

"Where is Goulash?"

Naomh remembered the grunt of pain and a brief search found the one member of their group who was hit. There were two bodies sprawled on top of him, he unceremoniously pulled them off. When he saw it was too late for the chef, he closed the eyes of the slumped body with words of regret. Rage filled within him, his face became a mask of fury, and Naomh turned on the Preacher.

"You were going to have us wacked. You wanted us dead like them."

He contemptuously kicked one of the very still gunmen in the stomach and a gush of blood erupted from the body's mouth. He marched across the room and laid his trembling hands on the bigger man and in his fury threw him to the floor. As he vented his rage on the Preacher, Naomh wondered.

"How am I going to salvage the situation and win the other faction leaders over to my side?"

At the edges of his infectiveness, he heard a sustained burst of gunfire behind him. Turning around, he saw the row of lined up captive's drop to the floor riddled with bullets from the rifles of the fallen gunmen. Finding the culprit and meeting her eyes, he demanded an explanation. Greta threw down the smoking gun and spoke in a voice as cold as stone.

"Their miserable lives were forfeit. They stood idly by while we were to be killed and all of them were in on it. You know the law."

Cahill as always backed her up straight away.

"She's right Tyro. This lot were a part of the intended betrayal. They wanted us dead too."

Their leader was in no mood for their reasoning. But on seeing the manic gleam in the blonde woman's eyes and needing allies, he relented.

"Besides I'm not sure that the crazy bitch would also turn on me?"

Naomh reluctantly nodded his head in agreement. He hauled the now visibly shaken Preacher to his feet. The man was bereft of his usual arrogance. Escobar pleaded with them for mercy, a commodity that he had in short supply, a few minutes ago.

"You cannot kill me. The movement needs me."

Greta moved towards him and produced a sharp blade. The focus of her attention broke down, babbling incoherently, the Preacher saw death in her eyes. She said to no one in particular.

"Let me finish him."

Her movement towards her victim was interrupted as another door opened and a youth that reeked of fanaticism came towards them. Her intended victim let out a roar of triumph, his ace up his sleeve had acted. The teenager revealed his stomach and the tell-tale form of a planted receiver. Cahill expressed the general consensus.

"He has a bomb surgically implanted."

The trigger for it was clutched tightly in one of his trembling hands.

"Let the Preacher go or I will press the button." Insisted his barely adult voice.

The reprieved Escobar gave a shrill laugh that echoed around the room and he gloated.

"We seemed to have reached an impasse. I told you God looks after his own."

His fear dissipated, his eyes reflected holy insanity.

"God loves me, he really does love me."

He crowed and then lectured for the benefit of his perceived victims.

"You see my devoted follower is a walking bomb and as my clever disciple among your faction would tell you, there are two types of explosive devices. Firstly there are the primary, which are easily set off and then there is the secondary type that is hard to set off. Guess which type he has inside him?"

Escobar's maddened eyes flicked towards the group and the would-be bomber. As they backed away from the unstable maniac, the Preacher seized his chance and bolted from the room's exit. With, his dupe between him and Naomh's crew, the fleeing man halted briefly and cast a malevolent grin at them. He raised his hand to show them something.

"Shit. Get out here. He's got a remote control." Said Cahill.

The betrayed youth, seeing that he was about to be left to his fate whether he wanted to or not, hesitated. The naïve idiot foolishly thought.

"I was supposed to retreat carefully through the door with my mentor."

Again, there came the hiss of the strange recoil and he was shot through the head in that instant of distraction. As he toppled to the floor, there was amazement evident in his unmoving features. The dead teenager had not even time to activate his lethal load. Greta urged her comrades to move as she put her weapon under her outfit.

"Quick. The Preacher won't trigger the bomb until he is clear himself."

Needing no other urging, the three of them ran for their lives as the body of the youth lay crumpled on the already corpse strewn floor. Cahill grabbed their confiscated M I M's on the way to the stairs. Minutes later, there was an all-mighty bang and the penthouse vanished in a ball of fire. The fleeing group had barely made it safely down a few floors, before the Preacher had activated the bomb. Brushing themselves free from pulverized concrete dust that had come pouring out from all vents, Naomh said matter-of-factly.

"Come on. Let's get of this mess and return to our own Contrib."

The Clerk and the Lenses looked startled as their comrades came running out of the elevator. Both of them had felt the explosion as it shook the entire building. Seeing only three of them, the pink eyed man asked, fearful of the answer.

"Where is Goulash?

Naomh shook his head sadly and replied to his question.

"I'm sorry. He didn't make it. The Preacher betrayed us."

Both men shook their heads in sorrow; they would miss the jovial chef from the Budapest Contrib. Cahill handed the pink eyed man, their dead friend's information unit and told him.

"Look after it."

Briefly staring back at the mayhem of the blazing building, the five RE-INSTATORS made their getaway. All of them knew that a war on another front had begun and this one would be even better than the battle against the Anschluss secret service, for this new conflict was against their own former comrades. Pushing through a gathering crowd of onlookers as the wail of sirens grew louder, the thoughts of this new conflict was to the forefront of their minds. Taking flight from the vicinity of the explosion, the five hooded survivors stepped on to a moving walkway that ran the length of waterway 223 and stayed on it till they reach the nearest shuttle station. From the Embankment, the group acted innocently and made their way to Heathrow Mag-Lev and then by their usual nefarious route, the fugitives began to make their way to the Dublin Contrib. When they were safely speeding away from the London Contrib, Cahill with his typical witticism in the face of adversary spoke the first words among them.

"I bet the penthouse does not look so fine now."

Greta snickered, but he did not bother to see if any of the other's showed any signs of mirth. Then, she asked philosophically.

"I wonder in the exact second that the bomber died; what he was thinking. Did the idiot even know that it was my bullet that killed him and not his device? It makes you think why these bombers do it, as they will never know the outcome. And what good is it if you cannot see the fruits of your handy work."

Her lover answered.

"Nobody will ever know. The idiot was carrying a live bomb and it blew him up and dead is dead. And believe me, the Preacher is next."

"By the way, where did you get those weird guns?" Interrupted Naomh.

"What guns?" Asked Cahill with malicious intent.

"The one that deceived their scanners."

He and Greta laughed at a shared secret.

"No, seriously, where did you get them?" Persisted their leader.

Both of the lover's nodded to each other and it was Greta who spoke.

"The Gaffer gave it to me, he said that it would come in useful sometime and as always, he was correct."

Naomh had at one point during the incident back in the apartment believed that the dreams were about to come true and he was about to be killed by his own side. But, now, he realised.

"Not in any dream had Greta made an appearance."

Then, the Clerk who had been mostly silent during the escape soberly asked.

"Why do you think that Goulash opened up to us? Do you think he had a premonition of his death?"

The good mood was severed and Naomh who had his fair share of loss lately replied.

"It was just a coincidence that's all."

To himself, he wondered.

"Will I ever cry for anyone again? For my father, tears came out of nowhere and then shut off, just like that. There is still soreness, but it is only a dull ache now."

The death of the amiable Goulash weighted heavily on their minds, but none of this lot would shed any tears. For now, escape from the Anschluss security forces was paramount and the battle with the Preacher would have to wait for another day. Once again the News channels told of another bombing. But this time, the reporters glorified in the extermination of a RE-INSTATOR terror cell. Broadcasted images showed mutilated bodies under wraps and then switched to previous photographs of the deceased. The narrator explained that the bodies were so badly burnt that D.N.A. had to be used. The fleeing survivors recognised the photo scans, especially the one of their friend. It made the Lenses wonder.

"Why when there are thousands of images of the dead men, did they use the most sinister ones? I for one have never seen that mean expression on Goulash."

Greta spoke in a hushed whisper.

"The Filth are taking credit for most of our handiwork."

The controller of that security apparatus was furious, he had seen the penthouse explode and his artificial skin went a sickly pale. He never knew that it could do that. But, the very relieved Chairman let out a deep breath when his screens showed Naomh and his group emerge unharmed into the London Contrib Street. His vow became loaded with recriminations.

"Shit, I've not had a scare like that for a long time. Whoever ordered that bomb to be set off will pay dearly."

Once the all-powerful and vengeful ruler made a statement like that, it was as good as done. If in the rare occasion that it would not, then those that failed him would suffer the consequences, just the same.

XIII.

GENEVA CONTRIB 2952 AD.

"Soon we will be approaching the thousandth year commemorating the predecessor of the Anschluss. One boastful ideology promised this length of a reign before and failed miserably. It has always been obvious that we are the only ones on this Continent who could ever deliver that pledge. The day when we took absolute power, now that's when the real festivities will commence. The celebration of the first achievement will begin in the year 2957 AD; not our measure of time, I grant you." Voiced the giant bulky man in a hoarse artificially enhanced means of speech that emitted from deep stained ruby lips.

Standing just shy of two metres tall, Ivan Tell, the Chairman was a heavyweight in more ways than one. At one hundred and twenty years old, he was the undisputed ruler of the Anschluss and was endowed with the keenest of political intellects. His was an appointed position that was unknown to the vast majority of the population. With recent events in mind, he added prophetically in his synthesised timbre.

"And of course, every crackpot from every radical organisation will try and fuck it up. What is their problem? We have brought them a new age of glory, peace and prosperity. We are the glue that holds this place together. Without us, the ordinary Plebs are less than nothing. Because of our continuity, this Continent has not seen a large conflict in a thousand years."

He was well aware that there was still a rotten underbelly of crime and terrorism out there in his supposed paradise. However, he and his kind had kept it to a minimum. In fact, he knew there was an alphabet soup of dissident groups among the billions of Anschluss souls in the crowded urban sectors that despised his government. This individual who practised total absolutism added smugly.

"I am in control. I could eliminate all of those radicals with a simple command."

That was the truth of the matter.

"But the normal Plebs turn to us for protection against these terrorists. So that makes my position stronger." Stated Ivan Tell with absolute certainty.

This was a man who had an inflexible agenda and been a necessary student of history, he would lecture to a select few.

"It has always been a fact when those who were been governed began to think the present system was failing them, they became disgruntled. Then these ignorant masses looked back on an old regime in fondness, even if it had been a despotic Monarchy, a totalitarian dictatorship or even a corrupt Democracy. Those of the disillusioned masses who had not

279

suffered personally soon forgot that the absurd leaders had ruled with an absolute mandate and done what they liked, heedless of the consequences. In opposition to the present system they would try and reinstate the ousted regime."

Granted, his kind ruled in a similar manner. But, then they had a goal and anyone who did not interfere in this were left alone to have a good standard of life. They did not mistreat the overwhelming part of the population, just because they could. Still, they were ruthless and downright sadistic to those who threatened their goal. The ambiguous ruler of the Anschluss carefully brushed imaginary dirt from the epaulettes on the shoulders of his archaic blue and red military uniform as he paced up and down on the rich carpeted floor of his office. The clothes that he wore in private could not have contrasted more with the drab grey suit; he was obliged to wear in public. Among his own, he became a strutting peacock, out amid the masses, he was a plain pigeon. His lair, the space he now occupied was a masterpiece of Gothic anarchy. It was perched on top of two hundred and thirty floors of his glass tower which itself stood on the manmade Genevan plateau. A huge spherical total mass damper, constructed of space mined asteroid metal on the hundred and eightieth floor kept the enormous structure stable, even in the strongest of gales; it was a lofty point indeed. To him and a few advisers, it was known as his.

"Bell Tower."

As with the fictitious character Quasimodo who inhabited the spires of the former Parisian cathedral of Notre-Dame, Tell could also reach down and pluck any miscreant into oblivion, abet by different means. For this high place above the constant milky strata was his nerve centre and from here, he also reached out all over the globe with suspicious tendrils of intrigue. He also was aware of another fact.

"My vantage-point is the ultimate challenge to the practitioners of the illegal sport of Base-jumping."

He gave out a large snigger, a sinister sound coming from transplanted chords. The man with a vicious sense of humour remembered the last Pleb who had tried it.

"How he got up unobserved was another story, still someone paid for that. The idiot leapt off the tall spire above me and hit a passing Wraith before his parachute opened. Clinging on for dear life, the failed base jumper never realised that somebody was in control of the flying machine."

Ivan Tell never had so much fun. He kept guiding the unmanned drone with its terrified passenger towards the façade of the adjacent tall buildings before swerving away at the last moment. Finally tiring of the game, he let it smash into a cluster of soon to be demolished structures down in the Milan Contrib.

"Some thrill seeker. I could hear his screaming all the time. Still, my

Bell Tower is a magnet to the rest of those masked miscreants. Despite him been smashed into pieces and found hundreds of kilometres away, his mysterious death has made the prize seem even greater. Well bring them on, I have plenty more Wraiths."

If the Brussels Contrib to the north-west was the centre of bureaucracy for the Anschluss, then his base in the Geneva Contrib was the heart of the political establishment. His place of operations was full of dark brooding opulence, a reflection of the man. A huge burning fire cast crackling shadows of perceived warmth, this was no electrical imitation, and it was a real log fire. Huge sumptuous red drapes enhanced the subdued colour of the Gothic gloom which was recreated from modern materials that were hidden behind the ancient wood and stone artefacts. All of these trappings had been appropriated from destroyed Cathedrals, Mosques, Synagogues and private collections. The Bell Tower's false coverings echoed age and stability, masking the steel and concrete that allowed this surreal construction to exist. The thin veneer coverings of his office mirrored the biology of the man. Perfect and flawless on the outside, hard, rough and slowly decaying on the inside. He had been at the helm of power for nearly eighty-years. To Naomh and his organisation, he was the ultimate despot and a master of concealment and deception. Among his own confederates, he liked to be called.

"The Kaiser."

He remarked to those in the know.

"The RE-INSTATOR'S are not the only ones who have a monopoly on appellations from the previous history of this Continent."

What you saw on the outside was the impeccable façade of regenerated skin that covered and concealed the dark ugly inside of cruelty and sadism that was very much his inner self. He was very courteous and indeed, quite charming in public. He was gifted with the instant handshake and a voice that reassured the perfect consummates of every successful politician. In private, his manner was of one whom had to be obeyed instantly and woe behold anyone who crossed or disappointed him; he had ways of crushing any dissent. His very efficient secret police known as PREVENTIVES and their flying Wraiths with their ever-watching eyes would keep the little people observed and removed from the equation, if needed. This unacknowledged department within the Anschluss security framework's main area of operation was to hunt down and eliminate political, religious subversives and in the infrequent case; of foreign infiltrators. This shadowy force was formed in 2343AD by a female Chairman (A leader of any sex still was known by that title.) who decided that the ordinary security apparatus in place was not sufficient. This clandestine organisation was responsible directly to the ruler of the Anschluss and not to the sham figurehead of the Prime Minster. Loyalty and expertise to the small cadre of the ruling elite was its main focus. Most of its best operators and superior officers were actually drawn from a selected gene-pool. Those of its members that did not belong to them came from incarcerated killers and those who had ruthlessly climbed the ladder of promotion. Its prime candidates had to be callous and merciless in any assigned task. These eliminators of government opposition had the best resources of the power block behind them. The only one of its targeted groups that were aware of them were the RE-INSTATOR'S and this was mainly because of the individual Rory Lynch. Somehow, this man never showed up on any imaging device and that made him impossible to track. Therefore, he constantly eluded them and at first this was put down to Human failure. The Wraiths on the other-hand were very efficient night flying helicraft. Silent, near invisible and deadly, these manned or unmanned craft observed and often eliminated any deviants, if the Chairman required it, but these too failed to track Lynch. Tell went over to the windows of his office and gazed out from their protective height. Specialised imaging devices allowed him to see through the ever present layers of pea-soup vapour discharges. The mostly flat urban belt with its sporadic clusters of tall buildings curved off towards the four corners of the compass following the curves of the Earth's circumference.

"This is my domain that I survey; all that lies beneath me is under my firm control."

From the height of his Bell Tower, he could afford to ignore the overwhelming the splotches of urban impact and decay which blighted the splendour of his Anschluss.

"It is far from been perfect, but then we are not here for that. This is only a step to the next level."

The clouds of foggy mist that were a constant companion of the urban dwellers began to darken and thicken; a sure sign of impending rain. His deep baritone voice commanded the background music to cease, so he could listen to the patter of the life-giving downpour outside the condensating glass panels of his luxurious watchtower. Highly sensitive listening devices allowed the rain to be heard inside, when it pleased him so. The pounding of the raindrops on to the ever vigilant receptors of the tower apex reflected the deep booms of thought that reverberated inside his skull. Looking down on the teeming masses of normal and inferior Humanity always brought home the simple fact that he and others like him were superiorly different from them. But still, the Chairman and his ilk controlled the Anschluss and everything within its borders.

"How will my kind judge me? Am I a Chancellor or a Charlatan?"

This was his private joke and he did not share this personal humorous witticism with anyone. Tell knew that his position of absolute power was not finite, if he failed in his appointed duty to adhere to the plan. He could not afford to show anything that could be perceived as weakness, it would be as if he had signed his own death warrant. As sure as the rain would cease, there were others who would usurp his position at any given opportunity.

"After all, it is their nature."

So far in his long reign, he had given no one that chance. There were many bodies sent to the recycling plants who had foolishly jumped the gun, thinking that they had outwitted him. Corpses of his own kind who had failed to usurp him dissolved spontaneously; that was more of what they were. He smiled at that. This relaxing diversion was scandalously broken by a shift in the intensity of the wind gusts that were a constant factor of life at this height. Even he could not control that. Large eye drops of frozen precipitation splattered against the glass panels in a drum roll and all that he observed faded from view with another command. Tell turned away from the windows, if he still wanted to watch the vista below, he could easily switch the glass panels to some other wavelength. But at the moment, the Chairman decided against this. The tall hairless figure went and sat at his huge desk. Just sitting there, he knew that he was at the pinnacle of the vertical political structure that ruled with an iron hand. From here, the tallest of summits in the natural or steel and concrete landscape was from where the real power that controlled the Anschluss spread its wings. His ruling elite achieved this universal mandate without the consent of the population. Contrary to popular opinion, the everyday governing administration was a sham. Outwardly, the political system was a Democracy, but in reality, it was a total Autocracy. Learning from history, these rulers had thought it.

"Ridiculous and absurd that once, actors and entertainers could assume the top position in a free society because of their popularity and not of their suitability.

The people did choose the Prime Minster to a forum with other elected officials, Tell had seen many. But in reality who ever held the position of the Chairman had absolute rule. In the rare event that the sham figurehead had not been the true ruler's selected candidate, then that person was usually eliminated along with family and friends and all the deceased were replaced with "Substitutes.". These doppelgangers underwent extensive plastic surgery to hide the deception. In the closed political structure of the Anschluss, a successful candidate not of the ruling elite's choice always earned the reward of an early death. After the Chairman, the next in the line of succession was the inner circle of advisors. Finally came the ineffective Parliament of the people, but you might as well be talking about ordinary Plebs as mentioning their miserable influence. He sipped his imported brandy and puffed on his Cuban cigar and in the background loud organ music played while he reflected on a seemingly minor problem. The audible score he was enjoying was one of triumphal, composed over seven hundred years ago. Flickering video units spied on those that needed watching and images of these criminals filled the screens. Numerous digital timepieces hung from the walls and displayed the exact time in the various Power-Blocks around the globe. The Chairman was at the fore front of the small per-cent of the population that was aware of the World outside the Anschluss; what he was puffing bore testament to that. Because most of these nations preferred isolation, each one's circumstances varied enormously; most had not exceeded a twenty-first century level of technology. Some like the Anschluss were a little beyond that while others had slipped into a twentieth century level. He knew that this state of affairs existed because Globalisation had been circumvented. Ideas and technological advancements were not been shared. But then, he and his kind preferred this. Unknown to the oblivious masses who still used the Gregorian calendar of the wider World, his kind used their own. To those in the know, the real year was 923 LY. This measurement of time began with the birth of their revered founder. The Anschluss kingpin rubbed the bare skin of his crown (He wore a detested wig in public and irritating false eye lashes.) as he idly marked off approvals of elimination on a hand held screen in this the tallest of buildings on the Continent. Behind him hanging from a vast wall were numerous video screens that with a push of a button caused the electric cacophony to disappear and become an ivory panelled wall displaying a huge ebony carving of the four horsemen of the apocalypse. This effigy was a constant reminder of all of Mankind's, but even more importantly, his kind's fate if he or his people failed in their task. This was their true symbol, not the one of the rising Phoenix that was displayed all over the Anschluss. For Ivan Tell and his kind were secretly known as LYUBINITES and this sinister sect had only one ultimate goal. This close knit and exclusive cult had ties that went way beyond kinship. They emerged on to the Global scene in the latter part of the 21st Century. Their revered founder was an eccentric Russian Doctor called Gregory Lyubin. He had been a self-styled mystic and a Professor of Genetics. He was idolised by his follower's cloned descendants, for that was what Ivan Tell was. They all took the surname and some like the present Chairman; the first name of the ten original gene-pool disciples. Born in crystal cryostats, they also differed from the majority of lesser Humans as the repeated process had divested them of any traces of bodily hair. This circumstance made them believe.

"Hair follicles are the mark of an inferior species of man and we are the next stage of Human evolution."

The long dead Doctor's giant statue lined the corridors of power along with his ten original followers. One of these smaller effigies was an exact likeness of the present Chairman. Lyubin himself had never been cloned, that would be done when the Aliens returned. Most of his cloned disciples privately agreed

"Anyway, if his Clone was present, then it would govern continuously, thus depriving us the descendants of his disciples any chance of ruling."

This suited them fine. They and the founder of their sect devoutly believed.

"Mankind had been created by extra-terrestrials over twenty-five thousand years ago and that all branches of Humanity had been originally created by the knowledge that the Aliens had in their possession.

THE GIFT OF CLONING."

They understood that man had abused this trust and engaged in sexual reproduction. Disgusted and betrayed, the Aliens had departed from the World. However, in their generosity, they implied.

"We will allow those who return to the old ways to join us out in the stars."

But something had to be acquired first to make this possible. Every generation of the Clones had searched for it, in vain and they, the practitioners of this God-like craft were closer to the truth than they knew. In search for the missing item, this elusive sect were always at the forefront of new innovations, but the sinister group had banned machines in the likeness of man. The LYUBINITES were true custodians of that mystery of life while the overwhelming majority of Humans had reverted to sexual reproduction. These true believers propagated by the methods of their creators. They were firm converts to the science of panspermia. But unlike the mainstream, they were fully fledged believer's knowing that the Aliens had put Human's fully formed directly onto the Planet and not the result of some micro-organism type of contamination from an impacting comet of meteor. The revered Doctor had been assassinated in 2094 AD outside a Parisian café. But he had already had a sizeable portion of his own genetic material frozen for preservation and his few loyal followers carried on his teachings and his arts. The Doctor had bequeathed them the artefacts and technology of cloning and it could only have come from an Alien race. Globes of light that spun complex webs at crystal cryostats created each new generation. They were only masters of activating the technology; they did not understand its mechanics. The LYUBINITES experiments in this widely abhorred field led to their downfall. Because of their quest for Human perfection and rejection of most of mankind, followers of the sect were systematically purged from society. With echoes of historical implications, similar to the Knights of the Winged One, they were imprisoned and murdered. Like them, they went into hiding and became a secret organisation that lingered at the fringes of society. Under this persecution, like a weed, their cause prospered. Through centuries of political intrigue, they now controlled the Anschluss. Those who believed that they had almost solved the "Secret." longed for the missing link and their own archives led them to believe that Lynch's line held the final piece in the biological jigsaw that was required.

THIS GOAL WAS THEY'RE RELENTLESS AND ALL CONSUMING TASK.

For without the secret, their improved version of mankind could not take its rightful place out in the stars. One drawback to their continuing dominance of the Anschluss was that each Clone had basically only his or hers own personality and when they perished, its unique memory vanished. These new reproductions had to start learning all over again. Because each new duplicate evolved quickly into adulthood; they did not grow as normal Human children did. Ninety-seven point nine per cent of all Clones were sterile, but though very rare, there were exceptions and some individuals could breed sexually. The original genetic material from the ten hosts had been used up centuries ago and now, a potentially cataclysmic problem occurred. As their scientists had been using material from each new generation, the substance of repetitive life had begun to prematurely degenerate. Abnormalities began creeping in to each successive creation, such as Tell's ruined voice. Most of the recent batches were so defected that when some escaped before they could be destroyed; they gave rise to the mutant stories that spread like wildfire around the populace. Those like the Chairman were outwardly ageing so quickly that a rare disfiguring skin disease marked their entire skin. The best plastic surgeons in the Anschluss discovered an artificial skin base that could be used to cover their horrifying appearance. But the membrane deteriorated and had to be renewed every decade. Still this malady was only skin deep; some of the LYUBINITES reached great ages. The Chairman himself was over a hundred and twenty years of age and mentally still in his prime. It was ironic that the only deformed people within his boundaries were himself and his kind as advances in genetics produced unflawed individuals among the normal Human population. And in the rare event of a defected embryo been produced, it was removed. So the majority of the inhabitants of the Anschluss had never seen an impaired person. Those that suffered horrific injuries through accidents or violence and where the severe damage could not be reversed, then those unfortunates always never recovered. The Clones held onto the reins of power tightly and underlings who knew nothing about the real identity and purpose of their mission carried out the everyday running of the vast power block. These menials interacted with the normal population and ran most of the bureaucracy of state, everything in fact except the espionage networks and foreign policy. The masses were ignorant of the State's true rulers. Only Rory knew of their far-fetched purpose and that nothing would stand in their way of achieving that goal. Through their unwitting servants and a technology that few were aware of, the LYUBINITIES had learnt a great deal about the RE-INSTATOR'S than Naomh or his father would have believed. The Chairman would boast.

"Anyone meriting my attention would be watched so astutely that I could stalk them while they eat, shower, shit and shave".

But inexplicably, this Rory Lynch vanished from view every time and his apartment in the Dublin Contrib was unmonitorable. Somehow in the rare event of getting someone in there, any surveillance device refused to work. There was a technology working there that none of the security force agencies understood and to Ivan Tell, it reeked of Alien influence. This led some of those in the know to acknowledge.

"We and the RE-INSTATOR'S might be separated brothers, both originating from those extra-terrestrial visitors. Only, those misguided individuals have taken a divergent path."

Now once again, the Clones had infiltrated Lynch's secret society with one of their own. The Chairman at last understood

"The missing piece to our cosmic dilemma lies in the hands of Naomh and not his father."

After recent events, his mole among his little faction was absolutely certain with Tell's assessment.

"This Naomh is about to undergo a transformation that will reveal the Alien technology and the knowledge of transferring the memory of a previous Clone into the new one. Thus insuring every LYUBINITE'S immortality."

THIS WAS THE TASK THAT THEIR CREATOR'S OUT THERE IN THE VAST COSMOS HAD GIVEN THEM. WHEN IT WAS COMPLETED, THEN, THEY THE NEW HUMAN RACE COULD TAKE its RIGHTFUL PLACE OUT IN THE STARS.

The great space plague had been proof that mankind was not ready yet. Humans were still impure. In the three early centuries of this millennium, the people of this Planet had conquered the surrounding Solar System. All the advanced Nations of the World had exploited the mineral wealth from the other Planets, their Moons and most important of all, the entire asteroid belt between Mars and Jupiter. Civilisation and technology only prospered now in the Anschluss because of the massive stockpiles that had been amassed and stored up when the true implications of the outer space pestilence set in. Mankind who thought they would be masters of space, glorified in its achievements. But Human beings had been so wrong. Some religions believed that God had cast man out of paradise until he atoned for its sins, but the holders of the Secret knew it was not a Deity; only the Alien race that had done this. In 2553AD, a plague swept through all space colonies eradicating nearly all of the Humans that lived off World. Then by some bizarre coincidence, a similar virus attacked all metals and alloys making large-scale space travel impossible. Every effort was put into curing the epidemic, but all efforts nearly failed. Then some boffin discovered that some small communities throughout the Planet that basically had stayed closed to outsiders and had a less diluted gene pool could survive in space. But these rural and mostly inaccessible closed off societies diminished in size and numbers as the centuries passed. Global migration had swallowed up most of these isolated groups. So now, the number of people that could endure space existence were few and far between, but a revolutionary but costly new construction of spacecraft allowed a few space flights a year. For now a fraction less that ninety nine point nine per cent of Humans were denied the experience of space travel. Most of the experts viewed it as a temporary setback and a cure would be found. After all, mankind had overcome worst epidemics since his creation. But that had been over four centuries ago and still no cure had been found. The descendants of Lyubin's disciples were positive their credo had the solution and it went back to the basics of their beliefs.

"Mankind will not be allowed back into the Solar System and further beyond until they have mastered the task given to them."

But alas, the LYUBINITES in their closed wisdom were also wrong. For their creators, the ALASTHA'I had no need of an army of resistance scattered throughout the Galaxy. The mostly departed Aliens had planned for a force of billions to be confined on the Planet's surface to confront the host of CRYSTALOID'I. So during Mescal's maddening paranoia, he had integrated a virus into the Hybrids genetic makeup that would not allow them prolonged access to space. In effect, the paranoid instigator of the outlandish scheme wanted the Hybrid army Planet bound as he informed his conspirators during a lucid period.

"If our creations do actually defeat the armies of mindless destruction. Then the last thing our passive race wants; is another bunch of rapid reproducing homicidal maniacs roaming around the Universe."

Of course, this was all unknown to the Chairman and his ruling elite. He and his kind had been paramount in interfering in the Anschlusss affairs for most of the thousand years of its life. Very few individuals outside his sect who lived in the Continental block even remotely knew the true history of the state. Naomh's father Rory did, but he was no more. He had been born while a form of the Anschluss was in its infancy and unsure of itself. In the beginning of its creation, the emerging European bloc had sided with a powerful and domineering Superpower across the western ocean. This Global power as they do; got embroiled in every major regional conflict on the Planet. Eventually in 2110 AD, such were its losses in Human life and prestige that it withdrew into complete isolation and left the rest of the World to fend for itself. With no Superpower to watch rogue states with their various excuses of economic, religious and political ideals, countless regional wars broke out around the Globe for the next two hundred years. In one case, Atomic weapons had been used. Europe was seen as a bastion of safety and tolerance. It became swamped by millions of refugees seeking a better life. The endemic peoples voted that enough was enough and a massive wire fence was constructed around its frontiers. This was the forbearer of the immense walls that now surrounded the Anschluss. Over time the barrier was replaced by concrete. During this time of global upheaval, the LYUBINITES consolidated their grip on the top echelons of power. They took on a far right perspective that was said among them.

"Only we, white Europeans of the promised race will be allowed out into space. After all, that is the colour of our brothers out there."

The wall eventually became a barrier to immigration. They then nationalised all foreign firms, seized their assets and repatriated its non-citizens. Other nations were certain that this illegal action would be the final coffin nail on the Europeans and their racist policies, but the so-called experts had been proved conclusively wrong. The new Power-Block prospered and others followed its example. Their agenda of reforming society began with them removing the smaller Religions and those minorities that were not the right colour or race. These State-makers used various nefarious schemes, mainly uncompelled sterilisation and genetically engineered offspring. Birth rates among those not deemed suitable decreased rapidly; while among those who were acceptable, large families became the norm. All those non–conformists that survived their genetic purges were transported out of the Anschluss or left voluntary. They became so skilled in the politics of intolerance, that within two hundred years their state had become exclusively white and Christian. Of course there was resistance from the targeted groups but this was used as an excuse for their differences and they were removed from the state even more speedily. Violent protests resulted in many deaths. Still, the LYUBINITES became extremely clever in isolating each group and their political experts did not repeat the mistakes of blatant rapid mass extermination of the other intolerant regimes of the past. Successive leaders just exiled all those that did not conform to unaccepting lands beyond the boundaries of the wall. As, the might of the emerging Power Block grew, its neighbours had no alternative but to accept the Anschluss's undesired. The new order that these strict rulers had created prospered until the space virus arrived. Ever the pragmatists, they used it to their advantage. Directing this disaster in their own deceitful way, these new state makers blamed God and removed the last obstacle on the path to their ultimate goal. The devious manipulators banished the last established Christian Religion from the state in 2573AD and sent its Priests, bishops and Pope into exile. The seat of the Holy see; the Vatican was torn down and its priceless treasures confiscated by the state; i.e., the LYUBINITES. Through education and deception, these art plunders had become the ultimate practitioners of eugenics. Having rid themselves of all of the non-conformists, they began to deal with the legacy of the ideas and physical structures the exiles had left behind. All religious and political assumptions deemed unacceptable were purged from most of the collective memory. Without regret from the ruling elite, buildings and memorials that could not be altered or given new histories were demolished with a Stalinist vigour. Having achieved most of what they had set out to do, the Doctor's disciples were now in complete control. Things settled down for them over the next few centuries and the worship of God became a forgotten memory among the majority of the Anschluss population. Then in 2609 AD, a calamity of their own making occurred. Some of their own kind, who had lost the plot created a super fertility drug that started out as a cure for the space virus. On hindsight, it was now known that it had been lunacy caused by the deterioration of the original gene samples. Trusting their own had become the most stupid code they had ever adhered to. Before the top echelon realised what this faction had done, it was too late. The twisted group within had indurated the entire population via the water system with the super fertility drug. The population of the Anschluss exploded from a billion to over five billion in two hundred years. It took their boffins another fifty years to stem the tide and find a method of contraception to counter act that incredible calamity. A new puritanical code enforced into them by the original Doctor Lyubin that ruled out mass sterilisation and terminations was now in practice. Obviously this drastic action did not apply to inferior races. The founder of their sect realised, even though it implicated him.

"Every person has a right to be born and besides, we are not certain who the Human will be that would blaze the path to the stars."

Caught in a web of their own devising and having no scapegoats to blame as in the past, all succeeding administrations put all of its efforts into controlling this enormous population. During the repression of every corner of opposition, the security agencies had discovered the existence of a shadowy group, which called themselves the RE-INSTATOR'S. So secret and closed was this faction, it took decades to build up a picture of them and what was revealed shocked the LYUBINITES to the core. A man whose origins and beliefs that were uncannily similar to theirs led this small band. But this leader appeared to be about nine hundred years old. He was not a clone, neither was he a charlatan.

THIS MAN HAD THE SECRET ALREADY.

Now at long last this present Chairman's agenda of infiltrating the small sect had succeeded and paid dividends. Tell had a Spy among them and this was only the second time that a covert operative had pierced the close knit ranks of Lynch's faction. A few weeks ago, the Spy had informed them that the long lived leader of the secret society had perished in the Chairman's betrayal and his confused offspring had received instructions to gather a technology that lay scattered all over the Planet. The report could hardly contain the excitement of the author. Tell too exulted.

"This is what we have been promised and the elusive piece will come within our reach. Naomh Lynch must be protected at all costs until his quest has been completed or should I say Tyro. Of course I know of their stupid appellations and who the titles belong to."

This was rich coming from the one who called himself, the Kaiser. In

290

the ironies of ironies, they, who were Naomh's most hated enemies, had been protecting his life since last November after his bitter fallout with his former comrades. If he needed conformation, Tell would have told him.

"On numerous occasions in the last few months, my elite squads have been eliminating your former friends while they were in the process of attempting to assassinate you."

The callous Chairman reflected.

"This Naomh. What an enigma. The fool has no comprehension of the forces; he would deliver to me. He only sees the little picture. What a pathetic dammed idiot? Ha, he wants to recreate the Anschluss in his own ideals. He cannot even see that the Anschluss is only a tool to the higher goal. Dam him and his arrogant father. Oh yes; this Naomh would be very surprised that we knew of his parent. When we learnt of his apparent eternal life, an attempt to entice him into our ways began. We put out the invitation over unusual lines and waited to see if he would accept it. A marriage between our two beliefs would have been the ideal solution. I remember that night twenty-three years ago when he entered the ball and I waited eagerly with our proposition."

The "Masquerade Balls." had become the social highlights of the Anschluss elite. These gatherings were the hottest tickets in town. The formal assemblies were a recreation of the fifteenth century masked Florentine balls, held in splendour amongst the favoured of that time, while the poor suffered and died. In the balls new guise, military regalia from the European Monarchies of the eighteenth and nineteenth centuries were the order of the day. A change from the drab clothing that the functionaries of the Anschluss wore in public life. For men, Royal reds, Prussian blues and rich Burgundies highlighted their outrageous baggy pants and long flapping sleeves. For women, similar colours with the odd yellow accented long flowing skirts and tight uplifting blouses that showed heaving bosoms to their full advantage. These official recreations of the masked balls were a favourite with the LYUBINITES as it protected their identities for obvious reasons. It would be quite a shock, to those that had been invited, if more than one of the same identical countenances were to appear in abundance. The wearers of the brightly coloured garb differed bizarrely with the original purveyors of those uniforms because the innovative owners of those styles always had the most outlandish and extravagant hair growths, especially sideburns, beards and moustaches. But now they were a bald parody. Normal Human guests were obliged to crop their hair in a similar manner to their hosts. Naomh's father with shoulder length hair had strolled past security, daring them to impede his entry. Monitoring devices once again failed to produce his image. If the scanners had, they would have seen that he was dressed in the most outrageous military costume, but it was from the twentieth century and totally out of contrast with the surrounding flamboyant costumes. He wore a black leather jacket and matching bulging trousers of the same material. A black leather cap with a prominent badge of an eagle at its peak topped off the ensemble. Heavy black and gold crosses around the jackets pockets and a red armband with a hooked cross on his left biceps contrasted with the entirely black shaded uniform. Rory did not give his name for public announcement and he strolled nonchalantly down the huge red carpet of the great ballroom. He made his way straight to the Chairman's table; he then clicked his heels together and raised his hand in a strange salute which was followed by the words.

"Seig Heill!"

When he finished his strange actions, Rory took an empty seat and sat down at the place that had been reserved for him. Without any show of respect or deference of been in the presence of the most feared and powerful man in the Anschluss, he spoke directly to Tell.

"Good evening "Baldies", so this is what the normal Plebs must mean by hobnobbing. What do you think of my uniform? Highly appropriate, don't you think. If you lot just had small black moustaches to go with those false hairpieces, then the setting would be highly apt for my outfit. Don't you think?"

Animosity laced his words. He would never forgive them for what they had done to him.

"So the verbal jousting has begun. He calls us "Baldies" because he thinks it is an effect of our genetic affliction." Ivan Tell decided. *"Or does he know of its true significance?"* Now, he was undecided. However, the others at the table were outraged at the man's front, people normally acted like they were threading around eggshells when in the great man's presence. All except one at the table did not recognise the uniform, but still each of them sensed the implied insult. The flouting of the banned Christian crosses was enough in itself to have a person incarcerated and made to disappear. Some stood up to remove this upstart, but with a look from the Chairman, these lackeys sat back down quickly. Ivan Tell knew of the uniform; the history behind it and the thinly veiled insult its wearer implied.

"So this is what he thinks of us?"

He clicked his fingers and motioned for a waiter. A hovering servant reacted instantly.

"Bring a drink for our guest and the finest Havana cigar."

His host wined and dined Rory with expensive liquors, rare treats and offered him the most beautiful women from their mist. But the man with the "Secret." seemed to scorn them and mock them with his eternal life. He raised his glass of an imported brandy, took a puff of a large cigar and gestured over to another table where the Prime Minster of the Anschluss sat.

"Is that the real one or one of your stooges?"

At this time, Rory knew their real nature. Later on in life, he had told his followers.

"The Chairman was the leader of the group that held the real and constant power. The office of the Prime Minster was always farcical."

He never divulged that they were also Clones. He knew that statement would be met with astonishment and disbelief. The acting Prime Minster returned Rory's salute, the uninformed man guessed.

"He must be someone important, if he is sitting at the Chairman's table."

Rory smiled at the puppet's ignorance and then he addressed those within earshot.

"I've noticed in my travels." (Travel's was a jibe, telling them that he could go out of the Anschluss without their permission or knowledge.) *"That those who rule prohibit certain freedoms to their societies, but not to themselves."*

"Oh we know about your little trips, unknown to you we have even thwarted some of your escapades." Ivan Tell sniggered silently.

The others sitting around the lavish table must have thought that Rory was talking about the luxurious items on the table in front of them, but the Chairman was certain that he was inferring to his own personal collection of banned books, art and other indulgences that the masses were denied. The big man responded to Rory's scorn.

"Certain things like knowledge and new ideas should only be used by those who are capable of putting them to good use for the benefit of all mankind. Information in the wrong hands is the worst crime that man can commit. We as the chalices of wisdom have a moral duty to protect the masses from themselves. Don't you agree or would you prefer a totally open society and all the disharmony it brings?"

Rory did not miss the reference.

"A chalice, so he jousts with a symbol of religious worship."

The Chairman in fine mettle continued.

"From what I understand, you rule your insignificant sect with absolute power and delegate little responsibility. Are we not the same, you and I? It's just a matter of perspective; I govern billions while you rule a couple of hundred misguided souls. My charges, the ordinary Plebs, by the way think that you are the bogeyman. These weak spirits do not like you; they fear your kind and look to us for protection."

"More religious references." Thought the leader of the RE-INSTATOR'S, but Rory did not respond. He resolutely held the view that secret society was not similar to the Anschluss rulers. For one, he did not treat his followers as sacrificial pawns. But he was well aware.

"These LYUBINITES are no fools, they have done what every great mind has failed to achieve. That was to conquer and unite the Continent of Europe under one government.

Although, I despise them, I have to admire them for that."

Those around the table enticed him into conversation, so they could see if he shared their beliefs. He did not. Then, still sitting at the Chairman's table, the proscribed group's leader then did an extraordinary thing. He clenched his fist and smashed a sesame seed cracker into smithereens and the crumbs were spread out in a large cluster on the white table-cloth. He picked at them randomly; devouring each selected fragment with relish and deviously asked the wisest among them.

"I know that the present means little to you, it's the future that compels your kind. You reach for the Stars, but will it be like it was promised when you get out there? Do you see this mess, I have just created? Is the Universe like this? Is each one of these crumbs, a Star or a Galaxy? As I devour each piece, it vanishes forever; does a Supreme Being do likewise with the Cosmos? Or as I heard you say the Universe is about using up the stuff left over after its creation and that stuff was put there for Mankind's benefit. Then I ask you once again what happens when all the stuff is used up? So many unknowns, don't you think? Are you not better to try and live for today?"

The irascible Kaiser had no answer for him and some of his underlings became red faced with the certainty.

"All these questions are mocking us and the "Great Secret."."

But the ALASTHA'I could have answered Rory's query. One of them would have mind-said in their enlightened way.

"Well, if all the lights went out in the Universe, we would attempt to re-ignite them again."

It was a cosmic paradox that the taking of life scared the passive Aliens to their crystal filaments, but a task of that enormity would be seen as a challenge. But that sort of science was way beyond Naomh's father's reasoning. The Chairman got to the point of the meeting.

"Enough of your babbling. I have asked you here tonight to join us. Think of what we can achieve together. Think of all the unknowns that we could solve?"

"Do you know that I was asked that same question, a long time back in Paris by your creator Dr Lyubin. And, I refused him." Replied Rory, putting the cat among the pigeons.

There were sharp intakes of breath around the table after the mention of that fantastic statement. To those in his immediate vicinity, it was like someone telling a Christian that they had met Jesus Christ himself. By all rights, the man before them should have been a revered member of their society. He harassed them further.

"Does that disturb you? That I had a personal conversation with your creator."

He was about to add that he had been nothing special, but he knew.

"That would push them too far."

Ivan Tell was the first to recover, he had already made this assumption years before.

"*That is all the more reason to join us.*"

Rory shook his head from side to side and bent close so only the Chairman heard his words.

"*After what you have done to me.*"

"*There are more of her.*"

This was whispered back.

"*I bet there is?*"

"*So why not join us? You can have her back again.*"

He ignored the offer and changed the subject.

"*There have been many types of government throughout history, all with their own names. Monarchies, Dictatorships, Democracies, Theocracies and so on. But what the fuck do you call one run by Clones. Especially as you are always trying to do each other over. Anyway how can you trust a government that cannot even trust itself?*"

Rory's jovial manner vanished. He gave the leader of the LYUBINITES a look of hatred that told of the hurt that they had caused him and accused.

"*You even sacrificed one of your own, who I had the misfortune to love.*"

"*Your son is one of us now.*"

"*He will never be; you will not find him.*"

At that moment, the Chairman guessed correctly.

"*This one will never join us. He has scorned our way all evening.*"

As if in confirmation of his words, Rory got up and left, but he gave a lingering glance of confusion at another table before his exit. Ivan Tell gave a delighted laugh; he was well aware who his departing guest was studying.

"*Look more closely; there is actually more of her here.*"

Security personnel were ordered to trail him and as usual, they lost him out on the streets. In his Bell tower, Tell had no regrets.

"*Yes. I am glad we eliminated him. What was it he said to me when he saw through my disguise and knew what I was? He said, just because you have lived a long time, it did not mean you were wiser than everybody else was. You could have lived in the same place and done the same things all your life. Thus going through a repetitive cycle of familiar events. Then, he rose from his seat and shouted at the selective gathering. Remember, a shroud has no pockets, even yours. Then, he had left. What the hell did he mean by those words? Yes, I am glad he is dead.*"

He was still bitterly disappointed that he had not seen his last moments. All that his hovering Wraiths had recorded was Naomh entering a dank alleyway. Then, he too vanished from the screens. Even his agent's false eye did not pick up his image. Twenty minutes later, it was as if the whole place was lit up and their blindness was cured. The narrow lane revealed a dejected Naomh with a smoking gun, but his father had vanished entirely.

"It is only because of my Spy that I know the bane of my security forces is indeed dead. But there is a mystery in that alley and it looks like the son has eliminated the father. Yes, Naomh is certainly one of us."

The Chairman had the last laugh. Some of the better-looking Clones had developed unnatural sexual appetites; this was weird considering the method of their birth. One of these gifted individuals had broken their taboo, with his permission of course. She had become Rory's lover and had given birth to Naomh.

"His father has been constantly outwitted by us. How would Naomh react, if he found out that he was one of us? And that the PREVENTIVE that had killed his parent had the same face as his mother. I would have paid over the odds to witness that surprised look on his father's face when he saw who our agent was. Yes, that was worth the decision alone to take the risk and eliminate him."

Naomh's mother had retrieved skin and hair follicles from her lover, but no scientist could clone his cells. The biology at his cellular level was so alien and complex, it was a language their adept geneticists did not comprehend. To the LYUBINITES, this had been further proof that Rory had been successful in gaining the mystery that was solely theirs. That is why she took it on herself to create a child in the repugnant way.

A few weeks later as he was going through reports from his Spy within Naomh's group, a slight cough from the shadows of his office drew his attention. Tell never heard the door to his office slide quietly open and someone enter. He had been expecting this individual, but he had not a clue of how long they had been in his presence. Naomh would be shocked to the core if he learned that this person was the exact duplicate of a member of his little cadre. Naomh's mother was not the only member of the LYUBINITES to infiltrate the RE-INSTATOR'S. The personage that had his attention was his private secretary, a position only second in importance to his. This person's unofficial title was the "Head of Protocol." and was well suited to the job as head of the Anschluss's espionage bureau. It was a position that this Chairman once held.

"Emotionally, this one in front of me is an empty vessel. And so cold hearted is this one, if I ordered it, they would throttle their own mother, if the Clone had one."

Tell was well aware of this types history.

"This particular series of Clone had not been an original member of the revered Doctor's disciples, but had only been accepted after the refusal of some nameless individual way back in the past. Their initial host had been chosen by default. So this one and my present Spy in Rory's organisation have more to prove than most. It had always been the way with them and could be portrayed as a major character fault.

296

The person who was now in his presence had only one overriding task and that was to eliminate any threat of their plans to join their creators out in space. Usually, the holder of this office would be the Chairman's successor, but Ivan Tell had another fantastic agenda and he silently snickered.

"With Naomh's help, my position will never again come available."

After been briefed by his agent, Tell had confided in his Secretary of Protocol and a few other senior Clones about the exact nature of Naomh's mission.

"This Pleb, who believes that we are his sworn enemy and who is also under our protection has to collect the pieces of our Creator's technology, which lie scattered around the World. And once it is assembled, this item will be the key that we have been seeking for nearly a thousand years. It will transform our existence; it is in effect the promise that had been made to us."

Aloud now, he continued in his musings in his synthetic voice for the secretary's benefit.

"This Rory was wrong. We are the true inheritors of the promise. Unlike those pathetic sentimentalists, we erased from our midst. We have no love of the past. Yes, we enjoy the trappings of power. That is our nature. We have our weapons. Atomic, chemical and biological. Our large security force and surveillance paraphernalia. But all of these things are only aids to the ultimate goal."

His annalist liked to hug the shadows from where this adviser's voice cautioned.

"The disasters of negligence are absolute."

Harshly, the Chairman turned on the owner of the voice.

"What does that imply?"

"Only that this Naomh is our only hope and like his father, he won't clone either. His skin and hair samples came back negative. He might not survive to deliver the key to us. We should use the same tactic, as our agent did with his father. Even though we do not understand why she did it. Our experts think it was another example of the degeneration. We should have another offspring as backup. We should use one of our good lookers and sexual experts; after all, it worked before."

Tell gave his advisor a dangerous look to see if he was been implicated.

"Are you saying that we should deliberately order one of our kind to break the taboo?"

Realising that a mark had been overstepped, the secretary backtracked.

"Well, it has already occurred before. And we might need the insurance of more genetic material from Lynch's seed. Dead is dead, after all."

The big man's sharp bark of a laugh rebounded on the speaker.

"You of all people should be very confident that our present operative will keep him alive until he has completed his mission."

"Of that there is little doubt." His secretary answered stiffly.

The infiltrator among Naomh's faction was from an elite branch of the security forces, made up entirely of fellow LYUBNITIES. The Spy's designation was simply; Agent XIII. This retention of ancient Roman numerals was a quirk of the ruling elite. It was their unique knowledge, which was not to be shared with the inferior masses. Plebs who saw these strange markings on ancient buildings were told that they were undecipherable. Any clever academic who solve the letters conundrum disappeared along with his or her findings. With knowledge of the past; connections could be made. The Chairman agreed with his advisor, associating pronouns instead of the moles name, it was their secret for now.

"Our Spy is very clever; Agent XIII can play dumb, passive, hard, very clever and fanatical to a cause. They are like the proverbial leopard changing their spots at will. In fact, they can be whatever Naomh wants them to be.

The Spy's genetic double had no doubt that the Chairman was referring to them as well.

"I take it; you have removed the main threat to Naomh without him guessing who was responsible." Enquired Tell.

"Need you ask? Paradise arrived early for him. The one who tried to blow him up is now with his so called Angels." Came the offended reply.

"I have studied this cell of the RE-INSTATOR'S from the information Agent XIII has given us. Take this list of his comrades that are to survive the purge. These people will give him the best chance at completing his task. You have a free hand to eliminate the rest."

The Kaiser handed over the file which was written on old-fashioned paper and his secretary scanned it. His second in command had also studied Naomh's cell and did not agree with Tell's choices.

"I have my reservations about some of them, but I will keep my opinions to myself. The Chairman's decisions are paramount, even if they are wrong."

In a rapid switch of thought that he was known for, a device designed to confuse antagonists and his secretary was a formidable opponent indeed, the supreme leader of the Anschluss questioned.

"Why do those countless masses out in our crammed urban sectors cry out for the preservation of things past? Is it when they see the primitive life their ancestors had, they can feel good and say, look how much more advanced and better off we are."

"Maybe it is because we have so much to learn from our ancestors." Hinted the shadowy figure.

Ivan Tell lost his composure and his normally monotone timbre rose slightly.

"Those primitive bastards rejected the true path to salvation and

caused the enlightened ones to reject this World and leave mankind to his own resources. If our Plebs have no idea where mankind is going, then why should they know about his past. The normal person is quite comfortable existing in ignorant bliss. So we, the keepers of the truth only allow some of the past to be remembered, so the masses can see how far we have progressed and know that our way is better."

Knowing the Chairman would lose his temper when anybody disagreed with him, the other person in the room agreed.

"Precisely, we have moved on."

Caught up in his contempt for the rest of Humanity, he told his second in command.

"Let me tell you something about those short sighted masses out there in the World and their ability to switch and change their short term view of things. Once on my travels, I came across a village whose existence seemed on the surface to be idyllic. The people led a simple, but prosperous life, farming fertile green pastures for generation upon generation. But the gifts from the fields were not inexhaustible and as long as it lasted, the villagers were able to afford some luxuries to supplement their existence, giving them a fairly well off lifestyle. And as the years passed, their fields were gradually losing their fertility and as each year passed, their lifestyle diminished a little bit. Then at a time of low crop yields, one of them discovered that below the topsoil lay a large seam of a much sought after and very valuable metal. Now, the villagers had a dilemma. Would they give up the life they had known for centuries and the fields that their past generations had loved and cherished and mine the soil to retain their comfortable way of life. If this generation did, then it would spell the end of their treasured community and usher in another way of life. Ties that had made them what they were would break and shatter the link with the past."

"It would depend on the individuals." Answered the other.

"Exactly, the younger generation would dig up the fields, but the older generation would perish in sentiment, wanting to keep the old ways."

His secretary was as intelligent as he was and with that renowned insight, the Chairman's advisor spoke.

"This is a lesson for us. We would dig up the fields."

Privately his second in command wanted to say.

"And get rid of those in charge as well."

But wisely kept silent. Ignorant, Tell nodded his bald head.

"Yes. Because this World that we were abandoned on has a finite amount of resources. It will fail to support the exponential growing population of mankind. After all there is only so much carbon, nitrogen, oxygen and other vital elements circulating around the Planet. The cycle of life will eventually fail because of the enormous amount of elements taken out of the system and stored in the Human population. This is what the

299

leader of the RE-INSTATOR'S meant about using up the stuff. He was really talking about this Planet."

"But what of the space resources? The quantity of materials out there appears to be inexhaustible." Demanded his confidant.

"We are reaching a crisis up there. The interbred who are capable of existing off Planet for long periods are dwindling rapidly. Our limited space existing gene pool has to be held in reserve for emergencies." Stated the Chairman.

The ruler of the Anschluss was referring to the discovery made centuries before that those people with limited gene pools from the isolated areas of the Planet were disappearing as the decades rolled by. These scarce individuals were able to tolerate the Space Virus much longer than most of the World's population. But through wars and assimilation, these ingenious peoples with their genes needed for space travel were decreasing. The continuous merging of the Human population was according to the LYUBINITES another straying from the true path. The Anschluss had isolated a certain amount of individuals still capable of existing off-world. In keeping with his honed ability to unsettle subordinates, the Chairman switched the focus of the discussion yet again.

"Do you know that Naomh's father was over nine hundred years old? I do not know how long he would have lived if he had not been killed."

"You jest?" Said his secretary, privately wondering.

"Is he taking liberties with his superior knowledge?"

Seeing his serious countenance, the doppelganger whistled.

"It's a pity that there was no trace of his body found."

"We will not go into the blame game about that." Replied an unusually forgiving Chairman.

"There were unusual circumstances."

Not taking the bait, Tell continued.

"About fifty years ago, a Clerk in the records ministry doing some routine research discovered it. The inquisitive bureaucrat followed the information trail back in time and was astounded at what it implied. The man informed his superiors and told them, that Rory had left a deliberate trail. It was as if he wanted to leave a message to us."

"What happened, when he reported this?" Asked the secretary, now fully engrossed.

"It was checked out and found to be true."

"And the Clerk?"

Tell sighed theatrically.

"His diligence was rewarded with elimination. We are always tying up loose ends."

Taking this as a hint, his underling withdrew. A few days later, Tell called his secretary back into his presence; he had decided to tell his assistant about the recent failure of their intelligence services. It was

300

something that he had not passed to his aide yet. The big man pursed his ruby lips and spoke in his husky monotone.

"There is a little matter that is puzzling our boffins. As you are well aware our mutual friend, now in the ranks of Naomh's party has a low frequency monitor that lets us know their location continuously. Twenty-four hours a day, seven days a week and so on. But the signal vanished a few days ago and it has not returned."

"But I know this system. It should be impossible to detect. The only other solution is that our agent was afraid of its discovery and disabled it." Replied his assistant looking very perplexed.

The Chairman remained silent, but was inwardly thinking.

"We both know the implications if Naomh has discovered our Spy. Our plans, centuries in the making could come to nothing. This time, I have no alternative schemes, if everything goes pear shaped. All our eggs are in the one basket."

"Why not send a communication to our mutual friend asking their opinion." Suggested his second in command.

"Negative. Such a transmission might now be intercepted. Our friend is only to be contacted, when there is no alternative. We have to wait for them to initiate any communication." Replied the Chairman firmly.

"Alright then. I will pay a visit to the Ministry of Communications and find a solution to the problem. That is our most pressing issue at the moment."

The secretary left the room with an expression on a face that said a grave error of misjudgement had been made. Regretting his candour, Tell requested the dramatic overture to continue from where he had stopped it the last time he was listening to its score. Not really paying attention to the background symphony, a brooding Chairman was left alone with unpleasant thoughts.

"Should I order my second in command to be eliminated. Was that one hinting that I might be fallible? Besides, it is well known that many of my predecessors had been removed in the past for what were perceived as misjudgements. Or did my clever and accomplished advisor guess that I sometimes used the RE-INSTATOR'S to eliminate any challengers to my position among our own ranks and take them out of the equation? Unknown to either group of course."

He turned the volume up as his final musings on the problem played in his head.

"Naomh might be proving even more resourceful than I considered. Then after all, is he not an overall part of the solution to the problem that was given to us from those out there. It only makes sense that he and his father would have advanced technology like us. It would just be different, that's all."

The bald ruler of the Anschluss began humming along the melody that encompassed his office as he went back to the viewing glass. A slight crack in his facial reflection reminded him.

"My Spy's own personal defect was seen too before that one began this mission and it would be at least another five years before such surgery is required again. It is ample time. But then when I succeed, there will be no more need for those adjustments anymore."

He also knew.

"This mission will be completed long before that time frame, for my agent has a zealous appetite for murder, deceit and betrayal. After all, that Clone is one of us and this sort of behaviour is in our genes."

Satisfied, the master planner commanded his hidden machinery.

"Open shutters."

The voice-activated machinery opened the seals fully. As the mechanical blinds unfolded silently and fluidly, he peered at the heavens above the murky lair of water vapour. He was looking for inspiration up there. Ivan Tell knew with certainty that if he failed, then there were many out there in the wings of his own ranks waiting to usurp his position.

"For are not my fellow conspirators spawned from the original gene pool's as myself and the original disciples. Obviously, some of them have the same talents to exploit, abet to a lesser degree."

The LYUBINITES operated in a climate of culpability and those who failed to deliver the required results bore the full responsibility of their deficiency. The reason for the removal of the location device by his Spy was indeed the obvious one. The RE-INSTATOR'S had indeed acquired advanced technologies, something similar to what their dead founder possessed an in consequence. Deep within their ranks, a pragmatic Agent XIII pondered.

"I cannot take the chance that something in the new inventory will reveal my transmissions. Still, time will tell. I will have to be more careful with them in future; they are becoming quite resourceful, even without the clever bastard, Rory to guide them."

XIV.

The Secretary of Protocol reported directly to the Chairman.

"You would have to admire their single-mildness; still they had more than a little help from us. Their vicious and unrestrained bloodletting is nearly over. The cloak and dagger assassinations have petered out to a minimum. A fragile truce is in effect. The internal and often bitter faction fighting has done what we were not inclined to; not yet anyway, it has made a serious dent in the number of RE-INSTATOR'S. Rumours are abounding that each cell has been so seriously depleted to the point that no group will prove a serious threat to the establishment in the foreseeable future. The laughable idea that they were an actual threat to the Anschluss is entirely their own belief."

Tit for tat killings had been the norm since the Gaffer's death and some of the newly formed splinter groups were irrevocably wiped out to a man. The Kaiser's aide put the proscribed group's death toll at 991 individuals with the Preacher and his following suffering the most horrifying demise of them all. After, the wily Escobar had fled from the exploding apartment in the London Contrib; his fluttering black cloak making him look like a bat out of hell, he raged at Naomh's survival from his unwitting Human bomb. A few days later after his failed murder attempt on his main opposition and vowing that the job would be finished, the vengeful follower of his God gathered together all of his faction in an obscure farming district in the Agriculture Sector not far from the Madrid Contrib. But unknown to him, the Chairman had sent out a punitive force in his wake. It was led by the Secretary of Protocol and this agent would not fail. This elimination squad whose sole responsibility was to tie up the Chairman's loose ends had tracked him down and these efficient killers were ordered to make an example of this non-conforming individual.

"Any danger to Lynch's son has to be eliminated and this Tobias Escobar is certainly the biggest threat to his continued survival. Remove him from the equation at once."

The Kaiser had raged when he had witnessed how close this Pleb from outside the Contrib's had come in killing Naomh with his suicide bomb. Heads had rolled over that debacle and those who had not seen the danger from the so called Preacher suffered more than most. High tech shadowy spectres moved into position with a buzz of radio traffic that was only audible to them. When the unit was ready, their leader gave the order with a cynical laugh.

"Let's give them some holy smoke."

Two biological dust bombs were hurled into the makeshift church where the Preacher and his faction members had gathered. As the orator began his sermon in the eager hall, his contralto voice punctured the hushed space as he read from his version of the scriptures. Anger was still at the forefront of his thoughts.

"I will make my flock plead for forgiveness tonight."

He began with great devotion; his voice trembled with passion. The Preacher beseeched his God, he begged and then prayed to be allowed to sit at his Creators right hand on judgement day; (The pious Escobar would not be so vocal in his request, if he realised that it was to be granted in a few minutes). Caught up in his self-importance, he was distracted slightly by a distorted purple gas that wafted around the hall.

"The incense is a strange colour today. I know that it is difficult to come by, but they could have done better than that. I will berate the procurer of the banned substance later."

The smoke grew thicker and thicker, it dancing plumes seemed alive somehow. Obnoxious fumes hemmed his parishioners in. The Preacher's oration faltered as he witnessed in disbelief, the demise of his flock. Through the thick haze, he saw scenes of the hell that he regularly sermonised about. Everyone in the packed hall began to vomit instantly and expressions turned to panicked horror as the green haze began dissolving the congregation's skin. The hall became a bizarre dance of pagan tetany as his flock lost the function of their legs and arms as each and everyone succumbed to the deadly gas. Some nearest the exits tried to escape, but the doors were barred. Nail scrapes in jagged blood formed on the soft wood as those at the closed entrances died in a more prolonged agony. None of the audience saw the Preacher's horrific death, as his entire flock had become fatty pools of melted flesh minutes before he finally perished to the same affliction. He had been last to die horribly as his pulpit was high above his departed flock. The regular orator liked to look down on his worshippers and one of his last sights was one of dissolved tissue. As the concocted malady gripped him, the door of the hall burst inwards in a hail of jagged splinters and a black figure strode towards him. Cloaked in a chemical protection suit, the secretary of Protocol reached him and knelt beside him. The dying man gazed at those features and instantly recognised them. In his losing struggle with death, all he could gasp was.

"You!"

That person left out a cruel laugh and then retreated from the scene. The Chairman orders to liquidate the Preacher's faction had been carried out literately. With his dying breath, (Curiously his mouth was the last piece of his body to dissolve.) the Preacher cursed Naomh. Seeing his killer's face had made him come to the wrong conclusion of who was responsible for his demise. Finally, his trademark black glasses fell to the floor and settled atop the pool of molten flesh. There were no survivors and two hundred odd souls had perished in that assault. With the mission completed, Tell's agent ordered.

"Turn the building to ashes; I want no evidence of what happened

here."

Although, the leader of the extermination squad would have preferred to leave the scene intact to remind those who opposed them, what their fate would be. However, the total destruction of the building was the agent's orders.

"Still I did enjoy the screams of despair."

Tell had also taken pleasure from the images of the massacre. He had a centre staged view, provided by a live video feed. Towards the end of January on the normal calendar, the new but disputed Gaffer was caught up in his own problems and had no idea that the Preacher had perished in such a horrific manner. He was preoccupied with his one certainty.

"This split among the remaining factions of the RE-INSTATOR'S is permanent and irreversible. So, I must plan for the future."

Naomh had lost a few good friends during the vicious feud, including a close associate of his, Tim the hat man. He had been a proficient assassin and a flamboyant character from the Athens Contrib. Somebody close to him had put poison inside the rim of one of the many trademark hats that he always wore. It was hinted that the only people who saw his baldhead were those he was about to kill. Tim always had his weapon concealed in his headgear and only removed it to use his pistol. After killing a member of another faction, he had put his hat back on unaware of the deadly concoction that had just been squirted into its inside rim. The poisonous acid had fused the material to his crown. Within seconds, he was screaming in fatal agony and for once he was trying to remove his head covering without the intention of murder. The lethal concoction ate through his scalp and dissolved his brain. An emotionally hardened Greta urged on by Cahill mentioned.

"It would have been classic, if he had not been Naomh's friend and one of our faction."

Others had been assassinated by more conventional means; bombs and bullets were the main reasons for their demise. Naomh pondered over the mess.

"Now it is up to me to paper over the cracks, but I have no idea where to begin."

Then, it came to him.

"Of course, the Gaffers place."

Having decided on this course of action, he went alone to his parents allocated living space, to gather information and hopefully to put his internal demons to bed. His father's apartment was also located in the Dublin Contrib, overlooking the largest green space in the area. The city park was dominated by a huge monolith. Its original dedicated appellation had been replaced by the one of the LYUBINITES. The flat was small and compact, so a tenant got the view instead of the space. But Rory always preferred to live here saying.

"It is large enough for a bachelor like me."

Before the incredible revelation, Naomh had often wondered why the man who he believed to be his uncle never married and it wasn't as if the opposite sex found him unattractive. It was quite the opposite in fact. He had never broached that particular subject with Rory. But now he believed that he knew the truth.

"My father killed my mother and this violent betrayal made him shy away from the opposite sex. Never mind the fact that he was a worm."

No matter what efforts the one part Mescal/Amulet put in to Naomh accepting his destiny, the son of two murdered parents could never forgive his father for that act. He himself had already come to terms with his own patricide. With a head full of new revelations, he entered the apartment and his eyes were drawn instantly to a photo-scan magnetically stuck on the back wall. Instant fury overwhelmed him and he charged towards the offending object and tore it from the partition. The erroneous orphan cast the captured image into a wastebasket. He stood there waiting for his intense trembling to subside. The object of his rage was a six hundred millimetre square image of himself as a toddler with both of his non-existent parents standing with broad smiles on either side of him.

"How many hours did I stare at that fraudulent lie, wondering if somehow I could retrieve some semblance of my lost childhood in the company of those dead parents."

His face briefly contorted in rage and he stamped his foot through the plastic frame of the false image as it protruded from the wrong recycling bin. Satisfied with his petulant act, he turned back to view the wall where the image had hung. However, the glaring print that had been protected by the frames back still mocked him. It brought forth awareness of the discarded photo-scan. Fuming, he went to a utensil cupboard and returned with a cleaning fabric. With a little too much effort, he scoured the wall. During this effort of eradication, the partition did a strange thing. The solid concrete barrier began to hum and vibrate and then to his bewilderment, the once very tangible wall had vanished completely.

"Shit." Said a startled Naomh as he dropped the cleaning cloth.

What really baffled him was that he was drawn to the space which was revealed, when he should have ran as fast as his legs would take him and fled the apartment, claiming out aloud that his madness had been revisited. Some sense within told him.

"This type of thing was normal for the Gaffer and nothing would surprise me anymore."

The Alien metallic voice returned and it urged him.

"Go in, cross the threshold."

He had become comfortable with it over the last few weeks. With uncalled logic, he demanded from the unsubstantial intruder.

"This has something to do with you, has it not?"

306

The voice confirmed his suspicions.

"You will find answers in there."

He took a deep breath and entered the newly discovered space. A confused Naomh found a room that was at least three times bigger than the rest of the flat.

"That's impossible." He exclaimed.

The black haired RE-INSTATOR had been wrong about not been astonished anymore, his emerging goose bumps grew more pronounced. He was intensely familiar with the layout of the building and assumed.

"There should be a small cupboard and then a public corridor at the other side of this wall."

Every member of the outlawed organisation checked out escape routes of the buildings that they regularly used, this was done more in the last few months. His heart jumped as the wall reappeared behind him with the same humming sound that heralded its original disappearance. Aware that he was now closed in and unsure of a getaway, Naomh's eyes were drawn to a huge unrecognisable V.D.U system that held a three dimensional unmoving image of a man in its limited field. The transmitted static figure hung suspended in a mid-air gaseous bubble with no visible attachment keeping it in place. The displayed image somehow belonged to the visualization and somehow, it did not. Its unmerging contours reminded him of oils viscosity with water. The amulet in his chest glowed briefly penetrating the fabric of his shirt like a red wound. The sparkling sphere responded to the cue and reactivated itself. The unfrozen image displayed a recording of a warrior from the past (Naomh had seen similar types of dress in a museum.) The image of a tall blond Aryan male with a braided beard in the very strange attire began a narration. Captivated, Naomh listened to his words. This was no ancient warrior from man's past, but a Human image superimposed on the features of Cathbad who was sitting in his Diadem fifteen thousand years ago. It was a recording carried by the line of the red jewel's holders. The image overlaid on the winged Alien from the post ice age regarded the stranger in front of him. If the representation was surprised to see another instead of Rory, he did not show it. Then Naomh surmised.

"It is a recording."

The antiquated warrior's false words told an unbelievable story.

"If you are viewing this chronicle and able to access it, then you are the next in line to bear the APOCRYPHA'I. You are the descendant of us, the first Humans to flee to this World. We fled from a malevolence so vile and ruthless that it defies comprehension. This master of deceit caused us, a race of perfect Human beings to mutate into insecticide grubs, so it would be able to feed on us."

Images of that false deception were displayed on the screen; new images showed the slow decay of a perfect Human into a creature that he had seen once before. For the one part Mescal/Amulet was feeding off of the Hybrid's jumbled emotions and concocting the only plausible story that this one would accept. Cathbad's interactive image in the guise of the warrior continued the fabrication.

"You are the last descendant of our esteemed leaders and only you can assemble the instrument of our enemies destruction. The voice in your head is part of this process."

This lie was close enough to the truth and the disguised image of Cathbad showed him the plan, the false Human explained.

"The Amulet in your chest is the key to mankind's salvation. It is called the APOCRYPHA'I. It assembles from seven single pieces of descending frequency to form a completed object. It is now disassembled and scattered around the globe in the hands of different Humans. This was done to keep them out of our enemy's pinchers. You must go in search of them and re-assemble it. Your red piece will guide you to the others. Our races future is in your hands."

The disguised winged being from the past last sentence was not referring to mankind; he was pertaining to his own Alien race. Under the influence of the red piece of the living jewel and its connections to the past, Naomh accepted the encompassed image of the Ancient Warrior's word's as the complete truth. Both of these technologies combined to superimpose his ego. It made him believe that he was destined for great things and what was more important than saving Mankind from a terrible fate. His father's transformation into a Human larva had convinced him of the reality behind the warrior's words. Great relief made him utter.

"The Gaffer failed and that's why that happened to him. He was not born like that."

Then in a flickering hiccup, the afore mentioned man's features superimposed themselves on the three dimensional representation. The image was so lifelike that Naomh felt infuriated at the semblance of his mother's killer and had to refrain himself from foolishly attacking his father's image. Rory's form was accompanied with various icons. The graphics offered a montage of various options. Listed on the screen were personal, contacts, equipment, etc. Naomh chose the first option. An interactive video of Rory appeared.

"How strange, he never allowed any images of himself to be taken."

It began.

"This message has to be quick; I will be able to lock it out briefly, so listen carefully. Naomh, my child. Yes, you are my son. I know this is going to be a hell of a shock to you. You are more than likely cursing me right now. You probably despise me. But my son, you will never know the joy; I had been your father. But our relationship had to remain a secret. We have too many enemies and some of them wanted you for their own schemes. Please forgive me. As you are viewing this, then I can be sure the thing has

decided that I am surplus to requirements. You are now the inheritor of the family secret and the fate of mankind now rests on your shoulders. But do not trust the voice, it has its own agenda. God bless my son."

Then, there was a short postscript.

"I hope you did not try and use that poisoned pill, I am nearly ninety nine per cent sure that it will not allow it to work. It has other plans for you."

The image of his dead parent faded.

"That's it; this short note was all that he left me. How can this explain all the hurt and pain that I am going through? He never told me why he killed my mother. There must be more."

Naomh was hurt and furious at his father's short message. He searched for more, but that was it. Everything else, he found with Rory's image contained technical information. That was the only personal file belonging to him that had slipped past the piece of the Mescal/Amulet. As soon as it had made contact with the three-dimensional information unit, it managed to corrupt other files and information that Naomh's father had amassed during his extraordinary and eventful long life. The ALASTHA'I wanted a clean slate on which to work upon. Its latest bearer would have no baggage from the past. Its host stayed in the unreal room and spent days reviewing what the blond warrior and his father's brief notes had told him. The one part Mescal/Amulet had come to the conclusion that this Hybrid was the one to reassemble it. With false recordings from Rory, it eventually convinced him that he had to travel the globe to reassemble the amulet. Naomh balked at the task.

"I have spent my entire life in the confines of the Anschluss and such a journey might as well be to the Moon. My friends and I know nothing about the outside World."

He was wrong, Tell's agent knew quite a lot about such things. The Alien voice with the assistance of the false image of the blonde warrior and Rory's false image put a plan together. An illegal map of the World appeared on the imaging device. He enquired.

"Where is the Anschluss?"

His homeland became tinted in green and it looked so insignificant to the rest of the landmasses. He would have thought it much bigger than that.

"Where do I have to go?" Was his second question.

The voice of the APOCRYPHA'I showed him where it had located the second segment; this area was highlighted for him as well. Intrigued his finger skimmed across the flickering contours of the imaging device and at the same time, his brain received images of a wall of tall buildings under a line of mountains on what must be a seashore. This unrecognisable spot was where he must go. Another image of Rory materialized and he removed his caressing digit as if he had received an electric shock. Showing no emotion, the representation of his dead father gave him a name of a contact who was familiar with the Nations outside the Anschluss. The man's name was Franz van DerKamp; a transitional resident of the Amsterdam Contrib. Naomh spent the next few weeks contemplating the impossible, leaving the only home he had ever known and going out to the hell World outside the Anschluss.

"I am not up to it. I would not know how to begin such a quest. I might as well be put on another Planet as venture beyond the walls of the Anschluss. There is no way; another option will have to be found. How can they entrust such an impossible search to me? This thing I have to assemble is scattered around the World outside. It would be easier to search for a needle in a haystack and I have seen the size of those in the agricultural sector."

The enormity of leaving his homeland set in and the doubting Thomas returned to the hidden room. Again he confronted the blonde form about the impossible task that he had given him, hoping that the image could reassure him. But the Ancient Warrior was only a recording and it gave him no more insight, it just kept repeating.

"You have to search for the rest of the APOCRYPHA'I or mankind is doomed."

Then, after another two days, the one part Mescal/Amulet directed him to a concealed space at the back of the hidden room. All that it contained was a single oily coloured glass like object about the size of a marble. This was the Guidex Sphere, a device created during the long voyage to the Planet of their temporary exile. In an unprecedented development, the invention was named after the individual who created the theory of warping space. By naming it after its creator, the ALASTHA'I had cemented the fact that they were no longer a unified commune. It's inside facets contained a mist of oily colours that pulsed in an unknown sequence. The one part Mescal/Amulet instructed its host to clasp his hands around the small sphere and concentrate. Naomh became lost in child-like wonder as the mist of swirling colours expanded and the globe began to increase in volume. He had no idea whether he was shrinking or it was growing. Finally when the mesmerising chimera reached the size of a man, it stopped enlarging. It was a wonder of flickering hues; something that might be found at the end of a rainbow. The fully emerged phantasm then did a Magician's trick. It seemed to suck in all the light of the hidden room, distort the air around it and in an instant, it vanished. Naomh had leapt back from it when it had suddenly disappeared. The internal voice told him.

"The Guidex Sphere is still there in the exact same place. The globe has gone through a series of refraction's and reductions. It has become invisible. On the wall of your father's hiding place are several bands of light. Take one of those and clasp it around your wrist. Focus the device on where the Guidex Sphere is. Press the correct sequence. This is the only

way; you can pass through the light shell."

Naomh went over to a shelf and found the previously mentioned bands. He picked up one. The seemingly plastic wristband was made up of seven square coloured crystal blocks that looked dull and lifeless. The voice told him.

"Press them in the order of the light spectrum."

The Hybrids were not capable of activating the sphere by mind-speech. Under instruction, he pressed the red, orange, yellow, green, blue, indigo and violet keys in that order. A narrow pencil of light shot out much like the coloured light of a flashlight. The missing circle of luminance responded and became visible again for an instant, then it mimicked the sequence of the visible light spectrum and vanished from Naomh's sight once again.

"Now leave it unseen and go to it."

He moved towards where he had last seen it and the voice within commanded.

"Enter the light absorbing sphere and behold the wondrous technology of our race."

The remnant of the ALASTHA'I did not mention.

"It had been a challenge to adjust the internal settings of the Guidex Sphere to the bodily chemistry of the Hybrid's."

Reluctantly Naomh approached the invisible globe and felt for it like a blind man suddenly finding himself in an unfamiliar locale. Feeling nothing, he stumbled and fell into it. Rory's son screamed out loud as he found himself enveloped in a space that could not be contained inside the confines of the globe. His mind was fast becoming confused.

"A space within a space that could not be there in the first place."

These unfamiliar transitions were playing havoc with his insides, he felt queasy. The internal presence calmed its host's rapid beating heart and his pulse began to return to normal. The now visible interior of impenetrable light was of a bland icy white reflection, but it was far from cold. After a confused inspection, he noticed that it was at least three times his height

"Expose the part of me. "

Naomh did as he was informed and bared the red jewel. The parameters of the incredible white space diminished in brightness and paled into a blank canvas. Like a ripple effect, red tesseral globules appeared at random spaces along its form and filled in where some of the blankness had been. Again, the voice of reasoning broke into his thoughts.

"Touching these red panels in various sequences will give you access to information and technology. As you gain another piece of the APOCRYPHA'I, other light frequencies of the spectrum will fill in and thus give you more access to the two before mentioned subjects."

"How will I know which ones to push?"

"This knowledge will come to you in time."

The presence of the mad exile was also confined to the limits and dictates of its Hybrid host; he too would only increase his knowledge as he merged with the other segments. Then the one part Mescal/Amulet guided him back to the entrance. Amazed, he passed through its transparent barrier and entered back into his father's hidden room feeling dizzy and light headed. Again, Naomh was flabbergasted. The Alien presence had a momentary feeling of pride at this basic piece of his race's technology and the awe emanating from its host. The masters of light technology had come up with the solution to the problem of the Preceptor- Bands by substituting them with the inferior technology for two reasons. The primary reason was that the Hybrid's brain waves were incompatible with the technology and secondly because of their creations unpredictability towards difference as anyone seen with a floating halo would be revered or killed outright.

"Now the hard part, illustrating what the sphere is to the Hybrid."

It explained to its host.

"This device is known to us as the Gudiex Sphere. It is a globe of concealment and protection that works on the principle that the amount of given space in a precise volume can be increased by compressing more volume into that existing space. But it has limits as the amount of space that can be compressed is proportional to the original surface area that is to be increased."

Naomh halted its explanation, when he slapped his forehead in an exaggerated gesture and mouthed.

"What the hell are you talking about? I went into a big white room that appeared from nowhere; just tell me what else it does."

The one part Mescal/Amulet wondered.

"Have we overestimated the intelligence of the Hybrids?"

His shade decided to simplify things.

"To put it plainly, the globe of concealment hides and protects anything that is contained within its parameters. The outside mass of the sphere can be shrunk to the size of a small pebble and enlarged to two metres when activated. It can withstand the impact of any type of weapon, even atomic, biological or chemical devices. When activated, the Guidex sphere cannot be detected by any instrument on this Planet."

Naomh told the voice.

"I have never heard of the weapons you have just mentioned."

The one part Mescal/Amulet realized it had indeed miss-judged the scope of this Hybrid's intelligence.

"How can a being from the race that created these terrible weapons, not know of them?"

But then, the distilled piece of the formally mad Mescal did not recollect his deceptions from his own race. The voice within Naomh stated simply with patience that it would not have needed for its own kind.

"The globe of concealment and protection can withstand impacts from

any weapon in the Anschluss's arsenal."

The Hybrid looked dubious while pondering the whole conception and then infuriated the one part Mescal/Amulet when he said.

"The name you gave it is too complicated. I will give it another label."

He thought deeply about the objects two priorities, protection and concealment and the answer presented itself. Two fairly common pets in the households of the Anschluss gave him his solution for a simple name. The first animal was the Chameleon, which was ideal in concealing itself and the second was the Tortoise, which had an outer shell for protection. Combining these two names, Naomh came up with the TORT-CAM.

"Yes, I rather like that name."

The ALASTHA'I within the amulet indulged itself in a bout of wry humour. It wondered why the Hybrids always had to name inanimate objects with the names of the fauna and flora of their Planet. Satisfied, Naomh spent the whole day activating and deactivating the Alien device. He entered and exited it continuously until he became very familiar with its operation. Somewhere during the uncounted translations, he asked a suddenly conceived question.

"Why didn't Rory use this technology? It would have made our battles a lot simpler."

"He wasn't ready for it. The Guidex Sphere needs you to activate it. Your gene-pool is more advanced than his."

Finally, Naomh was convinced of his destiny and with the help of the new found technology, he became resolute in journeying to those exotic places outside the only home that he had ever known and assembling the Amulet. He now believed.

"Completing this task will give me the means of overthrowing the corrupt regime."

The new leader of the RE-INSTATOR'S was slowly convinced that the picture had become bigger. He now had a unique task that dwarfed his previous ambition.

"I am the Human races only chance at redemption."

Naomh spent a long time considering his options and realised.

"I have little choice, this is the only path left open to me. Not only are the Filth seeking me, but now also, my former comrades have a vendetta against me. The truce will not last long. I am hunted from all sides and have very few contacts left. Only those I trust and the one name provided by my father."

He sent out coded messages to those that he wanted to accompany him, even to the associate provided by Rory. Naomh contacted the Pleb named Franz van DerKamp on his M.I.M and received a blocked out image. He explained to the voice.

"I am the new Gaffer and the old one is dead.

There was a long silence on the other side, the Amsterdam Contrib accent returned and agreed to help him. Taking a chance Naomh sent him a representation of the part of the World that he had to go to. If Rory's man had seemed astounded by the request, then his voice betrayed little. He ceased contact, but a few days later, Naomh's Frogs eyes received a message. His father's mysterious agent would arrange their departure from the Anschluss, but it would take a few months for a sea going vessel to go where he wanted to go. He could do nothing until then, but stay alive. The following Sunday, Naomh met all of the other survivors of the feud who he hoped to accompany him on his quest at a football match in the centre of the London Contrib. Only seven of those who he had sent feelers out to; turned up. He was slightly disappointed at the numbers. It appeared that most of the others were keeping their heads down and did not trust anybody, especially the one who had sparked off the killing in the first place. The sporting event took place in a huge stadium, one of the largest in the World, because after all according to one of the LYUBINITES.

"Every regime needed its Coliseum to keep the mob happy."

The game was between the London Contrib and the Madrid Contrib. Their hacker had got them the much sought after tickets. This venue had been chosen specifically, because like a huge flock of birds or a swarm of bees, their private conversations would be difficult to pinpoint in such traffic. This huddled group were any faces, in a sea of two hundred and fifty thousand individuals. But even now, electronic eyes in the sky were still watching them. The seven comrades that sat alongside him were the last of his true friends and were certainly the only ones, he could trust. Two surprised him, he had been unsure of them. Cahill, Greta and the Clerk had accompanied him to this rendezvous with the others. Here, the four of them met those who went by the aliases of the Prof, the Lenses, the Engineer and his large brother, the Persuader. Naomh told them.

"I have an incredible story to tell you. A way of ending the corruption of the Anschluss forever."

Needless to say, the others were more than intrigued. Their new leader received looks that said he was mad; the death of his uncle must have pushed him over the edge. But Naomh could not divulge the full truth about this far-fetched wild goose chase; that he was about to embark on. The current leader of the RE-INSTATOR'S explained his plan through their personalised M I M's. Their Frog Eyes did not look out of place in the stadium, for it was the only way to communicate in the vast crowd and most of the spectators used them for replays. A passing Barcelona wave interrupted their scheming as they joined in so as not to appear conspicuous. The exuberant celebration thundered around the huge stadium five times and then petered out. He went straight to the point.

"I have to go outside the Anschluss to complete a piece of technology that will give us the means of over throwing the corrupt regime that we are forced to live in."

Most of his stunned colleagues looked extremely sceptical. Still, the Prof who hailed from the London Contrib immediately agreed to go. This thirty-three year old Pleb got his code-name as he was perceived by all those except Rory, as being the cleverest among them. Edward Boyd, his real name was a lean man with a prominent Adams apple. He was the quintessential academic with his hooked nose, large old-fashioned spectacles that sat about high cheek bones and a slightly receding tuff hairline above them again. There were cures for that, but he did not bother with them. He would say when the subject came up.

"Baldness is not an ailment."

This high forehead gave an impression that he enjoyed intellectual challenges. His large wavy hair (where he had it) was balding and greying slightly; it contrasted sharply against the verdant brown of his pencil thin moustache. He was softly spoken and always emphasised his words. The Prof was fed up with the confines of the Anschluss and now Naomh was giving him a chance to follow his life-long dream and see the rest of the unknown World. He worked as a curator in a museum in which the only past portrayed was the one the LYUBINITES wanted. He told those sitting around him.

"One time when I was in a fit of depression over my closeted life, I took an unscheduled Mag-lev journey to the Kiev Contrib. I got as close to the eastern wall as I could. I spent over twelve hours staring at the obstacle and dreaming about what it was like on the other side. If I could have got through it I would have gone."

Been part of the Anschluss machinery, the wayward Prof was been tracked all the time from his implanted APS chip. This brought him to the attention of his superior's and subsequently Rory. With help from another within his cell; the Lenses, they were able to doctor the Prof's chip and the academic could now be wherever he wanted to be. It was a taste of freedom abet still in the confines of the Anschluss, but Edward Boyd was extremely grateful for it. The Lenses (Peter Kaliningrad.) on the other-hand disagreed with the necessity of leaving for foreign parts as the man from the Warsaw Contrib was well aware that he would be away from his beloved computers. The pink eyed man lived in a World of digital and wireless communication and rarely ventured out from his apartment. The thought of leaving his precious machines behind was too horrible to contemplate. Rory often said of the twenty-four year old Lenses.

"I can understand why he is wrapped up in technology. When you press the right icons, it does what you command it. It doesn't disagree with you or come up with different ideas or answer you back. Wrapped up with them all the time makes for a boring life"

But for all his wisdom, the Lenses was not quite sure that Rory understood about machines and the virtual plane. He would patiently explain the Gaffers failing.

"Computers also have personalities and can be just as awkward and unpredictable as people."

The Pleb from the Warsaw Contrib was under no illusions of his chances of evading the PREVENTIVES and certain capture without the others protection. He was also the youngest of them. Although the Lenses was the same height as the Prof, he had pink shaded pupils and would stand out in any crowd. The eye surgery had been performed by Rory, so that the appointed hacker could spend an unlimited amount of time accessing digital information without any adverse effect on his sight. So, Kaliningrad had little choice and agreed to go. The Lenses had a habit of wearing odd socks and his jumpers inside out. This annoyed the next member present, the brown eyed Engineer. Miguel Salvador from the Madrid Contrib would follow anyone who promised to bring back the banished faith to the atheist masses. The Engineer knew that the Anschluss had lost its soul and the deeply religious man firmly believed that Naomh and his uncle before him would re-establish the forbidden worship of Jesus Christ. The Engineer was an average sized man for the Anschluss, at nearly 183 cm, the same height as Naomh or Cahill, but taller that the Prof, the Lenses and the Clerk. He was embodied with a long serious face that reneged on the scant pleasures of life and for all that the rest of them knew, he was still a virgin, his God wanted him to remain celibate. The twenty-eight year old could not give his adoration to anything else, but his devout faith. Contradictory, he was a creative chemist and the group's pyrotechnic expert and some called him "The Blaster." He was an artist with explosives and he could boast that his bombs never harmed or killed innocent civilians, but the deadly devices still murdered or maimed members of the security forces. His wide set eyes made him study every possibility with a calmness that deserted others under pressure. Naomh was relieved that the Engineer had chosen to join him because the Preacher was his mentor and he had inherited his zeal of converting the entire Anschluss. His cupped ears showed that he liked to be in control at all times. By all rights, he should have joined the religious fanatic's faction. So devout was he in his beliefs, the Engineer wore a banned crucifix under his clothing. Rory had devised a synthetic leather looking pouch that hid it from prying x-ray devices. If the religious symbol was ever discovered, the man from the Madrid knew he would disappear from the face of the Anschluss. The committed Christian did not care about the consequences; the Engineer would give his complete allegiance to anyone who offered a return to the old ways. Naomh had taken the man from the Madrid Contrib aside and explained about the Preacher's betrayal. With a serious expression, the Engineer had listened in silence and went away. He thought long and hard and eventually seemed to accept Naomh's reasoning and would go with him. The other man that had stood protectively alongside the devotee of the outlawed sect was his brother Jose; also known as the Persuader. He was a giant of a man with a tranquil appearance enhanced by sculptured cheek bones and always done his adored older siblings bidding, his decision about leaving had already been made for him. His alias came about because of his massive size, strength and his broad chest. He was nearly 7cm taller and two years younger than his sibling, his massive girth made him seem more formidable than any one who approached his size. At a height of 190.5 cm and a weight of 120Kg, this solid bunch of muscle was far heavier that the 95kgs of brother. He was essentially their muscle man and had hands like shovels to emphasize this. The Persuader always had his squareish head shaven because of a prominent white streak of hair on his forehead. It was too much of a distinguishing mark; he also had a pronounced chin dimple. It was also no coincidence that the two brothers bore the same name as the Priest Salvador, for they were descendants of the same lineage. History was indulging in some peculiar connections. Greta was in the same boat as the giant, she knew that her lover would accompany Naomh to the gates of hell itself. So, of course she would go.

"Anyway, the heat is on and a few months outside the Anschluss might allow things to cool down." She said as if what they were planning was an everyday occurrence.

The Clerk had already agreed to go as he had the exact reasons as the Prof. He too had had enough of his regimented daily routine and longed for a different life. His erratic behaviour in the office had attracted the notice of his superiors and slamming reports would bring him to the attention of those that he would regret. The distracted man was never finishing any task given to him. Half way through something, he would leave it and start with another assignment. That would remain uncompleted too.

"Right, those of you that decide to go with me, meet me here in this warehouse tomorrow. I have something amazing to show you."

Suddenly, the Engineer and his younger brother left out a cheer; the Madrid team had just scored. The two brothers received dark looks from those around them. But straight from the restart, the London team equalised. The match ended in a draw and as the gang joined the buzzing throng leaving the stadium, Naomh gave them the location to where they were to meet next. Then, he pulled Cahill aside and whispered.

"Bring the most powerful weapon you have."

"Why?" Asked the red haired man.

"Just do it."

With those final words, the last of the true RE-INSTATOR'S dispersed to different locations around the Anschluss. Curiously, the watching Tell had a divergent thought.

"If I entered a team of Clones into the league, we would win it every year."

The next morning, Naomh called Cahill and Greta on the fixed video unit of their apartment and asked them.

"Come here before the others."

He sensed that he had interrupted something intimate between the two of them, but the couple had come straight over. Naomh knew.

"They have been fawning all over him since the Incident on the roof."

The demonstration that he had set up was to be held in an abandoned warehouse in a sector of the Birmingham Contrib that was soon to be redeveloped. No one would cry, when these once economic power houses of a long dead Empire vanished forever. The meeting place was located in a maze of dereliction; the doomed building was found by the Lenses and only for the map he had sent to their Frogs Eyes, none of those who were invited would ever have located it. When the conspirator told his two closest friends to expect the events of today to be so unconventional that he could not explain what was going to happen, their looks of incredulity were wider than his initial one. When pressed on the matter, he replied.

"Like the rest, you will just have to wait and see. But it will be worth it, that I can guarantee"

One by one, the other cell members arrived and he was delighted that everybody who had been at the match had turned up for his demonstration. None of them had let him down. Rory had selected all the members of his cell well; they were mostly orphans or children of indifferent parents. What it boiled down to was that nobody who really mattered would miss this errant group. Now that the new leader had his full audience, he took out from his pocket, what appeared to be a small glittering marble and showed it to the others.

"Very pretty." Said the Prof.

Smiling at a private joke, Naomh walked about fifty metres from his attentive friends and set the marble on the dusty floor of the unused building. Cahill gave Greta a bemused look, but there was a seriousness in her expression. So her lover just shrugged his shoulders and grinned. His eyes widened in amazement and the smile was wiped from his face. The object that Naomh had placed on the ground began to expand until it was nearly two metres high.

"Nice trick." Said an indistinct voice.

Then, Naomh showed them his newly acquired wristband and pressed the well-practised sequence. He walked up to the contraption. The circle of light responded and he appeared to be sucked into the sphere. In a confusing instant, the sphere vanished along with its Human victim. There were gasps of astonishment and open-mouthed gapes. Then everyone was on their feet and running towards where Naomh had disappeared. But the weird object reappeared before the charging group had reached it and a completely unharmed form stepped out from the illusion. He asked them.

"Well did it work?"

Everybody nodded in speechless acquiesce and all eyes remained fixed on the apparition in case it disappeared again. Feeling extremely confident now that the TORT-CAM had come through the first trial with flying colours, he decided to test its other alleged attribute. He enquired of a wide-eyed Cahill.

"Did you bring a launcher?"

Recovering slightly, his friend said.

"Yeah. I will go and assemble it. It took a few of us to bring the separate parts here."

Still disturbed at not been fully clued in, his friend left the warehouse for a few minutes and returned with the biggest portable missile launcher that any of them had ever seen.

"Where did you get that monster from?" Enquired the Clerk.

"Oh this. It is something I was saving for a special target. Like that treacherous snake, the Preacher for instance."

The Engineer gave Cahill a dirty look because of his reference to his former mentor. His comrade holding the launcher smiled sheepishly as he caressed the weapon fondly like a long lost friend. Greta gave a vicious laugh at her lover's words and a few of the others joined in on her merriment. Naomh became annoyed as his colleagues had regained their composure after his disclosure of the amazing TORT-CAM. He threw them off balance again and the smiles were wiped from every face as he said.

"Ok, Liben, Bonkers and I are going into that thing."

He pointed at the now visible globe and then he told the highly attractive blond woman who had ice water in her veins and insisted.

"Then you will arm the launcher, point it at us and fire."

Greta's face clouded over as if she was the butt end of an upcoming joke, she stammered.

"But-But."

Cahill cut her off with an edge to his voice.

"Alright Tyro, the vanishing trick was brilliant and it has its uses. But enough of this nonsense."

He thrust the launcher into the madman's hands.

"This mother fucking thing can penetrate any type of armour. There will be nothing left of that and subsequently you and me. There won't even be enough of our ashes to go to the recycling plant."

Naomh gave him a disarming look and said.

"Ok, we won't go in."

"Shit Tyro, you really had us going there." Said Cahill with visible relief showing on his face. All of the others had similar expressions. Then Naomh spoke with a finality that Rory once had as he thrust the weapon back into Cahill's shocked hands.

"I will just go in myself and you push the fire button."

"Why don't we just abduct two Anschluss troopers and put them inside. Then we can have as much target practice as we want." Asked a practical

Greta.

"That's not a good idea, because they will survive." Replied Naomh.

The rest of the crew joined in with other suggestions and the proceeding argument lasted for the next quarter of an hour. Then Naomh pulled rank and ordered Cahill.

"Just do it."

He point blankly refused.

"Come on my friend, I thought you are the Bonkers."

Still, he did not move, the hard man remained unconvinced. Then Greta said, seeing the commitment in her leader.

"I will do it."

Convinced that cold-hearted woman would comply, Naomh returned to the TORT-CAM and sealed himself in. Once inside the red interior and out of the others sight, he instantly regretted his confidant manner of a few minutes before.

"This is madness."

The one part Mescal/Amulet intervened and explained to him.

"Do not fear. You will not come to any harm. Now press your wrist band in this sequence red, green and red again. This will solidify the light shield. Quickly now. That female is very impatient and she might launch the projectile before the shield is in place."

Naomh complied and pressed the band in the correct sequence. There was a brief shimmering of the light barrier from the inside. Outside his perceived haven in the derelict warehouse, Greta calmly shouldered the launcher and aimed it at the visible globe. The others took forced gulps of air as she engaged the weapon. Cahill even turned away and started shaking.

"Don't do it." Pleaded the Clerk.

But she did anyway. The missile exited from the launcher at a frightening velocity, the confined space of the building making the projectile appear to travel even faster. The blur of light streaked across the dimly lit warehouse and impacted with the centre of the optical distortion. The warhead exploded with an ear-splitting boom that left all of the observers deafened. As the shocked group waited in the deadly silence, there was no movement from where the explosion had occurred; nobody dared move. Greta looked at the launcher with incredulity. She cast it aside as if the offending weapon had burnt her. The surreal quietness was enhanced as over a minute later Naomh emerged from the blasted space and the smoky haze of the detonations after effects. He was unharmed and had kept them waiting on purpose. An unrehearsed cheer went up from everybody present, excluding Cahill and Greta. Those two faces had become a picture. Naomh came back to them, a wraith emerging from the explosions aftermath.

"Well what do you think?" Suggested the survivor nonchalantly as if he

was discussing something as trivial as the weather. His best friend fixed him a look loaded with steel.

"You bastard, you knew all the time what that thing was capable of."

"No. I was only ninety per cent sure."

Cahill returned a look of horror.

"Only ninety per cent. Of all the stupid stunts to try. You could have been killed. And, I am called the nutter."

By now everybody else had gained a measure of composure and after Naomh's demonstration, all of them wanted a go in the amazing device. The eight of them experimented with the TORT-CAM and marvelled at its effectiveness. Their newly promoted leader told them the name he had given it. The Engineer soon found that the object could be shrunk with everybody inside it and one person carry them around in his or her pocket. Naomh handed each of them a similar band to the one he wore and told them.

"This small globe work's like a flashlight. It will reveal the invisible TORT-CAM while it still is concealed from sight. Don't lose them; the bands are your only way of finding it, once it is hidden."

Then amid their euphoria, he told them

"As you can see, things have changed and this fantastic device is only a fraction of the wonders that will be available to us if the search is successful."

His mystified friends wanted to know where it came from. Naomh became serious and cautioned

"Under my leadership, you will have to trust me and one day I will explain everything."

They were all members of an organisation that were used to having their questions unanswered, so they reluctantly agreed.

"Like father, like son." Whispered a dissenting voice.

The Lenses helped him when the pink eyed man said.

"This is what the Gaffer was working on. He told me that he had something incredible waiting in the wings. I knew that he was a genius, but this goes far beyond anything I expected."

Naomh gave him a grateful look. The others knew of Rory's inventiveness and became comfortable with this explanation. Then the Engineer asked some obvious questions.

"How long can we stay in it? Is there a time limit on oxygen for example?

The receiver of his questions got the answers from his internal source and replied as if the responses were his own.

"As long as we have enough food and water, then that is the only limit on our stay. The shimmering field surrounding the invisible space absorbs oxygen molecules, while excluding anything that is detrimental to our survival."

"That is some incredible piece of hardware."

"So we have to search the Globe for pieces of a technology that will give us more access to tools like this TORT-CAM." Enquired the eager Prof.

"Exactly. It is that simple and out there is the ultimate weapon to overthrow the corrupt regime." Answered Naomh.

After the meeting at the football match, some of their enthusiasm had waned, especially the part about leaving the Anschluss. Naomh's newly acquired second voice sensed this and intervened.

"Some of them are not convinced. Show me to them."

"I want you to see something." Announced its host to the others as he undone his shirt.

There were more astonished gasps of wonder as each member beheld the crimson shimmer trapped within his chest. The red sparkle grew with a hypnotic intensity and reinforced their bond with Naomh. As the brightness faded, it had worked its magic on them, their affinity to him had grown that little bit stronger and this tie would be reinforced with the acquisition of each piece. As the bearer covered up, the Prof asked.

"Does it hurt?"

"No!" Replied its bearer with a laugh thinking.

"That is such a typical concern of the timid scholar."

Turning to the wrist bands, he showed them how to operate them and once again they took turns in the vanishing sphere. Some even fired missiles at it with gusto and fragments of the shells ripped through the corrugated metal of the run down warehouse. The non-consulting Engineer noticed.

"The rays of sunlight piercing through the ragged gaps strike everything else and cause shadows, but the visible globe is an exception. It just absorbs the light completely."

There was a miniscule refraction of the rays, but no instrument of the Hybrids could measure that distortion. Naomh concluded the meeting.

"Return to your Contrib's, sort things out because we will be gone for a while and return to me in a week."

"How long will we be gone for?" Asked a curious Edward Boyd.

He received an exasperated look from his leader.

"I don't know, do I? As long as it takes."

Everybody nodded, said rushed goodbyes and went their separate ways. The Prof hurried back to his apartment in the London Contrib; he had a couple of pets to arrange homes for; two hamsters and an aquarium full of magnificent coloured fish. The Lenses had to erase sensitive files and destroy his illegal equipment. During the distasteful task, he thought.

"It's a dam shame; it has taken me years to assemble the parts for those machines."

The Engineer and his brother returned to the Madrid Contrib, to put things in order. Once there, they found out about the horrible demise of Escobar and his congregation. The two brothers brought the news back to the others and all of them incorrectly believed that they had been burnt to death by another faction.

"They were all shut in, men and women. No one escaped; the doors and windows had been sealed shut. Those that put out the blaze could not even find the ashes of the dead."

The Engineer's face bore an impassive front and Naomh harboured a doubt.

"He holds me responsible."

But the relived man from the Madrid Contrib put him at ease when he told him.

"I know that it was not you, Tyro. You, Bonkers and Greta would have gone in with guns blazing. I made the right decision to stick with you, if I had not then me and my brother would be dead now. We owe you our lives Tyro. It was God's will that we sided with you."

His new leader disagreed, but the practical Greta said.

"He is correct Tyro."

Then, the Persuader said.

"This TORT-CAM is the solution to all of our problems. We could use it as an assassination device. With our people inside it, we could get close to higher ranking targets, like never before."

"That's not its purpose." Said Naomh simply.

"Even if we used it like that, we would only be hoping that some of them chanced by." Cahill suggested.

"It's the system, we are against. The people at the top can be replaced." Added the Clerk.

The conceiver of the idea shrugged.

"It was only an idea."

Later on that day, Naomh brought Edward Boyd to his father's former residence after the older man had made sure that his pets had got a good home. He showed the man of learning selected files about the outside World stored in. The Prof was astounded and not just about the hidden room, the TORT-CAM had prepared him slightly for that. The lover of knowledge was like a kid in a candy store as he studied the real history of the state. He now fully realised the full scope of the insular and deceptive World of the Anschluss. Naomh told him.

"You must study the place where are going."

However, Rory's information was outdated, the last entries about it were over two hundred years old and because there were so many other places that captivated him, he never studied any in detail in his eagerness to proceed to the next one. The spectacled man's desire to leave his home and see the exotic places in the files grew tenfold. While his guest was engrossed, Naomh received an unexpected call on his F.V.U, (Fixed Video

Unit.) he was surprised at the identity of the contact. Against his better judgement, he answered it and the image of the caller appeared in his screen. It was Vladimir Illeau from the Bucharest Contrib. Through the two-dimensional image, he fixed his penetrating coal black eyes on Naomh. Most people were disturbed by that gaze; it was as if he was searching for something, only known to him. He wanted to rendezvous with him and again against his better nature, Naomh agreed to a meeting.

"What does that creep want?" Asked the overhearing Prof.

"I don't know, but let's find out."

"Call Greta and tell her to come over. Now that we are leaving, I think she would gladly put a bullet into his head." Suggested the other.

"Her and more."

Vladimir Illeau was disliked by all of Naomh's friends. If the Clerk was shy and introvert, then this guy was downright anti-social and a self-confessed misanthrope. This was an enormous advantage in his occupation. The sullen man worked in the body disposal units, where corpses were recycled and used mostly as fish bait or fertiliser. Very few people would have ate seafood if they knew what it was fed on. One hundred per cent of body disposition was done by machines and the efficient process needed no Human participation, just monitors; but Illeau had chosen this grisly occupation. How he had become a RE-INSTATOR, nobody knew. He was a sullen, cold and sinister character and code-named the "Mute.". Rory in a quirky humour had chosen this appellation. The others believed that the Gaffer had picked that tag because it was hard to get a word from the dour man. He informed them.

"That was not the reason."

He declined to explain the name to the others. All he said was.

"It is a word out of its time."

This did not faze Illeau; in fact he took pride in the label, especially since it was a title that none of the others understood. This tag did not describe his appearance, he was no freak, locked away to spare other people looking at him. No, the Mute was also extremely handsome with his dark brooding looks. He was fastidious and always clean-shaven, from his scalp to under his arms. This was a requisite for his occupation. Another prerequisite of his job were his pink latex gloves that he wore outside office hours, in fact he never seemed to have them off. But contrary to his neat appearance, people felt unclean around him. Most thought the reason for this was because of a slight inflection of saliva in his infantile words when he spoke. For the man based in the industrial sector had a distinct and lisping childish voice. If you had your back to him on the very rare time that he was addressing you, it would be a surprise to turn around and find an adult. Most agreed that this was the reason that he did not converse much. But this was not so, as the Mute had a grisly secret. He was a killer of Humans and he revelled in it. Some corpses that ended up on his assembly line had their lives cut short by him. The handsome murderer was fascinated by the exact moment of death and he yearned for the sight of that final instant. To him, there was a fundamental truth displayed in a person's last moment in this reality. His twisted thinking made him believe that he would find the answers to life itself in the final seconds of another soul. But Illeau was no killer of children; to him the non-adults had no conception of what they were losing. So the perverse being deemed it inconsequential and not worth the effort. How, he escaped the clutches of the PREVENTIVE recruitment agency was also a mystery. The Mute arrived at Naomh's door a few days later while the Prof was still his engrossed guest and the unlikeable man got straight to the point in his lisping voice.

"I know that something is up and that some of you are about to leave the Anschluss and I want in on it."

Naomh was flabbergasted.

"How did you know?"

"I have my methods." Another annoying trait of the Mute was that he was always reluctant to reveal too much. He nearly always answered a question with a whine of.

"I don't know 'oo."

Naomh spent the next couple of hours listening to his arguments and decided.

"God, that voice is really annoying."

He had never heard the man talk so much, so he finally agreed against his better judgement to him coming with them. He had two choices, either to whack him or let him tag along. Like the Prof had suggested, he knew Cahill and Greta would have chosen the former option. The man from the London Contrib had kept himself engrossed in his work during the Mute's visit; it was all that stopped him from laughing out loud at the others singsong voice. When the unlikeable man was gone, the academic said.

"The others are not going to like this and how did you listen to him for that length of time without even smiling?"

Naomh gave his friend a twisted smile and replied.

"It was dam hard."

On a sober note, he added.

"I had a strange premonition that he should be with us."

The Prof shrugged. Like the rest of his faction, he was aware of Naomh's gut feelings. He said.

"Well, you are our leader now and your decisions are to be respected. You know while you were talking to him, a notion came to me. Do you want to hear it?"

"Ok."

"Well you know how we are all orphans, we have no parents or family, but at least the Engineer and the Persuader are brothers."

Naomh nodded.

"Well since they're circumstance is slightly different than ours, then there should there then be a different name for them, not orphans. What do you think?"

"I think that going away will be a good thing for you, it seems that you have too much time on your hands at the moment."

The mention of the word orphan had slightly unsettled him.

"I cannot tell him that I have only become one in the last few weeks and I can certainly not divulge what my parent had been and how he died."

A few weeks later, the mysterious van DerKamp contacted him and informed him.

"Arrangements have been made."

It had been a long and frustrating wait, but eventually he had the means to get them to where Naomh wanted to go. He gave him a time, the date and the place where he would meet them. The place was out of bounds to the ordinary Pleb, so he would have to get the Lenses to work on the proper access chips.

Fourteen days later on a Friday morning, the nine remaining members of Rory's faction boarded the Mag-lev and headed south to the Atlantis Contrib. As the Prof had predicted, there were mumbled disgruntlements and downright hostility from the others when they saw the Mute. However, Naomh eventually persuaded them that he had to come with them. That was not the end of the argument about that matter, but it was put on the back burner. Illeau had been completely unbothered by the quarrel. The day of their departure from the Anschluss had finally arrived, thought it was a landmark event in their calendar; everybody else in the huge city-state remembered it for something else. Because during the night before, two people had the audacity to climb the granite plateau of the Geneva Contrib and to leap off the Chairman's tower and achieve "Base". Somebody had got video footage of the event and it was been transmitted to every M.I.M that desired it. Both of the free-falling bodies looked familiar and judging by Cahill's and Greta's broad smiles under their hoodies, Naomh guessed correctly that it must have been the two of them.

"The crazy bastards. They were lucky not to be caught. If they had been, I don't think that I would be making this journey now. I will broach the subject with them later."

Most of them were quite content in the early hours of that morning, foolishly believing that their familiar way of life would never change. On the start of this strange day, just over eight months since the death of the Gaffer, Naomh had looked at his apartment and wondered

"Will I ever see it again?"

Now he had to pack for a long journey, a thing he had never done before in his twenty-five plus years of life. The Prof left his place nice, neat and orderly. The Clerk being the Clerk left his apartment, well you know him, he had never looked after it when he was there, so why would he change now. Most of them were nervous, fidgety and suffering from a lack of sleep. Edward Boyd was different; he wanted to shout at the other passengers who were just commuting normally on their regular and mundane journeys.

"Where is your final destination? Is it the Athens Contrib or maybe the Oslo Contrib.? Well would you believe where we are going? We are leaving the Anschluss all together. What do you think of that?"

Naomh had been communicating with his father's contact, explaining to him what he required and the mysterious person replied.

"It will be done."

The Lenses had armed them with false documents for the trip south. So he, Naomh, Cahill and Greta took the Mag-Lev eastwards towards the London Contrib. There, the quartet would pick up the Prof. The rest of them would join the travellers in the Parisian Contrib. The workhorse of the Anschluss glided through the urban metropolis on a cushion of opposite polarity at a velocity of four hundred kilometres an hour in a shifting blur of concrete, glass, tunnels, culverts and bridges. The smoothness of the journey went unnoticed. The route took them from the Parisian Contrib to the Marseilles Contrib. At the Marseilles Contrib, the nine of them boarded a smaller version of the Mag-Lev and sped through the Atlantis sector. Only the Lenses forged chips allowed them access to this route. Hoodies were not allowed on this transporter, but they cared little. The exposed travellers would soon be out of the Anschluss watchers influence or so they thought. The nine commuters swiped the cards and boarded the special Mag-Lev. While it was standing room only on the normal conduits, these carriages were lined with plush seats of three aside facing each other and divided by a central passageway. The Persuader who usually found himself cramped voiced his approval.

"Now this is the way to travel."

Naomh, Cahill, Greta, the Clerk and the Lenses shared one booth while the Engineer; his brother and the Prof sat in the one across the aisle. Even though there were empty seats in both booths, the Mute sat alone. He had hated every moment of the previous journey down as he rarely travelled on the Mag-Lev. The unsociable man loathed all the jostling and inadvertent touching that those excursions entailed. Back in the Chairman's office, there were individual screens that held the image and relevant data of these nine travellers. If Naomh had known, he would have been astounded that except for the Mute, his companions matched the list that the Kaiser had given to his secretary of Protocol. The Mag-Lev broke clear of the urban wall as they left the concrete jungle of the metropolitan sector and in an instant found themselves travelling through a broad swathe of the two thousand kilometre wide agricultural sector. Sparkling sunshine immediately penetrated into the carriage causing the Mute to press the button to lower the blinds on his window. His travelling companions on the other hand glorified in the brightness. As each of them took turns looking out of the window, the landscape became wide open as they passed fields of corn, maize, potatoes, wheat, barley and every known vegetable in use in the Anschluss. Most of the fruit orchards, greenhouses and vineyards lay in the Southern sectors of the Iberian, Italian, Balkan and Atlantis sectors. Lone silo's, thirty stories high, large warehouses, irrigation systems and farm machinery stood out as the only non-living organisms in the huge open areas. After an hour, the passengers arrived at the port that lay in the shadow of the Mediterranean Sea wall. All, but one of them had never seen the huge concrete obstacle and the sea beyond. The group penetrated the close guarded docks of the Atlantis sector with the false identities that proclaimed them to be new dockworkers assigned for the next few months. At the gates of the dockyard complex, they were immediately shanghaied by a supervisor. The official looking man told them.

"Come with me. I am short-handed."

Reluctantly, the nine of them went with him. They could not afford to arouse suspicions and so they were put to work straight away. They were handed non-descript blue overalls and put them on. After eight hours of toil, they were told to knock off. The false dock workers began to search for the meeting point instead of getting washed, rested and fed in preparation for their next shift. The weary bunch had no intention of reporting for the next labour period. Now under the shadow of the mist shrouded vessel that loomed over them, the nervous RE-INSTATOR'S waited in a deserted warehouse for the contact, who would gain them safe passage aboard the enormous ship, which was been prepared for departure at this moment. Every warehouse in the complex had been marked with huge luminous numbers. Naomh had been told by his father's contact to find, number 1001. It had taken them over an hour on a shuttle that travelled along the massive dock-front to find it. The Mag-lev commuters found themselves in a profusion of brutal looking, but functional buildings. This virtual city of warehouses was one of the powerhouses of the Anschluss. From here its prized manufactured goods left the economic power block, destined for improvised nations that lacked the know-how, inclination or sufficient resources to produce such stuff. This helped enormously to spread its influence around the globe. The ordinary citizen would have been shocked to learn that the elite of the Anschluss in no uncertain terms adhered to the general policy of isolation that was inflicted on the vast majority of the general population.

It was a varied crew that lay hidden with Naomh in the warehouse on the waterfront. He was preoccupied with his thoughts.

"All except one has been through the mill with me. So I am quite positive that the others can be trusted with my life, but not with the secret I hold."

The ad hock group huddled close together in a perceived attempt at keeping warm. True to form, the Mute kept a measured distance apart from the others; he was used to the chill of the recycling plants. All of the rest were feeling the slight difference in temperature away from the heavily populated Contrib's. Removed from the billions of urban lights and close to the coast, it felt at least ten degrees cooler. The draughty interior of the dilapidated building they were hiding in did not help either. It was hazy, damp and gloomy, for there were no windows or skylights to break the enveloping confines of the place. The only air circulating around the warehouse came spluttering from knackered ventilation systems that played on frayed nerves with their constant clanking. Tottering on the edges of watery-torn vision lay vast stockpiles of some forgotten commodity that was left there to decay and mould. The stench of whatever it had been permutated throughout the entire warehouse wafting into everyone's clothes and after a couple of hours of this ordeal; it was the only smell they could remember. One particular nasty comment mentioned.

"It is probably for the best as we can no longer smell each other's fragment body odour after our day of travel and then working in the dockyard."

The floor where it could be made out under the mountains of refuse consisted of concrete that was chipped into thin uneven cracks. These indentures had undoubtedly been caused by countless years of footsteps and wheeled machinery crossing to and fro on forgotten tasks. Scattered puddles of dark oily stained liquid filled in any deep fissures in the etched surface of the floor. Empty plastic bags of some forgotten commodity lay strewn about the place like autumn leaves. Breaks in the warehouses wall caused the bags to dance gracefully in the swirling eddies that flowed through the gaps. To add insult to injury, an annoying light hanging above them flickered on and off and the constant sound of dripping water from somewhere stretched their already fraught nerves. On impulse Cahill wanted to put the offending light out with a burst of gunfire. He was warned off because everything had to appear normal from the outside. With a feeble attempt at humour and to diffuse the growing hostility towards each other, the Prof said.

"Why do you think they might send someone to fix it?"

This was greeted with muted laughter that gradually broke the increasing tension. As the covert group huddled together for what little warmth they could muster, each taking one hour stints at sentry duty. It seemed as the night progressed, the temperature this close to the coast and away from the urban sectors had dropped at least another five degrees colder. The vapour from that exhaled from their mouths testified to this. Some who liked the others to think that they were not bothered flirted in and out of restless sleep. In the middle of the Prof's turn at watch, a sudden clanking of the venting machine caused him to flinch. The Engineer noticed his nervous reaction and mockingly enquired.

"Never been one active service before. I'll even bet you have never been in an industrial complex or even strayed far from your comfortable Museum. Have you runt?"

Some of the others snickered silently. The Persuader caught in the mood added a jibe from the agriculture sector.

"He is about as useful as tits on a bull. He probably needs a wet nurse; he might even know what her teats are for."

Greta gave the large man a cold look and asked.

"Do you think that's all women are good for?"

However, the Lenses intervened to save the big man's flustered response.

"Leave him alone. He has done more than enough for the cause."

He more than any of them understood what his comrade from the London Contrib was going through. Edward Boyd absolutely abhorred violence; he had never shot, killed or wounded another Human being in his life. Most thought it strange that a man like him had made it into the organisation, but Rory had chosen him for his information skills saying.

"We have enough trigger men."

Why an individual like the timid academic surrounded himself with these killers, was something that he only knew. Having men like him and the Lenses around made their founder feel a more cleaner.

"What's it to you. Are you defending baldy?" Asked the Persuader, glad to have been deflected from answering Greta's challenge.

"You know, you make baldness sound like a disability, but did you know that hair comes from dead brain cells. And seeing that you have plenty of growth, even though you crop it regularly, what does that say?" Queried a mocking Prof.

Cahill left out a roar of laughter and said.

"Good for you."

He slapped the academic on the back while the others including the Engineer joined in on the merriment. A worried Persuader asked his brother.

"Is that true?"

He received a half-serious answer.

"Well Jose, the Prof is supposed to be the smartest among us, so he is probably right."

The Engineer turned away so his sibling could not see his mocking glint. Naomh did not interfere; he knew that the Prof was well able to stand up for himself, so he pretended that he was asleep. Before the big man's interruption, the intelligent man was going to reply to the Engineer's taunt. He was going to ask him.

"You are well known for doing dummy runs before a mission, then why

did you not do one before this. I'd also say that you are a bit out of your depth as well."

But as things had turned to mirth, the spectacled man let it go. Then Cahill turned to his leader, who lay alongside him. His best friend's face was full of emotion as he enquired.

"Are you awake?"

Seeing that he was, he spoke to his friend in a terse whisper.

"This is a fools earn. Let's give it up."

Not for the first time, Cahill advised returning to fight those who opposed them; the prospect of the impending sea voyage still made him uneasy. During the last few days, Naomh had also felt uncertainty about their new path, but the internal voice had eked into his psyche and he gradually accepted its logic. His closest friend on the other hand, had no such benefit and had experienced bouts of anxiety and a tightness of the stomach that came and went over the last twenty-four hours. Naomh thought it likely.

"This quest to unknown lands is frightened the living daylights out of him."

Cahill, like the rest of the group and indeed most of the Citizens of the Anschluss had never ventured outside the enormous Power-block. The rest of the World would have been as unknown to them as it had been to medieval adventures. This fear of the unfamiliar was eating away at him and his appetite for it was receding fast. Naomh received help from an unexpected quarter; Greta. She replied to Cahill's requests with simple logic.

"If the solution to our dreams lies outside the Anschluss in the vast unknown World, then we have an obligation to seek it out and use it."

At first she had been even more sceptical and hostile than Cahill, but Naomh had won her over with glimpses of the technology that the APOCRYPHA'I had already provided. She had agreed to undertake the journey and that counted her partner in; for he would never stray far from his beloved. To distract him, Naomh decided that it was time to berate him and Greta about the mad caper the two of them had pulled before they left. He called the two of them aside. The three of them rose and moved away from the others. Out of earshot, he demanded.

"That was a stupid stunt, the two of you pulled, the night before we left. What the Hell was that all about?"

An innocent Cahill said.

"What are you talking about?"

"Don't act the fool with me. I'm talking about the Base jump off the Chairman's tower."

"Oh, that." Answered a mischievous Greta.

As the two lovers giggled, the red haired one added.

"We decided to give the Anschluss, something to remember us by."

"You both could have been killed. Aside from the security forces that guard that place, it's also some drop."

"It's not the fall that kills you, it the sudden stop at the end." Retorted the blonde woman ignoring the mention of the PREVENTIVES. They both laughed again. Exasperated, their leader left them, but he took away one consolation.

"At least Cahill has taken his mind off the journey for a while."

Watch's went and changed, then during the early hours of the morning, when it was the Persuader's turn on sentry duty, the alert observer hissed in warning to the others. With clenched lips, the big man told them.

"Somebody is making their way towards us."

They all sought cover and removed anything that would draw attention to their presence and waited with baited breath for the stranger to approach. The shadowy figure came up to the door of the warehouse. The man halted in front of their hideout and unzipped his trousers and began to relieve himself against the metal cladding of the structure. Glancing left and right, he strained to see if he was been noticed. Just as the wary figure appeared satisfied that he was not been watched, he was yanked without ceremony through the briefly opened door. Realising his sudden peril, the man shouted the recognised password.

"Absent friends!"

In a rush, he added.

"I am the one you are here to meet. I am looking for Tyro."

After a brief command from Naomh who recognised the voice and the words, he was released only to stare directly into the gaze of eight nasty people who had even nastier weapons levelled at him. Raising his two hands very slowly, one of which appeared to be heavier and more cumbersome than the other. He was professionally frisked for concealed weapons and two automatic pistols were found on his body. One piece was strapped to the left arm and the other in the rear waistline of his unzipped trousers. Both of the lethal arms were taken off him as a chilling female voice looking at his still exposed manhood warned.

"Very impressive. Now zip it up before I decide to add it to my collection."

He hurried to comply with her demands, not quite sure what she meant but sensing the implied threat. Recovering his composure, the man walked straight over to Naomh and said.

"You are the leader. I can see it in you."

Registering the stranger's words made Naomh realise that he now acted and sounded like his deceased parent. The newcomer told them

"You have to move to another warehouse which has material that will be loaded onto the ship very soon."

But the most headstrong among them re-cocked his Flatpack and pointed at the man.

"Warning this weapon has been activated." Sounded the metallic voice of his gun as its circular magazine whirled around.

"How can we trust this stranger? He could be leading us into a trap. Why did this Pleb have us hide out in this warehouse full of stinking crap, when he obviously has another one more pleasant than this?" Challenged a sceptical Cahill.

The others nodded their heads and made no effort to move. The outsider looked at them with contempt glittering in hard eyes and replied.

"Look shit heads. I knew you lot have been hiding here for the last eight hours or so. What stopped me from coming in with a load of Filth before now? Let's get one thing clear. I have been called on to honour an old debt. I am to be your Guide and I will be the only one to help you, once you are aboard the vessel. The reason I put you in this one was simple. Nobody goes into this one unless they have no choice, so I knew that you would remain undiscovered until I could come and get you. You might be highly competent urban fighters, but let me tell you, out there, in the big wide World, you will be novices and probably useless. Also I am the only person here that can speak the language of the place where we are going. So stick your paranoia up your arse because I'm all you got. Be on the ship or don't. It's your choice and I really don't give a shit what you do."

With that, he turned and walked back into the night, daring Cahill to pull his trigger. The one part Mescal/Amulet interceded back into Naomh's awareness with vague memories of Rory's life.

"This person can be trusted. Your father saved his life and another's who he loved dearly and he was also a good friend of Rory's."

"Colourful use of the language, don't you think?" Noted Naomh as the stranger walked away. Then, he added trusting the amulets decision.

"His explanation seems plausible to me. Ok, let's do what the Pleb suggested and follow him."

Not waiting for a discussion, he moved off to follow the stranger; the other's had no choice but to follow their leader. The expanded group of nine men and one woman hugged the deep shadows and dark spaces along the sides of the warehouses that were cast by floodlights that seemed to be placed haphazardly between the buildings. The man had led them to warehouse 1010 and its interior was filled with clean plastic containers. It was a welcome difference from the last building. Their mysterious escort led them to the back of the warehouse and pointed to a container the size of a small apartment. He told them.

"Conceal yourselves in that."

His father's contact then turned to Naomh and with a sceptical look challenged.

"You told me that you have a way to get on the ship, unnoticed. Knowing the Gaffer, I am inclined to believe you. Once onboard, wait in the hold of the ship until two hundred hours and I will come to you. If you

are there, then from then on you will know me as the Guide."

It was not unusual for one of the Gaffer's associates to give a code-name and insist on it been used. The Prof thought.

"We are a paranoid bunch, that's for certain."

Then, the unfriendly man left them alone. Naomh ordered his crew into the container where each of them sorted their gear for the strangest trip that anyone on the Planet would ever make. Inside the metal prison which was full of tightly wrapped containers, they discussed the prospects of the journey and the idea of another language. To some of them it was ludicrous, to others it was a known fact. The curious Clerk wanted to break open one of the packages, but he was warned off by Greta.

"Everything must look normal in here."

They settled down in silence and waited for something to happen. Eventually after what seemed like an eternal silence, those hidden inside the container heard the frantic movement of men and machinery in the warehouse as the ship loaders blazed into action. Quickly Naomh brought out the unactivated TORT-CAM, still in its marble size. He smiled to himself at the memory of disbelief on the Guide's face that his charges could get on the ship undetected. Preparations to board the ship illegally began in earnest. The invisible shield was placed on the floor of the container, in a large empty space between packed machinery parts. The coloured marble grew to just over man size. This time, its inheritor let the Lenses activate it. The pink-eyed hacker pressed the squares on his band in the correct sequence and the device responded, the sphere enlarged and remained visible for a few seconds. This was the first time that the Mute had seen it and he appeared to be un-phased by the magic. True to his nature, he failed to be overawed, much to the chagrin of the sphere's owner. One by one Naomh's crew entered it and vanished into thin air. Then there was a humming sound and their leader told them that they were now invisible. Inside their red, but mostly white facet confines, the outside noise of the clanking warehouse machinery was lost to them. More importantly; they were relieved to find that the smell and the stinging aroma of the manure of the first warehouse no longer clung to their clothes. Passing through into the invisible shield had eradicated the offending molecules. As they waited for the den of obscurity to be loaded onto the ship, Naomh informed the others.

"The TORT-CAM is crammed with other items of the same advanced technology that will be revealed to us in piecemeal, when the need arises."

Another thing they had discovered during their experimentation was that the shell of the invisible shield could become transparent from the inside and allow them a perfect concealed viewing point. But as they were new to this amazing experience, Naomh decided to keep it opaque for now. It would be much like putting a blindfold over a nervous animal and keeping it calm. Later, he would let the Engineer and the Lenses free to discover if there were any other surprises of technology contained in it and how to make use of them. Those two were the most technically gifted among the group. Now that the Clerk was absolutely certain that they were invisible, he confided in his leader.

"When I was a kid, I used to dive under my blankets, pretending that I was in a space that shielded me from the outside World. Under my blankets I was convinced that no harm could come to me. This TORT-CAM was exactly what I had in mind."

The dockside began to buzz with activity. So comfortable cocooned in the unseen globe, the concealed companions never heard the security people checking the container with diligent patience or heard them sealing it with a yellow security tape. Neither did they sense the sounds of industry or feel the lifting of the container by large forklifts. The container, including its illegal occupants was brought to the dock-front and left in long narrow lines, along with thousands of others. Even in the harsh artificial light of the dockside, huge letters emblazoned on the ship's hull could be made out with little effort. The ship proudly proclaimed its name; it was the "ANS GREGORY LYUBIN.". Then, huge hover platforms with powerful thrusters lifted the containers high into the night sky and deposited them effortlessly into the hold of the huge ship. The lifting machines operator blissfully unaware that her load contained something far beyond her comprehension. These engines of industry were another piece of technology that the general population were ignorant of. By sheer coincidence or luck, the TORT-CAM had been in one of the last container's to be loaded onto the monstrosity of a vessel. Chance had nothing to do with it, their new benefactor had chosen well. Unknown to the stowaways, their hiding place would be nearer the top of the ships hold and it would not take that amount of effort to get them out. None of the illegal occupants even heard the great turbines rattle the ship as it began to build up power to set sail. It was berthed in a very deep dock that had been carved out of the sea bed, especially for craft of this magnitude. The huge vessel was held in place by "Magnetic Painters" inserted in the dock's wall. These sophisticated clamps were deactivated when the ship had generated enough power and it began to pull away from the harbour wall. When it sailed out of the harbour, its ignorant stowaways never noticed the motion of the great craft. They would have been grateful for that respite if they had known. The Anschluss had many smaller sleeker ships that glided over the surf, but because of its vast size, this gigantic sea going vessel did it the old fashioned way by sailing along the surface of the water. The vessel named after the father of the LYUBINITES bobbed up and down as it slowly passed through a gap in the Mediterranean Sea wall. When the ship was safely through, the channel was filled in the same manner as a drawbridge. In the fading light, the fugitives were leaving their homeland and for how long was anybody's guess. As if to help them on their way, the moon shone in full splendour, lighting the way ahead for the enormous vessel. For the first leg of its voyage, the ocean going craft would hug the sea wall of the Anschluss. An hour into the journey, the Engineer checked his watch and it was 1.30 am, it was time to get out of their hiding place and wait for the Guide. Naomh deactivated the camouflaged device and the now visible RE-INSTATOR'S entered the space of the container. They were all armed and on high alert for any treachery. Their weapons had been activated and held in readiness for any betrayal. Each person had been supplied with infra-red headlamps which banished the total blackness of the container. When everybody came out of the TORT-CAM, Naomh reduced it in size. Curses sounded as the sudden rolling of the ship threw them all back onto the floor of their hiding place. Regaining their feet, all of them, still rather unsteady made it to the door of the container. The Persuader opened its door cautiously and then satisfied there was nobody outside, the big man gestured for the others to follow him as he went outside into the hold of the enormous ship. The stowaways were on the roof of another container and it touched the side of the ship's bulkhead. Above them they could see a metal gangway that was just out of reach. Again the ship lurched and pitched them onto the container's roof. More curses, as the gang steadied themselves. Then, the Engineer motioned to his brother. The strongman approached him and his sibling put his foot into the cussed hands of the giant. With a mighty effort, the heavily muscled man from the Madrid Contrib flung his brother, gear and all, towards the gangway. The Engineer deftly grabbed the railing of the walkway and hauled himself over. Less than a minute later a rope came snaking down. The rest of his comrades climbed up the rope until they all stood on the solid metal. The ship passed through a rough part of the sea and the motion of the craft made their feet unsteady again. Swaying from side to side and finding it difficult to keep their feet, they finally made it to a doorway at the end of the gangway where Naomh advised the group to wait until their so-called ally made contact. Then the ship encountered heavier seas; whose waves were reflected back off the sea wall. The enormous ship might as well have been a toy as it pitched from side to side in rapid succession. Suddenly half of them became queasy and nauseated. Greta, the Engineer and the Clerk were suffering slightly less than those. The lurching of the vessel had hit the others hard. A few stomachs rebelled; their owner's faces contorted and turned a sickly pale colour. Some who had eaten recently regurgitated the meal and through mouthfuls of sweet sickly saliva swore perfidiously or in some cases called on divine intervention. The door slid open and only Greta and the Engineer were able to retaliate, both were seasick, but not in the same degree as the others. Those two pointed activated guns at the intruder, but it was their contact. Still, they did not lower the weapons. Seeing some of them half slumped over the gantry rails and vomiting and the rest with their heads between their knees to counteract the ships motion, he exploded into mirth. However, van DerKamp halted his laughing on seeing the dark looks aimed at him. Still with traces of humour glinting from his eyes, he spoke in a voice that said volumes of been there and done that.

"Take your time in getting to your feet. None of you have been on an ocean ship before and believe me it will take time to adjust."

On getting little reaction on his suggestion that they stand up, he ridiculed them.

"Shit man. Is this the most feared unit in the movement?"

Brushing aside their aggressive looks of hatred and frustration, he let them suffer another little bit and then produced a packet of pills. He offered them around with words of advice.

"Here take one of these and it will get rid of the sea sickness."

Through tear induced eyes, Cahill shouted.

"Don't touch them. He could be trying to poison us.

"Shit man. You take distrust to the heights of paranoia."

Seeing that nobody took the offered pills, the stranger with a sigh emptied the contents of the packet out on top of his jacket that he had just took off and thrown on the metal gangway. With both hands he mixed them up and told Cahill.

"Choose one."

Still suspect, he obliged and picked out one. The stranger told him.

"Put it into my mouth."

He opened his mouth wide and Cahill grudgingly flicked a pill into it. The confidant man swallowed it. Still no one took one. Naomh trusting the decision of the APOCRYPHA'I on the contact and feeling that this impasse might never be broken snatched a pill up before anyone could object. He gulped it down before any of his friends could stop him. Looking into the stranger eyes, he saw a look of grudging respect. Then, their Guide said to him.

"You did the right thing."

Instantly Naomh's discomfort eased and when his friends realized this, all of them scrambled forward to take a pill. The Mute got there first and snatched one out of the Guide's hands without a word of thanks. He swallowed it and his colour changed to a whiter shade of pale. Most of the others followed suit, even the pragmatic Engineer. Everybody except Greta took one. She would bear her slight discomfort rather than trust the stranger, no surprise there and because she did not take a pill, her partner also declined. The tall blonde woman whispered into her lover's ear and he smiled gratefully as he took one. The normally cold woman only ever showed compassion towards Cahill. When everybody had recovered enough to move, their Guide told them.

"Follow me. You cannot stay here."

Moving through empty pre-fabricated corridors, he brought them to a vacant galley. The Spy in the midst of the company smiled inwardly. Agent XIII had kept up the pretence and played their part well. This well-travelled person's seasickness had been an act. It was a sham for the benefit of the others and the stranger who had met them. This Pleb gave them an old fashioned metal key, a tradition that was still adhered to on Anschluss vessels. He showed them how to use the unfamiliar locking device and the opened door revealed a space that would be too small for a group their size. Their escort apologised.

"It was the best that I could do."

There were nine single sleeping cots. Naomh knew that Cahill and Greta would put their two together while the Mute would try and create as much distance between him and the others.

"Some happy family."

There was also a table, some chairs, an eating counter and some cupboards within the cramped space. The curious Prof checked their contents, but found nothing interesting. Disappointed, he shut them with a bang. The Guide got them settled in and left them alone again. He told them before he left them to their own devices.

"I will knock nine times when I come back, the same number as your crew, so that you will know, it is me. And, by the way there is no need to rise early; you will be on this ship for a couple of weeks, so relax."

That news left the Clerk and the Prof thrilled, their new life had begun already. The stressed out-group collapsed in a heap, exhausted, bewildered and uneasy at this strange place they now found themselves in. The fair haired Bureaucrat held the unfamiliar weight of the key. Despite the loud sound of the ship's engines, a few decks below them, all of them succumbed to sleep. Before he nodded off, the Clerk looked at his Frogs Eyes; it told the bleary eyed man that the date was the 4th of July 2952AD. Greta took unrequested sentry duty, she un-strapped her weapon, sat down on a chair and watched the door of the cabin and listened for any movement outside. She for one would not be caught on the hop. Like her sweetheart, the blonde woman still did not trust the man who called himself their guide.

"If he has any unpleasant surprises planned, then I will be ready with one of my own."

XV.

"ANS, THE GREGORY LYUBIN." 2952AD.

Naomh and all but one of his cast of desperate characters had finally done what most of them would have once thought was impossible; the nine of them had left the confined boundaries of the Anschluss and were now in the middle of the Mediterranean Sea. They were on an Ocean going vessel, the size of which would have easily dwarfed any in some of their imaginations. Besides, if any of them had seen what they were on from another angle, these givers of nicknames would have called it.

"A floating wedding cake with the wrapper still on."

This vast multi-tiered sea craft would become their home for the next few weeks and the fugitives would eventually gain some form of sea legs. The huge three and a half kilometre long ocean vessel was making steady progress towards the rising Sun. The ships huge solar sails that extended from its bow to its stern soaked up the power of the celestial furnace and transferred the captured energy to massive turbines under the ship's waterline. These enormous engines in turn propelled the giant craft's antipodes sluggishly over the waves. The solar sails that fanned out over the deck gave the ship the look of some exotic sea lizard with a membrane of stretched skin atop its chunky body. In the unlikely event of an attack on the massive vessel, these energy trappers could be retracted in an instant as the ship prepared to defend itself. A coat of dull metallic grey covered the entire hull of the vessel and its ascending forecastles. Unlike the smaller, speedier and more covert "Wave-Gliders." in the Anschluss's navy, its obtuse covering did not hide the vessel from detection. No, this power block's rulers wanted its competitors and allies to know where this craft was at any moment in time. This enormous contrivance of the waves was a symbol of their supremacy and arrogance. Its very presence was telling anyone that took notice that another force was in the process of regaining control of the high seas. The sea going vessel towered over two hundred metres high and was over a kilometre longer than anything else on the seven seas. It had a volume of over twenty million metric tonnes. Its hidden hangers on the second tier held over five hundred disc shaped warplanes along with two thousand amphibious craft, ready to be unleashed in minutes. The huge bulkheads of this city on the sea were also filled to capacity with every type of trade goods the Anschluss could produce and a honeycomb of passages inside the lacklustre hull inter-connected every space within like veins in a living body. Armoured gun ports festooned along the ship's hull mimicked the nodules of skin of the lizard's reptilian body. Its proud owners named the crafts type, Dreadnaut. They named this bizarre vessel, the flagship of their armada, the "ANS GREGORY LYUBIN". But unlike its ancestors of a similar type, this huge sea going monolith contained enough firepower to lay waste to entire cities and their hinterlands. Besides its onboard airforce and offensive forces, it bristled with 50.5cm guns that penetrated from its hull and rose in three levels above decks like a tiered cake. Its complement of Marine Corps numbered thirty-five thousand strong. The floating arsenal also had in its powerful array of armament, missiles that could reach any inland point on the Planet. It was also rumoured some of these arrows of destruction could even make near Earth orbit. Any of the Anschluss's minion states that strove towards an adjustment in their relationship always had a change of mind when this platform of gunboat diplomacy turned up on their shores. If that was the stick, then the vessel also had a carrot. It contained a palatial quarter of elaborate ballrooms, dining areas and luxurious suites to entertain visiting dignitaries. It was in these floating rooms of opulence, swaying rulers traded their souls. When the Anschluss sealed a deal here, some group, somewhere were about to pay in blood.

On their first night at sea, Greta had stayed awake guarding her eight cabin mates' slumber. Early in the small hours of the morning, movement outside caused her to alert her sleeping companions. Weapons were armed on silent mode. There was a slight activity at the door, followed by nine knocks. Naomh ordered them to wait and the sequence was repeated, this time more vigorously. The go-ahead was given to the Clerk and he put the metal key into the unfamiliar lock. He struggled with it, but it suddenly opened with a bit of effort from the outside. Those expecting a betrayal were left disappointed. It was the Guide, he was alone and had brought them food and hot drinks on a trolley. The grateful bunch took the sealed foil containers off him. This would become a regular routine and gradually most of them would begin to trust him over the coming weeks. Days of inactivity had given the mostly reluctant travellers time to dwell and they were visited time and time again with frequent bouts of recurring homesickness. The Lenses confided in the Clerk.

"As much as we hate the Anschluss system of government and its densely packed urban areas, it is still the only home that we have ever known."

Now, the small galley with one circular window seemed more of a prison cell than a new adventure. The Guide had warned them on their first night.

"Do not open the porthole as it might attract unwanted attention."

Only the Prof had no regrets with their new circumstances, his face beamed with the expectancy of new and wonderful sights. While the Lenses was used to small confined spaces, so a portable computer kept him occupied to the point of distraction. For the others though, even the regular games of cards played below decks in the confined galley had lost their appeal. At first, the players had enjoyed the shared camaraderie, but it soon petered away in petty squabbles and boredom as the Clerk won most of the time and besides Greta hated to lose. The enforced closeness in the cramped quarters began to play on the stowaway's nerves, trivial arguments and regular bickering broke out. One of the main grievances was the availability of the one toilet. When someone wanted to use it, it was always occupied. Another was snoring, in some extreme cases; the loud nasal noises threatened a riot. Cahill was this main culprit, he had his nose broken once and even though it had been healed, the loud snoring was a token of that painful incident. There was also a mention of the Persuader's big clumsy feet when he knocked over a card game and some drinks when the motion of the huge ship swayed in the opposite direction to which he was walking. Most of them preferred to wear earphones and listen to personal tunes. The Guide brought food when he could and on the first occasion of providing substance, he gave the Prof an exasperating look when the Pleb from the London Contrib asked him.

"Could my meals could be vegetarian? I don't eat meat."

Still, their mysterious benefactor complied with his request. The Mute who remained aloof got on everybody's nerves with his method of eating; it soon became a source of annoyance. The distasteful man nibbled away in a geometrical manner, usually in a circular method, no matter what type of meal that was put in front of him. Sandwiches did not bother the rest as much as other types of food. Biscuits were the most annoying fare.

"What a strange man. I'd like to see him try that with soup." The Prof thought to himself. But, he had to laugh at the Persuader, if he received a bag of treats. The big man just emptied them out of their package into one big pile and devoured them systemically. All of this unbalanced activity upset the Clerk the most, as his past life style was one of nine to five. He so desperately wanted to cast aside that former existence which had revolved around a fixed routine. He divulged to the Prof.

"I did not sign up for this enforced monotony. I had not bargained for this."

"Give it time, things will change."

He had also started to grow a ponytail in deference to the Guide's appearance and received quite a number of jibes about that. He did not care; it was his first step to remove the vestiges of the Anschluss. To add insult to injury the constant clanking of the huge ships turbines and crankshafts drove most of them to distraction, so everybody went back into the TORT-CAM when they required a quiet slumber. Even though the invisible globe was also a confined space, it did not have the same effect on them as the smaller expanse of the cabin did. The concealing device remained active and invisible in a corner of their new home. Whenever their assumed minder visited them, nobody inadvertently touch their bands. They made sure that it did not become visible. But Van DerKamp must have been perceptive, as his eyes always seemed to linger on that corner of the room. The watchful group were always careful to have a body between him and the apparently empty space. Eventually, the Guide recognised the signs of cabin fever. Curiously to him, the only one unaffected by the cramped conditions was the Lenses. So the only way to relieve the building tension among the close knit bunch was when he decided.

"You will take turns above deck, four and five at a time."

He acquired ill-fitting sailor's uniforms, which those going up put on. The grey woolly hats and white uniforms with flared bell-bottomed trousers gave them anonymity. He found it hard to find a set that fitted the Persuader, so the big man looked like he was going to burst out of them any second. Naomh, the Prof, the Lenses and the Mute were first up. Nobody on the huge ship took any notice of five more bodies going topside. The journey from their berth below to the deck above passed through a warren of strange structural design. It was a route of narrow corridors, steep metal stairs and heavy steel doors. Up above and away from the murky skies of the Anschluss and the bowls of the Dreadnaut, it was agreed.

"The Sun never looked so bigger and brighter."

As result of their confinement and their existence in the continually overcast skies of the Contrib's, the brightness hurt them at first. Still, the glassy sea fascinated all of them, but there was one notable exception.

It was Naomh!

Now that the bearer of a piece of the APOCRYPHA'I was integrated with the Alien chemistry of the ALASTHA'I, he had gained an irrational fear of the large body of salty water and its Human portion could not explain its antipathy. The surface of the sea sparkled with boiling silvery bubbles of sunlight and looked to Naomh as if it was a vat of acid. This was the first time that he had seen the sea in its full glory and something in the back of his mind distrusted this physical expression of the Planet. To the others, bar the Mute; it was a delight. All of them appreciated its endless expanse, its calm vastness and gentle hypnotic rhythm that was only broken by the foamy crests of the waves when they slammed against the hull of the huge vessel. In the distance, other types of ships going about their business wisely kept a wide berth from the sea going leviathan. These vessels seemed to be in a much greater hurry and usually sped past the lumbering ANS GREGORY LYUBIN. It was as if they feared to draw the attention of the huge Dreadnaut. The insular City-State dwellers began to appreciate the vastness of the World. Occasionally from their height, the excited voyagers would spot schools of Whales, Dolphins and other marine animals. The vessel was always accompanied by flocks of large sea birds that thrived on its food waste, which was ejected straight into the sea. The Anschluss rulers did not appreciate the fragile beauty of the Planet; it was only a tool to be exploited for their use, after all they would never be its custodians as their paramount ambition was to leave it. This melee of diving birds prompted the Prof to take out an optical recording device, so he could get close ups of everything new. Much to his delight, he filled chip after chip with unbelievable images. The recording enthusiast was fascinated by the large clumps of drifting seaweed that floated past to God knew where. He imagined been as free as the sea going plants, just to go where the tides and currents took him. The day brightened to reveal clouds that were a patch of white stucco on a blue canvas. Only the form of the ship told them, which way was up and which way was down. As the Prof took in the beauty of the horizons, he was sure as tears not caused by the tangy salt air threatened to spill down his awe filled cheeks.

"I have never seen anything that matches this?"

Taking his eyes away from the mesmerising liquid, Naomh studied the features of the Guide in this revealing light and saw that he had a well-tanned complexion. He guessed at his age.

"He is a little older than Rory. I'd say in his late-forties."

Then, something that he had not considered popped into his head.

"My father must have been very young when he had me?"

This Pleb from the Amsterdam Contrib was also taller than him and had a healthy mane of black hair that was tied back and tapered into an expansive pony-tail. In the short time that they knew him, he appeared to be more mature, very confident and most importantly, Van DerKamp seemed more worldly. Naomh found that he really liked the slightly taller enigmatic man. The novice voyager laughed to himself when he recalled the Persuader's comments when he first saw his long black locks. The big man whispered to the Prof.

"He must be really stupid."

"How do you make that out?" Asked the puzzled academic.

"Well look at the amount of hair he has."

The others hid stifled snickers at his naivety. The Prof was about to end the joke by telling him the truth, but a shake from the Engineer's head halted him. Naomh loved that naïve quality about the big man, the Spy just thought that he was nothing but a lummox. The Guide also called everybody

"Dude."

Or

"Man."

He now sported a set of orange flecked glasses. The spectacles intrigued the Lenses and he asked their wearer.

"Have they got some technical uses?"

To which, the other replied.

"No dude, just style. These Shades are for image only."

Kaliningrad did not believe him, until he was given them to wear. Then he saw that they were only ordinary sunglasses. Seeing that the others were distracted with the Shades, the Guide requested Naomh's presence over by the ships rails. Out of earshot, he simply asked.

343

"How did Rory die?"

His topside companion not daring himself to give an answer stood there silently and kept running his thumbs along the tips of his fingers. Anyone who knew Naomh well would have known that this was always a sign of nervousness and deep agitation. He stalled and then counteracted his question with one of his own.

"How come, we have never met before?"

"I was the Gaffer's ace up his sleeve. I was to be the safety valve, if things went wrong and that has certainly happened."

Mollified, Naomh told him the story about the betrayal at the arms deal and lied about Rory's death at the hands of the Anschluss forces. After he had finished, the Guide spoke.

"When you first told me; I became very distressed by your father's death. It was as if my whole World no longer made sense. I was literary shell-shocked."

The receiver of his sympathy believed him to be genuine. The newest member of their fellowship looked at him as if he was holding something back. But if he harboured any doubts about the fabricated end of the story, then the other man kept it to himself. Naomh suddenly realised what the Guide had said and spluttered.

"You said my father. How did you know that?"

"I knew him for many years. When I first saw you on my Frog's Eyes, the resemblance to him was uncanny. It was like I was looking at him from years ago. He was a great man. I had always been on my own and your father brought me into the fold and I met many wonderful people. Some who I loved died, but there were no regrets, they had chosen their own paths. There are some that I miss more than others, but that's life. What happened to him at that arms deal? I thought he was indestructible. I was in tougher scrapes with him and he always came out of them unscathed."

The fact that the Guide knew that Rory had been his parent shook Naomh to the core, but he was getting quite used to strange things occurring, so he recovered quickly and pleaded.

"Don't tell any of the others, he was my father. None of them know and for the moment, I want to keep it that way."

"Secrets Tyro?" Asked the Guide as he slightly raised a quizzical eyebrow.

He lied again.

"Just for now, Rory was betrayed and the Anschluss Filth killed him."

"Did you find out who the dirty Judas son of a bitch was?" Enquired the Guide.

"Yes. It was the Preacher." Answered Naomh, surprised at the biblical reference.

"That nasty piece of work."

His companion on deck felt no need to elaborate.

"You knew him."

It was not a question.

"Yes."

"Well, he is no longer with us."

"Good. Did you send him on his way or at least know who had the pleasure?"

"No, nobody knows who whacked him; it must have been a rival faction."

The Guide had a different opinion about who killed the Preacher, but he kept it to himself. Naomh was amazed that he no longer felt gutted when he mentioned his father's demise. But he had another very important question to ask the man who knew something of his parent's real past. He struggled with the words and eventually blurted them out.

"Did you know my mother?"

"No. I never met her."

"So, you don't know how she died."

The man from his father's past shook his head in the negative and he believed him. Seeing the disappointment in Naomh's eyes, the Guide looked for words of comfort.

"Still, she must have been a great woman if Rory loved her. You can be certain of that."

"So much that he killed her." Thought the younger man bitterly.

Naomh changed the subject; the memories of his own patricide were still too painful and he knew from the way that van DerKamp spoke about Rory.

"He would certainly try and whack me, if he found out that it had been me."

The Guide still on the same subject advised him.

"Since the Gaffer is no longer with us, you are no longer the Apprentice. You are now the leader, so why don't you take his Code-name? It would be a morale booster and it would also be a form of continuity."

"I would feel uncomfortable with that, but I will put it to the others. Let's go below."

The Prof was greatly disappointed and uttered.

"I will wait here until you bring up the others."

"It does not work like that. The number of the group has to remain the same and if anyone came by, how would you answer them?" Said the vexed Guide.

"I'd manage." Replied the academic sullenly and refused to be cajoled.

"Let's put it this way, if you don't move, then I will throw you overboard."

"Do as he says, he means it." Interrupted the serious Lenses.

As much as he loved the sea, he certainly did not want to be thrown into it, so he relented. The Prof would always remember his first day up on deck and his first glimpse of a sky free from the Anschluss. Down below in the vessels bowels; Naomh put the Guide's suggestion to his complement of Anschluss deserters. However, he had already come to his own decision and told them.

"Since we are no longer in danger because of who we are, I have decided to make a fresh start and revert to my name, all of the time. From now on, I am Naomh; nothing else."

Not to be out done, his life-time friend from the Glasgow Contrib said.

"Then, I will be Cahill."

Much to his delight, his lover said.

"I will be Greta from now on. Liben is dust."

She had only divulged her real surname to her red haired lover with a promise not to reveal it. Surprisingly, the rest of them stuck with Rory's appellations, even the Prof and the Clerk who hated their former land more than most. The Mute did not even answer. The Guide then took the other five up above. This became a regular routine and the groups became fluid, never really sticking to the same individuals. One day, the Guide wheeling a trolley of some sort told the confined group.

"There is rough weather brewing on top so you must wear this protective gear."

Those who went aloft to view the black sky came back wide-eyed and exhilarated from the wind driven salty spray. One who had been above, told those who had not been on deck during the ensuing tempest.

"I never felt so much alive."

The Prof had calculated.

"The amount of rainfall that drenched us went in tandem with the intensity of the wind."

The rest went up eager to see what all the fuss was about. Later on, Agent III was not so impressed with the excitement of the raw weather. The mole had seen it all before. This Clone had been on countless missions and had endured many hardships; from remote icy wastes to furnace like deserts. This expert in deception was the Kaiser's best operative bar one and he usually noted.

"This elite PREVENTIVE can act the part of a coward, a fanatic or even a confident. But make no mistake, this infiltrator is also ruthless, skilled in the arts of combat, language and covert operations. There is nothing that will bother this one."

So, it was highly irregular that the Spy was now on a mission of assistance instead of sabotage. Still, this Clone would waste anyone, including Naomh to protect the path to revelation. The mole bore a mirror image to one of the Doctor's original cadre. The long dead instigator would have recognised the features of the Clone immediately, but not the mind-set. Centuries of power playing had changed them irrevocably. The RE-INSTATOR contingent were never allowed to leave their cabin when the ship was anchored off a port and soon, the Guide began to take them up at night. When asked about this, he replied.

"Shift change."

In the darkness, the Anschluss side of the Mediterranean Sea was a long unbroken line of regular lights which marked out the line of its Sea Wall. The North African side had as many blotches of darkness as light. Naomh felt a bond growing between himself and the Gaffer's friend, so much so that he had a question only for the Guide when they were once again alone on deck.

"I want to tell you a thing that has me puzzled. About two weeks ago, you took me up here in the night time and we were passing a coastal city. It was just before the ship was re-supplying the Anschluss post, you called Isoa di Pantelleria."

The Guide thought back and remembered the city.

"It was Tunis."

"The name of it doesn't matter. The fact is that I felt somebody watching me from its lights. It was a man and it wasn't some solider or citizen. No, this felt personal. This person marked me and it was not a pleasant feeling. I felt a chill down my spine. It was a fear that I have not felt before."

Raising his eyebrows slightly, he did not dismiss Naomh's gut feeling.

"I had been around Rory for many, many years and those kinds of impulses had saved my life more than a few times."

Out loud, he uttered.

"Peel away the skin and you will find the father."

"What?" Asked Naomh.

"Nothing, I was just thinking to myself."

He asked the instinctive question.

"Did it feel like an Anschluss Spy or assassin?"

"No, as I said this felt different." Said Naomh as he mimicked the Guide's frown.

"Well there is nothing we can do about it now. We will just have to wait until that dude makes his move." Said the other, knowing

"We have left Tunis behind and will not be going back there again."

Standing on the prow as the tentative Sun rose from the east, Naomh squinted through a haze of foul smelling fumes. This smoke was not a discharge from the ships massive engines, but from a small cylindrical shaped object hanging from the Guide's mouth. His deckmate still had his miniature heating coil in his left hand and was puffing pleasurably from the smoking object. Although it bore a likeness to the harmless Cigs that were enjoyed throughout the Anschluss, his was something else. It had a very sweet smell. This "Joint." according to the Guide.

"Is a mild narcotic that relaxes the mind."

Naomh tried one when it was offered to him weeks ago and nearly choked to death. He gave his companion a black look and van DerKamp laughed as he said.

"It is an acquired taste."

When they took this time out from the confining holds below and as soon as the Guide lit up, he would revert to an archaic tongue from the late Twentieth century. When Naomh questioned the use of this addictive drug, the smoker just replied.

"Look dude. This weed just gets me mellow and shit man it gives me a positive vibration."

He had no idea what the Guide was talking about so the other filled him on the Nation which they were about to enter. It was a word that he was totally unfamiliar with.

"This Nation consists of a fortified enclave with its back to the sea. It is surrounded on all sides by a vast religious alliance that desires the total destruction of the place and the recovery of all of its land which they believe, belongs to them. A huge wall, similar but higher and thicker than the one that encloses the Anschluss separates the two antagonists. As long as this barrier stands, then this Nation will exist safe behind its ramparts. It also possesses an arsenal of Atomic weapons that it will use as a last resort, if it is overrun."

When the Guide explained to the ignorant Naomh what exactly these weapons were, he reproached him for telling him fairy tales. However, the inner voice declared.

"I have told you, there are such things."

The Human narrator lapsed into silence, met Naomh's eyes and admonished.

"You have really led a sheltered life."

The new believer in weapons of mass destruction shuddered. His companion asked him.

"What's the matter?"

"I just had a terrible thought. If the Preacher had got his hands on those things, he would have used them and killed tens of millions."

"You are probably right. But it's all hypothetical now. He is dead after all."

Going back to the previous subject, Naomh asked his deck mate.

"How did this conflict start?"

Swallowing a deep satisfying mouthful of tobacco smoke and exhaling, he said with a shrug.

"Mostly because of Religion."

Now, this was a subject his listener could warm to.

"You mean like the Anschluss prohibits it. Which side is against the worship of God?" Knowing when he got the answer, that would be the side he would support.

"Neither. Both of the antagonists believe in God."

348

Naomh gasped in confusion.

"I don't understand."

He really did not.

"It's straight forward enough. The Enclave is the land you know from the illicit Bible. Inside the wall are the people of Zion or as you would know it by; Israel. They are mostly Jews and number about a hundred and ten million souls. Outside the wall are the lands of the Prophet and their numbers are about three billion. Behind the wall is the Holy Land, where your Christ lived. Both sides believe fanatically in the existence of God, but not the same one and neither of them believe that your Christ is paramount."

"That's crazy. It doesn't make sense."

He was baffled from all this talk about more than one type of God. The Guide gave his charge an appraising look and if reaching some decision, he said.

"Look Naomh. There is a big place out there beyond the Anschluss. Although, there are eight billion people in our homeland, the rest of the World amounts to ten times that. Not everything out there is black and white, there are grey areas in between. You will see and experience a lot of weird stuff on your journey. Different sights, strange cultures. You will have to discard the preconceptions of what you think it is like outside the Anschluss. Because believe me man, you have seen nothing yet. And another thing dude, you and your crew might despise life back home, but believe me, there is a lot of far worse places out there in the big wide World."

Feeling chagrined, Naomh mumbled a reply and went silent as he tried in vain to picture a setting different from the Anschluss. The man from the European mainland was quickly sliding out of his depth from his unfamiliar surroundings. It felt like he was a small-lost boy that wanted to flee back to recognizable things. He focused on something tangible, another question he had never broached before.

"Did Rory have a codename for you?"

"Yes, he called me "Dutchy"."

"What does that mean?"

"It's a pun on what the area around the Amsterdam Contrib was once called."

"Oh, I see."

But he didn't, the Anschluss did not teach about the concept of nationhood.

"I'd still prefer to be called the Guide." Said his companion as he flicked the butt of his finished joint into the sea far beneath them. Neither of them saw the discarded Cig land in the water below, strong winds disintegrated it into tiny particles that became scattered forever. Having taken enough fresh air, the two men joined the other four and made their

way back below so the Guide could bring the other five topside.

Eventually, the long days and nights aboard the slow moving man-made levitation neared their tedious end. Although, the journey was taxing and tiresome, it had also been a time for reflection. On the penultimate morning of their voyage, Naomh along with the Prof, the Lenses and the Clerk took their turn with the Guide above deck. He had deliberately chosen the group without Cahill and Greta. He explained to nodding heads.

"Those two lovers do nothing but hold hands cuddle and steal kisses when they are up here. I'm not jealous, but it is annoying."

"Why don't you just tell them."

"Not a good idea."

The others nodded in confirmation. Changing the subject, the latest member of their group informed them.

"The GREGORY LYUBIN will make landfall at our final destination in the early hours of tomorrow morning. Then we will soon get off."

There were spontaneous cheers from all except Naomh. He replied to the news without much fuss.

"I guessed as much. In fact, I have been expecting it."

The speaker of the joyful titbit did not ask him how he was aware of this. The pony-tailed man just nodded in acquiescent. The younger man now asked a question that he had put on the back burner until now. It was as if he had been fearful of a particular answer.

"Is it as bad as I think it is outside the Anschluss? Unlike me, the Prof believes that our rulers are lying and it is a paradise beyond our walls."

"Your spectacle wearing friend is correct and in other aspects, so are you. I won't lie to you. Some places are indeed like Hell itself."

"And where we are going?"

"It is similar to our Homeland."

"That's a relief then."

"I said similar, not the same. It is far from that as you will soon see?"

Although, the reluctant seafarer was elated to be getting off the ship, it had been a safe and comforting haven and in one sense, he was loathe to leave it. Still, his destiny waited in the wings. His stomach tightened with the unpleasant realisation.

"We will be completely out of our depth in this new and exotic land. The Guide is the only knowledgeable one among us rookies. We will be certainly in debt to him."

He was wrong of course, Agent XIII had been there on many occasions. Later that evening as the nine of them partook of their full last meal aboard ship, there was little conversation shared as each person prepared themselves mentally for what lay ahead. Their meal provider brought them food from the ships huge galley, but declined to share it.

"I have to make preparations to get us off the ship, man."

The busy Pleb returned at nineteen hundred hours and told them it was nightfall, which surprised most of the gang.

"But it stays bright until ten o'clock at this time of the year." Stated the Clerk.

"This is not the Anschluss dude. I will explain it later. Now to important things. I have the false documents and official uniforms for us. These will entitle all of us to enter the country under a deal between them and the Anschluss. No questions will be asked. Now Naomh, you said you have something to show me."

Their leader gave the others a questioning glance and all but the usual suspects nodded their heads. The Guide did not miss the exchange.

"From the nods, I'd say, I have just barely past the test."

Without fanfare, the invisible TORT-CAM was activated and it appeared in the corner where it had been ever since the stowaways had settled into the cabin. The well-travelled man's eyes widened as the apparition focused into view, he had seen nothing like this before. Naomh went through its operation in a blasé fashion. He took the reluctant Guide into it and showed him around. For the first time since he had met Rory, the man of the World was at a loss for words. It got worse when some of the stowaways started to explain the TORT-CAM'S attributes, but eventually, he accepted their explanation. The long-haired man faced Naomh, gave him an appraising look and said.

"You are beginning to worry me, boy."

"Just a modern innovation." Replied Naomh innocently.

There were a few chuckles.

"Modern, my ass. That has something to do with your uncle Rory. Any more tricks up your sleeve."

"You will just have to wait and see."

He was pleased that van DerKamp had kept quiet about his true relationship with the Gaffer. Then Naomh tried to convince the Guide.

"Maybe, you should use the TORT-CAM, carrying the rest of us inside and enter the Enclave of Zion."

Although chuffed with the others trust, their escort ruled out that idea when he explained.

"Even if I go in alone, I will be followed everywhere that I venture in this land. And if the authorities discovered more bodies with me that they cannot account for, then all bets would be off and all of us would be detained."

He was asked.

"Why?"

"Lots of different people from around the globe do business around here. This place needs trade and commerce to prosper. They are not self-sufficient like the Anschluss. Anybody suspicious will be searched or even detained. So we will act like the regular type of personnel that is allowed to visit here and carry the normal gear of a guest to this land."

The fleeting visitor left once again, but returned at mid-night and took Naomh aside. He whispered a few words to him and they left together, but not before he had shrunk the TORT-CAM to marble size. All of the crew were sleeping outside the fantastic device that night. The Guide moved briskly and his charge hurried to keep up. The two men went from hold to hold of the huge ship. Naomh noticed that each enormous cargo bay held different items and one colossal hold that the two men passed through held large quantities of munitions. He asked the man in the know.

"Why so many?"

"Trade goods and gifts for the locals they want to influence. We will take what we need and put them in that contraption of yours." Explained the other.

"Will they be missed?"

"Probably, but we will be long gone by then."

The two pilfers had a busy night loading supplies into the gluttonous device. Naomh was surprised by one item which they loaded by the thousands. Small portable lifting machines made the task very easy. Besides that type of commodity, the two men loaded the sphere with familiar labelled tins of meat, vegetables, fruit and other non-perishables. Basic staples of rice, potatoes and bread were included in the rummage through the ship's cargo and most important of all, large plastic containers of drinkable water. When asked about the sizeable quantity of one particular commodity by Naomh, his fellow loader answered mysteriously.

"Just wait and see."

"I think we should go back to the weapons hold and take a selection of firepower."

"I was just about to suggest that."

With expert familiarity, the Guide selected an inventory of armaments and his companion in thievery agreed with his choices. There was one drawback however, only items of two metres high could fit into the fully expanded globe. The Guide asked a surprising question that nobody had posed before.

"How much weight can this thing hold?"

Unable to answer, he questioned the internal voice.

"Weight is not a factor. Only space is. You can only load as much as it takes to fill up its internal void."

With no limits, they filled the back of the weird compartment to the brim. Naomh realised.

"It will be very cramped until we start using the stuff."

Finally, everything the Guide deemed necessary was loaded into the TORT-CAM and it was shrunk back down to marble size. Its holder was amazed that the enormous quantity of materials put into it did not increase its weight by one gram. Naomh was at a loss to explain that, the voice told him.

"The explanation would be too complicated. Just accept it."

In no mood for something that would tax his tired brain to the limits, he let it go. Naomh returned to their hideout eight hours after the Guide had requested his aid, he was completely knackered and went straight to sleep. It would hit him later when he was free from exhaustion that the stocking of the invisible shield with that amount of supplies meant that they were definitely in it for the long haul. No sooner than he had closed his eyes, he was been shrugged awake. It was past daybreak and his midnight accomplice had returned. The others had been up for a while, but they had let him sleep. Now in the cold light of preparation, their escort motioned them to remove their normal clothing and put on the new uniforms he had brought.

"Gather up your gear and from this moment on follow my lead and do whatever I do. And give me your M I M'S. The communication devices will not work once you are away from the GREGORY LYUBIN."

Cahill became suspicious again, the Lenses looked outraged.

"Ok. Keep them if you wish. You will only be carrying excess weight."

All of them did. The Guide repeated again that they remove their outer clothes. The others nodded and began to strip off their own garments. They were amazed at the perfect fit. He was asked about that.

"I have a few talents of my own, man." Said the procurer of their new garments as he winked in a conspiratorial manner. When the crew were dressed, the Guide said.

"Ok, let's get this Gig on the road."

Gig was his name for their quest. The group left the small galley and entered the confined corridors that formed a maze throughout the ship. Nine of them headed in a direction different to any they had made during the prolonged voyage. A lift took them to an embarking area where their escort handed each of them legitimate access documents, which would allow them entry into this unfamiliar land. Each passport (The Guide called them that.) had their image and a false name; all matching their bio scan on a laser etched plastic card. The Lenses had supplied the counterfeiter with the necessary photo-scans. Some of them sat nervously, but none of these individuals showed any outward sign of the anxiety as they waited for their turn to leave the ship. Inwardly, the Mute was the most excited of the lot. Once off the ship, he could do what he had always done. All throughout the voyage, he had never been out of sight from the others and no chance to commit dark murder. Now, he was entering a place of millions and he rubbed his hands in eagerness. After what seemed an eternity, van DerKamp received instructions through an earpiece which he passed on.

"It is our turn to disembark."

Picking up their individual baggage the expectant group filed into a single line with the Guide in the front. Cahill and Greta took up the rear. The mostly apprehensive column moved out on to the ship's deck. Now,

353

the little group was exposed to a very warm sultry morning that done little to blow off the nasty smells of the floating vessel that they had been on for over four weeks. The stationary ship devoid of the trailing winds now seemed to absorb the heat. Blinded and stunned by the ferocity of the Middle Eastern Sun, the uncomfortable group followed the Guide to a moveable gangway that stretched from the deck of the ship to the floor of a smaller vessel below. The man who had been here before explained this.

"The GREGORY LYUBIN is too large to dock, so it waits off shore while smaller vessels come out to meet it. These transferring boats take off whatever has to go ashore."

The nervous group composed themselves as they were about to enter a new and exotic land. Stories and images of the Hell World outside the boundaries of the Anschluss lingered in the backs of these ignorant minds; so silence reigned. The Guide became worried by his charge's muteness, so he urged them with a whisper.

"Chat normally. We have to give the watchers the impression that we are part of the usual entourage from the Anschluss."

Understanding dawned on Cahill and he spoke out loud.

"Is it usually this hot?"

The Guide suppressed a wicked grin and answered.

"You must be joking."

The rest of the group relaxed at the news. Then, he added.

"Wait till the afternoon Sun gets up, then it will be twice as hot as it is now."

Already the Europeans were feeling their faces flush from the glare of the searing Sun, so none of the embarkees welcomed the news that it was going to get hotter. Naomh had other problems; again he was feeling a strange reluctance to the closeness of the seawater and the edginess increased as the mass of liquid got nearer. It felt as if it wanted to swallow him up. With white knuckles, he willed himself on. When the novice sea voyagers were half way down the moving platform to the smaller vessel and their gazes focused ahead, one of the group looked back at the huge ship, up at the darkened windows of the bridge where known to the intending double crosser, laid the Chairman. The supreme leader of the Anschluss had left the sumptuous diplomatic area of the huge vessel and sat at the helm. Ivan Tell was studying the group intently as they disembarked. The ruler of the Anschluss stood statue still and smiled grimly as Naomh, his Spy and the others boarded the smaller craft. He watched as the transferring vessel crossed the narrow stretch of water, went through a gap in the narrow sea wall and made landfall near a huge building that reflected the glare of the Sun. Still, the watcher kept his vigil until those he observed went out from his sight into the glass building of the arrival's hall. The Chairman had flown out on a luxurious flying craft with a few cronies that had blasted out from his tower on the Geneva

Contrib early that morning and landed secretly on the Dreadnaut. He was now paramount in the giant ship, it was an extension of his realm. For the Kaiser was the supreme commander of the Anschluss military forces with included, land, sea, air and the Space corps. The reason why the acting Admiral of the ANS GREGORY LYUBIN smiled to himself was simple.

"Naomh's group will have no problems with the custom points. The state below owes its very existence to the Anschluss. And to put it quite bluntly, its rulers would be in shit street without our assistance. So they will do what I demand of them."

Unknown to the confined population, the Anschluss was extremely suzerain and many states around the World paid close attention to what the Chairman desired. The self-centred and smug man also knew the RE-INSTATOR'S new secret. His agent had sent him images of the TORT-CAM during various stages of its operation and had even included footage of its strange red and white coloured interior. The mole had briefed him about the search for a device that would open the gateway to the stars.

"This amulet, Agent XIII called it, the APOCRYPHA'I. This is the culmination of our goal. And I will have it when it is completed."

His accomplished agents could not work out how those he was watching had got on to the huge ship, unobserved. But, he and his Spy were the only ones privy to that.

"As it should be."

He liked to keep his underlings guessing.

"Every journey starts with a first step and so it begins. Naomh has a guardian Angel watching over him and he does not even know it." He thought to himself as he departed the helm without a word to the crew. The arrogant ruler would have been shocked, if had had known how close his piece of wit was to the truth. His cronies filed in to line and followed him from the bridge. The Chairman had supreme confidence in his Spy among their ranks, who was receiving covert instructions all the time from his personal office. Tell boarded a large bellied Wraith that would take him back to the Geneva Contrib. High in the sky; he allowed himself a gloating smile that confirmed things were progressing well. Before his unwitting dupes had disappeared from his view, Naomh and his companions watched as the shoreline drew near. The Prof was awash in the thrill of growing excitement. He revelled.

"Another land and a different place."

All that any of them could make out was a smaller version of the sea bulwarks of the Anschluss and behind that meagre obstacle, a wall of tall indistinct buildings that stretched off in an uniformed line leftwards, rightwards and upwards. The line of high buildings only allowed a few glimpses of the background brown hills and lower sized structures that clambered upwards behind them. The shoreline configurations grew higher as the small craft got nearer. They stopped craning their necks at the enormous constructions when the angle of their necks grew too severe. The ferrying craft with the fugitives from the Anschluss reached the shore and the vessel's occupants disembarked at a large building. Naomh breathed a sigh of relief, the trip to the shore had been a nightmare and he had not spoken a word during the short junket. At the minute everybody's feet touched the solid ground, it seemed all of their legs betrayed them. It was like the whole Planet moved and left them behind. The Persuader had a flashback

"I once spent hours on the Stand ons. It feels the same after I got off; a bit wobbly."

The Guide explained their lack of coordination.

"It's because of the long sea voyage, give it time and you will get your old rhythm back."

"How long will that take?" Asked a queasy Lenses.

"It's different for everybody, anything from a few hours to a day."

"Great." Said the Clerk who was wearing the Guides odd shades.

He guessed that he would be one of those that would take the longest to recover. The Lenses gave a sudden gasp.

"My Frog's eyes have gone blank. It will not work."

Not taking his word, the rest of them checked their M.I.M's and found all of the units the same. They now agreed with the discoverer. A smug van DerKamp reminded them.

"Told you so, dudes. You are in a different World here."

Still, their sympathetic warden knew how each of his charges felt, none of them had ever felt so naked before, but they would soon get used to it. The Prof recovered first and spoke with reassurance.

"Well, this is supposed to be the start of a different life, so we won't be needing these anymore."

He took his off and threw it into the sea. He instantly felt better. The academic had removed the last vestiges of Anschluss paraphernalia and a weight fell away from his shoulders. Tell's agent thought to themselves.

"You will pay for that."

The others followed suit and removed their ear pieces, but the Lenses was reluctant to divest himself of his last vestige of technical equipment from his homeland and hoped.

"Maybe it's just a glitch and the lines will be restored."

"You haven't a prayer man." Said the Guide.

"I will work on it."

The Prof had an old fashioned digital timepiece with a leather wrist strap and he handed to the distraught Lenses.

"Here take this. It still works."

The grateful man accepted it; he looked at the date and it stated, the 7th of August 2952 AD It was correct. The Guide noticed the antiquated piece and uttered.

"God above! Where did you get that from?"

"I borrowed it from a museum."

The Engineer was again amazed at the ability to utter a religious connotation out loud without rebuke. With the fear of the unknown in his eyes the Lenses finally succumbed and removed his communication device. The pink eyed man strapped on the Prof's gift to the wrist without the band. The rest of his party had moved on, so he hurried to catch them up. As the group proceeded to the inside the arrival's hall, one of Naomh's cadre smiled an exact copy of the Chairman's mocking smile, this person was also aware of the intending betrayal when the search was completed. The small group were ordered by an automated voice to proceed through an enclosed area. The programmed timbre was in a heavily accented Anschluss. Their escort had previously briefed them.

"In this confined space, our group will be scanned with every surveillance device available to the Emigration officials of this land. If nothing prohibited is detected, then we will be allowed to proceed."

"What about the Lenses eye colour?" Asked the Prof of the Guide.

"If you are detained, tell them that it is inherent. They should accept that."

All of them fought an internal battle in the room, the Lenses more than most, as they did not know if the TORT-CAM would be discovered. This would be the first time that it would undergo such intense scrutiny since back in the Atlantis Sector's warehouse. The Guide's party had no need for this misplaced anxiety for two reasons. Firstly, its ALASTHA'I technology was too far advanced for the primitive detectors and secondly, the Chairman had already ensured that Naomh's party would be allowed entry with no interference. Unsurprisingly then, the nervous exiles passed through narrow corridors without any hassle and found themselves in another part of the massive building. A watching member of the Enclave espionage fraternity immediately recognised one of the gang and acknowledged.

"Trouble will follow that one."

She had orders to let them pass through unhindered. After rounding a narrow corner, the subjects of her scrutiny were in a huge glass and steel atrium of an exotic architecture that none but the Guide had encountered before. (The Spy never used normal channels.) Everywhere, there were images of this nation and some had the Anschluss script saying.

"Welcome to the ancient land of the Enclave."

If this encouraged looks of wonder among the companions. The sight of the diverse coloration of the many different races milling about under the roof of the foyer left them all speechless. (Except the Guide and the mole who had seen it all before.). People from the four corners of the Earth congregated here, a diverse bunch of olive browns to the ebonite blacks and strange sallow shades of the Human race. Been from the isolated

Anschluss where only white people existed, each one of them were both alarmed and afraid by the sudden enormity of the World. Automatically, they adopted the uniquely Human defence of believing that they were superior to the rest of these exotic peoples. Sensing his companions disquiet, the Guide spoke.

"It's ok. I was amazed the first time I arrived in this place. You will get used to it as well. Everybody here are people, just like us. They just look different, that's all."

Observing the group's expressions, the worldly man could see he would have a hard time convincing some of his charges. Greta, the Mute and the Engineer had looks of open hostility. He felt the three of them would always remain unconvinced, but as in time memorandum, some of the males among the group were already entertaining the thoughts of what the female bodies looked like under the weird clothing and certainly of sexual encounters. None, but the Guide noticed that the other foreigners were also sizing up the group and Greta with her tall blond locks and curvy figure was receiving many an admiring look. Seeing Cahill tight grip on her wrist, he relaxed. But when he saw the look of open fascination on the Clerk's face to the passing females while nudging the Persuader, a premonition warned him.

"We will have trouble with the slight built man. He will find a few admirers out here."

Back in the Anschluss, females normally ignored the Clerk, especially if he was in the company of his more handsome friends. Out here, it would be different. His slim stature and blonde hair combined with his deep green eyes would make him attractive to the females of this place and indeed other lands. Some of the cultures outside the Anschluss had a deadly response to any perceived insult to their female's honour, so the Guide decided.

"I will have to explain this to them as soon as possible."

At the far end of the atrium there was an abundance of automised eating and drinking stations. Their escort motioned the group to follow him in that direction and when they reached a sitting area, he told them to make themselves comfortable. With mixed emotions, the newcomers huddled at a table while the Guide and the shanghaied Persuader went to procure some refreshments. The two men returned with a large jug of coffee, another of juice and several synthetic cups. Both the coffee and the juice had a strong flavour and a smooth aroma, but it was pleasant enough. Then, the Lenses noticed a large glimmering timepiece on a wall. He looked at the one that the Prof had given him and told the seated group that it was wrong. The Guide explained with a glint of humour to the seating group.

"No dude. The time displayed is correct. The Enclave's time is an hour ahead of the Anschluss."

Most of the gathered group did not understand him, but the Prof did and he clarified it for the others.

"Time gains an hour when we go east and loses an hour when we go west from the Anschluss. The further we go in each direction the more it changes."

The others still did not comprehend and it started a heated argument. The Guide ended the discussion as he interrupted.

"Just accept it man."

When the coffee had relaxed them enough, the pony tailed man Pleb to two automatic doors at the opposite end of the building and said in a serious manner.

"Outside that entrance is a very different place. So follow my lead at all times. Now put these on. Each of you will find a set of clothes in your luggage"

He opened his large pack and pulled out another set of clothing.

"What this. Are we going to a fancy dress party?" Alleged Cahill when he saw the garments. The outfits were basically, an olive green sexless military uniform with black polished leather steel boots. The trousers and shirts had an abundance of pockets stitched in strategic places to carry all sorts of useful things. Males had to wear a small round cap of any colour on their heads, even under a beret, which was provided for both sexes.

"Bloody hell. You were not kidding when you said this was a weird place." Said an uncomfortable Engineer.

"Well, when in Rome you do what the Romans do." Replied the Guide.

"What are you talking about? We are nowhere near the Roman Contrib." Asked a baffled Clerk.

"Forget about it."

The Guide shook his head sadly as he remembered the one sided and biased education everybody received in the Anschluss. He had Naomh's father Rory to thank for enlightening him. Their comrade who was familiar with the ways of the Enclave pointed to male and female changing rooms and told them to go and change. They went in twos except of course the one female of the gang and the Mute. When, they all had come back changed, another round of coffee was requested. Everyone now wore a pair of black tinted sunglasses that topped off their Enclave ensemble. The new arrivals took all the time in the World to finish the beverage because of their reluctance to leave this perceived haven. Naomh was startled out from his rest when the internal voice's excitement hammered into his awareness, urging him to proceed at once.

"Why the hurry?" Enquired it's host.

"I can feel the next part of me. It is not far. Come follow me and we will become stronger."

Feeling pulled by the one part Mescal/Amulet, its bearer rose from the table as if it was his idea alone and urged the sitting group.

"Come on, if we don't make a move now. We never will get enough guts to go out there."

As if he had challenged them, the others rose from the seating and gathered their packs. As a group, they moved towards the doorway of another place.

"Nicely done." Whispered the Guide into Naomh's ear as he led the group outside. The doors slid open and suddenly the new arrivals were in another land. Instantly, each and every one of them felt the extreme temperature of the place, glad now for the sun block, hats and shades that the Guide had provided. Away from the air conditioned building, the heat became suffocating. But the sun protection denied the scorching Levantine Sun of any satisfaction of burning their pale skins. The ointment cooled their faces while they took stock of their new surroundings. The smell of citrus fruits wafted on the warm air bringing a pleasant aroma to the outside. This pleasing fragrance reminded the two brothers from the Madrid Contrib of the orchards of the Agriculture sectors. Suddenly there was a shattering supersonic bang and all of them nearly jumped out of their skins.

"What the Hell was that?" Demanded the jittery Lenses.

"It must be thunder." Said the Prof.

"No, that's their Air force. I forgot about them." Said the man who had been here many times.

"What! These people have flying craft out in broad daylight. But that is impossible. I never heard of such a thing." Was the Clerk's input.

Everyone else agreed.

"What's that then?" Quizzed the Guide pointing to a formation of seven silver disc shaped objects high in the sky. Looking up, the rest of them stared open mouthed at the wondrous sight high above them. The flat sleek looking planes were emitting powerful orange flares, while accelerating vertically. The noise of the flying machines was deafening. Then, there was silence as the engines were switched off and the planes fell like stones to the ground. Those from the Anschluss stared in horror at the falling objects, but at the last moment before the aircraft collided with the ground, their engines re-ignited and the flying disc's flew back up again and sped away until they were out of sight. The flying machines did not return and only their lingering vapour tails told them that the aircraft had been real and not imagined. Reluctantly all of them removed their gazes from the sky and took stock of the new surroundings. The Engineer felt cheated at the sight, which greeted them. Secretly, he had expected a land that the Bible had described, but it was a concrete high rise similar to back home. The Guide must have noticed the Engineer's disappointment and removing his shades; he raised a quizzical eyebrow and mocked.

"Well, what else did you expect?"

Still, the skyline was unlike any in the Anschluss. A lot of the structures were constructed of marbled white concrete and glass. Buildings lay tightly packed together in various heights and widths with very few spaces between them. Most had huge windows that were without glass and were fronted by balconies that hung precariously over the narrow shaded streets. The living quarters were separated from the hanging projections by wooden, metal and plastic shutters, which could be closed in the seasonal period of inclement weather. Some of the constructions appeared new, others ancient and crumbling, but all were occupied. Naomh who was still receiving instructions from the urgent internal voice started to head in a specific direction before he was roughly pulled back by a serious Guide.

"Where are you going?" Demanded the one who assumed that he was to be followed.

Startled from been controlled and somewhat confused, Naomh answered.

"I just know where to go."

The affronted Guide returned a hard look.

"How would you know where to go, man? You've only been off the boat five minutes."

"Actually. We have been here three hours." Said the Clerk factually.

If looks could kill, then the one that De Mere received from the Guide was terminal.

"Look people. There is a hotel I frequent during my trips here. Let's go and book in there. We can relax, get settled in and it will give you time to get accustomed to your new surroundings. Then we can plan a course of action."

The Persuader said in response to all of their baffled looks.

"What's a hotel?"

"Fuck man." Said the Guide and he explained the idea of a hotel.

"So these places are something like the Pleb's halls of the Anschluss, but you have to give credits to stay in them." Copped the Lenses.

"Yes. But the décor is not as functional." Replied the Guide with a concealed smirk.

Plebs in the Anschluss had no need for regular hotels or their like, because its efficient, speedy and twenty four hour running Mag-lev got anybody home in a couple of hours, no matter where one was or how long the journey was. Everyone else agreed on this course of action, most of the company were fatigued from the extreme heat and their taxing brains working overtime, trying to take in all the differences. A place to rest and take account seemed a perfectly good idea. Even Naomh relented despite an unheard voice of urgency against the suggestion. So, its bearer overrode it protests.

"The Guide is correct."

The chastised metallic voice of the APOCRYPHA'I went silent. The Guide took them around a narrow street where a lot of vehicles with bright neon lights stood formed into a line. Their escort motioned to the hired means of transport.

"These are called Cab's. For a fee they will take you anywhere in the Enclave you desire."

"Wow. That's amazing. Private transport is unheard of in the Anschluss." Said the know all Clerk.

Seizing a chance to put the smart alec in place, the man from the Amsterdam Contrib could not resist a gibe.

"That's not true. There are many types of private transport back home. You just haven't met the right people or looked in the right places."

The others laughed at their ignorance and the Clerk went bright red. The Cab was not large enough to take all of them and their perceivable luggage. So the group split into two manageable parties and two drivers agreed to take them to the given destination. The Guide, Naomh, Cahill, Greta and the Prof filed into one and once inside, the passengers found that they were separated from the driver by a transparent plastic screen. The Engineer, his brother, the Clerk, the Lenses and the Mute took the second Cab. Just before he had sat in their Cab, the Guide handed something to the Clerk and explained to him what they were for. In the first hired vehicle, van DerKamp told his companions.

"The screen is a security device. It's a throwback to the times when a driver could be robbed of his earnings."

The man at the helm spoke to them in an entirely incomprehensible language. The Guide answered in what must have been be the same tongue and he slotted about twenty metal discs into a drawer that appeared from the driver's side. He had added extra and the man smiled showing a broad grin of stained yellow teeth. The driver seemed satisfied, he darkened the Cab's outside windows as well as the one separating them from him and the contrivance took off. The other vehicle followed in their wake. Seeing the looks of consideration on his companion's faces about the strangeness of what had just happened, the Guide broke into private laughter and confirmed his private opinion.

"I told you man, you dudes would need me."

"What were those metal discs that you gave to the man in front?" Asked the Prof.

He for one never tired of learning new things.

"It is called money. To be more precise, Shekels. It is used here the same way as credits are taken from your account back home. For bigger transactions laminated plastic currency is swapped."

The Guide felt secure enough to speak the Anschluss's tongue as the driver had erected a privacy screen and was unable to hear their conversation. Then something had just occurred to Naomh. He concealed his astonishment well. Hiding his revelation, he smiled in encouragement at the Guide who mistook the intention that he was accepting him taking

362

the leading role. But this was not the case. For the bearer of the living amulet realised.

"I understood every word that had passed between the driver and the Guide. Stranger still, I can read the script of the Enclave, even though it reads from right to left and its Semitic characters should make no sense to me at all. Semitic; how do I even know that word?"

Naomh would have been even more alarmed, if he had known that another among the ten was also multilingual. It was the Anschluss agent. The ability to understand and converse in other languages was a benefit of been one of the LYUBINITES. Remembered language's came easily as each new generation of Clone seemed to retain one that was known or learnt by a predecessor. The new discoverer decided.

"There would be some awkward questions asked if I reveal to the others that I understand the Enclave tongue. I will keep this knowledge to myself. I am sure that it will come in very useful as the quest goes on."

However, one could only guess at the astonishment of the others including Naomh himself, if the Spy revealed their proficiently in the same language. The Guide had told the driver.

"We are a special unit back from foreign lands and are in need of rest and some fun."

Noticing their pale complexions, the man had sympathised with them.

"My brave countrymen, I will take you anywhere you desire."

The Alien voice interjected in the mind of its host.

"Who do you think gave sophisticated language to mankind? None, but us. Through me you can comprehend every speech mode in this World and some archaic tongues that have vanished long since."

Because of the darkened windows of the moving vehicle, the passengers could no longer view the strange metropolis as the hired vehicle sped through the narrow streets. It even went up steeply inclined streets; these ascending routes were relatively unknown in the mostly levelled Anschluss. An hour later the Cab stopped and the doors slid open. Its passengers alighted into a long narrow street that housed the same universal dwellings of the place, with one exception that the windows on the fronts of these buildings boasted no balconies. Each facade appeared to have only one entrance/exit, which lay at the top of various stair heights. Naomh's group waited until the other Cab had caught up to them and then everybody got out and stood in the street. The drivers wished them well and sped away leaving them alone on the street with its strange smells and atmosphere. The Guide told them to pick up their luggage and follow him. The group of Anschluss travellers ascended a flight of worn concrete steps closed in by two squat palm trees. The only person who knew what was going on indicated that the climbers wait at the top alongside a black painted and very solid looking metal door. The weary gang stood huddled at the stairs summit in full view of an imbedded surveillance unit, some left their packs rest on the ground. The Guide pushed his way up front, confronted the camera and spoke at it in the strange language. After what seemed like forever, the closed door slid open smoothly, belying the dilapidated state of the exterior. The efficiency of the door mechanism should have hinted at the sumptuous interior, but all except the self-confessed traveller were caught unawares. The faded light of the narrow streets dissipated into the brilliance of a summer day without the blistering heat. The inside of the foyer was crowned with a ten floored blue glass octagon whose diffracted light fed a virtual mini garden of paradise, complete with carved fountains and exotic flora and fauna. The latter consisting of brightly coloured singing bird life and cavorting pairs of small simians, leaping from branch to branch. The Prof stood in rapture to witness so many species in such a confined space. He laughed in delight as the caged birds scattered and he was treated to a feast of coloured plumage and undersides. The group was awoken from the vision of paradise by a loud happy greeting in a heavy accented Anschluss. A small leather faced rotund bald man embraced van DerKamp as he turned around to find the owner of the voice. The hairless man with a beard had grasped him in a massive bear hug while at the same time kissing both his cheeks. The others tensed at the perceived physical attack, but the Guide gestured that it was all right. The bubbly man released him and spoke in his weird accented Anschluss.

"Ah my devious friend Toni. May the grace of Allah be upon you and your friends."

"And may God bless your house as well Alieem." Returned the Guide.

The others looked shocked at the mention of a Supreme Being in such a public place, for such a thing would invite an interrogation and never returning, back home in the Anschluss. The Engineer frowned openly. The Clerk raised an eyebrow and pressed.

"So Toni is your real name?"

The Guide gave a wicked smile and replied.

"Just say, that is the name I use here."

Their jovial host never even batted an eyelid at this revelation, he was used to the intrigue of his guests and an unquestioning Proprietor made for good business.

"Come introduce me to your beautiful friends." Requested the man.

One by one they were introduced to the jolly proprietor and all were greeted in the same fashion which left them gasping for breath after the encounter. True to his word, their leader called himself Naomh, not Tyro. Not to be outdone, Bonkers named himself Cahill. But there was a problem; the usual one and this time it was doubled. Greta and the Mute steadfastly refused to participate in the greeting. The blonde woman had not even removed her dark glasses; the shades hid her dark look and angry glare. Her hand was itching for one of her concealed blades as the stranger approached her with opened arms. His face hardened slightly as she backed away from his intended embrace and took up a menacing stance. As a rule, Greta only made intentional physical contact with Cahill or with an opponent to be eliminated. Any other cases were accidental. The Guide flinched as he remembered the time at the Marseilles dock sector when she had that cold steel pressed against his groin. Their escort had not been prepared for this confrontation. Still, he reacted quickly; he stepped smoothly between them and whispered into the brown man's ear. Alieem relaxed and smiled; the jovial man dismissed the embarrassing situation with a wave of his hand.

"I understand. Please forgive me. I should have known. Come let me find you a place to sit and I will have refreshments brought to you." Offered the fast talking proprietor.

Funnily enough, he did not press the Mute's refusal of his greeting, one look into the others cold black eyes made up his mind for him. Alieem bowed slightly and he escorted them to a table close to the mini garden, much to the Prof's delight. The owner of the establishment snapped his fingers and a plainly dressed adolescent girl with a white silk scarf on her head came over to them. Her olive beauty was refreshment enough, especially to the Clerk.

"Ah Almas, my youngest wife. Bring refreshment and a glass of water for our guests."

The newcomer's were caught off balance by that simple statement as the young girl giggled and left with the remnants of a dazzling brown-eyed smile as she went away to do her husband's bidding.

"Youngest wife" Added someone in disbelief.

"Another thing you should know. Alieem is a follower of the Prophet and he is allowed many wives and whether those people engage in the practice is up to them. As you can see there is enough of Alieem to go around more than once, man." Explained the Guide.

"That is disgusting." Said the celibate Engineer.

The Guide did not press the matter as his old acquaintance returned and took his occasional guest aside. The Muslim proprietor asked him in a friendly, but anxious manner.

"Have you brought any goods for me? I know that you always think of your friend when you come here."

His Anschluss guest broke into a broad smile and replied.

"Alieem, you are going to love this."

When van DerKamp told him the amount and variety of contraband they had stashed in their belongings. The squat man assumed a pose of disbelief and reckoned if he did possess that quantity then it was all counterfeit. The haggling began.

"I think you are playing games with poor old Alieem." Insisted the innkeeper.

"Ok my friend. You will see tomorrow. Here I will give you a sample. You will see that I speak the truth." Returned the Guide.

He fished into a bag and produced something that was covered; he handed it over to the expectant man. It was a game they played, but never on this scale; normally the friendly haggling was over a few bottles. Just then his wife returned with the drinks. Alieem apologised to them.

"Your food will be served soon. Please excuse me, I have other customers to attend to."

He left clutching his prize, eager to sell the exotic and much sought after beverage. His youngest wife had left a tray with a large bottle of clear spirit that had the word "Elite." written on it in Anschluss script and several tumblers.

"Watch it, that stuff has a wicked kick." Said the Guide as he filled the small glasses with the aniseed liqueur. The Persuader downed his in one gulp and choked. He managed to ask in between watery tears.

"Shit, what the hell is that?"

"Arak." Replied the Guide.

After the big man's performance, the others treated their drinks with greater respect. When Alieem's young wife was out of earshot, Cahill questioned the Guide.

"What did you say to the fat man, that made him back off from embracing Greta?"

"I told him that she was a woman of God and had pledged her virtue to him alone."

"What does that mean? I don't understand." Said a perplexed Cahill.

The Engineer butted in.

"I do, he means a nun. The Preacher told me about them."

Fitting in with his inquisitive nature, the Clerk had other things on his mind. So, the bureaucrat asked.

"What goods do you have for him and where are they?"

"In the dobber." Said the Guide.

He had started calling the TORT-CAM by that name and so explained its context.

"It is another name for a marble."

This description of a plaything slightly irritated the presence within the Amulet. The Guide and Naomh both shared a conspiring smirk at hidden knowledge.

"When we took the dobber the night before we arrived, we slipped a few items into it."

He turned to his grinning accomplice.

"Shit Naomh. With that thing I could make us very rich indeed."

"Anyway tell that curious lot what you have." His co-conspirator returned.

"Well among other things. Mostly wine, whiskeys and mineral water,

distilled from the best northern river courses in the Anschluss."

"What?" Exclaimed the rest of the others simultaneously.

The Guide began to lecture them.

"Look man. Here in this part of the World, ninety per cent of all drinking water tastes worse than that shit there."

He pointed to what Greta was sipping and the distasteful expression on her face.

"It comes from de salination plants which uses sea water and man, that shit tastes pretty bland. But the mineral water from the Anschluss springs and unspoilt rivers of the frozen north and our regular rainfall makes our produce taste like manna from heaven to these people. So we have an awesome commodity to deal with; man. Especially now that I have given him a sample from the mineral water that runs off the Geneva plateau."

"How many bottles did you bring?" Enquired the Clerk.

"Bearing that ten bottles would probably cover our lodgings and food for the week. Well dude, when I discovered what that thing could do, I never had an opportunity like this so I packed six hundred cases of various beverages."

The Lenses did a mental calculation and whistled.

"Six hundred by twenty four. That's fourteen thousand four hundred bottles."

"Won't they be missed?" Asked the Clerk in a professional capacity.

"Well, if they find out, they can arrest me."

The Persuader slapped him on the back and proclaimed to the rest of the group.

"This Pleb is gifted."

Van DerKamp flinched at the slap and the man from the Amsterdam Contrib also thought he had been extremely clever. He boasted.

"There are millions of different items on the Anschluss vessel, this lot will not go amiss."

But unknown to him, the Spy had informed their superiors about the capability of the TORT-CAM, so the vintage wines and spirits were left in a convenient place for him to discover. Those in the know were well aware.

"Anschluss liquors made from the run off of cascading water from the Geneva plateau and the vast water-courses that ploughed through the urban areas were much desired throughout the places where the pressure on water resources is high."

Although, the City-State was deemed flat, that wasn't entirely accurate and water been liquid had to find its own level anyway. The huddled group broke out in merriment and the Guide was challenged on what else he had loaded the invisible shield with.

"A few other things." Was all that he would tell them.

Realising that they were now rich in this land, the Prof with a dreamy demeanour asked.

"*Tyro.*"

On seeing the others prompt; he corrected himself.

"*I mean Naomh. Could I purchase one of those fabulous monkeys or a spectacular coloured bird?*"

The Clerk had other fabulous olive skinned birds on his mind. The Guide clapped the Prof on his back and encouraged him by saying.

"*Whatever you desire shall be yours, my inquisitive friend.*"

The academic's beam was only matched by the wideness of the Clerk's grin. Alieem's youngest wife returned with nine steaming bowls of meaty chicken soup which was packed with exotic spices and fragrances. The travellers minus the one vegetarian dug into it with relish. The Guide ordered a vegetable dish for him. When the meal was consumed, they retired to rooms that were appointed to them. The exhausted travellers slept the night away. Well, Cahill and Greta did not. Much to the two lover's delight; they had a room to themselves. The group had spent two days and two nights of revelry at the hotel when Naomh approached the Guide on the third morning at his breakfast. None of the others had risen yet. Naomh insisted that he had to do something soon. The constant reminding by the one part Mescal/Amulet to proceed with the quest had finally galvanised him into action.

"*This might sound strange to you. But I have to meet somebody who I think knows that I am in the Enclave, but not where to find me.*"

The odd statement bothered the Guide and he showed it.

"*How do you know that man, is the little voice in your head telling you these things?*"

"*What!*"

The internal voice had never sounded so startled as it intruded straight away.

"*Does he know of me?*"

But, before its host tried to give an awkward explanation, the newest addition to their company added with a broad smile.

"*A joke dude. As you have not contacted anybody since we have been here, I figured that you must be getting your information from some crazy place, like a voice in your head.*"

"*Oh*" Replied a relieved Naomh.

Seeing that his matter of fact gag had went over its receiver's head and sensing the man at his table's urgency, van DerKamp became serious.

"*Ok man. Tonight some of us will go to the beach front for a few drinks. There is a multitude of drinking and eating places there. Whoever is seeking you will search there. That is where all the foreigners congregate*"

The two men were joined by their companions at irregular intervals over the next few hours. Some were still slightly hungover from the previous night's drinking and the Prof was proudly sporting a primate on his shoulder. The simian was a Capuchin monkey and unknown to the man flaunting the beast; it too like himself was not an original native of this place. It had been traded by a visitor for non-payment of a little bill. Naomh and the Guide waited until everybody had joined them and then the latter told the gathered group.

"Tonight some of us are going to leave the hotel and venture out into the Enclave, for some socialising, man."

There were a few objections about who would go. It seemed nobody wanted to stay, not even the Mute. After a compromise, the Prof volunteered.

"I will stay behind and guard the TORT-CAM. That's not my sort of thing anyway."

He was quite happy to remain in the Hotel with the animals and plants. Later that evening as the nine of them gathered in Naomh's and the room he shared with the pony tailed man; kit was extracted from the invisible shield that would be needed that night. The man familiar with the Enclave gave the go-ahead to pack some hardware.

"It is a negative on the use body armour. These places we are going to are establishments of entertainment; everybody in them wears as little as possible. Take the smallest weapons you have, ones that can be drawn quickly and pack a punch."

The Engineer gave a scorn, but his brother and the Clerk gave a different expression at the mention of scantily clad people. Greta must have been paying attention, because twenty minutes later, she turned out in such a body tight outfit that it revealed every contour of her fantastic body. It was a red skin-tight PVC outfit with numerous gaps revealing tantalising flesh. It was so curve hugging that the only place she could have concealed a weapon was between her ample breasts.

"Lucky gun." Thought more than one.

Noticing admiring looks from her male friends, she asked in an icy tone.

"What are you lot gaping at? We are here to impress the natives, are we not?"

The increasingly bolder Clerk answered for the others.

"They are certainly going to be that."

Then, he whispered to the Persuader.

"I certainly am."

As the revellers left to enjoy the nightlife, the Guide took a couple of bottles of whisky as a sweetener for Alieem. As a follower of the Prophet, van DerKamp was not sure whether the fat man partook of the alcohol himself.

"Well if he doesn't, the wily man will still make good use of it."

Naomh left instructions with the Prof.

"If we get into shit and nobody returns, you are to get out of here and return home."

Little did they know that the academic had no intention of returning to the Anschluss. He had finally escaped the confining shackles of the huge City-State and he wanted to discover the rest of the World that had been denied to him all of his life. He silently thought.

"If my comrades perish and I am the lone survivor, I will convert the Guide's stored up wealth into portable currency and with the TORT-CAM, take my leave and see the World."

He fed the monkey perched on his shoulder with fruit titbits that Alieem, the hotel owner had provided for a pilfered bottle of wine. The Prof became distracted by the feeding of his pet and hardly knew that the others armed to the teeth had departed the hotel. An hour later after a ride in a hailed Cab, the gang arrived at the beachfront. They got out of the hired vehicle and gazed at the wall of tall buildings that blocked any view of the beach and the sea. All around them, the ground floors of every building were lit up in rainbows of flickering neon glitter. The well-informed Guide explained.

"These are the pads, my man. If you are a main dude, you want to live here."

"What are you babbling about?" Asked the only female voice.

"These are the most sought after dwellings in the cramped Enclave, because of their great height and of course because of the cooling sea breezes that soften the blistering heat of this place."

"Why didn't you say that in the first place?"

"I believe I did."

There were so many bars and eating places along the neon strip that their long haired chaperone suggested.

"I don't have a particular choice, so Naomh why don't you pick one at random."

The metallic voice inside its host choose one for him, barley disguising its fever pitched excitement. So its bearer replied to his suggestion and pointed.

"That one is as good as any."

With a slight shrug, the Guide agreed to Naomh's choice and the excited group entered the premises named "Shekels.". Everybody could read its name because the lettering was written in bright light over the front in Anschluss script. The inside of the place was abuzz with noise and little of it was overheard conversation. Entire walls were covered with video projections that were emitting very loud music. Like the sign outside, the music was in an archaic form of their own tongue, much to the newcomer's amazement. The greenhorns took a seat and sat down. The Guide explained.

"People in the Enclave once dreamed of reaching the Promised Land,

which lay thousands of kilometres across the Western Sea. Though, the language of that land is similar to the Anschluss, it is slightly different, but close enough for us to understand."

The deep booming of sounds was making conversation, if not downright impossible, then difficult at least. To be heard, they had to shout. A sad Lenses wished he had a functional set of Frog's eyes now. He asked with great insight.

"Are the people across the Western Sea related to us then?"

"They were at first. It was said that their ancestors first originated in our lands before the Anschluss existed, then left in great numbers and made that land they went to the most powerful place on the Planet."

"What became of them?" Snorted Greta not believing a bit of this incredible story.

"In trying to bring their idea of peace and democracy to the rest of the World, they became entangled in too many conflicts and suffered greatly. So its great leader called, the President decided to let the rest of the World to their own devices and he isolated them from everybody else. They were once a proud race, but now are probably vanquished."

The one part Mescal/Amulet informed Naomh.

"The Guide's story is close to the truth. Your father travelled in that land many a time. It was one of his favourite places."

Events of its previous host's life were coming back to it. The row of seats, they picked to sit down backed up against a solid concrete wall. This was a well-practiced move; at least their backs would be protected. While the rest of the party took a seat, the Guide motioned for the Clerk to follow him to get drinks. The latter could not keep his eyes from all of the revealing exposed flesh that the female dancers seemed to be displaying. When the two of them returned with a tray of beer each, he told them.

"Relax and act like everybody else in the Club."

The blonde De Mere needed no second invitation and he leaped up to join the dancers. The Guide groaned in displeasure, but none of the other patrons appeared interested in them, mainly because there were numerous foreigners present. But then a good Spy would show no signs of eaves dropping. After a few beers were downed, a sweating Clerk returned with a gorgeous olive skinned beauty that wore a top that pushed her breasts up in front, so her two female charms were all you noticed. She appeared to be a bubbly confident character, but that could have been the drink or the heady atmosphere of the bar. The Clerk introduced his new companion.

"Her name is Beersheba."

With a forward smile, she enquired in accented Anschluss.

"I am sitting at the back of the Club, would the rest of you like to join me?"

The Clerk released the girl's hands momentarily and whispered to the Persuader.

"She has two more female friends. One of them is called Shoshanna and you should see her."

Her unflinching almond eyes challenged, again she insisted.

"Will you not join us?"

The big man got up instantly. Just as the Guide was about to refuse, Naomh heeding the instructions of the APOCRYPHA'I agreed. Still holding hands with his prize, the Clerk headed back from where he had been. Greta, Cahill and the Engineer stayed put with their concealed weapons close at hand in case of treachery while the rest of them rose from the table and followed. There was a powerful urge drawing Naomh. He became intoxicated with excited nervousness. The expectant man knew that in the next few seconds, his life would change forever and then he saw her. When his eyes locked with hers, something in his soul just clicked. It was as if he had been denied something all his life and he had just found it.

In an instant, he had been completed!

His passions were been mirrored in her eyes, it was a feeling of immediate and intense attraction. Trembling, the mesmerised man moved towards where she sat. He was now totally oblivious to anything else. He did not even notice the other two beauties sitting at her table and if Naomh was truthful, they were way better looking than the object of his attention. But his eyes never left hers as he sat down next to her. The man from the Anschluss had never been so close to such an exotic beauty before. Her skin was as brown as mahogany. She looked to be in extremely good shape and about the same age as himself. A slightly large nose with wide nostrils separated her brown eyes and her head was crowned with short auburn hair. He felt that this woman had been made for him. Speaking perfect accented Anschluss in an exotic tone, she said to Naomh as she stared straight into his eyes.

"You must come with me. Alone, with nobody else. My friends will keep your friends entertained."

The smitten man looked at the Lenses and the Persuader and knew that to be true. But, the Guide whispered to Naomh.

"That would be madness."

Hearing his words, the exotic woman intervened. She pointed to a disc similar to a pair of Frog Eyes and stated.

"My two friends, Beersheba and Shoshanna have a mobile link to me. As I said, they will stay as hostages if you like and he will come with me. You are armed, my friends are not."

The skimpy dressed woman skipped out of the Clerk's clutches and done a twirl.

"You can search me if you like."

Her large breasted friend said directly to the Persuader.

"Me too."

The big man blushed. It was obvious that neither of them carried a weapon. The olive skinned woman who was Naomh's only focus repeated her order for her companions to stay. They nodded in assent and continued flirting with their two delighted guests. The Guide whispered.

"How she know that we are packing and she sounds as if she is used to been obeyed."

The bearer of one piece of the amulet had an overpowering desire to be alone with her. Naomh felt destiny calling him; the voice inside him was drowning out every inclination except to accompany this exotic beauty. As their leader, he over rid the others anxiety.

"I will go with her and nobody is to follow. Agreed."

Reluctantly his companions acceded, it took the Guide longer and he also grudgingly relented. But, not before cautioning him.

"She could be the honey trap. We have used that tactic ourselves."

"No, this is different. Trust me."

"Ok. You might be right; after all we don't leave two hostages behind."

Having settled that, he got up with the beautiful woman and left with her. All of a sudden, he was out in the night air and alone with her. The two unlikely companions walked a short distance to a beachfront property and went into it. Taking her hand in his as if it was the most natural thing in the World, they both entered the lift side by side and ascended to the top floor. Naomh was pleased; she did not pull her hand away. Her touch was familiar; it was as if he had known it all his life. The woman from the Enclave took him into an apartment; its décor was unfamiliar to one born in the Anschluss. She led him to a couch and they sat down together. Face to face, the both of them had a million questions. Just as her guest was about to speak, she put her long thin fingers to his lips and said huskily.

"Tell me your name."

He answered a trembling voice.

"Naomh."

"It sounds like what I expected."

She smiled suddenly and he felt that he would drown in its radiance. Naomh returned the question. His companion looked him straight in the eyes. He stared back at the liquid pools of her orbs and saw himself reflected there. His heart leaped as she said.

"Miriam."

Naomh had vowed frequently that he would never be taken alive, he even once had a suicide pill, but now he found himself a prisoner of her eyes. The one part Mescal/Amulet shared its host's euphoria. Then Miriam said.

"I have something to show you. Wait here, I will return in a minute."

The shapely woman went into another room and a few minutes later, she returned dressed in a flimsy see through robe. Helped by the room's lighting, he could make out the delicious outline of her curved body. He felt himself becoming aroused and trembling for the want of her. The exotic beauty approached him and urged him to stand. As he faced her, Miriam opened her robe and let the gown fall to the floor. Naomh eyes were not drawn to her female charms but to the Alien object dangling between the paler breasts of her exposed body. Another piece of faceted light mirrored his own segment. The orange sparkle between her firm breasts was one more piece of the APOCRYPHA'I. Miriam was about to unclasp the object of his search and hand it to Naomh. With awe in her voice, she said reverently

"I have been safe keeping this for you."

The cautious man refused the gift for the moment, remembering the frantic thrashing of the first melding. But, the other voice intruded.

"It will not happen like that again."

He told her.

"I am not ready for it yet."

Sensing his trepidation, Miriam drew him into her naked embrace, she held him for a few minutes, kissed his cheek and then undressed him. Naomh put up no resistance. She gasped when she saw his red segment.

"I knew it to be true."

"Knew what?"

"When I first saw you that you were the one I have been waiting for."

Skin caressed skin, the red Amulet touched the orange piece, an electric shock percussed through both bodies. His impending lover turned to him and demanded passionately.

"Kiss me."

Naomh, trembling inside raised his hand and cupped her cheek. He was amazed at her softness. His throat tightened as he became intoxicated and light headed by her nearness. His heart was beating too fast. Her closeness felt akin to some powerful narcotic. It was the smell of her unfamiliar perfume, the sparkle from her coppery brown eyes, the colour of her olive skin and most of all, her touch as she tenderly stroked his arm. This simple action sent intense charges of eagerness shuddering through his entire being and he was trembling in anticipation rather than fear. He felt his body heave, as her soft lips sought his. He returned the embrace and accepted the kiss and her soft tongue found his. Naomh tasted the full pout of her lips as his other hand found the curve of her neck. In his eager search, his fingers found her the hardened nipple of her left breast and she moaned in pleasure. He carried her to her bedroom, where they made passionate love. Both took their time as they explored every contour of each other's body. Then, he entered her; it was a moment in time that neither would forget. As soon as Naomh thrust into her womaness, Miriam bit his ear and moaned. She cried out in a passion-induced cry.

"I am coming."

"So am I." Answered her sexual partner, shocked at the suddenness of orgasm.

Human fluids mixed and Alien energies combined. The two lovers climaxed together and in the magical instant, the separate parts of the APOCRYPHA'I joined. The two pieces of the Amulet's had coupled in that precise moment of ejaculation; they were sucked together with the released energy of an unbound rubber band. Miriam had completed her lives vocation. The hurriedness of it had startled both of them. When Naomh looked down; the Amulet had doubled in size and was a duo of pulsating colours, each one flashing in sequence. The now two parts Mescal Amulet was exhilarated; its experience of joining had been just as potent as the Hybrids sexual climax.

"I have more understanding."

Afterwards as the two lovers lay trembling in each other's arms, Miriam told him coyly.

"This was my first time. I have been saving myself for you. I knew that one day; you would come into my life."

He was surprised that she had been virgin and her inexperience went unnoticed. Naomh felt regret that he had not done the same and he lied to her.

"It was my first time as well."

His bed partner pinched him playfully and told him

"I do not believe you."

He had the good grace to blush and she laughed at his embarrassment. Miriam had been stroking his manhood during their conversation and he felt himself becoming aroused again. They made love again and again that night, neither of them tired of the experience. Both woke to the most wondrous dawn they had ever seen. She kissed his fingertips and he was aware that a bond had been created that would never be broken. From then on, the two lovers became inseparable and Naomh knew that the mystery of been in love had come to him finally. The day after their initial sexual tryst, Cahill saw them together holding hands and with insight he exclaimed.

"Oh!"

They had been relieved to find him unharmed. Still, the Clerk and the Persuader were disappointed to be divested of their two beautiful so called prisoners. Naomh showed all of them, the merged pieces of the Amulet and his companions were mesmerised. Then, he expanded the marble sized TORT-CAM and found that new orange tesseral panels matched the amount of red one's equally, the white colours had gone. A few hours after the revelation, an ecstatic Spy contacted Tell back in the Anschluss and briefed him.

"Everything is going to plan."

The new lover's went everywhere together. Naomh realised that he wasn't just captivated with this exotic woman, he was intoxicated. She was at his side constantly over the next few days, she never left him. Miriam explained her companionship.

"All military personnel involved in a forthcoming push have extended leave. So, I am totally yours, my love."

"I like the sound of that."

The man from the Anschluss had no idea what a big push was. But in his lovers company, Naomh never felt so alive. She showed him her World. The Old City in the centre of a district named after a place of legend; Jerusalem was a place of tall spires, onion-shaped cupolas and ancient stone. She took him to see the Holy places, the remains of the first wall built by King Solomon, renewed by King Herod and destroyed by the Romans in 70AD, the Dome of the rock that was built on its ruins between 685-705AD, from where the Prophet Mohammed ascended to heaven and the church were Jesus was buried before he also rose into heaven. Coming from a place that outlawed religious belief, Naomh gave credence to his amazement.

"How come the Enclaves authorities allow three separate faiths to be worshiped inside its boundaries?"

Miriam replied to his disbelief.

"That has always been the way. There are other sects as well. But even all combined they are an insignificant minority."

Holding her hand, left the Church of the Holy Sepulchre feeling subdued. Like the Preacher's sermons, he found that he lacked interest. As he knelt in the aisle and contemplated his beliefs, Naomh found that his heart was not in it. He quickly decided.

"I will not mention these places to the Engineer, because if he reacts the same way as I have, the devout man's whole World would come tumbling down.

The two parts of the Mescal/Amulet felt uncomfortable in the Christian holy places, as this faith unlike the other two had an abundance of images of beings with what could only be described as Preceptor-Bands over their heads. The two lovers then made a bus journey to the south and a place called Masada. This massive edifice of brown rock was situated in an area of flat barren lands and a salty inland Sea that was surrounded by wall of urban districts. Even though there was a cable car to the top, Miriam preferred to climb up the twisting paths of its steep slopes, so the two lovers made their way up the hard packed earthen ruts that had been worn down by countless feet. At the flat base of the forts summit and while Naomh was breathing heavily from unaccustomed exercise, his lover told him.

"This is the place where all defenders of the Enclave proclaim their promise to resist the foes of our people.

On the fourth day after their first tryst, inexplicably Naomh had become depressed; it was the inevitable reaction to the euphoria of gaining the second piece of the APOCRYPHA'I. For a time he suffered from dark moods and could not understand it, because he had never been happier. This upset him even more and then he remembered that his father had killed his mother. Rory's son raged that his life might follow the same dark path as his parent's.

"This will not happen to me. I would lose my own life before I would let anything happen to my love."

Sensing his disquiet, Miriam took him to the beachfront to swim; some of the others were already there and had laid large blankets on its goldenness. To those from the Anschluss, the beach was an unknown concept. Sandy shores were a playground for the elite only. All, except two had never seen the buff yellow sand or heard the soothing lapping waves or indeed the ancient aqueduct of another time that stretched along the seashore towards the lapping waves. Perched on its archaic concrete base was a giant statue that had a massive exposed manhood. Like adolescences, they had giggled at that. One sober voice said.

"I hope the Engineer does not see that thing?"

Miriam looked like a brown Goddess in her green swimming costume; her olive skin so accentuated in the sun dappled golden sand. When Naomh would not venture into the seawater, she ran pass him and jumped in with a loud squeal. The two pieces of the Mescal/Amulet was beginning to process more information and realised.

"The saline water is deadly to me."

It used all its reasoning to persuade its host to stay out of the lethal Sea. Beersheba who had already changed into a tiny two piece black bathing costume was frolicking in the water; her auburn curls glistened with salt water. Miriam urged Naomh to join them.

"It is refreshing my love. Come in."

He was rooted to the spot and declined, shaking his head.

"Oh come on, its only water. It cannot harm you." Urged his lover as she splashed some water towards him. Naomh froze as the arc of advancing water raced towards him. In an, he was no longer rooted to the spot; he was flying through the air and heading to the water. He yelled in panic.

"No!"

The Clerk who was now attired in the drab green military clothes of the Enclave had arrived along with the Persuader and the absolute gorgeous blonde beauty Shoshanna. For a laugh, the big man had pushed the unsuspecting Naomh into the sea. The voice within screamed in unison with its host at its immersion in the acid and was amazed when it discovered.

"My physical essence has not dissolved."

The Alien presence already knew that it could distance itself from its host's biochemistry and now to the growing whisper of the horror, it realised.

377

"Had I done so, I would have indeed dissolved. A resilience in the Hybrids make up merged and saved me."

As its hosts head came above the water and in between his spluttering, he heard the words above the mocking laughter of the others.

"Shit, Naomh, that was some scream. You would swear that you were going to be burnt alive or something."

The accumulating awareness of the Alien amulet quickly calculated.

"I should have estimated that the Hybrid female who was in tenure of my other segment was already familiar with the deadly liquid. That leads to the logical conclusion that she had been immersed in the saline mixture of Hydrogen and oxygen before. My former insanity allows me to live in the Hybrid's physical World, but in the immediate transition from one host to another, vital statistics are going astray and have to be evoked once again. Sometimes the missing information is minor, but this time it was a major incident."

Extremely relieved that the APOCRYPHA'I was unharmed, Naomh joined them in their merriment. Miriam swam over and put her deeply tanned arms around him and gave him a big salty kiss. His smile got bigger, but it was not as broad as the Clerk's when he noticed all the topless women sunbathers and their gorgeous tanned bodies. Shoshanna gave them a coy smile from her generous pout and also removed her top and displayed well-tanned busty breasts, firm hips and a flat stomach, which was pierced by some type of blue jewel. The really good-looking woman was as tall as Greta and with her fair hair; the female from the Enclave looked as if she had come from the Anschluss too. Her eyes were a reflection of her naval ornament. But, her cute dimples made her an entirely different creature from the normally exhibited straight face of Cahill's lover. The Persuader's smile when he saw the half-naked beauty became broader than the Clerk's grin.

"I could really get to like this place." Uttered the big man from the Madrid Contrib as he stripped off. He came flying into the shallow water and landed with a big splash alongside the bathers. The smaller blonde man followed an instant later. Naomh voiced an extension of the Persuader's words and ducked the grinning Clerk back under water when he came to the surface. Then, given the freedom of expression that they had enjoyed since leaving the Anschluss, the fair haired man swore.

"Jesus Christ, Naomh."

The Engineer who had just arrived with the Guide and the Lenses gave the Clerk a black look and censured him.

"Don't take the Lords name in vain."

The former bureaucrat was having too much fun and ignored the broody man's rebuke. Naomh, not caring where the Mute was asked rhetorically of one of the newly arrived swimmers.

"No, Cahill or Greta."

The Clerk winked as he answered.

"They prefer to be alone."

"Oh."

After frolicking in the water for an hour, the bathers came out to dry off and take the Sun. Shoshanna asked the Persuader coyly as she pinched one of his enormous biceps.

"You look the strongest; will you come and help me?"

Smitten, the big man nodded trying to hide his emerging blush. The two of them went to the vehicle that had brought her to the beach and returned with large portable foil freezers. The man from the Madrid Contrib done most of the carrying. When opened, the iceboxes contained much welcomed food and refreshments. Naomh sat eating the green flesh of a pistachio nut and watched the Persuader eat a large slice of yellow melon. The juice dripped down his face and Shoshanna laughed as she took a napkin and wiped the offending mess away. The big man got a ribbing from his friends about the way the glistening juice highlighted his chin own dimple even more. When Shoshanna said.

"I think it is really cute."

His mouth broadened into a large smirk. Like most of his group, the bearer of the uncompleted APOCRYPHA'I had never been as happy. With the uncorrupted Sun in his face, the overpowering smell of coconut oil on tanned bodies and the now familiar smell of the sea, spiced with the exotic foods of the picnic, he was surprised to see that the Engineer looked disturbed and sat away from the others. It was as if he was imitating the Mute. The sombre man frowned on the display of near nudity that was all around him. His brother knew that it was the presence of the half-naked women that caused his discomfort as he was always uneasy around the opposite sex. Greta was probably the only woman who was an exception to this. His big sibling was certain that his brother was also still a virgin. Under the rare influence of alcohol, he remembered him once saying.

"I am to remain celibate, that is the only way I can give a true commitment to God."

The Engineer kept his clothes on; it was a lifetime's habit of hiding his plain wooden crucifix. The devout man had also noticed that all of the Enclave people had a strange triangular medallion called the Magen David displayed proudly around their necks, but this did still not induce him to display his own religious emblem. Naomh went over to the Persuader's brother. The Engineer was the most religiously devout of the companions and Naomh silently believed.

"It is his closeness to the holy places of the Bible that is causing the conflict inside his mind. I was correct against telling him about the spiritual places I have seen. It would tip him over the edge."

Rory's inheritor sat down alongside the brooding man. Forgoing his friends Code-name, he asked him with a concerned look.

"What's the matter Miguel?"

With a strained expression, the Engineer took a deep breath and answered.

"I know that we are in a strange land and nobody here should be our enemy, but Naomh. I am deeply confused. Do not tell Jose, he seems quite taken with them, especially the very good-looking woman. She does not seem intimated by his size. But, these new friends and allies of ours are called Jews. Does the Holy Book not tell us that these people had Jesus crucified. So, how can we trust them? The Preacher said that we should not."

Internally, Naomh's mood darkened.

"Of all the ways for the normal superiority of the Anschluss to manifest itself. I have a problem here. I will have to convince him otherwise or this quest could be in trouble."

The two parts Mescal/Amulet came to its bearer's rescue. It locked onto accumulating memories and explained the solution. Naomh repeated it to the Engineer.

"My friend. Jesus forgives everybody. Did you not learn that from the outlawed Bible? Even while he was dying on the cross, the crucified Son of God even forgave his tormentors."

This appeared to mollify the Engineer and he went away for a stroll along the seashore to consider Naomh's words. Later as they left the beach and were walking back to Miriam's apartment, he took his leader aside and told him.

"Naomh you are correct about Jesus forgiving them. If he did it then so can I. As Jose really likes them, so I will try as well."

Naomh heaved an internal sigh of relief. Then, the Engineer gave Naomh a wry smile.

"Jesus tells us to forgive everybody, but I don't think he included the Anschluss rulers in that. They are beyond redemption."

His companion returned the smile with a loud belly laugh and said.

"That's for sure Miguel, that's for sure."

He was then drawn to another conversation that had been instigated by the Clerk. The curious bureaucrat had noticed that all of their Enclave friends had a non-removable ink design etched into their right shoulders. The blonde man asked them.

"What are they, some sort of controlling mark?"

"No silly. They are called tattoos. They are the symbol of our unit." Informed Shoshanna.

Of course, he then wanted one for all of the RE-INSTATOR'S. In an excited voice, he expressed his desires.

"Wouldn't it be great?"

The Guide put a halt to his plans, when he responded.

"I wanted a tattoo once, but Rory put a stop to it. He told me that we

were supposed to remain inconspicuous and something like that would draw serious attention to you. And, you know what that would mean?"

"Our long haired friend is right. We have to return home when this mission is over, so a tattoo is out of the question." Stressed Naomh.

A sulky Clerk mouthed flippantly, just out of earshot.

"Well I might not be going back."

The Spy laughed silently.

"Tattoo or no Tattoo, we know who you all are, already."

Another mini crisis popped up a few days later that accentuated the differences between the two allies. It occurred when they and their new friends were waiting for an Auto-bus. This was the most common type of public transport in the Enclave. The vehicle glided above a fixed rail in much the same way as the Mag-lev did. As the new friends were waiting at a stop, an Auto-bus arrived; it halted and sank to the ground with an inflated hiss. A group of disabled and handicapped people got off the settled transport contrivance. As these people made their way towards them, those from the Anschluss were horrified and every face showed its revulsion. Most of them actually backed away from the embarking passengers as if they had the plague or something. The Spy had the most appalled expression of the onlookers. This one wanted to turn away in distaste, refusing even to look at the misfortunes. Controlling an outbreak of shuddering, the mole stood fast and faced the horror.

"Are they Mutants?" Whispered the Prof.

"Excuse me!" Asked a hostile Beersheba.

"What kind of creatures are these?" Asked Cahill.

"They are freaks." Added the Engineer.

The Enclave woman was now furious; she struggled with the Anschluss language, but was unable to find coherent words. Eventually in a strained tone, she managed to utter.

"My friends. They are people just like us, they just have inherent disabilities."

The incredibly beautiful Shoshanna whose brother Gilliad was a life-long paraplegic scoffed at the incredulous looks. At that moment, she thought them arrogant and insensitive and not wordy of their companionship. She openly accused them.

"You would swear that none of you saw a disabled person before."

She was cut off by the blank looks on the faces of the Anschluss contingent. The Enclave woman was taken aback.

"You cannot be serious."

There were a lot of sheepish nods from the unacquainted company in answer to her surprised words. Her immediate superior, Miriam interjected.

"What a wonderful place your Homeland must be that your medical science is so advanced."

The rest of her compatriots agreed with her summation. Naomh apologised.

"I am sorry for our reaction, we were ignorant of such things."

The admission of guilt was accepted. Agent XIII could have told the others.

"It is not a wonder of medical science that make the Anschluss population free of disabled people, but a deliberate policy of eradication at the embryonic level."

The flawed Humans had also reminded Tell's infiltrator of their own kinds deformities and no genetically engineered Clone liked that sort of admonition of his or hers weakness.

"The Anschluss was right to remove these individuals from our midst. They are a burden on society." Silently hissed the one who belonged to a group of individuals who eliminated all of those who did not conform to their ideals. The LYUBINITES had not mellowed and this sect's capacity for zero tolerance of those who were different had grown in tandem with their own malformations.

XVI.

Paris, 2094 AD.

To any other patron of the small bistro of this European Capital who had been drawn in by the green menu chalkboard which stated that it allowed smoking; the lone man that sat at the table near the front door quietly sipping his earl grey tea and reading his imported newspaper looked slightly overdressed, even in this inclement weather. The contents of the broadsheet, he seemed to be reading held little appeal, for this individual was intently preoccupied with other matters. The man in the overcoat had scant interest in the wider World and Humanities petty problems. These typical everyday events no longer concerned him. A leading headline in the "London Times." reported that a suicide explosion had killed one hundred and eighty-nine people in the Yemeni City of Aden. A beleaguered American force had been the target. More printed columns told of further outrages across the diverse globe. He casually thought.

"Cod's wallop. There will be more people killed across this Union tonight and their deaths will go largely unreported. People in the west are trying to make out, that they live in the best place in the World. But little do they know of the true wonders out there."

The fact that this person was holding a newspaper and not a video information unit spoke of a man who preferred old-fashioned things and this café was a bastion for such people. This opinion would be enhanced by the rounded spectacles perched over his large broad shaped handle bar moustache, the cigarette holder in his left hand and that he drank out of a real china cup sat on a matching saucer. That would have been a fatal misconception, for this man did not cling to the past out of some perceived fancy; no this was the way he was. If someone thought that this eccentric would be a soft touch and an easy victim, then that too would be a deadly error. Earlier in the small hours of the previous morning, he had been lying on a soft bed with a thick mattress in his rented lodgings. His loaded hands were tucked under a folded pillow on which his head rested. In his ears and nose, two pieces of advanced technology kept him aware of his surroundings. These tools were certainly of a very old craft, but they were far from been outdated and had not been designed by Humans. The listening device implanted in his ears picked up the faint scrape of a boot outside his door. The pheromone device inside his nostrils detected the traces of anxiety and anticipation of those who were about to attack. His door burst open with a resounding crash, smoke canisters bounced menacingly across the floor and four black covered figures bunched tightly together materialised in his floor space. The hands under his fluffed pillow flashed out in a speeding arc and two pieces of steel vectored towards the intruders. Two of them went down instantly, the strange metal projectiles easily penetrating their up to date protective armour. Twitching fingers reacting in reflex fired one of the dead men's weapons. Another intruder died from his comrades guns, his back riddled at close range by a heavy calibre weapon. In the confusion, the man on the bed reached for a weapon that lay by his side under his blankets and a silent burst of light punched the final intruder from his feet. Rising from the bed, he now heard the sounds of many voices. He looked towards the small locker by the bed that he had just vacated and smiled ruefully. The bottle of brandy and Perrier water treat for himself had been smashed into shards by off target bullets.

"That's a dash inconvenient old boy. After all, there are some pleasures you cannot get back in Sanctum."

Taking a small but powerful rocket launcher, the master of his dark trade removed the partition wall of an adjoining room in an explosion of brick and plaster. Grabbing a blanket from his bed, he entered the devastated adjoining room, seeing two elderly bodies sprawled in agony and death. Without an inkling of remorse, their murderer left the room and the scene. Strangely, he made his way to the rooftop of the eight storey lodging house. The pursued man activated a small crystal and it became a floating Platform of Light. He threw the blanket over its glimmer and leapt on it. He glided towards an adjacent building and was soon lost among its roof angles. The deft man made his escape from there.

"I am lucky old man that they never brought a helicopter. I have been sloppy; the security forces must have traced my movements and found me here. I will have to be more diligent. My master does not accept failure."

The day before, he had assassinated another on the command of his God. This was over a matter that concerned the security of the hidden city, Sanctum. The man he had killed had been first, a former French legionnaire and then a soldier of fortune. Jurgen Klaus had been among a desperate bunch of mercenaries that had witnessed the location of the secret Priory during a rare malfunction of its protective shield. The other thirty-nine of his party never got out of the desert alive; they were systemically picked off by pursuing Knights. Klaus had been contaminated by the reactivating shield. That is how the assassin traced him. Five months later and back in France, the former soldier of fortune had no intention of ever going back to that part of the World. He had been incarcerated in a police cell in a small precinct over a drunken brawl. The argument began when a former soldier of Polish nationally did not believe the German's crazy story about the amazing place in the middle of the North African Sahara and rudely suggested.

"You have been smoking too much of the local wacky tobacco, my friend to come up with such a tale."

Things quietened down, but they flared up again when the drunken eastern European interrupted after Klaus started his incredible story once again.

"And people say you German's have no sense of humour. Well your great, great grandparents must have had, they invaded Stalingrad after all."

"Well, they made a right mess of your place on their way there." Countered the German.

He raised his glass and shouted.

"Prost. I think you are the funny one, Polskai."

The outraged Pole threw the first punch and an all-out brawl ended up thrashing the place. Both of them were locked up for the night and would be released in the morning. The local magistrate was getting sick of the German's brawling and menacingly informed him.

"You will go to prison for a year the next time."

While the two battered men were recovering in the promised cell, the assassin had stole in. He silently killed the five Gendarmes on duty and left himself into the cellblock. His target was behind bars with ten others; fellow brawlers and some petty criminals. The blearily eyed mercenary stared at him in horror; he had recognised the disguised moustache. The former soldier sprouted beads of panicked perspiration and then shouted out in alarm.

"Nein!"

The figure who stood at the other side of the bars took out a strange device, gave an evil grin beneath his large moustache and threw it between the gaps in the bars. The cellmates that were former soldiers recognised the explosive device for what it was; there was a mad scramble to chuck it out. The contraption suddenly expanded and grew in size, becoming too big for the bar spaces. Aghast prisoners stared at the thing in absolute horror and tried to smash it. But the device was indestructible. Their soon to be murderer departed the building to the sound of frantic wailing.

"Chin up my good fellows, that is no way for you to behave."

As the confident assassin swaggered away from the building, his handy work exploded. Imploded body pieces splattered against the wall, the confined vacuum bomb had done its grisly work. It destroyed flesh but left the surrounding metal and concrete relatively untouched. The German would no longer be a problem to the Winged One, everybody else had just been collateral damage. That and the previous morning's events had been stored in his memory. He had another task given to him by the one he owed his allegiance to. Outside the warm interior of the little café in the steady drizzle, a busy multitude of people of different colours and creeds passed by its foggy window. Faces from all over the Planet had made this cosmopolitan city of twenty million their home. Away from the footpaths, the wide streets and boulevards allowed a steady flow of motorised traffic. This would all vanish in the next two hundred years as the expanding European Union was hijacked by the emerging LYUBINITES and lost its liberal outlook. In every city, town and hamlet, their majestic Cathedrals and Churches, their grandiose Mosques and discreet Synagogues would in the future be demolished across the Continent as the believers in an Alien destiny removed all traces of God. It would become a land without spires or domes that professed no faith. The cosy bistro looked out over the majestic Eiffel tower that was under a grey and blue wash of a sky that was gradually turning black. On the inside of the café, a number of what could only be tourists were constantly gazing at the imposing metal structure from their window seats. But unfortunately for them, the dank autumn light and the low hanging clouds that started to blanket the city on this overcast day, also began to obscure its pinnacle. Still, brown and yellow leaves that seemed to be chasing each other in the swirling eddies appeared to hold the visitors interest. The fabricated steel tower had been the model of man's innovation when it had been erected and unveiled to the Parisian public. But the sitting man reading the newspaper had been unfazed by the boast of its creators, who insisted that the structure would last forever. Because this was no ordinary individual who sat here enjoying his hot beverage. The shadow of the tower cause him to muse.

"I was here in this city in another life when the long dead citizens of this place were actually building the foundations of that steel tower. I have also witnessed the birth of the motor car, mechanical flight, television, manned space flight, computers and mobile phones. However all of these inventions of man pale in comparison to the wonder of my master and his gifts.

This unassuming overdressed man was none other than the outlandish and flamboyant Captain Horatio Wesley himself. The former companion of Pamerstown and Clyde had accepted the fact that he had outlived all of the people of his time, but that belief had not always been the case. Around twenty-five years after the killing of the Explorer, the sceptical turncoat decided to call on a friend of his while on a mission in South Africa. His old oxford school chum was a high-ranking officer in the Boer campaign. He caught up with the main British column and was directed towards his friend Winthrope. Taking cover behind his horse, he watched the man go by. Wesley was shocked; the man was old and grey and looked in his mid-fifties. He pulled aside a young solider in his early teens, the baby-faced slip of a lad was carrying a handful of red flags and demanded.

"How old do I look boy?"

"Pardon sir." Said the puzzled range finder.

"I said, how old am I?"

Because Wesley was dressed in the uniform of his old rank, the lad stammered.

"About twenty five sir."

"Good answer; now go about your business and keep a stiff upper lip, that's a good chap."

The child soldier was greatly relieved to be released by the mad officer with the large moustache. As he scampered away, he saw a huge smile appear on the crazy man's face. Wesley was going to approach Winthrope and pretend to be his own son, but he decided against it.

"He might get wind of who I really am and then I will have to kill him."

The not fully converted disciple of an Alien God had no desire for that. Still, the former British solider had conformation of his longevity in the face of his old pal. He completed his mission and returned to the hidden city and began to believe.

"Now once again, I have another man to kill, a man who is the inheritor of something precious that had been stolen from the Winged One centuries before."

His God monitored him from crystal arrays and was intermittently linked with him by the mind-voice. Wesley had not been born in Sanctum, so the mind-contact over large distances was haphazard at best. His trademark-winged moustache of the Knights of the Winged One had been twisted back into an ordinary handlebar hair extrusion. It was a style not uncommon in the latter years of the twenty-first century where the ordinary individual took steps to stand out from the masses. His target was sitting directly opposite him and engaged in a heated debate with another man. Surprisingly, the former solider was more intrigued by this bloke, something about him nagged at another sense. Wesley's intended victim appeared to be a man of Slavic origin. He was none other than the father of the LYUBINITES; Doctor Gregory Lyubin. The sixty-five year old doctor was dressed in a buttoned down shirt, covered by a three-large buttoned tweed suit that had high angled pockets. His black cotton trousers ended with the finest Italian loafers; the vain man always dressed in the most expensive gear. The entire ensemble was topped off by a shaven head. The watcher admired his taste, once he would have revelled in such attire. The man in debate with Lyubin had already been alerted by Wesley's actions, his dress sense was atrocious. He was wearing the one-piece plastic jump suit that was currently in fashion for the masses, a cheap one at that. For the observant man had spotted slight nuances in Wesley's behaviour and dress that spoke of a man out of his time. The other man at the table was Rory, Naomh's father. The Knight of the Winged One had become irritated.

"My listening device that is normally one hundred per cent reliable is failing to broadcast their conversation to its imbedded receiver. Still, I have perfected another skill, lip reading."

The conversation on which he was eavesdropping was in standard English, this suited Wesley fine. The other man was a complete Anglophile and preached to his listener.

"This will be the language of the new order."

In a lilting Irish brogue, the man spoke to the clean-shaven and bald headed Russian with an air of finality.

"No, Doctor Lyubin. I disagree. We are on different paths. There is no way to eternal life."

Something in the doctor's demeanour changed, he studied Rory intently as if he was taking his measure. Then Lyubin inhaled a calming breath and began to lie slightly.

"I know what you are. I can't explain it, but I have been drawn to you. I have the technology; I located it on an expedition years ago. Together we can save the dream. I have gathered nine of my ten apostles. I want you to be the final one and the most favoured."

But Rory declared.

"Doctor I haven't a clue what you are on about. I am just a simple traveller. I am not interested in joining your cult."

The Russian stormed at the others definition of his cause.

"It is not a cult; it is the future of mankind."

Rory gave him a sceptical look that said.

"Save it for your usual dupes."

"There is a reason why I asked you to meet in this place. Look around you. What does this Café tell you? These people are afraid to change. That is why, they seek comfort here. You and me, we are not like them. Or the rest of mankind, they indulge themselves in the belief of God, which is been manifested in more extremity and prejudice. Well I tell you, our true creators will make themselves known long before any mythical being will reveal himself. Between the question of the existence of a supreme and my belief, I know which one will be answered first."

His guest's private opinion was.

"This sixty-five year old doctor is known to be eccentric because of his vast wealth, not mad as any man without riches would be considered to the rest of his peers."

The Russian's hugely influential father Alexander had started the trend, but he had disappeared mysteriously forty-nine years ago in the Far East. Rory would have been astounded if he was aware that Lyubin's parent used to put a green jewel around his neck while he was nothing more than a bottle sucking infant. The child was lost in its mesmerizing emerald light. His inheritor and son, Gregory had achieved enormous wealth with his cult that drew the rich and famous to him. Sadly he never attained the artefact that had vanished with his parent. He was able to stem the flow of age, to a certain degree and it was among these vain people that he found a following. Rory recalled a snippet of history.

"There was another who done just that. He rise was astounding and he had become the richest and most influential man on the Planet. But, he vanished suddenly and his technological Empire died with him. This was when I was still in nappies. Has the Doctor found the remnants of that? Or a trace of what I have maybe?"

The droll Doctor promised his followers eternal life. The dreamer gave these decadent people a fulfilment that the mainstream religions denied them. He had come alone to this meeting without any of his followers, for if it worked out the way he envisaged, the visionary would abandon them and form the true path. Lyubin had a list of his new apostles in his miniaturised laptop and the man with a master plan switched the computer on and brought up the names. He turned the screen to face Rory and he was certain the man opposite him would be impressed. Naomh's father scanned the list.

First name	Surname	Country
Rory	Lynch	Ireland
Elisabeth	Young	United States
Seigi	Ulrich	Denmark
Sandy	Bliehn	South Africa
Pawel	Ivan	Poland
Pablo	Nani	Portugal
Mary	Irvine	Canada
Ivan	Tell	Switzerland
Han's	Ernst	Austria
Serge	Sabatt	France

Rory recognised most of the names; each person on the list were all pre-eminent in their chosen fields. He also saw his own name at the head of the document. Been a quick study, he also noticed that the first letters of all of the surnames spelt out, LYUBINITES.

"What is that about? Has he put himself on a pedestal? If so then that would be typical of him."

The reader of the handpicked list also noticed that all of those on it were all Caucasian.

"Is the Doctor a racist?"

But Rory Lynch incurred Lyubin's wrath as he said.

"That's a lot of interesting names. I can see your reasons for choosing them, but why me? I am not in their league."

"You more than anyone are well aware of your own talents."

"Again, I tell you, I am nothing more than a simple traveller."

"Enough of your false tales. They might work with more gullible people, not me. Listen! I will tell you what has been revealed to me."

Lyubin told him with all sincerity

"Only me and my ten disciples are to be saved by the Alien race that have put mankind here in the first place. One day in the not too distant future, our Creators will return and take away the chosen few and our descendants."

"Doctor. I think you are entering the realms of absurdity."

"If I am then how come you are a lot older than you look?"

Rory became flippant.

"Plenty of moisture, shying away from the Sun, exercise and healthy

living."

Across the Café, Wesley's features twitched slightly as the once soldier in the servitude of Queen Victoria wondered.

"Have these two discovered the Master's existence. Is this why they are to be eliminated?"

The assassin now had no doubt.

"I must eliminate the other man as well."

Lyubin began ranting about Winged Aliens, not Angels, (Wesley had nearly lost his cool demeanour and upset his tea saucer at that.) cloning, hairless Humans (What was that about?) and how the true path would free them from the confines of this Planet. Most people hearing him would shake their heads and call him a crackpot, but to the listening servant of the true God.

"The bit about Winged Aliens is close enough to the truth for him to be a threat to his master. Yes. They will both have to die, old bean."

The killer had made his decision as he stroked his prominent hair growth. He also had a couple of vials to take the blood of his victims; this had to be brought back to the winged being. This taking of blood had been a common part of his missions, except on the first occasion with Clyde. (Zebulan did not infuse the blood of the insane, maybe he should have. He might have achieved his desire to kill, if he had.) The ancient Englishman was about to make good on his promise to put an end to the two conversationalists when the café door opened and several heavily armed Gendarmerie entered the little establishment. It was a favourite of theirs during breaks for lunch. Wesley silently cursed at the heavily armed policemen and women's entrance. Just then, Lyubin rose from his chair, his Slavic face flushed in anger and the irate man stormed out into the very unpleasant day. He turned towards the man who he had been sitting with and lashed out verbally.

"You will regret this."

Wesley had his first target chosen for him; he got up and followed the Russian out of the cafe. Rory, equally annoyed, closed his eyes for a brief second in a futile attempt to regain his temper and missed the exit of Wesley. The man who had been watching them had left his cigarette still smouldering in an ashtray. The Irishman swore, reached into his pocket and left more than enough money to pay the bill and he too hurried out the door. Once outside in the blustery day, he scanned the streets to see which direction the unrelated men had taken. A piercing scream sounded above the steady hum of passing traffic. He ran towards it. Rory was too late; the body of Doctor Lyubin lay sprawled in the pavement with a large winged handled stiletto protruding from his back. A pool of the Russians blood had spread to the concrete path and was joining the surface water flowing into a drain. There was no sign of the assassin and he was sure it was the oddly dressed man who had been reading the newspaper back in the cafe. This was Rory's first encounter with the Winged Knights and it was nearly his last. As he knelt down alongside the doctor's cadaver, the café he had just left erupted in a flash of light and then a ball of flame bellowed out onto the Parisian street. The explosion had been completely silent. Bodies smashed through a gaping hole where the café's facade had been seconds before and lay smouldering and blackened in the street. Bits of blue uniforms with bloody, grisly and meaty contents mixed with the fragments of video cameras from outside the destroyed premises and littered the smouldering street. As the smoke of debris settled, a stunned crowd gathered, some bloodied and battered from the debris of flying glass and mortar. People with make shift bandages from clothes and whatever came to hand assisted each other. Nobody staggered out of the ruined premises; there had been no survivors in there. Rory appeared to be one of these quick thinking people who began helping the walking wounded. As he assisted a good looking woman with blood flowing freely down her face and over her pouty lips, the helper nearly missed the faint trace of heat across his back. The slight tingle was enough of a warning. Rory suddenly twisted as three bullets smashed into the woman's body. There must have been another burst as more people around him dropped. Bystanders panicked and were scattering in every direction. Spurred into action, the target ran amongst the fleeing throng. Weaving between them and at the edges of his peripheral vision, he could see people dropping around him as spurts of blood erupted from their bodies. The running man made it around a corner and took a breath as he was no longer in the snipers sights. The approach of wailing sirens made him hurry up the street and melt into another crowd, who were totally oblivious to the carnage on the other street. He now felt daggers of pain and felt blood flowing freely inside his clothing. Rory put his hand under the plastic jump suit and his fingers came away covered in blood. The wounded man cursed.

"Shit. I've been hit bad. It must have been when I was helping that unfortunate woman. I better go back to my room and regenerate. I will not be able to give chase to the gunman."

Blood issued forth from his fluid filled mouth. Rory's unique healing powers were working at full power. The wounds he had taken would be fatal for anybody else. But as soon as the first bullet penetrated his flesh, his inherent healing abilities had kicked into overdrive. He rounded another corner by a white plastered building and leant against it for a brief respite. Leaving a bloodied handprint on the wall, the injured man found steps running down towards the Seine. Joining a bunch of tourists, he made his way down the stone stairs; his safe house was at the other side of the river that split Paris in two. The injured man looked behind and there was no sign of pursuit. He crossed the Alexander III bridge with its four pillars that were proudly topped off with golden statues of what looked like Pegasus and their mythical handlers to him. Hurriedly passing its array of highly decorated lamplights with the dappling blurs of gold from the river crossing's ornaments in his peripheral vision, he made it without incident to the other bank. There, the wounded man passed the Grande Palais, went down to the place de la Concorde and disappeared into the branch of merging streets. Back in his lodgings and stripped to the waist, Naomh's father did not look like a Human being. Muscles and sections of body had become grub shaped as Rory pondered the morning's events. The healing man had now no doubt.

"The heavily dressed loner sitting near the door was the culprit and had committed mass murder to get me or the dead Doctor. Was I the target or was it because I was sitting with Lyubin? Well if it was me, the assassin will have another try. All I can do is wait for him to make his move. And this time, I will be ready."

However, he was severely troubled by the efficiency of the assassin.

"Between the silent bombs, the knife murder and all the innocent people this guy has killed, this man must have some very powerful backers? Who the hell am I up against?"

It took the Rory/thing a couple of hours to regenerate. Shattered bones re-knitted, blood vessels regenerated and gaping holes sealed. When the patient was satisfied that he was healed, the uninjured man decided.

"I have to go back to the scene of the massacre and with special equipment and see what clues I can pick up about this mysterious killer."

This time, he wore a protective jacket that would stop most type of bullets and packed two automatic pistols of Israeli manufacture. Naomh's father had been foolish that morning, thinking that he was only meeting Lyubin and precautions were unnecessary. That lapse in judgement had nearly proved fatal. As Rory walked down the steps of his apartment block, his gaze locked into the look of disbelief on the features of a guy loitering across the road. The astonished man was the assumed killer of Lyubin and all of those people. On the other side of the street, Wesley could not believe it. Supremely confident in his own marksmanship, he uttered.

"This is a dashed inconvenience. That chap had been hit at least four times. He should be dead, old boy and now he his casually walking down those steps as if he hasn't a care in the World. It's as if he was going for a stroll. Something is not totting up."

While he was trying to recover his blade in the guise of helping the dead Doctor, he had found the other targets blood on the street. This confused him; this meant that his quarry had been hit and not wearing bullet proof protection and with a device of his Master's; he had tracked him here. However, his blade had remained trapped in the doctor's back. The body protection that he had been wearing failed in its purpose, but it did snag the Alien crafted knife and he had to leave it behind. The Knight of the Winged One had expected at any moment to come across the corpse of his second target even though the readings from the hand held device was telling him that his targets blood loss was diminishing. Determination gripped the hit man of the true God.

"I am not going to fail the Winged One or myself a second time. I will finish the job this time."

He reached for his concealed weapon that had been reloaded since the murder on the street.

"Well you had better do it now, old boy."

The two hundred and fourteen year-old man drew out his silent heavy calibre machine pistol. But Rory was a split second faster and two fully muffled magazines metal contents arced towards Wesley. With lightening reflexes, the Knight threw himself to the side. But the shooter had anticipated this and had fired slightly to the left of his target. A dozen projectiles hit the Englishman; at least six were mortal wounds. As the lifeblood oozed out of him, the long-lived man's final thoughts were.

"Strange I would have always thought that I would have copped it in some God forsaken arsehole of nowhere, not in the Frenchie capital. Well, you never achieved eternal life, old boy. But still you had a rather good innings old chap. It's a dammed pity though, I did not live longer. The World is getting very interesting, as they say."

Eyes that had first seen light during the advance of Empire over two centuries before, finally shut forever. If he had been allowed one final utterance in his wry humour, he would have said.

"It's a dammed shame that I did not get to finish that half bottle of brandy, old man."

The assassin's killer rushed over to the body and quickly scanned it with his own advanced technology, so he could study the images of his new enemy later. The mortally wounded man's apparent handlebar moustache had unfolded into a bizarre winged shape. Rory also took out a swab and took a blood sample from the dead man. For his killer had no doubt.

"There are more of them loose in the city. I have to get to the other apartment on the other side of the river as I can no longer stay in this one."

It was rented under an assumed name and his tracks had been covered. Rory walked to the nearest Metro station and made his way underground across the city. Television screens on the carriages showed graphic images of the slaughter that the mystery assassin had caused. His over working mind wondered.

"It is strange that there is no mention of the winged handled knife in the Doctor's body."

Between the Café and the street, there had been fifty-two dead and over thirty wounded. The Authorities were at a loss to explain it. Of course the usual suspects were claiming responsibility, especially since a number of Gendarmerie had been killed. Safely in his new apartment, Rory hooked his scanning device to a television unit. As the inquisitive man delved and X-rayed the lifeless three dimensional silhouette, he identified the advanced technology on the corpse. A niggling worry assailed him.

"There are other precocious player's out there in the big yonder"

He decreased the strength of the image to reveal the murder's naked body. The scan revealed a tattoo of an Angel on his heart and what looked like an ordinary handlebar moustache could in fact be untwisted into what definitely resembled wings.

"What's all this about wings? First Lyubin and now the assassin. Had the crazy doctor been on to something?"

Rory had taken a blood sample from the strange cadaver and now he analysed it. The results were astounding, the dead man had been at least two hundred years old, but had not looked a day over thirty. He was now convinced.

"There are certainly other players out there and they are engaged in a similar game to me."

The man that would be Naomh's parent searched for clues fruitlessly over the next century, but his search for his ruthless enemy reached a dead end. As the weird organisation never made another attempt on his long life, Rory assumed that they were another sect that had eventually faded away into the pages of history. In the Parisian flat, he stuck to his credo.

"If they don't bother me again, then I will not bother them. I am certain now that I was only a target because I listened to the dead Doctor."

Besides, the man who was far older than he looked had more pressing problems; as at this time, the LYUBINITES were making their first inroads into power. It seemed that he had been correct to ignore the mystery cult, but Rory could not have been so wrong, because Zebulan through his mind-contact with his servant had indeed identified the Amulet bearer, a circumstance that he had been unaware of up to now. The disturbed Alien had recognised.

"The Hybrid that originates from the island of the Watcher's base has a greater trace of the weaklings craft around him."

Its attraction was so great that it drew the DEFILED to it like a moth to a flame. Zebulan had ordered his vassal through the haphazard mind-voice.

"Forget the Doctor. Eliminate the other. In the process, see if he bears something unusual."

But, the supremely confident Wesley replied.

"I will deliver both of them to you master."

"My servant was too hasty and now the stupid Hybrid is dead. However, I have been proven correct. The other one is more dangerous than the Doctor and he has escaped."

Still, the few glimpses of Wesley's killer had given the false God some inkling of the plan of the ALASTHA'I. He was now assured.

"There are other components of the weakling's technology out there. I

must gather them."

At this juncture, the last remaining deviant lacked the knowledge and craft to locate a single piece. So Rory and the other carriers remained unfound and unmolested. Over the next few centuries, the gifted Alien began to work on a device that would alert him in the future, if any of his vassals came within reach of this mysterious technology. Still, by an opportune accident, Zebulan concluded.

"I now realise why the Master ordered me to remain behind. The trace of their craft is faint, but I have to be patient and prevent the assembly of what was created under the mounds."

Tunis, 858 years later.

It was extremely warm in the city this night. Most of its poorer inhabitants had deserted their various sleeping quarters in their stuffy, non-air-conditioned and unbearable bedrooms for the slightly cooler rooftops. Close to the urban centre, a dog howled a challenge to the annoyance of the outside sleepers and a chorus of its fellows instantly joined it. The four legged canines were still the ever-present companions of man. No true Human was privy to the meaning of those primeval howls. A warrior Knight who himself was not fully Human heard the bestial yowls and understood their meanings.

"Some are boasting of been the fittest male in the locality. The answering howls of the other males are disputing this and offering challenges to the upstarts. As it should be?"

This shadowy figure lay concealed in the dark recess between two unlit and crumbling ancient buildings that were located in the seedier quarter of the decaying North African Mediterranean port. The secluded assailant was silent and deadly patient waiting for his target to pass by. He was as unmoving as the concrete that concealed him. If any of the scattered RE-INSTATOR'S believed themselves expert trailers and assassins, they were incorrect as they paled in comparison to this master of the craft. Achmed could match the sound and step of his target and in the unlikely event that anyone saw him during his chase, his presence would be an acoustic shadow. He was close to the uncomfortable sound of the lapping Mediterranean, from where in the dimness he could discern with his extraordinary vision the grey monstrosity of the Anschlusss wall across the narrow sea. His feral yellow eyes easily made out the manmade obstruction that towered at the edges of the horizon.

"Looking at it, one might have crossed the barriers of time back to the middle ages, to a walled city that then and now had its bleak ramparts patrolled by vigilant soldiers. Except the ancients did not have the surveillance devices of those behind that concrete barrier. Maybe, they might have had old-fashioned versions of the wind powered generators

that are spaced every hundred metres apart, but on a much smaller scale.
Such a primitive power source compared to the technology of my God."

The man totally devoted to his God silently cursed the atheists of the Anschluss. Something drew him to follow the movement of a huge ship that sailed along the line of his vision, between the wall and the Golfe de Tunis. With his astonishing vision, the Knight made out the name of the sea going vessel; it was called the ANS GREGORY LYUBIN. With a sterile certainty; his yellow gaze locked onto the blue eyes of a standing figure.

"That one poses a threat to me and my Master. Somehow, he is briefly aware of me."

This puzzling discovery caused him to stroke his winged moustache. Unlike Wesley's hair extension, this was now an integral part of his constitution, much like a cats whiskers. The huge sea going vessel moved away like some kind of black/silver cloud, promising to deliver some portent of doom to those who waited at its final destination. There was an animal intelligence that lurked behind his hard cruel semi Human eyes. His finely tuned muscles quivered in anticipation as he knew with absolute certainty.

"Go now, but our paths will cross one day. And for you, it will be your last."

The glimpse at the sea going vessel had distracted him little; the assassin was still intently focused on the clandestine task at hand. It mattered not; that he had spent ten sweat soaked hours statue still, waiting for his opportunity to dispatch his master's enemy. Like his feline cousins, Achmed preferred to stalk his prey in the cool of the night and like them, he was possessed of a large heart, wider lungs and broad nostrils. These physical adaptations that enabled him to strike with blinding speed and strength were a gift from his divine Lord. When it came to the master's desire, his patience was boundless. He had taken the name of Achmed while out doing his master's service, a common enough address among the infidels. His proper title was only used in the Holy City of his God and by other Knights of his order. This servant's patience in the duty of his Deity was endless. Hours before and well into his vigil, a large black rat had approached him and paid with its meagre life for the negligible intrusion. A blade imbedded in the toe of his boot flicked out like a coiled spring and ended the unsuspecting rodent's foraging existence. Now its decaying carcass was been fought over by an army of filthy blood red cockroaches who had emerged from every niche and cranny in the walls of the narrow alley. The smell of death had drawn them. If the tiny scavengers were quick enough, he would leave them some larger prey tonight. During his vigil, many infidels had passed by; all of them were totally oblivious to the assassin hidden in the dark shadows. One fortunate individual even came into the narrow alley to relieve himself and he was so close that Achmed could have reached out and grabbed him, yet the man was totally unaware that he was sharing the alley with another. For this hidden shade was a master of stealth and murder, a product of thousands of years of meddling by his adored Deity. His divine briefing had been.

"The man to be eliminated in Tunis is a General and a leading politician of that poor Nation. Soon your target will cast the deciding vote that will make his country a vassal of the Anschluss and I do not want that union to pass."

The Winged One despised the larger power block. His devout and unworthy servant surmised.

"It is for reasons that my Creator is only privy to. I am sure it is because of their Godless society. "

The General was out celebrating with his well-trained bodyguards in anticipation of the next day's vote. This night, the politician continually boasted to those he met.

"Tomorrow will mark more prosperous times ahead and it is all because of me."

At last, Achmed's heightened senses detected the footfalls of his approaching mark. The man was not alone, the sound of raucous merriment testifying to this. The perfectionist was a little disappointed at the unprofessionalism of the guards. He voiced to himself.

"I would have preferred a better challenge. After all, I have made the effort in getting here. "This is not even a test. "

The assassin stepped out from his hideout and walked towards his prey. He was supremely confident in his honed abilities. All that the seven men coming towards him saw was a petite figure donned in a female's Burka. To their credit, the bodyguards within approaching group became instantly alert as it was unheard of an unaccompanied woman to be out alone at this time of the night, especially in this part of the World. Although, the one that they protected could not discern the perceived female's eyes behind the head covering, the macho man was certain that her attention was focused solely on him. Always a vain soul, the drink fuelled excitement that flowed through his body never allowed him to cast a doubt that she had been waiting for him.

"This concealed beauty desires me and the position that I represent. Only me, no one else."

As the leader of this country's armed forces, General Mustafa Affifi ordered his six bodyguards.

"Stand down, relax. After all, it is only an insignificant woman. "

"She still could have a bomb strapped to her, General." Replied a voice of concern.

"It must be really small then. "

Fingers relaxed on hidden triggers and relieved laughter broke the tension. But the genuine mirth became confused when the female did a strange thing. Achmed began his minuet. He raised his arms slowly and mesmerising; mimicking the fluttering wings of his master. The stopped group of revellers appeared bewildered. The confused general enquired.

"Is this another exotic delight to be sampled from the erotic fare, this quarter is well known for?"

Then, the mysterious dancer became a whirling dervish. Too late, all of the General's protectors went for their weapons. Flashes of speeding metal found all their targets and the seven bodyguards were dispatched in efficient murder. Men who were dead before they had time to be astonished crumpled to the hard ground, useless weapons clattering harmlessly alongside their now dead corpses. Affifi's eyes widened in shock, so much that it took him a minute to think of escape. He turned and fled and as his bulky figure put space between himself and the tiny terror. The devout killer took out his Anlace and it flew through the air in a sweeping curve. Gasping and wheezing from unfamiliar exercise, the unfit runner suddenly felt a wicked blow to the back of his legs. His knees buckled and in the next moment, he was lying on the ground staring at the night sky, wondering vaguely.

"Have I consumed too much alcohol?"

A beautiful flawless face with the ultimate cruel eyes cut off his view of the starry sky. It was the last thing the General saw as the moustached assassin expertly garrotted him. His slayer smiled in satisfaction at a job well done.

"Another who interfered in the Master's affairs has been dispatched."

He touched a hidden button under the embedded daggers hilt and two broad wings emerged from its razor sharp sides. When they were fully unfolded, a vial shaped space in the handle began to fill with blood. The servant of his God adept as any nurse filled the syringe for his Master with his victim's life force. When the infusion was completed, the wings folded back into the sides, he removed the vial and replaced it with an empty one.

"A gift for the living God. He will take the blood of the sinful, infuse the immoral taint and remove it from the existence of mankind. In essence, he is taking away the sins of the World."

Somewhere, lost in the distant past, Zebulan had made the transition from a divine messenger to God himself. The ritual of the Christian Templar's receiving the body and blood of Christ had been changed to the Deity accepting the blood of Mankind. Achmed's feeling of bliss at having served the living God so well was interrupted. A sudden intense emotion swept the feeling of satisfaction aside. One of euphoria set in; the diminutive Knight's Deity was bonding with him.

"The Winged One calls!"

He was receiving a direct communication from his Creator, who lay thousands of kilometres to the south. It came through no man made device. The contact issued from his Master's mind directly into his own unworthy conscience. The mind-voice instructed.

"Hurry back to the city, my servant. You are needed here."

With little regard for the sprawled bodies, the commanded killer moved swiftly and crouched by the wall of a nearby building. Finding easy purchase among its broken concrete, Achmed used these handholds to climb effortlessly to the roof of the building. Once on the rooftop, the Hybrid used his incredible agility, he landed on top of an adjacent two-storey building with a single bound. The climber noticed.

"The cities dogs have exhausted themselves with their prancing and barking. Silence is not ideal. I must rectify that."

In a high pitch screech, unheard by Humans, he left out a feline challenge and the ever-alert canines of Tunis went berserk. The howling racket covered any trace of his passing and any dozing denizen of that city only felt a shadow of his passing as he leapt to another building. Repeating this manoeuvre, Achmed silently crossed the rooftops until he reached the cities edge. He located his motorised vehicle and sped with haste to his master's lair. Zebulan had forbidden his vassals the use of his technology ever since Wesley's encounter with Rory. He had no idea, if the remaining ALASTHA'I could use transport staples like the Platforms of Light to trace him and he had no wish for Cathbad to discover him. His servant sped southwards towards the vast emptiness of the Libyan Desert, crossed the unforgiving sandy wastes and made his way back to the Hidden City to once again do his masters bidding. It took him three days of motorised travel to reach the edges of the desert fringe. He drove off the paved roads and stuck to rough tracks. The assassin was not travelling aimlessly; he knew his precise route. He followed a twisting meandering line of desert scrub, the water supporting the greenery was nowhere to be seen, but Achmed was aware that it was just below the ground. On these crude and often non-existent routes, it took him another nine days to reach familiar landmarks, which meant that his destination was close by. His secluded home lay far out in the middle of the Kavir. Surrounded on all sides by an inhospitable desert, it thrived in what the local Nomads called.

"The Empty Quarter."

After travelling non-stop without rest or nourishment, his four-wheeled vehicle brought him to the familiar rocky protrusions that erupted from the desert floor. These effects of nature were remnants from a time when the land was below the sea. The stony outcrops of fantastic shapes had been first sculpted by the tides and then when the land shifted by wind and rain and aeons of this erosion had resulted in their unusual and forbidding shape. Joy filled Achmed's heart at been so close to home and most importantly, he was near his beloved Master. Once, the hastily traveller was back in the citadel, he would discard the name that was used among the heathen. In these hallowed halls, he was Styarz, the Grandmaster and a Knight of the Winged One. This returnee was a direct descendant of

Wesley and something else. Even though he lived to serve the Master, the servant of God was always loathe to leave his home. As the Knight neared the hills and drove along a stony bed of a dried up river that lay waiting for the life giving rains that would make it whole again, he spied the citadel. He often dwelt on the comparison of the patient wait of the river and the Knight's relationship with their Master.

"We are fleeting like the rains, we come and go. The Winged One is forever."

The ruin that stood perched above had the look of the bleached bones of some long deceased sea creature. One that had dissolved into the mountain top creating a visual masterpiece with the contrast of the vibrant hues of the other peaks in the background. The bleak stark appearance of the ruined fortress belied the comfort of the haven in the valleys under its shadow. Their Life-giver dwelt under this paradise, deep in the bowls of the mountain away from the harsh sunlight. He abandoned his vehicle in a concealed cave, where it was looked after by a team of mechanics, for the next time he required it to do the Master's bidding. The returning wander started the long climb to the top and would arrive outside the fortress not even winded. Styarz harboured no doubts.

"I have been watched by my brothers, the moment I came within sight of the cluster of mountains."

He entered the gate guarded by the two winged statues and after a short climb, he approached the sulphurous haze of deception. Once past, he began the stairway to heaven. Styarz reached the first plateau where a piece of paradise lay in tranquil harmony with its accompanying surroundings, defying the harshness of the desert. He was gripped with ataraxia. Globules of dew glistened on the fruit of trees that showed no sign of decay. This was one of the miracles of his Lord. He was in the gardens of the God and uttered the benediction.

"Eden itself and its name is Sanctum."

This was the Master's gift to his chosen. Long lines of orchards, vegetable crops and vineyards lay side by side. The heady smell of their blossoms filled the plateau. As the returnee passed, he absently counted the flowers of the fruit trees.

"The harvest will be bountiful this year, all thanks to the Winged One."

In an instant, a light but steady mist fell from a cloudless sky, bathing the plantations with localised spray. Outside in the surrounding desert, it was fifty degrees above Celsius and no life sustaining moisture fell out there. Its inhabitant's did not know that with the technology available to his perceived Deity, it was a simple matter to produce such vast amounts of $H2O$. He passed the orchards of citrus fruits and as he got nearer to the hidden citadel, the fruit plantations gave way to manicured lawns of the finest emerald grass. Exotic flowers and shrubs with perfumed scents were a riot of colours in the borders of the lawns. In the centre of every emerald shape, bubbling water fountains adorned with bronze and silver castings of Cherubs lay quite content in the knowledge that they would grace any European palace if these water features so desired. Migrating desert birds flocked here on their flight south. Drawn to the sight of the numerous flocks, Styarz knew.

"The Winged One is kind to his lesser creations. Many of the migrating birds would not be able to cross the vast desert without Sanctum's presence. It is a much needed and welcome resource on the flight path across the desert to their winter feeding grounds."

The raptors birdsong and the soothing splashing of the fountains combined to create subliminal echoes of paradise. He located the secret entrance to the priory and the Master's keep. The returning Knight entered the honeycombed warren of cool tunnels that lay beneath the citadel. Their age long lore told them.

"These passageways are far older than antiquity and are perhaps the oldest intact inhabited buildings on the Planet. The underground borings date from the time when the living God had first set foot on the Planet to save his people from their follies."

It was close enough to the truth as the long departed Naisi's construction CRYSTALOID'I had carved out these subterranean tunnels, for a purpose that was also long forgotten. Zebulan's minions had enlarged and extended them in the years following their arrival. The cool refreshing air that circulated through the ancient spaces was a blessing, which was provided like everything else, by the Master himself. There was no fear of a build-up of lethal poisonous gases down here. He sped along the underground galleries that now became adorned with ancient frescos of what appeared to be Angels; there were no images of a crucified Christ here. The motifs were painted in rich vermillion and precious metals. The images were so old now that the gold's had minute cracks and the colour, once vibrant had faded to a flat yellow ochre. Down deeper, in shimmering halls of subdued light, there were more fantastic images, telling the deeds of former servants of the Winged One. These three dimensional works of religious art leaped out at the viewer and dragged him into the holy scene as if he were a part of it. No one, but their Creator knew how these heavenly images were created. Close to the Gods privy chamber, his fellow monk's altered Gregorian chants filled the halls with soothing melody. A gift, their Deity allowed. The singing was in Latin, the language of worship among the Winged One's servants. Styarz became aware that the God was agitated as he was summoned directly to an audience without using the proper protocols to appear in his presence. The Knight's heart thumped in trepidation at the Master's uneasiness.

"This means another journey."

The eager supplicant quickened his pace as he hastened through the subterranean corridors. He was about to meet the Lord of this place. The hurrying Knight made the transition to the Master's domain and into another World; a place of cold blue light. From his vantage point, the Winged God observed that the summoned Hybrid's breath froze slightly as it released plumes of white mist the instant he had crossed the threshold into his version of the Guidex Sphere. This was a result of the ingenious cooling mechanism that kept the temperature to the Alien's liking. However, it was proof to his servants that Zebulan was indeed the Divine Creator for a Devil used to bathing in the fires of Hell would surely perish in here. There was the holy smell of incense and Styarz discarded his usual superior attitude once inside the inner sanctum. Now in growing humility, he was in close proximity to his God. The shocked worshiper realised in astonishment.

"I have never before seen the Winged One so ungodly like?"

There had never been a time remembered when their Creator showed behaviour like he was now exhibiting. Nor was there even a hint of it mentioned in the Knight's ancient archives that lay nestled in carved out caverns to the east on another plateau. All of the orders functioning buildings lay cocooned around this sacred abode, on other levels in this underground World. On the immediate levels above their Master's living quarters, lay the spacious and very comfortable living quarters for the servants of the Winged One. Their Life-giver concealed the structures from inquisitive outsiders by a protective umbrella, which camouflaged the entire city. Very infrequently when a malfunction made the shield flicker and their marble city appear for a few moments, most of those who caught a fleeting glimpse dismissed it as a mirage. The few who equated the apparition with the myth of a lost city of wealth such as El Dorado, Shangri La or even the lost mines of Solomon perished if they tried to locate it, just like the survivor of the mercenary band that Wesley had dispatched all those years ago. Styarz always laughed at those dead fools,

"For there is indeed a treasure here, one beyond what any of those greedy and short-sighted infidels can perceive. It is the Winged God. A wealth above any other on the Planet or indeed within the Cosmos."

Styarz was the latest in a long unbroken line of Preceptors that served and revered the Master onto death. He was the newest that held the position that, David of Jerusalem, the Knight De Courcy and the soldier Wesley once held in service to the Winged God. Their credo stated.

"The Winged One was here when our primitive ancestors first started to walk upright. Our Master had seen the plight of these sub-Humans and in his infinite goodness, he took great pity on them. Our benevolent Deity saved us from a primitive existence from which man's ancestors would never have evolved beyond the cleverest simian that lives today. An eternity of grubbing for insects or fruit and fleeing from larger predators in the vast equatorial jungles would have been the Human race's lot. For without our God, there would be no pursuit of knowledge and

enlightenment."

The Alien being that he adored still abhorred the harsh light and heat that existed above ground and lived in his own freezing chamber far below the surface. From there, he sent Styarz and others like him out into the World to do his necessary work. Most of the time it was to eliminate a threat to his plans. His devout servants truly believed.

"For in his perfection the Winged One will not take any life, be it Human or animal."

To unquestioning Styarz, his Creator was the ultimate alchemist of Humanity and he intoned religiously many times a day.

"Praise and glory be to our God and Master and his gift of enlightenment."

Other religions and their worshipers were seen as ignorant short-lived deceivers.

"Those foolish infidels believe that their God is my God. How little do they know of my true faith?"

Generations of Zebulan's adherents had survived and even prospered alongside the followers of the Prophet, those Carpenter from Galilee and the inheritors of King David. His sect had used the others ways to their advantage. Because of their petite size and slender frames, these killers of men found it easy and convenient to go about their nefarious endeavours dressed in women's restraining and unrevealing garments. For thousands of years they executed appointed missions under unknowing eyes. Their bodies had become small and feminine, belying their abnormal strength and formable quickness. Many a foe had been fatally surprised before their secret was revealed. If this was not sufficient enough to protect the God then guile was another tool they had in abundance. Styarz had other concerns now.

"What in his unknown name could have occurred to agitate him so?"

Inside the God's chambers, which were known by his followers as the chamber of blue light, he now stood face to face with the discomforted Master. He took a deep breath and sighed.

"His pain is my pain. The God of the Christians sent his own son to suffer, we would not allow that. Any of us would have taken our Gods place. And all he has to do, is command."

The warrior monk snapped out of his musing in alarm, for the divine being had actually left his throne and was pacing to and fro. His huge wings were flapping in agitation and the rainbow perfection of his body was revealed fully to the Hybrid. His servant seeing his creator in his full glory, dropped to the icy floor in reverence and pressed his forehead firmly to its chilled embrace. Styarz was acutely aware that his Master had registered his presence, even though the prefect face had not betrayed any sign. As the God studied the imprinted Hybrid that cowered before him, Zebulan felt a warm superiority that momentarily intruded in on his worry.

The DEFILED was drawn towards his schemes concerning his vassals.

"I know from millennia of experience that the primitive life-forms on this rock have to be manipulated very carefully, for I am certain that if they ever discovered my true form and motives, they would tear me limb from crystal limb. That is the sole reason why I am shrouded in this distasteful mask of pure crystal with obnoxious Hybrid features etched on its fabric. Besides if they became aware of the fact that the overpowering smell of incense was to mask the smell of their carbon based bodies when they are in my exalted presence, I shudder to think of the consequences. Still, they are useful tools, so it is rational to let them think they are the real Humans and all the others will be eradicated when I am triumphant. They have no conception that their artificial evolution of mixing their genetic material with other mammal's genes was based on Seantanta's experiments. That their speed and quickness comes from a blending of different felines and the killer Primate. This one kneeling before me contains a small blending of the large communal feline of the southern plains.

His servant perceived his Halo change in colour, but was unaware of what it intended.

"Enough of this nonsense, I am been distracted."

Zebulan returned to the distressing events of the previous night when all of his millennia of counteracting the Watcher back in the past had been to no avail. It had all been a conniving diversion that he himself would have been proud of and he had played into the Cetheren's and the devious, but insane Mescal's light strands. Styarz's brief contact with Naomh had revealed again the existence of the ALASTHA'I artefact. But this time, the presence had been far more potent than the last encounter; the Alien had felt the connection more acutely. Ever since, he had detected it on the Hybrid that had despatched Wesley, he had had focused on the conundrum and his efforts had bore pulpa fruit. That was why, he had ordered Styarz back. But in the time that it had taken for him to return, just a few hours ago in fact, something momentous had occurred. Thousands of years of plotting against his own races schemes had been to no avail. Zebulan had finally discovered what his kin were up to.

"Once again, they have caught me unawares. Again, I have underestimated the mad Patriarchi. The anomaly that I am detecting is the life-force of Mescal. Incredibly, he is here in some form and part of some scheme."

The shock and enormity of this recent event had overwhelmed the DEFILED. For the first time since the splitting of the APOCRYPHA'I, he was aware and been drawn towards its presence.

"Segments of the arch-meddler are encapsulated in crystal energy spheres and have been separated. That is the reason I could not detect them until it was too late. Now, two pieces of this Mescal form have just been assimilated. Their existence show's up on my crystal arrays like the

presence of the powerful yellow Sun above my desert base. His presence is growing stronger."

It was now apparent that the most devious of them would be around to guide the Hybrid's against the CRYSTALOID'I legions. He had found humour at their choice of Cathbad, but that had been a clever ruse. If the vain Alien had been one to hand out compliments, he would have admired them, instead he raged.

"The rest of the mad ALASTHA'I must not be assembled. If the Hybrid's gain the knowledge held within his twisted mind, then my Master will hold me responsible. Well, if they mind think that I have underestimated them, then they are gravely mistaken. It is they who have miscalculated. I just have to sever the link between the assembling Elder and his host. It is as easy as that. And this one before me is well capable of that."

The unsettled God mind-spoke to the crouched figure abased before him.

"Styarz my beloved disciple, perceive and take note."

To his overawed servant, his God commanded and bubbling lights flew from him. Images began to appear within their forms. What the Knight was unaware of was that he was watching Zebulan's version of the Scrying Globes. The Preceptor was looking at himself back in Tunis, just before his killing spree. The images focussed onto the ship that had drawn his attention and now he could see the deck with pristine clarity. Two figures stood at the images centre, one was in his forties with long braids of hair, the other was clean *shaven* and younger in years, but a power radiated from this one. His God's voice broke the spell.

"I have a grave task for you, my devout worshiper?"

"All you do is command and your will, will be done."

"Your God is indebted to you."

He felt the physical adoration coming from his servant.

"How these few simple words affect these Hybrids. These primitive creatures would attempt anything for me; just for a few words of affection."

Still, he was well aware that they were a two edged sword.

"Have these killing organisms not hunted down and slaughtered inferior members of my own kind, including the hapless Setantana and Naisi. They killed, dismembered them and devoured their still inhaling carcasses. These are weapons that have to be used with extreme care."

Zebulan re-addressed his devotee.

"The man on the right is our mortal foe; he has in his possession, an artefact that was stolen from me, thousands of years ago. It is an item that will enhance the lives of my loyal worshipers enormously. I am sending you out to slay this mortal and recover a coloured jewel. Are you up to the task?"

"Of course. Where is this man now?"

"In the land called the Enclave. But I do not want you to enter there. Even with your prestigious talents, that would be an extremely difficult task."

"Still, if my God commands it, we will attempt it."

"I do not want my disciples to throw away their lives needlessly."

That was a lie, Zebulan had a few choice reasons, not to let Styarz and his Knight's to enter the land of his former base. First there was the possibility that traces of his presence still lingered around and he wanted nothing to affect his minion's adoration of him. He could give them advanced technology to penetrate the wall of steel around the Enclave, but now he was certain that emerging form of Mescal would detect it. Still in the mind-speech, Zebulan ordered the Hybrid.

"First enjoy a few nights with you comrades, then you will gather a few of our best disciples. The time has arrived for you to fulfil the vows your ancestors made to me. The long feared Evil has awoken and we must use all of our might to vanquish it and the one you have seen is its harbinger. He is Satan's minion on Earth. You and your fellow Knights will find a base outside the Enclave and when the thief moves, I will let you know."

Sudden holiness washed over Styarz.

"It is now up to me to confront my God's worst enemies. The Demons of hell have been unleashed and I will be the leader of the force sent to dispatch them. For certain. I must be the most favoured disciple the master has ever had, for he has laid this, the most holiest of tasks at my worthy feet."

As the Hybrid rose from his abasement, the God added.

"Go with my blessing, my most loyal follower and gather your brothers. Seek out this threat and neutralise it. I am your Creator and will be in constant contact with you during this mission. When you bring it back, I will bestow wonders on my people, the like of which you have never seen before. Now go with a good heart, for I am depending on you, my most faithful servant."

Tears of joy and devotion flowed from Styarz's eyes, as his vassal now understood clearly.

"My God had not been nervous, but excited."

The Knight still under the influence of been in the presence of his Deity hurried from the icy blue chamber to do the Master's bidding. He passed the magically lit passageways out into the acid yellow of the day. Already his agile mind was choosing those of his order that would accompany him on the holy mission. As he made his way down the corridors to his personal chamber, he indulged in a slight grin. The smile was because of where they must go. The devotees of the Talmud, the Bible and the Koran never realised that over the centuries, his brothers had lived among them and committed horrendous acts, which they blamed on each other. Thus these three faiths were always in conflict with each other. Styarz went to the bathing pools and ordered a servant.

"Bring two feisty females. I have a desire to copulate."

As the menial done his bidding, he silently acknowledged.

"Besides, the Winged One always needs more worshipers"

When both of his appetites of cleanliness and lust were sated, he dressed in a clean robe with a large cowl and made his way to the great hall. As he passed through the training hall, the leader of the order paused and watched as members of his sect practiced their fighting prowess. Bodies flew about; weapons were blocked and thrown at men and targets. A bunch of excited novices approached him and begged him to perform. The master of unarmed fighting agreed with a nod of his head. Five of the practicing combatants stood on each other's shoulders like performing acrobats, the topmost individual held a wooded board with outstretched hands. The Grandmaster reacted in a blur of movement and cats-tumbled forward in a series of rolls. At the arc of his final spin, he catapulted upwards and broke the displayed board with a precise kick. He landed easily on two feet to a round of applause. He bowed amiably and continued towards his interrupted destination. Huge timber doors made from wood that originated a thousand kilometres away swung easily on equally oversized black iron hinges. The long hall, the meeting place of the Knights was a creation of thirteenth-century Norman architecture. Large pillars held up equally large arches. The walls of polished marble showed through large hanging frescos. Each of the knitted scenes showed events of the God's life among them. Gone were the crucifixes and images of the Madonna and Child. Winged Deities were now supreme and the likeness of their God was everywhere depicting his sanctity. From the events in Jerusalem, the betrayal by the French King and the flight to their new home. Three men of their holiest legends accompanied the God in every physical image, the Semitic David, the Templar De Courcy and the Priest Salvador. The centre piece of the space was a long polished table that seated over two hundred Knights. This was known as the inner circle. On that long used board were the fruits of Sanctum. Its surface abounded with best of its produce. Large jugs of wine from their vineyards competed for space with platters of mutton, beef, pork, chicken and numerous edible fish. A wide variety of fruit and vegetables from their own fields and orchards were placed alongside loafs of freshly baked bread, all provided by the craft of their supernatural Lord and with minimum Human involvement. There was a black cloaked host already waiting for the Preceptor. One Knight rushed forward and embraced him, it was Staryc. His brother in arms was nearly a mirror image of himself and most guessed that they at least shared the genes of one parent. Both stood back and said.

"Salute."

The one that had been in the Winged God's presence told the other of the mission that he had been endowed with. Staryc told the Knight that he was to stay behind and govern in his stead, if the other was disappointed, then he did not show it. Instead, he said.

"This is a cause for a celebration, come tell us of your latest adventures in the lands of the infidels."

They joined the other Knight's at the table; one of the brothers raised his goblet and said.

"To the grace of the Winged One and all that he provides."

Everyone else followed suit, the feast began and stories in praise of their God were initiated. Back in his frozen chamber, the object of the prayers felt little relief in sending out his bunch of killers. The DEFILED surmised.

"The Hybrid that has assembled two parts of Mescal's form will prove just as adept in murder. I am certain that it was an ancestor of this one that slew the Knight Wesley."

Still, he had some faith in his servants; this present group had never failed him yet. If Zebulan had known that the completed Mescal/Amulet would contain all the knowledge of the ALASTHA'I and access to their superior technology, far more than the scant scraps available to him at this moment in time, then the false Deity would have had every right to be concerned. Even more alarming for the Alien manipulator was that unknown to him, something hideous also felt the two pieces of the APOCRYPHA'I come together. This despot who sat on a bone throne far to the deep south under a snow covered mountain and on a frozen Continent wrung his oversized six digit hands with glee. The monster shouted to the Heavens that he knew to be above him.

"Soon what was stolen from us, will be returned to us again. And all living things under the blue sky will pay for our humiliation and loss."

Every faction that desired the completion of the Mescal/Amulet for themselves should have stopped and took note. For what mouthed those words in that chilling voice was such an abomination that for once, Zebulan and those among the ALASTHA'I would have agreed.

"The owner of that spoken threat should be summarily destroyed."

But the warped creature also clutched a violet shimmer in its icy hands and this might have given Zebulan cause for celebration or more than likely, extreme terror. Because this thing of madness was convinced.

"Whoever is attempting to reunite the separate parts will have to come to me if they succeed in their quest."

Unfortunately for the searcher, the creature knew as it rubbed its misshapen hands together in glee while shouting to his cowering host.

"For whoever is assembling the stolen jewel, they and their sweet flesh would be just delivering the nearly completed source of our lost technology to me and our kind. And I am looking forward to that encounter. It is about time that these Humans revered us again."

The rest of his host bellowed in approval in their guttural language while their leader found ironic humour in the way events were working out.

"To think that we who do not dare leave our frozen Continent at this time have fretted for centuries on how to retrieve what was taken away from us. And it could be regained as simply as some stupid Human delivering it unsuspecting into my hands."

The thing was extremely pleased with this train of thought and it left out an insane bout of continuous laughter which echoed around his fragile ice palace. Some of the denizens who lived under his rule shuddered as shards of the ice construction dislodged and fell to the floor, shattering into a myriad of sharp pointed fragments. Watching his inferior's dodge the falling spears caused his merriment to grow. His insane laughter never abated and went on long into the frozen night. It took a long time to die away.

XVII.

THE ENCLAVE 2953 AD/6713.

It was nearly time to leave the Enclave, a place that had been Naomh's bunch of RE-INSTATOR'S adopted home for a year. He and his companions had arrived on the 7th of August 2952 AD and had been here much longer than they would have first anticipated. Unlike the internal voice, he had no regrets about the time spent in this foreign land. His head was full of unforgettable memories that he once would have declared as imagined fantasies. Some were more distinct than others.

FLASHBACK, SIX WEEKS, AA. (AFTER ARRIVAL).

As she adjusted the strap of the heavy stocked Uzi on her shoulder, it was pointed out by the female who had seen it before; to the other who was on his first inspection, that the long twisting wall that snaked up, down and along the irregular contours of the Middle Eastern geography separated the vast lands of the Prophet from the tiny coastal Enclave. This defensive structure that was a physical barrier to two different interpretations and claims of religion ran above another dividing line; a geological fault that parted two Continental landmasses. Thankfully, there had been no major earth shifting in millennia, though the wall still shivered from the daily pounding of explosive ordnance. Its imposing outline ran from the conquered land of southern Lebanon via the Golan Heights where it ate into Syria and Jordan. The Sinai peninsula was incorporated once again and now, the once deserts of the Hanegev were sheltered well inside its protected boundaries. To the enemy without, the biggest insult and cause for rage was the section that encompassed the land that had formally been Saudi Arabia. These new sectors ran south following the line of the Red sea and marked out a fair chunk of its seized territory and this was where the next assault into the desert would come from, into the land where the Prophet himself was born. To get to this daunting south eastern boundary of the Enclave, it had been a steady climb upwards from the lower western seacoast and its more densely populated areas. Both of them had gotten here by a method of private transport that Miriam had owned. This barrier that Naomh and his recent lover now stood atop was far higher and thicker that the one that encompassed the Anschluss's boundaries. Its European counterpart paled in comparison to the sheer aggressive nature of this one; it was all obtuse and irregular deflector angles. The two of them stood behind armoured perspex shields that allowed them a 270 degree view. This Middle-Eastern wall was not as straight or uniform as the much longer barrier to the north and it did not have wind turbines spaced every hundred metres. It did however appear a lot older to those who had actually seen the Anschluss one. Compared to its much older counterpart, this newer wall had been under a lot of duress and showed signs of frequent damage. As the visitor was been filled with this information, he was more inclined to enjoy the moment, of been in this incredible place. It was early morning and it was also a lot chillier up here than back on the surface, but daybreaks never smelt as fresh as this back in his homeland. Naomh had laughed off Miriam's suggestion that he wear warmer clothes and he was now regretting it. The two lovers had been on these ramparts since before light. They had watched as streaks of luminance seeped into the weakening blackness until a full dawn had crept up on them. After witnessing his first clear and unpolluted Sunrise over land in a life time of twenty-five years, he began to warm up. His Anschluss outcasts had been in the Enclave for more than month now. This was the first time she had brought him to the wall. Their vantage point's seventy year old surface was littered with blackened scorch burns, pocked marks and impact craters that in some places revealed its rust coated reinforcing steel that stuck out like exposed ribs. This immense fortification was the newest in an expanding line that approximately every half-century increased the living space of the Enclave. Each wall was constructed under duress; some had seen more vicious battles than others. The last one into the Prophet's homeland had been one of the worst. When one line of defence was secured; it was then made bigger and more formidable than the barriers that preceded it. This one was over a hundred metres high and ten metres in thickness. There were now fourteen lesser walls and one major wall surrounding the Enclave. Some of the first ones had been built on the highest mountains and the lowest desert flat pans that had been left behind by ancient retreating seas. Each wall had the names of those who had died during the seizure of its encompassing land embedded in a revered spot. These places had become shrines to the fallen and they were as significant as the original Temple Wall which still stood since antiquity. The fifth one had the largest number of plaques, over one hundred thousand souls in all. If the people of the tribes were triumphant tomorrow, then the latter would over time become another lesser wall. The shady sides of these demoted barriers were teeming with bird life; grateful for the shade and shelter, the once battle scared and pock marked, but now mainly weather eroded concrete provided. There were bigger holes caused by projectiles from long forgotten battles that had penetrated right through the lesser walls. These voids were home to the larger birds of prey and various climbing mammals and snakes. While on the Sun baked sides, reptile and insect life thrived making ready-made meals for the smaller raptors and flying mammals who in turn fed the ever hungry young of the flesh eating birds. There were no life-forms scraping a living on the first wall as constant daily battles removed any organism that had made scant inroads on its surface. Lofty watchtowers on top of the major wall rose like medieval turrets into the Middle Eastern sky. From these observation points on the solid ramparts, vast lengths of the perimeter of the Enclave's wall could be made out when the early morning Sun dissipated the lingering mist. Sea breezes laden with moisture wafting in from the not too distant coast collided with the massive walls and liquefied into dripping water that was collected in cisterns at their bases and distributed throughout the Enclave's water services. Long narrow metallic coils ran the vertical lengths of all the walls bar the outside one and were spaced every hundred metres. These coils were heated in winter and the now cold air coming in contact with them produced the same amount of water. This mechanically gathered liquid tasted slightly more potable than the bland desalinated Seawater of the eastern Mediterranean and Red Sea. All of the walls were constructed in the same manner as the Anschluss barrier, but unlike its drab grey shade, the Enclave's walls gleamed a translucent white in the midday Sun. Another difference between the two constructions was that the front wall of the Enclave could be manned with hundreds of thousands of troops in mere hours. Despite this; it was not seen by those who desired to pass it, as an impossible restriction. At the moment though, there were scant numbers of defenders present on its battlements. This barrier was a different type of obstacle, it was far more lethal. Thousands of kilometres of razor sharp concertina wire stretched out in parallel rows from its base as the first Human deterrent, the furthest one was over three kilometres out. The wall itself was brisling with automated weapons and surveillance devices that instantly registered any incursion. They were lined along the major wall and spaced every fifty metres apart in a grid formation. These countless unmanned automated gun ports jutted out like inflamed pustules; blemishing the walls smoothness and when the need arose, erupting as bursting blisters of concentrated fire. Programmed to a predetermined killing zone, these rapid firing and highly accurate gun ports of every calibre range would obliterate any perceived sortie across the wire. They were so effective that they could even target incoming fire of large ordnance and knock most of them out of the air. From the first line of defence to the wall, hundreds of millions of indiscriminating landmines lay buried. A single such exploding device would leave a potential infiltrator minus their lower limbs and cause them to die in slow agony under the harsh Middle Eastern elements. This excruciating death would serve as a warning to others, but the lesson went unheeded. In fact, the attacks had actually gained in intensity over the last few months. Those unfortunates that had already perished in the countless skirmishes lay testament to their failure by the virtue of their dead and mutilated corpses. The deceased and their equipment were left in charred lumps of twisted metal, cloth and bone, lying where they fell under the uncaring gazes of the automated gun ports. Those that perished recently were easily located from the canopy of carrion birds that shrouded the twisted bodies, pecking and biting, while feasting on the goblets of flesh and intestines that hung from deadly razor wire. The bloated carrion birds only dispersed from the grisly feast in dark black clouds when disturbed.

The virgin witness of this type of warfare thought.

"The Prof would not think his flying friends were so pretty now, if he saw them pecking the eyes out of those dead."

Some of the mortally wounded that were still alive and clinging to life knew the full horror of their fate when they finally succumbed to death. When Miriam saw that Naomh's gaze was transfixed by the flesh eating carrion birds, she told him.

"We call those the undertaker birds. They always appear in large numbers soon after a failed attack."

When a mine detonated, the explosive device was instantly replaced from a vertically stacked magazine system from below the ground, which contained hundreds of these lethal packages of destruction. The mines conveyer system automatically pushed up another mine to the fore, when the top one had detonated. Beneath the Enclave's side of the wall, the Hell outside was banished as the ground on the inside had been planted with countless orchards and farmlands. All seized land was initially used for the production of foodstuffs as it always contained unexploited nutrients which were turned into food growing plantations for the Enclaves cramped population. Another advantage of having fields between the first, second and third barriers was that if the enemy succeeded in lobbying any artillery over the first lofty wall, then most of the explosives would detonate harmlessly in these agriculture sectors. As Naomh and Miriam stood inside one of the staggered observation points that lay between every ten-gun ports just under the top of the major wall, the two lovers scanned the bleak vista beneath them. It was a hard place outside the walls perceived safety; the land was full of sharp stones, blasted stumps and gravel. Still holding hands at every opportunity, as new couples do, they both watched as the Sun burnt off the morning mist and the view before them focussed into clarity. Naomh made out a large level plain that ended in a line of brown hills that came looming out of the heat haze. Like his female companion, he knew that they were been scanned from there. He asked her.

"How is the land beneath the wall so flat?"

She explained.

"Ever since this wall was constructed, the Enclave has sent out armoured bulldozers to clear the land of obstacles and prepare it for the next seizure of territory."

He was amazed at the single mindfulness and determination of these people, but the foreigner thought he had found a flaw in her explanation.

"So how come your machines will not detonate all that buried hardware out there when they pass over them?"

Smugly, Miriam responded.

"All of our military hardware is recognised by the mines, so they can disturb or pass over them safely. New razor wire and tank traps are reset each time our bulldozers pull back."

Her lover noticed that she did not say retreat. But all the same, Naomh was highly impressed. The woman from the Enclave elaborated further.

"The first wall, a shadow of this was constructed nearly a thousand years ago. It stopped the fighters of the Prophet from entering our land, blowing themselves up and killing our people."

"Suicide bombers?" Asked her companion.

She nodded.

"Yes!"

"Just like the Preacher." Added Naomh, out loud.

"Sorry." Enquired his puzzled lover.

"It's just that we knew somebody that used that tactic in our fight against the Anschluss system."

Miriam gave him a look of distaste and asked.

"Did you agree with it?"

He replied quickly.

"No, of course not."

"Good."

She seemed satisfied with his hurried answer. As the morning dew solidified into life sustaining liquid, the constant dripping of the water down the wall's surface set Naomh's teeth on edge. He turned from the stain of the dead that littered the ground below and gazed into Miriam's wonderful brown eyes looking for an explanation for the senseless waste. His new companion recited a well believed belief among her people.

"Life is so harsh and cheap on the other side that every so often wave upon wave of so called Martyrs hurl themselves at the impenetrable barrier in desperation in an attempt to eradicate my homeland. They call it the wall of shame."

Her voice rose with patriotism as she emphasised this land of hers took generations of her people to build with their sweat and blood. She told him that.

"God gave us this land and no one but the Almighty will take it from us. He led our leader called Joshua from a land to the south called Egypt and brought us here to Israel. God told him that all of this land was ours."

Remembering his lack of belief after visiting the Church, Naomh asked his girlfriend.

"Miriam. Do you believe in God?"

"Of course. Yahweh is the one that put us here."

Suddenly a single round hammered against the armoured shield that they stood behind. As the sound of its ricochet faded away and the trembling shield stopped vibrating, a jittery Naomh asked.

"Was that fired from those hills?"

His lover nodded her head in conformation.

"Wow that was some shot."

The newcomer's words were interrupted as down below at the edge of the brown hills, plumes of dust began to swirl towards them. Miriam gripped his shoulder and he was surprised at her strength. She exclaimed excitedly.

"Look and see what happens."

As both of them watched through large optical devices that were rooted to the concrete, hundreds of motorised vehicles sped towards the Enclave's defences, kicking up mini sandstorms as the attackers crossed the flat terrain. Colourful flapping flags and pennants depicting crescent moons and strange calligraphy adorned all of the onrushing vehicles. The approaching motorised host were grouped in clusters and each knot contained a large vehicle with a strange pointed front that was chaperoned by several smaller craft.

"They are massive bombs. We call them torpedoes. Their crews are trying to bring down the wall. But their attempts have always been futile and still they come." Boasted Miriam.

"Why don't they conceal their attack with smoke canisters?" Asked the new student of conventional war.

"That sort of screen would not be effective against the guns sights and it would be more weight to slow their speed down."

As Naomh stayed focused on the nearing spectacle, his teacher added.

"There will be more food for the gluttonous birds today."

As she said those words, the flock of flying scavengers left their grisly meals; they had been disturbed by the onrushing commotion. The attackers easily burst through the first lines of wire, loud twangs of snapping steel coils smashing against metal went unheard from their observation point. Rapid firing machine guns cleared a path of mines, but still un-coming vehicles began to erupt in balls of flame as fast loading underground mines registered a target. From the surviving and still advancing vehicles, bright flashes that signalled bursts of fire arced towards the wall like swarms of metal wasps. Unprepared, Naomh was startled by the answer of thunderous sounds of heavy cannon. The wall's automatic weapon defences were activated by the rumbling movement heading towards them. The gun ports covering the vector of the oncoming vehicles answered and a rain of fire decimated the mobile attack, cutting the machines and their crews to shreds. Not one of the vehicles came close to the wall. The mobile bombs exploded in huge geysers of flame and oily black plumes of swirling smoke as they had been laden with high explosive. Men were thrown from the exploding vehicles, some in pieces, while others miraculously were still alive and left hanging on the lethal wire much like hapless insects on a spider's web. Those who had been wounded were left to die below in extreme agony as the automated defences switched off. As the noise of the guns petered away, it became hauntingly quiet. The screams of the dying and the pleading of the wounded did not carry to their vantage-point. Naomh understood about fighting an implacable enemy. But the scale of the slaughter that he was witnessing below invoked outrage. Miriam had a gleam of triumph in her eyes.

"Sometimes, the armies of the Prophet launch aircraft and missiles from their positions, but most do not reach their targets. The vast majority are shot down. The few that make it land and normally explode harmlessly in the Agriculture sector. That is why they attack like that or use those projectile weapons from a distance. But those methods are just as futile."

Not wanting to offend his lover, but he was unable to desist after witnessing the futility of the senseless slaughter.

"Maybe your people should try to make peace with those people." Suggested Naomh not thinking it strange coming from one who used violence to make his cause and would not comprise with his own relentless enemy.

"The hatred has gone on too long."

He then used the example of the Anschluss wall; saying that it was enough of a barrier in itself and no force was needed to stop anyone trying to get in. The citizens of the huge City- State had been told the lie that the people outside its wall did not want to co-habit with them. So they left them in peace to carry on with their own ideals and existence. As soon as the words came out, he realised the foolishness of them and that this was a different scenario. He had been reliably informed by the Guide.

"The Anschluss did indeed interfere with other Nations."

With a hard glint in her exotic brown exotic, she reprimanded him.

"Who do you think supplies us with most of our firepower? Naomh. None, but your own people. Our large neighbour to the north has an agenda out here that none are sure of."

Accepting her words to be true, mainly because of his conversations with the Guide, he faltered. But then as he recovered, Naomh thought that he had found another perceived flaw in the Enclave's defences. So, he gave voice to his observation.

"Why don't they attack by sea? That wall is a lot smaller, so it should be easier to breach."

"That is not true, because the sea along the entire coast is heavily mined with limpet charges that automatically seek out the hulls of ships in close proximity. The small wall contains countless sea going torpedoes and the rooftops along the seashore all have gun and missile ports on them. That combined with our airforce would obliterate any sea going armada."

Naomh did not know what an armada was, but he did not ask. Instead, he inquired.

"How did we get through then?"

"There are narrow channels that are free of mines. These so called safe passages can be closed in an instant if the enemy is spotted."

He ran out of questions, so he remained silent. But Miriam continued, her fierce patriotic words were spat out in contempt at the thought of handing all of this over.

"You are new to this land my love, but there is something that you must understand. The people of the Prophet have nothing out there in that wasteland. Look for yourself. So they want what we have. Our enemies want our hard worked fertile land. Our precious water and even our homes. You have seen how beautiful our land is."

He found another question.

"How many of them are out there?"

"Only Yahweh knows. As far as we know the lands of the Prophet stretch for thousands of kilometres from the north to the south and from this wall, the same distance to the east."

"So it is about the same size as the Anschluss, so its population must be the same." Naomh spoke with the naivety of a person from an insular society. He had discovered that most of the ordinary people of the Enclave knew absolutely nothing about the land within the Anschluss wall.

"From what you have told me of life inside your Anch, Anschluss."

She struggled with the strange word.

"I don't think so. Your homeland sounds like a virtual paradise compared to the lands out there. It is a place of decaying cities, wandering peoples and vast inhospitable deserts entirely unsuitable for civilised existence. Their women are uneducated and must appear in public covered from head to foot in sexless outfits which cannot expose one millimetre of Human flesh. The punishments for flouting the laws of the Prophet are extreme. Public execution by stoning or beheading for crimes of the flesh, cross amputation for theft. Hanging for betrayal and so on."

Naomh was left aghast by her tales and he still insisted in an overawed unconfident tremor.

"Still we must go out there."

Their conversation was lost in the roar of a deafening musical chant coming from loud speakers on the enemy side of the distant hills.

"What in God's name is that?" Asked a startled Naomh. The use of religious euphemisms was gathering momentum.

"That's they're Muezzin calling the faithful to prayer. He does it five times a day. They are praising their God." Answered Miriam.

The first time hearer was entrapped by the exotic sound, but as it faded away into eternity, a burst of gunfire from a high powered rifle erupted from somewhere on the wall. The heavy calibre projectiles ended the lives of some of the mortality wounded men hanging on the wire down below in the mined zone. From across the walls rampart's, Naomh traced the sound of the shots to a lone sniper. The firer was heavily cloaked, but there was something familiar about their manner. Even the RE-INSTATOR was horrified at the shooter's callousness. But then, he had shot men and women down in cold blood as well.

"Only when they were a threat, those wounded combatants were

417

helpless and no danger to anyone. Still, what goes on here is none of my affair."

He turned his thoughts back to the lands beyond the wall and wondered inwardly.

"This place, we have to venture into is nothing like the Anschluss. It appears to be more brutal and unforgiving."

The internal voice which had been silent for a while answered for his trepidation.

"I am now twice as knowledgeable. This land will not be a problem."

Naomh did not feel reassured and gripped Miriam's hand tightly. Mistaking his intention, she smiled in a way that made him weak.

"Maybe I should stay here with her and forget about the unattainable dream. I have never been at peace as I have been in the last few weeks living in the Enclave. There has been no killing by me, no hiding, just the enjoyment of life."

For the first time in Naomh's short and violent career and his constant war against tyranny, the young man realised.

"I now have something magical to lose. Miriam has become more precious to me than all of my companions, even Rory is not in the same league. It's ironic that I have found love in the most dangerous period of my life."

The Gaffer had always stressed that this was a weakness that the PREVENTIVES and their bosses could exploit. He had asked his underlings once.

"How would a potential partner react at news of your death, would it be worth putting someone through that."

Most of his members agreed, except Cahill and Greta, of course. But then, they had both chosen the same path. If one died, then the other would soon follow. The once willing martyr had never known that living life could be such a joy. The idea of staying was becoming more appealing. A hostile and outraged two parts Mescal/Amulet broke into his wishful longing.

"You will not be permitted to leave your task uncompleted."

An angry Naomh challenged it.

"What the fuck can you do if I decide to quit and walk away?"

The voice of the Patriarchi said in a cold metallic warning that was filled with certainly.

"Remember what happened to your father?"

Its host felt a cold rage suffuse into his being and in a dread internal voice, he challenged the speaking jewel.

"Are you trying to threaten me?"

"I have over-extended my wings. The emotions of these erratic bipeds are totally baffling to me." The two parts Mescal/Amulet silently decided.

He attempted to mollify the Hybrid and mind-told a lie.

"*No Naomh, you misunderstand. It's just that the process of change has begun and you will need all the pieces of me to prevent what occurred to your parent from happening to you.*"

Naomh's internal anger diminished and the bitter man acknowledged.

"*It has me by the preverbal balls.*"

He looked at the woman beside him, she had been unaware of the conversation. He knew for certain.

"*There is no way she would love a fucking insect or whatever I will become without the necessary completion of this APOCRYPHA'I.*"

Still oblivious of the turmoil going on inside his head, Miriam continued her narrative through fierce adoring brown eyes.

"*Your arrival could be not more fortuitous. Every fifty years or thereabouts, we launch an excursion into the Prophet's lands. The last one was seventy years ago and the next one is in six months' time. We, the people of Zion will begin an offensive a few kilometres into the east to gain new land for our expanding population. With our armoured legions, our forces will set up a holding area and defend it, while our engineer's build a temporary shield wall as a basis for another major wall. We will be in the fore and will slip away into enemy lands during the confusion of the battle.*"

Miriam looked unconvinced that they would survive the attack and somehow make it to the Prophet's lines. Her lover saw the hopelessness in her eyes and he reassured his love.

"*Don't worry. I have a way. When we are all gathered together I will show you the amazing things that are available to us.*"

Naomh had not shared the marvel of the TORT-CAM with her yet, it was not that he did not trust her, it just wasn't time yet. The owner of the Alien technology and those familiar with the wonderful device had noticed that after he had gained the orange piece from Miriam, its internal space seemed to grow in size. Looking directly into her amazing pupils, he found his own reflection there and it held her trust. His own eyes pleaded with her to stay behind in the safety of the Enclave. But no argument could persuade her.

"*I am a solider and besides I have waited all of my life to be with you and if we have only a few months left, then it will be together. Your journey is my journey.*"

If Naomh was really honest with himself, then he was quite relieved, as he could not bear to be parted for one instant from her. The two left the wall and went back to urban sector of the Enclave were they now waited for the onslaught by Miriam's army.

FLASHBACK, EIGHT WEEKS, AA.

Time passed and the lovers had now spent the best part of two months in each other's company and still the impatient voice within waited for headway. The quest had stalled much to the delight of most of his comrades as well. One day while they were alone together in Miriam's beach apartment, Naomh absently touched the now larger sized shimmer that was embedded in his chest with perspiring fingers. A blot of moisture formed an outline on his shirt and his lovers eyes were drawn towards the patch with a sense of reverence. Her partner had been transformed in the few months that the red and orange pieces had joined. His physique had become enhanced; his mental and physical capabilities were way sharper and within his green orbs lay a greater intelligence. Seeing where her eyes strayed, Naomh asked her rhetorically.

"You know what this is thing can do?"

In a reverent tone, she answered.

"My love, you forget that I have been wearing part of it most of my life and sometimes I used to get a whisper of what it can do."

He was about to reveal the connection between him and the Amulet, but the words did not come out. Again the metallic voice of the joined parts presided.

"That information is forbidden. Only you will know of my existence for the present. When the time is right then you can reveal all to your companions."

The bearer of the two pieces of the Alien life force had no reason not to believe the internal voice, but little did he know that the ALASTHA'I had no intention of any of their creations discovering the truth, not now or ever. Naomh found it simpler to explain.

"The merged Amulet makes certain advanced technologies available to me and that will give us the advantage every time."

"That is good to know, my love. Because this will seem an impossible journey. But with this, we will succeed."

An unfamiliar feeling of contentment washed over Naomh as he listened to her words. Embracing Miriam just for the feel of her closeness, he believed that he now knew more about the bond that Cahill and Greta shared. He did not like keeping secrets from her, so he revealed one of his own to her as he tapped his chest for emphasis.

"Miriam. I can understand your language. This allows me to."

She answered him in the language of the Enclave.

"I know. Your face betrayed you sometimes."

"Did it?" Replied her lover in the same tongue as if he had been born to it and used it all his life. Miriam could detect no accent.

"Yes my love, but don't worry about anyone else knowing. I don't think anyone else was watching you like me."

But the Enclave woman was wrong; Agent XIII knew too, the Spy was always watching Naomh intently.

"Anyway, how do you think myself and my comrades understand the Anschluss tongue?"

He shrugged.

"You learnt it and passed it on to the others."

"Yes, I taught them, but I am not that good of a teacher. It was my piece of the amulet that allowed them to become proficient."

"Do you remember when I told you that we will be safe during the assault into the desert?"

She nodded, but was still sceptical. He then began to explain his plan in her mother tongue about the use of the TORT-CAM of how she and her friends would go on the quest without appearing to desert their people.

"This seems to be a fantastic device."

"You don't know the half of it."

A meeting was scheduled for that afternoon, back in the hotel room. Even though a few of the companions stayed some days and nights away from Alieem's hotel, it was still their base. So they kept the rooms occupied and paid for, much to their hosts delight. Some of the others were in the middle of a small repast when Naomh and Miriam arrived. Most of them went without shoes or boots, even in the streets, their blackened feet testified to that. It was something that was unheard of back in the Anschluss, so that in itself was a good reason for doing it. Large chunks of bread were been washed down with cool bottles of Goldstar beer. Naomh had noticed that Cahill was drinking more than usual.

"It's his way of dealing with this new and strange land."

The people from the Anschluss found the food of the Enclave slightly different from theirs. There was little meat and when there was, it was mostly turkey or chicken or a ham substitute. Pork was forbidden by religious edict, this they found very strange, but this dietary law was accepted. The local bread was much nicer that the Anschluss equivalent, but the Clerk complained.

"There is just too much vegetables and fruit in the diet."

One thing, everybody liked was an imported fruit called a banana, although the Clerk and the Persuader sniggered had when they first saw it. When the two of them were asked.

"What is the joke?"

The smaller blonde man replied with tears in his eyes.

"It looks like a penis with no balls."

The Persuader could not contain his mirth and he also burst out laughing. The Engineer looked at the two of them in disgust and declared.

"The two of you are like silly children."

At this meal, the fare consisted mostly of a chewy brown bread infused with sun dried tomatoes. There were also slices of goat's cheese, pickled cucumbers and a meat substitute. Among the Anschluss gang, there were some who thought the food tasted different and these individuals were nostalgic for certain staples from back home. Both of the latest arrivals were offered a chilled beer and the brown bottles were accepted gratefully. Naomh was about to tell his companions about the events that were about to unfold in the next few days, when an enraged Prof stormed in. Nobody had seen the scholar for a while; he was spending a lot of time with a new friend called Solomon who had been introduced to him by Shoshanna on the first week of their arrival. He loved everything about this new country. To him, even the weeds on unswept footpaths looked more colourful than similar plant's back home. While in discussion with his new companion from the Enclave, the academic had discovered that the state had public libraries that held vast amounts of knowledge. Forbidden lore that had been censured in the Anschluss. These halls of learning had attracted him like a moth to a flame. He loved the musty halls with their smell of dust and ancient parchment.

"Real paper."

The Prof had grinned in delight as he had mouthed those words. As the reader lovingly fingered the tomes, abet with plastic gloves, the scholar delighted that the Anschluss had nothing like these.

"Only cold and impersonal electronic data."

However, as with everything each of them surmised about the Anschluss, he was of course wrong. For the Chairman had a vast private library of books, parchments and stone tablets that would have astounded the former curator if he had ever seen them. But today, the two of them had abandoned the claustrophobic buildings. The cooped up men had taken a break from the air-conditioned structures and went sight-seeing. Solomon had taken the Prof to the eastern wall for the first time. That was why; the man from the London Contrib had stormed into the room with Solomon trailing behind. Red faced from fury and not the Sun, he pointed at Greta and accused her in a bittersweet voice.

"Do you know what she was doing on the wall today?"

The Prof had engendered Greta's wrath and she returned a look of malice unseen by the others. But the raging man remained undeterred. Looking around at the others, the livid man said with evident outrage.

"She was using the dying men out there as target practice."

Naomh was not surprised at the revelation as he remembered the premeditated gunshots over four months ago when he and Miriam had first visited the outer wall. All of the others turned and looked at her; there was admiration in the Mute's eyes. In her defence, Greta shrugged off the accusations and said while munching a pickled cucumber.

"I know first-hand what it is like to be tormented. I was only putting them out of their misery. It is extremely cruel to leave them to suffer out there and dying in agony under the hot Sun. Could you imagine a slow death like that?"

Most of the others agreed with her distorted logic and the Prof's rage faltered as he thought about it. Swallowing his accusation, he said meekly.

"I'm sorry. I did not understand."

The tall blonde woman did not even reply to his mumbled apology.

Cahill, like the rest of the RE-INSTATOR'S had heard rumours of Greta's mutilation of Anschluss security personnel, but steadfastly believed.

"They were all unfounded. I have never seen her do anything really nasty to the ordinary rank and file, but the Filth, now they are a different matter. But after what she had endured at their hands, who could blame her?"

He now felt proud at her misguided effort to end the suffering of the wounded men and hugged her close. Still, one among them who was aware that she had a sadistic streak which thrived as a result of her horrific ordeal at the hands of the secretive Anschluss agency dared not speak out loud.

"I know she used to use her chosen codename Liben, but Black Widow would suit her well. Cahill should be wary; for I have no doubt that she would behave like the female spider and devour him completely."

The Mute was fascinated with death and was sorry that he had missed Greta's finishing off of the wounded soldiers, but then the cold killer amended.

"On second thoughts, I prefer to be up close and watch the light of their eyes go out. Still, it would be a bit of a distraction."

In the six months, they had been here; he was prone to wandering off by himself. He was not the only one, even Greta took time away from Cahill; the reason was now obvious. The Persuader spent a lot of time with Shoshanna, leaving his brother to himself. The handsome Mute began to spend many an hour on the Enclave's walls with a fresh-faced female soldier that his good looks had charmed. The young woman took him to the spots where one could see the lights of Damascus and Amman. Seeing that he had no interest in this, she took him to flash points along the wall and the carnage had pleased him.

"I will get her to give me a gun with a big sight, the next time."

The conversation turned to other things. The placid Prof went over to the Clerk; they had a falling out of sorts. The former bureaucrat had asked for a separate room from him. His room-mates pets were driving him crazy with their early morning screeching and clamouring for food and attention.

"So the shared bond within the group is starting to weaken. Cracks are beginning to appear. People are doing things separately. I knew it would not take long. There is only one person Naomh needs to succeed and that is me. He should forget about the rest of them." Reasserted the Spy to themselves.

Still, the Clerk and the Prof made up. Anyway, the man from the London Contrib was spending most of his time living in Solomon's place. This somewhat quiet man was not their only male acquaintance from the Enclave.

FLASHBACK, TWO WEEKS, AA.

Sixteen days after they had settled in this new place, it had been a Monday. Miriam had entered Naomh's room with six associates, two familiar women and four unknown men. Those from the Anschluss knew her female friends quite well. The two women had changed from the revealing outfits of their first meeting and the skimpy bathing suits that they wore on the beach when they had met them the second time. All of the seven, including the three men were dressed in olive green uniforms. Everyone of the men sported beards, with one of them having facial hair that nearly extended to his chest. Naomh and his Anschluss companions were also attired in the same military outfits. Miriam made the introductions.

"You have already met Beersheba, Shoshanna. The others are Moshe, Haim, Solomon and the Rabbi."

She introduced them to Naomh's companions one by one and there were handshakes all round. Each member of Miriam's unit nodded as his name was mentioned. The Rabbi whose real name was Aaron Kalwenixi was a man in his forties; he was a slightly tanned figure with an enormous black beard and long braided side locks that nearly put the Guide's ponytail to shame. His sloped brown forehead showed him to be a quick thinker. Like every male of Jewish persuasion, he also wore the small rounded cap. He had been born in the ancient Old City, a short distance from the wall of the Temple Mount. As a deeply religious Jew, he stuck to Kosher food and his version of the dietary laws. Moshe Stern was a small stocky man with a very dark brown complexion and a nasty scar that ran down the left side of his face; he was from a lineage of people who had come from the south a thousand years before. Haim Golan on the other hand was nearly black in colour; he was of lean stature, a little taller than any of his comrades and he had an enormous hooked nose with wide flayed nostrils. Because of his dusky skin, the whites of his eyes seemed more pronounced against his brown pupils. The other two men also had dark brown eyes like the majority of the Enclaves population. Solomon could only be described as a slightly younger Prof. It was in his attitude, not his appearance. This thirty-year old had been born in the coastal city of New Eliat. He was roughly the same size as the London Contrib man, but weighed at least thirteen kilos more. He also had a neatly trimmed beard and a full head of black hair. The feature of him that impacted most was that the outer corner of his eyes were lower that the inner ones. A sign of been a keen observer and it suited him well. As the introductions were completed, Miriam told the now larger group by four.

"These are the people I have been waiting for."

Her companions nodded their heads; they were a long time under the influence of Miriam's piece of the APOCRYPHA'I and understood. After that, all of them spent time in their company and they got to know them quite well. Eventually, the bearer of the living amulet would let them in on the real deal.

FLASHBACK, 13.5 WEEKS, AA.

A meeting was called and seventeen eager souls participated in it. Miriam stood up and spoke first.

"Now what you have revealed to me can be done in their presence. These six people will be going with us and I trust them with my life. Naomh, tell them what we are going to do."

He complied with his lover's request and explained to them briefly what must be done. Their new companions were experts in their fields and listened without interrupting until he finished. Miriam had argued a similar point until he had shown her the invisible shield two weeks after their first visit to the outer wall. Moshe spoke for these un-briefed listeners.

"It would be impossible for a group of our size and appearance to penetrate into the Prophet's lands unnoticed. We would be overrun quickly."

Haim and Solomon who had landed behind enemy lines in several commando raids disagreed in principle. The latter explained.

"We do not have the numbers or the equipment. We have been there with much larger groups. But they were lighting raids. We were in and out in less than an hour."

"It is as he says; a long stay with our meagre resources is out of the question."

The Prof smiled at their negativity.

"Ah, but we have something else."

Those from the Anschluss had knowing grins as a sombre Naomh held up his hand and said.

"Bear with me for a moment. First of all I have to show everybody this."

The bearer of the two parts Mescal/Amulet opened his green shirt and displayed the imbedded artefact. Miriam had shown her friends her piece many a time and they had become familiar with it, but this was something different. Hers had been solid and independent from her body. Everyone in the room was affected by its intoxicating allure and were soon under its influence. Like the Engineer, the Rabbi whose life was enthralled to his respective God was the hardest to sway; but gradually he accepted the inevitable and fell under its spell. It was the first time the Mute had seen the living Amulet and it had no affect what so ever on him. It was a personification of artificial life, so it held little interest for him. Naomh re-buttoned his shirt and then moved on to the next fantastic item. He took out the concealment device, enlarged it and went through operation of the TORT-CAM for the benefit of those not in the know. Needless to say, Miriam's six companions exhaled with the same gasps of wonder and awe that everyone else had when they first encountered the amazing object. The Rabbi proclaimed.

"This is indeed a marvel."

Naomh returned to explain his plan in more detail. He and his lover had discussed it a lot since the two pieces had joined. A nod from her allowed him to brief them further.

"On the morning of the Enclave's invasion into the lands of the Prophet, we will rendezvous with Miriam's troopers, board their armoured vehicles and take part in the armies advance. During the engagement with the enemy's forces, the seventeen of us will enter the TORT-CAM and wait until the battle is over. Night-time will be the opportune moment. Then comes the risky bit for us, this will be the time that we will make the attempt of crossing over to the Prophet's lines."

The gathered assemblage moved on to the serious business of achieving that. As the plans were discussed and personal inputs were either accepted or rejected, the Anschluss members of the group relaxed in the familiar checking of weapons and equipment. This had been an unnecessary chore during their stay in this new land. The soldiers of the Enclave had been amazed at the inflatable weapons of the RE-INSTATOR'S and had no idea of the kind of subterfuge lives their new friends had before they had arrived on these shores. Their own guns were functionally simple pieces, but extremely effective at killing people. No superfluous fancy voice commands for them. Final preparations would not be made until Naomh had all the information of when the Enclave invasion was to begin. As he checked his own rifle, it would not have been apparent to the others that he was having an internal discussion with the two parts Mescal/Amulet. The inner voice informed his host.

"As a consequence of having two parts of me, I now have access to more of the advanced technology Let me explain.

When their internal discussion had been completed to each other's satisfaction, a delighted Naomh addressed the gathered ensemble to tell them what himself and the Alien object had formulated.

"I have excellent news; this is going to be easier than anyone of us thought. The two parts of the APOCRYPHA'I has enabled me to discover another thing that the invisible device can accomplish."

He introduced his astonished listeners to the wonders that had just been revealed to him. Naomh addressed his rapt audience.

"The mother TORT-CAM is composed of interwoven strands of different frequencies of condensed light particles. This incredible structure can be for limited period's split up into a maximum of seven smaller units of a less denser and more malleable form. These shells, shall we say TORT-CAMLETS have numerous advantages and some disadvantages.

The speaker was chuffed at having come up with that designation.

"Give us the good news first." Interrupted the impatient Clerk.

Naomh pressed on, even though; he was slightly vexed at the blonde man.

"The plus side is that they are mobile and more importantly, these smaller versions glow with the individual colours of the Spectrum and have

the ability to penetrate any solid barrier."

He paused for any questions. His stunned audience stayed silent, even the Clerk gagged his smart mouth. The Engineer wanted to know.

"Who exactly who is briefing Naomh, he does not have such specialized abilities?"

But he too held his tongue with a silent promise.

"For now."

His leader continued.

"These TORT-CAMLETS can meld into any dense object with its occupants. Each individual sphere will pass safely through any barrier with absolutely no harm what so ever coming to them."

The technical people among them had an inkling of his explanation, but for the benefit of himself and the others, the Persuader asked.

"Could you explain it in simple Anschluss?"

"What he means is that the larger TORT-CAM can be split up into smaller versions and these new contraptions can move silently and invisibly and pass through solid objects." Answered his brother for those less mechanical minded.

Everyone in the room took this in. Again there was complete silence, until at last someone spoke, it was the Guide.

"And what are its disadvantages dude?"

"The downside is that while the smaller globes are static, their shield will last for about two days. But while in motion, the shield lasts only for twenty hours. Then the globes have to reform into the TORT-CAM and re-energise. This takes about twenty-four hours, but we can occupy it while this is occurring. Also the TORT-CAMLETS can only hold up to four bodies comfortably at a time. But because of our numbers, Miriam has divided us into this arrangement."

The Enclave woman spoke.

"These are the groupings. Remember them carefully. Naomh said that it will split up into seven coloured spheres. Naomh and myself are in the Red one. Cahill and Greta are in the orange one. The other two parings in the yellow and green spheres are the Engineer and his brother and the Guide and the Lenses. The last three, the blue, the Indigo and the violet will hold groups of three. These are as follows, Haim, the Mute and the Prof. Solomon, Moshe and the Rabbi. And finally, the Clerk, Beersheba and Shoshanna.

Cahill and Greta looked pleased at the statement. Some of the others did not, but held their peace. The Mute for one would have preferred to be alone. The Clerk on the other hand was absolutely delighted to be sharing with the two beautiful foreign women, especially Beersheba. The object of his desire returned the Clerk with a coy look that was loaded with suggestion. He positively beamed at the group, excused himself and departed to his bed in anticipation of pleasant dreams. The Persuader had grown quite attached to the beautiful Shoshanna over the last three months and the big man sighed in regret.

"As much as I would like to share a Dobber with her, it's not going to happen. I know that as sure as the Sun will rise in the morning; myself and my brother will be together in the same one."

There had been one problem with the arrangements; it was the Prof. The soft man was refusing to let his newly acquired pets behind, especially his monkey who he had named "Pricey." after a former work colleague. But, the issue was overcome eventually, when Solomon explained.

"They were tame animals. You cannot care properly for them on our travels. And if your pets escape, none of them have the necessary survival skills to last out there. They will perish within days."

Agent XIII added maliciously.

"Just like yourself wimp."

No one else was privy to those words. But Solomon had a solution.

"I have a friend that will look after them, but don't despair it will be a few months yet. You can spend more time with them until then."

Reluctantly, the Prof agreed to this, his urge to see more of the World overcame his attachment to his pets. Naomh secretly thanked the bearded man for his intervention. The Prof excused himself.

"I want to spend more time with my pets since; I will be leaving them behind when we finally move on."

Solomon went with him. When the spectacle wearing man had gone, the Guide spoke to those that remained.

"Of all of you. I don't think that the Prof is suited to this. There is a gentle softness in him and his mind is on other things."

There was no argument on that account from the others. On the next day which was a Sunday, Cahill and Greta approached Naomh. The latter spoke for the two of them.

"Why do we have to wait for the invasion? When we have the capability of the TORT-CAMLETS."

Smiling at his best friend's complete turnaround, their decision maker replied.

"I have already spoken to Miriam about that. She told me that if any of them vanished inexplicitly now, then they would be considered cowards and deserters and they will not bring that shame on themselves. At least when they don't return after the battle, it will have seemed that they had died while doing their duty."

"I see." Declared the blonde woman.

The Engineer returned, he had been about his business with his brother. The devout man had been at a mass. This had been a regular routine since the second month of their stay.

FLASHBACK, FOUR WEEKS, AA.

Sitting around one sultry day early on in their stay in the Enclave, the

Clerk seeing a strange pointed star around Shoshanna's neck remembered something. Fishing into his pocket, he took out a metal object and presented it to the Engineer. The man from the Madrid Contrib looked at the object in the giver's opened palm and his eyes widened. It was a small golden Crucifix, perfect in every detail, even down to a miniature crown of thorns. The receiver gasped.

"It is the most beautiful thing I have ever seen."

The former bureaucrat who had become very proficient at changing one item into other, told the amazed Engineer.

"It is over a thousand years old and made of precious metals "

He looked at Naomh slightly embarrassed and continued.

"It cost me three bottles of wine. The Engineer can put it around his neck and wear it openly around here. There are also Church's where people worship that image openly.

He pointed at the Crucifix that the Engineer now treasured.

"You must take me to these places."

Excitement now filled the eyes of the man long denied his religion. Ever since they had arrived, he had hung around their living quarters, but he now ventured out at the start in search of enlightenment. But all he found was the ruins of a long gone faith and a shut Church of the Holy Sepulchre. It had been three days after Naomh's visit, but the various sects sharing its hallowed halls had fallen out once again and it had been closed until the dispute was ended and no amount of bribery could get him in. Everywhere else, he found two different religions, the faith of the Jews and the Prophet. Devastated and lingering in disappointment, he stayed close to home once again and rarely ventured out. Now, he was aghast that he had missed out on the one thing that meant something to him. The Persuader who had spent a lot of time with one of the Enclave females tried to give Shoshanna a hard look and failed miserably. Still, he managed to ask her.

"Why did you not tell me of these places before?"

The gorgeous and indifferent woman shrugged while giving him a beautiful and woeful smile.

"I did not really know of them. Please forgive me."

The exquisite woman from the Enclave was forgiven instantly. It had been ignorance on Shoshanna's part, but Naomh had known about the Church's and had deliberately held back the information. He did not want the man from the Madrid Contrib to be as disappointed as himself. The Engineer looked downcast, but the Prof said.

"Solomon can show you these places to us?"

His bearded friend nodded in the positive and was good as his word. Although, the novice from the Anschluss had no idea what was going on during the services, he still participated and always felt a magic shiver when he took communion. He was always upbeat when he returned from practising his faith. As he explained his quandary to Solomon about not understanding the Word's, the Prof's friend told him.

"I can help you with that; well not me exactly. The Rabbi is truly a man of God and has studied other faiths. He can translate the words of your mass for you. Afterwards you can discuss the experience. He does so enjoy a good debate. He is away at the moment, but as soon as he gets back, I will ask him."

The Engineer looked grateful and a meeting was held two weeks later when the scholar had finished a tour of military duty. The Rabbi, the man with the huge beard insisted.

"I know of this Church and it is not far from here. Come, this place of worship will be still open and I will take you there."

The Engineer looked at him in gratitude and he and his brother left with the religious student. Privately, the big man wished.

"I'd rather spend more time with Shoshanna, but God forbid I mention that?"

Naomh was asleep; he was alone and in the Clerk's room in Alieem's hotel. Miriam had been called away on military duty for three days and at time like this, he liked to be in the company of his friends. Like his friends, he was amazed that there was no unemployment in the Enclave; their large standing army saw to that. At this time of separation from his love, he was inclined to sleep by the large wooden shutters and listen to the sound of passing traffic on the streets below. It was a comforting noise to one who had never been lulled by it before. Suddenly, he was aware of movement and one sleepy glance confirmed.

"It is still among the hours of darkness."

He glanced over at his luminous timepiece saw that it was just after midnight. The room lit up as someone activated the light sensors. Naomh sat up. A wide-eyed Engineer was shaking him awake and the large shadow of his brother was alongside him. The excited man needed to tell him about his new experience in the company of the Rabbi and the normally taciturn Persuader appeared to be as thrilled as his sibling. The former verbally recalled the public mass and receiving a real confession from an ordained Priest.

"The Rabbi translated the whole service and then explained that the Priest would receive confessions after the service. The Preacher used to make us do this in full view of the congregation, but this was a private affair. My Enclave companion could not help us with his translation. But deep down, I think the Priest understood my needs and I cleansed my soul of all its hurt and bad deeds. And Naomh, the Church was a place of wonder. There were all sorts of images of Christ and his mother, some were in gold and precious metals, others were painted and when I saw the huge statue of Jesus suffering on a wooden cross, I felt overjoyed. And then there was the smell of a holy place. The Rabbi told me that it was a pure form of incense."

Naomh thought.

"I am not pleased with the prospect of you telling a stranger about our business. But, I might as well let it go. The holy man did not understand your words. Still, if I mentioned this conversation to the others, they would probably visit the Priest and wack him."

The Engineer was oblivious to his misdemeanour as he continued.

"Oh Naomh, it was the most wonderful experience of my life."

The speaker's eyes lit up with fiery zeal as he promised.

"When we destroy the Anschluss, every Contrib will have its place of worship and the people will celebrate mass openly."

Then, he took out a wrapped bundle, opened it and reverently held two old fashioned books.

"After the mass, the Rabbi took us to his home. He has the most wonderful collection of religious books. He's like the Prof, he prefers paper. He says it brings him closer to God. He studies many religions, but mainly his own and the two other faiths of Abraham. He gave me these two holy books, one is a bible and the other is a mass book. Both are written in the language of the Anschluss. They are wonderful gifts."

He lingered on the much worn black leathered bible. Its pressed gold-leaf inlayed titles had been eroded a long time ago, leaving a poor yellow shadow of their once magnificent indentations behind. The Engineer believed that constant handling by devout hands was responsible. He opened the thick cover and showed Naomh the first page.

"Look at the inscription. The words are hand penned, unlike the machine print of its contents. Most of it is faded, the last bit in an illegible scrawl; all I can make out is the final line. It says your loving parents Tom and Mary, Cardiff 1870 AD. It must have been treasured by someone once. And the really amazing thing is that it originated in the Cardiff Contrib showing that our religion was once practised in the Anschluss a long time ago."

As the Engineer's voice trailed off, there had been an edge of fanaticism to it and his listener wondered.

"If I came into conflict with his growing beliefs, which way would he go? At the moment, it does not look good for my side?"

Before the man with a renewed purpose left, his voice became sombre.

"The Rabbi also told us that once over a thousand years ago, a large number of his people lived within the Anschluss boundaries. Nearly all of them were rounded up, put into detention centres. Then, the men, women and children were starved, shot and gassed to death. They killed over six million of them and other non-conformists. He believed it was because of their religion. That was wrong Naomh; Jesus would not have wanted that."

Illeau was next door and through the walls, he had overheard the conversation and as usual, the loner got the wrong message.

"What is so special about that? My recycling unit disposes of that amount of corpses every six months."

There were some more words uttered from next door.

"We will leave you to try and get back to sleep, but me and my brother can now face whatever comes at us."

The two men from the Madrid Contrib said goodnight and left Naomh to try and retrieve pleasant dreams, which of course meant, his brown eyed girl.

FLASHBACK, SIXTEEN WEEKS, AA.

After the revelation of the TORT-CAM, the whole group took the invisible shield to a Moshav owned by Shoshanna's parents. She told them.

"My family are away from the farm; in another part of the Enclave visiting relatives."

It was time to familiarise their new companions and their selves with the device and its new application. In broad flat furrowed fields of harvested cotton, they used various weapons on it. The Anschluss members began to familiarise themselves with the weapons of the Enclave which were very adaptable and could be used in many theatres of combat. Their own Flatpacks were only suitable for urban combat. They used the small squat "Uzi's.", the larger and longer ranged "Galil." with its curved barrel magazine and finally the 50 calibre "Beni." which fired 20 mm rounds from a long rectangular projectile holder and explosive 50 mm shells from a chamber under its long barrel. This was an amazing piece of technology, one that the Patriarchi's race might have been proud of. The internal voice addressed itself.

"It is no wonder that the Hybrid's best endeavours are product of death."

The heavy gun that even the Persuader would struggle to control hovered on cushions of air which in effect made it weightless to its operator. The Lenses called it.

"The Floating gun."

Each of the Anschluss personnel were also presented with black pistols called "Desert Falcons.". These were single action gas operated pieces that fired large bore .5 mm rounds. The magazine that fitted into the stock held twenty of these lethal projectiles. The crackle of small arms fire and the thud of contained explosions were not unusual in this wide-open space. What would be strange to an onlooker was that the shooters appeared to be firing at nothing. When the protective shield was first expanded, the Rabbi approached the man sized iridescent object and spoke some kind of ritual over it. He had donned a strange patterned shawl over his shoulders and held a small book in his hands. He put what could be only described as a small black box on his head. The religious man then circled around the inanimate object and began to chant in the Enclave's language. Miriam had asked for silence during this. Afterwards, she explained to the bemused

Anschluss observers.

"The Rabbi has blessed the TORT-CAM and asked God to protect and to keep safe any who rely on it."

Greta snorted with indifference, but the Engineer took affront. Not to be undone, he also blessed the object using the name of Jesus Christ and the sign of the cross. He also added a prayer that he had learned off by heart from the second book. To ease any apparent conflict, the Rabbi said diplomatically.

"I hope your God bestows the same protection as ours."

The Engineer returned the overture. Naomh had silently agreed with Miriam that respecting each other's beliefs was the basis for forming a new friendship. The captivated group even split it up into TORT-CAMLETS and operated them. To the Persuaders delight, he was allowed by his brother to share one with the object of his fascination; Shoshanna. They had a wonderful day out in the open that was finished off with a meal and cold beers. The Clerk had worn one of the skullcaps called a yarmulke and the Prof had laughed at him. The disgruntled copier slagged his mocker.

"You should try wearing one. It will cover up your bald patch."

Still in good humour, the spectacle wearing man answered the others retort.

"Sticks and stones. Well, you know the rest."

Then Cahill produced the adrenalin pills that served them well back in the Anschluss. When he explained to the Enclave crew about their purpose, each person shook a head in the negative.

"What's wrong with them?" Raged the one who had produced them.

Moshe explained.

"These high performance drugs might have been effective back in your colder climate, but our experts have found that out in the desert, they will quickly dehydrate you. You will become weak, disorientated and useless to those who will depend on you. Soldiers have also been known to form an addiction for them. No my friend, they are not a good idea."

"We will see." Responded the red haired man; not believing him.

He ignored the advice and during the next day's training, he secretly popped one. Half way through the exercise, precisely what the darker man predicted happened to him. An incoherent Cahill was treated immediately and when he recovered, he asked.

"What happened?"

"Exactly what Moshe said. You are so pig headed sometimes" Admonished his lover.

Someone could have said.

"And what about you and the Guides sea sick pills?"

A week later came the final test; half of them stole it into an artillery range the evening before a live fire session. Staying in it all night, its occupants waited inside it, alongside targets that would be hit the next day.

433

The invisible shield passed the test with flying colours. But as they emerged from their haven that evening with the intent to sneak back out, they were faced with a dangerous quandary. The immediate ground was littered with unexploded ordnance. The problem was solved by using the TORT-CAMLETS. The revealed sphere split into three and everybody re-entered them. A pressed sequence of the wrist bands activated motion. Like an unseen spirit, the moving globes glided over the lethal ground setting off unexploded shells in their wake. The gates of the firing range were shut; its thirty kilometre wire fence was as much of an obstacle. So it was an opportune moment to test their moving invisible shields most unbelievable attribute, its ability to pass through solid objects. With unheard commands outside the confines of the Alien devices, the three untraceable globes lined up at the fences perimeter. In each one, it was decided.

"Ok, let's go through it."

The invisible shields became mobile and the wire fence grew large and threatening. As it loomed before them, their occupants braced themselves for some kind of impact. Some even closed their eyes, but nothing happened and then they were on the other side of the barrier. The amazed and unique type of traveller's got out of the remarkable devices and waited as each third merged. Another sequence tapped into a wrist band and it became whole again. They located the vehicle that they came in and lost in the wonder of their shared experience, conversation was at a minimum on the journey home. The next day Miriam and Moshe had a long discussion with Naomh, Cahill and Greta. The latter two males kept nodding their heads throughout the conversation. The blonde woman said out loud.

"It does not matter, I will handle it."

Cahill used to his lover's over confidence (With good cause.) and her intractable ways answered.

"It's not for you my love; it's mostly for the others."

She relented and said without a hint of malice.

"You are right. They need the practice."

The five of them let the rest their colleagues into the dialogue. They let Moshe speak as he had the most expertise.

"My friends. We have been told that all of your combat experience consists totally of urban fighting. Well, where we are going, it is going to be entirely different. Outside the walls, the terrain is made of desert's wide open plains and bare hills. There are going to be very few places to hide, unless you know how to. We are going to take a few days every week to train you in this new form of combat."

The Rabbi gestured to Solomon and Haim, they took out a number of sandy helmets and the bearded communications expert explained to his foreign friends.

"As you know, neither of you were able to use our local version of your

Frog Eyes, the M I S (Mobile Information System.) simply because we use a different alphabet and language. But when we go into combat and are outside the walls, our armed forces use these."

He tapped a helmet for effect still speaking.

"An inbuilt microphone only broadcasts and receives radio traffic. There are no video images as inadvertent information stored on chips from a dead or captured solider could show our enemy the inside of the Enclave. So you my friends can use these."

He handed out one to each of them and began to show them, how to use the radios. None of the Anschluss had a problem with the simple devices operation. Over the next few weeks, the two diverse groups trained together in various landscapes and played out potential scenarios. They were becoming fast friends, so much in fact that Cahill broached what he thought was a serious question to one of them in the middle of a training exercise in a grapefruit orchard.

"Why have most people around here got large noses?"

The Rabbi donned in the same type of camouflage as the asker answered, not feeling one bit enraged at what some might consider an insult.

"It's the way we are made, it is like why have men Adam's apples and women do not."

"Oh, I see."

But, he did not. The Anschluss Spy who was in close proximity had an argument against the Rabbi's statement.

"I know of a LYUBINITE Clone who is female but has a prominent Adam's apple."

Of course, this titbit of information was never divulged. Time moved on and still, they practiced. It was during this period of waiting that the Engineer with Moshe's help designed portable showers and a toilet for the inside of the TORT-CAM.

"After all, we don't know how long we might have to spend in it."

Beersheba and Shoshanna made some curtain rails for the two devices, so any user would have privacy.

FLASHBACK, NINETEEN WEEKS, AA.

Weeks went by and all of them began to spend more time together. If they were not on the beach, then they were practicing as a unit. The visitors from the urbane Anschluss loved the trips to the sandy shores or the large lake in the north. Their favourite experiences were the open flamed barbeques and the unfamiliar smell of burning wood. These get-togethers only further advanced their shared feelings of comradeship. The Engineer's initial prejudice had long passed. It was during this time of waiting that Christmas was due. He had missed out on Easter, but he was going to participate in this festival. He insisted that the others from the Enclave accompany him for midnight mass in a Christian place called Bethlehem

435

and they did just to placate him. It was the most wonderful experience of the man from Madrid's life. Surprisingly, the Anschluss mole was also contrite, but for another reason all together. As December the twenty-fifth was also the birthday of the founder of the LYUBINITE, the revered Doctor Gregory Lyubin.

FLASHBACK, THIRTY WEEKS, AA.

Then came the day that the whole Enclave was waiting for, it arrived hot on the heels of a festival called Purim, the revelry was barely over, when the announcement was made, the 12th of August was D-day. The long awaited invasion would begin in earnest. From that day on, Naomh got to see his lover more infrequently, the same was said for the rest of their Enclave friends.

THE PRESENT, FIFTY-THREE WEEKS, AA.

The seekers of the uncompleted APOCRYPHA'I had now spent just over a full and memorable year in the Enclave. Miriam had received her final briefing that morning and informed her Anschluss friends to get ready. They all had a final get together and a video of the Enclave plan was studied. It showed an aerial view of the outer wall towards the south-east. There were two places where it bulged out to a length of ten kilometres, one in the north and one in the south. The object of the invasion was to connect a conclave-shaped wall to both salients and claim the land between. It looked a simple enough plan and it was discussed, then Miriam and her companions excused themselves.

"We have a lot to do before morning."

Naomh and his friends volunteered to help, but they were told that

"We want you there as little as possible, we need to keep you away from prying eyes, besides you would only get in the way. We will send for you in the early hours of the morning."

To ease his disappointment, his lover gave him a lingering kiss and whispered into his ear.

"Get some sleep and dream of me, my love."

Reluctantly, he released her and she left with her comrades. Then, one by one the others from the Anschluss excused themselves and retired until Naomh was left alone with the Guide. The leader of the band had guessed astutely.

"Something has been on his mind all evening and now that we are alone, he will tell what is bothering him."

He had been surprised, but secretly pleased that the other had hung around over the last twelve months. Now that van DerKamp had his undivided attention, the last person from the Anschluss to join their group dropped his bombshell. The man from the Amsterdam Contrib cleared his throat with a cough and announced.

"Naomh. I will not be going with you."

He pointed South-east for emphasises. A shocked Naomh started to protest, but he was halted by a raised hand.

"No hear me out dude. I have done everything here to speed you on your way. Now that you have found the contacts you have been seeking, you no longer need me. Anyway I would be useless out there; I know nothing of the lands beyond the wall. I have paid the debt I owed your father. So let me go and release me from that oath."

A disappointed Naomh privately understood.

"I have misgivings about the Guide been useless out there. But he has helped us out enormously in our transition from the Anschluss to this new and strange country. He made it possible for myself and Miriam to meet and continue the search together. His is right, he has done enough to help us and I have no right to expect him to risk his life out there in the unknown World."

The two parts Mescal/Amulet concurred.

"He has served his purpose and you no longer require his services."

The decision maker accepted both their reasons and smiled warmly.

"Of course my friend. You did everything possible to aid us and I now release you from whatever pledge you gave my father. You can go about your own business and when we have gone, take the cases of drink with my blessings. Who knows, we might be successful and I will call on you when we get back to the Anschluss."

The Guide looked relieved, believing Naomh was speaking from the heart. So he added.

"I could easily have vanished into the night during the last year without asking. Others might have thought that you would have ordered one of your lads to "whack" them, but not me. For my sake, I hope I have not misjudged you."

Naomh felt that he would choke with emotion if another word was uttered, so he just nodded his head. With that, Franz van DerKamp walked out of his life and he felt a strange loss. He suddenly felt drained emotionally and physically, so he retired to bed. His sleeping arrangements consisted of a large bed with a deep soft mattress. Sturdy legs kept its occupant about half a metre from the floor. It was an old style that spoke of a time when the bed's height kept the sleeper safe from marauding insects and other unwanted companions. It was an unnecessary precaution according to their host, Alieem was quite adamant.

"Let the Prophet be my witness. My hotel is free of such pests."

Secure with this knowledge, Naomh closed his eyes, but little sleep came that night. What did only intruded on an image of a prefect olive brown face with large brown eyes and the most wondrous smile. His thoughts flirted with the night before as they lay holding each other after a bout of passionate lovemaking. Then a cold shiver opened up the possibility that he and Miriam had shared their sleep for the last time. Abruptly, he was been woken by noises from another room.

"God. Is it morning already."

His delightful and troubling images of Miriam had vanished, to be replaced by dark regrets at the Guide's departure. He fell asleep again until his personnel alarm ended his lethargy. This time it was definitely daybreak as thin beams of morning's light wafting through the timber blinds laths testified. The roused man positively leapt out of from his sleeping arrangements, his good humour restored at the prospect of reuniting with Miriam. Most of the others had already risen. He checked in the forgone hope that the Guide had stayed, but true to his word the pony-tailed man had left. His bed had not been slept in and all his personal effects were gone. Naomh felt his previous melancholy return, but this was going to be a crucial day so he pushed it to the back of his mind. He told the others.

"The Guide has gone. He will not be coming with us."

There were some genuine gestures of regret. As they set eating breakfast each of them had their own reasons for continuing. To Naomh, the assembly of the APOCRYPHA'I was paramount. Cahill's promise meant that he would not leave him and as always that included Greta. The Prof had thought the Enclave a wonderful place, but its once mysterious allure had become mundane. He was now feeling confined in its finite space. The Clerk had the same sense of adventure. The Lenses had his own reasons and he would be lost without the others. Although, the Engineer was reluctant to leave the regular worship of his God, he knew that Naomh was the only one that would re-establish the faith back in the Anschluss. So he would continue the search and of course that included his brother. However, the Mute had most pressing reasons for getting out of the Enclave as quickly as possible. His natural instinct had taken over and he had drawn the attention of the law. Breakfast was hurried as everyone mulled over their departure. Some of them said goodbyes to Alieem and his family with the promises that they would return soon to resample his fantastic hospitality. None of them believed that likely to happen again. As the silent group of nine walked out into the morning heat, they found a duo of desert-camouflaged vehicles with two of Miriam's friends at the joysticks; Solomon and Haim. The former exchanged a broad smile with the Prof. Naomh and his compatriots, minus one, piled into the waiting transport and made their way along the narrow streets, from where the vehicles went underground to a road system that was only for military use. On the journey, the two drivers told them to change into the military gear in an accessible boot. They quickly dressed into the green uniforms, black boots and sandy helmets. A light at the end of the tunnel revealed a long snaking road that they had to climb to the captured heights of a previous invasion and at the top they found another wall. But all of the passengers were aware that this was not their final destination. Then, their two vehicles joined a large military column of similar types taking soldiers to the front and the first wall, by another tunnel network. None of them, abet the mole had seen such a gathering of military personnel and hardware before. The expectant gang had eventually arrived at what the overawed Engineer fearfully called.

"The gates of hell."

It was gloomy, stifling hot, noisy and incredibly dusty. The dim light was broken by the uncountable orange glows from the furnaces of huge armoured vehicles that could only be built for aggression. When the out of their depth bunch embarked at the designated one, there stood the Gatemaster of Hades himself. It was none other than the Guide; his newly grown forked beard was highly appropriate and he was lounging about as if he was without a care in the World. When the loitering man saw Naomh, he gave him a crooked smile.

"Well man, it's about time you got here. You dudes didn't think I let you wander off on your own. I might be old, but I still have my uses."

To say Naomh was astounded, but pleased was an understatement. Confused, he said to him.

"What are you doing here? You led me to believe that this quest was madness and should be abandoned."

"Well you know man. You should know by now, to do, as I say, not by what I do. Our journey up to now has been mainly uneventful, but it looks like that is about to change."

Naomh gave the pony-tailed man a sarcastic laugh and uttered.

"Shit man, if you think the last few months have been uneventful, then you have a weird sense of humour. Besides, you are scaring me shitless at what's behind those walls."

With a broad grin, the other said.

"Be afraid Naomh; be very afraid. If it were not for your box of tricks, I for one would not set foot out there beyond this wall."

The younger man joined in with his friend from the Amsterdam Contrib's graveyard humour. Both of them laughed confidently and all of a sudden, Naomh's World felt a lot better. The Guide would have been even more happier, if he had realised the enormity of his decision. The Anschluss Spy among their ranks had already reported him to the Chairman and at this precise moment, a snatch team was already been prepared on board the ANS GREGORY LYUBIN. The oblivious van DerKamp was to be lifted for questioning after the others had left the Enclave. Once back in the Anschluss, he would be interrogated by Tell's experts, just to tie up loose ends. Afterwards, orders would be signed for his elimination by the man in his comfortable aviary. If Naomh ever returned to his homeland, he might have never known the fate of the man from the Amsterdam Contrib and he would have lost a great friend and comrade. It had been a close call for the Guide, but the Spy among them was the only one that knew it. The thwarted traitor fathomed silently.

"If the opportunity ever arises, then I will take that chance and do away with the pony tailed poser myself. And I will take great pleasure in taking out that smart Alec."

This one of the LYUBINITES was glad to be leaving the Enclave, the deceiver had told the Anschluss ruler during a covert communication.

"There is too much religion and too many hairy men around here."

Miriam approached Naomh gave him a hug and a quick peck and then all business-like said.

"We have to load up the T0RT-CAM with supplies. None of us know how long we will be out there. Come with me."

The Guide and the Rabbi went with them; the latter had special dietary items to include on the inventory. At that very moment, the body of a young female soldier was found on a lonely part of the wall's ramparts away from the main trust of the invasion. A division of defending reservists who were taking up positions for the upcoming attack had found the contorted form. It was immediately noticed by men who were no medical experts that all the indications pointed to the fact that she had not died a natural death.

"She has been strangled."

The recently deceased had been half-naked and choked with her own pink underwear. Her swollen purple tongue could not speak the name of her killer and her M I S had been missing, assumingly disposed of by her murderer. A tracking device located it outside the outer wall and there was no way of retrieving it. The hardened veterans of the wall's ramparts knew that the unfortunate girl had been murdered by someone from the Enclave. Careful scrutiny of the immediate area showed that no one had infiltrated the wall from the Prophet's side. The body was taken away to be examined later, it was not a priority, there were going to be many dead today and sadly the cause of their demises would easily be known. Strangely, a few days later, it was found after the girl's body was examined that there had been no evidence of a sexual assault. Further analysis had discovered that the deceased female had been at the height of her menstrual cycle and the coroners guessed wrongly that this may have put her perverted killer off from raping her. But then none of the State pathologists knew who her murderer was of his motives. The metallic dog tags on her cold body had identified her as one Rabi Geller or as Naomh's party would have known her before her untimely death, as the female companion of the Mute. A few hours after her killing, the perpetrator was back among them. The Devil with the face of an Angel was his usual self and acting as if nothing out of the ordinary had occurred. As if in the middle of a mundane inventory, he began to scroll letters into a personalised M.I.M. Somehow, he had got his working again, Although it was unable to be used for communication, it could store information and been an individual of no friends, this is what he usually had utilized it for anyway. The unsociable man had no inclination to pass on this knowledge of operation to those he was with. The Lenses believed.

"That weirdo is just stubborn and will not give up on the useless contraption. If I could not work mine, then how could he?"

If anyone came near him while he was looking at the device, he would turn it away from their sight, thus proving the latter's point. The Clerk became too curious and he was harshly warned off. It was as if he had come too near a dog chewing a bone. If all of his companions, bar one could have read the stored information on the device, they would have been horrified. Because it held a list of his victims and Rabi Geller had been the latest and the one thousand, nine hundred and eighty first entry in it. Twenty-five of those men and women had been murdered during his year long stint in the Enclave. All of his victims had been killed at random and until now there had been no trail leading to him. Rabi Geller had been a mistake; his uncontained murderous urge had overpowered him and now anyone investigating her death would find a path leading towards him. But now it did not matter, he would be gone by tomorrow, away from the enforcers of this jurisdiction and he would never pass this way again. The disturbed man sitting amongst the companions allowed himself a gloating smile at his own cleverness and silently uttered.

"I should have been more productive?"

XVIII.

The mustering troops expected nothing but a bitterly fought battle; there would be no quarter given on either side. There was a general consensus among the soldiers of the Enclave.

"After all, we are about to annex more of the land of the Prophet's birthplace. The enemy will do everything to stop us. And if needs be, we too will die for our country."

The Anschluss dissidents thought that an absurd and ridiculous ideal. The Guide scoffed.

"Imagine dying for those bastards who rule us?"

All bar the Spy agreed with those words. Internally Agent XIII was livid and vowed.

"You will all pay dearly for that belief. That I guarantee you."

The discussion faltered as Naomh and his really out of their depth motley crew of exiles became humbled at the sight of the endless lines of armour that lay side by side at their marshalling points under the shadow of the outer wall. Three storeys high, machines of a type unknown to most of them stretched off in each direction as far as the eye could see. The huge thickly armoured tracked contraptions that overawed them were heavy, bulky and muscular objects; totally different from the normal light and streamlined machines of the Anschluss. But then, these were engines of war and had only one set of purposes, death and destruction. The only thing that they had encountered from their homeland that resembled this type of construction was the ANS GREGORY LYUBIN. Agent XIII knew exactly what these aggressive instruments of war were for and so did one other among them; the Guide. The great machines of metal were deployed in a vast underground chamber under the area between the two final walls. To most of the Anschluss company, this was a hellish space of constant noise and activity. The Prof, although keen for new experiences was full of distaste.

"A place full of vulgar sounds and an episode that I could have done without."

Above this artificially created underground space and under the blue-sky lay long stretches of orchards that were a vision of agricultural bliss devoted to living things. Tall cypresses enclosed rectangular plantations of much smaller fruit bearing trees. The Doctor's disciple among them was sympathetic towards the much taller plants. It was a real life metaphor for the way the clusters of their tall buildings looked out over the vast low level skyline of the Anschluss. While underneath these life generating spaces, there lay the nightmare of industrial output whose sole purpose was death and destruction. On the outside of the wall, there was another World that was somewhere in between the other two. It neither teemed with life, but it was littered with other manmade devices faithful in their obligation towards death. Soon this indistinct and unproductive region would mature into another growing place devoted to crop management, but not before a violent birth. Enormous concrete and steel gates spaced every quarter of a kilometre along the long wall blended seamlessly with their supporting structure and provided a link between these two incompatible spaces of darkness and sunlight. These massive doorways would open effortlessly when the command to advance was given. The war machines would then trundle up the ramps and snarl into action. The ten metre high; thirty metre long and ten metre wide "Tanks." as Moshe called them reverberated with frightening roars of animal mimickery. Huge blue coloured six pointed stars, formed by superimposing one inverted triangle upon another were emblazoned proudly on the metal skins of the two hundred and fifty-nine tonne machines. The exiles from the Anschluss were well used to the symbol of the Enclave by now. There were also numbers of a familiar script etched into the hulls in smaller white figures. Miriam's one had the digits 2927 on it. Naomh and the Spy were secretly shocked at that. In the growing climate of excitement and trepidation, none of the others had noticed that it was the year of their leader's birth. Troubled, the bearer of the Alien presence asked the internal voice.

"This is taking the piss, right?"

"It's just a quirk of reality, that's all."

"Some coincidence?"

Composing himself, Naomh returned his scrutiny to the rest of the war machine. The entire four sides of the Tanks bristled with gun bores of various circumferences and lengths. The mechanical machines were a much larger and highly sophisticated image of the first such contraptions that appeared on the battlefields of Western Europe nearly a thousand years ago. As with their inferior predecessors, these armoured vehicles would inspire the same terror among their enemy. Anyone in consistent contact with the machines wore heavy overalls and ventilation masks. The smell from their noxious discharges was overpowering. The Tanks used a cocktail of chemicals and high-octane fuels to power their monstrous jet powered engines. Huge track assemblies studded with metal nodules gave the machines momentum. The crews of the huge armada of the armoured mechanised vehicles which had reinforced sections of a new temporary wall attached to the fronts and backs of their hulls by robust metal arms waited in excitement for the order to board. The fifteen metre high temporary wall sections were constructed from the toughest high-grade chromium steel and were easily more durable that the Tanks hulls that were manufactured with plastic polymer coated steel. These payloads were a metre thick and gave impenetrable protection to the front and back of the armoured vehicles while they were still attached. Jutting and swivelling turrets on the sides and tops of the barrier holders contained revolving cannons that could vector their killing fire around and above the domineering steel wall sections. The tallest person in the thronged assembling area barely measured to less than a fifth of the height of the metal behemoths. Up this close, the serrated teeth on the tracks looked downright vicious and it was easily understood the damage they would do to unprotected flesh. It was impossible for Naomh and his friends to tell which was the front and which was the back of the machines. The curious Engineer asked for more details. The lean bearded Haim took off his face protection and replied as if he was reciting out of a technical manual.

"These Tanks are of the Dian class, named after a legendary Enclave leader; those of their crew call them the Wall-makers. Complex hydraulics provide their muscle. The Tanks have two steering columns which can be reversed at will, so either side of her can be the front or back. Each vehicle weighs over two hundred and fifty metric tonnes and can reach a maximum speed of ninety kilometres an hour. Most of the large guns are of a 200-mm calibre and have a rapid rate of fire of a hundred rounds a minute. When the Wall-makers reach their allotted position, the front wall section is put in place and then the huge metal arms arc over the Tank with the rear piece and this is slotted on top of the first piece."

Moshe interjected.

"In other words either side can be the front or back."

The methodical man from the Anschluss was highly impressed. Haim also explained.

"Each Tank has several layers of metal armour with thin sheets of plastic explosive sandwiched in between them. When a projectile hits each layer of this reactive armour, the sheet of plastic explosive will detonate and render the lethal force of incoming fire ineffective. But enough direct hits would deplete the protective armour and destroy any Tank, for these heavily armoured vehicles are not indestructible."

Seren (Company Commander.) Miriam Meir commanded one of the vehicles and told them.

"My crew and I are part of a division that is known as the Holders of the line. We like the rest of the army have been mobilising for months in preparation for the big push."

When all of the Anschluss crew had met her a few hours ago, they were amazed at the transformation in her. Her auburn hair was tied up in a bun by a neat green band and a slender microphone was projecting from her mouth. She looked every millimetre the company commander. Even her new uniform was worn with the arrogance of one used to command. A doubtful Naomh wondered.

"Do I really know Miriam at all?"

Still he was aware that she was a soldier and during the time spent together, he had missed her when she had to report to do her military service. These frequent and regular separations hurt him deeply; sometimes she was gone for a week or more at a time. He would spend those absences drinking with his friends and renewing his bond with them. But the highlights of his stay in the Enclave were her anticipated returns and their first moments of contact after her release from duty. Early that morning, just before they had been collected, he had approached Cahill. He had something to tell him and he prepared for conflict. He asked his friend.

"Would you have a problem if Miriam became my second in command during this next stage of the journey?"

Although slightly hurt, his friend agreed when Naomh told him his reasons.

"It will cause less tension between our two different groups. It will give her people a reference of command."

He made his best friend his third in command, above the Guide and this placated him. Rory's old friend had no complaints; he recognised the wise decision of an emerging leader. Now that Naomh saw the solider that his lover was, he was positive that the correct choice had been made. They were also told by Miriam that their other companions had military ranks as well.

"The Rabbi is a Rasar (Master Sergeant.), Solomon is a Rav Turai (Corporal.) and the rest of my crew are Turai (Privates.)."

As she finished with the new introductions, an automated cart pulled up alongside them. It was loaded with bulky protection gear. Rav Turai Solomon spoke to the uninitiated.

"Put these on. It is standard Tank gear and once you are covered, it will allay any suspicions. Each of you will look like a member of a Tank crew as you board."

Following their comrades from the Enclave's lead, they began to dress in the supplied uniforms. Large heavy padded jackets that even fitted the Persuader were put on. Sections of plastic body armour that doubly protected more vulnerable areas covered their initial layers. The main piece of the manufactured protection covered the trunk and legs. Fire resistant gloves and boots finished off the ensemble. Extremely durable laminated helmets and equally tough emerald plastic visors protected the head and face. The military head coverings were also emblazoned with the five pointed star and had micro-phones embedded in their reinforced layers. These communication devices were a very basic version of their non-functioning M.I.M's. Each helmet had the name of its owner, in Enclave script incorporated on its helm. When told that, the curious Clerk asked.

"What is my name?"

"Shlomo Olmert." Beersheba translated and added with a smirk.

"A former boyfriend of mine."

"Nice one." Replied the butt of her joke with a broad smile.

None of the others were as inquisitive as him; they were more interested in the uniform itself. This protective gear would take a lot of punishment before it allowed its wearer to be seriously injured. It would not save them from large projectiles or close range fire of a heavy calibre. Surprisingly, the newly donned apparel were of an olive green colour that would give little camouflage out in the barren wasteland of no man's land. The military clothing was also baggy and lined with numerous pockets. Miriam, her crew and now their Anschluss compliment also had a red beret tucked into one of their breast pouches. The Prof who had seen the outlay of the land beyond the outer wall questioned the Serene.

"Why green uniforms? It is all brown desert and scrub out there."

She lovingly caressed the metal of her command and replied.

"The colour is mainly because of tradition; our armies had always worn this shade of green. And even if anybody is caught outside their vehicle, there is nowhere to hide or is there a chance of survival. So a desert-camouflaged uniform is irrelevant. That is also why we also carry no survival equipment in these pockets. If you have to leave the protection of "RUTH", then you are dead."

She grabbed her empty pockets and squeezed them for emphasis.

"What is this thing, RUTH?" Asked a puzzled Lenses.

The sultry Haim explained.

"It's our name for our Tank; it is named after, the Rabbi's mother. All of the war machines are given a name by their crews and it is normally female. Out there in the middle of the action, RUTH will be more important to her crew than a member of their own family. Her protective hull, like the womb of your mother will be all that remains between you and death. So it is only right to give her a name."

The huge machines by contrast to the green uniforms were the colour of the outside desert; a blend of dry browns, tans and yellows. Each vehicle bristled with narrow gun ports that rose above the marble shaded metallic wall sections that were attached to their front and back chassises. Unstoppable mammoth sized tracks supported their main frames which were just as lethal as their gun ports. Anything, whether it be flesh or metal would be crushed or slashed into pieces, if it went under those whirring chains of linked metal. The armoured vehicles were the products of immense underground assembly lines and an army of the Enclave's people toiled twenty-fours a day in eight hour shifts to produce these frightening machines of aggression. Most of the raw materials to create these monsters of war came from the Anschluss. From the steel ingots and even the huge induction welders that fabricated metal parts, down to the sophisticated software that ran all of their systems. What the LYUBINITES got in return for this vast investment of hardware was anybody's guess, but it was rumoured it was a sweetener to prevent the Enclave from using its vast nuclear stockpile against its hostile neighbours. If the Chairman had ambitions to expand his territory to the south east, then a radiated wasteland was not an option. The admiring group from the Anschluss and especially the Engineer were distracted from their appreciating scrutiny as they heard through ventilation ducts, the roar of another wave of low flying warplanes from above. Their supersonic signature crowding out the brutal tune of the revving armour as the flying discs flew off to clear any visible enemy positions from the immediate vicinity. The ground shook with the sound of massive explosions, this percussion of distant thuds had been going on all morning. With their missions finally completed the warplanes returned minutes later to refuel, rearm and revisit their targets. This constant bombing from the air insured that the Enclave invaders would meet depleted and unorganised resistance during their invasion. The supersonic bangs of the aircraft had just alerted Naomh to a new sense. The bearer of the APOCRYPHA'I had just discovered another of his heightened senses. With the two parts Mescal/Amulet, the changing being had now acquired a greatly enhanced Doppler effect and knew instantly whether a warplane was moving away or coming towards him, just from the sound it was making. On a different subject, the Engineer had a question about the loud rumbling noises of the Tanks.

"Why are they so noisy? These machines could easily be made to run silent, so the enemy could be surprised if they did not hear them coming."

Again, Haim answered.

"The reason the Tanks are so loud is because it is to instil fear in the Prophet's forces. Their roar will increase out there. When the entrenched enemy armies hear RUTH and her friends rumbling towards them and shaking the very ground itself, it scares the living daylights out of them. Besides that, our advancing salient would already be detected by their surveillance devices, even if we did run silent."

"So you use their own fear against them." Worked out Greta.

"Yes, that is so." Agreed Haim.

The plan Naomh and Miriam had concocted to get them to the other side of the Prophet's lines appeared sound. That is to someone who knew that they had the use of advanced technology of the TORT-CAM. Their design took full advantage of the blitzkrieg tactic the army of the Enclave had prepared. After the sustained and prolonged bombardment from the air and from the deadly gun ports of the Enclave's wall, the mechanised forces would race out in a many pronged attack. While the enemy was in disarray from the barrage, the mechanised forces would form a temporary barrier of steel that would move rapidly to encompass a new area of occupation. This annexed land would measure a fifty-kilometre long strip by an eight kilometres wide band that would run adjacent to the most outwardly points of the outer wall and fill in the bulge between them. Moshe told them.

"It will take approximately five thousand Tanks to form the barrier. This will be our most ambitious attack yet. There will be three initial lines at the vanguard totalling fifteen thousand Tanks and one hundred and five thousand crew."

The new encircled area of four hundred square kilometres would be designated as the "Transit Sector.". This defensive zone would then be held against any counter attack from the opposition forces until a new and more solid wall was constructed. Then over the next few years, huge sections of the new barrier would be hauled out by gigantic armoured tower cranes and put in place. Naomh had questioned Miriam about the reason for a daylight attack, when a night assault would achieve fewer casualties. Her reply was in the form of a scorn.

"We are not cowards. Our forces will face the enemy with the Sun in our eyes and the wall at our back and sides; there is no hiding out there. If a Tank is destroyed, then more than likely, so will its crew. It will be a case of do or die."

In the past these temporary barriers had to be defended against fanatical resistance and there was little optimism that it would be any different this time around. For under the hills in the distance, just out of visual range lay vast manmade bunker complexes that hid a vast army of the enemy. This was from where the soldiers of the Prophet who called themselves Mujahedeen launched their repeated attacks against the Enclave. The people of the tribes only found out about these tunnels when over eight centuries ago their armies launched their fifth expansion eastwards into lands ruled by the Hashemite Kingdom of Jordan. This invasion was achieved by overwhelming military might and the transit sector was secured easily enough as had been the case with the previous instances. Or so their generals thought. During the first night of occupation, countless soldiers of the Prophet poured out from the hidden underground bases in the new transit sector and engaged the entire invading army. Vicious close quarter fighting, including hand to hand took heavy tolls of the attackers and defenders alike. The Generals behind the fourth wall had no choice but to call in a massive air strike that lasted a full week until all in the trap were destroyed. That included friend and foe. Very few of their own forces made it back to their original lines. The awful price paid for that expansion had a subvene outcome, for the terrible loss of life incurred eased the pressure on the living space within the Enclave for over a hundred years. So no further expansion was needed for that century. But as the population increased again, its thirst for more land grew and further expansions were made. Its craving for new living space would never be quenched and it was now time for another enlargement. Naomh kept a thought to himself.

"I'm not sure that it is coincidental that our group happened to arrive in the Enclave at this precise moment in time? It would be at least another fifty years; depending on the outcome of this one, before the next onslaught."

The internal presence had no views on the matter. The Rabbi ruefully explained.

"The people of Zion cannot not loose either way, for if this seizure of land is successful, then the Enclave gains a new sector. And if we fail, then

the Human losses will ease the pressure for more living space."

Naomh was appalled at his cold logic, but he kept silent as this was not his fight.

"This major outbreak of hostilities is only a side-show to us, as it serves our purpose in getting into the Arab lands undetected."

Still, from what he was told by Miriam and her friends, his former rulers had made it their business. To him, this was more proof of the callous interference of the Anchluss in other Nation's affairs. Realisation came in an instant of awareness as he made the next progression in logic.

"They supply both sides in this conflict to keep them at each other's throats, so they can continue their evil designs unhindered."

New hate for his old foe suffused in him at their casual meddling of their two southern neighbours. He promised to himself.

"Soon the callous rulers of the Anschluss will reap the harvest of all of their misdeeds."

As the clairvoyant in him finished those words of intent, the engines of the Tanks were powered down in preparation for the final ignition, when the machines would speed out into no man's land. All was not quite though; a hive sound of voices mingled with the sound of the overhead warplanes making their sorties still filtered down to where the invading force was gathered. Naomh began to explain the final plan that was concocted by himself, Miriam and the voice within the amulet.

"It is simple in detail, but it relies on perfect timing. We will be aboard RUTH at the vanguard of the huge invading force. Our vehicle will continue on passed the limits of the new transit sector when all the other Tanks halt. Seren Miriam will ignore any orders to pull back. And when our armoured vehicle is out a reasonable distance from the new barrier, Haim and Solomon will then release a few harmless smoke canisters to make it appear as if we had been hit. When the concealing vapour is at its fullest, then the two men will throw out a few lifelike dummies to make it look like the crew leapt from the apparent burning vehicle. Under the guise of been hit and under the cover of the billowing fumes, our squad will pile into the mini TORT-CAMLETS while we are still inside the Tank. Then we will wait for a timer to set off the explosives that Moshe has planted to blow the armoured vehicle to smithereens. The seventeen of us will then sit out the battle until it is deemed safe and then the mobile invisible light shields will move through the outlying verges of the confused lines of the Prophet's army."

Miriam continued for him.

"Before any of us leave the haven of the TORT-CAMLETS, each one of us will dress ourselves in the enemy's uniforms. Then we can mingle with the rank and file of the Prophets forces once we have left the safety of our indestructible havens. We will be ignored in the confusion and as false Mujahedeen; we will retreat behind our enemy's lines. But before that,

each concealed group will wait until everybody has resumed contact and gathered together. Then, our re-assembled troop can set off together to locate the third piece of the APOCRYPHA'I."

"Simple as that man." Uttered the sarcastic Guide.

Naomh was confident of success. Even though, he knew nothing of the lands beyond the wall; he would know which direction to go in. The voice within was still guiding him. A deafening silence ensued, the warplanes had finished their tasks and the sudden quiet was disturbing. For the last few weeks of their time in the Enclave, they had to endure the constant noise of the warplanes overhead. But now there was a maddening silence. Then, the hush ended just as abruptly, a siren sounded, stretching through the surreal tranquillity. It was time to board the waiting throng of armoured vehicles. Anticipation gripped the Anchluss outsiders; this was going to be an unique experience. Other crews approached rising platforms and mounted them like well-rehearsed band marchers while Naomh and his people were slightly out of step. They were not conspicuous as other crews still remained on the ground and those that did now stood to attention. Then loudspeakers placed above every mechanised vehicle broadcasted the same encouragement from the Chief Rabbi. (Who at this time in history was also the Enclave's President.).

"Soldiers of the barrier. The day has arrived to make Israel proud. This is going to be a tough fight, for once again we are about to seize more of the land of the Prophet's birthplace. They, our hereditary enemy will fight with the last drop of their blood and so shall we."

There was a great roar, the President continued.

"You, our sons and daughters will venture out into hostile land and hold the line. Of that I have no doubt. For the people of Zion and the Tribes, do your duty. Victory for God and his people. We salute you. Now strike while the iron is hot."

Then as the vocal and passionate voice of the President faded, patriotic music in the Enclave tradition filled the airwaves in each attacking vehicle and in every radio receiver in the mobilized forces. The listening Tank crews were full of enthusiastic expectancy and took their private oaths. Spirits among the well-trained crews were at a high, death or failure was not an option. Today, was the day of the big push, the first in seventy years, the only one in a generation. All around the Enclave, its people stopped their everyday actives, gathered around information units and held their breath. Naomh and his friends were also holding their breaths, even though the RE-INSTATOR'S were veterans of many a small-scale skirmish, none of them had ever taken part in a battle on this scale and that included the false one among them. The out of their depth Anschluss clique were told by the machines commander.

"Take up positions inside the vehicle and do not to interfere in its operation. You are to sit tight until it is time to put the plan into action."

Then, there came a loud sound of curved horns. Miriam must have got some kind of order through her ear piece during the wailing; she turned to her enlarged company and said.

"The shofars have sounded. Let's go."

The Guide added.

"Ok people, let's boogie."

"What?" Asked Shoshanna.

"Let's rock." Amended the speaker.

She understood that.

"Oh."

The only way into the foreboding war-machine was by a hatchway that lay two metres above its huge tracks. A mechanical rising platform connected to the Tank by thick hydraulic arms lay flat on the ground. All who were about to enter the war machine, stood on it and a press of a button caused it to rise with its Human cargo. When it reached the level of the hatchway, they stepped off and entered the foreboding space of the machine's innards. Another push of a button and the platform would become the door as it filled in the gaping hole in the vehicle's side. For the platform would become an integral part of the Tank's hull. When RUTH'S unusually numbered crew had boarded the war machine, everybody sat in their allocated places; Haim showed the unfamiliar Anschluss people where to sit. Those familiar with the procedure strapped each of them in as the heavy metallic door of the vehicle groaned noisily shut. It slammed closed with a sudden bang and a dread feeling of confinement washed over them. The Guide felt like he had been interred in a metal coffin, he decided not to utter his misgivings to the rest of his compatriots. As none of them had any idea what a coffin was. When one died in the Anschluss, the body was wrapped in a sterilised celo-wrap after the cause of death was established. Autopsies were completed at the death scene. From there, the deceased was taken straight to the body re-cycling plants, where their remains had the unfortunate pleasure of meeting the Mute and his ilk. The metal machine of war's hatch had clanked shut and sealed them in tighter than the lid of a steel drum. Among the hundred thousand plus crewmembers from the Enclave, some of the interred were of a similar mind to the Guide and prayed that they had not also entered an iron tomb. As lights began to flicker on, the unfamiliar bunch of Naomh's gang found that the inside of RUTH was so different from the interior of the TORT-CAM. Firstly, there was the overpowering heady smell of engine oil. It also stank of other lubricants and hydraulic fluids too, the spaces inside their invisible shield were odourless. The machine had no curved slender walls of soft blue light, but harsh functional angled lines of welded metal that encompassed a dank electrical lit mechanical world of switches and display lights. Magazine loaders that held vast amounts of miniature shells were fed to the twenty guns of varying calibre by long belts that served as the Tanks offensive and defensive firepower. The small size of the shells was deceptive as each individual compact explosive round packed an almighty punch equivalent to two hundred kilos of T N T. These high velocity shells would penetrate through any armour of the Prophet's armies with devastating consequences. Sensing Naomh's discomfort, Miriam came over to her strapped in lover and squeezed his hand. She smiled through her battle visor. He felt a weight lift, because of the confidence his woman displayed. His lover regretfully let her grasp go and moved to her battle station. The rest of her legitimate crew followed suit and strapped their new comrades into a row of seats intended for soldiers. Her genuine compliment took up positions like the cogs of a well-oiled machine. Seren Miriam Meir sat at the helm, where she would give the commands. Turai Haim Golan was the driver and he powered up the massive jet engines. Rasar Aaron Kalwensixi was the navigator/radio officer and he done a brief check of his array. Turai Moshe Stern was the shell loader; Rav Turai Solomon David and ordinary Turai's Shoshanna Fine and Beersheba Goldstein clasped heavy-duty joysticks as they took up various weapons positions. The automated voice of Ruth's computer commanded them to prepare its systems and make ready for the order to advance through temporary openings that would soon appear in the wall. The Anchluss members of the crew fidgeted as they waited in trepidation, mostly from inactivity and a feeling of been surplus to requirements. Cahill had muttered when he heard the artificial voice.

"I hope that's not the real voice of the Rabbi's mother."

Some of his friends tittered nervously. Their uneasy demeanour was in total contrast to the cool professionalism of the Serene's crew with their specific tasks to do. The accustomed commander of Ruth ordered everyone to put on headphones. Those now under her directive complied. The Spy was grudgingly impressed with Miriam's voice of command. There was a crackle in the radio reception and a voice of decree gave the order to advance over the airwaves. Outside the hulls, powerful gears whirred into action and the two hundred tonne gate sections of the outer wall moved swiftly away from their apparently seamless joints. Elaborate ropes of metal strand wires connected the gears and trundles of the gates moving apparatus to a counter box in a sophisticated mimicry of the ancient Trebuchets that had once tried to knock down the walls of the Enclave's Holy City. The huge counter levers moved the gate sections fluidly over the growling Tanks. In an instant, the mechanised killing machines roared into action, the noise was deafening as the pent up energy of a hundred thousand machines was released. The power of each two hundred litre engine shook the ground as the vast armada of machines sped through the gaps in the outer wall. RUTH was the foremost vehicle in the vanguard of the massive motorised invasion force that swept out into enemy range. As the armada of war broke from the three sides of the outer wall, the clanking and cranking of the shaking machine rattled their teeth to the bone. It seemed like an unstoppable tsunami of metal as the propelled pile of armour churned up all the detritus from previous attacks that lay strewn in the killing zone. Both machine and Human parts were ground into fragments of dust from the massive weight of the heavily armoured vehicles and serrated tracks. It had rained the night before and the stampede of iron churned the mixture into the beginnings of fertilisation for the new land. It was a good omen and a fine start for the eventual orchards that would spring up in the near future. History was been written for another generation of Enclave children. The population of the encircled nation were witnessing the Genesis of a new sector within the expanding nation and in the years to come, a person would be asked.

"Where were you on that day?"

This attack would become such a landmark event in Enclave mythology that a person's life could be marked from this event. Exhilaration gripped the crews of the invasion force as wave after wave of heavy armour poured out from the gaps in the outer wall and raced to form the new temporary barrier some twelve kilometres distant. All along the salient, the "Tanks" came out from the gates in rows of five. Behind the first wave, came another five, behind them another five and so on. The war machines poured out from the gates in an endless stream of congested metal. The broad swathe of armour became an unstoppable force. As the flowing metal contrivances broke further from the total security of the wall, the wave of machines behind the vanguards swept out to the left and to the right of the leading vehicles, to form lines of ten then twenty, thirty, forty and so on. The alternating Tanks began to fill in the gaps between each machine of war. Then, there was one line of a moving steel wall rushing out to fill in the salient perimeter. The co-ordinates of the new barrier now lay eight kilometres away from the advancing metal hordes position. There had been no response from the opposing army, but each Tank member knew.

"It will only be a matter of moments."

Deep down under a distant smoke covered ridge, the army of the Prophet had soaked up the rain of death that fell from the skies. The waiting force remained relatively intact inside armoured bunkers that lay deep down under the protective rock of the embankment. The airborne barrage had little effect on the Prophet's forces; anti-aircraft fire had even taken down a number of the flying discs. The combined Arab armies had been busy over the years since the last Enclave expansion. Eventually, its generals accepted that their enemy had total dominion of the skies, so they went back to an old strategy. The people of the Prophet built an underground line of defences that ran the entire length of the Enclave's wall. Secret re-enforced concrete tunnels that originated ninety-eight kilometres away, in urban areas deep in the Prophet's land connected the underground defences to a constant supply route. An immense battery of anti-aircraft weapons kept inquisitive Enclave planes away from discovering the tunnels entrances. Before Tell's investiture, the Anschluss satellites had located the earthworks, but in their duplicity, those in charge failed to tell their Enclave allies.

"They will come to us like whipped dogs."

Then in a massive feat of engineering, railway lines were constructed in the tunnels and supplies of men, weapons and munitions were brought up to the front lines. Out here, and only kilometres from the outer wall of the Zionists, vertical shafts were cut to the surface. Gun platforms, housing multi-barrelled artillery pieces and their crews would shoot to the surface via these vertical tunnels. Propelled by powerful jets built into their bases, the gun platforms would rise rapidly. Then, their gunners would catch the enemies Tanks out in the open and obliterate them. The Prophet's generals watched through periscopes that had replaced those optical devices that were destroyed by the bombardment and studied the line of armour that faced them in silent affronted rage. There was a shared loathing of those machines. Because of the Enclave's overwhelming air superiority had left them with little aircraft and a non-existent airforce, they had to confront these dread machines with inadequate ground forces. The ordinary soldier was in fear of these metal monsters with their narrow gun slits with extendable metal strips that protected the gun crews from offensive fire. The soldiers of the Prophet never got to see the faces of the enemy; thus the machines became dehumanised and infused great terror in their forces. To make matters worse, the ground shook with the thunder of the advancing armour and this unnerved the soldier's even more. The ultimate terror came when their heavy guns fired and the shells ploughed men apart. This inspired greater fear as the victim's blood and body parts showered surviving comrades. But now they were ready for their enemy, concentrated fire and geographical intelligence had shown them where to mass their forces. Just in case this assault was a devious ruse, they still spread out the majority of their armies along the entire length of the hated wall. The eerie silence within their own bunkers only lasted a few eternal moments and then the Prophet's generals gave the order. Seconds later, there came a deafening whistling sound as volley after volley of high explosive rained down and slammed into the advancing metal line. Thousands of plumes of black oil smoke filled the landscape like uncountable whirling Dervishes. As the smoke of war enlarged in chemical combustion, visibility of the battlefield with the naked eye vanished. Both sides reverted to artificial devices. The invading line stood firm as it soaked up the rain of high explosive. A similar order was given on the Enclave's side and as one the entire armada of defensive armour responded in a synchronised broadside. Inside every Tank, well-trained gunner's let the automated firing systems take over as electric cannons whirled and responded. The outgoing arcs of fire flowed around and over the attached wall sections. Inside RUTH, Naomh and his company watched in fascination as the mechanical loaders clicked into action. Empty shell cases began to fill up the vehicle at an alarming rate as each red-hot shiny compact metal case flew from oiled breaches. Moshe shovelled the ejected shells into large steel buckets of cooling liquid and the steam for this effort began to fill the confines of the Tank. Reacting to the condensing mist, a ventilation system kicked in and sucked the fog to storage bins under the floor. These spent rounds would be jettisoned later when it was safe to do so. In this engine of war, however, it would be done soon; to make it seem that it had been irreparably damaged. Every vehicle in the entire circle of metal fired its hardware simultaneously into where their weapon systems were indicating where the enemy fire originated. The largest bores swivelled to a ninety degree angle and arced downwards until they were level with the wall section, then the adaptable hardware rose again and the manoeuvre was repeated. The falling barrel had the devastating effect of many rounds impacting on a target at the same time. The rolling fire was joined by every artillery piece that lined the great wall. The entire ridge in front of them was decimated and vanished in a wall of smoke and fire. Visibility was further clouded as the dust and rock from hundreds of thousands of explosions filled the very air of the battlefield. But the answering symphony of death barely changed its response and a deluge of high explosive still rained down on the armoured line. RUTH began to be buffeted with striking shells detonating against her armoured protection. To her unfamiliar occupants, it felt like they were back on the Anschluss Dreadnaut and moving through heavy seas. Gun platforms were been destroyed and men were dying in the mist of this downpour of high explosive and shrapnel. The Enclave forces suffered losses too. The Prophet's gunners were now using night sensitive equipment since their targets were obscured by the smoke and dust. Inside Miriam's vehicle it now felt that they were under a corrugated sheet of metal that was bearing the full front of a tropical hailstorm. The exploding armour and tough metal skin of most of the Tanks were holding. All the machines in the line were taking an almighty pounding, but their crews prayed their layers of protection would hold until the wall sections were lowered into place. Inside RUTH, the Prof felt an almighty thirst, his lips had become dry and his throat was raw, so he clamoured for water. Solomon handed him a container. The grateful man gulped the cool liquid down. Then a direct hit took out their weakest point, the imbedded cameras of the metal hull. The crew of Miriam's command now had to rely on the limited vision of the more primitive armoured glass ports. Inside the battered machine, the heat began to rise. The Prof's throat became even more parched and then all of a sudden Miriam cursed through her microphone.

"This is going to get nastier than any of us thought. Their forces are

too well dug in. They have learnt a lot since the last invasion. We better get moving."

Infused with high-octane aggression, she ordered Haim.

"Push the engines to their limits."

Her driver complied and he ignited the war machines back up engines. RUTH moved ahead of the converging line and motored towards the Prophet's lines. High above on the outer wall in their observation towers, the watching Generals could hardly believe their monitoring equipment when a single vehicle broke formation and headed towards enemy lines. Zig-zagging as it accelerated towards the ridge where the vast majority of the Prophets forces were dug in, it raced to certain doom. All across the line, a number of Tanks responded to the manoeuvre and other mechanised vehicles followed suit and joined in on the crazy attack. They had passed the co-ordinates of the new line. But thankfully most of the well-trained drivers and rigid commanders obeyed their orders to hold the line. Engines ceased their turning and the rumble of advancing thunder abated considerably. Quickly, they began to form an unbreakable metal line between the two outer points of the curving salient. In all, about twelve-hundred crews formed a three-kilometre phalanx behind the first vehicle that broke formation. Inside the leading vehicle Beersheba looking through a rear view lens, told Miriam.

"Serene Meir, some of the other crews are following in our wake. They have not held the line."

RUTH'S commander felt utter despair.

"Those trailing crews will be decimated when their armoured vehicles get closer in range to the enemy guns. The nearer they get, the more penetrating power the enemy's guns will have. I cannot break radio silence to warn them as it will give the game away."

Miriam felt like a fraud.

"Those brave crews do not know about the protection afforded to us."

Incoming fire arced over the wall sections and once again found their hull. Suddenly, there were harsh popping noises. White hot metal fragments cooled to glowing splinters as the metal fragments penetrated the armoured skin of the vehicle. Most missed the occupants by a hair's breadth but one hit Cahill's gloved hand and scalded him. His body armour had failed to stop the impact of the white-hot splinter entirely. The injured man pulled off the offending gauntlet and cursed as an angry red welt caused him extreme discomfort.

"That's going to hurt later."

Oddly, the blood that trickled down his injured hand felt cool compared to the furnace heat of Ruth's inside. Through the pain, Cahill guessed correctly that he was going to be left with a nasty scar. He was extremely lucky as his body armour probably prevented the shrapnel from taking his hand off completely. Dusty pinpricks of light flashed through the metal skin of the Tank. Both her real crew and its adopted company did not feel so protected now as the jagged holes let the outside in. Their Serene insisted.

"Naomh, Put your plan into effect immediately. If we wait any longer, we will be dead or seriously injured before we can get into the TORT-CAMLETS. My baby is not going to take much more of this pounding. So all non-essential personal pile into the shields now."

It was her command and she expected to be obeyed. Another voice enforced her will.

"You heard her, get into the dobbers, dudes."

The Enclave crew released their safety harnesses and then did the same for their comrades from the Anschluss. It was now time to put the well-practised drills carried out on the farms and firing ranges into action. The crews of the seven bubbles had already been decided. Miriam and Naomh would share the final one. Activated wristbands revealed each designated sphere and all within the Tank piled into their assigned TORT-CAMLET'S until her commander was the last at its controls. She took one final look at her dependable machine and went to join Naomh in his unseen shield. Like him, she had removed her headgear and sweat began to drip down her brow. Her second half had not moved into the globe of invisibility and protection yet, he was waiting for her. As she came to him, he pressed the correct sequence on his wrist band, and the lifesaving piece of technology instantly appeared alongside them. The soldier from the Enclave found herself instantly in a haven of coolness; tranquil red and orange tiles replaced the hell of her former command. There was an astonishing silence away from the furnace and deafening noise of a moment before. Her sweaty forehead dried right away. She did not even see, feel or hear the machine that had been part of her life for five years been blown to smithereens. Her dependable Ruth was pulverised and went out with an almighty bang as solid steel was turned into a shower of hot iron fragments. Minutes after her destruction, Mudassar Hassan's rocket crew stuck their heads out of their buried fox hole. A damaged tank swivelled towards them; the enemy were totally oblivious to them. His men sighted their armoured piecing weapon at the sitting target. The Syrian gave the command to launch, at the same time thinking of the glory that would be bestowed on them. His battery of missiles streaked towards the war machine to the shouts of.

"Allahu Akbar."

Incredibly, the deadly explosive heads vectored off in another direction and missed their target completely. Hassan looked through his laser sights in disbelief; there was nothing to be seen. The attempted strike had drawn the attention of the targeted Tanks automated systems and Mudassar's crew got their second wish, they achieved martyrdom in a bust of Hell's brimstone. What none of the dead men knew was that the missiles had

457

struck one of the invisible TORT-CAMLETS and none of the occupants had been harmed; in fact they were totally oblivious to the strike. The few hundred other Tank crews who joined the charge had not been so lucky; their armoured vehicles ran into the wall of fire and most of them brewed up in temperatures of 3,000 degrees centigrade. All of the crews, to a man and woman of those flaming machines perished in a burst of incineration. Back in the observation tower that contained the Enclave's War room, the overall Commander of the operation of the seizure of land swivelled in his "Battle chair." and stared at the icons on the battle computer in disbelief as the cohesiveness of his attacking formation was broken. Aluf Abner Kaufmanns was the supreme commander of the Enclaves assault forces, a position achieved from his tactical brilliance and his battle-plan had been altered. An artificial mechanical eye filled his empty right-sided socket. The career soldier had lost it and his two legs from a fluke event. Years before as a lowly Turai, he had been jogging in the agricultural sector between the two final walls when a shell had come over the barrier. In the middle of the onion fields, he was sure that his life had ended. All that Kaufmanns remembered was a blinding flash, incredible pain and oblivion; but he had lived. That brief bombardment was very rare; it had been instigated by a solider of the Prophet who had lost it. The hidden army knew that such a circumstance would reveal their positions and be subsequently destroyed and that was the result in this case. The maimed Enclave solider had been only twenty-five. Refusing to believe his military career was finished, the strong willed man began to study tactics. His superiors realised that Kaufmanns had a God given gift for organisation and strategy. He rose through the ranks and at young age of thirty-nine, he was the supreme commander of the Enclaves offensive forces. Realising instantly that his formation had broken up, Aluf Kaufmanns ordered more Tanks held in reserve to speed out and plug the holes left by the still advancing machines. The Commander punched up the number of the first machine that had broken ranks and it showed him who the crew of the itinerant vehicle was. The face staring at the screen was astonished.

"That crew was among the most efficient and most decorated company that our army possessed. I have even handed out medals to them myself. Still, there were reports of them in the company of Anschluss spies. And the secret service had kept a watch on them. This is not kosher." Kaufmanns told one of his junior adjutants.

There was more going on than his rank allowed him to know. He hoped it would not affect the seizure of more living space. The Commander was a student of history and the military planner found it ironic that his people were mimicking the strategies of their mortal foes from the past.

"Such are the repetitions of history."

He returned to the courageous, but futile charge of the breakaway group and then the inevitable happened. All of the Prophets guns zeroed in on the unfortunate vehicles and they vanished in a cloud of destruction. Well aimed rounds ploughed into the armoured vehicles sides and even cleared the attached wall sections and found the tops. Turrets were torn off by the ferocity of the fire; their smashed and broken operators never knowing how they died. Pieces of machines flew into the sky, only to fall back in a metal parody of long needed precipitation. Then, the Commander shook his head in admiration and exclaimed.

"The majority of the enemy forces artillery have targeted the breakaway group and have ignored the majority of the wall constructing machines. This has given them precious time to complete the artificial barrier."

He watched as the other vehicles in the armoured brigade crews released their wall sections which slid into each other and locked into place between the northern and southern walls. Taking less fire, the powerful hydraulic arms then placed the rear sections of wall on top of the sections of barrier that were already in place. The rest of the Tanks that had held the line were now solidly behind the impenetrable wall of steel and safe from harm. Incredibly some of the ones that had broken formation and received the concentrated fire from the enemy had survived. These burning machines managed to limp back towards their own lines, but they were now on the wrong side of the barrier. A helpless Aluf Kaufmanns watched as each armoured vehicle was picked off one by one by the duped Prophet's gunners. In contrast, the outer side of the temporary metal wall became a death trap for those brave crews. The destroyed war machines billowed up in plumes of black acrid smoke. The charging group had been an insult that the Prophet's army did not dare ignore, but their rashness cost them dear in lost territory. Now a new wall was completed and the Enclaves Tanks had detached themselves from their wall sections and had formed a formidable obstacle. Realising their error, the Prophet's artillery concentrated on the metal wall and millions of tracer rounds slammed in the new barrier. Impact rounds sparked off the temporary wall like flies been zapped in a blue light incinerator and had as little effect. Different types of vehicles now filtered out from the gaps in the Enclave wall and from pre-arranged assembly areas, these new types of machines launched millions of mines into the new killing zone. These huge and even more heavily armoured Tanks were mounted with electric catapults that were fed with assembly lines of mines. This grim planting brought the seeds of death to lay on the desecrated soil, waiting for their harvest of death and destruction. Great anger broke out among the Mujhadeen as they beheld the completed barrier. An ant-like charge of men and vehicles alike poured out into the open from their defensive positions and charged towards the temporary wall in an effort to remove that dishonourable stain from the Prophet's land. (By their bare hands if necessary.). This charge of frustration was the ultimate folly. The overall commander of the Prophet's forces, Sheikh Ben Saudi Mohammad was filled with dismay as his sections of his converging army were shattered in the mined plain. The Enclave's Generals could not believe their luck as waves upon waves of the enemy forces had broken from hiding and came across the plain. Kaufmanns ordered immediate Air strikes. Within minutes of been called in, the aircraft were in flight and the exposed Mujahedeen were decimated. Huge precision guided napalm bombs, their bellies full of burning jelly rained down from above. Caught out in the opening, tens of thousands died in minutes and their engines of war were pulverised into red hot cinders. Like a wave of seawater, the onrushing wave of Mujhadeen was broken against the breakwater of mines, artillery and the metal barrier. Shell shocked and decimated, the counterattacking army began a much disorganised retreat under the spiralling plumes of black smoke. It was a false cover, not many of the machines and men involved in the rash attack made it back to their own lines. The observing political leaders on the Prophet's side began to fume and vowed.

"Whoever was responsible for the reckless bombardment on the relatively few breakaway vehicles that had instigated the rashness charge would pay with their worthless lives."

The commanders of the Prophet's army watched as the survivors of their once proud army retreated in disarray. In stark contrast, the Enclaves war staff broke out in spontaneous cheering. The first stage of the expansion move was a huge success with minimum losses, far less than was expected. The re-deployment of the new wall had been a calculated success. This initial loss in Tanks along with 8,400 souls was an acceptable price to pay. In all, the causality figure would not exceed forty-thousand compared to the hundreds of thousands of the Prophet's armies. There would be far fewer grieving families than was originally anticipated and the list of names to be etched into the new wall was considerably less than what was foreseen. All thanks to the posthumous charge of the first crew and the others that had drawn the enemy fire. Kaufmanns swore in God's name.

"I will make them hero's, never to be forgotten as long as our people prosper."

Little did anyone watching realise, on either side of the divide, that all the occupants of that vehicle were very much alive and well. Those presumed dead lay hidden in invisible protection besides the fist-sized smoking and scattered fragments of their vehicle's remains. Shortly before it was obliterated, all of the crew and passengers had piled into their pre-assigned coloured TORT-CAMLETS and became safe from the projectiles and the subsequent explosion that followed. The smaller globes like their parent were mini bubbles of inpenetration. Some of the groupings were content with their partners, others were not. A bitter Prof mentioned this to the Mute. The macabre man responded in his whinny voice.

"Well, you can go outside, if you want to."

That was the end of that discussion. Safe and secure Miriam grieved for the crews of the other Tanks who had perished in their misguided charge.

"Eight thousand- four hundred dead."

She had loads of time to do just that as the plan was to wait until the enemy's war machine dispersed after its failure. They waited for two hours and then Naomh resumed command and through an untraceable communication device ordered them.

"Move towards the Prophet's lines."

The invisible globes moved forward at a steady speed of ten kilometres an hour, an action instigated by a sequence on their wristbands, two greens and two blues. An alert spotter on the Prophet's side noticed that a line of their own defensive mines was detonating in a sequence that vectored towards his position. He was puzzled that his screens revealed nothing visible or even a concrete threat.

"Have the Enclave some secret weapon that can see our mines and is causing this spontaneous explosions? Or is there something that we cannot detect moving through there?"

To make certain that it was not his second guess; the experienced fighter ordered a barrage of high explosive to rain down on what he was observing. When the smoke of the falling shells cleared, the trail of creeping detonations had ceased. He shrugged.

"Allah has been merciful. We must have got whatever it was."

What he did not know, was that the invisible TORT-CAMLET'S had crossed the minefields and were no longer revealing their movement. With the attacking wave been decimated and any chance of stopping the new wall having failed, some of the more strategy thinking among the Prophet's leaders ordered their forces to retreat back to the cities and lands away from the dishonour of the Enclave. But the bulk of the besieging army remained. The leaders of those that were leaving were aware of the political consequences.

"Our nations will lose political clout among the Muslim Confederation."

They would only leave a few observers. But the Enclave's war staff had another surprise coming. Now that the enemy's guns had revealed their position and knowing that forces aligned against them would splinter and break up, they could plan a devastating counter attack. Their information network told them that the Muslim Confederation was loosely held together and their failure today would cause huge rifts in the alliance.

"Now was the time to strike" Aluf Kaufmanns decided.

But over the next three hours, he and his staff remained on the defensive as the regrouped Mujhadeen launched wave after wave. With enormous losses, these suicidal attacks made a few minor breaches in the new wall and caused heavier Enclave causalities. These were quickly repaired and the Prophet's army was driven back repeatedly, but not without more losses. Back in the Geneva Contrib, the Chairman was watching the unfolding events as they transpired from highly focused satellites in space. The Kaiser had already known about the TORT-CAM from the information his Spy had been able to supply him with. So the head of the LYUBINITES figured.

"As I have had not heard from my agent, our unwitting dupes must be unable to move."

Taking a decision, he contacted a member of the inner circle, who was aboard the ANS GREGORY LYUBIN. An image of a striking woman appeared on his screens. With indifference, he ordered the Anschluss forces to interfere. On board the huge vessel, his subordinate gave the orders. Majella Irvine's commands were obeyed at once. Although, the captain was master of his ship, the seafarer obeyed this woman without hesitation. Back at the conflict, Kaufmanns and his staff now realised that the attacks had been waning in ferocity and it was now time to strike. But in the instant of giving the go ahead, the entire Prophets line erupted in a cataclysmic series of detonations. The Enclave war staff had never seen explosions of such a magnitude before.

"My God has someone used Nuclear bombs!" Exclaimed a member of Kaufmanns staff as he witnessed the obliteration of the distant hillsides. An observer in the command centre who was dressed in the uniform of the Anschluss interrupted.

"My dear General. We decided to lend you a hand. Our gift to our loyal ally of the Enclave. Just a few extremely powerful laser-guided block-bursting bombs. Have no fear, there will be no radiation." Susan Irvine said as if she was a grown up talking to a child. The career solider hated the arrogance of the Anschluss. However been the pragmatist that he was, he also knew that his people needed them. None, but those in the know would be aware that this woman was the identical of the one who had given the order to attack on board the Dreadnaut. The Enclave General hid his shock well, better than the rest of his staff in fact; maybe it was because his one eye revealed less expression. His people were also uneasy because none of their detection equipment had registered the Anschluss's warplanes. The flying discs had come from the huge warship, which still lay off the shore of the Enclave in the Mediterranean Sea. The Clone observer smiled to herself.

"My government did not interfere because of the reason I gave you General. No, it is much simpler than that. Our Spy out there must have contacted our superior and told him that the Army of the Prophet lay between her crew and what they are seeking. And as a consequence, the Chairman decided to remove that obstacle. After all, we need to flex our military muscle once in a while."

The Kaiser's observer hissed into the commander's ear. Her voice filled with satisfaction.

"Launch your aircraft now. It must appear that your airforce carried out the attack. We must not be implicated."

Still in a state of shock at the scale of the destruction, Kaufmanns ordered his planes to launch. From his vantage-point, a few seconds later, he heard the deafening super sonic booms of the aircraft, realising that the planes had already passed him on the way to their objective. The precision bombs and secret ordnance easily penetrated the now alarmingly exposed underground bunkers and brought a terrible rain of death down on those who had not the foresight to flee. Some of the discs were shot down by desperate anti-aircraft fire. No one gave much hope to the ejecting pilots, their bombing ensured their fate. The exposed enemy were easy meat as the Anschluss craft had removed the entire range of hills and cracked the solid concrete bunkers as if they had been eggshells. Now that the perimeter had been secured and the assailants were in complete disarray, the next wave of precision machines lumbered forth. Huge armoured cranes, which resembled medieval siege towers, came towards the breastwork of Tanks sandwiched between the metal barriers and took up positions behind it. These cranes would build the next outer wall and all workers and machines would be under constant attack until the wall was completed. As each armoured vehicle was replaced by a huge wall section, it would retreat back behind the original barrier. Personnel would have to be replaced during the construction and ferrying them and their replacement crews would now be the most dangerous task. It would take the best part of two years to fully erect the new outer wall and upgrade it to the standard of its preceding companion.

Protected in the TORT-CAMLETS, Naomh and his compliment had already engaged another feature of the Alien devices. It was called limited circular motion. The mini invisible shields could travel in a modulating manner, while keeping their contents confined in a centrifugal field for a few kilometres. Under the control of their wristbands and its own steam, the Alien technology moved towards the decimated army's frontier. The moving invisible shields in built guidance systems would not fail them. Crossing the Prophet's lines, many of the dying Mujahedeen felt the slight whisper of their passing and been on the threshold of death, the doomed men were certain that it was a host of Angels of death present on the battlefield that had come to take the martyrs away. Many were already counting the amount of virgins that they would receive in paradise, even those without the lower halves of their anatomy. The seven invisible moving bubbles of invulnerability passed across the former lines of their foes and penetrated ten kilometres behind vanished lines. Here, they halted near a narrow ravine and waited for a lull in the battle. The seventeen survivors rested and to some sleep came quickly. Foam filled sleeping mats had already been put into the invisible shields. By mutual consent, all views to the outside were cut off. The immediate landscape shook with the power from the Anschluss bombs and unfortunately the Guide's and the Lenses mini TORT-CAMLET slid off firm ground and came to rest at the bottom of a ravine. When they awoke many hours later and opened the viewing slots; the two men faced a scene from hell. Ghoulish faces and the leachate of the dead poured around the contours of their haven like some hellish rain of blood and gore. They were submerged in a sea of death leaving a red film as their vista to the outside World. Where there was normal light in between the crimson, they wished that there was not, for these spaces made grim viewing. While both had slept deeply, the Prophet's army had cast hundreds of its slain and charred warriors into the pit and bulldozed over them. Unfortunately for them, they got their first close up look at the soldiers of the Prophet. All were bearded and had some sort of head scarf on their heads, those that still had heads of course. Dead, decaying bodies and earth lay piled on top of them, mangled corpses and ruined faces pressed up against the lair of light. So close in fact that the Lenses believed that he was one of the dead. Kaliningrad freaked out and went into hysteria as he imagined the bodies hitting the TORT-CAMLET and forming a chain that would keep him in the netherworld forever. The Lenses continued wailing, so his companion gripped him hard and insisted.

"Chill out dude, its going to be alright."

This did not stop the screaming, so the Guide hit him as hard as he could and knocked the computer hacker out cold without causing him serious injury or even killing him.

"The real thing is nothing like what you were used to when you played your games back in the Anschluss." Admonished van DerKamp to the unhearing man.

Then, he cursed aloud.

"Shit, he is the only one of us who knows how to operate this thing. I will have to wait until he comes around."

His self-inflicted quandary was interrupted when the Engineer's voice came over the communication device embedded in his helmet. He explained their predicament as calmly as he could.

"We appear to have landed in a mass grave. The Lenses went ape-shit on me and so I had to forcibly calm him down."

"Stay put, we are able to track you. We will come to you."

"Hurry up. I don't want him waking up until we are out of here."

"We have to wait until dark."

The voice on the other side went silent. However, he was much relieved.

"They are coming for us and it will not be long."

The Guide knew at least how to reactivate the opaque shield and he did just that. Now he waited for the others with his oblivious partner. When the Lenses had come too, the others had regrouped and located them. All, but the Prof, he refused to come out into what he called the fields of carnage. The peaceful scholar had no desire to see the horror on the faces of the dead or their burnt, dismembered and bloodied bodies. He would stay inside his oblivious haven until they were far from here. In the dark of night, broken by orange flashes and muffled explosions, the Persuader dug them out with another of Naomh's fancy new gismo's that incinerated the soil and the layers of dead without any tell-tale signs of smoke or light. Thankfully, it also removed the rotting stench of the bodies as well. The pit of death held no interest for the Mute and he wondered what all the fuss was about. The depraved man had seen enough piles of corpses waiting unceremoniously to be disposed of in the recycling plants. Some might have wondered would the obnoxious man have been so cocky if it had been him under all of the bodies. But then, no-one knew what the macabre individual got up to on his shifts in the body disposal business. No, it was the precise moment of death that intrigued him; still a part of him regretted the sinful waste of the non-recycled corpses. The jittery numbed Lenses were dragged from the TORT-CAMLET and he came out of his lethargy with a scream. It was quickly muffled by Cahill's hand before anyone might hear the panicked sound and investigate. Still shaking violently, he spat out a gobble of blood speckled phlegm. Beersheba handed him a soakage pad, which he took gratefully. The Rabbi gave him a sedative, which rendered him calm and relaxed. When he was sufficiently calmed, he asked the Guide.

"Did you have to hit me so hard?"

Van DerKamp shrugged and said.

"It seemed like a good idea at the time, dude."

The injured man had a black shiner around one of his pink eyes, so the Guide gave him his favourite pair of his flecked sunglasses. The Lenses was delighted, the Clerk scowled, he had always coveted a pair of those. Then everybody dressed in the uniforms of the enemy and wore the same checked hear covering. Miriam on Haim's advice decided.

"We should move a few kilometres away from the pit and set up a temporary base camp. There we can gather our strength for the long trek that lies ahead of us."

Much to the Lenses relief, the move was done. When a suitable site was found, Moshe and Haim climbed to a high point with a powerful optical device and a saucer shaped antennae. Meanwhile Naomh began to reassemble the TORT-CAM from the separate pieces that his comrades released from their possession. Reluctantly, the Mute gave up his globe; he was imagining the corrupt uses that he could use it for and voyeuristic murder was paramount in his mind. The seven TORT-CAMLETS had already been made visible and as Naomh pressed a combination on his wrist band, each separate sphere merged together like bubbles of viscosity until the original single shield was reformed. The Prof went inside to check on something. Two minutes later, the inquisitive man came out and asked the others.

"Were any of you sharing space with the supplies?"

As everybody shook their heads in the negative, he continued.

"So where did everything go, when it was separated into its different components?"

No one had an answer.

"But when it was reformed, everything was still there. It doesn't make sense."

Perplexed, he looked at Naomh an answer. The owner of the wonderful device said.

"I don't know either."

He shrunk it down and put it into a pocket of his strange uniform. The two parts of the Mescal/Amulet did, but decided.

"My explanation will be too complicated for my host?"

So, he remained silent. In the meantime, Moshe and Haim had returned and both had excited expressions on their faces. The smaller man was so excited; he began babbling in the Enclave language. For those who did not understand, Solomon translated.

"We went to the top of the outcrop and focused our lens westward. We saw the shiny metal wall. Our people have done it. They have completely enclosed the new living area."

There was a cheer from the Enclave members. A misinformed Haim added.

"And the only major causalities were the Tank's that followed us. And what's more from the radio traffic we picked up, it was our charge and those that followed us who tipped the balance. Only for us, the invasion would have been a failure and there would have been a huge loss of life on our side."

A sombre Miriam said.

"Then, their deaths were not in vain. Ok, let's move out."

The hurt was still in her eyes, she wanted to put as much distance between the dead that she still felt responsible for. Looking like the rest of the bedraggled Mujhadeen, the company marched eastwards for a couple of hours. Anyone that saw them had their own worries and the false soldiers of the Prophet passed through the long lines of defeated soldiers without incident. When it was judged safe, the gang moved off a flat road and slipped into the darkness. In a natural culvert Naomh formed the TORT-CAM. Gratefully the questors all left the desert night and re-entered their haven. Even thought they had slept for a long period while waiting for the Prophet's forces to retreat, most of them found that they were still exhausted and sleep came quickly for them. Unlike the eternal slumber of the dead outside, these sleepers would soon have to wake and continue their quest for the next piece of the APOCRYPHA'I. But one among the hidden found sleep an elusive goal; it was the Anschluss Spy. This person had tolerably enjoyed the full-scale battle and the mad high-octane rush towards the Prophet's lines. The scale of the engagement had been dazzling and the mole felt invigorated while images of explosions and death and the eruption of the entire ridge filled the agent's sleepless attention.

"Now that's what I call a war, not the pathetic shit the RE-INSTATOR'S had me involved in. Their fire fights against the rule of my kind were nothing more than a minor fracas."

The next morning just before daybreak, the seventeen of them stood out on the exposed desert road, the TORT-CAM had already been miniaturised and put back into its host's pocket. They held council and it was decided.

"We have lingered here far too long. We are now rested and will risk travelling for a few hours in the cool of the morning to make up some ground. Any objections?"

There were none. As they huddled together, still dressed in uniforms of the Prophet's army, Naomh told them about the vague pull that he was feeling.

"I am being drawn south. It feels a long way away, so that's the way we will go for now. We will leave the road for a while and head in that direction."

"We will be safe; our airforce will not pursue the retreating enemy. They have achieved their purpose. Our leaders have gained what they set out to achieve and will not risk any more losses." Said Haim.

"Speaking of the causalities. We are now presumed dead and our names will be etched into the new wall." Announced the Rabbi.

"I would like to see that." Added Solomon.

"What about our families and friends? They will think us dead too." Said Shoshanna.

The enormity of what they had done now sunk in. The Enclave members became subdued.

"For all we know. We might have been if we did not have the TORT-CAM. It is the reason that we are still alive and breathing."

"Imagine their delight when we come back from the dead." Said Beersheba.

This restored their good humour. But Miriam had a dark thought that she kept to herself.

"This quest is not over yet and who is to say that any of us will return to prove the names on the wall to the contrary."

As the well-prepared and heavily armed band moved off the road into desert scrub, the Lenses once again checked the date on his antiquated timepiece. It stated that it was the 13th of August 2953 AD, so he mused.

"Unlucky for some?"

He picked up his pace to catch up with the others who had got slightly ahead. Even the rising Sun seemed to inherit their urgency as angry welts of red streaked across the bluing sky. The growing gashes of reddening allure in the day breaking vista grew more akin to the whiplashes that invoked more effort from a flagging slave. Reluctantly, the little troop who was now really much more out of their depth filed into line and moved off in the direction Naomh gave them after consulting with the voice within. Most of them were unsure about the long unknown journey ahead, but for a few, expectation hung in the air and these people looked forward to what it might bring. Alone, the Mute had not blanked his screen and spent the hours of waiting scanning the battlefield. Images of the dying and dead enthralled him and he looked forward to more of the same bloodletting. He for one was glad he left the Anschluss as the opportunities to kill had increased tenfold and his diary of death was becoming larger and more interesting. The random killer decided.

"If I get the right opportunity, I will possess the concealing device for myself.

After all, the former morgue attendant was in this quest for reasons that only he was aware of.

XIX.

Once the lingering smoke from the aftermath of battle was left far behind, those who were eager for new experiences found themselves amongst dark and desolate highways, away from the lifelong comfort of artificial luminance. Flickering lights of encountered towns and villages promised havens of normality from the all-encompassing darkness, but these were the places of the enemy and to be avoided at all costs on this journey into the unknown. One of their numbers had passed through his own gates of purgatory with shut eyes. Still, he had certainly achieved his version of paradise on the other side and it was even more wonderful than he could ever have imagined. These last days of August and early September had been the happiest of his life.

"A wilderness with the wonderful sound of the desert wind and the musical chirping of the locusts and crickets at night. With its patchy scrub and fleeting glimpses of Desert Ibex, White Sand Gazelle and Orgynx. This is why I left the dreary Anschluss and its urban monotony. To be out here in this place and to behold its wonder."

The happy fugitive was drawn to reciting prose out loud; not caring if any of the group heard him. The enthusiastic scholar had learnt from Solomon the names of the odd beasts and even stranger plants that existed out here. His new horizons were places where the air was fresher the spaces were bigger and most important of all to those who found themselves there, it was free from Anschluss control; or so, all but one among them thought. Skies that did not fill in with the murky mist of billions of water vapour discharges glowed with a raw and passionate beauty of their own. The regular infringement of flying craft and subsequent spreading plumes on this different medium only added to the feeling of escapement. The newcomers listened to the silence of the near desert foothills. What a strange thing, what a striking change it was to most of these travellers, these new frontiers had opened up their minds. To see and behold a vista, empty of any visible manmade artefacts. To them, mankind had no influence out here, but the ignorant travellers did not realise that man had already made a considerable impact on this landscape. What looked to them like normal hills and natural bumps on the land's surface, hid their true origin. Some of these protrusions were in fact artificial and thousands of years old. Abandoned or destroyed mud brick enclosures had been absorbed by the landscape and elements to take on another semblance. Once these worn down mounds and walls had been the bases for forts, walled towns and simple compounds that stretched over a time period from antiquity to medieval times and on to what man called the beginning of modern times. The footsore questors had no comprehension of the importance of these forgotten undulations as they tramped over them in a hurry to make more ground. An endless concoction of armies had

469

attacked or defended these barely discernible structures; from Assyrians, Babylonians, Egyptians, Greeks, Romans, Crusaders, Ottomans, British, Israelis and Arabs. The list was as endless as the manner of warfare. Only natures struggle to reclaim the land made the lost fortifications appear to be natural outcroppings. The only Alien observer in their midst knew.

"Even the concrete metropolis of the Anschluss would eventually be reclaimed and swallowed up by the relentless force of nature, if the Hybrids ever vanished from the Planet. Nature was very patient in her relentless makeover."

Of all of them; only the Guide, the Spy, Haim and Solomon had ever ventured so far into a land devoid of obvious manmade structures. Even Miriam and the rest of her crew never strayed far from the reassuring concrete of the Enclaves outer wall. The comforting barrier of their home was always in view of Ruth's rear view cameras on the few limited incursions into No Man's Land. Shoshanna joked.

"A swim in the sea is the furthest I got."

For obvious reasons, the Persuader laughed the loudest at her quip. This new frontier challenged them, but all were supremely confident in their abilities and Naomh's bubble of wonder; even if it was cramped with supplies. They were well stocked with provisions, enthusiasm and purpose. With no cloud cover over their route, the fierce heat of the day radiated out into space, leaving the nights bitterly cold. But their excellent Enclave military clothing spared them much more discomfort during the hours of travel. They were unaware that the TORT-CAM became even more efficient at maintaining their physical well-being. The red and orange tiles now fixed on each individual and provided the most comfortable temperature for them. The first twilight that these strangers of open country had ventured out from the haven of the unseen shield was the most remembered. The night sky was amazing, it had thousands of eyes and all of them were natural. When the searchers looked up into the desert night, myriad pinpricks of white pierced the blanket of the night sky, but the slender crescent moon outshone all of the flickers. They had known about the quantity of Stars contained in the sky, but the sparkling heavens out here belittled the drab sight of an Anschluss or Enclave night. It was more impressive for the Northerners; their sky was constantly dampened by the ever present and vast urban glow which was reflected on to the ever present murky mist over the population centres. Those who had been in the Agricultural Sectors had a little inkling of the wonder of an unspoilt sky. As usual of all of them, it was the Prof who was affected the most. Out here, free from his past, he felt so small that he began to question his place in the overall scheme of things. The quarter moon was even visible during the day, but it was dwarfed by the giant of the Solar System. Just before the dawn each morning, some of them took a slight chance to linger on the vast emptiness of the open desert and the clear blue sky that its days produced. These people were all over-awed at the sight, for never in their confined lives had any of them seen such an open expanse of vista unbroken by building after building. When the rhythm of travel was broken, such as now, the Clerk loved these unexpected boons, his life more than the others had been so predictable. This unfamiliar feeling of freedom and irregular hours had a profound effect on him and he actually glorified in it. The wiry man wanted to be different. As a number in the civil service; he always had to be smart and clean-shaven and most of all obedient to his superiors. Unlike most of the others, the former Registrar had to conform to the standard, otherwise he would have been brought to the attention to the Ministry of Protocol and nobody wanted them breathing down their necks. Victor de Mere had been a nonentity, who had lived in a nine to five existence. As an act of defiance against his lifetime of conformity, the Clerk constantly wore his desert khaki uniform, even in the confines of the invisible globe. He now sported a beard similar to Haim's, Moshe's and Solomon's. He halted his rebellion at that; the Rabbi's hair growth was a bit too extreme for him. This petulant act against the dictates of his former life was carried out by the erstwhile bureaucrat simply because the Anschluss had frowned on all types of beards, moustaches and long hair length in men. Those in authority and the Spy among them deemed these expressions of hair growth a primitive custom. Any breach of this enforced etiquette brought the attention of the security forces down on you and to any member of the outlawed RE-INSTATORS, that would be fatal indeed. The Clerk had been amazed when he had first seen the Guide's long locks, but experience now told him.

"Only certain rules applied to certain groups in the Anschluss."

One day during a rest stop, he and the Prof were lying on their backs, engaged in a new pastime; cloud watching. In conversation with his companion, they were been watched by one of the parties sentries. As a moving shadow briefly blocked off the heat of the Sun; he told the academic while tugging on his new hair growth. The chin hairs had been irritating at first, but that had soon passed.

"If my former office mates could see me now? Those boring conformists would probably think me mad and I would be hauled away for reassessment. Well fuck them, I prefer it this way. What do you think Prof?"

His companion had also grown a pencil thin moustache that required regular attention; he concurred with him and said.

"This outdoor life is agreeing with you. You look healthier, fitter and more relaxed. And you have even got a colour."

The Clerk positively beamed. But the Prof was becoming more captious in nature, so he added mischievously.

"Did you notice that all of the Enclave men are circumcised, it is a big

part of their religion and culture. Why don't you try that Victor, then you will be really different."

"I am definitely not going that far." Replied the other man from the Brussels Contrib when he actually found out what circumcision actually meant. He winced at the thought of it. He even went weak at the knees. The Prof confided in the Clerk.

"I asked Solomon if it hurt when it was done. And he told me; it was done when they were babies. So nobody had a remembrance of it."

"Why do they do it?" Asked the Clerk.

"He said because of their faith and cleanliness." Answered the other.

"Shit. I hope if the Engineer forms his new religion back home, he does not insist on that. Otherwise, I am not joining it."

The academic chuckled out loud.

"Me too. Nobody's interfering down there."

But privately, he always worried about the Engineer's thinking.

"What kind of Deity allows one of his followers to go around blowing up people to further his goals?"

If Edward Boyd had a belief in a God, then it would have been a pacifist being. Even Solomon's overlord demanded blood now and then. The Clerk joined in with the Prof's mirth. The third oldest of the newly enlarged band of companions was another who revelled in his new lifestyle, far away from most of the trappings of civilisation. While the intellectual had proceeded with his scholarly career in a restricted museum, his heart had not been in it; he had to correspond with official doctrine. The Anschluss's version of the past was absolute and his individual conjectures were frowned upon. As a result of his inquisitive nature, the seeker of new learning had been confined to a backwater department of little consequence. Remembrance made him mutter.

"There had been little chance of field trips or even working in an historical theme park, abet the Anschluss's version. No! Just a dusty basement office with poor ventilation had been my lot."

But down there away from prying eyes, he indulged in his one passion. He used to stare at an illegal laminated map of the World that had escaped censorship. Unfortunately, it had been in a language, he could not understand. Rory had told him.

"It is French, but I too have no understanding of it."

This had been a deliberate lie. The Gaffer could have told him the names of the places on it, but decided against it. He still had the map and was tracing his route across it with a bright red marker. The World was now his oyster and he was looking forward to adding more lines onto the chart. He was witnessing sights and things that no pen and ink drawing could display, things such as Snakes, Lizards, huge insects and the like, stuff that most of the other exiles could have done without. The Prof was gob smacked when he first saw the giant cacti of these lands, some grew

472

over a metre high; he had miniature versions back in his London Contrib flat. He exclaimed in wonder.

"I had no idea that the prickly plants could grow so big."

He also did not realise either that the scant plantings of Cypress's and Eucalyptuses that they gratefully took shade under were imported over a thousand years ago and were not natural to this part of the arid landscape. There was one blot on his idyllic circumstances and that was that the travellers were using up their supplies as the days went by. The discarded packaging and plastic containers were buried, so as to not leave any evidence of their passing. This environmental vandalism was not to his liking, but he did understand the need. The Lenses joined them, just as the Prof took a deep gulp of the pristine desert air. The academic actually enjoyed taking breaths and asked the other two.

"Do either of you feel the same?"

The Clerk nodded in the affirmative while the man from the Warsaw Contrib was non-committal. Only, the Mute soon discovered that he hated the desert. Much to his annoyance, the unliked man developed a bad case of hay fever. His handsome features were soon ruined by a constant runny and red nose. The Rabbi carried every type of tablet in his medical satchel, but their appointed medical officer had never accounted for this simple allergy. So the unfortunate Mute was left to suffer. On the other side of the coin, Haim was intrigued with his new friends from the Anschluss's practice of giving themselves code-names. The man from the Enclave asked them.

"Could you give me one?"

The Guide, the Clerk, the Prof, the Lenses and the two brothers from the Madrid Contrib formed a separate huddle from the rest of their comrades and through much mirth and silent giggling, the laughing bunch came up with the name.

"Pecker."

The man with the big nose was delighted with the strange sounding word and asked what it meant. Straight faced, the Guide lied.

"It is the name of a person who controls the automated systems of travel back home."

Haim who was intrigued with mechanical things liked that and so the appellation of "Pecker." became his new name among his European comrades. His clued in friend Moshe was a vendor in a family owned ice-cream business and he wisely kept silent about that.

"God only knows what they would have called me."

The seventeen seekers of the APOCRYPHA'I had been travelling on a southeastwardly vector for two weeks now and were deep into the Prophet's domain. Progress became slow and monotonous as they encountered a landscape of soft weathered black shale, it made tough going. Naomh also relished in its challenge. He had never been so free, so alive and he lived for the next day. The measure of the advancing kilometres on their instruments mattered little, for to both the Anschluss and the Enclaves people distance was relative. Their measure of distance depended on the mode of transport used in their respective societies. Hundreds of kilometres were measured by mechanised travel and in minutes, so neither group had any actual concept of any real expanse. Shoshanna had already plotted their course; the group would make their way on foot and hug the Red Sea coastline of the Arabian mainland for a short spell. Then, the travellers would leave the narrow tihama of the coast and make a broad semi-circular sweep of the Nafud desert back to the coast again until they reached the Asir highlands. The main reason for crossing the inhospitable desert to where the two parts Mescal/Amulet drove Naomh was because their small party would avoid the major population centres of Medina and Mecca. At first it was tough going for the Europeans, been from a metropolis with moving walkways and not having the military training of the Enclave members of their company. Most of the group was not used to travelling long distances by foot or over tough, rough and uneven ground and in the heat that would reach over fifty degrees centigrade in the height of summer, the effort was exhausting. The marchers became footsore and fatigued from the sun-baked ground as they travelled over the stony beds of dried up wadis. But its effects were limited, thanks to the durable boots with their toughened Velcro straps, the unwitting Enclave quartermasters had provided. Still there were complaints of blistered feet, but these irritations soon callused and the re-hardened skin was not so easily abraded. Moshe and Haim insisted.

"Everybody must drink a litre of water during each hour of our march."

Both Enclave men called for a halt at an arbitrated time and watched as the others drank. When they were satisfied that each and everyone had complied, the trek was resumed. They called this hydration and it was a necessary task. It also became a sore point of debate among those less affected as some of their number kept calling for a break to relieve themselves. Those who did not answer the call of nature took up covering positions around who had scrambled for privacy. For the first week of marching over the uncompromising terrain, the most unaccustomed hikers collapsed when a halt was called. Notably, the Lenses, the Clerk and the Prof. These three were knackered and went straight to sleep, not even pausing for something to eat. When the trek was resumed, the stiffness and soreness of their muscles took a long time to dispel. The three mentioned had to be woken up and dragged out of their slumber every time. Each of them would have a dishevelled look and eyes full of sleep, but the promise of encountering something new overcame their reluctance at rising. But as the subsequent days passed on and the band progressed over the uneven terrain, their stamina and speed increased. The fatness of the Anschluss was burnt off and all of its former citizens were now able to keep up with Miriam's unit: even the three sloggers as the Guide called them were matching the others pace. Still, even they were delighted when the Rabbi informed Naomh on one evening.

"We will not be moving the next day."

"Why?" Asked their leader.

"It is a very important day in our religious calendar. It is the time of Tishrey and time for our new year. To us, this most holiest of days is a time for prayer and reflection."

The impatient internal voice was against it.

"More delays, we have already spent the better part of a year in the Enclave."

But the bearded man was adamant, so Naomh relented. The next day, their Jewish contingent moved away from them and went about their business. Strangely, the men and women separated in two different groups. The inquisitive Prof wanted to spy on them, but he was warned off. The Engineer was also intrigued, but surmised.

"Their ritual does not belonging to the true faith and therefore, I have no interest in it."

Still, his unusually perceptive brother did mention.

"Is it not strange that those men and women had to live and die together in their Tank? But when it comes to religious worship, they separate."

His older sibling had no answer for him as he had been a follower of the Preacher and he had similar views about women's participation in religion. The Rabbi and his little flock would always take time out for such occasions. A few days later, their Enclave companions celebrated two more such holidays, one religious and one secular. The first was called Yom Kippur and the other was when the second barrier had been completed. The next day, the group reassembled and moved forward again. After two more weeks of coastal travel and avoiding any settlements, large or small, they left the heights of the seashore with their dressings of individual foliage and descended into the desert proper. The Engineer was saddened by this change of direction as now there would be no towns or settlements out there. The religious man had become intrigued by the loud calling from the muezzins to the faithful when they passed near towns and villages. The tuffs of green on the rugged red hills now gave way to a brown maze of sandstone with speckles of dark shade which offered scant protection from the searing Sun. Out here on the great swaths of sand and rock that was the desert floor, the wind fought the principal star for dominance. During the daylight hours, the glaring heat continued unabated, it radiated up from the desert floor giving them little respite. All of them really appreciated the regular temperature of the TORT-CAM and retreated into it when the oppressive heat of the Sun became unbearable and the large hundred litre drums of bland Enclave drinking water that Miriam had loaded into it were really appreciated now. Ironically, the headdresses of the Mujahedeen became a necessary boon. There were two periods of brief respite from the harsh Sun, the first was in the early hours of the morning and the second was in the solitary hour before darkness. But these brief respites diminished as the trudged southwards. Haim, a veteran of tactical design advised.

"When we are camped outside the TORT-CAM, one person should always remain on guard with a heavy calibre weapon inside the invisible shield. That will always give us the advantage of surprise."

It was agreed that Haim's suggestion be put into operation at all times. Another problem that cropped up was radio transmission. Except for the Spy, all of them had only small Enclave radio mikes and any communication between them would be easily tracked by the Prophet's forces. So it was agreed that these could only be used in an extreme emergency. Naomh questioned the APOCRYPHA'I about this. The naive Human still thought that he was conversing with one of his own race.

"Surely, your people have invented advanced communication devices that would remain undetected and could be used by us."

The two parts Mescal/Amulet did not know how to reply, as the ALASTHA'I communicated solely by the mind-voice and three-dimensional Missives via their Preceptor-Bands. Other artificial means were never required. But its interaction with the Hybrids enabled it to tell falsehoods.

"This will come with the next piece of my form."

Naomh accepted the white lie. Beyond the flat barren land that glowed in the changing colours of the desert Sun and at the limits of their optical devices, the travellers observed a horizon that melted into the sand and boasted scattered clumps of weather worn peaks that jutted out of the flat landscape like mountain tops that protruded above a sea of clouds. But this type of vista belonged to the highest points above sea level, not somewhere distant in these slightly lower than sea level altitudes. The inexperienced wanderers were about to cross a nine million square kilometre ocean of sand, dirt, shale and stone of many shades and textures. The untried gang would have to endure blistering temperatures during the day and the paradoxical cold at night with little relief or respite. Without the boon of the TORT-CAM, they would have had little hope of success and would have perished from any number of things. Their desiccated bones would lie there for centuries, maybe to be found by some inquisitive traveller far into the future. Someone, such as the Prof or Solomon. If the seventeen of them travelled by day, then they would have to endure the life sapping stifling heat that reached fifty degrees centigrade and made the sand and rocks hot enough to scald skin. This unbearable heat was mixed in with the added danger of high water and salt loss. So it was decided to listen to the expertise Haim.

"We will use the safety of the temperate interior of the invisible shield during the blistering heat of the day and travel in the lesser of two evils, at night. This method of travelling will also make it harder for us to be tracked."

Out in the endless ocean of sand, Naomh missed the comforting sound of the crashing waves and the regular rhythm of the sea with its salty taste from their trek along the coastal highway. The Watcher back in the past could have explained to him why these Hybrids felt this way about the closeness of the liquid expanse that dominated their Planet. It was an inherited memory from a time even before the interference of the ALASTHA'I in the Primates evolution. For the barely evolved simians had spent 50,000 years hugging the coastlines of the Continents as their augmenting race spread out to encompass the World. By living on the Planet's shorelines, the Primates had a ready supply of food and easier travel to new horizons. The ancient Being in another time frame noticed.

"The ancient Primates first steps to move into the interiors of the Continent's and leaving their comforting coastline echo's this group of Hybrids trepidation at heading into the unknown. Have we changed them much? They still seem to possess their original fears of ignorance."

Then, Cathbad remembered the time when he, a being of an immensely superior race had been afraid to enter a dark tunnel on board a spacecraft.

"But then, it is not us who are going to confront the warped CRYSTALOID'I, the Hybrids are."

Still, moving away from the sea gave them an advantage. The desert travellers could move faster and they had escaped from the hundred per cent humidity of the coastal areas. For out here away from habitation and the main coastal arteries, there was no constant flow of traffic or sighting of people, from which they had to hide from, when approaching headlights warned them to take cover away from the roads. Some nights the wary gang had moved at a crawl as they had to keep leaving the traffic arteries to avoid the oncoming vehicles. This constant scramble for cover slowed them down and had left them short tempered when opting for the safety of the invisible shield numerous times in a single night. One evening, an endless military convoy had caught some of them unawares and they had failed to make it into their haven. Squatting down in the vehicle driven dust for eight hours did not improve anyone's temper. It was determined that five of them would travel at any one time, the rest would stay in the tranquil red and orange World of the globe. A rota system was worked out. Naomh who carried the marble sized haven was excluded from this; he had to trek across the sand wastes every night. The Spy was disgruntled with this arrangement; the mole did not like the bearer of the Alien artefact to be out of sight for too long. Meals were taken in the cool of the night and before Sunrise. Everybody, except the Mute took turns with the cooking.

The Rabbi had a stock of special foods and would only consume items that were deemed Kosher. Foodstuffs were brought out from the TORT-CAM and the fare was adequate and filling. It consisted mostly of dried meats and vacuum packed vegetables, olives and fruit, hard biscuits and a never-ending supply of coffee. It was standard military fare, full of protein and capable of generating plenty of body heat. After one fairly bland meal of chicken, rice and bitter olives, prepared by the Clerk and the Lenses, it caused Cahill to comment wishfully as he spit out a chewed olive pit.

"I will bet that this is nobody's favourite menu. Do you remember the meals Goulash used to serve? Man, that Pleb knew how to cook."

Taking a swallow of his own average fare, Naomh agreed, while the Persuader gave a loud burp and was reprimanded by the others. The big man ate any type of food with gusto. When the utensils were finished with, they were put in a plastic container that was filled with water. A sterilising tablet was dropped in to clean the plates, cups and cutlery. The Clerk preferred to wash his cup the way he had seen Moshe do it. After one of the first meals, the stocky man filled his cup up with sand and cleaned it the old fashioned way.

"After all our water might become precious."

Beersheba still took the cups off them and dropped them into the cleaning fluid anyway. It was during these meals that plans for the next day's travel was discussed. While the clamour of decision making held little interest for the Prof, the sounds of the open desert drew him like a magnet. This curious wanderer always liked to put a little distance between himself and the others whenever possible. Solomon always accompanied him; they were inseparable since they had first met all those months ago. Victor Boyd truly believed that the others were oblivious to the wild beauty that surrounded them. His favourite time was at the nights when the group encountered difficult terrain and found it difficult going and decided to rest early. Then from the concealment of the undetectable shield, he and his close friend used its invisible surveillance to study the desert creatures at night. He was amazed how it came alive after dark. Using powerful headphones, the Prof could also savour the wonderful noises and complex behaviour of its inhabitants. He was like a child when oblivious large animals came close enough to touch. Then one day, Solomon tripped and broke his ankle; he could not accompany his friend for a while. All alone on his vigils, the inquisitive man soon discovered that if he left a light source naked to the desert sky, it would attract thousands of insects and these in turn caused predatory bats to orbit the beam, snatching the hapless creatures from spiralling mass caught in the allure of the light emission. The amateur ecologist then discovered the specialists of the desert, the Lizards. He was amazed by their numbers and variety. But his method of attracting the desert wildlife was soon put to an end. The Guide was furious at the Prof, when it was discovered, how reckless he had been with their safety. The scholar challenged the man from the Amsterdam Contrib and said.

"But we are invisible, no one can find us."

The pony-tailed man shook his head at the Prof's stupidity and educated him.

"Anyone seeing the light from your torch would become suspicious and could be waiting for us when we emerged. They could have an ambush set up for us. People that live out here are not stupid."

It hurt him that nearly everyone else including Solomon agreed with the Guide and then the Prof was then given a dressing down in front of the rest of the small company. But one person took his side. The Lenses became flippant, he reckoned that those from the Anschluss was been divided into three camps. There was himself, the Prof and the Clerk in one group and the others on the other faction and the Mute by himself, so he asked the Guide.

"Don't blame him; we are only learning about these new lands and state of affairs out here. You might as well blame whoever gave him the lamp or then again, you could the blame the person who made the torch. People make mistakes."

The Engineer stepped into the argument.

"That is the most stupid reasoning I have ever heard. The Guide is right, this is not a game, and the danger out here is as real as back in the Anschluss. Sometimes you might not get a second chance."

A few days later, Haim gave the Prof a little gift that he was delighted with. It was a florescent lamp that lit up the night and could only be seen by an adapted pair of lenses or insect antenna. As the journey progressed, the scholar became more confident with the desert surroundings and preferred to spend more time outside with his mini recording devices. His outings were conducted while the others slept or rested and he never used a visible light source again. He was getting really good at concealment and was able to study the wildlife without been observed. On this particular morning, the spectacle wearing watcher sat on a large boulder under the shade provided by a cliff overhang that was still cool from the passing desert night. His hideout was also protected by the cover of a large quince bush. The inquisitive man had already picked some of the greenish yellow pear shaped fruit, but did not taste them. Solomon had already warned him.

"Even though you might see some animals or birds eat various seeds and remain unharmed, they could still be deadly poisonous to Humans."

He noticed several small colourful birds out on the baked earth of the desert floor. (The rains were a fleeting and distant memory for the parched ground). The winged animals were squabbling over the remains of a small skink. He felt guilty about the enormous stockpiles of food that was carried within the TORT-CAM, so he fished into his pockets and retrieved a handful of nuts, biscuits and dried fruit that he always carried as a snack to

479

ease his hunger during his long vigils. He slung the titbits out towards the raptors. Startled the birds flew off; croaking in alarm. But such was their desperation for any source of nourishment in this brutal land, they were soon returning to feed upon this unexpected bounty. The large coarse biscuits were reduced to crumbs within seconds. A melee for the food began in earnest and it was soon joined by larger birds. The newly arrived flying creatures started to gobble up the kernels and slices of fruit in frenzied haste while their smaller cousins scampered between their towering legs and fought ferociously for the scraps missed by the larger raptors. The smaller birds were pecking at crumbs that were no longer visible to his naked eye. The Prof laughed in delight at the spectacle that he had initiated. Neither, the Human observer or the desert avains noticed the gliding shadow high above. Little did either the man or the hungry creatures know that something with razor sharp eyes had seen the commotion. Attracted by the squawking and scramble of the feeding birds, a large desert bird of prey swooped down and the predator ended forever one of the bigger bird's need for forage. It happened in the blink of an eye. There was a choking gurgling squeal and all the surviving birds scattered to the four winds while the predator flew off mouthing a triumphal shriek with its prize clutched firmly in its killer talons. All that was left was a small patch of blood on the desert floor. Moisture was so precious here that even the blood of a victim could not be wasted. The Prof's stomach turned, for he was the cause of the beautifully patterned bird's demise. An accented voice from behind him made him jump, it was Solomon and he was hobbling. The Prof was overjoyed that his friend was up and about.

"It is not wise to interfere in the normal way of things, my friend." Said the Semitic looking man in rebuke.

"But that predators young will not go hungry today." Riposted the Prof.

"Touché."

Solomon agreed with his assessment. Both men smiled and their eyes met briefly, there was a bond been formed that would grow stronger. The Prof confided in his friend.

"I never dreamed that it would be like this."

"I know what you mean. Is it not wonderful and awe inspiring?"

"More than anyone will ever know. I am really glad I left the Anschluss."

Then Solomon surprised him as his hands done imaginary measurements.

"Surely this must be the source of all the dirt in the World. It makes you wonder why the surrounding peoples begrudge us a little land when they have so much empty space out here. If I owned this land, I would share it with the Prophet's people and turn it into a place of plenty for everyone."

"Yes it would be paradise. A person could begin here again, far from

the dictates of any government." Agreed the Prof.

"What a fantastic challenge, would it not, just to live out here and turn back the desert in pursuing such a dream." Sighed a wishful Solomon.

"Why do they call this place a desert? In between the tufts of scrub or under any rock. There is more diverse life here than anywhere in the sterile Anschluss. There are even Saltbushes on the moving dunes" Asked the other.

"And it is natural life, evolved to exist out here. I have heard that far to the south and west there are deserts of nothing but gigantic shifting sand dunes and still there is an abundance of life out there. And even farther to the south, there are grass savannahs on which millions of great beasts survive." Solomon told him.

"I am going to see that someday." Vowed his companion.

Then the Prof showed him a recording unit with all of the animals, plants and anything interesting he had amassed during the time that his friend was out of action. He told him.

"It was to be a surprise."

The two men who were fast becoming more than friends spent the rest of the morning observing and taking notes until the accumulating heat had them reluctantly call it a day. As they made their way back to the camp, the Prof rather shyly asked Solomon if he would help him in gathering data from now on.

"I would be honoured my friend." Said Solomon.

After that conversation, the two friends became even more inseparable and spent most of their free time together studying the wildlife and collating the data they collected as they travelled daily towards the groups intended destination. It did not take long for the others to spot their growing closeness. A few days later, the Guide told Naomh as the two of them sat out in the heat of the day checking their weapons and watching both of them. In this moment of time, only these four were outside the invisible shield.

"Do you see what those two are doing?" Asked van DerKamp.

Naomh noticed that some of the others including himself were beginning to look up to the pony haired man, seeking his advice and appraisal. The real leader of their company told Cahill earlier.

"It's because, the Guide looks a similar age to Rory and behaves a little like him. And every one of us probably needs a new Gaffer in our lives. Especially out here, far from the familiarity of home."

Naomh replied to the question.

"Those two are just studying the land and making harmless observations. It just a hobby after all. It keeps them occupied."

The questioner shook his head from side to side, his companion continued.

"As I said, it's just something to take their minds off the journey."

Replied an indifferent Naomh, thinking that it was just their way to forget about their homes and what had been left behind. He was still not fully clued up to how much the Prof despised the Anschluss.

"No dude. You could not be more wrong. Let me tell you a lesson from man's history. Do you know that all Empires and colonial powers used such information that those two individuals are amassing? These greedy governments used it as preparation for conquest. Enlightened people like the Prof and Solomon travelled out from the confines of their society into unknown lands to study and then published thesis on the wonder of it all. Most of these explorers fell in love with the lands and societies that they encountered and tried to preserve the beauty and uniqueness of it. But these enlightened people became the very tools of destruction of all of what they treasured. The "Think Tanks." back home read between the lines and saw the potential resources that were there for the taking. These foolish romantics even described the terrain and the strength of the opposition that their armies would encounter."

His student interrupted as he grasped what the Guide was implying.

"In short. These misguided romanticists provided a detailed plan of logistics for the exploitation and eventual subjugation of what they had cherished."

"Exactly. Armies of conquest and subjugation followed in their footsteps. These well-meaning people eventually brought a form of the same thing that they were escaping from to the new places they settled." Agreed the history lecturer.

"So you think somebody in the Anschluss will use their notes for conquest one day?" Asked his listener.

"Who knows? I doubt it though; those devious bastards are well informed already. But if the two lads knew that, would either of them desist from what they are doing?" Challenged the Guide.

Naomh just shrugged and replied.

"Both of them seem to love the wonder of new landscapes and daily discoveries. So I doubt it too."

"Let me tell something else about the behaviour of Governments." Suggested the teacher becoming unusually serious.

"I lied when I told you that I had never been outside the Enclave before. A long time ago when I was about your age, I was with your father down in Africa."

Rory's son became quite and pensive. He had never heard anybody talk of his parent outside members of the RE-INSTATOR'S.

"It was in a nation at the edges of the sub Saharan desert."

Naomh looked bemused.

"It is far to the South." The Guide said while shaking his head.

"Oh." Replied the other.

To himself, the man from the Amsterdam Contrib added mentally.

482

"I might as well be talking about the moon. I will get the Prof to show you the place on his map."

The narrator continued without his usual colourful language.

"The country we came across was very poor and destitute. There was appalling poverty and famine. Your father raged against this waste of Humanity and vowed to change it. It would serve as a lesson to the other poor Nations that were at its borders and these countries could follow its example. Rory went to their leaders and convinced them that he had a way to turn their fortunes around. Your father could be quite persuasive when he wanted to. Rory devised a plan and put it into action. He found local resources that the natives of this country had been unable to exploit before. Its people were brought back from the brink and your father began organising their economy. In a decade that Nation was exporting food and commodities and became extremely wealthy and living standards rose substantially. Soon their factories even began importing goods from their poorer neighbours and passed on some of their wealth to them. Your father and myself believed that his intercession was a resounding success."

The Guide paused for breath and surprisingly, Naomh felt very proud of his parent. But then the speaker's tone changed. It became bitter with disgust. His listener became puzzled.

"I met your father a few years ago and asked him, did you have any news from there. Rory gave me a vicious laugh and told me. The surrounding countries became jealous and formed an alliance. Then these envious people invaded their prosperous neighbour, citing that they were the reason their own people were poor and destitute. Their armies invaded on four fronts and raised the country to ashes. The people of the Nation that Rory had helped were nearly exterminated off the face of the Planet and the few survivors fled with what little possessions they could carry. These people had become dispossessed and became wanderers. No other country would take them in."

Naomh was horrified.

"Rory investigated and found out it's was the Anschluss's doing. Representatives of the ruling elite had approached the leaders of the other Nations and beguiled them with falsehoods. These consummate politicians convinced the ignorant leaders that the country, Rory had helped was responsible for all of their woes. The Anschluss supplied the antagonists with modern weaponry and the rest is history."

The Guide had nearly finished his story.

"You know, he blamed himself at what had happened. He told me that he should never have interfered. He believed that the Anschluss's meddling was an act of petulance against him personally."

Naomh privately found.

"I believe his implausible tale, because of what Miriam told me about the Anschluss supplying weapons to her people and besides, the treachery

reeks of them."

His companion had finished his unusual story, so they both sat in silent contemplation. Naomh broke the silence by asking his opinion about another of their crew.

"And what about the Lenses. How is he coping?"

"I don't think he will ever change from what he is. Where the Lenses finds himself, he will lock himself away in a room of computers. His World will always be the same, no matter where he ends up." Spouted the Guide.

True to his words, the Lenses on the other hand had shunned the outside desert, more than not, the strange eye coloured man spent most of his time inside the TORT-CAM studying its operation. When the hacker first saw its keyless technology, he became fascinated with it and been the Lenses; he had to solve its nuances. The fascinated man would work out the theory and the Engineer would put the acquired knowledge into a practical use.

"I don't think, he will ever come out of there, I am certain that he will be unaware that we have been travelling half way around the globe. If we are successful and get back home, I am sure that he would totally oblivious to the wonders that we will have seen."

"That's for sure."

The two men laughed at the implications of the Lenses ignorance. When the laughter had died down, the Guide gave Naomh a calculating look and then sighed as he had made a momentous decision. All serious now, he told his old friend's son.

"Naomh, I lied a while ago. When I told you about that it was fifteen years ago down in Africa, it was more like eighty."

"What! That's impossible."

A sceptical Naomh recovered from the Guide's anecdote and said.

"I'd say now you are lying or pulling my leg."

"How old do you think I am?"

"In your forties." Answered the other without hesitation.

"You are wrong; I will be a hundred and twenty-two on my next birthday."

An open-mouthed Naomh found himself becoming repetitive.

"That's impossible!"

"Never the less, it is true. Ever since I became a companion of your father, my aging process has slowed down. I realised that it was because of been in close proximity to your father. It was the same with Rory; he never aged a day since I knew him. You must believe me; this is no far-fetched tale."

The metallic voice confirmed the Hybrid's words.

"He speaks the truth, it is an effect of been around me. Your father's age measured in centuries."

"You are right, nothing about my father should surprise me anymore."

Astounded by the implications, Naomh became unusually silent. Gaining a new perspective, he eventually said.

"If you say so, then I believe you."

Both men became lost in thought. Unknown to the pensive duo as they discussed the Lenses and van DerKamp's previous escapades, those outside the invisible shield had just been sighted by a solider of the Prophet. Major Alwi Zaid lowered his binoculars and could not believe his luck. He knew that any stragglers would head south and his company were there to intercept them. But these soldiers were different; the Major had not expected to encounter these types of men. Zaid was the commander of the most feared section of the Prophets army, the discipline and infringement of Doctrine Squad. The satanic looking officer dressed in an all-black uniform and head scarf was the military Kadi of the Prophets forces. He was the judge, jury and executioner of who he himself deemed to be a criminal or deserter. This lover of death and position judged everybody unworthy. The Major and his subordinates were the most dreaded and hated people in the discipline squad. He and his men travelled among the armies with a miniature crane hooked up to his all-terrain vehicle. The converted killing apparatus was easily assembled and from its solid metal frame, hangings were carried out regularly, some were public, some were not. His unit had an impartial mandate to execute all deserters and criminals within the Prophets forces. Each solider in his command achieved perverse satisfaction from inflicting cruel and deadly punishments on any whom failed in their duty to God and his Prophet. Zaid rubbed his hands in eager anticipation on seeing the group of bedraggled Mujhadeen.

"Judging by their uniforms and black and white checked Smaughs, this huddled group are members of the Al Qud's Brigades. These ferocious fighters are usually untouchables, descendants of the original people of the Prophet that had lived in the lands behind the Enclave wall, before they had been cast out."

Now, these men had committed an infraction that even they could not escape from, the Kadi's sadistic bloodlust. He had an excuse prepared in the unlikely event of him been found out after their hanging.

"I deemed them to be common deserters. It was evident that those ragged scum had stolen the uniforms and headscarfs off of the dead."

Whether they were stragglers or genuine deserters did not matter, he and his soldiers would torment them until the World was rid of their miserable existence. The Major and the Mute had a common lust for the demise of others except that the Prophet's executioner hooded his victims and never got to see their eyes as death overtook them. The former also needed their fear while the handsome murderer cared little for that emotion; it was like a by-product of his homicidal activity. The Mute had also killed women, regretfully, the Kadi as a military enforcer had not. But the Major was in for a shock, just because the men below were dressed in the Al Quds brigade uniforms, it did not mean that the four were soldiers of the Prophet. As eager as he was to finally lay his hands on this elite group, the Kadi should have been more cautious. The Major and his men were about to make a fatal error. Zaid and his troop of thirty men quickly surrounded the group. They left the crane a short distance away as he delighted on bringing it forward when his victims were cowering in terror and helplessness.

"I do so enjoy the looks of terror my victims display when they see it, for they realise instantly what it is for."

Zaid strode forward and lowered his radio microphone over his mouth. Secure in the knowledge that his men had him covered and he was in instant communication with them, he gained in stature. In a loud, but contrite voice, the expert tormentor addressed them and smirked at their imagined dismay. Solomon had spotted the approaching Major and whispered harshly.

"See the mike at his mouth, that means there are others about and watching us. The three of your unshaven faces are not typical of the Mujahedeen, so cover up."

Naomh, the Guide and the Prof began hastily covering their faces so as not to betray their European heritage. The three of them watched the man striding forward from under covered faces. The others were still in the TORT-CAM and the appointed sentry must be seeing what was going on.

"A sure sign of guilt." Observed Zaid as he watched them conceal their faces.

One had the audacity to get off his knees instead of cowering. He came walking towards him while the rest stood their ground. It was Solomon and he had experience of his heredity foes structure of command and tongue.

"How can we be of service, Major?" Asked the man in a strange accent.

The Kadi was taken aback by the strange inflection. But, then he dismissed it as the Prophets lands were vast and some among them did not even speak the tongue of God as a first language. Still, the man's words told him what had guessed.

"They are deserters after all. I am familiar with the true owners of the uniforms accent. It is regrettable that we will not have the pleasure of hanging one of the arrogant Al Qud's brigade.

To the upstart, he barked.

"Silence! Why have you not joined the retreating army who are at this moment regrouping in the east?"

The officer demanded a really good explanation. His eyes searched the immediate area and he insisted.

"And where is the rest of your unit? All I can see is you wretched creatures. I also see that none of you are wearing your standard

communication equipment. Trying to disguise yourselves?"

"We got lost. And because our radios were damaged during the fighting, we were unable to contact our unit." Shrugged Solomon.

Major Zaid became more than slightly annoyed at this soldier's indifference as any stragglers his troop encountered usually crapped themselves by now. His black uniform was always a giveaway. The veins in his forehead bulged in affronted outrage.

"No, I don't think so. That is a common lie among your kind. I find it incredible that your four radios are destroyed. It is obvious that you are deserters and you will be punished. Those uniforms you wear are not your own." Claimed the Kadi.

The executioner had already made his verdict from the first moment he had seen them. Still, the man appeared unruffled by the portent of his words. Zaid spoke into his mike as he ended his proclamation. All of his men appeared from their cover and came to stand alongside him. Weapons with curved magazines covered the four false members of the Al Quds brigade. Still the man who had come towards him showed no fear and did not even try to explain about the stolen uniforms.

"He must be unhinged. There will be little fun with this one. But the other three have already shown fear by trying to hide their faces. I will start with them, maybe then he will understand the gravity of his situation."

Suddenly an armed solider appeared from thin air. A baffled Zaid rubbed his eyes in disbelief.

"By the beard of the Prophet, my eyes are playing tricks on me, the man has no beard."

Then a second clean shaven man appeared with another bearded man. Gunfire filled the air and his men started to drop all around him. All of the apparitions had light machine pistols except one who was equipped with a floating heavy calibre machine gun and she was massacring all of his men. Too late realisation came to the shocked Major.

"A woman with a gun and wearing a uniform of the Mujahedeen. Not deserters, but spies. Only the Enclave use women and clean-shaven soldiers."

From the edge of his peripheral vision, he noticed a head fly into the air like a punctured balloon. He saw the gun of a swarthy bearded man traverse towards him and a burst of fire knocked him from his feet. Within a few seconds all of the former ambusher's were down. The ordinary foot soldier of the Prophet's army would sleep easier tonight if they had known that Zaid and his sadistic bunch were no more. Certain that all of the enemy lay dead, Greta lay down her smouldering Beni and it hovered unassisted. The blonde killer demanded from the four who had been outside the safety of the invisible haven.

"Do I always have to save your hides?"

"That's why I brought you along." Grinned Naomh viciously.

Her red haired lover also laughed.

"Get rid of the bodies." Ordered Miriam.

One of their antagonists was feigning a fatal injury; his weapon was trained on the gathered bunch. Just as he sighted his targets and was about to squeeze his trigger, his back erupted in a cluster of bullet holes. The oldest among them had seen him just in time. The Anschluss infiltrator was disgusted, the mole had realised that during the fire-fight.

"I got cocky and now the Guide has saved me from taking a bullet. If my benefactor thinks that I will be grateful, then he is mistaken. If it is possible, I hate him even more now."

Unknown to him; he had witnessed a flaw in the Clones character and the LYUBINITES did not like to be in debt to anyone.

"Yes. I will deal with you when the time comes."

In the silence after battle, someone groaned. It was the sound of somebody in mortal pain.

"This one's also still alive." Said the Lenses pointing at a sprawled form.

It was the Major.

"We must help him." Insisted the Prof.

The Rabbi and Solomon agreed. The Mute had beaten the others to the mortally wounded Kadi. The expectant freak knelt down beside the dying Mujhadeen; he wanted to be there when the man expired his last breath. The lover of death waited for the transition from life to nothingness. He knew that the Major's final whistle of breath was at hand. But in the final moment of his life, the Mute was abruptly pushed away. Major Zaid's mouth was incredibly dry even though blood flowed from his lips. His tortured body hurt like hell. He tried to focus and saw a beautiful Angel of death float across his vision. While the others were arguing, Greta shot him straight between the eyes. She had used her infamous catch phrase as she ended the major's life.

"You're dust."

The Mute was furious; the Major's death had been too quick and her bullet had shattered the dying man's head like an exploding melon. He had missed the glint of life go out. Aggrieved and unwilling to lose his cool, he moved away, sat down and made another entry into his murderous diary. One of Major Zaid's corporals and three privates went into the next entries after the Enclave female solider. Greta with her heavier weapon had gotten most of them. The Prof was even more enraged at the killing. Some of the dead men had small holes the size of marbles in the front of their bodies and on their other sides; the exit wounds were as big as footballs. He knew this to be the work of Cahill and Greta.

"Those two sick bastards idea of foreplay is to file down the tips of ordinary rounds and turn them into fragment rounds. It is hard to discern

which one of them should be called Bonkers."

The infuriated pacifist pointed at the Major's body and then to those who had committed the murder and said.

"That's your solution to everything."

Disgusted and still ranting, the embittered Prof stormed away from them. He always thought that discretion was the better part of valour and hated the confrontational attitude of his companions.

"Naomh, I told you he was too soft for this game." Admonished the Guide.

Others agreed, but Solomon defended his friend.

"Compassion is not a sign of weakness."

The Spy secretly disagreed with his words.

"Of course it is. Anything that effects your judgement has to be."

Their leader told them.

"Comply with Miriam's orders and get rid of the bodies."

Solomon was about to follow his friend, but Naomh intervened.

"Let me go after him."

The man from the Enclave nodded. Naomh chased after the Prof, he was a good distance ahead. He called after him.

"Wait."

The disgruntled man slowed down and allowed his commander to catch up to him. As he reached him, the visibly upset man turned around and faced him. With tears threatening to spill from his eyes, he demanded from his leader.

"Haven't we seen enough killing? What have we become Naomh, even the Mute was showing some compassion when he knelt down to comfort the dying man. We had a chance to save that man's life. He could have received medical attention from the Rabbi and we could have set off a flare to bring his own people. Then all of us could have waited in the TORT-CAM until he was rescued."

Naomh had a big argument against those words, but it went unsaid. He put his hand on the academics shoulder and gripped the shoulder blade in a comforting pinch. He told the grief stricken man like a parent mollifying a non-understanding infant.

"Edward; There will be a lot more killing before this is finished. We have already lost friends and companions back home and I cannot guarantee others won't die as well."

"I don't know if I can carry on." Said the Prof as his tirade ended and he became full of abject despair.

"Listen to me. The prize at the end of this is so wonderful that there will be no more killing. The Human race will move on. Violence will be a thing of the past. I promise you this." The bearer of the amulet was really sincere in his words and something in them made the Prof believe.

"That is a goal worth pursuing."

He agreed.

"I will keep you to that promise."

"And I will hold you to it. Come on, let's go back."

As the two men made their way back to the others, neither of them had the benefit of hindsight. If they had done it the Prof's way, Major Zaid was so hated among the ranks of the Muslim army that the former Kadi would have died a terrible death of torture and mutilation at the hands of his fellow Mujahedeen. The dead men would have never known that Greta and the rest of the shooters had done them a favour of a quick death. A fate that Zaid's murders had denied many a man in the Prophet's army. When Naomh and the Prof got back, the others had finished the dirty work of dragging the bodies away and leaving them piled unceremoniously on top of each other in some scrub that Moshe had found a few metres away from the brief fire-fight. They had divested the corpses of useful items, such as their communication devices and anything that would improve their disguises. The Engineer callously kicked a severed head, minus its mike, towards the heap of carrion and it landed amid the gore. Someone said.

"Good shot. You could make the Madrid Contrib team."

The Prof's disgust returned. When Greta saw them return, she spoke to Cahill in a loud enough volume, so she would be overheard.

"Why is he so upset about them?"

She pointed to where the dead lay.

"These carrion would have done the same to us. Anyway, all these bodies can now feed his precious animals."

Greta was certainly not one for displays of remorse. If the returning man had heard her words, he did not react to them. Solomon went to the Prof and put his arm around him and led him away. Cahill's lover hurled one final insult.

"Touching."

Miriam and Beersheba had gone to see if there were any more soldiers around. The Persuader and Shoshanna headed off in the opposite direction. The four scouts came back ten minutes later; the latter reported nothing unusual. But, Miriam had a different story.

"It looks like this bunch arrived in a motorised vehicle and left one of their number to guard it. But as soon as he saw the two of us approach, the man jumped into it and drove away at high speed."

Beersheba gave a wicked laugh.

"I never had that effect on a man before."

Her Serene told them in a professional capacity.

"He certainly has a radio device in his vehicle, so we had better move away from here, enter the TORT-CAM and lay low for a while. Whoever he finds will come looking for us and there will be a lot of them."

Bloodlust was high, so some were up for the fight. But the sensible amongst the rest of her party agreed. They packed up and marched over the desert scree for an hour. When it was decided that they had left the scene of slaughter far enough behind, Naomh re-formed the invisible shield and went to get the Lenses who had re-entered its confines before the ensuing trek. The Engineer went with him into the insular sphere.

"I need to check on his progress."

Their friend from the Warsaw Contrib had tried to stay inside the globe before the brief fire-fight. The engaged man said to them as they prepared to go into battle.

"I am examining something interesting. I am fully confident that the rest of you can handle whatever is happening outside without me."

Much to his annoyance, he was given a weapon and dragged out anyway. Once inside the now familiar red and orange light, the two men found him near a white chamber, which had emerged behind a pile of boxes. An excited Lenses told them.

"I was messing around here and found this treasure throve of technology."

Naomh questioned the APOCRYPHA'I.

"What is this place? How come we never came across it before?"

The two parts Mescal/Amulet answered.

"It is a place of the craft which created my parts. In this section of the Gudiex sphere, there are items of advanced technology that will help you in your quest. As you gain more parts of my essence, then more sections will open up and these compartments will reveal more devices."

As far back as the two parts Mescal/Amulet and his fellow ALASTHA'I remembered, the Hybrids thrived on a reward system. So this was the method the deceitful Aliens now used to keep their creations on the right path. Naomh told the Lenses what it was and suggested. *"You and the Engineer should experiment with the stuff that you will come across. Do an inventory to utilise anything you find."* As an afterthought, he added. *"Be very careful with it, we don't know what's in there."*

The Lenses and the Engineer put their heads together and came up with a name for that section of technology. The two technical men called it, the LAB-CELL. The two parts Mescal/Amulet approved at this technical abbreviation.

"If it had been left to one of the others, only the Creator knows what the Hybrids would have called that section of the Gudiex sphere.

While the concealed group stayed put under the impenetrable blanket of the invisible shield, the fascinated duo spent the rest of the day away from the others studying the newly discovered LAB-CELL and the contents that it unveiled. The Persuader brought them refreshment now and then and the non-technical man was always ushered out of their presence. The two men never felt the passing of time until Cahill entered and told them that they had to move on. Both knew that when Naomh shrunk the TORT-CAM to marble size, then whoever was still inside would have to remain put until it was enlarged. This time though, after the skirmish with the soldiers of the Prophet, they needed every available hand. So the two men reluctantly came out into the normal light of day.

Meanwhile, nobody had come looking for the Major and his men or those that killed them. The lone surviving solider driving the hanging crane had come across a group of stragglers and in a grave error of panicked misjudgement stopped alongside them. When the retreating soldiers had seen the hanging vehicle and realised what unit he was from and more importantly that he was alone, they decided on a little justice of their own. The gleeful men had hung him up, castrated him and left him still alive for the vultures; not before he had told them what had happened. The vengeful men also gleefully burned the infamous hanging crane, delighted in the knowledge that its infamous owner would never torment one of the rank and file again. Unaware of these events and the unlikelihood of pursuit, the questors marched along that night. Those at the back of the single file kept a watch on their rear. Little zephyrs of change carried on the wind currents hinted at an end to the brown barren desert and its cracked baked clay. The sparse growth was giving way to lush and more numerous vegetation. Towards dawn, the landscape, the marchers were traversing became as verdant as any either of them had seen since coming into the Prophet's lands. Smelling as if it had rained recently, the vista ahead as far as the eye could see was carpeted in an emerald green covering. It had not in fact rained; the reason for the lush landscape was manmade. Huge reservoirs of desalinated sea water were strategically placed around the desert and these irrigational systems simulated seasonal rainfall that only naturally fell in winter time. It was an attempt to keep the Nomadic lifestyle, the very lifeblood of the people on this Arabian Peninsula, alive. Vast herds of sheep, camels and sprinkling of goats formed blots of mottled browns and whites on the newly flourishing grasslands. Numerous large tents of the nomadic people who eked a living on this seasonal bonanza sprouted from between the livestock. Armed men in motorised vehicles patrolled the herds from predators and rustlers. As the intrigued group watched the activity of the Nomads, the Clerk asked.

"How do we get pass this lot?"

"We will wait a few days my friends and these wanders will be gone. Their herds will exhaust the grasses and they will move on to richer pastures." Informed a knowledgeable Solomon.

The Prof's close comrade and Haim called everyone in the group

"My friend."

This really annoyed the Anschluss Spy. The mole insisted silently to themselves.

492

"Why do these people call me their friend? I am not their friend. They are only an end to a means; this bunch of foreigners means nothing to me."

Miriam pointed to a blurry object on a distant hill.

"Do you see that old fort over there? We will use it as a place to wait and rest until the Nomads move on."

Once the climbers had reached the ruins heights, the Guide, the Rabbi and the Persuader went out to scout and set up a warning perimeter. The Enclave man confided in his two companions.

"I like this tactic of evading the enemy, before we would have set up a defensive perimeter and if a hostile force approached, a fire fight would ensue. Now we just disappear and wait until any potentially hostile force is gone. Yes it is much better."

The fort that Miriam had directed them towards was about five kilometres away and out of view of the nomadic camp. The stark structure was on the far side of the surrounding hills of the massive nomadic encampment and their teeming masses of domesticated livestock. The questors arrived at the fort without been observed. The building like all in this scorching land whether they were of modern concrete or mud brick ruins was coated in a finish of white alabaster plaster. So ancient was this construction that its flat roof had collapsed centuries before and it now had a make-shift canopy of bramble and twigs from the plants that availed of its shade. All of its once fine and rare timber had been burnt in many a nomadic campfire. The fleeting traveller that availed of the fort's shelter cared nothing for the beautifully decorated wood, only that it provided warmth and dry fuel for their cooking fires. Two once impressive marble columns mined from distant islands in the Western Sea and brought here at great expense, tethered drunkenly at its entrance. The lintels of the same material that once rested on top of the columns, now lay shattered upon the ground, covered by the ever shifting sand. The strange calligraphy that adorned their entire circumference was made illegible by time and climate. Mud brick coin parapets that crowned the once proud walls appeared chipped and gapped like misused teeth. The inside walls bore testament to the sooty scorch marks of the past campfires. Red brick and terracotta tiles once used in its construction now formed crudely built fire circles. Amongst the carbonised ashes lay fragments of animal bone from the many feasts that had been consumed in the courtyard under the gaze of the circulating stars.

"It must have been abandoned a long time ago." Stated Haim.

"So what's new? Every building we passed in this desert was derelict." Said the Clerk.

"As we told you many times already, these people do not know how to use the land." Beersheba pointed out with her inbuilt Enclave prejudice.

The folk from the tribes might have been surprised to learn that the

493

ancestors of the forts inhabitants had once brought civilisation to the Western World. While the ancestors of the Enclave and the Anschluss lived in crude straw huts, these people lived in places surrounded by learning and civilisation. Piped water meandering through aqueducts brought running water to their houses to supply ingenious fountains, bathing pools and toilets. These travellers would not be so free with their bigoted attitude against the people of the Prophet if they were aware of what this place had boasted in its prime. Even after twenty centuries of neglect, the fort still had a working water service and its leaking pipes provided the moisture for a bunch of fruit trees that stood in the centre of the long abandoned courtyard. The non-tended plants had precious few leaves in this season, but they still retained clusters of small yellow fruit clinging perilously at the tips of their gnarled limbs. Each one of the sallow produce was speckled with splotches of brown decay that spoke of a rotten core. But another season of rain would cause young buds to erupt from its branches and start the life cycle again. Suddenly, the irrational nature of this place conspired against them. They were about to be hit by what the natives called a Shamal. Sand laden winds suddenly blew up out of nowhere, speckles of dirt, grit and then small stones began to fall and in an instant, a full blown sandstorm was upon them. One minute, clear blue skies, then darkness smothered them as the wind began to shiver and howl. The ensuing assault of windborne particles caused them to retreat from the fury of the instant tempest to the deeper shelter of the ruin. The remaining fruit tumbled to the floor and the Prof ran to gather it. As the scrambling man began scooping the round fruits up, the gale became so fierce that some of the forts crumbling masonry fell to the ground and the bare tuffs of climbing weeds clinging to the ancient walls danced wildly as the sandstorm increased in ferocity.

"Quickly everybody get into the TOR-TCAM." Advised Solomon.

The Guide, the Rabbi and the Persuader had not returned from their reconnoitre; so the Lenses with permission from Naomh risked a transmission. He put on the Enclave helmet. The pink-eyed man contacted them by the Enclaves broadcasting devices. The Rabbi answered and said.

"The three of us have found shelter in a secure cave and will sit out the inclement weather."

The call lasted ten brief seconds; it was not long enough to be traced. Naomh brought forth the TORT-CAM and those inside the trembling structure got out of this violent aspect of nature. As always the transition was profound, the silence of the insular World was more acute this time. When the squall had abated and faded into a light shower of fine spray, Shoshanna who was on point saw the Persuader, the Rabbi and the Guide at the translucent perimeter. The three men's faces were agape, a curious look etched across their faces. What was more puzzling was the fact that all of the men were staring directly at them and none of them had activated their wristbands. The Persuader had the butchered carcass of a dead animal slung over his shoulders. It had been a sheep. As those in the invisible shield came to greet them, the Guide gestured that they had a problem. He said as he pointed at a glistening outline.

"Look."

The others did so and soon discovered what he was talking about. In the dark recess of the fort, the falling sand was revealing the shadowy outline of the TORT-CAM. For the gravity driven grit did not penetrate the light barrier but flowed around its invisible curves. Naomh shrank the globe, wiped it and reactivated it. Without its revealing shroud of fine particles, it once again performed its intended operation flawlessly. Intrigued by the discovery, the Engineer took out a canteen of water and poured it over where he assumed the vanished shield was. To cries of dismay, the flowing liquid once again exposed their havens shadowy parameters.

"We will have to be careful where we hide from now on. Any falling dust or rain will reveal us." Said Cahill.

The Persuader had other things on his mind, his belly in fact.

"My two friends and I thought that this group could do with some fresh meat. We found this stray meal wandering around; it must have got separated during the storm.

"It is a gift from God." Interrupted the Rabbi.

"Not the Nomads?" Asked Moshe.

The three hunters grinned at the others. The unfortunate animal had been professionally butchered by the Rabbi who told the Enclave members.

"I cut the sheep's throat after the Persuader had run the stray animal down and caught it with his bare hands."

"So it is kosher." Advocated a delighted Haim.

A nod from the butcher confirmed his assumption. The dubiously acquired meat was skinned, cut into large chunks and put into a stew of vegetables. It was left simmering on a smokeless heating unit. The aroma wafting from the stew was mouth-watering. Moshe fetched bread from the Enclave out of the storage area of the TORT-CAM and all except the Prof enjoyed one of the best meals any had ever tasted. The committed vegetarian peeled the fruit that he had gathered and cut away the rotten bits. His intense effort gleaned him a miserable few pieces of edible pulp. He offered them around, but the others declined. He decided to save them for his animal friends. So good was the meal and the camaraderie that Haim told a joke. The big nosed man began.

"Centuries ago, the army of the Enclave faced a similar sized force of the Prophet across no man's land. Two lines of opposing trenches faced each other. Every morning at 7.oo am; Yossi from the Enclaves army used to shout across at the Prophets lines.

Is that you Achmed?

An Achmed would stand up and answer.

It is me.

Yossi would then shoot him dead.

This continuous verbal abuse went on for a few weeks until a sergeant on the Prophets side went to his commander and told him what was happening. The commander considered the situation and then told the sergeant.

I have a plan.

Next morning at 6.50am, you will shout across to the enemy's lines. Is that you Yossi and when someone replies, you will shoot him. The sergeant thought this a brilliant plan and told his commander that he was very wise and that was why he was their commander and he a lowly sergeant.

So at 6.50 the next morning, the sergeant shouts across to the Enclaves lines.

Is that you Yossi?

He got no reply.

Again he shouted and still he got no answer.

Frustrated, the sergeant kept shouting and got no reply. Then at 7.ooam, a voice came back.

Is that you Achmed looking for me?

The sergeant shouted back in anger.

It is.

Then Yossi said, fuck you Achmed and shot him through the head."

Those from the Enclave busted out laughing even though they must had heard the joke many times. However, the brand of humour was lost on Naomh's people and most of them laughed politely. Amazingly, all but Greta, who laughed in genuine mirth. This surprised her closest friends.

"It must be because we are out in the open sky away from our built up areas. The freedom is even touching her."

The rest of the seekers agreed with him when the subject of Greta's outburst of laughter was broached. Of course she was not around at the time. Another believed; he knew the reason for her good humour.

"She found it funny because someone got to shoot somebody."

As the Persuader and Shoshanna packed away the plates, Greta noticed a horrible looking spider making its way across the sandy floor relentlessly towards the remains of their meal. The grotesque eight-legged insect had a huge humped back. She made to stamp on it, but the Prof's expression made her hesitate.

"Don't harm it." Said the academic as he touched the rim of his spectacles.

The blonde woman ignored him, gave him a dirty look and squashed the hapless arachnid with the heel of her boot. The dead spider's body exploded in a spray of tiny organisms and suddenly, her statuesque form was covered in thousands of little spiders. The miniature host was in her face, her hair and for the first time in their lives; her comrades saw Greta lose it. They had found the chink in her armour. She ran away from them screaming as she frantically tried with flailing arms to brush the countless offenders away. Cahill chased after her and went to his lover's aid. The two of them eventually managed to get rid of the tiny spiders with a container of water that was unceremoniously dumped over her. Witnessing her loss of demeanour; the Clerk and the Prof had collapsed into fits of laughter. None of the others had dared to express their amusement openly as the Prof through tear filled eyes said to his companion in mirth.

"I told her not to."

The academic was apt in making trivial comments.

"I did hear you."

The Clerk nearly bit his tongue in an attempt to stifle his hilarity as he saw Greta return with Cahill. But she had seen them smirking.

"Did you think that was funny little men?" Demanded the enraged woman coldly of the duo, her voice was laden with icy venom.

The infectious smiles were instantly wiped off the two men's faces. Both of them rushed to stammer an apology.

"No, no, not at all."

The disgruntled female appeared satisfied at their sudden meekness. The Mute had also been laughing at Greta's plight; his sense of humour was always at someone else's misfortune. Unlike the other two, her threat had no effect on him. The next day however, the butt of their humour had a revenge of sorts. A large colourful black and yellow insect landed on the Lenses arm. With an expression of disgust, the pink-eyed man brushed it away. It buzzed around and then resettled back on his arm. The Prof told him.

"The insect will not hurt you. Leave it alone, it will fly off in a few seconds."

It did as he predicted, but no one saw where it went to. Then, the so-called expert left out an almighty roar as another insect of the same variety had stung him. Pain filled his face as he lifted up his jumper and discovered a large red welt and a trapped yellow wasp. The offending insect flew off. Greta and the Mute were delighted at his misfortune. The latter nearly choked on a nut that he was chewing, while the former's cruel laughter hurt more than the irritating swelling. But the more galling thing was swallowing the pills the Rabbi gave him against infection. It was like gulping down his pride at his lack of knowledge of this new environment, he found himself cast into. But their doctor's remedy had immediate effect and the swelling decreased noticeably, so his mood lightened a bit and eventually he found humour in what had happened to him. They had been far enough away from the nomadic camp that the motorised herders had not heard the commotion. But the very next day, an adolescent male and female came up to the fort and engaged in an illicit coupling. The questors had hastily covered up their presence and scampered into the TORT-CAM. But they had no need to worry as the two inexperienced lovers were so absorbed in their love making that the youths did not spot anything out of the ordinary. If they had, it would have been their last moments on Earth as Greta had them in her sights. The muzzle of her rifle protruded slightly from the invisible shield. The liaison lasted briefly; it was hurried, urgent, inexperienced and dangerous because if the un-betrothed couple were missed and assumed to have been together, then dreadful repercussions would be visited on the two of them. As quick as the two hurried lovers had come, the teenagers left one at a time and headed back to their camp in different directions. The male nomad took a roundabout route where he had tied up a single lamb, his reason for been up here. The female Nomad headed back directly and on her way gathered some pretty flowers that their livestock had missed, this was her excuse. The two youths returned the next day to the same place and engaged in the same act of passion. It was the Mute's turn at the trigger and he itched to kill them from his hidden vantage-point. But lost in their animal urges, the copulating couple would have been oblivious to their last moments and this stayed his hand. Besides the missing couple would draw a search from the thousands of people below. The evil man was twisted, not stupid. Three days later during Solomon's watch, there were signs of urgency in the nomadic camp. Livestock was been rounded up and tents were been loaded on to vehicles. The next morning during the Prof's vigil, the entire camp moved off in a swirling trail of dust. The sentry informed the others about the change. The brief verdant plain had been left silent and bare and once again waiting for the seasonal rains to return in time and renew it. Bits of discarded rubbish and tattered rags and a few dead animal carcasses which were been fought over by scavenging dogs and hovering birds were all that told of the temporary encampment that had stood here. The hidden questors could move at last and be on their way. Out of curiosity, the Clerk looked at the date, it was a year and two month's since they had left the Anschluss. It caused him to ponder.

"When I was on the Mag-Lev going south, I could have never imagined where I am now. And the sights I have seen since. What is the next year going to be like? I'd bet that it is going to be even more interesting."

On that account he was going to be correct and the eager man might have wished that he had indulged in common sense and he had stayed in his boring job and never left the Anschluss. A few hours later, the searchers of the APOCRYPHA'I crossed the former sight of the nomadic camp scattering the miffed carrion eaters and headed where the two parts Mescal/Amulet guided Naomh. Their direction was still southwards and into harsher lands were only the hardiest plants and animals survived.

XX.

MEDINA, THE HOLY CITY OF THE PROPHET 2953 AD/ 2331.

To this man of great stature and knowledge, the warm dry humidity was stifling. But Sheikh Mohammad Ali Ben Sulimani took no notice of the inclement heat and bore the indignity of its effects with the same bearing as he ignored the annoying biting insects that hovered around him.

"No, I have more pressing things on my mind!"

Above his long white Thobe and underneath his red and white checked Ghuta, the leader of his people was almost frothing at the mouth; as he sat in pride of place, in full view of the packed stadium and the recording cameras that were broadcasting his image to the billions of the Prophet's followers throughout the Muslim World. For those watching eyes, he forced himself to appear solemn and repentant. Still, he was furious at his state of velleity. *"This is to be a public humiliation carried out in the sacred city as a result of my officer's perceived incompetence. A rush of blood filled passion; a moment of indecision, this is to be my shame and their kismet."*

To the watching audience, he sat still and stone faced. There was no betrayal of the fury raging within and the agonising eroding of his self-esteem. The only indication of his agonising frustration was a slight tugging of his neatly trimmed square beard and the hard glint in his nearly black eyes that were set above his not too prominent hooked nose.

"No, I will not give the mob or the other Caliph's gathered here, the satisfaction they crave."

While he and his entourage endured the heat in spartan conditions, other despised rulers sat in air-conditioned luxury; sipping cool drinks, nibbling at titbits and looking forward to the spectacle.

"How dare they!"

Seated around him were portions of his large family, members of his inner circle and their relations.

"These members of my tribe are to share in my humiliation as well."

Not only was the Sheikh, a Sunni Muslim and the Caliph of his people; he was also their Ayatollah. Sheikh Ben Sulimani was a youthful looking man in his late forties; his uniform beard was neatly trimmed with a pencil shaped moustache to augment it. His crown was still covered with a full head of hair which still remained pitch black. He was also a flamboyant and charismatic leader, much loved by his subjects and envied among other rulers.

"And now I am about to lose my best officers because of their love for the ways of the Prophet and their hatred for the People of the Tribes. We failed once again, even though, our strategists knew where the attack was going to come from. Our enemy's occupation is a tumour that has to be

499

removed from the lands of the Prophet. And now, the malady is getting bigger."

The enduring hatred among the followers of the Prophet for the Zionists had grown into a festering rage over the last ten centuries. He took account of historical reality.

"*We have endured insult upon insult, shame upon shame and still the affront remains. The expanding Enclave has broken all of its treaties and re-conquered the lands of Palestine and Gaza. Not content with that, they now encroach into Lebanon, Syria and most of Southern Jordan. The two great cities of Damascus and Amman have shifted eastwards, so their inhabitants would not have to look at the wall of shame. And, now after the latest incursion, they were deeper into the borders of the Prophet's own soil. And still the arrogant Zionists bite deeper into our sacred lands. I also have failed again at the foot of the wall of shame. And now because of the ineptitude of our armies more of the Prophet's land was in the greedy clutches of the Zionists.*"

It was discovered that it was the forces under his command that fired the first shots on that accursed leading Tank. The blue star on its turret still mocked him.

"*I still cannot believe that all the other artillery units followed my gunner's example and every heavy gun, howitzer and mortar zeroed in on the few advancing vehicles instead of targeting the main line of advancing armour with the wall sections. Those vital moments lost while our artillery pummelled the breakaway group had turned the tide of battle against us. It had allowed the enemy vital time to complete their steel barricade.*"

He felt no pleasure that the offending vehicles had been wiped from the face of God's Earth.

"*Their crews had died hero's deaths, while my brave men have been branded cowards and the villains of the defeat. A sensible order to retreat was given but a worst debacle followed when tens of thousands of Mujhadeen had lost their heads and charged the wall, only to be slaughtered in numbers that defies belief. It was sheer stupidity. For every sensible commander knows the futility of such an aggressive manoeuvre in attacking such an obstacle. None of the men under my command had taken part in that disastrous action.*"

As a well-versed student of battle; he had ordered the retreat of his command in a disciplined fashion just before a section of their defensive positions went up in a huge explosion exposing their forces. To him, the Enclave had used new types of powerful bombs that removed the top of the hills they had been entrenched under. The other leaders of the Muslim confederation had ignored his warnings and the effects were disastrous. The battle had been turned into a slaughter of great magnitude and to cover up the insane charge, the blame was laid with those who had first targeted the break-away Tanks.

"And now some of my best men are to pay for that decision with their lives."

The Sheikh had lost very few people in comparison to his allies. Looking at his doomed officers, he uttered contritely.

"It would have been better for them to die smashing against that unbreachable wall or buried in the underground bunkers, than the fate that now awaits them. But then I would have lost a great number of my forces."

The other leaders and military rulers from the Prophet's nations had demanded.

"You must make an example of your men as it was their initial actions that resulted in the farce of trying to halt the Enclaves ever-creeping advance into the land of the Prophet."

To alleviate the shame of the hoards of the Muslims, his finest officers were to be executed live on camera and the scene broadcasted into every coffeehouse, souk, palace and hovel in the lands of the faithful. The handsome Caliph rose, fell to his knees and touched his forehead to the uncarpeted ground of his central tier as the Muezzin's voice came over the loud speaker in a call for the faithful to pray. At the end of the recital, the holy speaker of God asked.

"Allah (BLESSING BE UPON HIM.); forgive the condemned."

The Sheikh was certain.

"My men will be received favourably in paradise and many golden haired virgins will be waiting for them."

The loud hailer trailed away to silence and a respectful hush swept around the packed tiers of the stadium as the doomed officers were led out like common criminals. The grip of rage tightened in the Sheikh's inner being as he saw his men had their hands tied behind their backs.

"This is designed to humiliate me further. How they die is to reflect on me."

All of the condemned officers were known to him, some were even his distant kin. Again, he repeated.

"How they die is to reflect on me."

His ill-fated men were led to the centre of the pitch where a line of black hooded swordsmen waited. Decapitation was to be their fate. They would have preferred a soldier's death, even by firing squad. But this was to be denied to them. If the other Sheikhs had their way, his men would have been hanged. In a fury, he advised them.

"If this occurs, then by the will of Allah, (BLESSING'S BE UPON HIM.) the rest of you will have to destroy my tribe and nation completely."

Knowing that they risked pushing him too far and as most of them had been weakened as a result of the war; a comprise was agreed. Execution by beheading. The Sheikh had once witnessed the botched beheading of a rapist when an incompetent executioner had performed it. It had taken several crude blows to sever the neck until finally the remaining muscles and tendons attaching the neck had to be cut off with a sharp knife. It had been a messy affair. He silently prayed.

"Allah (BLESSINGS BE UPON HIM.) give my men a quick and painless passing to paradise. "

The Sheikh knew that it was more than a political decision to have his men executed; it had been a religious one as well. Some of the Mullahs and Imams were been queried at a grass root level, if the numbers of the Muslims had reached their pinnacle. There had been no expansion of the Prophet's lands in centuries, the faithful had been excluded from the atheist Anschluss among other nations and questions were been asked among the faithful, especially since the Enclave was nibbling away at the Western edges.

"Has the spread of Islam reached its zenith? Will the holy Religion go into decline? Will we be left alone in a Godless World?"

The Imam's also needed to reassure their flock's commitment to the faith. The best way to achieve this was to reproach others and so, the Sheikh's officers were blamed in failing to do their duty to Allah. As he sat in his seat, his posture rigid, Ben Sulimani surmised.

"Some of the other warlords are hoping that even now, I will object to the decision and cancel the executions. Thus showing weakness and strengthening their standing while at the same time undermining my own influence among the followers of the Prophet."

He hated those faction leaders with deserved passion. For at this time, as always, the nations of Islam were far from been united. Many of the once larger Nations had fragmented into Fiefdoms and the Sheikh was the leader of one of these entities; down in the south-western corner of the Arabian Peninsula. The North African countries refused to take part in the assaults on the Enclave and make it a two front war. The Turks who had once guided the nations of Islam had once been part of the Anschluss, but ceded when it turned atheist. The non-believers held on to the land on the European side of the Bosporus and in a decision that reeked of blasphemy tore down the remains of the great mosque of Suleiman after a series of earthquakes destroyed most of the buildings fabric. The following destruction of former Church of Hagia Sophia and the other great mosques started a religious war that ended badly for the Anschluss's enemies. After fierce battles and a nuclear stand-off, (The Anschluss been the only ones with the weapons of mass destruction that were willing to use them.) the Turks and their allies sued for peace as they still lived under the shadow of the Anschluss walls. Since then, its rulers had a policy of appeasement towards their much larger neighbour. There was also no proof that the LYUBINTIES had indeed been responsible for the demolition of the religious sites. They proclaimed their innocence and blamed the destruction on the final massive earthquake. The World of Islam as a consequence was not united in a cohesive front in the campaign against the

Zionists. Most of the time they involved themselves in petty localised conflicts and squabbled amongst themselves. Some of the North African states were even courting the Godless Anschluss. He promised to himself and Allah that those fence-sitters would also pay for his humiliation. The Sheikh had sworn a Fatwa against the Enclave.

"God willing, I will destroy it and return the Kubbetes-Sakhra back to the faithful."

Of course, he had not yet delivered on his promise to the one God. With this in mind, he watched as each prisoner was marched to their fate with heads held high and locking their gazes with him, their spiritual leader. His men were proud to die for him, so he could redeem his honour. He cursed inwardly.

"Such a fine waste of men."

Also in the same breath, he vowed.

"Those cowards hiding behind the Enclave walls will pay for this. I will see their leaders and Generals marched to a gallows and publicly hanged in front of all of the Nations that serve Allah (BLESSINGS BE UPON HIM.). And their vanquished people cast into the sea. They can sail back to where ever they had come from."

If he could deliver on such a promise, he would certainly become the supreme leader of the Muslim peoples and the new Mahdi would spring from his seed. Ben Sulimani and his descendants would unite them under one banner and even take on the mighty atheist Anschluss. For all his hatred of the Tribes, at least the Zionists shared a belief in the one God.

"But these are dreams of the future."

Stuck in this melancholy mood, the Sheikh longed for the company of his favourite offspring, his eldest daughter Ayesha. This beautiful pearl was his eldest child from his first wife and she had something in her possession that could not be risked away from the safety of his desert stronghold.

"Many of those fools think it is because of her chastity that she is not here. If they only knew?"

He had many wives and daughters, because he was cursed to have only female children spring from his loins. The Sheikh was absolutely certain.

"This is a punishment from above because of my failed vow to rid the Zionists from the Prophet's lands. Until this is achieved, there will be no male heirs and no Mahdi. Many lesser rulers and indeed some of the stronger ones believe their families can strengthen their standing among the faithful by marrying their unworthy sons to my beautiful flower of the desert. But God willing, I will bring the Enclave barrier down and be rewarded by the Prophet himself, who has ascended to paradise from behind those very walls."

What would the Sheikh have thought if he became aware as the executioner's blades flashed brightly in the sunlight and then fell in swift silver arcs to end the lives of his men that a resolution to his desires would soon pass his way. While the blood thirsty crowd cheered as the heads of his devoted followers fell to the emerald grass of the arena with fountains of red blood spurting from their severed necks, that he would soon come closer to his dream as it was possible. If he only knew as the headless bodies of his men toppled sideways, that the crew of the Tank that had caused his humiliation were on the way to him. By a strange twist of fate, he had ownership of what they wanted and these people had in their possession the means of breaching that accursed wall. As the loyal blood of his men seeped in to fill the dried cracks of dirt along the cracked parchment of the arena's centre circle; the Caliph had little realisation that the tool he desperately required was slowly approaching him and the carrier of that device was far from been a servant of the Prophet as he had often imagined. Not wanting to prolong his shame, a moment longer, he stood up.

"The dirty deed is done; I will not discredit myself any further. They have got their kilo of flesh."

With a clap of his hands, Ben Sulimani gathered his entourage together as his men's dismembered remains were been loaded on to a single battered vehicle that spoke of been formally used as a livestock carrier. Rage again threatened to overwhelm him at the snide smiles that were directed his way.

"Some of those gloating dogs will pay for this day's events. I swear that on the Prophet himself."

The Sheikh and his subjects quickly left the arena. He would not stay and watch the other rulers revel in his shame. Still moving, he arranged for his men's bodies to accompany him. Outside the arena, a convoy of armed land rovers were waiting to take him to his fleet of helicopters. The flying craft took him and his retinue to his palace complex and summer retreat far out in the desert south of the city of Taif and his beautiful flower of the desert; Ayesha. There, those who had kept his honour intact would get the burial they rightfully deserved and their families would be generously compensated.

Meanwhile, the seventeen seekers of the APOCRYPHA'I were camped well outside the Holy City of the Prophet. Arrangements were about to be made for them to enter the forbidden zone when the internal voice informed Naomh.

"The holder of the next piece of me still lies southwards."

As the nine flying craft with long slender rotating blades flew pass, the Alien voice updated its info.

"Somebody in one of those has been in close contact with the third part of me. It was this person that I felt, but he is not the holder. We must go in the same direction as them."

Hidden from the heat of the midday desert Sun in the comfort of the

TORT-CAM their plans were changed. Thankfully, the pursuers moved away from the fringes of Medina and back out into the desert. An uneasy Solomon had expressed his doubts.

"I am not confident that we can intermix with the large Muslim population without drawing suspicion."

Out here in the sandy wastes, off the main transport routes, there were few that might spot this unusual company, but still it was a risk they dare not take. So sticking to their well-practiced routine, they continued travelling during the cool of the night and resting during the heat of the day. This still suited the fair skinned European members of the party nicely, especially the Lenses and the Mute. The gang had been travelling over five weeks since they had left the safety of the Enclave, just to get this far, it had been tough going. Then, the LAB-CELL provided them with much more superior equipment to ease the hardships of travel. The internal presence had directed Naomh to it, in its eagerness to proceed more quickly. The Lenses and the Engineer were solving its mysteries too slowly. First its inventory provided outfits that would adjust to the new environments they progressed through. Each person would be snug inside their covering, no matter what the external conditions were outside them. The Mute, for one was grateful, even if he never mentioned it. The pale man was sick of the infringing heat. The colour of these wondrous suits would also blend with the surroundings; it would not make them invisible, just hard to see. So after these clothing innovations, it was decided to risk the hardships of daytime travel as well. Their stops for rest became less frequent and the questors began to cover ever more ground in their daily marches, but even at night time, each one of them was consuming a lot of water. During one long swig of the refreshing liquid, Haim said.

"Best invention ever."

At the moment their desert outfits were worn under a set of combat fatigues which were identical to those worn by the Mujhadeen. Still, the Arab clothing could be whipped off at any moment, if their other suits offered a better advantage. It was decided by one of their few experts.

"As we are far away from the War Zone and since then we have had a number of close encounters with groups of retreating stragglers, which are growing more common by the way, we can also pass ourselves off as retreating Mujahedeen. And if any of the passer's by get too curious, some of us can converse in Arabic."

They still displayed the arsenal of weapons that had been taken from the dead Kadi and his men, so the mixed company were as prepared as they were going to be. A few days later, just as daylight was fading it was decided to break the routine and rest that evening. As Naomh and the Guide snatched a view of the terrain they would cross the next night, the unfamiliar novice questioned the experienced traveller.

"Are you sure that you have never been outside the Enclave's walls and

in the lands of the Prophet before?"

The Guide shook his head and replied in the negative.

"Shit no. Isn't it fantastic man? It makes any dude feel so fucking humble to see such a vast emptiness. Even in Africa there had been trees, like big time. This is like, far out man."

Naomh was still looking through the laser sights of a viewing device and he realised.

"He must be smoking one of his ever-present joints as my long haired companion always reverts more than usual to that archaic twentieth-century speech when he is puffing."

Sure enough an instant later, he smelt the familiar sweet waft from them. Miriam joined them. His partner ruined their contemplation of life's mysteries as she interjected with mortal concerns and a familiar gripe amongst their foreign companions.

"It makes you think, that with their millions upon millions of square kilometres of empty space which our enemy don't inhabit, by the way, they wouldn't miss a few hundred square kilometres that we need to survive."

After a debate between the Anschluss members of the group, all of them agreed to side with the Enclave members when any of their new allies expressed distaste at anything their heredity enemies did. So as neither of the two men was willing to upset their new colleagues from the coastal land, they both agreed with her. She became suspicious at the two men's easy acceptance of her words, but as she caught Naomh's eyes, her heart softened. The Guide noticed the adoring looked in her brown eyes, so he knobbed his cig and said to the two, that had eyes now only for each other.

"I'll leave you two love birds alone man and help with the meal that the others are preparing. See you later alligator."

He left them to their own devices. Miriam lowered her voice to a conspiratorial whisper and asked.

"Naomh. What does he say? Sometimes, we find it very hard to understand him. Does he not speak the same tongue as you?"

Her lover failed to stifle a laugh as he answered her question.

"Sometimes."

Now that she had discussed one of his companions with him, Miriam broached the subject of another.

"My love, I feel that the Guide is a good person and so are the rest of your friends, but that one you call the Mute is different. My friends do not like him. Even Moshe said that his own mother or father would not trust him."

A slight change appeared in Naomh's eyes, it was for a brief instant and then the expression vanished. Still Miriam had seen the hurt in his eyes.

"My love what is the matter, does it upset you that none of us like the Mute?"

"No, Moshe is right that man is a rat, but like the rest of us, he is an orphan. Most of us had our parents killed by our government, Greta knew hers, but they were murdered in front of her."

She never heard his un-mouthed words.

"What would Moshe think about me, if he knew about my killing of my parent?"

"I am sorry my love. I did not know. Will you forgive me?"

"Of course, I do. I would forgive you anything."

He relaxed in her company and felt pregnant with possession every time she was near. He drew her closer and kissed her full on the lips. Lost within his desire and with half closed eyes, he glanced into her fully shut orbs and was amazed that this person trusted him so much. The want of her, engulfed him. The passion filled couple finished their love making out in the watchful desert evening. One of them wondered between the deep breaths of post sexual activity.

"Are we been watched like that Nomad couple?"

At this precise moment they were, the turncoat rarely left the bearer of two pieces of the amulet out of their sight. Revelling in the moment, Naomh was another one, who was glad he left the confines of the Anschluss, but he was certain that he had to return when the mission as completed. Indulging in a bit of wishful thinking, he thought.

"Then I can show her the wonders of my society, one without those murderers who call themselves rulers."

The Questors had already picked a secluded spot for their camp that would hide them from the air and if they happened to be discovered on land by hostile forces, then the seventeen of them could immediately pile into the TORT-CAM. As the two lovers returned, Haim and Moshe waved them through their sentry post. The invisible Persuader was also watching with a heavy calibre machine gun. They found the rest of the group gathered around a mobile cooker that received its power from light rays of any description. Tonight, the unhindered moonlight was enough for its operation. There was a hot meal simmering on it for them, it smelt spicy. The others had already cooked theirs and were eating sizeable portions. Solomon was supervising the cooker and its contents, a spicy chicken and vegetable stew. The Prof had done himself a separate broth without meat. After everybody had sated their appetite, they retired to the invisible shield for concealment and rest. Naomh missed the time that he and Miriam had spent together in the intimacy of the TORT-CAMLET away from the others. It had been Heaven even though Hell had been on the outside all of the time. Now the stacked boxes within the confined space gave everybody a modicum of privacy. After sharing with Miriam and fully aware of the growing dependence between them, he was no longer slightly envious of Cahill's and Greta's bond. But he was also blind to other relationships that were forming around him.

It took the group another two weeks of travel in this alternating existence of harsh yellow sunshine and comforting tiles of red and orange to reach a close proximity to the third piece of the APOCRYPHA'I. Naomh for one had wished that it would never end. The times when he was lying with Miriam and nestled in her arms, whether it was during the fiercest heat of the day or at other rest times that were mostly called when fatigue encroached had become the most treasured moments of his life. The only blot on this landscape of bliss was the continued intrusion of the internal voice urging him to proceed more quickly as they were nearing another part of it every day. This mental harassment was always conformation that these blissful times were nearing the end. During the first weeks of travel through the desert, Naomh had reckoned.

"I could easily accept this existence which ends every dawn in my endless repetition of anticipating of spending the entire day snug against the sleeping body of the woman that I love."

Now that his sleeping arrangements had altered, he looked even more forward to the shorter periods that he and his lover were resting together. So when the two parts Mescal/Amulet informed him one night just before Sun-up.

"We will finally reach our goal during the next nights travel."

He became sullen. Miriam's lover knew that his weeks of contentment were over. The travellers had been nearing a mountain range that grew larger by the day. That morning, just before the company were about to crash out and prepare the camp, he sat off ahead, a few metres away from the others. He was left to himself, fully armed and dressed in his new attire. Anticipating a new divergence in the company's circumstances, he thought about the larger picture, it suddenly overwhelmed him.

"I am supposed to travel the World, go to strange places and recover seven pieces of a talking amulet. This would give me the power to overthrow the Anschluss. How ridiculous it sounds? I don't even know where they are? Yet all of my friends are no fools and still they travel with me."

In a perverse moment of judgement; Naomh then wondered what his travelling companion's real motives were.

"Well, the Prof really seems happy out here. He had always wanted to see the wonders of the Planet. It is that simple with him. The Lenses, well he was known by the Anschluss security forces and would not survive alone without our protection. The Clerk, he too had always been sick of his limited life and now seemed a much more confident man. The Engineer's reason is not so easily found, he had been once a devotee of the Preacher, but now follows me as he believes that I can bring his God back to the Anschluss. But, the Persuader's reason is easy enough; he always follows his brother. Cahill is my friend since boyhood and even though he felt ill at ease at the prospect of leaving the Anschluss, he has also made a solemn

vow to me. Greta's reason was as simple as the Persuader's was, like him with his brother; she would not let Cahill out of her sight. The Guide's reason seems to be loyalty to my father, Rory and now me. Miriam, well she was part of the equation and her people follow her. The only real puzzle is the Mute and I haven't a clue of his motives and something tells me that I don't think I want to know."

He returned to the TORT-CAM a little bit wiser and found most of the crew asleep. Naomh went to the already sleeping form of Miriam and quietly undressed and nestled close to her. This was for body contact and not for warmth as the temperature of the red and orange interior was forever pleasant and constant.

Sure as the Sun would come up and boil the desert surface, a day later on the 12th of Sept 2953AD, the desert trekkers reached what must have been the mother of all Oasis's. Spirits became buoyant; there would be no more monotonous rocky plateaus or great sandy deserts. The observers lay crouched down on a rugged foothill and watched the miracle of nature through laser sights. This ocean of greenery in what was normally an unforgiving desert stopped them in their tracks. Many a traveller that had copied a similar journey without the comforts these people enjoyed must have been euphoric at the sight of it. In the middle of this lush vegetation that lay in the shadow of the spine of green and red mountains that straddled the western coastline of the great desert peninsula, manmade objects were visible to the prying eyes. There lay for this part of the Planet, a substantial watercourse which flowed into a large shimmering blue lake. Situated on an isle in the middle of this watery Eden lay a huge white alabaster fort, surrounded on all sides by fairly stout walls. Bulbous golden domes and tall thin minarets decorated the compound haphazardly. This was where the next target spent his winter retreat, but he had fled to it now as a haven of isolation and away from accusing fingers and wagging tongues. From this distance, the fort and its encompassing greenery appeared to nestle in the bosom of the over powering mountains, but the complex was actually seven kilometres away from the natural buttress of rock. Here, it could take advantage of an intrinsic paradox and still be safe from an aerial attack. For the eastern side of the escarpment was also a virtual paradise. Its slopes abounded with in forests and wildlife of many species. There were also many anti-aircraft batteries hidden among its crags and caves. The Sheikh hunted wild boar and big cats in the foothills. Its western sides in contrast were a barren red desert. The wall of mountains turned cool sea breezes into falling rain that regularly bathed these eastern escarpments. It was pretty much the same effect as the Enclave walls that helped replenish its water supply, but on a much grandeur scale and for far less people. The walls encompassing the fort were like some small prodigy of the Anschluss or Enclave's barriers and some among Naomh's party were not impressed. Fluttering in the weak wind were many flags and pennants signifying whom ruled here.

"This is not good. I know of this ruler, my friends. He hates the Enclave more than any other." Said one of Miriams co-horts.

Quickly, Moshe explained

"This man swore a blood oath in front of the fifteenth wall. He stood directly in front of the walls guns, but just out of range. The man who is represented by those symbols promised passionately through a loud hailer to eradicate the whole lot of us. He must have survived the bombs from the planes that were sent out to put an end to his affront. And that is no mean feat, many a dead corpse can testify to that."

The gist of a plan began to form in Naomh's mind or was it more interference from the APOCRYPHA'I; he wasn't able to tell anymore. He asked them.

"Tell me all you know about this leader."

In between the bits of information that the Enclave members of the group gave him, Naomh began to build up a profile of the Prophet's servant. He came up with an idea. It was so simple that it was the perfect plan and it was staggering in its simplicity. The beginnings of the scheme was outlined to the rest of the crew.

"Firstly. Our friends from the Enclave cannot come with us. Because you will be recognised for what you are."

Their leader held his hand up to halt the expected protest, but he only received one and it was from an unexpected source.

"I am coming; I can easily pass for one of you." Said Shoshanna.

"Are you sure?"

Her friends nodded, so Naomh relented.

"We will get as close to the fort as we can and use the TORT-CAMLETS to infiltrate the place. Once inside, we will reveal ourselves and confront him with our bargaining chip."

One of Miriam's crew caught on quickly enough. Haim advised them.

"You could pretend to offer him the technology of the invisible shield, with its ability to penetrate the Enclave's defences. That is his dream and it would make him a leader of great standing among his people. Our downfall would be his stepping stone to greatness."

"And the proof that you are not dreamers or madmen will be that you are already inside his own defences. Even inside his own quarters or even better still, inside his Harem." Added Moshe.

"What's a Harem?" Asked a puzzled Clerk.

When it was explained to him by one of the girls, his eyes widened and he whistled in appreciation. The new gigolo sniggered.

"Well, we had better hurry up then. I would like to see his face when he realises that we by passed all his security."

"Are you sure you don't want to go just so you can see this Harem." Asked the Engineer with a slightly raised eyebrow. He was still at ease

with this alien concept of many wives, never mind concubines. The others began to laugh at the religious man's serious words and their mirth became contagious, so he joined in as well.

"Fuck man. That would be a sight to see."

That was the Guide.

"Far out!" Added the Clerk.

That restarted the whole bout of laughter again. Greta had reverted to her usual self and did not share the others good humour. The Mute wondered what it would be like to have one of those forbidden pretty necks between his hands. None of his victims had been from such a privileged or pampered background. He liked the idea of that; these indulged women had more to lose than others did. Then a serious Miriam pulled Naomh aside and levelled her concerns at him.

"You are not really going to let the TORT-CAM fall into the enemies hands. Are you? That is a device that my people have no defence against. Groups of suicidal fanatics could be smuggled into the Enclave at will. They could even get a fairly large army behind the walls. We cannot let that happen."

"Of course not. It is only the bait. This Sheikh will never even get to see it. That I promise you." Replied Naomh.

She accepted her lover's words and he reassured her.

"Trust me."

His brown eyed lover did. The onlookers spent the day observing the compound, taking note of the sentry's movements, its defences and how far they could approach before entering the TORT-CAMLETS. The Guide, the Persuader and Shoshanna moved off to circumvent the fortress. Miriam stayed close to Naomh all day, she was uneasy about their impending separation. It would not be their first since their time in the Enclave, but it would be the first risky parting. Moshe spoke for all of them when he voiced their assumptions and scoffed at the defences.

"Brute force could take that place easily; it could be taken without warplanes. It is only capable of defending itself against small forces."

To himself, the soldier of the Enclave added.

"Maybe, when this quest is over and we return home, I will request a large mobile force that can be airlifted quickly to this leader of the Prophet's armies and eliminate them. In one swoop, my people can rid itself of this bold and implacable foe. I will also be a warning to our other enemies."

Although, everybody accepted the sultry man's assessment; that was not what they were here for. Those who were going to pierce its walls still had to use the mobile versions of the invisible shield, so their infiltration of the Sheikh's complex would go unnoticed. The three scouts returned from their exploring mission. The Guide spoke for them.

"All of the forts defences appear to be uniform; there is no weakest

point as such. There are an inadequate number of sentries patrolling the walls. But in saying that, it might have detection devices that we are unaware of. There does appear to be some sort of garden complex on the south side. That would be the best place to penetrate its defences."

The seventeen of them crowded close and as usual, all but one had an input. A plan was agreed. During the discussion, Haim gave the Anschluss members a contribution that was totally strange to them.

"Anyone entering that compound must not be dressed in the Prophet's uniforms. If any of you are captured or overpowered, you will be considered spies and shot out of hand."

"I do not understand, even the Filth take prisoners." Said Cahill.

A bitter Greta gave her experienced insight.

"But those scum eliminate them after their usefulness is over."

"I do. In a conflict between opposing Nations anyone caught in the others uniform are shot out of hand. It is an agreed fact." Clarified the Guide.

Those that were to enter the compound decided to dress in plain blue overalls. The infiltrators engaged the plan and pressed ahead. Naomh, the Lenses and the Prof were in one TORT-CAMLET; the Engineer, his brother; and Shoshanna would share another, much to the big man's delight. That left the Guide, the Clerk with the Mute while Cahill and Greta were in the last one that was to penetrate the fort's defences, as always the couple preferred it that way. Miriam, Moshe, Haim, the Rabbi, Bersheava and Solomon were to remain close by in the remainder of the invisible shields. Before, they set off; Shoshanna fiercely hugged each one of her compatriots. Then the stunning woman took off her Magen David with its chain, kissed the cool silver metal and handed it to the Rabbi. With wry humour, she said.

"Look after that for me. Something tells me that I won't be needing it down there amongst our enemy."

Naomh also kissed and hugged Miriam and told her.

"Everything would be fine."

"Promise?"

"With all of my heart."

As the intending infiltrators moved off, the Rabbi cautioned.

"Be very careful my friends. Down there is a place ruled by the words of the Prophet and the script of the holy Koran."

Despite her lover's promise, Serene Miriam ordered those remaining behind

"Set up a pattern of covering fire in case things go wrong."

These six expertly set up camouflaged firing positions of portable mortars, heavy Beni's and highly accurate missile launchers. Meanwhile, the whole of the infiltrating force moved undetected to within a kilometre of the fort's walls. This easy done manoeuvre caused the watching Moshe to utter.

"I told you that its security is laughable. It is a building for show, not defence."

He kept watching as the four mobile and invisible shields were activated. The globes lit up for a brief few seconds, undetected by those within their target. Vanishing instantly, the unseen globules moved forward at a fluid pace towards the compound. Their remaining Enclave comrades had not a slight whisper of a clue, where they were now. It was decided not to cross the open water of the moat, because of the incident with the rain revealing their shapes. They had no idea if the encompassing body of water would have a similar effect. The invisible globes moved across a black marbled bridge with exaggerated arches that straddled the moonlit sparkling water of the fortress's moat. The four moving unseen apparitions dropped silently to the grassy embankment of the moats opposite bank. Following a pre-planned route, the unseen infiltrators reached the point of incision. The Alien devices easily passed through the fort's solid defences and in a blur of liquid penetration, they found themselves in the verdant courtyard that the Guide had pointed out. By sheer luck or providence, the Sheikh was out walking alone in the cool of the evening. So certain of his safety, he always went without bodyguards as he sorted out his private thoughts while taking the night air. Besides the two ever present things that normally preoccupied him; the Enclave and the absence of a male heir, another intertwined issue was more prominent this evening.

"I want revenge against the rulers that attempted to humiliate me!"

Earlier, he had tried to rectify the second predicament. The handsome Caliph had chosen from his harem, a teenage beauty with exquisite child bearing hips for tonight's copulating and Allah (BLESSINGS BE UPON HIM.) would relent and ensure him a male heir. Still, he did not get his hopes up. Lost in his musings, Ben Sulimani nearly jumped out of his skin as several armed and hooded assailants dressed in blue uniforms appeared from nowhere. At first, encouraged by their sudden transition, he thought them fabled "Afreet.". But that instant flight of the imagination had passed and recognition made him utter.

"They are mere mortals like me."

He breathed easier. Inside her invisible cloak, Shoshanna had recognized him for what he was and moved out of her undetectable shield. Her armed companions followed suit. The shadows quickly surrounded him. The Sheikh was about to shout in wild alarm at the intruders, but a strong hand clasped his mouth, making it impossible for him to yell in warning. It would be useless anyway; all of the sentries on this section of his complex by his private garden had their focus on the outside. This need for his family's privacy might now cost him his life. Somebody gave commands and he was dragged and half-carried to the unseen area by the wall by a very powerful man. Unable to resist, he inwardly believed.

"Assassins! Have some of the other Caliphs made their move? No! That is impossible. No person under the Prophets sky could infiltrate this fortress without a major battle. My palace has a vast array of defensive weapons. How is this possible? Treachery! It has to be an inside betrayal."

Naomh addressed the outraged Sheikh; his voice became heavily accented to his comrades as he spoke fluently in the Language of the Prophet. Another tool given to him by the two parts Mescal/Amulet. His shocked crew stared at him, while Shoshanna gave him the strangest look. In her own language, he whispered into her ear.

"I will explain later."

Those unaccented words baffled her even more. He continued talking to the prisoner.

"We are not here to harm you. We seek allies and have been directed to you. We are in the possession of something that will interest you greatly."

Gathering his composure, Ben Sulimani nearly choked out the words.

"What Devils are you to appear from nowhere?"

He had recognised them for what they were, for when the one who was obviously the leader ordered him to be taken towards the shadow of the wall, the man had spoken in Anschluss, but then he had also used Arabic. (It was a good thing that he had not heard Naomh's hushed Hebrew words to Shoshanna.). The Sheikh had also spoken the European tongue in reply. Again in the Anschluss language, the Arabian Caliph insisted.

"I am Sheikh Ben Sulimani, the lord of this place. Again I demand, who are you and what are you doing here in my private garden?"

Naomh was impressed at the man's intelligence and courage.

"Even though he is our captive, he is now asking the questions and in our first language. Besides, he could have told us that he was someone else."

Despite, the dialogue, the impasse held. No-one was about to yield ground and give in. Naomh and the Sheikh glared at each other in ambivalence. Then Shoshanna stepped forward, removed her hood and spoke slowly in the Prophet's tongue.

"It is known that you do not harm women and we seek your hospitality."

Taken aback by her strange beauty, he had nearly gasped out aloud. The Sheikh took a deep breath as he took in her large blue eyes. As his own dark orbs studied her, he became intrigued and agreed with her request.

"Though you have entered unlawfully. By the will of Allah, (BLESSINGS BE UPON HIM.). I will offer my hospitality. Now put away your weapons."

Nobody did as he asked. Shoshanna took command.

"Do as he asks. He is a man of honour. He has sworn an oath to God."

514

The Guide agreed, he told those that doubted.

"He offers us his hospitality and by his laws he cannot harm us."

Naomh nodded to the others to lower their weapons. The intruders complied and removed their head coverings. Ben Sulimani counted eight men and two beautiful blonde women, a rarity in his Kingdom. The Sheikh was very intrigued at how easily this strange group had penetrated his security.

"And as true as the Prophet, I am going to find out how they have done this?"

He brought them to the main buildings and found some of his house staff. If his servants were surprised at seeing the strangers, they did not show it. He commanded them.

"Take these guests to suitable quarters, but disarm them first."

None of them objected to their weapons been removed, they had plenty more in the invisible shields that a proper security search would have revealed as colourful baubles. Before the menials led them away, the Sheikh said.

"You will change and bathe. We will meet later, at a banquet to be held in your honour. I am sure that you have an intriguing tale to tell me. My servants will come and get you. Until then."

With that he strode away, but not before sizing Shoshanna up. She stood firm under his scrutiny. His staff led them towards their assigned rooms. None among the Europeans knew what servants were, except the Spy and the Guide that was. When the latter explained what they were, the others from the Anschluss were aghast. The Clerk and the Prof had some affinity with the servants; the slight difference was that these two were formally in servitude to a bureaucratic machine and not an individual. But the bondage of these lowly people was light years away from their former predicament. Then Shoshanna added.

"They are the lucky ones, there are many out there in the Prophets lands that do not have the same comforts as these servants. They look well clothed and fed and have a nice roof over their heads."

Still, those not used to the idea shook their heads in disagreement at the menial's plight. The Guide believed correctly that those escorting them had no knowledge of the Anschluss tongue. But just in case, he advised them.

"Speak about trivial things."

As he and his colleagues were been led through a labyrinth of corridors, the servants only seemed interested in getting them to their appointed rooms. The escorted group passed through vaulted halls of elegant marble walls and ceilings of elaborate scrollwork with strange calligraphy painted on ceramic tiles which to these uninitiated were staggering in their complexity. Intricate timber partitions that were more space than wood contrasted with the fullness of the studded tiled walls. The Prof marvelled in delight and promised to himself, that one day he would be able to read

515

those words. From the books, the learned man had read with Solomon's assistance in the Enclave libraries, he knew this type of architecture was called Arabesque. Out loud, he said.

"Interesting. I wonder; if the Sheikh has a library."

Then as if on cue, they passed through a hall with polished wooden panels and gold and silver guild-work that showed many reflections of each passer-by. This room lined with expensive timber was filled with books, scrolls and manuscripts of many ages. It was an oasis of learning. The Prof was certain that he had died and had gone to the Heaven that the Engineer was always talking about.

"Interesting. I wish Solomon could see this."

When the guests arrived at their quarters in a section of the sprawling complex that often housed exotic diplomats from other Nations, the servants insisted that the women take a separate room from the males.

"Interesting" The Prof announced when he heard about the arrangements.

Tempers flashed, eyes blazed and temperatures boiled over. But the unfazed servants refused to be budged from their orders. One of them spoke in Arabic.

"Masters, normally the women would be placed in a different building entirely, the Sheikh does you great honour by allowing them into the same guest wing as you."

Reluctantly, Naomh agreed after been advised by Shoshanna that non-compliance was fruitless, So the men were split from the women.

"Interesting. The Sheikh is been flexible for us. We must have his attention." Said the Prof.

"Not us. Her!" Said Greta pointing at the Enclave woman.

The blonde women responded, catching the glint of the Persuader's eyes.

"I seem to have that effect on men."

Cahill held his tongue in silent fury at the mention of separate quarters, but he too complied after his lover advised him.

"It will be alright."

The tall blonde beauty gave him a lingering kiss, much to the distaste of the servants, who were unused to displays of public affection. There was another male who longed to kiss the beautiful Shoshanna, but knew.

"Miguel would only scorn me."

The two women were shown to their sumptuous quarters in the west wing of the palace. An unspeaking servant had led them through a warren of passageways until they had arrived at their assigned quarters. Shoshanna sighed in ecstasy at the extravagances that had been provided by the place staff. When the Enclave woman saw the huge and beautiful enamelled sunken bath, she jumped out of her bland uniform and leapt in to the foaming and perfumed water with a squeal. Her sole female companion undressed with a little more dignity, but she soon joined her companion in the bubbling bath. Unknown to the two bathers, their host was watching the two naked females through a spy hole. One of the exquisite blonde women intrigued him; he could not stop thinking about her. Ben Sulimani had only eyes for her and her naked body confirmed his desire.

"I must possess her; she will make a fine addition to my harem."

He watched them for a half an hour, until they left the bath and dressed in clothes provided by his staff and chosen by him. An hour later, Greta and Shoshanna left their luxurious room and made their way unhindered to the men's quarters. The Sheikh had ordered his staff not to impede them. The Enclave woman was impressed with the ease that her companion found the men's quarters. The Persuader was on guard at the door when the two knocked on it. He let them in with a whistle. Startled by the shrill noise, the others looked and saw that the two alluring women had removed their bland blue uniforms and now wore very feminine clothing that accented every delicious curve of their fair skinned bodies. The two piece dresses, one of blue silk and the other green revealed a good deal of their midriffs and thrust ample exposed bosoms into their companion's eyes. Knee length skirts exposed long legs that ended with high-heeled shoes. All of the males stood open mouthed at the beautiful dresses that they wore and the way the garments highlighted their bodies. Although the men had seen these women in far skimpier bathing suits, Greta and Shoshanna never looked more desirable to most of the unattached males. Besides, they were the only members of the opposite sex, they had seen in the last few weeks and they had always been dressed in drab military attire, even down to their sexless underclothes.

"Do you like it?" Asked the beautiful Enclave woman.

She did a twirl to tease the gaping men. Her skirt lifted to show shapely thighs and a silver chain that she had added herself.

"Interesting." Said the Prof.

But the others exclaimed, the Persuader's voice been the loudest.

"Wow!"

"Put your eyes back into your sockets. We can use this to our advantage." Said Cahill and then he glared at the Prof. *"And by the way, if you keep saying interesting, I will personally rip your tongue from your mouth."*

Greta laughed viciously, her large bosom quivered noticeably in the muslin dress. The Prof bit his tongue to stop himself from saying interesting again.

"You will definitely get the Sheikh's attention in that outfit." Said the admiring Clerk, stating the obvious.

"That's the plan then." Said Naomh. He was wondering what his brown skinned Miriam would look like in that type of clothing.

"Alright, I will keep the Sheikh distracted with my obvious charms."

517

Shoshanna giggled as she shook her ample bosom and continued.

"But for this sort of venture, you should be using Beersheba and not me. She has the talent for this."

The Clerk who had partaken of the mentioned woman's charms silently agreed with her, but out aloud, he said.

"You are far prettier than her."

"Liar." Giggled the receiver of his advances.

The Persuader not happy with the idea of her flirting with the Sheikh put his large forearm around her and said.

"No, he is right. You are the most beautiful woman in the World."

She gave the big man a coy smile that had him grinning like a Cheshire cat. His brother had already noticed that his sibling had a crush on her; he looked towards the Heavens and whispered.

"That's all I need."

Uncomfortable with the way the conversation was heading, he had other more practical things to do, so he went into an adjoining room. The Mute who had no appreciation of beauty silently mocked.

"You all look the same when you are dead."

Then, the men and women made plans. Shoshanna recollected something about Naomh.

"How is it that you can speak the Enclave tongue as if born to it?"

"Why do you think?"

"Oh?"

"I also know the Prophets words."

"That will come in useful then."

Meanwhile, the ruler of the fort was baffled; none of his spying devices were operational. His technicians were scurrying about trying to locate the massive fault, but the Sheikh's eavesdroppers would never find it. The Engineer and the Lenses had discovered the blocking device in the LAB-CELL'S inventory. The questor's conversation would remain between themselves. The Guide turned to his female companions and said.

"We were not able to warn you, but your room is been monitored as well. I hope you were discreet"

"Well, the Sheikh definitely got more than an eyeful then" Said Greta.

She and Shoshanna laughed wickedly, while Cahill and the Persuader scowled. So neither woman said anything about the large bathing pool. The Engineer walked into the room from a side door; he had been availing of the Sheikh's hospitality. He had been filling containers with water from the palace's supply, he was already thinking about the next stage of their quest. Of course, the owner of the precious liquid was completely unaware of this. Cursing his bugging equipment and its operators, Ben Sulimani decided that he would glean no information this way, so he had to do it the old fashioned way. He would match his wits against them.

"It is time for the banquet. Go and get my guests."

A servant did his bidding. Greta and Shoshanna had gone back to their own rooms and found a much different set of clothing for them. It was the same in the men's quarters, white robes of traditional Arab garments were laid out. Not wanting to upset their host, they put the Thobe's on. Only the Clerk revelled in his new appearance. The Sheikh entertained them in a gigantic canvas tent that had been erected in one of the huge courtyards of the palace. Funny enough this large enclosed space was fully blanketed with desert sand.

"A relic of the way my ancestors once lived when they were Bedouin and were truly close to Allah (BLESSING'S BE UPON HIM.) and which I have grown accustomed to." Ben Sulimani said proudly, comfortable in his long lineage and customs of a feudal society where everybody had their place. The interior of the tent was a wonder of silk and carpet. The former type of decoration hung from tent poles while there were two types of the latter; both of which adorned the sandy floor and the canvas walls. All of these were beautifully embroidered with colourful calligraphy that mesmerised an uneducated scrutiniser. Luxurious red velvet ottomans were laid out in large circles and at their perimeters lay slender, but sturdy iron braziers. The glowing stacks radiated a pleasant warmth that warded off the chill of the desert night. Lulled by the comfort and hoping to catch his reluctant guests off guard, the Sheikh asked of Naomh a question that had been niggling him.

"How is it that you and one of the women can speak Arabic and the others cannot?"

"We were once a part of the espionage section and the language of the Prophet is one of a few that the two of us can speak."

"I see."

He appeared satisfied; he had met agents of the Anschluss before. Many of the Sheikh's people lounged about; all the males wore military uniforms and chequered headscarves. Some shielded their eyes with dark sunglasses. The women were few and far between, but those that were present had their entire bodies covered with a muslin cloth that only allowed their eyes to be seen. Greta and Shoshanna were obliged to wear the Abaya's as well and had changed out of their revealing garments at the bequest of a servant who had a female voice for a man. A black veil called a Boshiya for the lower part of their faces completed the Arab ensemble. Surprisingly Cahill's companion had no objections to this article of chauvinism. This time, she quite liked to remain hidden behind the rigid clothing and delighted in her anonymity. It was also much easier to conceal her weapon. The men of their party were dressed in their unfamiliar garments; the Sheikh wanted them at a disadvantage. A clap of his hands and all of them were seated at a long table covered in fine silk tablecloths, Ben Sulimani was at its head and his guests were spread out on either side of it. Heavy plates with blue opals around their rims, ivory handled cutlery and highly decorated silver tea pots with hunting scenes etched into them were laid alongside very ornate china cups and saucers that echoed similar motifs. Servants were always at hand, fluttering about and seemingly invisible to all but the questors. The menials were filling cups with cool water, fruit juice and steaming tea to those who requested it. Those that followed the Prophet's ways did not take alcohol in public much to the regret of Naomh's company. Still, some of them did enjoy the pungent tea. While the servants were leaning over their shoulders, refilling any empty or half empty glasses, one attendant stood out especially for the traitor in their midst. The servant had recognised another Anschluss mole and had given a hand signal that was only known to the most trusted among the LYUBINITES. The traitor responded with an exact duplicate of the gesture, signalling to the other Spy.

"I will contact you later."

Events became even more bizarre still, Shoshanna's people also had an agent in the Sheikh's staff and their presence was unknown to the Anschluss Spy. Unbelievably, the Enclave operative had been a good friend of hers during their school days and he had recognised her instantly as she sat in close proximity to the Sheikh. Sacha Fine alias "Abu." (Servants did not have second names.) surmised.

"My compatriot must be on her own and I must not jeopardise it by contacting her."

Fine had been in the palace complex for over two years and was still a lowly servant. The Enclave agent wondered.

"How has she got that close to the Sheikh? I have never seen her here before."

The answer was obvious to the silent schemer.

"Then again the Sheikh was always a sucker for a pretty face."

Like the Anschluss Spy, Fine would stay put and glean as much information as he could. A mouth-watering aroma of roasting lamb that turned on huge spits over crackling flames wafted into the covered space. As his guests enjoyed the Sheikh's hospitality, Naomh asked his exotic host as he indulged in a mouthful of stuffed pear shaped brown fruit.

"What am I eating? They have to be the most succulent things I have ever tasted."

The Arab imparted his knowledge.

"These fruits are called figs, a gift from garden of Eden itself."

While the two very different men chewed the palm fruit, the topic of the recent war came up. Naomh feigned complete ignorance of it. Their host told them about the single Tank that had broken formation and had prevented the United Muslim Forces from halting the expansion of his enemy.

"That cursed vehicle ruined our plan. But still they were brave and died hero's deaths."

A poker-faced Naomh stared at the Sheikh.

"What would he do if he found out that we were in that Tank? He would have us killed in a fit of rage, I'm sure."

The oblivious Ben Sulimani then clapped his hands and servants brought in platters of what looked like fried insects.

"Try these delicacies my friends. These Locusts have had an abundant year and are feeding on our crops. So in return, we eat them."

Not to insult their host, the Anschluss native hid a grimace, picked up one of the large Arthropods and bit on it. Surprisingly, the gross object was delicious. In between crunchy mouthfuls, he asked their entertainer.

"Have you ever heard the story of Troy?"

This was a memory from an ancestor who fought at the ancient city; it had been brought forth by the two parts Mescal/Amulet.

"You mean where the ancient Greeks got into the walled city by means of a wooden horse." Replied, the educated Sheikh as he put down the remains of a locust.

"Precisely. Well, we have a modern version of that horse in our possession and it will be of great use to you."

The Guide was impressed with both of their knowledge on that very old tale. His leader then bent close, whispered into Ben Sulimani's ear and began to explain how they got into his private gardens unobserved. He was so close to the Sheikh that neither the other Anschluss Spy or Sacha Fine heard him. When Naomh finished his fantastic story, the Arabian man looked at him with an incredulous expression. Still, the cogs in his mind turned.

"I still have no conceivable explanation how these people got into my palace unobserved. Could this fantastic tale straight out of the Arabian nights be true? Added to this, there is the failure of my spying devices. If it is, then this is indeed a wonder. Surely Allah (BLESSING'S BE UPON HIM.) has delivered these people to me."

Out loud, Ben Sulimani wondered.

"Where is this miracle now?"

"Only I can reveal its presence."

Naomh's listener was no fool and under the pretence of been delighted, he was also plotting.

"What do these Kuffars from the Anschluss really want from me? If I imprison them, my tortures will get it out of them. But I do not know what I am dealing with yet."

So the wise ruler decided against that course of action, for now. He was not going to dismiss this fantastic tale just yet. The Sheikh put on a charade that he was over the moon and the Arabian ruler clapped his hands for the musicians to play a well-rehearsed tune. While his servants brought around more trays packed with delicious chocolate, honey and almond coated biscuits, a dancer appeared on to the floor. She got the Clerk's attention immediately. Her feminine form was draped in numerous veils of different coloured silk. The lacy material was placed strategically over her body, which showed as much of her dark brown skin as they concealed. She was an exotic flower, emboldened with eastern promise. Her brazen outfit showed her narrow waist and ample cleavage to full advantage. She began to belly dance, much to the delight of most of the men present. The swaying of her exotic curving hips to the beat of the music became hypnotic. The sensual dancer discarded her veils, titillatingly and provocatively. Each fluttering piece of heavily perfumed silk was greeted enthusiastically by her male audience. Her rhythmic gyrations were lithe and supple; an emerald jewel pierced into her navel drew the enthralled men's eyes and mesmerised them. One of the Questor's wondered.

"Is that the next piece?"

However, the seeker of the living amulet was not drawn to her and the voice within had already informed him.

"The next segment is yellow in colour."

While the others appreciated her obvious seductive charms, Naomh's attention was attracted like iron towards a magnet to a veiled and muslin covered female who had just entered. The intriguing figure sat alongside the Sheikh in an air of familiarity. He knew instantly.

"Underneath her concealing robes, there is a piece of the APOCRYPHA'I pierced into her belly button. I cannot make out her features, but her eyes tell me that her beauty surpasses the dancer and maybe even Greta and Shoshanna."

All of her slender and nail varnished fingers were adorned in exotic rings of blue opal and white gold. She was the Sheikh's beloved daughter; Ayesha and the closeness of the next piece of the living jewel seemed to burn a hole in her Boshiya like a well advanced pregnancy. He forced himself not to stare at the Ben Sulimani's daughter. The presence of the Sheikh's oldest issue was not unusual. She was always at his side when her father was dealing with other leaders, dignitaries, etc. Ayesha could read their intentions; glean falsehoods that gave him an advantage over his political and economic rivals. His daughter could also converse with her father's mind, unheard by anyone else. It was all, because of the piece of heaven, she wore. He devoutly believed.

"A gift from Allah. (BLESSING'S BE UPON HIM.)".

He had come into the possession of this spiritual artefact through Ayesha's mother. Her ancestors had taken it as a spoil of war when their armies had totally vanquished another warlord, leaving none of his people or kin alive. A young son of the victor had been drawn to the body of its former wearer by a voice that was not from this Earth. From then on it was passed through the female line. As negotiations stalled; Ben Sulimani received the yellow jewel as his dowry. If he had a son; he would break tradition and it would be his inheritance. His insightful daughter had been scrutinising the people from the Anschluss. Silently; her father asked her.

"Is there falsehood here?"

"No father. I can find no untruths on their behalf."

What the female holder of the piece of the yellow piece did not know was that Naomh's two segments of the Mescal/Amulet were blocking the influence of her single part. Both of these were aware of the other conversation, but it was akin to a private Missive and the words remained unheard. Still, the merged piece tipped off its own host.

"Forgive me. I do not want to appear untrusting. But why come to me? You know we also have a proverb that goes like this. It says that one should be aware of Greeks bearing gifts." Said the Sheikh intruding on his guest's scrutiny of his daughter.

The ruler of this place was used to that, his flower of the desert always had that effect on people. Naomh took a sip of ice cool fruit juice and answered with all the sincerity he could muster. It was not too difficult as he kept as close to the truth as possible, he just twisted it, here and there. Of course there was no mention of the APOCRYPHA'I.

"As you have already ascertained, we come from the Anschluss. It was a difficult journey to get here. We went over the wall in the eastern border by the Bosporus straights and made our way down the Levant. A large number of our brotherhood died in getting here."

"Of course." Nodded the Sheikh.

A slight shrug showed that this did not impress him. Naomh's eyes suddenly hardened with indisputable fanaticism.

"We have appropriated this device under the noses of the rulers and fled for our lives. All of us have sworn to destroy the Anschluss."

"Why?" Questioned the Sheikh as he silently pondered.

"There is genuine hatred in his soul. The word Anschluss coming from the foreigner's voice sounds much like myself using the word Enclave."

This was where the Rabbi had advised Naomh on how to win the Caliph over.

"The government of the Anschluss has no soul. They in all their cursed wisdom deny us the worship of God and his Prophet." Spat out Naomh.

This got the devoted man's undivided attention, for this was the only truth, he would accept.

"Are there many like you in the Anschluss?" He enquired.

"Alas; there are tens of millions of lost souls denied their faith." Replied his guest in regret.

To his daughter, he asked in the silent way between them.

"Does he still speak the truth?"

"Yes father."

But out loud, he countered, trying to catch the stranger off balance.

"Ha! But the God of the Europeans is Christian. The last of my brothers in faith were driven out centuries ago."

Naomh continued the deception.

"Yes, we were once, but this God of Jesus has failed us by letting the Atheists triumph. He is not as strong as the God of the Prophet is. For your God has not forsaken you as ours has. Inshallah."

He had used the words of the Koran in the proper way; again it was coaching from the Rabbi. The two of them had practised this until he had gotten the right inflection. The latter was unaware of his acquired language skills.

"Again I ask. Why me?" Said the Sheikh.

He was wavering now.

"My strange guest must be sincere, for no man would use the word of God as a falsehood, not even those Enclave curs. Besides, Ayesha is confirming his sincerity."

The Arabian ruler had a lot to learn about those not of his faith and his trust in an Alien artefact that had its own agenda. Listening to what he knew were lies, the Engineer had kept silent and resolute. He still believed his Christian faith was supreme among beliefs. Naomh had warned him to say nothing; it would jeopardise the mission. The man from the Madrid Contrib could not disguise his religious fervour, so his silence was the best option.

"After we deliver the Enclave to you. We will need the vast armies of the Prophet to march on the infidels and sweep them away." Asserted Naomh with real passion.

Some of what he said about the rulers of his homeland was indeed the truth.

"But the Anschluss is technically superior. Your presence here proves that. It would be suicide to make war on them and that is a sin in Allah's eyes. (BLESSING'S BE UPON HIM.)." Countered the Sheikh again.

Naomh decided it was time to up the ante and take an educated guess.

"I feigned ignorance before. We know about your war with the Enclave. We could not get to you in time to impart this information. The Anschluss supplied the bombs to your enemy which destroyed your underground bunkers."

"That is impossible; they provide the armies of the Prophet with most of their firepower." Said a confused Sheikh.

"Yes. Its rulers play the game of nations with little regard to individuals. As long as they keep the two of you at each other's jugular, then neither of you can look towards the west. But the leaders of the Anschluss are very weak and a popular uprising will sweep them from power. And the words of Mohammed, (BLESSINGS BE UPON HIM.) and the worship of Allah should be the focus of that rebellion."

This was certainly not the truth. The Chairman's firm grip on reins of power was not so tenuous, it was absolute. Sheikh Ben Sulimani's head spun with delusions of grandeur at the implications. For he firmly believed that he would be the father of the Mahdi, the one who would forcibly unite all of mankind to Islam. Conquering the atheist Anschluss would deliver billions of more worshippers for Allah and set his line on the path to the Unifier.

"All of the great leaders throughout the millennia have failed to convert the Europeans. And it could be me Sheikh Mohammad Ali Ben Sulimani that delivers them. With that many numbers, the rest of the World will not be a problem."

His own feeling of self-importance convinced him to take this new divine messenger at full value. He did not even question why of all the rulers of the Muslims were these strange people drawn to him.

"This is what I was born to do. I will take the jihad, first to the Enclave and its Zionist masters and return the Haram to the people of the Prophet. Then, the holy jihad will be taken to the Atheists of the Anschluss. It shall be written thus?"

The debacle at the Enclave's wall was already forgotten. Ayesha squeezed her father's hand; it was a sign that her part of heaven was in agreement. Then there came an incident which clinched the deal and made the Sheikh truly believe. Greta was drawn towards a particular servant and decided that there was something suspicious about him. The edgy orderly was moving towards their table. The tall blonde woman had made a decision. She rose in a flash, whipped out her concealed and altered Desert Falcon pistol and shot the servant straight through the head with a single 0.5mm round. As he toppled to the floor in an audible thud, the huge marquee erupted into mayhem. The Sheikh was surrounded instantly by his bodyguards; they would be his living shields. Outraged shouts filled the confused air.

"Assassin."

There were a lot of weapons now pointing at Naomh's group. Other guards had Greta covered, but they hesitated, she was too close to Ayesha. Through clenched teeth and shocked gasps, the killer of the servant tore off her Boshiya said.

"Check the body."

Shoshanna translated her words to the frantic guards, the furious Sheikh nodded.

"Do as she says."

Someone leant down and examined the servant's body. The officer felt something that was out of the ordinary. He sliced opened the dead man's robe with a blade and there were gasps of amazement. The slain waiter had been wearing a surgically implanted explosive receiver. His dead fingers had only been millimetres from the detonator. Someone had wanted the Sheikh dead and would have succeeded only for Greta's intervention. Ben Sulimani although shaken, recovered and commanded.

"Put away your guns, this woman has just saved my life."

There were whispers amid the awed silence. The intended victim demanded from his blonde saviour.

"How did you know woman?"

"Just call it female intuition." Replied their saviour in a voice laced in sarcasm.

The Sheikh rose and dismissed nearly everybody with a clap of his hands. When he was alone in the huge tent with Naomh and his companions, the lord of the palace asked.

"Where did she get that weapon from?"

"Same place as the rest of us." Acknowledged Cahill.

Each one of them opened their clothes to reveal various weapons. Ben Sulimani realised.

"Any of them could have murdered me at any time."

His belief in them became steadfast. Now the Sheikh was very interested in Naomh's offer and he issued the foreigner with a challenge.

"I will give you a test and if you succeed, then we will talk further. Within the week, you will try to penetrate the security around my bullion room and if you are found in there. Only then will I believe your incredible story. It is the most protected room in my palace. There is an ancient book of the Koran in there said to have once belonged to the Prophet himself. If you bring that specific tome to me, then we will have a pact. It will be sworn on that holy book."

"Agreed." Compromised Naomh, but a growing insight informed him.

"You are lying. The bullion room is not the most guarded place in your palace. Not by a long shot. The private quarters of Princess Ayesha is the most secure space in the stronghold. For she has a treasure that you do not fully understand, but believe that it is a part of Heaven."

The ALASTHA'I had certainly succeeded in convincing the Hybrids that their Churigna were indeed Godly. The Sheikh clapped his hands again and servants appeared.

"Go with them, they will take you back to your quarters."

Throughout all of the commotion, the Mute kept staring at Greta; he was intrigued by her perception. He asked himself.

"She had seen the look of a man who had already resigned himself to death. He was a willing participant to that circumstance and that is an experience I have never before encountered. Has Greta some sort of mystical power?"

After the Caliph had dismissed the foreigners, he called for his head of security.

"Were they searched before they were allowed into my presence?"

"No Excellency. You said they were honoured guests and to offer them respect." Replied the man.

"You are correct, I do not hold you responsible for that, but the bomber is another matter."

526

"Yes, Excellency."

"Place yourself under arrest, I will deal with you later."

The man bowed and was led away. Meanwhile, his guests did not dally; they acted within hours of the Sheikh's challenge. The TORT-CAMLET'S energy reserves were running low and if the devices failed, then the eleven of them would be trapped behind the Sheikh's walls with no plan "B". However, before their assault on the next piece of the APOCRYPHA'I began, the Guide asked Greta.

"How did you know that servant was a bomber? And none of that crap that you gave the Sheikh."

The statuesque woman shrugged.

"As I met his eyes, he had the same distant look as the guy back in the penthouse in the London Contrib. I knew that he was about to blow himself up."

The Mute stifled an unheard gasp.

"She saw death before it happened."

"But, what if you had been wrong?" Hissed the Clerk.

Cahill answered for him.

"She wasn't."

Then, the two parts Mescal/Amulet that had only one focus told its host.

"It would be better if someone else came in contact with my other portion. The effect of the female with the piece and you been in close proximity cannot be calculated for. I am not sure what will occur if you handle it without her consent. You could start spasming again. Another of you comrades will have to retrieve it and we can see what will occur when we are in a safer environment."

Taken aback, Naomh thought long and hard about who he was going to choose. He surprised himself with his selection. He told the others.

"It will be the Clerk."

The former bureaucrat beamed,

"I am chuffed that you have this much confidence in me. I swear that I will not let anybody down."

The plan was put into action. Shoshanna would depart and visit the Arabian ruler's private quarters. She was to use her female attraction to distract him. The Enclave beauty had already told them.

"The lecherous Sheikh has already slipped me a hand written note. It was just before his attempted assassination."

"Maybe I should go and cut his balls off." Volunteered Greta.

"Keep her in tow." Demanded a horrified Naomh of Cahill.

"It was only a suggestion." Smiled his red haired friend viciously.

"But a proper one." Stated the Engineer.

"Be careful Shoshanna, for this shrewd ruler would expect such a ploy." Warned the Persuader.

She went over and gave him a lingering kiss.

"I will. Will you miss me if I don't return?"

"More that you will ever know. But don't talk like that."

She promised huskily.

"Then I will have to come back."

Greta was given the task of watching events transpire in the Sheikh's room and to extract their comrade when it was time. The Engineer, the Persuader, and the Lenses were to make a believable attempt at the treasure room, while the Guide, the Mute and Cahill would take up strategic defensive positions around the Citadel. From their hidden shields, they could lay down an invisible spout of fire. Meanwhile, Naomh and the Prof were to guard the Clerk as he entered the princess's room to retrieve the next piece of the APOCRYPHA'I. However a serious problem had just cropped up; the Mute had already taken one of the invisible shields and absconded. Plans were redrawn.

"I'll kill the bastard." Vowed Cahill.

Changes were made; Naomh, the Prof and the Clerk would share the first shield. The two women had to have their own as they would be in another part of the complex. That left Cahill, the Engineer, his brother, the Guide and the Lenses in the final one. The questors of the living jewel set off to reach their objectives. All three of the TORT-CAMLETS had breezed through walls, doors and detection systems unopposed. Energised pluses from the invisible shells knocked the surveillance devices out. There had been dead guards at every juncture. The Mute had been busy; he had cleared the way for them. Surprisingly there had been no alarm. Naomh and his two companions were outside the target's room; the three men had taken up concealed positions and waited. Others were deep into their missions and no one knew what the Mute was up to now. The Clerk was already in the Princess's room. He lurked in the shadows behind a large wooden dresser, he had shrunk the invisible shield and it was in his pocket. Lights came on and he retreated deeper into a corner. A side door opened and the Sheikh's daughter entered. Ayesha went to a large gold rimmed mirror and removed her Boshiya. The twenty-one year old woman, supremely confident of her beauty stood in front of the looking glass, still veiled and in her red undergarments. She admired her figure and so did the mesmerised Clerk. With bated breath, he uttered.

"Unfortunately. I am not here for that."

He located Naomh's amulet between the two pieces of her silk underwear. The yellow object of his leader's desire was like the belly dancers jewel, pierced into her navel just above her hourglass waist and firm buttocks. Open mouthed, he watched in fascination as the undressing girl removed her veil. He gasped at the perfection of her features. Her wide brown eyes matched the exotic girl's dusky skin pigment, her perfect nose stood proudly above a full pout of ruby coloured lips. The exotic perfume of her jasmine scented body drove him wild with desire and the sliminess of her busted frame overpowered his senses. The man from the confines of the Anschluss was certain.

"I have never seen such a naked foreign creature before; even Bersheava pales in comparison. This is why I left to travel. Sights like this are what I had in mind."

As the lust filled watcher's desire grew; the Clerk nearly forgot why he was here in her room. The oblivious Ayesha moved to her bed, pulled back a large blanket and covered herself. It was as if a bucket of cold water was thrown over the Clerk. He leapt out of the shadows and charged across the room to her bed. Her assailant had his hand over her mouth before she could react. He gazed into her large brown terrified eyes as he searched for the piece of Naomh's amulet. Ayesha struggled, got loose and was about to scream. But the blonde intruder had his hand over her mouth again. She was biting his hand. He whispered through clenched teeth.

"I have never hit a woman before, but if you don't stop struggling, I will make an exception in your case."

The beautiful Arabian creature must have had an understanding of the Anschluss language for she stopped resisting. Her gorgeous brown eyes shone like a trapped animal. In that instant of stillness, he stuck her with a hypodermic dart and she became instantly motionless, but still aware. Her eyes widened in disbelief as he lifted her bed covers. He looked at the perfect body and gazed at the yellow Amulet fragment that was pierced into her navel. Tracing his trembling hand across her flat bellybutton and fully aware of her heaving bosom, inviting thighs and what lay between them, he fought his growing desire and removed the jewel. The Clerk gently recovered her with the blanket, he was no rapist. But the removal of the Amulet must have countered the effects of the sedative, for the shock at losing her lifelong sixth sense caused her to overcome her terror and cry out in fright.

"Intruders!"

In an instant, the room filled with her protectors. Dedicated and armed eunuchs, whose sole purpose was the safety of the princess piled in from another room. Ayesha's scream of alarm had the whole palace complex buzzing like a swarm of angry hornets and armed men filled the halls. But outside the room, the Clerk's back up team had already been alerted by the cry of alarm and burst into the princess's room. Bursts of fire from Naomh's weapon dropped the guards, but one had got behind him. Another short burst of fire and the hidden assailant fell to the carpeted floor, his blood mingling with the millions of finally woven knots. The Prof stared at his smoking gun in disbelief; he had actually killed a man and he did not think it interesting. Shocked fingers let his weapon fall to the floor as he was dragged out of the room by the Clerk. Naomh followed suit and they walked into a virtual army outside in the corridor who were in no mood to take prisoners. The three men were heavily outnumbered and out gunned. On a command from his leader, those that were still armed dropped their weapons and raised their empty palms. No sooner had they their hands held high, the whole of the enclosed hallway echoed from a thundering and the unrelenting sound of a large calibre weapon. The Sheikh's guards died in the prolonged burst of fire. The Mute emerged from thin air besides his shocked comrades; he had laid down the arc of fire from a hidden TORT-CAMLET ahead of them. Their saviour promptly disappeared again. Those who the loner had rescued recovered and made a mad dash down the hallway where they reached the doorway of the palaces priceless library. A rocket whizzed by the two men's heads and exploded within the fantastic literary collection. The hall of irreplaceable learning started to go up in flames. The Prof watched in growing horror as the inferno greedily rushed forward to gobble up ancient parchment and paper. In minutes, all of the exquisite artwork and calligraphy would be non-descript ashes. Books full of divine colour were no more. The man of learning was disgusted as their space filled with black suffocating smoke. The Clerk realising that the three of them were trapped by the inferno took out the miniature cloaking device and activated it, by pressing the correct sequence on his wristband. Himself and Naomh shone their recognising beams and with a leap vanished from sight. The Prof still stood transfixed. A hand appeared from nowhere and grabbed the unmoving man and propelled him into the separate space. Inside the haven, each one of them caught their breath. Outside their sanctuary and along confused corridors, explosions were set off in sequences. The Engineer was orchestrating mayhem and the Sheikh's halls ran red with blood. In another realm of obscurity, the Clerk held up the yellow piece of the APOCRYPHA'I. Wide eyed, he handed it to Naomh, who snatched it out of his hands in the blink of an eye. Surprised at his roughness, he ordered.

"It is time; we were out this wasps nest. Tell the others to get the hell out of here as well."

As the Prof was still addled, the Clerk gave the order to the other globes. The possessor of the three parts never even realised that the yellow piece had no immediate effect on him as he sped on his way in the bubble of invisibility and to the relative safety of the outside desert.

At the first sound of gunfire, Greta had burst into the Sheikh's room, his outside bodyguards were dead, killed by her, but Shoshanna had everything in hand. The beguiled Arabian Caliph lay bound and helpless as a result with his infatuation with the one he assumed was an Anschluss woman. He had enticed her to his rooms, thinking it had been his idea. Now he mumbled in rage through his gagged mouth.

"One look into her pretty eyes and a sharp pain, then oblivion. What a fool I am."

He had not heard the silent gunfire outside his private quarters. But the sound of other automatic fire and explosions were loud enough. The drugged man had come around quickly. In her haste, Shoshanna had not administered the sedative correctly. The enraged Sheikh began to struggle against his bonds. Greta was about to put a bullet into the helpless prisoner, but the Enclave woman stayed her hand as she draped her body over him for protection.

"No! There is no cause for that."

Robbed of her victim, the cold-eyed blonde woman took another course of vindictive action. She rubbed salt into his wounds.

"While you lie there helpless, there is something that you should know. We were the crew of that Tank that destroyed your plans. What was the number on its side again, oh yeah, 2927."

That number had been ingrained on his soul, he countered confusedly.

"But they were blown to smithereens?"

"I don't think so."

Ben Sulimani saw the truth of her vile words in the face of the one that saved him. Greta opened the door; the two women left the tied up Sheikh, so they could re-enter the TORT-CAMLET unseen. The Enclave soldier followed Greta through the maze of corridors, but the duo of them ran into a wall of armed men. In a blur, the Anschluss woman activated their invisible shield and dived into the shell, but her companion went down. Secure in the hidden globe, Greta saw that Shoshanna had suffered a mighty head wound. She lay crouched in silent pain as her blood pooled on to the marble floor of the hallway. Beside her lay her discarded weapon. With deliberate and grim determination, Greta left the safety of her impenetrable shield and tried to get to her wounded companion. Bullets zipped by her head like a swarm of angry wasp's intent on seeking revenge for some affront. It was useless and Shoshanna was probably dead anyway. There was nothing Greta could do for her and with incredible agility she back flipped into the TORT-CAMLET. She left the scene of her companion's demise and the trail of the Enclaves woman's blood on the ancient marble floor. Those inside the Engineer's invisible shield had seen her brave, but unsuccessful attempt to save her companion.

"Let's get out of here now. They either have or not have the next piece by now and the energy of the shields is running low."

As they moved away, gun battles still erupted. Naomh's company and the Mute were still active. The Sheikh's private army dropped smoke canisters and donned night vision apparatus. Shadowy circular outlines appeared and fire was directed at them. But these tactics were of no avail. Fighting their way through smog filled corridors in their invisible and impenetrable shells of light, the invisible attackers gunned down hundreds of the Sheikh's disadvantaged personal guard. It was the Human equivalent of a turkey shoot. Unhindered, the spheres of death moved through the fort's solid walls and out into the oasis night. The bridge connecting the complex was too far away, so it was decided to the risk revelation and cross the open water. The alerted sentries on the walls saw a strange sight, ripples formed on the surface of the water, but there was not even the slightest breeze. A moving circular sheen was revealed by searchlight. Guns blazed and a torrent of fire arced towards the strange object. But the well-aimed ordnance had little effect and the unknown thing reached the other bank and promptly disappeared. During the prolonged escape, the Sheikh had been discovered and released from his bonds. As updated reports came to him, his rage became tighter than the plastic ties that had incapacitated him. Unbelievable accounts came flooding in. Ayesha's hysterical mother, the only survivor told him.

"Your entire Harem has been slaughtered by the one who had not spoken at any time in your presence."

Thankfully all of his children were safe; they had been in another part of the palace. Then came the worst news possible, his precious daughter's quarters had been violated and by the grace of Allah, His cherished offspring was unharmed, but her piece of heaven had been stolen. Ayesha was in a state of shock. He could get nothing responsive out of her.

"My piece of Heaven has been robbed by thieves of the night. That is what the devils had come for. Everything else was a lie."

The Sheikh's rage towards those thieving sons of pigs now surpassed even that of the Enclave. Survivors among his guard told him.

"There was fire that came from nowhere. It decimated our ranks and strange moving shapes that soaked up everything directed at them."

All the deceivers, except one had vanished without a trace. He ranted and raved to himself.

"Those jackal curs have stolen my piece of Heaven."

His hatred of the Anschluss now knew no bounds. Still, he had a quandary of sorts.

"They have left a wounded comrade behind and she will survive. That woman should pay for their treachery. But she has saved my life. The one with the cold eyes would have surely killed me without her intervention."

He gave commands.

"Get every soldier of mine out into the desert night to seek out those deceivers. I want them alive"

His forces began a massive sweep of the immediate area; precious helicopters were even used.

"By the grace of Allah (BLESSING'S BE UPON HIM.). I want them living and breathing."

Out at the edges of the verdant oasis, the successful questor's began to re-assemble the TORT-CAM. The comrades, they had left outside had taken up covering positions as Moshe had noticed the chaos inside the fortress. Solomon had realised from the start without saying to Miriam.

"The six of us could have entered the complex with our friends. We

could have stayed in the invisible shields and come out if we were needed. Still as a strategist, I know that these covering positions are the best option. My Serene thinks with her heart where Naomh is concerned and would have insisted on going."

As the visible globes appeared one by one and materialised alongside them, relief swept in. First to arrive were the Engineer, the Persuader, the Guide, Cahill and the Lenses. Next came Naomh; then the still shaken Prof and finally the Clerk. Second last came Greta and finally the Mute had arrived; he had revelled in the concealed murder of the Harem and the slaughter of the guards. He was so wrapped up in the carnage that he had left his departure until the last possible second. As the killer of a lot of men and women appeared, Cahill was about to make good on his recent promise, but his hand was stayed by the Lenses.

"He saved the lot of us."

Serene Miriam noticed instantly that one of her crew was missing. The second that the Mute had come out of his invisible shield. A cold feeling came over her. Hoping that she was still within one of the wondrous devices, she demanded.

"Where is Turai Shoshanna?"

Then, the sobering news brought by Greta that Shoshanna had been mortally wounded during the short and mostly one sided gun battle took all joy from gaining the third piece of the APOCRYPHA'I. All of the thieves had been light headed with success, but it was now tainted with sadness, grief and regret. Tears flowed openly among Miriam's people and their anguish even touched the most of the Anschluss members of the quest. The Persuader looked like he had run into a concrete wall and come off the worst. Helicopters buzzing overhead shook them out of their lethargy.

"Let's get out of here; we will deal with our grief later." Said the Rabbi looking up at the flashes in the night sky.

"We have to go back for her." Insisted the biggest among them.

"That is not possible; we will not throw more lives away."

The Commander of the Sheikh's forces reported back, the expert tracker was baffled.

"Those, who we searched for have vanished into thin air. There is not a whisper of their passing anywhere."

The Sheikh swore.

"Those curs have used the secret device that enticed me. It is not a fabrication after all. Such a thing does exist and I will have it along with the stolen gift of heaven."

A few days later, far away in the Enclave Commander Kaufmanns stared at the information that had come up on his screen. It had been sent from the espionage section and stated.

"An operative of ours named Sacha Fine, who had been planted in Sheikh Ben Sulimani's household had seen Shoshanna Wiseman in the

company of a number of Anschluss citizens in the palace. Hours later, the whole complex had erupted in a battle. There had been hundreds of the palace staff killed."

Aluf Kaufmanns was perplexed. He requested the information of the losses during the construction of the barrier and found her name along with the rest of her Tanks crew as killed in action.

"For God sake. I was at their funeral; they were heroes. It was their breaking away from my plan that had been the master stroke. Their names will be inscribed on the new wall. Should I visit their families and tell them that their loved ones are still alive?"

He decided against it.

"No! That would give rise to too many questions and I don't need an investigation on that scale."

Then, the Enclave officer remembered the reports logged in the back of his mind.

"Her crew had also been in the company of Anschluss personnel before the invasion."

He checked the video records prior to the assault and counted Tank 2927's complement has been unusually high. Focusing in on some of the individuals showed a surprising number of blonde haired personnel. Been the career soldier that he was, the Commander knew.

"There is more going on than I need to know. It stinks of Anschluss involvement and if someone up above wants me to know what is going on, I will be informed."

The commander's thought's turned to other pressing matters.

Back in the invisible TORT-CAM, a kilometre from the Sheikh's palace, yellow tesseral were added to its inside contours. However, most its occupants bar two were oblivious to the superimposing transformation. Each of the others were trying to cope after the loss of a comrade. After the reported death of Shoshanna, the wilderness and its sky that had looked so alive to the Prof became dark and decayed, promising that all of them would eventually be buried under its uncaring gaze. Deep down, he came to the realisation.

"It's just the same as the Anschluss out here, but worse. It promises you unlimited freedom, but it can snatch it away and deal death as quickly as any PREVENTIVE unit. Things have changed and the great adventure has become soiled."

Miriam and her friends were devastated; never in a million years did any of them think their death would come in such a strange and faraway place. However, it was the Persuader who took the reports of Shoshanna's demise the hardest, he was inconsolable. When he broke from his silent grief, the helpless man with tears streaming down his cheeks urged.

"We have to go back, even if it is to recover her body."

Deep inside, the big man knew that this was not an option. His brother's heart went out to him as it now dawned on the man who only had a spiritual love for his God that the relationship between his sibling and Shoshanna had been more that platonic.

"They must have been lovers, though for the life of me, I cannot see what that beautiful woman saw in Jose."

He frowned on promiscuously, but decided that it might have been a good thing for his brother. The Persuader had never been so happy when he was in her company.

"Still, now he has to deal with this loss, he will turn more to prayer now."

But ironically, it was a man of another faith who put the big man at ease. The Rabbi took him aside and explained the facts to him. Aaron Kalwenixi was from a long unbroken chain of belief and had many an experience of comforting the relatives of the recently deceased. To him, the Engineer and his fledging religion was just a novice. If he took offence at the other's intrusion, then the Persuader's brother kept it to himself.

"Are you all right?" Asked the bearded man.

His tearful reply was nearly inaudible.

"No, I am not."

The Rabbi told the visibly upset man.

"It's only the ones that are left behind that feel the sorrow. The dead have no need of grief, they are with God now. She is at peace now and the real beauty of her was in the lives that she touched. You have to realise that death is part of life and we have to accept it. That is the way of God. The initial shock of loss will be regulated with time."

"I don't think so." Came the mournful response.

Greta also appeared upset that she could not have saved the Enclave beauty. Cahill felt proud when the Guide told the others about her attempted rescue. Still the cool woman took her failure badly and for the rest of the comrades, the illusion of invincibility was wiped away in the cold safety of the TORT-CAM. The Mute only regretted.

"I did not see her die and watch such a pretty light go out."

The mostly grieving company of the search for the uncompleted APOCRYPHA'I now numbered sixteen. Naomh told the Enclave crew.

"I feel responsible for her death as she had joined my quest and it has killed her."

But surprisingly, the Rabbi told him.

"We are not sure if our comrade is dead and even if she is, it is not your fault. From what Moshe and Haim told us, the invasion would have been a failure and we would have been killed anyway. If anything, you gave all of us a few weeks of borrowed time. And, we thank you for that."

His remaining crew members nodded in agreement and Naomh turned away, so they would not see his watery eyes. A few hours later, the Persuader was caught trying to go back for Shoshanna. The big man was fully packed and armed to the teeth. It was his brother who confronted him at the boundary of their hidden haven. He put his hand on his younger sibling's shoulder.

"Don't be a fool Jose. It would be a suicide mission. You might as well put one of the Preachers bombs on you and blow yourself up."

"Still, I must go. She could be still alive."

"I cannot let you go."

"You do not understand love; all you have is that strict God of yours. Now let me go."

"This is more about my love for you."

"I have to do this thing. I am feeling useless Miguel. The rest of you have your talents, all I had was my strength, but that is nothing now. I could not save her the first time, so I will go back and try again."

The Engineer was taken aback; his dejected brother had never gone against his wishes before. But he did not relent. Then inflamed with grief and anger, the big man said.

"Are all your stories of Jesus untrue then? After all, you are fond of quoting the story about the shepherd risking the whole herd in going back for one lost sheep."

His brother cursed.

"You can always find a passage in that Bible to justify your thinking. Well not this time?"

The smaller man sighed and gave a nod to someone behind the big man as he uttered.

"Forgive me my brother."

The Lenses stuck the big man with a needle. It was the same stuff that Shoshanna had used on the Sheikh and the Clerk had used on the princess. The big man's knees buckled and his face expressed shock at the betrayal as he collapsed to the Alien floor. The Engineer kissed the unconscious Persuader on the forehead and it took four of them to carry him back to his sleeping place within the TORT-CAM.

"My brother is going to hate me when he wakes up, but as I have saved his life, his resentment will be bearable."

Those carrying the dead weight offered no words to the contrary. Time was passed in silence. Through its host's influence on the others, the uncompleted APOCRYPHA'I used its growing empathy and symbiotic relationship with the companions to reduce the power of grief among the sixteen and a powerful emotion that should have affected most of their efficiency was put on the back burner. Its manipulation of them was growing stronger. The Engineer could not believe it, but hours later when his brother awoke, his suicidal tendencies had evaporated. Although, the big man was still aggrieved, his pain at Shoshanna's loss had diminished noticeably. Even among her compatriots, the bouts of weeping were getting fewer and farther apart. The presence of Mescal was been severely tested at keeping the Hybrid's focused and it eventually got them moving again. They now played a game of cat and mouse with their chasers. But one evening disaster struck while the pursued were snaking across a dried up wadi. Weapons were pointed at the banks and night vision goggles were revealing the path of the gorge ahead. A few days ago thunderclouds had rumbled and billowing clouds had deposited a huge unseasonable downpour on the coastal heights and the cascading torrent had done what the Sheikh's men could not. It found them. The highly alert group heard the surrounding rumbling and stood dumbfounded; most of them had no clue at what was happening.

"Are they using Tanks?" Asked Beersheba.

Naomh's possession of the Doppler Effect made him inform his jittery comrades.

"Whatever is making the noise is coming from behind us."

Weapons were pointed in that direction. But lucky for them one among them knew of the calamity that was approaching. Moshe screamed in panic, not caring if any of the searching soldiers found them.

"For God's sake get out of this dried up river bed. We've no time to get into the Dobber."

Without hesitation, everybody reacted to his warning and tried to get up to higher ground. A rapid flow of water covered their dust stained boots making the footwear gleam as if new. Behind it came the main body of liquid. Previous flash floods had washed away all of the soft topsoil of the exposed riverbed and the hard packed earth along its route caused the advancing water to reach a speed of an inter-city shuttle. The main body of the flash flood was travelling at over a hundred kilometres an hour and the wall of water; mud and plant debris was on them in an instant. The watery avalanche snatched three of them away. When everybody regained their senses after the wall of water had left them clinging to dry ground, it was found that the Guide, the Lenses and the Rabbi had been carried off by the rapid cascade. The remainder of the group stood on the slopes on what was now a river. As, each of the fortunate escapees took deep breaths, Naomh knew that they had no choice but to use their communication devices to locate their missing friends.

"I don't noo- if this is a good idea, we will be found." Said the Mute in his whinny voice. He received a number of dirty looks, especially from Cahill who still had a bone to pick with him over his antics back in the Sheikh's fortress. Their missing comrades beat them to the decision.

"Come in. Can you hear me?" Crackled a voice over the airwaves.

Two kilometres away, a battered and spluttering Guide had dragged the pounded Rabbi ashore through a shallow mud filled trench. The religious man had been struck by a flying log. His night vision equipment had been shattered to pieces and his helmet had undoubtedly saved his skull from been smashed. He gasped in pain and held his bruised or broken ribs.

Coughing up a mouthful of muddy water kicked up by the silt-carrying cascade expanded his chest wall and he yelled again in discomfort. The Guide removed the injured man's packs and the Rabbi grimaced in relief. The Lenses found them; he had heard their Enclave comrade groan in the night's silence. He had swum ashore only a few hundred metres down from them. The second he put his foot on the sandy bank, he cursed in pain. His ankle was badly swollen. He hobbled over to the other two and with grimaced teeth, the man of technology said.

"We have no choice; we have to break radio silence."

The Guide concurred; the two of them could not carry the Rabbi. He found a spare communication device in his salvaged pack and put it in his ear. He got through to the others instantly and he was told.

"Stay put while we come to you."

The broadcasted communication was picked up and the Sheikh's soldiers and hundreds of troops vectored in on them. The three battered survivors of the raging torrent were in deep trouble; they had no invisible shield to hide in. If they were found first by the searching soldiers before their friends got to them, then the unsteady men would have to try and evade their chasers the old-fashioned way. A short time later, anxious voices came from behind them and then there were sounds from in front of them. The three men found a group of rocks and prepared to defend themselves. There were now voices all around them; carried clearly on the desert air.

"We are trapped!"

The three seekers had become the hunted and there were no avenues of escape open to them. The surrounded men would make a fight of it, but the precarious situation was useless. Ben Sulimani had flown out on a helicopter, the moment his technicians had located the source and the vector of communication signals. Two groups were converging towards each other. Like his experts, their ruler was puzzled.

"How did the defilers of my hospitality get this far without been detected?"

He was on the ground now and he revelled in the chase. It was the Human equivalent of a boar hunt and it thrilled him. But his growing enthusiasm for the chase disappeared when one group of his prey vanished into thin air. Not for the last time, he cursed.

"Not again."

But to his joy, the other bunch had been trapped in a cluster of rocks. His men swarmed towards them like bees to a honey pot. The noose tightened as the night lit up into brilliant day. Blinding yellow searchlights revealed the three crouching men to the Sheikh. An impatient shot rang out, it took the Guide in the shoulder and he fell back in pain. His protective jacket had taken most of the impact and little blood had been drawn. An answering round from the pink-eyed Lenses took out the offending sniper, that guy was not so lucky. All hell broke loose, the desert night air filled with automatic fire.

"I want them alive." Screamed the Sheikh down his communication line.

The Guide clutched an explosive grenade; he for one would not be taken prisoner as he had seen what happened to such individuals before. His two trapped companions agreed and followed his example. The Lenses should have been prepared to bite down on his poisoned tooth. But been the former coward that he once was; it had been removed years ago. The enemy forces were only metres away. Fingers tightened on the explosive devices trigger. The Rabbi began chanting in his own language.

"I have them now." Thought Ben Sulimani jumping the gun.

Twenty of his best soldiers burst into the rocks and found them gone. A second before his men made contact, there had been an amazing flash of bright light and every night goggle and scanning instrument became obscured for a micro-second. In the confusion, the Guide, the Lenses and the Rabbi had been hauled into three mini TORT-CAMLET'S and were saved at the last moment. As the exhausted and relieved Guide looked into the face of his saviours, he gasped in pain.

"About time."

Still, he knew.

"It had been a close call."

His two rescued companions echoed similar sentiments about dying after been discovered in the nick of time. Just then, three primed explosive devices which each of them had discarded detonated along with the Sheikh's men. Safe in their invisible sanctuary, they never heard the screech of rage and threat's that followed as Ben Sulimani realised from the sound of the simultaneous crump's that he had been thwarted once again. However a few days later one of their number did hear the menacing words of the furious leader. The enraged Sheikh charged into his prisoner's recovery room and demanded answers from her. But Shoshanna was feeling the strain of her injuries; the wounded Enclave woman was totally drained. She had little energy and was unable to focus on anything. She once again relapsed into unconsciousness. The Sheikh wanted to shake the answers from her, but he knew that would probably kill her. As he left the room, he vowed.

"By the holy words of the Prophet, (BLESSINGS BE UPON HIM.) that Anschluss woman is going to give me all the correct responses, one way or the other."

XXI.

By an un-agreed consensus, there had been no celebration at the gaining of the yellow piece. However, ever since the time the wanderers had left the Anschluss and been in the Enclave, birthdays had come and gone. All of them were now a year older and except for the Guide and the intending betrayer, it the first time in their lives that any of them had celebrated the event in another land. It had been the same for the Enclave crew and this time in an ironic twist of fate, it was the missing and presumed dead; Shoshanna's. A muted celebration was held in her honour, but it became more of an impromptu wake than a festive occasion. Thoughts were on the preceding events. The reduced compliment of sixteen seekers of the APOCRYPHA'I were now far away from the Sheikh's domain. The company had a last few nerve-racking days. Every moment of the last seventy-two hours had consisted of making enough ground between themselves and the frantic searchers. Surprise packages left behind by the Engineer took a fearful toll among the chasing soldiers and heightened their rage. All, except the injured duo of the Rabbi and the Lenses ducked and dived making their way southwards along the spine of the western mountains, finding cover among the crags and trees of the mountain slopes whenever discovery heralded. Whether, it was night or day, the hunted contingent moved. Flirting in between the outside World and the TORT-CAM, the crew finally escaped from the clutches of their pursuers. Eventually and unknown to the hunted, they had crossed a boundary into another rulers domain. Utterly frustrated and boiling with rage, Ben Sulimani had to give up the chase. If the border of that Sheikhdom were crossed by his troops, then he would be at war with his neighbour and his allies. It was a risk that the Caliph of his people could not take, but the decision to back down had been a close run thing. The urge to regain the piece of Heaven was overpowering, but the fact that he was losing too many good men ultimately swayed his decision. The chase was called off. It was only now after the heat had died down and the pursued were no longer under the cosh that they could mourn the loss of a friend and comrade. An impromptu wake/birthday was held for Shoshanna amid tearful recrimination.

The heavily strapped Rabbi again helped them with their grief and a modicum of peace was found among the lamenters. After all, this was a group well used to death. The man of religion gave his Serene the silver Magen David held in trust and told her.

"Keep it safe."

She thanked him and replied, though not really believing it.

"I promise, after all I might be able to return it to her one day."

"That's the spirit."

It was during this period of despair that the bearer of the three pieces of the Alien technology was hit with a double whammy. The atmosphere of gloom and the inevitable "Downer." following the gaining of another segment affected Naomh more than the previous two times. This night, he had become short tempered, argumentative and depressed. Knowing little about his affliction, the others left him alone with the grieving Miriam. The next morning, the Prof stirred awake. The committed pacifist was having a crisis of conscience. He had killed a man and he was full of remorse. The loss of the beautiful Shoshanna played heavily on his disheartened mind as well. Surprisingly, the night before, the Persuader sought solace and comfort from him. The big man had told him after he was well inebriated.

"I can't get the last look of her beautiful eyes out of my head. They were full of life and now, she is dead."

Even though, the living amulet was working its magic, he threatened to break down again.

"Why don't you talk to your brother?"

"Miguel does not understand the love between men and women. He has only time for his God. He would only tell me that she is waiting in heaven for me."

Death always brought out the worst in the Prof, whether it was a Human or a pet. But now he was full of bitterness at his own act. To rub salt into his emotional wounds, he had been involved in a skirmish that had ended up with a beautiful library been burnt to the ground. It mattered little that he had taken a life to save Naomh from certain death.

"Am I still a man of learning? I am not like the others; killing comes easy to them. But if it had required me to slay another Human being to have saved Shoshanna's life, I would have done it as well. My friends have become a liability. There are changing me. I am becoming like them. Maybe, it is time to go a separate way."

He silently weighed up his options to himself and knew.

"Deep down, I cannot desert them. They are my only friends after all."

He looked over at the place where Shoshanna used to lie and sighed. The Prof decided.

"I will seek out the comfort of my animal companions. It is only when I am among them that I can find true solace."

There had been no pursuit for a week now and it was judged safe by all to leave the invisible haven, if one was careful that was. To confuse any chasers, they had vectored back out into the open desert. It was in the early hours of the morning and he tried in vain to wake his best friend to go out and find consolation in nature. Solomon was too depressed and had taken too much alcohol the previous night. The man from the Enclave begged off. He was still red eyed from the tears he had shed for his dead friend. Like the rest of the Enclave crew, his friend was inconsolable, but the Prof remembered the homily that the Rabbi had given for Shoshanna. The edge of sorrow in his voice was pronounced.

"I know that we have no body to grieve over and there is a chance that she might still be alive."

Greta who was still upset at her failure to save her shook her head at those words. The Rabbi's voice rose.

"But, if our beautiful comrade has perished, then she is with God. We are the shock troops of the Enclave and each one of us always expected to die and if we did it would be together in our Tank." The Rabbi softened his voice. *"Our beloved sister has just gone ahead of us that's all. And more of us might join her, if that is God's will."*

His words brought a little comfort to his people.

"God's will my arse, I plan on staying alive for ever." Thought the Spy.

This member of the LYUBINITES had a different outlook on life and death was not included. The Prof had shed a few tears for Shoshanna, more than some it must be said, while the others drowned their grief in alcohol and cigs. The intellectual had been surprised that the Mute had even got drunk. The loner had stood up at one stage, swayed and fell into a heap with a silly grin on his face, much to the amusement of the others. But thankfully, they were ignorant of the pleasant thoughts that the twisted man was indulging in. Not having drunk as much as the others the night before, the man from the London Contrib went out himself. He cast his eyes about at the sleeping mass as he passed through the TORT-CAM'S sphere of influence. Outside the brightness of the day was always more intense than inside the now red/orange/yellow Alien World of the concealment device. He strolled towards a water hole that the fleeing group had passed the night before. Through constant observation by him and Solomon, they had learned that it was the best spot to observe any wildlife.

"Every animal that ekes a living out in this harsh environment of the open desert needs to drink. Predators know this as well. Is that what I have become, a hunter. No, that type of animal kills for food that they need to survive out here in these harsh lands."

The burgeoning naturist located a shrubby bush, made his way towards it and squatted down behind the man-sized plant. As was the norm, the Prof had not taken any body armour. He had even discarded his protective helmet, because he liked to feel the chill of the morning and live the conditions that the wildlife endured daily. All, he took was a flask of coffee and an image-recording device. Edward Boyd felt useless unless he had a cup of the stimulating drink first thing in the morning. He also deactivated his Enclave back up communication device as incoming calls always caused the wildlife to bolt. It was to prove to be a fatal error. Under the plants covering, the fascinated academic spent the next few hours observing the water hole, sipping occasionally from the coffee flask while he took some amazing video footage. He thought ruefully.

"Solomon would have been a help. I have no idea what some of the

creatures I have seen are called. He might."

However, his heart was also not in it; a beautiful face and a dead man's features kept intruding. Feeling the wind pick up, the hidden man cast his eyes skyward just as the shadow of a passing nebula of clouds ghosted by, threatening to herald a sudden storm. He hoped it would rain and maybe the chilled water might wash away the stain of blood from his hands. Crouching behind the thick gorse bush, the watching man was juggling with a decision.

"It's about time to call it a day. I have only brought a video recording device and no other essential equipment. Not even weather gear. I could get soaked out here."

The Prof was now feeling the sudden chill as the weeks spent in the heat had acclimatised his body to the normal heat of the desert day. Even the sips of the hot compliment were only providing brief respites from the drop in the temperature. A pathetic looking bush had got his attention; the lack of rain in this part of the desert had caused all of its lilac petals to fall around its base like fallen butterflies. Not caring what its real name was, the amateur biologist named it.

"Lingering Wings."

The lifeless plagiarism of that beautiful insect caused him to mutter.

"I am really morbid today. I could have come up with a better image than a reminder of death. Still, that is the mood that I am in."

Suddenly, all the animal life around the water scattered in alarm. Excitement renewed itself, as he was certain it was the approach of a large predator. His waning enthusiasm was reinvigorated. The hidden observer noticed movement to his left and felt a momentary disappointment. He saw a member of their group walking along the rim of the waterhole. Unknown to him, he had found the worst sort of man killer. Although, the Prof had little in common with the person he was watching, he still was about to call out a greeting. But something stayed him. Then for a laugh, he thought it might shake him out of his depression, he decided to record their movements and play it back later in front of the gang. In a frozen instant all of his intended mirth dissipated when he saw that person bend down and take a communication device from a bulky pocket and converse in Anschluss. He immediately recognised the Frog Eyes.

"That M I M still works. How could that be?"

Then, he heard words that shook him to his core.

"Come in, PREVENTIVE control. This is Agent XIII. Put me through to the Chairman."

Edward Boyd was astounded at the conversation and for a decisive moment did not believe what he was hearing. The Prof froze like a trapped rodent that he was so fond of watching.

"This is unbelievable. I have to get out of here and warn the others. They have no idea what kind of danger they are in."

The concealed observer kept his recording device pinpointed on the traitor. It would be proof enough. With this evidence, he was sure the rest of the group would believe him. He didn't accept it himself. But as the hidden witness moved to get a better angle, he inadvertently snapped a dry twig. The hard cruel eyes of the traitor flashed to him. The Clone had been alerted by the sound of the broken stick and located him from the glint of his recording device. The Prof cursed himself for coming out unarmed and more importantly without communication. He saw certain death in those eyes. He tried to flee and scrambled from his hiding place in an impetuous dash.

"Why run, you will only die tired" Laughed Agent XIII.

As the Spy aimed their rifle, the zigzagging Prof could only lament.

"We've all been fools. Never in a million years would I have thought that one was a turncoat. I have to let Naomh know; otherwise he hasn't got a prayer. I have to survive this."

The weaving runner felt a wicked blow as death caught up with him anyway. He crashed into a thorny thicket, oblivious to the blood ripping barbs. As the mortality wounded man lay face up, his lifeblood quenching the deserts thirst, he wondered abstractly.

"Would it rain after all or will the scavengers fight over my corpse?"

One racking cough, a soft whistling wheeze and the former museum curator's quest for knowledge was over. The secret of the traitor's identity died with the dead man. The scholar passed from this World with a final gurgle of blood that issued from his lips. Edward Boyd had died at the age of thirty-five and his life experience could have been compared to a mayfly. He had spent the vast majority of it like a grub, but over the last year, he had flown free like the adult insect that only lived for a day. Would he have stuck to his monotonous life back in the Anschluss, knowing the final outcome of his great adventure; no, probably not. The traitor was annoyed at the stupidity of been discovered, but relaxed in the knowledge that.

"My weapon had been on silent."

The Spy had realised early on that the TORT-CAM did not allow radio traffic alien to its parameters to be broadcast from inside it, even simple location messages were out of the question. So the Anschluss's agent among them had to go a distance from the others and contact Tell from there. The intending betrayer callously stood on the discarded video recording device belonging to the deceased Prof and ground it into pieces. The dead man's inactive communication device was torn from his bloodied lobe and treated similarly. The body of the Prof was hefted onto the killers shoulder and carried a fair distance away from the murder site. All of the LYUBINITES carried a flesh dissolving agent to destroy the molecular evidence of their Cloned background. It was fished out and poured over the body. His flesh began to dissolve and break down. In ten minutes, there would be nothing left. The on-going chemical reaction was hastily covered. Just as the gruesome task was finished, the murderer heard somebody approach. The Anschluss agent recognised the man that approached. The Spy itched to kill him as well, but the killer was well aware.

"Two simultaneous disappearances would be unexplainable. Besides, the Prof had in his possession a small globe which he thought that I had not noticed. Retrieval of this is a priority as I don't know what is in it. I've no time to dally with this one."

So Agent III rushed back to the TORT-CAM to find it. This item had not bothered the traitor before; they did not give a dam about the weak man and his fantasy's. But now it was a priority. Another member of the sixteen had also come out in order relieve themselves and puff on a cig. The others had complained about the stench from his vice, so when it was judged safe, their comrade from the Amsterdam Contrib smoked outside. It was of course, the Guide and he much preferred to use the open desert than the recycling system of the confined globe. Twenty minutes before, he had been lying in his bed after just waking up; he stretched and yawned with an exaggerated effort. The Guide was reluctant to get up, but imminent bodily functions and the need for a smoke won the argument. The pony-tailed man rose; left the invisible shield and went out into the open desert. He walked for a bit enjoying the fresh air and lit up. By the pool, he found a place to relieve himself. As the Guide squatted down to do his business, he was by chance near the murder scene. The street wise man instantly noticed the recent disturbance and read the signs telling them of the Prof's demise.

"Shit man, this does not look good. No man, this looks fucked up."

The sleuth had seen the evidence for traces of blood on the tips of thorns that had scratched the Prof's body as he had tumbled into the desert gorse. The Guide unhooked his weapon and went over to the bush where he found the crushed video unit and communication device. The ear-piece had dried blood on it. Then, with rifle pressed into his shoulder, the armed man retraced the indents of the killer's heavy boot steps, located the trail and continued following it for two hundred metres. A strange smouldering green mist drew his immediate attention. Then to his horror, the shocked member of the company located the crumpled body and the smoking form of the Prof. The remains appeared to be dissolving. Quickly, he used the butt of his weapon, turned the corpse over and saw its bloodied face.

"Ah no! Exclaimed the discoverer.

Then, the dead features vanished forever as the skin cracked like dried parchment and boiled away into a liquid pool. The shocked discoverer took stock and did not like what the evidence pointed to.

"The bad news is that the footwear has revealed that the person responsible for the Prof's demise is one of us. The boot is regular issue among the squad. But its print will not give up the owner's identity as it is

standard Enclave military issue and everyone of us wears the same identical type. This extremely tough footwear has a hard plastic sole that will not wear away and they have no individual thread marks. So the boots have no distinguishing features. I haven't a clue who was responsible for this shit, but it stinks of the fucking Anschluss."

Bitter frustration made him swear profusely.

"Shit, shit, shit, man!"

The Guide realised at the moment.

"Only myself and the perpetrator of this atrocity knows what has happened. I cannot arouse the suspicion of the killer by checking everybody's boots. Also, most of our crew have similar sized feet, including the females. Still, the Persuader could be ruled out, he has massive ones. But the big man cannot be confided in, in case his brother is the killer. After all, I not so sure they are even brothers, they look so different from each other."

This unwanted turn of events make him question everything.

"Miriam can be ruled out also, as she had handed over her piece of the amulet willingly. So beside myself; the Persuader, Miriam and of course Naomh, everybody else including those from the Enclave could be the assassin. I cannot dismiss Miriam's people either as those devious bastards of the Anschluss could have planted one of them a long time ago."

Churning emotions implied there was at least one traitor among them. As the implications dawned, there was a sudden deterioration of darkness, signalling rain. A brief, but violent downpour broke and it was upon him in an instant. The almost horizontal squall lasted a few minutes and then moved away to the fringes of distant hills. But the squall had done its damage; for the brief duration of the heavy downpour had impaired his sight. If the killer had been out there, he would never know now. More importantly, it had also erased the footprint trail of the assassin and thus any evidence to point at the traitor. He was suddenly inspired.

"The killer would have been caught in the shower too. I've got to get back to the Dobber. Muddy boots will reveal the traitor or at least cut down the number under suspicion."

When he arrived, the discoverer found to his dismay that everybody else had been caught in the falling rain.

"I have no choice man; but to wait until the dude who has put an end to the Prof makes their next move. I haven't even got a body to show them."

He greeted them with a smile, thinking.

"The murderer must not know of my discovery."

The Guide was highly saddened at the spectacle wearing man's demise and he repeated an old maxim to himself.

"You were told once, never make friends because then nobody can let you down. And what makes this doubly worst is that the murderer is still

among our group and is also a friend of mine, unless it had been the Mute. I will not tell Naomh of my suspicions of an Anschluss assassin among us, for three reasons. He is the only one who can assemble the amulet, the double agent could have made a successful attempt at any time, so he is safe at the moment and thirdly, his reaction to the news might alert the killer. No; like the murderer, I will let everybody else assume the Prof just left to pursue his dream and abandoned us."

Back inside the invisible haven, all but two were oblivious to the events outside in the desert. The killer of the Prof was furious; the Spy could not locate the intellectuals recording. Agent XIII had frantically searched for the small globe, but in a method without drawing attention to themselves. Solomon had taken a nap after the brief shower and was now awake. Everybody was eating a meal. The bearded man frowned and asked the others about his close friend.

"Where is the Prof?"

The Guide's heart skipped a beat.

"Out with his precious animals. Where else?" Said Cahill.

A very concerned Solomon replied.

"But it was over eight hours since he tried to wake me. He could not be gone that long? It's not like him, he usually only spends about three hours by himself. Five at the max."

Some of the crew now began to worry for the academic's safety. Heavily armed search parties were sent out. By choice, the Guide picked the Mute and he steered his prime suspect towards the place where the Prof's body had dissolved away

"Now, I will see if he betrays himself by his actions."

But Illeau was either a good actor or he was totally oblivious that the decomposed profile of Prof's body was close by. On the other hand, the murderer had already decided.

"If the one who accompanies me discovers the corpse, then they too will be dispatched. I will fabricate some story about us been attacked."

Luckily, the killers search partner never made the grisly discovery. But what those not in the know realised was that dissolving agent had disposed of the Prof's corpse entirely, there wasn't even a bone left. Even his clothing became a constitute of the dirt. Out here in the barren wastes, the smell of blood and death travelled speedily to highly toned orifices. Scavenging animals who had hurried to the corpse backed away in bitter disappointment, unable to digest the chemical muddle. The dead Prof was even denied that small gift to the animals that he loved in life. All of them returned to the TORT-CAM safely and they were downhearted. The search had ended fruitlessly. As the discoverer of the Prof's demise had surmised, the general consensus was that he had finally departed their violent company. The scholar must have gone AWOL. Agent XIII now regretfully decided to put the plan to do away with the Guide on the back burner.

"There would be too many questions."

Miriam delved into the missing man's personal effects, but as with the Spy, she could find nothing to hint at his fate. Everybody was baffled, because if he left, he would have left a message where it would be easily found. The absconded man was still their friend after all. The mostly puzzled group were drinking coffee and in heated discussion about the Prof's mysterious disappearance when a loud buzz sounded. An apparition holding the three dimensional image of the intellectual appeared in the middle of them as if he had been a ghost. Been the closest, Illeau had been the most startled and he had not been alone.

"Shit." Said the Clerk as he nearly dropped his plastic mug with the fright.

But the cool headed Greta had her weapon trained at the flickering disturbance in an instant. So had Naomh, the Guide, the Engineer and Moshe. The others had been as startled as much as the Clerk and reacted that little slower. These people had jumped back in reflex. Recovering, most of them swore at the sudden appearance of the man from the London Contrib; while the Lenses laughed out loud as he guessed.

"The Prof must have become familiar with using the advance technology of the TORT-CAM. This message must have been on a timer."

The three dimensional translucent figure of a sombre Prof, began his narration with a hint of sadness glazed in his eyes. With his London Contrib accent, Edward Boyd addressed the recording device that was now displaying his image to his startled comrades.

"My friends. I have put this image recorder on a timer and it will activate itself after a certain time period if I am not here to halt it. After much deliberation and soul searching, I have decided to leave you and search out my dream. Unlike the rest of you, I am not suited to the constant killing and now even my own hands are soiled. I am just a man of learning and I would become a burden and hindrance to the rest of you. Good luck with your journey and when you complete it, you will find me. Oh as the Lenses has just realized after viewing my speech, I have learnt a few tricks. One that will be very useful to you, as it will be to me is that located in the LAB-CELL is a device that reproduces every precious metal and gem on the Planet. It can also produce any document or plastic currency. Goodbye my friends, especially you Solomon and may your God keep you safe."

The little academic gave instructions on how to use the useful device, he signed off with a deep sigh and his image vanished. There was stunned silence, Solomon was devastated. The killer and the finder of the Prof's body knew well that the artificial representation of the dead man might as well have been a spirit from the netherworld as they both had just witnessed a voice from the grave. But one of them did not believe in the afterlife. The close knit group waited all day in case the Prof had a change of heart, but he never returned. Solomon was inconsolable, he had lost two friends in less than a few weeks and he insisted.

"The Prof would never do such a thing?"

However, the Lenses disagreed and surmised.

"He has killed another Human Being. To him, that was unacceptable and that is why he left."

The Guide continued the lie.

"The Prof had the capability to make precious metals, so he is well fitted out for his trip."

The Mute was asked his opinion and true to form, his answer was brief and non-committal. *"I don't know-."*

Some of the group agreed, while others disagreed. His killer was secretly delighted when they all reluctantly consented that the Prof had upped and left. All of them would have preferred if it had been Illeau who had departed. The Lenses added.

"As we have no idea of the full inventory of the Dobber's contents, we do not know what he took with him. And judging by his use of the hologram, he was probably more familiar than the rest of us with its inventory."

The following morning as the group assembled and greeted the new dawn; there was a subdued atmosphere among them because of the Prof's abrupt departure on top of the death of Shoshanna. The Guide was haunted by his discovery and his forced silence. He knew that the seekers had a rotten apple among them. Once again, he asked himself.

"Who among us is the killer? It could be anybody, even someone from the Enclave. But why did they kill the Prof?"

Eventually, the answer came to him.

"He must have discovered something significant about them. A thing so important that they murdered him."

The man from the Amsterdam Contrib had one likely candidate; it was of course the Mute. *"I will watch that sinister dude very closely from now on. If he even looks at any one else cross-eyed, I will blow his fucking head off."*

But, Rory had always stressed upon him.

"Do not always accept the obvious."

So, he looked at the other members of their small contingent.

"I can rule out, Naomh and Miriam and the other members of her crew. There was no way that the filth had planned that far ahead. Cahill and Greta, no! Their hatred of those in charge was not put on."

Then it came to him.

"The turncoat must have been offered something that they could not turn down. With the Engineer, a return to the faith would sway his hand, his brother would follow him. The Lenses and the Clerk could have been offered important positions. That's ironic, because the same could have been said about the Prof. No, it is none among them. It has to be that

leech; the Mute. "

Six hours later back in the Geneva Contrib, the screen with the Prof's image and fact-file was switched off with a shrug from the Chairman. His now, more careful agent had contacted his office and updated them. The Kaiser was not too bothered, he knew.

"Naomh's group was only as strong as the weakest link and Edward Boyd had certainly been that."

The next day dawned and again they waited for the missing man. The evening followed in its wake and there was still no sign of the absconder. Reluctantly, the fifteen travellers moved on. Solomon was told.

"If the Prof changes his mind, then he will follow us. Each morning before we retire to the TORT-CAM, a coded message will be sent to the Prof's communication device and if he is so inclined, he can eventually locate us."

Two days later; Naomh had awoken with a nagging sense of confusion. He did not feel the same; something within him had altered. Opening his bleary eyes, he was confronted with Miriam gazing directly into his own.

"She still looks at me with the same level of love and trust. So, nothing has changed."

But, the nagging feeling of transformation persisted. He could not rid himself of the certainty that something had.

"Of course everything has changed."

He had absorbed the third part of the APOCRYPHA'I and even now in the background of his mind; Naomh could feel it ticking away. Its constant presence had stepped up into another gear. He was finding it increasingly more difficult to banish it to the edges of his awareness. The metallic voice was intoning religiously.

"The fourth part of me lies to the north east, high up in a land of mist and mountains."

With some considerable effort, he removed it to the outer limits of his mind. Regaining control, he asked Miriam's people did any of them know about the lands to the east.

"Those places are known as Asia. Those lands are many times larger than the Prophet's and the population more numerous." Said Haim.

"It doesn't matter how big they are, the jewel can guide us to where the next piece is located."

Moshe took over.

"We first need to go south to the coastal cities of this landmass. From there we can find the best way of making our way east."

The rest of the company agreed and their leader showed them the three pieces imbedded in his chest. Once again, the other members of the company were affected by its physical presence; each of them could feel the power of the living amulet. It was the main reason that their grief for their two missing comrades had faded away into a palpable regret. As they moved along on that day, Naomh now knew the truth about the nagging feeling. His physical stature had improved greatly; his reflexes and intellect had advanced considerably. He decided to put his theory to the test. Cahill had always been the stronger of them, so he challenged him to a wrestling bout.

"Let's have a contest."

While his suggestion was been digested, he kept a bland expression refusing to betray his growing suspicion.

"What you and me?" Asked his friend jovially, knowing what he was requesting.

For this was the way it always began. He reckoned it was time for some fun to compensate the desertion of the Prof and the loss of Shoshanna.

"Yeah. Why not?" Agreed the red haired man.

Then, both Cahill and Greta snickered. The Guide asked.

"What is so funny?"

"As long as we have known the two, Naomh has never won a bout." Said the Clerk in reply to his question.

Noticing the change in Naomh's physical stature and prowess since they had first met all those months ago in that dingy warehouse, the Guide gambled.

"I'll make a slight wager on Naomh. Any takers?"

The Persuader who was very fond of the Guide's cigs wagered.

"I will beat the winner in return for a few."

The procurer of them accepted on the condition.

"Only if you will do my chores for a month."

The big man agreed instantly, so sure that he would win the bet. Now if Cahill's strength was prestigious, then it was nothing compared to the Giant from the Madrid Contrib. But there was a glitch in the agreement. An equally confident Cahill refused outright to bout with him.

"Whoa. You have not beaten Naomh yet." Reminded the Guide.

Greta's lover just shrugged as he sized up the shaven headed colossus.

"God. What am I letting myself into?"

The Persuader showed a toothy grin.

"Ok Naomh; lets rumble." Said Cahill.

The two combatants squared off and circled each other. It was over in two point five seconds. The red haired contestant shook his dazed head from the kneeling position that he suddenly found himself in. Greta was gobsmacked. All of the Anschluss members could not believe it, except the one who had betted on him.

"You got lucky for once in your life." Said the loser, slightly enraged at the ease in which Naomh had dropped him to the floor. Rising quickly, face flushed, he slapped his hands together and spat into them. He motioned for another bout.

"Ok, let's do it."

His face must have missed the comfort of the sand, because he reacquainted himself with it once again. He ended up sprawled on the earth even quicker than before, if that was possible. Cahill tried again. The same thing occurred five more times before Naomh's opponent acknowledged defeat with little grace, it must be said. Then, the giant among them spoke.

"Enough. It is my turn. I will show you how it is done"

His brother turned to the winning gambler and with a mocking glint in his eyes asked.

"Is the wager still on?"

As the big man removed his upper clothing, the Guide observed his massive upper body.

"Surely you jest." Insisted the man from the Amsterdam Contrib, now silently realising.

"I have made a serious error of judgement."

The hundred and twenty kilo giant spat into his huge calloused hands, rubbed them together and advanced menacingly on Naomh. Yet to everybody's astonishment, the big man ended up lying stunned on his hands and knees on the desert floor in a slightly longer time than it took Cahill. Then surprisingly, Haim offered a challenge. The first looser gave a snort of derision and said.

"If I or the Persuader could not beat him, what chance do you have?"

"Yeah, little man." Added the second defeated opponent.

Haim moved towards the speaker with purpose. The big man saw his intent and met the provocation. Smoothly, the Enclave soldier made a deft action and the Anschluss man ended up eating dirt again. Cahill attacked him and he too lost again. The Rabbi laughed.

"Oh, we probably forgot to mention that Haim is an expert in Krav maga."

Those from the Anschluss gave ignorant looks. So Beersheba told the astonished cadre.

"It is a form of unarmed fighting."

Greta admonished her disgusted lover.

"He has a low centre of gravity and used that against the two of you."

"You mean; he is small and stocky." Said the largest among them.

The Persuader was not a graceful loser either. Haim and Naomh squared off and although the large nosed man put up a much better fight than the previous two, he too was easily defeated. The bearer of three parts of the APOCRYPHA'I felt elated and he had not even broken a sweat. The victor of the bouts noticed his companions look of fear and awe that their unbelieving eyes now held. His company were now fully under his thrall. The mole had noticed this change as well.

"The others follow him around like little ducklings following their mother. Well, let them, the rest of them are fools. I am not!"

The Guide reached into his pocket, fished out some of his Cigs and handed them to the defeated big man anyway. This little gift eased the pain of his recent humiliation, Cahill was still red faced from his two defeats, but he would get over it. Haim was content, he knew a better opponent when he saw one. The Rabbi and Solomon who had scant knowledge of this part of the World told them.

"The best way to get to Asia is south to the coast and try to get a ship from there."

It was the only plan they had, so their leader went with it. Later that night as the fifteen of them crossed southwards over the dusty dunes, Naomh wanted to test the Lenses and walked alongside him. Asking the cleverest man among his Anschluss friends (Now, that the Prof had run out on them.) to test him on any subject he choose. Again, he astounded them by answering every question the computer hacker gave him. The pink eyed man looked chagrined. Naomh kept his thoughts to himself.

"I have always reckoned that the Lenses were one of the smartest people I had ever encountered. But he has a real limited expanse of knowledge and is now a child compared to me."

Then, he turned to the wisest among them, Solomon. Naomh had an ulterior motive for this; he wanted to draw the man out of his enforced silence. As he conversed with the Prof's close friend in his own language, he became dizzy with the implications of his newfound abilities. His mind became awash with possibilities. Over the next few days, he noticed.

"While I have been the leader of the squad since the Gaffers death and the others follow my orders, it has somehow become different. Their relationship with me has changed. Now everybody really accepts my leadership without question. They are mine. Each and all of them."

Of that fact, he was sadly mistaken. Most of his comrades would follow him to Hell and back, if he wanted them, but there were serious exceptions. Also Naomh did not comprehend that the now three parts Mescal/Amulet was influencing their feelings of obedience. The creature that had been formed by the mix of his Humanity and the Alien personality was increasing its authority over the two individual characters. Eventually, it would be neither one nor the other, but something else altogether different. If Naomh was to realize anything, then it was time for him to be afraid, for his Humanity was slowly and inexorably slipping away.

Somewhere far to the south lay other Beings that had a similar genetic makeup as familiar as the one he was attaining. But these creatures walked a very different path in their evolution. The bearer of three parts of the living amulet's new found elation would have been submerged if he knew of the danger they would pose in the near future. Never in a million years could he imagine the threat that awaited him. The nightmare, he would confront one day was as excited as Naomh was, for it knew that another piece of the APOCRYPHA'I had merged and soon it would be on its way to him. Another bout of insane laughter echoed around his Kingdom causing all of his subjects to cower in subjugation, but all this was for the future.

Unknown to Naomh, there was a closer and potentially, a more immediate threat. Hard, cruel and feral yellow orbs looked southwards. It was dark ahead of the searcher, but there was still a faint trace of brightness back behind him, in the west. The owner of those eyes was none other than Styarz. He had a company of twelve warriors with him. After the holy command from their master, they had left the city of Sanctum and spent time among the heathens on the red sea coast of the Egyptian mainland in a city called Hurghada. Here, the Preceptor had become Achmed once again and he bided his time until his master commanded him to move. Following the decree from their God, Styarz and his fellow Knights were unable to enter the Enclave, so they had to wait until their prey came out. A few weeks ago, the Winged One had told them that a piece of the stolen technology had been activated in the lands of the Prophet. They had travelled to that point by crossing the narrow sea by ferry and then in quad bikes. But in the massive confusion of the battle aftermath, it was hard to find a trail. The leader of the other twelve's tenuous bond with the one who he sensed back in Tunis told him to head south. There one of his men picked up the indents of Enclave boots and the chase began. Stalking, evasion, camouflage and attack, this was the credo that the Knight's of the Winged One adhered to. The followers of Zebulan were the ultimate ambusher's and these pursuing killers crept ever closer to Naomh's company. Because of their nefarious activities and exceptional eyesight, no communication devices were required among them. Hand signals were all that was needed. Styarz and his contingent slept during the heat of the day as all of his band of altered Hybrid's succumbed to the influence from the blend of nocturnal predator locked into their genetic makeup. These hunters much preferred travelling during the hours of darkness. Once the Knight's became still and unmoving, their speckled cowls shimmered with a concealment that made them almost invisible. The cloaks enabled them to hug the shadows and be on top of their targets, before they could react. The instant the day's light faded into blackness, the Knight's came out of their sleepy but instantly alert state. The band of very accomplished killers rose from their slumber, prayed to their God and ate a sparse meal. All of Styarz's men had exceptional night vision, an advantage over Naomh's crew, who had to rely on artificial enhancement equipment for their night-time marches across the open desert. It had taken the minions of Zebulan, a few weeks to close the gap on them. Now they were only a few days behind their quarry and Styarz told his gathered brotherhood.

"Soon we will overtake them and dispatch them."

The Winged One had given him a device to track and locate their targets. It locked on to something that had been stolen from the God when the Deity had first taken sinful man under his wings. The Preceptor pointed the pulsating globe southward.

"The connection is stronger. We are getting nearer."

His belief was slightly correct, but it was his quarries gaining of the third piece that improved the link between the two Alien devices. Back in his desert city and out of view from his followers, Zebulan became even more agitated. Suddenly, one of the trackers sniffed the desert night air. Then the Knight revved up a gear on his Quad and followed a corridor of scent. The others never hesitated and sped behind the vanguard. After a kilometre, they halted at a bunch of desert scrub. Under its scant woody canopy, they discovered a band of nocturnal canines. The excited scavengers were fighting over the remains of some Human corpses. Their scent and excited yapping had carried on the slight night breeze and had attracted the attention of their tracker. A blood-curdling yowl from Zebulan Hybrid's caused the nervous canines to scatter from their prize. The Knight's had found the chewed up bodies of Major Alwi Zaid and his command of military police. Examining the scene of the brief fire fight, Zebulan's followers were all puzzled at how these soldiers of the Prophet had lost the upper hand. To all purposes the dead men had set up a professional ambush and should have at least caused a few causalities among their targets. The signs showed that this was not so, they had not even fired a shot.

"But why had this had happened?" Wondered a confused Styarz.

Another mystery was that a number of their target's tracks had appeared from thin air.

"It is puzzling. But then the master had warned us to be extra wary as the ancestors of these people had stolen something very precious from the Winged God."

As the Knight pondered the facts, Styarz accurately guessed that their quarry must have in their possession some type of concealment device.

"No wonder the Winged One desires the return of this object. Just think of the use the brotherhood could put it to. We would be able to penetrate places that hitherto were impossible."

Digesting this information, he ordered his men to increase the pace. As the chasing band followed the trail and read the signs, the leader of these murderous Knights told his men.

"When we encounter the God's enemies, do not attack until we are sure that they are all in view."

But this would be difficult, the Knight's were unsure of how many they would face as all of their targets wore the same identical footwear, except the one with the huge feet. Some of them kept appearing and disappearing, the task that he had given his men would be extremely difficult. As the leader of the chasers pondered this, it was surprising that Styarz never wondered how it had been possible for anything to be stolen from his God. But his devotion to the Winged One entered the realms of fanatic intolerance. His adoration was so intense and uncompromising that he would have believed that like Adam and Eve, someone once had betrayed the trust of God. They tracked their targets to the Sheikh's fortress. Their Master's device had told them that they were somewhere in the immediate vicinity. While they were observing the huge complex, all hell broke loose. There were so many patrols out that their progress had been impeded. Styarz's force had to stay hidden during the uproar and it taxed even their considerable skills to remain unnoticed. They began to fall behind their targets, as patrol after patrol crossed their path. The size of each armed party numbered more than they could possibly overcome without drawing some serious attention to themselves. Frustrated, inactive, they had to stay concealed until the hullabaloo died down. With startling insight, Styarz knew.

"These frantic patrols are also searching for our quarry."

Like them, the Preceptor would have been equally upset if he knew that those he sought were making their way slowly south-westwards in the TORT-CAMLETS. Styarz had no inkling how his prey were travelling. After piling into their invisible shield, the questors also sat it out. But, then on a dark night, when the orbiting moon was a pale shadow of its full brightness, they emerged from their fantastic hideout and proceeded to move away from the turmoil. When things quietened down and their cowled tracker's picked up the trail again. It was evident that their targets were no longer close by and had escaped the Sheikh's wrath. Styarz now realized that his company were more than two weeks behind their targets. The Sheikh's men had also discovered their three wheeled vehicles and they were now on foot. The thirteen Knight's made haste and went after them. A few days later and another enigma. Alongside a small water hole, his men had come across the site of the Prof's demise. Again, the chasing band read the signs.

"These we pursue are internally divided. One of them has dispatched this one and only left a stain of a body. It does not matter why, but it weakens them."

To Styarz, the Prof was just another dead and melted corpse; he had no interest in the dreams or the plans of the man that had been eradicated forever in a burst of gunfire. However, his men had found something missed by his killer, a small swirling globe that screamed of the Winged God's craft. His lagging band moved on and a day later, the pursuing Knight's came upon a truck depot, it was in an intersection, where tracks became roads and eventually highways. Styarz made a tactical decision.

"We require faster transport, if we are to shorten the distance between our quarry and us."

The Knight's approached the truck depot with blood on their minds. Those who had stopped for rest and refreshment were going to get more than they ever envisioned as the silent killers surrounded the depot. With a signal from Styarz, his men went into action. They quickly and efficiently dispatched all who had been in the wayside complex. There were no survivors or witnesses to their dark deed, men women and children died, killed by cloaked executioners. The bodies of the slain were left where they sprawled. With a couple of newly acquired vehicles, the pursuers speeded up the chase and started to make up ground on their unaware quarry. They were so close now; the twelve Knights' of the Winged One under Styarz's leadership were only a few hundred metres from the camp of their targets. The band of Zebulan's servants had approached with headlights switched off and left the vehicles behind in a gentle depression about a kilometre away from their prey. Before, he and his company started to hunt this group, their leader had wondered why his God had needed this many Knight's to eliminate such a small bunch of enemies. The supremely confident assassin was certain that he alone could eliminate this group. But now, he had an inkling of why these people were a threat, it crept into his thinking often during the chase. Away from the abandoned vehicles, the Preceptor commanded his men to kneel and he began the intercession with their Creator. Lately Zebulan was always with him. Styarz was a bit confused by this, as the Winged God had never needed this amount of contact before. Still, his diminutive servant glorified in the continuous presence of his divinity.

"In the holy annuals of our order, this mission is certainly unique."

Then, he responded to his God.

"Lord of our humble brotherhood, we are ready to attack. But we must be sure how many of them there are."

Zebulan had become increasingly jittery since the Hybrid had acquired the third piece of the APOCRYPHA'I, so he ordered.

"Go ahead, attack without haste. I can sense the one that has what was stolen from me. I have supreme confidence in your abilities."

The impatience of the DEFILED was about to cost his servants dearly. Although Styarz had not determined how many targets there were, he was never one to question his God. The supremely confident commander of the Knight's raised his Anlace with his right hand and held it aloft to the night sky. This was a re-enactment of the Knight De Courcy's original pledge to Zebulan, over sixteen centuries ago. The polished blade seemed to reflect the silvery moonlight and it shone as bright as the space rock itself.

"A good omen, and with the Winged God's blessing already received, our task would be concluded in a few heartbeats." Felt Styarz with his

kind's usual air of arrogance and belief. Silently, the ambusher's worked their well-practiced routine and moved to within metres of the encampment. His band moved silently to well-chosen vantage-points. The accomplished killers fanned out and quickly surrounded the temporary-resting place of those they had finally caught up with. None of the Knight's would use projectile weapons, they were that confident in their abilities. They would rely on surprise, speed, their martial skills and cold steel. Blending with the deep shadows, their victims were unaware of their impending doom. There were fourteen targets, eleven men and three women. All of them were sitting out in the clearing conversing and apparently oblivious to their fate. There was no sign of the concealment device. An over confident Styarz believed.

"Nearly the same amount as us. What a simple task for my group. I could do this alone?"

The leader of the ambusher's raised his hand just as the light was fading and dropped it in a chopping motion; it was the signal for attack. Like coiled springs, his men sprang into action. Human/feline shapes bounded into the open space. With enhanced physical capabilities, their agility and speed was mesmerizing. Despite this, the leaping and twisting Knight's were cut to pieces. An arc of tracer fire came from nowhere. The lethal spray of death originated from thin air. Some of his men reacted to where the fire from the invisible weapon originated and responded. The Lenses had been firing the heavy 50 calibre "Beni." from the cloak of the TORT-CAM; it had been his turn at the helm and he had been ready for the attack. Thinking he was safe, the hacker had not bothered with body armour. But incredibly, Styarz's people had found a weakness in the questor's defence. There happened to be a small gap of a few millimetres around the barrel and a small tungsten dart managed to find this cavity. It took the Lenses in the eye. He fell back with a scream and his weapon ceased firing. But the hovering gun had done enough damage; the wounded man had personally taken out at least seven attackers. The rest of his companions had reacted the moment the pink eyed man had opened fire. Their weapons had also cut through the ranks of Styarz's Knights and the battle had become uneven in those few seconds. However, against these incredible odds, two of the bounding attackers managed to reach their foes with their incredible twisting and turning. The Preceptor had reached the leader, the one his master had directed him to. He knocked his weapon from his hands as he flew passed the startled man. The Feline/Hybrid halted on his light feet and back flipped towards him. Bullets whizzed by him, but he connected with his enemy's head. The Knight landed on him, bowled him over, his feet registered the jarring impact. It was a mighty blow. There was a loud crunching sound and his shocked opponent toppled to the ground. But as the attacker crouched and was about to finish his opponent off, a bullet smashed into his shoulder and hurled him into the undergrowth. It was a tall blonde female that had wounded him. Dazed and bleeding profusely, the leader of the Knight's crawled to safety; satisfied that he had delivered a mortal blow to his God's enemy. Out of the corner of his eyes, he had seen another of his men impact a mighty whack to a big man before he too was cut down by two shooters who held close quarter rapid firing weapons. Realisation dawned.

"They were waiting for us!"

Though mortally wounded, those of his men that still breathed life fought on. But the valiant Knight's were eventually dispatched by angled close targeted fire. Another person crawled away from the conflict; he was at the opposite side of the clearing from Styarz.

It was Naomh!

His head pounded while his vision swam. He gurgled and spat up blood stained sputum from his mouth. His throbbing head made it painfully difficult to think. The dazed man knew by right.

"I should have been killed. If I had not twisted a slight fraction before the blow connected, the impact would have been fatal. My newly acquired abilities have undoubtedly saved my hide."

He was badly shaken, but his friends had been stirred into action in the moment of attack. His company had been warned and were expecting the ambush, but the speed of it was frightening. It wasn't just scary, it was awesome. The seriously injured man decided.

"I can do nothing for my friends now. I have to get away from them. None of them can know the monster that I will transform into."

He stumbled away from the fire-fight and fell into a two-metre depression in the desert. From the instant, he had been injured; the harmed man felt his body regenerating itself. The three parts Mescal/Amulet's healing abilities went into overdrive, it had taken over his bodily functions and within micro seconds of the blow, it started to repair the damaged cells, blood vessels and nerves. His flesh started to bubble and spasm as his blood temperature dropped. Every fibre of his body burned with the coolness of regeneration as the healing process soothed the fiery pain. Naomh was recovering fast and awareness of the attack flooded back.

"Our attackers had moved with blinding speed. But who were these men; they are definitely not the Sheikh's people."

Then half way through his accelerated healing, he realized something profound.

"I am not healing like my father did; I am not turning into a worm. By God, I am not like him after all."

The healing man felt euphoric despite his injuries. Some part of him knew that it would take the remainder of the night to recover fully, so he lay down on the cool desert floor and closed his eyes. Across from him in the clearing and away from his awareness, a hysterical Miriam demanded.

"Where is Naomh? I cannot locate him. His communication piece is

down and there is no sign of him. "

Tears flooded her shocked eyes and spilled down her cheeks. Another of the group was as equally tear filled as Miriam, but he reacted differently.

It was the Engineer.

His brother had been felled with an identical blow as Naomh. The big man was unconscious and his breathing was ragged and faint. Again a frantic Miriam demanded.

"Where is Naomh?"

Her growing anxiety filtered away, all of her reliable attributes of command, common sense and steadfastness. Even the normally stolid Greta appeared to be in the same agitated state. Of the group, only the Mute appeared indifferent. The blonde woman told Miriam.

"I took out, Naomh's attacker, but he still connected with him, then I lost sight of him. "

Noticing their second in command's inability, the Guide took command of the still shocked group.

"This is not over yet. Some of our attackers might be still out there. Form a defensive cordon and get the Persuader into the Dobber. "

Battle experience took over. The Guide, Cahill, Moshe, Beersheba and the Clerk took up a defensive perimeter. A dry eyed Miriam took over at the point.

"I will be the first to welcome Naomh back when he returns. "

She refused to believe that anything bad had happened to him. The Engineer, Solomon, Haim, the Mute and the Rabbi gently lifted the comatose and bloodied Persuader into the safety of the TORT-CAM. He was a dead weight and they struggled. Inside the three coloured haven, the men discovered the wounded Lenses. He was unconscious and a sharp object was imbedded in his eye. Blood dripped from the dreadful wound. The Rabbi checked his injuries and decided.

"The big man has priority. "

Their appointed Medic gave the wounded Lenses an injection that would keep him out. Checking that he was breathing regularly, the Rabbi gave Solomon a padded disinfected bandage and told him.

"Clean around the eye. Keep it moist. "

He then went to his more critical patient, knowing that it was hopeless. Outside the makeshift, but sterile operating theatre, the others scanned the clearing with night vision goggles and only counted the dead attackers. None of them could risk going out into the desert, there might be more of their assailants out there. They failed to locate Naomh, but to their relief they did not find his corpse either. Double-checking still turned up nothing. The anxious gang waited out the night and as soon as the first rays of the morning sun illuminated the clearing, their missing comrade walked in. The few hours of darkness had seen him completely healed. When Cahill saw his friend, the relieved sentry said.

"Thank fuck."

Their leader took stock of the grim faces that greeted him and realised.

"Something is dreadfully amiss."

When Miriam saw him, she rushed forward and threw herself into his arms. Tears of relief were evident in her features. Groggily, he explained his vanishing act.

"I must have been knocked out. I have just come around. Is everybody alright?"

Greta looked at Naomh dubiously. She had seen the blow that he had taken and he had no right walking in without any apparent injury. Besides, the companies fruitless nearby search did not find him either. Still, they had other priorities now. The tall statuesque woman said.

"No. Everybody is not. The Persuader took an almighty wallop. He will not survive it and the Lenses got clipped. He took a piece of shrapnel in the eye. The Rabbi gave the little man a sedative and he is unconscious. There is nothing our doctor can do for the big man and he is dressing the Lenses wound."

Naomh inwardly knew.

"If the Persuader has indeed taken a blow similar to the one I took, then unfortunately Greta's assessment is true. Because, only the imbedded amulets intervention has saved me."

The completely recovered man was gutted. He surmised that his gravely ill friend had only hours to live. Sensing its host's disquiet, the internal voice interjected.

"There is healing equipment in the LAB-CELL that will save your friend. It is a similar method that allows me to heal you."

Sensing a reprieve, he took in the information and leapt into the TORT-CAM. The Rabbi had a defibrillator in his hands and looked reluctant to use it. When Naomh saw the grief stricken Engineer standing over his brother, their eyes met and the tearful man said.

"He is not going to make it. I am praying for him."

Surprising to Naomh at least, the Mute also had never left the side of the stricken patient. He was gaining new respect for the repulsive man. Then, he told them.

"There is a chance."

A tiny glimmer of hope sprung into the Engineer's face. With a fierce passion, he clung to Naomh's words.

"How? In God's name how?"

"There is very advanced medical equipment in the LAB-CELL. The Rabbi will be shown the know-how on its operation. As our medical expert, he will be given the tools and knowledge to perform the necessary surgery."

The bearded man looked uncertain. He took Naomh aside and

whispered critically.

"I have only a basic knowledge of field wounds, the Persuader has suffered massive trauma, his skull is crushed, there are probably fragments imbedded in his brain and he is bleeding internally. This type of surgery is way beyond me. He needs a professional surgical team. I cannot even cure the Lenses; he will be blind in one eye."

"Trust me." Naomh said as he gave the APOCRYPHA'I the go ahead to instigate the procedure. On instruction, the Rabbi stripped to his waist and the three part's Mescal/Amulet glowed briefly. A globe of indigo light came out of nowhere; suddenly the nimbus surrounded the Enclave medic, his head jerked back as if he had received a sudden slap. Then, the glow spread and bathed the unconscious Persuader. The big man's sweating body absorbed the light and his face softened. A liquid screen like an oily raindrop materialized in front of the Rabbi and his patient. The apparition was accompanied with round spherical globes the hovered within the light shell that enveloped them. It showed a spectra-graph of the near fatally injured man displaying an Alien representation of his anatomy. Somehow the Rabbi began to understand the complex imagery and the procedure for the elaborate surgery to heal the Persuader. Concentrating, he saw that there were many colours in the screens silhouette image. He quickly ascertained the red areas showed the most damaged areas, the yellow areas the next level of damage and the blue areas, the undamaged parts. His goal was to turn the spectra graph entirely blue. He began to manipulate a set of surgical lasers, for that's what the globes were. A rheobase image showed up and the lasers began to elicit a response from the damaged tissue. He told them.

"Everybody leave except the Engineer."

An hour later, the Rabbi came out of the LAB-CELL. There was no evidence of blood on his clothes. He looked at the expectant group and shook his head in wonder.

"Such an amazing thing. Our patient will live and recover as if nothing has happened to him."

There were gasps of relief as they realized that the mortally wounded man had been brought back from the brink and each and everyone rushed in to see the miracle.

"Something else guided me and I was able to return the sight of the Lenses. He too will be cured. Now, anyone else that is injured, come with me."

Haim and the Guide were slightly bloodied and their confidant doctor led them away. The internal voice warned its host.

"Do not let him examine you with the healing device; he would not understand what he is looking at. Because of me, your biology is different now."

Naomh panicked.

"I am not a worm, am I"?

"Of course not, your capabilities have just been enhanced."

Its relieved host accepted that. While the Rabbi was performing the surgery, Naomh and the others had gone to inspect the dead attackers; it would take their minds off of the operation. What they found was very strange. All of the assailants had been garbed in identical shimmering black cowls. They were all small sturdy built males and possessed large wing shaped moustaches with long flowing locks. Even more inexplicable was none had a projectile weapon of any type. Still if they had not been fore-warned, it was doubtful that they would have inflicted such carnage among the bounding shapes. Naomh knew.

"We had been extremely fortunate, if Solomon had not been looking out for the return of the Prof, we would have never known that they were coming."

The Enclave man had refused to believe that his friend had abandoned them and he did not give up hope that he would return. During one of his regular vigils, he had seen the glint of steel from Styarz's dagger in the soft charcoal gloom and had sounded the alarm. Instead of hiding in the TORT-CAM, the arrogance in their abilities had nearly been the end of them. After their encounter with the Major Alwi Zaid, the over confident bunch decided to play the ambush game and turn the tables on those approaching. So, if they had not that massive advantage of been prepared for the attack, the consequences would have been horrifying. The fifteen men and women had been lucky. Back in the camp, the Mute was once again disappointed that some ones last moments had been denied to him. That was why he had kept his vigil alongside the big man. He did not care for that healing machine at all. Naomh assessed the situation with those who were not injured and all agreed that it was time to move southward and put as much room between themselves and the site of their near defeat. The internal voice advised its bearer.

"You too need time to rest and recover. You have to stay in the TORT-CAM for a few days. Someone else will have to carry the Gudiex sphere while you recuperate. The healing process is new to your body functions."

The custodian of the uncompleted APOCRYPHA'I was caught in a dilemma, who to choose? His selection became obvious, he asked Miriam and she agreed. While he was recuperating in the Alien space, the metallic timbre intruded on his musing once again.

"I was trying to get your attention, but your thoughts were focussed on other things."

"It was concern for our new enemies."

"And you should be alert. This was no random skirmish. The wing shaped blades, moustaches and the attackers incredible agility form part of my memories. I have been searching through my past and found that one such man with similar features tried to kill your father hundreds of years *ago in the Parisian Contrib. The man had of course failed, but luckily his type was never encountered again during Rory's long life.*

"And now they are back."

"Yes, they have been searching for you for a long time now."

"Why?" Asked its host.

"We were never able to figure that out."

"I have. They could not know about me, these people must be after you."

The three parts Mescal/Amulet became deeply disturbed with all the symbolism of the wings.

"It means that whoever is after my form knows something about my race or is it pure coincidence?"

A day later, one who did not believe in chance had just finished recovering out in the desert. Styarz had cut the bullet out from his sinewy shoulder blade and expertly stitched the wound. While he was recuperating, he took stock of the events. Now the lone wounded Knight knew why the Winged God had been so agitated during his audience.

"All of my command has been slain. This is incredible. These were foes far greater than the ordinary rank and file of the Knights of the Winged One and it is certain that the Cabal had never encountered enemies such as this before. The Master has given me a great task. Besides, they are without their leader now."

The next morning however, he had walked into the camp, none the worse for wear. This was a near repetition of events across time. Styarz's ancestor, Wesley had the same unbelieving expression on his face, the last time these bearers of Alien gene pools had crossed paths. But unknown to the Preceptor, he had survived, while his forefather had not. Concealed under his speckled cowl, the hidden watcher saw the way his quarry vanished into thin air and re-emerged time and time again. So the hunter was now aware of their secret. Standing up, he flexed his body. Satisfied, the Grandmaster resumed the chase and loped off in pursuit.

"I will avenge my brothers and return what was stolen from my Master. It is a cloaking device that wants retrieving."

But there was now something else for himself.

"The women were a wonder. I have never encountered such feisty females. They had fought magnificently. Especially the tall blonde one. I will take one of them back with me; she will make a great mate and what a gift our offspring will make for the Winged One."

In the camp, Naomh had similar problems to Styarz. After the near defeat, the cockiness of easy victories dissipated.

"That small man would have killed me if it had stayed one on one".

The seekers moved on and their shadow followed. To throw anyone off the trail, every so often, they reduced the invisible shield into its moving parts and travelled incognito. Unaware that his targets were still moving, the Knight fell behind again. Every morning since the incident and as the hangover from the attack had diminished; Naomh went out alone away from the others and began to practice his fighting ability.

"I need more strength, speed and agility."

Benefiting from his enhanced physique, his martial skills began to develop, until he was sure, he would be a match for more of those nimble assassins. His speed and agility grew with every passing day. The improved fighter had no doubt.

"At least one of them remains at large and he will attack again. But the next time, it will be my unknown assailant that will come off the worst. I promise myself this."

When his internal discussion was finished, something else bugged Naomh about the events leading up to the attack, until he realized what it was. He sought out his partner and took her aside.

"Miriam, can I ask you something?"

"Yes my love. Anything."

He took a steady breath, wondering how to phrase what he was about to say to her without causing offence.

"You know that we came through the ambush because Solomon was still watching for the Prof."

She nodded.

"I have known Edward for many years; now don't get me wrong, I am really upset that he left us to seek out a new life. But how can I put this?" He paused briefly; then continued. *"Well it just seems that your comrade is more disturbed than any of his old friends at the Prof's desertion. Is there something here that I am missing?"*

"What do you mean? The two of them were just good friends and shared an interest in knowledge. Solomon is a sensitive person; it is not unusual for him to care for another."

"He's not that sensitive, he can kill just as well as the rest of us." Thought Naomh inwardly.

Out loud, he said to his lover.

"So you don't think there was something more to their relationship."

"Like what?" Queried Solomon's compatriot.

Naomh became uneasy and shrugged.

"You know!"

"No. I believe that I don't" Replied Miriam, a little confused.

So, he hinted.

"Well, they only knew each other for little over a year. So, they should not have been that close, unless something else was going on."

Miriam's eyes widened slightly, her dark eyebrows seemed to grow larger with that gesture.

"Oh!" Was all, she said.

The Enclave woman returned his original shrug and her tone grew harder.

"I don't know if there was, but if there was, then so what?"

Naomh became embarrassed as he tried to find the right words.

"Well, because that type of behaviour is frowned upon in the Anschluss."

"We are not in your homeland now." Rebuked Miriam dryly.

He got the hint not to pursue it any further, so he just said.

"Ok, but don't tell any of my people about my suspicions as most of them might not understand."

Then, his confidant added with a sly smile.

"Don't mention it to the Rabbi either; he does not understand that type of behaviour as well."

Her lover then switched the discussion to two more of their friends.

"Concerning the Clerk and Beersheba. I am surprised that the two of them have not become a couple after their initial liaison."

"It had suited both of them at the time and they have just moved on." Replied Miriam.

Now, it was his time to utter.

"Oh!"

Two days later, Naomh and his two wounded companions had recovered completely, though one of them would never be the same again.

It was the Lenses.

The strange surgery the Rabbi had performed on him with the LAB-CELL'S intervention had altered his appearance forever. His left eye now glowed with a rainbow pupil. Far from been upset with his new predicament, he was delighted. Using one of the Guides phrases, he explained.

"It helps me when I am accessing the LAB-CELL'S memory bank. It speeds everything up and I understand the working of it easier. Besides I think my eye looks really cool now."

To the rest of them, he looked mighty strange with one pink eye and one multi-coloured orb. Beersheba told him.

"We will have to get a patch made for you, if we encounter any more people, your appearance will give rise to some awkward questions."

What nearly pleased him as much was that every old scar and blemish on his twenty-six year old body had vanished. The still recovering Persuader found himself in the same predicament. The Rabbi said.

"I can do it for anybody else who requires it."

Unsurprising; the Engineer, Greta, the Mute and Naomh reneged. The Clerk too refused outright. No one knew the man from the Madrid Contrib reasons; it probably had to do with the body been the temple of the Holy Spirit. Greta simply said.

"I have none."

Cahill backed her up on that score. The Clerk said his marks were well-earned battle scars and nobody knew the Mute's reason, nor cared. Naomh's changing molecular structure was his reason. The Rabbi became a very busy man over the next few days. The Guide was delighted to have an old appendix scar removed. Cahill had a few war wounds attended to, especially the nasty scar he had received in RUTH. But the best reaction came from Moshe, he had been living with his facial scar for five years, it was caused during an industrial accident and now it was gone. Their bulky night vision equipment was replaced by small oily flux coloured monocles that fitted snugly to the wearer's eyes. The Lenses had found these among the LAB-CELL'S broadened inventory. These monocles were so light that their weight was unnoticeable and their effectiveness was far superior to the old ones from either the Anschluss or the Enclave. But the major benefit of gaining the third piece was the acquisition of element fabrication. The Prof already had a working model set up. This marvellous contraption consisted of a tripod of globes fixed onto a crystallized frame. When activated, its light seeped into the ground and the air gathering trace elements that were formed into precious metals and gems. They now had a form of hard currency which would come in very handy on the next legs of the journey.

The three parts Mescal/Amulet still urged Naomh eastwards, but he was proceeding with Haim's plan of going south first. The travellers avoided the few towns and smaller settlements as they progressed perpendicular to the rising Sun. But now because of Naomh's recently broached language skills, they travelled openly. The rich clothes that had been given to them by Sheikh Sulimani's servants had become a little worn, but it still marked them out as been wealthy.

"It is time for a different disguise." Said the Guide.

A few days later, Naomh, Solomon and Haim armed to the teeth approached a tribe of nomads and bartered for women's clothing and on Moshe's advice, a herd of goats and sheep. It would complete their disguise and make them appear as an authentic family unit. The Tribesmen sold them what they wanted for an exorbitant amount of paper currency called Riyal's and the deal was sweetened with a few choice gems created by the mining equipment. It did not matter as the money had been taken from the bodies of the dead Major and his men and there seemed to be a lot of it. But, they were curious to see if the artificially gems passed the test, they did. The women of the poor, it seemed wore a more restrictive set of garments than the loose robes of the Abaya. This time remaining females took offence at been covered from head to toe in a Burka as it would encumber their response if they need to be stirred into action. The Enclave female soldiers also saw them as repressive. Greta was the most galled at her lack of mobility. She relented however when it was pointed out to her by Beersheba.

"You most of all will stand out like a sore thumb. And after all, it did

not encumber your reactions back in the Sheikh's palace."

With great expertise, the male Anschluss members had their fair hair and complexions dyed by the Enclave women to resemble the Prophet's people. But the Clerk's and the Mute's extremely blonde features had been impossible to disguise. It was decided to dress them up like the women. Both men accepted it with good grace. The Lenses had also been forced to wear his eye patch whenever the travellers encountered people. An inquisitive person might have asked why there were no children among them. The disguised travellers joined the vast throng that was migrating back to the Arab cities. To passer-by's, the fifteen looked like a large family unit, too poor to own a vehicle. Many were on foot like them. It appeared to the military experts among them that all motorized vehicles had been commandeered by the defeated armies. As every moving contraption that passed them was full of soldiers, they leapt to the sides of the roads. They did not want to answer any awkward questions that military types asked. During the arduous trek on the dusty and sun-baked roads, the Clerk confided in the Lenses.

"It seems that every place we go to has a different form of currency. Laminated notes and metal discs. I am going to collect them and if we ever return home, it will be my proof that we were outside the Anschluss."

"That is a very good idea." Replied his confidant, wishing that he had thought of it first.

Cloaked in their new disguises, the footsore group reached the hearth land of the Arab cites after thirteen days of travel. The huge urban areas on the southern coast that progressed eastwards following the curve of the Arabian Peninsula were vastly different from the desert communities in the middle and in the Western side of the enormous desert isthmus. Each nation blended into one another much like the Contrib's of the Anschluss, but they did not amalgamate seamlessly. The independent Arab nations had borders that were sealed and permission was needed to cross them. The quality of life varied in each one, those farthest to the east were the wealthiest. On the outskirts of these crowed urban areas, the Rabbi butchered their herd animals and preserved the meat according to the Enclaves sacred dietary laws. His compatriots like those from the Anschluss would eat most things, but the man of religion would not. Haim mentioned to him.

"We are soldiers first."

As they approached the built up area; the evening sunshine glanced off the white buildings making the city shine in the Sun. This vast urban sector of the southern coast was a wonder to the travellers. Rich and outlandishly ornate residences mixed with squalor even though there was always a compound of large walls separating them. Gleaming high rises of glass lined the shorelines, many in the shape of sails. Really old buildings nestled alongside newer constructions. Every district had a large domed and minaret building for worship called a Mosque. No matter how poor or impoverished the community was, the religious buildings were always huge and fabulously decorated. The Guide gave his companions a titbit of history.

"Our Anschluss had fantastic Cathedrals like these once. That was before our rulers tore them down."

"We will build them again." Vowed the Engineer.

He was mightily impressed by the magnificent places of worship and still enthralled that people could gather and pray openly. It was in these cities, especially among the poor housing stock that the people from the Anschluss had seen their first diseased and malnourished people. Begging was a way of life; this concept was alien to nearly all of them. They saw deformed individual's without limbs; people that were blind and some with horribly disfigured growths all over their bodies. Sickness seemed to have crept into the population and made its permanent home there. The Guide seeing his friend's looks of disgust and pity said.

"This is the real World, welcome to it."

As before Naomh had a master of the tongue and he took the lead. Asking for directions, those far away from their homes found adequate lodgings. The owner had been wary of them at first. But once the hard cash was flashed, his demeanour changed noticeably. Most of those that encountered them noticed straight away that these outlandish Nomads had no information devices in their ears and instantly surmised.

"They must be of some strange sect that prohibits such things."

After settling in, he requested food and a man guided them to a large secluded seating area that was in the middle of a walled courtyard. Haim advised them.

"No one is to ask for alcohol here, it is forbidden and the punishment is severe. Now that we look like followers of the Prophet, it would look very strange."

All of the cliental of the establishment were focused on broadcasted images that nearly caused the newly arrivals to make a mistake. Video screens dotted around the premises showed footage from the attack on the Enclave wall. The images of war were accompanied by exotic and rhythmic music and an excited narration in the Prophets tongue. Miriam stared dumbfounded at the surreal footage as she saw her beloved RUTH blown apart. The number 2927 on the side of the leading Tank had instantly drawn her to the screen. It all looked unreal and then she saw the fate of those crews that had blindly followed them. As a guilt-ridden survivor, the former Enclave Serene held her head in her hands and silently grieved. Those that saw her actions; just thought that she was a woman weeping for a lost father, son or brother among the Mujahedeen. How wrong these onlookers were? The battle scenes lasted an hour; they tried hard to ignore them and concentrated on the food that was ordered by the

Rabbi. After the ridge exploded, the images switched to a group of men been be-headed. Horrified, most of them turned away from the graphic scenes. A whispering Engineer nudged Naomh and hissed.

"Look up."

His leader did and saw the stone-faced image of Sheikh Ben Sulimani. He was taken aback like the rest of them. Wanting to get away from the face of the man they had betrayed, Naomh said.

"Come let's take a stroll and take in the sights."

Leaving the face of the Sheikh behind, the fifteen of them went out to the narrow streets. The meal bill was added on to the cost of their lodgings. A strong pungent waft of coffee, food and spices permutated through the crowded streets. It was early in the evening and the heat of the day had abated, people used this time to shop and go about their business. Aggressive vendors accosted them and tried to sell them everything from the practical and impractical. They passed a coffeehouse and men were smoking out of a strange tubular contraption full of water.

"We have to try that." Urged the Persuader after inhaling some of the white smoke that an old man blew into the air. The original purveyor of the inhalation of Cigs agreed. The two of them and Haim sat down on plastic seats under the shade of a palm tree while the others continued on. The Enclave man did the talking for the two Anschluss men. The patrons of the eating house were all intrigued by two players of an ancient board game called backgammon. It was over two hours later when the others came back. Everywhere they had been, it seemed that the stern face of Ben Sulimani stared out of countless screens, there was no way of avoiding his image. Out of earshot, the Guide told the returnees.

"Haim has been talking to the old men and has found out that there are ships that commute regularly across to a place called India and we can purchase tickets for the journey. We have to find the port city of a place called Aden."

They went back to their lodgings for sleep, the Guide told the Lenses.

"You are to take a photo-scan of each of us."

After he took them, he appropriated the Clerk. When asked, he replied.

"We need the proper documents for the other side. Also lay out the clothing the Sheikh gave to us. From now on we must appear rich."

They spent the best part of a week in the coastal city, until the Guide was satisfied that they were prepared to move on. When Naomh awoke bright and refreshed the morning of their departure, the internal voice within urged him eastwards, it had not been happy with the delay. The seekers of the APOCRYPHA'I checked out of their lodgings and reached the dock fronts by a public bus that actually rolled over the ground. Here, they found that a ship would take them across the sea to a place called India. Jewels and gems were traded for a new currency called Rupee's in small banking establishments along the dock-front. It would be easier to exchange these on the other side. Then fifteen tickets were purchased by the Clerk with Haim's assistance and their new identity documents passed the test at the departure point. It said that they were from a place called Kenya and were travelling to meet distant kin. Their disguises had been reinforced with a plausible story; the Clerk and the Mute had become women again. The reluctant voyager's boarded the ship. The ramshackle, paint flaking rusty craft was crowded to the rafters, it was thronged with pilgrims and defeated Mujahedeen who like themselves were in disguise. Some were returning home to lands were they were in the minority. As before, their wealth bought them better off quarters. But the berths were not private; the group had to endure the company of other well off patrons. The journey aboard the insufferable ship took a few days across a large sea that was vast and empty and blue. Occasional distinctive dhows, relics from a bygone age passed their bow in what was once the busiest ship-ways in the oceans. But the vast majority of the oil reserves that had fuelled the global trade had run out hundreds of years ago. People on board the vessel called the waterway; the Arabian Sea and the company were mighty glad when land was sighted. The Sun was just rising in the eastern sky when the ferry closed in on the shoreline and a line of ancient crumbling buildings that still bore traces of garish colours lined the dock front. The air though hot smelt fresh, a hangover from the recently ended monsoon. The relieved group disembarked and passed through the customs point with ease, it was the 5th of October 2953AD. They had arrived in the post monsoon season, they could expect some days of rain on the journey north, but these would be infrequent compared to the season they had missed. Temperatures in the south were about 20 to 25 degrees and would fall to about 10-15 degrees on the journey north. The officials did not question them too much and accepted their contrived story. A partisan bureaucrat wrongly guessed that the men were defeated Mujahedeen and his sympathies lay with them. All at once the travellers were amazed at the throngs of people that infested the crumbling city. They were greeted with a dizzying mix of sights, sounds and colour. The clothing of the natives in this new land seemed a lot gaudier than the lands of the Prophet and there were a lot of different styles in evidence. Audacious reds and equally loud yellows were evident on passers-by. Women wore the Dhoti or a Sari, both style of the one-piece flat cotton or silk garments were fastened by a knotted Stanupatta at the back. A lot more brown and black coloured flesh was been exposed here than on the other side of the sea. Men wore the traditional Dhotis or Kurtas tops with Sahvar pants. There were also echoes of familiar attire among the throng. Among the various head coverings, a blue or black spot on the forehead was the most prevalent. The enclosed Enclave and the overpopulated Anschluss easily contained as much people, but here on this exotic port, the density of the people seemed more obvious. To their collective horror, disease and disfigurement seemed more prevalent on this side of the Arabian Sea. Naomh found that he easily understood this new language of Hindi; it was one of the oldest in the World. Another thing that astounded them was the structure of the majority of communication devices. They were small flat hand held screens, of a type that had long since vanished from the Anschluss. People spoke into them and viewed images on their screens. Some natives that looked more affluent had various earpieces and other bright discs replacing the spot on the forehead. Seeing one individual press the item in the middle of his head and begin talking confirmed that they were indeed more advanced devices about. They booked into a hotel and rested for four days. After a little searching and to keep up the ruse of them been curious travellers, the new arrivals found Money-Changer's that readily changed the notes of the Prophet's people, for a commission into the local currency. No questions were asked where this apparently affluent looking group got such large amounts from. The Clerk asked.

"Why don't they use electronic credits like the Anschluss?"

The well-travelled Guide explained.

"Most nations do not openly trade with each other; their banking systems are not compatible. So most places have reverted back to using notes and coins. A lot of people prefer it. They feel comfortable having something substantial in their hands."

One delighted Money-Changer told them the best way of travelling north; the direction that the internal voice was now pushing towards. It was by what appeared to be a primitive Mag-Lev that moved on metal rails. It was called a railway and great chuffing machines called Locomotives ran on it. These engines were powered by efficient thirtieth century steam boilers, but due to overcrowding, they only ran at a speed of 65 kilometres an hour. Purchasing first class tickets, the fifteen of them boarded the contraption. The gang was amazed that the language used by the railway staff resembled a form of accented Anschluss that they could understand with a little bit of effort. An official outfitted in a strange black hat and uniform of large shiny buttons with a shrill whistle in his mouth advised them.

"The end of the northern route finishes in a city called Agra and the train will take about five days to get there. You will have to make several changes on the way and endure a long wait for connections. An on-board intercom will tell you about these."

The helpful official brought them over to a cluster of heavily scratched black boxes that housed video screens. At a touch, the gadget showed the entire railway system of the Sub-Continent and from it they could plan their route north. It was an old fashioned relative of the Mag-lev route planners that abounded in the Anschluss. While the intending users were studying it, Naomh approached the Engineer and the Lenses, ushered them aside and asked them.

"I need the two of you to stay in the TORT-CAM and try to locate anything that might be useful to us in these strange new lands."

When both men heard of the long, dusty, stifling and episodic journey ahead of the gang, the Engineer who was proving himself to be the brains of the outfit readily agreed. However, the Lenses was slightly reluctant. He pulled his leader aside and voiced his doubts; his initial euphoria had waned since his eye transplant.

"Naomh, I am used to circuit boards and VDU's. This light show, you use is way beyond my capabilities. The new eye is excellent in accessing information, but it will take me awhile to master it. And I have found nothing useful since."

"I don't want to fix anything. It's your analytical mind we need. Just get into its memory and inventory; then find what we want. Practice makes perfection."

The Lenses was chuffed at his leader's confidence in him and replied.

"I will try my best."

"Good" Said Naomh as he clapped him on the back.

As the train pulled off every available space on it was taken up. Every carriage except the first class ones had people hanging from their sides and the roofs were covered in a lining of humanity. Secluded in their first class carriage, they spent the following days without venturing outside. Meals were brought to them and a toilet just outside their seating arrangements served their needs. Due to their heavy tipping, delighted train staff jumped to their every need. The window of exact dimensions showed them, when they were awake, a moving landscape of yellows greens and browns and nameless people going about their labour intensive efforts as they had done for millennium. Judging by the scenes that flew pass, the agricultural system looked primitive compared to the Anschluss or the Enclave. It was overloaded with domesticate livestock and antiquated machinery bearing the blunt of the work. They shook their heads in disdain and this feeling was enforced when the train went over a bridge spanning a river and they saw hundreds of brown skinned washer women beating their coloured linen against the stones exposed by the water course. Somewhere along the route of their journey the rail travellers passed the boundary of the tropics. Nearly five days later after waiting for overcrowded and late arriving trains, unheard of in the Anschluss; the Locomotive passengers reached their final destination and gratefully got off. The questors had arrived at the last city on the northern frontier. All the line changes had taken place at night and they were done with a brusqueness that spoke of a desire to reach their destination and except for Solomon, the travellers had little interest in their different surroundings. The groups curiosity of local traditions had waned with the absence of the Prof. The time endured on the platforms was spent mostly stretching inactive limbs, eating titbits, drinking refreshments and smoking cigs that were purchased in small kiosks. Several strange three wheeled motorised contraptions took them from the final railway station to the centre of the city. To the new arrivals, it looked like they had arrived in the middle of a religious festival; the city was a riot of colour. Every window, the travellers passed was lit up with the soft glow of numerous tiny clay lamps. They were correct, it was the middle of October and the Hindu festival of Diwali was in full flow, commemorating the defeat of the God Rama by his counterpart Ravana. It was a good thing that nobody among the travellers asked questions about this strange religion, with all its deities and animal Gods. One could only imagine what the Engineer and the Rabbi would have thought. A mighty river flowed through the city and its banks were thronged with a sea of people. The waters were full of brown skinned bathers and other people who were fully clothed washing themselves at the riverbank. Heavily worn manmade steps at the river's edge were full of people blowing horns and others holding flaming brands. The harsh horn sounds were accompanied with tinkling bells. Strange floating platforms full of flowers were pushed into the river as offerings to the river God. In the dull of evening, the reflected orange glow of the torches made the river appear as if it was on fire. Cows wandered around and were treated with great respect by the indigenous people. They had found out about this strange custom soon after they had first entered the sub-Continent. Nothing about the World surprised them anymore. It would be hard to find sleeping quarters in this thronged city, people were camped everywhere. So Cahill advised.

"It will be virtually impossible to use the TORT-CAM; there are just too many eyes in this place. Someone will see us."

Eventually a modest block of flats with rooms to rent was found and as always the cost of lodgings was not an issue. When the greedy concierge found out what they were willing to pay, he evicted a few guests and reimbursed them with a fraction of what he received from the Clerk. After they were safely in their room, Naomh expanded the invisible shield and entered it. He found the Lenses and the Engineer in the LAB-CELL. The two men were totally engrossed and barely acknowledged him. The multi coloured orbed man told him.

"You were right. This is sophisticated simplicity. Once you get the hang of it, it comes easily. Now leave us, we have a lot to get through."

Unchagrined by their dismissal, Naomh departed the TORT-CAM, leaving it whole and he joined the others.

"The two of them can come out when they want to."

The duo never did and took their meals inside the shielded space. Most of the fare in this strange country consisted of various types of rice, tangy relishes and bright coloured vegetables. They took repast in different places; some did not serve beef while others did not serve pork. Lean chunks or strips of lamb and poultry were available in all of the establishments. The next day, Naomh questioned the caretaker of their building about the north. The concierge who told them his name was Sanjeen Thaper returned a look as if they were mad. But he had seen many an adventurer pass through here in search of the God's knew what. The man told them.

"I will make enquires."

Later that afternoon, he sent them with a ragged boy called Valimik Bhaskar to a reliable contact that would direct them Northwards. The urchin brought them to the most fantastic building that any of them had ever seen. It was a mausoleum, built for love by a Mogul Emperor called; Shah Jahan. Their contact called it the Taj Mahal. The Lenses scoffed at such foolishness. The huge white building had a large edifice of white marble with inlays of semi-precious stones, huge windows and it was topped off with a large bulbous dome. Four tall minarets completed its imposing presence. To those from the Anschluss, it had no practical function and it stood alone at the end of a large oblong reflecting pool of water that had two parallel red paved walkways running the length of its course. Cahill gave the boy a handful of large denomination notes and thanked him for his assistance; Valimik Bhaskar's eyes widened and the cash disappeared in a flash. The boy took off in a blur in case the strange people wanted their money returned and the crowd swallowed him up. The urchin moved with a light step, he was already making plans what to do with his new found wealth and one of those thoughts was not to reveal his fortune to his boss back at the inn. Their contact, Sanjay Patel had noticed the exchange and said in Hindi.

"Goodness gracious. That was a foolish thing to do, Sahib. Many around here have never seen that amount of money. His life will be in danger."

Naomh sat down alongside the man and noticed that he had the most amazing blue eyes that contrasted heavily against the swarthy skin of his face. Cahill was intrigued about the building constructed for love. Greta asked her own lover.

"Would you build something like that for me, if you had the means?"

"Of course my love. We will have a look around Naomh while you sort out what's happening." He replied.

The rest of them, except the Guide who stayed with Naomh joined Cahill and Greta in the sightseeing. As the others left, the contact that had heard the Anschluss words spoken to them in the same language.

"Shit, does everybody in the World speak Anschluss?" Demanded Naomh.

"It was one of the old tongues of this land, spoken by the powerful people. And so because of the respect it gets, it is still used by the educated and those seeking to better themselves."

The Guide speaking from experience whispered into Naomh's ear.

"Naomh, on my travels, I have met many people that speak like us.

Once it was a language of power and poor people around the World learned it because they believed it would help them. It was seen as a way out of their misery.

The negotiations began in the same language. The contact directed them to a small town about two hundred kilometres westward from Agra and the name of an inn where somebody else could direct them onwards. Satisfied with the man's information, Naomh believing him to be genuine; went over the top with the payment. The man's eyes widened as much as the boys had and it vanished into his robes just as quick.

"Thank you Sahib. You are most generous."

The Guide seeing the brief glimpse of naked hunger in the man's eyes as he received the money could not resist a jibe.

"How come your life will not be in danger as the boy's will?"

"I am much cleverer than the urchin Sahib. But, I will give you a bit of advice. You must stop flashing money about, like you are doing. There are many desperate and greedy people in this land."

With that he said his good-byes and departed. When the rest of the crew returned, they made their way back to the inn. Naomh took out the shrunken TORT-CAM, enlarged it and released the Engineer and the Lenses from the concealment device; the two men reluctantly came out. The women spent the day purchasing only fresh fruit and vegetables that they recognized. On the morrow, the trek northward began. Surprisingly the fifteen questors encountered little traffic and very few people. They were also back to walking again. The ignorant adventurers did not know if these new lands they travelled were hostile, but soon found out. After a few days and a few skirmishes, it was discovered that these strange places were harsh and lawless, where any sign of weakness or a chance for gain was eagerly pounced on. All of them now carried weapons openly. The Guide informed them.

"Remember now. We are not to trust strangers. It is not an option."

The Lenses gave him a mocking look and in a slightly sarcastic tone said.

"Were you not a stranger before we met you?"

"You know what I mean?" Returned an exasperated van DerKamp.

The rest of the gang hid their silent laughter. Unlike the Prophet's lands, not all of the women covered themselves and by contrast some men did. The few people they encountered were of a slightly browner complexion than those from the Enclave, but were not as dark as the people from the south. Those from the Anschluss covered up more. Constant washing had removed the false tanning colours which had not been renewed. When looking for directions, Naomh did all the talking. One comfort was that alcohol was available in the many inns and taverns of the small villages, they passed on their way North. Though the locals were wary of them, these people did accept their currency in exchange for clothes, goods and information. The armed strangers usually made the locals think against attacking them. In the few instants where it did not, they left bodies behind. The inns were easily located from the gaudy florescent lighting above their doors and windows. One night the weary travellers finally reached the village, the contact in Agra had told them about. The travel worn group found the establishment he had mentioned and now stood outside its threshold. The name of the premises was displayed in a strange calligraphy under an image of a regal brown man, who was shedding tears copiously. The man was wearing what looked like a bandage on his head. Naomh translated the sign.

"The tears of the Mogul Emperor."

"Is he crying because he has been wounded?" Wondered the Lenses.

Some of the others guffawed.

"No you fool. That is a style of outfit" Responded the Guide.

The reason for Kaliningrad's ignorance was explained because he and the Engineer had spent most of the journey through the sub-continent confined in the TORT-CAM and had not sussed out the local customs. The two men had been lost in a place of advanced technology and had not noticed the days fly by. This was the first time either of them had seen the strange headdress. During their confinement, they had fashioned an incredible looking synthetic eye patch for the Lenses and of course, the Clerk wanted one. He was refused his request, due to its impracticability and he sulked. Moshe opened the door to reveal a bar with mirrored ceilings and yellow stained marble walls. The aroma of stale coffee and some other sweet smell wafted in the air. They entered the establishment and were greeted by a wall of impenetrable smoke, a cacophony of noise and music that pierced the soul.

"What in hells name is that awful racket?" Demanded the Clerk.

"Shut it. We don't want to antagonize the locals over some stupid reason." Ordered the Guide.

Seated around its table's were groups of men with thickly muscled, tattooed forearms and sporting various hairstyles, from close-cropped hair to long flowing locks. Some could have been female; as dotted among the patrons were some individuals that kept on their head coverings, not revealing their features for various reasons.

"Definitely a gathering of Human flotsam from surrounding areas." Thought the Spy.

The Guide sniffed the smoke filled air that permutated and wafted around the premises. In an instant, a beam of pleasure crossed his features.

"Shit man. Can you sniff that?"

"Of course. We can smell that stink. You would want to have your olfactory lobes cut off, not to notice that odour." Responded the Clerk.

The Persuader pushed passed the blonde speaker and he also formed a wide grin.

"Is that shit? Everybody's smoking grass in here." Said the big man excitedly.

The haze cleared momentarily and the male members of the squad stood transfixed, for prancing about on platforms dotted around the floor like little islands were numerous scantily clad female dancers. The Guide advised the Anschluss members.

"Keep your head coverings on. Your pale features might give rise to unwanted questions."

Those from the Enclave with their various shades of brown skins would arouse less suspicion. Haim opted for seats in a part of the premises where their backs were protected by a solid wall; not so as it worked out that the lads had an unobstructed view of the erotic dancers. Needless to say the men were delighted. Another high breasted slinky clad female approached their table and spoke to them in a rapid flowing speech which left nearly everyone bamboozled. However, Naomh now had an understanding of every tongue on the Planet, thanks to the growing influence of the three parts of the APOCRYPHA'I.

"She asking us what we would desire from the establishment." Translated Naomh.

Catching the Clerk's eyes straying to her nearly exposed cleavage, he gave him a look of consternation and rebuked the lecher.

"She is not offering that, you idiot."

De Mere laughed and Beersheba gave him a friendly cusp across the head. This made him chuckle even more. Cahill had begun to notice.

"He has changed immensely since we first left the Anschluss. He is no longer the shy and timid person from the Clerical class. He has turned into a very loyal and confident man. The Clerk is especially more comfortable around the opposite sex now."

Naomh addressed the sitting group, translating the serving girl's words as quick as she uttered them. The waitress was a quick study and she worked out that he was the only member of the group who understood her. This was not strange to her as many different types of people crossed her path. So she directed all of her questions at him. When he ordered for them all, she asked him what kind of currency they had. He showed her some gold bars; Sanjay Patel had told them.

"Paper monies are useless up there."

Her eyes widened at the size and amount and she left to fill the order. Naomh did not feel like eating, but to look like a bunch of weary travellers, they had to appear eager for nourishment and relaxation. The threat of poison or unwanted narcotics would not pose a problem as each of them now carried sensors that would alert them if the food had been tampered with. These had been one of the new items that the Engineer and the Lenses had found in the LAB-CELL during their long search. The waitress returned with ice cold drinks that were strong in alcohol and a few cig's which the Guide had requested. He reached for one, smelt it, then lit up the large joint and inhaled a deep drag. The man from the Amsterdam Contrib sighed in ecstasy. The Persuader eagerly followed suit. Soon after, the food arrived and it was served by numerous other half-naked nubile women. There were exotic platters of meats and vegetables and saucers of spices and sauces. The aroma emitting from them was mouth-watering. Anybody, who thought there were not hungry, soon forgot that their appetites had been recently sated as their sensors registered the food clear of any contaminants. The Clerk had acquired a taste for exotic foods and he beat them all to the meal. As he took a mouthful of meat, rice and sauce, his easy smile vanished beneath his cowl and he tore it off to reveal a bright red face. He tried to speak, but choked on his words while pointing at his mouth.

"Water, Water." Croaked the blonde man.

For a split second, all of the company thought the detectors had failed and the Clerk had succumbed to poising. But some of those from the Enclave started laughing and the others relaxed when Moshe told them.

"The food we have been served is very, very spicy. That is the source of his predicament.

"Serves you right. You greedy bastard." Admonished Cahill.

He then realised that some of the clientele had been staring at De Mere's pale features. Then as if they lost interest, these people turned away to continue what they were doing before the Clerk's impromptu performance.

"When we are finished the meal, ask the serving girl where we would get information about the lands to the north east. Give her a bribe." Advised the Guide to their only speaker of the local language.

While the rest of the patron's seemingly ignored the group, one shady character did not. He was watching their every move from beneath his shoddy cowl. This unscrupulous individual sensed a golden opportunity to get him out of the downturn in his luck. Jamair Khan was one of the new generation of "Pariah's." and he had fallen on hard times. When he heard Naomh asking about the lands to the north, he would not turn down such a God given chance to earn some cash. The untouchable deviously schemed.

"I will send them to the one that will pay me well for delivering these naive gold-flashing travellers into his hands."

Those who had crossed his wormy path knew Khan as the "Snake Charmer". It was because of his sneaky ways rather than any proficiency with the flute and the legless reptiles; who were the noblest of beasts compared to him. What Jamir Khan did not know, the display of wealth by the group was a ploy concocted by the Guide to encourage assistance on their journey and it seemed greed always came up trumps. Another thing that Khan was unaware of; was this bunch of what he assumed to be harmless and vulnerable travellers was in fact the most accomplished

579

bunch of killers that would ever cross his miserable path. The occasional cut-throat took the final swig from the glass of strong spirit that he was nursing all night and rose from the table. With an awkward gait in his step, he accosted the group. Nearly all of Khan's face was covered with a dirt-stained face cloth of some kind, only his un-trusty wide eyes and mouth remained visible. With a harsh labour-intensive effort and severe breaths, Khan told Naomh.

"Sahib, through no fault of my own, I have overheard that you wish to travel north. Well good fortune must be smiling on you, for I know of a tribe that regularly crosses the lands that you are seeking. For an agreed price, I will be telling you all I know about these places. If you are more generous, I will take you to meet a person who can take you there."

Naomh agreed even though the stranger had nervous twitching eyes that darted everywhere except at the person he was in conversation with. Khan began his narrative and hid his pleasure at the amount of gold, he had received. For the Anschluss crew had no idea of the value of precious metals in these impoverished lands, been that they came from a society that dealt exclusively in computerized credits. Those from the Enclave knew that they had an inexhaustible supply of this resource. They took no notice of the other greedy shifty eyes that lingered on after the transaction had been completed.

"The lands to the north" Khan began in a ruined voice, while Naomh translated for the others.

"Are called the Scab lands or Blasted Lands. It depends who you are talking to. These places are boiling hot during the day and freezing cold at night."

He was interrupted by a snort of derision from the Clerk.

"We can safely say that after our previous trek across the desert, they will hold little hardship for us."

Although, he could not see the full face of Khan, Naomh was certain that the stranger returned a superior look of mockery.

"If you speak of the Prophet's lands? Then, I am telling you that they are a land of milk and honey compared to this place. I will be letting you know about them, then."

He paused for effect, lifted their communal pitcher of beer without asking and poured a generous measure into his own empty glass. The masked man took a long swig and wiped his lips before continuing.

"Once over a thousand years ago, there was a mighty power here with a billion people within its borders."

He waved his hands in a broad circular motion, to emphasize this.

"This land was ruled by a Queen who lived far away in the west. But the people rebelled in a peaceful manner and the great power left. Now, the people left behind did not agree with each other. They fell out and divided the one large nation into three. All three argued that they did not

receive a fair amount of land and the two largest went to war continuously. Always at each other throats, I am telling you. The rulers let their people live in poverty as they spent vast amounts of money on weapons. Eventually both had developed weapons with the power of Suns. Their armies used these terrible weapons on each other and millions died in an instant. Huge cities became large craters in the ground. The great mountains were vaporized and sheared in half. The Northern cities of New Delhi and Amritsar along with the whole of the region were reduced to wastelands. Millions died in the detonations, but most had already fled south during the initial stand-off."

"Enough of this nonsense." Interrupted Naomh. *"If we wanted to hear outrageous tales, we would have hired a storyteller."*

Khan trembled in outrage and spoke in a clenched voice.

"You do not believe me?"

Some of the group snickered, but the mole knew that his words were true. That was enough for the stranger. He rose from the table and removed his cowl. The growing laughter ceased. Standing before them was a man or was it a man. It was difficult to tell, his face was ruined. It was covered in layers of blisters. Some oozing pus. Abnormal growths protruded from his forehead, his nose was a ruin. The monster screamed at them as he limped away.

"This is what the land does to you."

The three parts Mescal/Amulet urged its bearer not to let the stranger go and he rose from the table to chase after the departing figure. He called after the fleeing man.

"Wait!"

The Guide gripped his leader's shoulder and warned.

"Be careful Naomh. I know a sneaky bastard when I see one. Jose, you go with him."

Naomh smiled and replied.

"I'm touched. You actually care what happens to me."

Jamair Khan was shrewdly assuming.

"These conscious people are weak and gullible fools. They will have sympathy for me and that win them over to choosing me for a guide over somebody else."

The horribly disfigured man had used this ploy of being a pathetic Human Being to his advantage on numerous occasions. Usually with fatal consequences for those he lured into trusting him. The Snake Charmer smiled inwardly as he saw the man and another of his companions run after him. His well-practiced ruse had worked again. He made as to turn back, stopped for a split second and then continued on. Again, he heard the shout towards him. So the man with the ruined face halted and let him catch up. Acting with barely suppressed rage, Khan demanded from the chasing men.

"Goodness, why should I be helping you? I saw the looks of disgust on your faces. You think me worthless of your attention."

Naomh had gotten too close for comfort and nearly gagged on stink of the man's rancid breath. A lingering sour odour about him turned his stomach, but he was careful not to show any revulsion. They needed this man to guide them to the Mountain Kingdom, the internal voice had told him about.

"Look I'm sorry about the others behaviour. Let's triple your normal price." Said Naomh in a conciliatory tone.

Outwardly, Khan answered.

"The amount of money does not matter."

If anybody knew the Snake-charmer well, it was always the most important consideration.

"Four times then. Do you accept?" Asked Naomh.

"Agreed. I will return at Sunrise and meet you on the edge of town by the crossroads and we will travel to one that regularly crosses the Blasted lands." Replied the disfigured man.

Naomh instinctively knew.

"We cannot trust this unscrupulous man. But the assurance of a reward will make him take us to where we want to go."

"Oh I nearly forgot. We will be needing supplies, so I will be requiring some money up front." Said Khan believing that he was now in control.

He proposed an outrageous figure. Naomh reached into his pocket and handed over some gold without even bothering to count it. The Persuader also gave him the various currencies; he had in his pocket. In the middle of the bundle, a large ruby fell out. Khan's eyes locked on to it as it fell to the ground. His look towards the big man enquired; what about that?

"Keep it."

He did gleefully. The three men parted, each going in an opposite direction and both parties oddly content. But it was the Snake-charmer that was the most pleased, he had a fairly substantial amount of hard currency and a jewel that was worth a fortune. The greedy thug would make contact with his murderous acquaintance on his hand held device.

"I will become even wealthier. These people have no conception of the value of gold or jewels and that must mean they have lots. My luck has surely changed."

In an extremely good mood and on a roll, the creature who thrived on others misery thought that maybe his friend might let him pleasure himself on one of the women before they met their unenviable fate. He had only seen one of them clearly and she was a beauty. The next morning, Khan returned saying.

"My contact will be agreeing to be meeting you. I will take you north to him. It will be a journey of many days."

But Naomh and his companions had agreed the night before.

"We do not want such a treacherous rat travelling north with us. It would slow us down and we would not be able to use the TORT-CAM, if the occasion crops up."

To these ends, he softened the argument with Khan, against him accompanying them. The blonde man who had nearly choked on his food produced a case with an enormous amount of gold, jewels and a large bungle of Southern denominational notes. Khan stopped himself from whistling out loud through ruined lips.

"This small gift is a reward, if you give us the name and whereabouts of your man. And also, if you keep our business with him secret."

"Agreed!"

Although, he was disappointed in not going with them and sharing the women with his northern contact, the amount of riches he had just received more than made up for it. Khan was now a very wealthy though still an ugly man. He would easily find many agreeable whores that would even accept him now. The sneaky rat handed over the name of the man they were to meet and directions to an inn in a town on the borders of the wasteland. Naomh paid off Khan and the shifty man drifted away knowing

"I will still receive more from Singh when that vicious Mother-eater has disposed of them."

Growing in the ways of the Hybrid's, the three parts Mescal/Amulet intruded.

"He thinks; he has successfully betrayed you."

Its host replied.

"Do you think?"

Later that night, Khan's sightless eyes stared at the gaudy mirrored ceiling of the bedroom in the pleasure house. He had chosen the palest prostitute in the premises; it would make up for missing out on the white woman. During his drunken and drugged revelry, he had shown the pretty young whore the enormous amount of riches he had received; thinking it would impress her. The intoxicated man had not been wrong; the cunning whore realized instantly that such an opportunity would not pass her way again. She had knifed Khan in his drunken slumber. As the woman was packing her bags to return south and dreaming of the small business by the sea that she would buy, she looked at the revolting corpse and knew.

"I will never have to pleasure such monstrosities again."

His death and her flight would go unreported. Life was cheap up here and a dead Pariah and a missing whore was of little interest. The quarries outside the town were full of bodies such as him. It must be asked, did Naomh know Khan's eventual fate when he gave him such a vast sum of money? Back at the site of the Taj Mahal, he had listened to Sanjay Patel about the danger the street urchin had been in when he had given him the paltry sum of notes. It seems that Naomh had certainly worked out what kind of dirt bag Jamair Khan had been and when the Anschluss agent

583

found out about his deviousness, they were not surprised.

"After all, I know something about his past that he is oblivious to."

XXII.

Happily entwined around the form of his lover, unwanted sounds of reality began to make inroads into his Alien realm of slumber, shrill bird noises and the like. But the more pressing disturbances were the droning hums of passing vehicles that swept by in a rising and falling crescendo of discordant movement. Listening to the sound of moving traffic on the wet road below them, Cahill had a flash of inspiration; he wasn't third in command for nothing. The gang had set up a make shift camp and were overlooking the narrow transport route just a few kilometres north of the town where they had left underhanded Khan. The concrete highway thundered with the odd overloaded vehicle moving ponderously along its artery at speed much greater than their walking pace. Ever since Naomh had put Miriam in second command, there had been a competitive rivalry between the two of them; both had been fighting for influence from their leader. From their vantage point, the hum of the passing traffic irritated those from the Anschluss, who only knew the silence of the Mag-lev.

"Why don't we see if we can purchase or steal one of those vehicles? We are sick of walking and tired of travelling in things that are out of our control. Anyway, it would speed things up and if we are still been followed, we can leave them farther behind."

All of his companions agreed with his suggestion and he was chuffed.

"Well, he was due one." Said the Lenses well naturedly.

He got a heavy slap on the back for that.

"It would be better if we bought one, so we can be shown how to operate it and what it runs on." Advised Haim who had just become the groups appointed expert on motorised vehicles. After all, the Enclave man had driven a Tank for years. Except for the Spy who wasn't going to mention it, no one from the Anschluss had any experience, not even the Guide. But the long haired man was a quick learner.

"And another thing, we need supplies of food and fresh drink. All the food that the Guide took from the ship is gone and the stuff that Miriam supplied us with is running low. There is enough preserved meat, but that is for the Rabbi, he won't eat anything else." The Clerk said after doing an inventory.

"Well, I thought the Enclave was your final destination. How was I to know that you dudes would have me travelling half way around the World?" Replied van DerKamp in his defence at what looked like bad planning on his behalf.

Everybody else agreed with Haim and the turban wearing Clerk, he had bought the hear-gear the previous night. So, it was up to their only speaker of the local tongue to acquire the vehicle at the next town. Fortunately, the next village was a day's march along the road. Passing traffic ignored them, but as it whizzed by, it did buffet them with strong gusts. Naomh,

Haim, the Persuader and the Clerk went into the town to acquire the motorised vehicle. A few hours later, the others stared in disbelief at the contraption that the group had purchased. It was a large twenty-seater vehicle with eight large rubber wheels, the height of the Persuader. Its gaudy appearance, with bright garish colours and ornamental bars twisted in fine scroll work, which were placed on the body haphazardly made the Enclave members laugh until the tears flowed down their cheeks. When the buyer of the vehicle climbed inside and closed the curtains along its windows, they collapsed in a heap and were unable to move. Naomh, like the rest of the Anschluss members having no experience of private transport felt insulted by their reaction to his choice. Beersheba scolded Haim.

"I thought you would have more sense."

"It was the best of a bad lot, you have seen the others. Anyway, it will do the job. This thing will get us going a lot faster and the engine is sound."

The truck, that's what the seller had called it, ran on an old-fashioned methane gas engine, from a fuel source which was stored on its roof in a large bubbleous bag. The visible noxious gases emitting from a battered exhaust pipe in the back made them feel queasy. But as Haim had indicated, it was a lot better than walking. The gang clambered into it and when the Enclave man engaged the engine, the truck rattled twice as much as his former command. The appointed driver soon mastered its controls and the vehicle set off North westwards following the road signs to the town that Khan had directed them to. The truck had a primitive built in map system and the Lenses had programmed in their destination. Its maximum speed was a slow seventy kilometres an hour. Soon the rocking motion of the truck lulled them into a sense of complacency; the questors entered an existence of stops and starts. Faces stared at them from passing traffic, some were from excited children and curious passengers, but most of the drivers seemed disinterested unless they perceived a fault with their drivers operation. Angry glares, voiced profanities and beeping horns were met with intents of immediate aggression until, the Rabbi calmed them down. Been from the Enclave and experienced with private transport; he explained.

"Ignore them. They are only gestures."

Other times, they were so close to passing vehicles that they could have clambered out and got into them. To avoid these collections of stares, the curtains were pulled down and privacy was restored. A smugly vindicated Haim let the others know.

"Not so stupid now."

As the kilometres flowed by, to those in the front, oncoming shadows appeared blurred. But as the distance was closed, these indistinct images at the sides of the roads cleared and became trees, signs, people and even livestock. When it rained, the Persuader became fascinated by the globular raindrops that flowed down the windscreen and until they intercepted by its wipers and obliterated. They continued northwest along winding roads that were for the most part unpaved and unsigned. The map that Khan had given them was now their only guide as the system in the truck became outdated. Many of the passageways were just wide enough to accommodate two lanes of traffic. Eventually even these roads gave way to narrow mud churned tracks. What little vestiges of civilisation the group had encountered was vanishing in their rear view mirrors. Most of them took turns driving the truck. All but one was eager to learn, as the Mute could not be bothered. They soon agreed however that the Persuader would be discouraged from driving. He sped along like a manic, totally oblivious to the dangers. After he ran over some sort of animal that had been caught in the headlights, he was told that was it. The bang had awoken those who were sleeping.

Weapons were flashed, but those who were awake told them to relax. They got out to see what had been hit; it was some kind of wild pig. The Mute looked at the wide eyes of the dead animal and reassessed his opinion.

"This vehicle has some potential after all."

The others slept or rested, when they were not driving. Everybody took shifts at the front, two at a time and they kept moving through the night, thanks to the large headlights that illuminated the blackness ahead. There were no mounted front or rear view cameras or night viewing sights either; primitive mirrored glass showed the unseen spots. So bad were the roads that they were encountering, the truck was only making an average of thirty kilometres an hour. At some stage through the endless black, they came up to a checkpoint; a solider with a strange head-dress accosted them. He had no interest in searching the vehicle since it was heading out of his jurisdiction. Besides, he was not even fully aware where that point was on the map, the Indian government relinquished control somewhere along this line. The solider gave them some official advice through the opened window.

"This is a lawless place, you are best advised to turn around and go back."

Naomh answered for all of them.

"We have pressing business out there."

The solider with a fully cleared conscience shrugged and motioned for them to proceed.

"After all, I have given them the obligatory warning and it is up to them to heed it or not." He went back to his warm post as the strangers re-started the motor and drove passed. All throughout the truck journey, the Clerk was transfixed by the passing landscape and most of the time had his face pressed up against the cool window. He told the others as he scratched

587

his neatly trimmed beard.

"There is something to be said for private transport, with its freedom to go anywhere and at any speed you want. No fixed timetables or destinations. Now that's what I call life."

The Engineer responded with a snort of derision.

"But we can't go anywhere we want. We have to go where Naomh is been directed. So we don't have any freedom with our movement. We might as well be on a Mag-Lev."

"You know what I mean."

"Not really! No."

"Oh forget about it."

During the night, an inbuilt heater kept them warm and in the day's heat, an air conditioner kept them cool. In his half sleepy state, the Clerk listened to the mechanical click of the air conditioning unit as it began its endless cycle of cooling the warm air. The relaxing rhythm of its smooth rotation was ended, when Cahill located an in built radio and then the crew were treated to monotonous chanting of something that tried to resemble music. After fiddling with its tuner, they found something akin to the tunes that they were familiar with. The music system had the ability to play pre-recorded stuff, but they lacked the necessary input devices. While most of them dozed during the long journey; the Engineer sat in the back with his brother; both of them were fully awake. The big man had fully recovered from his near death experience. The two siblings were in deep conversation. The religious man had asked his brother repeatedly since his recovery.

"Since you were very close to death, did you have an out of body experience? Did you see the gates of Heaven? Was there an Angel of God beckoning you on?"

The Mute was fascinated with the conversation; he too wanted to know if the big man had caught a glimpse of an afterlife. The Persuader shrugged as he replied.

"I don't remember anything. It was just a blank. There was nothing."

His brother seemed, not for the first time, disappointed. The other wanted to put the bad experience behind him and wished that he would be allowed to forget about it. The twisted listener mouthed silently.

"I knew it. If the big ox had seen such a place, his eyes would reveal it."

Moshe whose turn it was at the wheel slowed down; this action roused the sleepers. The engine of the garish truck was switched off and the strong smell of gas became more noticeable. All of them got off the vehicle and scrutinised a sign which bore the name of their search in the script that Khan had written. It lurked under the feet of the massive mountains that encompassed it.

"This is the place as far as we can tell. It seems to match the

characters." Said Moshe, pointing to the writing and the sign. They looked down on the settlement that was half way down on the other side of another mountain.

"*It looks like a toytown.*" Added Beersheba.

"*And it looks a long way down.*" Said the Guide.

"*You can't be seriously thinking about driving down there.*" Exacted, the nervous Clerk as he pointed to the narrow twisting road that led downwards to obscurity and to him; certain death.

"*Of course, it is the only way down.*" Said Moshe, matter of factly.

"*You're kidding, right.*" Stated the nervous blonde man.

"*He's not.*" Laughed Cahill.

"*Shit.*" Was what the Clerk finished with.

The passengers got back into their purchased vehicle, the reluctant registrar was last. Haim took over at the helm; he was their most experienced driver and advised.

"*Hold on.*"

With a wicked smile, he then proceeded carefully down the narrow twisting road that appeared to be the only way to reach their destination. This precarious route had a few of them holding bated breaths and muttering silent prayers. At one sharp turn, the driver had to reverse the truck and half of it stuck out over the edge. Those in the back looked out the rear window, saw the drop that was revealed by the brightening sky and went pale. Half way down, the Clerk nearly promised the Engineer full complicity in his religion, if he assured him that they would get down intact. But, their Enclave driver had a mastery over the truck and they arrived at the bottom safely and much relieved. The only way into the place was by a large suspension bridge, which stretched over a deep and narrow gorge. Once the chasm must have been the town's natural defence. The twinkling lights on the other side were fading as the dawn's stronger light superimposed itself on the artificial luminance of the town. The day began to brighten noticeably as the vehicle drove across the bridge. Taut slender wire cables bore its enormous weight, the only things that stopped the bridge from tumbling into the gorge below. Although the Engineer had calculated that the structure was safe; Haim still drove across it at high speed. On the other side of the span, the town that was gradually revealing itself clung to the edges of the Blasted Lands, surviving on the illicit traders, who were brave, foolish or desperate enough to cross those lethal lands. Despite its shabby appearance, vast sums of wealth were exchanged behind its closed doors. It was essentially, a centre of illicit goods, such as cannabis, opium and arms. Even people's lives were bought and sold in some quarters. Slavery, assassination and expulsion were a much bargained currency that was constantly exploited. The grim town boasted many a new and old construction. But the tattered appearance of hastily built and half-finished buildings spoke of a large influx of new people or from the rusted re-enforcement bars protruding from horizontal and vertical planes, it may have been the opposite and most of the population had fled. Older works spoke of care and attention to detail with their superior stone work polished to a smoothness that only the passage of time could produce. The shabbiness of the newly poured mass concrete, that frayed at the corners exposing its honeycombed make up, outnumbered the older residences by ten to one. All agreed it was a place to be viewed only from the back window of their vehicle. But they needed information about how to get around the mountains and according to Jamair Khan, their contact was here, so they had little choice, but to enter. The vehicle and its fifteen passengers drove through the town and with a little help from inquisitive locals; they found the inn they had been seeking. The inhabitants were friendly enough, the town relied on trade and it was used to strangers. Haim parked their vehicle outside its front entrance and Moshe and the Rabbi guarded it. The rest of them reluctantly entered the ragged inn and took their concealed weapons off safety. The premises was cosy enough on the inside, but still, even at this early hour in the morning, it was noisy, rough, messy and full of lingering odours. Naomh heard one of the patrons call a drink, he also ordered refreshment and his words came out all gobblely gook to the others. When the travel weary group were seated and a person brought over the drinks, Naomh asked the server.

"We are here to meet a man called Raj Singh."

The waiter's eyes widened slightly, but made no sign that he recognised the name. He seemed nervous and looked like he wanted to leave their company as quickly as possible. Although, the person they sought called himself Singh, it was nothing like his real name. Even Naomh with his new found mastery of language would still have found it difficult to pronounce. Up here, it was a common enough name for him to remain unnoticed. The man who used clandestine names like the RE-INSTATOR'S had heard them. He was a cloaked shadow, perfectly at home in the dark alcove that he had chosen to sit in. Again Naomh asked the server.

"Is Raj Singh here?"

Seeing the insistence in his customer, the serving man trembled and pointed to the dark recess where the man he was looking for, sat. The Clerk gave the man a large silver coin and he gratefully left the table. Naomh and the Guide got up and approached the unlit corner, the former asked in the common language of the sub-Continent.

"Raj Singh?"

The man answered in a hoarse voice,

"Who wants to know?"

Naomh went straight to the point.

"Jamair Khan sent us. He said that you could be of assistance to us."

"Then, if the Snake Charmer led your path to me, I am he."

Each of the travellers had been around enough people who gave a false name to recognise that this so called Raj Singh was one of them. The hooded stranger removed his cowl and gave a smile that displayed a row of metal teeth. Two large earrings hung from his extended fleshy ears. Besides two ice cold blue eyes under heavy lidded eyelashes; that was all that was visible of his face. Singh wore a cloth mask, like all that thrived in the Blasted Lands. It was a measure against the harsh Sun and high radiation. Seeing the two men gawk at his face covering, wondering if he also hid his features for the same reason as Khan, he said.

"Sit."

The mysterious speaker gestured to the seats in front of them. He saw that the two men were still taken aback by his unusual appearance, so he tried to put them at ease.

"The mask is an occupational hazard of living in the Blasted Lands, my friends. I am so used to it, that I always wear it. And, it is a custom of my people."

This native of the radiation zone wore the mask for another reason than Khan. He was not disfigured as the other was. His entire skin had a red tinge, much like a severe bout of sunburn. The reason for this went back to the time of the atomic detonations. The Indian government had stockpiled all of their space-mined iron ore's in the northern part of the Sub-Continent. The intense blasts had broken it down into a fine layer of dust that was now covered over by a thin layer of top soil and pebble screed. In some places vast areas of the terrain was still exposed and these areas were known as the "Rusty Lands". All sources of drinking water were infused with fine amounts of the red pyrite and got into biological systems, thus giving most life-forms that red tinge. Singh continued.

"Khan told me that you would arrive before I set off north, so we delayed our travel plans to see if we can be a help to you."

This was a complete lie; Singh had hung around the town, waiting for them to arrive. Khan had sent him a text message; this was the only type of communication that this man who had a taboo against Human images would receive. He would not pass up this golden chance to increase his fortunes and like the other rat; he too sensed an opportunity too good to miss.

"My friend Khan told me that you needed someone to guide you north towards the Mountain Kingdom. Well my friends you could not have found anyone better. My people know these places like the back of our hands. You have certainly found the right person."

"You will take us?" Asked Naomh.

"That depends on the price." Said the other.

The fee was agreed, the haggling was non-committal on Singh's side. It seemed that he was eager to have them along. They had a long chat about the arrangements while the Guide had remained silent for obvious reasons. Their new travelling companion got up and said.

"I will finalize things on my side and send someone to the east of town in the morning. Be there at 5am."

The man that knew the road ahead rose and offered his hand. Naomh took his firm handshake and privately thought.

"There is something unclean about his touch."

Hiding his distaste with a wide grin, he said.

"In the morning then."

Singh left brusquely, bid his farewells and turned, just as a drunk accidentally bumped into him. The very intoxicated man got affronted and was about to confront the clumsy fool who had upset him and more importantly his drink. But when the sot saw who it was, the drunken man sobered instantly.

"Please forgive me. It was an accident. I didn't mean it." He pleaded.

Normally Singh would have gutted the offender, but he sensed.

"A show of random violence here would not hold steady with these soft foreigners that I have just done business with. The usually reliable Khan said these people had enough wealth to make it worth my while. In fact, by the flow of the Snake Charmer's words, he has never seen so much and when it comes to money, his is never prone to exaggeration. Still it is not strange that I am unable to contact my devious southern contact over the last few days. I'd wager the leech is probably spending all the money these people had given him on pretty whores. He will contact me when he needs me to settle our account."

As Singh left the building, the very relieved drunk rushed to the bar ordered, a large glass of spirit and downed it in one gulp. His hands were trembling visibly and the measure of alcohol did little to halt the shaking. As soon as he was sure that the violent killer was not waiting for him outside, he would leave the premises, vowing to never return again. None of the seekers of the APOCRYPHA'I missed the brief exchange and its underlying meaning. Because of his association with Khan, each and every one of them knew that this guy could not be trusted. The curious Guide approached the proprietor and had a brief conversation with him. It appeared that the man had a basic understanding of Anschluss. The owner was a large moustached man with a huge belly. He kept shaking his head in non-compliance until van DerKamp handed something over discreetly. A hushed conversation then began. After a few minutes, their companion returned to them and sat down.

"From what I've gathered, Singh is one nasty and a very dangerous customer. The Barman told me last night that our new friend was involved in a fight with another hard man. Singh easily overpowered his opponent and held him over a table in a vice like grip. Then he picked up a bottle of powerful spirit and poured it over his victim's head. The man begged for mercy."

"That sounds really nasty." Scoffed their own head-case.

The rest joined in with his merriment. The Guide, who had experience of Cahill when he lost it, held his hand up and said.

"I don't think you realised the gravity of the man's predicament. Singh then took a lighter from his pocket. He struck it and produced a naked flame and he set the man's head on fire. This guy ran out screaming in agony into the night with his head ablaze. Singh then threw a knife into the fleeing man's back. His dead and charred body was found outside later, minus the blade."

The others laughter was cut off like a tap.

"We had better be careful around him then." Said Greta.

"I should think so." Added her lover.

The Mute thought Singh a brutal savage.

"What's the good of going through all that effort if you cannot see the eyes? Still the screams might have been interesting."

With these words, the twisted man had a revelation.

"I was correct. Travelling with this lot has given me a clue. It is possible that death screams are a message to the other side. To get ready for a soul. I will have to pursue this theory."

The only way for him to do that was to make his victims suffer more. To look like normal travellers and not to arouse their intending guide's suspicions, a room was booked for the night. The truck was parked in a safe place, Moshe and the Rabbi joined them. The usual suspects stayed below to enjoy the atmosphere of the drinking area while the remainder made their way upstairs to a common sleeping place. Miriam told those who stayed behind.

"Don't be too long, we have an early start tomorrow."

The others came up two hours later and looked none the worse for wear. The Persuader explained to his brother.

"We just had a few sociable drinks."

The temperature had plummeted drastically after nightfall as was the norm in these frigid altitudes so close to the Himalayan mass. The log fire in the blackened grate had been reduced to embers sometime during the bitter night. Most of the company lay huddled together, cocooned in a mass of communal warmth. All except three; Cahill and Greta, lay away from the rest, isolated in a corner of the rented lodgings. The Mute had also put as much space away from the others as was possible in the cramped room. The itch to kill one of the strangers had been over powering, but he resisted the urge. As the hour of Singh's return approached, the Guide was gaining the urge to venture from the scant comfort, the threadbare room had provided. He had been cocooned inside buildings, their vehicle and of course the TORT-CAM for most of the last few weeks, the cooped up man needed some fresh air. The crew had been unable to use the invisible shield this night as their sleeping quarters was shared with strangers. They had to make it appear to Singh that all of them had spent the night in this hotel.

No matter how much wealth they offered the proprietor, he would not throw anybody out into the freezing night. So, if anybody wanted a room, it had to be communal. Such were the laws of hospitably and honour out here at the edges of the Blasted Lands. Intact and roofed buildings that offered lodgings were few and far between. However, all of the strangers had rose and left in the last hour of darkness. As their unwelcome roommates departed, the Persuader set up an alarm perimeter and took sentry duty. The others could sleep safely now. After their long drive north, most of the questors were bone weary and availed of the opportunity to sleep in. The Guide lost his battle to stay put, the pressing need to relieve his full bladder won the argument once again. Still fully clothed, he lifted the blanket as he rose. Freezing air intruded on the warmth of the slumbering bodies under it. Somebody near to him swore. To appear as inconspicuous wanderers, their body armour was discarded before they had bedded down. There had been too many eyes here, but it was highly unlikely word of their whereabouts could travel back to the Sheikh. The pony tailed man had not been able to sleep during the night and his tired bleary eyes tried to accustom to the insulated darkness of the cramped room. The armed Persuader who had kept watch over them acknowledged the Guide and when he suggested that he take over the watch, the sentry gratefully agreed. Before, he retired, he told him.

"Solomon has already gone out, he should be back soon."

The man from the Amsterdam Contrib still desired the outside, so when the big man finally fell asleep, he fumbled for the remote sensor deep in his pocket and de-activated the sensor for the warning systems of their alarm system. He left the overcrowded and rank smelling room as the invisible infra-red sensors switched off. He halted for a brief moment and reactivated the warning device. Those that noticed his departure just turned over and tried to get more sleep. He found a toilet on a narrow landing and availed of its nearness and comfort. Longing for a deep breath of mountain air, the risen and emptied bladderd man left the room and descended down an unpainted rickety staircase with the desire to also view the majestic mountains. Still half asleep, he rapped his knuckles against the cornice of the wall as he made an unsure decent. He felt a sharp stab of pain and cursed.

"Strange that I did not notice how steep this is, last night. But then I was slightly high."

He pushed the shoddy glass door and it resisted, so he shoved it with his shoulder. The door gave way abruptly and with a tired creak and the Guide found himself outside in the bitter dank twilight, just as the first rays of dawn rose over the colossal mountain tops. Clouds licked over the sharp edged mountain peaks and snowmelt boiled off in thick white puffs that seemed eager to join their celestial cousins. His eyes were drawn to the enormous summits; it seemed to him that the snow draped over the mountains like a suit of white rumpled robes. He loved this time of the new day, the quietness of the morning where each sound was more pronounced, had its own individuality and did not merge with other noises. So he was unaware of the presence of Solomon. He took a deep breath of pristine mountain air; he even basked in the bitter chill. Ever since, Rory had acquainted him with the wonders outside the Anschluss, he had promised to himself, he would see the glory of every dawn when possible, no matter where he awoke and found himself. Unlike the dead Prof, the Guide had had not been denied sights such as this. He was aware that there were billions of souls living under the murky skies of polluted streets and short vistas that were encroached on every angle by concrete and glass who would never behold this wonder. It started to sleet, but he left his hood down and ignored the icy wetness that intermingled with the tears of awe on his chilled face. Bitterness affronted him with the Anschlusss coda, that their cities were the supreme areas on the Planet. Still, he also underestimated the single-mindlessness of the LYUBINITES. If the Doctor's disciples wanted to and given enough time, they would surely level these heights in a similar manner as the European Alps. To himself, he said.

"They know nothing."

Aloud, he said.

"Surely these are the aristocrats of all mountain ranges."

Another voice agreed and startled the Guide in the process. It was Solomon.

"Shit. He is still not on the lookout for the Prof, is he?" He thought, knowing that he would never return. But all he said to the pensive man was.

"You're up early."

Solomon replied in his accented baritone.

"I find that early in the morning, I am more alert and I can focus my mind more clearly. So it is a good time to rise."

The man from the Amsterdam Contrib agreed. He was of the same mind and believed that all of the others did as well.

"Well except the Persuader and Moshe when they had indulged in two much Cigs the night before." He amended.

"And myself as well." He was in a generous mood this morning.

"That is some view." Said the man from the Enclave pointing upwards.

The Guide decided to try a little humour on Solomon as he lit up a joint.

"You know what the Persuader said when he first saw the mountains with their icy white tops and the green trees around their bases?"

His early morning companion shook his head and replied.

"No, but please tell me."

"He said that they look like huge ice-cream desserts."

They both chuckled as all around the shantytown; cheap electric lights flickered on, illuminating the frosted glass windows to let you know that the occupants of the flimsy dwellings had awoken to begin a new day. The Guide knew what the Prof would have said, if he were still with them.

"Behind every one of those light's is a unique and different story."

Although, the people up here appeared to be very poor by the living standards of the Anschluss, their rustic lifestyle appealed to him. Then, the mouth-watering aroma of freshly baked bread wafted towards them as the wind shifted in direction. Caught in its assault on his senses, Solomon asked his companion.

"Yes, this simple life might not be so bad after all. Is this the kind of lifestyle you envisage when Naomh completes his search and the Anschluss is no more?"

"It will, but it will be a lot more comfortable." Replied the other early riser.

Puffs of smoke spiralled into the brightening sky from well used soot stained chimneys as the occupants that had risen cooked a warm and fortifying meal to ease the rigours of their working day. He longed for the day of the simple life, with no more worries or problems. The two men stayed looking at the fantastic view in silence and then the Guide asked what he believed was the real reason for the quiet man been up this early.

"You still don't think the Prof done a runner? Do you?"

The other man just shook his head.

"No. Edward did not abscond. Something must have happened to him. Between you and me, I think he encountered the small men with the winged shaped moustaches. In avoiding them, he was unable to catch up with us and fell behind them. So now he is making his way towards us. But there is another possibility that I do not want to think of."

"That the Sheikh captured him."

"No."

"That, he left of his own accord."

Solomon shook his head; he eyes said the words that he was afraid to utter. He longed to tell the bearded man the truth and put him out of his misery, but he knew that would make him a target for the killer.

"So why did he leave us those holographic images?"

"They were on a pre-set timer and were activated when he did not turn up to stop them."

"Well I hope you are right."

The Guide let him think that in the worst case scenario that the weird men that had nearly put an end to the Lenses and the Persuader had caused the Prof to lose them. But he realised that the man from the Enclave did not need to hear his speculative thoughts, especially as the perceptive man might see through his lies. He softened the blow with the accepted view.

"Well. You do not know him as long as the rest of us. But more than

any of us, he despised the Anschluss and anything that it stood for. We his friends even reminded him of it, so to feel completely free of it; he probably decided to make a clean break. I think that it was the first time that he killed somebody and the Prof was not prepared for that."

"I hope you are also right my friend as the alternative does not bear thinking about." Replied Solomon.

"Still you seem very sure that he will catch up with us if he is not in the Sheikh's clutches. I don't want to disappoint you, but we have travelled a long way overseas, deserts and thousands of kilometres. Surely the Prof cannot find us now."

Solomon gave the Guide a measuring look and then having made a decision, the man from the Enclave confided.

"I'll let you into a little secret, my long haired friend. The Prof gave me a tracking device from the LAB-CELL. He has another like it and it can find me anywhere."

He showed him a tiny shimmering globe that was more white than red.

"I have worked it out. The two colours vary; the bigger the white section, then the closer he is to us and vice versa. So that is how I know he is still alive."

The man from the Amsterdam Contrib shook his head and said.

"The clever dude!"

"Yes, he is that."

"I better go up and wake the others." Said the Guide, wanting to change the subject.

He had a mental flash of all of the deceased's paraphernalia smashed in the desert scrub and then the smoking corpse.

"Somebody else has got the other tracking device."

Images of small cloaked men with strange moustaches imposed themselves over the site of the dead Prof. He mistakenly thought.

"No. We wiped those small dudes out. None of them could be following us now."

He returned to wake up the rest of their party while Solomon returned to his lonely and useless vigil. Once again he relieved himself in a fairly clean toilet area. He rushed up stairs and de-activated the alarm and stifled a breath as the odour of so many bodies crammed together in the small room overcame his awoken senses. Looking at the sleeping forms, he smiled a perverse grin and re-activated the alarm. He walked straight through the invisible beams grinning.

"This will wake up the lazy bunch."

The warning system went haywire and pandemonium broke out. People went berserk at been suddenly jolted from their slumber and in an instant the Guide faced a line of activated weapons, all of which were pointed at him. He raised his hands in panicked submission, with a look of fear etched into his white face. He had momentarily forgotten how highly alert and well drilled this lot were. The general consensus was.

"You stupid bastard. You were nearly blown away."

The redness of his wind-flushed face had turned pale with the fright as he forgot that many of his companions slept with weapons in hand when outside the TORT-CAM.

"Shit, shit." Grimaced, the well-travelled man.

The now not so clever individual swallowed hard as he knew that he had been milliseconds from death. Feeling a cold shiver down his spine, he turned and came face to face with Greta's and Cahill's mocking grins that spoke volumes about how they had been watching him ever since he had entered the room. Remembering his thoughts about who was the most vigilant among their group, he quickly amended his thinking.

"As the Lenses would say, those two are always on the cursor, they miss nothing. Still, we should be grateful for that."

Everybody calmed down, there was still a few muttered grumblings and they were about to go back to sleep again when Cahill suggested.

"Since everybody is now awake, we might as well stay that way."

His words were met with a few groans and not a few dirty looks in the Guide's direction. There were a few sarcastic mutters of.

"Nice one Bonkers."

Those with quicker reactions made a sudden dash to the limited toilet facilities and left those that had overindulged in beer and hash to groan in dismay. As they sorted themselves out, the room became a hive of activity as each person made their own preparations for the next leg of the unknown journey. Everybody had slept in their clothing in case of an altercation during the night, so some of them badly needed to freshen up. A few days before, the three parts Mescal/Amulet had told his host.

"There is indeed a lethal presence of radiation about many of the people here."

So the LAB-CELL provided a wondrous containment layer against molecular degradation. It was a pill that had to be taken orally. The anti-radiation sheen fitted like a layer of sweat giving them an unseen protective lustre that coated their skin. The internal voice explained.

"It will act like a glossy TORT-CAM and like the interior of the Gudiex Sphere; your internal temperature will remain constant despite outside fluctuations. But it will offer no protection from a projectile of any calibre or range. A pill has to be taken each morning and discontinuation of this soluble process will cause the protection to fade away."

Because of its defensive frailties, they wore ordinary body armour over the sheen giving the false impression that this was their main radiation gear. However, the common protective clothing of the Enclave too underwent a fundamental change. Each person was required to step into a polarised beam of light that altered the molecular constitution of their armour. Its protective capabilities increased, the suits now seemed more durable, plastic and fluid. Movement underneath their constraints became more carefree and less confined. This caused Haim to utter.

"It feels like I have nothing on at all."

"Will I fire at it and see if it does the same job as before?" Asked a malicious Moshe.

"I think I can make do without that experiment."

This caused the others to laugh; even the Mute nearly broke into a smile. Beersheba called Miriam aside and she explained something that had been bugging her. Then, the two of them approached Naomh and the others. Out loud, so everybody could hear, a mini conference was held. The auburn haired woman asked them.

"Don't you think it strange that nobody tried to attack us during the night for our wealth? It has been a major problem before and the people up here seem more desperate than most."

"They seemed to fear that freak Singh and would you blame them. You saw the way the other patrons reacted when the drunk bumped into him. Even the staff looked afraid. Maybe we are under his protection." Suggested the Guide.

"That's probably it. Agreed those in discussion.

"Another thing that is even more worrying is that he is prepared to accept his fee after he has delivered us to our destination." Added the Clerk, now that they were on the subject.

"That's just good business sense." Said the Engineer.

"No what I mean is, if the lands are so hard up there, then you would think that he would demand an advance, so he could buy some luxuries or even necessities to take back."

"Good point, I'm beginning to get worried." Voiced the concerned Guide.

"Right, we will have to be careful around him. We have to use him; he is the only one who can take us there. All of our new body armour must be worn all of the time, when we are outside the invisible shield." Said Naomh taking command.

"We will have him think that we are just curious travellers." Added Solomon.

Then, the Lenses came up with a great plan. He put it forward to the others.

"What if two of us stay inside the TORT-CAM all the time. We will have the surprise of having two extra members that he will be unaware of. If his lot try anything funny, then we will have the advantage."

The others considered it a good plan and he picked himself along with Beersheba. After all it had been his idea. The Clerk instantly became jealous and the rest of the party laughed. Their leader moved things move forward.

"Alright Cahill and myself will go outside town, meet this Singh and

bring him back here."

"Ok, but be careful as you go through town." Advised the red haired man's partner.

"Of course. That goes without saying." Replied Cahill.

"I cannot afford to lose either of you over a few baubles." Said Greta as she tried to inject some humour. Her lover chortled with genuine mirth as he gave her an affectionate peck, while Naomh gave her a measuring look. Then, the Clerk who was their unofficial quartermaster informed them.

"We need to acquire more drinking water, our supplies are diminishing and we do not know how long the next step of our journey is."

"Or the quality of the local water." Suggested the Rabbi.

"Ok, Victor, take Solomon, Moshe and the Guide with you, these three might make themselves understood. I will go with Cahill and meet this Singh."

Haim butted in.

"Since we are now going onwards with these strangers, every one of us needs a big pack to be believed. We must make it look like that we are ordinary travellers and everything that we need is with us."

Miriam agreed.

"You are right. They must not even gain a hint of the invisible shield. That is our main advantage. You go with them and get what you think each of us would need."

It did not take the four men long to purchase a sizeable quantity of drinking water and a little longer to get Haim's supplies. The rest of the gang went back with them and carried the plastic containers of liquid to the room. The proprietor did not bat an eyelid; he knew where they were going. Before the water was loaded into the TORT-CAM, the Rabbi put sterilising tablets into each one.

"Just to be sure."

The Clerk had gone off on his own after the supplies had been brought back to their rooms and now came back sporting a blue stone pierced into his nose and asked.

"Well, what do you think?"

His companions were well used to his copying antics by now and just shook their heads. Two hours later, Naomh and Cahill returned with Singh. The strange man looking more fearsome in daylight told them.

"I have finished the preparations for the crossing of the Blasted Lands."

Their leader told their new guide.

"You will be well rewarded, when you get us to our destination. We will arrange a big bonus for you and your people."

Singh smiled at those words and thought to himself.

"Don't make foolish promises, my friend, especially as they will come

back to haunt you."

As the rest of the questors came out to meet Singh, their dubious guide was secretly rubbing his hands in glee. It was because, his intending victims were attired in the best anti-radiation gear, he had ever seen. The peculiar garments looked plastic and gave the strangers the appearance of been robotic. Even the strange material that covered their faces was far superior to the flimsy filter cloth masks that he wore. He also admired the heavy squat weapons that they carried. The guns looked highly modern, efficient and well looked after. Singh had made the mistake of thinking that just because their weapons were pristine, they had rarely been used. He gloated to himself.

"By the elephant God, I love those rifles and their garments; they will make fine clothing for me. I must warn my men to be careful not to damage such magnificent goods when the betrayal comes. These outlanders must have more wonderful items in their baggage. It will enhance my standing among my people to relieve these people of such never before seen luxuries. Surely my luck must be changing; the animal God's are smiling upon me once more. I think this time that the Snake Charmer has found the mother lode."

If Naomh had been privy to Singh's musings, he too would have warned the other about foolish promises. The heavily, but inferior covered man quickly noticed.

"Two of their number is missing; it is a man and a woman."

He had counted them while they were lounging about the truck, the night before. Suspiciously, he asked.

"Do we have to wait for the other two?"

"No. They have decided to return home. Neither of them fancied this journey. They have seen enough of the World. There are only thirteen of us now. I hope that you don't believe in unlucky numbers."

Singh thought to himself.

"You should. They are two wise people, though neither of them will ever know it. But they will wonder what happened to you when you never return to wherever you came from."

Their new untrustworthy guide asked them.

"Did you sell the truck?" I informed you last night that only pack animals can cross the land we are about to traverse."

Naomh lied when he told him.

"That deal has already been done."

Haim had just abandoned the vehicle in a dark dingy street. Singh silently sniggered.

"Good, those monies will be mine also."

The man with the cruel eyes led them across the road to his waiting comrades. Cahill silently counted the numbers of their fellow travellers and whispered.

"Not good odds."

"Still we cannot back down." Responded his companion.

The fifty members of his company wore the same face mask as Singh and some were holding the reins of strange animals that had the appearance of domesticated cattle. The beasts were large, covered in long black coarse hair, except in the tail and flanks where it hung in a long fringe. They had however unnatural looking long red maws and the same rusty tinge where skin was exposed. Though it was the most primitive form of equipment conveyance, the beasts did appear sturdy looking and capable of the required task. But the animals also had an overpowering musky smell about them. Singh led them to four of the livestock that had no baggage and showed them how to strap on their gear. Moshe ran his hand along the muscled packed flanks of the animals and said to the others.

"These strange looking cattle are built for endurance and not speed. They are also very well insulated, so it must be cold where we are going."

With an exceptionally wide smile, Singh addressed the gathered company not of these lands.

"Come my new brothers and sisters; let us begin this journey while the mother Sun still shines upon us. We are about to cross the shattered remains of the Hindu Kush. Long ago many Suns fell on top of them shearing away their sides to form the mother of all cliffs. Some say they are more beautiful now."

The Anschluss infiltrator had noticed something troubling.

"Singh and his people are wearing scraps of a special unit of PREVENTIVE clothing and equipment. The shards of garment are from the elite espionage unit and that specialised gear is especially designed for the covert department. The only way they could have attained this was if the operative has perished. These people must have killed the agent and that was no mean feat, especially since the dead agent did not even get a chance to use their dissolving agent. Yes. We are dealing with some dangerous customers indeed. I will have to watch them vigilantly."

What Naomh and his companions did not know was that Singh's plan was to climb the highlands, up where the tallest peaks hid behind the clouds. Then skirt along the Hindu Kush, which was the wrong mountain chain, the questors were seeking and come near to the secluded valley where his people lived in between the massive rent created by man's aggression. Singh knew that some of his people that had journeyed south with him would regret leaving the warmth of these comfortable lands, so he kicked them into moving. His cut-throats jumped into action. The pack animals protested and their flayed hooves crunched the compacted gravel of the road as they reluctantly rose. It was a sound that would become as familiar as their own voices over the next few weeks.

A week later and the huge pulverised break in the mountain chain allowed the frigid Katabatic winds to funnel down from the gale blown wasteland of the north. At this stage of journey, Singh was indeed baffled.

"Neither the chill of the dawn or the hovering above zero temperatures of the noon, nor the creeping cold of the evening has any effect on the soft strangers."

He became equally puzzled and curious as they climbed higher that the increasing bitter cold of the night altitude had no physical impact on them either and every morning, he found them refreshed and in such good spirits. He would even go out on a limb and bet that even the harsh glare of the poisonous Sun that they would soon encounter around his homeland would have little effect on their complexions, if he could see them under their face coverings. The slender eye sized polished discs of their silvery eye pieces spoke of a technology far in advance of the goggles he had taken from that lone military man that had slain quite a few of his people before succumbing. Singh came to the logical conclusion.

"It is the special clothing that they are wearing that is been responsible for their unflagging endurance. Even the dirt refuses to stick to them. Just their outfits alone would be worth the price of many betrayals. Yes there is more to them than meets the eye."

The leader of the mountain travellers continued his train of thought.

"I will have to fight some of my people for the prizes this unique group carry. Still that is no problem."

His line of thinking was confirmed when one morning they awoke to an exceptionally freezing dawn; the stinging cold even brought icy tears to his eyes. Fires that had burned low had fuel hastily added to them. As their glowing embers flared up, Singh went around and kicked his people awake, forcing them about their business. All were aching with the bitter cold and cramped muscles. Singh silently cursed when his thirteen guests came out of their canvas shelter ill affected and suffering little or no discomfort at the recent hardships.

"It is a fact; I am thinking that last night's freezing fog and bitter chill had little effect on them."

But then, he reprised his resentful thinking.

"This is a good thing, for soon I am thinking that their possessions will soon be mine."

He called a greeting to them and the air in front of his mouth formed a cloud of steam. One of his guests responded with a minimum breath of frozen air. Just then there was a fall of snow and it seemed that his charges were fascinated by the snowflakes dancing in the swirling eddies. Singh realised.

"They must have never seen falling snow before or it is a rare occurrence for them."

He was correct with his assumption, those who lived in the Anschluss Contrib's murky skies never witnessed a full fall of snow while in the Enclave, it only fell on the Golan. An experienced Haim told them.

"None of you would enjoy it so much, if you had not got on this protection gear."

The Spy and the Guide silently concurred. The "Caravan." as their intending betrayer called it made its way through the diminishing warmth of following days, but rested each dusk and a meal was consumed before sleep. As the cavalcade climbed more into the mountains to the pass that Singh knew, he was aware.

"The weather will grow steadily bitter, the higher up we venture."

Soon the coldness became more noticeable from the plumes of breath that were forced out of the pack animals nostrils from their endless exertion. They were now greeted every day with blizzards and icy winds. Ponds were now covered in a thin icy lace. The caravan had entered a region of freezing mists and tall pinnacles, bare rock faces, ice sculptured valleys and jagged ramparts of frozen canyons. Their route was nothing more than precarious tracks etched into the mountains sides, indistinguishable trails that crossed over uncertain wooden bridges that stretched across harsh looking azure icy cold streams. These gravely water courses were full of small pebbles, large rocks and invisible grit that had been carried from higher elevations. The meandering Human constructions seemed as old as the mountains themselves. None of the questors knew how Singh's people found these paths without the benefit of technology. The flat landers from the Anschluss gazed in stupefied awe at the incredible landscape. All, but Agent XIII had never heard the wind howl with such intensity, it was if the mountains roared their defiance at them. Taking in the imposing heights, the Guide who was something of a seasoned traveller wondered as nearly all of the Anschluss's ancient heights had been levelled off in building the great wall around it.

"I have never seen anything to compare with this. These mountain peaks must be the highest elevations on Earth."

The well briefed Spy knew that these ranges were not, for had the seasoned operative not scaled the highest peaks on the Planet during their rigorous training. High above these was the roof of the World where Mount Everest towered to 8,848 metres above sea level. But of course their intending Judas said nothing.

"The others must think that these lands were new and exotic to me as well."

At heights of around 4,000 metres and above, they found something to break the monotony of the hard trek and cause laughter. Solomon spotted a close knit herd of grey brown mountain sheep with white bellies that were sure footed among the precarious slopes. Their guide called them Shapu. The cause of their merriment was that each animal had a tuff of beard at its chin that caused Haim to utter.

"One of them must have been the Rabbi's father. The resemblance is remarkable. Don't you think?"

The butt of the joke took no offence and joined in on the laughter. Singh was always tempted to poison their guests, but the strangers never took meals with them. His charges always ate alone and made their camp away from his people. But the most persuasive argument against that manner of killing, he told himself.

"Myself and my people would be denied the pleasure of live captives. I am thinking that would not make me a popular leader among my murderous tribe. And that Greta is the most incredible woman I have ever laid eyes upon."

Although, he had not caught one sight of her face since the start of the journey, Singh still remembered it from the one glimpse he had got when he caught her adjusting her mask before they had set out. The pale beauty of her face spoke of an unblemished milky skin hidden under her clothes. He had already noticed her long legs and firm buttocks. She was a well-built woman, way taller than the diminutive and squat females of his tribe. Singh could hear her screams even now.

"I will bring her to her knees. Oh how I will hurt her before she succumbs?"

The pack animals (Solomon found out that they were called Yak's.) which were the popular choice of transport in these lands just crumpled to the ground every night after hearing a certain command from one of the animals minders. The punishing journey still took a lot out of the beasts. But after a night's rest with food and water, the pack animals were as resilient as ever the next day. The beasts of burden were fed by a leather basket that was tied around their scarlet maws. A simple command would get them up and going the next morning. The Prof's close friend from the Enclave had regained some of his inquisitive nature and he was amazed at this. He tried to learn the command and affect the same response. Each evening after hearing the order to rest, the pack animals formed a rough circle and bore the brunt of the cold. At the centre of this crude circle of living insulation, small cooking fires were lit and their scant heat provided a modicum of comfort against the worst of the wind's chill. Most of those from the Anschluss enjoyed the smell of the crackling wood; it was a fragrance that had been denied to the majority of them until the barbeques back in the Enclave. One morning, there was a breather from the routine; just as the day was breaking, Singh led them to a precipice and showed them the lay of the land they were about to traverse. On one side far off in the distant eastern haze lay the enormity of the unseen Himalayas, the direction they should be going in. While the questors were no experts on mountains, something about the far off ranges looked abnormal. The three parts Mescal/Amulet informed its host of their guide's deception.

"The man Singh is leading us in the wrong direction. The fourth part of me is calling from the direction of the eastern mountain range."

"Obviously, we cannot go there directly; it must be a roundabout way.

Another thing; I cannot make out their language, you said that I could understand every tongue." Enquired Naomh.

"It is odd; these people must have invented a new dialect. I will work on a solution to it."

The many peaks of the mountain chain which jutted out of the high altitude misty sea of clouds seemed similar to their lower island counterparts that barely kept their heads above sea level. In contrast, Singh pointed to the deep ravines with their pencil paths that meandered like hairline fractures along their steep gorges. The tree line lay banished to the bottom of these deep places as if to lay credence that should foolish mortals ever venture to these forbidden heights that were the sole preserve of the Gods, then it would be at their own peril. Soon, the path ahead was forever covered in a layer of snow and the going got tougher. The caravan left an indelible trail of footprints and hoofprints across the white landscape that would be smoothed over after the next fall of snow. On these higher elevations, the loud shrieking gusts of mournful wind bore testament to the bones revealed from previous avalanches. The flesh of the frozen corpses remained mummified in the constant subs zero temperatures, making it impossible to tell when their departed owners had perished. It might have been last week or centuries ago. Singh's tribe were repulsive opportunists and there were a lot of de-fleshed bodies out there that they knew exactly when they had perished; for he and his tribe of man eaters were responsible for their murder. The frozen heads that were preserved impaled on wooden stakes back at the cannibals village still had looks of horror and betrayal etched into many of their features. The grimacing skull's expressions of hopefulness directed at the mountain peaks enhanced the belief that these enormous creations had been folded by grief. But the real horror that was thankfully denied their sightless eyes was when victims were brought back and their dead torso's put on butcher blocks or hanging hooks waiting to be carved up at the monsters leisure. He and members of his tribe could not afford to buy live flesh from the traffickers back in the southern town. They used Kahn to direct victims their way by giving him a share of whatever they acquired. Singh told his confidents during one rest stop.

"But, if the Snake charmer is right this time, I might even go into the people buying market. Imagine it, I could pick out a tasty morsel myself and for once not rely on what comes our way."

Singh's way of life was a result of a basic and barbarous necessity, but what he didn't realise was that his next intended victims were endowed with a brutalisation of 30th century efficiency. The next day, the Cannibal leader told them.

"My friends, the caravan has reached the highest point of our trek and it will be mostly downhill from here."

Up to now, they were making roughly twenty-five bone weary

kilometres a day, but it would increase much faster now. Naomh's crew were delighted as the tough going was bringing them close to exhaustion. Even though they did not suffer from the hardships of the weather like Singh's people, they were not used to such exertion at such altitudes. The high mountain air was causing fatigue, so tired footholds loosened and they hung onto the surefooted pack animals to stop from slipping. Noticing their growing weariness in the latter half of the day and comparing it with their freshness in the morning, Singh weighted up his options and told his deadly cohorts.

"Our impending attack has to be done at night and down in the lowlands. Up here a single shot could cause loose boulders or compacted snow to sweep us all away."

Then such an event happened and the outcome truly amazed the normally unfazed Singh. As the members of his caravan were threading through a difficult path, there was an unfortunate accident. One of the Cannibals slipped and a rifle belonging to this man was discharged accidentally. There was an instant deep rumbling after the fourth sharp crackle and an avalanche of thundering snow swept a number of the party away, including the owner of the offending weapon. Five of his band and two of their charges were carried away in the frozen torrent. Haim and the Guide had been buried under the mountain of snow.

"The white death has struck again. There is no hope for them. What a waste." Said Singh with finality after assessing the accident scene. He was sorely aggrieved that some of the precious gear had been lost among the wasted meat of the corpses. The beast of the mountains knew that the falls of snow were becoming more frequent, what he did not know was that it was the gradual heating up of the Planet that was the cause. But Naomh and his people scampered down the newly formed ramp of heavily compacted snow and the Engineer fished up hand sized burners from his baggage. Singh had no idea that they had location devices for their friends. He watched as the burners made short work of the snow and incredibly they found the two of them alive, but Man-eaters were not so lucky. All of them were dead, as they had suffocated under the weight of the fallen snow. As the two survivors of the fall were dusted of snow, Singh remarked again to himself as he gazed at the lifeless scarlet features of his people. Their face coverings had come off during the fatal accident. He saw the surprise on some of those he was escorting; they had never seen such angry red faces. He had an answer for them.

"Your burning things must have done that to them. The coverings that your two comrades are wearing must have deflected the heat."

His explanation was grudgingly accepted, they did not want to go into details about their own protection gear. Singh though was still privately intrigued.

"Their outfits are definitely more remarkable than I had been thinking.

They do not even look wet after been in all of that sopping snow. I will become more feared when these things are in my possession."

Out of earshot, he told the rest of his men.

"Preserve the victims of the avalanche; these unfortunates will be the main meal at the tribe's victory celebration over our live meat."

Over the next few days, the men and animals of the caravan inched they're pace across the snow and ice, fearful of another avalanche until they made their way down from the heights and reached a ragged tree line. The plants at the edge of the living barrier were little more than stunted stumps; similar to those caught out in no man's land between two opposing armies. The lone undersized trees were the vanguard of this patchy greenery and their sharp pointed needles provided scant nourishment for the few species that existed here. As the mountain crossers penetrated the non-existent canopy, spirits increased in the miserable forest, when Haim delved into the snow under the frozen firs and revealed greenery. The uncovered plants made a pleasant change from the never ending snow blinding whites and stark greys of the higher altitudes. When they probed deeper into the forest, the greens became brilliant yellows and reds. The trees also became larger and healthier. After a few more days, the sky was banished under a flourishing canopy of brown pine needles. As the caravan descended, the frozen snow turned into icy streams and rivulets. The Clerk took off a ribbed glove and dipped his hand into one and swore.

"Man that's freezing."

The others in his company took his word for it. Further down the steep slopes, thousands of waterfalls poured out over tree lined rocky outcrops forming a myriad of shallow pools of sky reflected water. The trees themselves appeared to defy gravity by the way the plants exposed gnarled roots clung precariously to the jagged ridges. The shaggy branches of the needle trees had the appearance of unruly hair. The wonder of this wilderness took the foreigners breath away and again Naomh believed.

"The Prof took the wrong decision in leaving us. Still what wonders is he encountering?"

Suddenly, there came a whisper of noise and as they got closer, the sound became a deafening roar. It frightened the very wits out of Naomh's group. Unstringing weapons in a fluid motion, those that were in unfamiliar lands rounded the corner from where the noise originated. Singh immediately noticed how professionally his charges had acted and reappraised his opinion of them. As the Cannibal still admired the shiny guns they possessed, he realised.

"We will be definitely taking them unawares. Still, I have the ultimate confidence in my people's abilities at ambushing any Human prey. And soon these very nice weapons will be mine."

The wary and alert group halted and stared in stupefied awe as each one of them was greeted with one of the most spectacular sights that Mother

Nature could provide. The fearful noise was from the thunder of millions of litres of water cascading over a huge precipice every second. It was the largest waterfall, they had ever seen. Its icy snowmelt had taken tens of millions of years to produce this incredible wonder and the water dropped unbroken for seven hundred metres. At the bottom, the pressure caused a fair proportion of the tumbling liquid to be blown away as a fine spray and amongst this mist. There lay a sparkling rainbow, placed there as if it was a gateway to an enchanted realm. Singh's charges were captivated and fascinated at the spectacle. He wordlessly scorned them.

"Foolish idiots. It is only a flowing of water."

Solomon produced a video-recording unit and took the image of the crew with the majestic waterfall in the background.

"Just for the Prof when we see him again."

The malicious Cannibal laughed silently at the image taking.

"I will throw the recording device on the cooking fires with their bodies."

Singh's people had a taboo about devices capturing their images. At the mention of the Prof, Naomh was also wishing the curious academic could have seen this fantastic sight. Because of the melancholy that he was feeling in remembrance of his friend, the bearer of the APOCRYPHA'I felt the strangest emotion emanating from the presence within. If the three parts Mescal/Amulet had deemed to explain, it was positive that its host would be unable to comprehend. Because it was a feeling of enormous loss. For this was one of Cetheren's and Cathbad's favourite places to come and reflect when the ALASTHA'I had lived on this Planet. The shades of Mescal were certain at this precise moment in time that its hosts two feet were embedded in the snow exactly above where the two winged Aliens had laser etched their own footprints into the rock in a moment of reckless fun. The two brothers had copied the antics of the missing Cupix. Much to the annoyance of the older generation of Elders, he used to leave traces of their script around the globe. Celtair defended him to his students.

"After all, it is a trait of recklessness that we desire."

One such etching in a place the Hybrid's called Columbia marked the meridian of the Equator. The indigenous natives worshiped it and called it the centre of the World. (How did these primitive people know that?) Once their kind would not have even considered this low form of interference on another Biosphere, the long separated Assirah and his group would have testified to that. But something like those impressions was now insignificant on the scale of their meddling. In its flight of fantasy, the three parts Mescal/Amulet could tell the Hybrid.

"Brush away the hard packed hydrogen oxide under your feet. This action will reveal etchings that had been created thousands of years ago."

The presence within the Amulet decided against it.

However, I then will have some awkward explaining to do about the origin of those Alien footprints."

A few days later, the inert beauty of these upper heights was banished forever to memory as the process of education continued for the questors. The Engineer who had been constantly monitoring the air passed on his findings.

"It is becoming even more contaminated."

A nightmare World would soon be encountered in the lowlands between the two mountain chains. Singh pointed to the wretched lands the caravan was about to cross. One look under the glow of the pallid Sun where apparently shining stars had impacted, told them that even the Kavirs of the Prophets lands were benign compared to the harshness of this place. The greenness of the Indian sub-Continent had altered into harsh browns and dark reds. The soil itself wore its desolation like the down trodden poor that eked a living in dingy slums alongside more affluent neighbours in many metropolises on the Planet. The live air crackled and hummed as if the land wept in a constant strangled wail or in utter frustration at what the tiny insignificant Humans had done to it. The scarlet horizons of the flat western sky were abnormal in their intensity. Like the land, it seemed that the sky was also on fire. Silhouetted hills appeared to cower down, afraid of another nuclear strike and its precursor, deadly radiation. The falling acid rain did little to cleanse the desecration and outrage; it was more akin to rubbing salt into a wound of blistered and festering skin. What little plant life that struggled on the scantily covered hillsides twisted up in scarlet horror from the soil as if trying desperately to escape contact with it. The land below appeared silent of animal life, nothing could live here, but they were wrong. Unknown, even to Singh and his tribe, there was one former plant here that had purchased an existence in this desolation. Its survival was a detriment to anything that crossed its path. The thing lay lurking five metres below the soil and it mimicked the survival methods of the bipeds. It too had become an eater of flesh and had evolved an animal intelligence. The warped organism had meshed the ground together to form a blanket of scree. It had evolved this strategy for two reasons, for protection against the harsh ultra violet light of the unforgiving sun and secondly for ambush. Once, it had been a normal Plasmid with a bleached furry stem that had fed on small insects. But now, it had mutated into a bulky redness and looked for larger game. The fine white hairs that trapped unsuspecting insects and leeched out their life fluids meant that it no longer relied on photosynthesis for continued existence. So it had retreated underground and the intense radiation had changed it as it metamorphosed and grew over the centuries. The carnivorous plant now took larger victims. Nobody knew its name, as it acted with a lightning speed to snare its victims and drag them in a split second underground. Those who saw it for an instant before it paralysed them could never warn others of the terrible fate that awaited them.

Beneath the soil in their living tomb, it kept the warm bodies alive and fed slowly off of them. It hid among the labyrinths of a frozen forest that was made up of calcified trees which had been petrified in time by the edges of atomic detonation. From a lot of these stumps, there hung crudely fashioned metal chimes which rang out in a futile attempt to banish the mad wail of the air.

A day later and deep into the Blasted Lands, the intensity of the falling red flecked snow increased as the wind from the Northeast whipped up the life sapping blizzard to an impenetrable darkness. Singh had no choice but to wait out the deadly precipitation and he was once again annoyed as he noticed the biting chill of falling flakes and its inherent radiation had little effect on Naomh's crew. The caravan settled into the ruins of an ancient monastery. Once it had been beside gently sloping verdant hills. But the greenery had been vaporised and now the monastery stood out in the open on orange coloured dirt; unshielded from the brunt of the ruined lands weather. This was a resting-place that the eaters of Human flesh had used frequently and where many a grisly torture and feast had occurred. The now deserted ruin had witnessed countless events since its founding. The excitement of its infancy, the solidness of its maturity, but it only bore the scars from the day the fire fell from the sky. If bricks and mortar could speak, these inanimate objects would tell of the day when two multi nuclear warheads containing a hundred warheads each launched from opposing directions careened into each other and veered off course and crashed into the Western Himalayas. The resulting detonations sheared away the sides of the great peaks leaving a two kilometre high vertical precipice around the south and western faces. The million to one accidental collision brought the two sides of the conflict to their senses and an uneasy truce was called. But it had been too late for the exposed states; these political entities along with their entire communities of millions had been obliterated, becoming wastelands. The monastery had been directly below ground zero and had remarkably survived relatively intact, unlike its inhabitants. The Engineer told them.

"The air contamination is at its worst here."

The Clerk noticed strange abstract imprints of Humans in startled postures along the walls of the monastery and was baffled at their creation. He was mystified at how the artist had created such perfect outlines, so he asked the others.

"How do you think such images were created?"

None knew the method and if they had been told, not one of them bar one would have believed the explanation. The figures that looked so life like to the questors had been real people once who had been vaporised in the instant of nuclear detonation and had left their shadows on the walls. These horrifically created etchings had now been softened over time to their present likeness. After breaking fast the group retired to their canvas tents, to rest the night away. As always, the crew posted guards and they all took turns at guarding their section, not only against an external attack, but mostly against an internal one as well. During this tension filled night was Naomh and Cahill's turn. The full brunt of the crackling snowstorm hit them around midnight and the two sentries had no option, but to retire inside their large tent.

"Great that's all we need." Complained Cahill.

This was said for the benefit of those watching them, because with the protective clothing and viewing devices, they were not as blind and helpless as Singh might think. Still, Naomh was pleased with this radiation filled inclement weather, for he was sure this was where their intending ambusher's would make their move. The Mute had noticed Human bones and bloodstains on the eroded stonework and had told Naomh about his observations. At the start of the trek with Singh's people, the normally uncooperative man had warned the others.

"Do not take any food offered by them, especially the meat."

The clueless Clerk had asked.

"Why? Do you think they might drug or poison it?"

"No 'oo. I think it might be Human."

There was shocked silence among the rest of the questors as their blood ran cold on hearing his revelation. All of the gang avoided even walking near the cooking fires of Singh's people and if any did, their respirators were on so they could not smell the obnoxious odours. The Rabbi, the Engineer and Solomon shunned them more than the others, if that was possible. The caravan was holed up in the ruins for three days as they waited for the weather to break. The conditions were so bad that Singh was unable to proceed with his planned outrage. On the third morning the heavy orange snow turned into light tanned drizzle as the wind changed and brought a new warmer weather system from the west. Naomh emerged from their canvas shelter as the murmuring rain trickled down the remnants of the ruined wall face that the tent was backed up against. Now that the weather cleared up slightly, he took a good look around their surroundings. The rising and harsh sunlight filled in the shadows of the buildings brickwork. Its walls stank with the potent smell of old fires. Surely it was a testament to its faded importance. The pathetic weathered un-repaired stonework showed no vestiges of its former glory. The ramshackle gate openings were long bereft of the large proud doors and the intricate carvings they once boasted. Now the crumbling towers and watchposts lay ruined in defeat to the passage of time. Uncountable crimson weeds and lichen that looked and felt abnormal obstructed the stone work in many places, where it gained purchase without succumbing to the harsh gales that regularly blew up. These substandard stains were an inferior replacement for the colourful bunting that once adorned the structure. Only when they briefly flowered with unchained abandon during the short summer did they give a meagre hint of the past splendour. Naomh imagined.

"Somewhere back in time, on a morning such as this, it would have been a beacon for tired and weary travellers. The same kind of rainy day as today minus the crackling background of radiation would have enticed them into its sanctuary with the promise of safety, warmth and a hot meal."

He was brought out of remembrance of things past by movement from Singh's people. Several of them were further demeaning the building by relieving themselves against one of its sheltered walls. Hot steam could be seen rising into the night air, in stark contrast to the cool moisture falling in the opposite direction. His amplified hearing had picked up the sound of them urinating. Naomh focused on the reason for him been here.

"The demise of this once important building could be a metaphor for the Anschluss and I will be the one to piss on its ruins."

His mood lightened. But the experienced three parts Mescal/Amulet could have debated.

"What you are going to replace the Anschluss with might go the same way?"

The next day the caravan entered a corrupted-forested area of unnatural stunted trees that evoked wariness in the group. It was not so much the desecrated woodland, but Singh's people's behaviour. They appeared to be familiar with the land and moved with briskness that nothing would surprise them here. That night the seekers conferred and concurred that whatever mischief Singh had planned would happen tomorrow.

"We should stay in the TORT-CAM and wait it out. When they can't find us, then they will move on. Said the Clerk, who was anxious to avoid any confrontation. But most of the others bloodlust was up.

"Anyway, look how many innocent travellers we will be saving by ridding the earth from a few of these scum." Countered Greta.

The Engineer and the Rabbi agreed; the men of two different faiths had for once the same credo.

"They are a stain on God's creation and if we can speed up their journey to the fires of Hell. Then so be it."

The odious Mute as usual said nothing, but he was secretly up for it. He liked nothing more than a little murder and mayhem. Serene Miriam took over.

"Right then, here is the plan. We will post no more guards outside our tent. Every night from now on, Singh's people will see no one at the entrance and they will begin to think that we trust them. You can be sure that's when this scum will make their move."

The questors played out this tactic for the next two nights, but the attack never came. One of the reasons for this reprieve became evident the first morning. Naomh and his gang woke up one morning to find the

Cannibals extremely disturbed. Unknown to the most of the Questors, two of Singh's people had been found with their throats cut. It happened while they were relieving themselves. The Mute had been up to his nefarious endeavours again and not that he cared, but the murderer had delayed the confrontation. Then one of Singh's people went to him and swore.

"I have seen two people with them. Neither one, I have seen before. They were of a different form than those we have been watching. I could not tell what sex they were?"

The Cannibal leader became troubled.

"Are they the two that were left behind? They must be trailing us, but that would be impossible. Those two soft foreigners could never have made that trek on their own. Well, just in case, two can play at this game, I will give them a nasty surprise."

He ordered six of his men, to fall back and watch for anybody trailing them. If they saw anyone, they were to kill them instantly.

"I will leave their bloodied flesh stripped torso's up ahead. Then I will see how the clever bastards handle that."

Then Singh remembered something.

"A few years back; we ambushed another white skinned man who was alone out in the wastes. Even though, we had the element of surprise, the man had killed a fair number of us. Are these of the same kind? No, for he wore a distinct type of uniform and carried different equipment."

Over the next couple of days, his party of ambusher's never encountered anybody. He called the one over who had told him the wild tale and flattened him. The six men who stalled behind were called back to the main group. That night, the Cannibal leader was having an enjoyable dream.

"The blonde woman was stretched out over two makeshift poles. The heads of her companions were on sharpened shafts around her. Her bloodied and naked body was lashed to the stakes by leather straps. She was screaming. The main reason for this was that he had sliced off her nipples and had eaten the tasty treats in front of her eyes. (Obviously, he did not know the woman he was tormenting, Greta would not scream.)

He took out a large knife and was about to relish the next few delicious hours. Once again he advanced with his knife."

Someone was calling him, Singh woke and cursed. He hated to be disturbed, especially from such pleasant dreams.

"Still, they will be real enough very soon."

The man who had dared wake him told him.

"One of the softlanders gave the men a few large bottles of very strong spirits. There was a fight between them and Zungi is dead."

"They might be cleverer than I thought."

He looked at the man.

"Any more injuries?"

"Just a few knife wounds."

"Well you know what to do with the body. At the rate you idiot's are been killed, we will soon have enough meat for a sizable feast."

Two days later, the blood froze in the questors adrenaline filled veins as the noise from the forest played havoc with their senses and drowned out the background radiation. The caravan had entered another forest of chimes and it appeared that the noise was part of the landscape. Their escorts thought the music was exhilarating. By Singh's upbeat mood, the crew guessed the attack would come very soon. The chimes were a primitive superstition created by the tribe of Cannibals. They foolishly believed that if the lethal radiation could not be heard, then its effects would be diminished. The caravan made camp that night in another bunch of blackened ruins. The searchers of the APOCRYPHA'I had noticed that there were a lot of those in the last few days. While sitting out in the open and gathered around a flickering fire, Greta observed that the scant firelight had illuminated the dark recess under a broken sill. A spider's web dangled under the lintel and ensnared in the trap was a piece of leaf. The twisting leave's vibrations along the silken threads would alert the predator and when it pounced, it would be sorely disappointed when it discovered its catch. Smiling grimly, the tall blonde woman knew.

"It will be a lot worst for that cockroach Singh when he springs his trap as the spider will live to try again. The Cannibal will not. He will be dust."

Naomh ordered Beersheba and the Lenses.

"You are to fall back and come at them from behind."

On the pretence that they were delighted with Singh's tale that their journey would be soon over, the Guide gave them twenty bottles of strong spirit. This was done openly, so that the Cannibal leader would have to share them out that evening. It was a clever ploy, for more than likely the man-eaters would be drunk, fight amongst themselves again and be easier to take out. The bushwhackers made their move in the middle of the night, shortly after they had downed the last of the spirits. Spurred on by the alcohol and the promise of more, Singh struggled to control his people as they called for the attack. To the company, whose senses were on heightened alert, the accidental colliding of so many bodies converging on them sounded like the drumbeats of a war chant. So sure that their numbers would overwhelm the questors, the man-eaters had already decided that the time for silence was over. Forty-three men with murderous intentions surrounded the tents, armed with guns, cutting knives and rocket propelled grenades. The attack began in earnest, the assailant's glee, lasting exactly two minutes. A sobered and bloodied Singh was running panic stricken. The killer of mostly easy victims could not believe it.

"What went wrong?"

The fleeing Cannibal leader replayed events as he careered away from the slaughter.

As his freaks surrounded the tents of their intended victims, Singh smacked his lips in anticipation of the forthcoming delights, especially the fun he was going to have with the pale female. Just as they were about to move in, one of his dimwit villagers did a stupid thing and fired an improvised rocket at the small cluster of tents. The rest of his murderous crew got carried away and also opened fire on what they surmised was defenceless sleepers. The canvas shelter exploded and everything inside it was blown to smithereens. Huge holes in the tent's canvas material testified to the mayhem that would be found inside. Singh was stunned; all of his sport and booty was in an instant taken away from him. The beautiful pale woman was now more than likely a charred corpse abet a tasty one. Livid, the fleshy lobed beast killed the incumbent who had fired the first rocket out of hand with a curved dagger. The idiot fell to the ground, gurgling on his own blood as the raging killer told his men.

"Carve him up later. I will personally eat his heart."

As two of the bushwhacker's picked up the corpse, a withering burst of fire from behind started taking out his men. Both of the carriers of Singh's victim dropped their prize and toppled on to the dead man. A tribesman's head exploded to the left of him as he dived to the ground in reflex.

"Thud, thud, thud. thud,"

Others went down to the sound of a heavy calibre weapon and did not rise. Their blood wasted on the crackling ground. Then, as the smoke cleared where the tent had been, all of the strangers emerged out of the surreal haze totally unharmed. They came out with guns blazing. There was a she-devil at their head and she was coming for him. The blonde woman had removed her head covering and gave him a blood-curdling look that he normally reserved for his victims. She had special plans for him and none of his men remained standing. Her blue eyes target him and she promised.

"You are dust."

In this ruined land, Greta should have said.

"Radioactive dust."

Singh got the message anyway. Unmanned, he had run for his rotten life. The apparently soft strangers had wiped his people out in a blink of an eye. The man who had the tables turned on him was running for his life, away from that terrifying female devil. The panicked pack animals, some with their slain riders still dangling from their backs stampeded in his direction. The distressed beasts of burden trampled him into the ground in their maddened flight. Singh went down under their flailing hooves. But he rose unhurt, alive and more importantly, he was out of sight from his pursers. The Cannibal's leader could not believe it; he would survive this unexpected turn of events. Regaining his composure, he screamed in defiance as he ran into the forest of calcified stumps.

"I will be back with ten times more of my people and you will pay for his outrage. They have heard the noise of battle and will soon be here."

No sooner had he finished those boastful words; the ground beneath his feet trembled slightly. The fleeing man gave it a confused look and realised that his groggy state was affecting his senses. As he shook his head in a bid to clear the fuzziness, the flesh eating creature snapped from under the soil in a blur of ambush and yanked him underground with crimson claws that had once been pale thorns. He had vanished into nothingness as suddenly as the stranger's had appeared from nowhere. The apex predatory organism had taken an uncharacteristic risk, it normally only attacked lone victims as it had an inbuilt sense that if it was seen by Humans, then they could dig it up at their leisure and destroy it. The Plasmid knew that if it was located, it would be defenceless. But the overpowering smell of blood detected by its tendrils had been intoxicating and it had reacted to its growing frenzy. Still alive, Singh was injected with nervous neurotoxions and digestive enzymes; he would provide the living fodder for the next generation of killer plants. Was it ironic that the man with many names was going to suffer horribly to death by a plant that had no name? Nature had used one monster to rid itself of another, for the flesh eating plant was an obscenity created by herself. The eater of Human meat had received much worse than a taste of his own medicine. For his victims were dead when they were consumed, he would not be. The Clerk had been the only one who had seen the demise of Singh; it had been so quick and sudden that he wasn't sure that it happened. During the next few days of travel through those lands, he refused to leave the safety of the TORT-CAM. Nobody believed his fantastic tale of red hued tentacles. They assumed that Singh either escaped of was killed during the firefight. Once days later, when he overcame his terror, the blonde man saw a shrub with its branches flailing in the wind, it seemed alive and it was coming for him. Just like what had happened to Singh. He fled screaming, back into the safety of the protective shield, activating his wrist band as he ran. The Mute, who knew the look of terror well and judged the Clerk's tale to be true as the blonde man vanished out of sight. He also fantasised at what it would be like to be such a creature lying in wait for potential victims. He knew about the Indian belief in reincarnation and if it were true, he would enjoy coming back as such a thing. He began to dose and enter his twisted World, where none but him and his victims were welcome.

"Coward." Groaned Greta in disgust at the Clerk's reaction, her lover agreed, Cahill was a little less subtle about it, but then neither of the two lovers had seen the monstrosity that took Singh. One day, well into the future and in another guise, some of them would encounter that creature again, but that was for another time and circumstances. Now back in the present, the searchers of the APOCRYPHA'I had other concerns, for

Naomh's party had lost another member of their group. The intrepid travellers were now only fourteen strong.

XXIII.

Once again the winds of change and chance had soiled their harmony. This fickle circumstance of fate shook them out of their growing complacency and slapped them into reality. As if in response to their chill of incredulity, a frigid wind came from a northerly direction. But those that were standing around the scene of the immediate battle were unaffected by its assault. Like the weather, most of the questors were in an ugly mood, while others were in a similar state to post sexual activity. These two individuals had enjoyed the one-sided fire-fight and it was of little consequence that one of their number had been killed during the confrontation. A palpable cloud of depression hung over those that cared. Singh and his treacherous villagers who had brought them over the mountains had bitten the radio-active dust and the questors had been forced to resort to their own devices yet again. More than one of the survivors of the brief fire-fight thought.

"Is it my imagination or do the foul bodies of the man-eaters smell worse than normal dead."

The three assailants that had survived the massacre had fled to gather reinforcements. The village of the cannibals was close by and those bloodied trio would be back soon with an enormous force of vengeful carrion eaters. An over confident Singh had coveted Greta and their advanced equipment, but he had perished in a more horrifying manner than all of his many victims. His former comrades who cared nothing for sentiment; only survival in this harsh and unforgiving wasted land would have hoped eat his rotting corpse. But they would never find it. Naomh decided that if the Clerk's story was true, then there was a certain poetic justice in his demise.

"Singh and his people were opportunists; waiting for their victims and if what the Clerk told us is correct, then it looks like Singh was snatched by a better opportunist than himself."

Greta did not believe the Clerk's crazy story and the beautiful blonde woman did not suffer fools gladly. But that budding argument was put on the back burner as a series of unfortunate events had led tragically to one of Miriam's comrades been mortally wounded in the firefight. He had died instantly from his wounds.

It was Haim!

The big nosed man had taken the full impact from a volley of rockets launched by a panicked villager. He went down in a heap and his body armour had failed to protect him from such close range explosive fire. The Alien film that guarded them from the fluctuations of temperature could not provide the same safeguard against projectiles. It had been ripped apart like tissue paper. As it was moulded to the body's constant movement, it had not the same effect as the impenetrable TORT-CAM. It offered little comfort that Haim's killer had died as he had pulled the trigger, his head erupting in a spray of blood. Two of the mortally wounded man's compatriots had rushed over and ripped the burning fabric from their comrades tortured body. But the man from the Enclave was dead before his friends could hasten him into the LAB-CELL and attend to him. Miriam's pleading with the Rabbi to save him fell on helpless ears. Now the dead man's former commander sat on the hard ground with his unprotected sagging head held gently in her hands. She had watched the faint spark of life fade from his pain filled eyes. The raging Mute had missed it; he was too busy finishing off the wounded tribesmen. As Miriam cradled him in her arms, the Rabbi checked in vain for his vital signs, but there were none. As she caressed his bloody forehead, she demanded from their appointed doctor.

"You have to save him. You were able to heal the big man and his injuries were no greater than Haim's."

Through his own haze of grief and tears, the heavily bearded and pious man told his distraught commander.

"The healing technology will only work if there is even a minuscule of life left. It cannot bring back the dead. Only God in heaven can do that."

Shocked resignation set in.

"There must be something else in there that can save him." Choked Miriam with a sob, the distressed woman was clutching at straws.

The Rabbi sadly shook his head.

"No, Miriam, think about it. If there was even a little hope? Would I not be the first one into that wonder of healing?"

Overflowing tears spilled down her cheeks.

"Let him go Miriam. Haim is no longer with us." Advised Solomon.

Moshe and Beersheba nodded in solemn resignation. The former did not think that his joke about the body armour's effectiveness was funny now. Taking in each of her compatriots eyes in turn, she tearfully relented and gently closed his sightless brown eyes. The grieving Enclave woman would never forget her last smell of him; coppery blood mixed with the salt of her tears and the metallic fumes of explosive chemicals. The intimate contact of his skin was denied to her as a result of the Alien film protecting her body from the radioactive terrain. To most of Haim's surviving companions, their friends death was another wake up call. Some of them might have taken that extra and more foolish chance in the belief that the miraculous technology of the LAB-CELL would save them. But from now on each one of them would be as careful as possible. There would be no crazy risks. All of them were no strangers to death and would recover quickly, especially around the influence of the Alien artefact. So it seemed that Mother Nature took time out from the horror of what had been done to her, to grieve for their fallen comrade. The clouds wept remorsefully, shedding their grief with blood red acid rain and thus scouring the land from the murder that had taken place. Tributaries of flesh and gore from where the slain lay twisted in death seeped into the sodden ground to form blood scarlet streams that flowed down the hill to be gone from the memory of what had happened here. The people from the tribe's insisted on adhering to their beliefs and the Rabbi stated.

"Haim has to be buried in the ground. A funeral ritual has to be performed over his body."

This was alien to those from the Anschluss, where bodies of the deceased were disposed of mechanically with little ceremony and then they ended up as compost for the vast agriculture sectors. Singh and his scum were left for the carrion eaters which of course included his own people. The Anschluss members wanted to make haste as the survivors from the clash would return with more reinforcements, but the people of Zion were insistent that their ritual had to be performed. They needed an outlet for their sorrow and they were also were grieved that Shoshanna had been denied this ceremony. Haim would not travel to meet his maker without his friend's goodbyes.

"I think that people from the Anschluss are taught to deal with other people's grief callously. We will have our funeral for our friend, but it will not be here in this tainted soil." Insisted Moshe.

He did not know that the influence of the APOCRYPHA'I had greater effect on them and it was diluting weaker emotions. When the Engineer explained.

"We can accommodate our grieving friends. There were some among the RE-INSTATOR'S who sometimes used a ritual, when a body of one of their fallen escaped the clutches of the Anschluss's mopping up squads."

Armed with this knowledge, his impatient comrades relented shamefacedly. An hour later, they found a small oasis of greenery on higher ground. The mournful Rabbi compromised.

"This will do."

The sky darkened even more and the weather turned against the mourners. Visibility went down to a few feet. While a grave was dug for the unfortunate Haim; RUTH'S crew carried out a series of strange duties. Solomon began to carve the unique writing of the Enclave on a flat stone. They could at least read both sets the numbers on it. These were in the same script as Anschluss and the inscriptions stated, 2924AD-2953AD. The other numerals stated 6682-6713. The rest of its meaning was explained by the red-eyed Beersheba.

"It is his name, his rank, the place where he was from, the time of his birth and the date of his death. The second set of dates are our lunar Hebrew calendar."

Those from the Anschluss nodded, the Rabbi had explained to them once that the Enclave and the Prophet's Nations used different measures of time. If Haim had been one of the latter; then the second date would have been 6716. To speed things up, the Engineer whispered to his brother and the big man went away. The Persuader returned with a large laser burner and melted a rectangular hole in the ground. Although, the religious novice was intrigued by the upcoming ritual, he too sensed his leader's urgency. The Enclave five were pleased at the gesture, for the cleansing fire from the burner sterilised the corrupted ground that would inter their fallen comrade. The Rabbi went to his pack and returned wearing a black and white shawl and some sort of square cube on his head. He also had a black book in his hand. He looked a different person to his Anschluss counterparts. The Rabbi was their spiritual leader and he read from the Torah. Miriam and Beersheba reverently wrapped the body in a shroud of patterned linen. Solomon, Moshe, the Persuader and the Engineer lowered the package gently into the ground with hemp ropes. The two Enclave women tore at their hair wailed in grief much to Naomh's anxiety. He cringed, in case Singh's people heard them. Then, their equally loud Rabbi began to chant in the ancient Semitic language of the Enclave. The bonded crew of RUTH held hands tightly during the his prayers from the Kaddish. This made the Guide privately utter.

"They were prepared for death at any time."

The Anschluss Spy privately ridiculed this open and outpouring display of grief as much as they despised the religious ritual.

"Weaklings."

But then this hard-hearted person believed.

"When this mission is completed, immortality will be mine and death among the chosen few will only be a memory. For us, there was never a ceremony like this and soon there will never be a need for one. If one of the LYUBINITE perishes, it is presumed that this individual is not worthy of participating in the great return. For simple logic tells that they have not brought this event about. So, they are smoked as failures with little pomp."

On the other hand, the three parts Mescal/Amulet always wondered about these Hybrids need for physical contact outside the mating ritual. Companionship and close proximity was not enough; their creations constantly needed this touching. It had always intrigued its Alien race. The Patriarchi Celtair had mentioned to him once.

"It is because they do not have the meld of the mind-voice and this is their way of cementing bonds."

The Hybrid intercessor with the Great Mathematician continued with the closing words.

"The spirit has left the tabernacle."

Naomh fervently hoped there was none of Singh's people nearby.

"Between the women's wailing and the Rabbi's booming voice, the Cannibals must surely hear us?"

When the ceremony had concluded, the hole in the melted earth was re-filled until it was level with the surface of the original ground. Solomon, Moshe and the Persuader had done the digging throughout the sodden weather. The heavy stone marker was placed on top of the grave in a horizontal position with the writing facing the heavens. Then each person from the tribes picked up a small pebble, kissed it and laid it on the flat stone as they paused for a few moments to silently voice words of regret and sadness. Miriam with tears still evident asked the Anschluss members of the squad to do the same. They did and even the Mute complied with their comrade's request, death was his familiar and constant companion. The ceremony had touched some of them to the core of their being. Especially, the Engineer. Solomon produced a small plant cutting of a Cyprus tree and reverently planted it alongside Haim's grave. Out loud, the Rabbi said.

"This is a piece of our homeland. May it flourish out here far away from the land of Zion."

Then Miriam started weeping out loud again. With tears in her eyes the Enclave woman appeared inconsolable; she told her lover her concerns.

"Those Human carrion eaters will locate the grave and dig up Haim's body and desecrate it and there is nothing we can do about it."

Something about the ceremony must have touched the uncompleted Mescal, for it told Naomh.

"The technology that created my form can conceal the dead man's grave with a smaller and simpler device akin to the TORT-CAM."

When its host explained this to Miriam and her people, they were overjoyed. The Lenses went to get it from the LAB-CELL. While he was doing this, the continuing crackling rain grew heavier and began to obscure the immediate landscape around them. In seconds, the visibility went down to a few metres. With nothing but mist in their vicinity, it seemed that they must have travelled with Haim to the next realm. The Rabbi had ceased his chanting. In a trembling husky voice, the Engineer asked.

"Was that his soul you were performing that rite for?"

Tears still glinting in his liquid brown eyes, the Rabbi replied.

"Haim has gone to Heaven. If our sister Shoshanna has also perished then he is now with her. He will no longer feel the pain and the want of this World. He will be with God forever as it was promised in our holy book."

The simple ceremony appeared to affect the Engineer more than anyone. He felt that the strange religion of the Enclave was akin to his own. The Spy among their ranks was extremely sceptical and dismissive at the ritual. That person privately believed that Haim had just become wormfood, but had taken part in the absurd funeral so as not to arouse any suspicions. Turai Haim Golan had died at thirty years of age and was buried far away from his beloved mountains that he was named after. Then an abashed group which included, the Guide, the Engineer, the Clerk, the Lenses and the Persuader told the others.

"The name we gave him did not mean the driver of a Mag-Lev; it's what we call a big nose."

A tearful Beersheba smiled briefly.

"Haim knew what its meaning was all the time and he just played along with you." Suddenly shouts of outrage cut through the gloom and the mourners heard an army of raised bickering voices carried on the wind. The acidic downpour impaired their vision and they had no idea where the commotion was originating. But they knew it was directed towards them. It was time to flee, but in which direction. Even Naomh's improved hearing could not pinpoint where their attackers were. What happened next, was later according to the Engineer; a miracle. A hole in the overcast sky allowed a beam of light to strike the stone of Haim's grave and it lit up the mist-shrouded day for a few brief seconds. What the gift from the Heavens revealed caused urgency in the group. Hoards of maddened screaming Cannibals were converging from the western heights towards them. If the light from the grave had not serendipity glanced in that direction, they would have been quickly overrun and overwhelmed. Naomh placed the concealing device on the grave and Haim's final resting place vanished from sight. All of them, then hurriedly gathered their equipment. Naomh shrunk the TORT-CAM and pocked it. As those been chased fled northwards, Miriam glanced back and could not see the vanished marker. She nodded in satisfaction. After they put a lead of a kilometre between them and the howling mob, the order was given to pile into the invisible shield. It would have to be done in a hurry, the horde of man-eaters were only minutes behind them. The Guide halted behind the stump of a shattered tree and placed his rifle on the hollow trunk and aimed in the direction of the fast approaching tribesmen. The Persuader also had his heavy calibre weapon out and had ducked behind a large boulder. The two men laid down a burst of suppressive fire at anything moving towards them. The muscle bound man's head stuck out above the rock and his bare forehead was caressed by the chill wind driven rain as he and the Guide prepared to buy their friends a few seconds to reach the safety of the unseen sphere. The leading bunch of chasers went down as the two men's covering fire decimated their ranks. A bullet took the Guide in the leg and shattered the ankle bone. As he screamed in pain, Cahill stumbled back to the two men who were laying down covering fire and roared above the noise of the withering gunfire.

"What are you doing?"

"Tell Naomh to find some covering before he activates the Dobber. The rain will reveal its shape." Grimaced the Guide.

"Shit we forgot about that."

A minute later, their red haired comrade returned, ducking the incoming fire.

"We have found a small cliff overhang that is out of the weather, come on lets go, we will be safe there."

The Persuader fired another burst and three shadows went down.

Relieved, the two men who were buying time ceased their fire. However, the other side did not. The big man carried his wounded comrade and followed Cahill. Inside the dim light of the cave, Naomh had already thrown the marble sized TORT-CAM on the earthen floor. Away from the bright glare of light at the overhang's entrance, it expanded and revealed itself instantly and had vanished just as quick. Cahill, the Guide and the Persuader rushed into the darkness and revealed the whereabouts of the invisible shield by pressing on their wristbands. The Clerk called from the safety of the invisible haven and the three men who had been behind them quickly entered its assured refuge. Greta had been manning the rapid firing Beni at the juncture between two realities. The concealing device was shut down and it shrunk. Its floating colours abruptly vanished from view. They were safe once again in their red, orange and yellow World. There were howls of outrage from their pursuers as the maddened Cannibals surrounded the cleft in the rock and found nothing. The chasers had been fully sure that their quarry lay underneath it. Three tribesmen entered the darkened clef and one sprayed bullets into its unseen confines. Amazingly some of the projectiles ricocheted off the invisible shield and careened into the firers two companions. They died instantly and he fled out of the cave like a bat out of hell. Improvised explosive devices were hurled inside the opening and balls of black smoke issuing from the entrance testified that there would be no resistance. So their shock at discovering an empty space once again was palpable. Searches were carried out for bolt-holes, but this too proved fruitless. One of the unaware tribesmen's feet was only a centimetre away from them. Inside the invisible bubble of viscosity, those been pursued were infinitely more safe that a babe in a mother's womb. The future parent's soft skin could easily be penetrated, unlike the impenetrable layer of the TORT-CAM. The enraged mob left the cave and resumed the chase. After a few hours of futile pursuit and howls of outrage, frustration and bafflement, the protagonist host gave up the hunt and went back to their hidden settlement, where the fight for Singh's vacant leadership would begin in earnest. As was now the norm, once inside the impenetrable shield, the questors always proved to be elusive to their pursuers. The wounded Guide was rushed into the LAB-CELL and healed in minutes. The hunted passed the remainder of the night tucked in the bosom of the Alien device and by mutual agreement stayed put until the dawn of the next day broke. The first of them to venture out that morning was greeted with a fine mist, the type that irritates the person with the eternal question.

"Will it stay like that for the rest of the day or would it just rain heavier and get it over with?"

It did make them all agree to return to the shelter of their haven and take breakfast. All were amazed at their hunger and the fare was consumed rapidly with little conversation. After the hastily prepared meal was over,

Miriam took her partner aside and told him

"Myself and my friends are really grateful for you disguising Haim's final resting-place."

He replied.

"It was the least that I could do."

Then she left out a sob and held her lover tightly. Through her anguish, she pleaded.

"My love; I always thought that I was a more than capable Serene, but I have already lost two of my old friends and maybe one of my new friends. I think that this quest is beyond me. You know that the Rabbi said that we were already prepared to die in our Tank, but now I think that was all bravado. None of us really expected to die, other crews yes, but not us."

As Naomh comforted her, he replied.

"Hush my love. Nobody expects to die. If anyone has failed in keeping our friends alive, it is me. After all it is my quest. We knew that it wasn't going to be easy and some of us might not make it. There was nothing that we could have done to save Shoshanna and Haim. And let's hope that the Prof really did just leave us."

Wiping her tears, Miriam said.

"You are right my love. We are soldiers and death is an occupational hazard. But it is still hard to lose my friends."

"I know."

He held her tighter and hoped to God that he would not lose her. That was the one thing that would finish him and he had no wish to discover what sort of person he would become if that unthinkable event happened. But now they were now only fourteen strong. Naomh did the calculations.

As far as I know, two are dead and one has fled. I have three segments of the APOCRYPHA'I, but I have also lost three good friends in gaining those pieces. I fervently hope that I will not keep losing those that I love and respect at that ratio."

Unknown to all, but on behalf of one of the searchers; three days later the LYUBINITES had gotten them revenge for Haim's death. It was not done for some attachment to the Enclave man, but to remove the stain of the slain PREVENTIVE operative. That was an indignation that the Anschluss elite would not suffer lightly. The covert agent went out alone on the excuse of scouting and away from the others and contacted the Chairman with the approximate co-ordinates of the tribesmen's village. The mole had estimated its distance from the time it had taken for the chase to begin. The Spy had also seen the expectancy of attack in the eyes of Singh's people and guessed that their village was very near. Within minutes of the long distance conversation, the revenge strike was initiated. Less than two hours later, back in the Cannibal village, there was bitter disappointment at the way things turned out. But at least the eaters of Human flesh had the remains of their comrades who had been slain by

Naomh's company and the business of selecting a new leader would begin. This always sparked off a good fight. The younger villagers eagerly looked forward to it as Singh had ruled for thirty-five years, ever since he had bush-whacked the previous Headsman. Besides, they had not witnessed such a free for all during their hard and short lifetimes. Many were disgruntled that the headman's corpse could not be found as Singh had been a mighty leader. For the eaters of Human meat firmly believed that if they consumed the flesh of a person, then they would ingest that person's soul and thus the craft that person had when they were still among the living. The Cannibals grisly feast was interrupted by a flying disc that materialised above them in the smoke filled air. Butchered bodies were left turning on spits, choice cuts were abandoned on chopping boards. The villagers had seen these flying objects before. The sleek silver craft was welcomed with broad smiles of filed and metal teeth as it usually showered them with food; medicines and supplies of cover and warm clothing. These were sporadic gifts from the government of the south who still were plagued with guilty consciousness of the north's devastation and this was a way of easing their collective guilt. Many of the man-eaters were still crunching bones and chewing Human gristle as the plane hovered silently above. But the Cannibals should have been more careful, because this flying craft was very different. It was infinitely more advanced, bore different markings and it had flown a long way at five times the speed of sound. Instead of hiding, the villagers gathered around out in the open to fight for the bonanza that was about to float down from the sky. Those with keen eyesight saw its silver doors open and a large metal container fall from it. The assembled throng was puzzled as no parachute opened. A wizened elder spoke above the hush.

"Surely whatever is in the metal casket will be smashed to smithereens?"

However, their collective bafflement lasted an instant. For the second time in a millennium, the Blasted Lands were rocked by a nuclear detonation, though this explosion of one mega ton was far less than the previous ones. It mattered little to Singh's people. For the entire village, its occupants and twenty square kilometres of land were obliterated and vaporised in a flash of blinding light. Far away in laboratories around the World, seismic recorders registered the blast, but this inconsequential area was known for strong tremors, so the data was just filed away only to be retrieved as a curiosity. Such was the punishment for killing one of the Anschluss inner circle. Out of harm's way, it was the Clerk's turn at sentry duty and he went over to the TORT-CAM'S viewer to replace Beersheba. He rubbed her head as he asked her.

"Was there anything unusual during your watch?"

"Now that you ask. Yes. There was a blinding flash to the south and a deep rumbling, but whatever it was; it did not affect anything near us."

As he relieved her, the Enclave woman gave him a hug and a peck on the lips and she went to get some rest. The Clerk settled in to his watch and was greeted with a flat vista that led to a line of bushes. Mesmerised, the replacement sentry gazed intently at the cluster of static plants. A slight breeze picked up the thermals and suddenly all the foliage seemed alive. The plants swaying in the wind grew more frantic as the gusts increased and in a moment of recall, they appeared threatening to the observer. The increased jerking of the plants mimicked automation. The Clerk left out a howl of terror and turned off the viewer. He fled to the middle of the three coloured sphere and sat there quivering. Greta left out a snort of derision; she still did not believe his testimony about the killer plant. But Beersheba went over and put her arms around him. She held him tight and patted his hand as she had now lost two friends and the brown woman needed holding just as much as the Clerk. It took the former bureaucrat nearly two weeks to overcome his phobia and fear. Late in the afternoon, they agreed to venture on, but after a short trek, the fine mist cooled and turned into a powdery snow. This put paid to any kind of travel as their footprints would reveal to any of the deceased Singh's people the direction they were travelling in and make it simple to track them. The Spy could not reveal that these precautions were now unnecessary, as their pursuers were no more. The falling snow also had another drawback. To keep the TORT-CAM from been revealed like their footprints, they had to keep the invisible barrier covered in snow. So if any of them ventured out, they would have to pass through the veil of icy wetness and the wintry covering had to be dug away. When whoever went outside re-entered, it would have to be packed up again. So it was decided that none of them would leave the haven until it was time to move on. The plunging snow increased in intensity from the heavens and covered the bleak nakedness of the ruined forest as if in a futile attempt to secure the trees modesty. It was briefly successful and each branch stump was soon outfitted in a pristine white. But the weight of the falling snow on the suffering wood soon caused the nakedness to reappear again and restart the cycle as long as the snow fell. The grounded Questors soon got bored with the unchanging outside and locked it away for another day; the internal three hued space was much more preferable to the outside white blanket. Three days, the gang remained inside the TORT-CAM, as there was no respite from the snow. Some felt guilty, others remorse when they looked at the empty spaces where Haim and Shoshana used to lie. There was no sadness for the Prof; he had made his own choice. But once again the uncompleted APOCRYPHA'I was working away in the background of their emotions and dissipating their mostly collective grief into the recesses of acceptability. What had started off as a residual loyalty to its purpose was now an overwhelming compulsion, but some still had over-riding issues that would come to the fore. The Mute had problems of his own; the enforced inactivity niggled at his core. If there was no movement soon, he might kill again and if he did, the murderer knew that it would be all over for him. The twisted man was under no illusions of surviving if he killed one of them; he could flee, but to where. But Illeau was like a drug addict looking for a fix and the urge was getting stronger with every passing day and to hell with the consequences. But to his immense relief, it was judged safe to move on the next day.

Over a hundred and fifty kilometres behind them, a similar type of killer to the Mute hunkered down in the chilled ruins of a burnt out building. He had read the physical signs of the Human flesh eater's demise and was aware that two had escaped. Back in the Arabian Desert, he had been caught in unusual shadows of indecision. In desperation, he pleaded to his God.

"I cannot find them. They leave no trail."

Zebulan sensed the technology of his race about his servant.

"Show me what you have found."

The contrite disciple held the globe up high. His Deity knew at once what it was and explained.

"It is a bonded globe. It is connected to another; you can use that to find them."

His joy was immense; he would not fail his God. The next day Styarz had passed the village of the man-eaters; he had avoided their patrols easily. Surprisingly, the deadly radiation of the blasted lands had no effect on the feline/Hybrid mix. As the Grand master loped on, he saw the blinding flash that obliterated the village; it caused him to reconsider those he hunted yet again. He himself had just been out of the localised danger zone.

"My targets must have some powerful friends. Still, they do the Planet a justice; there is no place for scum such as them."

Again, because of the invisible shield, he had not been surprised at the inevitable outcome. Those that he pursued had overcome adversity, they had enraged another massive force and this time they wiped them from the face of the Winged God's earth. He was beginning to grudgingly respect them, but they still had to die.

"They are enemies of my God. For that there can be no forgiveness."

The Knight rose and continued the chase. Ahead of him, the falling snow ceased to decorate the landscape where the TORT-CAM lay hidden, so the seekers of the APOCRYPHA'I decided to move on. They packed away the translucent defence, donned their protective gear and struck out in the direction that Naomh was been drawn towards. It was perpendicular to the route that Singh had been taking them before his attempt at double crossing them. As the crew headed in that direction, there was a heated debate about that.

"We know Singh was a back stabbing bastard, but how do we know he

was taking us in the wrong direction." The Guide questioned after Naomh advised them of the route they were going. Most of the others agreed with the well-travelled man, nodding their heads in assent.

"*That man-eating scum was definitely taking us the wrong way.*" Insisted their leader.

"*Of course, that foul animal was leading us astray.*" Miriam backed up her lover.

"*I agree with Naomh and Miriam. He was taking us towards his tribe.*" Added Greta and if she did, then so did Cahill.

"*But, it still might have been in the same direction.*" Maintained the Guide.

"*Maybe we should go back to his friends and politely ask them for the proper directions to the Mountain Kingdom.* Challenged Naomh sarcastically to those who disagreed with him.

That put an end to that debate. They travelled over the flat crackling landscape for two weeks, all of the company sorely missing the vehicle. No matter how absurd, it had looked, it was way better than walking. But out here in the Blasted Lands, it would have been useless, as there were no roads where the determined trekkers were making their way. The lie of the land seemed to be steadily gaining in altitude and getting slightly healthier. Their leader came to decision.

"*No one is allowed to use the comfort of the TORT-CAM; every eye and gun is needed in these harsh and unforgiving lands. There might be similar tribes to Singh's out here in these devastated places and some might even be more desperate.*"

Eventually, the fourteen came to an enormous rift that stretched away in either direction as far as the eye could see. The Engineer took out a pair of enhanced oblong viewing globes. After studying both directions, he concluded.

"*It looks like the ravine goes on for many a kilometre in either direction. The only way across is by a flimsy bridge, about two clicks south.*"

The group made their way to the only crossing.

"*Cross this, you must be joking.*" Mouthed the Clerk.

A rickety rope bridge lay before them. It was in a dire state of repair and it could not possibly hold anyone's weight. Moshe volunteered to cross first; the Persuader followed him. The big man said logically.

"*If it can support me, then it will be easy for the rest of you.*"

He looked at his sibling for conformation and the other nodded his assent. The Clerk was privately puzzled.

"*It is strange that he would let the big man risk himself so?*"

Still, the less brighter man word's made sense to the others as they hedged their bets. The Engineer knelt down beside the precipice and fumbled at the Velcro of his backpack as the two volunteers put their feet tentatively on the wooden boards of the frail structure. There was a slight gasp of relief from Moshe as the first wooden board held. The two men edged out slowly and reached half way across the chasm without any mishap. Their friends on solid ground exhaled sharply at every step. Suddenly, when the two men were nearly half way across, the bridge creaked and swayed alarmingly. The untreated timber lath that Moshe was standing on immediately gave way and with a yell, the Enclave man went through the bridge floor with a loud curse. He was saved from certain death as the Persuader had grabbed his hand. Moshe clung on to the strong man's vice like grip while frantically shouting.

"For God's sake don't let me go, pull me up."

But there was another loud snap of timber as the two men's combined weight sent them crashing through the bridge and they plummeted to their doom. The others screamed in shock, but the Engineer flung something towards the falling duo. A blur of ethereal light sped towards the flailing men. It coalesced into something solid and formed a steady platform that glided under them. The flailing men became stuck to it like iron filings to a magnet. Their two comrades were saved! The gliding objects of light brought the two-shaken men to the other side of the natural gash in the landscape. Everybody, except the Lenses looked at the Engineer in stupefied awe. The latter was standing with another small globe in his hands and the others guessed rightly that he had been controlling the object that had saved his brother and Moshe.

"Just something I was keeping for the proper occasion." Nonchalantly replied the operator.

"Well, why did you not use it before?" Demanded an aggrieved Cahill.

"The opportunity never came up and I wasn't a hundred per cent sure it would work."

"You're taking the piss, right?"

"Yes." Answered the Engineer, but his eyes betrayed his relief.

He produced more of the spheres and told the others.

"Come, let's follow them across."

The crew were well used to the surprises of the LAB-CELL by now and stood on them without any hesitation. Glued to the objects, the recovered questors surfed effortlessly across the gorge. Of course some did not look down while others kept their eyes closed the whole way across. At the other side, they were amazed at how easy; it had been to cross such an impassable obstacle. On the other side, the Lenses spoke.

"We call them, "Skimmers"."

"Magic Carpets, man." Said the Guide.

"That's a stupid name. Where did you get that from?" Asked the technical driven Engineer.

"Never mind." Replied the exasperated pony tailed man.

The well-read Rabbi grasped his shoulder and said.

"I have read the story and know what you are talking about."

A few days later the questors arrived at the vertical escarpment of the shattered Himalayas. This part of the mountain range had been shaped by more than nature; man's destructive energy had a significant hand in its present appearance. Aeons of geological layers were exposed like a laired cake. Each person who stood in front of the sheer magnitude of the vertical escarpment, halted in awe and frustration. The seekers had come up against the preverbal brick wall, except that it was here physically in front of them and right in their face. Nobody had a clue how to scale this immense barrier. It made the high walls of the Enclave look like a miniature obstacle of a modelled city. Nature had taken hundreds of millions of years to form the massive snow topped peaks in the thin altitude as the Indian tectonic plate shoved against the Eurasian plate. But in an instant of Human madness, the beauty of nature had been scared forever. The biggest waterfalls on the Planet flowed over its unnatural ledges, far higher than the natural one that had enchanted them back on the mountains to the south. As the gargantuan flows of water cascaded over a drop of a kilometre, there was nothing majestic about them. The flowing water fell down like pus oozing from a blister, the drop was so high that vast sprays of water at the bottom formed into flimsily froth and floated in the strong wind like the bubbles of methane on the ALASTHA'I Home World. The majority of water gathered at the foot of the cliff face and flowed away in a broad scope barely a few millimetres deep. Nine hundred years was not enough time to form a deep river course. This reworking of nature was all lost on the travellers; they had only one concern.

"How are we going to get over that? Singh must have been taking us in the right direction, despite his intended treachery." Admonished, the Guide to Naomh.

His perplexed leader had no answer. The smooth cliff face housed no nests or dens, but the ground beneath their feet was stained with bird droppings and adult carcasses. There were no tell-tale signs of their residency such as twigs, clusters of feathers or dead young that fell from nests, but white streaks of guano hardened on the cliff face. No, they nested somewhere else. Solomon spied them out as he pointed at a bunch of black shapes in the sky.

"See those birds up there; that is the only way up this."

The rest glanced at the flying animals. There was nothing graceful about the bird's flight as each flying speck was expending great energy and effort flying in the irregular wind currents, in order not to be dashed against the cliff face. This was another hazard awaiting here. The wind was funnelled between the two great mountain ranges; the invisible force of nature flowed through the valley, all the time building, until it had reached a crescendo and smashed against the glass face of the Himalayas. It was as if this natural force was trying to reintroduce nature's irregularity on this land that had turned its back on the natural order. The wind howled and screamed at them and buffeted them against the cliff face. It was all they could do, to keep upright. The wind seemed to shriek.

"No mortal should bear witness to this defamation."

The Clerk commented on the bird's appearance, they were all beak and talons.

"God's aren't they the ugliest birds you ever saw."

The rest agreed. But Solomon pointed out.

"They are scavengers, they are designed for life here, looks are not important to them. They live off the birds that are smashed against the cliffs."

"A bit like the Snake charmer and Singh then. Ugly bastards, but suited to the life out here."

"Exactly."

"But none of this explains on how we are to get up there." Interjected the practical Greta.

Then the Engineer and the Lenses laughed outrageously.

"I told you, they would come in useful at some stage. It looks like we will be needing them again." The Engineer said to the oddly eyed man. The practical man from the Madrid Contrib saw an obstacle as a challenge and this cliff barrier was the biggest physical impediment, he had ever faced.

"I think now is that time you were waiting for, but are you sure they will help us now. They might not climb to that altitude." Said the Lenses, continuing their private conspiracy.

The other party reached into his backpack and emerged with five of the strange spheres of light that had saved Moshe and the Persuader and allowed the rest of them to cross the ravine.

"These Skimmers will get us up there." Emphatically asserted the man from the Madrid Contrib.

"Think of them as far sleeker and superior versions of the hover thrusters back in the docklands of the Anschluss."

The excited man placed them on the hard grey stony ground that had been shaped by Atomic detonation and not scraped away by ice and water. He activated them with the use of another sphere and the light shells merged in a fluid viscosity, coalescing into a ten metre circular and solid block of dense light. He advised them.

"Put our gear and yourselves on the round platform."

The others complied and their boots clanked with a firmness that spoke of the magnetic properties of this Platform of Light. The Engineer activated his globe and the large creation with its occupants began to rise slowly and steadily upwards. The wind gave out an incensed outcry; it had little effect on the vertical travellers. Steadfastly upwards, they rose and the higher they got; the brighter the Sun reflected off the glassy surface of the cliff edge. Cahill shouted at the rising group.

"Put on your eye protection, the brightness could blind us."

The others did as he said and all eyes were blocked by mirrored discs. Seven minutes later, they were at the top. As the mesmerised flyers dismounted the Platform of Light at the escarpment's summit, the Engineer re-activated the globe and the singular object of light buzzed off and separated into individual spheres. He packed them away. The effortless climbers now faced a long bleak stony plateau. Nature had still not worked out an ecological strategy for this newly formed landscape. The barren setting stretched on and ended in a line of even higher mountains, but their instruments told them, that it was clean at least. It was a weird, wonderful and most importantly, a healthy landscape which stretched out in front of them. The ground no longer hummed and cracked. Solomon pointed to the distant peaks and spoke in awe.

"The roof of the World must be up there somewhere. There could be no place higher in God's creation."

"Our own Golan looks like tiny sand dunes compared to these." Voiced Beersheba.

The three parts Mescal/Amulet privately confirmed Solomon's assumptions to Naomh that these indeed were the tallest of mountain ranges. But the Alien presence knew that the mountains back on CRYSTALIOS near the holy city of Zedenia were five times as high. He sighed as he amended.

"The former city, for now it is no more, but the heights are still there."

As the Engineer de-activated the Platform of Light, the APOCRYPHA'I directed its bearer to the LAB-CELL and explained in its metallic timbre.

"These high altitudes could be lethal to all of you. All of you come from relatively low lying areas, especially those of you from the Anschluss. Most of the heights of the Anschluss and the Enclave have been levelled over the centuries and these elevations will take a severe toll on your health. All of you could perish without even been aware of it. Each one of you needs to augment the pills that you have taken against the radiation of the lower lands."

He gave the Rabbi directions for dispensing pills to combat the altitudes effects and regulate their physical well-being. Everybody took one after the hazards were explained; even Greta. Their leader took a deep breath and said to the gathered group.

"Let's go."

Before the group moved on, all of them looked back to the west, the sky was a wash of reds from some celestial impressionist palette, it was further enhanced as the horizon became aflame with incessant lightening.

"Come, a storm approaches. Let's get away from the edge before it hits us." Said Solomon with a worried glance at the western sky.

With the adrenaline induced pills working their magic, the little group moved off with a swagger and proceeded up the high roads. They did not get far, it looked like their journey was going to be impeded again. At a place where these highlands looked the same, where wastes of rock and scrub that had been chiselled by natural forces formed a natural bump on the surface, the travellers came across a bizarre make shift structure. It was half buried in the mound, a montage of tin and sandbags, a sorry looking place from where even more sorrier armed figures emerged. The watchers had been observing the group's progress for a while now. Moshe recognised it for what it was. It was a border post. A flag based on two separate pennants, flown above each other fluttered defiantly in the strong mountain wind. Through his viewing monocle, Solomon described it.

"It has two pictures on it, something that looks like a white Sun or star and a horizontal crescent moon like on the Prophets banners. The two motifs appear against a red background and it is all surrounded by a blue border."

He finished his description and Cahill asked the question that was on everybody's mind.

"Do these people belong to the nations of the Prophet?"

The Rabbi replied.

"Even though there are Nations of the Prophet in this part of Asia, these people are not among the faithful".

"Then we can relax."

"I don't know about that. There is an armed man coming towards us."

As Miriam pointed that out, some of them fingered concealed weapons and waited for the approaching man to make his intensions known. Pem Dorjee, the solider of the government outpost was amazed that anyone had come from that direction. The man who lived under the tallest pinnacles on Earth was certain that nobody could have scaled the vertical cliff face, even with specialised climbing gear and this lot appeared to have none. He made the only assumption possible; he would never believe the real method of their ascent.

"They were probably dropped by helicopter and thought that it would be spectacular to slip into the country by the back door. They have to be here for the Tournament? Only someone that daring would make such an effort."

He went to meet these strangers who were covered by his men in the post.

"We can make a good impression too."

Naomh and his crew saw the solider wave and as had become the norm, he would speak. Still, he gestured for the others to fan out. Greta and Cahill moved to the right flank and the Engineer and his brother moved to the left, the rest stayed in the rear. The man did not appear to be threatening; his Chinese manufactured Burp gun was slung over his back and his green military uniform was in a poor state of repair. The approaching soldier had a slim mike that covered his mouth. Naomh surmised.

"Vocal communication seems to be the lot of military types."

The man under his scrutiny raised his mike up.

"Welcome, are you here for the Tournament." Politely enquired the slant eyed solider with the long drooping moustache.

"Of course." Answered Naomh taking the cue, not knowing what the hell a Tournament was, but after Singh's people, he was glad that he understood the words. He no idea that the language he spoke in was called Nepali until the moment he uttered those words. As the bearer of the APOCRYPHA'I conversed with the armed man, the Guide fished into his pack and brought out four bottles of whiskey and a couple of packs of Cigs and offered them to the solider. The customs guard eyes brightened as nobody ever crossed through their post. In fact as far as he knew these people were probably the first in a long time. The man from the highlands had been here six months and had never seen anybody come from that direction, nor had any of his predecessors. Bribes were very few and far between for any custom post in the Kingdom and they were non-existent in this one.

"Up to now, that is." Muttered the delighted receiver to himself.

Sergeant Dorjee invited them to take shelter from the bitter cold and the creeping storm. The travellers agreed and they came out of the weather. There were ten men manning the post. If any of the soldiers decided that these border crossers were easy pickings and had other goods to be taken, then the fact that some of these travellers were entering the Tournament talked them out of any rash decisions. The commander had already judged them.

"Besides, they looked well-armed in any case; even though I do not recognise the make of their weapons."

The questor's and border guards spent that morning huddled over a gas stove and shared the whiskey which one of the soldiers put into a strong coffee. Other bottles were dished out as the soldiers had eagerly consumed the lot the Guide had given them initially. It was soon discovered that some of Pen Dorjee's men spoke Anschluss and a few separate conversations broke out. Naomh had to intervene in each one. The Lenses kept his eye patch on, but his strange eyes would not have disturbed the soldiers much, for many peculiar men/women entered the Tournament. As the two companies relaxed, one of the slant-eyed men brought out a bizarre object of pipes and buttons. It was a musical instrument. Before he played, he explained.

"This is a tune about the high altitude meadows and the terraced hillsides below them."

He began to play it and the other soldiers clapped and broke into song.

One jolly soul among them that had consumed a good deal of the strong liqueur stood up and danced what could only be described as a local jig. When the good-humoured highlanders finished, most of their guests applauded the strange rhythm. One of the singers, Girija Prasad Koriala asked with a broad smile on his face.

"Do you have a tune from your country?"

The Guide produced a guitar from his backpack and began playing.

"I've never seen him with that before." Said the Clerk.

Moshe took out a mouth organ from one of his packs and joined in. The Guide sang in a soft drool, which did not do justice to his playing. Then Beersheba caught up in the mood began to sing, her voice was wonderful and haunting. The rest of the crew joined in, all except Greta and the Mute; she did not like displays of abandonment and he had no interest in music, to him it was just awful noise. The pious Engineer preferred songs that gave praise to his God, but he added his tenor voice. The night passed away in good company and most of the guests were surprised to see the rising dawn. The approach of day was the signal for the questors to depart and some among them regretfully said their goodbyes. The weather was still bad, so the soldier's bid their guests stay until it broke. But, the constant movers had other ideas.

"We have to go, we have an appointment." Announced Naomh.

"The Tournament."

"Of course." Lied the receiver of the question.

"We understand. Good look and I hope you do well."

He pointed to a battered video unit and added.

"We will watch out for you on that. You will be victorious."

Privately, Pen Doorjee did not think so as he told one of his men.

"These strangers were mostly very nice people, but they lack the killer mentality needed to survive the Tournament. Still, I will cheer on whichever one it is on our battered video unit."

The other border post solider believed.

"The giant looks naïve, so it must be the small man with the strange eye patch."

"You could be right? Appearances can be deceptive and that is certainly true when it involves the Tournament."

As the fourteen of them parted company with the border guards, the Clerk fished out more liqueurs and Cigs and handed it to the soldiers. Pem Dorjee and his platoon were really grateful, as it would make some of the long nights of their unenviable watch more bearable. Been from a tribe of honey gatherers, the officer took out a slab of the amber nectar and handed it to the Clerk. It had been his last luxury, but thanks to the stranger's gifts, he was able to part with it. The company was given directions to the city in the clouds, where the Tournament was to be held. The soldiers called the place; Kathmandu. The border post was soon left behind and travellers began to ascend higher up on the rooftop of the World. Here they began to encounter a different landscape of tree lined gorges, exposed rock and thin winding roads. Although, they were getting higher, it did not appear that the land was getting bleaker; in fact the opposite was occurring. After a short time, the border post at the edge of the World was only a memory. Conversing while they were moving was commonplace and Moshe said to the others.

"Have you noticed that all the armed forces we have encountered since we left the Enclave have no female soldiers. Are the Enclave and the Anschluss the only ones?"

The Guide answered his question.

"No. On my travels through the African Continent, there are many female and even child soldiers."

"Children. You are kidding us. Right." Said a shocked Cahill.

The well-travelled man shook his head sadly.

"No, I'm not. Some of these fighters are as young as eight. The military commanders of these rag tag militias can get these children to do things and commit horrible atrocities that most adults would not do. I told you dude that there is one fucked up World out there."

"Well if we ever come across these children and they are hostile, we will eliminate them." Said an ever practical Greta.

"That's for sure; I'm not having my ass shot off by some kid." Concluded the Clerk.

This silenced the conversation as all of them contemplated such a situation and how they would react if it ever came up. The sinister Mute reappraised his proscription on killing children.

"Those battle hardened and murderous youths might be worth the effort."

Their small band was struggling with their heavy backpacks down a narrow road as travelling light would arouse suspicions. Several vehicles had gone by, but none stopped. Then a large truck passed them and the air was filled with an obnoxious waft.

"What the hell is that horrible smell?" Asked the Clerk.

The two brothers knew having spent most of their lives in the Agriculture Sector.

"That truck was full of pigs." Said the big man.

"No wonder we are forbidden to eat them." Said the Rabbi, still holding his nose with two fingers.

"Those filthy animals must taste horrible" Agreed Solomon.

"You don't know what you are missing." Said Cahill.

The Anschluss members disagreed with their Enclave friends and an argument begun. The slagging match only ended when a vehicle with many glass windows passed by. The transport contrivance was fully laden with people. The odd looking piece of machinery halted and the driver got out. He went over to the exhausted group and spoke to them.

"What's he saying?" Asked the Clerk of the only one of them that could understand him.

"He said that this is his "Bus." and for a price he can take us where we want to go." Answered Naomh.

"This must be something like the Autobus back home." Said Beersheba.

"Well what are we waiting for?" Demanded the Clerk.

In a rush, he threw his baggage on to the Bus. The driver gave a gapped gold toothed smile as the blonde man gave him a bargaining advantage. A practical Miriam told her lover.

"Ask him how much it was to Kathmandu? That is where we need to go."

He did as she requested and the driver told him the price. Naomh looked perplexed. As he negotiated with the man, the other kept shaking his head. Miriam wanted to know.

"What's the matter?"

"He wants the fee in paper money that is unique to this land." Answered their mediator.

"Well, we are sick of trekking, so give him what he wants." Said the Clerk as he made himself comfortable on the Bus.

"We don't have any of that." Said the Lenses.

Naomh continued haggling with the driver, he offered him gold and then gems, but the man shook his head each time. Up close, the Engineer admired the vehicle with Moshe. It had a bulbous metal front and a high bonnet. Low down it had six enormous head lights and higher up, it possessed two huge mirrors that projected out from the front like two ears. These allowed the driver a rear view. A large window with long black plastic and rubber wipers finished off the front of the vehicle's appearance. The Engineer thought that the front gave the vehicle an individual appearance, much like a person. A mountain of dirt and dust obscured whatever colour it had been originally. But the oddest feature of the bizarre vehicle was its wheels. These typical of antiquated locomotion were huge gas filled inflated rubber rings that totally concealed the bottom of the Bus and came up above the height of the roof. A curved roof finished at a door in its rear. The bargaining with the driver was going nowhere and an increasing irritated Naomh gave the Clerk an exasperated look as the blonde man had already made himself at home on the motorised vehicle. Then Beersheba noted something about the driver's smile and whispered her discovery to their leader. Her pleased leader suddenly kissed her on the cheek. He called the Clerk to come over to them, but the comfortable man refused thinking that he was about to lose his easy ride. The blonde man was dragged ceremoniously off the vehicle by the Persuader who had obeyed Naomh's command. He was told about the Enclave woman's suggestion and he shrugged his shoulders as he fished into his pockets. He came out with two miniature balls of platinum. The driver nodded in delight and snatched them from the Clerk; it was an immense fortune to him. He then did the usual thing for this part of the World; he bit into them and grunted in satisfaction. But then the driver did something bizarre. He took out a small device, attached a heavy cable to it from his machine, He activated it and placed the small marbles of metal into it. He closed its lid and the thing glowed white hot. A minute later the thing had cooled sufficiently and the machine spit out four of what could only be described as metal teeth. The driver gathered them up and filled the gaps in his mouth with them. He then picked up the device and gave them a nearly complete metallic smile. The beaming man motioned for them to board his vehicle. Shaking their heads, the fourteen questors got on and they were grateful that there would be no more walking. The gang made their way down a long narrow central aisle and found five rows of unoccupied seats at the rear. Their view outside was blocked by the huge wheels, but a window could be opened and a blind could be pulled down to block the wheels presence. The driver turned the ignition and the vehicle jerked into action. The huge wheels kicked up a massive dust trail as it moved off. The plume of dust was a constant companion of the Bus as it used up dried riverbeds and long unpaved roads as its route. The Lenses noticed immediately that the other passengers used the same hand held screens for communication as the majority of people back in India. Half way through their journey, the Guide whispered to those who were not asleep.

"Everybody on this thing wears their wealth on them. They all have gold teeth and the women are adorned in jewellery of precious metal and stones."

"So why did the driver not take any of these items when they were offered. He could have traded them for the paper money he originally requested." Wondered Moshe.

"I think he knew that we had something more precious on us and he just held out. How, I don't know?" Said the Rabbi.

He was right, the driver of the Bus had his fortune told that morning and the palm reader told the superstitious man.

"You will encounter strangers that have in their possession the one thing that you value most of all."

That was platinum and the now beaming Pen Peinja was absolutely certain that his horoscope had been correct.

At the precise moment of this conversation, Styarz had come to the ravine with the shattered rope-bridge. Taking a grappling hook from his backpack, the Knight tied a wire of a few millimetres circumference around it. The unperturbed Hybrid flung it with a mighty throw across the gap. It landed on the other side and snagged in the ruined supports of the bridge. He pulled it taut and lashed it around one of the wooden posts on his side. He had formed a span of a few millimetres. Leaping on top of it, the Knight ran across the strained wire with a balance and dexterity that would make all trapeze artists look like novices of their trade. At the other side of the gorge, he took out his Anlace and severed the wire from the grappling hook. After putting the hook back into his pack, the Grandmaster continued his chase. A good distance to the east, the slowness of his targets vehicles journey was maddening. It stopped regularly and let off passengers and then the driver would wait to see if he could pick up more. There were glances of impatience exchanged among the band, but it was still better than walking. The Clerk and Beersheba passed the time on the moving vehicle by trading gems and gold for the laminated paper money that was in use in this land. The currency notes were of green, blue, red and brown and were of various denominations. Each note had the image of a regal old man on one side and pictures of the tall mountains on the reverse. Delighted natives were only too eager to exchange their notes at the rate of gold and precious gems that they were getting. The two opportunists had soon amassed a substantial wad of the paper money, funnily enough, the entirely different looking currency was also called Rupee's. After one stop that lasted nearly three hours, the searchers of the APOCRYPHA'I were not so sure that they should stay on the Bus much longer. The final straw came when the passenger vehicle halted at a recent rock-slide. The driver informed his passengers.

"It will take many hours to clear it. I have radioed to the nearest village and they are sending a Bulldozer."

Naomh and his weary comrades got off to relieve themselves and purchase some hot food at a roadside vendor who had been clever enough to set up a temporary shop at this juncture. This seller took the notes off them and handed them back small coins. In between mouthfuls of some type of hot vegetable and meat roll, the Clerk asked.

"What in this forsaken place is a Bulldozer?"

The Enclave members of the group knew along with the Spy and the Guide. So did Naomh as Miriam had told him about those machines back on the Enclave wall. Moshe filled in the bemused Clerk and those others who did not know.

"It is a land clearing machine. I used to drive one before I joined Serene Miriam's crew."

"Don't you mean, after you were promoted?" Said the Rabbi with a twinkle in his eye.

Moshe, Solomon, Miriam and Beersheba laughed at the long bearded man's words. It was a private joke among the survivors of the crew of RUTH. Bulldozers were called sector-recycling automations in the Anschluss and like all of its heavy machinery including agricultural vehicles; they were huge and usually took a crew of twenty to operate them. They were in essence mini mobile factories; the Anschluss always avoided the notion of private transport. While the interrupted travellers were enjoying their repast, a strange shaven headed man dressed in orange garb with a florid face and a petite version of the Guide's ponytail approached them. Everybody's path that he crossed fell to the floor and bowed their heads.

"Who is he?" Asked an unimpressed Greta.

"He must be someone important." Whispered the Rabbi.

The brightly garbed individual introduced himself.

"I'm am a monk and you must come with me."

Some of the abased people looked chagrined that none of them showed the monk the respect that he deserved. The man looked weak and pampered, but his movements betrayed an inner strength. A gut feeling within Naomh urged him to tag along and strangely, for once it was not the three parts Mescal/Amulet. The internal voice urged him.

"Do not follow this man!"

But for once, something deeper within the bearer of the APOCRYPHA'I made him ignore the internal advice. Their new guide led them to a trail that meandered high above the village. Eventually, the climbers arrived at a strange stone and wooded structure that hung on the side of a cliff. Its tightly packed seven stories clung precariously to the mountain edge. A long winding stairs of hand carved worn stone steps formed the threshold between the building and the mountain slope. The steps centre's had belly shaped from the centuries of climbing pilgrims. No two stones had the same indenture. The Lenses began to address every tread out aloud as he put his foot on them, much to the others annoyance. He proceeded upwards towards the crisp air without flagging his count.

"One, two, three."

At the top, the ragged breath of the counter announced.

"Two thousand, five hundred and fifty-four."

Up here, between heaven and earth, they met the Lama. The Holy man was waiting at the top of the flight of steps for them; He was full of decorum and good manners.

"Welcome, honourable guests. My name is Tunee Waewnokyoong. I am the Lama of this humble place."

The Mute for one did not care for him at all; he was aware that the Holy man could see into his soul. The man appeared ancient with long locks of wispy white hair and a huge pointed beard of the same manner. He looked painfully thin under his large scarlet robe, but in reality, his frame was heavily toned. His long-lived eyes betrayed no senility; there was an unknown intelligence lurking behind them.

"Welcome, I have been waiting for you."

The serene man looked only at Naomh.

"Please, come and follow me." Said Tunee Waewnokyoong.

As they did, the Lama showed them around the monastery. Strange figures with haloes of light above shimmering forms adorned the walls of the monastery. Some looked Alien, others appeared Humanlike. Passing the prayer hall, the subdued questors heard the soothing sound of the Monks sutras. But the arrogant Spy in their ranks thought it sounded more like an angry hornet's nest. There was a meal laid out for the guests, it was set for fifteen people, exactly the same number as the Lama and the questors combined. Their contaminant sensors told them that it was safe to eat, but no-one indulged, not even the ever hungry big man among them. As if sensing this, their host reached into the Mute's fare and selected a tasty titbit and ate it. The spread consisted mostly of red rice and chillies. There was no meat much to the Persuader's chagrin; still it was tasty enough. There was water and yak's milk to wash it down but most of them stuck to the water. The sullen Mute had left his food untouched after the Lama had sampled it. After the meal, the strange monk requested a private audience with the bearer of the Alien presence. His companions already had their hackles up and insisted that Naomh should not be alone with the strange man. But their leader disagreed and over ruled them. He was intrigued by the holy man's demeanour. He left the others in the company of a few monks and went with the Lama. The three parts of the Mescal/Amulet was becoming frantic. The Holy man was another of those unexplained anomalies that had cropped up throughout the ages without the knowledge or interference of the ALASTHA'I. This man of reflection had reached the Panna, the third and highest level of Buddhist learning. The Lama brought Naomh to a chamber covered in mosaic circles. The two vastly different men went to the centre of the confusing room and the Lama motioned his guest to sit on its smooth floor. The lord of the monks told him.

"You must relax. There is no threat here."

He did so and suddenly the three parts Mescal/Amulet was banished to the fringes of his awareness. Its host nearly panicked, but the soft voice of the Lama said.

"It is alright. He will return when we are finished. Now I have a question for you. What colour is Heaven?"

An absorbed Naomh thought about it and could not give a certain answer. Although. he was now the cleverest among the questors, he was positive that the Engineer or the Rabbi could have answered this riddle. He responded to the holy man's conundrum.

"I cannot be sure."

"There is one who follows in your footsteps who knows."

He did not understand those words.

"Who does this old man mean; is it one of my companions? The Prof maybe?"

The bearer of the APOCRYPHA'I had no idea that the Lama was referring to Strayz. If the Winged Knight who hunted them was asked the same question, he would have replied emphatically and without hesitation.

"Frosty Blue. For that is the colour of the God's chamber and where the Winged One dwells is surely a reflection of paradise."

The circles around the enclosed space began to move with their own accord, slowly at first, then with a mesmerizing speed. They were entering Samadhi, a state of total collectedness. Some part of Naomh's awareness told him this was impossible, the blocked Alien part, but he accepted it. He floated in a psychedelic trance and entered another reality, one that was filled with winged demons, men encased in shields of light and billions of souls been extinguished and flying towards the source of creation. Naomh saw himself like reflected images in a mirror that entrapped the future and held it for a brief instant. The Lama shared in the vision of the inevitable, for that what it was. These events would come to pass. The old monk smiled ruefully as he gazed upon the harbinger of the World's destruction.

"All the portents were true; here in front of me is the herald of death and the destroyer of all that my order cherishes. How simple it would be for me to crush his windpipe. But this is not his destiny. He will bring a reign of death to the World, the like of which it has never seen before. It will be another mass extinction, but on a scale and speed the Planet has never witnessed in its four billion year old life."

The Lama's order was only there to observe and not to interfere. The wise monk thought.

"I am absolutely certain that if I did attempt to strike this one down, some unseen force would not permit me to do it."

He brought Naomh out of his enforced slumber; he would not remember any of the visions. The glimpse of the future was not for his benefit, but for the Lama's. Again and out of the blue, the Holy man demanded from him.

"What colour is Heaven?"

He had the answer now.

"It is whatever colour you want it to be."

Tunee Waewnokyoong smiled, it appeared that the answer had satisfied him. Naomh talked long into the night with this mystic man from the east. He spoke of his journey here and the enemies that tried to impede them. The monk was aware of all of this and he could have told him about the fate of Singh and his villagers. He could have also told the spirit of the dead Cannibal that in a Cosmos based on circles, what comes round goes round. The mystic man showed him strange things. He could levitate and spirals of energy danced around him. As he witnessed the sparking energy surround the monk, Naomh believed that he now understood the strange murals of people with glowing nimbi around them. But, he was wrong, if he had examined them more closely; the astonished man might have recognised himself and some of his comrades in the images. After, he had passed the storytelling wall, the Alien presence returned and it was now even more disturbed. Something unknown to it had been changed within the Hybrid. It had also got a glimpse of the Lama's mind as it was shut out. It observed the monk's credo and society and it was astounded.

"How could such a violent species achieve this level of existence? This is what Celtair and I strived for during my moments of clarity. A society devoted to learning, contemplation and the mysteries of the Cosmos while still been able to resort to violence if necessary."

As his guests departed the next morning, the Lama knew.

"This visit has signed the death warrant of our order. One day these people will return in different guises and extinguish this place and one of the last lights in the Cosmos will go out.

Naomh did not know it, but that brief encounter and the night spent learning from the Lama would save his life in the near future. He was also puzzled that this devotee of peace had given him a weapon shaped in a five pointed star telling him that he would need it soon.

"What a strange gift from one such as him."

Down below at the vertical escarpment formed from nuclear detonation, Styarz confronted the obstacle that faced him. Once its face was a smooth glassy wall, shaped in the instant of Atomic fusion, but nearly nine hundred years of erosion had carved minuscule cracks in its facade. He knew instinctively that his targets had gone over that vertical obstruction. The Knight of the Winged One just grunted and tested the face for footholds. Satisfied, he began to scale the precipice. Without any fuss, he slowly and inexorably climbed. Toughened fingers that killed or paralysed found purchase and held him with their vice like grip. Half way up the vertical precipice, the storm front slammed into him. The howling wind must have thought that it would be more successful in knocking this one off, than those that had the affront to overcome its obstacle before. The force of nature increased in fury, the higher the mortal climbed, but unperturbed, the stubborn Hybrid ignored it. Up above, Gunta Shalimar sat close to the burning brazier in the border post. He hated the cold and was sure that he was descended from the peoples far to the south.

"This must be the most cursed place in the whole Kingdom? I despise this miserable bone chilling place"

His only highlight during his tour of duty was when the foreigners had given them the spirits and cigs. But he and his companions had consumed the alcohol in a bout of bored gluttony.

"Still, I have a packet of cigs left. I will enjoy them later."

Then, he heard another solider say.

"I don't believe it, there is something else moving from the cliff face."

Their commander took the optical device from his subordinate and made out the approaching shadowy figure.

"By the Buddha's large belly, I have to go out in that again."

Still, he took comfort that this person might have some gifts for them as well. He stepped out into the inclement weather to greet the stranger. At the top of the vertical escarpment, Styarz was breathing heavily, but he was far from exhausted. He shook the small amount of water that clung to his cloak. Taking in his surroundings, straight away, he noticed the lone structure that failed miserably to blend in with the landscape. Pen Dorjee confirmed that it was another stranger coming from the direction of the escarpment.

"By the Robes of the fat Buddha, this place is becoming very busy. Still, I have just smoked my last Cig and hopefully this approaching man would be as generous as the last bunch that had passed this way."

Styarz was about to go around the border post, but it was too late. An armed man was advancing on him. The man was gesturing in a strange tongue. The Winged God's assassin reacted; negotiation was not in his makeup. As the man died, from a thrown blade, a burst of mechanical fire arced in his direction. It came from the isolated structure. He picked up the dead man's Chinese made weapon, a rather out dated piece, the time for stealth was over. Styarz meandered into action and men went down. He had taken a small explosive device from one of the dead guards and threw into the structure. The border guard who was manning the heavy calibre gun heard the clunk of the grenade. He was caught in the flash; he felt the most pleasant sensation of heat, just before he became a smoking husk. Gunta Shalimar would never be cold again and Girija Prasad Koirala would never sing again, unless it was with some heavenly beings. Their cowl wearing killer took out a small pebble sized globe and twisted it. Lights within it began to shimmer like a trapped electrical storm. He placed it on the ground and walked towards the bunker. Behind him, the globe expanded and disintegrated in a bright flash of concentrated Electric Magnetic Pulses. All of the posts recording devices were wiped clean. There would be no evidence of his murder spree. The Knight of the Winged One looked eastward; all within the border post were dead. On investigation, the ruthless killer had discovered the shattered empty alcohol bottles and the blackened cig packets. It confirmed what he already knew.

"My quarry has recently passed this way. That is good because the chase will end up here high upon the roof of the Master's World. I long for its completion and my return to Sanctum, where I will be back among my God and my brothers. I will bring blood that is worthy of him."

Without even a backward glance at his act of destruction, he then loped away on the trail of his Deity's enemies. The wind that lived in these high places howled loudly and he wanted to mimic the primeval sound. Something in his mixed genes bade him so, but his cautious Human part resisted the urge. The determined Styarz increased his pace, for he knew as soon as the gale died down, the rain would come again and a part of his genetic makeup had no love for it. Still, he moved on relentlessly and began to eat up the gap that separated him from his quarry.

XXIV.

THE GOLDEN CITY. 2953 AD.

To those that bore witness to the event, it appeared that the Sun had risen in the west that morning hundreds of years ago. The Mountain Kingdom of twenty-five million souls had been extremely fortunate on the day the nuclear weapons had fallen to earth. The missiles of mass destruction had slammed into the Himalayan Mountain mass and the prevailing winds had blown the dirty radiation clouds westwards and southwards. It seemed that the little poverty stricken Nation with an area of 140,797 sq. km that had always cursed its position at the top of the World was now very fortunate because of exactly that reason of geography. The descendants of the survivors of that fateful day now celebrated that event every five years with a twisted celebration. As the cycle of events came around once again, today was the beginning of the final countdown to the eagerly awaited Tournament. From all across the ancient capital city, listeners heard the sudden fanfare of the huge fifteen hundred-year-old brass trumpets and the equally dated drums that accompanied them. The citizens of the city that lay kilometres above the lowlands and thousands of metres beyond the gorges were filled with the same gusto as the booming instruments and all eyes looked in the direction of the arena. One of the ancient large brass musical pieces had a visible crack that effected melody and it gave life to a bitter note. The harsh tune echoed off the many golden domes of the ancient city that shone brightly in the lofty backdrop and close proximity of its surrounding mountains. Gold, it seemed was an integral part of the cities religion. It had been five years since the city had this non-indifferent sound reverberate around its narrow streets and lanes. It's growing resonance matching the swelling excitement of the Mountain Kingdom's population. The tainted melody came from the arena and this building that held pride of place in the cities heart would be the centre of its inhabitants focus over the next week or so. From any vantage point in the city, colossal holographic projections perched on its conclave roof could be seen in the weeks leading up to the event. These images of warriors and previous champions would remain lit up until the Tournament ended. So overcrowded was the city during the five yearly event that daily life spilled out on to its streets. Countless stalls selling a wide selection of goods vied for customers. Everything was for sale, from food and snacks, to memorabilia depicting fighting scenes and portraits of former champions. The closer one got to the arena, the more the stalls tended to sell items associated with the Tournament. Those lucky enough to afford and secure places in the arena waited in anticipation of upcoming events. The inside of the vast domed arena contained a circular pit that was surrounded by a mezzanine and ten upper balconies. It held a hundred thousand standing souls in a cauldron of fierce passion and a sea of emotional fluctuation. But infinitely more than that would watch the event on video units all over the globe. Then in an instant, the heavy sound of brass and percussion petered off, making the arena silent except for a few bursts of individual isolated voices. The continuous background din of chanting and baying from the excited spectators had ceased like a flow of water cut off when the trumpets had first sounded. The musical announcement had brought a sense of expectation to the crowd. It was standing room only and some of those lucky enough to be in attendance had children perched on their backs. Most of the assembled throng were dressed in traditional colourful hats and woollen clothing, but there was evidence of a few foreigners among the host, different styles of outfits testified to that. Naomh and his crew were amongst these outlanders. They had eventually made their way here. It had just finished raining when they arrived; the latest of the slightly unusual heavy downpours for this time of year had started twelve hours ago. Now, the departing clouds parted to reveal glistening domes, splendid in their golden sheen. The heavy cloudburst had removed the lingering film of dirt and scum that had built up over the last few dry months. It was as if the many golden domes of the city had spruced themselves up for the Questor's arrival. As the searchers took in the sights and sounds and the cultural domination of the fighting contest, the Rabbi wondered, especially after their encounter with the Lama.

"How can such a peaceful people with such a passive religion have come up with an event like the Tournament?"

In the city and on the way here, everybody they met had been eager to tell them about it. Men and old boys had the same glint of anticipation in their eyes when they spoke of it.

After leaving the monastery, a different monk brought the questors back to the scene of the landslide where their previous journey had been halted. Something bugged Naomh and the niggling feeling insisted that the rock-fall had not been an act of nature. To the gang's surprise, the Bus was still there and the requested Bulldozer had just arrived.

"Now that is some coincidence." Thought Naomh.

He asked the driver of the Bus.

"Does the Bulldozer usually take this long to get here?"

The much patient driver used to such occupational hazards nodded.

"These narrow and twisting mountain roads are frequented by avalanches and rockslides. It might have cleared several such obstacles to get to this one."

Huge gasps of laboured effort in the form of water vapour came from funnels in the machine's bonnet. But the sluggishness of the earth moving machines motion belied its efficiency as it effortlessly cleared the rubble obstruction off the road and into the gorge below. Plumes of dust and debris danced all the way to the bottom where it settled to form another part of the landscape, far below and out of sight. Once the larger pieces of rubble had been cleared, the Bus delivered them to the city in the clouds without any other diversion. It took them another day and its passengers arrived just before ten in the morning local time. The date was the 6th of December 2953AD. The city of Kathmandu lay at the northern foot of the Mahabharat mountain range of the Eastern Himalayas. The climbing Sun at this high altitude captured the elegance of the ethereal dance of the ghostly white colour of the swirling fog as it rose from golden domes and less ornate roof tops. This urban setting on the roof of the World was abuzz with the excitement of the forth-coming Tournament. In the thronged bars and eating establishments, the questors found out more about the event. Delighted locals once again told the inquisitive foreigners about the games. Old men boasted that they had the privilege of seeing the best fighters. All explained that they were a five-year occurrence that pitted the competitors against each other in a fight to the death. Haim asked.

"Why would anyone do that? How can these people sit around and gather enjoyment from such a thing."

The Rabbi agreed with him, but the Mute could have given him his answer.

"For the pleasure of watching the light of the soul go out."

"For fame, glory and the prizes that come with winning." Answered a local in accented Anschluss when asked the same question. Though the very idea of fighting for recognition and riches made no sense to these idealists, but some among them privately wondered how they might do in such a Tournament. Solomon was not so inclined.

"I think the idea is abhorrent and I know that if Edward was still with us, he would be equally repulsed."

During the conversation, the three parts Mescal/Amulet astounded Naomh.

"You have to enter the Tournament. It is necessary in order to gain the next part of me."

"You can't be serious?"

But, he knew that the internal voice had no sense of humour when it came to unifying itself.

Its host objected.

"There must be another way. Maybe, we can steal it, the same as we did back in the Sheikh's fortress."

"No. This is the only way."

Eventually, Naomh relented and informed the others. Greta, Cahill, the Engineer and the Persuader offered instead. The Mute could have done it, but he did not like to kill in public and under such scrutiny. But their leader answered them by saying.

"Thanks for the offer, but I am the most skilful fighter here. I will have the best chance of winning this Tournament. "

The traitor among them privately thought.

"That's what you think."

The days wore on and the gang had finally made it to the arena, but not before booking a room in the overcrowded city. It took them considerable time and effort to acquire lodgings and it was only the fact that Naomh mentioned that he was entering the contest that finally secured them a place to stay. The proprietor told them three days later after seeing their inaction.

"Your fighter must go to the arena and register himself for the competition."

The Tournament Dome was an insignificant piece of architecture compared to the enormous stadiums of the Anschluss. The Clerk did a quick calculation and imparted his findings.

"At a guess, it probably holds about fifty thousand seating."

The amount they offered for entrance tickets tempted enough people to part with their cherished places. Inside there were very few seats, it was a free for all. They bunched together and waited for events to begin.

"I think there is definitely more than fifty thousand here."

The Engineer had reappraised the Clerk's original estimate of the arena's assemblage. Then the King, the Queen and the other members of the royal family of the small Mountain Kingdom entered the arena and took their places in the seating area. The entire ruling family of the tiny realm was in attendance. The royal entourage contained the members of the ruling Dynasty; the Ranas. None of the religious fraternity was present, due to their peaceful Buddhist beliefs. During the fighting contest, the Lamas, the Monks and the Priests were encouraged to retreat to isolated monasteries and seek enlightenment. Naomh gazed at the royal entourage, splendid in their pomp and ceremony. It was a strange concept, Monarchy; the Sheikh was the only other sovereign that ruled by divine right, that he had encountered. In the Anschluss and the Enclave, leaders were chosen by the people, but in the case of the corrupt regime of his homeland, Naomh now knew this to be a farce.

"Presidents might change, assemblies might be elected, but the Chairman was the real power and he never changed during his lifetime. Only death removed him from his position."

This unfamiliar concept of ruling by divine right tugged at desires within Naomh. Encouraging him, the three parts Mescal/Amulet voiced its bearer's desires.

"One day, you shall rule like them, but your Kingdom will be enormous. It will encompass the globe."

Full of self-indulgence, he bearer of the APOCRYPHA'I pledged.

"This is indeed my destiny and I vow that I will rule as a servant to the people."

Something at the edge of his awareness and unheard had different ideas about his plans for the future.

"Such naivety. My people have no need of democracy and good intentions, now that our very survival is paramount."

Naomh would never voice this train of thought to his friends as they would certainly believe him of having large delusions of grandeur. Especially, those from the Enclave. Then a loud splitting noise cracked the respectful silence. The eyes of the crush shifted towards the direction from where the ear shattering sound had originated. It came from the killing floor of the combat zone. This was located in the sunken area in the middle of the thronged arena. Plumes of coloured smoke rose from its depths and a faint mechanical sound was heard. Three pedestals began to rise from the misty depths of the pit. One of the platforms rose quicker that the other two; but even that was ascending in maddening slowness. The first into the audience's sight held the huge three dimensional shaven head of a caricatured announcer. It became attached to an under proportioned body. The primitive holographic projection caused the Alien within the amulet to compare the technology of its race.

"Its flickering erraticism would be painful to a Preceptor-Band. The clearness of a Missive is like comparing night to day."

The swelling animated graphical effigy was standing erect with his suited barrelled chest pushed out in front of him and a long trestle of black plated hair swinging at hip level. As the created image cleared the mist. He lashed into a booming commentary. Naomh translated.

"Welcome my friends. To the top of the World and the greatest martial combat competition on the Planet; where the winner takes all."

The large crowd cheered enthusiastically.

"Do you want to see the rewards for the victor?" Asked the announcer loudly, knowing what the mob's answer would be. The answering roar of the rank and file was deafening.

"Yes." Chanted the gathering as one.

"Are you sure?" Quizzed the Hologram, playing to its audience.

Another mighty cheer erupted and reverberated around the enclosed dome.

"Yes!"

The atmosphere became electric, the very air in the arena crackled in anticipation as the first prize emerged from the purple haze. It lay on top of the second pedestal and contained a vast wealth in precious metals, jewels and paper money. It was more than enough to live out the remainder of your life in absolute luxury here in the Mountain Kingdom. It failed to move the seekers of the APOCRYPHA'I in the same manner as the avarice spectators, although two of Miriam's people whistled aloud. For the device within the LAB-CELL could now produce any precious metal found on the Planet and some that were not. But when the second "Prize." was revealed, it became a different matter entirely. The crowds cheering faded in direct proportion to the rising of the third pedestal. Its top was formed into a dais and on it was the Adonis of female perfection. Her exotic beauty was intoxicating and she was easily the most completely formed female that any of the questors had ever seen. The males in the arena were stunned into silence at the impossible dream of possessing this vision in a way that only a male could, while the female part of the audience became half-silent in envy of such a dazzling image of woman. The sallow skinned beauty oozed concupiscence. She was covered in a sequined yellow fabric that made you doubt that she was not entirely naked. This second skin accentuated beyond doubt, every delicious curve of her female form. Even the Persuader, who once thought that Shoshanna had been the most beautiful woman in the World, now revised his opinion. The Clerk stared open mouthed, even the devout Engineer showed a blush that betrayed his thoughts. The Mute became full of his usual desires. He had a different type of longing; he only desired to see the seductive twinkle in those mesmerising painted eyes go out. Only the arrogant fighters among the assemblage remained cold and outwardly, seemingly unaffected by her physical radiance. Each of them had the supreme belief of one that had never tasted defeat and were confident at the end of the Tournament, she would be theirs. All of them held their excitement in check, in anticipation of that time. As the vision returned to the depths, the holographic announcer made a lewd comment.

"Who would not like to spend one night with that?"

If Miriam had misgivings about Naomh putting himself in danger by entering the competition, it now doubled at the sight of the prize. Now when he won, it might be his faithfulness she might lose, the Enclave woman felt almost boyish compared to her. She saw the way the men were affected by the woman's beauty.

"Even Cahill who has eyes only for Greta appears flustered by just a dazzling smile aimed in his direction."

The blonde woman had his hand gripped firmly and Miriam was surprised to realise that she clutched Naomh's in the same manner. She definitely did not want to leave her man alone with this woman, even if it meant gaining the fourth piece of the amulet. The sexual magnetism the woman was emitting was overpowering and if she as a female could be affected by it, then only God knew what it was doing to the men's hormones. She need not have worried. The three parts Mescal/Amulet had plans for both of them in the future and in its desire to be whole again, it would make Naomh cut her pretty little throat if need be. Then Greta broke the spell as her twisted humour came to the fore.

"I bet you, she breaks wind just like the rest of us."

Naomh was oblivious of her joke, he was studying the beautiful woman intensely and his reason was not the obvious one.

"She has the fourth part of the APOCRYPHA'I on her body. And like

the Sheikhs daughter, she does not wear it openly."

With an effort, he averted his gaze from the beautiful woman and focused it on the line of combatants. He did not fear these killers of men or even women as he was certain.

"I am now the quickest and strongest mortal on the Planet. I will overcome them no matter what type of weapon they carry into the arena."

The Guide apprehended an official and asked in Anschluss.

"Where can one of us enter the Tournament?"

The man pointed to a door. It was a flickering screen displaying a multitude of languages. About half way down, it proclaimed in European words, "Tournament Entrants." Even the script of the Enclave and the Prophet was displayed. The two Semitic languages lay side by side as it declaring their equality, much to the annoyance of the Enclave party. Two huge muscle-bound men with red sashes around their waists stood at either side of the screen. A hastily formed queue had been formed. There was always a flood of new entrants at the last minute. Many had a rush of blood to their head, believing in their own invincibility, but it was always the beautiful girl that tipped them over the edge. The organisers of the games used these unfortunates as fodder for the experienced fighters and to wet the blood appetite of the crowd. Any adept fighter who wanted to enter the lethal contest had made up their minds a long time ago. Naomh left his party and went and joined the line. The row moved quickly and then he was standing in front of the two guardians. He told them.

"I want to enter the Tournament."

The burly men stood aside and let him enter; the screen flickered and vanished. He entered an opulent office and a man sitting behind a chair introduced himself as crown prince Birendra Gyanendra.

"Welcome. You wish to enter the Tournament?" Asked the Prince formally in Anschluss, he had been watching him on a recording unit.

Naomh thought it a stupid question and contemplated privately.

"I would not be in this room if I didn't."

But all he said was.

"Of course."

Prince Birendra was not surprised, as there was usually a flurry of late applicants, especially when they saw the woman and thought with their balls. All business like, the heir to the throne said.

"Every entrant has to put up a surety."

Naomh agreed even though he had no idea of the value.

"All combatants are allowed a weapon of choice that is not projectile in nature."

He concurred once again and a contract was signed. The Prince's eyes hardened as he said.

"There is no way out of this now. If you fail to participate, you and your entourage will be taken to the metal mines and believe me, death in

the arena is immeasurably more enjoyable than those dark and unlit places. Two armed guards will now accompany you until you are called. Someone nominated by you will come back and settle the contract. May your God wish you luck?"

The Prince dismissed the competitor, not before handing him a copy of the contract which to Naomh's amusement was printed in Anschluss and on old-fashioned laminated paper. Hiding an outward display of his mirth, he found two armed men immediately by side. He had entered the Tournament, not by virtue of his fighting prowess, but rather by an entrance fee. He was certain it was a large amount, but wealth seemed to vary in all the lands that they had travelled through. The victor would receive all of the loser's gambits, a huge prize fund and the beautiful temptress. But all he desired was the fourth part of the living jewel.

Back inside the room, the heir to the throne wished that this interviewing of idiots would come to an end. He had more pressing business. Reports had come in a few days ago of a cessation of contact from their most isolated border post high above the Blasted Lands. A search and rescue party had found the bunker destroyed and the soldiers slaughtered. All of the posts recording devices had malfunctioned and he had not received one image of the attack. Every now and then, a shadowy force that called themselves Maoists emerged to cause upheaval in the Kingdom. They were armed and supplied by the Russian Federation, a huge Nation to the North that had returned to the revived ideology of Communism. It was an isolated attack, but he had ordered more troops on to the streets, in case of a spectacular event. Meanwhile, Naomh went back to his friends, he was accompanied by his new minders and told them.

"These two guys have to stay with me. They have accepted me as an entrant. One of you has to pay this amount in precious metal or gems."

He handed them the contract. The Clerk had purchased some sort of sandwich and crumbs spilt to the floor. Studying the paper, he said in between mouthfuls.

"I will get it."

The blonde man searched their packs and measured out the exact amount. He turned to the Persuader and said.

"I might need muscle. Come with me."

The big man went with him. A half an hour later, the two men returned. The bureaucrat among them had been studying the contract and the rules. The Clerk told them what he had learned and began explaining the code to them.

"Naomh has to enter a cell below the ground at sundown. He will sit there and wait until his door opens up. He will then enter the fighting pit and face an opponent. Only one of them will leave the pit alive. He will keep fighting until he is dead or victorious. There is something else that is worrying. This exact location of the arena and fighting pit is not by

chance. This building is perched on top of a special mountain. It is made of a rare black mineral that by its very presence and abundance blocks all radio traffic. Once Naomh is down there on the killing floor, we will not be able to contact him."

The competitor looked at his companions and saw the worry in some of their eyes, especially Miriam. He was supremely confident.

"Have no fear, I will win."

Then, the Clerk told Greta.

"Another thing, Women are not allowed to enter the Tournament."

Scowling, she replied.

"Chauvinists. I could easily defeat any man I have seen trying to enter that competition."

Cahill for one believed her. Naomh took his woman aside and talked to her in hushed tones. The two lovers spent the rest of the day together; well except for his two burly minders who never left his side. At sundown, his two chaperons told him it was time to go. He kissed Miriam passionately and told her not to worry. The rest of his friends clasped his hand in support. As he was escorted away, one of the impassive minders thought that their charge was a very foolish man.

"This man has a beautiful woman and enough wealth it seems, so why is he throwing his life away. Perhaps, it is for the fame and the glory. Yes! He is indeed stupid."

But of course the burly man could not know Naomh's true purpose. The two minders took him below ground and he was let into his cell. Before this, he had to reveal his weapon of choice to a screen and then he was scanned to make sure that he carried nothing else. The place of his temporary confinement was circular in shape; it had no corners or angles of any type. The door shut behind him and blended seamlessly with the rest of the incredibly smooth wall. He now felt very alone. His wary eyes took in a wooden bed with a crude mattress covered in a woollen sheet. Alongside it, there was a latrine and a basic sink under a small mirrored cabinet. Curious, he opened it up and found it full of basic medical supplies. There was also a large water container with paper cups and that was the only furniture in the tiny space. He thought the presence of the toilet odd, but then he amended.

"Then again, I don't know how long I will be in here."

Unlike the other competitors, he was not completely alone. All they had were their thoughts, he had his internal voice.

"I'm completely cut off from the outside World."

Separated from his companions and indeed the rest of the city, Naomh studied the round wall of the cell, it was smooth and shiny and disorientating. Up above, his friends considered the fighting pit from another perspective. All noticed immediately that it was isolated from the crowd of spectators by a see through barrier. The Engineer rapped on it. He then placed a small globe on its slender film that was concealed by his rubbing hand. Satisfied, he gave his assessment.

"It is constructed from a type of reinforced transparent plastic which is so impenetrable that bullets and other projectiles will bounce harmlessly off it. Naomh is all alone down there, if he gets into difficulty, none of us can help him."

"What about the T0RT-CAMLETS." Asked Moshe.

"They are too slow, if Naomh gets into trouble, it will happen in an instant." Answered Cahill.

"We could use them and get down there before he starts to fight." Said Miriam looking for any advantage for her lover.

"It would be no good. I have detected over a hundred video devices focussed on this area surrounding the pit. Those watching would know at once that we vanished into thin air. Imagine the sensation that would cause. The TORT-CAMLETS would not have enough power to get us out of this city. No whether we like it or not, we have to have confidence in Naomh and do it his way." Advised the Lenses.

"We could go outside and come back in." Suggested the Rabbi.

"Nobody is allowed out now, it is the rules and anyway all the exits are closed. I have already checked." Said the Guide.

Naomh's companions had no choice but to grin and bear it. It was common knowledge among most of the spectators that sometime in the past when the tourney was in its infant stage, some aggrieved punters had decided to push the odds to favour their fighter. They eliminated some of their own combatant's competitors with silenced sniper shots. That was why the reinforced transparent barrier was put up at a great cost. The questors split up and mingled with the crowds while each of them waited for something to happen down in the pit. They met back together and the Engineer had something interesting to report. He explained.

"We found an information unit that explained a lot about the Tournament. Naomh is in a cell; he is isolated from everyone and everything, as is all the other combatants. Each cell is above an automated track that circles the arena. It is behind the wall of the pit and under us. The cell has two doors, the one he entered in and the one leading to the fighting pit. Two cell doors will open and two fighters will face each other in the arena. The victor returns to his cell. The empty cell is filled by another fighter from another row of cells that follows the circumference of the first line of cells. The outer one moves in tandem to the inner one depositing a fighter in to any empty cell in the first circle. This rotation of the two circles continues until the outer one is empty. Then the inner circle keeps rotating until there are only two fighters left. Nobody knows who will be facing each other, the choice is totally random."

The Rabbi said insightfully.

"It sounds like some weird amusement ride of death. These people are

really messed up."

What the information screens did not reveal to the questors was that this tiny Kingdom had few natural resources and been on top of the World, it was little use to any other power block in the area. So to survive and prosper, one of its former rulers came up with the Tournament idea. The Games brought in massive wealth from gambling, video rights from neighbouring nations and tourism. Billions around the World tuned into it; legally or illicitly. Even the Chairman and his ruling elite watched it back in the Anschluss; ninety-nine per cent of the Plebs had not this option. The Spy who had seen it all before pretended to be just as ignorant as the others. It brought out a growing bloodlust that was entering the genes of the LYUBINITES. As Naomh sat on the crude wooden bench in his bland cell, boredom kept bringing his confused thoughts back to the vision of beauty.

She plagued him!

The provocative woman had picked him out from the throng and she looked so vulnerable. She had given him the impression that she wanted him to fight for her and win her heart. This female was easily the most beautiful creature he had ever seen and she had a piece of the living amulet about her.

"Could I not feel the same level of love for her as I do for Miriam? After all, they both might be promised to me. In the Prophet's lands, a man has many wives."

The three parts Mescal/Amulet interjected.

"Naomh. It is the part of the APOCRYPHA'I in her possession that is making you feel this overpowering attraction to her. This woman is not like Miriam. She would dispose of you in an instant and take your segments for herself. That female is no more shy and insecure than you are a coward or a pacifist."

"Nobody that pretty and innocent could harm anyone." Answered a besotted Naomh.

As the infatuated man pondered this, he felt his cell shift. It was moving forward, a small bit at a time. Cathbad back in the past went into panic mode.

"The female Hybrid is intently using the fourth piece of the APOCRYPHA'I to enhance her sexual magnetism, so that no other individual of her species, whether it is male or female that she desired can resist her obvious charms. But in Naomh's case it is extremely perilous; for the segments have to obey their programming to join together at all costs. For all we can project, the female could end up with the four segments and that is not conducive to our scheme.

The three parts of the Mescal/Amulet understood this too, but like Naomh it was losing itself to the allure of completion. His cell shifted again. It moved three more times. Both of their growing desires were put on hold when a screen brightened on one of the walls. Somebody's image told him it was his turn to enter the fighting pit. The representation looked like a computer depiction; it was not a real man. The door to the pit opened and impatiently Naomh rose and strode through it. He entered a silent and surreal place. He gave a look up at the baying crowd, but was denied this by an opaque barrier.

"So, they have completely cut me off from my friends above."

But his comrades were aware of every move that he would make. They had purchased front row positions and had stood anxiously watching the preliminary rounds and waiting for Naomh. Most of them were aghast at the senseless bloodshed. The insightful Spy knew.

"The organisers are using the unknowns to blood the more experienced killers."

Solomon and the Rabbi refused to watch until their companion came out. The Mute was in heaven; he revelled in the spectacle of senseless killing, confident eyes been dimmed forever and the close ups on the video screens.

Then Naomh entered the pit!

A door of exact proportions as that which he entered opened from another side of the arena and his opponent stepped out to face him. It was a tall sinewy black man with a longer slender blade in his hands. His opponent was slashing the blurring steel to the sides of him with lightning speed. The swordsman advanced on the unmoving Naomh and swiped down with the razor sharp blade. Incredibly, he caught the flat sides between the palms of his clasped hands and held it tight. The astounded man could not free his weapon and as he struggled, Naomh whipped his legs from underneath him. The man fell heavily to the arena floor and his blade remained in his opponent's grip. Naomh reversed the sword and plunged it into the man's chest. He died with a gurgle of blood. Before the victor had time to take an effortless breath, a hole opened in the floor underneath the corpse and it fell into fire. Incinerated into ashes as it had never been.

"So that's the loser's fate." The winner realised.

Naomh had not even used his primary weapon, a seven pointed metal star given to him by the Lama. He was directed by a video image to go back into his cell and he did so. Up above, Prince Birendra Gyanendra judged Naomh's prowess and moved him out of the rudimentary rounds.

"I have misjudged him, he has incredible talent."

The bearer of the APOCRYPHA'I waited a substantial length of time until he was called into the fighting pit again. If, he did not know better, he would have thought that the organisers had forgotten about him. Strangely, he did not use the toilet facilities during his long wait. He did drink, but did not eat. Then his screen lit up and he was commanded to enter the pit again. From the other side of the sunken arena, his opponent also came out.

He was a giant of a specimen; bigger even than the Persuader. He stood over two metres tall with biceps as large as a man's legs. His upper body hinted at prestigious strength. The man's eyes were slanted and his oiled skin was sallow in colour. Various blue inked tattoos covered his body and face. A long black trestle of knotted hair flowed from his shaven scalp. He stood akimbo with a huge saw toothed blade in his right hand. The fearsome man roared a mighty challenge for the benefit of the unseen crowd and charged. Flushed with his increased reflexes, he easily side-stepped his attacking opponent with a turn of blinding speed. Naomh's hand and eye co-ordination had increased ten-fold. As the man went passed after missing him with a swipe from his weapon, there was a flash of a hidden blade across his foe's throat and the large man fell to the floor of the pit gurgling in his own blood.

It was over before it began.

The victor needed no prodding to retreat back to his cell this time. As the door closed, the body of the huge fighter was consumed by the flames. The winner was completely oblivious to the crowd's reaction above and had no inclination that all the cheering and baying had ceased instantly. There was complete shock in the arena as the man had been a former champion, enticed back into the pit to relive his former glory. He had also wanted to taste the charms of the female prize; he had such a time with the last one and this one looked even more desirable. The prodigious fighter had been expected to win the tourney once again or at least make it to the final round. Besides Naomh's companions, the only other happy people at the outcome were the bet takers. Disbelieving punters tore up their betting slips. A lot of money had been wagered on the huge man. There was one happy individual who had bet on his friend, it was the Guide of course. He had found out about the gambling aspect of the Tournament and had wagered on his friend. The Clerk seeing all the envious looks from the other punters and the admiring looks from the females in the crowd directed at the Guide rushed forward to bet again on Naomh.

"Forget it man. After that display, you will get no more odds on him anymore. It's a shame really man, for I should have had words with him before he went down there."

"Why?" Asked a disappointed Clerk.

"Because I would have told him to make the fight last longer. Ma-an! We would have really cleaned up and all those lovely ladies might have been real appreciative of our knowledge."

"Oh yeah" Chorused all of the male members of the group, well except the Rabbi, the Engineer and the Mute.

"Are all of you for real? Naomh's life is at stake down there." Shouted Miriam.

She was still angry at the idea of her man been alone with that beautiful harlot.

659

"Get real, Miriam. There is nobody on the Planet that would take Naomh." Said the Clerk.

Cahill nudged him hard in the ribs and whispered in the gasping man's ears.

"You idiot. She is afraid about what will happen when he wins. He will be alone with the prize."

The Clerk's eager green eyes widened as sudden understanding came to him.

"That would be horrible, to be in that situation."

But the longing in his eyes betrayed him. Another person, thousands of kilometres away nearly choked on his imported Australian brandy when he saw Naomh enter the fighting pit. It was the Chairman. The ruler of the Anschluss had just tuned in to watch the former winner's bout. That ill-tempered fighter had been a favourite of his and a worthy champion. He called aside his Secretary of Protocol.

"We will have to get our Spy in their ranks to enter the Tournament. Our agent can eliminate most, if not all of his opposition."

"But if they do that, will our infiltrator not have to lose against him?" Enquired his underling.

He gave a dismissive shrug; compassion was not in his nature. After all this was the person who ordered the obliteration of the ridge where the Prophet's army was gathered and he also sanctioned the destruction of Singh's village with the stroke of a pen.

"The secret is paramount and the only ones allowed to kill LYUBINITES or order them to die are ourselves."

He glanced at the replays and then saw how easily Naomh had dispatched the vicious killer.

"Cancel that directive. He is easily capable of winning the Tournament without our agent's assistance or sacrifice."

The big man returned to his guests and said.

"Anyone care for a slight wager."

The Guide, the Clerk and Ivan Tell were greatly wide of the mark. There was one who could defeat him and was waiting eagerly for his chance. This one had no doubt that it would be him and Naomh in the last two. Back in the Tournament complex, Styarz laid waiting in a cell in the same underground complex as Naomh. He too was not alone, he was lost in religious ecstasy and the presence of his God was all about him. At long last, the Winged One had given him a task worthy of his commitment and talents.

"When I have killed and disposed of my Gods primary enemy and recovered what was stolen from him, then a whole new future waits for us, his chosen people."

The tracking sphere had led him here and lost among the crowds, he watched his main target and his companions, waiting for the time to strike.

As he witnessed Naomh entering the fighting contest, he realized that this was golden opportunity. The Grandmaster also entered the competition and his entrance fee was a number of fantastic gems (Not of this World) that had been gifted to him by his God for when it was necessary to exchange them for some purpose. Prince Birendra, a shrewd judge of fighting ability sensed something very unusual about the strange small man called Achmed and had dismissed him from the first rounds. As he sat in his cell, the Knight did what came naturally to him, waiting. He was his usual confident self and he relaxed with the memory of the first task the Winged One had given him.

When he had been a youth, the God had him flown on a golden chariot of light to a lush Savannah deep in the interior of the African continent. The tableland with its coarse grass and scattered tree growth was easily verdant than the barren wastelands that harboured his home. But it was, as the desert compared to the bounty of his God's Eden. There on the vast Serengeti, he was confronted with a pride of lions lazing the afternoon away in the scant leafy shade of a few trees. As he neared them, the challenge from the roar of the large mane'd male shattered the calm of the pride and the lazy afternoon. The huge male was a victor of every threat to his harem. The male rose and darted towards him as Styarz had crossed the point of no return. The lion gave out a ferocious roar and bared his razor sharp canines as his lips retracted in warning. Something in the Hybrid's conscience told him he also used that gesture when threatened. Styarz ignored the hint and when the male attacked, he killed him quite effortlessly. The females and their cubs came towards the victor and smelled him. The pride relaxed around him and accepted him. That's when he knew, his God had given him wondrous powers.

Sitting in his cell, he flexed his feline/Hybrid muscles in anticipation. He had supreme confidence in his feral skills. His enemy was no match in strength and agility or guile to him.

"No wonder my God wants the elimination of his first creations. It is a fact that he reviles these Humans, as unlike my kin, they lack the imagination, the Winged One has bestowed on us."

The Knight was called to enter the fighting pit by the same video image as Naomh. Arrogantly, the being born to fight strode into the pit. He looked at his opponent in contempt and disdain. The siren wailed, impatient for the combat to begin, he circled his opponent.

Styarz became a blur.

The fight was over in a split second; the other man in the pit had his larynx crushed from the power and speed of the blow. The Grand-master had not even drawn his Anlace. It had ended quicker than Naomh's two battles. Up above, the bearer of the uncompleted amulet friends recognized the small cloaked combatant instantly.

"It is one of the small moustached men that had nearly destroyed our

company, back in the desert. Shit where did he come from?" Demanded the Guide.

The Lenses went real silent and unconsciously touched his eyepatch. His now sombre friends watching from above now realized that their leader might not survive this after all. Their initial exuberance was fading into a solemn vigil and knowing that all of them were helpless to intervene. Of them all, the Persuader paled with the most at the memory of what this diminutive man and his companions had done to him. The big man gripped his seat with suppressed rage and not a little fear. After viewing and assessing the initial rounds, the organizers agreed that Styarz like Naomh should go into the seeded pool. The marital skills displayed by him impressed and it stated that he was no amateur. The Prince had judged him correctly. The two heredity enemies created by a race that were far from been God's avoided each other over the next few rounds of the Tournament. Then Styarz faced his next opponent. His feline senses confirmed.

"There is nothing exceptional about him."

But, the small slender man had poison darts in his knuckles that had evaded all sensors. Each hidden projectile was tipped with deadly strychnine. This covert killer had already used four and had dispatched that number of victims. Styarz's opponent griped his left hand into a tight fist. He then flicked one of his fingers outwards causing a small lethal and undetectable dart to fly unerringly towards him. The Knight had seen the intention in the man's fear filled eyes. With his incredible agility, Zebulan's tool twisted and avoided the poisoned projectile with ease. The firer panicked and discharged again. Once again, he missed as Styarz dodged the needle sharp projectile. Without realizing, he fired the remaining four in a sustained volley and failed to his target. As he died, he regretted leaving another ten darts in his cell.

Like Styarz, Naomh studied his next opponent and like the Knight before him, he could find nothing remarkable about him. One detail that did stand out was the way the man removed his gloves from his hands. It was done with a care that spoke of a deadly weapon. Up above, his friends could have warned him, his opponent had a lethal and poisonous touch. They had watched this man's first bout with fascination, he had gripped his opponent's fingers in respect and held tight. The other fighter screamed in agony as if he had just put his hand in an open fire. The ungloved viper released his hold. His victim's palms sported ugly black bruises; he held them up in disbelief and collapsed. He was dead before he even hit the floor. The man with the deadly touch moved away, the floor opened and the body fell into the fire below. He now offered Naomh his hand. His friends above screamed in dire warning. They had no need to worry, their comrade refused. The devious combatant was prepared for that eventuality; he flexed his fingers in a menacing manner, held them above his head and slowly advanced on Naomh.

"So this Pleb wants to wrestle me."

The two wrestlers clasped hands. Naomh's friends above gasped in disbelief. Their leader felt a burning sensation as his opponent released his grip.

"Poison." Warned, the three parts Mescal/Amulet.

"But, it is not a problem. I am now extremely familiar with your chemistry."

The smug man backed away waiting for his self-produced bane to do its work. To his astonishment, his foe remained unaffected from the deadly toxins. Naomh's alien biochemistry had now made him immune to all toxins and diseases. He did not give his opponent time to recover from his fatal mistake. He flung his weapon of choice, the five-pointed metal star given to him by the Lama and it imbedded itself in the toxic man's temple. The man with the deadly touch died and his body fell into the burning fire and the metal star flew back to Naomh's clasp. A peculiar spectrum of gases wafted up as his strange chemistry burned.

"This is getting too easy." Thought, the victor as his cell door opened.

But his penultimate bout was not so easy. He faced another non-descript man, but this fighter must have shown Prince Birendra something special because the organiser of the Tournament had given this man a bye until this round. Naomh was startled; his opponent was only wearing a skimpy pair of black briefs and stood there with his hands clasped behind his back. The puzzled man from the Anschluss could not see what he was holding. The man was heavily tattooed on his right forearm with large black script. It was three numbers 666. He knew what they signified from conversations with the Engineer. The two combatants squared off; there was a blur and Naomh was now facing six opponents. Startled, he made a lightening attack on one of them and instead of the expected contact, he met thin air. One of the images responded with a swipe of a heavy wooden club and knocked the wind out of Naomh. Kneeling down and gasping, the six figures advanced on him, their hands once again behind their backs. Again he charged one of the solid looking images and still he passed through emptiness. Another blow from the solid cudgel connected with his head and opened up a wound in his forehead. Blood flowed freely from his scalp and he backed away. His opponent never finished him off; he was making an extravagant bow. The fighter was playing to the crowd. His victim was becoming panic stricken, another serious blow would cause the inbuilt healing process to begin and although Naomh would not become a monster, he had nowhere to hide. He would be helpless as his body recuperated and he could image the horror of his lover, friends and the crowd of watching spectators. Up above, his comrades were in shocked silence; his easy victories were quickly forgotten. Miriam, white faced with fear was gripping Beersheba's hands, her worry about him spending time with the beautiful woman banished as she realized the love of her life might not even survive this bout. Each time, from their vantage position, they could see which image had the club behind his back and thus which was the real opponent. Twice now, he had chosen the wrong one. Down below, something had just occurred to Naomh, the blow on the head and the blinding flash of pain had clarified his thinking. This had drawn his attention to a peculiarity of his foe.

"At the instant of my failed attacks, only one of the images produced the weapon, but which one? I need a way to anticipate the correct one or this guy with the reflected images will slowly pummel me to death."

Then, the answer came to him.

"Reflective images!"

He prepared to attack, freed his star shaped blade and rushed forward. Going for a definite image, Naomh dummied and swiped at another catching it across the throat and he was showered with blood. The club fell to the floor with a palpable thud. All five other images vanished and only one dead body remained. He retreated back to his cell as the body fell into the fire. He had fought the opponent with reflected images and won with brainpower as well as muscle. There was a huge cheer from the crowd and a much-relieved one from his friends. Miriam could not stop herself from shaking in relief, then as she recovered, she asked the obvious question.

"How did he know which was the real one?"

None of the cluster of companions came forward with the answer. Then Greta guessed.

"He must have got a glimpse of the club."

"That must be it." Said the Lenses.

The other's agreed, but the sneakily smiling Mute shook his head in disagreement. A disgusted Cahill said.

"What do you know?"

The efficient serial killer replied in his whinny voice.

"Naomh saw what I saw."

"And what was that?" Asked Solomon.

"The man was using reflected images of himself, think about it."

"So! We kind of saw that"

That was the sarcastic Clerk.

"It is simple, the Pleb had 666 on his arm, but his images had the reverse, 999 and they were on his left arm."

"Oh." Was the general consensus as realization dawned.

There was newfound respect for the unlikable man. Except from the Guide who silently thought.

"That's something that a PREVENTIVE agent would have spotted."

Styarz's next opponent was just as agile as him. He was a fighting monk of the Shaolin order. The once enlightened spirit had become an outcast among his sect for his sense of superiority and preferring the mortal vices instead of the spiritual. During a practice bout, he had killed the chief monk and the sects most accomplished fighter, just to prove that he was the most skilled among them. He also had stolen away the most precious relic of his order, a black mask made from an impenetrable substance. It was even known to stop bullets and now this martial combat was the best way of proving that he was the most capable fighter on the Planet. He had already dispatched five opponents during this Tournament and was revelling in it and of course the prizes would be a welcome bonus. He had grown tired of the frugal living and the enforced celibacy. Yes, the former monk really looked forward to enjoying the charms of the female. The outcast's weapon of choice was an unusual thing to the watching company. It consisted of two pieces of metal rods connected by a linked steel chain. The extremely adept warrior flailed it around with amazing dexterity and bore down on his diminutive rival. Though, he was a highly adept fighter, he had not the speed or fluidity of Styarz's feline constitution. The Knight now had crystal claws fitted over each digit on his hands and bare feet that retracted in the same manner as his feline cousins. Far superior to any metal or alloy; these killing extensions were another gift from his God. These incredibly durable talons had enabled him to climb the high cliff face at the edge of the blasted lands with such ease. He responded to his opponent's moves in a majestic moving blur. Avoiding the deadly weapon of his opponent in a fluid twirl, the warrior of a vastly different sect opened up the monk's impenetrable mask with a swipe of his claws. His shocked opponent staggered back and put a hand to his face. It came away in a stripped pattern of blood.

"Impossible!" Stated the fighting monk.

Blinded by the flowing blood and dented mask, the outcast's movements lost their fluidity. Although to a normal opponent, it would have gone unnoticed. The Grandmaster went for the jugular and finished him off quickly with a swipe of his feet. The automated screen told Naomh that he was in the final, there as only one opponent left. It was Styarz, the feline Hybrid and the Lord of the Knights of the Winged One. Naomh studied the cowled figure in front of him. Again, he saw nothing remarkable about his rival.

"But, he must be something special. After all, he has reached the final."

The bearer of the APOCRYPHA'I saw the cloaked Knight pull down his hood to reveal a large wing shaped moustache. He nearly faltered; he forgot all of his former bravado about meeting this attacker again. Thoughts of the pain that he had endured at the hands of this diminutive man flooded back. As the eyes of the two Aliens dupes met, their two masters had conflicting emotions. Zebulan had taken the unprecedented step of incorporating an image recorder on his servant's irises. His Knight's opponent was drawing him in and he knew what he was going to

665

discover.

"He basks in the presence of my most despised adversary. But the insane Elder is un-completed and he must not be."

The three parts Mescal/Amulet also looked into Naomh's opponents eyes and saw a fanaticism for a cause that he envied. There was also a familiar presence in the background that withstood conformation.

"If my host could only have that devotion?"

The presence within the living amulet would have been even more astounded if it had learned that this commitment was to one of his own race. For, it had no idea that the leader of the DEFILED was still on the Planet. The Grandmaster who was normally non-conversant during a fight found the urge to taunt his opponent.

"It is one on one now. You have no hidden shield to retreat into and come out like a reptile. Your cowardly advantage is gone."

Styarz retracted his lips in warning and pounced. The Knight had moved even faster than Naomh. He barely dodged the blows; he was on the back foot. But still, the Patriarchi's host managed to counteract the oncoming assault. His attacker noted.

"He has learnt from the last attack. Good, this is a fight that will go into the lore of our order. "

Then, the Knight realised.

"If I had used the claws out in the desert; my mission would have been completed then. It's no matter; the chase will be over soon enough."

Naomh had other ideas. The searcher of the seven pieces enjoyed great satisfaction as he felt one of his blows connect. Styarz was stunned; never in all of his years of murder had he been hit like that. Like all bearers of feline genes; he had no toleration for his own pain. Out of form, he left out an animal squeal. Still, his Human side recovered instantly and he flipped into a fighting stance. But the damage had been done. Naomh no longer believed that the little man was invincible. The sudden pain was diminished as he received his master's thoughts. Styarz's blistering retaliation had opened up Naomh's clothing and revealed the Alien artefact. Feral eyes were drawn instantly towards the sparkling presence. Zebulan distracted his servant during the revelation and ordered his menial.

"You must retrieve the object within his chest. This is what was stolen from me and must be returned at all cost."

The agile Knight catapulted with his enhanced feet aiming for his opponents head. This time however; Naomh was ready for it and twisted away from the impact. The astounded attacker was aggrieved; he had never missed with this tactic before. Blow for blow was traded and blocked as if they were enacting some well-choreographed routine. They appeared even until; Naomh let his metal disc fly. It ricocheted off of Styarz's crystal covered fingers and flew back to him. But it still sent a shock wave up the deflecting arm. Seizing the initiative, the thrower pressed his attack. It nearly proved fatal. A lethal swipe from the other set of crystal talons nearly ripped him asunder. A twist of his neck had taken most of the momentum of the blow, but the diluted force of the backhanded attack knocked out his monocles. His opponent backed off, but not before noticing the strange filament discs that tumbled to the arena floor. With God learned insight; Styarz knew what they were. It gave him an opening. The feline Hybrid had another secret weapon that until now, he had no reason to use. It was another gift from the Winged God.

"It will serve me well."

A flick of his right wrist revealed a small orb and he twisted it. A strange blue mist wafted from it and floated upwards.

"More poison" Wondered Naomh.

"No, this is something else." Warned, the three parts Mescal/Amulet.

The mist swelled like a balloon and penetrated the video monitors; it got into the electrical system and along fibre optic conduits. It spread like a virus. Suddenly all the lights went down, along with the video images. The entire arena complex was in blackness, but more worrying for the bearer of three pieces of the APOCRYPHA'I, the centre of the imponderable inkiness was the fighting pit. He had lost the boon of his sight enhancers. The audience in the arena went hysterical. Prince Birendra automatically assumed that it was a Maoist attack and ushered the royal family away. The new monocles of Naomh's companions automatically switched frequency and every one of them could still see the fighting pit. High up on the Geneva Contrib, Ivan Tell became furious, he had been enthralled by the explosive clash, especially now that he had a vested interest in the outcome. He insisted the images to be returned. His technicians told him.

"The problem is at the other side."

To the Chairman, their helplessness was irrelevant; he demanded answers not excuses. Back in the pit, the object of his concern was blind; Styarz was in his element. For the darkness did not exist for him. The Knight's night vision was as good as any feline predator. The pupils of his feral yellow eyes became large and visible as he advanced on the hapless enemy of his God. He had an easy victim; his opponent was in total despair and backed against the wall. All that Naomh could remember was the terrible blow to the head that this small man had inflicted previously. He flinched, expecting another similar strike at any moment. Two dancing points of yellow light similar to the headlights of the vehicle that brought them to Singh was his only point of reference. But when he was at his nadir, the voice of the Lama came to him.

"Now is the time, use what I have imparted to you."

Peace flowed in his soul; he relaxed with a supreme effort. His mind locked onto a technique that had been imprinted into his psyche. Incredibly his body began to rise from the arena floor. His lighter than air form scraped up the side of the pit's wall until he hung in mid-air. Styarz checked his advance as he saw Naomh rise from the floor.

"Such a miraculous thing. Still he must die; he is an enemy of my God. I will ask the Winged One to teach me this when I return home after this business. I have to move fast and retrieve the jewel before his dead body falls into the fiery pit."

The warrior Knight took out his Anlace. He had been reluctant to use it up to now, on what he considered inferior beings. Up above in the systems control room, a frantic technician got a semblance of operation. The machinery of the arena went into haphazard random fluctuation. All the separate panels of the floor opened at once, while the shield barrier at the top opened completely. Styarz checked his advance on his helpless victim and leapt for the side-wall of the fighting pit with the biggest leap, he had ever done. Incredibility, he hit it half way up. But now, the gift from his God betrayed him. His Alien constructed talons were so sharp that they begin to rip through the smooth wall of the fighting pit like a razor sharp knife through a curtain of silk. He began to slide down its torn face as if it had become butter. Frantically he swiped at the wall over and over again, but he could gain no purchase. As he fell into the searing inferno, the flailing Knight was incinerated instantly. He had no time to ask his God's forgiveness for his failure. Unlike, the negative Clerk, the pragmatic follower of Zebulan had never factored inconsistency into the equation and had paid the ultimate price. All that Naomh had seen were the erratic movement of the feral orbs and then their extinguishment. Suddenly, the lights came back on, sections of the floor reappeared in an irregular fashion and the protective screen above the pit began to open. Getting no sight of his agile opponent, he guessed what had happened. When the barrier above was opened fully, the Guide screamed at his leader below.

"Up here."

Naomh took in the scene instantly. He came out of the trance, dropped to a section of solid floor, hopscotched along static pieces that instantly vanished after he left them and after gathering enough momentum, he catapulted skywards. The strong hands of the Persuader grabbed him. Then, he was hauled over the parapet and was safe. Naomh had survived the pit and had won the competition. He had left a realm of chaos below and entered one of pandemonium. Meanwhile, the mob of former spectators had gone "Ape shit." when the arena's systems had failed and now that the lights had come back on; they panicked as they sought escape. The hysteria spread like wildfire. People were pushed into the pit during the crush to get out of the arena. Flailing bodies went through the air; some crunched on pieces of floor, while others went straight into the furnace below. Naomh, the champion of the games stood with his friends, who were an oasis of composure amid the turmoil. The security forces had begun to restore order with brutal efficiency. Eventually, there was a calm of sorts. The victor's former escorts came over to him and Naomh and his company were quickly surrounded by a wall of troops. The encompassing armed force was not a threat, but a protective escort. The fourteen companions were led to the ruler's throne. King Gyanendra had returned to the arena, his son was satisfied that the strange malfunctions were nothing to do with a Maoist attack. The supreme monarch beckoned Naomh to approach his throne and then ruler of the Mountain Kingdom proclaimed him the victor. The divine ruler was delighted with this year's Tournament.

"It has been the most amazing contest ever and more importantly revenues from the event will soar to unprecedented levels."

He did not know where all of the strange fighters had come from, but he was delighted with the winner. He seemed to be the most normal of them; obviously he had not seen him float in mid-air. There was a great cheer among those who had escaped without harm or loss from the uproar. Two very different people observing the events had two equally different emotions. The Chairman's connection had been restored and he was jubilant as he saw the King congratulate the victor. The ruler of the tiny Mountain Kingdom had little comprehension of how lucky he and his twenty-five million subjects had been. Because, if Naomh had perished, he would have been on the end of a massive nuclear strike. The LYUBINITES dream would have been over and their petulant nature would have required, someone or something to blame for their failure. The Kaiser had also wondered where all the freaks had come from; this was a strange statement considering his cloned background. The other was the Lama and as he came out of meditation, his pondering was disturbed.

"I introduced him to the power of the mind. Have I interfered with the natural order of things, was I a tool for something I do not understand?"

The holy man re-entered the other plane; he had much to think about. Back in the stadium, Naomh had become the champion of the bloody games and was paraded around the arena like he was no longer mortal. He had been separated from his companions as he basked in the glory and adulation of the mob. Garlands made of many perfumed flowers were flung at him and one of these fragrant bouquets was draped over his neck. He was showered with the material gifts and the pleadings of women to bear his offspring. When he got close to his friends, he whispered to them.

"Eventually they will bring me alone to be with the female prize. Once there I will send for you all."

"We had better use a password, so we will know that it came from you." Advised the Lenses.

"Good thinking. What will it be?"

"Use the nickname you gave to Haim. We are the only ones who would know that." Suggested Moshe.

Without mentioning it, in case somebody overheard it, they all agreed on that idea. After a couple of hours of been paraded in front of the cheering crowd, the grateful winner was brought to the room of the beautiful temptress, while his friends were given different quarters where they were wined and dined with exotic food and drink. As companions of the victor, they were also offered male and female company as well.

"If we don't accept it, we would be insulting their hospitality." Said the Clerk who had become quite the libertine. The blonde man put his hand around one of the taller females, who had most of her ample breasts showing and she led him upstairs. The three women questors refused point blank, any of the male lovers offered to them. But the men enjoyed the female company. (Well, except the Engineer, Solomon and the Rabbi.) Ten minutes later there was a howl of outrage from upstairs and the Clerk came running down taking the steps two at a time. His face was indignant.

"What the fuck is a Lady boy? That wasn't a woman, it was a man. She, I mean he had balls."

"Serves you right." Said the Guide who had his arms around two real female beauties.

All the others laughed at his deserved predicament, even Miriam whose mind was on other things. In another part of the arena complex, the escort left Naomh inside a luxurious room and departed. He had been bathed by a frolicking group of pretty girls and was now wearing a green robe and flowing black pants. The Prize sat at the centre of a space full of walled and ceiling mirrors. Ignoring the lavishness of the quarters, he was drawn towards her; he felt an insatiable desire. The APOCRYPHA'I had already sensed its other part. She was reclining on a divan, in a pose that set Naomh's pulse racing. Her beautiful head was resting on a fluffy pink pillow. She was attired in the most outrageous dress, the man from the Anschluss had ever seen. It was a see-through body tight one-piece garment that clung to every delicious curve of her body. The woman had a sparkling radiance that blossomed with eastern promise and she smelt of flowers in bloom. Deep down, Naomh was losing this battle of another kind.

"Greta's figure is every bit as shapely as this woman's and Miriam is everything I want in a female. But still, I am drawn to this temptress like no other."

She was in his blood; the flames of his passion were well and truly stoked. Her eyelashes, lipstick and nail lacquer were all a shade of green, it was confirmation enough that she was in possession of the fourth segment. The smell of flowers would not go away. Naomh had just entered the lair of the ultimate sexual predator, the Human equivalent of a female black Tarantula. Her tempting lure was the certainty of the ultimate sexual encounter. The Prize and the bearer of the fourth part of the living Amulet looked at this winner of the Tournament; her heavily painted eyes glittered with barely suppressed excitement. This vibrant vessel of womanhood had seduced many winners, but she knew instantly, the first second she had seen him in the arena that this was the one she had been waiting a long time for. She had no title, her name never seemed important to anyone who got this close to her. This woman who was sizing up Naomh and turning his blood to water was far older than her beautiful and youthful appearance suggested. As the latest bearer of this piece of the living amulet, this woman had been waiting centuries for this one. Incredibly, she was hundreds of years of age; but did not look a day over eighteen. She had acquired her piece by murder. The former holder of the green segment had fatally overindulged his sexual appetite. He had taken six beautiful women to his bed for an orgy. He had exhausted the other five, but his efforts had left him wide open for her attack. Something drew her to the amulet around his sweating neck. Before he realised it she had killed him. Every five years since the Tournament began, this greatly gifted courtesan had put herself up as the prize, because the bearer of the fourth piece knew one day, that this one would be drawn to her. Her excitement had been held under a tight leash when she first saw him in the arena. Now she exulted.

"And now it has happened. He is here at last."

During every contest since its inception, the gorgeous female changed her appearance slightly, to continue the deception that she was a new and different Prize. Supremely confident in her femininity, she motioned with her long sculptured nails for Naomh to join her on the couch.

"Come to me."

The husky passion in her voice commanded him. Instantly enraptured, her pawn did as he was bid. At this moment, he would die for her, if she decreed. His mind blanked. Naomh became lost in a fog of obsession and all he knew was that he wanted this woman. Her fragrance and her beauty were over riding his self-control.

"God's I must have her."

He had no resistance to her magical allure. If Naomh could see past the beauty of her face, he might have noticed the malevolent intelligence and wisdom gleaming in her eyes. Sitting alongside her, she began to unbutton the robe he was now wearing. Her long nails felt like electric shocks of titillation. She saw the multi-coloured amulet and nearly gasped in wonder. The three parts Mescal/Amulet was troubled. The power of the fourth piece was intoxicating to the Hybrid; its charge was fading under the power of her sexual allure. It was losing him. In desperation, the internal presence shoved the image of Miriam to the forefront of Naomh's mind. It was like a slap in the face for his host. The harlot had instantly noticed his change of demeanour. All of a sudden, this male was resisting her charms, he obviously desired her, but something was preventing him from falling into her thrall completely.

"No, not something, it is someone." Amended the sexual manipulator.

Quickly she realised.

"He has a soul mate below and this bond is interfering with my ambition."

The long-lived courtesan was a lover of both men and women and her sexual appetite was legendary; both sexes were enthralled with her sexuality. She decided.

"I will send for his lover, dominate her and then him."

The courtesan clapped her hands and a servant appeared. She explained what she wanted and the man hurried away instantly to do her bidding. The messenger stood before the companions and addressed them.

"The Champion of the Tournament wishes for his woman to join him."

The Questors looked disturbed as this was not part of Naomh's plan. Besides, the menial had not given the agreed password.

"Did he say anything else?" Asked the dubious Engineer.

The messenger shook his head in the negative. The Guide dismissed him and told him.

"Wait outside a few minutes dude and we will get back to you."

"Something's wrong, he did not use the code." Said the Lenses after the man departed.

Miriam was about to stand up and go with the messenger. But van DerKamp put a restraining hand on her and whispered.

"The Lenses is right, something is up. I can feel it. Let someone else go."

All of them agreed and a hushed debate began. Finally, Greta cut them short, she glanced at Cahill for conformation and he nodded. His lover said.

"I will go. I am the best at this sort of thing and after all, they are expecting a woman. So we had better not disappoint them; had we?"

Reluctantly Miriam agreed; the Enclave woman had no wish to see her soul mate in the arms of another. She was certain that nobody could resist that young woman's charms. The messenger left with Greta. The tall Anschluss beauty entered the room; she took in the scene immediately. The Harlot was semi clothed and when she saw the winner's lover, she rose to greet the new participant in her sex game. As if on cue, her top slid gracefully to the floor, revealing two full bosomed breasts of perfect proportions. Greta scoffed.

"This hoar thinks; I will fall for her charms."

The Prize turned her full lustfulness on to Greta. Suddenly, the woman from the Berlin Contrib became aroused, much to her astonishment. In that moment of uncertainty, the temptress was alongside her, kissing her and fondling her busty bosom. Greta felt her own breasts been exposed and a slight wetness caress them. Her nipples hardened with the attention. The woman looked up, her lips sought Greta's and to her astonishment, she responded hungrily. The Asian beauty only came up to her chin, but it was her that was bending down to seek her mouth. Her tongue eagerly sought the other woman's and soft moans escaped his friend's lips. From his vantage point, Naomh saw Greta's clothing fell to the floor to reveal the

672

neatly trimmed blonde triangle of her pubic hair. From the divan, the voyeur felt his manhood rise; he was watching two of the most beautiful women he had ever seen making love. He was fit to burst; these two were teasing him with their lovemaking. Naomh thought abstractly.

"I should be doing something else, like trying to get control of the situation."

But he could not break the spell of their erotic performance. The sallow woman from the Mountain Kingdom was stroking his friend's private parts and Greta seemed to be enjoying it immensely. The very air of the room buzzed with enormous sexual resonance and the contrast of the woman's complexions. Then, the two highly aroused women were completely naked and advanced on him. Naomh had an erratic thought.

"I'd bet the Clerk's head would explode, if he witnessed this performance. Mine sure the hell is."

The harlot supremely confident in her sexual dominance made Greta stand still as she began to caress and stroke Naomh. She finished undressing him with a skill and sensuality that had every erotic point on his body aflame. Once again, her long nails sent electric shocks through his body. She held the taller woman's hand and stroked it up and down her leaders swelling manhood while his own fingers were caressing her silky pubic hair. With her own dark haired womanhood thrust out, the experienced courtesan removed Greta's hand began to straddle Naomh. The man under her was lost within the moment; his erect penis entered her. As he slowly penetrated her, he looked into her eyes and was in bliss. She looked at Greta and bid her to join them. The highly aroused woman did as she was urged. The sexual bombshell got off Naomh and regretfully, he removed his hand from her thrusting buttocks. Supremely confident in her abilities, she motioned for Greta to assume the position she had been in. This embodiment of sexuality enjoyed watching others perform the sexual act. She relished been a voyeur herself. She bent down and kissed Naomh's lips. Her tongue seeking his while one of her hands stroked his manhood. An aroused Greta sat on Naomh and also stroked his penis. Her inviting fair haired triangle was only millimetres away from his manhood. The harlot was waiting for the moment when he entered his lover, but it never happened. Suddenly, the temptress eyes widened in shock and she slumped forward on to Naomh's chest. The sexual bombshell was dead and it was Greta who killed her. The blonde woman straddling him had a knife in her hand. Naomh was shocked out of his desire and regained his senses. Her companion in the sexual frollickry thought it funny as he looked at the corpse of the beautiful woman with the blood trickling from the corners of her mouth and staining her lips.

"I'll be dammed, but her ruby red lips look even more voluptuous now."

The three parts Mescal/Amulet urged Naomh.

"Quickly, find the next piece of my form."

He scrutinised the body of the dead temptress, but he was unable to locate it. It was a mystery, because its presence screamed about her person. Then with sudden clarity, he knew where it was.

"If the Green piece enhances her sexual desirability, then there is only one place it could be."

He studied the form of the dead beauty and his hand reached towards her still form. The fourth part of the APOCRYPHA'I was secreted in her sex organ. He put his fingers in and found it straight away. He shuddered; the temptress's vagina was still moist and inviting. Her femininity that moments before had been the most coveted object in his World was nothing now. He roughly removed the green sparkle and touched it to the three pieces imbedded in his chest. The flap of skin covering it opened and it instantly melded together. The shock of their joining was decreasing each time; the physical effort this time was barely noticeable. But the mental joy of the now four parts Mescal/Amulet was overpowering, he fell to his knees and gasped. When he opened his eyes, a few minutes later, he found Greta staring at him with an unreadable expression on her features. She was looking at the now four-coloured taint. Her eyes left the amulet and met his and the still naked blonde woman said.

"We had better get out of this room."

Greta stood up and again he was appreciating her full-busted nakedness. She wanted to leave the place of her embarrassing weakness behind as fast as Naomh removed his gaze from her exposed curves and uttered

"No, we have to stay here; we will get the others to come to us. Otherwise it will appear suspicious."

The two former sexual partners still naked took the body of the harlot that was now staring at the mirrored ceiling to another room and covered it with a heavy blanket. The two un-consulting lovers now seemed extremely mortified at the interaction that had occurred between them. They both made a spoken promise.

"We will not mention what had happened in the room to any of the others, especially to Miriam and Cahill. Explaining to our real lovers that it was the effect of the fourth piece of the APOCRYPHA'I that had got us into that predicament will not go down well with them."

"Agreed."

Both of them dressed hurriedly and Naomh went to the door. He called for a servant and told him.

"Fetch all of my friends up here; it is time for a celebration. Say this word to them; Pecker."

The man obeyed of course, the victor was now master of this place for a year. However, he was slightly aggrieved that he did not get a glimpse of the beautiful Prize, especially, if she had been naked. He hoped.

"Still, she might appear when I have finished with his request."

He hurried away to do the champions bidding. As the two of them waited silently, Naomh thought remorsefully as he stole glances at the room where the female body was.

"Did Greta have to kill her and how did she snap out of the sexual trance? I could not?"

He realised at the time there had been an overpowering compulsion to gain the next segment of the amulet and he would also have snapped out of it. He now understood that the proud blonde woman was sorely angered at the way the temptress had easily manipulated both of them and it probably reminded her of another time when she had been just as helpless.

"She just reacted to the situation. But where the hell did Greta get that blade from? She was completely naked and either one of us would have spotted it."

Been very close to her completely exposed form, there was only one possibility of where it came from, the same place as the green jewel and he did not want to dwell on that. The bearer of the now four parts of the living Amulet came to the conclusion.

"She and Cahill must have some very interesting foreplay."

XXV.

The red moon hung low in the high altitude sky. The wind howled; another effect of nature was letting him know, it too was about.

He ignored it's mournful sounds, he had more pressing concern's.

Unperturbed, it wailed again.

Still, he seemed oblivious to it.

The wind became bolder, now it mocked him.

That touched a raw nerve and got his attention. He roared in defiance at its unwanted intrusion.

"Are you screaming at me? Dam you!"

Extraordinary events had conspired to reach this unforeseen impasse that the bearer of the uncompleted APOCRYPHA'I was now facing. As a consequence, events had become static and the leader of the fourteen questors collided with this apparently immovable barrier head on. What he did not know, caught in this time of indecision was that things were about to get even weirder still. As he fought against this unsolvable obstacle, a fierce spring tempest blew up from nowhere. Now, the wind carried a malicious intent within its bosom. Ordinarily, the creatures of this region would seek shelter on an inclement morning such as this. No living thing would be standing out in the bitter chill of this wind that was infused with a fine spray of mist and hail. The fall of the icy particles intensified and the globules of frozen liquid grew larger and more numerous. The intense squall lasted for a few minutes and the drum roll of the falling hail faded as the icy droplets melted as the morning warmed slightly, allowing the mist to become the dominant weather feature. It appeared that this mini-tempest of persistent rain was solely directed at the lone figure who was standing erect on the bleak hillside and who was intently focused throughout his vigil. This mortal who had the audacity to ignore nature's fury basked in the thrill of the inclement weather. His impervious clothing deflected the bitter cold and the stinging frozen moisture of this grisly mountain season and kept in the heat. He wanted to tear off his clothes and let the wind scour away the perceived blood that he had shed during his bouts of the Tournament. The murder of the beautiful vision of womanhood played on his thoughts the most. His participation in that ugly event had left him feeling unclean. He had already decided.

"If nature has a personality; then she was in a crusty mood today, a bit like me."

As if the puny mortal stood there in defiance to test her limits, the wind, an extension of herself howled in greater rage at this lack of respect for her power. She hit him with her full fury once again. Naomh looked out across the entire landscape with his newly enhanced monocles that made a mockery of the storms poor visibility. With another hue added to the inner skin of the LAB-CELL, the Engineer and the Lenses had fabricated these

676

superior versions. Consisting of two wafer thin optics that formed a watery film in each orb, these advanced devices transmitted three dimensional images and sounds directly to the wearer's brain. At long last and unknown to the Hybrids, they had a method of sending and receiving primitive Missives. At the moment, the highly developed viewing device provided him with a clear and unobstructed image of the surrounding terrain in front of him. The scene ahead held a grim vista of large boulders and splintered sized pebbles. Tuffs of greenery were few and far between, those that could be made out were hunkered down between rocks and under ridge overhangs. This muddled panorama matched the growing turmoil within his mind. He was as unsettled as the sharp rocky terrain ahead of him. It looked like his and his comrade's relentless search for the pieces of the living amulet had come undone. He was waiting for inspiration, but it did not make itself known. Doubt's crept in; he was struggling to accept the situation than he was now in.

"Has it all just been a false hope? Is our dream of over throwing the corrupt rulers of the Anschluss, just that, a fantasy born from a need to flee our homeland and the relentless assaults of the Filth."

Finally, the weight and enormity of the quest pressed down on him and the experience was suffocating. The usual depression after assimilating a piece of the APOCRYPHA'I set in, but this time, the dark mood was more pronounced. Even the flickering on of the green tesseral failed to lift him. He had braced himself for the usual downer and not this intense helplessness. He knew.

"This is strange as for the first time since absorbing Miriam's piece; I have not lost a cherished comrade."

Thinking of his lover made him realise that he could not keep his hands off her since the events in the Harlots quarters. Every moment it was possible, he had copulated with her. The inner voice could have told him.

"This is the effect of gaining the green piece, it will wear off soon."

Eventually his sexual urges had returned to normal. The bearer of the four parts of the living amulet had not come out here all alone to scan the terrain that lay ahead of them. No, Naomh was out here away from his companions simply because he was brooding. This silent and pensive watcher had made excuses to his lover and comrades requesting of them.

"I need time to myself. It can become overwhelming."

Most of his friends understood, even his beloved Miriam, as all of them including Tell's mole had witnessed his fluctuating moods every time he gained another piece. At this moment in time, the sharp and jagged landscape held little worry for him. No, his immediate concern was the lack of contact with the voice within and the peculiar depression that he now found himself in. As, if to add insult to injury, the normally talkative voice of the APOCRYPHA'I had become unusually silent and non-undemonstrative. Naomh had not heard from the metallic accent in days.

Its host was beginning to wonder in growing dread if it had ceased to function. His situation triggered a memory. He remembered once when he was having a bad time with the futility of the RE-INSTATOR cause. His then uncle, Rory took him aside and asked him.

"What is the matter? You look like the weight of the World is all yours."

When Naomh explained to him his concerns, he replied.

"There is nothing wrong with that. It is better to be pessimistic than optimistic."

"How is that, surely it is better to feel the opposite way?" Said the other.

"Well if you always expect something to turn out for you and it doesn't, then you will be very disappointed. If, however you expect the worst and it does not happen, then you will have got a bonus. Think about it."

He cast his thoughts back on the events of the last few days. After the killing of the beautiful temptress of the Mountain Kingdom, he had gathered his small band together in her room and made plans to flee. The companions fled the Golden City like thieves in the night. Before that, he had called a servant and told him.

"None of the staff in the victor's quarter are to bother us for a day or two."

This was not an unusual for their guest of immeasurable importance; other victors of the fighting contest had wanted to be left alone with their trophy before. The former winner that Naomh had so easily dispatched had spent two weeks with his female trophy before he had ventured out of the pleasure room and that was only for a request by the King to attend a public audience. The palace staff complied with the requisition while they concealed the naked body of the dead temptress with the same device that had hidden Haim's grave back on the cold mountain top. If the servants found them gone and discovered the dead woman, then all hell would break loose. The clever Lenses had also managed to reproduce the Hologram that the Prof had used and he left several false images of them in the harlot's quarters. This way, there would be nothing suspicious for the servants to report for a while and the departed group would avoid a similar ducking and diving as when they were chased by the Sheikh's troops. The escapee's had used the TORT-CAMLET'S to get them out of the palace complex and into the city proper. Here, the streets were buzzing with extra troops, but the fugitives went unnoticed as they mixed with the celebrating crowds; none had remembered such a bizarre outcome as this year's Tournament and spirits were high. The secretive gang were covered up in stolen clothing as the clued in population would instantly recognise the man of the moment or indeed any of his companions. When they were at the outskirts of the high altitude city, the fleeing group stole a large well used private transport vehicle. The Persuader smashed its window with a gloved fist and its wailing alarm was silenced promptly by Moshe, who then quickly started the engine. The vehicle stealers took the first road out of the capital, not caring for the moment which direction they were going in. All through the flight, there had been no word from the internal voice. This was unusual, as it would be normally euphoric at gaining another segment of itself. A sudden thunderstorm made driving impossible, they had to pull over and wait it out. The rain was not the problem, their optical devices could penetrate its opacity; no, it was the strong winds that was a part of its physical embodiment. Otherwise they could go crashing over the hills. They did not generate the TORT-CAM within the pilfered vehicle as it was on a blind spot. They had no wish to lose their comfortable method of transport and start walking again. Nor could they activate it out in the rain, it would be easily seen. They had no choice but to set up defensive perimeters, guard the vehicle and wait out the heavy downpour. Needless to say, nobody was happy with the sentry duty. The Engineer wondered why as their superior protective outfits would stop anybody from getting wet. The driving rain increased in vigour until it sounded like crashing waves on a rocky seashore. The tempest lasted most of the day and an unsaturated crew were glad to move on. Now three days later, out here in the weather and away from the others, its bearer was trying unsuccessfully to re-establish contact with the alter ego. The Alien voice had been a constant presence in his mind ever since that fateful night in the Sarajevo Contrib and though he had wished it gone on numerous occasions, its host was now surprised at how frightened he had become by its continued silence. Over the last few days, he was lost without its continued influence. Naomh desperately searched the recesses of his mind for it. But there was still no interaction with it. He was now becoming quite frantic and trying to find something to cling on to.

"I will not succumb to failure, ever since this fantastic quest has been forced on me, I have not looked back. I have a strong compulsion that this search is both righteous and the correct path to follow. I would know if it was wrong or evil. This is the reason that I exist and in following the path of assembling the APOCRYPHA'I, I have grown with every step. I have only four parts of it, it is not complete yet and it will not end here in this God forsaken place."

His heart pounded with indecision. If this was now out of his hands and the end of the search, he knew that he would sink into utter despair. Once again, Naomh entreated to the non-co-operative voice within and still there was no accommodation. He raged.

"No, this cannot be the end. There have been too many sacrifices. Too many deaths; too much lost and changed. No, I will not let it end here, do you hear me. A father that I never knew as a parent is gone. Goulash, who never even knew about this crazy journey, is dead anyway. The beautiful Shoshanna and the strong and loyal Haim have perished and they had

believed in the quest. Even the Prof was changed by it; he could not take the killing anymore and fled. I have nearly been killed twice and the Persuader nearly suffered the same fate. No for the sake of my dead and suffering comrades, I will not abandon this quest. Now answer me, dam you."

He knew that the rest of his company looked up to him and trusted him with his decisions. Naomh was almost certain that none of them knew the full extent of his secret agenda.

But sometimes, the Guide, the Engineer, Greta and even the Mute looked at him as if each of them had an inkling of the true nature of his quest. It was nothing specific, just the odd glance that would be directed at him from the four mentioned. Again, he made demands from the A.W.O.L living amulet.

"Where the Hell are you? Answer me!"

One thing inbuilt into Naomh's character was that he was persistent. He would not give up calling for it until he got an answer. Suddenly, the bearer felt a faint trace of its presence; it was a suggestion, nothing more. Bouyed by that whisper, he probed deeper.

"So, it is still a part of me."

Relief flooded in and the contact became stronger. So in tune was Naomh now with the internal awareness that he was amazed to find that the other presence was confused. This was new to its host. The voice had always seemed to be in control, never flagging or surprised by any challenge or obstacle. He requested a response from it.

He received no reply.

Naomh threatened it; this always worked in the past.

Still, no answer.

He tried coaxing it.

No response.

A trace of panic laid its chill grip on his spine. Was the presence of the uncompleted APOCRYPHA'I fading because of that very reason of not been whole?

"I cannot return to what I was before it."

Then Naomh had an idea born from desperation.

"It is always there when I need to be healed."

He took out his throwing star, bared his right forearm to the chill and with clenched teeth prepared to slice his wrist.

"That will get its attention."

The fluctuation within its host's chemical balance, due to his anxiety must have awakened it, for it replied in a sulky attitude.

"Put away the weapon, I have no time for this nonsense."

"Why have you gone silent? What is the problem?" Demanded a very relieved Naomh as he sheathed his blade.

"It is the fifth piece of me. I cannot locate the blue segment." Replied

the four parts of the Mescal/Amulet in a completely baffled tone.

"I have been scrutinising the entire Planet's surface using my people's technology without even finding a slight trace of it. I have been searching since the fourth piece assimilated, but it has been a fruitless task."

"Are you sure?" Asked its troubled bearer.

The presence within did not even bother to answer that question. Naomh was been influenced by its indecision as he made his way back to the rest of the troop who were in the vicinity of the TORT-CAM. He had a suggestion

"Maybe, one of them can help?"

As he shared the living amulets melancholy, his train of thought took an unusual turn. Naomh suddenly realised with clarity.

"Compared to the lands that we have passed through over the last year, the Anschluss is not so bad after all. The poverty, desperation and sickness that we have encountered on our travels convinces me of that. Those everyday hardships just don't exist back home. My homeland had many faults, but such blatant neglect of the majority of its citizens is not one. Only those who refused to conform are treated differently. It could be a paradise and a role model for the rest of the World. All we have to do is to rid it of its corrupt system of government and its leaders. And we need the completed APOCRYPHA'I for that."

The Alien presence within him did not like this train of thought. As the Hybrid absorbed each part of it, he was supposed to adhere more rigidly to his programming and become focused on the course the ALASTHA'I had set him on. Their pawn would not be allowed to deviate from their desired outcome. (But what the incomplete Mescal/Amulet did not realise was that the mix with the Hybrid was changing its make up as well.) Naomh be might well able to make his own decisions for the betterment of his race contrary to what it required. But the Winged Aliens had a back-up plan; it had been used before and more recently with his parent Rory. It could at any stage reactivate its host's inactive sperm and Miriam could produce his successor. If he was made to perish, she could with difficulty absorb the four pieces and hold those in trust until her offspring was born. She would be reduced to a babbling infant or a doddering wreck, but her fate was of little consequence in its quest for completion. The individual red segment of the living amulet had caused this circumstance on a few occasions when its bearer was not conforming or had not met its expectations. For the plan of the ALASTHA'I was paramount and their tools were just as expendable as the Chairman's underlings. Although haste was essential, it was not foremost and it had been wrong before about its host's potential. Relieved at re-establishing contact with the living amulet, Naomh made his way back to the others. At the camp, Beersheba was trimming Solomon's beard; the busy woman had just finished grooming Moshe's and the Clerk's chin growth. The Rabbi had steadfastly refused to have his extensive tresses attended to. Miriam had been waiting for him and she handed her returning partner a mug of steaming coffee while giving him a look of loving concern. His devotion for her was growing stronger, but he still felt remorse about his liaison with the temptress and Greta. He knew that those events had been out of his control, but he still felt guilty about his stimulating participation. Shortly after their escape form the city, a confused Naomh had caught the tall blonde women alone and asked her.

"What the Hell went on back there?"

She seemed to be as embarrassed as him and soberly advised.

"Look, let's forget about it. Circumstances were out of our control. We had no power over those events."

"I know that we agreed not to, but should we tell Cahill and Miriam what happened?"

He sounded like he needed to ease his guilty conscience. His recent bouts of love making with Miriam seemed a farce. Two other naked bodies always intruded. Greta shook her head slowly and replied.

"No Naomh, think about it, it would serve no purpose and only cause tensions. Imagine how Cahill would react? As I said, let's forget about it. Nothing happened. Ok!"

Her relieved conspirator agreed, but as he walked away from her, he could not get the image of her nakedness out of his mind.

"Forget about it. Ha! How could you not think about that?"

The Clerk had witnessed the hushed conversation and wondered what that was about. But he did not ask. Now in the present, he took the hot drink off his partner with a grateful smile, he still could not look at Greta directly and if he did, his eyes would be drawn towards her obvious attributes. Even though she was now clothed, he still remembered every fine detail of her naked body and especially her firm buttocks. Refusing to be distracted by these conflicting emotions, Naomh gathered the group together and revealed the apparent insurmountable problem to them. He spoke in a low voice.

"I cannot locate the next piece of the amulet. With the means given to me, I have searched and searched but I have no inkling of what direction to head in."

"What do you mean that you cannot locate it?" Contested Cahill, his leader's words were unpalatable to him and the rest of the crew.

Don't worry, give it a few days and it will come to you." Said the unperturbed Guide.

There were different reactions from the rest.

"Was that it? The end of the quest."

This was the unbelievable consensus from the others, except the Mute. The serial killer appeared indifferent to the importance of the search for the technology that would overthrow the Anschluss rulers.

"Was it all for nothing?" Voiced Cahill after Naomh's earlier

deliberations.

In an expression of temper, his best friend hammered the ground forcing earth up from the edges of his fist. There was utter disbelief among some of the others; even the laconic Greta became upset. The Engineer saw his dreams of a return to religion go down the spout. The Clerk also lost his cool, the former bureaucrat began to shout and rant while he waved his hands in an angry gesture.

"After all we've been through. The friends we have lost. Shit, I think the Prof had the right idea. Naomh, you better come up with something, maybe you're not trying hard enough."

"Have you or any of the others any better ideas? Well I'm all ears." Demanded, the bearer of the four parts.

"I don't know. Maybe, it's out in fucking space or somewhere just as mad."

The red faced speaker turned and kicked a utensil into the air; it just missed the Rabbi by a whisker, a bushy bearded one at that. The elder gave the offender a hard look, but the perpetrator was too angry to apologise. Naomh just ignored the contempt in the Clerk's voice as he watched the plastic pot sail through the air. Something went click in his mind as he listened to the blonde man's tirade. He looked open mouthed as he stared up at the Heavens. Suddenly Naomh broke into a broad grin. He grabbed his astonished friend by the cheeks and kissed him on the wary forehead. Amazingly, the answer had come from an unusual source.

"You're a bloody genius Victor. That's why I cannot find it. I was looking for it in the wrong place. If it's not on Earth, then it has to be off Planet. It's that simple."

The four parts of the Mescal/Amulet had become disturbed that its race's tools had determined the location of his next part, while it had eluded it. But it quickly put that down to the fact that it was not complete. With urgency, it cast aside its concerns and directed its attention into space. The Moon was the first object to be inspected, but that search turned up negative. Then, it focused on the space junk of the Hybrid's that littered the voids in between the planets of this solar system. Again the search proved negative. Next, it was the turn of the Red World, the fourth from the Sun. The four part's Mescal/Amulet felt a whisper of itself. Concentrating from where it felt the connection, it was attracted to a specific place. It informed its host.

"The next piece of me is on the Red Planet."

"Mars. That's where it is!" Yelled Naomh out loud.

Even, the uncompleted APOCRYPHA'I got caught up in the Hybrid's excitement. *"Affirmative. Now that I have located the next piece of me, its signature grows stronger. It is calling to me across the vacuum of space."*

Then a sombre Guide hawked and spat as he asked the hundred million-credit question.

683

"Sorry to put a dampener on your spirits man, but how the fuck are we going to get into space? That place has been off limits since the space virus made it impossible. We are still goosed man. Even more so now."

The growing elation stalled, but then the smiling Lenses took centre stage, the former computer hacker came up with the solution.

"That is not exactly true. One of the things I hacked into in the Anschluss secret files was that our beloved government still have a clandestine and active space programme. They still have people that are resistant to the disease. And from that sensitive information, it is also clear that other power-blocks around the World do not have the same capability anymore. The sector where the spacecraft are launched is in a place called Guiana."

"Where is this place called Guiana?" Asked Moshe.

The Enclave man was not the only one who had not heard of it.

"Across the World on the South American Continent." Replied the Guide for everyone's benefit.

"That's on the other side of the Atlantic Ocean." Said Solomon.

"And how do we get there?"

Cahill wanted to know and so did everybody else.

"By a couple of very long sea voyages." Answered the Guide with a vicious grin.

All of the Anschluss members of the group groaned, it was clear that they had gained little affection for sea travel. As if to compound their misery, their pony tailed comrade said in a likewise vein of humour.

"We have been on dry land too long; a good long sea voyage will clear the cobwebs from the brain."

"And not to mention the stomach." Said a disgusted Clerk.

The mole knew the weird eyed man was correct with his synopsis on space travel and decided.

"On that information alone, you will be eliminated after the quest is concluded."

It had now become a regular event when Naomh gained another segment of the APOCRYPHA'I, the Engineer and the Lenses with his unique connection would trawl the new inventory of the LAB-CELL. As always, a few new and highly interesting items of advanced technology would crop up, they had already discovered the advanced Monocles. Again both enthusiasts were not let down. This time, the two men struck the jackpot. Among the useful additions were firstly, small coloured globes that attached to the ear and like Naomh let the wearer understand most of the spoken languages on the Planet. Now, everybody became multi-lingual and none of them would have to rely on their leader for communication when they found themselves in a strange land. Those like the Spy who were proficient in more than one language found an increased ability in these tongues. The second of these useful arrivals that was unearthed was a truly wonderful device; it was an aerial three-dimensional contour map of the World. It displayed every physical feature of the Planet, from the seven Continents, the oceans, geological configurations and even the urban districts of man. The enthralled group found themselves staring at the Planetary palette, from its turquoise oceans, the brown deserts to it's the green jungles and forests and the grey cities. If they focussed in at the correct angles then individual buildings could be made out. Now for the first time all of them had a clear picture of the immensity of the places outside the Anschluss and the Enclave. Where once, they had only the confined spaces of their respective homelands, the whole Planet was now their oyster. With this navigational wonder, the now more knowledgeable travellers could plan their routes and not rely on local information. The map was a live three-dimensional image projected from the undetected ALASTHA'I technology still orbiting the Earth. The Mole who had vast experience of satellite imaging was amazed at the accuracy, the detail and the clarity of the device. This one knew.

"This is a step beyond in advanced technology."

Using this imaging globe and after much debating and discussion, an acceptable route was finally planned out from their immediate position to Guiana.

"Ok let's find the nearest port and make our way to these America's." Said Naomh as he traced his finger along the rim of his beaker. He took one last sip of his now cool beverage from his mug and flung its remaining contents to the ground. The Lenses interrupted, as an idea came to him.

"Could you imagine what the Prof would have thought of this living map? I reckon that he would have brought it back to the Anschluss and shown the sceptical Plebs there about the rest of the World. That would open up there insular and closed minds."

Agent XIII privately reinforced an earlier assessment.

"Yes, that one's ideas are dangerous. If the weird coloured eyed man survives this quest, he will have to be eliminated."

Some of the Lenses words had an effect on Solomon, fingering the small object given to him by the Prof; he stayed intently focussed on the scientific marvel. He wondered if it would connect to the device and reveal his missing friend's location. Unfortunately, it did not. He did not know that its fellow piece now lay at the bottom of the fiery pit, unharmed, but forever unmoving. The resurgent questors packed up their gear and began a long trek back into the Indian Sub-Continent. By going Eastwards first, the company avoided the Blasted Lands and it caused the negative Clerk to comment.

"It would have been much easier to come this way the first time."

A bitter Beersheba responded.

"If we had, then Haim would be still alive."

The Rabbi removed that melancholy thought.

"We had no idea where we were going; we were relying on that treacherous rat Singh."

"True." Was her sad reply.

During the same time as this leg of their journey, events were rapidly transpiring back in the palace in the Mountain Kingdom. A technician had brought an unusual video to the King. It was footage of the final battle of the Tournament, just after the lights went down. It showed the eventual winner hovering unassisted in the air as his opponent fell into the fire and was incinerated. The royal ruler became outraged, because he knew of only one grouping that was capable of that feat.

"Are the religious orders plotting against me? Is the winner one of them?"

He ordered his soldiers.

"Fetch the Champion and his companions into my presence."

They came back with a strange tale.

"Getting no answers to our demands, we forcibly entered the winner's room and found transparent images of those that were sought. They were all gone along with the beautiful prize."

The King was astounded, but wisely decided not to act against those who he still blamed; it would tear his country apart. A few days later during a rest period and a brief meal, the Lenses and the Engineer had discovered another useful thing about the TORT-CAM. The multi-coloured eyed man explained to the others while they were taking lunch.

"Myself and the Engineer discovered something about our invisible shield that is very practical. Do you know the way the LAB-CELL is a separate entity from our living space by the fact that is separated by a wall of opaque light?"

Those that were interested nodded. So, he continued.

"Well, we can now split the interior into separate quarters using these walls of light. At last each of us can achieve some degree of privacy."

Now that he had everybody's attention, the rest of the gang were delighted with the Lenses discovery. The Spy was the most pleased of all. This communal living among inferiors was getting to the traitor and this new form of solitude was belatedly welcomed. The meal was finished and they arrived at the border between the Mountain Kingdom and India. To one side flew the flag of the country they were leaving and a hundred metres away the flag of the Sub-Continent challenged for attention. Their vehicle was stuck in a slow moving line. Eventually after five hours of crawling, they were at the front of the line. Armed soldiers motioned them to pull to one side. Seizing a chance to test his new language abilities, the Guide said.

"I have experience of this. Let me deal with it. Everybody get out."

A suited turban wearing man approached them as van DerKamp tried out his skills. He had a whispered conversation with the official, something

686

was passed between them and the pony-tailed man came back to them.

"It's sorted, get back on the vehicle."

They all re-boarded their means of transport and Moshe re-started the engine. Their motorised vehicle was ushered through the frontier without further mishap. With the Enclave man at the helm, they started the long descent, down winding and twisting roads and eventually they reached the first destination on the planned route. The fourteen travellers got off the ramshackle truck that had got them this far and were now facing the huge metropolis of Calcutta. They travelled through the turbulent streets, making their way from its outskirts to its centre, through the constant noise and bustle. It appeared to be a black hole of a hundred and fifty million souls. Using their newfound mastery of the languages of this ancient metropolis, the new arrivals rented a room in the overcrowded city. There were definitely more people crammed into every square kilometre here than any other place they had been and that included their Homelands. Densely packed buildings fought each other for space and sunlight, much like the trees of a forest eager for the sky. The crush of Humanity, the variety of their transport vehicles and even their livestock in this compact space was overwhelming and it was not the bland sterile atmosphere of pure urbanisation that permuted around. The abundance of stenches that mixed in close proximity was only matched by the constant noises of its everyday activities. The rooms that they eventually found were located in the east side, close to the cities dockfront and the frantic bustle of the thriving port matched the rest of the city in its never ending rhythm of commerce. They booked out a whole floor. Half of them stayed in the rented rooms, eating food from their supplies, while those that were inclined towards the exotic went down into the streets to sample the local fare. Finding seats in a restaurant in a winding street that came out of a history archive, these seven sat down to their meal. The dark waiter who must have been originally from the south brought them a menu, which each of them could now read. A chicken or meat curry dish accompanied with japati bread and basmati rice became their choice. Bottles of cool beer were also ordered to wash down the meal.

"Dam, this is hot." Voiced the Clerk while gulping down a mouthful of the cold beer.

No one felt inclined to take in the sights, so when the meal was finished and the thrill of soaking up the character of the quaint location had been satisfied, they retired back to their rooms. After a little chat and use of the toilets, everybody crashed out. It was Beersheba's turn at guard duty. She activated the alarm system and sat in a chair on the landing with a fully loaded Uzi across her lap. Tomorrow, they would find passage Southwards. Three hours into her watch, the sentry thought she felt an unusual movement of the landing. The armed Enclave woman shrugged at her giddiness and put the strange sensation down to tiredness.

"I must have nodded off for a moment." Decided their guard.

She took a swig from her water bottle to regain her concentration. The liquid had a bit of pep added to its mixture. Alert now, she thought nothing of the previous odd feeling. Then, there came a strange rumbling from outside and the building began to shake violently. Suddenly Beersheba understood what was happening as she witnessed fine jagged cracks whip-lashed along the cement plastered walls of the room. It seemed as some nonsensical scribing's were been etched by some invisible hand. She cried out a warning to her comrades, but Naomh beat her to it. He had been at the edges of deep sleep with his body folded around Miriam when the internal voice intruded with great urgency.

"The Continental plates that meet at this point have shifted slightly. Do as I say and get everybody into the safety of the Gudiex Sphere."

Naomh shouted the command, just as Beersheba stormed in his room. She shouted in unison with her leader. Her voice trembled as much as the apartment floor.

"It's an earthquake, everybody get into the TORT-CAM."

"What is happening?" Cried someone.

"The building is dancing." Came the answer from the Persuader.

All of the crew had left their rooms and were in the hallway.

"Do as Beersheba advises. Get into the protective shield." Ordered Solomon.

He also knew what was happening. The room shook again, this time with even greater force. Jagged cracks grew in diameter. They did not need more urging and as one the group dashed into the activated shield. All but one of those from the Anschluss had even the slightest idea what an earthquake was. These tectonic plate movements happened rarely in their homeland, the last one was in the Athens Contrib over seven hundred years ago. That force of nature had brought down the wall, but the loss of life was low and the authorities in typical fashion suppressed all knowledge of it. Its rulers could not be seen to be helpless, even against the ravages of nature. The rent was quickly repaired and the hushed up incident was quickly forgotten about. Safely inside their impenetrable shield that now had green tiles added to it, none of the room's occupants noticed the growing intensity of the vibrations. Aged and poorly constructed towers began to topple like giant trees in storm shaken jungle. Like their timber counterparts, the falling buildings brought down others in their descent. Then came the massive shock, it measured seven point three on the Richter scale. None of the cocooned questors felt the vertical drop of nine floors as the eleven-storey building's columns bucked, sheared and toppled sideways. Nor did they hear the thud of the separate floors hitting each other as each level collapsed like an accordion, killing many of the occupants. In seconds, the poorly constructed building had become a heap of twisted metal, concrete, bloodied corpses and ruined lives. The once tall structure was now piled up at three stories. The TORT-CAM and its fourteen unharmed occupants ended up in a hollow space in the mess of the building's smoking debris. There were tons of rubble above, below and all around them. The viewer showed only a dusty cave, they had limited visibility through the swirling haze.

"Shit. What are we going to do now?" Asked the Persuader in a shaken voice.

His brother came up with the solution this time. He modified the burners that had dug Haim's grave. The others copped on to his scheme. Solomon and the Persuader strapped them on and armed with air filters to stop them choking, the two of them left the safety of their shield. Increasing their effectiveness, the two sturdy men burned their way out of the living tomb with beams of fiery heat. Their pace was maddenly slow as they checked the walls of their newly created burrow after each burst. The heat seemed to liquefy the parameters of the tunnel into a solid mass and held its confines together. Satisfied, that their newly created tunnel would hold, Naomh reduced the TORT-CAM to marble size and returned it to his pocket. They followed the duo out of the underground tomb. Outside the pile of rubble, the temporary subterraneous dwellers were greeted with a scene of devastation. On the streets, it looked like some petulant giant had thrown a tantrum. Buildings that were not toppled sideways lay in heaps of rubble. Trees, neon signposts and electric poles were scattered around like matchwood. Cracked concrete was filled in with water from busted mains and sewer pipes whose rank stench was on the foul air. Loud wails from survivors and alarm devices filled the surrounding vicinity. Traumatic people were immovable and transfixed in shock. Naomh saw the Mute bend down alongside a dying woman. He wrongly believed that he was trying to help her. He never saw the blade.

"What the hell happened? Is this country at war? Was it an air strike?" Moshe fired off the three questions in rapid succession. He had been in a deep sleep before the earth shattering events and had moved with the others in an orderly reflex. Solomon put him right.

"No. It was a natural disaster. What you would call an earthquake."

"Wow!" Was the reply from his compatriot.

Suddenly the ground began to quiver again and Miriam responded to the situation.

"After shocks. Quick, everybody back into the TORT-CAM again. It is not over yet."

Her lover re-activated the concealment device and the entire group scrambled into it. Unknown to them, they had been seen by a local street beggar. Kable Padji was still shell shocked from the traumatic after effects of the massive earth tremor, but his fluid filled eyes had not lied. Dazed with congealed blood on his shaven scalp, the result of falling masonry, he had seen the strangers disappear into thin air. The ruined buildings began to rattle again and bits crashed to the ground. The lethargic survivors suddenly gathered their wits and tried to flee. But falling masonry buried most of them and drowned out their squeals of panic. Padji who had spent a lifetime on these unforgiving streets was a born opportunist and he had only one choice. The street beggar leapt into the air where the last person had vanished. He was a second behind the last man and crashed into his back. Recovering, he found himself in an unknown place of safety and many colours. Strong arms pinned him down and the homeless man was blinded by a powerful light. Unfortunately, when the beam was switched off, he found himself looking down the muzzles of several weapons.

"Kill him." Said one of the armed people.

It had been a tall blonde female.

"No! You cannot violate this sacred space." Pleaded Naomh's internal voice.

"Use a sedative."

The unwanted guest heard another speak. One with the voice of command said.

"Do it Solomon's way."

Kable Padji felt oblivion, but he awoke alive and well in the middle of the devastation. Sprawling bodies and limp limbs hanging out of piles of rubble convinced him that he had made the correct decision. The strangers and their invisible World had vanished and miraculously he had survived. This amazing event had a profound effect on him.

"I have been saved by servants of the God's who took Human form."

Sensing a golden opening, Kable Padji became a wandering Holy-man over the next few years and told anyone who would listen about his divine rescue. Travelling the land with a retinue of followers, dressed in the finery of an orange robe, the new Guru never revealed that his saviours had pointed guns at him and one of them wanted to end his wretched life. Instead the self-appointed "Sadu" told a different tale.

"When I awoke in paradise; the servants of the God's judged me unworthy. The vengeful ones wanted to slay me. But the wisest among them sent me back to redeem my life."

This added to the fact that Padji had been the only survivor in that city area that had borne the blunt of the tremor added credence to his testimony.

"We should have killed him." Said the Mute in his whinny timbre, now that they were a kilometre away from the rescued man, his blood lust had barely subsided. Greta agreed.

"He will be able to tell others about us."

"Who will believe him?" Said the dismissive Lenses.

Another far-fetched tale that could have been told was that the Atomic bomb dropped by the PREVENTIVES on Singh's people could have started a delayed chain reaction in a seismic fault that was now only released in this innocent city causing the deaths of two million people. The dynamic group left the shattered metropolis and travelled their way down the eastern side of the Sub-Continent in a newly purchased vehicle. The Clerk had paid an exorbitant price for it and though monies were inconsequential to him, the former registrar was galled on principal. On the way south, they encountered a lot of traffic going in the opposite direction and in the skies above flying craft moved with great urgency. Their vehicle passed many checkpoints manned by armed soldiers. By covering themselves up, added to their proficiently in the language allowed them to bluff their way through these hastily erected barriers. Day after day passed by as they traversed the outskirts of Visha`khapatnam, Ra`jahmundry, Vijayawada and Guntur. Travelling down the narrower tail of the Sub-Continent, each alternating driver avoided the cities of Chirla, Ongole, and Nellore until they finally reached a place called Madras. The inhabitants of this sprawling port city were as black as coal to the questors. Settling themselves in to a hotel, the cramped travellers abandoned the vehicle and just left the engine running. Gathering information, it was found out that there was a regular voyage to a place called South Africa which had been the next place on their planned route. Consulting their three dimensional map, it was in the right direction. The office of the ticket seller offered them various routes and some included a brief stoppage in the cities of the Prophet. Needless to say, this was avoided at all cost. It meant a longer time at sea, but the questors were comfortable with that. The searchers of the APOCRYPHA'I once again took reluctantly to the Ocean. Their vessel passed through the Palk Strait and made port in Colombo, the largest city on an island called Sri Lanka. Here the ship let off and picked up more passengers. Then the vessel took to the open sea by passing clusters of islands called the Maldives and the Seychelles. After many days of travel, the sea going craft rounded a huge island called Madagascar and then it was within striking distance of the African mainland. Passing by the Cape of Good Hope, it arrived at its final destination, Cape Town. Here was a large city that nestled under the shadow of an enormous table shaped mountain. Its tall tower-blocks competed with the natural heights in reaching for the sky. From here, the questors had to find a vessel to take them across the vastness of the Atlantic Ocean. As usual, they went to the dock front and split up into groups and trawled the surrounding area for the necessary information. The now experienced travellers encountered a hotpot of various races. It was a mosaic of different peoples, but most of its inhabitants were a different shade of black. Ironically, now that it did not matter, everybody spoke a very accented version of Anschluss. Here things went against them; they could not find a vessel to take them across to the America's. The fourteen split up after much persistence and time spent in and out of waterfront bars (Some did not complain about this.), the Guide eventually found one man that offered them some sort of passage. But, there was a major hitch; its owner could only take them so far. He asked of those wanting to hire his ship.

"Why don't you fly there? It would be a lot quicker and less costly."

"We don't want to announce our arrival."

"I understand." Replied the man who was familiar with such operations and decided that the price had gone up.

"So we have a deal?"

"Come tomorrow and we will discuss it."

The ship was tiny compared differently to the Anschluss Dreadnaut and the various ferries that they had travelled on before, but it was built for speed. The vessels name was proudly displayed in Anschluss script along the prow. It was called.

"The Flying Assegai."

The sleek craft was so named because the ship had a similar design to the slender iron tipped ancient spear of its owner's forefathers. The Captain of the coastal clipper was an unusual man. He had a white name for a black man. He had a shaven scalp and if it was possible, he appeared to be more muscular than the Persuader. He was not as tall and he had a wicked scar along his left cheek, caused by a man who immediately met his maker. Frank De Boer was a jolly man and most of them enjoyed his company and infectious laugh, but the captain was far from been a fool. The Ocean goer said as he showed them a sea chart and traced a route with his finger.

"I can take all of you as far as a sparsely populated island cluster on the North western side of the Continent. There you can bargain for passage across the wider Ocean."

The Lenses and the Clerk consulted their own three dimensional map and when the two men returned, one of them nodded to Naomh.

"It is in the right direction, but it is in spitting distance of the Anschluss."

De Mere like his friend the Prof had become sick of the needless killing of people, especially when they put the temptation of great wealth in front of them. So, the former bureaucrat put a plan into action. He discussed his scheme with the captain and an equitable arrangement was agreed on by both parties. The former registrar whispered into his friend's ears and said.

"We are just putting incredible temptation into his path. So my way is insurance against treachery. And I really like this man, so it would be a shame for one of you to kill him."

The Mute thought.

"It would be no bother at all."

So when the final deal was done, the Clerk, the Persuader and De Boer went to a local bank and deposited a substantial sum in a currency called Rand's which the blonde man had already acquired. When their purser was satisfied that the captain had completed his part of the bargain, he would then call the bank with a special number and it would free the monies for the returning sailor. They were certain that the captain was an honest man, but now they could relax. The black man turned to them with a serious grin and mentioned.

"I like the way you do business. This way, there is no mistrust. That is good for you, for I like you. And because I am a Zulu that is also good news for you. If my people get on with you, we will be the best of friends, if not then I will stab you in an instant."

The dusky individual took out the head of a wicked looking spear and showed it to the two men. When he saw the worried faces on the other two, he gave a wicked laugh and slapped them on the back.

"But then you have no need to worry, I feel that we will get on famously."

The duo joined in his mirth, though it was a little forced. The rest of their compliment were waiting on the dockside when the three men got back. They boarded the ship and the captain soon made sail. His vessel was capable of hitting four hundred and eighty knots an hour. Early in the morning as the day heated up, the stretching synthetic materials of the deckhouse creaked with the rising temperature. Although the rest of the ship was constructed with light and durable alloys, De Boer preferred the touch and the aroma of the malleable wood. Inside the deckhouse, there was the familiar array of thirtieth century instruments, especially the blue Nav-visor that he wore. But one dominating thing stood out, it was a huge circular wheel made of white timber and brass plates. De Boer spent most of his activity adjusting this wheel, every now and then turning it to the left and the right. Other times, he moved it fast or slow. Moshe spent a lot of time with the Captain in the bridge; the Flying Assegai fascinated the Enclave man. The Zulu even let the wide-eyed man steer the craft occasionally. The lesser darker man told him.

"I have never controlled something that moves this fast before."

"Not many people do my friend."

He clapped the stocky man on the back for good measure. Most of the gang had enjoyed the Captain's company and the black man was full of a lifetime's conversation. But for a moment, he became unusually serious. He pointed to the bleak coastline on the starboard. Intense heat appeared to radiate off the whiteness

"That place is called the Skeleton Coast, man. If you ever found yourself stranded out there, do yourself a favour and put a bullet in your head. It would be the sensible thing to do. Nobody unfortunate enough to be shipwrecked there has survived in a thousand years."

But then, the jolly black man did not know about his passengers amazing equipment that made light with the harsh rigours of extreme conditions. De Boer had also twisted the facts slightly. This stretch of coast got its name from the countless shipwrecks that stuck out of the shallow water with their metal ribs exposed from stripped away sheeting. These unfortunate steel and wooden carcasses and their crews had been driven aground by the ferocious weather that regularly battered this shoreline. Far faster than the weapon it was named after, the Flying Assegai sped through the wave tops at two hundred kilometres an hour or as the captain measured; three hundred and seventy knots. The Clerk knew he had left his life of drudgery far behind. He had exchanged his tiny office cubicle and was now skimming across a blue Ocean at lightning speed.

"Yes, this is far better; more than I could have ever dreamed."

After the better part of a day of skirting up the coastline at the exhilarating speed and the wind constant in their lives, the white desert of the coast turned green and the climate became humid and insufferable. Now, they and the crew were greatly thankful for the breezes that flowed as a result of the ship's momentum. The speeding craft rounded the Continental horn and headed in a slightly Westerly direction. Eventually, the greenness of the mainland became brown and then sandy desert again. The prevailing Atlantic breeze became a blessing to the ship's crew. They had not the option of retiring to the coolness of the TORT-CAM. Finally, the vessel arrived at their destination, just as a dense plume of mist began rolling in. It was a cluster of seven volcanic islands called the Canary's that lay 113km off the North West coast of the African Continent. The ship made its way to the largest one, Tenerife. Again thirtieth century technology kicked in as the craft easily made its way through the seemingly impenetrable shroud. Suddenly, the ship was past the wall of fog and its passengers and crew were staring at a primeval sight that the ALASTHA'I would have recognised. The islands large volcano, Pico de Teide had become active again in the last few hundred years. There was a constant plume of dirty smoke and ash spewing from its 3718 metre high crater and sometimes there were orange flickers of fire within that smoking cloud.

"Jesus wept." Said the Mute in his whinny voice.

"We have arrived in Hell itself." Stated the Engineer as he gave Illeau a dirty look.

He was certain the repulsive man had uttered those words, just to rile him.

"That's the Lord's truth." Added the black Captain.

Both the Clerk and the Lenses had noticed the large plumes of smoke when they had consulted the real life map. Not bothering to close in, the two men thought it was a result of some industrial process. The Canary Islands had once been a paradise, but after achieving its independence from its European masters over nine hundred years ago, its situation changed drastically. In retaliation for its actions, the emerging nations of the Power-Block banned their citizens from holidaying there. This was the source of the islands previous wealth and arrogance. As their economy withered and died, it begged to be readmitted to the fold, but it was left to wallow in its own fate. This was a lesson the Europeans wanted the rest of its bickering regions to learn. These once lucrative pieces of real estate were now barren dust rocks. The dregs of humanity hid out here on the isolated islands and they became a base for piracy. De Boer spoke.

"You will find many ships that will take you across the Ocean in one of the waterfront taverns. You don't mind if we don't berth here, this place leaves me and my crew with a sick stomach and I am not referring to all the ash around here. Now about our deal, I have done my part."

The Clerk went to the ship's radio and arranged for the account to be opened. De Boer got confirmation and was satisfied. There were firm handshakes all around and as they were leaving the ship, the captain called after them.

"Be careful here, about who you choose to befriend. The sea dregs that have crawled ashore here are not as nice as me or my crew. I would not like to hear that you ended up in Davy Jones locker."

With that, the man who had just deposited them in the arsehole of nowhere gave an enormous belly laugh which sounded as loud as the rumbling of the volcano. The Captain and his command disappeared out of their lives. Once again they trawled the bar of a foreign dockfront. The establishments of this place were rough and untidy and a different language was spoken, a form of Spanish. But their newly acquired language translators made this circumstance irrelevant. After a short search, numerous shady captain's agreed to take them across to the other side of the ocean. They eventually picked the most trustworthy and that was not saying much for this character. There were no places to deposit money and use the same arrangement as they did with their former carrier. The new captain would only accept precious metals. So half was put up front and the captain would get the rest at the end of the journey. Some dodgy individuals noticing the deal had tried to con and rip them off or offered other opportunities. These people were discouraged with harsh words and the flash of armed weapons. The more adventurous that tried to mug them in the narrow streets made the final mistake of their wasted lives and an extra few bodies floating in the harbour was no big deal. The next morning, they rendezvous with the captain. As they boarded the vessel; the sullen crew did not inspire trustworthiness in the manner of the compliment of the Flying Assegai. The Engineer thought it ironic.

"The black captain inspired more trust than this white one. I would have judged those two people very differently at the start of this quest."

There were no greetings or conversation; in fact the only one who addressed their questions was the captain. Moshe asked him in the old European tongue.

"How long will it take to cross the ocean?"

"About twenty four hours." Replied the seafarer.

The shifty captain was lying; he had never made the journey to the other side of the Ocean and had no intention of doing it now. Inwardly he voiced.

"But I wouldn't worry about that, if I were you?"

The ship went southwards and west of the Cape Verde islands. Half way through the sea crossing, a slight mid Atlantic drizzle started, its wetness barely kissed the wooded deck, but it did make the varnished timber sparkle in newness. This vessel was different to the one that had brought them to the islands; its owner called it a Catamaran. The main body was supported on two large skis' that cut through the waves at speeds of two hundred kilometres an hour. It was only slightly slower than De Boer's sleek craft. From his bridge in the wheelhouse, Captain Hose` Maria Antonio looked up to the night sky; he had not decided when the betrayal would come. The weak shower dissipated, it seemed that the piebald clouds were noncommittal and the weather was as undecided as himself. His passengers had already paid him a fortune. But his greedy crew believed that there was more to be had and some like the deceased Singh desired the three women. Antonio even believed.

"Shit, I reckon that some of those perverts even have the same carnal desires on the blonde men."

It would not be the first time these treacherous seafarers had taken such action, Davy Jones locker would testify to that. Most of their victims had been taken easily with drugged food, but this lot stuck to their own fare. One of his crew reported that he had seen a sizeable amount of edible supplies along with large containers of water on the table in their cabin. This amazed the Captain as he was sure.

"Their meagre baggage could not have contained much more than excess clothing. I am at a loss from where they obtained their food and water from. They are a careful lot and are also heavily armed and look like they know how to use those weapons."

From his first mate, he had prised out the information about one of their missing crew.

"Baptiste had tried to jump them with a band of cut-throats he had met in a bar while he was ashore. That hombre never turned up for this trip and that says to me, he failed. He is now more than likely floating amid the flotsam."

Antonio was thinking twice about taking them on.

"Man, I have a bad feeling about this one."

As the fast ship skimmed over the wave tops at its maximum speed, the pondering Captain still looked up into the approaching night sky for inspiration. He was confident that his sleek bullet shaped craft could out run most coastguard vessels, but decided against taking out his passengers on an isolated shoreline, just as they were putting them ashore. He knew that out in the emptiness of the Ocean, there were very few eyes watching. Most nations Navy's hugged their own coastlines and any vessel out on the open sea took its own fate into its hands. The day ended and the small yellow moon had a spattering of clouds around its aurora giving him scant light to work on. Inexplicably, his engines stopped abruptly and a fail-safe mechanism activated automatically. The vessel de-accelerated until it was at full stop. His instrument panel was going haywire, he was baffled.

"This ship has never broken down before."

She was always regularly maintained, for more than not, he regularly needed a quick getaway. But it now lay helpless and was bobbing around on the ever-moving sea. The pirate captain had heard of the place where many ships had inexplicably disappeared, but that mysterious area was over two thousand kilometres from their position. There could only be one other reason for this malfunction, his paying passengers. Antonio was now very worried and he had a right to be. He had guessed correctly. Below decks, the mind-voice of the Patriarchi had startled Naomh with an unusual and urgent request.

"You have to stop this vessel now. The next piece of my form is not on the Red Planet, that's the sixth piece; the fifth segment is in the depths of the Ocean. In fact it is right below us."

"I don't understand. What do you mean?" Demanded its perplexed host.

"The next piece was also hidden from me. I could not sense it before. The barrier of sea water prevented this. But as we passed over this area of Ocean, there came a strong and desperate connection."

The ship was sabotaged by a beam of light from Naomh's wristband. The living amulet in its urgency had acted without its host's consent. As the vessel remained static, the bearer of four parts now felt a faint connection. But, neither he nor the uncompleted APOCRYPHA'I knew exactly where it lay, for the sea-water refracted the connection much like its density bent light waves. All they had was an approximation. In the meantime, Antonio had come to a decision. He gave the key to the arms locker that was in an effect, a larger version of a glory hole to his Bo' sun. The wily captain never told him or his crew about his misgivings, not that any of them would have listened. Anyway, he surmised.

"If they overpower the strangers, then good, I can share in the spoils. If not, then I can say that my crew's actions were nothing to do with me. I will not move from the bridge."

Antonio appeared satisfied as he watched his first mate handing out a variety of firearms. The Bo' sun along with the rest of the crew of blackheart's attacked and died as Naomh's orchestrated death squad responded to the attack. The crew's lifeless bodies were thrown overboard without any fuss. During the altercation, Solomon had slipped on some engine oil and was knocked out cold. The Rabbi immediately rushed him to the LAB-CELL and set to his injuries. The captain had not participated in the attack and had stayed in the wheelhouse. He heard the sound of sinister weapons and knew that things did not look good for his scuppered crew. There was a fleeting spectre at his viewer and one of the passengers had a weapon pointed at him. He raised his hands and said.

"I had no part in this."

The shadow shrugged and put a bullet in his forehead. The captain slumped over the controls and his blood filled the spaces between the knobs and buttons. The assassin stared at the dead man for a while and then slipped out. Minutes later, the others came into the cabin and found the dead man. But now they had nobody to pilot the vessel.

"Shit man, we needed him alive to steer the vessel. Who done this?"

No one volunteered the information, but the pony-tailed man had his suspicions.

"It is not a problem, we can work out how to sail this vessel." The Engineer said after studying the helm in the bridge. Moshe nodded in agreement.

"How is Solomon?" Asked the Lenses.

"He will be fine, but he took a nasty whack and will be out for a while."

"Ok, let's see which one of you can control this ship. Let's get on our way then." Insisted the Guide.

"No! We are stopped here for a reason. The next piece is below us, under the sea. It is desperate somehow." Stated a shocked Naomh.

Cahill gave him an incredulous look. His unsubtle voice became laced with sarcasm.

"You mean to tell me that in this huge ball of liquid; hundreds and thousands of square kilometres across, we have just passed over it. Man; that's what I call fortunate."

"We are not that lucky. I don't know exactly where it is." Replied his leader.

"How do we search down there?" Asked Beersheba.

"I don't know, we do not have the proper equipment. We do not have time to search, it is urgent that I get to the bottom. There is something happening to the fifth piece."

"Maybe the same pills that put the coating over us back in the Himalayas might work?" Suggested the Lenses.

"Who is going to try that? The pressure will crush you like an eggshell, if it does not work." Said Moshe.

While the dubious gang were discussing their options, the four pieces of the APOCRYPHA'I reached out to its fifth part. The underwater segment responded to the contact like a drowning man gasping for air and the majority of it did not like what it had to say. With great urgency, it told Naomh.

"The TORT-CAMLETS could descend to the Ocean floor and you can spread out and search for it."

Shadows lengthened as preparations were made. Finally, it was agreed that Naomh and everybody else except the Engineer, the unconscious Solomon and the Lenses would use the separated TORT-CAM and trawl the seabed. The Clerk refused to go down into the depths. In rush of urgency, the unseen shields went over the edge and instantly turned visible on contact with the saline liquid. The four coloured globes descended to the sea floor and their occupants were amazed at the diversity of fish that swam past. Farmed fish socks had enabled the Ocean's life to recover from the millennium long damage that had been done to it by reckless fishing Nations. The sea-life was oblivious to the search; they had only thoughts of eating or not to be eaten. Besides some of those Ocean going scavengers were already feeding on the weighted down bodies of Antonio and his crew. Each visible globe fanned out and searched the murky depths. The deeper they descended, the more pronounced the marine snow of plankton size organisms got. Most of them only recognised the pale shrimp like creatures and the shapes of bigger fish feeding amongst the living soup. Once again, it was announced.

"The Prof would have loved this."

His murderer was getting pissed off of hearing that and would have enjoyed telling them.

"No, he would not. He is dead, you deluded fools."

It took two hours and it was the globe with the Persuader and Moshe that found the wrecked submersible. It was revealed as an eerie portrait through the gloom. The rest of the searching globules rendezvous with it. Naomh and Miriam's sphere touched up against the wrecked craft. But, the two structures, one of light and the other of metal refused to marry seamlessly. The female occupant stated the obvious to those who were listening.

"I don't want to be an alarmist, but we cannot penetrate the hull. The film of sea water is having an effect on the merging."

They kept trying, but it was useless. The visible shield kept bouncing off and moving away.

"We need another solution." Said the Rabbi.

Naomh came to a decision.

"The rest of you return to the surface, there is no point in risking all of us now that we have located the wreck."

It was the sensible choice and the others agreed. The two lovers watched as the rest of the spheres drifted to the surface and they both felt incredibly alone even though they were in constant contact with the others. Up above, a storm blew up, a kilometre down; they were oblivious to the atmospheric conditions. This time the battle was against non-Human foes, it was against gravity, pressure and such. The submersible was precariously balanced on a ledge that fell away in a chasm of blackness and such magnitude that if it tipped over, then it would be lost forever. Incredibly, there was a meagre spark of life within its confines. Inside the submersible, the Australian man who wanted to explore the whole World had finally run out of luck. If the man from down under was still conscious, he would have known that his dreams had turned sour. Jimmy Rooney had always been an adrenaline junkie and now the odds had finally caught up with him. He had done it all, he had climbed the tallest mountains, traversed the barren deserts and the icy Arctic. He had found the azure artefact on a dying man, deep in a cave on Easter Island. The wonderful blue jewel had always given him the edge. He had become incredibly rich through wise investments. Bored with his playboy lifestyle, he sought out adventure. His success in the financial World was mirrored in the record breaking one. His exhilarating challenges were always met and faced with a cock sure attitude. This earned him the admiration of some and hatred from others. But up to now, his worst moments had come when he was crossing the frozen wastes of Antarctica in a flight of terror. At dinner parties, held in his honour, he would tell his guests.

"Something unmentionable had chased me, I never saw it, but crikey mate, I knew if I had faltered, then I would have copped it mate."

Still the "Shadow terror." as he called it lingered in the recesses of his darkest nightmares. He was in the middle of attempting the fastest underwater crossing of the Atlantic when disaster struck. He was thinking about a forbidden race in the inaccessible Anschluss called the Span. He had been astounded by the trouble he was now in; the blue amulet had never warned him. Rooney never knew that the mass of salt water was impeding its effectiveness. The sudden seismic activity had toppled the undersea mountain side and killed his crew. It pushed his submersible along until it tottered precariously over another ledge and this dropped into an unimaginable abyss. This huge hole in the Ocean floor was not natural. It was created over seven hundred years earlier when mankind was fighting a losing battle against global warming, rising sea levels and coastal erosion. The levelling of the Alps and the creation of the Atlantis sector was not beneficial to helping the problem either. Not that anyone unaffected cared, but some Pacific islands had been submerged completely by the rising seas. An idea born from desperation was muted. It was never quite clear who the reckless Nation had been, but several nuclear bombs were detonated in the same spot in the middle of the Ocean. The Atomic charges were placed in holes that were bored a mile under the sea floor at the edge of the mid-Atlantic ridge between the Atlantis fracture and the Barracuda fracture. The massive release of energy created a huge underground cavern of hundreds of miles across and of an unknown depth and above it, a thin crust of a sea floor. The enormous weight of the sea mass began to penetrate this slender layer above the pulverised rock and commenced to drain slowly into the cracks that started to appear all over its surface area. So precise were the calculations of detonation that no Nation encountered an expectant Tsunami. The tides hitting the Anschluss sea wall rose to an all-time high, but the unexceptional rush of water was deflected off its concrete mass. Did it work? It instigators said yes as the sea level fell by a metre over the next few years. The drowned Pacific islands returned, but there was no one who would go back to them. This brought a reprieve to the rising sea levels as new forms of energy practice and consumption halted the old destructive ways. Not that he cared otherwise; the Australian was now hanging over these once cynical measures of tackling global change and nobody knew how deep the chasm was. This underwater misadventure had happened over a week ago and now, he was mortally wounded and unable to move. The bodies of his crew floated around him like some horrific bloated water rings. The living amulet had quickly put up a blue shield for his protection. But the seawater was gradually eroding it away. He knew that the blue jewel was working overtime to keep him alive, but it was trying for the impossible.

"I am going to die here mate. I always took too many risks and the odds have finally caught up with me."

It was keeping him in stasis; its will to survive was apparently stronger than his. The whole of the underwater craft shifted again, but it did not go over the edge. Rooney's piece of the APOCRYPHA'I went into panic mode. The egotistic thrill-seeking Hybrid had put his races millennium long plan in jeopardy. It was stuck under a kilometre of dreaded sea water with a dying host and totally unreachable. It could hear the gloating of the long dead Naisi, telling it.

"I told you not to rely on the stupid creatures."

In the moment of its final despair, there came a familiar presence. Something recognizable was calling to it. The fifth piece of the Mescal/Amulet decided to shut down its host from Perth primary functions to preserve itself. Like its latest host, it had no option, but to take a gamble. It adopted the Hybrid trait of total optimism. The Australian's mind ceased to operate; it needed his energy just to keep itself functioning. Its state of desperation increased as time moved on relentlessly, the Universe would not apologise for failed deadlines or dashed hopes. Those on the surface came up with a very risky idea. It was put to Naomh.

"There are explosive canisters in the cargo hold of this ship. We can modify one of these charges. It can be dropped alongside the sunken vessel. Then on your command, it can be detonated by remote control. The blast will punch a hole in the side of the vessel and you can enter into it. But there is a good chance that the blast might knock the vessel over the edge."

The highly concerned four parts Mescal/Amulet told its host.

"Time is running out for my other part."

Naomh had no choice.

"We will go with the plan."

The square drum was dropped over the edge and it was swallowed

701

whole. It began to sink quickly into the depths. Whoever dropped the depth charge was highly accurate. The contained explosive device landed about two metres away from the ruined craft. Naomh had explained where it lay to those above. The Engineer switched on its magnetic capability and the device clamped to the side of the hull. He was receiving information from those below and he appeared satisfied with the position.

"Ok, when you are ready, give me the order to detonate."

His nervous leader complied and there was a blinding explosion. From above, they could hear the anxious voice of the Guide.

"Are you alright. Come in."

"We are Ok."

There was relief on the surface.

"We can see inside. It worked; there is a gaping hole in the side."

Just then the ship began to shake violently. The TORT-CAMLET floated in through the jagged hole and it was met with a grisly sight. Bloated bodies scraped by and then they saw one glowing. The Alien globe manoeuvred towards that one. The invisible shield touched the shinning figure and the two lights merged. The former bearer of the fifth piece came awake for an instant and Naomh met his eyes. He saw regret and an ironic smile in them as the man expired his gurgling breaths in bubbles of released oxygen. He was considering an attempt at rescue when the shaking of the craft grew more violent. The movement dislodged the dying man and he disappeared into the darkness of the stricken vessel.

"We have to get out of here." Insisted Miriam insisted.

They were barely out when the vessel gave a loud groan and toppled into the abyss. It was a pity that the Australian had expired, for his dead carcass was truly on its way down on a memorable journey. Naomh joined the blue piece with the rest; he now had a five coloured Amulet. Then in the moment of their triumph, the motion of their haven went dead. They were now stranded in the bubble of their protective shield; the pressure of the weight of the salt water would crush them, if they tried to leave it.

"What happened? Why are we stalled?"

Naomh repeated Miriam's questions to the internal voice. The Patriarchi replied.

"The sea water has drained the power of the split Guidex sphere quicker than was anticipated. This would not be a problem to the completed shield."

The assembling ALASTHA'I was becoming prone to making Hybrid errors.

"Come in. come in." It was the Clerk's anxious voice.

Naomh explained the situation.

"Shit!" Was the reply.

The calm voice of the Engineer came on a few seconds after that.

"Hold tight, we will think of something."

"I will use another TORT-CAMLET and go down and rescue them." Said Greta.

"No, the same thing will happen to that." Said Cahill.

Down below the shield of protection began to flicker and they were using up their oxygen reserves. This life sustaining gas was not been replaced and precious time began to elapse. Up above, Naomh's voice sounded deeper and huskier. Panic set in, they had no way of hauling them up. The two entombed lovers were fading fast. Naomh gave his lover a weak smile and managed to get out the words.

"It will be alright. Our friend's will get us out of this."

The Engineer thought long and hard and then he knew what to do.

"Of course. It is a property of the light shields."

It took him three frantic hours and the growing tension was unbearable. He turned the ship into a giant electric magnet. Lucky for them, the ship had a lot of metal in its holds. Without asking, the Persuader activated the improvised device and the air hummed. Metal flew from everywhere, just missing them. The cabin walls creaked and groaned.

"Switch it off. Switch it for fuck sake." Shouted everybody as they dodged flying metal.

The Engineer managed to get to the switch before anybody was killed or injured. The big man got looks of exasperation from his cowering friends. The magnet was strapped to two lifeboats and pushed out a bit from their vessel. It was reactivated and the stalled under-water shield sped to the attracter. The trapped couple felt the movement and became relieved. The motion began to produce oxygen and their breaths became stronger and deeper. Something monstrous was awoken and stirred in the depths. It was all crustaceans and dusty particles. Like the Plasmoid back on the Asian wasteland, it too was born from nuclear detonation. The huge sea creature that might have been once, an Octopus or Squid had been perched on a ledge, just where the submersible had plunged over the edge. Its lightening quick tentacles had snatched at the falling machine and grabbed it in a limpet like grip. But it instantly released its vice like hold when it felt the unliving metal and plastic. Its attention was now aroused and the sea creature floated upwards. Its underwater senses locked on to the rising effervesce of transparent filament that held the two Questors. Knowing that the oily bubbles of light were something it could digest, the thing gave chase. The TORT-CAMLET'S occupants could not be got at, but the monster was capable of swallowing them whole through a large orifice in its main trunk and retreating back into the depths. This would still prove fatal as the now visible shield's power was fading fast. However, unknown to any of them, including the eager sea monster, as they rose, a huge piece of metal wreckage was following in their trail. The jagged section of hull with the still visible lettering of HMS ATL, had lifted from its sandy coating and trails of its eight hundred-year garment of encrustation trailed away into a plume of debris. The rising shield popped through the water's surface like a bobbing apple. The Engineer disengaged the magnet as soon as he saw the blue sphere break the surface and the drop in magnetic charge caused the rising metal to change in direction. The momentum of attraction decreased, but it was still speeding upwards. The trailing comet imitation was now heading towards their vessel and it would surely penetrate their hull as it spiralled in their wake and plunge them back in the watery mass again. A relieved Miriam looked down through the transparent floor and instantly saw the danger. The mutant creature was nearly upon them. She shouted an alarm into her speaker.

"There is something huge and ugly on a collision course with the ship. Quickly, turn the vessel."

The frightened woman did not know whether she spoke in Anschluss or Enclave. It was inconsequential, for they understood all tongues now. Moshe who was the helm quickly turned the vessel. The metal projectile skewered the sea monster and directed the now impaled creature towards the ship. Both objects; one inanimate and the other now thrashing in its death throes glanced off the side of the hull, throwing everybody forward. But thankfully, the metal and fleshly mass failed to penetrate the metal of the hull and only caused a long scratch in the paintwork. The surface of the water filled with a dark oily liquid and the viscous scum spread out quickly. Their two rescued comrades were brought on board still inside the flickering sphere.

"Do not come out of the segment of the Guidex sphere. Merge it with the rest, it will enable you to depressurise."

Naomh passed on the instructions.

"It is to stop us getting the bends."

The dead creature began to degenerate in the night air to the accompaniment of the Clerk's words.

"What the hell was that thing?"

"I don't want to know, just get us out of here." Voiced a jaded Miriam from inside the improvised decompression chamber. Her lover agreed. The inside circumference had gained another hue, it was blue. The remainder of the voyage westwards was relatively incident free, their vessel passed few ships and those that they did ignored them and their high-speed trail. Solomon had recovered and they told him the amazing tale of how they had gained the fifth piece. However Naomh had regrets.

"I would have liked to have met the bearer of the fifth piece. Something tells me that he could have been one of us. I think I would have liked him."

Scratching his beard, the healed Enclave man asked the beaming accomplishers.

"Why did you not use the burner's, that would have kept the craft below stable and you could have rescued him."

The others looked at the Engineer and through gritted teeth, he said.

"Well, nobody's perfect."

Naomh told them the colour of the fifth piece.

"It is blue. Someone or something has a weird sense of humour leaving this piece to be found at the bottom of the sea."

"It's just a coincidence." Informed the internal voice.

Two hours out from the blurry coastline of the New World, they at last found a warship that confronted them. When they did not answer the warnings issuing from a large hailer, the coastguard vessel opened fire on their ship. The first shot was fired across their bows and still they ignored them. Then tracers hammered into the side of their hull; the other craft's commander had lost patience. The appropriated pirate craft was holed and began to take in water. The questors used the Skimmer to get off the sinking ship. One by one they leapt onto the activated technology. Water splashed onto them and they lay flat against its shimmering surface. The ensuing explosion hid their escape as they sped out of sight from those that had sunk them. The Engineer had set his Monocles to far range and looked open mouthed as they approached the shore. Suddenly he stood up and gaped in awe. On top of the highest mountain, there stood the tallest statue he had ever seen. It was a huge effigy of Christ and he was waiting to greet them with open arms. For a minute, he thought.

"I did not get off the ship. I'm dead and my soul has travelled to Heaven."

But to his joy, he was still alive and the apparition was real. Had the devout man found at long last what he had been searching for all of his life, a nation that worshiped his God? (When Pope John Paul the eleventh had been exiled here in 2340 AD, he moved the Vatican and the centre of Catholicism to this city. An exact replica of the religious institution had been built in this hotter climate.). Unaware of this historical incident, the Engineer dared to hope. As if to confirm this, the rays of the Sun reached down from behind a solitary cloud as if they wanted to grab him and lift him up into the heavens. He stared at the gleaming polished buildings of the beachfront and wondered if these were indeed the gates of heaven. Unlike the Anschluss or the Enclave, this city was free of their encompassing walls or impediments. Like the opened hands of his God's effigy, the place was inviting him in. But cowering behind these pristine structures lay the habitat of the dammed. Huge sprawling "Favela's." covered the once verdant hills. Ramshackle structures constructed of the cheapest, salvaged and discarded materials closed in narrow streets whose unpaved centres were open sewers. Even paradise had its ugly side and once again, the Anschluss would not look so bad. It was advised by the Lenses.

"We should land in a stretch of jungle to the north-west of the impressive city."

Once ashore and under the canopy, the new arrivals found themselves between the shade and the sea. The rustling of the trees leaves signalled the arrival of rain, just before they felt the first splatters. Naomh activated the TORT-CAM and under its canopy of red, orange, yellow, green and now blue tesseral, they would rest for a while and regain their strength. A new chapter in their quest had begun.

Another individual who would be waiting for them at the Anschluss base had also crossed the Atlantic Ocean, but in a far quicker time and more comfortable method of flying transport. The Secretary of Protocol did not just fly in first class; the Chairman's agent was first class. The Kaiser's second in command had been assigned this mission to make sure that everything progressed according to his plans. Because like all Anschluss outposts, the Spaceport was mostly staffed by locals at the lower levels, the less its Plebs knew about the outside World, the better. As the private craft sped over the unseen Ocean far below, the Spy's double enjoyed the view of the puffy clouds and the clear light of their cruising altitude, knowing that they were only one of the privileged few from the enclosed society that would get to see this celestial sight in their lifetimes. The pilot for once had been glad of the speedy trip.

"This is one dangerous individual that I want to be rid of quick."

He had nearly shit himself when he found out who his passenger was. People had been known to disappear for upsetting this cold figure of command and when the plane touched down in the South American Spaceport, he breathed a sigh of well-being. His landing had been immaculate; there wasn't even a bump on contact with the ground. As their unwanted superior departed across the tarmac, a heavy downpour struck. He held back a laugh as his former passenger was caught out in it.

"It's a good thing, we got down before that."

His crew agreed and to their immense relief, they were informed over the coded airwaves.

"Your plane will not be taking this passenger back to the landing site on the Geneva Contrib. You are to return home immediately, another trip has been scheduled for you and your crew.

The captain was extremely grateful to that unknown bureaucrat. Then, one of his crew advised him with a nervous laugh.

"Let's get out of here before we get blamed for the weather or something else?"

The experienced flyer nodded and silently thought

"I pity the poor pilot and crew who are to make the return journey with that high ranking bastard. For if their unknown reason for been here does not go well, then those unfortunate crew members will pay dearly. And from whispered rumours among the Flying Corps and other branches of the military, that will more than likely prove fatal."

XXVI.

SOUTH AMERICAN CONTINENT 2954 AD.

Loud church bells announcing that it was eight o'clock in the morning heralded their arrival in the most western of hemispheres. The angelic resonance called out to one of them in particular. The Engineer was euphoric.

"I have at last found what I have been denied all of my life."

The fourteen seekers of the APOCRYPHA'I had made landfall in the America's. In the history of the Human race, this embarking was immensely more significant and definitely more spectacular than Columbus's landfall on Hispaniola in 1497AD. If there had been any of the same superstitious Aztecs around on this day; the 28th of February 2954AD who had thought that Corte's and his band of cut-throat Conquistadors were the returning emissaries of the Sun God Quetzalcoatl who were once again walking the Earth, then those aboard the Platform of Light would have convinced them even more so. The Spanish and Portuguese had transformed this New World into an imperfect model of their own society, but it would be a footnote in history compared to what one of these arrivals would achieve on a global scale in the near future. The fourteen global travellers stepped off their advanced transport device and on to a secluded sandy beach armed with the language of the place. Early that morning, two hours before the Sunrise, they had remounted their fantastic travelling contrivance and hugged the coast. As dawn broke, white clouds skimmed over the dark mountain tops in a paradoxical upheaval of the surfers back on the waves who had caused them to dismount and walk. The three dimensional map showed them that their path lay northwards. But it was decided to rest for a day or two in this amazing city. It was on the insistence of the Engineer that they stay for a while as the intrigued man wanted to find out more about the people that worshiped his God openly. The group found a luxury hotel and booked in. The main type of communication device on this Continent was a dark visor that reflected darkness and was worn over the eyes when needed. The locals called them. *"Shades."*

Fourteen pairs were bought fourteen to blend in with the indigenous population. The Lenses guessed correctly.

"They're for the bright Sun."

The next day, they took a moving contraption known as a cable car to the top of Sugar Loaf Mountain and from there they continued up to the heights of Corcovado Mountain and looked with awe on the huge effigy of the "White Christ." The Engineer spent hours staring at one of the seven manmade wonders of the World and vowed to himself.

"I will erect a bigger one back in the Anschluss. In fact, there will be

one in every Contrib."

Three days later and after touring around the city called Rio de Janeiro, the new arrivals found out that it was not paradise at all. The contrast between the rich and poor was mind boggling and could not be more pronounced. Been from two societies where most people were equal (Or so they were made to believe.), the questors became disgusted with the place and decided to leave. Although the natives adored their religion enormously, even the Engineer became disillusioned with the city and some parts of the shanty town were so dangerous, even they avoided them. However, the Mute killed three people during their short time there, but still, he did not sate his appetite for murder. He for one thought it a wonderful place. Life was worthless here on the mean streets and dead bodies turning up in the gutters were two a credit. Then everything changed for the Engineer, he found what he was looking for. If the statue of Christ was the largest Christian effigy in the World, then the pinkish white marbled building he was looking at was the largest church he would ever see. He and his brother had followed a converging crowd. Clasped crucifixes and rosary beads among the throng had immediately drawn his attention. Then, along with the pilgrims, they emerged into a large horse-shoe piazza whose surface was made up of an array of bluish cobble-stones, red bricked borders, larger white slabs and rarer ones with faces and inscriptions. One at his feet had the letters "Levante." inscribed on it. A tall obelisk and four ancient lighting devices sat at the centre of the plaza. This tapering pink hued stone that was now topped with a cross was a replica of the one that the Emperor Caligula had taken from Egypt nearly three millennia ago. The original structure back in the Roman Contrib now bore the remembrance of an achievement of one of the LYUBINITES. The cast iron lamp-posts had stone basins under their splayed metal feet that issued forth clear drinking water under the inscription; "ANNO MDCCLII.". At the edges of the paved open space, there were two ornate fountains spewing out pure gurgling water whose sound alone eased the discomfort of the suffocating heat. Two large semi-circular colonnade buildings formed an enclosing circular magnificence. All around its top were numerous shining statues looking down in judgement. The chiselled images even sat in alcoves carved from the buildings stone and above them, the replica dome of Michelangelo that seemed to float in the air independently of the main structure. The two brothers pushed their way to the flight of steps that led up to the buildings frontal façade. Wooden railings blocked an enclosed seating area that looked up to a white structured speaking platform that was marshalled on either side by two giant statues. Receiving answers to his questions, he found out that the glorious structure was called the "New Vatican.". The awe inspiring building was a near exact replica of the one that the rulers of the Anschluss had torn down centuries ago. The only differences were in the locally sourced materials and the majority of its original pieces of its artworks hung in the inheritors of its destructors private apartments. This was where the Catholic Church had fled in banishment and ever since that dark day in November 2553AD, its Popes named themselves Pope Exile. They also issued a new doctrine that they would return to the European Continent and re-establish the faith. The current head of the church was named Pope Exile the sixty fifth. The massing crowd was drawn to the front of the square in anticipation. Everywhere and upon everyone was the symbol of the banned crucifix. The throng of people waited patiently for something to happen. Then an elderly man dressed in a white gown and a white circular cap similar to the ones that his Enclave comrades sometimes wore topped his head approached the speaking platform. All around him were strangely dressed men in clothes of red, yellow and black lines. Each of these men were armed with automatic weapons. This imitation of the ancient Swiss Guard protected him from an attack by the LYUBINITES. Though, the Pope had little realisation that if Ivan Tell wanted him dead, then he would be. The Engineer grabbed the stranger alongside him and with the power of the lingual device asked him.

"Who is that?"

If the man thought it strange that a person wearing the crucifix asked that question, he ignored it and said reverently.

"That is Pope Exile the sixty-fifth. The risen Christ's representative on Earth."

The crowd began to sing and during the heavenly sound, Miguel Salvador had come up with a God inspired plan.

"Faith has led me to these shores. I know what to do."

When the crowd dispersed, the Engineer approached the building. But on each attempt, he was refused an audience with the Pope by indifferent security personnel who were well used to such crazy fanatics. There was only one way for it and he approached Naomh for permission to use the TORT-CAMLETS. Seeing the fanaticism in his eyes, his leader reluctantly agreed with his friend's uncompromising desires.

Pope Exile the sixty-fifth was startled out of his sleep by two figures standing at the edge of his enormous mattress laden bed. One was a huge man while the other stared at him intently. The smaller man dropped to his knees and had a fierce look of devotion etched into his features. This one proclaimed.

"Your eminence, we are here to offer you assistance."

God's bishop on Earth guessed that these were no assassins; he saw the strange crucifix's and was now wide awake. Saint Peter's inheritor asked.

"How can I help you my sons?"

The Engineer still on his knees explained.

"We have come from the Anschluss and must have been directed to this place by divine accord."

His eminence became intrigued and listened to the man's words.

"We are on a mission and when it is completed, we will return home. There is a huge underground of people waiting for God's words and we can bring it to them."

The Pontiff was intrigued.

"Many of my predecessors of this holy office had tried unsuccessfully to get missionaries into the Atheist Anschluss. All of their emissaries had never contacted them again. Can you get back into the Anschluss with such an envoy?"

"As easily as we got in here."

The Pope got out of bed and went over to a writing table. There he wrote some words on a sheet of paper and used his signet ring to seal it with a stamp. He handed it to the Engineer and told him.

"Come back here in two days."

Then, the larger intruder touched a band on his wrist and a ball of light appeared in the corner of the bedchamber. Both men vanished into it and it disappeared. The Pope was left the feeling that he had been visited by a heavenly vision.

"No, they were men enough."

He had much to do after listening to the strange tale and he summoned his secretary to make the preparations. Two days later, the brothers passed through the huge complex with ease and respect. Once again, they knew that they were in a Holy place; the smell of incense was overpowering. If the main Basilica which was in the shape of a traditional Latin cross intrigued them, then its interior which was bathed in pervasive golden light made one of them think instantly of paradise. If the Lama had asked the Engineer about the colour of Heaven, he would have answered.

"I am now looking at it."

The letter literary opened up all of the doors until they found themselves in the presence of the Pope and a small gathering of Arch bishops. Then began a morning that the Engineer would never forget. The Holy-men made him a priest and ordained him in a small but private ceremony. Another man approached and kissed the Pope's ring.

"This is Padre Pious. An Exilian. He will be my papal nuncio. He will accompany you back to the Anschluss and help you to reconvert the people."

The two original questors returned to the others with their new companion. There was open hostility against the man accompanying the brothers, but when the Engineer made it clear.

"If Padre Pious is not allowed to go with us, then Jose and me will abandon the quest and try to make our own way home."

Naomh relented. The Nuncio was to be their newest companion. However, the Spy had no intentions of letting the papal representative reach the Anschluss.

"When I get the chance, he will die like the Prof. His ideas are infinitely more dangerous."

From here, the seekers of the APOCRYPHA'I booked passage to a place called Cuba. Since they had departed the Mountain Kingdom, it had taken them a couple of weeks of sea travel in numerous ships of varying descriptions to get this far. They had made their way from port to port, from Asia to Africa and across the wide Atlantic Ocean to the New World. Crossing the Atlantic was the first time that they had been on such a broad expanse of water and out of sight of land for such a long time. All their previous voyages had been coastal hugging trips and only once when they crossed the Arabian Sea had they been out of sight of land for more than a day. From half a World away, the now seasoned travellers had leapfrogged on sea craft that were nothing more than small boats compared with the ANS GREGORY LYUBIN. This leg of the journey was to be made on a transatlantic liner that was an epiphany of extravagance and even bigger than the Anschluss Dreadnaut. Its name was "OUT OF HAVANA." So luxurious was life on board the vessel, that none of them were ever obliged to use the concealing shields. On this leg of their journey, each of the questors had discarded their military paraphernalia and carried small-silent concealed pistols about their persons. Still, each weapon packed powerful fragment rounds. On board the city sized liner there were a wide variety of well-stocked shops in glittery malls that catered for any number of items. As they had an absolute fortune in precious stones and metals and a method of producing an endless supply of currency, purchasing items was not a problem. All the males soon found out that shopping was a thing that the women loved to do. Even Greta joined Miriam and Beersheba on their excursions to the shopping malls on board the huge ship. The Clerk joined them on one spending trip and came back wearing the most outrageous clothes they had ever seen him in. Standing alongside the others on their balcony, he wore a loud red and white striped suit with a glowing tie, topped off with a banded Fedora. He was taking his inkling of fitting in with the locals to the extreme.

"What do you think?"

He had asked the others while doing a twirl. Hands over mouths did not cover the ensuing laughter. The brightly cloaked peacock looked chagrined and threw the soft felt hat at the Persuader as he was laughing the loudest. His movements must have loosened his pouch that held his collection of coins. His purse flew over the edge of the balcony and landed on a deck way below. When it hit the ground, it burst and the metal and plastic pieces flew like shrapnel exploding from a fragment grenade. Passing children grabbed them up and fled the scene. The Clerk was gutted.

"Never mind, you can always get more." Consoled the Lenses.

The Engineer went into the room and returned with a fistful of the lost items and handed them to the distraught man from the Brussels Contrib.

The grateful receiver beamed as the benefactor told him.

"It always pays to have a backup plan."

The women also came back loaded with items, as the Lenses newest duplicating equipment easily reproduced flawless paper currency of any description. Monetary unit's known, as American dollars seemed to be the most desired among the shopkeepers, bars and eating places on the liner. So, they had used precious stones and gold in exchange for laminated currencies, which the Lenses then easily counterfeited. Unable to control his blood lust, the insidious Mute found other pursuits aboard the giant vessel and hence, a few passengers found themselves in Davy Jones locker. The murderer was not prejudice, but he concentrated his killing spree on the poorer classes below decks as nobody cared much about them. The Nuncio and the Engineer began to spend all of their time in their cabin, discussing a shared doctrine. The man from the Madrid Contrib began to see that his former mentor, the Preacher's system of belief differed enormously from the Vatican's. Still, both men had one thing in common; they blamed the Jews for the murder of the Christ. The Nuncio disliked the Enclave people, simply because of that. He kept his opinions private and taking a leaf out of the Mute's book, he rarely spoke to them. The mole among them despised the Nuncio for a lot of reasons, chiefly because of his religious adherence and his long untrimmed nasal and earlobe hair. It appeared that he was more interested in his soul than his physical presence. Heated debates began as they found a rift in their doctrine. The Engineer had only ever heard of the first two commandments back in the Anschluss. The other eight laws of Moses, he had found out about in the masses back in the Enclave and he was shocked that he had broken quite a few of them. Still, he reasoned.

"Since I had been unaware of them, I could not be at fault. I can make a new start now."

It was during a bitter remark by the well-travelled Guide, that the Engineer began to respect the Vatican's agent. The pony tailed man spoiling for an argument questioned.

"If God treats everybody as an equal; then why is there such a gulf between the rich and the poor in your city? It is a place of palaces and slums."

The scarlet wearing skull capped man replied.

"Think of the poor people and the way they exist, that is their purgatory. And if they truly redeem themselves, then like us that have a better life and thus they will live in better circumstances. But alas, there is too much sin among them yet. They have not truly given themselves to God and must suffer in accordance."

The Guide believed that he was spouting bullshit, but the eager learner among the gang vowed to do better with his devotion. Not wanting to seem ignorant, but still wanting to know, the Engineer asked.

"What does this name, Exilian mean?"

Hiding his scorn, the Nuncio explained about his order, its founder and how it was formed after the church was banished from the Anschluss. There were other orders like, the Dominicans, the Benedictines, the Franciscans, etc and of the female ones, Carmelites and Silesians. The Engineer wondered what God wanted from this variety of followers, but kept it to himself. Naomh knew however that if the Nuncio knew of his internal presence, the Papal envoy would consider it; the voice of his Guardian Angel or madness. He also disliked the Priest. It had only taken one incident to confirm this. When he had found out that he was from Sao Paulo, he wanted to find out about the place mentioned in his favourite song. But when the other knew of his reason, he said with a shake of his head.

"I have no time for such foolishness."

This did not endear him to the bearer of the living amulet. One morning while the Clerk and Moshe stood above decks, taking the salty air, the former registrar said to his companion.

"Moshe, is it my imagination, but all of the lands we have been in, the ports and even the train stations have their own individual smell."

"In what way?" Replied the other.

"It's hard to say, but it's like a train station smells the same no matter where we were and even sea ports have their familiar aroma."

"Yes. I see what you mean." Moshe agreed.

He then took in a deep breath of the salty air as if to confirm his friend's theory. The liner progressed northwards stopping at places for those who wished to visit. The questors had lost their appetites for new and exotic places, so they stayed on board. There were enough distractions on the massive liner anyway. The Guide had found a gambling place and he, the Clerk and the Persuader spent a lot of time there. Everybody had their own space, so the Anschluss mole lost themselves easily and was making regular contact with Ivan Tell. For the last few days, an announcer on board had begun a countdown to their arrival. Now on this beautiful balmy morning, one that made you glad to be alive, the questors had joined most of the passengers lining the deck for a view of their destination. They were not disappointed; the liner had berthed in a manmade paradise, its beachfront looked even more opulent that the Brazilian city. It was an island state that the locals called Cuba and they had arrived at its capital, Havana; the same name as the ship. It had beautiful white plastered buildings, roofed in bright red cement tiles and fantastic glass covered hotels that boasted swimming pools surrounded by exotic plants and palm trees. What most of the ships occupants did not know was that this too was only a façade. Behind the hotel blocks and out of view lay squalor and poverty, the lot in life for most of the island's inhabitants. Unlike Rio, they would not be allowed to see this. They embarked off a gangway, similar to the one in the Enclave all that time ago. But now there was a confidence in their attitude and posture, which only the Guide had displayed during that first time. They were getting use to been in unfamiliar places now. Having no identification, they were ushered into a small room by a white suited man and his armed escort, their confidence quickly dissipating. A large old-fashioned fan circulated the growing warm air with a great effort. A rather sweaty official wearing bifocals scrutinised them. But the nervous bunch had no need to worry; these island rulers did not care where people came from, only that they had enough wealth to last them during their stay. The guards were dismissed. The customs man mentioned this and after a large donation in dollars to him, documents entailing them to stay in the country were quickly produced. They shook hands with the bribed man and he directed them to one of the better hotels lining the seashore.

"I have a cousin there, he is the manager and he will look after you. Just tell him, I sent you."

With a conspiratorial wink, he gave them his relative's name and directions to the hotel.

"Greedy bastard. If they are all like that around here, we will have no problem." Voiced the Persuader.

"Don't judge him too harshly; bribes are the lot of poorly paid officials. Said the Clerk to the big man.

After booking into the hotel recommended by the official, Naomh decided.

"We will spend six weeks here."

The worn out-group needed to stay put in one place, to recuperate. He was amazed that the internal voice had no objections. The five parts Mescal/Amulet explained why to Naomh.

"This is ideal as we have to wait until the two Planets come in close conjunction and that will not be for at least two months. Otherwise, it will take half a year to get there."

The incomplete Mescal's knowledge of the primitive means of space travel possessed by Hybrids was outdated by centuries. He assumed that it would take months instead of days to get to Mars. So, he had calculated the best time for lift off. When Naomh told the others, a loud cheer went up. Most of his crew were delighted, except for Tell's Spy who had no time for this period of relaxation. Agent XIII just had to grin and bear it and pretend that they were as excited as the rest of them. Naomh actually felt relieved that he could ignore the mission for a short period. The gang spent the next weeks in heaven. It was in a closed off complex by the beachfront. The enforced rest and recuperation worked wonder on all of them; even the Mute refrained from his casual killing, it took great effort on his part. There would be uproar in the private complex, if bodies were to be found. The cruel killer was not mad; he knew that he would be quickly identified. One Friday as they all sat on the steps of the hotel foyer, a bizarre procession passed them; it was the brass band playing in the middle of it that drew their attention. Everyone in it was dressed in black and six of them carried a wooden coffin with large brass handles and a tall ugly and dignified coloured man holding a large black umbrella, led it. With his voice loaded with distaste, the man from the Holy See said.

"It is a blasphemous funeral cortege. It is a twisted version of the true rite and the man in front is mixing a pagan belief with the proper faith."

"Who is he?" Asked the Persuader about the charismatic man that was at its head.

The Priest from Rio gave Illeau a strange look and said to him.

"You tell them. He has your namesake."

The killer from the Bucharest Contrib appeared unsettled. He shook his head and uttered.

"I don't know-.

The Exilian looked confused and frowned.

"Why, he is the formal attendant, otherwise known as a Mute."

Instead of being outraged at Rory's cruel joke, Illeau smiled secretly.

"Yes, I am the one to lead others into the afterlife."

The others did not get it; they had always thought he had been given the name from his reluctance to converse and his sullen demeanour. Then, the time of waiting was up; there was a deadline to be met. Most of the company left the Caribbean island with huge regret, all that is except the five parts Mescal/Amulet and the Anschluss Spy. Both of these were impatient for the search to continue. There was only one vessel that sailed to where the questors wanted to go and having no choice, they booked passage on it. On the ship which journeyed to the mainland that was nothing more than a floating rust bucket, they met a fellow traveller who became a wealth of information. He gave them some useful advice.

"The people in this port we are sailing to are wary of strangers, so you are better off dressing and acting like them. Speaking their language is a bonus. Do any of you speak Spanish?"

In a previously agreed suggestion from the Guide; the entire group shook their heads in the negative. They did not want this passenger to know about their newfound language skills. The man that was volunteering information might have found it ironic that if it were not for the translation device, the Engineer and the Persuader who were born in what was once Spain had no knowledge of their ancestral tongue. He told them.

"Luckily, I can help you with one thing. I have for sale enough outfits for you. At least you can look like the locals."

He sold them bright shirts, colourful trousers and dark glasses. Now conscious of entering a different and probably dangerous leg of the quest, the Engineer presented the Pope's man with items of their advanced technology. The Nuncio refused outright.

"The Lord God will see me safe; after all I am about his work."

After a short sea trip, they arrived on the South American mainland. The port of Cayenne could not have been more different than the heaven they had left a few days ago. All of them were constantly amazed at the contrasts of lifestyles they had encountered on their journey and the conditions people were subject to appeared to be getting worse. Again Naomh thought.

"Our homeland is not so bad and it can be the ideal for the rest of mankind."

But unlike the Spy, he did not know that the whole of this place was an Anschluss Enclave. It was formally known as French Guiana and it's far away rulers wanted it to appear as deprived as possible. If it had the same living conditions as the Anschluss, then it would draw millions of people from the surrounding countries into its heartland. But as a result of this deliberate policy of the LYUBINITES, its neighbours believed it a worst place than their own and none had the desire to cross its boundaries. Those that did quickly retreated from the squalor. The fifteen travellers stepped off the boat, outfitted in the same manner as the locals, thanks to the salesman. The whole dock front was used as a refuse dump; it lay cluttered with dead and decaying matter. Swarms of insects hovered over the waste that formed a thick layer of scum on top of the water. Brown rats and other types of rodents unknown to them could be seen climbing and leaping on any solid object among the filthy debris. Tidal plants clung to the quay walls in splatterings of bright garish colours that was mimicked by the colour of the scummy water. The Guide voiced his opinion.

"This is the pits man. Never in all our travels have we seen such a rundown place."

"We can count ourselves lucky that each of us has been immunised against every known disease." Stated their medic.

"Although, we are probably going to come across one here in this cesspool that has not been discovered yet." Added Moshe as an afterthought.

Months of been in the outdoors and especially lounging around in Havana gave them all a fine tan, which made the squad blend in with the locals. A lot of them seemed to have a European heritage. There was many a splattering of blonde and fair heads among the majority of the black haired crowd. The plusses of dressing like the locals had one huge drawback; the clammy humidity of the city on the edge of the jungle was overpowering. It seeped in under their clothes and even felt like it got under the skin. Cold sweat trickled down their faces, only to be instantly heated up. This state of circumstances was extremely uncomfortable and even though, the group was only a few minutes off the boat, their morale was eroding quickly. Swarms of insects tickling their ointment-exposed faces found their foreign blood a delightful treat and the new arrivals found themselves swatting at real and imaginary pests. Those from the Enclave were slightly more tolerant to the insect irritations than those from the Anschluss. The first to start whinging was as always the Clerk.

"This has to be the worst place we been yet. We better find shade, because I won't be able to take much more of this." Cribbed the blonde man.

Another bite from an unseen insect made the Persuader agree with him. With the advice of the traveller, not to stand out and draw attention, they had to forego on the protection sheen pills as it would look mighty strange if they were the only people that the insects ignored. To top it all, a fall of tropical warm rain confounded his misery when it came suddenly from nowhere. In less than a minute, the clear sky had turned black and rumbled with deep thunder. The Clerk continued with his moaning.

"Shit. What the fuck is this? Rain is supposed to be cold, not warm."

Taking their cue from the locals, the new arrivals ran for cover as the downpour intensified. It grew heavier and heavier until they could no longer hear each other under its deafening noise. In all their travels, they had never witnessed such a deluge. It lasted a full three hours until it abated; its strength never waned during that time. The rainfall had ended as quickly as it had begun. It was like as if some celestial being had just switched it off. By then all of the crew had become stiff from inactivity and pissed off by the Clerk's moaning. Naomh was ignoring his constant whinging as his attention was drawn to the weirdest sight. Two figures on a footpath sat on their haunches and were completely covered by heavy-corded smocks and wearing the widest brimmed hats he had ever seen. Rivulets of water flowed over the edges of their broad head coverings. The two had sat out the entire storm out in the open. The squatting men seemed intent on a crowd of people hurrying up the street in an effort to beat the next downpour. Two swarthy men dressed in black suits, large white collared shirts with dark shades covering their eyes pushed ahead of the mob. They were carrying two red suitcases. Suddenly there was a crack of a single bullet and one of the men carrying the luggage fell to the ground as his head exploded. There was a split second of silence, then another crack. Naomh and his people had already found cover after the first bullet whizzed by. The second man fell like the first, clutching his head as if he accepted the inevitable after seeing his mate fall. The two squatting assassins discarded their wide brimmed head coverings, rose and approached the dead men. Each gunman pumped a full magazine of bullets into them and calmly walked away from the riddled bodies. Then three, two wheeled vehicles sped towards them. The killers of the two men jumped on them as passengers and drove away. Before, they set off, one of the drivers got off the remaining contraption and placed a paper notice on both of the deceased chests and plunged a large dagger through each note. He remounted his two-wheeled motorised vehicle and sped off in the others wake. Exercising his newfound language skills, the keen eyed

Solomon read it aloud.

"Don't fuck with the Sombreros."

The two slain men were left lying in the deserted muddy street and the cases they carried opened to reveal a white powder. Trails of blood mixed with the flour like substance and formed a bloody pulp. The Guide whistled when he saw the contents.

"Man, that is some serious shit."

"What is it?" Asked the Lenses.

"That stuff will blow your mind."

"Is it that good?" Wondered the Persuader.

The user of the Cigs became unusually serious.

"No, that stuff would fuck you up, big time. Keep away from it."

"Alright." Said Naomh as the big man's gaze still lingered on the narcotics *"This is the plan; some of us will purchase a vehicle, while the others find the usual place where those who like a drink hang out."*

They had found from experience that no matter what part of the World they were in, there were always places where buying a few drinks could get a local to impart some information. The translation globes had become very useful, now they could split up and go about their business without Naomh. The technical members of the group, the Engineer, the Lenses and Moshe went to acquire the vehicle while the others went in search of a drink. They soon found a place; it was called a "Cantina.". They entered the premises and it was as shabby as any place they had frequented in the last year. The patrons of the bar suddenly stopped their conversations and the barman gave them a hostile look through the silence. Unperturbed, the Guide went straight to the counter. He ordered beers and then said to the surly barman.

"My friends and I have had a little luck and we would like to share it. So why not give everybody here a few beers, on us. Imported beer, sir."

He handed a large sum of dollars over the counter.

"Tell me when that runs out."

The barman's face brightened and his customers cheered. The silence might have never been as conversations resumed. The beers only came in glass bottles. The barman opened them and cleaned each one with a grubby cloth. The Guide with help from a pretty young waitress carried the frosted bottles to the table where the others sat. The Nuncio did not drink beer. As they had no wine, he requested plain water. Pools of liquid formed at the bottle's base and the varnished wooden table. A lot of craved initials and rude suggestions on the bench's surface diverted some of their attention. The barman handed out the free drinks to the ten or so people. He raised his own bottle and the customers followed suit. He turned towards Naomh's crew and said.

"Salute."

The questors responded in the same fashion. After a few more drinks, paid for by them, the talkative patrons gave them the information they had searched for. One of the customers who liked to be the centre of attention, especially to those who were buying him beer, told them.

"There is such a place, deep in the jungle amigos. It is surrounded by a fence and patrolled by guards. Anyone that gets too curious about what goes on behind it disappears. My cousin and a few of his friends desperate for work went there, but they never returned. No seignior, it does not pay to get to curious about that place."

While, he was giving them directions, the Engineer and his group returned.

"Man, I could do with a cold beer." Said the Lenses.

The serving girl brought over three. As they gulped down the chilled beverage, Moshe told them.

"We have bought three vehicles, suitable for the terrain ahead."

Viewing them from the window by their bench, they saw large jeeps, outfitted in kaki green and a lot less garish than the one that had been acquired back on the road to the Mountain Kingdom. Catching Naomh's eye, the Rabbi said to his fellow compatriot.

"Good choice."

Beersheba turned to them with something she had noticed.

"These people are a friendly lot; it makes me think that the guy on the ship fed us a lot of bullshit to sell us these clothes."

They said their goodbyes to the owner and patrons of the Cantina. They left enough money to cover the bill for more drinks and left to a resounding cheer. The travellers divided themselves among the three vehicles and made their departure. As soon as they drove out of the shabby town, all of them except the Nuncio began changing into their protective outfits; he would not wear the trappings of violence. It was difficult enough to change in the cramped and humid space of the jeeps crowded interiors. Tempers flared at the unintended jostling in some of the four wheeled craft, especially in the one that held the huge Persuader. Over the sounds of swearing on the air wave, Naomh could not resist returning the Rabbi's jibe.

"Not such a good choice now?"

In his defence, like an echo of another time, Moshe said.

"It was all that I could find at such short notice."

The Rabbi had given them a glowing pill, again the Nuncio declined and the protection sheen warped around their skin. Much to everyone's comfort. The persistent biting of the insects was banished to a bad memory and their sweaty skin soon cooled. Then, the inevitable happened; they were attacked a few kilometres outside the port town. As always, it was because of the wealth they flashed around. Whether someone in the bar decided to take them or told a friend, it did not matter. The questors reacted instantly as bullets whizzed towards the first land rover, their Enclave acquired deflection jackets took a few impacts, but those who were hit remained unscathed. Fire was returned and their attackers were not so lucky. The firefight lasted a few minutes and the ambusher's fled, leaving a few dead behind. They did not even bother to check the causalities and left them in their wake. The attack caused Solomon to mouth as he pointed at the dead bodies.

"We will have to stop flashing our wealth around. This is getting quite ridiculous."

"What's wrong with it?" Said Greta. *"It keeps us in practice."*

Her lover and the Mute agreed with her assessment. The Enclave man sighed in exasperation at the tall woman as he remounted his vehicle. The green and tanned vehicles travelled southeast for two days on unpaved roads. The routes got narrower and the jungle became more verdant and lush. Trees got bigger and their wide buttressed trunks seemed immovable. At times a canopy of leaves formed by intertwining trees on opposite sides of the road blocked the sky for long distances at a time. In these tunnels of greenery, the hiss of the rain on the leaf canopy became more intense and every morning, the view of the road ahead was obscured by a wall of rising mist that came from the steaming jungle. It rained every minute of the two-day journey in the cooking cauldron. The weather was certainly trying to make them miserable. Rain crackled on the leaves like an imitation of some giant popcorn maker. The jungle abounded in a great variety of animal life and it caused Solomon to mention.

"Edward would have loved this place, he would have never left. He would have spent months; no years here."

The Clerk put his hand on the Enclave man's shoulder and gave it a gentle squeeze. He said.

"Maybe, he has found a place as wonderful as this?"

"Hopefully"

The Guide whose eyes locked on to a bunch of feeding maggots turned away from the conversation; his clenched teeth nearly betrayed him. The third day out from the port; the 26th of April 2954 AD was a day when Naomh was about to meet someone who would have a profound effect on him and his quest. Some of the men stood in the undergrowth at the edge of the dirt road relieving themselves. Sick of been confined, they did not bother with the invisible shields facilities. Their discharges adding to the bubbles of moisture that had already settled on the green foliage waiting to be evaporated when the heat of the day built up. Even in this verdant paradise, death was never far away. Pristine trees contained decaying leaves, half green and yellow with underbellies that had gone completely brown. The cause was huge parasitic vines that would eventually suck the life force from their hosts as they crawled towards the sky. Away from the sound of their transport's engines, the sound of the jungle was overpowering. Ear piercing animal whoops, Primate screeches and bird whistles fought for dominance in the leafy canopy. The inquisitive Solomon wandered off into the tangle of green. Behind giant mahogany trees that were being slowly ensnared and strangled by creeping Liana's, he saw something that brought him to an awed stop. A short time later, he returned breathless and told them of some wonderful sights ahead.

"Come, let's have a look. We need to stretch our legs anyway and you must see this."

The one time sidekick of the Prof had stumbled upon ruins that were smothered by the jungle. The hidden debris lay close to the edge of a silent green pool. Down in its murky depths, on subterranean ledges and its sandy bottom lay generations of clay, stone, copper and gold figurines, all inlaid with precious metals. These were once offerings to Mescal's race. Strange statues of winged beings fought for supremacy with the jungle vines and creepers on the ancient temple walls. As Solomon cleared away some of the jungle growth, the images of these Alien creatures became more pronounced. The five parts of the Mescal/Amulet was astounded. He was looking at rough effigies of his exiled race. The long dead Hybrid carvers had built this temple of adobe and on to these scarlet mudbricks, they had engraved images which had depicted his kin as the Gods of their people.

"By the moons of CRYSTALIOS, some of these Hybrids did remember our time on this Planet. How can that be possible? Did, the DEFILED instigate this? I will have to wait until I am completed to solve this riddle."

The five parts Mescal/Amulet wondered if the whole of the ALASTHA'I scheme was snowballing and careening out of their control. Its host sensed the unease of the living amulet and said.

"Come let's go from here; we have no time for this. Sightseeing is not high on our list of priorities right now."

With regret Solomon followed his companions back to the vehicles. Then as to increase their leader's edginess, there was a strange gust of wind that rustled nearby trees. The bearer of the living amulet was about to meet another man that was going to have a profound effect on him, more so than the Lama, for he was about to share in the quest itself. Through the curtain raiser of living foliage; a figure stepped out of the shadows. In a flash, weapons were pointed at the man who seemed to have appeared from nowhere. Naomh was drawn towards the huge stocky and brown skinned man who was dressed in military style clothing. This strange person bore the craggy countenance of his face with a proud resolve. Numerous shadows under the angles of his face made him appear to be in his early fifties. His braided jet-black unruly hair was immediately noticeable; it was parted in the centre and hung over both of his cheeks in spirally braided pigtails. These winding twisting braids were laced with feathers and beads of many colours. On his bared forearm, there was an ink tattoo of a winged shape, similar in design to the moustached men who had attacked them back in the Arabian Desert.

"Is he connected to them?" Asked Naomh of himself.

The man who confronted the questors walked the road of the medicine man. He was the Shaman of his people. He thanked the runes that he had cast a month ago and the trances whose visions had brought him to this encounter, far from his desert home in the north. Here the spirits told him, he would meet the people who would redeem the honour of his tribe.

"And the spirits were never wrong."

Naomh noticed the lone stranger's eyes were totally focussed on him and as he returned the eye contact, he instantly realised that the man was no enemy. So the bearer of the living amulet silently mouthed.

"Oh no! Not another one."

Then, the voice within interjected.

"You must go to him. There is an unusual, but familiar anomaly about him."

Naomh's heart leaped.

"Could this strange man have another piece of the APOCRYPHA'I?"

Somehow another utterance; the voice of reason did not think so.

"It would not be that easy?"

Its bearer did what the internal presence suggested and confidently approached the man. The others still had Naomh covered with their weapons. The weird man standing with his burly arms folded had already guessed that these were no drifters and he seemed unfazed by the guns pointed at him. They had a purpose about them, one that he could assist them with. The dusky coloured man spoke in a strange brash dialect of Anschluss.

"I am Chief Dan George of the Anasazi, but you can know me by the name of the Shaman."

"I am Naomh." Replied the one who had went to him.

The Indian accepted this to be true.

"We share a common path at the crossroads of our separate destines. You search for the frozen rainbow and I am here to offer my words of wisdom."

The stranger put him to the test. He spoke in the ancient and exclusive language of his people. Without hesitation, Naomh greeted him in that tongue. Too late, he realised his mistake after responding in the same rhetoric.

"What does the white man know of the tongue of my father's? You are blessed with powerful medicine. But I can see that the good spirits are within you. Come sit with me and we will exchange words."

Chief Dan George sat down and crossed his legs; he motioned for Naomh to do likewise. Sensing no threat, he also sat down. Then, the man with the two braided pigtails told his story, the words came out in the form of a musical chant.

"The spirits of the earth and sky have aided me in my search for you. I am of the Anasazi. Long have we been thought vanished from the Mother, even longer, have we warded the secret. The shattered Totem of my ancestors was stolen by the soldiers of the Union. It was held in trust by us until the one who is destined for it arrives."

Naomh was now certain that this enigmatic man had the sixth piece of the APOCRYPHA'I.

"Open your shirt and show him the truth." Commanded the five parts Mescal/Amulet.

Its host was reluctant to show his secret to the stranger, but he relented and done what the internal voice requested. The Shaman's eyes widened at the sight of the uncompleted Alien technology embedded in Naomh's chest.

"The Spirits were right. You are the one." Intoned the Indian.

The brown man moved forward reverently and reached towards the multi-coloured jewel. As he laid his heavily callused hands on the revered shimmer, Naomh resisted the urge to pull away. But the Shaman's touch caused an unexpectant reaction within the bearer. The Indian had reached into his soul and discovered the Alien presence within. The living amulet seemed to approve of his tactile approach, but was unaware of the Indian's discovery. The Anasazi withdrew his hand and unbuttoned his jerkin. Around his neck was a strange painted ceramic vial. It depicted winged beings and a violet jewel. Remembering the last person who had that symbol about his presence, Naomh became uneasy, but again the internal voice enforced its original assessment.

"He does not have the next segment, but I feel a connection to him. He can lead us to the last piece of me. And for the moment, this peculiar man is no danger to us."

Sensing Naomh's uncertainty, the stranger simply stated.

"I am now one with your search. Come, we will go and do the Spirits bidding."

The two of them rose and went over to the others.

"Lower your weapons, he will be coming with us."

Reluctantly, his comrades did as he commanded. The Shaman was introduced to the company, some shook his hand, others held back. They did not need this intrusion in their close knit group. Surprisingly, it was the Nuncio who protested the most.

"He is a primitive savage. He has no part of this and should be told to go on his way."

Naomh gave the Priest a hard look and said with an air of finality.

"He comes with us."

When their newest member heard the Guide's name, he said.

"You are the Pathfinder, I am an Indian."

"What's an Indian?" Asked the fascinated Clerk.

"A name given to us by the white man."

Some of them were confused, had they not left India thousands of kilometres behind in the east. When this was explained to the brown man, he just laughed.

"No, I am not from there."

"Then, how come you share the same name?" Quizzed the Lenses.

"Well, thousands of years ago, one of your ancestors went looking for India in three ships. He sailed west instead of the usual eastern route. When he arrived in my Continent, the seafarer believed that he was in India, so he called us Red Indians and the name has stuck since."

The Mute thought it a stupid story, but did not say so. He was uneasy around the strange man. The Indian thought him.

"The epitome of the real Paleface."

Then, the unusual man invited them to eat with him. Suddenly there was the smell of a fire and the mouth-watering aroma of cooking fish and stewing coffee. Naomh thought it strange that he had not noticed these potent whiffs before. The Nuncio sulked and went back to the jeeps, the Engineer followed him. The Shaman led them into a shallow overhang, where he had an open fire going. There was a spit over the flame and it held several roasting peacock bass that he had caught during his vigil. The fish was delicious and the fare was consumed with relish. During the meal, the curious Clerk asked the Indian.

"You are not red."

"I know." Replied the big brown man matter of factually.

"We have seen real red men, back on the high mountains in Asia. They were the colour of raspberries."

He began to tell the stranger about them. When the repast was finished, everybody boarded the jeep's and they were on their way again. With the big Indian, one of the vehicles became even more cramped; needless to say, it was not the one with the Exilian Pious. The newly enlarged group of sixteen souls arrived at the town that lay about fifty kilometres from the secluded area. They went to the nearest Cantina and again asked questions after buying more drinks for the clientele. One of the locals told them.

"That area is out of bounds, but there is a lot of noise and activity at night time."

A scrawny lad who looked about twelve and was sweeping the floor of the drinking room approached Naomh, his tired eyes full of hope.

"Seignior. My name is Manuel Alfosno. Do you go there in search of work?"

The Guide nudged Naomh under the table.

"Yes. My friends and I are in search of work."

"If you could help me. I would be very grateful. About a year ago, my papa went there for work. We were a very poor family, but Santa Maria must have smiled on father as he found employment there. Every month, he

sends money to us. We are very grateful for his sacrifice, but we would like to see him again. So if you come across him, would you pass on my message? Please seignior.

Something in the youth's plea touched a chord in Naomh, he too knew what it was like to be deprived of a parent and his heart went out to the young lad.

"Of course, if I meet him, I will tell him how he is missed."

The lad's eyes lit up; he handed Naomh a laminated picture of a thin swarthy man with a very black moustache and equally dark locks. Overjoyed, Manuel said.

"Gracious Seignior. His name is Alfredo."

He left them with a spring in his step, just as a man approached them and offered hash for sale. To the Persuader's delight, the Guide smelt it, then took a little taste and purchased a couple of kilos. The dealer then took out small bag of white powder and winked.

"Amigos, why not try this delight? It is like a piece of Heaven on earth."

He was told nicely by van DerKamp.

"No, thanks. We are not interested in that shit."

"But Amigo's it is the finest powder in the America's" Insisted the dealer.

The Guide's voice hardened.

"Go away."

With a serious expression, he added while he dismissed him.

"You sell any of that stuff to my friends and I will kill you."

The petty drug peddler saw the steel in his eyes and retreated. The Persuader looked disappointed and asked the man who always shared a buzz with him.

"Why can we not try that stuff? The man said it was way better than hash."

The Guide gave the big man a stern lecture.

"I'll only tell you this one more time. That stuff is highly addictive and dangerous. It will fuck you up. Keep away from it."

"He is right, that stuff is bad medicine." Said the Shaman.

The Persuader seemed to respect the view of the strange man, so he let them believe that he lost interest in the stuff.

"You are right. I get enough kicks out of liquor and hash."

"And don't forget the ladies." Added the Clerk.

"Listen to the expert." Said Beersheba sarcastically as her eyes went to Heaven.

The Lenses was eating some bland tasting cashew nuts and commented on their tastelessness. Miriam sprinkled a lot of salt on the white kernels and told him.

"Try them again."

He did and mouthed.

"Much better."

The aggrieved Engineer chastised his sibling.

"Why don't you be like him Jose and enjoy the simpler things in life?"

An hour later the Guide went to relieve himself, his stomach was acting up and he spent quite a time in the dingy toilet. Truth to tell though, he probably took more time cleaning the dodgy china toilet bowl than actually reliving himself in it. When he had finished his lengthy ablutions, he returned to his companions to find them leaning over a convulsing Persuader. He had been gone about thirty minutes. The big man was having some sort of seizure. His nose was full of blood and vomit was erupting from his mouth in irregular intervals. The Nuncio stated.

"The wages of temptation."

To his God, he silently implored.

"Is this my test? Am I in the company of the Devil's minions?"

Ignoring him, the Guide demanded.

"What happened?"

"We don't know. He disappeared for fifteen minutes and then he came back and sat down. He started mumbling and giggling; then he was out of his tree. Then all of a sudden he collapsed to the floor. This fell out of his hand." Answered his distraught brother.

The Guide saw the little satchel of white power. There was fury in the man from the Amsterdam Contrib's eyes, he knew what had happened. He was seething as he said.

"Do what you can for him; I'll be back in a minute."

The Engineer went with him; he had an idea what he was about. The two men left the others to their ministrations on the gravely ill man. Once again, it took the Rabbi all of his newfound skills to save the big man. He had to tend to him on the spot; they could not risk exposing the TORT-CAM. It was difficult enough, but his patient also suffered a hangover from the serious injury inflicted by the Winged Knight. But their medical expert managed to resuscitate and save him; he had a good deal of help from the Indian. The Persuader came out of his paroxysm and opened his eyes. He was like a reprieved drowning man and gasped for air. The Rabbi took the Nuncio's bottle of water and said.

"Drink that."

There was a huge sigh of relief among his friends as he gulped the liquid down. The Guide and his brother returned and both gave the dishevelled Persuader a withering glance.

"You stupid idiot. Why did you do it?" Said the Engineer, but his relief was evident. His recovering sibling had the good grace to look ashamed; he asked for more water and downed about two litres in as many minutes. Then still wobbly, he replied to his brother's question.

"For a different buzz."

"I told you that stuff was dangerous." Said the Guide.

The white-faced man looked apologetic and belatedly said.

"It won't happen again."

"Narcotics are Satan's vice." Recited Padre Pious.

The Mute who had been engrossed in his diary of death before the incident now returned to his grisly reading. The glazed eyes of the big man had not interested him and he silently mouthed.

"If you want the ultimate buzz big man, then you should do what I am doing. No controlled substance can give you that thrill."

As they left the Cantina and came out on the paved street, the emerging gang encountered the body of the drug dealer who had tried to sell them the white powder. The peddler's corpse lay sprawled on the ground with a small round bullet hole in his forehead. His blank uncomprehending eyes stared fixedly into space and judging by the pool of blood around his head, the back of his skull was blown completely away. Passers-by ignored the body, deciding that he had rightly paid for his infraction. The others looked at the Guide and jumped to the wrong conclusion. The object of this scrutiny simply replied.

"I told him the consequences. And it seems, this is the way things are done here"

The companion who had gone with him intervened.

"It was not the Guide who killed him, it was me."

Most of the crew agreed with the killing, but the Mute was in a foul mood.

"I should have thought of it first."

It would have been ironic, in doing what he done best, the weirdo would have gained credence with the rest of them. The Nuncio looked at the Engineer in horror and admonished him severely.

"What have you done? The taking of life is against God's commandments."

"Sometimes it is necessary."

The man from the Madrid Contrib was in no mood for a sermon. The young lad from the bar ran over to them and grabbed the Guide's hands.

"You should leave quickly seigniors. His amigos will not like this and they will come looking for you."

Leaving the town to avoid an unnecessary gunfight because the of the Engineer's slaying, the cadre of sixteen drove the fifty miles from the locale to the barrier of the Anschluss base. Through their laser sights, the companions scanned the perimeter of an electric fence that had an outer circle of a watery moat. Cahill spoke aloud to no one in particular,

"Why does the Anschluss surround everything with barriers?"

"It is their way." Said Greta.

"The white man has always build forts on land that was not his."

The Shaman made the point from the perspective of the conquered. The gang split up into three groups, Naomh and the Guide went one way. Miriam and Beersheba went in the opposite direction while the rest set up a base camp hidden in the cover of the jungle and waited for the reconnoitring parties. The owner of the invisible shield activated it and split it up into its seven parts. He took the red unit, entered it under the watchful eye of the Guide. It vanished and he waited to see him on the other side of the fence. But to his surprise, the thing materialised alongside the open trench. It refused to cross the water. The sphere moved back and vanished and in a few seconds, it reappeared alongside the astonished Guide. The man from the Amsterdam Contrib explained to an equally perplexed Naomh about what he had seen. The inner voice worked out what had occurred.

"The water is charged also. This energy barrier is playing havoc with the Guidex sphere's mechanisms. That is why the separated modules cannot pass through. I am certain, it is a result of the mixture of the high humidity, the falling rain and the electric fence itself."

Naomh never finished listening; he called his lover straight away and was relieved to hear her voice. He told her.

"Neither of you touch the water, it is electrified. Make your way back to us."

"Ok. We are on our way."

As the mobile shields could not penetrate the strange energised barrier, then they would either go over it or under it. The two men skirted the electric perimeter in an Eastward direction looking for a weakness. They had the same result with every colour at every place. Another sudden downpour caught them unawares. Then on the other side of the fence, they heard the approach of motorised vehicles. The two friends ran back to the edges of the tree line and took cover while they waited until the others came for them. Totally protected from the intense squall, the Guide looked up into the canopy of the huge trees. He sighted a bunch of red haired monkeys with large bulbous noses that lay huddled in the branches above. He chuckled with delight as he saw that each individual primate held a large leaf over their heads for shelter from the deluge. He poked Naomh in the shoulder and pointed.

"Look."

His sheltering companion looked to where the Guide had directed.

"I think they have more sense than us." Suggested his friend.

The rest of their group appeared to have more sense as well, for they did not come to them until the downpour had eased considerably. He showed the rest of his friends the huddled troop of monkeys and Cahill sighed.

"What is the matter?"

The man who had pointed out the Monkey's wanted to know and the other acquiesced.

"It just that at times like this, I wish the Prof had not run out on us and could share these moments."

Naomh also became melancholy at the realisation.

"He is probably having a better time."

As always, the Guide hid his sadness at the turn in the conversation; he was still focussed on the one certain individual who he thought killed the academic. But Illeau had done nothing yet for him to betray himself. The Guide was also wrong when he thought that only two in the concealed group knew for certain that the Prof was definitely not alive, himself and the murderer. For another among them had guessed at what had happened to the man from the London Contrib. The intending infiltrators of the Anschluss spaceport observed the fence that hindered them; taking turns in two-hour shifts. It was during this period of inactivity that the Engineer offered the Shaman the items of advanced technology that the Nuncio had refused. The big brown skinned man accepted them gratefully. As he showed the Indian how to install them, he said.

"A gift for helping to save my brother."

Each person on watch noticed that heavily armed motorised patrols passed every half an hour. Having ruled out the use of the TORT-CAM technology, Naomh's crew had to find another way. The Engineer came up with the answer to the problem; it was staring them in the face. They would use his babies.

"We will use the rising Skimmers." He said with a shake of his head, as if there was another alternative.

"Will they work? Won't the fence interfere with them as well?" Asked Moshe who usually learnt from experience.

"There is only one way to find out." Said Greta.

"I have to inform you that there is an even greater problem." Announced the Rabbi who was the group's medical expert.

"And what is that?" Asked the Clerk who was looking forward to the unique experience.

"We have to find out which of us can actually go out into space. We have no idea if any of us is immune to the space virus. No-one from the Enclave has been up there in hundreds of years."

"How can we do that?" Queried the Lenses.

"The LAB-CELL has the necessary equipment. We will go there and find out, if any of us is immune."

The voice within told Naomh.

"You are. Do not let yourself be scanned. They will see the changes in your biology."

He was not over enthusiastic about that news.

"I do not want to make this fantastic trip alone. I really hope; others are immune as well."

They all entered the Rabbi's domain. Each member of the Quest stripped to their undergarments and stood in front of the glowing screen. The examiner initiated a bio scan. He checked the results and to everybody's surprise, especially the Anschluss Spy, only the Shaman and Greta passed the scan. There was uproar; Miriam, Cahill and a livid De Mere were the most vocal among the protesters. The bearer of the APOCRYPHA'l silenced the protests.

"This argument is stupid and pointless; the disease is fatal to you all. You cannot go; it is as simple as that. Only Greta, the Shaman and myself can go out there. End of discussion."

"Can you find something in that magic box of yours to immunise us?" Asked Beersheba of her compatriot, the Rabbi.

The Guide secretly had other ideas.

"This is a recipe for disaster. I do not think it is a good idea to leave the irrational Greta and Naomh alone on this crazy mission. And, none of us knows anything about the Indian. But the man of the World sensed that the Shaman could be trusted. The wise Anasazi spoke to the emotional group.

"This is why the Spirits led me to you. You will need my strong arm and council out there away from our Mother. Now on her sister Planet, we will be three and not two."

Still most of them believed the trip would be the hardest part, according to the Lenses briefing, nobody was alive on Mars. The Red Planet had been abandoned a long time ago. Naomh assumed that.

"There is no need to be alarmed. It would be something similar to retrieving the piece from the bottom of the sea. Whoever wore it now would be dust and bones."

The five others pieces did not want to alarm its host, but it could have voiced the facts.

"As the indigo piece still exists, then its host was also alive."

It decided to keep silent on the account. Despite all the vocal reservations, the gang made plans anyway. It was eventually agreed that the three of them would go over the fence in the early hours of the morning when activity around the base would be sluggish. A huddled group consulted the living map about the best place to land, when they came back. The LAB-CELL'S three-dimensional map showed a vast desert to the south of the Continent. It had large open flat tracks of terrain to land on and more importantly the place appeared isolated. It was agreed that when the three of them returned, they would land there. So the others had to make their journey to the barren land. The Shaman decided to import some humour into the subdued atmosphere.

"Let me tell you a story my friends. Centuries ago, in the infancy of Space travel, the government of my land was in great rivalry with another nation called the U.S.S.R, for the dominance of space. The spacemen on our side were called Astronauts and on the other side were called

Cosmonauts. *My government spent millions and millions of dollars more than their rival. Many years later when the rivalry had cooled down, two of these people were talking to each other about the merits of each other's experience. The Astronaut told the other that his agency had spent millions of credits on developing an ink pen that could write upside down in zero gravity."*

The Lenses interrupted.

"What was the point of that?"

"This was in the days of zero gravity; there was no artificial atmosphere in spacecraft. Anyway, the Cosmonaut showed him something and said, this is what we used and it did not cost us a single credit."

His listeners were intrigued and the normally non-interested Persuader asked.

"What did he show him?"

The Shaman smiled and took a primitive lead pencil from his pocket and said.

"This! Sometimes people look for complex solutions when there is an easier option staring them in the face."

"You have an easier way."

"For this trip. No, my friend. Unfortunately this time, it has to be done the hard way."

Then the time of parting was upon them and they said their goodbyes; Naomh and Greta's farewells to their lovers were the most poignant. Cahill unstrapped his favourite weapon, a small squat and stocky rapid-firing rifle that was used for close range fighting and handed it over to Greta.

"I hope you don't need it, but it will remind you of me."

Naomh nearly choked on his own words. He did not like this idea of parting very much. He had also left the marble of the invisible shield in Miriam's charge. The internal voice had told him.

"This version of the Guidex sphere was not designed for the conditions of another World."

Naomh also advised her not to show it to the Exilian unless it was unavoidable.

"He will not understand it."

It was also agreed that from now until the three of them returned, there would be no radio contact as Anschluss listening posts might overhear them. Miriam would always remember that parting, she had clung to her man with the overpowering sweet smell of damp foliage, the most prevalent sense in her memory. Over the next few weeks, that odour of separation would taunt her until the day of her lover's return. Both of them had tears of grief and frustration that mixed with their constant kisses. Finally, the two lovers broke apart.

"Don't worry my love, as sure as the Sun rises in the morning, I will come back to you." Naomh whispered through his tears. Then, he gathered

himself together and said his goodbyes to the rest of his little bunch. The others were also taking the separation badly, all except the Mute and the Brazilian. Both appeared indifferent, an empty Planet held little interest to them. The Guide told Naomh.

"Look after yourself and the other two. I'd like to get to know the Indian dude a bit better."

Through their advanced Monocles, those who were not going watched the other three rise. Naomh, Greta and the Shaman stood on a Platform of Light. It was not affected by the electric/water fence and it rose over the barrier effortlessly. In less than a minute, they were on the other side and once again back in the Anschluss domain. Halting for a brief moment, they looked back at their friends with expressionless faces and moved away into the base. The trespassers sprinted across the open ground towards large hanger like buildings in the distance. The required spacecraft was visible through their all-purpose Monocles. As the three infiltrators neared the spacecraft, they inadvertently disturbed someone; it was a man in blue overalls. The startled worker was about to shout an alarm, but Greta was a blur. She spurred into action, her blonde locks flowing. The man's warning shout never came; it was cut off as her blade took him fully in the throat. He slumped to the ground face up. Naomh went numb with recognition; it was the guy in the photo image. He had found Manuel's father and was now staring into his sightless eyes. The man who promised to pass on a message to his son shuddered with regret. Greta and the Shaman dragged the body away and hid it behind some plastic drums. The only woman among them fixed a pair of shrewd eyes on him.

"We will be long gone when they discover him. It had to be done, he was about to give the game away."

The Shaman agreed with her. Naomh gave a rueful smile; he knew that she was right, as Greta always was. If it had been left to him, they would more than likely in the middle of a gun battle at this moment.

"Am I getting soft? That man had to be silenced. Just because I knew something about him does not matter."

He suddenly remembered the Prof's words about all of the needless killing. Sneaking around a large expanse of tarmac, they soon discovered that a spacecraft was all powered up and ready for take-off, it was awaiting its crew. The lit up and humming craft had no guards; the security only surrounded the periphery of the base, in their arrogance of not believing that anyone who did not belong would get this far into its protected area. Like the ANS GREGORY LYUBIN, this Anschluss contrivance also had a name emblazoned on its sleek silver side. It said in broad letters;

"THE MARY IRVINE."

The three intending hijackers moved quickly and silently towards the large craft. If the Tanks of the Enclave looked like giant squat beetles, then the spacecraft of the Anschluss appeared as a long thin flying insect. The

Watcher back in the past could have explained to Naomh.

"The invertebrates of the Planet had been evolving for hundreds of millions of years and in the time, they have found the perfect frames for flight. Thus any Hybrid invention would eventually simulate the insect's solution to the problems of movement in this medium."

As the infiltrators commandeered the spacecraft, Greta addressed a concern.

"This has been too easy."

"I agree." Responded Naomh.

"The Spirits have been with us." Was the Shaman's opinion.

The traitor among their ranks could have enlightened him, for the Anschluss elite needed him to complete his mission, if they were to fulfil their long awaited destiny and the Chairman would assist him whenever it was possible. The mole had already contacted the necessary people and the easy access to a space ship had been allowed. The callous security agency had even engaged in the ancient act of perdu and even left the lone local worker as a sacrificial lamb so not to allay suspicions that it had been all set up for them. They had not selected Manuel's father deliberately, that had been an uncanny coincidence. All around the base and hidden from the trio lay hundreds of concealed and heavily armed men and women, watching and listening, but above all they were their just to make sure that the two RE-INSTATOR'S and their unlikely ally boarded the craft safely.

Outside the base, the tropical rain clouds had parted for a few hours giving everybody a clear view of the spacecraft's take off. The accelerating spacecraft lit up like an exploding firework as it traversed the night sky on the night of the 1st of May 2954AD. Back on the ground and over a kilometre away from the Anschluss base, the rest of the Earthbound Questor's watched the flickering light rise into the night sky. It sped upwards until it merged with the other twinkling stars and became indistinguishable from the heavenly points. For a while it outshone the celestial lights and then it was gone. Now it could be any of the millions of stars above in the black sky. Then, what was left of Naomh's small army here on Earth went back to the land rovers to begin the long journey south-westwards towards the meeting-point. There was subdued silence among them; each lost in their own thoughts. Even the Clerk made no attempt at his usual humour. Five hours later, another light sped towards the heavens. They did not see this one, as the Earthbound questors were already in their vehicles and heading westwards. The Chairman had ordered the launching of a second ship; it was much larger than the one that Naomh and Greta travelled in. It contained over a hundred elite PREVENTIVES. Even the traitor among them was unaware of this event, but they would have approved of it. Tell had informed his second in command.

"Something sinister and unexplainable has happened on Mars and now was the time to find out what was going on up there."

The Kaiser was privy to information that others were not. Centuries ago there had been a classical betrayal by the LYUBINITES. Hundreds of scientists, none of whom was a clone of the doctor's Apostles were left to rot on the red rock. Darwin Otis was the head of the scientists who were rising fast through the echelons of power. But he had been outfoxed by his rivals and left stranded on the Red planet. Those deliberately forsaken on Mars were quickly forgotten as the centuries passed. Without regular trips from re-supplying craft, they would only have lasted about a year, two at the very most. But now the Chairman was receiving reports that there was some sort of unusual activity up there and what was more worrying was the fact that Naomh was drawn towards the Red Planet. He told his Secretary of Protocol before his second in command had crossed the Atlantic.

"This is a chance to kill two birds with one stone. What one might call a double whammy."

The Anschluss were the only power block, still capable of space travel and even they had not put anyone on Mars in over two hundred years. Unaccountably, there had been too many unexplained events and lost craft and personnel and accidents did not account for all of them. The Chairman was certain that this niggling little mystery would be solved once and for all. He fully expected his back up force to find and report back that they had found the desiccated remains of the scientific colony. He knew that Human flesh decayed slowly in the non-bacterial and low oxygenated air of Mars.

"I might even order Bliehn to bring back Otis's body. I could put it on display in my office. Yes, that would shock a few people."

Tell laughed out loud at his own cleverness. He proceeded to contact the commander of his Space Corps who was already on her way to Mars on another craft and order her to do that.

XXVII.

"Five, four, three, two, one."

"Engage engines."

A different type of metallic voice was now giving the commands; for one thing it was female. Then a touch sensitive instrument panel received a long slender Human finger and the crafts engines roared into action.

"Ignition." Announced the craft's artificial voice.

Those on board cringed and waited for the shouts of alarm. A convinced Naomh uttered.

"The game is up now. Hordes of Anschluss troops will pile out of the buildings and swarm all over us trying to stop us."

The commandeered spacecraft's control panel lit up even more as it sped down the runway, accelerating to two hundred kilometres an hour in a matter of seconds. The ten kilometre long concrete runway did little to dampen the violent shaking of its mechanical parts as it launched from the spaceport at the fringes of the South American jungle with its three illegal passengers. Naomh felt ill at ease in the cockpit of the MARY IRVINE; even though he was told that the shuttle would take them to Mars of its own accord. The onboard computers were programmed to arrive on the Red Planet in a little over five days. This was quicker than the normal journeys of a few weeks or even longer depending on the conjunction of the two Worlds. The aggrieved incomplete semblance of Mescal was upset, because he got his calculations wrong.

"My information on their space-crafts capabilities was outdated. The knowledge was from an old host. These anomalies could jeopardise my calculations. The sooner that I am complete; the better."

The Spy had known, but Agent XIII was in no position to tell anyone. The distance of the journey came up on the screen. The Patriarchi recovered.

"This is the reason that I delayed you. The journey is short, because at this time, the two Planets orbits are as close as they would ever get."

"Short. You have to laugh. It is 37,260,000 million kilometres away. I remember when one end of the Anschluss to the other was the longest distance possible. And now I am travelling across the space between Planets."

"You should try traversing whole Galaxies." Said the pompous sounding Alien voice.

"Maybe someday."

"Not if I can help it."

Its host never heard that.

"Wow, this thing can really move. We are about to ride the wind." Mouthed the Shaman.

The uncompleted Alien form expressed mirth at the Hybrid's pride in the antiquated craft.

"My own race had once commuted between these two Planet's in a matter of minutes."

The three hijackers had a specific window of opportunity to exploit; otherwise the journey could take months. Twelve hours later, another craft had used the same time frame of extent to take off and follow the MARY IRVINE. These first time inter-planetary travellers had back up and were unaware of it. The Anschluss used nuclear engines in their fleet of spacecraft to propel them through space. Controlled atomic explosions in a fission reactor converted metal into electrified atoms. These miniature particles spun at enormous speeds, hurling them out of a powerful nozzle in a jet stream to speed the spacecraft through the Solar System. Each detonation in the engine area was equal to 10,000 tons of TNT. Huge shock absorbers mounted on heavy pusher plates controlled the force and heat of the explosions. The Anschluss scientists had perfected the Ion drive. The spacecraft generated its own magnetic field to protect its crew from the lethal solar flares that periodically erupted from the distant Sun. The on board detection computers gave sufficient warning of such a solar event and metal shields would slide smoothly down over the viewing ports, protecting the crew from the deadly radiation. The craft also rotated along its axis as it sped through the blackness, creating an artificial gravity in its enclosed space. Naomh felt akin to one of the whirling bullets of his gun. He fervently hoped that he would not be ejected at the same velocity. The bearer of the living jewel looked over at his female crewmate, the personification of calmness; Greta. Feeling obliged to swear, now that the Engineer would not hear him, he uttered.

"Shit! Does anything faze her? I am crapping buckets."

However, he still looked out the window and saw the World spiralling away and then they were in near Earth orbit. The reluctant Astronauts had no idea when the transition between going up and now travelling across space had occurred and they had equally no idea that the ship had passed through the Van Allen Radiation belts. Naomh's heart, though beating fast nearly skipped a beat as he looked longingly back at the blue orb of his Home World. The side of the Planet they had come from was shrouded in blackness. He could make out the point where day and night melded on the globe below, a thin line that circumvented the azure sphere with such precision that it could have been drawn by a compass. In the side illuminated by the Sun's rays, he could see the Continental landmasses and the vast Oceans far below. Weather patterns blocked out patches of sea and land. He saw the totality of the World, free from the censorship of the Anschluss. It was a wonderful sight that reminded him of a larger scale of their living map. In awe, the Shaman called it.

"The Mother."

Naomh asked him why, he had named it so.

"She gave birth to us all."

Even the urban incubus of the Anschluss was pleasing to the eye, when viewed from this height. Privately, the native North American did not think so.

"It looks like a large carbuncle on the Mother's skin."

The entire concrete desecration of the Planet was concealed by the ever present water vapour mist that hovered overhead its urban areas, stubbornly refusing to be burnt off by even by the Summer Sun. But, its encompassing wall was clear to see. It was a similar story all around the globe; the encircling walls of the paranoid Power- Blocks came to the fore and were the most visible of manmade objects. Within minutes, the increasing acceleration of the craft away from the Planet revealed a blue sphere that stood out proudly against the patchy blackness of space. Its glowing spherical shape contrasting against the blackness of the Cosmos. The incomplete Alien stifled a mind-gasp within Naomh's chemistry.

"Oh, how I have missed the beauty of space. Even, the Hybrids Planet is magnificent in its blueness and apparent tranquil charms; even more so now. How I yearn for one single moment where I could once again view my Home World CRYSTALIOS from such a vantage-point."

The crew of the craft knew that it was still racing into space, but the ratio of their acceleration was augmenting as they saw the sphere fade away in to a decreasing speck. The three Astronauts flew pass the dark side of the moon, until finally they were engulfed in the darkness of inter-planetary space. The blackness became unsettling, as there was no focal point of distance or position. The internal voice calmed and reassured its host.

"Space travel had been the norm among the ancients."

But its bearer did not feel comforted and replied.

"I am sure that, if God had wanted sentient beings to fly; then surely, he would have given them wings."

"You are closer to the truth that you know." Muttered the Alien presence ruefully.

Near earth satellites had locked on to their flight path as they left the Earth's influence and then the craft was picked up by similar Anschluss technology as it passed the Planet's moon. When it entered the void between the two neighbouring satellites of the Sun, it became harder to track. Life on board the MARY IRVINE settled down to a normal routine. The Spacecraft ran itself, so there was little for the three hijackers to do. Naomh slept a lot; his female companion kept herself busy while the Indian meditated. He was surprised that neither of them became claustrophobic as the small-enclosed space had become their whole World. Greta and the Shaman weren't very good conversationalists and it was hard to get a long drawn out discussion out of them. There was a mini gym on board as physical exercise was essential to stop the muscles from turning to jelly during longer trips through the vacuum of space. This was used regularly. Greta spent most of her time awake studying the craft's operation. The blonde woman was a quick learner and soon she became adept in controlling it.

Behind them and following in their vapour trail, the pilot of the chasing craft also named after one of the LYUBINITES had no such problems. The commander of the "SANDY BLIEHN.", Captain Zola Bliehn was a Clone and an inheritor of the original disciples' genes. She was also a veteran of the Space Corps and had countless near Earth orbits behind her. The space captain was excited with her mission as inter-planetary trips were a rare event these days. She was exhilarated at being given this task, especially since her command was named after the original owner of her own D.N.A cells. The other ninety-nine personnel aboard were elite soldiers of the same regiment. These highly competent military people were the PREVENTIVES best.

"Tell has pulled out all the stops for this one, so I better be successful."

Like all of the ruling elite, she had a morbid fear of failure. Back in his gothic fancy, her leader knew.

"The MARY IRVINE will soon be out of range from the moon's tracking stations and will not be picked up by their Martian equivalent. These other planetary monitoring systems have ceased to be operational some time ago. This is part of the Martian mystery and the main reason for my back up ship that follows in Naomh's wake. Bliehn will now be my eyes and ears, just like my Spy within his company."

Five days later, as the leading ship drew nearer to the Red Planet; the voice within the Amulet got unusually excited.

"I have located the next piece of myself. There is a large gash across the Planet's surface. Even from orbit, you cannot miss it. The canyon stretches for over four thousand kilometres and it is over seven kilometres deep. At the bottom of this geological feature, there is a habitable complex. This is where, it is."

The approaching Red Planet did not appear as welcoming as the blue orb of the Hybrids Home World. The three Humans stared at it in trepidation. To the five parts Mescal/Amulet, born on a crystal based sphere, it was of no consequence.

"It is not so different to the Hybrids Planet. It is also a rock, only smaller in mass and all it lacks is the fluctuating combination of hydrogen/oxygen, an ozone lair and active geology."

The on-board synthetic voice gave out the essential statistics and composition of the smaller World.

"It is the fourth Planet from the Sun with a diameter of 6,790 km, its thin atmosphere was mainly carbon dioxide and temperatures ranged from −120 to 16 degrees Celsius. Its rotation period was 24hr's 37 min, slightly longer than an Earth day and it has a sidereal revolution of 687 days. It

also has two moons called Phobos and Deimos".

Through the connection of the APOCRYPHA'I with his father's past, Naomh learned the history behind man's conquest and abandonment of the Red Planet. Surprisingly, it was not the Anschluss who first stepped foot on its dusty surface, but a state called the Russian Federation. Cosmonaut Alexander Puvin was the first man to leave the imprint of a boot on the Planet's surface, way back in 2025AD. Other rival nations followed and eventually the fourth World from the Sun's surface was carved up among the competing nations. But the event of the Space virus made most countries abandon their space programs until only the Anschluss had the capability or inclination to continue on. The surface of the Martian World was littered with the abandoned debris of exploration and exploitation. The Questors craft was about to land in a sector that was still claimed by the Anschluss, not that anyone would challenge a claim of sovereignty, if they ended up in another region claimed by some other Power-Block. The spacecraft hurled through the thin atmosphere at an enormous velocity. Powerful reverse thrusters ignited to slow its descent and suddenly there were through the emaciated cloud lair and observing the Red World at first hand. The craft sped along through the Planet's thin atmosphere in a lazy shuffling motion designed by Anschluss engineers to burn off excess speed. But the spacecraft experienced little buffeting from the wind; the terrain below seemed as familiar as any desert landscape on Earth, but its surface was utterly lifeless. Its wind chiselled features looked craggy and worn and there was evidence of really ancient water-courses that had long since evaporated into space. As they flew over rugged canyons, it still looked pleasant enough, but appearances were deceptive. The trio were looking at an Alien land of no compromises. During the day temperatures reached a hundred plus degrees Celsius and at night under the star filled sky, they fell below minus two hundred degrees as the furnace heat of the Martian day radiated out into space having no cloud cover to retain the warmth. The normal cramped and bulky protection suits worn by Anschluss miners and the slightly less lighter ones used by the Space Corps would be substituted by a sleek body fitting suit of light crystal, provided by the LAB-CELL'S Alien technology. It would mould into their body contours and fit like a second skin. It was more efficient that the garments they had worn since teaming up with Singh. The brassy toned voice of the on board computer advised them that it had selected a landing site a few kilometres from the massive canyon that cut a distinctive gash along this hemisphere. The MARY IRVINE would land to the south of a huge dormant volcano called Olympus Mon's and its three lesser neighbours. It had not in fact made the decision itself; it was only reacting to Greta's programming. As the craft came closer to the tear in the Planet's surface, the true size of the rift which the on-board voice named "Marnier Valley." dawned upon them. Naomh questioned his pilot's choice.

"Why don't we just land at the bottom of it? It seems wide enough to take this craft."

"There are too many unknowns, such as wind currents, the smoothness of the surface below. Neither of us is skilled enough to take over from the computer completely." Insisted Greta.

The Watcher back in the past could have told her.

"The bearer of the APOCRYPHA'I could easily pilot this primitive craft under its guidance. But that might give rise to awkward questions. This is the first time that Naomh has ever seen a spacecraft, never mind been in one."

Their stolen craft touched down away from the large Martian abscess as powerful supercharged thrusters caused it to land vertically. Once it was on the surface, all non-essential systems were powered down. Their female companion brushed away two dangling blonde fetlocks, it was as if her hair was trying to betray her. It made her seem more girlish and not the cold killer that she was. It brought back the memory when once Naomh and Rory were discussing her. The dead Gaffer confided in him.

"She is a tragic beauty. She should not be involved in this game. She should be happily married and raising children."

Privately, Naomh had disagreed.

"I could not imagine her doing anything else."

Back on Earth, the internal voice had him retrieve a small globe from the LAB-CELL'S inventory. When the mission to Mars was been planned back on the South American landmass, the five parts Mescal/Amulet had been caught on the hop with its Hybrids stooge's necessity to enter the vacuum between Worlds. This eventuality had never been figured into Mescal's, Cetheren's nor Cathbad's calculations. Besides that, the Elder Celtair and the council of Patriarchi had insisted that their creations could never leave their blue World. Still, the Hybrids had managed this engineering feat and the ALASTHA'I fail safe: the Space virus had curtailed mankind's proficiency enormously. Off-World protection had never been a priority and now it was a necessity. The uncompleted Alien presence had to now circumvent its ethos and interface with the technology that created it. The two Hybrids; who were slowly gaining a slight mastery over the contrivances of the LAB-CELL would take too long to try and design the requested protection. The merging APOCRYPHA'I obliviously had not that sort of time, so it used its host. Much to the chagrin of those two, the internal presence quickly adjusted to familiar mechanisms and accessed the inventory far quicker than the fledgling Human operatives thought possible. In seconds, Naomh was holding a blue jewel, the product of Alien labours. Now inside the confines of the spacecraft, it explained what it was for and how to operate it.

"You got to be kidding?" Was its host reply.

"There is no other way."

"Shit!"

Naomh called the other two to him. He tried to get the words out, but he hesitated and stuttered.

"What is it?" Asked the only female.

This seemed to upset him more.

"I have just found out how to operate the protection against the Martian atmosphere and I don't think either of you are going to like it."

He faltered again.

"Out with it." Insisted Greta.

He took a deep breath and did as she said.

"It means getting naked again."

"Oh!"

"Each one of us has to strip to the bare essentials and this globe has to be run along every part of the body."

He showed them the device. Greta shrugged and began to strip, so did the Shaman.

"It's not like you have not seen it before." The stripping beauty acknowledged.

Naomh felt himself becoming aroused as she began to undress. With sudden clarity, he remembered her nakedness and their sexual contact back in the Mountain Kingdom. He closed his eyelids; then opened them and once again, the beautiful blonde woman was naked before his eyes. He hesitated as she nagged.

"Get on with it and stop gaping."

With trembling hands, he touched the globe to her arm and activated it. Her hand began to transform into something that resembled blue latex. He hurried through the rest of her body and had a major problem with her breasts, buttocks and private parts. Regretfully, he finished the job and Greta stood there in her full splendour. The new blue skin accented every curve in her perfect figure. To Naomh, she looked even more appealing; her Alien azure form appealed to something within him. She sensed this and gave him a sceptical look. Miriam's lover smiled, despite this and said to break the moment.

"Cahill is a lucky man."

Her features softened and she replied mockingly.

"I know."

The moment passed and they were back to the business of preparing to go outside. Greta said.

"I will do you two."

Grimacing at the implication of those words, Naomh also stripped and stood before her with the naked Indian. The operator of the globe glanced at the crotch area of his body and retorted.

"I think that maybe; Miriam is a lucky woman too."

Then, Greta looking at the Shaman, added conspiratorially.

741

"I think his woman is even more fortuitous."

She laughed and Naomh was astounded as he never heard her express genuine mirth before. Her humour was usually cruel in origin and at someone else's detriment or expense. As if to tease him, she worked on the Anasazi first, leaving him to stand in full view of her for as long as possible. When she began on him, he closed his eyes and hoped that he would not betray himself. The adapted Martian wear differed from the sheen of the painted on shield they had used in the Blasted lands. It was more solid and could be removed easily, but it still did not give them protection from physical impacts. In one of the cargo holds, there was a vehicle suitable to the Alien terrain; this was a boon from the Anschluss. The three of them loaded it and drove it down a ramp to the strange World's surface. To Naomh, the fragrance of the Red Planet smelt different, but how he knew this was baffling. The Alien space suit filtered the small amounts of oxygen and water vapour in the atmosphere and maybe this was what he sensed. It was a bland and static sky, not like the constant motion of the Earth's medium.

"By the Spirits, Mother Earth's cloak has a fine personality compared to these threadbare skins." Pronounced the Shaman.

Naomh watched as Greta took the wheeled vehicle for a trial run under the huge shadow of Olympus Mon's. Her proficiently with it amazed him.

"She must have studied its operation during the trip. The Engineer's ways and the Enclaves soldiers' preparation must be rubbing off."

Plumes of red dust rose up from its rubberoid wheels as she swerved over the Martian surface. The tall blonde woman reversed back at high speed and stopped a few centimetres from him. He had never seen such carefree delight on her features. Her joyous mood was infectious and with a glad heart, Naomh and the Red Indian boarded the vehicle. As the off-Worlders travelled across the Alien landscape, a slight breeze caused a swirling dust devil to vector towards them and the converging vehicle. The three Earthlings braced themselves for impact from the Alien weather front. But they were all astounded as the swirling helix had little power compared to its Cosmic cousins on the blue Planet. It lacked sufficient moisture to have the same effect as a comparable event on Earth. Without further mishap, the vehicle reached the edge of the huge fissure. Parking their contrivance behind a large rusty boulder, it was covered with a similar red coloured canvas that the Indian had found in the hold. Peering down into the seven-kilometre depths, each of the amazed lookers were unable to see the geological fractures floor. It brought out a flight of fancy in the five parts Mescal/Amulet; he longed to be whole again, back to his winged fullness. On seeing the vast drop; he would have savoured gliding down to the bottom. Naomh activated a Platform of Light. To his relief it worked and the three of them stepped onto it. But, the lesser Martian atmosphere seemed to affect its performance; it had lost its magnetic hold.

Thankfully, that was its only malfunction. The single-minded preciseness of the ALASTHA'I became a hindrance; their advanced technicians had designed the travelling devices for the exact tolerances of Earth gravity and not any other Planet in the Solar System. Its passengers would have to be extremely careful during its descent. It was best advised by the Shaman that.

"It would be wiser, if we sit down on it instead of standing up. We were not meant to fly and it is a long way down."

The other two concurred. As the hovering device descended, Greta clung to Naomh with a powerful grip and that really surprised him.

"As long as I know her, Cahill is the only one she ever touched in familiarity and companionship. Well, except back in the Mountain Kingdom, but she had no control over that. That was the effect of the green piece."

He enjoyed her closeness and the affinity of one of his own female kind on this Alien World. He also tried to hide an embarrassing thought at been pressed up against her accentuated curves.

"Shit. I hope I don't get a hard on. Excusing the pun, but it would really stand out in these suits."

Oblivious to Naomh's idle concerns, the Shaman sat cross-legged in front of them. It was a nerve-racking plunge to the bottom, but the Indian never even blinked, but he was thinking.

"By my ancestors, I always wanted to soar like the great eagles of the mountains and drop like an arrow to the ground. I pray to the spirits that now is not the day that they grant me my wish."

During the descent down the layers of bare geological past, the brown man looked at the revealed Planet crust and compared it to the Mother. To him the dry red layers with liverwort blemishes looked like the aged dry parched skin of a really ancient elder or even a mummified body. In comparison, even in his desert homeland, the layers of rock contained the richness of fossilized life and still living things. This World had no evidence of past life. The Platform of Light halted a half a metre above the canyon floor and about a kilometre away from the manmade structure that clung to the rift's wall. It skimmed in that direction. On the Shaman's advice, the still activated hovering device was left hidden at the cliff base about five hundred metres from the opening of the uninviting entrance.

"Just in case we need to get out of here in a hurry."

It was a wise move considering that had been the case during the last three searches for the APOCRYPHA'I. Gathering themselves, the three Earthlings proceeded towards the man-made modules, weapons at the ready and not quite knowing what to expect.

Precisely twelve hours later, the pursuing ship landed on the other side of the giant fissure. It took that crew way longer to set up as they were burdened with heavy and cumbersome equipment. Captain Bliehn scanned the crater bottom with laser sights and was amazed to find newly indented footprints etched into its dusty surface.

"How did they get down there so quick?"

It took her crew most of that Martian day to set up their base and abseiling equipment. But finally, her company reached the bottom too. But now they were at least twenty Earth hours behind their quarry. The small army had enough fire power and were supremely confident that there was nothing here that they could not handle. The Anschluss outfit were seriously wrong with their assumptions. The armed group took up covering positions outside the base and waited. Ahead of them and twenty hours earlier, the three searchers of the Alien technology had just approached the door of the manmade module. Strangely, it had once been welded from the outside, but someone had blown it open after they removed the red earth and piled it to one side. The second door of the air lock was still sealed and in pristine condition. The Shaman stated the obvious.

"People have already been here. It is impossible to tell how long ago."

He picked up a discarded plastic shell; it had strange calligraphy on it.

"It looks like Chinese."

Meanwhile, Greta motioned them to be prepared and in response, both of her male companions aimed their pieces at the air lock. The blonde woman pressed the panel to open the door. The icon lit up and the door opened efficiently. Nothing leaped up at them, except a blast of stale air. The gas that supported life was almost visible and it made an audible hiss as it sought release from its confinement. The three of them entered reluctantly.

Drip, drip, drip.

Water was not a natural sound on this parched World. Now cold calculating eyes watched them. Then, there were whispers of a language. One that was unfamiliar to Naomh, but the analytical mind of the five parts Mescal/Amulet found it tauntingly familiar. It was like some sort of machine communication. The three off-Worlders had left the harsh reddish brightness of the crimson Martian day and entered the darkness of the tunnels. A blanket of dimness greeted them; the three explorers switched on the lights of their close quarter weapons and activated their monocles. The bright beams of light revealed a tunnel wall that had not been carved by some really ancient geology. No, this was manmade. A few hundred meters in, the reluctant space travellers heard faint noises and then silence.

Again faint traces of movement.

Then silence.

"There are Evil Spirits in here and we have to chase their wind."

Whispered the Shaman as his voice broke the ghostly quietness.

The other two had no idea what he was on about. They went deeper into the gloom and then they heard more scraping sounds.

Drip, drip, and drip.

The sound of water was becoming stronger. There was running liquid somewhere in the murky tunnels and its resonance was increasing in vigour. The lights of their weapons penetrated the inky blackness and scoured the cavern trying to locate the origin of the scraping noises. The constant dripping began to grate on their edginess. Just as much to confirm that his two companions were still alongside him, Naomh commentated as he rubbed his hand along the tunnels wall surface.

"These tunnels are in a bad state of repair. Look at all the holes in them. Water erosion?"

"Look again! Those are footprints." Said Greta.

"What the hell?" Gulped Naomh.

"They are not cracks, those patterns look like footprints and they run along the floor, the walls and the ceiling of the tunnel." Repeated the striking blonde woman.

"What's going on Greta?"

Hunted looking blue orbs caught his eye, but it was his second companions words that froze him with an internal chill that even his special suit could not allay for.

"Whoever or whatever lives here is not Human. This place has the smell of the shadow World."

Naomh's blood chilled at the Anasazi's words and cold apprehension filled each of their beings. There was another whisper of movement and something-sped pass in a chunky blur. Silhouetted against ceiling, it was using the roof of the tunnel as its pathway.

"That explains the footprints!"

There was a loud thud as something ahead of them dropped to the floor. The now very nervous questors saw fleeting shadows and then a figure confronted them. Its bulky form blocked the way forward. It looked only part Human. Metal appendages appeared to be grafted onto parts of its body. Greta's borrowed gun blazed in a loud and murderous arc of fire, but incredibly, she missed. The thing moved with fantastic agility and then it was gone in another blur of speed. The tunnel ahead was empty once again. It made the three of them wonder if they had imagined the spectre. The Shaman uttered.

"This is not good for us. I think we have definitely entered the abode of the Evil spirits."

The superstitious Indian was beginning to get on the already twitchy Naomh's nerves. Besides, the brown man was wrong, for the apparition had been as real as themselves, it was no ghost and it was not alone. The Anschluss had abandoned the shadows on the Red Planet a long time ago for some forgotten infraction. Once, hundreds of years ago, the phantoms had been the Power-Block's pre-eminent scientists. Then these questors of more knowledge began dabbling in a field that was forbidden by the Chairman of that time. None of them had even been considered for cloning, their gene pool had not come from the original Apostles. But their leader; one Doctor Otis had an air of panache and had a strange influence over everybody, including the LYUBINITES. Those in the know attributed this air of charisma to the indigo jewel that he always seemed to touch. But, for all of his brilliance, the profound mind was unaware of their secret. Still, the Doctor's disciples feared him, but were also envious of his expertise and the strange power he seemed to hold over other people. As with everything they feared, the descendants of Lyubin and his cronies made sure that he would be no threat to their long-term plans. These men and women of learning had been left to their doom as a result of false promises. The scientists were promised unlimited scope and resources on this Planet, but through a series of betrayals (The currency of the LYUBINITES.) the highly educated men and women were abandoned and left to starve and suffocate on the World of limited resources. One of the betrayers estimated.

"Within a year, those who were a threat to us would only be a distant memory, nothing but mummified flesh."

However, the Anschluss manipulators had miscalculated. This rare misjudgement would cost them dearly. Deep below their excavations, the intellectual castaways located a huge store of underground oxygen and stagnant water that kept them alive. They came upon it just as their own reserves were petering out. Their brains had been affected by oxygen starvation and the one with the piece of the APOCRYPHA'I had strange ideas thrust upon him. Been in close affiliation with the Doctor's suffering had affected it too. The living Amulet needed the closeness of living Hybrids or else it would perish. It needed to preserve its bearer's mortal coil, just as the Australian's piece had when it host was about to perish in an extreme environment. This had never had been a problem on a Planet full of Hybrids. On this World with a limited stock, the presence in the indigo jewel decided that the Human body alone was too frail to survive in the Martian atmosphere. Doctor Otis under the influence of his piece of the Mescal/Amulet and its paramount desire to exist until it rejoined the whole devised the solution of replacing frail organic body parts with durable metal. This was a common construction material used in the fabrication of the outpost. As the flesh of the forced colonists became weak, it organic structure was deteriorating fast, their leader made what appeared to be a sensible decision. A member of the abandoned colony was sacrificed for their life giving tissue. (Once an equally mad, but whole Mescal had cannibalized materials for information units. Now a part of him went far beyond the pale and into a realm that it could never have envisioned.) Members of Otis's group had already perfected the necessary anticoagulants, antihistamines and rejection drugs for the process. The cannibalizing started with the lower grade technicians. But their harvested numbers had been depleting over the years. Every female survivor had her reproductive system subverted by drugs, for the forced colonists could not support any population growth. Once there had been twelve hundred of them, but their numbers had dwindled to a hundred and twenty-three individuals over the centuries. Now, these sibilant voices whispered in glee.

"Intruders, intruders!"

"They have been delivered to us."

"We must avail of their fleshly parts."

"Take them quickly and intact."

The twisted Scientists had availed of such an opportunity once before. Three hundred years before, the Chinese had sent a subterfuge mission to the Planet. Otis and his kind had lured the Taikonauts to their deaths and they had over fifty bodies to cannibalize. Two hundred years ago, the last of the very rare Anschluss visits had stopped and now after such a long time, more had come. The ships that could have taken them back to Earth were destroyed every time by self-destruction mechanisms. The machine things that were once men and women of learning scampered across the ceilings of the caverns with one purpose. To ambush this new gift of Earthlings and harvest their organic body parts and if possible to save their ship and return to Earth. Back in the tunnels, Naomh, Greta and the Shaman had crossed some sort of open sewer and after leaping over it, the Indian examined it. The rancid pool was swimming with some type of metal excrement. It bubbled and steamed like some sort of alchemist's concoction and the Anasazi guessed correctly.

"It has the coppery stench of blood."

Next, they encountered a larger but similar underground lagoon; this one had a rusty metal gangway over it. Greta stated the obvious.

"Sure signs of present or former habitation."

Passing over it, the three of them entered a chamber and to their horror found countless dismembered Human skeletons, a lot with clumps of flesh attached. The stale air of the subterranean caverns had mummified the gruesome body remains. Greta noticed something very ominous.

"It is very strange, but all of the carcasses appear to have specific pieces removed. Look, those ones over there have had their arms and legs amputated; with surgical precision, mind you. And that lot over there have had their eyes plucked out, as well as internal organs. All those splayed chest cavities testifies to that."

In the moment of viewing this horror, five bulky figures attacked. The three questors responded with loud bangs of fire, but their bullets bounced off metal parts and the onrushing assailants knocked them to the floor.

Captured!

But the Shaman was not among the prisoners; the Anasazi had escaped in the confusion, leaving one of the monsters cursing. It had the Indian's tomahawk buried in the metal of its forehead. The things had moved too fast and had dropped from the ceilings. Greta had been partially right about the denizens of this place. What faced them in this warren of tunnels on the Alien World was a mixture of Human and machine. The ones that had attacked them had a complete metal frame for a torso and the burst of fire directed at them had bounced off harmlessly. Still firing weapons had been knocked from their hands and they were set upon at close quarters. They had no chance in the confines of the tunnels. A bloodied bruised and battered Naomh and Greta had been brought to a large room carved out of the Planet's red rock. The walls and ceiling of this sub-terrain chamber were lined with pipes and vents that sprayed hot gases made visible in white plumes of super-heated vapour. The blast of these discharges was toxic and would have been lethal to the two terrestrials, if not for their protective suits. But their abductors blossomed in this poisonous atmosphere and every one of them had a smoking metal venting pipe grafted to the back of its neck. The monsters when studied up close by their prisoners seemed to shuffle about as if they carried a great weight. All of their movements were exaggerated and these Demons were now the antithesis of what they had once been. It was more a physiological guilt that made them move around so, for as they found out to their disadvantage, that the things were highly mobile if they wanted to. While the two questors were chained, those who were no longer completely flesh or indeed Human were in a heated discussion about their fate. Their abductors were also sharing out the edible fare from their ration packs. None of them had tasted real food in centuries. These long-lived stranded beings existed mainly on the bland fungi of the cavern's walls. There had also been dark rumours that some of them had even eaten the meat of those that had been cannibalized for parts. Their leader was once one Doctor Darwin Otis and he was the present bearer of the sixth piece of the APOCRYPHA'I. He had come by it with the murder of a mentor. At the time it had been a rational decision for he firmly believed that he could change the World and end the misery of its poorest inhabitants. The creature that Dr Otis had become was now involved in a discussion with his board and he was insisting.

"Our two captives must remain alive and intact at least until my new plan succeeds. And you can be sure that it will. Why do you still doubt me?"

He had a strange accent, plastic lips emphasised every syllable. His main opponent, Dr Edith Thomson disagreed. She had drawn the short straw and was one of the next selected for the cannibalization of her body parts. These two prisoners would give some of them another fifty years reprieve. Through well practiced techniques, nothing of their flesh would be wasted. The monster who had the Shaman's hatchet still buried in his head returned.

"We have chained them up and put them in a contained room, it has a

slightly enriched atmosphere, but they can only tolerate it for a while. We have added more oxygen to assist them."

"How long precisely?"

"About two days."

"Kill them and be done with it." Insisted Thomson.

Otis slammed his metal fist on the table and over the resounding clanging addressed those who would be swayed in his rasping voice.

"No! We need them alive. Edith, you are looking at the short-term solution. This is a fantastic opportunity. Look at the big picture. I will force the self-destruction codes of the craft that brought them here out of them. Also to relive the agony that I am going to inflict on them, I will encourage them to send for more people. And within a few weeks, we will have more than ample body parts."

Another twisted scientist agreed with Otis. His power of persuasion was already influencing the others, after all this was his gift. More of his kind were going over to his side.

"Our leader is correct. We had lived so long in this place that our present body organs would not sustain us on Earth. If those two are made to contact our former home and bring more people, then we can harvest them." Said one female in a gravely voice.

"Think of it Edith. We can return home where there is an endless supply of fresh body parts. Just think of it, we can leave these dusty halls and with our new eyes and lungs, we can see the blue skies, feel the rain and once again taste real food. There will even be pools of water. No! Not just pools, but rivers and Oceans. We, all of us, can see this miracle of nature once again."

Otis's eyes brightened at the thought, but still a few of his opponents still remained unconvinced. Then, with sudden inspiration and his power of persuasion, the former Doctor found the decisive factor to switch the argument in his favour.

"Back on Earth, we will become strong, multiply and get our revenge on the Anschluss elite. Whoever the current Chairman is, his lickspittles and his underlings will become body parts for us. It matters not that these are not the same people that left us here to rot. They are inheritors of the system and will pay for the crimes of the past. We will have our revenge and we will rule in their stead."

Those among his colleagues including his main antagonist who had opposed him moments before now switched to his line of thinking at the promise of retribution from their arch enemies. Even Dr Thomson's eyes burned fiery red at the promise of reprisal on their betrayers. It was agreed to follow Otis's new contingency plan.

"Super. Come let us question our two guests. They might even explain how the other one escaped from our clutches and how he still eludes us."

An hour later and the interrogation was not going to plan. Otis was outraged; his people had tried to remove the intruder's spacesuits by cutting them off, but failed miserably each time. He was advised by an expert.

"Even cutting tools of Gas and metal are useless. Our hated enemies must have come a long way since our betrayal. I have never seen such technology before."

For physiological impact, the monsters had worked in total darkness, the two prisoners appeared blind to their every ministration. But they did not know about their monocles, even in this Alien light of obnoxious fumes, their prisoners could make out a semblance of their abductors. The strange thing was that their two captives refused to co-operate; both of them even insisted.

"Although, we are from the Anschluss, we despise its rulers."

Otis was so familiar with that festering hatred that he actually believed them. Besides that, there was something about the man that drew the scientist towards him. The male specimen had something underneath his strange suit that called to the Cyborg. After the initial communal interrogation, Otis draw by that anomaly went back alone to interrogate their two captives. Naomh had immediately felt the presence of the next piece of the APOCRYPHA'I on their lone interrogator during the first questioning. Sharing the same affinity as his male prisoner, Otis had dismissed his companions, when he was also sure of the mysterious presence. Their leader wished to examine them himself.

"Maybe I can achieve better results on my own?"

Suspiciously, his people retired and left him alone with the captives, but not without questions. He had to pull rank to get some of them to leave. Potent lights came on as the machinery of the lab powered up. Blinded initially, his two captives gradually regained their sight as their monocles adjusted to the change in light frequency. They both looked around the underground room, boiling hot gases and flames spurted out from corroded pipes at irregular intervals. Naomh guessed correctly.

"Even though they won't protect us from blows, it is our blue skins that protects Greta and myself from a scalding or even worse.

The instruments and valves of the lab buzzed and crackled with the same noises as a similar establishment in Victorian London during the infancy of electrification. The presence within guessed correctly this was a result of the limited resources available to the apparitions. Its host looked at the Machine/man and for the first time in a long time, he felt utter despair. He was helpless and out of ideas. He was lost in a cloud of dread on a World devoid of any type of nebula.

"Our only hope is the uncaptured Anasazi."

The monsters told them that the Indian was dead, but Naomh secretly knew.

"He is not. If the Shaman was indeed gone from this World, then I have

no doubt that these freaks would have shown us the body."

Greta appeared terrified of the monsters and he was beginning to share her dread. The one that was toying with them now had a discoloured nametag that said Otis. The owner of that name on the other hand had absolutely no fear at all; he was immeasurably stronger than the two frail Humans were. His grafted metal arm could shatter bones as if they were dry twigs. He had some inferior parts though, his heart, it was still flesh and a metal plate protected his brain. He switched on two powerful lights and focused both beams on his two helpless prisoners. In the artificial light of the interrogation room, Naomh and Greta got their first good look at one of their abductors. The machine/man was Human in stature and appearance. Its metal parts were of a rancid metal, due to the long exposure in the underground Martian caverns. Even, its fleshy parts had taken on a bromidic character of yellow parchment. Its grating voice questioned in a heavy reedy timbre.

"Again I ask you. Why are you here?"

The rasping sound grated the ears of the two complete Humans. His two helpless prisoners winced. His oily breath stank of some industrial process. Sweet smelling lubricants mixed with his blood powered the artificial parts of his frame. Their reaction annoyed Otis. His tone became menacing. Again, he stipulated.

"Why did you come to the Red Planet?"

He received no answers and an unheard Naomh had an unspoken wish.

"Why can't I come up with a short jibe like Cahill would, if he were in the same situation?"

But terror and a dry mouth prevented him from replying. However, his blonde companion did it for him.

"We came here for the sightseeing. We heard it is good at this time of the year. What do you think, been a local and all that?"

The twisted Doctor advised them.

"Good, you retain your sense of humour. But, I have other ways to make you talk, some pleasant and some not so pleasant. Which would you prefer?"

Both of his prisoners realized that they were going to be tortured. The jailer retreated to a wall that held dozens of wicked looking metal implements. He shook his head menacingly, after all these instruments of torture would be useless against the unknown material of their suits. Making a deliberate show, the twisted scientist picked up a long needle and pierced some type of vial with its point. He squirted out a thin stream of liquid from it. Then satisfied, he put the concoction back on the table. Totally in control of things, like a lab technician with a helpless lab rat, he picked up two electrical electrodes and sparked them against a metal door. Sparks of energy flew from the two polarized connections. Pleased, he also put the anode and diode back on the table. First, he tried to inject a truth serum of his own devising into his male captive, but the point would not penetrate. Then after thinking for a while, a smiling and all surgical like Otis stabbed his male prisoner with sudden ferocity. It worked; the suit was not designed for a close headlong and forceful impact. His study of their cuts and bruises had implied this. His powerless victim grunted in pain and the machine/man grinned as his drug entered his prisoners bloodstream. But he did not know that the wearer of the five parts of the APOCRYPHA'I was immune to the effect of drugs as his Alien chemistry kicked in. Otis waited and waited, he soon realized it was having no effect. The master of chemistry became frustrated at his concoction's failure to produce results. He tried a different approach with Greta, he used brute force. He punched her with his metal fist, she grunted at each blow, but would not yield.

"You're a stubborn bitch. Let's try something else."

Otis connected up electrodes to her body and applied electric shocks. The charges easily penetrated her suit. As she began to spasm, her tormenter uttered

"Super."

But his joy was short-lived; once again she bore the pain and refused to talk. The tall blonde closed her eyes tightly, clenched her teeth and endured her torture. She became the epiphany of Martyrdom. A disturbed Naomh was highly aware.

"She will die before she utters a sob, a scream or a plea."

Greta had been in a similar place before and had been forever changed by that horrific experience. To all knowledge, Cahill was the only one of them to ever see her cry and that was on his first encounter with her. His heart went out to her. Otis was flabbergasted

"My truth serum has no effect on the male and the pretty girl is made of steel. She should be screaming by now, but there isn't even a tear. She would die rather than give in. But there is hatred there. I will be able to make use of that."

Their jailer had to leave them or his rage would get the better of him and he would squash them like bugs. The real irony of the situation was that if he had switched methods on his victims, it would have yielded results. Greta would have surrendered to the truth serum and Naomh would have eventually succumbed to the physical violence. Otis departed; he was quiet literary fuming,

"I will let them stew for ten Martian hours, so they can think about the hopelessness of their predicament."

Leaving a bunch of sharp pointed needles in full view of his captives, the Machine/man left a vicious threat before he withdrew.

"It seems that a sudden jab of a sharp object implied with force can penetrate your suits. I will go and think on suitable applications."

The sinister Being left, but returned within a moment to issue an even more ominous threat.

"By the way, my colleagues want to cut you up for body parts and unless you help me, I will let them."

Then, he really left his two captives alone. The highly oxygenated air was making him erratic. The two prisoners were left in silence, but continued to struggle against their bonds. Although Naomh's strength was prestigious, these manacles had been designed for the Machine/men. This implied that all was not rosy among their jailers. They might be able to exploit this dissent, though neither of them had a clue on how to do that. Both he and Greta had spotted the recording devices, so they had remained silent throughout their isolation. Their Alien looking suits kept their bodies regulated, supplied them with oxygen and water and the necessary nutrients to keep them alive as well. In their World of silence, they had no idea how much time had passed. It could have been days or hours when the two incarcerated RE-INSTATOR'S heard the shuffling movement that told them, another of the monsters approached. This member of the outcasted group had sneaked in when Otis had retired. He had an insatiable hunger, he desired the flesh of the female in a way that none of his fellow scientists envisaged. He had deactivated the recorders; he wanted to be alone with these two. Cornelius Butt was as horny as a bull among a field of cows in season. He often complained.

"All of the females in the colony had been plain or even downright ugly and that was before their flesh had been replaced with metal parts."

He had studied the female captive through the surveillance devices and rightly concluded.

"Even through her strange film, she appears absolutely gorgeous and she showed no fear during her interrogation by Otis."

This intrigued him as well as the fact that he had not been this close to a beautiful woman in centuries.

"Even before their transformation, my female colleagues had been an ugly bunch anyway, but I still had done it with some of them."

This sexual predator had sexual intercourse with some of them even after their alterations. He had to touch her; he had to feel the silkiness of natural skin again.

"It has been a long time since I have caressed such soft flesh."

In a shuffling movement, he was alongside the female captive. The monster had his greasy hands all over her, but he could feel nothing but the strange blue film.

"Shit, this must be a nightmare revisited for her." Thought Naomh remembering how it was when Cahill had first found her.

Greta looked at the monster; his one good eye had a glint that she was familiar with; desire. The other orb was just dangling there, like some loose slinky toy. There was a strange sound of clicking motors every time the freak moved. She did not know if his loud grunting was his normal laboured breath or a symptom of his lust. Using it to her advantage, she said in a husky voice, hoping he would fall for her sensuous bait.

"Release my hands only and I will show you real pleasure. Would you not like to see my unclothed body?"

The machine/man gave her a measured look. He might have been a pervert, but he was no fool. Still, he was now only thinking with one part of his body. Butt noticed the used needles on the table and surmised incorrectly that Otis had given the woman a truth serum.

"One of the drugs side effects is to make the receiver as horny as hell. After all I have used it before on some of my unsuspecting colleagues when they had been whole. And none of them even vaguely compares with this woman."

Naomh's despair waned, Greta was looking for an opening and he was amazed at her audacity. He quickly amended.

"Then again, she is not the same weak girl that Cahill had rescued all those years ago."

His female friend continued her baiting.

"My legs are still secured, how could a little girl like me harm such a fine specimen as you?"

Still, the lustful monster held back. She quizzed him as if she understood his hesitancy.

"Oh, you are afraid of the one that was here before. Maybe, he wants me himself. I don't mind, anyone will do."

"Clever girl. She has guessed his weakness; this one wanted to displease his leader as much as he wanted her body. Not for parts, but for his sexual gratification." Surmised her fellow captive.

However, an opinionated Butt had his own false synopsis.

"Shit, Otis must have given her some dose; her sexual appetite has gone off the Richter scale. She want's it bad, really bad."

The twinkling gleam of hunger in the Machine/man's one Human eye became more pronounced. It moved forward and freed her shielded hands. The randy scientist already knew.

"I will not get such a chance again. The others who have no regard for the wonders of the flesh will cut her up and share out her body parts. Those prudes have no appreciation for such fragile beauty."

Looking into her masked enticing reflected blue pupils, Butt said aloud.

"You are correct, what could a puny girl like you do to me. You will submit to me."

His growing lust had won the argument. The helpless woman flashed her eyes and huskily said.

"Of course."

He released her hands and backed off slightly. As her legs were still restrained, Greta calculated.

"I need to entice him closer."

The beautiful blonde woman smiled at the grotesque figure hungrily. She lowered the shield that had frustrated Otis and slowly removed the top of her one pieced suit. Her inflicted bruise's enticed him even more. Butt sneakily noticed that a jewelled band on her wrist activated it.

"I will tell Otis about that later. It will deflect his anger from me."

The monster stared at her unsupported bosom. Greta now had his undivided attention. Her generous breasts were exposed and in full view. Butt's one good eye nearly popped out of his head. It was a long time since he had seen or partook of that sort of soft flesh. Uncontrolled desire was getting the better of him.

"By the metal tits of my female colleagues, I want to reach out and squeeze her substantial Melons and stroke her hardened pink nipples."

The ogling monster liked that name. It reminded him of some forbidden fruit or to be more exact, it was another thing that he had not tasted in a long time. Faster that the eye could see, he suddenly seized her hand in a vice like grip and directed the soft flesh towards his groin. Unperturbed, Greta smiled lustfully and stroked his crotch.

"That part is real." Muttered, the compliable female as she felt the Cyborg get aroused.

The rhythm of her stroking got quicker and the fumes from the vent pipe of the highly aroused monster began to cloud the lab.

"Faster." Demanded Butt.

He had taken his eyes off her and he was lost in his passion. Seeing his distraction, Greta steeled herself.

"I will only get one chance to strike."

In an, she seized it. Her eyes hardened and suddenly a razor sharp blade appeared in her hand. The now armed woman hacked off the hosepipe in its chest. Reddish fluid spurted out from the severed artificial artery and the creature toppled to the floor gurgling from the lack of life fluid. With a strength she should not have possessed, Greta had also his ripped off the crotch in her other hand. The acidic steam of gore that spurted from the thrashing Machine/man would have killed her, if her protective film had not been covering her lower half. But the scalding blood vapour's ate through her leg manacles and weakened them enough for her to snap them off. The freed woman ran towards a hatchet with flecks of red paint on its handle, snatching it up she turned towards the spluttering monstrosity and loped his head off. He was dead in seconds, his body lay in a huge pool of acidic blood and every drop had been drained from Butt's flesh. A ghoulish slinky eye stared at her and she ground it into the floor with her right foot. Greta was untroubled by her vicious assault as she spat into the corpse's face.

"That's what a puny girl like me can do to you, you fucking monstrosity. You are not a man. You are a ----?"

Butt's aggrieved killer stalled. She stalled, searching for an appropriate word and then she found it

"A fucking Flue Stack. That's what you are, nothing but a Flue Stack."

"Where the hell does she get the blade from?" Wondered Naomh, still shocked from her frenzied assault.

His satisfied female companion grabbed a durable container, filled it up with the smoking blood and poured it on to her fellow prisoners bonds. After a few grimacing seconds, he too snapped his constraints with ease.

"We have to deal with Otis; he has the sixth piece of the APOCRYPHA'I." Said Naomh.

"These walking pieces of plumbing must be destroyed. Every last one of them." Insisted Greta.

She wanted her revenge to be final and absolute at their treatment of her, but her superior maintained knowing that all of this must have brought back painful memories of another time of humiliation.

"We don't have the time for that and anyway discretion is the better part of valour."

"Well, you should make time." Came a sinister voice.

Both of them turned to face an amused Otis. The metal monster Doctor glanced casually at the deceased intellectual and picked up the unattached penis.

"Super. That solves the body part problem for a while. Though I don't think any of us wants that."

He cast aside the offending organ and appeared to considered things.

"Now what am I going to do with you two? But first things first, what was this about a sixth piece? I must say you really now have me intrigued. That means you must have another five, simple mathematics and all that, you know. Is this what you have come for?"

He showed them his indigo piece of the living Amulet, a glowing beacon against his sickly hued form.

"Well, I have solved the conundrum of your presence. It looks like you came to get the sixth piece, but it looks like I will have them all now."

Inside Otis could not contain his joy; he imagined the power he was going to have with that amount of segments. He looked at the female whose large breasts were still exposed making Greta aware of her semi-nakedness.

"Super. But I'm going to rip them off you and give them to one of my female colleagues. They will make fine additions for Edith."

Otis had long since rid himself of such lustful baggage, now spiteful revenge dominated his whole existence. The warped once Human advanced menacingly. But this time Naomh was prepared. The leader of the abandoned scientists made a grab for him, but he dodged passed the Machine/man. Otis made a similar grab for Greta and cursed. A blade stuck out of his fleshy hand and acidic blood flowed freely scalding his non-metallic parts. With a backhanded swipe, he floored his assailant. The receiver of the blow slumped to the manmade floor of another World. She appeared to be unconscious. He picked her up and tossed her around like a rag in a dog's mouth. His victim flew through the air and hit the cavern wall hard and rolled off its face where she slumped to the floor. She did not move. The monster advanced on her still body; intent on inflicting more harm. He never got to her; suddenly there came the dull sounds of explosions and gunfire. The crew of the SANDY BLIEHN had begun their attack, they had waited too long and the sight of one of the monsters searching for the Shaman had tipped their hand. Startled by the loud thuds and crackle of automatic fire, the Machine/man turned his attention back to Naomh. His notorious temper was getting the better of him. Moving with lightning speed, he grabbed his cornered opponent by the throat. Otis was about to tear him limb from limb just as the Shaman burst in and cannoned into him. The Cyborg let go of Naomh as he crashed to the floor. The Indian opened fire and as his machine emptied its load into the monster, sparks flew where the bullets hit metal parts, but there were clunking sounds where flesh was hit. The Anasazi's weapon was empty and still the Machine/man advanced on him. The Indian took out a huge knife and prepared to meet his ancestors.

"Quickly, show him five the parts of me." Came the internal metallic voice.

Like the uncompleted APOCRYPHA'I, Naomh sensed that their interrogator had been drawn towards the pieces imbedded in his torso. It had to be used to gain an advantage. He shouted at Otis, the enraged Cyborg turned from the Indian and came once again at him, Naomh opened his suit. He openly displayed the five parts of the living amulet.

"Is this want you want?"

He was mimicking Greta's previous act of enticement. While Butt had eyes only for female flesh, Otis on the other hand was drawn towards the living amulet. Its pulsating flux of red/orange/yellow/green and blue caused far more excitement than fragile flesh. The monster's eyes widened at the sight of the shimmering technology, he instantly understood at what he was looking at.

"Super."

But Naomh's gambled nearly backfired. The five parts Mescal/Amulet was caught in a quandary of its own making. It debated amongst itself.

"Is this mixture of Machine/Hybrid the way to proceed? It is certainly much stronger and durable than the ordinary Hybrid. But, it also has its disadvantages. However, in weighing up the cost in resources to complete the necessary numbers of such an organism would be counterproductive. Besides the female Hybrid had dispatched one of them easily enough."

As the Alien presence pondered its dilemma, the Shaman's voice entered the realm of the APOCRYPHA'I.

"Naomh is the one. He is the chosen. You cannot deviate from the plan

of the ancients?"

Shocked by the Anastai's awareness of him, the separated five parts of the Mescal/Amulet made its decision. Otis's piece betrayed him. Its desire to be re-united with itself took precedence and it came to the logical conclusion that it would be simpler for one part to meld with the majority of the whole than vie versa. It began to shut down Otis's vital systems. But would it be quick enough to save Naomh from the scientist's murderous rage. The Alien presence got help. While the Doctor was distracted, Greta who had been feigning unconscious leapt on top of him; she had a thick oily towel in her hand. The topless woman stuffed the material down his mechanical exhaust pipe and then rolled away under a heavy metal table to safety.

"Take that, you fucking Flue-Stack."

The semi-Human's vent pipe began to block up and it stopped fuming. Otis frame began to shudder. The Cyborg realizing what was happening to him screamed with a ragged breath.

"No-oo!"

But it was too late; no sound emerged from his plastic mouth. His internal pressure had reached boiling point and Otis quite literary blew his top. He exploded internally and his fleshy parts deteriorated as organic clumps began to drop to the floor. Naomh quickly ripped the indigo jewel from the disintegrating body as vapours of obnoxious gases filled the caverns artificial air. Otis's fleshly chunks dissolved in minutes and only corroded metal parts remained. But the hard metal shell that protected his brain case and other vital organs survived in similar casings. At the finish of decomposition, a half-completed matchstick etching with metal casings protruded from the sandy floor. Greta covered herself up as Naomh merged the pieces. This time he immediately felt the overwhelming satisfaction of the joined amulet. The three seekers of the sixth piece of the APOCRYPHA'I did not waited to witness the climax of their grisly work; they fled down the tunnels with their prize. The sound of conflict was drifting away from them. The escapee's came across the body of an Anschluss solider, his space helmet was shattered and his head had been ripped from his shoulders. Greta recognised what he was.

"The Filth! They must have followed our stolen Spacecraft."

Hatred filled her eyes, she looked like she wanted to go back and fight her implacable enemy. Naomh grabbed her by the shoulder; she whirled around and nearly struck him.

"We have no time for them; we have more important things than a few Anschluss soldiers."

Snapped out of her hatred, his mercurial blonde companion agreed.

"You are right, let's go."

The dead man must have being a sapper as Greta found a satchel full of high explosive charges strapped to his back. She snatched them up and as luck would have it, they passed the oily river; they were going in the right direction. The possessor of the explosives halted, set the charges and timer and then threw them in the volatile mixture. It would take seconds for the highly vaporous mixture of gases to ignite after the initial explosion. The three of them ran for their lives. It would be close. Outside in the red dust, the Shaman made towards a boulder fifty metres from the entrance and the hidden Platform of Light had already been activated.

"You've been busy." Said Greta to him.

"I thought we might need a quick escape. So I moved it closer." Replied the Shaman.

As the hovering contrivance rose up the red rock canyon wall, their little present went off. Even in the less dense atmosphere of this World, the bang was impressive. They heard the deep rumble from below ground and as the tunnels were engulfed in flame; its oxygen-fuelled ferocity was sucked towards the Martin atmosphere like ferrous metals to a magnet. Looking down, the two from the Anschluss and the Indian saw the ground shake and the spouts of superheated oxygen shoot out of the tunnels like liquid flame from a nozzle. Greta laughed with abandon.

"Those Flue-Stacks are only scrap metal now."

Naomh joined her, but his mirth was more of relief. In an instant; their laughter was abruptly cut off. Confused smiles were still frozen on their faces. Five Cyborgs emitting howls of outrage had made it out of the caverns and the steep walls of the canyon were proving no obstacle to them. Each clambering horror had captured oxygen canisters and space helmets about them. The Machine/men were scampering up the cliff face and closing with frightening speed and agility. They were still scientists and intellectual pride at been outwitted had got the better of them. The five were heedless to reason and it proved fatal. The Shaman took out, what appeared to be a detonator and waited a few seconds and then pressed it. The whole cliff underneath them collapsed in a heap and the ensuing landslide took away their pursuers who consequently smashed to pieces at the bottom of the huge ravine. The shock of the explosion buffeted the rising platform and Naomh lost his balance. Just as he was about to go over the edge, the Indian caught him. The Shaman had saved his life for the second time. Greta admired his work and acknowledged.

"You really have been busy."

At the top, Naomh disengaged the Platform of Light and the three of them ran to their camouflaged vehicle, mounted it and drove to their spacecraft. Now came the difficult part, the spacecraft needed to take off on a long stretch of runway and although the ground in front of them was level enough, it was not as even as the concrete runway on Earth. Still, it was their only way off the Planet. Greta took over the cockpits controls, while Naomh and the Red Indian manned its weapon ports. As the inter-Planetary craft sped down the bumpy terrain, the former looked at the

Shaman and said.

"Thank you for saving my life back there."

The Anasazi replied.

"That is why I share the same path as you."

The MARY IRVINE reached the take-off velocity and made for the blackness of space.

At this point, Naomh realized.

"Nearly everyone that has joined the quest has at some stage saved my life."

He was beginning to believe in fate. They were battered and bruised, Greta the most of all. But he had acquired the sixth piece of the APOCRYPHA'I and now there was the small difficulty of getting back home to the Earth again. But, the bearer of the living amulet had another major enemy and this one too would confront him in the future.

Back at the scene of their triumph, Doctor Thomson regarded their booty. The Cyborg horde had overcome the PREVENTIVE force and found their spacecraft on the opposite side of the great fissure to the one that had escaped them. The arrogant Blien had been so confident of victory; she had not even set the auto destructive device on her spacecraft. Altogether the twisted scientists had lost twenty of their own number; they had gained over eighty bodies in various states of disrepair and twenty live captives. Otis's second in command looked at the mangled corpses and whole bodies lined out in front of her. Thomson gave an evil laugh; she recognized the face on one of the terrified living captives. It was a visage that was etched into their collective memory. One like this had been instrumental in their abandonment on this dead World. A person with her face had been the one that had sealed them in.

"Is it her?" Asked the machine form of a colleague.

"Well, if we have stayed alive this long, who is to say, our betrayers have not discovered a way."

"We will soon find out anyway, one way or the other, this one will pay."

Thomson remembered that this person had taken immense pleasure at the time of their betrayal and had given a loud gloating laugh at their fate.

"We see, who will be laughing now. Bitch."

But she was still mighty confused.

"How could this be? The one that I remember should have been dead a long time ago. She must be a likeness of those who betrayed us. Still, she has also left us a present of a way of getting back home again. Have our enemy's brains become soft over the centuries? If so, it will make our task easier."

Grabbing the chin of Bliehn in a forceful grip, she said to the trembling woman.

"Do you remember me?"

This agent of the LYUBINITES looked at her in blank astonishment; she had no idea who her weird looking capturer was. The Clones retained some innate memory of their previous incarnations, but not specific ones. Thompson promised herself.

"Such a pretty face, I must have it."

Then, the attractive face became distorted with horror as the Machine/men set about their gruesome business of harvesting body parts. The living captives watched as blood was drained from dead bodies and appendages were removed with the precision of surgeons. Then, the living prisoners were taken away and locked in a cell. Days later, Bliehn was confronted with a nightmare, one that she desperately wanted to wake up from. One of her dead subordinates was now looking at her, his face had been transferred onto one of the monsters. The thing turned to one that must have been female once and a debate began. Finally, the once woman spoke.

"Harvest them. Their parts will be easier to store."

Thomson stared at the terrified commander of the Anschluss Space Corps and in a chilling voice said.

"Keep their commanders face for our leader's reconstruction. He will appreciate the irony of that. I will have her pretty breasts though. Mine have always been flat and boyish looking. I am certain that her ones will look good on me, don't you think?"

Bliehn screamed an animal sound as the monsters closed in to harvest her body. The vital organs of Otis were saved and he would be made whole again. His followers needed his insight and clear thinking, now that there circumstances had changed for the better. Revenge that had once only been a pipe dream was now within their reach.

"Humpy dumpy would be put back together again, but he would have the face of an Anschluss space corp. Now that will scare the living daylights out of them."

The twisted scientists had enough body parts and now had the means to leave their five hundred-year-old prison. The Chairman's underling suffered the most; there was no clean death for her. First, they had taken her breasts and the one that now wore them, came and showed them to her. The horrified woman could still see the newly formed scars.

"Don't you think; they suit me better that you?"

She screamed. But then, her torment had only begun. A few days later, a leg was taken, and arm and so on until a functioning stump was left. Each time she screamed again for the release of death. The vindictive creatures kept her alive for weeks until the final moment when they removed her head and brain. Bliehn talked before her dismemberment and now the twisted machines knew the secret of the LYUBINITES. The more efficient Cyborgs would soon be back on Earth again and they had a few old scores to resolve. They also had one new score to settle, one that Dr Otis would insist on when the Anschluss spacecraft was operational again. His hatred for the three that had stolen his essential jewel far eclipsed that of his desire for revenge against the Clones. Naomh's list and variety of enemies was definitely growing longer and equally more bizarre. Unknown to him, his adversaries now came from many Worlds. Another enemy within his company had also come to a decision. The mole had worked out what the completed APOCRYPHA'I would be.

"It is a communication device. This is how we will contact the Aliens. Once it is activated, they will come to us and fulfil their promise to us. And once it is completed, the others will be of no use to us."

If the six parts of the Mescal/Amulet had been aware of this assumption of its purpose, then it would have scoffed.

"You primitive life-forms have no idea really, have you?"

XXIII.

The hijacked Spacecraft was about to planet-fall; in minutes it would penetrate the Earth's canopy. Their brief foray on another World was over and the craft's three astronauts were about to return to the World that had birthed them or the Mother as the Shaman called her. They had been gone for the best part of twelve days, it had taken five days to get there and five more to return and they had spent two days of hell on the Red Planet's surface, well under it to be precise. Five days ago as the crimson ball fell away, their destination of Earth had seemed a dot in the void, but after the long space voyage, Naomh, Greta and the Shaman could once again behold their Home-World in its full splendour. It just as magnificent as the first time they had witnessed it. The Shaman took joy in the fact.

"No matter how many times one beholds her; the beauty of our Mother will never lose her allure to those of us born within her womb."

The bearer of the six parts of the Mescal/Amulet was on his way back to his Planet armed with a purposeful vengeance. Naomh had gained a new resolve and incorrectly imagined.

"This quest for the APOCRYPHA'I will be completed and the Chairman will be overthrown. After all, what could be harder that this last mission? Nothing else we will encounter will be as difficult as regaining this indigo piece of the amulet."

However, if he had thought more about it, he would have not have jumped to those conclusions. After the Shaman had saved his life, he began to believe that success had been pre-ordained from the start. The list of his saviours had grown and he had found a new enemy, but the Cyborgs were no threat to him down here.

"Against all the odds, I now have six segments. How could such an unlikely bunch like us come together? It has to be fate."

The naïve Naomh knew nothing of the Chairman's original selection of his companions or the elimination of those Tell had judged, not-suitable. The returned Spacecraft would touch down as the Sun's rays came over the Earth's sphere. This was a highly dangerous and often deadly manoeuvre. Once again, Greta proved herself to be a highly competent pilot. What she did not realise was that Naomh could step in at any moment, if any difficulties occurred. It was another result of now possessing six parts of the APOCRYPHA'I. Besides, they had already chosen an old landing site; the Alien intruders had used out here in the extreme desert. Back then when Mescal's presence had been as a physical being, the western edge of this Continent had been frozen under a kilometre of snow and compacted ice, a result of the larger glaciers that had existed in the infancy of the Hybrids creation. The landing site was located under the shadow of the impressive spine of mountains that straddled the Continents Western coastline. Just under two weeks ago, Naomh listening to the five parts

Mescal/Amulets guidance had given the others who had not ventured into space, the co-ordinates of the landing site. Breaking radio silence an hour ago had confirmed that their companions would be waiting for them at that exact location. The living map had been extremely useful in getting them to the required destination. The Chairman had also been waiting for that communication and he was now alerted. He had been extremely anxious for information. Another space crew had apparently vanished on the Red Planet and he was at least relieved that Naomh had made it back to Earth. Very soon, the Spy would soon fill in the ruler of the Anschluss about the events on Mars. The thirteen that had remained behind had rushed towards the meeting point. All but two taking turns at the driving to ensure a continuous journey. Even though there were the strong personalities of the Guide and Cahill among them, it came as no surprise that Miriam had taken command of the Earth-bound group. Within hours of their arrival, a communication channel was opened and now was the first time, it received a transmission. Hearing their friend's voices brought immense relief to the returning space travellers. The three on the fast descending Spacecraft were even more relieved that their companions were exactly where they hoped they would be. As they hurtled through the blue line of the atmosphere, those on board crossed over the "Terminator boundary." and passed from night into day. Far faster than a bullet, they came in from the Pacific side of the Southern Continent, flew over the huge wall of the Andes and descended towards the meeting point. A few scattered cotton ball clouds unveiled themselves, then minutes later, the desert below began to light up and on its surface was revealed huge images of strange creatures and even weirder signs and symbols. These ancient etchings on the barren floor were truly meant to be seen from space. Images that were a long gone people's invitations to the Gods called to one in particular.

"The Hybrids did remember our cherished race; they left these signs for us. This is really astounding." Realised, the six parts Mescal/Amulet as he interpreted the etching meanings.

"Messages to the God's." Was the Shaman's vocal opinion.

Naomh's other and usually sceptical companion did not scoff at the Indians words. She too had no other plausible explanation for the drawing's existence. On board the descending craft, he had really ached for his lover and he had no doubt that Greta missed Cahill as much as he desired to be with Miriam. While, it appeared that the Shaman's immediate concern was just to get back to Mother Earth.

"Only a few more minutes, my love." Whispered Naomh.

Miriam and Cahill had spent the last five days looking into the night sky towards the fiery yellow point in the stars where the Shaman told them the World of Mars looked down on the Earth. Down in the Atacama Desert, the Engineer had modified some large lenses and the two separated lovers focused on the red ball as if they could remove the layers of obscureness and discover their three companions. But it was to no avail and they had waited for this day until their soul mates returned. For their returning partners, part of their very beings lay behind on that Alien Planet. As the space vehicle hurtled over the desert floor, a fast arriving localised weather pattern obscured the land and its images. The rapidly descending crew hoped that their friends had provided markings for a safe landing. In response to sudden obscurity, the inky blackness of the desert floor became illuminated with a circle of pinpricks of fiery light that formed the sketchy outline of an improvised landing area. Greta hit the thrusters and the resulting detonations slowed the Spacecraft to a manageable speed. The internal voice had already explained to Naomh.

"Your spacesuits are so effective, there will be no need for a period of recuperation as is the norm for all other space travellers of this Planet."

The bearer of six pieces of the living amulet glanced over at one of his crewmates and felt that the expedition to Mars had changed them forever. It was as if he had known the Indian all of his life and of course, he had known Greta for years. This thought prompted a moment of clarity; it was from the time when they had been shared lovers of the Himalayan harlot. He blushed suddenly. The blonde woman who was in his thought's sapphire eyes had been studying him. She gave him a wry smile as if she had been thinking along the same lines. For a moment, he held her gaze and then turned his attention to the instrument panel. He had seen the twinkle in her eyes and he felt that their shared experiences since leaving the Anschluss had especially drawn the two of them closer. This was something he could not have said before this incredible journey had begun. Thankfully and with a little regret perhaps, they were able to remove the ALASTHA'I suits themselves and Naomh was spared the sight of her naked body once again.

"Not that I would complain, if I did."

The battered Spacecraft and its equally bruised crew touched down with a noticeable bump and a huge parachute slowed their acceleration across the wind-flattened desert. The metal spacecraft frothed and snorted like a panting racehorse as it vented the gases of re-entry. It would take a few minutes for the inter-planetary craft to cool down. Its passengers alighted from the space craft and the Shaman dropped to his knees and kissed the dusty grit, to him it was the sweetest taste imaginable.

"Praise the Spirits, we are home."

Though this place was considered one of the driest parts of the Planet, the three astronauts could taste the scant moisture in the foggy air. Eleven of the twelve of their companions mobbed towards them, at the front was Cahill and Miriam. Their emotions were evident, by the tears and looks of relief etched into both faces. When Naomh saw his Enclave lover, he felt a catch in his throat and the tears well up in his eyes. He braced himself for a flood of weeping, but the sobs never materialised. All previous thoughts of a naked Greta were brushed aside. The onrushing pair hurled themselves into the waiting embraces of the two astronauts while the others surrounded them and clapped the returnees on the backs. As usual the Mute took no part in the shared camaraderie. Everybody else was smiling and touching. The Shaman began chanting. The six parts Mescal/Amulet felt a twinge of regret.

"I have none of my kind waiting for me. My people are light years away in the vastness of space."

Miriam clung to Naomh and refused to let him go. When everybody had calmed down, Greta had noticed something.

"Where is the Nuncio?"

The Guide filled them in.

"Bad news, I'm afraid. You know that he refused to wear body armour and during an ambush, he was killed. Still, the bullet took him in the back of the head; the protection would not have mattered."

Naomh sought out the Engineer's features and offered his condolences.

"Sorry."

The religious man shrugged as if it had been no loss at all.

"He has taught me enough, I can bring the truth back to the Anschluss, even without him."

The Nuncio had not been a favourite of the others and if any of them had checked the body in detail, they would have found out that he had been shot at close range. The Guide changed the subject.

"How did it go?"

Their leader unbuttoned his shirt and showed them the newly added Indigo shimmer, the dead man was forgotten immediately. As always there was awe on the faces of those who saw the living amulet. The questors spent two nights in the desert, celebrating and sharing the events of the past week. Inside the TORT-CAM, indigo Tesseral were added to its luminance. The Shaman told those who were not on the Red World, the fantastic tale of the recovery of the newest piece. There were looks and gasps of astonishment and truth to be told most of them had been glad to miss out on that adventure. Illeau was one who was not.

"Oh, how I crave to take the lives of those desperate creatures. Otis and his kind have gone to drastic measures to stay alive and that means, they hold a great value on life, more than most mortals. I envy Greta's killing of the lustful monster; I would have enjoyed seeing the light of that one's eye go out."

As always, when they dallied, the internal voice urged Naomh on. A meeting was called; the Shaman called it.

"A Pow-wow."

Then, to everyone's amazement, he said.

"The next and final piece of the frozen rainbow lies far to the north and I know exactly where it is to be found. You will follow my path to it."

The bearer of the six parts felt.

"He is not telling us the whole truth; the Anasazi is concealing something from us."

Two weeks later, the Posse as the Shaman now named them had crossed another border and arrived in a country called Mexico. It was the southern neighbour of the Anasazi's land. This Nation and another few islands in the Caribbean were all that the Government of the United States of North America allowed certain members of its citizens to visit. This Power-block was the Shaman's Nation and where the next piece of the APOCRYPHA'I lay. In the year 2176 AD, the United States and Canada merged into one union. Its rulers had decided to withdraw from the World stage. This huge nation started the policy of isolation that many others were to follow in the coming centuries. But unlike the Anschluss, its leaders did not stick rigidly to the isolationist policy. Only the rich, the famous, the well-connected and the adventurous were allowed to know of the extrinsic delight of foreign travel. That was how the Shaman was able to leave his birthplace and meet them in the tropical jungle. This time, the LAB-CELL enhanced their communication devices. Now, a three-dimensional image of whoever was contacting them dominated the parameters of their vision. It was as if they were alongside them. It was a wonderful device, but Solomon warned.

"If any of us are in a fire-fight, use sound only. Otherwise, these devices will block out what is happening around you. And no sight means no life."

On the journey through Mexico to the American border, they passed a land of dramatic mountain peaks and jungle valleys. The fascinated travellers were greeted with countless images of the countries past. Most of it showed great temples dedicated to Gods whose images disturbed the Patriarchi. It was if these relics from the Hybrids past were calling out specifically to him. When their vehicles had stopped in a small town of white cinderblock houses for a break from the long journey, the questors wandered around, taking in the sights. As was the rule in populated places, they wore no protection sheen against the biting insects, been inconspicuous was the order of the day. After a really painful nip, Cahill cursed.

"What kind of a place is this Continent? It's all biting things."

Aggrieved at the description of his side of the World, the Shaman spoke in a huff.

"Well, none of you were on the Red Planet. This is just a slight discomfort"

"Well, I don't think there was anything up there to bite you incessantly." Retorted Cahill.

"No, there was just a bunch of Flue Stacks that tried to cut us up for our body parts."

An unusually subdued Greta uttered. It was rare for her to take another's side against her lover, but Mars had affected her deeply. There was some sort of religious festival going on. Captivated, the outsiders became riveted to a commencing spectacle. In the centre of a cleared area, a large vertical pole stood at the centre of a gathering crowd's attention. At the top of its slender height, there were several ropes attached. The throng parted as several men wearing brightly coloured adornments of bird plumage rushed forward and shimmied up the pole. The men were a blur of rainbow shimmer. At the top, all of the performing natives secured themselves to the connecting ropes. Releasing their grips from the pole, they hung suspended in the morning air. The Shaman felt an affinity towards the dangling men. Then as one, they began to whirl around the pole's circumference. Their momentum picked up and they became faster and dizzyingly faster. The flying men were called "Voladores." and to the ancient presence within, these flying acrobats were simulating the flight of the ALASTHA'I.

"The Hybrids do remember us." Voiced the six parts Mescal/Amulet as his mind went into overdrive at the implications of this revelation. *"Do they know of our plan? Some seem to have an inclination. The Shaman for one and the Holy man from the east certainly did. But these two Hybrids are assisting the bearer; it must be part of Cetheren's overall programming of their kind. "*

The questors tiring of the spectacle of spinning men found a nearby Comedor. It was a small stall that sold spicy food that was rolled up in some sort of bread pouches. Some of the hungry group purchased portions and a bottle of strong liquor distilled from sugar cane; it was called Aguardiente. The drink had an incredible kick to it. Again the Mute annoyed some by his manner of eating. After leaving the small town, they travelled by the Atlantic coastline route until it ended up in a seaside resort similar to the one in Cuba. Like that place, the group rented hotel rooms by the beachfront and relaxed. The three that had recently been in space needed the rest more than the others. All the members of the quest were gathered in Naomh and Miriam's room of the hotel that they were staying in. A Pow-wow had been called; the Shaman's name had caught on. The five-sided fifteen-story hotel looked out over a deep blue swimming pool that led to a golden sandy beach and white crested waves. Naomh became slightly melancholy.

"Somewhere out there in its unknown depths lays the body of the bearer of the fifth piece." The bearer had wondered about that man. Except for Miriam's orange jewel, all the other bearers of the segments of the APOCRYPHA'I had wanted his pieces and would have removed him from the equation.

"I will never know whether that person who lies at peace in the depths of the Ocean would have been an ally or a foe in the search for the

remaining bits. Instinct tells me however; he would have become one of us.

A flippant Clerk mouthed.

"Well, it's all water under the water now."

He got a dirty look for that. The view over the coastal beach and the serious surfers out on the swelling waves made the smart talking blonde man remark.

"That's the only sand; I ever want to see again."

Most of the small band laughed. Greta's expression of mirth was one of the loudest.

"She is really coming out of her shell." Thought someone.

The Shaman got serious and informed them of what lay ahead.

"I have already told you that the next piece of what we seek is in the United States of North America. Even though, I have been smuggled out, I can get myself and the rest of you back in. I know the right sort of people. But once we are on the other side of the border, each of us will need the proper documents. I have none; they were the price for me been smuggled out. But I have a scheme to get us the correct identification. Then we can forge them."

"Why do we need documents, if we are to be smuggled in? And vice versa, why do we need people traffickers if we have the proper identification?" Asked a perplexed Solomon.

"We cannot use the forgeries to actually enter the land as every legal departure is recorded on a government mainframe that we have no access to. So we would not be registered as American citizens. And once we are within its boundaries, we are liable to random checks."

The Lenses waded in with his expertise.

"But an enforcement officer could check our false documentation on a mainframe and we would be still be busted."

"I am sure that a man of your talents, once you got access to the mainframe, will be able to make us, official citizens." Correctly assumed the Engineer.

"You know me too well."

"Then, the plan is to seek out and befriend an American tourist. And unknown to him, we will borrow his travel documentation and other identification necessary to move about without attracting notice on the other side of the border." Advised the Shaman.

"How do we do that?"

"We will use two of the girls as bait. Our female companions will fraternise with a male tourist. They can use their obvious talents, get them aroused and drunk; then go back to his room and relieve him of the documents."

The Rabbi added.

"Just jab him with the same stuff we used on the Sheikh back in the Prophet's lands."

Beersheba and Greta volunteered while Miriam said.

"I am useless at that sort of flirting."

The contrast between them, one petit and olive skinned and the other tall and ivory coloured would surely set any red-blooded man's pulse racing. The two beautiful women sat at the bar dressed provocatively for the evening. In little over a few minutes, they were approached by an eager male. The man wore a large white hat; a suit of a similar shade and a boot laced tie that was the same colour as his shirt, black. His brown leather skinned boots had some sort of metal spike attached to them. To them it might be some type of weapon that the wearer was proficient with. They would watch his footwear carefully. He was some wealthy landowner in some place called Texas, a state over the border in the United States. This individual was exactly what they were looking for, so both women encouraged his advances. He had a really loud drawl that annoyed Greta and which Beersheba called fetching. The Texan told his two female companions.

"God dam! I really like your accents."

Both women giggled inanely. The two girls got him very drunk with Tequila and went back to his room in apparent fits of giggles. The mark thought incorrectly that he was going to have one hell of a night. He slung his wide brimmed hat on the floor and said.

"Hot dang! I think I will leave on my boots for you two mares."

The drunken American tottered on the edge of the bed with a silly grin on his face as one of the women began to lift her top over her head, he said.

"Shucks."

But he never saw the promised delights; the other conspirator knocked him unconscious with a jab. There, they lifted his documents. The Engineer was outside the door; he did not approved of this scandalous flirting, but he took the booty and went straight to the LAB-CELL where he and the Lenses made perfect copies for the men. He would add the Biometric information later. Then, the cards were returned to their unconscious owner. As the two women departed the Texan's room, Beersheba bent over and kissed the oblivious man on the forehead.

"You will never know what you missed out on."

Back with their friends, the practical Clerk said.

"We need more examples, just in case the Texans ones were forgeries. The Shaman has only used his once so he is unsure of their appearance."

"Well if you did not need them all the time you lived in you homeland, then why do we?" The Mute asked the sly question. Not liking Illeau, because he felt the stench of decay around him, the Indian replied.

"I am one and outside the law. A group of our size will draw attention."

The next night; the Clerk and the shy Persuader plied the same trade with a fairly good-looking middle-aged woman. She had taken a fancy to the big man and the gamely Californian had got more intimate than he had bargained for, before she had succumbed to the drug. He came out of the room blushing while the Clerk was grinning like a Cheshire cat. The questors had all the documents they were going to need to make them legitimate citizens of this United States. Naomh's small company arrived at the border; it was an electrified fence that stretched from the Atlantic Ocean to the Pacific Ocean. The Shaman told them.

"It is thousands of miles long."

Only the two usual suspects among them knew what a mile was. Unlike the Anschluss, the Americans needed a regular supply of cheap labour, so they did not construct an impenetrable barrier. The Red Indian who did not want to enter the country through proper channels told them.

"It's time to round up a few traffickers. They have tunnels that go under the border. Be careful around this lot, they are a bunch of vermin."

The Shaman brought them to a dingy joint that was located in a small town north of Monterrey that had sprung up on the Mexican side of the border in the last few centuries. Ironically, people from both sides needed to cross and an army of smugglers called "Coyote's." accommodated them.

"I will do the talking, none of you use Spanish. That will make them suspicious."

The Shaman went to a table and met a man that was surrounded by a group of what could only be called cut-throats. They had enough experience of recognising that type of person by now. As he watched the Indian make the bargain; Naomh was beginning to find this scene repetitive. He whispered to the Guide who was the closest to him.

"It's like watching myself make the deal with Singh. The Shaman is right, there is no doubt that theses shady characters can be trusted, but we will go along with them."

"I agree."

The Anasazi agreed a hard won price with the Coyote's to use their tunnel and it had to be paid in American dollars. He came over to his friends and went back to the trafficker's table with the Clerk. Half of the money was handed over and the rest of the price would be settled at the border. Under the mask of a small moon, they drove to a crossing point with their untrustworthy hosts and disembarked in a lonely place besides the large electrified fence. Naomh's crew were on high alert, they were well experienced in the currency of betrayals and besides the body language of those that accompanied them was false. As the mixed group loitered about, it was soon evident that nothing was happening. The men of the border town made their move.

"Amigos we seem to have a little problem, the price has just gone up and I have a hunch that you have more than enough monies to pay us, seniors and senioritis." Said their pocked marked looking leader while

giving an extravagant bow. It was a given signal and more armed men appeared around them. The questors were about to act, but the leader had been lightening quick on the draw. In an instant, he had two silver guns to Naomh's head and he was about to pull the triggers. He now had the eyes of a psychopath and the Guide knew.

"Shit, this guy is hopped up on the white powder."

"I am going to make an example of this one hombres; so you will know how serious I am. Buena sera amigo."

None of his friends could save him in time, the Coyote's eyes said that he was going to do it. Suddenly, the pistol totting Mexican's eyes widened in shock and he fell to the ground with a knife in his back. His spine had been severed and the inconspicuous Mute was right behind him. So precise had been the mortal wound that nerveless fingers had never even squeezed the triggers. Seizing the initiative, a gun battle broke out and their adversaries were wiped out to a man. During the close quarter fighting, three of Naomh's small force had received some injuries; those that had been wounded were rushed into the LAB-CELL and attended to. The bearer of the uncompleted amulet could not believe it and neither did the Guide.

"The Mute has saved my life."

The man forever suspect of him declared to himself.

"He needs Naomh alive until he completes the jewel."

The person he saved looked at him in a different light. He thanked the cold man and Illeau just shrugged. When everybody had been judged fit and well, they reassembled at the fence. Naomh's saviour was sitting down on a large boulder and putting some sort of entry into his M I M. The Shaman said pointing at the electrified barrier.

"Our friends that have passed on to the happy hunting grounds in the sky were supposed to show us a way through that."

Nobody knew what he was talking about. Seeing the blank stares, he clarified his thoughts.

"Go and look for some tunnels."

They did but the search proved fruitless. Moshe put words to what all of them were thinking.

"Our dead amigos were telling lies or else they are hidden well, I'd stick with the former."

"Let's try the TORT-CAMLETS."

They did but they still would not work in the vicinity of a charged barrier.

"We have another way." Said Moshe.

"The Skimmers." Replied the Lenses.

"Of course that would have been the obvious choice. But, there is a valid reason why I went to the smugglers in the first place. We will be seen by the countless surveillance devices and someone watching will be very

interested in our unusual way of getting over the fence." Informed their new guide.

"But they were never seen back at the Anschluss's spaceport." Said the Lenses.

The man from the Warsaw Contrib was wrong, they had been seen; the bases security forces were ordered to let them through on that occasion. Once again, the Engineer intervened.

"I have devised something similar to what I seen the small winged shaped moustached man use back in the arena in the Mountain Kingdom. It will do the same job."

Miriam decided for them.

"Do it."

On the Enclave woman's command, Naomh activated their strange method of transport. Using the Platforms of Light, the little group prepared to cross the border at night. The man from the Madrid Contrib used a variation of the same technology as Styarz had and threw a flickering globe into the air above the fence. There was a blinding flash and an invisible pulse knocked out any watching surveillance equipment for over a kilometre. The border guards had been alerted to a whole section going down and ordered appropriate action. But within a few minutes, it became operational again and mobilising crews were ordered to stand down. In the same time frame and out of sight of the watching devices, Naomh's small force was on the other side of the water course called the Rio Grande. They were now in Southern Texas. The border infiltrators marched towards the nearest town, guided to it by its blanket of amber streetlights. The Shaman took the lead. Dawn showed its face as the new arrivals crossed the town line. In this border town, the purchase of vehicles was uncomplicated. Looking around, the lifestyle of these Americans was certainly at the level of the Anschluss and if you counted their freedom, it was higher. Communication devices were in the form of L.C.D screens that extended on a metal rod over the eyes. They originated from the ears in a telescopic motion. It appeared to be a peaceful and civilized land, but some people carried weapons openly.

"Are they at war?" Asked those from the Enclave.

"There is no external conflict. It is their right." Said the man from this land.

"What do you mean?" Queried a perplexed Beersheba.

"The ordinary citizen can defend themselves against foreign invasion or even their own government, if it came to that." Explained the Anasazi.

All, but one of the RE-INSTATOR'S thought the latter reason was an excellent one while the concept of turning against your own was alien to those from the Enclave. The inhabitants of this nation spoke a language similar to Anschluss, but to make sure there were no hints of their foreign identity, the questors used their translators. Its people were of every race and colour and clothes of denim and cotton was the chief attire of many who passed them. Of course, the Clerk would purchase some as soon as possible, especially, the broad rimmed hats that were so prevalent. This new land appeared to be a microcosm of the World. But there was one big difference, measurement. Kilometres were miles, metres were feet, litres were gallons and kilograms were pounds. Everything seemed to be for sale in this place and it often came in big portions. The preferred method of transport of the Americans amazed them, the vehicles were known as "Hover-cars." Powerful thrusters allowed the craft to glide along the ground at about a metre high. Looking longingly at sleek vehicles with names like Ford and Chrysler, built for speed and luxury, some were disappointed at the Shaman's choice. He called it.

"A Winnebago."

The automobile that they had bought was ideal. It had five beds and a little kitchen area, complete with cupboards, a cooker, a fridge and various cleansing units. Tables and seating could be unfolded when necessary and they could substitute for sleeping places. The vehicle had encrypted digital licence plates that allowed it to be located at all times. So the Lenses quickly broke the code and he could change its identification at will. It also connected him to a mainframe and he promptly made them false citizens of the state. In the driving area, a satellite guidance system displayed a three dimensional map of the country. The display was a primitive version of their living map. After a quick study, the Engineer declared.

"Navigation will be simple, just tell us where we have to go, Shaman."

The six parts Mescal/Amulet was drawn towards the Arizona desert exactly were the Indian pointed out on the digital chart. The Lenses studied the map and punched in their route. As they headed towards the setting Sun. The Indian told them.

"We call anybody sitting up front with the driver; Shotgun."

After that, nearly everybody wanted to ride alongside the driver. The hover drive across the vast countryside seemed to drag on forever; they stayed rooted to the "Glideways.". These were large eight lane concrete roadways that were exclusive to hovering transport. The transport arteries travelled in level lines, mountains were tunnelled under, rivers and gorges were bridged. Every physical thing was resculpted for the priority of the roadways. As they flashed by highly visible neon signs showing off ramps to various urban areas, the Clerk had impulses to visit every stated destination. Afterwards, he only remembered a few name places of the indicating neon signs of the journey on the route through Texas, New Mexico and Arizona. They were San Antonio/ Houston, El Paso, Albuquerque and Phoenix. The informative on-board information unit told them that a famous Glideway called "Route 66." passed around here, but none of the weary travellers were interested. The skies were huge and full of vapour trails of higher flying craft. The questors found the Glideways fascinating at first, but soon the endless horizons with no sight of an end to their journey began to annoy them and the heat of the Sun caused those who were not driving to doze intermittently. At least there were countless buildings that provided them with fuel, refreshment and toilet facilities. An L.C.D screen in the vehicle allowed some of them to watch an endless variety of programs. One thing that amazed the watchers was that anybody and anyone could criticize their government without any repercussions, a concept unheard of within the Anschluss and to a lesser degree in the Enclave.

"That's the way we want it to be." Said the Guide.

Unheard, the Spy muttered.

"In your dreams hairy man."

Like the time on the ANS GREGORY LYUBIN, the constant travelling was grating at the small group's nerves and inevitably some minor squabbles broke out. One that came to a head was that the Guide and the Persuader were smoking more and more dope. Early in the morning while the others were asleep, the two men got the inevitable munchies. The famished men raided the communal stores and inadvertently ate a sizeable portion of the Rabbi's remaining kosher food. There was outrage about this. The bearded man folded his arms and said with clenched anger held in check.

"My personal store has been reduced."

Solomon and Moshe were more vocal in their anger at what had been done.

"All of the inconsiderate things to do. There are mountains of ordinary food there and you ate the Rabbi's."

"We were hungry and just went for the first stuff that we found."

This infuriated the Enclave men even further. The two miscreants were abashed and kept apologizing. Seeing how upset they were, the Rabbi relented and said with one of total belief.

"The Lord God will provide."

The Engineer envied the total belief of the devout man.

"I do not think his words of prophecy would come about this time. After all, we are thousands of kilometres away from the Enclave and on the other side of the World."

But a few days later, the Almighty did deliver and the impressed Engineer was speechless. He asked after witnessing the event.

"Does your God give out miracles?"

"If one believes so." Replied the Jewish adherent.

"Then why did he not save Shoshanna and Haim? That would have been a far better request than mere food." Silently mouthed a sceptical Clerk.

What had happened was that during a rest stop, the Rabbi noticed something about a town below that brought a smile to his heavily bearded face. With delight etched into his features, he had seen a wire that stretched along a perceived religious enclosure of his own faith. He told Naomh.

"I have just spotted an Eruv. We have to go down there."

"A what?"

Solomon explained what it was. Down below, in familiar streets, those from the Enclave found what they were expecting; a large Jewish community. Familiar writing appeared in windows and above doorways. The Rabbi began to purchase large quantities of supplies and in some cases he left some small storekeepers, especially the bakers with empty shelves. Still none of the vendors complained, his dollars were real enough. The bearded man was like a kid in a candy store. While the Rabbi had been stocking up, the Clerk and the Lenses had spotted a shop that specialised in selling all sorts of chips on information. Entering its wide-open floor plan, they were astounded at the variety of subjects available. There was everything from fiction, non-fiction, other languages etc. The United States of America and Canada choose to isolate itself from the rest of the World, but did not allow its citizens to become ignorant of it. Looking at a cover that displayed exotic animals and destinations, the Lenses said to his friend.

"The Prof would love this country. All of this stuff is forbidden back home."

Three days later, while hovering through a vast open plain of scrubby grassland, there were thousands upon thousands of what looked like very hairy cows. The Shaman called the large shaggy beasts.

"Buffalo."

Then added to some of the intrigued.

"The white man is doing some good to restore the balance. In trying to bring back what was lost is a worthy cause and it pleases the spirits. It will be my goal too with the help of you the protector's of the Amulet, to bring back what is close to extinction."

The Mute thought to himself.

"What a foolish man. If he thinks that we give a dam about his pathetic animals. We have lived in a huge City State and get on well without them. Besides there is no pleasure from killing a dumb beast."

Suddenly, the buffalo scattered in every direction. They were been chased by large hairy dogs.

"These are Wolves and you are watching the endless dance." Intoned the Shaman.

The weary group entered a rest stop on what was termed an Indian reservation. Here the inhabitants began to resemble the Indian and people called him Chief Dan George.

"One journey is ending and soon we must begin another."

The Indian added as his travelling companions entered the cool ventilated air of its shop.

"We must get some supplies for my people."

The Anasazi brought strange items, for the most part; they were sweets and confectionery.

"For the little ones."

He also purchased liquor and tobacco and strangely, a huge tank of water that was fitted to the back of the Winnebago. He said about the alcohol and Cigs.

"For the old ones."

He paid for the large amount of items with dollars supplied by the Clerk. The storekeeper was at first suspicious and bore a stern manner. The sultry purveyor checked the laminated bills and on finding no in flaw in them, his demeanour changed. He even provided assistance in strapping the purchased items to the roof of their vehicle. Powerful thrusters lifted the load with ease. A large tarpaulin of some synthetic material was used to cover the loaded roof top supplies. The Shaman took them on the final leg of the journey; they left the highway after two hours for a narrow slip road. They travelled on that for four hours, then left that for a dusty track. Huge Sawannas loomed out in front of the vehicle. The giant cacti were over ten metres high.

"Wow if the Prof were only here to see them."

Eventually they left any type of road and glided cross-country during the hours of darkness.

In an instant of uncomfortable braking, the gliding contrivance halted. The unannounced stop was accompanied by numerous oaths. Solomon had been at the helm.

"What's up?"

"Look at that thing."

A weird looking lizard with bead like scales of orange and yellow was caught in the headlights.

"That's a Gila monster. It's a nocturnal and poisonous lizard and it eats small mammals and eggs." Said the Shaman.

As the stout bodied reptile moved away, there was a sarcastic comment.

"Thanks for the nature lesson."

Solomon restarted the vehicle and it glided on. Finally as the dawn broke on the 2nd of June 2954AD, the Winnebago reached a line of secluded hills far from any inhabited area. An L.C.D screen appeared in front of the Shaman's eyes and the Anasazi made a non-video call in his own language. All of them understood what he was saying, but anyone else picking up the transmission would be ignorant of the words. As soon as the questors got near the blank wall of red stone, a camouflaged screen parted and they glided into the darkness that was revealed. Headlights switched on automatically in the gloom and the vehicle was through the dark in minutes. The Indian's charges had arrived in a narrow dirt valley surrounded by steep walls and large overhangs. Under the natural formation of the mesa's, beautiful white plastered ancient buildings covering structures of adobe bricks, some as tall as five stories hung precariously to manmade ledges. The village looked as if it had been carved out of the cliff's face itself.

"How quaint." Said Solomon.

The engine was turned off, the vehicle settled to the compacted ground and as its last purring faded into silence. People of all ages emerged from the cool interiors of the alabaster buildings and soon the gang was surrounded by excited children and yapping mongrels. The inhabitants of this cloistered place were dressed in the most bizarre clothing, strange even to most of what they had encountered on their long search. Tipped off by the Shaman's message, the tribe were attired in their finest regalia. It was the feathered headdresses on the male's crowns that stood out immediately. Tearing their eyes away from the impressive items, the questors saw that the men wore tanned leather breechcloths over white coloured leggings that were tied with a leather belt. Shirts were decorated with intricate quillwork and beadwork. The women wore patterned buckskin dresses, concho belts, various bodices and shawls. Both sexes wore sturdy leather moccasins. The Shaman shooed both the children and dogs away, but one child remained clutched to him. He patted him on the head and told his travelling companions.

"This is my son, Little Owl. His mother, Gentle Spirit, has passed on to the other World."

The Engineer, who had learned that the Shaman was the Holy man of his people wondered.

"This is another faith that allows its Priests to marry and have children, but as the Nuncio said, it is a primitive one. If this is the way of things, then my new order back in the Anschluss has to be the true one. My God only expects total devotion and does not allow his Priest's to have female ties. And that's the way it will be."

The adults remained and greetings for their prodigal son began. His welcoming people performed a ceremony to cleanse the Questors and win favour with the Spirits. There was a lot of chanting, rattle shaking and drum rolling. Suffice to say, the Engineer was unhappy with the pagan ritual. He sat prone with eyes averted. Old men with wrinkled skins and white flowing locks approached the Shaman and his guests. These village elders demanded a sign that Naomh was the one. The Engineer had noticed that some men from the tribe had already unhitched the water tanker and had taken it away.

"That means water must be precious out here. I have an idea."

From questioning the Shaman, he was informed.

"Our water wells and storage cistern's are at a low capacity as it has not rained in two years. Our precious crops and livestock were using most of the limited supply. The water that we have brought will be accepted

graciously, but it will only be a drop in the Ocean."

The Engineer came up with an idea and put it to Naomh. He, in turn consulted the APOCRYPHA'I and the internal voice agreed. The schemes initiator took the miniature TORT-CAM from his friend and asked for some privacy.

"I need the Lenses as well."

These two were let away to a secluded room and returned a half an hour later with a circular shimmering globe. One of its creators handed it to his leader. Then, Naomh stood up and told the Shaman.

"Gather your people together."

Without hesitation; he did so and the holder of the orb quickly found himself in the centre of a curious audience. Years later, the old ones would tell the tale.

"The promised one stood in the middle of the group and raised the shimmering globe to the sky. Our people began to chant, Hi ya, hi ya. A nimbus of striking colour that none of the Elders had encountered before shot from it and headed straight through the gap in the cliffs above and into the night sky. There, the Spirit Beam; began its work."

Billions of isolated hydrogen and oxygen molecules came together and formed into a dark localised cloud that revealed itself by obscuring the white pinpricks of the distant stars. The nebulous crackled and thundered and then it burst. An immense localised downpour began, forcing everybody to take shelter. The deluge lasted an hour and it filled the hidden tribes near depleted cisterns to the brim. Needless to say the tribe became instant believers. An Elder approached Naomh and said.

"You are the Rainmaker; your companions are the Rainmaker's companions."

The Anschluss Spy felt much consternation, not liking to be relegated in authority. Drums started to be pounded; the tribe began to chant and dance in gratitude for the gift from the strangers. A meal was prepared and a fatted cow was butchered. As the questors sat as guests of honour, food was served in beautiful glazed pottery with each piece decorated with beautiful abstract colours. After the meal of beef, rice, chilli and beans was consumed, a pipe with a powerful smelling tobacco was passed around. Strangely none of the guests refused even those that had an aversion to smoking. The voice of the uncompleted Patriarchi told Naomh.

"There is a powerful narcotic in the pipe, but I sense no treachery. The Indian is using some strange power compelling all of you to agree to take this pipe. But I will negate its effect on you."

Spirits soared on puffs of smoke and into the night sky, where the Shaman and his guests walked the plains of another realm. Here where there were no lies, the mystic of an ancient faith encountered the Questors in different guises of the animal World and looked into each of their souls. He now knew.

"The Rainmaker has indeed the most powerful medicine. The drug has no effect on him; he is not on the spiritual plane."

However, the others were lost to a clustered spiral existence. Colours of every hue flashed by as the drugged companions entered the Spirit World. There was calmness and then a sudden jolt and they were on another plane. The voices of the shades told the Shaman that some among the group were perpetrators of dark deeds and one of the comrades was at least suspect.

"In the ancient lore of my kin, this one should be named as the Trickster."

But those on the other plain also told him that Naomh needed this one and the Shaman always done what the Spirits asked of him. He said nothing of the enemy within.

"The seeds of their betrayal are well planted."

They came out of their trances, sad to have been dragged from their spiritual contemplation. The traitor was disturbed, but did not show any outward consternation. The others looked at the Shaman with newfound respect. The Persuader actually beamed with positive energy.

"Man that was the best trip, I ever had. I became a huge black bear."

The Guide agreed; he had become a fox. Miriam with wide eyes told them.

"I transformed into an eagle and soared through the sky."

Her lover lied and said.

"I was a Lion."

A puzzled Cahill had become a wolf while Greta had also glided through the heavens as a falcon. The Engineer had been a beaver, the Mute a vulture, the Clerk a magpie and the Lenses a mole. On the Enclave side, the Rabbi took the wise form of an owl, Solomon, a salmon, Moshe, a prairie dog and Beersheba, a sleek ermine. The Indian who was wise in the way of the netherworld knew that like Naomh, the traitor had lied about what form their soul had taken. That person had manifested into the guise of a cuckoo. Even the Engineer appeared to lose his surliness over been initiated into the pagan ritual and became intrigued with his surroundings. So he asked the man who had brought them here a few questions.

"I can see that your village is a master of concealment, but how do you actually fend for yourselves."

Some of the village elders leaned close as the Shaman answered. They took for granted that all of Naomh's people understood and spoke their ancient tongue. These wise men knew that it was a gift from the Totem.

"There are other little caverns with ledges where we cultivate corn, maize; beans and other such staples, there are usually plenty of underground springs for water for this. But we have found large deposits of rare gems that we use to trade for essentials. Still, we would like the gift of money making that would stop all the awkward questions. Some foolish men had followed me in the past hoping for this wealth and now their *bones feed the desert."*

The Questor's nodded. Beersheba said.

"We have encountered much of that on our travels."

Naomh looked at the Lenses and the strange eyed man complied.

"You shall have as much of these dollars that your people need."

"That is one problem solved. Now, my brothers and sisters, I have something to show you."

On the way, Solomon asked the big Indian another question.

"You population seems so small. How has your tribe survived, been isolated and with such few numbers?"

"We take wives and husbands from the other tribes, such as the Pueblo, the Navaho, the Apache, the Comanche, the Sioux and so on. The Shaman of the other peoples know of the bad medicine and the ghosts of the past. The Spirits choose those who enter our tribe, those who would be worthy of the task."

"I see." Replied Solomon, but he did not.

The Shaman led them to a darkened room, where a video unit was set up. He told them.

"You must sit and watch. This is the trail that must be blazed."

Then, he spoke softly; deep sorrow had found his furrowed eyebrows.

"This is what happened to some of our youths, our young braves who without the knowledge of our Elders tried to regain the Totem and end our shame."

The screen came on as the lights of the room dimmed. It showed ten smiling youths, faces painted, armed with automatic rifles and outfitted in brown camouflaged uniforms for some task. The video showed one of them boasting that they would retrieve the Totem.

"That was Peter Fleeting Foot and such is the naivety of youth. Still, it was for a noble cause." Said the Shaman in a voice over.

The footage continued and showed the youths breaching a wire barrier and arriving at huge steel gates at the side of a mountain. Dan George told the fascinated watchers.

"This is where the stolen Totem is kept."

Back on the screen, the youths found a large air duct. The ten infiltrators lowered themselves down into its dark depths by a steel rope and pulley system. They were still smiling for the recording device. The youths had found a sewer system, but the flowing mass was devoid of any type of effluent. It was unclogged with any waste; people had not used the bases facilities for a long time. The flowing water was crystal clear. The youth's spirits brightened at the sure sign that the base was uninhabited and some chanted with abandon. This was evident in the grinning faces that filled up the video image. A voice said as they jumped into the liquid.

"Our journey was not wasted. The tribe will have plenty of water now."

Throwing caution to the wind, the youths of the Shaman's village increased their pace through the waist high water. The gradient of the sewer system gradually decreased and the flow of water became sluggish. With a sudden rumble, a section of wall behind them slid silently out and blocked their retreat. The skin of the temporary dam opened up to reveal a giant fan, which whirred into action and the water they were immersed in started to bubble and boil. The frothy liquid carried away five of their number that did not react quickly enough while the others had managed to cling to the sides of the tunnel. They were "Peter Fleeting Foot.", "White Feather.", "Soaring Eagle.", "Growling Bear." and "Crazy Tunes."

As the five who were taken unceremoniously overcame the sudden shock at been carried away by the fast flowing water, they began to enjoy the ride. Seconds later as they rounded a bend, smiling faces turned to horror and boisterous laughs turned to screams of panic and desperation. Two huge silver grinding cylinders blocked their path and began to suck them in. There were five sounds of crunching bone and sinews as each of the youths were ground into minced meat. Some of the viewers closed their eyes in horror. Others were fascinated or repelled, but kept their eyes on the unfolding drama. Within the confines of the grisly recording, the remaining youths had heard the screams of their comrades and one of them shouted to the others.

"Wait until the fan swings back in place."

The section of the wall must have heard his plea. It began its robotic motion and the water became still again. The surviving, but shocked youths retreated back beyond the fan section. Crazy Tunes took command.

"We will wait till the section moves out again and enter the space it leaves behind it."

Five nervous boys waited and then the section of wall began its automated procedure again. The youths of the tribe rushed into the space and found themselves in a shallow pool of water. To their relief, the survivors found steel steps that led up to a door. This was a maintenance duct. The heavy impediment was opened, but it took the combined effort of them all to push it. Then, they were in a steel supported three metre high dry tunnel with a gently sloping concrete floor. Artificial light illuminated the way. Cautiously and now fully alert, their bravado had vanished with the deaths of their friends. A few minutes after the remaining five entered the corridor, their hushed whispers died on flabbergasted lips. There were looks of disbelief and then a thunderous rattle of whirring gunfire and the lustre of the screen went dead. All that remained on the screen was a hazy distortion. There was an unnerving pause among the watching audience and the Clerk's voice broke in.

"What the fuck happened to them?"

"We do not know. None of them returned. All we have is this broadcasted film that came from each of the braves."

The Engineer interrupted.

"It sounded like a revolving cannon."

Incredibly one of the youths survived by hurling himself down a ventilation shaft, but the fall damaged his broadcast device and all the viewers got was audio. Crazy Tunes; the last of the braves deep breathing and continuous narration went on for ten minutes. The listeners heard him say.

"I have entered a big cavern; there it is. I have found it. It is more fantastic than I could have imagined."

As he moved closer, his attitude changed.

"There is something wrong here. Why is it doing this to me?"

His immediate euphoria subsided; there was a long silence until his sobbing voice returned. It sounded like he had lost all reason.

"It is useless, what was the point of all of this. Been the only survivor, I will look like a fool in front of the tribe. I will be blamed for the others deaths. I will become ridiculed. This jewel was not worth the lives of my dead companions, people that I knew all of my life."

He wailed in despair and the fascinated listener's heard a sudden bang. So intense had they been concentrating, some of them jumped at the sound. The Shaman spoke.

"All that the video unit recorded from there on was silence. So none of us know what happened to our youths. A Pow- wow was called and it was agreed that none should go there until the spirits brought us aid. And you my friends are that help. But, because of their raid, the place is like an Ant's nest. We will wait till things die down."

"Have you forgotten about the TORT-CAM?" Asked Beersheba, certain that he had not.

"Look outside."

They did and saw the beginning of the rain that was out of season.

"It is a vast open space out there and the rain reveals the form of the invisible shield. We will have to wait until it fades and that could be in days or weeks. Come let me show you where you are sleeping."

Everybody rose and the Shaman guided them to two rooms in the warren of buildings and told them.

"For the moment, there is nothing we can do. So, bed down for the night."

The Lenses went into the LAB-CELL to produce the tribes required dollars.

"After all, we are going to be guests and it was only fair that we pay our way."

Surprisingly the alabaster buildings were very comfortable, so Naomh and his companions slept a peaceful night on plump mattresses while the Shaman and his people kept vigil. Incredibly, the unnatural rains lasted three weeks. The village's cisterns were filled to the brim and were even overflowing. Their deep wells had reached more than the most bountiful

Winter's depth. Then on the 22nd of June 2954AD, the Shaman had news.

"There is a break in the clouds and though our weather forecaster is confused, he is sure that it will last a few days. So as the white men who use to forge metal would say, now is the time to strike while the iron is hot. We will set out when the rooster crows next."

The following morning as the Mother Sun rose over the mountain tops and as dawn's silvery tongue licked away the last vestiges of night, the questors rose to find the Shaman still guarding their place of slumber. Still immersed in a feeling of tranquillity, Solomon voiced.

"This is such a wonderful place, I know that Edward would have stayed here forever after he had seen the World and wanted somewhere to spend his final days."

Most of the others agreed with his assessment. The Spy did not and privately thought.

"This place is full of filthy primitives and unworthy of the Alien's promise."

The Clerk had stayed up all night with the Indian. Victor de Mere had certainly left his former life in the Brussels Contrib far behind. His friend's stared open mouthed at him. The Engineer gave a nasty curse, but his bigger brother had an amused smile which he concealed from him. What caused these conflicting views was the fact that the former blonde man was now attired in the manner of the Anasazi. He wore numerous beads and feathers in his long hair and he had shaved off his beard. The Clerk had spent an enjoyable night with some unattached Squaws and they had done this to him. Now, both he and the Shaman had painted their faces. Their friend told the others.

"It is war paint."

The Guide who had once been the subject of the blonde man's infatuation thought.

"Monkey see, Monkey do. I think he should be given a new codename. The Mimic would be appropriate."

"I hope for their sakes, they did not make him one of their tribe." Interjected the Lenses.

The others laughed as the Red Indian pointed at the Clerk.

"My brother has a new name among my people. It is Victor Who Has Many Faces. Come let us breakfast. It is good to set out on a full stomach."

He led them to the morning meal and even the Rabbi's tastes were catered for. While eating his fare of fried bacon, maize and bread, the big Indian told them.

"I have cast the runes and the omens are good."

"What are they?" Asked a curious Moshe.

The brown skinned man put an ancient leather pouch on the table, untied two laces and poured its contents on to the table. To the others, it looked like an assortment of old bones, Human and animal.

"These predict the future." Snorted a disbelieving Engineer.

"Not exactly, they just point to the omens." Said, the advocate of a belief that the man from the Madrid Contrib would never understand. Just then the Mute turned up, he had been missing all night and nobody had bothered to find him. While the others found peace, he had found torment. Driven by trance induced visions of himself in a place where blood flowed like wine, he had drifted from the others and found himself in a familiar place where death took precedence. Illeau had been drawn to the mummified bodies of the tribe's Elders. He was captivated by the living dead and had spent hours just gazing at them. He wanted to find out about the process and had enquired about it. Those of the tribe, who he spoke to, called them.

"The Dry Ones."

A really wizened old man explained more.

"These are the remains of our former Shaman. They remain here because the task that they committed themselves to remains uncompleted. They are trapped between this World and the happy hunting grounds until someone succeeds in ridding us of our shame."

The ancient's account had fascinated the weird soul even more. While eating the morning meal, the Shaman insisted.

"You will rid yourselves of your vehicle; I have better ones for the journey ahead."

After breakfast, he brought forth four Humvies. To the wanderers from across the great Ocean, they were essentially tiny Tanks that were highly mobile and adequately armed. The Humvies also hovered above the terrain, much like the Winnebago, but their thrusters seemed more powerful. Moshe liked what he saw. Five of the Shaman's people were also going with them; the others had seen them around. He introduced them as.

"Ron His Enemies Fear Him, Dave Whose Car Is Called Ford, Peter Who Strides Quickly, Jim Fat Bear and Mike Porcupine."

In all their travels, these were the strangest names any of them had ever heard. All of the Indians had their faces painted like the Shaman and the Clerk. Preparations were made in earnest. The entire group, including the Anasazi were now outfitted in the body hugging suits from the LAB-CELL. The Indian's were also given a set of the advanced Monocles. Moshe explained about the clothing's effectiveness, remembering Haim's death.

"They will not stop armoured projectiles, but will stop small arms fire up to a distance of twenty metres, but not at point blank range. And anything between those two scopes will wound you. They are mostly a protection, in case the land is contaminated."

The Indian's understood and Jim Fat Bear spoke.

"So it is wise not to get hit at all."

"Precisely!" Replied Beersheba, the Anasazi's humour was lost on her.

The Indian's weapons had the familiar look of all guns and were called M-65's and Magnum's. Moshe approved them.

"Fine weapons."

"Let's go."

They boarded the four Humvies and sped out to the wilderness. Dave Whose Car Called Ford drove one while Moshe was at the helm of another. Greta was in charge of the third and Mike Porcupine drove the fourth. They proved to be the ideal vehicles when they were out in the desert heart. Just then there was a loud rumble of thunder over the plains, the Shaman said.

"It is a good omen; the Spirits are awake and interested in us mere mortals and our efforts."

"I thought that you said it would not rain." Said the astute Engineer remembering the inadequacies of the invisible shield.

"The omens say it will not."

Two miles away from their starting point, the fleeting rain had little effect on the topography and the hot desert Sun had rid itself of its influence already. To the Indians amazement the downpours had been localised over their hidden city, the rest of the desert did not receive one drop.

"It is an effect of the magic that the Rainmaker done." Stated Mike Porcupine.

The Shaman agreed with his Tribesman's assumption. One look at the barren land and Naomh turned to Greta and said.

"Great, this place looks like Mars."

His companion in the off-World terror nodded in confirmation at his quip and she mocked.

"Let's hope that we don't run into any more Flue Stacks."

He recalled the Red orb with a sickened smile, knowing.

"If she really thought that she was going to encounter them, she would not be so carefree with her words."

But Naomh's comparison between the two landscapes was wide of the mark. For while the countenances of the two inhospitable terrains appeared similar, this barren land in the centre of the North American Continent abounded in life forms that originated on its sandy earth. Life clung to shaded areas under cliff overhangs and outcroppings or behind rocks and boulders and it thrived beneath the cool blanket of earth. There were plants out there that held miniature pools of water in their cupped leaves. These tiny lakes supported diminutive Worlds of their own. Unlike Mars, this land was still been sculpted by an infrequent force that the Red Planet had not witnessed in millions of years; water. Ancient rivers had broadened and deepened causing small canyons to snake along through the soft topology.

The sky to the west appeared to be on fire and the land itself had been reddened by the wind. Huge scarlet weathered erosions shaped by the elements projected out of the desert floor. The spires and pinnacles reminding the seekers of destroyed city blocks with the rubble of their destruction coned around their bases. These natural erosions of weathered stone were the colour of copper and brass. Peter Who Strides Quickly said.

"We call these places, The Painted Lands."

Like all deserts that had not seen regular rainfall for a long time, its earth had become concrete hard and in some places, there was a scarcity of life for there was no soil to hold water, even if the seasonal rain came. Some years, it did not. They sped over arrow straight dirt tracks with their thrusters leaving plumes of dust in their wake. Out in the centre of the waterless sea, the small army encountered a steel wire fence that stretched for eternity. From an advantage point, the advanced monocles allowed them to view the obstruction without they themselves being observed. There were signs with pictures of skulls and crossbones and writing that warned.

KEEP OUT, CONTAMINATED ZONE.

TRESPASSERS WILL BE SHOT.

"Not very inviting. Is it?" Said Cahill.

Ron His Enemies Fear him told them.

"We have to go through that without been seen. It was put there by the military. These anonymous individuals lied to the people and told them that the land beyond it is contaminated by deadly radiation. There are video units all along its perimeter. They also patrol the enclosed area to arrest and keep unwelcome visitors like us out."

The others laughed when the Lenses replied.

"Not through it; but over it."

The fierce looking Indian produced a large steel hatchet called a Tomahawk in his hands and challenged the multi coloured eyed man.

"Are you mocking me, white man?"

"I think I like him." Said the Guide as the rainbow eyed man backed away; his oily smirk replaced with terror. Heedless of the banter; the Engineer took out the biggest version of the Platforms of Light and it instantly distracted the fierce looking Anasazi from his prey. The Persuader produced what looked like a weapon of sorts. It had an enormous muzzle on front of an equally large cylindrical barrel. He explained its use.

"It fires disruption devices called E M P's. That short for Electrical Magnetic Impulses. Each round as it detonates will knock out any surveillance devices for kilometres and the disruption will last for hours. Those who are monitoring the area will think that a massive lightning strike brought down their equipment."

"Or something else." Said Jim Fat Bear.

"Don't mind him; he is always the wearer of bad medicine." Added Peter Who Strides Quickly.

When the intruders were ready to approach the fence and go over the top, the Engineer produced another surprise. He took out an indigo globe of light, aimed it at the four Humvies. Their presence blurred and in an instant, the air powered vehicles were gone from sight. The Shaman's people jumped back with curses. Recovering, the Anasazi reverted to the craft of their ancestors and began to hide all traces of the group's tracks. This took a while and when the Indians were finished, the Persuader fired the first round. A circular ball of light flew out from the disrupter gun and exploded in a rainbow of colours ahead of them. The gang rushed forward and used the Platform of Light to go over the top of the fence. On the other side of the barrier, the Persuader fired a salvo of beams at different ranges to make sure their path remained unobserved. With the Shaman at their head, they charged forward into the desert night. Resting on a cliff edge, the infiltrators looked down at two massive steel doors in another flat and chiselled cliff face.

"It is under there." Said the Shaman.

"Not more holes in the ground." Mumbled their leader.

"How do we get under there?" Asked Beersheba.

"We have something." Replied a smug looking Lenses daring Ron Whose Enemies Fear Him to challenge him. It was in this part of the quest that he and the Engineer came in to their own and proved their worth. The rainbow eyed man told Naomh.

"We have finally unlocked the LAB-CELL'S secrets .You request a specific item and the thing helps you design it. It can achieve anything. There is one mystery though; it will not produce real flying objects. Hovering items it will, but not high altitude craft. As I said it is a mystery, but we are working on it."

"One that you will not solve." Came an unheard voice.

The Engineer took out strange weapons that floated like their Beni and gave them to those who wanted them.

"These guns have been designed by me; their explosive projectiles can be detonated at will. Bullets or shells can pass through solid objects without exploding or if you miss a target, you can detonate as they pass by. There are two thousand rounds in each circular magazine"

Most of the questors took one of the amazing guns. All of the native Indians did as well, but Greta and Cahill declined. The two lovers still preferred their own familiar arsenal of weapons. Recollections from the caverns of Mars made Naomh utter.

"This place looks abandoned of life and not just Humans."

The reason was not as obvious as the Shaman guessed.

"Since we have not been challenged, your disruption devices must have worked. But there is another peril here besides man."

Beersheba and the Rabbi were to remain topside and warn them of any external danger. The Lenses with Moshe's help had placed a globe of light on the floor. It expanded to form an oblong crystal projectile. The tip of it began to revolve independently from the rest of it until it glowed white-hot. With the Persuader's help, the strange contraption was pushed against the cliffs edge. The spinning head melted through the rock like a red-hot knife through butter. It created an open tunnel with no spoil and was a lot faster and more efficient than the burners. The Engineer put on a strange visor that allowed him to see ahead of the machine. Inside the culvert the cutting machine had just opened, pencil beams of light showed swirling clouds of dusty particles. They left the "Borer." get a distance ahead of them; switched on their weapon lights and proceeded in single file down the newly created tunnel. As always Miriam was at her sweetheart's side. Eventually, the machine broke into tunnels that had already been created. The Engineer halted the boring machine.

"We will use these manmade corridors; they will lead us to the heart of this complex."

One of the Shaman's tribe bent down and examined strange tracks on the dusty floor. Jim Fat Bear spoke.

"Man, there is something strange going on here. These tunnels seem to be used by something. They are markings that I am unfamiliar with. I would say at a guess that they were left by something manmade."

"You are right my brother, this place is dirty, but it smells clean. And there are no vermin tracks or even their carcasses." Said Mike Porcupine.

"Sh'ss"

He was cut off by a harsh whisper from Greta. These tunnels had reminded her of the Martian caverns and the blonde woman had been on heightened alert. She half expected the Flue Stacks with their smoking pipes to emerge from the dark depths.

Well, she was half-right.

As if enamoured with a sense of déjà vu, there came another set of Alien noises. But these sounds had a smooth whirring mechanical efficiency about them. They were about to come face to face with one of the things that had dispatched four of the young Braves of the Anasazi. There was a louder droning sound and a weird contraption that stood on eight short metal legs appeared. On its flat rectangular base, it had a huge cylindrical form that resembled a jet engine. This squat artificial thing was at home in these underground corridors. The group ducked back into the tunnel they had created. Just in time as there came the thunder of mechanized gunfire. The automated sound was deafening in the confines of the underground tunnel. A hail of precision firing red-hot lead pounded into the Engineer's tunnelling machine. The boring contraption thrashed around like some giant white maggot on the end of a fishing line. Something had identified the drilling machine as a foreign object that did not belong and took appropriate action. Some of the lethal hail ricocheted into them, but their protective armour made the deflected projectiles ineffectual. Still, it knocked the wind out of a few of them and some doubled over as if they received a stomach punch. Beersheba sighted her weapon and fired a salvo. Her selected projectiles rounded the corner and zeroed towards the gun platform. But the rapid firing contraption knocked them out of the smoky air. Two large square expressionless lenses mounted on a large slender rod acted as its eyes and they searched for the source of the attack on it. Ron Whose Enemies Fear Him spoke.

"I think this is one of those occasions when my people say; we are up shit creek without a paddle."

"What is it?" Asked Cahill.

Moshe answered his query.

"A gun mounted platform. Our army experimented with the concept, but they were unreliable. Because of their many failures, the program was abandoned."

"Well it looks like someone got it right." Surmised the Clerk.

"Man. I've heard of looking down the barrel of a gun, but this is just downright ridiculous." Was the input of the Guide.

Agent XIII knew that Mankind had once flirted with the sciences of Robotics and enhanced artificial intelligence, but then divested themselves from that path. The forever meddling ALASTHA'I had been influential in diverting them off of that track. Dependency on Robots would reduce the number of Hybrids on the Planet and this was not conducive to their overall scheme. Still, some Governments pushed right up to the limits and this United States was one. The piece of the Mescal/Amulet wondered.

"Had Naisi been right all the time? My host and his comrades appear to be ineffectual against these automations and they are extremely primitive compared to the altered CRYSTALOID'I."

The Engineer came up with a desperate idea.

"Jose will launch one of those disrupter shells and while it is confused we will all fire together, some of our shots might get through."

The big man fired a shell; it exploded in a confined blinding flash. It had been shot out of the air like a clay pigeon. Three more were launched and received the same treatment.

"Any other ideas?"

"Everybody fire together, we will hit it with everything we've got."

Their new weapons fired and a barrage of the same magnitude as the gun platform arced out and curved towards the target. The mechanical apparatus recovered quickly and sensing the threat, it opened up in a sustained burst of fire. Speeding projectiles from the machine were blocked by the questors' fire while other bullets proceeded towards their target. This tactic of interception happened at a mind-boggling rate until such was the rate of their fire that projectiles eventually got through to the gun platform. The machine exploded sending white fragments through the air. The Shaman was the first to stick out his head to see if the Engineer's desperate plan had succeeded.

"By the pony tails of my ancestors, it worked."

He clapped the innovator on the back and told him.

"Your strategy was brilliant; it was just like the game of football that they play in my land. Or as the "Grey Hairs" from my tribe with their simple wisdom would say it was like two rams head butting each other until one gave in."

Then, one of his people put his arm on his spiritual leader and said.

"Two of our friends have gone to the hunting grounds in the sky."

Jim Fat Bear and Ron His Enemies Fear Him had been killed in the firefight. The former's air of cynicism had been borne out. The Shaman went over to the deceased and uttered a mournful chant. Finishing the ritual, the Red Indian jumped out of their hiding place and pottered up to the destroyed machine. The others followed him and moved out from their hiding place and examined the smoking hulk. The Clerk been the only realist among them stated the obvious.

"Fuck. We were lucky that time, how the fuck are we going to get passed more of these things."

Mike Porcupine thought of his two dead kinsmen and did not think they had been so fortunate.

"We have to come up with a new strategy. Anything else in the magic bag of yours?"

"Why not gather up pieces of that, get a picture of another one, then bring it back to the LAB-CELL and construct another." Suggested the Clerk.

"That's brilliant." Said the Guide.

"I don't understand?" Declared Cahill.

Solomon answered for him.

"It will enable us to get up close to another one and destroy it before it realizes the deception."

"And who is the lucky bastard who gets to try it."

"Since the Clerk came up with it, he should put it into action." Answered Greta with a wicked laugh.

The feathered haired man went pale, but the equally colourful Shaman saved him protesting.

"There is no need for Victor Who Has Many Faces to risk himself. I will volunteer; it is my burden."

His similarly attired Anschluss comrade gave him a grateful look while Moshe suggested.

"I have an improvement on your plan. Why not set up the TORT-CAM in this tunnel and from its protection knock out one of the automated gun platforms. Then we can quickly repair it and use that one."

"Turai Moshe's plan is better and poses less of a risk. Greta, you are the best shot. Go into the safety of the Dobber and take that thing out." Commanded Serene Miriam.

After all, it was a military decision. Inside the invisible shield, their confident sniper sighted her weapon as another gun mounted platform approached. The Engineer had spotted where the machine was to be hit from.

"There is a flexible fibre optic filament connected the huge revolving gun to its rectangular base. Sever that."

The whirring moving gun platform advanced on eight legs, its limited machine brain was confused by the debris ahead of it. It guns were ready to fire at a moment's notice. A single shot took out its cerebral connection. It went dead with an audible powering down. Satisfied, Greta had done her job; they piled out of their concealment device. The gun platform was converted to their cause in a matter of minutes. The only Humans still alive in the complex followed the gun-mounted platform as it took the lead. Naomh's internal presence became self-righteous at their success against the machines and with borrowed Hybrid enthusiasm it shouted at the long dead Naisi in adopted nuances.

"Bring on the CRYSTALIOD'I."

It recovered instantly from its outburst; the Hybrid emotions reflected his previous madness. Ten minutes into their descent, another machine was encountered. The Shaman stayed put on the captive device, his finger on a makeshift firing button. The others retreated to a relatively safer distance. The inquisitive machine knew that the thing that was vectoring towards it was one of its type and should be present in the tunnels, but its signal of recognition was distorted. Before, it could investigate further; a withering burst of gunfire ended its electronic deliberations. The advancing group protected by their deception encountered and destroyed two more gun platforms and then they reached a juncture that held six lifts. The Lenses had them operational in minutes. All of the crew scrambled in and they descended deep into the bowls of the earth. As the lift halted and its doors opened automatically, two disruption globes were thrown in. But, there was no waiting reception. Still, like Crazy Tunes before them, the questors had found the piece of the APOCRYPHA'I. It had been removed from its host and sunken in a bath of chemicals. The violet jewel lay in the centre of a vast open planned floor; the large area was well lit and monitored. At its base like some macabre offering was the body of one of the youths from the Shamans tribe. The young warrior lay spread-eagled with a pistol that had fallen from nerveless fingers at his side. A pool of dried blood testified that he was no longer of this World. The Shaman was aghast, from the clues; it looked like Crazy Tunes had blown his brains out. But that was not possible; suicide was not in his people's make up. His race were warriors and death by one's own hand was not an option. Watching cameras abounded, but the Engineer's globes had made them temporary ineffectual. Bursts of well-aimed fire then made them obsolete entirely. Time was needed for what they were about to do. Crossing the open plan floor warily, all of them were suddenly hit by a wall of what only could be called depression. Everybody staggered away from what felt like a physical blow.

"Back!" Shouted the Shaman.

Retreating out of range from the strange effect, they all slumped to the floor, puffing and panting. It had been as if some enormous pressure was taken from them.

"We must ponder this."

"What strange medicine is this?" Asked Dave Whose Car Is Called Ford.

The Shaman had sat cross-legged for an hour, murmuring a soft chant that caused resounding echoes around the chamber while he applied more paint to his face. He rose to greet the others with a striped pattern of vibrant reds, neutral blues and flat yellow ochre's. They also noticed that he now had a large knife strapped to his side. The blade looked ancient and it had an ivory handle with strange cravings of angels etched into it. The warrior unsheathed the blade and faced towards the chemical bath. He held the metal and bone high and made a vow. Then, the Anasazi spoke directly to Naomh.

"I have a measure of what has passed this way. The Totem is not whole. Though my people were always aware of this thing, I now fully understand this. Since the Totem has been separated from its host, it has been emitting rays of depression and many scientists studying it have inexplicably committed suicide. Men and women with bright careers ahead of them, full of zest for life started to brood, then came the dark moods and even darker bouts of depression. Eventually so many succumbed to sad death that the "Great White Chief" and his advisors decided that machines should watch over it until a solution could be found. So an army of gun mounted platforms were given the task to guard this secret base. That is why there are no people present. That was over four hundred years ago. Only I can take it from here, but when I call for you, you must also enter the battle. It will be a fight of wills."

Watching the actions of the rest of the crew, the bearer of six parts of the living amulet agreed with the Shaman. They were unusually jumpy, nervous and all had panicked expressions emblazoned on their faces. None would cross that invisible line of mental attack. Naomh agreed with the Indian, he knew that he could not absorb this seventh piece of the APOCRYPHA'I, something felt different about its presence. The Shaman understood why.

"The Spirit voices told me to keep this from you until it was time. It is only half of the piece."

"What?"

"This piece was split from another, thousands of years ago. I also know where that is, but we must first gain this one. Then we must go there. This is the reason why it causes such despair; it's longing for its other half. My people have lived with it for a long time; we have built an immunity of sorts to it. It does not take us so easily. But still our young brave was overcome simply enough. So if I can separate it from the chemical bath, I must wear it until we seek out its other half."

Inside his thoughts, the six parts Mescal/Amulet agreed.

"He is correct; this is not a complete part of me. It will destabilise the rest of the whole. We cannot risk trying to meld it together with the rest of my parts."

Naomh and the others were sorely disappointed, all of them had been certain that this was the final piece in the jigsaw.

A communal despair set in.

The Spy was especially peeved; this person's returning moments of triumph to the Anschluss was now delayed indefinitely. The tortured piece of Mescal's altered form was still sending out probing tendrils of hopelessness. The Shaman moved into the half pieces sphere of influence and resumed his cross-legged position. He sat down with an effort and began the mental confrontation. Again, the wise Indian chanted, sweat began to form on his craggy face as the internal battle began. Safe from the weird conflict, the others watched, not daring to interfere. After twenty minutes, the trembling Shaman called for Naomh. Without hesitation, he rushed forward and sat alongside him.

"Open your spirit."

Naomh used the knowledge of what the Lama had imparted to him. The Shaman felt the strength of his will and nodded silently. Three minds fought for domination, two Human and one Alien. Still, the two earthly combatants were losing the battle; the tortured piece refused to allow them forward. It failed to acknowledge the mastery of the six pieces. It hit them with the oppressive dark deeds of their lives. The immersed half-piece was gaining the initiative. They were now fighting for their sanity and ultimately their very existence.

They were both failing!

Just as the sands of time were running against them, they were saved from an impossible source. Out of the blue, the Mute strode forward through the impenetrable barrier of depression and simply walked over to the bath of chemicals. Reaching in, he grabbed the half piece of the living amulet. Contact with Human flesh ended its battle with Naomh and the Shaman and they snapped out of the potentially lethal conflict. The big Indian was the first to recover and he moved towards Illeau. He demanded.

"Give the Totem to me."

The Mute gave him an indifferent look and handed it over without a moment's thought. The weird man was wondering what all the fuss was about. Naomh was astounded.

"How did he do that?"

All that the Shaman knew was that the Spirits were never wrong.

"He is not like us. It had no effect on him."

The retriever of the piece simply said in his whinny voice.

"The thing was distracted by your battle with it. Anyone of us could have marched forward like me and took it. It's just that I thought of it first."

This explanation satisfied the others, Naomh and the Red Indian were not so sure. They were right to question. For Illeau had absolutely no regrets about his long line of dark deeds, so the twisted piece of the APOCRYPHA'I could find no chink in his emotional armour. All deliberations were put aside as their communication devices crackled and an image of their crouching two comrades who were left behind appeared. Beersheba and the Rabbi who were still above ground warned them.

"There is a lot of activity out here. Several flying craft are speeding towards us as I speak. You need to get out of there now or there is going to be one hell of a pitched battle."

The instant the surveillance devices of the underground base went down, the President of the United States was awoken in the Whitehouse and advised of the situation. Giving the go ahead, a squad of elite airborne commandos had been dispatched to assess the cause. Several of the flying craft landed and hundreds of heavily armed and well-equipped soldiers began making their way towards them. Peter Stride Quickly picked up the body of Crazy Tunes and carried it on his back. The infiltrators began a frantic rush back up the tunnel they had created. Here, they also recovered the bodies of their two dead comrades, so according to the Shaman.

"The three of them can be given the proper rituals. It is regretful that we cannot find the others."

Naomh had the TORT-CAM out and was ready to activate it at the last moment. The fleeing group just reached their two sentries in time. The invisible shield was activated and they fled into it just as the land was over-run with soldiers. The Shaman's people were memorised by the calmness within.

"Have we entered the Spirit World?" Asked Mike Porcupine certain that he was going to meet Ron His Enemies Fear Him and Jim Fat Bear.

"No! But we are as safe here as a young Buffalo calf surrounded by a wall of adults. No marauding wolf can touch us here." His medicine man told him.

Like all of those they had taken a piece of the APOCRYPHA'I from, the forces of the United States set upon a frantic search. But it was to no avail. A mystified commander reported back.

"I have bad news to report. We encountered no resistance, but we

found that all of the gun platforms were destroyed. My troops were able to get to the centre of operations. And, they found the thing gone. We found some old dead bodies and fresh blood in one of the corridors, so whoever took it, is still close by."

"Find them." Ordered the President.

Those that the Special Forces searched for stayed within the invulnerability of the TORT-CAM for three days and waited. As the hullabaloo died down, they emerged one night under the pale moon light of the desert night and floated over the electric fence lightening quick and into safety. Their four Humvies were made to reappear, they were about to board them and head back to the hidden village, but one of the Anasazi intervened. It was Peter Who Strides Quickly. The usually silent Indian went to the first vehicle and activated it and let it speed out to the open desert. He then went to another and repeated the procedure. Ten kilometres away, a fast moving light sped through the cloudless sky. Two invisible streaks sped from the flying object and the two driverless vehicles were incinerated in sudden balls of flame.

"Wow!" Said Cahill.

"Back into the TORT-CAM" Commanded Miriam.

As the concealment device was been activated, the Guide threw four explosive devices into the remaining Humvies, two into each one.

"They won't know how many there are now."

When the last person was safely in the hidden shield, the two vehicles erupted in explosions of crimson fire. Now they had another problem, the concealed group were still hidden in the invisible haven, five days after the destruction of their escape vehicles. Searching soldiers had found their burning remains and officers posted guards on the charred metal. Constant uninterrupted shifts of twenty armed men and women watched over that patch of scorched desert. Only fifty metres away, the hidden questors had had enough. It was time to devise a plan to get them out of here.

"The Sentries are going nowhere, we will have to take them out, split the TORT-CAM into TORT-CAMLETS and make our way out of here. If not we could be here forever."

It was agreed and on the fifth dawn against a background of dark blue and purple sky that promised poor visibility, they made a move. They had no choice, if it rained; then the unseen shield would be revealed. Weapons were fitted on silent and the Indian braves unsheathed their large knives. The Anasazi and Illeau went first, fanning out to take out the five sentries on the peripheries. As soon as they were down, wolf calls would alert the three snipers, Greta, Cahill and Moshe. Minutes later, five calls came one after another and the remaining Americans bunched together over a luminous warmer died without even knowing it. Before their blood was absorbed by the sandy sponge of the ground, the invisible shield had been split up into its smaller mobile counterparts and they were away. Days later and after another bout of hide and seek, they arrived back at the hidden village foot sore and very weary. Sleep came to them easily enough in the tranquil hideout. While they slept the sleep of exhaustion in the Anasazi village, the Indians dead had their ritual and passed to the happy hunting grounds. After that solemn occasion, a great celebration was held. There was much dancing and chanting.

"Hi ya, Hi ya." Sang the gathered tribe.

When the questors awoke, the Shaman proudly displayed the long lost Totem or the penultimate piece of the APOCRYPHA'I. Speaking to the Heavens and the gathered throng, he proclaimed.

"The shame of the tribe is half removed."

Hard liqueur and a milder form of narcotic was passed around. Tomorrow, they could worry about the last piece. Amid the euphoria, the Anschluss Spy in their ranks had been disturbed for a while. This mission was becoming complicated; the cuckoo's tangled web of deceit was becoming undone. The infiltrator needed to talk with the Chairman. This false member of the cadre was beginning to have a grudging respect for the rest of the questor's. However, the inbuilt prejudices of the LYUBINITES were still paramount.

"They are proving resilient in overcoming any type of challenge. Naomh and some of his crew would make a fine addition, not only to the Anschluss security services, but dare I think it, even the inner circle of disciples. Of course the brown skinned people would never be accepted, especially the savage."

The two-dimensional image of the Chairman appeared on the deceivers concealed communication device. The predicament of the mole was explained and fell upon un-sympathetic ears. Agent XIII's supreme leader listened like the great father whose genes he had inherited and then reinforced his Spy's flagging resolve. Ivan Tell spouted their coda.

"Only those of us who have the original genes of the Doctor and his disciples are judged to be the inheritors of the secret. The rest of mankind have been evaluated and found lacking and cannot be allowed to participate in the great reward. There is no room for any of them; not even Naomh."

The talk with the Chairman had renewed the enemy's within resolve.

"By the shaven head of our founder; I will see the mission through."

Privately, back in his tower, the Kaiser had made another decision.

"Not another flawed one. After they have completed the mission, my Spy will have to be eliminated. Agent XIII has strayed from the true path. If my little cuckoo goes outside my parameters, then Spy or no Spy, they will suffer."

Once again, the Questors were ready to resume the search for the amulet and spirits were high. This was finally the last piece. The living map was consulted, but this time it was the Shaman who was drawn towards the half piece.

"The path is open to me. I am been led all the way to the tip of the South American Continent and then across the south sea to another landmass of frozen ice."

The Anasazi had been expecting this journey. There were no cities on this land at the bottom of the globe. During this stage of planning, the Shaman was once again assaulted by melancholic un-joined violet piece. He barely resisted its depressive attack of suicidal inclination and fell into a coma. His frantic Tribesmen and the Questors attended him at the moment of his collapse. Both had conflicting methods of saving him. The Rabbi's decision of rushing him into the LAB-CELL was rejected by Naomh's internal voice.

"You cannot. The separated segment will corrupt all of its mechanisms."

"But he was already in it out in the desert. It had no effect then."

"That part of me went into stasis when it was taken from the chemical concoction. It has recovered and is now aware of its separation. It is not thinking logically and will not until it is joined with its other segment."

He passed on this information to the others; the Lenses understood the implications more than most. It was decided to let their catatonic travelling comrade in the care of his own people. The medicine men of the Anasazi fought the infliction for three weeks; they had help from another Holy man far away in the Mountain Kingdom. Through the spirit pathways, the Lama had joined the battle for the Shaman's life. The Tribe's elders were well aware of the danger from the violet half-piece of the frozen rainbow. One of them told them during their vigil.

"Once in the days of our ancestors, long since past; it had corrupted an Elder of the Anasazi. He responded to its abnormal demands and sent out parties of warriors to murder local farmers and their families. The slain bodies were gleaned of every ounce of flesh. Roasted bones were smashed for their marrow and the grim harvest consumed over open fires. When his atrocities were discovered, he was slaughtered in a popular uprising and the piece was given to another. From then on, the bearers were watched carefully and would be slain out of hand if they became erratic."

"This could be the Shaman's fate?" Asked the dread Clerk.

A nod answered his rhetorical question. There was a lot of chanting and billowing smoke until finally one of the healers came out and proclaimed.

"We have won the battle for the life of our brother."

The mostly relieved bunch were allowed to see him. From the corners of the group, the Mute scrutinised the features of Chief Dan Brown. He had never known a man to be at death's door for so long and he wanted to see if there was an imprint of his seeking in the Indians eyes. He did see something there, but he did not know what it was. The man under their worried observation was just about awake and smiled weakly at the intrusion.

"Are you Ok?"

"I am well. It seems as if the Spirits have need of me yet."

"We have reason to be grateful to them then." Replied relieved Naomh.

The Engineer wanted to say.

"Don't you mean Jesus?"

But he held his tongue. It took the Shaman nearly four months to recover fully and as he was the only one who could withstand its continued assault, they had no choice but to wait. This was not entirely true however; the Mute could have carried it. But the bearer of the other six parts was unable to trust him. The tribe's elders eventually judged Dan George to be free of corruption and he was allowed to proceed with the questors.

The fourteen seekers of the APOCRYPHA'I left the village of the Anasazi under the full moon in the month of October. Taking two vehicles, they headed south and into the unknown. Finally, the weary questor travellers arrived at the frozen tip of the South American Continent after a soul tiring and energy-sapping journey of thousands of kilometres. They had passed through steaming equatorial jungles, bypassed large cities and eventually crossed Patagonian tundra where mountains loomed over plateaus until they reached this bleak and dreary place. Driving over highways of every state and description, from six lane motorways to muddy tracks, they eventually crossed over swathes of rural terrain that had no discernible manmade courses. The route they had taken was known as the Trans Continental highway. The Engineer fitted a new fuel source in the form of a swirling globe and engines of their vehicles got their power from the Sun's light. Its efficiency allowed them to make the journey without refuelling once. On board on of the Humvives, the Shaman remembered the tangible disappointment among the tribes Braves that he would be going to the bottom of the World alone with Naomh's party. The three survivors of the raid on the underground complex, Dave whose car is called Ford, Mike Porcupine and Peter Stride Quickly took it the hardest. He told them.

"The great sky Spirits have willed this way. But, you my people will know the moment of joining."

The Shaman knew why it was only he that was accompanying them.

"My destiny lies in the snow-covered land at the bottom of the World."

With their help, he was about to re-write a wrong and fulfil an ancestral pledge, some infraction that his forefathers had committed. When asked about it, he became vague and non-committal. He touched his half segment of the living amulet and said in a tone the bore no argument.

"I will not speak of it anymore."

He kept his wall of silence. On the six week long drive down, the Red Indian had vexed those that shared his vehicle. Been from a land that seldom saw the rains, he used to let his window down, so the sound of the

799

falling drops could come in to the vehicle. He loved the shifting melody when sudden wing gusts amplified the vigour of the falling downpours. The Clerk brought a smile to his craggy features when the blonde man called the clouds.

"The Mothers blankets."

The Guide in a vengeful mood did not speak aloud. He knew the smart remark at the tip of his tongue would upset the Indian.

"What do you call the rain then, The Mother's piss?"

Eventually, though as the questors went more southward, the temperature chilled and the rain turned into sleet and snow. That was enough for the Shaman and he kept his window closed. The others were content with that state of affairs. The Guide had also irritated his fellow passengers with his cig smoking, so they made other arrangements. All those that enjoyed a puff had to share a vehicle. Finally, they reached a land where the sharp angle of the Sun provided little sunlight for tree growth. It had taken many weeks to get to this point and the wind scoured lands of Patagonia did not look inviting. The northerners were confused, their calendar told them that it was late spring, but it seemed that they had arrived in mid-winter. The Shaman also wondered why these questors did not try and acquire a flying craft; it would have cut their journey time enormously.

"Perhaps, they know it is safer to travel on the ground. What we possess should not be chanced on the fickle fate of flight."

The impatient Spy had always been thinking along the same lines about acquiring such a craft. But as they were sure they were the only one capable of piloting such a machine, so they let it go. After all it would lead to awkward questions. The reason for not flying was simple. The internal presence diverted Naomh's thoughts from powered flight; it was not in the ALASTHA'I plans. It had been aggrieved that flying into space could not have been avoided, so it planted a phobia of flying into its host's physique. So even if others had brought the question of flight up, he would have rejected it. In due time though, the weary group reached an impassable range of icy glaciers and their vehicles had to be abandoned altogether at the edges of a glacial spout. Looking through powerful viewing devices, Haim spoke.

"It will be a long hard slog to cross that inhospitable terrain."

"Still, we have to go over it."

The Engineer and the Lenses conferred. They instantly agreed.

"Naomh will bring his pieces of the Amulet into the LAB-CELL, it might reveal something useful to us."

They emerged with a new and improved Platform of Light that easily accommodated all of them with room to spare. It was exactly the same type of transport device that Naisi and his company were on the day back in time that they met their grisly end. The exposed TORT-CAM stuck to the base of the hovering mass like something soldered seamlessly. The journey ahead became easier; their larger conveyance could soar to thirty metres above solid ground. Three people would guide the hovering beam by their bands while the others stayed out of the weather in the now visible shield. Unfortunately, the Anasazi had to always be one of them; they could not risk his piece inside. He accepted this circumstance with his usual mind-set. All of them would take turns on the point. The Shaman looked down on the passing terrain and told the Clerk.

"Victor Who Has Many Faces; we are cloud riders."

Solomon was fascinated by the rumbling avalanches caused by the moving glacier far below them and knew.

"It would have been a time consuming and capricious crossing without the use of our wondrous technology."

As if a test to the Enclave man's theory, it happened on the Guide and the Persuader's watch with the Shaman while the others dozed in the sanctuary of their comfortable haven. When the moving platform was gliding up a steep incline, there was a sudden jerk in its ministrations. It began to shimmer, dim, then blacken and finally to power down. The pony-tailed man kept pressing the correct sequence on his seven-coloured band, but to no avail. The bearer of the uncompleted amulet was drawn out of his secure sanctuary. The rest remained inside.

"What is happening?" Demanded Naomh from the one who really understood their travelling contraption.

"There is something in the air impeding the Platforms operation, you must land or it will fall from the sky." Answered the voice within.

The un-complete shade within the amulet thought this very strange.

"Only my race should have the technology to cause this problem."

They descended to the glacier with a bump and got the others out of the TORT-CAM. Some were miffed at the rude landing and enquiring eyes demanded an explanation. Their leader explained what had occurred as they stamped around on the frozen ground.

"We really have a spanner in the works." Said the Engineer.

The Lenses added.

"There must be a glitch in the machine."

The Shaman had the most impractical answer.

"It's the Evil Spirits, but the omens have been good, so there is nothing to worry about."

Needless to say, they were not impressed with his faith in imaginary beings. Especially, the Engineer, he was getting annoyed by the Indian's calm belief in a bunch of old bones, make believe spirits and superstition.

"Only God himself can predict the future."

As the Rabbi was agreeing with his religious counterpart, their transport contrivance floundered completely. It ran out of energy and just switched off. The reluctant marchers had at least another couple of hundred kilometres to go until they reached the coast, but thankfully the gliding machine had cleared the most impassable rivers of frozen ice.

"We have to walk, we don't know how long it will take to recharge and it is also draining energy from the TORT-CAM."

"So be it, the Good Spirits will guide us."

"I'll bet your runes did not see that coming." Muttered the Lenses.

Everyone pitched in; they began to organize provisions and more adequate clothing for the hazardous passage through the edge of the glacier. The Clerk argued to stay in the comfort of the functioning shield, but the six parts Mescal/Amulet advised Naomh against this.

"I do not know, what is affecting the Platform of Light, it could have the same adverse effect on the Guidex sphere."

Ten days later, the weary trekkers had arrived at this point in the dead of night and after their arduous journey of ragged kilometres, all of them were clearly exhausted. It had been a long slog. They had come from the Northern Hemisphere, passing at first through Mexico, then the sub-tropical lands of Guatemala, Honduras, Nicaragua and Costa Rica. At the Equatorial zone, they encountered the lands of Colombia, the steamy jungles of Brazil, the bleak tablelands and desert regions of salt marshes of Bolivia until they reached the wide pampas of Argentina and finally the wild and broken fiords and off-shore islands of southern Chile. Taking in the scenery, most thought that they were on another World. It could not have looked so different from their respective homelands. Now, under the subdued light of dawn, they huddled together on a narrow peninsula in a mock parody of nesting penguins overlooking the chilly Ocean. The wind drove into them howling like a banshee. One powerful gust nearly knocked them off their feet. Using his communication piece as normal conversation was impossible; the Anasazi told them over the howl of the buffeting wind.

"This is where we must cross to the frozen Continent."

Pointing to the even bleaker island mass of Tierra del Fuego that was separated from them by the Strait of Magellan, the Persuader asked more in hope than logic.

"Could it not be that place over there?"

Answering his question rhetorically, he said with a long sigh.

"I didn't think so."

His brother once again took out the Platform of Light and tried to activate it, but he got no joy. Disappointed, he told the others.

"It looks like we will have too this the hard way."

In her own language, Beersheba said.

"Tell me something new?"

The Clerk who was scanning the immediate area with his optical device rapidly exclaimed.

"I don't believe it. There is a cluster of dwellings over there."

Incredibly, he had sighted a fishing outpost nestled between two cliff promontories in a forbidden cove. Its make shift structures of wood and salvaged metal under the overcast sky made it the most desperate and forlorn settlement in the America's. Reluctantly, the jaded travellers made their way down to the place at the edges of civilization. As they neared, the ramshackle buildings of the settlement appeared huddled together in a futile resistance to keep the bitter chill at bay. Although plumes of smoke emitting from metal soot coated chimneys promised a warm reception in their interiors. The locals called this abysmal place, "Penguin Shores.". As luck would have it, there was a Cantina here in this miserable outpost of Humanity. The only liquor available was a harsh and locally distilled spirit that none of the weary group wished to sample. A smiling Guide went to the bartender and took out several bottles of Anschluss liquor and other types of spirit that he had picked up on their travels. His translator had already registered the local dialect of the serving man.

"Here try this."

The Cantina owner recognized good quality stuff and poured a sizeable quantity for himself. Swallowing the glassful of amber liquid produced a beatific smile on his weatherworn features.

"Have these as gifts from me and my friends." Said the Guide as he pushed the lot towards the man who instantly became suspicious.

"Why would you do this for me signor?"

"We need your help."

"For these I will try my best." Replied the beneficiary as he took the bottles off the counter.

"Where can we purchase a craft to take us across to the frozen Continent?"

The few customers of the tiny inn looked at the Guide as if he were mad. The barman said shook his head as if he had not heard him correctly the first time.

"Across the frozen sea. Is that what you said seignior?"

One of the patrons who was drowning his woes heard the conversation and his outlook immediately brightened. He did not care if they were mad.

"Santa Maria, I have just what they are looking for and it looks like they will pay my price. After all they look like they have come a long way."

He stood up and said.

"Amigos. It looks like we might be able to strike a deal."

In another drinking establishment in the far corner of the World, the questors had come up trumps again. Here they purchased a small hover boat off of the desperate man. They had no idea that he had been looking at the end of his fishing career. Ailing health, advancing age and not been able to afford a crew was about to finish him. The fisherman used these air filled contraptions as it meant that they could fish all year round and did not have to wait for the weak rays of the short summer Sun to melt the ice bound cove. As always, money spoke, they paid the seller enough that he would never have to put to sea again. The purveyor of the hover boat did not want to know their reasons for crossing the sea to the frozen Continent. He advised them after completing the sale.

"Only the best seafarers in the World can cross that Ocean."

The Guide sweetened the deal with a case of American liquor. Once aboard their newly acquired sea vessel, a whimsical Solomon said.

"Now, who is going to sail this thing?"

This time, their acquired means of transport seemed to float upon a large bag of air or gas. Moshe volunteered to be the skipper.

"After all; I sailed the Pirates vessel all the way to the South American coastline."

The Enclave man stared at the Spanish scripted instrument panel for about ten minutes. He then powered up the hover boat and its airbags filled up. The sea craft lurched out of the frozen harbour like a drunken person. Watching from the shoreline, the former owner of the sea craft blessed himself in the Catholic fashion and uttered.

"I will never see those foolish people again."

A kilometre out from Penguin Shores and the slightly warmer sea currents had dissolved the frozen water. At first the solid mass of glacial ice hugging the Patagonian coast gave way to a sea of mirror shards of glassy ice and then to ice free open water. The boat which was basically a work horse made hard work of crossing the choppy seas. Enormous waves forced them to constantly adjust the height of the craft's flight in order not to be swamped. They had entered the latitude known to generations of sea voyagers as the roaring forties and soon they were about to pass into the screaming fifties. Growlers of various sizes bobbed past them making their headway extremely hazardous. Then, their craft encountered the parents of the smaller obstacles as it entered a sea of crowded fields of pack ice and bergs. The cynics aboard had their doubts that it would ever reach their intended destination intact and it would more than likely condemn them to a watery grave. Huge wave swells battered the boat and crew and all of them winced every time the groaning of the ships metal frame resonated in sharp crisp air. Ice and snow froze to the hull and structure of the hovercraft. Amongst the ship's inventory were several large gas bottles with harnesses attached. They took turns melting the accumulating snow and ice, for if the weight increased, it would surely sink their vessel. There would be no frost bitten hands, the bone chilling cold had little effect and their protective gear served them well. Then disaster struck, it was an unpredictable event that took the wind out of their sails, a large block of ice came heading their way. It was the month of December and Summer was in full swing. The annual seasonable thaw cracked and split the ice sheet. It was followed by more of its kind; some of the floating obstructions were over a kilometre long. Each sculpted creation was unique, moulded by its journey around the Southern Sea's.

"Shit man, how are we going to get pass this lot?" Asked the Guide.

The flow of icebergs became denser and Moshe was unable to manoeuvre the hover boat around the river of frozen giants. Just as the boat was about to be crushed, they had no option but to scale one of the floating behemoths. One by one, each of them climbed up one of the icebergs, just as a loud groaning heralded the end of their boat. It was smashed into metal and wood splinters. The crew were marooned and adrift on a melting iceberg. Panic set in quickly. For the first time in a long time, they were utterly helpless. The lone voice of Solomon stated their quandary.

"What are we going to do, if we had the Skimmer operational, it would be easy?"

"Try one." Commanded Miriam.

The desperate group huddled around the globe that the Engineer had placed on the white surface of the ice-berg. It stayed black and inactive. There were groans of disappointment.

"Get into the LAB-CELL and find something that can help us." Demanded Cahill of their two appointed experts.

"We are rightly up shit's creek without a paddle now." Mentioned a not so helpful Shaman.

Three day's passed and nothing helpful was found and to further compound their dire situation, the iceberg moved into a warmer current. It was beginning to diminish noticeably. But more worryingly, their shrinking base was drifting away from the main cluster of floating bergs. They would have to act or every one of them would end up in the freezing water or marooned forever at the bottom of the sea in the Alien bubble of impenetration. The mobile TORT-CAMLETS were a delaying option. But they would eventually power down and their occupants would receive a watery grave, just like the bearer of the fifth piece of the APOCRYPHA'I. One of their number was fuming. The Spy was about to come clean. The traitor had waited for this extreme decision until all hope had faded and all other options had run out.

"It is time to call in a back-up squad; a fast aircraft could be here from a monitoring ship in minutes. It galls me to call for a rescue party, but there is little choice now."

Agent XIII was distracted briefly. Feeling the pressure of a full bladder, the Persuader moved away from the others, unzipped his fly and began to relieve himself. Hot steam rose up from the iceberg. The Clerk seeing this went hysterical and screamed at the perpetrator.

"Excuse the pun, but we really are on thin ice. Is it not melting quickly enough for you?"

A war of words broke out; everybody had something to say. All except the Mute and the Engineer. The latter was engrossed with a swirling globe. Now that they were in serious trouble, cracks began to appear in their togetherness as reflections of the splitting ice. Tell's mole was about to make contact with the watching vessel when the Engineer shouted.

"I have a solution!"

Unknown to all but one, the call for assistance was never made. The others listened to his idea and it seemed that the man from the Madrid Contrib might have come up trumps once again. A highly relieved Naomh wondered.

"What would we ever have done without him?"

"I sent up an observational globe and discovered that this flow of icebergs tails all the way back to a huge landmass. So all we have to do is to come up with something that will allow us to leap from one to the other."

"Much like stepping stones in a river." Said the Shaman.

"Exactly."

"As all the technology we are using seems to be based on the properties of light, I have come up with something that might work. One of light's properties is electro- magnetism. So here's my scenario. We fire a projectile to the next iceberg in the chain. On it is a light attracter. We will wear light belts of the same frequency and once the attracter is activated we will be drawn across to it. There are two problems though. Firstly, I could only come up with one attracter, so the shot is going to have to be accurate every time. And, if someone ends up in that freezing water, they will survive with our protective clothing. But for how long, I do not know. Added to that, they will be swept away by the drifting current."

It took him half an hour to set everything up. There was no debate about who was going to take the shots even though every one of them was more than competent marksmen. It would be Greta, she was better than the rest of them. The Engineer handed her his contraption and explained its use. The unfazed blonde woman took the heavy looking device and knelt down. The attracter's firing part was mounted on a sturdy tripod. Cahill gave her shoulder a tight squeeze while the others waited with batted breath. Although, most of them were satisfied with her capabilities, it still seemed an impossible shot. The next iceberg was over two kilometres away and was a speck to the naked eye. There were too many impossible variables for the shot to land true, wind, distance, poor visibility and unfamiliarity with the launching device. A howl from a sudden intense gust of icy wind seemed an obstacle to mock her attempt. She took aim; there was a madding delay until she fired. The projectile speed across the blue sea and to those watching, the globular light seemed to take forever until it hit another iceberg with an audible clump and a spray of frozen chips. Someone cheered; Greta gave them a glare and uttered.

"Did you ever doubt it?"

"I will go first. The rest of you make sure that you deactivate your belts seconds before you hit the receptor. " Said the Engineer.

He activated the attracter and it hummed on. They could see the bright light clearly on the other iceberg. He also turned on his belt and instantly flew through the chilled air. This time, there was no modicum for error; he was guided straight for his target. At the edge of the island of floating ice, he deactivated his belt. He landed away from it and rolled causing a cloud of snow to rise up. He got up and waved, he was alright. The others followed until all fifteen of them were safely across. For Naomh, the jump across had been a confusing experience, in fact he did not remember it at all. Unknown to him, the ALASTHA'I within came to the fore. The presence of Mescal was exhilarated by the short flight across the deadly Ocean.

"It was a far cry from my past life, but still, it was a brief taste of the freedom of flight. How I wish that the leap had lasted longer?"

His host landed upright on the ice and with more grace than those that had preceded him. Now, it was time to get the weapon to them. The Engineer fetched out a large durable tarpaulin of stretchy material and told two of his strongest companions, the Persuader and the Indian.

"You are to hold this up when I tell you."

He pressed another sequence on his belt and the firing weapon detached from its previous position and flew towards them. When it was a couple of metres away, its designer shouted. *"Raise the sheet and catch it."*

They did and it was undamaged. Greta then sighted the next iceberg in the sequence and the process was repeated. This one was only half the distance away. The markswoman methodically shot their escape route. At one stage, their shooter scared the wits out of a group of speckled leopard seals. The sluggish mammals stumbled into the frozen sea and in their preferred medium; they sped away from those who had disturbed them. It took a day and more to reach the rugged ice sheet that clung around the solid rock of northern Antarctica. The ice leapers gained more confidence with each flight through the air and howls of glee filled the chilled air. The Shaman was really flying like an Eagle now. As the ice-berg hoppers neared the frozen Continent, the icy Antarctic Sea took on a greenish cast. The icebergs bunched together forming a lacy sheet and some began to look like crazy ice sculptures. There were no more death defying leaps, they had simply hop scotched over the meandering trail of bobbing slabs of floating ice. They did however disturb more basking seals, walruses and penguins. Gradually, the bluish green spaces of ocean became less and less. Now the exhausted group could walk across large distances until they needed to use the attracter again. By this spasmodic route, the weary questors had reached the frigid threshold of the Weddell Sea to the Ronne Ice Shelf and the attracter became surplus to requirements. The frozen ramparts of the new land bore testament to the very cold latitudes that lay ahead. They mounted the frozen snow and traversed the ice bound bay until they reached the Antarctic land mass proper. The Shaman told them when there was solid land under them, how he knew was anyone's guess.

But they were shattered and were grateful for the halt in their long journey. There was no night at this time of the year in these southern latitudes, but the bone weary crew decided that they would sleep and rest before they set foot on the frozen over Continent. Sleeping blankets were taken from the trustworthy shield. The next morning, their time pieces stated that this was the hour of the day. The Clerk found that as usual, the Shaman was up before them. The Indian was kneeling down and facing north. The man from the Anschluss listened to the words that were coming from his mouth. They were in the Indians ancient tongue. Though, he understood the words with the aid of the translator, he could feel the elemental power of his incitement.

"Oh Great Spirit, whose voice, I hear in the winds."

"Whose breath gives life to all the World."

"Hear me."

"Let me walk in beauty and make my eyes ever behold the red and purple Sunset."

The once blonde haired man felt overawed at the beauty of the poem and asked.

"Where did that come from?"

"Those are the words of a long dead Sioux Chief called Yellow Hawk."

Chief Dan George felt the repetition of history.

"These old words were composed during a time of transition, where the author was aware that his old World would never be the same again. My life too is about to change, out there in the frozen wastes, something beyond our wildest nightmares eagerly awaits us."

The night before, the mystical Shaman had cast the runes and now the omens did not look so good, especially for himself. The big Indian just shrugged at his intended fate.

"It is the will of the Spirits."

He would not tell the others of their portent.

XXIX.

ANTARCTICA 1912 AD.

Frigid icy particles locked within the gale force wind gave its repeating howl an unique depth as the man in charge of the ponies of the failed expedition looked around the flimsy shelter of the canvas tent. His intelligent eyes glanced briefly over his frozen moustache at his comrades, who were sleeping the sleep of the near dead. Like him, their exhausted bodies had just sat down and waited for death. Digging deep into his mental reserves, he rose, having made his decision.

"There are not enough supplies for all of us. Our stash of pemmican is all but consumed; the whale and seal meat is a forgotten luxury. Even the horsemeat has gone."

The Englishman realised that one less persons demands on their frugal amount of stores would make all the difference and having failed to keep the equines alive; it was up to him to make the ultimate sacrifice. Just then, the power of the buffeting polar wind buffeted the tent shaking the canvas and rattling the metal and rope supports in an effort to blow its Human filling out into the unprotected night. This sudden and more intense gust enforced the judgement; he had made moments ago. Before, the doomed explorer went out to the freezing polar blizzard; he paused for a few seconds and stood silhouetted against the Antarctic whiteness. The weary man uttered to the worn out men words, which were to become immortal to those soft readers of newsprint who thrived on the hardships of others from the comfort of their normal everyday existence.

"I'll be sometime."

Oat's hobbled away from the tent on his gangrenous leg; out into the windy wastes and hoped he would perish quickly. He didn't even pull down his heavy snow goggles to protect himself from the freezing snow and ice. Stinging tears flowed down his cheeks. He was so weak that he expected to expire within minutes; but his end was long in coming.

"Maybe, I should go back to the others."

The relative comfort of the inadequate tent looked very inviting as his well-honed survival instincts kicked in. Despair gave way to hope.

"We can overcome this! We will eat the surviving dogs, if we have to."

His words of encouragement were cut off as something huge and alien hidden in the veil of snow rose up from behind him. The dark shadow had moved across the ice and stormed through the blizzard in an erratic gait to intercept him. The thing had been in a frenzy since it had smelt warm Human blood. It knew that the man-meat was tainted; but it was desperate for nourishment. That explorer never returned to the tent, but the others lived to tell part of his heroic tale. Back in the Northern Hemisphere and amongst the trappings of civilisation, the survivors of the failed expedition regaled others of their fight against the elements in books of popular fiction. But none of the Antarctic explorer's had even the slightest inclination that they had unwittingly escaped from a fate worse than any of them could have imagined.

SOUTH POLE STATION 2099AD.

The last few devoted scientists were in deep trouble, these twenty dedicated men and women had opted to stay for the final winter. It would be their final chance to amass essential data. There would be no landing aircraft for six months. These devoted men and women were on their own until then. The main sponsors of the century old explorations had pulled the plug on their operations and this would be the last evacuation. Due to the growing mistrust between Nations and the frequent disappearances of personnel, the bases were been abandoned. Strange rumours of attacking giants had spread like wild fire among the residents and those less dedicated had left. The leader of the Scientists, a professor of geology named Philip Browne could have understood the descriptions of huge forms, if they had been on top of the World instead of the bottom. Chief supervisor Browne who was not an expert on ecology would have said without hesitation.

"Polar bears. Somehow the enormous animals have lost their fear of us and are gathering in packs and picking off individual Humans."

But been on the opposite pole, he put the deaths down to accidents and miss-adventure.

"After all, how many people die in civilized places and you have to take into account that this is a more hazardous environment."

Unfortunately, Browne in his last moments knew.

"I have been dreadfully wrong, the shadows are real and attacking the base."

There were nerve-racking clunks and scrapings outside and these were no misplaced or transported Arctic Bears. The metal sheeting of the base was creaking and groaning as its rivets were popped one by one. Those inside knew that this assault on the fabric of the base was no wind effect; but something alive that was forcing their way in. There were only ten men and women of learning left, their experience with weapons was limited and to their collective horror, all types of communication had ceased. The ten survivors were cut off from the outside World. Not that it mattered; help could not come in time. The outer aluminium skin of the bases wall buckled and sharp claws poked through at many points. Panicked shots were wasted and huge forms entered between the enlarged gaps. The screams began.

Across the globe, unperturbed radio monitors' put the cessation of communication down to secrecy or an experiment. Months later during a break in the weather, the returning Boeing aircraft and its crew found no living thing. The insulated aluminium walls of the structure had long thin

810

scrape marks, rented holes and the inside walls were covered in blood. The leader of the rescue team found that all recording devices had been destroyed and brought the wrong assumption back to his commanders.

"It had to be an attack from a hostile Nation or terrorist organisation."

MOUNT TERROR, 2954 AD.

Now nearly a thousand years later, the huge things that had been on the ice sheet on those two far apart fateful nights became awake. Some event had snatched one of them from its insane mutterings and ended its fitful sleep. This group of monsters were real and had a pecking order. Their appellations were in simple numbers and he been the leader was named "One". His immediate subordinate was "Two" and so on. The others of its kind lounging around the great hall chewing on the bones of seal flesh, long since cleaned of decent meat seem to be affected to a lesser degree. They were more preoccupied with the scarcity of warm-blooded food. It would soon be time to leave their underground caverns and go out to the ice sheet and hunt again. These long-lived beings preferred the easy catch of mankind. In the last thousand years, Human's had been coming to the frozen Continent, but unexplained disappearances had kept their numbers low. Most of those who vanished mysteriously had ended up in the larder of these creatures. But their ruler was certain.

"The time long foretold in our oral histories has arrived. The thief is here!"

What was stolen from them by the deceitful Hybrids had just set foot on the diminishing ice sheet. The presence of all the other parts of the lost technology screamed about its person. The thing exulted.

"Soon it would be returned to us, that which the filthy, devious and untrustworthy Hybrids had stolen from us, because they refused to recognise that their time in the scheme of evolution had passed and it was time for the new order."

Every muscle in the thing's face twitched in anticipation of the restoration of the proper order. Some of its facial sinews did not derive from the normal biology associated with a land mammal of this Planet. This being knew.

"My people's inherent madness will be banished into oblivion once the rest of the secret is delivered to us. Then we will go out into the wider World once again and recover it from the inferior Humans. There will be no room for men on this place that was promised to us."

Unknown to the six parts of the APOCRYPHA'I; it was their craft that had brought down the Platform of Light back in Patagonia, a trap that had been set for millennia. One wanted a tired enemy to confront for he knew that these small Hybrids had an unpredictable strength and brutality about them. His kind had learnt that a long time ago. The remaining members of Naomh's group that had just landed on the Antarctic land mass only saw a land of ice that stretched into a confused panorama. Its breath-taking bleakness overawed them. Cold sunlight fell upon them as deliberations were made. Enhanced monocles had turned into shades of black giving their wearers a protection against the whiteness and not least of all a demonic and soulless looking appearance. An old two-dimensional map brought by the Shaman informed them they had landed on a place called the Ronne ice sheet. The Lenses fetched their advanced version and switched it on with a press of his wristband. When it expanded, it seemed that its clarity and colour in the pristine chill air was more pronounced. Their three-dimensional version gave them the advantage of height and depth and it showed a perpetually snow covered land mass of 13,209,000 sq. kilometres resembling an open fan. Most of its mountains occurred near the coasts and from its snowy desert heartland, rivers of ice inched towards the sea. From the questor's vantage point, all around them was only the whiteness of the rugged icescape. However, even in this most inhospitable place, life thrived. Some hardy mosses survived in the outer rim. But the most visible forms of life were the thousands of Emperor penguins that competed or were eaten by the whales and the fur and hair seals that lived in close proximity to the ice/sea boundary. It was a land of savagery and solace. Ridges of snow, which had been whipped up by a recent blizzard, filled the sterile landscape. Because of the well-insulated outfits, they wore; the group was oblivious to the bitter chill and the way below zero temperatures that would normally freeze the sweat of ill-prepared explorers. As the Continent was tilted towards the Sun at this time of the year, the gang were spared the fifty degrees below temperatures and over a hundred kilometres an hour winds. Not that these extreme conditions could have had any influence on the well-shielded questors. The ferocious freezing gales would now only be a slight hindrance to their movements. Never before in all of the previous searches did the six parts of the Mescal/Amulet experience such a naked pulling. The urge to be whole again had even crept into its Hybrid tool and caused great urgency. But if it was possible, the Shaman's half piece showed even greater exigency. When it was reunited with its twin, then a completed violet piece would join the whole. The completed brilliant mind of an untainted Patriarchi Mescal would be present once again on the Blue orb.

"This is the last piece." Said the internal voice to its host.

Soon all the learning of his race would be present again on this mudball of a Planet. With the intelligent and murderous weapon, he controlled (The Hybrids); the lost beauty of the ALASTHA'I Home Worlds would be restored again. Sharing in the Hybrid experience had convinced the six parts Mescal/Amulet that their creations were more than a match for the tainted CRYSTALOID'I.

"Yes, it will get quite a shock, when its minions are destroyed by our ruthless creations." Of that, the incomplete mind had no doubt. Its bearer focused on the living map and then Naomh pointed to a place that he was

drawn to. Consulting the map, the Shaman nodded.

"It is in the Ross ice sheet in the Mc Murdo sound. The bad news is that it's on the other side of the Continent."

"Typical."

That was the Clerk's voice. A manmade form stood out on the bleak landscape and the searchers found a long abandoned corrugated metal structure. It had been ransacked once; a whistling sound made by the jagged holes in its walls had drawn their attention. Inside, its ancient and scattered contents looked remarkably preserved. Timeless frozen blood stains still covered its solid walls. The place left a bad taste in their mouths, so they hurried on until a vast icy ridge lay before them. Here, the group halted and took account while Naomh focused his attention Northwards or was it Southwards. He was not sure down here. Like the search for the other pieces of the APOCRYPHA'I, this would have taken them decades to locate without the connection between the segments. The internal voice informed Naomh that the original surface of the Continent laid a couple of kilometres below the ice covering.

"I am been drawn deep underground. That is where the final piece of me lies."

He imparted that information to his colleagues and the Shaman who too shared the bond agreed with his assessment. The impetuous Clerk decided to mimic Naomh's reaction when he received such news.

"Oh no. Not more holes in the ground."

His leader glared at him and he shut his trap instantly. Cahill turned towards one comrade in particular and queried.

"I don't fancy walking across that terrain. Especially after that long haul when the big Skimmer went down. Is there anything in your magic box to make things easier?"

One of their technical men replied.

"I am sure that I can accommodate you."

The Engineer produced another strange set of devices from the LAB-CELL. The three globes expanded to vaguely resemble the large projectile shaper borers they had used in the Arizona desert. He pressed a side facet on one of them and to his relief, they became operational. None of them were aware that the blocking device was toned down a bit. The thing that waited deep underground had become an impatient servant to his erratic nature and now eagerly wanted to confront them. A barely discernible panel in the working device slid open and revealed a screen of coloured light. He pressed a code and the contraption expanded to a size capable of seating six people on its exterior. The Light Sled as the Engineer named it hovered a meter off the surface of the frozen ice. He done likewise with the other two and instantly achieved the same result. The long deceased explorer who perished all those centuries ago could not have imagined the equipment available to Naomh and his compliment. If he had seen their marvels of technology, then he would have voiced the opinion.

"If it was that easy, then there would have been no point in doing it at all."

For the questors, there would be no slow and dangerous trek across the frozen wastes or loss of direction. This company would be dependent on dogs and sleighs, mindful of the hazard of thin ice and plunging to their doom in nameless crevices. There would be no frostbite, snow-blindness, hunger or the constant shadow of the bitter cold dogging their every step. All of the companions boarded the contraptions. Naomh, Miriam, the Clerk, the Guide and the Mute mounted one. As always, the man from the Amsterdam Contrib wanted Illeau close. Cahill, Greta, Beersheba and the Rabbi took the second one and the final machine seated the Engineer, his brother, the Lenses, Solomon, Moshe and last but not least their newest companion, the Shaman. Miriam, the Engineer and Greta were at the helm of each contrivance. The controls were fairly basic, they were speech operative. The machines were commanded to move forward and they gradually picked up momentum, as their operatives became familiar with their concept. With the swiftness of thought controlling them, their manoeuvrability was astounding. Speeding along and covering ground effortlessly, Cahill realised.

"If I close my eyes, I could be on some fantastic carnival ride."

The Light Sleds worked on the same basic principal as the Mag-lev, but unlike the former, a fixed route did not confine them. The two big men of their multi-cultural alliance were talking to each other in excited conversation. The Indian and the Persuader were fast becoming good friends. They had the same build, the same temperament and both said a lot without actually using many words. There was another among them who viewed the Shaman in a different light. He was not so much looking for a friend, but an ally against the deviousness of their original and implacable enemy. The Guide was raging an internal debate on whether to let the latest member of their group into his lonely secret.

"I know that the Anschluss is a scheming beast, but it is near impossible that the Shaman is one of their agents. When this part of the mission is over, I will confide in him about my suspicions. And if he agrees, then the Mute is history."

The man from the Amsterdam Contrib had no inclination that the Shaman knew precisely who the traitor was. But the Spirits had told him to stay quiet and not to break the harmony of the group. The Anasazi was a prisoner to their commands. He was also aware the long range plans of the cuckoo's kind. He thought that it was ironic that his people were bound by the same object. But his tribe knew that circumstances altered and he could have told the LYUBINITES with their unflinching credo

"Nothing remains constant; except change itself. Once the frozen rainbow is whole, then the burden of my tribe will be removed. Unlike the

rulers of the Anschluss, it is not the ends to the new beginning that they desire."

The Light Sleds flowed across the inhospitable terrain of glaciers and dry valleys with relative ease and Human spirits soared on the high adrenaline powered ride. The oncoming landscape became whiter and icier, but the use of the monocles made them unaware of this extreme of geography. Somewhere on the journey, they began travelling North instead of south. Eventually hours later, the whispering voice of the APOCRYPHA'I drew them to a river of ice that flowed from a high peak. It was the largest glacier on the Continent. Nobody cared that the first layer of the frozen liquid had been deposited tens of thousands of years ago, long before any of the ALASTHA'I had even set foot on the Planet. The searchers had reached the other side of the Continent and stared out at a place of three mountains. They had arrived on the coast of Victoria land in the Mc Murdo sound. Their final destination lay on a place called Ross Island that appropriately lay in the Ross Sea. According to the map, its co-ordinates were 77 degrees south, 168 degrees east. Ross Island consisted of three Volcanoes' in an area of 2,460 sq. km. The Shaman consulted his laminated map and told them the name of the peak that was drawing Naomh.

"This White Mountain is called Mount Terror."

"Tell me why I am not surprised by that." Muttered the Clerk, he was becoming an irritating master of sarcasm. Mount Terror was a one million year old basaltic shield situated on the eastern side of the island. Numerous cones and domes stood out on its flanks. Most of it was under snow and ice. The Shaman folded his arms and scrutinised the inhospitable elevation with the undesirable name. He told the others.

"We must go under that."

The Engineer simply mentioned, in case anyone had underestimated his ingenuity.

"I have combined the boring feature into these machines, so it will not be a problem for us."

The technical man pressed touched a blue panel and told the other drivers to do the same. Sharp tips at the front of the machines began to rotate independently from their bodies, until they glowed with a white hotness indistinguishable from the surrounding landscape. The radiant tips were pointed downwards as the rear of the glowing devices rose like the trick of levitation that the Lama had taught Naomh. The churning machines burrowed through the frozen ice like a red-hot knife through butter. The manner of locomotion also created an air pocket that followed them downwards, deep into the unknown. It took about a minute to bore through the millennium old permafrost and reach the hard soil of the buried land that had been only seen by drilling scientists and something else. The stubs of the burrowing machines glowed brighter at this juncture and they dug through the frozen basalt rock with relative ease. The angle of descent the shearing light excavated brought them into a gigantic cavern at its floor level. As luck would have it, the descending machines had chosen the perfect angle of inclination. Otherwise they would have found themselves free falling through the empty space from the top of the underground chamber that they now found themselves in and according to the Clerk.

"That would have been nasty indeed."

Huge tapering stalagmites and equally impressive stalactites of erratic dimensions covered the large space. Each unique creation fed from above by the endless dripping water that seeped from the melting ice sheet. Some of the natural sculptures had even joined together and formed solid pillars that suggested falsely that they were holding up the cavern's roof. Naomh ordered them to dismount and keep silent from now on. Low whispers and hand signals were to be the manner of communication from here on in. Leaving the de-activated boring machines in the huge underground space, the wary group entered this Alien World under the volcanic mountain, comforted by a view through weapon sights. The highly alert potholers moved out into a small side channel and found themselves in a labyrinth of frozen chambers. The APOCRYPHA'I guided Naomh to where it was drawn and the tunnel he chose seemed indifferent from the rest. Eventually, the vigilant and heavily armed group worked their way into caverns that were not the result of natural geology. Smooth tunnel linings appeared to have been carved by similar devices to the Engineer's boring machine. The Persuader and the Shaman who had taken the point suddenly raised their hands to signal a halt. There were undecipherable noises up ahead and once again three of them were reminded of the caverns of Mars. But the shapes that were exposed to their scrutiny bore no resemblance to the Flue Stacks or were ever likely too. At first, all except the Indian thought that they had encountered giant Humans of a primitive culture, who dressed in ritual outfits with miniature wings attached. The extremely tall figures, all over three metres high that they were watching moved with pronounced titillation. So from their gathered experience of different cultures, they falsely came to the relieved conclusion that they were actually watching two people, one mounted on the shoulder of the other. But their disbelieving eyes soon confirmed the impossible and it was more incredible that their first assumption. For the inhabitants of this underground place were not Human at all. No, more monsters stirred in these depths and the questor's had just encountered their weirdest and most dangerous adversaries yet. These creatures were entirely alien looking and their stunted wings were real. The colour of these being's skin was a pale blue with blotchy dark patches at irregular spacing's. The Shaman whispered fearfully to his companions.

"Behold these Demons are the shame of my people. Our ancient forefathers called them Gods and worshiped them. But long ago, there was

a parting of our tribe. We know from the words of our ancestors that those who stayed with the Gods suffered a horrible fate, while my descendants fled northwards and continued on the wheel of life. The Anasazi know these creatures as the "Droko.".

The rest of them, thanks to the language globes had a complete knowledge of the Shaman's tongue knew this to mean "Flying Lizard." The Anasazi did not view the three metre high Demons as divine, but the tribes handed down legends did see them as all-powerful and they had a rational fear of them. Young misbehaving children were threatened by a visit from them, if they did not heed the words of their elders. The child Dan George remembered many a sleepless night when he dreamed of these monsters. But, another was caught in an unbelievable quandary. A highly disturbed Agent XIII was not prepared for this, not this early on in the mission or so soon.

"Are these the beings that the great doctor promised who would deliver the secret to us? The Chairman said that we have to get the completed amulet and then call out to them. After receiving our transmission, they would come down from space and save us. But the communication device has not been completed yet."

Then, something clicked.

"The promised ones have to come from space. These creatures cannot be them, they are already here."

The relieved Anschluss Spy was satisfied with that. The being's that could have been the LYUBINITES saviour's minutes before had now become an implacable enemy. The turncoat had also adhered to the doctrine that the Aliens would be Humanlike in appearance. The nearly completed Mescal/Amulet was also unbalanced as it stared aghast through the eyes of the Hybrid, as its presence was drawn towards one of the figures. The shades voice gasped, even its host felt the shock. The being in the Amulet was looking at "Abominations.", creations of half Hybrid and half ALASTHA'I. The APOCRYPHA'I locked and uncompleted mind of the Patriarchi locked reeled at the implications, the absurdity and most of all the impossibility. The primary abhorrence that sat high above its fellows reminded him vaguely of the long departed Cetheren. It was sitting on a throne of bone made from numerous species including Hybrids and directly under a huge mechanical timepiece that had hands made of entire Human skeletons. Its skin was the colour of translucent white. It was not a complete albino; it did have the black splotches of its parent race. The Alien mind wondered.

"Is this abuse of the laws of creation one of Zebulan's warped schemes, left on the Planet before he departed? No, even the DEFILED could not create such a profanity."

While Zebulan did not create these monstrosities, he did know of them. His Hybrid servants had encountered them before and had even named

817

them. His worshipers called them.

"The Rafaim."

Around three thousand previous planetary cycles around the Sun, before the birth of his servant David, some of these Abominations came searching for him. His use of ALASTHA'I technology had drawn some of the more adventurous of these ice dwellers to him. Those that had left their ice bound Continent found him in the narrow coastal area of the Levant. This surprised the seekers as they rightly assumed that whoever they found would have, like them, a dislike of the heat. The Rafaim had a higher toleration to the climate extremes as they were half Hybrid. These migrating ALASTHA'I/Hybrids had an inherent fear of Zebulan. He represented something that disturbed them and the fact that the Winged Alien was kin to their murdered parent. Afraid to confront the DEFILED directly, the Abominations cloaked themselves in black armour and set up a Kingdom on the cooler mountain tops of the Middle East and waged war on neighbouring tribes. Eventually, they subjugated a tribe of sea peoples called the Philistines who had settled in cities along the coastline. At over three metres tall and clothed in Hybrid semblance, they became formidable warriors and were considered to be giant's among those of smaller stature. In their false guise, these mixed species interbred with the Hybrids and their offspring became more and more Human-like. But these diluted mixtures of genes began to have shorter life spans than their parents and their stunted wings vanished into nodules. Because of the conflicting mix of Alien genes, the giants became more aggressive and hostile to their fathers. The original expedition of surviving ALASTHA'I/Hybrids were no match for them, so their creators returned to the ice sheet and those that were left behind became known as the Rafaim among the Hybrid tribes. Over the next few centuries, the bastards evolved into a warrior class, huge in stature and fearsome in appearance. It was mainly because of the strange growths on their faces. Six fingers on each hand (A part of their Alien heritage) became a sign of their divinity. But the Rafaim were few in number. Insufficient offspring were born alive and their scant numbers were depleted in combat with the Hybrids and amongst themselves. Eventually, there was only one left, his name was Goliath and he was the foremost warrior in the land. This giant warrior had no peers and his mere presence on a battlefield guaranteed victory. Back in Jerusalem, Zebulan at last understood the enormity of the Abominations and like the shade of his fellow ALASTHA'I thousands of years later, he was aware that they had to be destroyed. The Winged Alien knew that these absurd creations could be more of a threat to his master's legions of CRYSTALOID'I. The DEFILED knew of the Giant's weakness. So in the guise of an Angel, (A ploy he had used for centuries) Zebulan manifested in the presence of a Hebrew shepherd boy named David, a vassal of the King, Saul. The last of an Alien race had to eliminate the final one of the Abominations, so he tolerated the cooler climate of the winter hills. Cloaked in his heavenly form of duplicity, he gave the Hebrew boy a special stone for his sling; it was a fragile crystal marble laced with deadly seawater. The false Angel then told his enraptured believer how to defeat the Philistine warrior. On the day of the battle above the valley of Elah; two sizeable armies faced each other from opposite hillsides. The huge Rafaim stood alone demanding single combat from any warrior of the opposing army.

None took up the challenge.

As the sun rose higher and the heat of the day intensified, Goliath kept taunting the Hebrews by thrashing his huge spear against his equally large metal shield.

Still none among his foes took up the challenge.

Then to the horror of the Hebrew king, a small untrained peasant left the ranks of his massed force. The ill-equipped youth made his way down the hillside to confront the giant Philistine warrior. Saul was aghast as the two sized up, the comparison in height and physique was laughable. The Rafaim warrior was heavily armoured. He had a wicked looking sheathed sword, his six knuckles greaves held a large heavy spear and a priceless iron shield, while the shepherd boy was unprotected and carried only a leather sling. There was great laughter from his enemy's hillside at their foes champion. As the unwitting tool of a false messenger of Jehovah confronted Goliath in singe combat, the former animal herder turned warrior launched the stone from his leather sling. It struck his huge imposing protagonist in the centre of his forehead and shattered, covering Goliath's face with acidic sea water. There was still enough of the ALASTHA'I make up the "Rafaim" and he went down in a heap, screaming and clutching at his steaming face in agony. David rushed over and decapitated the agonised Philistine before he could recover. The poor shepherd boy became the leader of his people and built a great walled city over Zebulan's base. The Winged Alien was astounded by the belief he had instilled in the Hebrew boy.

"They can overcome any obstacle, if they believe that a Deity commanded it."

The last of the DEFILED was convinced the he had now rid the World of the Abominations, but he had been wrong. He knew nothing of the host back in the frozen Southern land mass. Supreme in his arrogance, he never even questioned at how they had come about. He had thought them some Hybrid mutation that their creators had not accounted for. Now, five millennia later, the six parts Mescal/Amulet using the Hybrids senses began to collate data from their surroundings and it noticed from their covert position that these creatures had a basic version of his races technology. The uncompleted Patriarchi had to access it. Unlike Zebulan, he had to find out, how these Abominations came about. Then, he would use the Hybrid under his control to destroy them and this infernal place.

The unsettled voice within advised Naomh to remain covert until it decided on the best course of action. Time wore on as if it tried to put its tattered fabric together until all the ALASTHAI/Hybrid's appeared to fall into a fitful sleep. In fact, some link through their initial contact with the sought after technology allowed them to search for those who they knew to be on the frozen Continent. The twisted creations had no inkling that the questors were already here and were focusing their attention in the wrong place. It was time for the infiltrators of this Alien domain to proceed about their surreptitious business. Using valuable energy, the uncompleted APOCRYPHA'I over rid his host's conscious and shut out his presence. To the others unaware of the switch, they became astounded when a pencil thin beam of multi-coloured light emerged from Naomh's chest and shot towards a bank of strange frozen formations behind the grotesque throne. Some of his companions were about to interfere, but were stopped by the Shaman.

"This is supposed to happen. Leave the Rainmaker be. We will watch out for him."

"You heard what he said, take up covering positions." Miriam ordered.

Naomh's companions took up a defensive cordon around their trance like leader. On another realm, the six parts Mescal/Amulet commanded the information system to operate, fully believing that the machine would obey his instruction.

It refused to comply.

Unperturbed, it tried again.

Still no reply?

Again, it ordered the machine to allow it access.

Nothing!

The presence within the amulet pondered why the machine was refusing it and with insight the answer came to it. These creatures were a mixture of ALASTHA'I and Hybrid.

"And that was supposed to be genetically impossible." A long ago voice reminded the former Patriarchi.

But what was once infeasible was now a fact. So the six parts Mescal/Amulet needed the combined might of his and the Hybrid's being to access the machine. The Alien presence released his host's confined conscious, joined his uncompleted mind with his tool and together both intricately different beings commanded the machine to operate.

"It works!"

Intrigued now as the acquirement of new information, no matter how unpleasant was still in the life vapours of an ALASTHA'I. The combined conscious proceeded and the information unit whirred into action. Globes of varying hues appeared and one was selected. On command, it gave up the information of the origins of the Abominations. The cavern vanished from view; its volcanic formed background was replaced with the scene of the brightness of his races last day, minutes from departure from this Planet. To re-witness that morning so many millennia ago with such clarity and all the familiar faces touched the six parts Mescal/Amulet to the core. The once ALASTHA'I faltered. The combined intellect saw a resigned Cathabad standing alone with his beautiful wings folded on the snow covered plain watching many blurs streaked through the sky, seconds before leaving the atmosphere. The six parts Mescal/Amulet missed his own wings as much as he missed his kin. The Alien part shared Cathbad's pain, then realised.

"If the other hundred of my race have remained behind as planned; then my former friend must be still on this World, simply because of his longevity. So; he must know I am assembling. Why does he not seek me out?"

Something within the internal voice told it that it might not want the answer. Then, the reason dawned.

"I must be complete."

The required information had correlated. The image shifted to the orbital craft as they docked with the Spacegrub that was hidden behind the moons of Jupiter. The six parts Mescal/Amulet was confused.

"How could this bastard unit have that information?"

On board the EXPECTATION, everything was prepared for the next stage of their flight from the "INIQUITY.". Those who were supposed to be were aboard, so the hyperspace drive was initiated and the craft started its approach into deep space. Sometime during the acceleration as they were passing the last rocky Planet of the system, a monumental event occurred. The huge ship began to break up and tear itself apart. The six parts Mescal/Amulet could not take his awareness from the unfolding tragedy. It shared Naomh's horror as the ship was engulfed in a massive explosion and disintegrated. Its nuclear core slammed into the outer World on the very fringes of the yellow Stars influence and the orbiting rock shattered in a cataclysmic eruption. The mini nova filled the emptiness of space and the Solar System changed in appearance. The furthermost out Planet split into numerous icy rocks of varying sizes.

"This cannot be. Our technology is infallible."

But there was salvation as one pod broke free as the Mothership was no more. Cetheren had been preparing to go back to the Planet, for his task had consumed his own soul and he had to see it to the end. The part creator of the Hybrids still had his dark secret, for against his nature, he had withheld a piece of the APOCRYPHA'I. Without that segment, their whole plan would be to no avail. He was in the process of ejecting in a pod as the ship exploded. Unknown to Cetheren, he; the intended saviour of his race had caused their ultimate destruction. The emerging EGO had latched onto his dissatisfaction like a beacon guiding ships home. It influenced the very disturbed mind to launch at the critical time of hyper drive initiation.

Firmly entrenched in madness, the devious Entity caused him to abandon protocol and operate the forbidden system. The backlash of power during the prohibited launch was responsible for the Spacegrub's annihilation. Back on the Planet, Zebulan, thousands of years back in the past was riveted to the scene; his master made him watch these events that were occurring in real time to him. It was a lesson of its power and it frightened the life out of its servant. Unknown to his expired kin, the deviant knew that Cathbad and ninety-nine of his former race had been left behind to monitor their plan. He could not enter the mound, so he intercepted communications from the Spacegrub to them. He would continue doing so until the agreed time of transmission cessation began. In a split second, circumstances had changed; he now had a different task. The EGO'S servant would convince the Earth bound Aliens that their fellow ALASTHA'I were still alive and as all their energy was focused inwardly on the Hybrid's World, his task was made simpler. Along with Zebulan, the visual narrative of the bastard information unit far into the future followed this single pod. The shade of the uncompleted Patriarchi was not able to continue, so it paused the image as profound shock gripped its encapsulated soul, intending to send it back to more terrible madness than before. Mescal's presence was unable to continue. The gelded Hybrid part urged it to discover what happened, with the vulgar optimism of their bastard race.

"We have only seen this single image and we can be sure other escape pods left the ship."

Clutching to this train of thought, as the alternative would crush him; the Alien presence commanded the video image to continue. Both beings followed the recorded narrative of the surviving pod back towards the Planet; it had just departed from. But as the escaping vessel was streaking away from the doomed Spacecraft, pieces of the fragmenting vessel cannoned into the pod just before it attained orbit. Out of control, the escape ship hurtled through the atmosphere and smashed into the frozen southern continent in an eruption of light. Zebulan who had been in a similar situation knew from the craft's velocity that no-one could emerge alive from that sort of impact, so he left the scene. From the hissing and smouldering wreckage crawled a vapour leaking Cetheren. Mescal's former student was in luck; he had landed in a place with a temperate climate. Just as he was dragging himself to safety, something with the odds of millions to one occurred. One of the Cryostats from the genetic engineering labs of the obliterated Mothership came speeding towards the Planet with a series of sonic booms and survived the re-entry. But the combination of speed and passing through the Earth's protective shield changed the micro-organisms aboard. The small chamber impacted away from Cetheren and above ground, but a localised mist of its mutated cargo infused into every pore of his tortured body while he remained oblivious.

The staggering Alien had entered a state of chromosomal aberration. He was unaware of the profound occurrence as he had become unconscious from the loss of life giving vapours. The radiation from the localised explosion spread out in a centralising mist across a twenty kilometre radial of the frozen Continent. A few hours after the invisible barrier coalesced and as the light of the short Antarctic Autumn day was fading fast, a group of fur clad Hybrids appeared. Their curiosity awoken by two stars falling to earth. One of them insisted.

"Our verbal legends told us that the God's had brought us to this place by flying shards of hardened ice. And now, those that we worship must have returned."

The inquisitive hunters entered the same condensed mist that bathed Cetheren, unaware that it had the same profound effect on their genetic makeup. The normal process of evolution of the Planet had been circumvented once again, though this time it had been accidental. The natives rescued their Deity and brought him to their nomadic village at the edge of the ice sheet. Cetheren never fully regained his entire faculties and remained forever in a state of delirium.

This was the origin of the horror.

The Hybrids built their divinity a permanent home of stone carved out of solid rock. As the comatose God lived out his life in an endless sleep, the short-lived Hybrids subsisted generation after generation and continued to worship at his feet. Centuries later after the initial contact; one of their Shaman's had a vision and he explained its portent.

"Our slumbering God needs a wife. This will allow him to converse with us mere mortals."

So it was decreed that one of the females was to marry the Deity and when her life expired, then another of their women would be chosen. The selected young female was shaved of all body hair and painted blue with dark splotches over her feminine areas. This ritual was performed for the next few hundred generations of the ice dwellers. It brought prosperity to the tribe and its numbers increased tenfold, but the God never spoke to them. Then, the good years changed, as it was with fickle deities. At this time of desperation, an extremely pretty young girl appropriately called "Blue Seal." was the latest bride of the God when disaster struck. The animals of the Ocean that came on to the ice sheet to rest, breed and rear their young began to decrease and then vanish altogether. The animal's counterparts in the freezing blue sea also began to decline. The loss of the seals in particular was a disaster, for their flesh provided food, their skin provided clothes and their blubbers provided their oil for cooking and light. All in all, the basic necessities for survival on this harsh land were eroding fast. The tribe faced annihilation and would be forced to move back to the other Continent from which they originally fled from. None of the tribe knew why their ancestors had settled here, their oral histories were vague about that. This would be a major hardship as their descendants had walked across the ice sheet and now there was a narrow channel of open sea between the two landmasses. The Elders were beside themselves with worry, they were no seafarers. Their seal skinned kayaks hugged the frozen shore and never crossed open seas. The Shaman pleaded with their sleeping God for salvation, but he did not answer. When things were at their nadir, Blue Seal had a revelation that would save her people. The dream voice told her.

"You must lie with the God and his child will save the tribe."

The teenage girl could not reveal her plan as it would be treated as sacrilege and in all probability her life would be forfeit. She resolved on a fait accompli.

"If the tribe are confronted the seed of the Winged God been in her blessed womb, then they dare not harm her or my child."

She decided to let her two sisters, "Little Penguin." and "White Seagull." into her audacious scheme. They were of the one mind with her and their role was to entice the two guards that watched over the Gods chambers away while she performed the coupling. Over the intervening weeks her two siblings wormed their way into the affections of two of the regular guards, "Sleek Albatross." and "Large Mink." During one flirtation, the former unable to subdue his lust told one of the sisters of a night that he and his friend would be watching over the God. This was betrayal of the most serious kind, for both men were already married and infidelity was punished severely. So secrecy was paramount. The two lustful guards were mindful of the consequences, if they were discovered. But the promised delights outweighed the risk and their male hormones were in overdrive. The two unmarried sisters were also the two most beautiful women of the tribe, at fifteen and sixteen summers; they were well into womanhood. The night that they and the two guards had chosen for the illicit rendezvous turned out to be an appalling one; weather wise. White Seagull had slipped a drug into the evenings sparse meal of the now rare Muktuk and the rest of their family were in a sleep that would last till early morning. Neither girl had partaken of the whale blubber; their stomachs were too tight with anticipation. The two kinswomen waited an hour to be certain the drug worked and then they would make their way to Blue Seal's stone dwelling. As the Gods bride, she dwelt in his abode known as "The Grotto." This, the only permanent construction of the ice dwellers was the home of the God; fifty smoothly polished steps led to a cave that had been cut out of the chilled mountain rock. This stone had permanent permafrost icing even during the short season of what passed here for summer. Centuries later, far to the north and in another landscape, the dwellings of the Anaszai's hidden village would mimic this structure. The falling snow battered the sprawling tent village and a chilling Antarctic fog shrouded the vicinity as the two sisters emerged from their father's tent and made their way between the skin covered dwellings. The two women were sure they would remain unobserved as nobody would venture out on a night like this. Just to be certain, both females clothed themselves in white fur seal skins and wore their newest mukluks; footwear that was so soft as to muffle their footsteps. Blending in with the snowy night, they skirted across the encampment like a wind driven snowdrift and they arrived at the Grotto's entrance unseen. After climbing the stone steps that were continuously brushed of falling snow, White Seagull pushed the skin flap aside. Fiery braziers hung at either side of the opening, the orange flame constantly fuelled by precious Whale oil. The two women left the flickering fires to struggle against the howling wind and entered the quietness of the Grotto. Blue Seals living quarters were inside the Cave, but adjacent to the Gods. She was only allowed into her divine husband's presence when accompanied by the Shaman of the tribe. These adulterous men who they were to tryst with stood tall in front of the God's chambers anxiously awaiting the night's promise. Their older sister waited entirely naked, in silent anxious excitement behind the precious timber door of her room for her sisters to distract the guards. The inside of the Grotto smelt of the wood that it was built from, this extremely scarce resource came from driftwood that the various currents brought to their shores. Looking into an even more priceless metal mirror that hung man high from a wall (One of the benefits of been the God's bride.), she admired the perfection of her glistening blue skin and her small heaving bosom. Her brown teats stood hard and pert, mainly because of her growing excitement and not from the cold. Blue Seal like all of the brides of the sleeping God before her had all vestiges of Primate hair removed from her statuesque figure. Her tattooed skin also mimicked the hues of her betrothed. She trembled, not for the first time that night as the mysteries between man and a woman were unknown to her. She then realised that the involuntary shudder came from a cool breeze infringing on the warmth of her room as her two sisters had just opened the main door to the Grotto. The oldest of her female siblings closed the entrance door. Then, both temptresses stood there and faced the two sentries. Brazenly, they beckoned for the men to come over to them. But now, both of the guards became caught between their sworn duty and the offered delights. The sentries remained steadfast and refused to move. The two desirable women became unsure, as the two men now seemed intent on their duty. Then as if from a choreographed routine, both girls smirked at each other, positive in their womanhood and turned away from their admirers. With deft fingers they undid the sinew strings that held each other's garments together. The clothes slid easily off their oiled and heavily perfumed bodies and fell to the wooden floor. Two rounded pale buttocks greeted the two open-mouthed guards. Their erotic display was too much for any red-blooded male, especially since the men of the tribe outnumbered the females by three to one. Leaving their posts and discarding their heavy spears, they ran to the naked girls. The older sister had left the timber door slightly ajar and she waited until she heard the frantic sounds of coupling. Then, the God's bride opened the door fully and slid silently into the corridor. With baited breath, she risked a glance towards the fornicating couples. Four frolicking ivory skinned bodies greeted her. Her two sisters lay astride the now two naked guards, who were only intent on one thing. Soft moans escaped from her sister's lips. Excitement flowed through her sexual organs at the sight of the lovemaking; it only enhanced what the evening held for her. She hurried to the Gods chambers intent on consummating her marriage. Blue Seal gently pushed open the door and it creaked noisily. She froze in place, expecting shouts of alarm from the cavorting guards. But those two were lost to a males basic urges. She entered her husband's chamber. The pale blue winged God looked magnificent in his slumber and she wondered.

"Will his body be warm?"

She hesitated, now her naivety in the ways of man and woman came to the fore. For Blue Seal was undoubtedly a virgin. The dominant female of the village, the Chief's haggard wife had expertly checked this out, before any of their females could become the beloved of the God. But desire overcame her trepidation. Like every pre-sexual adolescent, she knew the theory, but lacked the experience. Then she became perplexed.

"Does the God have the right tool for the job?"

Looking down on the prone immortal, she removed the loincloth that covered his private parts with trembling hands. Blue Seal stared aghast, for there was no manhood to be seen. After all, nobody in the tribe ever mentioned seeing it.

"But they always referred to the God as a man and a woman could not become the bride of another woman."

Instinct took over and the young adolescent climbed on top of the inert form and straddled above where she assumed his sexual organ to be. Blue Seal rubbed her sex rhythmically against his icy soft body. She gasped at the shock of the cold of her husband's form and then forced a huge intake of breath again as a large crystal penis emerged from somewhere inside his body. (That the Hybrid's and the ALASTHA'I shared the same organ for procreation was a source of discomfort among the Aliens and a fact that they did not like to dwell on.) The God's manhood was she guessed at least three times larger than the most endowed man of the tribe. She had watched couples mating without their knowledge and she knew that the females of the village would rant in envy at her lover's impressive specimen. She mounted the erect member and stifled a grunt as it penetrated her and broke her hymen. Blood flowed freely between her legs and oozed on to the God and entered his pores. Far into the future, the watching six parts Mescal/Amulet screamed at this ultimate violation. Back in the past, the pain of penetration gave way to an unbelievable pleasure as Blue Seal thrust more frantically on top of the huge organ. The penis could not enter her womb fully; it was just too big. The God's manhood went limp and the straddling female betrayed her orgasm with a scream, just as she heard the climaxes of the two guards outside the chamber. In the moment of Cethern's ejaculation, his piece of the APOCRYPHA'I split in half. Far into the future, its other parts screamed, especially the Shaman's violet piece. Chief Dan George staggered back at his segments reaction. The bearer of the other half part stirred awake with a start. A large smile crossed the bastard life-forms features.

"At last! The fools are here."

Far back in the past, Blue Seal let her ragged breaths subside. Reality kicked in, for now it would be time to atone for her actions. Her mind raced at the implications of what she had done.

"I have the seed of our God inside me."

Of this she was certain, as she had felt his maleness shoot into her as her vaginal muscles had clamped around his manhood. Blue Seal fled back to her room. But the now two dressing guards saw her and more unfortunately for them, so did the tribes Shaman who had risen from a fitful sleep that urged him to check on the God. He saw them all. The long dead spiritual leader saw the flushed naked girl coming from the sacred room and with horrified insight, he knew what had happened. He shouted an alarm; Large Mink panicked and threw his spear at the priest. It struck him in the chest and killed him instantly. Other warriors rushed in, saw the mortality wounded man and overpowered the two guards. The murderer of the Shaman and his accomplice were put to death, more for failing to watch over the God than for their infidelity and the killing of their holy man. They were bound and gagged and hurled into the frozen sea. Both of the unfortunate men's wives and possessions were given to two unmarried males, Blue Seals sisters were disgraced and would spend the rest of their summers as spinsters, but as she had rightly assumed the tribe were afraid to punish her. She, like Cetheren had inherited the genetic changes of the localised mist that had been emitted from the falling chunk of space debris and they had become sexually compatible. The watching Mescal was unaware of this incredible fact. Within two months the girl had become noticeably pregnant. A Pow-wow was called to resolve the issue of the God bearing female. Some thought the girl's actions were right while others refused to worship the unborn life-form. The tribe split and went to war. On one side were those who believed in the mating of the God and his wife while on the opposing side they were those that abhorred the idea. (Those that rejected it were the forefathers of the Chief Dan George's people). Each of the two parties, now sworn enemies had a piece of the shattered piece of the APOCRYPHA'I. The six parts Mescal/Amulet agreed with the Red Indian's ancestors: for different reasons, it must be said. Those that disagreed were in the minority and were driven inland to the frozen wastes. On the day of Blue Seal's labour, vast shoals of fish and seal herds returned. The villagers believed the birth was blessed with this gift and they had made the correct choice.

A year later, hunger had made those that had fled inland return to the coast for reconciliation. What they found made some of them run back in to the interior and certain death. Others built boats of hide and attempted to cross the frozen sea from the other side of the Continent. This desperate course of action was given to the new Shaman by a voice from the Spirit World. Following Blue Seals example, all of the females of the tribe had mated with their sleeping divinity and in that short time, the new children had matured into fully formed adults. There were now many Gods, but no people. Chewed Human bones that lay scattered among animal remains offered a clue to what happened. The Gods who had become adults in that short year and had killed and eaten their relatives for sustenance. The growing God's had inherited a madness at their creation and a taste for flesh. Those that had escaped by sea with their half of the APOCRYPHA'I reached the tip of South America and never returned to the ice World again. These descendants of the Anasazi numbered two hundred and ninety three men, women and children. Those that remained in the interior of the frozen landmass were systematically chased down and devoured by the new race, they had inadvertently created. When the last of the tribe that remained on the icy Continent was hunted down and consumed, the Abominations then retreated into these huge underground caverns that had one exit from where they ventured out to find prey. With all the other Hybrids killed or fled, they fed on the ice sheets natural wildlife. They multiplied and set up this Kingdom of madness. Their leap into advanced technology began with the discovery of Cetheren's globes and his violet half-piece of the Mescal/Amulet. Somehow, these twisted creatures managed to access the wonders within and with their Hybrid ingenuity and ALASTHA'I genius, these mixed beings built an advanced outpost of technology. It was superior to all models on the Planet, except two, Zebulan and Cathbad's exiled group. But the madness of what they were lurked around the very fringes of their existence, becoming more extreme as the centuries passed. The ALASTHA'I/Hybrids built no lasting cites or monuments. They were stuck in a circle of decay waiting for the return of what had been stolen from them. The fact that they raged against this perceived crime was a twisted impression that they had retrieved from the madness of their father. Then, the six parts Mescal/Amulet witnessed the final horror. A century later, in a fit of rage and insanity at their limited existence, the leader who named himself; One smashed the crystal body of his parent to bits in a tantrum that owed itself to its Human half, or did it? The Hybrid part within the melded watcher intruded with its own assumption.

"If you live by the sword, then you die by the sword."

The advanced Being could find no fault with that primitive logic and the grieving Patriarchi knew.

"There will be no more days of tranquillity for Cetheren, watching the falling globules of methane refracting into prisms of many hues on the shoreline of his cherished ocean. My temperamental student will never again swim in the Endless Sea of greenness or glide through the air."

As he grieved for another of his race, the revelations got worse. The ALASTHA'I without a physical presence located the creed of their beliefs and the six parts Mescal/Amulet was shook to the core of its preserved being. The Abominations had the final half piece of him, but these creatures of madness desired the rest, so they could escape from the insanity that afflicted them. But the uncompleted APOCRYPHA'I knew it was a futile hope.

"Their inherited derangement would consume me and I would revert back to a madness greater than the one that I have freed myself from. These Abominations have to be destroyed and the Hybrids under my influence will be the tools for this necessary act of extermination."

With this new purpose, it began to sever the connection with the information until that had revealed so much grief. His watching comrades saw the beam of light retract and retreat back into Naomh's chest, the six parts Mescal/Amulet had learned all that he had wanted to know. It had been the Abominations technological craft that had brought down the Platform of Light and the source of it had to be destroyed. The Hybrid host had shared in the unfolding events and he asked the presence within.

"Are those winged monsters part of the threat to mankind?"

For only the second time the APOCRYPHA'I failed to answer a direct question from Naomh. It removed all traces of the revelations from its host.

"We must find the source of their power and destroy it."

A logical guess was that sunlight was the source of their power. Moving cautiously around the large underground chamber, the questor's found the source of the Abominations power. It was a huge triangular crystal prism. But as they debated on how to destroy it, one came flying through the air on stunted wings and sharp talons. The thing possessed of titanic strength moved with incredible speed despite its disordered gait. It ploughed into the group knocking them over as if they were skittles of flesh and bone. It spoke in an ancient Human language; the Shaman recognised it without the aid of a translator.

"Where is it?" Demanded the thing.

It attacked again; hardened crystalline talons ripped through Naomh's protective garments and revealed the living amulet. The monster paused in its fury and stared at the uncompleted APOCRYPHA'I in wonderment. But One knew it was not whole. Twelve Alien fingers reached for it and the other six parts shuddered. In a scream of despair, it popped out of Naomh's chest. It was now in the creatures hands. Its original bearer flopped to the rock floor, he became an empty vessel. His recovered comrades aimed their weapons at the monstrosity, but the Anasazi shouted.

"Don't shoot; if it dies we have no idea what its effect would be on the frozen rainbow."

The new holder's shout of joy turned into rage, its heirloom would not assimilate. As six and one half segments tried to meld, the uncompleted piece caused a backlash and knocked out the three metre thing in a flash of stunning light. It stumbled away and fell down a borehole and vanished from sight. The Shaman leapt forward and grabbed the violet shimmer and the block of six pieces from the thrashing monster before it went over the edge and into oblivion. He knelt alongside their unmoving leader and reinserted all of his original pieces, Naomh jolted to life like a recharged battery. The Indian joined his two violet pieces and retained them. The Patriarchi within and its dazed host exclaimed.

"Treachery!"

They had no time to confront the situation. All of them heard the sound of a vengeful host coming towards them. The Humans opened fire with everything they had, but their fire seemed to hit a shimmering shield and vectored towards the tunnels walls. The Droko had a version of their TORT-CAM. It did appear to be a limited curve and not a complete sphere and it was pushed ahead of the converging host. Some of their explosive rounds were getting through. Due to the scope of the tunnel, very few of the stunted winged monstrosities were been taken out and they were inexorably closing the gap on them. The Engineer had one explosive device left, but it would only take down a few of the weird creatures. Then, the Lenses had an idea; he whispered it to their munitions expert. The man from the Madrid Contrib nodded in agreement and turned towards the Clerk.

"Give me your collection of coins."

"What?"

"Your pieces of metal."

"No way!" He had already lost his first collection.

"They are useless baubles and will be no good to you if that lot catch up with us. I can use them as shrapnel."

The inhuman shrieks behind the shield grew louder. Those frightening howls immediately convinced the Clerk and regretfully, he handed over his precious collection of hundreds of discs contained in his own globe of light. He held one single token back. Quickly, the Engineer fashioned a crude bomb, loaded it into the chamber of his gun and fired it at the ceiling in front of the advancing shield. To the approaching Droko, it appeared to be a dud; it stuck in the tunnel ceiling without going off. Then, the devious firer made it look as if his weapon was misfiring and threw it to the ground. The gleeful host surged forward. When the mob of tightly packed Alien things was exactly under the failed charge, the Engineer retrieved his weapon and pressed a panel on the gun. In an instant, there was a deafening blast and quite a number of the Droko were pepper dashed with numerous currencies from the questor's travels. The red hot pieces of the alloys cut through them and halted the chase. Suddenly, there was a great rumble and the frozen basalt of the tunnel lining cracked like parchment, collapsed and blocked the Alien chasers. The reprieved and isolated questors fled upwards to where they had left the tunnel excavators. The borers in the underground cavern were mounted quickly and sped up through the already cut escape route. Out on the surface, the escapee's remounted their Light Sleds and hurried towards the coast. At the shoreline of a peninsula on the edge of the Larsen ice-shelf that looked like a spine that had been stripped of its flesh, the Shaman took out his joined violet piece. Naomh was expecting a confrontation, one that he did not want. But thankfully he and the internal voice had misjudged the Anasazi. Since the brown man had melded them, the feeling of abject despair emanating from each of them ebbed away in what felt like a long sigh of relief. There was total exultation as it became one with its separated half. In an act of reverence, the Indian handed them to their intended host. He explained.

"It was up to me to join those two, the violet piece is now ready to merge with the whole. "

A contrite Naomh received the violet hue and joined its pulsating form with the other six pieces and the preceding elation was washed away into insignificance.

THE SEVEN SEGMENTS OF THE APOCRYPHA'I HAD BEEN JOINED AND THE WHOLE WOULD BECOME GREATER THAN ITS PARTS.

Patriarchi Mescal was complete again and his madness was banished into a bad memory. Although he still had no physical presence, his great mind had been returned to sanity again. His host echoed his Alien counterpart's sentiments with a physical rapture.

"I am completed!"

When the bearer of the seven parts of the unified item of their quest recovered, Cahill asked.

"Can we return home?"

"Yes. Our quest has finally finished."

There was communal joy; then a sudden noise alerted them to danger. The huge form of One stood facing them blocking their escape route to the sea. During its plunge, its stunted wings had broken its fall. But the impact had stunned the creature. He had sped here in a violent rage to confront them. Behind them came the howl of hundreds more of the Demons, they had found another way around the tunnel blockage. Trapped between the hammer and the anvil, the frantic questors were transfixed. Miriam ordered a defensive line while Naomh and the Anasazi turned to confront the towering Abomination that blocked their escape. Immediately, the frozen air filled with the sound of a fire-fight, gunfire was a rare sound to this frozen Continent. Red fire sparked from their guns. The maddened Droko had no shields and the odd one started to go down, but their erratic movement was making them hard to hit. Likewise the single monstrosity that faced their two other comrades dodged most of the projectiles and was once again on top of them. Standing at the vanguard of the bearer of the APOCRYPHA'I was the Shaman. The Indian stood with open arms, his flailing brown jacket covering his sides like a wing. To the man behind him, Chief Dan George looked like a Human version of the thing that buzzed towards him. The man from a culture that Naomh could once never imagined turned to him and uttered the most serious words that he had ever heard from him.

"Now my journey is ending. You must take the frozen rainbow and show it to my people. So they will know that their shame is ended."

The Shaman looked a changed man; before Naomh could stop him, he issued forth a war cry with the name of a former chief of the Chiricahuh Apaches.

"Geronimo."

Emboldened by the chant, the warrior charged the bane of his people. Despite its colossal strength, the Shaman grappled with the Droko and he was holding his own. Like his long bloodline, he was strong and resilient; he was the epitome of the noble savage. While man and monster were intertwined, Naomh was trying to get a clean shot. The One took out a swirling globe and focused it at him, he recognised a familiar technology.

"Oh, oh!"

That was all he had time to utter, his weapon fell to the snowy waste and once again he fought a battle of the mind. The orb that was trying to pull the completed APOCRYPHA'I from his chest and it was beginning to succeed. Naomh despaired.

"If the thing achieves its ambition, then we are doomed."

But, the Shaman like the ancient king of Israel also had a secret weapon; salt water. He had concealed this from the others, mostly because he was unsure of its effect. It had been in the curious vial that hung around his neck. Snatching and smashing the vial, he rubbed the saline liquid into the Droko's face as the talons tore into his body. The half Alien collapsed clutching its face, but the Indian was still in its embrace. The Shaman had countless cuts to his body and his insides were busted up. He knew he was dying, the Spirits were never wrong. His wise; but pain filled eyes looked at Naomh. He grimaced.

"I cannot hold it much longer; it is getting the upper hand. I am your sacrificial lamb. You know what to do."

"I do!"

Naomh despaired as his hand gripped the shrunken TORT-CAM and brought it forth. The stunted winged ALASTHA'I/ Hybrid hesitated; it was mesmerised by the lost technology. Seizing on the monster's indecision, he flung it at the startled Alien who still clutched his friend. As it flew through the icy air, the visible shield expanded and it impacted on the two of them. The globe of light sucked them in. The chest wrenching pressure was off Naomh; he rushed forward, shrunk the cloaking device and hurled it into the icy depths of the southern sea. Contact with the saline water made its interior transparent. Still entwined with the beast, the Shaman appeared to be at peace and as he vanished from sight his last pain filled words to the companions were.

"Do not grieve for me. A river has an ending as well as a beginning. I have run my course, achieved my destiny and made peace with our dead. I have erased my people's transgression and put it to rest. The Spirits are contented at last."

With those words, his eyes saw the beauty of the World for the last time as he waited for the passing to the happy hunting grounds in the sky. The Guidex sphere sank to the bottom of the Ocean and the Anasazi was really gone. Seeing the leader alone, the remainder of his bunch retreated to his side, still keeping the maddened horde at bay. Then with great urgency Naomh told them as he pointed to the icy sea's frozen depths where the Shaman and the monster had been interred.

"We must leave this place before the other Demons get here and rescue that thing from the TORT-CAM."

The internal voice responded.

"They cannot, the saline water is deadly to them. Quickly activate the Platform of Light, it will operate now."

As the hoard of the Droko came over the ridge, Miriam gave the order to fire and weapons thundered. But it took a lot of firepower just to bring a few of them down.

"We cannot hold them, they will break through, let's get out of here."

Then the frozen air filled heavy arms fire and thundering artillery arced towards the converging host of monsters. They began to go down in greater numbers.

"What the fuc--!" Mouthed Cahill.

"Who cares, let's get out of here." Roared Greta.

The Engineer had already activated the Platform of Light, he had responded to Naomh's command. He was extremely relieved when it worked. What all but one did not know was. *"Another squad of camouflaged PREVENTIVES have engaged the Droko."*

The covert attackers had parachuted here while the questors were underground on the orders of the Chairman. None of their intended saviours wore a recognisable uniform, so the Spy was the only one who was aware of who the rescuers were. But their arrogant saviours had made a terrible mistake. They had let the host get too close before opening fire and like the last squad, that had come to their rescue on Mars, they too were been decimated. The ever adaptable monsters picked up fallen weapons and turned them on the Anschluss soldiers. The beleaguered defenders took advantage of this unexpected intervention. Miriam took command and repeated Greta's advice.

"It's time to get out of here."

Just before, they leapt on board the hovering platform; the Clerk bent down and snatched something from the ice. It was the remains of the beaded necklace of the Shaman. He put it into a pocket and leapt onto the hovering light. As the escapee's glided over the icy water and out of hearing of the enraged Demons and the firefight, the Mute was doubly disgusted by the loss of the TORT-CAM. He had planned to steal it and use it as a place of ambush and murder. Still, he was grateful, he had seen the demise of a Demon and that nearly made up for the loss of the invisible shield. The Clerk was equally upset about the loss; he had been taking holo pictures and collecting currency units from all of the strange lands they had been in. It would be proof to those in the Anschluss that he had been outside its boundaries. But these had been left in the expanding globe and were now at the bottom of the icy sea. Still, he had one single currency token from the Mountain Kingdom. The remaining fourteen questors were now down to the bare essentials, all they had was what was in their packs. Luckily for the Rabbi, three of them contained his kosher food. It he used it sparingly, it would last a few weeks. They had lost their irreplaceable sanctuary, it had served them well, but what neither of them knew was that the trapped Droko was stuck at the bottom of the sea till the end of its days. It could not venture forth as the ALASTHA'I parts of its make-up would perish in the salty sea and by the same consequence, the others of its kind could not rescue it. Unheard, One roared in madness from the inside of its underwater prison. There was an equal howl of rage far away in the sandy wastes of North Africa as Zebulan's uncharacteristic outburst caused his cabal of Knights to cower in terror. His master's enemies had gained an invaluable tool in their war against his patron.

As the Platform of Light and its fourteen passengers sped away from the frozen Continent with the questors and the now completed APOCRYPHA'I, the Alien presence imbedded in Naomh's physique now knew the answer to the riddle of the images in the temple and etched into the Chilean desert.

"The Hybrids did not remember us; it was a memory of the ALASTHA'I /Hybrid that had terrorised the people who had once lived on the shores of the large southern land mass. When they fled across the icy sea and found new homes, the aboriginal people cast images in stone and sand in a bid to appease the terrible Gods, so they would not come in search of them. What the Hybrids did not know was that they were relatively safe in their steaming jungles. But the Shaman's people with their piece of the Amulet had scattered even farther and had for a while interbred with the natives to

conceal their lineage and their possession of a piece of me."

It felt to Naomh that its semblance seemed more complete.

"You are now a who not an it."

"I am!" Exulted the true mind voice of Mescal.

Hours later, the lighthouse keeper outside Penguin Shores was shocked to see the Platform of Light glide over the thawing out sea and head inland a kilometre down the rugged coast. Back on the furthest tip of South America, they were delighted to see a facade of colour again. Deciding to avoid the settlement as there would be too many awkward questions, they glided over the frozen glaciers and when they broke clear into the sparse vegetation that found purchase on rocky scree, the reds, yellows and browns were magnificent. Gone were the endless frozen wastes, the white and flat landscapes and now the other surviving questors had a tiny inkling of what the three visitors to Mars had been through. The loss of the TORT-CAM which had been the real jewel in their crown and the craft of the Shaman caused much difficulty on their travel North. The Rabbi would have to curtail his diet; he could store large quantities of food no longer. As they reached more temperate climes, they even availed of squalid digs, staying put in the invisible shield was not an option now. They paid for any type of accommodation that kept them firstly out of the cold and as they progressed, out of the heat. Gone was their endless supply of wealth, so the Clerk and the Guide had to bargain with what they had left. In one of these ubiquitous hovels, Naomh came to a decision.

"We have to go back to the Shaman's people and show them the assembled jewel. Call it one last adventure before we go home."

It was in one of these safer places that Cahill and Greta approached Naomh and requested a private Pow wow. The urgency of the appeal was highlighted and he agreed. Away from the others, his male friend spoke for the two of them.

"Greta has brought this to my attention. We discussed it and agreed that you should be made aware of the situation. Both of us find it strange that you have been saved twice now by a large force of armed combatants, once on Mars and now once again on the frozen Continent."

Greta jumped in with his suspicions.

"I think and he agrees with me that somebody back in the Anschluss knows what we are about."

The seeker of the living jewel did not like the implications.

"You are saying that we have a traitor."

They both nodded.

"And you know who it is?"

The tall blonde woman took the hint.

"We believe it is the Mute. He is the only one who has an operational MIM."

"But, he saved me at the border fence."

Once again, Greta spoke.

"So did the two intervening parties. That must be their mission, to keep you alive. They must know what you have and desire it for themselves."

The worried bearer mulled this over for a while and then decided just like the Guide had.

"Ok, keep silent about you suspicions. But watch him like a hawk."

"Why don't we turn him to dust?" Asked a hard eyed Greta; that was her solution to everything.

"No, not until we are sure."

Ironically, now that they had in their possession what they had been seeking, the journey had actually become tougher. Without the invisible shield and its endless stock of supplies, what was once simple became extremely difficult. Enduring many hardships, it took many weeks until they arrived in the hidden village of the Anasazi. Some among them had advised.

"It will be too difficult to get there, we should go straight back to the Anschluss."

Naomh's reply was.

"I made the Shaman a promise."

That was the end of that argument. Unknown to them, the Anschluss Spy had facilitated their journey. What seemed like incredible luck in finding vehicles and avoiding trouble was not down to fate or chance. The co-operative people that they regularly bumped into, willing to assist them were in fact, disguised Anschluss agents or in lexicon of Agent XIII; "Assets.". Through the Chairman, the Spy had arranged these operatives to be precisely at the leg of where one of their journeys ended and the next leg started. They made it the whole way without ever firing a shot. They had no idea that they were been protected by an elite squad of their original foe's. When they saw the desert walls of the concealed village, the subject of their long but uneventful trip was broached by Cahill. A naïve Naomh put it down to his possession of the completed APOCRYPHA'I.

"It has the power of making us innocuous and making people assist us. That must be one of its benefits. I told you it would do anything for us."

"You wish. You only made it here because of my efforts." Thought the mole privately.

In the desert village, they were aware of Chief Dan George's passing. Peter Who Strides Quickly told them.

"The Spirits have told the Elders that the Shaman has vanished from the Earth, but he had been at peace when he went to the happy hunting grounds."

The Spy once again had a different outlook on events.

"Bullshit. You just made that assumption because the big savage is not with us and logic would tell you that something must have happened to him."

Naomh went to talk to Little Owl. He had accepted his father's passing on to the Spirit World and he would now practice the ways of a Shaman. A tribal gathering was held and the Bearer as he was now called showed them the completed frozen rainbow. Their shame was lifted, it was with its rightful owner and the celebration lasted well into the night. They stayed a week amid the tranquillity and then it was time to return to their home. Now it was the turn of the hidden tribe to fit them out with currency and supplies for their journey home. One Elder told them.

"When you gave us those gifts, it was like the grey squirrel burying his hoard until he needed it again."

The only place where Anschluss ships docked in the Americas was a huge port a hundred kilometres east of the spaceport. Huge quantities of tea, coffee and chocolate beans were loaded in place of the machine parts that had been brought over to the other side of the Atlantic. Without the TORT-CAM, sneaking about was more difficult, but the intending stowaways made it aboard with more than a little help from the Spy. After an uneventful crossing, they were back where the Quest had begun and to where Naomh was promised it would end. To the apparent chagrin of the Clerk, they were once again dressed in Jumpsuits and appropriated Frog Eyes were functional once again. He was an ordinary blonde Pleb again, but his singled fingered coin told him this was not the case. As he adhered his communication piece to his ear, the sombre Lenses privately remembered with regret.

"You were correct Edward; you were never going to use your piece again."

As much as those of them from the Anschluss hated its intransigent master, they were still delighted to be reconciled with the only home that the majority of them knew. It took them two months since leaving the ice sheet. The master of this domain was just as anxious to have them back and his long tentacles of assistance had benefited them enormously. Those that had saved them back on Antarctica were now food for the Droko, they were lucky compared to most of those who had been on Mars. Although, they had died with huge gaping wounds, they had not become the living dead of the Machine/men. As the cargo ship approached the western sea wall of the Anschluss in the full light of day, all of the questor's were up on deck. The Rabbi and Solomon had dropped a bombshell a few days out from their arrival. The heavily bearded man gathered the close knit group together and told them of a decision the two of them had made.

"My dear friends, I am leaving to return home, my part in this journey is over. It is my spiritual duty to return to my people and their six thousand-year-old struggles. The Guide has arranged for me to remain aboard this vessel. It is exchanging cargo and in a few days it will reach the Enclave."

Solomon simply said.

"I am going to look for the Prof."

No one among them would be able to change his or the deeply religious man's mind; so with heavy hearts they accepted their choice. The Guide wanted to tell Solomon of the Prof's demise, but he kept his silence. Everybody hugged and kissed them and what was even more surprising than their intended leaving was that Greta did as well. The Engineer would miss the practitioner of a different fate; the bearded man had taught him to respect all religions. Then during this parting, the most bizarre event of the quest occurred. The Rabbi went over to hug the Mute, but Illeau backed away from him like a man faced with a deadly rattlesnake. In a slow motion incident, a huge piece of machinery fell from the top of the ship and to the unbelieving watchers his entangled body toppled into the foaming sea and was gone forever. The others stood in open mouthed shock and Greta reacted like it had been an attack. Her weapon trailed along the upper deck, but there was no one there. If the dead Illeau had not moved that few metres to avoid the Rabbi's embrace, the falling object would have missed him entirely.

"Well that's the problem of him solved." Whispered a recovered Cahill to Naomh.

Illeau had his murderous list in his hands at the time and the M I M. toppled to the deck floor. The device had always intrigued the Guide, so he rushed forward and picked it up. It was code locked, so he gave it to the Lenses to decipher. It took the computer wizard nearly one week to open it and the contents shocked everybody. Digital information revealed that the nefarious Mute had been a serial killer of immense proportions. The video log started with an image of the man from the Bucharest Contrib. He spoke in his whinny voice.

"If someone else is watching this, then I am dead and this is my legacy. Ever since I knew, I have been fascinated with the last moments of Humans. My quest began when my two parents locked me in a room as they both cut their wrists and I was forced to watch them slip away. But I was a weak child and closed my eyes and I missed the blissful moment of their death. One week locked up with their corpses convinced me that I had to look for the secret. I knew that if I looked close enough at dying people in their last instances of breath, then the great secret of "Why?" would be revealed to me. For the eyes are the mirrors of the soul. From now on, you will hear my thoughts about those I have helped to make the transition from this miserable World to the next one.

Victim 1. Olaf Helb. 19 years of age. Unlikeable Classmate. Poisoned.

Victim 2. Mrs Shank. 32 years of age, my gym teacher. Strangled her during intercourse.

Victim 3, 4, 5, 6. Barman and staff who refused me drink. Blew up the premises."

The list of murder seemed endless, the memory counted hours. It would have to be studied at leisure.

"He was the dark side of us." Was the opinion of Beersheba.

"I'd say he was a fucking lunatic." Said the Clerk.

"Me too." Added the Lenses.

"Well, he got his comeuppance." Announced the Guide, certain that he had paid for the murder of the Prof.

Naomh confided in Cahill and Greta.

"Well, it looks like that really is the end of our Spy?"

They both agreed. Later that night, the Guide had finished scanning the extensive death list and was troubled for the name of Edward Boyd was not on it. That information sent a cold shiver down the pony tailed man's spine.

"That means that the traitor is still with us."

The disturbed man had been certain that Illeau had been the rotten apple in the barrel and he was now in a bone chilling quandary. Now that his chief suspect had been eliminated, he looked at the faces of the others and had no idea of who it could be. During his murderous career, the Mute had been personally responsible for the death of eight hundred and ninety-three individuals. But in one particular murder, he had saved the bearer of the APOCRYPHA'I and changed the fate of mankind. Indirectly, the twisted Human being had helped to usher in the new age of death. It would be likely that if he had known, he would have been well pleased.

Back in his high lair, Ivan Tell had become a worried man since the death of Illeau. The Mute had played both sides of the fence, he was sure of that. The disturbed killer had come to their attention during an investigation into two mysterious deaths. Background checks on the victim's movements turned up his name. Under interrogation, he showed no fear and brazenly revealed.

"I am a RE-INSTATOR. I will spy on them for the government if I am allowed to continue with my murdering."

The Chairman had agreed; he needed someone to watch Rory closely. This vile man knew that his agent had infiltrated them. Tell had promised the killer a position in the termination divisions, if he accompanied the questor's. Needless to say, he agreed. After it was over, the weird man would spend his days giving the condemned lethal injections.

To say there were mixed emotions among them as the huge sea gates slipped open fluidly would have been an understatement. Naomh had just crossed his symbolic Rubicon. This was the final leg of the journey and against impossible odds; they had completed the task and assembled the living amulet. Once again the Clerk looked at his timepiece, it was the 15th of March 2955AD, and they had been gone nearly three years. With help from the Guide, the Rabbi and Solomon transferred on to the Dreadnaut that would take them home. Their great adventure was over, but a new one was beginning for the others and Naomh was the only one who had an inkling of what to do next. Another in their mist had informed the Chairman not to have a squad of PREVENTIVES waiting to apprehend them as they disembarked. Some gut feeling told the traitor that the completed APOCRYPHA'I would be useless to the LYUBINITES until some sort of ritual was completed. Reluctantly, the true ruler of the Anschluss agreed, but he warned his secret agent in the lexicon of official speak.

"Do not to fuck up."

His Spy resisted the urge to blurt out a familiar retort that was only used amongst the identical Clones.

"Keep your mask on."

A curious Agent XIII also asked.

"Did you have the Mute taken out?"

The Chairman never gave an answer and the screen went blank. Alone and unheard, he added.

"Beware the ides of March, my returning friend."

The traitor returned to the others with a smile that was misinterpreted by them, they believed that it was because of their success. The mole stifled a giggle.

"Well, they are half right, because of them, they could now be looking at the next Chairman. Imagine; if any of them realised the implications of my good humour. Now that would really put the cat among the pigeons, if those clueless dupes ever found that out. Still, if they did find out, I could take them all out without them ever knowing, but where would the fun be in that."

The returning fugitives made it safely to a safe house in the Lisbon Contrib and it was there that their leader was going to drop a bigger bombshell than the Rabbi or Solomon had. Considering what they had all been through, he felt guilty about the secret of his ancestry.

"It is time to tell the others about the identity of my father. They deserve the truth. It is the least that I can do."

The metallic voice intruded and spoke mind words of reality.

"This is not the time for that revelation. There is a lot more to be achieved and neither of us needs your companions to be distracted by this news. It will cause a great split."

Reluctantly, his host agreed, but vowed.

"I will tell them soon."

However, the final secret that he had been his father's killer was one that he would never reveal. He would tell no one; not even his beloved Miriam. The revelation of his patricide would come from another. Oblivious to this future event, the bearer of the completed APOCRYPHA'I sighed.

"After all, how could they respect or even follow anyone that murdered his own parent."

HERE END'S ALIEN REFORMATION; BOOK ONE OF THE HYDRO-CARBON STRATAGEM. BOOK TWO; HYBRID ASCENDANCY CONTINUES WITH NAOMH'S QUEST FOR WORLD DOMINATION.